PENGUIN CLASSICS

DON QUIXOTE

Miguel de Cervantes Saavedra, the son of a poor Spanish surgeon, was almost certainly born in 1547. He served in Italy in 1570, and as a regular soldier he fought in the naval battle of Lepanto and other engagements, until he was captued by pirates while returning to Spain in 1575 and taken to be the slave of a renegade Greek in Algiers; he attempted unsuccessfully to escape several times, and was finally ransomed in 1580. For the rest of his life he was preoccupied with the difficulties of making a living, and spent two periods in prison. He had already written some plays and a pastoral novel, *La Galatea*, when in 1592 he offered to write six plays at fifty ducats apiece. He had no success until 1605, when the publication of the first part of *Don Quixote* brought him immediate popularity. The *Exemplary Stories* were published as a collection in 1613, and in 1615 appeared the promised continuation of *Don Quixote*. Cervantes died in 1616.

John Rutherford is a Fellow of The Queen's College, Oxford, where he teaches Spanish, Spanish-American, and Galician language and literature. He has also translated *La Regenta*, by Leopoldo Alas, for Penguin Classics, and (with others) *'Them' and Other Stories*, by Xosé Luís Méndez Ferrín, for Planet Books.

Roberto González Echevarría is Sterling Professor of Hispanic and Comparative Literatures at Yale University. He is the editor and author of numerous books on Spanish and Latin American literatures. His *Myth and Archive: A Theory of the Latin American Narrative* (Cambridge) won awards from the Modern Language Association of America and the Latin American Studies Association. In 1999 he was inducted into the American Academy of Arts and Sciences.

The Ingenious Hidalgo
DON QUIXOTE
de la Mancha

MIGUEL DE CERVANTES SAAVEDRA

TRANSLATED BY
JOHN RUTHERFORD

WITH AN INTRODUCTION BY
ROBERTO GONZÁLEZ ECHEVARRÍA

PENGUIN BOOKS

PENGUIN BOOKS

Published by the Penguin Group

Penguin Putnam Inc., 375 Hudson Street,
New York, New York 10014, U.S.A.

Penguin Books Ltd, 80 Strand,
London WC2R 0RL, England

Penguin Books Australia Ltd, 250 Camberwell Road, Camberwell,
Victoria 3124, Australia

Penguin Books Canada Ltd, 10 Alcorn Avenue,
Toronto, Ontario, Canada M4V 3B2

Penguin Books India (P) Ltd, 11 Community Centre, Panchsheel Park,
New Delhi – 110 017, India

Penguin Books (N.Z.) Ltd, Cnr Rosedale and Airborne Roads, Albany,
Auckland, New Zealand

Penguin Books (South Africa) (Pty) Ltd, 24 Sturdee Avenue,
Rosebank, Johannesburg 2196, South Africa

Penguin Books Ltd, Registered Offices:
Harmondsworth, Middlesex, England

This translation first published in Penguin Books (U.K.) 2000
This edition with an introduction by Roberto González Echevarría
published in Penguin Books (U.S.A.) 2001

5 7 9 10 8 6 4

LIBRARY OF CONGRESS CATALOGING IN PUBLICATION DATA
Cervantes Saavedra, Miguel de, 1547–1616.
[Don Quixote. English]
The ingenious hidalgo Don Quixote de la Mancha / Miguel de Cervantes Saavedra;
translated by John Rutherford; with an introduction by Roberto González Echevarría.
p.   cm.
Includes bibliographical references.
ISBN 0 14 04.4804 7 (pbk.: alk. paper)
I. Rutherford, John, 1941– II. Title.
PQ6329.A2   2001c
863'.3—dc21   2001021439

Printed in the United States of America
Set in Columbus MT

CONTENTS

INTRODUCTION

Miguel de Cervantes Saavedra's masterpiece has endured because it focuses on literature's foremost appeal: to become another, to leave a typically embattled self for another closer to one's desires and aspirations.
This is why *Don Quixote* has often been read as a children's book and
continues to be read by or to children. Experience and life's blows teach
us our limits and erode the hope of living up to our dreams, but our
hope never vanishes. It is the soul's pith, the flickering light of being,
the spiritual counterpart to our DNA's master code. When the hero regains his sanity at the end of Part II, he dies. As the last chances of living an imaginary life disappear, so must life itself. Don Quixote's serene
passing reflects this understanding; he knows that the dream of life is
over, and as a Neoplatonist and Christian, his only hope now is to find
the true life after death.

Stories endure because they either express an archetype or create a
new one. The epic and other oral narratives, including tragedy, retell
known stories: think of Ulysses, Oedipus, Roland, the Cid. *Don Quixote*
creates an archetype that is, appropriately, the archetype of type—the
founding story of printed literature.[1] It is the tale of the reader, who indulges his imaginative needs not in a collective setting such as the theatre or the public square, but alone with his private yearnings, listening
to his inner voices and those to which he gives life in his soul's stage as
he scans the pages. Because of print the reader is more educated; his
memory is not only his or his people's, but that of many other individuals and cultures. Unlike those listening to singers or actors performing,
the reader can go back and replay a scene, relish again what he liked,
giving his own tempo to the unfolding of the story, taking time to let

the pleasure of his imaginings sink in slowly or flipping the pages quickly to come to the end of an adventure and learn his hero's fate. This is what we, the readers of *Don Quixote*, imagine that the hero himself did as he read his cherished romances of chivalry. It is what we ourselves do as we savour our favorite passages, rereading isolated episodes, suspending the malleable time of fiction to postpone or really just forget our own inevitable demise.

Alone with ourselves and a book we can be children again. You cannot get up in the theatre and challenge an actor, and you would be smothered by the crowd if you interrupted the minstrel's performance. But in our own private space, huddled under the cloak of our fantasies with the book, we can counsel our hero, sigh for a damsel, shout insults at the wrongdoers, and enter the fiction in soul, if not in body. This last thing is, of course, what Don Quixote attempted to do: to bring his reader's imaginings to the bruising world of tangible reality and to the withering present. The book's archetype would not be complete if the hero remained in the ideal world of literature. Human desire is all too human; it longs for actualization in bodies and things, in the here and now of the sensory and the sensual. These are, of course, not as pliable as our fantasies and the world of books, and therein lies *Don Quixote*'s power—and the frontier between children's stories and those for adults.

There was nothing even remotely like *Don Quixote* before 1605, when the novel appeared. There were chivalric, pastoral, and Byzantine romances; epics in the style of Ludovico Ariosto's; stories like Giovanni Boccaccio's or, closer in time, Matteo Bandello's; and of course, picaresque novels since the publication in 1554 of *La vida de Lazarillo de Tormes* and in 1599 the defining *Primera parte de la vida del pícaro Guzmán de Alfarache*. Shakespeare and Molière worked within established theatrical conventions dating back to the Greeks, as did Cervantes when he wrote plays. But *Don Quixote*, which drew from all the prose genres that preceded it (and some poetic ones, too), had no beaten paths to follow.[2] In fact, such is the book's novelty that this novelty is incorporated as an issue into its own fabric. Don Quixote is too old to be a picaresque anti-hero, an epic champion, a pastoral lover, or a knight, and as a petty nobleman of the lowest rank he would make an unlikely courtier. So much for the available literary roles. Protagonists his age, even in Cervantes's other works, were usually husbands cuckolded by their younger wives or sages beyond desire or adventure left to voice useless warnings to the young. As much else in *Don Quixote*, the parts do not fit, provoking laughter, to be sure, but also wonder that leads to profound reflection. This is why Georg Lukács calls the novelistic genre, whose founding was *Don Quixote*, "the epic of a world that has been abandoned by God," and adds that "the objectivity of the novel is the mature man's knowledge that meaning can never quite penetrate reality, but that without meaning, reality would disintegrate into the nothingness of inessentiality."[3] It is as difficult to overstate *Don Quixote*'s originality as it is to relive the surprise of its first readers when it reached their hands.

Postromantic habits of thought have led some to make Cervantes into a rebel or an outcast, if not the member of a religious minority chafing under oppression. How could the author of such an original book, so deviously ironic, not be working against established authority? The paucity of documentary evidence about Cervantes's life has allowed for no small amount of speculation along these lines, fueled by commonplaces about the Spain of the Counter-Reformation, redolent with hooded inquisitors, and by the racial and religious strife of our own era. It is just as hard to disprove as to prove anything about Cervantes, given how little is known, but what we do know, together with a sensible reading of his works, makes it reasonably clear that the author of *Don Quixote* was a loyal Spanish Catholic, and a patriotic one at that. Spaniards did not have to stop being Spanish or Catholic to be audacious and modern. Younger than Cervantes, Diego Velázquez, a genius in his art, was a court painter, and his contemporary, Pedro Calderón de la Barca, a major playwright also at the court, wrote more than a hundred *autos sacramentales* celebrating the eucharist. Like them, Cervantes probed pitilessly into the human condition, speculated about the nature of his own art, and produced masterpieces in sharp dialogue with the greatest works of the Western tradition. One of the outstanding features of Cervantes's Spain was the plethora of artistic and literary luminaries, sometimes within a few blocks of one another in Madrid: El Greco, Lope de Vega, Francisco Zurbarán, Tirso de Molina, Luis de Góngora, Francisco de Quevedo, and many others. This is why it is called the Golden Age in conventional literary histories. We will never know what

produces a talent like Cervantes's, but commonplaces about rebellious-
ness in the contemporary sense should be the first to be discarded.

Cervantes's life, though far from easy, was relatively ordinary for
someone of his class and background. His commonality, in fact, is relevant to the genesis of *Don Quixote*, to his career as a writer, and to literary history. It was new for someone who lacked social rank and a
thorough humanistic education to dare to become an author. With Ma-
teo Alemán and Lope de Vega, Cervantes belongs to the first generation
of writers who attempt to make a living from their craft, creating new
literary genres that deviate from Renaissance theory and practice.[4] Lope
de Vega, writing prolifically and mostly for the theatre, succeeded. Cervantes did not, and he had to depend (futilely and sometimes patheti-
cally) on the support of aristocratic patrons. This precarious professional
status, which undermined his authority as a writer, is why Cervantes so
often incorporated himself in his fiction and the humblest cause for the
notorious self-reflexivity of his work. With what authority, other than
the weight of my own mundane experience, do I dare to write this
book? How can I, a lowly being, dare to pretend to be the source of
these inventions? Are they mine, and if so in what way? Cervantes realized that he was his own most alluring mystery, and that his story as
writer was the most interesting of all. *Don Quixote* is the tale of the
reader because it is also that of the writer.

Even if Cervantes led a fairly ordinary life, it was rich in experiences,
and it is projected not only onto obviously autobiographical stories, such
as the captive's in Part I, but onto nearly all the lives told in *Don Quixote*.
It also informs the overall structure of the book, which tells Don
Quixote's life by adhering not to Renaissance poetic formulas about
well-wrought plots but rather to the picaresque *vida*. A life told by someone like Cervantes, who had lived almost his own entire life, is a shape
understandable to all, not just to those steeped in the classics and their
commentators. Cervantes being Cervantes, however, tells the life of Don
Quixote as the character he wills himself to be, with little or no information about his "real" life, meaning his family background and how he arrived at the decision to become a knight-errant. But all the stories in *Don
Quixote* are subsumed into that of the hero's life as the novel unfolds toward its natural and expected conclusion in his death. Cervantes's trans-

mutation of his own experiences into the stuff of literature has its specular image in the hero's efforts to elevate his life into fiction. Cervantes and Don Quixote find each other in the book.

Throughout his life Cervantes met with repeated failures and misfortunes; when literary recognition at last came, it brought few worldly or spiritual rewards—it was as ironic a turn of events as those in his fictions. Born in Alcalá de Henares, a university town a few miles east of Madrid, probably on September 29, 1547, Miguel was the forth of Rodrigo de Cervantes's and Leonor de Cortinas's seven children. Had his family been wealthy or enjoyed exalted aristocratic status, his not being a firstborn male would have added to Cervantes's woes later on. But Rodrigo, though he belonged to the gentry like Don Quixote (an *hidalgo*), was a man of modest means who was once even incarcerated for nonpayment of debts. In 1564, when Miguel was seventeen, Rodrigo stated in a document that he was a "surgeon," a profession that was then barely above that of barber and that neither required much education nor produced much income. Nothing definite is known about Miguel's early education, but it has been inferred that he studied with the Jesuits in Córdoba and Seville and with the humanist Juan López de Hoyos in Madrid. He was then in his late teens and early twenties, had published some poems, and had had his first scrape with the law for wounding a man in a duel. As a result of this incident he left in 1570 for Rome, where he joined the retinue of Cardinal Julio Acquaviva, having duly given proof, as was required in Spain, that he was of "clean blood" (having no Jewish or Arabic ancestors) and an *hidalgo*. Italy, where he enlisted in the Spanish forces deployed there under John of Austria, was a decisive intellectual experience for Cervantes; but nothing was as traumatic as his military exploits, which literally marked him for life. At the naval battle of Lepanto, fought against the Turkish fleet in 1571, Miguel went on deck for hand-to-hand combat and fought bravely though he was ill with a fever. A harquebus shot to his left arm maimed him for life and led, in the Spanish-speaking world, to the rhyming epithet by which he is known to schoolchildren: "el manco de Lepanto," the one-handed man from Lepanto.. He was proud of his wound, a badge of courage and loyalty that he boasted about as late as the prologue to Part II of *Don Quixote*, which appeared in 1615, a year before his death. From then on,

Cervantes also frequently petitioned rewards from the Crown for his distinguished military record.

In spite of his injury, Cervantes continued his military service, but when he was finally furloughed in 1575 and had begun his trek home, he suffered a greater misfortune: he and others were seized by Barbary pirates and taken hostage to Algiers. Hostage-taking was rampant in the contested Mediterranean. The letters attesting to his military exploits, which Cervantes planned to use in his pleas before the court, led his captors to believe that they had stumbled upon a greater prize than they had expected. After three failed escape attempts, he was finally ransomed in 1580 and made his way back to Spain. He was twenty-eight when he was captured, thirty-three when he regained his freedom. Cervantes had wasted his late twenties and early thirties as a slave in Algiers, an experience that would enrich his fiction, but at a great price.

As if trying to make up for lost time, Cervantes wrote several plays upon his return to Spain, among them *La destrucción de Numancia* (his best) and *Los tratos de Argel*, both staged in Madrid in 1581. He also wrote and published in 1584 a pastoral novel, *La Galatea*, which met with relative success and shows hints of what was to follow in the mixture of styles and the intrusion of erotic violence in the ideal world of the shepherds. Or, as Richard L. Predmore eloquently put it, "he began to see how myths could be deflated with injections of real life and real life ennobled in mythical robes; he began to explore the possibility of catching the complexity of human life in a net of ambivalence."[5] But Cervantes was already thirty-seven years old; his work for the theatre—the only profitable literary activity—was only modestly successful, and he had to earn a living to support his new wife Catalina de Palacios Salazar Vozmediano. It was not his only responsibility. As a result of a liaison with another woman, Ana Franca de Rojas, Cervantes also had an illegitimate daughter, Isabel de Saavedra. And so he obtained a position as commissioner and tax collector in Andalusia, around Seville, as the Crown was stockpiling wealth and supplies for what would be the disastrous Armada of 1588. Cervantes suffered terrible ordeals in this job, then as now an unpopular one. Disputes over the handling of his accounts landed him in Seville's jail, and he was once excommunicated by the general vicar of that city. Throughout his forties Cervantes was imprisoned several times, resulting in more experiences that enriched his work, but again at a steep price. He claimed in the prologue to Part I of *Don Quixote* that it was in Seville's jail that he first had the idea for *Don Quixote.*

In the waning years of the sixteenth century Cervantes was in Valladolid, though he also spent time at Esquivias, where his wife owned vineyards, and he shuttled back and forth to Seville because of his job. He was by then writing *Don Quixote*, which went to press in 1604 and appeared early the next year. Cervantes was about to turn fifty-eight when the book was published, always an advanced age to begin making your mark as writer, but particularly then, when it was rare to live to be sixty. He had only ten years of life left, but they were as productive and successful as anyone could hope for. *Don Quixote* went through several printings and was soon translated into English and French. Publishers were suddenly interested in printing not only Cervantes's fiction, but also his theater. In 1613 the *Novelas ejemplares*, a splendid collection of twelve short novels, was published, as was *Viaje del Parnaso* in 1614, a long poem in which Cervantes surveys the literary scene of his time. That same year, an apocryphal second part of *Don Quixote* appeared, signed by someone calling himself Alonso Fernández de Avellaneda. Cervantes, who was halfway through writing his own second part, was spurred to finish. It appeared in 1615, as did a volume of his plays. He was ill and rushing to complete what he thought would be his masterpiece: the Byzantine romance *Los trabajos de Persiles y Sigismunda*. He did finish it, but he did not live to see it published, dying in Madrid on April 22, 1616.[6] The *Persiles* was published posthumously the next year. In its moving prologue, Cervantes bid farewell to his friends and mused with humour about his late-found fame with the same composed tone of Don Quixote's parting words on his deathbed.

Cervantes's irony, elegant self-mockery, and disclaimers of authorship are certainly at the core of his mind and work. In *Don Quixote* the author pretends to be merely the translator of a manuscript written by Arabic historian Cide Hamete Benengeli. He dramatizes this by stopping the action in Chapter 8 of Part I, protesting that he has run out of text and then telling an elaborate story about how he found the remaining chapters and secured the services of a translator. Thus the rest of the novel would be the work of this translator, who is intrusive enough to append impudent comments about the characters or the plausibility of their speech. There are also remarks by the author about the translator's comments, as well as on the incongruity of the high-flown rhetoric of certain passages. Many segments are parodies of recognizable literary genres, such as the chivalric romances and the pastoral, as well as the rhetoric of the courtly love tradition, full of paradoxes and trite figures. And so there are layers upon layers of discourse, commenting on one another, blurring the source, intention, and ultimately the legitimacy and truth of the final product. Further ironic distancing is provided by the blatantly literary nature of the "found manuscript" device, which makes the whole thing appear to be a sham from the start, and by allusions to Cervantes's other works, such as *La Galatea* in the episode of the scrutiny of the knight's library. If the Cervantes mentioned by the priest is the same as the one on the cover of the book we read, is he a fictional character in *Don Quixote* or its author? Is the whole of reality a book whose characters we are and the author of which is too grandiose for us to fathom? If we are on the same level of reality as this author-character, the inescapable conclusion is that we, too, inhabit a fictional realm. But if Don Quixote's inability to distinguish literary fiction from reality is what makes him a madman, where does that leave us?

We are aware, of course, that all this charade is in jest, but knowing it is also part of the game. Yet we do continue to play it, and there is the rub and the road that leads to the deepest and darkest recesses of this series of interlocking ironies: does Don Quixote really believe in his fictions, as when he emerges from Montesinos's cave in Part II and tells a tall tale that he insists others should believe, or does he act in the knowledge that it is all bogus? The mirror play leads to a disquieting questioning of the self's coherence, of the mind's very existence as a thinking, feeling, and willful entity to which we can attribute our actions and beliefs. Joaquín Casalduero maintains, in a disturbing insight, that at the Duque's house, when Don Quixote is finally treated like the knight-errant he wants to be, the hero has a distanced, ironic perception of himself as a parody of his desires: "Don Quixote, a spiritual man, sees his own image as a knight-errant, which he had heretofore always contemplated in the purity of his own actions: it is an image of his external self. The honors, social status, the fame that society can grant a man of the spirit are nothing but a burlesque image, a distortion of his inner life."[7] It is at this level that irony's humour becomes serious indeed, and Cervantes's disclaimers as author acquire a deeper meaning, one that affects the very nature of *Don Quixote*.

In Cervantes's delightful prologue to Part I he calls himself stepfather to the book, yet he tells the reader how he is hard at work writing the very prologue that he is reading because he truly does not know how to legitimize his relationship to t(his) creation. A helpful friend then appears (Cervantes always favours dialogue, as the splitting of his authorial self here attests), and tells him to make up what today we would call "an index of names" or bibliography, to lend authority to the book. By suggesting that the tradition from which *Don Quixote* presumably emerges can be fabricated, Cervantes is subtly underscoring the book's and his own originality. The literature produced by the new writers will be new, therein its value in every sense, including monetary.

Consideration of *Don Quixote*'s composition is not limited to the prologue and to the passages mentioned about the origins of Cide Hamete's manuscript and the commentaries by the translator and the author or transcriber: it is embedded in the games of chance, improvisation, and error that are so much a part of the book. It is a play that takes us outside the fiction. One topic of *Don Quixote* criticism since the publication of Part I in 1605 has centered on Cervantes's various gaffes or oversights. Though there are others, the most blatant is the appearance of Sancho on his donkey when it had been stolen from him in an earlier episode. Cervantes makes light of this in the prologue to Part II, though he did make hurried emendations of the book between printings of Part I. But the errors feed right into the issue of authorship, authorial intention, irony, and the structure of the novel. In short, they undermine the authority of the author and highlight his ironic stance before the final product. Is this mine, the issue of my imagination, or is it partly the product of chance? How much of its creation obeyed my intentions? Should I not humbly accept the role of chance in the composition of the book and admit with humility my crass errors, where my limited powers could not totally master the universe of fiction that I tried to invent?

So effective was Cervantes's ironic stance that it allowed him to deal brilliantly with the biggest threat to face him as author: the publication of Avellaneda's spurious *Don Quixote*, purporting to be a continuation of the original. It now seems as if Cervantes wold have had to invent Avellaneda had he not existed (it is not known who this author really was, for it is fairly certain that he used a pseudonym). Cervantes was writing Chapter 59 of Part II when the rival book appeared in 1614. Avellaneda had misread Cervantes's masterpiece, as did most of his contemporaries, reducing it to its comic elements. He also insulted Cervantes, mocking him for, among other things, his physical handicap, and boasted that his book would ruin the sales of the real Part II if and when it appeared. But Avellaneda had only played into Cervantes's hand. His response was, as Stephen Gilman put it, "to encompass [Avellaneda] in a web of irony."[8] He absorbed the fake book and pirate author into the fiction of his own, even having his novelistic characters attest to the counterfeit nature of their doubles. Avellaneda became another one of Cervantes's characters, one of the fictions that play at undermining Cervantes's authority, while at the same time strengthening it.

Cervantes's own doubts about his agency as author tend to lend credence to a theory about the genesis of *Don Quixote* proposed in 1920 by the noted Spanish scholar and philologist Ramón Menéndez Pidal.[9] Characteristically, as the greatest expert of Spanish popular balladry, Menéndez Pidal maintained that the source of the book was an *entremés*, a comic one-act play, in which a man goes insane trying to reenact the exploits of great epic and chivalric heroes sung about in the *romances*, or Spanish ballads. This *Entremés de los romances* would have given Cervantes the idea for a short novella, like those he published in 1613 as *Novelas ejemplares*, about a gentleman who suffered the same fate as Don Quixote trying to imitate the actions of knights in the romances of chivalry. Be that as it may, the most significant part of the theory is that *Don Quixote* was going to be a novella that would end with the hero's first return home, when he is picked up by his neighbour Pero Alonso while babbling lines from a ballad about Baldwin and the Marquis of Mantua, characters in the Charlemagne cycle. If that were so, the rest of *Don Quixote* grows out of this narrative kernel, being made up as it goes without model or plan. The fortuity of the narrative structure, which depends on chance encounters at roads and inns, would mirror this fortuitous beginning, sharing with it a delicate balance between chance and invention. It is the blueprint for errancy and error, as well as for the questioning of authorial design.

The most significant addition to *Don Quixote* as the plot proceeded beyond the first sally was Sancho Panza, whose presence allowed Cervantes to indulge his penchant for dialogue and multiple perspectives. Sancho gives a voice to the world of slovenly inns, innkeepers, prostitutes, muleteers, criminals—a whole panoply of people living in the present as they had for centuries—that Cervantes had adapted from picaresque fiction and observed first-hand in his travels as a tax-collector and in the jail. In terms of the development of the novel as genre, Sancho is as important as Don Quixote because he develops as the plot progresses and circumstances place him in new situations. A topic in Cervantes criticism has been that Don Quixote becomes Sanchified and Sancho Quixotized as their lives intertwine. Cervantes removed from picaresque fiction the inherent penchant for evil of characters drawn from the lower classes, and Sancho is the prime example, but only one of many. Maritornes, the grotesque prostitute at Juan Palomeque's inn, is kind and tender to Sancho and Don Quixote, and Ginés de Pasamonte is a clever rascal but not malevolent by nature. Sancho governs his bogus Island of Barataria with common sense, honesty, and compassion. Through him Cervantes shows that any man can rise to the occasion on the strength of his God-given wit and goodness.

But Sancho's most important role is as foil to the knight's deranged plans, warning him of his wild misperceptions. "What giants?" asks Sancho when Don Quixote points to the windmills and rejoices in the anticipation of adventure. Of course, Sancho becomes enmeshed in Don Quixote's fictions not only because he is gullible but also because of the need to lie to get out of difficult situations. He winds up defending the existence of Dulcinea in Part II to cover earlier prevarications and falls for the Duque's contrivances. All of this is hilariously funny, particularly in the original because Cervantes had an uncanny ear for the variations of Spanish according to social class and region. The point is, however, that Sancho is not in possession of the truth because of his simple nature and common sense. Neither he nor Don Quixote is ultimately right, as the episode of Mambrino's helmet shows: the reader knows that it is a barber's basin, but from outside the fiction and aided by the narrator. In the fiction, as no doubt in the reader's own world, the truth is a matter of negotiation and compromise. Sancho is as befuddled as Don Quixote because he, too, is human and he also has a penchant for error and self-delusion in the midst of a changing reality. Together Sancho and Don Quixote sketch the shape of the emerging modern self.

If the Renaissance, or early modern period as it is now called, meant renewed faith in the human capacity to make, organize, and control—from politics to urban design, from painting and sculpture to architecture—*Don Quixote* signals that the resulting new science and philosophy have also led to radical doubts about the self. Sancho's island is the distorted version of utopias such as Thomas More's and well-run kingdoms like the ones envisaged by Niccolò Machiavelli. The wooden horse Clavileño may not have soared to real heights, yet his flight mocks the limitations of ancient conceptions of the cosmos, with solid spheres and fixed stars. The boundlessness of the universe discovered and contemplated brought about a crisis whose names are Galileo Galilei and René Descartes. The emerging modern self experiences a frightening freedom when, armed with its limited if autonomous powers, it faces the immensity of the universe. It is Don Quixote setting out alone on his first sally, at dawn, heading aimlessly toward the broad Castilian plain. It is the starry night sky seen by the characters through the ramshackle roof of Palomeque's flimsy inn, which offers no shelter and provides no limit. Descartes's relentless questioning left him only with a self that exists because it thinks and poses questions. Literature allowing more margin than philosophy to speculate, Cervantes ventured further, questioning the nature and cogency of that self. This is the issue raised by Don Quixote's madness. What is a sane self? Cervantes begins where Descartes leaves off. His response to this quandary was a comical hero too old to be enmeshed in his family romance (there is nothing about his parents) and an author too jaded to have confidence in the effectiveness of his own will and intentions to create.

The elusiveness of Cervantes's irony has led some to think that he was a follower of Erasmus and to view *In Praise of Folly* as an important influence on *Don Quixote*. Whether Cervantes had read the Rotterdam humanist or been a follower of his many disciples in the Peninsula is difficult to prove or disprove.[10] But it is clear that Cervantes's irony goes further than Erasmus's. *In Praise of Folly* is an elegant exercise in double-speak: everything Folly says in her monologue is played off against the sane way a Christian should approach faith and doctrine. There is no stable truth against which to measure Cervantes's irony, which whorls in a spiral of infinite evasiveness. This, of course, is more daring than Erasmus's presumably sacriligious ideas (such as reading the Bible directly in Hebrew and Greek). In *El pensamiento de Cervantes*, Américo Castro went as far as to call the author of *Don Quixote* "a skillful hypocrite."[11] Castro masterfully argued in that book that Spanish humanists had kept up with philosophical and scientific developments elsewhere in Europe, particularly in Italy, and had devised a method to absorb their findings without provoking the Church. It was a system of double truth: the universe was guided by its own laws, free of God and religious doctrine, which however enveloped it all, including potential discrepancies and contradictions. One's individual opinions were left out, as if the whole thing could not affect personal faith. It was a gesture similar to the formula by which laws sent to the New World irrelevant to local conditions were received: "se acata, pero no se cumple" (obeyed, but not enacted).

It is worthy of notice that of the two literary archetypes created during Spain's Golden Age, Don Quixote and Don Juan, it is the second that has been most often taken up by later writers, not to mention by composers. Don Quixote's musical legacy cannot compare to Don Juan's. Perhaps this is so because eros will always be more appealing than the reflective humour of Cervantes's masterpiece and the desire of the protagonist to be other than himself. But the disparity is obvious only if one takes the mad gentleman to be the sole archetype in the novel. From within literature, however, the most important character in Cervantes's novel is the narrator, the implicit author whose ironic games concerning his product are the foundation of the modern novel. This was understood immediately by writers such as Alain-René Lesage, Laurence Sterne, and Henry Fielding, who picked up Cervantes's legacy explicitly, and by every novelist who has put pen to paper since then. A host of modern Latin American writers—Jorge Luis Borges, Alejo Carpentier, Gabriel García Márquez, Carlos Fuentes—have understood that Cervantes, more than Don Quixote, is the origin of narrative fiction and have turned him into a character or a problem in their works.[12] Don Quixote, of course, has heirs of his own in Stendhal's Julien Sorel, Gustave Flaubert's Emma Bovary, Herman Melville's Captain Ahab, and James Joyce's Leopold Bloom. In a memorable book, René Girard argued that desire mediated by literature harkened back to *Don Quixote* and was the essence of the novel as genre.[13]

Leo Spitzer and Erich Auerbach coincided in locating what is "Cervantine" in the difficulty of pinning Cervantes down on any given topic, in his play of perspectives. Auerbach states that "the theme of the mad country gentleman who undertakes to revive knight-errantry gave Cervantes an opportunity to present the world as play in that spirit of multiple, perspective, non-judging, and even non-questioning neutrality which is a brave form of wisdom."[14] Spitzer's brilliant analysis of linguistic perspectivism in *Don Quixote* (beginning with the uncertainty about the mad gentleman's last name: Quesada, Quejana, Quijada) concludes that "in our novel, things are represented, not for what they are in themselves but only as things spoken about or thought about; and this involves breaking the narrative presentation into two points of view . . . the only unquestionable truth on which the reader may depend is the will of the artist who chose to break up a multivalent reality into different perspectives. In other words, perspectivism suggests an Archimedean principle outside the plot—and the Archimedes must be Cervantes himself."[15] But, of course, we have already seen how elusive Cervantes the author is. While agreeing with Spitzer's definition of Cervantine perspectivism, Ciriaco Morón Arroyo comments that the author of *Don Quixote* was no relativist when it came to morals and adds the following: "Perhaps we ought to point out here that perspectivism is inherent to Christian thought. Perspectivism as a form of modesty that recognizes the limits of all judgement and human knowledge is, indeed, Christian humility and intelligence in its strictest sense: the capacity to perceive the limit of our own creations: *eironeia*."[16]

To my mind the "Cervantine" is found in the ease, the elegance and apparent effortlessness, with which the intertwined and complicated stories, happening in different levels of the fiction, resolve themselves, with multiple suggestions about a variety of profound themes, none of which is mentioned directly or in abstract terms. A case in point is the episode in which Don Quixote attacks the wineskins while dreaming that he is in pitched battle with Pandafilando de la Fosca Vista, the giant made up by Dorotea when she concocts the story about being Princess Micomicona. This story is a translation into chivalric fiction of what happened to her with her suitor Don Fernando, whose name cleverly rhymes with that of the giant. Like the giant, Don Fernando is a voracious lover of all; the Greek *pan* and *philos* give the clue here. Fernando and the giant are "Panphilanderers with a Menacing Gaze"—the gaze being the mark of lasciviousness and will to possess. As Javier Herrero, whose superb analysis of this scene I am following here, observes, the fact is that Don Quixote has by his actions slain the giant and brought to a happy conclusion Dorotea's ordeal.[17] This is all very funny, no doubt, except to the innkeeper whose wine has been spilled, but at the same time it is worthy of profound reflection. Here is a madman solving a real conflict while engaged in a dream battle with a giant who is the product of a lie. Don Quixote has become the instrument of a weird kind of Providence. An equally masterful, if even more complicated, design is the Pageant in the Forest in Part II, when Sancho's lies about Dulcinea result in a baroque performance in which the imaginary lady (a "metacharacter" invented by the other characters) materializes as a beautiful page who is playing her role. This transvestite Dulcinea opens a Pandora's box of suggestions and suggestiveness worthy of the most modern and daring of writers. As in Pandafilando's story, one senses here the presence of an ironic and elegant creator unwilling to show his hand any more than he has to, aware of the significance of it all yet feeling that it would be unworthy of him to point it out. The reader, this reader, gratefully understands, and humbly marvels at the unsurpassed mastery.

—ROBERTO GONZÁLEZ ECHEVARRÍA

NOTES

1. See Ian P. Watt, *Myths of Modern Individuality: Faust, Don Quixote, Don Juan, Robinson Crusoe* (New York: Cambridge University Press, 1996).
2. The genres mentioned are incorporated into the fiction of *Don Quixote* as characters afflicted by the same malady as the hero attempt to play out in real

life roles drawn from books. Hence Marcela and Grisóstomo the pastoral, Cardenio the courtly lover, Ginés de Pasamonte the rogue and picaresque author, and so forth. In some cases, such as Grisóstomo's, the result turns out to be tragic.

3. *The Theory of the Novel: A Historico-Philosophical Essay on the Forms of Great Epic Literature* [1920], tr. Anna Bostock (Cambridge, Mass: MIT Press, 1971), p. 88.

4. See Otis H. Green, "Originality: The New Literary Genres," in his *Spain and the Western Tradition*, vol. 4 (Madison: University of Wisconsin Press, 1968), pp. 210–85.

5. *Cervantes* (New York: Dodd, Mead, 1973), p. 107.

6. The reader will note the proximity with the date of Shakespeare's death (April 23, 1616), but England had not adopted the Gregorian calendar, so the death of the two writers is separated by several more days.

7. *Sentido y forma del Quijote (1605–1615)* (Madrid: Ediciones Insula, 1949), pp. 294–95.

8. "The Apocryphal *Quixote*," in *Cervantes Across the Centuries*, ed. Angel Flores and M. J. Bernardete (New York: The Dryden Press, 1947), p. 247.

9. There is an English version of this paper in *Cervantes Across the Centuries*, ed. Flores and Bernardete, pp. 32–55.

10. Spanish Erasmianism was studied by Marcel Bataillon in his monumental *Erasme et l'Espagne* (1937). The Spanish translation published in 1950 and 1960 by the Fondo de Cultura Económica in Mexico as *Erasmo y España* is an expanded version of the original.

11. Américo Castro, *El pensamiento de Cervantes*, Anejos de la Revista de Filología Española—Anejo VI (Madrid: Imprenta de la Librería y Casa Editorial Hernando, 1925), p. 249.

12. See my "Cervantes y la narrativa hispanoamericana moderna: Borges y Carpentier," *Unión* (Havana), 10, no. 37 (1999): 4–13.

13. *Deceit, Desire, and the Novel: Self and Other in Literary Structure* [1961], tr. Yvonne Freccero (Baltimore: Johns Hopkins University Press, 1965).

14. *Mimesis: The Representation of Reality in Western Literature* (Princeton, N.J.: Princeton University Press, 1953), p. 357.

15. "Linguistic Perspectivism in the *Don Quijote* [1948]," in *Cervantes*, ed. Harold Bloom (New York: Chelsea House, 1987), p . 22.

16. "La historia del cautivo y el sentido del *Quijote*," *Iberoromania* (Tübingen), 18, (1983): 103.

17. Javier Herrero, "Sierra Morena as Labyrinth: From Wildness to Christian Knighthood," *Modern Language Studies* 17, no. 1 (1981): 55–67.

FURTHER READING

TEXTS

Miguel de Cervantes, ed. Roberto González Echevarría. CD Rom by Primary Source Media, Orange, Connecticut, 1998. Contains, keyed in, the first edition of every work by Cervantes, the best critical edition, and an English translation, in addition to the entire *Tesoro de la lengua castellana* (1611) by Sebastián de Covarrubias, introductions, bibliographies and more than one hundred illustrations for *Don Quixote* drawn from editions from the early seventeenth century to the present.

Don Quijote de la Mancha, ed. Francisco Rico et. al. Barcelona: Instituto Cervantes, 1998. Two volumes and CD Rom. Heavily annotated Spanish edition, with commentaries, bibliography, and ample contextual information.

BIOGRAPHIES

William Byron, *Cervantes: A Biography*. Garden City, New York: Doubleday, 1978.

Malveena McKendrick, *Cervantes*. Boston: Little and Brown, 1980.

Richard Predmore, *Cervantes*. New York: Dodd, Mead and Co., 1973.

COLLECTIONS OF ESSAYS

Juan Bautista Avalle-Arce and E. C. Riley, *Suma Cervantina*. (London: Tamesis, 1973.)

Miguel de Cervantes, ed. Harold Bloom (New York: Chelsea House, 1987.)

Cervantes Across the Centuries, ed. Angel Flores and M. J. Bernardete (New York: The Druden Press, 1947).

Cervantes: A Collection of Critical Essays, ed. Lowry Nelson, (Englewood Cliffs, N.J.: Prentice Hall, 1969).

BOOKS

John Jay Allen, *Don Quixote: Hero or Fool? A Study in Narrative Technique*. Gainesville: University Presses of Florida, 1969.

Frederick A. de Armas, *Cervantes, Raphael and the Classics*. Cambridge: Cambridge: Cambridge University Press, 1998.

Aubrey F. G. Bell, *Cervantes*. New York: Collier Books, 1961.

Edward Dudley, *The Endless Text. Don Quixote and the Hermeneutics of Romance*. Albany: State University of New York Press, 1997.

Manuel Durán, *Cervantes*. New York: Twayne, 1974.

E. C. Riley, *Cervantes's Theory of the Novel*. Oxford: Oxford University Press, 1962.

P. E. Russell, *Cervantes*. Oxford: Oxford University Press, 1985.

Ruth El Saffar, *Distance and Control in Don Quixote: A Study in Narrative Technique*. Chapel Hill: North Carolina Studies in the Romance Languages and Literatures, 1975.

JOURNALS

Anales cervantinos (Madrid)

Cervantes (Cervantes Society of America)

BIBLIOGRAPHY

Dana B. Drake and Dominick L. Finello, *An Analytical and Bibliographical Guide to Criticism on Don Quijote* (1790–1893). Newark, Delaware: Juan de la Cuesta, 1987.

Dana B. Drake, *Don Quixote in World Literature: A Selective, Annotated Bibliography*. New York: Garland, 1980.

TRANSLATING *DON QUIXOTE*

It seems to me that translating from one language into another, except from those queens of languages, Greek and Latin, is like viewing Flemish tapestries from the wrong side, when, although one can make out the figures, they are covered by threads that obscure them, and one cannot appreciate the smooth finish of the right side.

(*Don Quixote*, Part II, Chapter LXII)

Yet another *Quixote* translation? Isn't it an act of quixotry to write the thirteenth English version of the great Spanish novel?

Several of the earliest translations of Cervantes's masterpiece (those by Thomas Shelton, 1612 and 1620, John Philips, 1687, Peter Motteux, 1712, and Tobias Smollett, 1755[1]) are still of interest because they recapture much of the vivacity of Cervantes's writing. But they are inaccurate: their authors had only the most rudimentary dictionaries and other reference books, and their style of translation was much freer than is acceptable now. Motteux, for example, removes entire sentences or even paragraphs, and adds others of his own. He has a particular fondness for inserting his own jokes, which are more scurrilous than funny. He is an example of what we could call the cavalier tradition of *Quixote* translation.

Charles Jervas, whose translation was first published in 1742,[2] is important for initiating a different tradition. He follows the original text as closely as he can, and this is a welcome innovation. But his version lacks the energy and wit of Cervantes's prose, and turns *Don Quixote* into a solemn book. Jervas thus initiated the puritan tradition of *Quixote* translation, which was strengthened by the Romantic reading of the book, according to which Don Quixote is no figure of fun but a noble hero fighting for his lofty ideas in a hostile and uncomprehending materialistic world. Like so much Romantic thought, this view of the book has remained influential to the present day. It's a misreading because it underplays the fun; yet, as Anthony Close has shown,[3] it was what was needed to establish *Don Quixote* in modern times as a world classic.

Despite the Romantic revaluation, almost a century and a half passed without a new *Quixote* translation into the English language—and then three appeared in seven years in the 1880s. The puritan tradition, with its great strengths and its great weaknesses, is to be found at its best in these translations by Alexander J. Duffield (1881), John Ormsby (1885), and Henry Edward Watts (1888).[4] Each of these meticulous scholars devoted immense efforts to ensuring that every detail of this translation was as correct as he could make it, and Ormsby was particularly successful; but this was again at the expense of the humour. The twentieth-century English translations remain, on the whole, within the powerful puritan tradition.[5]

My intention in this latest addition to the large family of *Quixote* translations is to combine the virtues of the puritans and the cavaliers, and to avoid their vices.

But literary translation is difficult work, and translators often make it even more difficult by an understandable but mistaken attitude of reverence for the original artist, beside whom it's all too easy to feel like humble artisans who can only ever aspire to produce a pale shadow of the original or the reverse side of a tapestry: a self-fulfilling prediction. So whereas the artist dares to make the familiar unfamiliar and create fascinating strangeness, the timorous artisan-translator removes the strangeness and makes it all familiar again. Here is an example. Cervantes gives the alert reader the chance to catch a telling and amusing glimpse of the brash young graduate Sansón Carrasco's sharp-witted malice, and of Don Quixote's bumbling innocence, in a deft parodic reversal of a conventional formula for leave-taking at the end of Chapter VII of Part II: "Sansón embraced Don Quixote and begged to be sent news of his fortunes, both good and bad, to rejoice at the latter or grieve over the former, as the laws of friendship required. Don Quixote promised to do so." One of the twentieth-century translators shies away and writes: "Sampson embraced the knight and begged him to let him know what his luck might be, so that he might either rejoice or mourn, as the laws of friendship required." Another recent translator also refuses the fence and says: "Then Sampson gave our knight a farewell embrace, begging him, as the laws of friendship required, to send news of his luck, whether good or bad, so the one could be rejoiced in and the other be grieved over." The joke has disappeared.

Literary translators must conquer these fears. If, as we've been told over and over again, we're attempting the impossible, it follows that we aren't humble hacks but heroes. So I had to try to write as Cervantes did, and to be as creative and as playful with language as he was. By undertaking this translation I'd chosen to rub shoulders with the great man, so that was what I had to do, not grovel at his feet.

This is less immodest than it might seem. The original author's creative energies had to be spread over a vast area as he wrote his novel: the creation of characters, the construction of plots, the description of settings and the development of themes, as well as the writing of expressive sentences. But the translator can focus his creative energies on the sentences because the rest is, in a sense, given. He does have to use his imagination in these other areas because the novel must be for him not a string of words but a world in which he lives; yet this readerly re-creation is less of an effort than original creation. It is, however, an effort that translators must make. The translator is not a machine into which the original text is fed, to emerge in another language but in all other respects identical. This is Don Quixote's concept of translation, and it is why he holds translators in such low esteem: 'I should be prepared to bet a tidy sum that where it says in Italian *piace* you say "pleases," and where it says *più* you say "more," and that you translate *su* by "above," and *giù* by "beneath" ' (Part II, chapter VI). What I tried to do was different: to let the Spanish words construct in my mind's eye the world of the novel, and to live in that world; to see and hear Don Quixote and Sancho and to make them my best friends (some loss of sanity is a price that any artist has to pay); and only then to search for the English words with which to describe what I found in my imagination.

I therefore had to reject the notion, implicit in the puritan tradition, that the translator must never impose anything of his own on his translation, and must use a neutral, transparent language through which the first author's brilliance can shine. This idea of the invisible translator depends on the discredited metaphor that presents language as the clothes for the body of the thoughts and the feelings. Watts expresses it with eloquence in his introduction:

The translator should efface himself, for it is not he whom the public have come to see, but the author. To intrude one's own nineteenth-century personality into such a book as DON QUIXOTE, is an offence as gross against good manners as against art. A worse crime than this, however, is to deck the author as well as his book in your own colours − to put on him your livery − to make him speak after a set manner − to torture and twist his character, as well as his work, into conformity with some fantastic idea in the translator's brain.

But this self-obliteration, however admirable the modest sentiments underpinning it, is impossible. All that the principles outlined by Watts can achieve is a surreptitious imposition of their own dullness on the translator and the translation, which is the worst crime of all. The translator of the *Quixote* has no option but to deck the book in his own colours and make the author speak after a set manner, and it is better if he first decides what kind of *Quixote* he wants to write. In translating every sentence he must choose between a multiplicity of possible solutions, and his choices should be governed by his vision of the whole. This ideal of his doesn't need to be fantastic, and is more likely to be a reflection of current critical opinion, if the history of *Quixote* translation is anything to go by. My *Quixote* reflects a contemporary view that is a synthesis of the two opposing readings of the past, and that makes it possible, thanks above all to the work of Sir Peter Russell,[6] to see this novel as a funny book without this recognition interfering with its status as a world classic.

One instance of the unconscious imposition by translators of their own livery on Don Quixote is, as Russell has shown, the English translation of the most famous of the titles by which Don Quixote is known, "el Caballero de la Triste Figura." This title originates in Part I, Chapter XIX, as a jocular coinage by Sancho, after some shepherds have stoned his master and knocked many of his teeth out of his head. When Don Quixote asks his squire why he has given him this new title, the reply is: "I was just looking at you by the light of that poor bloke's torch and the truth is that at this moment you're the sorriest sight I've ever clapped eyes on. It must be because of being tired after your fight, or else losing all those teeth." But Don Quixote disregards Sancho's explanation and accepts his new title as an appropriately lofty expression of his noble suffering, a heroic epithet rooted in the long and glorious tradition of the knights errant of olden days. Translators have decided that this ambiguity is untranslatable and have suppressed the joke: the early translators give us Sancho's jocular meaning, "Ill-favoured Face" and "Rueful Countenance"; and later translators, under Romantic influence, give us Don Quixote's solemn, heroic meaning, "Sorrowful Figure," "Sad Countenance," doubly unfortunate because it puts literary language into the mouth of an illiterate rustic. Yet "The Knight of the Sad Countenance" is what has stuck in people's minds, a telling example of the power of translators: two badly translated words have perpetuated the false Romantic image of Don Quixote in the English-speaking world throughout the twentieth century.

To write my English *Quixote* I also decided that I must free myself from the insidious influence of the conventionally literary language of most nineteenth-century and twentieth-century English versions of the great novel, and use modern English, just as Cervantes had used the Spanish of his own day, not only in dialogues but in the narration. If my Quixote and my Sancho were to speak with living voices they had to use the varieties of contemporary spoken English that men of their age and background would use today, except where, for purposes of parody, Cervantes wrote a Spanish that was already archaic at the beginning of the seventeenth century.

It's absurd, for example, to have Sancho address his master as "Your Grace" or "Your Worship," literal renderings of the "vuestra merced" that he always says in the original. Sancho uses this form because it was inconceivable for a servant to address his master in any other way. In the Spanish of the early seventeenth century there is no hint of archaism about it. To make Sancho employ those archaic English forms is to ensure that he's born dead; the same is true, for the same reason, when Quixote is made to call Sancho "thou," as a translation of the "tú" that he uses except when he is angry with him and moves into the more distanced "vos." The only form of address available in modern English to translate "vuestra merced," "tú" and "vos" is "you," and the different degrees of respect and familiarity expressed by the three Spanish terms must be conveyed in other ways.

Yet Cervantes's text imposes limits on modernization. It's impossible to present some of its non-modern features from seeping through into any faithful translation. One example of this is its narrative redundancy.

All narration contains redundancy, as does all language, since neither the conditions of reception nor the human memory is perfect. *Don Quixote*'s redundancy is, however, like that of other narrative texts of its period, more extensive than in modern novels. In part it reflects the rhetorical practice of those times. It may also be that with an extra four hundred years of accumulated novel-reading experience we need less help to follow the narrative thread than Cervantes's first readers did. It's also true that Cervantes wrote his novel with a listening audience in mind, as the heading of Part II, Chapter LXVI shows: "Concerning what he who reads it will see, and what he who has it read to him will hear." There's more interference in oral reception than in visual reception, so the redundancy must be greater. Pleonasm is an insistent stylistic feature of this novel, most often taking the form of pairs of synonyms. Recapitulations are also more frequent and insistent in the *Quixote* than in modern narratives. Although the translator can do something to reduce the intrusiveness of the synonymous pairs and the recapitulations, he can't eliminate them and be true to Cervantes's text.

So I couldn't be consistent, and totally modernize the *Quixote*. Nor would it have been desirable to do so. Any translated literary work ought to retain marks of its origins, of its otherness in time and in space, of its historicity and its foreignness. Some of the unusualness to a modern ear of, for example, this novel's oaths and insults and its expressions of courtesy needs to be retained: it would be inappropriate to reduce the rich variety of religious and parental references in the characters' swearing to the unimaginative, repetitive scatology and sexuality of contemporary English expletives, or to turn graceful seventeenth-century courtesy into twentieth-century callowness. And many of *Don Quixote*'s themes and motifs are inescapably old-fashioned: there's no modernizing its concern with rank and with family status, or with feminine chastity.

Another non-modern, and non-English, feature of this novel is its many long and complex sentences. Now this is one aspect that it would be easy to modernize and anglicize, by dividing Cervantes's long sentences into the short ones preferred in contemporary English prose. This practice simplifies translation, and maybe makes for easier reading, but it destroys rhythms and emphases and relationships. It's wrong to take even those occasional long sentences in the *Quixote* with loose structures, and subdivide, tighten and correct them because they are not instances of stylistic carelessness but examples of Cervantes's masterly creation of realistic dialogue: his amused observation of the deleterious effects of natural verbosity, or of passionate interest in the subject under discussion, on the speaker's grammar. One of Cervantes's many innovations is his exploitation of linguistic register to give all characters, even those who make the briefest of appearances, their own distinctive voices.

Chopping up the other kind of long sentence, the one formed with meticulous precision, is equally mistaken. Such syntactical structures are also projections of mental structures, and in particular of *discreción*, central to the value-system underlying the *Quixote* and much seventeenth-century Spanish thought. *Discreción* is manifested in speech in the ability to express profound and complex concepts in an appropriately complicated yet lucid manner, conveying a sense of the multiple relationships between them. Dividing a far-ranging sentence of this kind into a succession of simple short sentences overlooks this important fact underpinning the formal elegance.

So the translation of *Don Quixote* does turn out to be logically impossible, after all. The translators must both make his text modern and keep it old, make it English and keep it Spanish. There can be no coherence or consistency. But this doesn't matter. All creative literature exists as a defiance of rational logic. There's nothing more illogical or irrational than a metaphor, saying that something is something else.

Translation is only impossible as any worthwhile enterprise is impossible: impossible to perform with the perfection that we desire. What translators must do, like modern knights errant, is to come as close as we can to the impossible goal.

—JOHN RUTHERFORD

NOTES

1. *The History of the Valorous and Wittie Knight-Errant, Don Quixote of the Mancha*, trans. Thomas Shelton (London, 1612) (Part I); *The History of Don Quichote* (London, 1620) (Parts I and II); *The History of the Most Renowned Don Quixote de la Mancha and his Trusty Squire Sancho Panza*, trans. John Philips (London, 1687); *The History of the Renown'd Don Quixote de la Mancha*, trans. Peter Motteux (London, 1712); *The History and Adventures of the Renowned Don Quixote*, trans. Tobias Smollet (London, 1755).

2. *The Life and Exploits of the Ingenious Gentleman Don Quixote de la Mancha*, trans. Charles Jervis (London, 1742).

3. In *The Romantic Approach to 'Don Quixote'* (Cambridge, 1978).

4. *The Ingenious Knight Don Quixote de la Mancha*, trans. Alexander J. Duffield (London, 1881); *The Ingenious Gentleman Don Quixote de la Mancha*, trans. John Ormsby (London, 1885); *The Ingenious Gentleman Don Quixote of La Mancha*, trans. Henry Edward Watts (London, 1888).

5. *The Ingenious Gentleman Don Quixote de la Mancha*, trans. Samuel Putnam (New York, 1949); *The Adventures of Don Quixote*, trans. J. M. Cohen (Harmondsworth, 1950); *Don Quixote of La Mancha*, trans. Walter Starkie (New York, 1964); *The History of that Ingenious Gentleman Don Quijote de la Mancha*, trans. Burton Raffel (New York, 1995).

6. P. E. Russell, 'Don Quixote as a Funny Book', *Modern Language Review* (1969); *Cervantes* (Oxford and New York, 1985).

Thanks, from the bottom of my heart, to TITA RUTHERFORD, to whom this translation is dedicated, for your wifely forbearance; to PETER RUSSELL, because you showed me, and so many others, how to enjoy *Don Quixote*; to PETER CARTER, because you showed me how to write a novel; a RAMÓN, MARUJA E PILAR CANCIO, pola sombra da vosa figueira e mais pola luz da vosa amizade; to LIZ KENDALL, DAVID LONGRIGG, IAN MICHAEL, VÍCTOR RODRÍGUEZ GESTO, LAURA RUTHERFORD, MARUXA RUTHERFORD, ROSA RUTHERFORD, XOANA RUTHERFORD, JANETTE SWAIN, and RON TRUMAN, for all your kind help; to the legion of *Don Quixote* scholars, who made it easy to write the explanatory notes; to my fellow translators JOHN ORMSBY and HENRY WATTS, for many useful suggestions; to all the friends and colleagues who unconsciously contributed so much to the development of the characters' voices; to the UNIVERSITIES OF A CORUÑA, CORK, and OXFORD, and in particular to ANTONIO RAÚL DE TORO SANTOS, ADOLFO LUIS SOTO VÁZQUEZ, TERENCE O'REILLY, DAVID MACKENZIE, IAN MICHAEL, and COLIN THOMPSON, for giving me audiences on which to try out my ideas; to the UNIVERSITY OF OXFORD and THE QUEEN'S COLLEGE, OXFORD, for allowing me the sabbatical leave without which I could not have completed the translation; to PAUL KEEGAN and PENGUIN BOOKS, for giving me the enormous privilege of being a translator of *Don Quixote*; and to DON QUIXOTE and SANCHO PANZA, whose ebullient company kept my spirits high throughout this long, long pilgrimage.

JOHN RUTHERFORD
Ribadeo (Galicia) and Oxford (England)
March 1999

CHRONOLOGY

His brother Rodrigo is ransomed

Birth of Flemish painter Rubens

1578 Third attempted escape

1579 Fourth attempted escape

First permanent theatre in Madrid, the Corral de la Cruz, opens

1580 Ransomed for 500 ducats paid by his family and by Trinitarian monks, returns to Madrid

Montaigne, *Essays* published

1581 Travels with Philip II's entourage to Portugal, newly annexed by Spain

1582 Death of St Teresa of Avila

1583 Sir Walter Raleigh's expedition to Virginia

1584 Marries Catalina de Salazar in Esquivias, La Mancha

Illegitimate daughter, Isabel de Saavedra, born

1585 *La Galatea*, a pastoral romance, published

Cervantes sells two plays (both now lost)

Death of his father

1587 Appointed king's purchasing agent in Andalusia, responsible for provisioning the Armada against England

1588 El Greco paints the *Burial of the Count of Orgaz*

Defeat of Spanish Armada

1590 Unsuccessfully petitions Council of the Indies for post in the West Indies

Adds Saavedra to surname

1592 Charged with fraud, he is briefly jailed, but later cleared

Signs contract to write six plays at fifty ducats apiece

1593 Death of his mother

1594 Briefly in Madrid, then returns to Andalusia as a tax collector

1595 Wins first prize in a poetry contest in Zaragoza

1597–8 Spends several months in prison in Seville, on account of discrepancies in his tax accounts; likely that he conceives *Don Quixote* during imprisonment

1598 Death of Philip II and accession of Philip III

1599 Birth of painter Velázquez

The Globe playhouse opens in London

1600 Birth of dramatist Calderón de la Barca

1603   Death of Elizabeth I

1604   Cervantes and his family move to Valladolid, briefly the capital of Spain

         Finishes writing *Don Quixote* (Part I)

1605   *Don Quixote* (Part I) published

1606   Cervantes and family return to Madrid

1612   Thomas Shelton publishes the first English translation of *Don Quixote* in London

1613   *The Exemplary Novels*, a collection of short stories, published

1614   *The Journey to Parnassus*, a long allegorical poem, published

         The 'false' *Don Quixote II* appears, under the name of Alonso Fernández de Avellaneda

         The first French translation or *Don Quixote*, by Césare Oudin, published in Paris

1615   Cervantes published *Don Quixote II* and *Eight Plays and Eight Interludes*

1616   Finishes writing novel *The Trials of Persiles and Sigismunda*

         Death of Cervantes in Madrid

         Death of Shakespeare

1617   *The Trials of Persiles and Sigismunda* published posthumously

A NOTE ON THE TEXT

This translation follows the text of the first editions (Juan de la Cuesta, Madrid, 1604–5 and 1615), as presented in the useful modern edition by Luis Andrés Murillo (Clásicos Castalia: Madrid, 1978)—except in the treatment of the narrations of the loss and of the recovery of Sancho's donkey, in Part I. These passages were omitted from the first edition, through the oversight of either Cervantes or the printers, so that the reader suddenly finds Sancho without his donkey, and later in possession of it again, without any explanations, as Cervantes makes both Sansón Carrasco and Cide Hamete Benengeli remark in Part II (Chapters III and XXVII). In Cuesta's second edition of Part I (1605), the loss and the recovery are inserted, in Chapters XXIII and XXX respectively, but the former is the wrong place because Sancho continues in possession of his donkey for another two chapters. So following Juan Eugenio Hartzenbusch's edition (Rivadeneyra: Argamasilla de Alba, 1863), I have, like several modern editors, inserted the loss where it belongs, in Chapter XXV.

There are many other less important inconsistencies in the early editions. Some chapter headings, for example, don't belong to the chapters that they precede. I have left all these, without comment, for readers to spot and ponder on for themselves. Some critics think that they could be one of the games that Cervantes enjoys playing with his readers.

The original, in common with most books of the period, has hardly any paragraphing within chapters, so this has been my own work, often coinciding with Murillo's decisions.

The 1604–5 *Don Quixote* is divided into four parts, but the 1615 text is presented as Part II. When I refer to Part II, I mean the 1615 text.

This translation includes everything that appears in the first editions and that was written by Cervantes, except the formal dedications: the first one seems not to have been his work, and the second is purely conventional.

Just before going to press, the critical edition directed by Francisco Rico (Barcelona: Instituto Cervantes, Crítica, 1998) became available, and its informative footnotes were used to make some important corrections.

The Ingenious Hidalgo

DON QUIXOTE

de la Mancha

CONTENTS

PART I 11

CONTENTS

CONTENTS

CONTENTS

CONTENTS

CONTENTS

CONTENTS

PART I

PROLOGUE

Idle reader: I don't have to swear any oaths to persuade you that I should like this book, since it is the son of my brain, to be the most beautiful, elegant and intelligent book imaginable. But I couldn't go against the order of nature, according to which like gives birth to like. And to what can my barren and ill-cultivated mind give birth except the history of a dry, shrivelled child, whimsical and full of extravagant fancies that nobody else has ever imagined – a child born, after all, in prison, where every discomfort has its seat and every dismal sound its habitation? Tranquillity, peaceful surroundings, the pleasures of the countryside, the serenity of the skies, the murmuring of the springs and the quietude of the spirit – these are the things that encourage even the most barren muses to become fertile and bring forth a progeny to fill the world with wonder and delight.

It can happen that a man has an ugly, charmless son, and his love blindfolds him to prevent him from seeing the child's defects: on the contrary, he regards them as gifts and graces, and describes them to his friends as examples of wit and cleverness. But although I seem like Don Quixote's father, I am his stepfather, and I don't want to drift with the current of custom, or beg you almost with tears in my eyes, as others do, dearest reader, to forgive or excuse the defects that you see in this my son; and you are neither his relative nor his friend, you have your own soul in your own body, and your own free will like anybody else, and you are sitting in your own home, where you are the lord and master just as much as the king is of his taxes, and you know that common saying, 'Under my cloak a fig for the king.' All of which exempts and frees you from every respect and obligation, and so you can say whatever you like about this history, without any fear of being attacked for a hostile judgement or rewarded for a favourable one.

I'd have liked to give it to you plain and naked, undecorated by any prologue or the endless succession of sonnets, epigrams and eulogies that are usually put at the beginnings of books. Because I can tell you that, although it was quite an effort to write the book, producing this preface that you're now reading was far worse. Many times I picked up my pen to write it, and as many times I put it down again because I didn't know what to say; and once when I was in this quandary, with the paper in front of me, the pen behind my ear, my elbow on the desk and my cheek in my hand, wondering what I could write, a friend of mine burst in, a lively and clever man who, on seeing me so thoughtful, asked me the reason, and I didn't keep anything from him but said that I was thinking about the prologue that I had to write for the history of Don Quixote, and that it had reduced me to such a state that I didn't want to write it at all, still less publish the exploits of this noble knight.

'Because how do you expect me not to be worried about the opinion of that ancient legislator called the general public when he sees that after all this time sleeping in the silence of oblivion, and burdened by the years as I am, I'm coming out with a book as dry as esparto grass, devoid of inventiveness, feeble in style, poor in ideas and lacking all erudition and instruction, without any marginalia or endnotes, unlike other books I see that, even though they are fictional and not about religious subjects, are so crammed with maxims from Aristotle, Plato and the whole herd of philosophers that they amaze their readers, who consider the authors to be well-read, erudite and eloquent men? And when they quote the Holy Scriptures! Anyone would take them for no less than so many St Thomases[1] and other doctors of the Church; and here they maintain such an ingenious decorum that having depicted a dissolute lover on one line they provide on the next a little Christian sermon, a pleasure and a treat to hear or read. There won't be any of this in my book, because I haven't anything to put in the margins or any notes for the end, still less do I know what authors I have followed in my text so as to list them at the beginning, as others do, in alphabetical order beginning with Aristotle and finishing with Xenophon and Zoilus or Zeuxis,[2] even though one was a slanderer and the other a painter. My book will also lack sonnets at the beginning, or at least sonnets whose authors are dukes, marquises, counts, bishops, ladies or famous poets; though if I asked two or three tradesmen friends of mine, I'm sure they'd let me have some, every bit as good as those written by the best-known poets in this Spain of ours. In short, my dear friend,' I continued, 'I have decided that Don Quixote shall remain buried in his archives in La Mancha until heaven provides someone to adorn him with all these attributes that he lacks – I'm not up to it, because of my inadequacy and my scanty learning, and because I'm naturally lazy and disinclined to go hunting for authors to say for me what I know how to say without them. This is why I was so perplexed and distraught when you arrived, my friend: there is justification enough for it in what I've just told you.'

When he heard this my friend slapped his forehead, burst out laughing, and said:

'Good God, my dear fellow, you've just corrected a misconception I've been labouring under all this time I've known you, considering you to be sensible and judicious in everything you do. But now I can see you're as far from being that as the heavens are from the earth. How can matters that are so trivial and easy to remedy have the power to engross and perplex a mind as mature as yours, accustomed as it is to demolishing far greater difficulties? I assure you this isn't caused by any lack of ability on your part, but by an excess of mental indolence. Do you want to find out whether I'm telling you the truth? Well, pay attention, and you'll see how in the twinkling of an eye I destroy all your problems and remedy all those deficiencies that, you say, are perplexing you and discouraging you from publishing the history of your famous Don Quixote, the light and mirror of all knight-errantry.'

'Tell me,' I replied once I'd heard him out, 'how do you intend to fill the vacuum of my anxiety and turn the chaos of my confusion into clarity?'

To which he replied:

'Your first problem, about the sonnets, epigrams and eulogies written by important and titled people that you lack for the beginning of the book, can be remedied if you take the trouble to write them yourself and then christen them and give them whatever names you like, fathering them on Prester John of the Indies, or the Emperor of Trebizond,[3] of both of whom I know there's evidence that they were famous poets; and even supposing that they weren't, and some pedants and academics start their backbiting and their nit-picking about whether this is true or not, you mustn't care a hoot about that, because even if they do find out that you were telling lies they aren't going to cut off the hand with which you wrote them down. As for references in the margins to the books and authors from whom you take the sayings and maxims that you include in your history, all you have to do is to stick in a few relevant bits of Latin that you know by heart, or at least that you can look up without too much trouble, such as, when you're writing about freedom and captivity:

Non bene pro toto libertas venditur auro.[4]

And then, in the margin, you mention Horace or whoever it was that said it. If you're dealing with the power of death, you can trot out:

Pallida mors aequo pulsat pede pauperum tabernas,
Regumque turres.[5]

If you're talking about the friendship and love that God tells us to feel for our enemies, go straight for Holy Scripture, which you can do if you take just a little care, and quote the words of God himself, no less: Ego autem dico vobis: diligite inimicos vestros.[6] If you're dealing with evil thoughts, go for the Gospel: De corde exeunt cogitationes malae.[7] If your subject is the fickleness of friends, there's always Cato, ready with his distich:

Donec eris felix, multos numerabis amicos,
Tempora si fuerint nubila, solus eris.[8]

And with these scraps of Latin and other similar ones you'll be taken for a scholar, at least; and that brings no little honour and profit nowadays.

'As for providing endnotes, you can easily do it like this: if you include a giant in your book, make him Goliath, and this alone, which will hardly be any trouble for you, will give you a splendid endnote, because you will be able to say: "The giant Golias, or Goliath, was a Philistine whom the shepherd David slew with a stone from his sling, in the vale of the terebinth, according to what is narrated in the Book of Kings," in the chapter where you'll find it written.[9] After that, to show that you're erudite in the humanities and a cosmographer, you should contrive to name the River Tagus in your history, and there you have another fine endnote: "The River Tagus was so called by a Spanish king; it has its source in such-and-such a place, and it flows into the Atlantic Ocean, kissing the walls of the famous city of Lisbon, and it is said to have sand of gold, etc." If you deal with robbers, I'll tell you the story of Cacus,[10] which I know by heart; if it's whores, go to the Bishop of Mondoñedo and he'll lend you Lamia, Laida and Flora,[11] and this particular endnote will bring you great credit; if it's cruel women, Ovid will let you have Medea; if it's sorceresses and witches, Homer has Calypso and Virgil has Circe;[12] if it's valiant captains, Julius Caesar will lend you himself in his *Commentaries*, and Plutarch will give you a thousand Alexanders.[13] If love is your subject, with the slightest smattering of Italian you will find Leone Ebreo gives you full measure.[14] And if you don't want to go wandering in foreign parts, here at home you have Fonseca, *On the Love of God*,[15] containing everything that you and the cleverest of writers could ever want to find on the subject. In short, all you have to do is contrive to mention these names or touch on these stories in your own story, and leave it to me to provide the endnotes and marginalia; I swear by all that's holy to fill your margins, and use up reams and reams at the end of your book.

'Let us now consider the list of authors cited, which other books include and yours lacks. The remedy for this is simplicity itself, because all you have to do is look for a book listing them all from A to Z, as you say, then copy this list into your own book; and even if your deception is plain to see, this won't matter in the slightest, because you hardly need to use the authors anyway, and there could always be someone stupid enough to believe that you have used them all in this simple, straightforward story of yours. Even if it serves no other purpose, your long list will at least lend your book an instant air of authority. Besides, people aren't going to take the trouble to check whether you follow your authors or not, because they haven't anything to gain from doing so.

'What's more, unless I'm much mistaken, this book of yours doesn't need any of those features that you say it lacks, because from beginning to end it is an invective against books of chivalry – which Aristotle never dreamed of, St Basil never mentioned and Cicero[16] never came across; nor do the niceties of truth or the observations of astrology fall within the scope of its fabulous extravagances; nor are geometrical measurements of any relevance to it, or the confutation of arguments employed in rhetoric; nor is there any need for it to preach at anybody, mixing the human with the divine, a motley in which no Christian understanding should be dressed. All that has to be done is to make the best use of imitation in what one writes; and the more perfect the imitation the better the writing. And since this work of yours is only concerned to destroy the authority and influence that books of chivalry enjoy in the world and among the general public, there isn't any need to go begging maxims from philosophers, counsel from Holy Scripture, fables from poets, clauses from rhetoricians or miracles from saints, but rather to attempt, using expressive, decorous and well-ordered words in a straightforward way, to write sentences that are both harmonious and witty, depicting what is in your mind to the very best of your ability, setting out your ideas without complicating or obscuring them. You should also try to ensure that the melancholy man is moved to laughter when he reads your history, the jovial man laughs even more, the simpleton is not discouraged, the judicious marvel at its inventiveness, the serious-minded do not scorn it nor the wise fail to praise it. In short, always have as your aim the demolition of the ill-founded fabric of these books of chivalry, despised by so many and praised by many more; and if this is what you achieve, it will be no mean achievement.'

I listened in profound silence to what my friend said, and his words so stamped themselves on my mind that I accepted them without any argument and decided to use them for this prologue, in which, gentle reader, you will discover my friend's intelligence, my good fortune in finding such a counsellor at a time of such need and your relief on finding that there will be no deviousness or circumlocution in this history of the famous Don Quixote de la Mancha, reputed among all the inhabitants of the Plain of Montiel[17] to have been the chastest lover and the bravest knight ever seen in those parts for many a long year. I have no desire to extol the service I am rendering you in introducing you to such a noble and honourable knight; but I do want your thanks for making you acquainted with the famous Sancho Panza, his squire, in whom, I believe, I give you a compendium of all the squirely fun scattered throughout the whole troop of vain books of chivalry. And so may God give you health and not forget me. Farewell.

TO THE BOOK OF
DON QUIXOTE DE LA MANCHA

Urganda the Unknowable[18]

If you, O book, are duly hee—
To seek the company of pu—,
You won't be told by some prize du—
That you are but a fumbling gree—.
But if you aren't on pins and nee—
To go off into fools' posse—,
You'll no doubt see, when least expe—,
It is the wrong horse that they're ba—,
Although they will all be so fra—
To show that they're extremely cle—.

And since, of course, it's common kno—
That he who finds a tree that's lea—
Is well protected and well shie—,
So your good fortune kindly o—
In Béjar[19] a stout oak that's ro—,
And that gives princes as its a—,
And on which dukes were procrea—;
And one's a modern Alexa—,
So go henceforth to seek his sha—,
For Fortune always aids the bra—.

You will recount the sad adve—
Of a hidalgo, good and no—,
Who read during his idle mo—
And ended up mad and deme—.
Ladies and arms, loves and knights e—[20]
So made him swell with fond emo—
That, like some Orlando Furio—,
But tempered by his loving fo—,
By force of arms he went and co—
Fair Dulcinea del Tobo—.

Don't print recondite illustra—
On the front page, on your fine scu—:[21]
Low cards can often win the ru—
When court cards are what all are pla—.
Be humble in your dedica—,
And you won't find some joker hoo—,
'Look, here is Álvaro de Lu—,
Look, here is Hannibal of Ca—,
Look, here is the new French King Fra—,
Complaining that Dame Fortune's stu—.'[22]

Since it was not the will of Hea—
That you should have the erudi—
Of that wise negro Juan Lati—,[23]
You must avoid Latin expre—.
So don't you try to be too cle—
Or make out that you're some great thi—,
Because, with a dismissive gri—
From ear to ear, the knowing pe—
Who sees through all your bluff will mu—,
'And just who do you think you're tri—?'

Don't go for needless complica—,
Or poke your nose in lives of o—,
Because when something's off the su—
What's wisest is to be eva—.
Those who indulge in random ja—
Will get a dose of their own me—,
But you must devote all your e—
To conquering renown and ho—,
For he who publishes his no—
Will leave it in this world for e—.

You must remember that it's cra—,
If a greenhouse is your dwe—,
To go and pick up stones and pe—
And throw them at your next-door nei—.
The wise man should be most painsta—
And should proceed very discree—

In all the works that he relea—
For he whose fictional crea—
Are for young ladies' entertai—
Writes without any rhyme or rea—

Amadis of Gaul, to Don Quixote de la Mancha

SONNET

O you who lived the life of deep distress
I lived, far from my love and in disgrace,
Reduced to penitence from happiness,
Upon the Peña Pobre's rugged face;[24]
O you, whose drink flowed freely from within
The salty reservoir behind your eyes,
And who scorned silver, pewter, plate and tin,
To eat on earth the food that earth supplies:
Live on, secure that while the ages last
– At least, so long as that brave charioteer
Apollo drives his steeds in the fourth sphere[25] –
Your clear renown for courage must stand fast.
Your land in all lands will as first be known,
Your learned author stand unique, alone.

Sir Belianis of Greece,[26] to Don Quixote de la Mancha

SONNET

I cut and thrust and hacked and meddled more
Than all of chivalry's most valiant knights,
Was brave and proud and skilled in arts of war,
And set a hundred thousand wrongs to rights.
I left my deeds to perpetuity;
In courtly games of love I was no fool;
The hugest giant was a dwarf for me;
And I obeyed the duel's every rule.
I made Dame Fortune grovel at my feet,

And my control, by calculating skill,
Of Opportunity was so complete
I dragged her by the forelock at my will.
But, though my luck soared up to highest space,
I'd love, O Quixote, to be in your place.

The Lady Oriana,[27] to Dulcinea del Toboso

SONNET

O Dulcinea, I so wish I could
Transport, and thereby banish all this care,
My Miraflores to the neighbourhood
Of El Toboso, moving London there;
    And then adorn my body and my soul
With what you wear, and what you long for, too;
And watch the famous knight whose heart you stole
Win some stupendous battle, thanks to you.
    And then if I could chastely take my flight
From my Sir Amadis, as you have done
From your Don Quixote, courteous and polite,
And so I'd envied be, and envy none:
Be sad no more – be happy without measure:
Not pay the bill, but still have all the pleasure.

Gandalín, Amadis of Gaul's Squire, to Sancho Panza, Don Quixote's Squire

SONNET

Hail, famous hero! It was Fortune's will
That you should be a squire; so she contrived
To shape her plans with sympathetic skill,
And you, triumphant and unharmed, survived.
    No longer does the errant enterprise
Regard with scorn the sickle and the spade;
To haughty knights who'd trample on the skies

Your unassuming modesty's put paid.
  I envy you your donkey and your name;
I envy you your food and wine galore
In saddle-bags that pregnantly proclaim
Your providence, O Panza. Hail once more!
Our Spanish Ovid's homage is unique:
To kiss your hand and let you cuff his cheek.

From the Witty Poet Streakybacon to Sancho Panza and Rocinante

  I am the squire called Sancho Pa—;
I took French leave, and scarpered pre—
To live a life of indepe—
Far from Don Quixote de la Ma—;
For Villadiego, though so gua—,
Would summarize all his state rea—
In the convenience of retrea—,
As is made clear in *Celesti*—,
A book than which none is divi—,[28]
Though of the human so revea—.

TO ROCINANTE

  I'm Rocinante, the world-fa—,
Great grandson of the great Babie—,[29]
Who, for my sins of macile—,
Into Don Quixote's power was ta—.
When last wins, I win all the ra—;
But when it mattered, I moved sma—:
I never missed my feed of ba—,
For this I learned from Lazari—
When all that wine the lad was stea—
And gave the straw to his blind ma—.[30]

Orlando Furioso to Don Quixote de la Mancha

SONNET

Among a thousand Peers you are our peer;
Though you are not a Peer, peer have you none,
Nor is there room for one while you are near,
Unvanquished victor, great unconquered one!
    I, Quixote, am Orlando, one who, harried
By sweet Angelica,[31] roamed far seas, where
To Fame's high altars as a prize I carried
What valour dull Forgetfulness could spare.
    I cannot be your equal. This respect
Is owed to both your exploits and your name,
Although, like mine, your sanity's suspect.
But you will be my equal if you tame
The haughty Moor and our fierce Scythian foe:[32]
Love binds us in a fellowship of woe.

The Knight of Phoebus[33] to Don Quixote de la Mancha

SONNET

My sword is not to be compared with yours,
Phoebus of Spain, strange courtier in disguise,
Nor with your glorious arm my arm that pours
Forth rays in which the day is born and dies.
    I scorned all empire, and I scorned the throne
That ruddy Orient offered me in vain,
To see once more the fair face of my own
Most lovely dawn, my dearest Claridiane.
    I loved her in a rare and wondrous way,
And, absent and beset by tribulation,
I tamed hell's fiends, who cringed under my sway.
Through Dulcinea, though, your reputation,
Great Quixote, is eternally secure,
And she, through you, is famous, wise and pure.

Solisdán[34] to Don Quixote de la Mancha

SONNET

Although absurdities have always played
Their havoc on your poor disordered mind,
There's nobody, Don Quixote, who'll upbraid
You, sir, for being abject or unkind.

      Your deeds themselves will be your judge and jury:
You righted wrongs, you freed the galley slaves
And in a thousand beatings felt the fury
Of many a wretched crew of arrant knaves.

      And if your Dulcinea were to slight
You or to play you false in some base way
Or were not sympathetic to your plight,

Your comfort in your woe would be to say
That Sancho had no pander's arts to move her:
A fool he, callous she – and you no lover.

Dialogue between Babieca and Rocinante

SONNET

B.   Why, Rocinante, are you thin and worn?
R. Because I'm overworked and underfed.
B. Are you not given any hay or corn?
R. No. Quixote wants to starve me till I'm dead.
B.   Your manners fill me, sir, with equine shame:
    It's ass's work to strike at one's sustainer.
R. Whoever's born an ass will die the same:
    See him, an ass in love. What could be plainer?
B.   It's folly, then, to love?   *R.* It's none too bright.
B. You're metaphysical!   *R.* My belly's rumbling.
B. Complain about the squire!   *R.* Why, in this plight
    Of mine, waste time on moans and grumbling
    When both my master and that squire of his
    Are hacks as much as Rocinante is?

CHAPTER I

Concerning the famous hidalgo Don Quixote de la
Mancha's position, character and way of life

In a village in La Mancha, the name of which I cannot quite recall, there lived not long ago one of those country gentlemen or hidalgos who keep a lance in a rack, an ancient leather shield, a scrawny hack and a greyhound for coursing. A midday stew with rather more shin of beef than leg of lamb, the leftovers for supper most nights, lardy eggs on Saturdays, lentil broth on Fridays and an occasional pigeon as a Sunday treat ate up three-quarters of his income. The rest went on a cape of black broadcloth, with breeches of velvet and slippers to match for holy days, and on weekdays he walked proudly in the finest homespun. He maintained a housekeeper the wrong side of forty, a niece the right side of twenty and a jack of all trades who was as good at saddling the nag as at plying the pruning shears. Our hidalgo himself was nearly fifty; he had a robust constitution, dried-up flesh and a withered face, and he was an early riser and a keen huntsman. His surname's said to have been Quixada, or Quesada (as if he were a jawbone, or a cheesecake): concerning this detail there's some discrepancy among the authors who have written on the subject, although a credible conjecture does suggest he might have been a plaintive Quexana. But this doesn't matter much, as far as our story's concerned, provided that the narrator doesn't stray one inch from the truth.

Now you must understand that during his idle moments (which accounted for most of the year) this hidalgo took to reading books of chivalry with such relish and enthusiasm that he almost forgot about his hunting and even running his property, and his foolish curiosity reached such extremes that he sold acres of arable land to buy these books of chivalry, and took home as many of them as he could find;[1] he liked none of them so much as those by the famous Feliciano de Silva,[2] because the brilliance of the prose and all that intricate language seemed a treasure to him, never more so than when he was reading those amorous compliments and challenges delivered by letter, in which he often found: 'The reason for the unreason to which my reason is subjected, so weakens my reason that I have reason to complain of your beauty.' And also when he read: '. . . the lofty heavens which with their stars divinely fortify you in your divinity, and make you meritorious of the merits merited by your greatness.' Such subtleties used to drive the poor gentleman to distraction, and he would rack his brains trying to understand it all and unravel its meaning, something that Aristotle himself wouldn't have been capable of doing even if he'd come back to life for this purpose alone. He wasn't very happy about the wounds that Sir Belianis kept on inflicting and receiving, because he imagined that, however skilful the doctors who treated him, his face and body must have been covered with gashes and scars. But, in spite of all that, he commended the author for ending his book with that promise of endless adventure, and often felt the urge to take up his quill and bring the story to a proper conclusion, as is promised there; and no doubt he'd have done so, and with success too, if other more important and insistent preoccupations hadn't prevented him. He had frequent arguments with the village priest (a learned man – a Sigüenza graduate no less) about which had been the better knight errant, Palmerin of England[3] or Amadis of Gaul; but Master Nicolás, the village barber, argued that neither of them could hold a candle to the Knight of Phoebus, and that if anyone at all could be compared to him it was Don Galaor, Amadis of Gaul's brother, because there was no emergency he couldn't cope with: he wasn't one of your pernickety knights, nor was he such a blubberer as his brother, and he was every bit his equal as far as courage was concerned.

In short, our hidalgo was soon so absorbed in these books that his nights were spent reading from dusk till dawn, and his days from dawn till dusk, until the lack of sleep and the excess of reading withered his brain, and he went mad. Everything he read in his books took possession of his imagination: enchantments, fights, battles, challenges, wounds, sweet nothings, love affairs, storms and impossible absurdities. The idea that this whole fabric of famous fabrications was real so established itself in his mind that no history in the world was truer for him. He would declare that El Cid, Ruy Díaz, had been an excellent knight, but that he couldn't be compared to the Knight of the Burning Sword,[4] who with just one back-stroke had split two fierce and enormous giants clean down the middle. He felt happier about Bernardo del Carpio, because he'd slain Roland the Enchanted at Roncesvalles, by the same method used by Hercules when he suffocated Antaeus, the son of Earth – with a bear-hug.[5] He was full of praise for the giant Morgante because, despite belonging to a proud and insolent breed, he alone was affable and well-mannered.[6] But his greatest favourite was Reynald of Montalban,[7] most of all when he saw him sallying forth from his castle and plundering all those he met, and when in foreign parts he stole that image of Muhammad made of solid gold, as his history records. He'd have given his housekeeper, and even his niece into the bargain, to trample the traitor Ganelon in the dust.[8]

And so, by now quite insane, he conceived the strangest notion that ever took shape in a madman's head, considering it desirable and necessary, both for the increase of his honour and for the common good, to become a knight errant, and to travel about the world with his armour and his arms and his horse in search of adventures, and to practise all those activities that he knew from his books were practised by knights errant, redressing all kinds of grievances, and exposing himself to perils and dangers that he would overcome and thus gain eternal fame and renown. The poor man could already see himself being crowned Emperor of Trebizond, at the very least, through the might of his arm; and so, possessed by these delightful thoughts and carried away by the strange pleasure that he derived from them, he hastened to put into practice what he so desired.

His first step was to clean a suit of armour that had belonged to his forefathers and that, covered in rust and mould, had been standing forgotten in a corner for centuries. He scoured and mended it as best he could; yet he realized that it had one important defect, which was that the headpiece was not a complete helmet but just a simple steel cap; he was ingenious enough, however, to overcome this problem, constructing out of cardboard something resembling a visor and face-guard which, once inserted into the steel cap, gave it the appearance of a full helmet. It's true that, to test its strength and find out whether it could safely be exposed to attack, he drew his sword and dealt it two blows, with the first of which he destroyed in a second what it had taken him a week to create. He couldn't help being concerned about the ease with which he'd shattered it, and to guard against this danger he reconstructed it, fixing some iron bars on the inside, which reassured him about its strength; and, preferring not to carry out any further tests, he deemed and pronounced it a most excellent visored helmet.

Then he went to visit his nag, and although it had more corns than a barleyfield and more wrong with it than Gonella's horse, which *tantum pellis et ossa fuit*,[9] it seemed to him that neither Alexander's Bucephalus nor the Cid's Babieca was its equal. He spent four days considering what name to give the nag; for (he told himself) it wasn't fitting that the horse of such a famous knight errant, and such a fine horse in its own right, too, shouldn't have some name of eminence; and so he tried to find one that would express both what it had been before it became a knight's horse and what it was now, for it was appropriate that, since its master had changed his rank, it too should change its name, and acquire a famous and much-trumpeted one, as suited the new order and new way of life he professed. And so, after a long succession of names that he invented, eliminated and struck out, added, deleted and remade in his mind and in his imagination, he finally decided to call it *Rocinante*, that is, *Hackafore*, a name which, in his opinion, was lofty and sonorous and expressed what the creature had been when it was a humble hack, before it became what it was now – the first and foremost of all the hacks in the world.

Having given his horse a name, and one so much to his liking, he decided to give himself a name as well, and this problem kept him busy for another eight days, at the end of which he decided to call himself *Don Quixote*, that is, *Sir Thighpiece*, from which, as has already been observed, the authors of this most true history concluded that his surname must have been Quixada, and not Quesada as others had affirmed. Yet remembering that brave Amadis hadn't been content to call himself Amadis alone, but had added the name of his kingdom and homeland, to make it famous, and had styled himself Amadis of Gaul, so Don Quixote, as a worthy knight, decided to add his own country to his name and call himself *Don Quixote de la Mancha*, by doing which, in his opinion, he declared in a most vivid manner both his lineage and his homeland, and honoured the latter by taking it as his surname.

Having, then, cleaned his armour, turned his steel cap into a visored helmet, baptized his nag and confirmed himself, he realized that the only remaining task was to find a lady of whom he could be enamoured; for a knight errant without a lady-love is a tree without leaves or fruit, a body without a soul. He said to himself:

'If, for my wicked sins or my good fortune, I encounter some giant, as knights errant usually do, and I dash him down in single combat, or cleave him asunder, or, in short, defeat and vanquish him, will it not be proper to have someone to whom I can send him as a tribute, so that he can come before my sweet lady and fall to his knees and say in humble tones of submission: "I, my lady, am the giant Caraculiambro,[10] the Lord of the Isle of Malindrania, vanquished in single combat by the never sufficiently praised knight Don Quixote de la Mancha, who has commanded me to present myself before Your Highness so that Your Highness may dispose of me as you will"?'

Oh my, how our worthy knight rejoiced once he'd spoken these words – even more, once he'd found someone he could call his lady! The fact was – or so it is generally believed – that in a nearby village there lived a good-looking peasant girl, with whom he'd once been in love (although it appears that she was never aware of this love, about which he never told her). She was called Aldonza Lorenzo, and this was the woman upon whom it seemed appropriate to confer the title of the lady of his thoughts; and seeking a name with some affinity with his own, which would also suggest the name of a princess and a fine lady, he decided to call her *Dulcinea del Toboso*, because she was a native of El Toboso: a name that, in his opinion, was musical and magical and meaningful, like all the other names he'd bestowed upon himself and his possessions.

CHAPTER II

Concerning the ingenious Don Quixote's first sally

Once he'd made these preparations he decided not to wait any longer before putting his plans into action, encouraged by the need that he believed his delay was creating in the world: so great was his determination to redress grievances, right wrongs, correct injustices, rectify abuses and fulfil obligations. And so, without telling anyone about his plans or being seen by anyone, one morning, before dawn because it was going to be one of those sweltering July days, he donned his armour, mounted Rocinante, with his ill-devised visor in place, took up his leather shield, seized his lance and rode out into the fields through the side-door in a yard wall, in raptures of joy on seeing how easy it had been to embark upon his noble enterprise. But no sooner was he outside the door than he was assailed by a terrible thought, which almost made him abandon his undertaking: he remembered that he hadn't been knighted and by the laws of chivalry shouldn't and indeed couldn't take up arms against any knight; and that even if he had been knighted, he would, as a novice, have been obliged to bear white arms, that is to say a shield without any insignia on it, until he'd won them by his own prowess. These thoughts made him waver in his plans; but, since his madness prevailed over all other considerations, he decided to have himself knighted by the first person he chanced upon, in imitation of many others who'd done the same, as he'd read in the books that had reduced him to this state. As for the white arms, he resolved to give his lance and his armour such a scouring, as soon as an opportunity arose, as to make them cleaner and whiter than ermine; and thus he calmed down and continued on his chosen way, which in reality was none other than the way his horse chose to follow, for he believed that in this consisted the essence of adventure.

As our fledgling adventurer rode along, he said to himself:

'Who can doubt but that in future times, when the true history of my famous deeds sees the light, the sage who chronicles them will, when he recounts this my first sally, so early in the morning, write in this manner: "Scarce had ruddy Apollo spread over the face of the wide and spacious earth the golden tresses of his beauteous hair, and scarce had the speckled little birds with their harmonious tongues hailed in musical and mellifluous melody the approach of rosy Aurora who, rising from her jealous husband's soft couch, disclosed herself to mortals in the portals and balconies of La Mancha's horizon, when the famous knight Don Quixote de la Mancha, quitting the slothful feathers of his bed, mounted his famous steed Rocinante and began to ride over the ancient and far-famed Plain of Montiel"?'

And it was true that this was where he was riding. And he added:

'Happy will be the age, the century will be happy, which brings to light my famous exploits, worthy to be engraved on sheets of bronze, carved on slabs of marble and painted on boards of wood as a monument for all posterity. O sage enchanter, whomsoever you may be, to whom it falls to be the chronicler of this singular history, I beg you not to overlook my good Rocinante, my eternal companion in all my travels and wanderings.'

Then he turned and said, as if he really were in love:

'O Princess Dulcinea, mistress of this hapless heart! Great injury have you done me in reproaching and dismissing me, with the cruel command not to appear in the presence of your wondrous beauty. Vouchsafe, my lady, to be mindful of this your subject heart, which suffers such sorrow for love of you.'

He strung these absurdities together with many others, all in the style of those that he'd learned from his books. This made his progress so slow, and the sun was rising so fast and becoming so hot, that his brains would have melted, if he'd had any.

He rode on almost throughout that day and nothing happened worth mentioning, which reduced him to despair because he was longing for an early encounter with someone on whom he could test the worth of his mighty arm. Some authors say that the first adventure that befell him was that of the Pass of Lápice, others claim that it was that of the windmills, but what I've been able to discover about this matter, and indeed what I've found recorded in the annals of La Mancha, is that he rode on throughout that day, and that at nightfall both he and his nag were exhausted and half dead from starvation; and that, looking all around to see if he could spot some castle or shepherds' hut where they might retire and find some remedy for their great hunger and dire want, he caught

. an inn not far from the road along which he was travelling, which
.s as if he had seen a star leading him not just to the portals but to the
very palace of his redemption. He quickened his pace, and he reached
the inn as night was falling.

Sitting by the inn door there happened to be two young women, of
the sort known as ladies of easy virtue, on their way to Seville with some
muleteers who'd chanced to break their journey that night at the inn.
And since whatever our adventurer thought, saw or imagined seemed to
him to be as it was in the books he'd read, as soon as he saw the inn he
took it for a castle with its four towers and their spires of shining silver,
complete with its drawbridge and its deep moat and all the other accessories
that such castles commonly boast. He approached the inn that he took
for a castle, and at a short distance from it he drew rein, waiting for some
dwarf to appear upon the battlements and announce with a trumpet-blast
the arrival of a knight. But finding that there was some delay, and that
Rocinante was impatient to get to the stable, he rode on towards the inn
door and saw the two dissolute wenches sitting there, and thought that
they were two beautiful maidens or fine ladies taking their ease at the
castle gate. At this point a swineherd who was gathering together some
pigs (begging nobody's pardon, because that's what they're called) from
a stubble field happened to sound his horn to round them up, and Don
Quixote thought that his wish had been fulfilled and that a dwarf was
announcing his arrival; so it was with unusual satisfaction that he reached
the inn and the ladies, who, on observing the approach of a man dressed
like that in armour and clutching a lance and a leather shield, started to
run in terror back into the inn. But Don Quixote, conjecturing their fear
from their flight, and raising his cardboard visor to reveal his dry and
dusty face, addressed them with courteous demeanour and tranquil voice:

'Flee not, nor fear the least affront; for in the order of knighthood
which I profess it neither belongs nor behoves to offer any such, much
less to high-born maidens, as your presence testifies you to be.'

The girls had been peering at him and trying to make out his face,
hidden behind the ill-made visor; but when they heard themselves called
maidens, a term so much at odds with their profession, they couldn't
contain their laughter, which was so hearty that Don Quixote flared up
and exclaimed:

'Moderation befits the fair; furthermore, laughter which springs from a petty cause is a great folly; but I say this unto you not to grieve you nor yet to sour your disposition; for mine is none other than to serve you.'

This language, which the ladies didn't understand, together with the sorry figure cut by the knight, only redoubled their laughter and his wrath, and things would have come to a pretty pass if it hadn't been for the appearance at that moment of the innkeeper, a man who, being very fat, was very peaceable, and who on seeing such an ungainly figure, with such ill-matched equipment as the long stirrups, the lance, the leather shield and the infantryman's body-armour, was more than willing to join the maidens in their merry-making. But he was also intimidated by all these paraphernalia and, deciding to address the knight in a civil manner, he said:

'If, sir caballero, you're looking for somewhere to stay the night, you'll find plenty of everything you need here – all except a bed that is, we haven't got any of those.'

Don Quixote, observing the humility of the governor of the castle, for they were what he took the innkeeper and the inn to be, replied:

'For me, sir castellano, anything will suffice, because

> My arms are my bed-hangings,
> And my rest's the bloody fray.'[1]

The host thought that Don Quixote had called him castellano because he'd taken him for one of the Castilian conmen, whereas in reality he was an Andalusian, a prime picaroon from the Playa district of Sanlúcar,[2] no less a thief than Cacus, and no less an evildoer than any experienced page-boy, and he replied:

'In that case,

> Your bed must be the hard, hard rock,
> And your sleep to watch till day

– and that being so, you go ahead and dismount in the certainty of finding in this humble abode plenty of opportunities not to sleep for a whole year, let alone one night.'

And with these words he went and held Don Quixote's stirrup, and the knight dismounted with the greatest difficulty, not having broken his fast all day long.

He then instructed the innkeeper to take great care of his horse, for a finer steed had never eaten barley. The innkeeper looked at the animal, which didn't seem half as good as Don Quixote had claimed, and, after housing it in the stable, went back to receive orders from his guest, whom the maidens, now reconciled, were helping out of his armour. Although they'd taken off his breast and back plates, they couldn't fathom how to disengage his gorget or remove his imitation visor, tied on with green ribbons that would have to be cut, since it was impossible to undo the knots; but he would by no means consent to this, and kept his helmet on all night, making the funniest and strangest figure imaginable. As these trollops unarmed him, he, thinking they were illustrious ladies of the castle, wittily declaimed:

'And never sure was any knight
So served by damsel or by dame
As Quixote was, one happy night
When from his village first he came:
Maids waited on that man of might,
Princesses on his steed, whose name . . .³

is Rocinante, good ladies, and mine is Don Quixote de la Mancha; for although I had intended not to discover myself until the deeds done for your benefit and service should have made me known, yet the necessity to accommodate this ancient ballad of Sir Lancelot to our present purpose has been the occasion of your knowing my name ere it were meet; but a time will come when you will command and I shall obey, and when the might of this arm will manifest the desire I have to serve you.'

The girls, who weren't used to such rhetorical flourishes, didn't answer, but just asked if he'd like a bite to eat.

'I would fain eat anything,' replied Don Quixote, 'for, by my troth, much good would it do me.'

It happened to be a Friday, so there was no food in the inn except a few helpings of what is known in Castile as *abadejo*, in Andalusia as *bacallao* and in other parts of Spain as *curadillo* – in other words the humble salt cod; but in these parts it was strangely called *truchuela*. They asked him if he'd like some of this troutling, because that was all the fish there was.

'If you have a goodly number of troutlings,' replied Don Quixote, 'they will serve me as well as a trout, because it makes no difference to me whether I am given eight separate reals or a single piece of eight. What is more, it might even be that these troutlings are like veal, which is better than beef, or like kid, which is better than goat. But whatever this fish is, let it be served; for the travails and the burden of arms cannot be borne on an empty stomach.'

A table was set at the door of the inn, where it was cooler, and the innkeeper brought a dish of inadequately soaked and worse cooked salt cod, and a loaf of bread as black and mouldy as the hidalgo's armour; and it was a source of great mirth to watch him eat because, since he was wearing his helmet and holding up the visor, he couldn't put any food into his mouth with his own hands, and somebody else had to do so for him, a task performed by one of the ladies. But when they tried to give him some drink, they found this an impossible task, and he wouldn't have drunk a drop if the innkeeper hadn't bored a hole through a length of cane and put one end into his mouth and poured the wine into the other; and Don Quixote suffered it all with great patience, so as not to allow his helmet-ribbons to be cut. In the midst of these activities a sow-gelder happened to arrive at the inn, and as he did so he sounded his pan-pipes four or five times, which convinced Don Quixote that he was indeed in some famous castle, and that he was being served to the accompaniment of music, and that the salt cod was trout, the bread baked from the whitest wheat-flour, the prostitutes fine ladies and the innkeeper the lord of the castle; and it all confirmed that his decision to sally forth had been a wise one. Yet what most bothered him was that he hadn't yet been knighted, because he knew that he couldn't lawfully embark on any adventure without first having been admitted to the order of chivalry.

CHAPTER III

Which relates the amusing way in which Don Quixote had himself knighted

And so, troubled by this thought, Don Quixote made short work of his meagre lodging-house supper, and then called for the innkeeper and, shutting himself up with him in the stable, fell upon his knees before him and said:

'I shall ne'er, O valorous knight, arise from where I kneel, until your courtesy vouchsafes me a boon which I desire to beg of you and which will redound to your own praise and to the benefit of humankind.'

The innkeeper, seeing his guest at his feet and hearing such pleadings, gazed down at him in perplexity, not knowing what to do or say, and kept telling him to stand up; but he kept refusing, and the innkeeper had to promise to grant his request.

'No less did I expect from your munificence, sir,' replied Don Quixote. 'Know therefore that the boon which I have begged and which your liberality has vouchsafed me is that tomorrow you shall knight me; and tonight, in the chapel of this your castle, I will keep the vigil of arms; and tomorrow, as I have said, what I so desire shall be accomplished, so that I can legitimately roam through the four corners of the world in quest of adventures for the relief of the needy, as is the duty of chivalry and of knights errant such as I, whose desire towards such exploits is inclined.'

The innkeeper, who, as I've said, was something of a wag, and had already suspected that his guest wasn't in his right mind, found his suspicion confirmed when he heard these words and, to have something to laugh at that night, decided to humour him; so he said that he was quite right to pursue these objectives, and that such desires were natural and fitting in such a knight as he seemed to be and as his gallant presence testified; and that he himself in his younger days had followed the same honourable profession, roaming through different parts of the world in search of adventure, without omitting to visit such districts as Percheles and Islas de Riarán in Malaga, Compás in Seville, Azoguejo in Segovia,

Olivera in Valencia, Rondilla in Granada, Playa in Sanlúcar, Potro in Cordova and Ventillas in Toledo,[1] and many other places where he'd exercised the dexterity of his hands and the nimbleness of his heels, doing many injuries, wooing many widows, ruining a few maidens and swindling a few orphans, and, in short, making himself known in most of the law courts and tribunals in Spain; and that he'd finally retired to his castle, where he lived on his own means and on those of others, accommodating all knights errant, whatever their status or position, solely because of the great affection he felt for them and so that they could share their wealth with him, to repay him for his kindness.

He also told Don Quixote that in his castle there wasn't any chapel where he could keep the vigil of arms, because it had been demolished to build a new one, but he knew that in case of need vigil might be kept anywhere, and Don Quixote could do so that night in a courtyard within the castle; and in the morning, God willing, the proper ceremonies would be performed to make him into a knight, so very thoroughly that no knight in the whole wide world could be more of a knight than he.

He asked Don Quixote if he had any money on him; Don Quixote replied that he did not have so much as a single real, because he had never read in histories of knights errant that any of them had ever carried money. To this the innkeeper retorted that he was deluding himself – even if it wasn't written in the histories, because their authors had considered that there wasn't any need to record something as obviously necessary as money or clean shirts, that wasn't any reason to believe that they'd travelled without supplies of both; so he could take it as true and proven that all knights errant, of which so many books are full to overflowing, kept their purses well lined in readiness for any eventuality, and that they also carried shirts and small chests full of ointments for curing the wounds they received; because there wasn't always someone available to treat them in every field or desert where they engaged in combat and were injured, unless they had some wise enchanter for a friend, and he came to their aid, summoning through the air, on some cloud, a damsel or a dwarf with a flask of water of such magical properties that, on tasting just one drop, they were instantly cured of their wounds and injuries, as if they'd never been hurt. But, just in case this didn't happen, the knights of old had considered it wise to see that their squires were provided with money and other necessities such as lint and ointments to dress their wounds; and if any such knight happened not to have a squire (a most unusual occurrence), he himself would carry all these supplies in small saddle-bags that were scarcely visible, on the crupper of his steed, as if they were something else of much greater importance because, except in such circumstances, carrying saddle-bags was rather frowned upon among knights errant; and the innkeeper therefore advised Don Quixote – although he could, if he wished, command him as the godson that he was about to become – never again to travel without money and all the other supplies just mentioned, and he'd discover when he least expected it how useful they could be.

Don Quixote promised to do exactly as he'd been told, and then he was given orders to keep the vigil of arms in a large yard on one side of the inn; and he gathered his armour together and placed it on a water-trough next to a well, and, taking up his leather shield and seizing his lance, he began with stately bearing to pace back and forth in front of the trough; and as his pacing began, night was beginning to fall.

The innkeeper told everyone in the hostelry about his guest's insanity, his vigil and the knighting that he awaited. They wondered at such a strange kind of madness and went to watch him from a distance, and saw that, with a composed air, he sometimes paced to and fro and, at other times, leaning on his lance, gazed at his armour without looking away for some while. Night fell, but the moon was so bright that it competed with the source of its brightness, and every action of the novice knight could be clearly observed by all. And now one of the muleteers staying at the inn decided to water his animals, and to do so he had to remove from the trough the armour placed there by Don Quixote, who, on seeing him approach, cried out:

'O rash knight, whomsoever you may be, coming to lay hands on the armour of the most valiant knight errant who ever girded sword! Take care what you do, and touch it not, unless you wish to pay with your life for your temerity.'

The muleteer wouldn't toe the line (it would have been better for the rest of his anatomy if he had); instead, grasping the armour by its straps, he hurled it to one side. When Don Quixote saw this, he raised his eyes to heaven and, fixing his thoughts, as it seemed, on his lady Dulcinea, he said:

'Assist me, dear lady, in this first affront suffered by this breast that is enthralled to you; let not your favour and your succour abandon me in this first moment of peril.'

And with these and other similar words he dropped his leather shield, raised his lance with both hands, and dealt the muleteer so powerful a blow to the head that he fell on the ground in such a sorry state that had it been followed by another blow he wouldn't have needed a doctor to treat him. Then Don Quixote replaced his armour and continued pacing to and fro with the same composure as before. After a while another muleteer, not knowing what had happened (because the first one still lay stunned), also came to water his animals and, as he went to remove the armour from the trough, Don Quixote, without uttering a word or asking anybody for her favour, again dropped his leather shield and raised his lance, and didn't break it over the second muleteer's head but rather broke the head, into more than three pieces, because he criss-crossed it with two blows. All the people in the hostelry came running at the noise, the innkeeper among them. When Don Quixote saw them, he took up his leather shield and, with one hand on his sword, declared:

'O beauteous lady, strength and vigour of my enfeebled heart! Now is the time for you to turn the eyes of your greatness towards this your hapless knight, on the brink of so mighty an adventure.'

With this he felt so inspirited that if all the muleteers in the world had attacked him he wouldn't have retreated one inch. The wounded men's companions, seeing them in such a state, began to rain stones on Don Quixote, who fended them off with his leather shield as best he could, unwilling to move away from the water-trough and leave his armour unprotected. The innkeeper was yelling at them to let him be – he'd already told them he was a madman, and as such would go scot-free even if he killed the lot of them. Don Quixote was shouting too, even louder, calling them perfidious traitors and the lord of the castle a poltroon and a base-born knight, who allowed knights errant to be treated in such a way and who, if he had been admitted to the order of chivalry, would have been made to regret his treachery:

'But to you, vile and base rabble, I pay no heed; stone me, come, draw near, assail me as best you can, for you will soon see how you are made to pay for your folly and your insolence.'

He spoke with such vehemence and spirit that he struck fear into his assailants; and this, together with the innkeeper's arguments, persuaded them to stop, and he allowed them to remove the wounded, and continued keeping the vigil of arms, with the same composure as before.

The innkeeper wasn't amused by his guest's capers, and decided to put an end to them by giving him his wretched order of chivalry before any further calamities occurred. And so he approached him and apologized for the insolent behaviour of that rabble, about which he'd known nothing; but they had been properly punished for their impudence. He said that, as he'd mentioned before, there wasn't any chapel in the castle, and in any case there wasn't any need of one for what was left to be done; because the essence of being knighted lay in the cuff on the neck and the touch on the shoulder, according to his information about the ceremonial of the order, and all of that could be done in the middle of a field if necessary, and his guest had already fulfilled the bit about keeping the vigil of arms, because two hours of it were quite enough, and he'd been at it for over four. Don Quixote believed every word; he was there ready to obey him, and could he please expedite the process as much as possible, for if he were to be attacked again, after having been knighted, he did not intend to leave a single soul alive in the castle except those whom its lord commanded be spared and whom, out of respect for him, he would not harm.

The castellan, thus forewarned and now even more concerned, hurried away to fetch a ledger in which he kept the muleteers' accounts for straw and barley and, accompanied by a lad carrying a candle-end and by the two maidens, he came back to Don Quixote and ordered him to kneel; and, after reading for a while from his ledger, as if reciting some devout prayer, he raised his hand and cuffed him on the neck and then, with Don Quixote's own sword, gave him a handsome thwack on the shoulder, all the while muttering as if praying. And then he commanded one of the maidens to gird on the novice knight's sword, a task performed with much grace and discretion, with which she needed to be well provided so as not to burst out laughing at each stage of the ceremony; but the exploits that they'd watched him perform kept their laughter in check. As the good lady girded on his sword, she said:

'May God make you a most fortunate knight and give you good fortune in your battles.'

Don Quixote asked what was her name, so that he should thenceforth know to whom he was indebted for the favour received, because he intended to bestow upon her a share of the honour he was to win by the might of his arm. She humbly replied that her name was La Tolosa, and that she was the daughter of a cobbler from Toledo who lived near the Sancho Bienaya market stalls, and that wherever she was she'd serve him and regard him as her lord. Don Quixote replied that, for his sake and as a favour to him, she should thenceforth take the title of a lady, and call herself Doña Tolosa.² She promised to do so, and the other maiden buckled on his spurs; there ensued almost exactly the same dialogue as with the lady of the sword. He asked what was her name, she said it was La Molinera, because she was the daughter of an honourable miller from Antoquera, and Don Quixote also asked her to take a title, and call herself Doña Molinera, and offered her further services and favours.

Now that these unprecedented ceremonies had been performed, at top speed, Don Quixote couldn't wait to be on horseback sallying forth in search of adventures, and he saddled and mounted Rocinante and, having embraced his host, made such extraordinary statements as he thanked him for the favour of dubbing him knight that it would be impossible to do them justice in writing. The innkeeper, concerned only to be rid of his guest, replied to his rhetoric in no less high-flown although somewhat briefer terms, and was so delighted to see the back of the man that he didn't demand any payment for his stay at the inn.

CHAPTER IV

About what happened to our knight when he left the inn

It must have been about daybreak when Don Quixote left the inn, so happy, so gallant, so delighted at being a properly dubbed knight that the very girths of his horse were bursting with his joy. But remembering his host's advice about the essential supplies that he should take with him, and in particular money and shirts, he decided to return home and equip himself with them and with a squire, resolving to take into his service a neighbour, a poor farmer who had a large family but was well suited to the squirely office. With this in mind he turned Rocinante towards his home village, and the nag, half sensing its old haunts, began to trot with such zest that its hooves seemed not to touch the ground.

He hadn't gone far when he thought he could hear, coming from a dense wood on his right, faint sounds as of someone moaning, and he said:

'I thank heaven for the favour it now grants me, providing me with such an early opportunity to fulfil the duties of my profession and gather the fruit of my honourable intentions. These cries come, no doubt, from some man or woman in distress, who stands in need of my protection and assistance.'

He turned right and rode over to where he thought the sounds were coming from. A few steps into the wood he saw a mare tied by the reins to an evergreen oak, and tied to another a lad of about fifteen, naked from the waist up, and this was the one who was crying out, not without reason, because a burly farmer was flogging him with a leather belt, accompanying each blow with a word of reproof and advice:

'Keep your mouth shut and your eyes open.'

And the lad replied:

'I won't do it again, sir, by Christ who died on the Cross I swear I won't, I promise that from now on I'll take more care of the flock.'

When Don Quixote saw what was happening, he fired up and said:

'Discourteous knight: it ill becomes you to assault one who cannot defend himself; mount your steed and take up your lance,' (for the man also had a lance leaning up against the oak to which his mare was tethered) 'and I shall force you to recognize that your actions are those of a coward.'

The farmer, seeing such a figure bearing down on him, encased in armour and brandishing a lance under his nose, gave himself up for dead and meekly replied:

'This lad I'm punishing, sir knight, is one of my servants, and his job is to look after a flock of sheep for me, but he's so careless that every day one of them goes missing; and although what I'm punishing is his carelessness, or his wickedness, he says I'm doing it because I'm a skinflint, so as not to pay him his wages – but I swear by God and by my eternal soul that he's lying.'

'You dare to use that word in my presence,[1] you villainous wretch?'

said Don Quixote. 'I swear by the sun that shines down on us that I am minded to run you through with this lance. Pay him immediately, and do not answer back; otherwise, by God who rules us, I shall exterminate and annihilate you this very instant. Untie him.'

The farmer bowed his head and, without uttering a word, untied his servant, whom Don Quixote asked how much his master owed him. The reply was nine months at seven reals a month. Don Quixote worked it out and found that it came to seventy-three reals, which he told the farmer to hand over there and then, if he didn't want to die. The fearful countryman swore by the tight corner he was in and by the oath he'd already sworn (he hadn't sworn any oath at all), that it wasn't as much as all that, because an allowance and deduction had to be made for three pairs of shoes he'd given the lad, and one real paid for two blood-lettings when he'd been ill.

'That is all very well,' replied Don Quixote, 'but the shoes and the blood-lettings will be set against the flogging you have given him without due cause: for if he has done some damage to the hide of the shoes that you bought him, you have damaged his own hide, and if the barber bled him when he was ill, you have done the same to him in good health; so that on this account he owes you nothing.'

'The problem is, sir knight, I haven't got any money on me; if Andrés would like to come home with me, I'll pay him every single real I owe him.'

'Me, go with him, ever again?' said the lad. 'No fear! No sir, I wouldn't even dream of it – so that as soon as we're alone again he can flay me like St Bartholomew?'[2]

'He shall do no such thing,' replied Don Quixote. 'My command will be sufficient to ensure his obedience; and provided that he gives me his oath by the laws of the order of chivalry into which he has been admitted, I shall allow him to go free, and personally guarantee the payment.'

'Think what you're saying, sir,' said the lad. 'My master here isn't a knight at all, and he's never been admitted into any order of chivalry – he's just Juan Haldudo, the rich farmer from Quintanar.'

'That is of little consequence,' replied Don Quixote, 'there is no reason why someone with a plebeian name should not be a knight, for every man is the child of his own deeds.'

'That's as may be,' said Andrés, 'but this master of mine, what deeds is he the child of, seeing as how he refuses to pay me any wages for my sweat and toil?'

'I'm not refusing you anything at all, my dear Andrés,' replied the farmer. 'Please do be so kind as to come with me – I swear by all the orders of chivalry in the world to pay you, as I said, every single real I owe you, and with brass knobs on too.'

'You may dispense with the brass knobs,' said Don Quixote. 'Pay him in silver reals, and that will satisfy me; and take good care to do exactly as you have sworn to do, for otherwise, by that same oath, I swear that I will come back to punish you, and that I will find you, even if you hide yourself away like a lizard. And if you wish to know who is issuing these commands, so as to be the more obliged to obey them, know that I am the valiant Don Quixote de la Mancha, the righter of wrongs and injustices; and God be with you, and do not forget for one moment what you have promised and sworn, under pain of the penalties prescribed.'

And as he said this he spurred Rocinante, and before very long he had got under way. The farmer followed him with his gaze, and as soon as he was certain that he'd ridden out of the wood and was out of sight, he turned to his servant Andrés and said:

'Come here, my son, I want to pay you what I owe you, just as that righter of wrongs has ordered.'

'I swear you will, too,' said Andrés, 'and you'll do well to obey that good knight's commands, God bless him, because he's such a brave man and such a good judge, by all that's holy, that if you don't pay me he'll come back and do what he said he'd do.'

'And I swear I will, too,' said the farmer, 'but, since I'm so very fond of you, I think I'll increase the debt first, just so as to increase the repayment.'

And seizing him by the arm, he tied him back to the evergreen oak and flogged him half dead.

'And now, Señor Andrés,' said the farmer, 'you can call upon your righter of wrongs. As you'll see, he isn't going to right this particular wrong in a hurry. But I don't think I've done with the wronging quite yet, because I'm feeling the urge to skin you alive, just as you feared I would.'

But at length he untied him and told him he could go off in search of his judge so that this gentleman could carry out the sentence he'd pronounced. Andrés crept sullenly away, swearing that he was going in search of the brave Don Quixote de la Mancha to tell him exactly what had happened, and that the farmer would pay for it sevenfold. But, for all that, Andrés departed in tears and his master was left laughing.

This was how the valiant Don Quixote redressed that wrong; and delighted with what had happened, and considering that he had made a most happy and glorious beginning to his knight-errantry, he rode towards his village full of satisfaction, and murmuring:

'Well may you call yourself fortunate above all women who dwell on this earth, O Dulcinea del Toboso, fairest of the fair, for it has befallen your lot to hold subjected and enslaved to your every wish and desire a knight as valiant and far-famed as is and shall be Don Quixote de la Mancha, who (as all the world knows) was but yesterday admitted to the order of chivalry and today has righted the greatest injury and wrong ever devised by unreason and perpetrated by cruelty: today he has wrested the scourge from the hand of that pitiless enemy who was so unjustly flogging that delicate child.'

As he was saying this he came to a crossroads, and this brought to his mind those other crossroads where knights errant would pause to consider which way to go; and, to imitate them, he remained motionless for a while; but after careful thought he let go of the reins, surrendering his will to that of his nag, which followed its original inclination – to head for its stable. After a couple of miles, Don Quixote spotted a throng of people who, as it afterwards transpired, were merchants from Toledo on their way to Murcia to buy silk. There were six of them, each beneath his sunshade, accompanied by four servants on horseback and three footmen. As soon as Don Quixote saw them, he imagined that here was the opportunity for a new adventure; and, wishing to imitate in every way he believed he could the passages of arms he'd read about in his books, he decided that one he had in mind was perfect for this situation. And so, with a gallant bearing and a resolute air, he steadied himself in his stirrups, clutched his lance, lifted his leather shield to his chest and, taking up his position in the middle of the highway, awaited the arrival of these knights errant, for this was what he judged them to be; and when they came within sight and earshot, Don Quixote raised his voice and, striking a haughty posture, declared:

'You will none of you advance one step further unless all of you confess that in all the world there is no maiden more beauteous than the Empress of La Mancha, the peerless Dulcinea del Toboso.'

The merchants halted when they heard these words and saw the strange figure uttering them, and from the figure and the words they realized that the man was mad; but they had a mind to stay and see what would be the outcome of the required confession and one of them, waggish and sharp-witted, said:

'Sir knight, we don't know who this worthy lady is; do let us see her, because if she's as beautiful as you claim she is, we'll most freely and willingly confess that what you say is true.'

'If I were to let you see her,' retorted Don Quixote, 'what merit would there be in confessing so manifest a truth? The whole point is that, without seeing her, you must believe, confess, affirm, swear and uphold it; if not, monstrous and arrogant wretches, you shall face me in battle forthwith. For whether you present yourselves one by one, as the order of chivalry requires, or all together, as is the custom and wicked practice of those of your ilk, here I stand and wait for you, confident in the justice of my cause.'

'Sir knight,' replied the merchant, 'I beg you, in the name of all us princes gathered here, that – so as not to burden our consciences by confessing something never seen or heard by any of us, particularly since it is so detrimental to the Empresses and Queens of La Alcarria and Extremadura – you be pleased to show us a portrait of that lady, even if no bigger than a grain of wheat; because the skein can be judged by the thread, as they say, and this will leave us satisfied and reassured, and leave you pleased and contented; indeed I believe we are already so far inclined in her favour that, even if her portrait shows that one of her eyes has gone skew-whiff and that sulphur and cinnabar ooze out of the other one, we will, just to please you, say in her favour whatever you want us to say.'

'It does not ooze, you infamous knaves,' replied Don Quixote, burning with anger. 'It does not ooze, I repeat, with what you say, but with ambergris and civet kept in finest cotton; and she is not skew-whiff or hunch-backed, but straighter than a Guadarrama spindle.[3] And you shall pay for the great blasphemy you have uttered against such beauty as that of my lady!'

And so saying he charged with lowered lance at the blasphemer in such fury that, if good fortune hadn't made Rocinante trip and fall on the way, things would have gone badly for the reckless merchant. But Rocinante did fall, and his master rolled over the ground for some distance, and he tried to get up, but he couldn't, so encumbered was he by his lance, his leather shield, his spurs and his helmet, together with the burden of all the rest of his ancient armour. And as he struggled in vain to rise he cried:

'Flee not, you paltry cowards; you wretches, bide your time. 'Tis my horse's fault and not my own that I am lying here.'

One of the footmen – not, it seems, a very well-intentioned one – on hearing all this bluster from the poor fallen fellow, couldn't resist giving him an answer on his ribs. And coming up to him he grabbed his lance and, breaking it into pieces, took one of them and began to give our Don Quixote such a pounding that, in spite of all his armour, he ended up as well threshed as the finest chaff. The muleteer's masters were shouting to him not to hit so hard, and to stop, but the lad was by now so caught up in his game that he wouldn't leave it until he'd played all the cards of his fury, and, picking up the other pieces of the lance, he shattered them, too, on the poor fallen man who, in the face of the storm of blows raining down, never stopped shouting as he threatened heaven and earth and those brigands, as he imagined them to be.

The lad grew tired, and the merchants continued their journey, supplied with enough to talk about throughout it on the subject of the poor pounded knight. Once he found himself alone, he again tried to get up; but if he hadn't been able to do so when fit and well, how was he going to manage it now that he was pummelled to pieces? Even so he considered himself lucky, in the belief that this was a fitting misfortune for knights errant, and he blamed his horse for it all; and it was impossible to get up, so very bruised and battered was his body.

CHAPTER V

In which the story of our knight's misfortune is continued

Finding, then, that he couldn't move, it occurred to him to resort to his usual remedy, which was to think about some passage from his books; and his madness brought to his memory the episode from the story of Baldwin and the Marquis of Mantua in which Carloto leaves Baldwin wounded in the forest,[1] a tale known to every little boy, not unfamiliar to youths, celebrated and even believed by old men, yet with no more truth in it than the miracles of Muhammad. It was perfect for the predicament in which he found himself; and so, with many manifestations of extreme suffering, he began to writhe about on the ground and to say in the faintest of voices what the wounded knight of the forest is said to have said:

> Where are you, mistress of my heart?
> Are you not pained by my distress?
> Maybe you know not of my plight,
> Maybe you're false and pitiless.

And on he went reciting the ballad right up to the lines that go:

> O noble Marquis, gentle sire,
> My uncle and my lord by blood . . .

Fortune decreed that at this point a farmer from his own village, one of his neighbours, happened to be returning home after taking a hundredweight of wheat to the mill. Seeing a man lying there the farmer came up and asked him who he was and what was the matter with him, moaning away like that. No doubt Don Quixote thought that this was the Marquis of Mantua, his uncle, and so his only response was to continue reciting his ballad, informing the man of his misfortune and of the love that the Emperor's son felt for his wife, exactly as the ballad relates.

The farmer was astonished to hear all this nonsense; and, removing the man's visor, which had been battered to pieces, he wiped his face, which was covered in dust. And once he'd done wiping he recognized him and said:

'Señor Quixana,' (for this must have been his name when he was sane and hadn't yet turned from a placid hidalgo into a knight errant) 'who's done this to you?'

But he continued to reply with his ballad to everything he was asked. Sizing up the situation, the farmer took his back and breast plates off as best he could, to see if he was wounded, but couldn't see any blood or signs of any hurt. He managed to lift him up, and with great difficulty hoisted him on to the donkey, since this seemed the more tranquil animal. He picked up the armour and arms, including the fragments of the lance, and tied them on to Rocinante, which he took by the reins, and taking his donkey by the halter he set off in the direction of his village, deep in thought as he heard the nonsense being spoken by Don Quixote, who was no less pensive and so badly bruised that he couldn't keep his seat on the donkey, and every so often breathed sighs loud enough to reach heaven; so that the farmer again felt he should ask what was wrong, and it must have been the devil himself who made Don Quixote recall tales to fit the events, because at that moment, forgetting all about Baldwin, he remembered Abindarráez the Moor being captured and taken as a prisoner to his castle by the Governor of Antequera, Rodrigo de Narváez. So that when the farmer asked him again how he felt and what was the matter with him, he replied with the very same words and arguments used by the captive Moor to reply to Rodrigo de Narváez, as he'd read the story in Jorge de Montemayor's *Diana*,[2] making such appropriate use of it that the farmer wished himself to the devil for having to listen to such a pack of absurdities. He realized his neighbour was mad, and hurried on to the village so as not to have to put up with Don Quixote's interminable harangue more than necessary. It concluded like this:

'You must know, Señor Don Rodrigo de Narváez, that this fair Jarifa I have mentioned is now the beauteous Dulcinea del Toboso, for whom I have performed, do perform and shall perform the most famous deeds of chivalry that have been witnessed, are witnessed and shall be witnessed in this world.'

The farmer replied:

'Look here sir, as I'm a sinner I'm not Don Rodrigo de Narváez, nor the Marquis of Mantua, but Pedro Alonso, your neighbour; and you aren't Baldwin, nor Abindarráez, but the honourable hidalgo Señor Quixana.'

'I know who I am,' retorted Don Quixote, 'and I know that I can be not only all those whom I have mentioned, but every one of the Twelve Peers of France, and every one of the Nine Worthies as well,[3] because all the deeds performed by them both singly and together will be exceeded by mine.'

With these exchanges and other similar ones they approached the village at nightfall, but the farmer waited until it was darker so that nobody could see the battered hidalgo so wretchedly mounted. When he thought the time had come he entered the village and went straight to Don Quixote's house, which was in an uproar: the priest and the barber, great friends of Don Quixote's, were there, and his housekeeper was shouting:

'And what's your opinion, Father Pero Pérez sir,' (for this was the priest's name) 'about my master's misfortune? Three days it's been now without a trace of him, his nag, his leather shield, his lance or his armour. A fine pickle I'm in! It's my belief, as sure as I was born to die, that his brain's been turned by those damned chivalry books of his he reads all the time – I remember often hearing him say to himself that he wanted to be a knight errant and go off in search of adventures. The devil take all those books, and Barabbas[4] take them too, for scrambling the finest mind in all La Mancha!'

The niece said much the same and even more:

'And let me tell you this, Master Nicolás,' (for this was the barber's name). 'My uncle would often be reading those evil books of misadventure for two whole days and nights on end, and then he'd throw his book down, grab his sword and slash the walls of his room, and once he was exhausted he'd say that he'd killed four giants as big as four towers, and that the sweat pouring from him was blood from the wounds received in battle, and then he'd drink a pitcher of cold water and feel calm and well again, claiming that the water was a most precious draught brought by the famous sage Squiffy,[5] a great enchanter and friend of his. But I'm the one to blame for it all, not telling you gentlemen about my uncle's madness so you could have done something about it and burned those unchristian books of his before it came to all this; he's got lots and lots of them, and they do deserve to be put to the flames, like heretics.'

'I agree with that,' said the priest, 'and I swear that before another day has passed they'll be put on public trial and condemned to the flames so that they can't make anyone reading them do what my friend must have done.'

All this was overheard by Don Quixote and the farmer, who could no longer have any doubts about his neighbour's illness, and so he began to shout:

'Open up to Sir Baldwin and the Marquis of Mantua, who's sore wounded here, and to the Moor Abindarráez, brought captive by the valiant Rodrigo de Narváez, the Governor of Antequera.'

These shouts brought all four running into the porch, and as the men recognized their friend, and the women their master and uncle, who hadn't dismounted from the donkey because he couldn't, they ran to embrace him. He said:

'Stop, all of you, for I am sore wounded through the fault of my steed. Carry me to my bed and, if you are able, summon the wise Urganda to heed and tend my wounds.'

'Just look at him, in the name of the devil!' cried the housekeeper. 'Didn't I know in the marrow of my bones what was wrong with the master? Up you go, sir, up you go to bed, we'll cure you well enough without any need for that there Ugandan woman. Damn those chivalry books, damn the lot of them, getting you into such a state!'

They took him to his bed and, examining him for wounds, couldn't find any; he told them that it had been a general, overall battering sustained when he and his steed Rocinante suffered a terrible fall as he was doing battle with ten giants, the most lawless and reckless giants to be found almost anywhere on the face of the earth.

'I see, I see!' said the priest. 'So there are giants in the game as well, are there? I swear by this Holy Cross that I'll burn them tomorrow, before the day is over.'

They asked Don Quixote a thousand questions, and his only reply was to request food and to be allowed to sleep, for this was his greatest need. And then the priest asked the farmer to tell him exactly how he'd found Don Quixote. The farmer told him the whole story, including the nonsense that on being discovered and transported the knight had uttered, which made the priest even more anxious to do what the very next day he did do: call on his friend the barber Master Nicolás, with whom he walked to Don Quixote's house.

CHAPTER VI

About the amusing and exhaustive scrutiny that the
priest and the barber made in the library of our
ingenious hidalgo

Who was still asleep. The priest asked the niece for the keys of the room
where the books, the authors of the mischief, were kept, and she was
happy to hand them over. They went in, the housekeeper too, and found
more than a hundred large volumes, finely bound, and some small
ones; and as soon as the housekeeper saw them, she ran out of the room
and back again clutching a bowl of holy water and some hyssop,[1] and
said:

'Here you are, reverend father, you take this and sprinkle the room
with it, just in case there's one of those hordes of enchanters from those
books in here, and he puts a spell on us as a punishment for the torments
they'll undergo once we've wiped them off the face of the earth.'

The priest laughed at the housekeeper's simple-mindedness, and told
the barber to hand him the books one by one so that he could see what
was in them, since he might find some that didn't deserve to be committed
to the flames.

'No,' said the niece, 'there's no reason to let any of them off, they're
all to blame. Better throw the whole lot of them out of the windows into
the courtyard, and make a pile of them, and set fire to them, or take them
to the backyard and make the bonfire there, where the smoke won't be
such a nuisance.'

The housekeeper said much the same, so anxious were both women
to see those innocents massacred, but the priest wouldn't agree without
at least reading the titles. The first one that Master Nicolás put into his
hands was *The Four Books of Amadis of Gaul*, and the priest said:

'This is a strange coincidence: I've heard that this was the very first
chivalry romance to be printed in Spain,[2] and that all the others have
their origin and beginning in it; so it seems to me that, as the prophet of
such a pernicious sect, it should be condemned to the flames without
delay.'

'No, no,' said the barber. 'I've also heard that it's the very best of all the books of this kind that have ever been written; and so, being unique in its artistry, it ought to be pardoned.'

'You're right,' said the priest, 'so its life is spared for the time being. Let's see that one next to it.'

'This,' said the barber, 'is *The Exploits of Esplandian*,[3] Amadis of Gaul's legitimate son.'

'Well, to be sure,' said the priest, 'the excellence of the father isn't going to be of any avail to the son. Here you are, ma'am, open that window and throw it into the yard, the first faggot on the bonfire we're going to make.'

The housekeeper was delighted to do so, and the good Esplandian flew out into the courtyard, where he patiently awaited the flames with which he was threatened.

'Let's see the next one,' said the priest.

'This,' said the barber, 'is *Amadis of Greece*, and all the books on this side, I think, are members of that same family.'[4]

'Then out into the yard with the lot of them,' said the priest. 'Just to be able to burn Queen Pintiquiniestra, and the shepherd Darinel, and his eclogues, and his author's devilish, contorted language, I'll burn the father that begot me, too, if I catch him going about as a knight errant.'

'I agree,' said the barber.

'So do I,' added the niece.

'That being so,' said the housekeeper, 'let's have them here, and out into the courtyard they all go.'

They gave them to her, and since there were so many of them she spared herself the stairs again and flung them out of the window.

'And what's that monstrosity?' asked the priest.

'That,' replied the barber, 'is *Don Olivante de Laura*.'[5]

'Its author,' said the priest, 'also wrote *The Garden of Flowers*, and to be frank I couldn't say which of the two is more truthful – or rather, less mendacious. What I can say is that this one shall go out into the yard, for its arrogant nonsense.'

'This next one is *Florismarte of Hyrcania*,'[6] said the barber.

'Oh, so it's Señor Florismarte, is it?' replied the priest. 'I can tell you he's soon going to end up in the yard, too, in spite of his strange birth and famous adventures. No other outcome is feasible, given the clumsiness and dullness of his style. To the yard with him, and with this other one as well, ma'am.'

'With pleasure, sir,' the housekeeper replied, and joyfully she did as she was told.

'This is *The Knight Platir*,'[7] said the barber.

'That's an old book,' said the priest, 'and I can't find anything in it deserving of mercy. Let it join the others without leave to appeal.'

And it was done. Another book was opened and they saw that its title was *The Knight of the Cross*.[8]

'With such a holy title as this book has, it could be forgiven its ignorance, yet as the proverb goes, "Behind the Cross lurks the devil": to the fire with it.'

Taking up another book, the barber said:

'This one's *The Mirror of Chivalry*.'

'I know this gentleman,' said the priest. 'Here we'll find Sir Reynald of Montalban and his friends and companions, worse thieves than Cacus, and the Twelve Peers, with the true historian Turpin.[9] Yet the fact is that I'm inclined to condemn them to nothing worse than perpetual exile, if only because there are among them some of the creations of the famous Matteo Boiardo, from which the Christian poet Ludovico Ariosto also wove his tapestry – though if I find him in here speaking any language other than his own I won't show him any respect at all, but if he's speaking his own tongue I'll take my hat off to him.'

'Well, I've got that book in Italian,' said the barber, 'but I don't understand a word of it.'

'Nor would it be a good thing for you to understand it,' replied the priest, 'and we could have done without that captain bringing it to Spain and turning it into Castilian,[10] because he left behind much of what was best in it, which is what happens to all those who try to translate poetry: however much care they take and skill they display, they can never recreate it in the full perfection of its original birth. I say, then, that this book, and all others we find that are about these French matters, shall be thrown out and deposited in a dry well until, after further deliberation, a decision is reached about what to do with them – all except a certain *Bernardo del Carpio*[11] who's skulking about here somewhere, and another book called *Roncesvalles*,[12] because these will pass straight from my hands into the housekeeper's and from there to the flames, without any remission.'

This was confirmed by the barber, who thought it all very fit and proper, since he considered the priest to be such a good Christian and lover of the truth that he couldn't tell a lie if he tried. Opening another book he saw that it was *Palmerin of Oliva*,[13] and next to it was another one called *Palmerin of England*, and when the priest saw this he said:

'Let the olive be chopped into logs and burned, and not even the ashes remain. But let the palm of England be kept and preserved as something unique, and a casket be made for it like the one Alexander the Great found among the spoils of Darius and designated as a case for the works of the poet Homer. This book, my friend, deserves respect for two reasons: because it's excellent in its own right, and because it's said to have been written by a wise king of Portugal. All the adventures in Princess Miraguarda's castle are superb and splendidly contrived; and the speeches are courtly and clear, and have due regard for the character of the speakers, with great precision and sensitivity. I propose, then, that so long as you agree, Master Nicolás, this book and *Amadis of Gaul* should be saved from the flames, and all the rest should perish, without any further enquiry.'

'No, my friend,' replied the barber, 'because this one I've got here is the famous *Sir Belianis*.'

'That book,' replied the priest, 'and the second, third and fourth parts, too, need a dose of rhubarb to purge them of their excess of bile – and that section about the castle of fame and other more serious nonsense will have to be removed, for which purpose they are granted a stay of execution; and whether mercy or rigorous justice is applied to them will depend on how they mend their ways. Meanwhile, you keep them in your house, my friend, but don't let anybody read them.'

'All right,' said the barber.

And not wanting to weary himself any more reading chivalry romances, the priest ordered the housekeeper to take all the big books and throw them out into the yard. His command didn't fall on deaf ears, because she'd rather have been burning those books than weaving the finest and largest piece of fabric in the world, and, seizing about eight of them, she heaved them out of the window. But because she took up so many of them together, one fell at the barber's feet and, curious to know what it was, he saw: *History of the Famous Knight Tirante the White.*[14]

'Good heavens!' cried the priest. 'Fancy Tirante the White being here! Give it to me, my friend: I reckon I've found in this book a treasure of delight and a mine of entertainment. In it you'll discover Don Quirieleisón de Montalbán, a most courageous knight, and his brother Tomás de Montalbán, and the knight Fonseca, together with the fight that the brave Tirante had with the mastiff, and the witticisms of the maiden Placerdemivida, and the amours and the trickery of the widow Reposada, and the lady empress in love with her squire Hipólito. Let me tell you this, my friend: as far as its style is concerned this is the best book in the world. In it knights eat and sleep and die in their beds and make wills before they die, and other such things that are usually omitted from books of this sort. But in spite of all this I do have to say that the man who wrote it deserved to be sent to the galleys for life, for not knowing what he was doing when he was writing such nonsense. Take it home and read it, and you'll see that what I say is true.'

'That I'll do,' replied the barber, 'but what about these other little books here?'

'They can't be books of chivalry,' said the priest, 'but books of poetry.'

And, opening one of them he saw that it was Jorge de Montemayor's *Diana* and, convinced that they were all of the same sort, he said:

'These don't deserve to be burned with the others, because they aren't and never will be as damaging as those books of chivalry have been — these are books for the intellect, and do nobody any harm.'

'Oh sir,' cried the niece, 'please have them burned like the rest, because it could well happen that once my uncle gets over his chivalry illness he starts reading all these other books and takes it into his head to become a shepherd and wander about the forests and meadows singing and playing music and, what would be even worse than that, turn into a poet, which they say is a catching and incurable disease.'

'The girl's right,' said the priest, 'and it'll be a good idea to remove this dangerous stumbling-block from our friend's way. And as we're beginning with Montemayor's *Diana*, it's my opinion that it shouldn't be burned, but that the parts about the wise Felicia and the enchanted water[15] should be cut, as well as nearly all the poems in Italian metre, and that the book should be welcome to keep its prose and the honour of being the first of its kind.'

'This next one,' said the barber, 'is also called *Diana*, the second part, by an author from Salamanca. And this other one has the same title, too, and it's by Gil Polo.'[16]

'Well,' replied the priest, 'the Salamancan one can go to join and swell the ranks of the books condemned to the courtyard, but the one by Gil Polo must be safeguarded as if it had been written by Apollo himself. Look lively though, my friend, let's hurry up, it's getting late.'

'This,' said the barber, opening another volume, 'is *The Ten Books of the Fortune of Love*, written by Antonio de Lofraso, a Sardinian poet.'[17]

'As sure as I'm in holy orders,' said the priest, 'no book as amusing and as fanciful as this has ever been written since Apollo was Apollo, the muses were muses and poets have been poets. In its own way it's the best and most singular of all those of its kind that have ever seen the light of day, and anyone who hasn't read it can reckon that he's never read anything worth reading. Let's have it, my friend: I'm happier to have found it than if I'd been given a cassock of finest florentine.'

He put it to one side with great satisfaction, and the barber went on to say:

'These next ones are *The Shepherd of Iberia*, *The Nymphs of Henares* and *The Undeceptions of Jealousy*.'[18]

'Well,' said the priest, 'all you have to do is hand them over to the secular arm of the housekeeper, and don't ask me why, or we shall never be done.'

'The next is *The Shepherd of Filida*.'[19]

'That's no shepherd,' said the priest, 'but a clever courtier, to be cherished like a precious jewel.'

'This big book here,' said the barber, 'is called *The Treasury of Divers Poems*.'[20]

'If there were fewer of them,' said the priest, 'they'd be better thought of. This book needs some weeding, to rid it of certain vulgarities among its splendours. Keep it back, because its author's a friend of mine, and also out of respect for other more heroic and sublime works he's written.'

'This,' said the barber, 'is López Maldonado's *Book of Songs*.'[21]

'The author of this book,' replied the priest, 'is also one of my great friends, and when he sings his own verses his listeners are lost in admiration, because he does so in such a sweet voice that you could say he chants and enchants all at once. His eclogues are rather long, but then you can never have too much of a good thing. Keep the book with the chosen few. But what's this other one by its side?'

'*Galatea*, by Miguel de Cervantes.'[22]

'That fellow Cervantes has been a good friend of mine for years, and I know he's more conversant with adversity than with verse. His book's ingenious enough; it sets out to achieve something but doesn't bring anything to a conclusion; we'll have to wait for the promised second part; maybe with correction it'll gain the full pardon denied it for the time being; so while we wait and see, you keep it a captive in your house, my friend.'

'All right,' said the barber. 'And here are three more, all together: *Araucana*, by Alonso de Ercilla, *Austríada*, by Juan Rufo, the magistrate from Córdoba, and *Monserrate*,[23] by Cristóbal de Virués, the Valencian poet.'

'Those three books,' said the priest, 'are the best ever written in heroic verse in the Castilian language, and they can rival the most famous Italian ones. Preserve them, as the finest pieces of poetry Spain possesses.'

The priest grew tired of looking at books and ordered all the rest to be burned in one fell swoop, but the barber had already opened another one, entitled *The Tears of Angelica*.[24]

'I'd have shed them myself,' said the priest when he heard the title, 'if I'd had this book burned, because its author was one of the most famous poets in the world, not just in Spain, and an excellent translator of Ovid.'

CHAPTER VII

About our worthy knight Don Quixote de la Mancha's second sally

And now Don Quixote began to bellow:

'Come, come, you valiant knights; 'tis now you must display the worth of your mighty arms, for the courtiers are getting the better of the tourney.'

They ran to see what the commotion was all about, and this put a stop to the scrutiny of the remaining books; as a result it's believed that *Carolea* and *The Lion of Spain*, together with *The Exploits of the Emperor* by Luis de Ávila,[1] went to the flames without any trial at all, because they must have been among the remainder; and perhaps if the priest had examined them they wouldn't have received such a severe sentence.

By the time they reached Don Quixote's room he was out of bed, shouting and raving, laying about him with his sword in all directions with slashes and backstrokes, as wide awake as if he'd never slept. They wrestled him back to bed, and once he'd calmed down a little, he turned to the priest and said:

'Indeed, my Lord Archbishop Turpin, it is a disgrace for us, who call ourselves the Twelve Peers, so meekly to allow those knights courtiers to carry off the victory in this tournament, after we knights adventurers had won all the honours on the previous three days.'

'Hush, my friend,' said the priest, 'God will grant a change of fortune so that what is lost today is won tomorrow, and for the moment you should look to your health – you seem to be overtired, if not sore wounded.'

'Wounded I am not,' said Don Quixote, 'but weak and exhausted I am indeed, for the bastard Roland has been pounding me with the trunk of an evergreen oak, and all out of envy, because he can see that I am the only man who opposes his bravado. But my name would not be Reynald of Montalbán if, as soon as I rise from this bed, I did not make him pay for it, in spite of all his magic spells. For the present, however, bring me victuals, for they, I know, will be more to my purpose, and leave it to me to seek my revenge.'

And that's what they did: they gave him some food, and he fell asleep again, and they fell to marvelling at his madness.

That night the housekeeper burned to ashes all the books in the courtyard and the house, and some must have perished that deserved to be treasured in perpetual archives; but fate, and the scrutineer's laziness, wouldn't permit it, and in them was fulfilled the proverb which says that the just sometimes pay for sinners.

One of the remedies that the priest and the barber had prescribed at that time for their friend's malady was to have his library walled up and sealed off, so that he couldn't find his books when he got up – maybe if the cause was removed the effect might cease – and to tell him that an enchanter had carried them off, with the library and all; and this was done without delay. Two days later Don Quixote did get up, and his first action was to go and look at his books; and, since he couldn't find the room in which he'd left them, he wandered all over the house searching for it. He kept going up to the place where the door used to be, and feeling for it with his hands, and running his eyes backwards and forwards over the walls without uttering a word; and after some time doing this he asked his housekeeper where his library was. Well trained in her answer, she said:

'And what library do you think you're looking for? There's no library and no books left in this house, because the devil himself took them away.'

'No it wasn't the devil,' replied the niece, 'it was an enchanter who came one night on a cloud, after you'd gone away, and he climbed off a serpent he was riding and he went into the library and I don't know what he got up to in there, because a bit later he flew away over the roof and left the house full of smoke; and when we made up our minds to go and see what he'd done, we couldn't find any books or any library. All we remember is that as that wicked old man flew away he shouted that because of a secret grudge he bore the owner of the books and the library, he'd done the house the damage that we were about to discover. He also said that he was called the sage Munaton.'

'Frestón[2] is what he must have said,' said Don Quixote.

'I don't know,' said the housekeeper, 'whether he was called Frestón or Piston or whatever, all I know is his name ended in ton.'

'That is indeed his name,' said Don Quixote, 'and he is a wise enchanter, a great enemy of mine, who bears me much malice, because he knows by his arts and his learning that the time will come when I shall engage in single combat a knight who is a favourite of his, and defeat him, without his being able to do anything to prevent it, and for this reason he tries to make as much mischief for me as he can; but I can promise him that he is powerless to gainsay or avert what heaven has decreed.'

'Who can doubt that?' said the niece. 'But uncle, why do you have to go and get involved in these arguments? Wouldn't it be better to stay quietly at home instead of looking for better bread than what's made from wheat, and forgetting that many a man's gone out shearing and come back shorn?'

'My dear niece!' replied Don Quixote. 'How wrong you are! Before anyone shears me I will pluck the beards off the chins of all those who even contemplate touching a single hair of mine!'

Neither woman answered him back, because they could see that he was growing heated.

And yet he did stay quietly at home for a whole fortnight without showing any signs of wanting to re-enact his former follies, and during this time he talked all kinds of amusing bunkum with his friends the priest and the barber, as he declared that what the world most needed was knights errant and a rebirth of knight-errantry. Sometimes the priest contradicted him and sometimes he gave in to him, because if he didn't make use of this tactic it would be impossible to restore his sanity.

During this fortnight Don Quixote set to work on a farmer who was a neighbour of his, an honourable man (if a poor man can be called honourable) but a little short of salt in the brain-pan. To be brief, Don Quixote told him, reasoned with him and promised him so much that the poor villager decided to go away with him and serve him as squire. Don Quixote told the man, among other things, that he ought to be delighted to go, because at some time or other he could well have an adventure in which he won an island in the twinkling of an eye and installed his squire as governor. These and other similar promises persuaded Sancho Panza, for this was the farmer's name, to leave his wife and children and go into service as his neighbour's squire.

Don Quixote immediately set about raising money, and by selling one possession, pawning another, and always making a bad bargain, he scraped together a reasonable sum. He also found himself a little round infantryman's shield, borrowed from a friend, and, patching up his shattered helmet as best he could, he told his squire Sancho the day and time he intended to set out, so that he too could obtain whatever he considered most necessary. Don Quixote was particularly insistent on saddle-bags, and Sancho said that indeed he would bring some, and he'd bring a very fine donkey of his too, because he wasn't all that much given to going very far on foot. At this Don Quixote hesitated, racking his brains to try and remember if any knight errant had ever been escorted by a donkey-mounted squire, but none came to mind; yet for all that he decided that Sancho should ride his donkey, proposing to provide him with a more honourable mount at the earliest opportunity, by unhorsing the first discourteous knight he came across. Don Quixote stocked up with shirts and everything else he could, following the advice that the innkeeper had given him; and once all these preparations had been made, without Panza saying goodbye to his wife and children, or Don Quixote to his housekeeper and niece, they left the village unseen one night, and by daybreak they'd ridden so far they felt certain no one would be able to find them however hard he looked.

Sancho Panza rode his ass like a patriarch, complete with saddle-bags and leather bottle, longing to be the governor of the island his master had promised him. Don Quixote happened to take the same road he'd followed on his first sally, across the plain of Montiel, with less discomfort than before, because it was early morning and the sun, being low, didn't bother them. Sancho Panza said to his master:

'You'll be sure, won't you, sir knight, not to forget what you promised me about the island. I'll be up to governing it all right, however big it is.'

To which Don Quixote replied:

'I would have you know, my good friend Sancho Panza, that it was a custom much in use among the knights errant of old to make their squires the governors of the islands or kingdoms that they conquered, and I have determined that such an ancient usage shall not lapse through my fault. Quite on the contrary, I intend to improve upon it: for those knights would sometimes – more often than not, perhaps – wait until their squires were old men and, once they were tired of serving and of suffering bad days and worse nights, give them some title, such as count or at the most marquis of some valley or paltry province; but if your life and mine are spared, it could well be that within six days I shall conquer a kingdom with others annexed, any one of which would be perfect for you to be crowned king of it. And you must not think that there would be anything extraordinary about that: incidents and accidents befall us knights in such unprecedented and unimagined ways that I might easily be able to give you even more than I have promised.'

'And so,' said Sancho Panza, 'if by one of those miracles you've just said I became king, then Juana Gutiérrez, my old woman, would be queen no less, and the kids would be princes and princesses.'

'Who can doubt it?' replied Don Quixote.

'I can,' retorted Sancho Panza. 'To my mind, even if God rained kingdoms down on this earth none of them would sit well on my Mari Gutiérrez's head. Look here, sir, she wouldn't be worth two brass farthings as a queen – countess would suit her better, and even that'd be hard going for her.'

'Commend the matter to God, Sancho,' replied Don Quixote, 'and he will give her what is best for her; but you must not be so daunted that you agree to content yourself with anything less than being a provincial governor.'

'I shan't do that, sir,' replied Sancho, 'not with such a fine master as you, who'll be able to give me everything that's good for me and I can cope with.'

CHAPTER VIII

*About the brave Don Quixote's success in the dreadful
and unimaginable adventure of the windmills, together with
other events worthy of happy memory*

As he was saying this, they caught sight of thirty or forty windmills standing on the plain, and as soon as Don Quixote saw them he said to his squire:

'Fortune is directing our affairs even better than we could have wished: for you can see over there, good friend Sancho Panza, a place where stand thirty or more monstrous giants with whom I intend to fight a battle and whose lives I intend to take; and with the booty we shall begin to prosper. For this is a just war, and it is a great service to God to wipe such a wicked breed from the face of the earth.'

'What giants?' said Sancho Panza.

'Those giants that you can see over there,' replied his master, 'with long arms: there are giants with arms almost six miles long.'

'Look you here,' Sancho retorted, 'those over there aren't giants, they're windmills, and what look to you like arms are sails – when the wind turns them they make the millstones go round.'

'It is perfectly clear,' replied Don Quixote, 'that you are but a raw novice in this matter of adventures. They are giants; and if you are frightened, you can take yourself away and say your prayers while I engage them in fierce and arduous combat.'

And so saying he set spurs to his steed Rocinante, not paying any attention to his squire Sancho Panza, who was shouting that what he was charging were definitely windmills not giants. But Don Quixote was so convinced that they were giants that he neither heard his squire Sancho's shouts nor saw what stood in front of him, even though he was by now upon them; instead he cried:

'Flee not, O vile and cowardly creatures, for it is but one solitary knight who attacks you.'

A gust of wind arose, the great sails began to move, and Don Quixote yelled:

'Though you flourish more arms than the giant Briareus,[1] I will make you pay for it.'

So saying, and commending himself with all his heart to his lady Dulcinea, begging her to succour him in his plight, well protected by his little round infantryman's shield, and with his lance couched, he advanced at Rocinante's top speed and charged at the windmill nearest him. As he thrust his lance into its sail the wind turned it with such violence that it smashed the lance into pieces and dragged the horse and his rider with it, and Don Quixote went rolling over the plain in a very sore predicament. Sancho Panza rushed to help his master at his donkey's fastest trot and found that he couldn't stir, such was the toss that Rocinante had given him.

'For God's sake!' said Sancho. 'Didn't I tell you to be careful what you were doing, didn't I tell you they were only windmills? And only someone with windmills on the brain could have failed to see that!'

'Not at all, friend Sancho,' replied Don Quixote. 'Affairs of war, even more than others, are subject to continual change. All the more so as I believe, indeed I am certain, that the same sage Frestón who stole my library and my books has just turned these giants into windmills, to deprive me of the glory of my victory, such is the enmity he feels for me; but in the end his evil arts will avail him little against the might of my sword.'

'God's will be done,' replied Sancho Panza.

He helped his master to his feet, and his master remounted Rocinante, whose shoulder was half dislocated. And talking about this adventure they followed the road towards the Pass of Lápice, because Don Quixote said they couldn't fail to encounter plentiful and varied adventures there, as it was a much frequented spot. But he was dejected by the destruction of his lance, and he told his squire so, and added:

'I remember reading that a Spanish knight called Diego Pérez de Vargas, having broken his sword in battle, tore a weighty bough or trunk from an evergreen oak, and did such deeds with it that day, and thrashed so many Moors,[2] that he was nicknamed Machuca, that is to say, the thrasher; and from that day onwards his surname and that of his descendants was changed to Vargas y Machuca. I have told you this because from the first oak tree that comes before me I intend to tear off another such trunk, as good as the one I have in mind, and with it I intend to do such deeds as to make you consider yourself most fortunate to be deemed worthy to behold them, and to witness that which can hardly be believed.'

'God's will be done,' said Sancho. 'I believe every word you say. But do sit up straighter, you're riding all lopsided, it must be that hammering you got when you fell off your horse.'

'That is indeed the case,' replied Don Quixote, 'and if I do not utter any complaint about the pain it is because knights errant are not permitted to complain about wounds, even if their entrails are spilling out of them.'

'If that's so there's nothing more for me to say,' replied Sancho, 'but God knows I'd like you to complain if anything hurts. As for me, I can tell you I'm going to moan like anything about the slightest little pain, unless that stuff about not complaining goes for knight errants' squires as well.'

Don Quixote couldn't help laughing at his squire's simple-mindedness, and declared that he could moan as and when he pleased, whether he felt any pain or not, for he had not yet read anything to the contrary in the order of chivalry. Sancho pointed out that it was time to eat. His master replied that he didn't need any food yet, but that Sancho could eat whenever he liked. So Sancho settled himself down as best he could on his donkey and, taking out of his saddle-bags what he'd put into them, he jogged along and munched away behind his master, and every so often he'd take a swig from his leather bottle with such relish that the most self-indulgent innkeeper in Malaga would have envied him. And as Sancho trotted on, drinking his fill, he didn't remember any of the promises his master had made him, and reckoned that going in search of adventures, however dangerous they might be, was more like good fun than hard work.

To cut a long story short, they spent that night under some trees, and from one of them Don Quixote tore a dead branch that might almost serve as a lance, and fastened on to it the iron head that he'd taken off the broken one. He didn't sleep in all the night, thinking about his lady Dulcinea, to conform with what he'd read in his books, where knights errant spent many sleepless nights in glades and deserts, engrossed in the recollection of their ladies. Not so Sancho Panza who, with his stomach full, and not of chicory water either, slept right through until morning; and, if his master hadn't called him, neither the rays of the sun, falling full on his face, nor the songs of the birds that, in great throngs and with expansive joy, greeted the coming of the new day, would have been capable of awaking him. He got up, had his breakfast swig and found his leather bottle rather slimmer than the evening before; and his heart sank, because it didn't look as if this lack was going to be remedied as soon as he'd have liked. Don Quixote refused breakfast because, as we know, he had decided to subsist on savoury recollections. They continued along the road to the Pass of Lápice, and at about three o'clock in the afternoon they sighted it.

'Over there, brother Sancho Panza,' said Don Quixote when he saw it, 'we can dip our arms right up to our elbows in what people call adventures. But take note that, even if you see me in the greatest peril imaginable, you must not seize your sword to defend me, unless you should see that those who attack me are rabble and common people, in which case you can most certainly come to my aid; but should they be knights and gentlemen, it is on no account licit or permitted by the laws of chivalry for you to assist me, until you yourself be knighted.'

'You can be sure, sir,' replied Sancho, 'of being fully obeyed there, specially since I'm a peaceful man by nature and don't like getting involved in rows and brawls. Though I do have to say that when it comes to defending myself I'm not going to take much notice of those there laws of yours, because divine and human justice both let anyone defend himself against attack.'

'I do not disagree in the slightest,' replied Don Quixote, 'but as regards assisting me against knights, you must keep your natural impetuosity under control.'

'I'll do that all right,' replied Sancho. 'I'll keep that particular promise as strictly as the Sabbath.'

As they talked away like this, two friars of the order of St Benedict appeared on the road, each seated upon a dromedary: their mules were no less tall than that. They came complete with their riding masks and their sunshades. Behind them was a coach with four or five horsemen escorting it, and two footmen walking. In the coach, as was later discovered, there was a Basque lady on her way to Seville to join her husband, who was going to America to take up an important post. The friars weren't travelling with her, they just happened to be on the same road; but as soon as Don Quixote caught sight of them he said to his squire:

'Either I am much mistaken or this will be the most famous adventure ever witnessed; for those black figures over there must be and no doubt are enchanters abducting a princess in that coach, and I must redress this wrong to the utmost of my power.'

'This'll be worse than the windmills,' said Sancho. 'Look here, sir, those there are Benedictine friars, and the coach must just be taking some travellers on their way. Look, look, do take care what you're doing, this could be one of the devil's own tricks.'

'I have already told you, Sancho,' replied Don Quixote, 'that you know next to nothing on the subject of adventures. What I say is true, as you will soon see.'

So saying, he rode forward and planted himself in the middle of the road down which the friars were plodding and, when he thought they were near enough to hear him, he cried:

'Diabolical and monstrous wretches, release this very moment the noble princesses whom you are abducting in that coach, or prepare to be killed this instant as a just punishment for your wicked works.'

The friars reined in their mules and sat there in astonishment at the figure cut by Don Quixote and at the words he'd spoken, to which they replied:

'Sir knight, we aren't diabolical or monstrous at all, we're just two Benedictine friars going about our business, and we haven't the faintest idea whether there are any abducted princesses in this coach.'

'Soft words will not work with me, for I know you only too well, perfidious knaves!' said Don Quixote.

And without awaiting any more replies he spurred Rocinante and charged with levelled lance at the friar in front with such determination and fury that, if the friar hadn't thrown himself from his mule, the knight would have brought him to the ground sore vexed and indeed sore wounded, if not stone dead. The other friar, seeing how his companion was being treated, dug his heels into his castle of a mule and made off across the plain faster than the wind.

Sancho Panza, seeing the friar sprawling on the ground, slipped off his donkey, ran over to him and began to strip him of his habits. And now two of the friars' servants came up and asked what he thought he was doing stripping their master like that. Sancho replied that the clothes were rightly his, the spoils of the battle his master Don Quixote had won. The servant-lads, who lacked a sense of humour and knew nothing about spoils and battles, seeing that Don Quixote had gone off to talk to the ladies in the coach, fell upon Sancho, knocked him to the ground, gave his beard a thorough plucking and his body a merciless kicking, and left him lying there breathless and senseless. Without pausing for an instant the friar remounted, terrified and trembling and drained of all colour, and spurred his mule in the direction of his companion, who was waiting a good distance away to see what would be the outcome of this nightmare; and not wanting to stop for the conclusion of the incident they continued on their way, making more signs of the cross than if they had the very devil at their backs.

Don Quixote, as has been said, was talking to the lady in the coach, and saying:

'You may now, in your ineffable loveliness, my lady, dispose of your person as best pleases you, for the pride of your ravishers lies on the ground, o'erthrown by this mighty arm of mine; and that you may not pine to know the name of your deliverer, be informed that I am Don Quixote de la Mancha, knight adventurer and errant, and captive to the peerless and beauteous Doña Dulcinea del Toboso; and in requital of the benefit you have received from me, all I desire is that you turn back to El Toboso and on my behalf present yourself before that lady and inform her of what I have accomplished for your deliverance.'

Everything that Don Quixote said was overheard by one of the squires escorting the coach, a Basque; who, seeing that the man didn't want to let the coach continue on its way, but was saying that it must turn back at once to El Toboso, rode up to Don Quixote and, seizing him by the lance, said in bad Castilian and worse Basque:

'Go on way, knight, and go with devil. By God made me, if not leaving coach, you as killed by Basque as stand there.'

Don Quixote understood him perfectly, and with great composure he replied:

'If you were a knight and a gentleman, which you are not, I should already have punished your folly and audacity, you wretched creature.'

To which the Basque replied:

'Me not gentleman? I swear God you lie as me Christian. If leaving lance and taking sword, soon see you monkey making! Basque on land, gentleman on sea, gentleman for devil, and see lie if other saying.'

'"Now you shall see," quoth Agrages,'[3] quoted Don Quixote.

And throwing his lance to the ground, he drew his sword, took up his little round shield and set upon the Basque, intending to kill him. The Basque, seeing the knight advance, would have preferred to dismount from his mule, which was a hired one and therefore a bad one and not to be trusted, but all he had time to do was to draw his sword; and it was lucky for him that he happened to be next to the coach, from which he was able to snatch a cushion to serve as a shield; and then the two men went for each other as if they were mortal enemies. The rest of the party would have made peace between them but they couldn't, because the Basque was saying in his topsy-turvy tongue that if they didn't let him finish his battle he'd kill his mistress and anyone else who got in his way. The lady in the coach, astonished and terrified at this sight, made the coachman drive a safe distance off, and then settled down to watch the desperate struggle, in the course of which the Basque dealt Don Quixote such a mighty blow on the shoulder, over the top of his shield, that if he hadn't been wearing armour he'd have been split down the middle. When Don Quixote felt the impact of the terrible stroke he cried:

'O lady of my soul, Dulcinea, flower of all beauty, succour this your knight who, through his desire to satisfy your great goodness, finds himself in this dire peril!'

Uttering these words, gripping his sword, raising his shield and launching himself at the Basque was the work of a moment, as Don Quixote resolved to venture everything on the fortune of a single blow. The Basque, seeing Don Quixote advance, could see from his spirited bearing what a brave man he was, and decided to follow his example; so he stood his ground, well protected by his cushion but unable to turn the mule one way or the other because by now, exhausted and unaccustomed to such pranks, it couldn't budge a single step.

So Don Quixote was advancing, as described, on the well-shielded Basque, with his sword aloft, determined to split him in half, and the Basque was awaiting him with his sword also aloft, and upholstered in his protective cushion, and all the bystanders were terrified and wondering what was going to be the outcome of the prodigious blows with which the two men were threatening each other; and the lady in the coach and her maids were making a thousand vows and offerings to all the images and holy places in Spain for God to deliver their squire and themselves from this great peril. But the trouble is that at this very point the author of this history leaves the battle unfinished, excusing himself on the ground that he hasn't found anything more written about these exploits of Don Quixote than what he has narrated. It is true, though, that the second author of this work refused to believe that such a fascinating history had been abandoned to the laws of oblivion, or that the chroniclers of La Mancha had been so lacking in curiosity that they hadn't kept papers relating to this famous knight in their archives or their desks; and so, with this in mind, he didn't despair of finding the end of this delectable history, which indeed, with heaven's help, he did find in the way that will be narrated in the second part.

*Second Part of
the Ingenious Hidalgo*
DON QUIXOTE
de la Mancha

CHAPTER IX

In which the stupendous battle between the gallant Basque and the valiant man from La Mancha is brought to a conclusion

In the first part of this history we left the valiant Basque and the famous Don Quixote with naked swords aloft, about to deliver two such devastating downstrokes that if their aim was true they would at the very least split each other from top to bottom and cut each other open like pomegranates; and at this critical point the delightful history stopped short and was left truncated, without any indication from its author about where the missing section might be found.

This worried me, because the pleasure afforded by the little I had read turned to displeasure as I considered what an uphill task awaited me if I wanted to find the great bulk of material that, as I imagined, was missing from this delectable tale. It seemed impossible and contrary to all good practice that such an excellent knight shouldn't have had some sage who'd have made it his job to record his unprecedented deeds, something never lacked by any of those knights errant

> Who go, as people say,
> Adventuring their way,[1]

because every one of them had one or two sages, made to measure for him, who not only recorded his exploits but also depicted his least thoughts and most trivial actions, however hidden from the public gaze they were; and such an excellent knight couldn't have been so unfortunate as to be totally lacking in what Platir[2] and the like had more than enough of. So I couldn't bring myself to believe that such a superb history had been left maimed and mutilated, and I laid the blame on malicious time, the devourer and demolisher of all things, which had either hidden or destroyed what was missing.

It also struck me that, since modern books like *The Undeceptions of Jealousy* and *The Nymphs and Shepherds of Henares* had been found in his library, his history must also be a recent one, and that, even if it hadn't been put into writing, it must live on in the memory of the people of his village and others near by. All these thoughts left me feeling puzzled and eager for exact and authentic knowledge of the complete life and works of our famous Spaniard Don Quixote de la Mancha, the light and mirror of the chivalry of that land, and the first man in our times, in these calamitous times of ours, to devote himself to the toils and exercise of knight-errantry, and to the redressing of wrongs, the succouring of widows and the protecting of maidens, those maidens who used to ride about, up hill and down dale, with their whips and their palfreys, carrying their maidenhead with them; for unless raped by some blackguard, or by some peasant with his hatchet and his iron skullcap, or by some monstrous giant, there were maidens in those times gone by who, at the age of eighty and not having slept a single night under a roof, went to their graves with their maidenheads as intact as the mothers who'd borne them. I say, then, that for these and many other reasons our gallant Don Quixote is worthy of continuous and memorable praise – which shouldn't be denied me, either, for all the hard work and diligence I devoted to searching out the conclusion to this agreeable history; although I'm well aware that if heaven, chance and fortune hadn't helped me, the world would have been left without the pleasurable entertainment that an attentive reader of this work can enjoy for nearly two hours. And this is how I found the missing part:

One day when I was in the main shopping street in Toledo, a lad appeared, on his way to sell some old notebooks and loose sheets of paper to a silk merchant; and since I'll read anything, even scraps of paper lying in the gutter, this leaning of mine led me to pick up one of the notebooks that the lad had for sale, and I saw it was written in characters that I recognized as Arabic. Although I knew that much, I couldn't read them, and so I looked around to see if there was some Spanish-speaking Moor in the street, and it wasn't very hard to find one, because even if I'd been looking for a translator from another better and older language,[3] I should have found him, too. In short, chance provided me with a man who, when I told him what I wanted and put the book in his hands, opened it in the middle and after reading a little began to laugh. I asked him why, and he replied that he was laughing at something written in the margin of the book by way of annotation. I told him to tell me what it was and, still laughing, he replied:

'As I said, this is written here in the margin: "This woman Dulcinea del Toboso, so often mentioned in this book, is said to have been a dabber hand at salting pork than any other woman in La Mancha."'

When I heard 'Dulcinea del Toboso' I was dumbfounded, because it immediately suggested that the notebooks contained the history of Don Quixote. So I told him to read me the title-page that very instant and he did so, making an extempore translation from the Arabic, and it said: *History of Don Quixote de la Mancha, written by Cide Hamete Benengeli,[4] an Arab historian.* I had to draw on all the discretion I possess not to reveal how happy I felt when I heard the title of the book; and, getting in ahead of the silk merchant, I bought all the papers and notebooks from the lad for half a real; and if the lad himself had had any discretion and had noticed how much I wanted them, he could well have expected and indeed exacted more than six reals. Then I went off with the Moor to the cathedral cloister and asked him to translate the notebooks, or at least all those that had to do with Don Quixote, into Castilian, without adding or omitting a single word, and I offered to pay him whatever he asked. He was satisfied with fifty pounds of raisins and two bushels of wheat, and promised to make a good, faithful translation, and to be quick about it, too. But to ensure the smooth working of our agreement, and not to let such a find out of my sight, I brought the Moor home with me, and in little more than a month and a half he translated the whole text just as it is set down here.

In the first notebook there was a realistic picture of Don Quixote's battle with the Basque, with both of them in the positions described in the history, their swords aloft, one protected by his little round infantryman's shield and the other by his cushion, and the Basque's mule so lifelike that you could tell from a mile off that it was a hired one. At the Basque's feet were written the words *Don Sancho de Azpetia*,[5] which must have been his name; and at Rocinante's feet were these other words: *Don Quixote*. Rocinante was depicted in such wonderful detail – as long as a wet week and as lean as a lath, with a jutting spine and far gone in consumption – that it was easy to see how appropriately he had been named Rocinante. Next to him stood Sancho Panza, holding his ass by the halter, and at his feet were the words *Sancho Zancas*; and he must, to judge from the picture, have had a short body, a plump paunch and long shanks, these last two features being expressed in the words Panza and Zancas respectively, because he's given both these surnames at different points in this history. Other details could be observed, but none of them is important, or relevant to the truthful narration of this history – and no history is bad so long as it is truthful.

If there is any objection to be made about the truthfulness of this history, it can only be that its author was an Arab, and it's a well-known feature of Arabs that they're all liars; but since they're such enemies of ours, it's to be supposed that he fell short of the truth rather than exaggerating it. And this is, indeed, what I suspect he did, because where he could and should have launched into the praises of such an excellent knight, he seems to have been careful to pass them over in silence, which is something he shouldn't have done or even thought of doing, because historians should and must be precise, truthful and unprejudiced, without allowing self-interest or fear, hostility or affection, to turn them away from the path of truth, whose mother is history: the imitator of time, the storehouse of actions and the witness to the past, an example and a lesson to the present and a warning to the future. In this history I know that everything anyone could want to find in the most delectable history is to be found; and if anything worthwhile is missing from it, it's my belief that it's the dog of an author who wrote it that's to blame, rather than any defect in the subject. At all events the second part began like this, according to the translation:

The keen-edged swords of the two valiant and enraged combatants, thus raised aloft, seemed to be threatening the very heavens, earth and watery abysses, such was the determination displayed by both men. The first to deliver his blow was the wrathful Basque, and he did so with such force and fury that, if his sword had not twisted in the course of its descent, that stroke alone would have been enough to put an end to the fearful fight and to all our knight's adventures; but fortune, which had better things in store for him, turned his opponent's blade aside so that, although it struck his left shoulder, all the damage it did was to disarm him on that side, carrying with it a large part of his helmet together with half his ear, all of which tumbled to the ground in hideous ruin, leaving him in a sorry state indeed.

By God, who could describe the rage that took possession of the heart of the man of La Mancha on seeing himself treated in this way? All that can be said is that it was so great that he rose at last in his stirrups and, gripping his sword with both hands, brought it down with such fury full on the Basque's cushion and head that his admirable protection was of no avail and, as if a mountain had fallen on top of him, blood began to trickle from his nose, and from his mouth, and from his ears, and he started to slide off his mule, from which he would no doubt have fallen had he not clung to its neck; but even so he lost his stirrups and dropped his reins, and the animal, terrified by the awful blow, began to gallop this way and that, and soon bucked its rider off.

Don Quixote was calmly watching this scene, and when he saw the Basque fall he jumped from his horse, ran up to him and, putting the tip of his sword between his eyes, told him to surrender or he would cut off his head. The Basque was so stunned that he could not reply, and his fate would have been sealed, so blind with rage was Don Quixote, if the ladies in the coach, who had been watching the fight in consternation, had not hastened to where he stood and pleaded with him to do them the great kindness and favour of sparing their squire's life. To which Don Quixote, haughty and grave, replied:

'To be sure, fair ladies, I am well content to do as you request; but I insist on one condition to which you must agree, which is that this knight promise me to repair to the village of El Toboso and present himself on my behalf before the peerless Doña Dulcinea, that she may dispose of him according to her pleasure.'

The fearful, disconsolate ladies, without stopping to think about what Don Quixote was demanding or even asking who Dulcinea was, promised that the squire would do whatever was required of him.

'Since you have given me your word, I shall do him no further harm, even though he richly merits it.'

CHAPTER X

*About what happened next between Don Quixote and
the Basque, and the peril with which he was threatened by
a mob of men from Yanguas*

By this time Sancho Panza had struggled to his feet, somewhat mauled
by the friars' servants, and had stood watching Don Quixote's battle, as
in his heart he prayed to God to be so kind as to give his master the
victory and let him win some island of which he could make his squire
the governor, as promised. So once Sancho saw that the fight was over
and that his master was about to remount Rocinante, he went over to
hold his stirrup and, before he started climbing, knelt down before him
and, grasping his hand, kissed it and said:

'Don Quixote sir, please make me the governor of the island you've
just won in this dreadful battle. However big it is, I'm sure I'll be strong
enough to govern it as well as anyone who ever governed islands anywhere
in the world.'

To which Don Quixote replied:

'I would have you know, brother Sancho, that this adventure and others
like it are not island adventures but roadside adventures, in which there
is nothing to be won but a broken head and a missing ear. Be patient,
for there will be adventures that will enable me to make you not only a
governor but something greater still.'

Sancho thanked him profusely and, again kissing his hand, and the
skirts of his armour too, helped him on to Rocinante, and himself mounted
his donkey and set out after his master, who, without a word of farewell
to the ladies in the coach, rode off at a brisk pace into a nearby wood.
Sancho followed as fast as his donkey could trot, but Rocinante's speed
was such that Sancho fell further and further behind and had to call out
to his master to wait for him. Don Quixote did so, reining Rocinante in
until his weary squire caught up with him, and said:

'What I'm thinking, sir, is that it'd be a good idea to go and take refuge
in some church somewhere, because that man you fought is in a really
bad way, and it wouldn't surprise me if we were reported to the Holy

Brotherhood[1] and they came to arrest us. And by God, if they do that, we'll sweat blood before we get out of prison.'

'Not at all, Sancho,' said Don Quixote. 'Where have you ever seen or read of a knight errant standing trial, whatever outrages he is accused of?'

'I don't know anything about getting out of rages, I've never been in one in my life – all I do know is that people who go fighting in the fields are dealt with by the Holy Brotherhood, and I'm not going to poke my nose into that other thing you said.'

'Do not worry, my friend,' replied Don Quixote, 'for I shall rescue you from the Chaldeans[2] themselves if need be, let alone the Holy Brotherhood. But tell me, pray: have you ever seen a knight more valiant than I on all the face of the earth? Have you ever read in histories of any knight who is or has been more spirited in the attack, more persevering in the pursuit, more dexterous in the wounding or more skilful in the unhorsing?'

'To tell you the honest truth,' replied Sancho, 'I haven't ever read a history, because I can't read or write, but what I will dare bet is that in all the days of my born life I've never served a braver master than you – and I pray God these braveries of yours aren't paid for where I just said. And what I pray you to do is to see to that ear of yours, you're losing a lot of blood from it. Here in my saddle-bags I've got some lint and white ointment.'

'All this would have been quite unnecessary,' replied Don Quixote, 'if I had remembered to make a flask of the Balsam of Fierabras:[3] for but one drop of it would have saved us both time and medicine.'

'What flask and what balsam is that?' said Sancho Panza.

'It is,' said Don Quixote, 'a balsam the recipe for which I carry in my memory, and if provided with it one need not fear death or contemplate dying from any kind of wound. And so, once I make some and give it to you, all you have to do when you see that in some battle I have been cut in two (as often happens) is to take the part of my body that has fallen to the ground and, before the blood congeals, neatly and carefully place it on top of the part remaining in the saddle, being quite sure to make it fit exactly. Then you will have me drink just two mouthfuls of the balsam, and I shall be as sound as a bell.'

'If that's so,' said Sancho, 'I here and now renounce being governor of the island you've promised me, and all I want in payment for my many good services is for you to let me have the recipe for that wonderful potion – to my mind it'll fetch more than two reals an ounce anywhere, so it's all I need to live an honourable and easy life. But first I'd better know if it costs a lot to make.'

'For less than three reals you can make twelve pints of it,' replied Don Quixote.

'Strike me blind!' replied Sancho. 'What are you waiting for, why not make some here and now and show me how?'

'Enough of that, my friend,' replied Don Quixote. 'I intend in due course to show you even greater secrets and do you even greater favours. But now let us see to this ear of mine, for it is hurting more than I should like.'

Sancho took lint and ointment out of his saddle-bags. But when Don Quixote saw his broken helmet he was on the point of going berserk, and, placing his hand on his sword and raising his eyes to heaven, he said:

'I swear by the Creator of all things, and by the four evangelists and all their holy writings, that I will lead the life led by the great Marquis of Mantua when he swore to avenge his nephew Baldwin's death, and until then "ne'er at table to eat bread nor with his wife to lie", and other such things that, although I cannot remember them now, can be taken as spoken, until I have exacted full vengeance on the perpetrator of this outrage.'

When Sancho heard this he said:

'I'd just like to point out, Don Quixote sir, that if that knight has done as he was told and has gone to present himself before my lady Dulcinea del Toboso, then he's done his duty and doesn't deserve another punishment unless he commits another crime.'

'You have spoken well and to the purpose,' replied Don Quixote, 'and so I hereby annul my oath as regards exacting fresh vengeance on him; but I swear anew and confirm that I will lead the life I have just described until I wrest from some knight another helmet at least as fine as this. And do not imagine, Sancho, that I am doing this without a solid basis, for I have a clear model to follow: exactly the same thing happened, down to the very last detail, with Mambrino's helmet, which cost Sacripante so dear.'[4]

'You just send all those oaths of yours to the devil, sir,' retorted Sancho, 'they're bad for your health and worse for your conscience. Or else tell me this – supposing days and days go by and we don't come across anyone in a helmet, what then? Have we got to honour the oath, regardless of all the inconvenience and discomfort, always sleeping in our clothes, never under a roof, and those hundreds of other penances in the mad old Marquis of Mantua's vow, that you're so set on reviving? Just think about it, sir – it isn't men in armour you'll find on these here roads but carters and muleteers, who not only don't wear helmets but have probably never even heard of them.'

'You are mistaken about that,' said Don Quixote, 'because before we have been riding along these highways and byways for two hours we shall see more men in arms than fell upon Albracca to carry off the fair Angelica.'[5]

'All right, then, so be it,' said Sancho, 'and please God we come well out of all this and the time soon arrives to conquer this island that's going to cost me so dear – and then I can die happy.'

'I have already told you, Sancho, not to worry about all that; for if finding an island presents any problems, there is always the kingdom of Denmark or the kingdom of Soliadisa,[6] which would fit you like a glove, and still more so being as it is on terra firma, which should make you even happier. But let us leave these matters until it is time to deal with them; and now see if you have anything to eat in your saddle-bags, so that we can go without delay in search of some castle where we can stay for the night and make the balsam about which I have told you; for I swear to God that my ear is very painful.'

'There's an onion here, and a bit of cheese, and a few scraps of bread,' said Sancho, 'but that isn't food for a valiant knight like you.'

'How mistaken you are!' replied Don Quixote. 'I would have you know, Sancho, that it is an honour for knights errant not to eat for a whole month, and if they do eat, it must be what they find readiest to hand, and you would know this well enough if you had read as many histories as I have; for in all those very very many that I have read, I have not found any mention of knights errant eating, except when it happened that some sumptuous banquet was held for them, but otherwise they used to live on next to nothing. And although it is evident that they could not have gone without eating and satisfying all the other needs of nature, because, after all, they were men like us, it is also evident that since they spent most of their time wandering in woods and wildernesses, without cooks, their everyday food must have been country fare, like that which you are offering me now. And so, friend Sancho, do not be afflicted by what pleases me; do not seek to build the world anew, or to turn knight-errantry on its head.'

'I'm sorry I'm sure,' said Sancho. 'Not knowing how to read or write, as I said before, I haven't been able to find out about all these rules of knighthood. From now on I'll put all sorts of nuts and raisins into the saddle-bags for you, being as you are a knight, and for me, not being one, I'll put in feathered provisions of greater substance.'

'I am not saying, Sancho,' replied Don Quixote, 'that it is obligatory for knights errant not to eat anything other than those nuts to which you refer; but that they must have been their usual sustenance, together with certain herbs, known to them and to me, which they found in the fields.'

'It's a good idea,' said Sancho, 'to know about those there herbs. I fancy we're going to need that knowledge one fine day.'

Then he took out what he'd said he'd brought, and the two men ate together in peace and good fellowship. But anxious to find somewhere to stay that night they didn't linger over their dry and frugal meal. They remounted and hurried on, to try and reach a village before nightfall, but both the day and their hopes of doing so came to an end as they were passing some goatherds' huts, and they decided to spend the night there. Sancho's sorrow at not reaching a village was matched by his master's delight at sleeping in the open air, because he considered that each time he did so he performed an act of possession that provided fresh proof of his chivalry.

CHAPTER XI

*About what happened to Don Quixote with
some goatherds*

He received a hearty welcome from the goatherds. Once Sancho had
accommodated Rocinante and the donkey as best he could, he set off on
the trail of the smell being given out by some chunks of goat meat that
were boiling in a pot over the fire; and, although he'd have liked to find
out there and then if they were ready to be transferred from the pot to
the stomach, this wasn't possible, because the goatherds took them off
the fire and, spreading some sheepskins on the ground, made haste to lay
their rustic table and, showing great goodwill, invited them to share their
meal. There were six goatherds using that fold and they all sat down
around the skins, after begging Don Quixote, with rough ceremony, to
sit on an upside-down bowl that they placed there for him. Don Quixote
did so, and Sancho stayed standing to serve him the drinking horn. When
Don Quixote saw his squire on his feet, he said:

'So that you may see, Sancho, what great good there is in knight-
errantry, and how close those exercising any of its ministries always are
to being honoured and esteemed by the world, it is my wish that you
should come and sit by my side in the company of these excellent people,
and be one with me, your natural lord and master – that you should eat
from my very own plate and drink from my very own cup: for of
knight-errantry may be said what is said of love, that it makes all things
equal.'

'What a great honour!' said Sancho. 'But just let me tell you one thing,
sir – if I had plenty to eat, I'd eat it as well or even better standing up
and by myself as sitting down next to an emperor. The truth is that what
I eat in my own little corner without any fuss or bother, even if it is only
bread and onions, tastes much better to me than all the fine turkeys on
other tables where I'd have to chew slowly, drink hardly a drop, wipe
my mouth all the time, never sneeze or cough if I felt like it, or do all
those other things that being by yourself and free and easy lets you do.
So, sir, as for these honours that you want to confer on me for being a

follower and servant of knight-errantry, which is what I am as your squire, I'd rather you turned them into something more practical and useful, and I renounce all your honours from here to eternity – though I'm very grateful to you I'm sure.'

'You shall sit down all the same; for he that humbleth himself shall be exalted.'[1]

And seizing Sancho by the arm he forced him to squat by his side.

The goatherds couldn't make head or tail of this gibberish about squires and knights errant, and they just sat there eating in silence and staring at their guests who, with great elegance and even greater appetite, were stowing away chunks of meat as big as their fists. Once the meat course was finished, a quantity of sweet acorns was spread on the sheepskins together with half a cheese, harder than if it had been made of mortar. Meanwhile the drinking horn was being kept busy, circulating so often (now full, now empty, like a bucket on a water wheel) that it soon exhausted one of the two wineskins hanging near by. After Don Quixote had satisfied his stomach he took up a handful of acorns and, gazing at them, held forth as follows:

'Happy the age and happy the centuries were those on which the ancients bestowed the name of golden, not because gold (so prized in this our age of iron) was then to be obtained with ease, but because men living in such times did not know those two words *yours* and *mine*. In that blessed age all things were held in common; no man, to gain his daily sustenance, had need to take any other pains than to reach up and pluck it from the sturdy oaks, liberally inviting him to taste their sweet and toothsome fruit. The limpid fountains and the running streams offered him their delectable and transparent waters in magnificent abundance. In the clefts of rocks and in the hollows of trees, diligent and prudent bees formed their commonwealths, offering to every hand, without requesting anything in return, the rich harvest of their sweet labours. The sturdy cork-oaks, without any other inducement than that of their own generosity, shed their thick, light bark, with which men first covered their houses, supported on rustic poles, only as a defence against the inclemencies of the heavens. All then was peace, all was friendship, all was harmony; the heavy coulter of the arching plough had not yet ventured to open and enter the tender womb of our first mother, for she, without any compulsion, yielded from every part of her broad and fertile bosom everything to satisfy, sustain and delight the children then possessing her.

'Those were the days when artless, lovely shepherdesses roamed from dale to dale and from hill to hill, their hair in plaits or flowing loose, clothed in no more than was necessary to conceal with modesty that which modesty has always required to be concealed; and their ornaments were not those now in fashion, luxuries of Tyrian purple and martyred and tormented silk, but verdant burdock leaves and ivy intertwined, in which perhaps they walked as fine and elegant as our court ladies do now in the bizarre creations that idle curiosity has put before their eyes. In those times the amorous conceptions of the soul were expressed as simply as they had been conceived, without any search for artificial circumlocutions to enhance them. Fraud, deceit and malice were not yet intermixed with truth and plain dealing. Justice kept within her own bounds, and favour and interest, which now depreciate, confound and persecute her, did not dare assail or disturb her. As yet the judge could not make his whim the measure of the law, because there was nothing to judge and nobody to be judged. Maidens and modesty roamed, as I have said, wherever they wished, alone and mistresses of themselves, without fear of harm from others' intemperance and lewd designs: their ruin was born of their own will and desire. And now, in these detestable times of ours, no maiden is safe, even if she is hidden away in the depths of another Cretan labyrinth:[2] for even there the plague of love, with all the insistence of its accursed importunity, finds its way in through some chink, or wafted through the air, and infects and ruins her and all her seclusion. It was for the protection of such ladies, as time went by and wickedness increased, that the order of knights errant was founded, to defend maidens, protect widows and succour orphans and the needy.

'This is the order to which I belong, my brothers, whom I thank for the most friendly welcome that you have given me and my squire. For although every man alive is obliged by natural law to assist knights errant, it is nonetheless meet that, knowing as I do that in ignorance of this obligation you have welcomed and regaled me, I should acknowledge your goodwill with the utmost gratitude.'

This long harangue (which could well have been dispensed with) was pronounced by our knight because the acorns he'd been given had reminded him of the golden age; and so it occurred to him to offer these useless arguments to the goatherds, who listened without uttering a word, bemused and bewildered. Sancho kept quiet, too, and ate acorns, and paid frequent visits to the second wineskin, hanging from a cork-oak so that its contents could be kept cool.

It took Don Quixote longer to finish talking than it took the others to finish eating, and then one of the goatherds said:

'So that you can more truthfully say, sir knight errant, that we've welcomed you with a ready goodwill, we want to offer you some pleasant entertainment by getting a companion of ours, who'll soon be here, to sing to us – he's a bright lad, fond of the ladies, and, what's more, he can read and write and he plays the fiddle as prettily as can be.'

The goatherd had hardly finished speaking when the sound of the fiddle reached their ears, and soon after that the fiddler himself appeared, a well-graced lad of maybe twenty-two. His companions asked him if he'd had his supper, and when he replied that he had, the goatherd who'd offered Don Quixote the song said to the lad:

'In that case, Antonio, you could give us the pleasure of hearing you sing, just to show our guest here that there's someone among us who can, and that in these woods and forests there are people who know music. We've told him about your abilities, and now we want you to air them and show that we're right; so go on, sit yourself down and sing us that ballad about your sweetheart that your uncle the priest made up for you – everyone in the village thought it was very good.'

'All right,' the lad replied.

And, not needing to be asked again, he sat down on the stump of an evergreen oak and, after tuning his fiddle, soon began, with great charm, to sing this song:

Antonio

Although, Olalla, you love me,
You never say you do,
Not even with those pretty eyes,
Mute tongues that love speaks through.
I know that you're a clever girl,

So I'll say it yet again,
For once true love has been revealed
It never ends in pain.

    It's true enough, Olalla dear,
You've sometimes made me feel
Your snowy bosom's made of stone,
Your soul is made of steel.

    And yet amid your coy rebuffs
And modest dressings-down,
From time to time hope lets me see
The borders of her gown.

    My hopes swoop on the fair decoy
And yet they've never savoured
The sadness of not being called
Or the joy of being favoured.

    If love is kindness, as they say,
You're so endowed with this
That the conclusion to my hopes
Must be the longed-for bliss.

    If loyal services can help
To turn a breast benign,
Some of the things I've done for you
Must surely make you mine.

    For if you have been watching out,
You often will have seen
Me wearing my best Sunday suit
On Mondays, neat and clean.

    As I well know, fine clothes and love
Walk down the selfsame way:
I've always wanted, in your eyes,
To look gallant and gay.

    I shall not mention dancing, or
The singing, for your sake,
Of serenades, from darkest night
Till crowing cold daybreak.

    I shall not mention all the praise

I've spoken of your looks;
It's true enough, but it's put me
In other girls' bad books.

　　Craggy Teresa said, when I
Said you're as lovely as can be:
'There's them as thinks they loves a saint
When what they loves is a chimpanzee.

　　Just look at all her flashy gewgaws,
Hair from someone else's head,
Just look at all her phoney glamour:
Love himself could be misled.'

　　So then I told her she was lying;
Her cousin took her side;
He challenged me, and you know what
He did and I replied.

　　It's love not lust I feel for you,
For it's not that I'm inclined
To slap and tickle, stuff like that:
I've better things in mind.

　　The Church has got a solid yoke
Tied firm with silken twine,
You stick your head in your own half
And I'll stick my head in mine.

　　If not, I swear it here and now
By my dead kith and kin:
I'll only ever leave these hills
To be a Capuchin.

　With this the goatherd brought his song to an end; and, although Don Quixote asked him to sing them another one, Sancho Panza wouldn't agree to it, because he was more in a condition to sleep than to listen to songs. And so he said to his master:

　'You settle yourself down straight away where you're going to spend the night, because the work these good people have got to do all day long doesn't let them spend their nights singing.'

　'Yes, I understand, Sancho,' replied Don Quixote. 'It is plain to see that the visits to the wineskin demand requital in sleep rather than in music.'

'We all of us enjoyed the wine, thank God,' replied Sancho.

'I do not deny it,' replied Don Quixote, 'but settle down now wherever you like, for it is better for those of my profession to watch than to sleep. Nevertheless it would be a good idea if you dressed this ear of mine again – it is hurting more than it needs to.'

Sancho did as he was told, and when one of the shepherds saw the wound he told him not to worry, he'd apply a remedy that would soon cure it. And the shepherd picked a few leaves of the rosemary that was growing there in great plenty, chewed them and mixed them with a little salt, applied them to the wound and bandaged it tightly, assuring Don Quixote that no other remedy would be necessary; which proved true.

CHAPTER XII

About what a goatherd told Don Quixote and the others

And now one of the lads who brought provisions from the village appeared and said:

'Hey, do you know what's happened down in the village?'

'How are we supposed to know that?' replied one of them.

'Well, it's like this,' the lad continued. 'That famous student-shepherd Grisóstomo died this morning, and it's rumoured he died of love for that fiendish Marcela, rich Guillermo's daughter, that girl who wanders about all those God-forsaken places dressed up as a shepherdess.'

'Marcela you said?' asked one of them.

'Marcela I said,' the lad replied. 'And the best part is he's left in his will that he wants to be buried out in the wilds, like some Moor, at the foot of the rock by the cork-oak spring, because rumour has it that's where he first saw her, and they say he said so himself. And he's left other things to be done, too, but the village priests say they won't be done, and that it wouldn't be right to do them, because they're more like what pagans get up to. To all this, that great friend of his, Ambrosio – you know, that student who dressed up as a shepherd with him – replies that it'll all be done just as Grisóstomo ordered, and the village is in an uproar about it, but, to judge from what everyone's saying, they're going to end up doing what Ambrosio and all his shepherd friends want, and tomorrow they're coming to bury him with great pomp and ceremony where I said. And it's my belief it's going to be well worth seeing – at least I'm not going to miss it, not even if it means that I can't get back to the village tomorrow.'

'That's what we'll all do,' added the goatherds, 'and we'll draw lots to see who'll stay behind to look after the goats.'

'A good idea, Pedro,' said one, 'but there won't be any need for that, I'll stay behind with everybody's goats. And don't put it down to virtue or lack of curiosity on my part, but to me not being able to walk, because of that broken branch that went through my foot the other day.'

'Thanks all the same,' replied Pedro.

Don Quixote asked this Pedro to tell him about the dead man and the shepherdess, to which Pedro replied that all he knew was that the dead man was a rich hidalgo who lived in a village in the sierra and who'd been a student at Salamanca University for many years, after which he'd come back to the village with a reputation for being wise and well-read.

'In particular, people said he knew all about the science of the stars, and what the sun and the moon do up there in the sky, because he used to tell us exactly when the clips were going to come.'

'*Eclipse* is the word, my friend, not *clips*, for the obscuration of the two great luminaries,' said Don Quixote.

But Pedro, not troubling himself with trifles, went on with his story:

'And he also used to predict whether a year was going to be fruitful or hysterical.'

'You mean *sterile*, my friend,' said Don Quixote.

'Sterile or hysterical,' replied Pedro, 'it all boils down to the same thing. As I was saying, with all this predicting his father and his friends grew very rich, because they believed him and did as he advised when he said: "Sow barley this year, not wheat; this year you'd better sow chick-peas, not barley; next year there's going to be a bumper crop of olives, but the following three there won't be any at all."'

'That science is called astrology,' said Don Quixote.

'I haven't the faintest idea what it's called,' retorted Pedro, 'but what I do know is that he knew all this and more besides. In the end, not very many months after he came back from Salamanca, he took off his long scholar's gown one day and appeared dressed as a shepherd, with his crook and his sheepskin jacket – and this other man, his great friend Ambrosio, who'd studied with him, he dressed himself up as a shepherd too. I was forgetting to say that Grisóstomo, the dead man, was very good at writing poems – he even used to write the carols for Christmas Eve, and the mystery plays for Corpus Christi[1] that the village lads performed, and everyone said they were brilliant. When the people in the village saw the two scholars suddenly dressed as shepherds they were amazed, and couldn't work out what had led them to make such an odd change. By this time Grisóstomo's father had died and he'd inherited piles of property – royal estate, goods and cattles, cows and horses, sheep and goats, as well as masses of money, and the lad was left the absolute lord of it all, and the truth is he deserved it, because he was a fine companion and very charitable, a good friend to all good men, with a face like an angel. Later it was known that he'd only changed clothes to wander all about these wild places after that shepherdess Marcela the young lad mentioned before, because poor Grisóstomo, God rest his soul, had fallen in love with her. And now I'm going to tell you, because it's something you should know, who that lass is – it's possible, and more than possible, that you won't hear anything like it in all the days of your life, even if you live to be older than noses.'

'*Moses* you should have said,' interrupted Don Quixote, who couldn't abide the goatherd's word-mangling.

'Noses have been around for quite a while, too,' retorted Pedro, 'and if you're going to be picking on every other word I use, sir, we shan't be done in a twelvemonth.'

'Forgive me, my friend,' said Don Quixote. 'I only mentioned it because there is such a difference between noses and Moses; but your reply was an excellent one, for noses are indeed older than Moses; and do continue your history, and I will not interrupt you ever again.'

'I was about to say, my dear good sir,' said the goatherd, 'that there was one farmer in our village even richer than Grisóstomo's father, and he was called Guillermo, and God had given him not only vast riches but also a daughter whose mother, the most honourable woman in all these parts, had died giving birth to her. I can see her even now, that lovely face of hers with the sun in one cheek and the moon in the other. And what a fine housewife she was, and so good to the poor – I do believe that at this very moment her soul must be enjoying God in the other world. Guillermo was heartbroken at the death of such an excellent wife and he died, too, leaving his daughter Marcela young and rich and in the care of one of her uncles, a priest in our village. The girl grew up so beautiful that she put us in mind of her mother, such a great beauty herself, although everyone thought that her daughter was going to be even lovelier. And so she was, and by the time she was fourteen or fifteen all who set eyes on her praised God for making her so beautiful, and most fell hopelessly in love. Her uncle kept her shut up indoors, very bashful and demure, but the fame of her great beauty spread far and wide – and this, and her fortune, brought the men not only of our own village but of all the villages for many miles around, the very best of them too, flocking to ask, beg and pester her uncle for her hand in marriage. But even though he'd have liked to marry her off straight away, since she was of the right age, being a true and good Christian he was unwilling to do so without her consent – and no, he didn't have an eye on the gains to be made from delaying the girl's marriage and keeping control of her property. This, I can promise you, was said in praise of the good priest in more than one circle of commentators in the village. For I should tell you, errant sir, that in these tiny places everything's discussed and everything's gossiped about; and you can be quite certain, just as I am, that a priest has to be a saint to make his flock speak well of him, especially in a village.'

'That is quite true,' said Don Quixote, 'but do continue, for the story is a very good one, and you, my dear Pedro, are telling it with a certain stylish grace.'

'It's the grace of Our Lord God that I'm in need of, which is more to the purpose. Anyway, what happened was that although the priest described to his niece, in detail, the qualities of each one of her many suitors, begging her to choose and marry whichever she preferred, all she ever replied was that she didn't want to marry yet because, being so young, she didn't feel strong enough to bear the burden of matrimony. Faced with excuses as good as these appeared to be, her uncle stopped pressing her, and decided to wait until she was older and able to choose a companion to her taste. For as he said, and said rightly, parents shouldn't provide for their children's future against their will. But lo and behold, like a bolt from the blue, meticulous modest Marcela appears one day converted into a shepherdess, and, despite all the efforts of her uncle and the other villagers to dissuade her, off she goes into the fields with the other shepherdesses in the village to mind her own flock. And once she came into the public gaze and her beauty was exposed to all eyes, I couldn't tell you how many rich youths, hidalgos and farmers dressed up just like Grisóstomo, and wandered about the fields wooing her – among them, as I've said, our deceased friend, who people said no longer loved her, but adored her.

'But you mustn't suppose, just because Marcela has given herself over to this free and easy life, with little privacy or rather none at all, that she's done anything to bring the least discredit upon her modesty or chastity; quite the opposite, she watches so closely over her own honour that of all her suitors and pursuers not one has boasted, or could boast without lying, of having been given the slightest hope of fulfilling his desire. Because although she doesn't avoid the company of shepherds, and treats them with courteous friendliness, as soon as any of them reveals his intentions, even if in a proper and holy proposal of marriage, she hurls him from her like a boulder from a catapult. And in this mood she's wreaking more havoc on these lands than if they'd been invaded by the plague; because her affability and beauty encourage those who know her to serve her and to love her, but her disdainful destruction of their hopes drives them to the brink of suicide; and so they don't know what to say, and only cry that she's cruel and an ingrate, and other similar words that describe her character all too accurately. And if you were to stay here awhile, sir, you'd hear these mountains and these valleys echoing with the laments of the broken-hearted wretches who pursue her.

'Not far from here is a place where there are almost two dozen lofty beeches, and there is not one on whose smooth bark is not engraved the name of Marcela, and above some a crown with which a lover affirms that Marcela wears and deserves to wear the crown of all human beauty.

Here a shepherd sighs, there another moans; here songs of love are to be heard, there dirges of despair. There's one who spends every hour of the night seated at the foot of some oak or crag, and there, never allowing his tear-filled eyes a moment's rest, sunk and lost in his thoughts, he's found by the morning sun; there's another who, finding no relief or respite for his sighs, stretched out on the burning sand in the racking noonday heat of summer, sends his complaints up to merciful heaven. And over every single one of them the lovely Marcela triumphs, footloose and fancy-free, and all of us who know her are waiting to see where her arrogance will lead, and who will be the fortunate man to tame such ferocity and enjoy such perfect beauty. Since everything I've narrated is the proven truth, I can well believe that what this young lad here said they're saying about the cause of Grisóstomo's death is also true. And so I advise you, sir, not to miss his burial tomorrow – it'll be well worth seeing, because Grisóstomo has lots of friends, and it isn't a couple of miles from here to where he said he wanted to be buried.'

'That is indeed what I intend to do,' said Don Quixote, 'and I thank you for the pleasure you have afforded me by telling me such a delightful story.'

'Oh no!' replied the goatherd. 'I don't know half the things that have happened to Marcela's suitors, but it could be that tomorrow we come across some shepherd who can tell us about them. And now it'll be a good idea for you to go and sleep under cover, because sleeping in the damp night air could be bad for your wound – though the remedy you've been given is so effective that there's no fear of an infection setting in.'

Sancho Panza, who was wishing that the goatherd would take his endless talk with him to the devil, also asked his master to go and sleep in Pedro's hut. He did so, and there he spent most of the night remembering his lady Dulcinea, in imitation of Marcela's suitors. Sancho Panza settled down between Rocinante and his donkey, and there he slept the sleep not so much of a star-crossed lover as of a hoof-hammered squire.

CHAPTER XIII

Which concludes the story about the shepherdess Marcela,
together with other events

But hardly had the day begun to show itself on the balconies of the east when five of the six goatherds got up and went to wake Don Quixote, to ask him if he still intended to go and see the famous burial of Grisóstomo, and to tell him that if he did they would keep him company. Don Quixote, who was longing to go, rose and told Sancho to saddle the horse and fit the pack-saddle on to the donkey immediately, which he did with great diligence; and with the same diligence they all set out on their way. And they'd ridden less than a mile when, as they crossed another path, they saw half a dozen shepherds coming towards them clothed in black sheepskin jackets and with wreaths of cypress and bitter oleander crowning their heads. Each had a stout holly stave in his hand. With them came two gentlemen on horseback, splendidly dressed for travelling, accompanied by three servants on foot. When the two parties met they exchanged courteous greetings, and when they asked each other where they were going they discovered that they were all on their way to the burial, so they travelled together.

One of the horsemen said to his companion:

'It seems to me, Señor Vivaldo, that we're going to count however much time we spend on this famous burial as having been time well spent: it is indeed going to be famous, considering the extraordinary things these shepherds have been telling us about the dead shepherd and the death-dealing shepherdess.'

'I think so, too,' replied Vivaldo, 'and I'm not talking about taking just one day over it, either – I'd happily take four days off for the sake of witnessing it.'

Don Quixote asked what it was that they had heard about Marcela and Grisóstomo. The horseman replied that they'd joined up with the shepherds earlier that morning and that, seeing them in such mournful attire, they'd asked why they were dressed like that; and that one of the shepherds had told them all about the secluded life and the beauty of a shepherdess called Marcela, and about the love she inspired in the many men who wooed her, and about the death of that Grisóstomo to whose burial they were going. In short, he told them everything that Pedro had told Don Quixote the day before.

So this conversation came to an end, and another one began when the man called Vivaldo asked Don Quixote what it was that prompted him to ride about such a peaceful part of the world armed in that fashion. And Don Quixote replied:

'The profession that I exercise does not allow me to ride in any other way. Easy living, luxury and repose were invented for effete courtiers; toil, disquiet and arms were created solely for those the world calls knights errant, of whom I, unworthy as I am, am the very least.'

On hearing this they all concluded that he was mad; and to make quite certain, and to find out what sort of madness he suffered from, Vivaldo went on to ask him what knights errant were.

'Have you not read,' replied Don Quixote, 'the annals and histories of England, which treat of the famous exploits of King Arthur, commonly known in our Castilian tongue as Artús, who, according to an ancient tradition divulged throughout that kingdom of Great Britain, did not die but was, by sorcerer's art, turned into a raven, and who, in due course, will recover his sceptre and kingdom, and reign again; for which reason no Englishman has ever been known from that day to this to kill a raven? Well, in the days of that good king the famous order of chivalry of the Knights of the Round Table was founded, and the love between Sir Lancelot of the Lake and Queen Guinevere was consummated as is there recorded, the go-between and confidante being that honourable duenna Quintañona,[1] all of which gave rise to the ballad that is so well known and so highly praised in Spain:

> And never sure was any knight
> So served by damsel or by dame
> As Lancelot, that man of might,
> When here from Brittany he came,

with its smooth and gentle unfolding of its deeds of love and war. Well, from that time onwards, handed on down the generations, the order of chivalry gradually extended and spread throughout many different parts of the world, and its members were famous for their exploits: the valiant Amadis of Gaul with all his sons and grandsons to the fifth generation, and the valorous Felixmarte of Hyrcania, and the never sufficiently praised Tirante the White, and the brave and invincible knight Belianis of Greece, whom we have very nearly been able to see and speak with and hear in our own times. This, then, gentlemen, is what it is to be a knight errant, and this is the order of chivalry, in which I, as I have said, although a sinner, have professed; and I do profess everything professed by the knights of whom I have told you. And so I roam these lonely and deserted places in search of adventures, with the firm intention to employ my arm and indeed my whole person in the most perilous adventures that fortune sends my way, in aid of the weak and needy.'

These words showed the travellers that Don Quixote was indeed out of his wits, and they could now see what kind of madness had taken him over, which astonished them as much as it did everybody else who made this discovery. And, to while away the time during the short journey said to remain, Vivaldo, who was a clever man with a cheerful disposition, decided, when they reached the sierra where the burial was to take place, to provide him with the opportunity to expand on his nonsense. So he said:

'It seems to me, sir knight errant, that you profess one of the very strictest professions in the world, and it's my belief that not even being a Carthusian monk is as strict.'

'It may be that it is as strict,' replied our Don Quixote, 'but whether it is as necessary to the world is something that I am within a hair's breadth of doubting. For, if truth is to be told, the soldier who carries out his captain's orders contributes no less than the captain who gives him those orders. What I mean to say is that monks, in peace and tranquillity, pray to heaven for the well-being of the world; but we soldiers and knights put into practice what they pray for, defending the world with the prowess of our arms and the blades of our swords, and not under cover but in the open air, the targets for unbearable sun-rays in the summer and for the piercing frosts of winter. So we are ministers of God on earth, the arms through which his justice is executed here. And since the business of war and all its associated activities cannot be conducted without guts, sweat and toil, it follows that those who profess it must labour harder than those who in tranquil peace and repose are forever praying to God to favour the weak and defenceless. I do not mean to say, nor does it even cross my mind, that the life of a knight errant is as virtuous as that of a cloistered monk; I merely want to argue, from my own sufferings, that it is, without a shadow of doubt, more laborious and more buffeted, hungrier and thirstier, more wretched, ragged and louse-ridden; for there is no denying that the knights errant of the past suffered much misfortune in the course of their lives. And if some of them rose by the strength of their arms to be emperors, I know that it cost them dear in blood and sweat, and if those who did rise to this degree had not had enchanters and sages to help them, they would have been baulked in their ambitions and cheated of their hopes.'

'That's what I think, too,' said the traveller, 'but there's just one thing, among lots of others, that I don't like about knights errant, and that is that when they're about to undertake some mighty and perilous adventure in which there's a clear risk of losing their lives, it never occurs to them to commend themselves to God, as every Christian's meant to do in such moments of danger, but instead they go and commend themselves to their ladies, with as much spirit and devotion as if their ladies were God himself – which seems to me to have a smack of the pagan about it.'

'My dear sir,' replied Don Quixote, 'it cannot be otherwise, and the knight errant who conducted himself in any other manner would be committing a grave misdemeanour, for it is an established custom in knight-errantry that the knight errant whose lady is present when he undertakes some great feat of arms turns his eyes to her with gentle lovingness, as if to implore her to favour and succour him in the parlous straits into which he is about to enter; and even if there is nobody there to hear him, he is obliged to whisper a few words in which he commends himself to her with all his heart; and of this we have innumerable examples in the histories. And one cannot assume from this that they do not commend themselves to God as well, for they still have the time and the opportunity to do so in the course of the subsequent action.'

'All the same,' replied the traveller, 'I still have my doubts – I've often read how two knights errant have words and, one thing leading to another, they lose their tempers and turn their horses and take up their positions a good distance from each other, and then, without any further ado, they charge, and in mid-career they commend themselves to their ladies – and what usually happens in these encounters is that one of them tumbles back over the haunches of his horse, pierced through and through by his opponent's lance, and the other one would fall off his, too, if he didn't hang on to its mane. Now I can't see how the one who died could have had any chance to commend himself to God, with everything happening so fast. It'd have been better if, instead of using up his words commending himself to his lady as he charged, he'd employed them on what he ought to have done as a Christian. What's more, it's my belief that not all knights errant do have ladies to commend themselves to, because not all of them are ladies' men.'

'That cannot be,' said Don Quixote. 'What I mean to say is that there cannot be any knight errant without a lady, because it is as natural and proper for them to be lovers as it is for the heavens to have stars, and it is quite certain that there has never been a history in which one can find a knight errant without a lady-love; because his lack of one would in itself be sufficient for him to be regarded not as a legitimate knight errant but as a bastard who had gained entry to the fortress of chivalry not through the main gate but over the wall, like a thief and a robber.'

'All the same,' replied the traveller, 'if I'm not mistaken, I think I can remember reading that Sir Galaor, the brother of the valiant Amadis of Gaul, never had any particular lady to commend himself to, and this didn't make people look down on him, and he was a very brave and famous knight.'

To which our Don Quixote replied:

'My dear sir, one swallow does not make a summer. Furthermore, I know that this knight did secretly burn with love, apart from the fact that, as everyone knows, he lost his heart to all those ladies who took his fancy, a natural inclination towards the fair sex that he could not overcome. But, in short, it is very well attested that he did have one special lady whom he made the mistress of his heart, and to whom he did indeed commend himself very often but very secretly, because he prided himself on being a secretive knight.'

'So if it's essential for every knight errant to be a lover,' said the traveller, 'we can assume you're one, too, this being part and parcel of the profession. And so long as you don't pride yourself on being as secretive as Sir Galaor, I beseech you, with all the urgency I can be permitted, on behalf of these good people and myself as well, to tell us all about your lady's name, home town, rank and beauty – I'm sure she'd count herself lucky to have the whole wide world know she's loved and served by such a knight as you appear to be.'

Here Don Quixote heaved a deep sigh and said:

'I cannot affirm whether or not my sweet enemy is pleased at the whole world's knowing that I serve her; all I can say, in response to what is so courteously requested of me, is that her name is Dulcinea; her homeland El Toboso, a village in La Mancha; her rank that of princess at least, for she is my queen and lady; her beauty superhuman, for in her all the impossible and chimerical attributes of loveliness that poets ascribe to their ladies become reality: her hair really is golden, and her forehead the Elysian Fields, and her eyebrows rainbows, and her eyes suns, and her cheeks roses, and her lips coral, and her teeth pearls, and her neck alabaster, and her breast marble, and her hands ivory, and her complexion snow; and the parts hidden to human gaze by modesty are such, I do think and believe, that wise consideration cannot find comparisons for them, but only extol them.'

'We should like to know about her family, lineage and ancestry,' said Vivaldo.

To which Don Quixote replied:

'She is not of the ancient Curtii, Caii or Scipios of Rome, or of the modern Colonnas or Orsinis, or of the Moncadas or Requeséns of Catalonia, nor yet of the Rebellas or Villanovas of Valencia, the Palafoxes, Nuzas, Rocabertis, Corellas, Lunas, Alagóns, Urreas, Fozes or Gurreas of Aragon, the Cerdas, Manriques, Mendozas or Guzmáns of Castile, or the Alencastros, Pallas or Meneses of Portugal; she is, rather, of those of El Toboso de la Mancha, a lineage that, although recent, is such that it could well be the generous rootstock of the most illustrious families of future centuries. And let no man contest this except on the condition placed by Zerbino under the trophy of Orlando's arms and armour:

> Let no man move this armour or this sword
> Who will not prove his prowess with their lord.'[2]

'My own lineage is the Cachopíns of Laredo,' replied the traveller, 'but I'm not going to be so rash as to compare it with El Toboso de la Mancha, even though, to tell you the truth, this is a surname I've never heard of.'

'Never heard of it my foot!' retorted Don Quixote.

The others were all ears as they listened to the conversation between the two, and even the goatherds realized just how crazy our Don Quixote was. Sancho Panza alone thought that everything his master said was true, having known him, and known what sort of a man he was, ever since childhood; and Sancho only hesitated a little when it came to the part about the lovely Dulcinea del Toboso, because he'd never heard of such a name or such a princess, even though he lived so near to El Toboso.

As they continued on their way engrossed in this conversation they saw, coming down a gorge between two great hills, about twenty shepherds, all wearing black sheepskin jackets and crowned with wreaths some of which were later discovered to be of yew and the others of cypress. Six of the shepherds were carrying a bier covered with a great variety of flowers and branches. At this sight one of the goatherds said:

'Those men over there are bringing Grisóstomo's body, and at the foot of that mountain is the spot where he said he was to be buried.'

So they hurried there, just in time, because the shepherds had placed the bier on the ground and four of them had begun digging a grave beside a hard rock with their sharp pickaxes.

The two parties exchanged courteous greetings, and then Don Quixote and those who had come with him went to examine the bier, and on it, covered in flowers, they saw the corpse, dressed as a shepherd, of a man who seemed to be about thirty; and even though he was dead, it was plain to see that in life he'd had handsome features and a gallant disposition. Scattered around him on the bier there were some books and many papers, some open and some folded up. The onlookers, the grave-diggers and all the others kept an extraordinary silence, until one of those who'd brought the body said to another:

'You'd better make quite certain, Ambrosio, that this is the place Grisóstomo said, since you're so concerned for everything in his will to be carried out exactly as he instructed.'

'Yes, this is the place,' replied Ambrosio, 'because it was here that my unhappy friend often told me the story of his misadventures. He told me it was here that he first saw that mortal enemy of the human race; here that he first declared his love, as honourable as it was ardent; and here, at their last meeting, that Marcela sealed her scornful rejection, which led him to put an end to the tragedy of his wretched existence. And here, in remembrance of so many misfortunes, he wished to be laid in the bowels of eternal oblivion.'

And, turning to Don Quixote and the travellers, Ambrosio continued: 'This body, gentlemen, that you are contemplating with compassionate eyes, was the dwelling-place of a soul in which heaven placed an infinite portion of its riches. This is the body of Grisóstomo, who was unmatched in intelligence, peerless in courtesy, perfect in politeness, a phoenix in friendship, generous beyond measure, grave without presumptuousness, joyful without vulgarity, and, all in all, the first in virtue, and second to none in misfortune. He loved and was hated; he adored and was disdained; he entreated a dragon, pleaded with marble, chased the wind, cried out in the wilderness and served ingratitude, whose reward was to make him the prey of death in the midst of the course of his life, which was ended by a shepherdess whom he wished to make immortal in the memory of mankind, as those papers at which you are looking could demonstrate, if he had not instructed me to commit them to the flames as soon as I have committed his body to the earth.'

'If you do that,' said Vivaldo, 'you'll be treating them with even harsher cruelty than their owner himself, because it's neither just nor proper to carry out the wishes of a man who orders something that no rational arguments can justify. Augustus Caesar would have been out of his mind if he'd agreed to what the divine Mantuan poet ordered in his will.[3] And so, Señor Ambrosio, even though you are committing your friend's body to the earth, don't commit his writings to oblivion; for if he was so aggrieved as to command it, you shouldn't be so foolish as to obey him. Rather let these papers live, and Marcela's cruelty with them, for ever, as an example to the living, in times to come, so that they can avoid such pitfalls; because I and these friends of mine know the history of this enamoured and desperate friend of yours, and we know about your friendship, and what caused his death, and the instructions he left when he died; from all of which lamentable history it is easy to judge how great was Marcela's cruelty, Grisóstomo's love and your faithful friendship, and also to see what happens to people who rush headlong down the path that delirious love places before their eyes. Last night we learned that

Grisóstomo had died and was to be buried in this place, and so, moved by curiosity and compassion, we departed from our route and agreed to come and see for ourselves what we'd been so sad to hear about. And in recognition of this compassion, and of our desire to do something about it if we could, we beg you, O Ambrosio, – or at least I for my part beg you – not to burn these papers and to let me have some of them.'

And without waiting for the shepherd to reply, Vivaldo stretched out his hand and took some of the papers closest to him. Seeing which Ambrosio said:

'Courtesy obliges me, sir, to let you keep the papers you've just taken, but it would be vain for you to think I shall not burn the rest.'

Vivaldo, longing to see what was written on the papers, opened one of them and saw that its title was *Song of Despair*. On hearing this Ambrosio said:

'This is the last thing the unfortunate man wrote. And so that all can hear, sir, to what a pass his misfortune had brought him, please read it aloud: there'll be time enough to do so while the grave is being dug.'

'That I shall do with pleasure,' said Vivaldo.

And since all the others were equally curious, they gathered around him, and he read the following in a clear and ringing voice:

CHAPTER XIV

*In which the dead shepherd's verses of despair are given,
together with other unexpected events*

Grisóstomo's Song

Since you would have me publish, cruel maid,
From tongue to tongue, in this and every nation,
The news of your implacable disdain,
I'll call on hell itself to come and aid
My grieving breast with howls of lamentation,

And bend and break my voice with grief and pain.
And as I strive and labour to explain
My sorrow and your cold and heartless deed,
Forth shall the terrifying clamour stream,
And in it fragments of my bowels shall teem
To make my torture exquisite indeed.
So give me your attention: listen now
Not to harmonious sounds, but to the row
That from my bosom's depths in desolation,
Stirred up by bitter frenzy without measure,
Flows for my pleasure and for your vexation.

The roaring of the lion; and the raging
Howl of the vicious wolf; the scaly, craven
Snake's dreadful hissing; and the awful groan
Of some horrendous monster; the presaging
And cautionary croaking of the raven;
Across the tossing sea the gale's wild moan;
The furious bellow of the overthrown
And wounded bull; the pitiful lament
Made by the widowed dove; the dreary whine
Of the much-envied owl:[1] let all combine
With shrieks from the infernal regiment
To clamour forth from my tormented soul,
So mingling in one vast, tumultuous whole
That all the senses are soon overpowered;
For novel tones are needed to declare
This deep despair by which my heart's devoured.

The doleful echoes of such great confusion
Shall not resound on Father Tagus' banks
Or famous Betis'[2] olive groves: for I
Shall spread my miseries in sad profusion
In mountains' deepest caves and steepest flanks,
With a dead tongue yet with a living cry;
Or in some hidden vale, or on the shy

Shores that from human dealings still abstain,
Or where the fiery globe was never seen,
Or where vast hordes of noxious creatures glean
Their baneful living from the Libyan plain;
For though, unto the barren wilderness,
Uncertain echoes of my heart's distress
Take word of your unequalled cruelty,
They shall, by favour of my wretched fate
Reverberate all over land and sea.

Disdain is death; suspicion, false or sound,
Defeats the patience of the firmest mind;
Base jealousy destroys with its despair;
Interminable absences confound
Our lives; faced by neglect, our hopes for kind
Or happy fortune don't reduce our care:
Inevitable death lurks everywhere.
And yet – a miracle! – I don't expire,
Jealous, disdained, far absent, fully sure
About suspicions that I can't endure,
Neglected by the one on whom I feed my fire;
And, racked by all this torture, I can't spy
A glimmer of those hopes that pass me by,
Nor do I, in my grief, seek hope – no, never:
Instead, to magnify my misery,
I swear to be bereft of hope for ever.

But is it possible to hope and fear
At once, somehow? And is it for the best
When arguments for fear have much more weight?
Why shut my eyes when jealousy stands here
And, through the thousand gashes in my breast,
Is something that I have to contemplate?
Who would not run to open wide the gate
To disbelief, when right before his eyes
Disdain's revealed, and wavering suspicion

Is changed to patent fact – Oh sad transition! –
While limpid truth is turned to murky lies?
Fierce tyrant of all Love's imperial lands,
O Jealousy, place cold steel in these hands!
Give me, Disdain, a rope of twisted thread!
But grief has gained a cruel victory:
Your memory, I fear, is long since dead.

    I die, and I despair of being blessed
In life or death with any joy at all,
So I'll persist in my fantastic dream.
I'll say that he who loves the most does best,
The freest man is he who's most in thrall
To Love's tyrannical and ancient scheme,
And my eternal enemy I'll deem
To have a soul as lovely as her face;
Say that forgetfulness is my desert
And that, by means of this most dreadful hurt,
Love builds his empire on a solid base.
With these ideas, and with a well-tied knot,
I'll put an end to my poor mortal lot,
Destroyed by her disdain and heartlessness.
I'll give my soul and body to the air
And know I'll bear no future palms of bliss.

    With your unreason you make manifest
The reason forcing me to bring to bear
This force on my own life, a baneful blight;
So, since this mortal wound deep in my breast
Is proof that must make anyone aware
How gladly I succumb to my bleak plight,
And if by chance you recognize my right
That the clear heavens of your lovely eyes
Should darken when I die, you must control
Your grief: when I leave you my shattered soul
I don't want kind responses as some prize.

Instead, with laughter on that grim occasion,
Show that my dying is your celebration; ◄
But this request's a foolish waste of breath
For I well know it will increase your glory
That my life's story ends in sudden death.

And now the hour has struck: from deepest hell
Come, thirsting Tantalus, to my ordeal;
Rolling your mighty stone along its way
Come, Sisyphus; come, Tityus, come as well,
And bring your vulture; Ixion, bring your wheel;
Come too, you sisters toiling night and day;[3]
And now let all of you as one convey
Your mortal anguish to my breast, and sigh
(If it's allowed to victims of despair)
Your harrowing laments over my bare
Carcass, refused a shroud in which to lie.
Come, three-faced guardian of the dreadful gate[4]
And all hell's brood of fiends, and celebrate
And sing the doleful descant of your grief;
No better tribute can, I think, be due
To lovers who have won death's cold relief. ◄

O Song of Desperation, do not grieve
Now that in desolation I must leave;
But rather, since the cause that gave you birth
By my misfortune grows and grows in gladness,
Be free from sadness, even in the earth.

The members of the audience quite liked Grisóstomo's song, even though the reader said he didn't think it accorded with the account he'd heard of Marcela's modesty and virtue, because Grisóstomo complained about jealousy, suspicion and absence, all to the prejudice of Marcela's good name and reputation. To which Ambrosio replied, as one who knew his friend's most hidden thoughts:

'To satisfy that doubt, sir, I should tell you that when this unfortunate man wrote this song he was far from Marcela, having taken himself away to see if absence would have its customary effect; and, since there's nothing that doesn't worry an absent lover and no fear that doesn't assail him, Grisóstomo was worried by imagined jealousies and suspicions that he feared as if they were real. And so everything that fame affirms about Marcela's virtue is true: except for some cruelty, and a little arrogance, and more than a little disdain, there are no faults at all for envy itself to find in her.'

'That's true enough,' replied Vivaldo.

As he was about to read another of the papers he'd saved from the fire, he was halted by a miraculous vision (that was what it seemed to be) which came before their eyes: on top of the crag by which the grave was being dug the shepherdess Marcela appeared, so beautiful that her beauty was even greater than it was famed to be. Those who had never seen her before gazed at her in silent amazement, and those who were used to seeing her stood in no less awe. But as soon as Ambrosio saw her he said, with indignation in his looks:

'Have you come, perhaps, fierce basilisk of these mountains, to see if your presence will make the wounds of this poor man slain by your cruelty spout blood? Or have you come to gloat over the achievements of your barbarity; or to contemplate from those heights, like another pitiless Nero, the flames of burning Rome; or to ride roughshod in your arrogance over this luckless corpse, as the ungrateful daughter did over her father Tarquin?⁵ Tell us now why you've come and what you want; because knowing that Grisóstomo's very thoughts never failed to obey you when he was alive, I shall ensure that, even though he's dead, you'll be obeyed by the thoughts of all those who called themselves his friends.'

'I haven't come, Ambrosio, for any of the reasons you've mentioned,' replied Marcela, 'but to defend myself and to demonstrate how wrong are all those who blame me for Grisóstomo's death and for their grief; and so I beg all of you here to give me your attention, because it won't take me very long nor shall I need many words to bring the truth home to people of good sense.

'You all say that heaven made me beautiful, so much so that this beauty of mine, with a force you can't resist, makes you love me; and you say and even demand that, in return for the love you show me, I must love you. By the natural understanding which God has granted me I know that whatever is beautiful is lovable; but I can't conceive why, for this reason alone, a woman who's loved for her beauty should be obliged to love whoever loves her. What's more, it could happen that the lover of beauty is ugly, and since that which is ugly is loathsome, it isn't very fitting for him to say: "I love you because you're beautiful; you must love me even though I'm ugly." And even if they are well-matched as far as beauty goes, that doesn't mean that the attraction's going to be mutual, because not all beauty inspires love. Some beauties delight the eye but don't captivate the heart; just as well, because if all beauty did inspire love and conquer hearts, people's affections would be forever wandering this way and that without knowing where to come to rest – there's an infinite number of beautiful people, so the affections would be infinite, too. And, according to what I've heard, true love can't be divided, and must be voluntary, not forced on you. If this is so, as I believe it is, why do you think I should be obliged to give in to you, just because you say you love me dearly? Or else tell me this: if heaven had made me ugly instead of beautiful, would I have been right to complain about you for not loving me? What's more, you must remember that I didn't choose this beauty of mine – heaven gave it to me, exactly as you see it, quite freely, without my asking for it or picking it. And just as the viper doesn't deserve to be blamed for her poison, even though she kills with it, because nature gave it to her, so I don't deserve to be blamed for being beautiful; because beauty in a virtuous woman is like a distant fire or sharp sword, which don't burn or cut anyone who doesn't come too close. Honour and virtue are ornaments of the soul, and without them the body, even if it is beautiful, shouldn't seem beautiful. Well then, if chastity is one of the virtues that most embellish the soul and the body, why should the woman who's loved for her beauty lose her chastity by responding to the advances of the man who, merely for his own pleasure, employs all his strength and cunning to make her lose it?

'I was born free, and to live free I chose the solitude of the countryside. The trees on these mountains are my company, the clear waters of these streams are my mirrors; and to the trees and the waters I reveal my thoughts and my beauty. I am the distant fire and the far-off sword. Those who have loved me for my looks I have disabused with my words. And if desires are kept alive on hope, I have never given any hope to Grisóstomo or fulfilled any man's desires, so it can truly be said of all of them that they were killed by their own obstinacy rather than by my cruelty. And if it's objected that his intentions were honourable and that for this reason I should have been more responsive to him, I reply that when, in that very place where his grave is being dug now, he revealed those honourable intentions of his to me, I told him that mine were to live in perpetual solitude and to allow nothing but the earth to enjoy the fruits of my seclusion and the remains of my beauty. If, after I'd spoken as plainly as that, he still chose to persevere against all hope and sail against the wind, is it surprising that he sank in the middle of the gulf of his own folly? If I'd encouraged him, I should have been false; if I'd gratified him, I should have been acting against my own intentions, better than his. He persisted although disabused, he despaired although not hated: and now you tell me whether it's just for me to be blamed for his grief! Let the man I deceive complain, let the victim of broken promises despair, let the man I entice nurse hope, let the man I accept rejoice: but let me not be called cruel or murderous by any man whom I have never deceived, made promises to, enticed or accepted.

'Heaven hasn't made it my destiny to love, and it's vain to think I'd ever love out of choice. Let this general warning serve for the individual benefit of each of my pursuers; and let it also be understood from now on that if any man dies because of me, he isn't dying from jealousy or mistreatment, because a woman who doesn't love any man can't make any man jealous, and disabuse must not be confused with disdain. He who calls me fierce and a basilisk can leave me alone, as something evil and dangerous; he who calls me an ingrate can stop courting me; he who calls me distant can keep his distance; he who calls me cruel can stop following me: because this fierce basilisk, this ingrate, this cruel and distant woman is most certainly not going to seek, court, approach or follow any of them. If Grisóstomo was killed by his own impatience and uncontrolled passion, why should anyone blame my modest and circumspect behaviour for that? If I keep my purity in the company of the trees, why should anyone want me to lose it in the company of men? As you all know, I have wealth of my own and I don't covet anyone else's; I live in freedom and I don't like to be constrained; I neither love nor hate anybody. I neither deceive this man nor run after that; I neither toy with one, nor amuse myself with another. The innocent company of the village shepherdesses and the care of my goats keep me happy. These mountains mark the limits of my desires, and if they do extend any further it is only for the contemplation of the beauty of the heavens, the way along which the soul travels back to its first abode.'

And as she said this she turned and disappeared into the thick of a nearby forest without waiting for an answer, leaving everyone astonished as much at her intelligence as at her beauty. And some of them, wounded by the powerful arrows of the rays flashing from her lovely eyes, made to follow her, heedless of the clear warning that they'd heard. Don Quixote, seeing this, and thinking it a good moment to make use of his chivalry by succouring a maiden in distress, cried in a ringing voice and with his hand on the hilt of his sword:

'Let no man, of whatever estate or condition, dare to follow the beautiful Marcela, under pain of incurring my furious indignation. She has shown with clear and sufficient reasons that she bears little or no blame for Grisóstomo's death, and that she is far from reciprocating the desires of any of her suitors; for which reason it is right that, instead of being pursued and persecuted, she should be honoured and held in esteem by all good men, for she has shown that she is the only woman in the world who lives such a chaste life.'

Whether because of Don Quixote's threats or because Ambrosio told them to finish what they were doing for their dead friend, none of the shepherds left the spot until, with the grave dug and Grisóstomo's papers burned, they placed his body in it, not without shedding many tears. They sealed the grave with a thick slab of rock, to be replaced in due course by a tombstone which Ambrosio said he was going to have made, with the following epitaph engraved on it:

> In here, earth's cold and paltry prize,
> The body of a lover lies,
> A shepherd who was cruelly slain
> By one who paid love with disdain.
> Ungrateful, haughty, cold and fair
> Was she who drove him to despair:
> More triumph for man's deadly foe
> As tyrant Love's dominions grow.

They strewed flowers and branches over the grave, condoled with their friend Ambrosio and took their leave of him. Vivaldo and his companion did the same, and Don Quixote said goodbye to his hosts and to the travellers, who begged him to come with them to Seville, because it's just the place to find adventures – on every street and round every corner they're simply waiting for you, more of them than anywhere else in the world. Don Quixote thanked them for the information and for their disposition to extend such courtesies to him, but said that for the time being he did not wish to go to Seville and indeed could not go there, until he had rid all those sierras of foul robbers, with which they were said to be infested. In view of his firm intentions the travellers decided not to pester him any more and, repeating their farewells, they left him and continued their journey, during which they weren't short of things to talk about, what with Marcela's history and Don Quixote's mad deeds. He resolved to go in search of the shepherdess Marcela and offer her all the services in his power. But events didn't turn out as he expected, according to what is related in the course of this true history, the second part of which ends here.

Third Part of
the Ingenious Hidalgo
DON QUIXOTE
de la Mancha

CHAPTER XV

*Which relates the unfortunate adventure that came
Don Quixote's way when he came the way of some wicked
men from Yanguas*

The wise Cide Hamete Benengeli says that as soon as Don Quixote had taken his leave of his hosts and of everyone else at Grisóstomo's burial, he and his squire rode off into the forest where Marcela had disappeared; and, after they'd wandered about it searching for her in vain for over two hours, they reached a meadow of fresh grass, with a cool, tranquil stream running alongside, which invited and indeed compelled them to spend the hours of early afternoon there, because the heat was beginning to be excessive.

Don Quixote and Sancho dismounted and, leaving the donkey and Rocinante free to graze as they pleased on the lush grass, they ransacked the saddle-bags; and, without ceremony, in peace and good fellowship, master and servant ate what they found in them.

Sancho hadn't bothered to hobble Rocinante, safe in the knowledge that the nag was so meek and chaste that all the fillies in the pastures of Cordoba wouldn't lead him astray. But as fate – or the devil, who isn't always asleep – would have it, there was also in that valley a herd of Galician pony-mares belonging to some muleteers from Yanguas, whose custom it is to take their siesta with their animals wherever there is grass and water. And that place where Don Quixote happened to find himself suited these men from Yanguas very well.

It happened, then, that Rocinante felt the urge to enjoy some fun and games with their ladyships the pony-mares and, abandoning his natural habits and his normal gait the moment he scented them, without requesting his master's permission, he broke into a lively trot and went to inform them of his needs. But it seems that they must have been feeling more like grazing, because they gave him such a welcome with their hooves and their teeth that his girths soon snapped and he was left saddleless and naked. Yet what must have affected him most was that when the muleteers saw the attack that was being made on their mares, they ran over with their walking-staffs and gave him such a good hiding that they left him sprawling on the grass. At this point Don Quixote and Sancho, having witnessed Rocinante's thrashing, arrived breathless on the scene, and Don Quixote said to Sancho:

'From what I can see, friend Sancho, these are not knights, but base and low-born men. I say this because it means that you can freely help me to take due vengeance for the affront to which Rocinante has been subjected before our very eyes.'

'How the devil are we going to take vengeance,' replied Sancho, 'when there are more than twenty of them and just the two of us – or just the one and a half of us, more like?'

'I am the equal of a hundred men,' retorted Don Quixote.

And without further thought he seized his sword and attacked the men from Yanguas, and so did Sancho Panza, encouraged by his master's example. Don Quixote dealt one of them a blow that slashed open both his leather smock and a large part of his shoulder.

The muleteers, seeing so many of themselves so rudely handled by only two men, resorted to their walking-staffs, surrounded the pair and began to lay into them for all they were worth. The truth is that with the second blow they knocked Sancho to the ground, and Don Quixote went the same way in spite of all his eager dexterity. As fate would have it, he fell at the prostrate Rocinante's feet, from which one can judge the furious pounding that walking-staffs can give when wielded by wrathful rustic hands. When the men from Yanguas realized what they'd done, they loaded their animals as fast as they could and hurried on their way, leaving the two adventurers looking a sorry sight and feeling in an even worse temper.

Sancho Panza, lying by his master's side, was the first to start groaning, and he said in a feeble, doleful voice:

'Don Quixote sir! Oh, Don Quixote sir!'

'What do you want, brother Sancho?' replied Don Quixote, in the same weak, languishing tones.

'If it's at all possible,' replied Sancho Panza, 'I'd like a couple of swigs of that Fairy Brass's drink, if you've got some handy. Maybe it's good for broken bones as well as for sore wounds.'

'If I had some here, wretch that I am, what more could we want?' replied Don Quixote. 'But I swear to you, Sancho Panza, on my word as a knight errant, that before two days have elapsed, if fortune does not ordain otherwise, I shall have some in my possession; given a modicum of luck I shall manage this in the turning of a hand.'

'And how long do you think it'll be before we can move our feet?' replied Sancho Panza.

'For myself,' said the battered knight Don Quixote, 'I must say that I cannot tell how long. But I am to blame for it all, for I should not have drawn my sword against men who are not knights, as I am; and so I believe that, as a penalty for having broken the laws of chivalry, the god of battles has allowed me to be punished in this way. For this reason, Sancho Panza, you must always bear in mind what I am about to tell you, because it concerns the well-being of us both: whenever you see rabble of this kind offering us some affront, do not wait for me to draw my sword against them, for I shall most certainly not do so, but you draw your sword and punish them to your heart's content; and if any knights come to their aid and defence, I shall then defend you and attack them with all my power. You have already had a thousand signs and demonstrations of how far the powers of this mighty arm of mine extend.'

This was how arrogant the poor gentleman had become after his victory over the brave Basque. But his warning didn't impress Sancho Panza enough to prevent him from responding, and he said:

'I'm a peaceful man, sir, meek and mild, and I can overlook any insult, because I've got a wife to support and children to bring up. So even though it isn't up to me to give any orders, you bear this in mind, too – in no way am I going to draw my sword against anyone, peasant or knight, and I hereby, before God my Maker, forgive all affronts that anybody ever has offered me or ever will offer me, whether the person who has offered them, offers them or will offer them is of high or low birth, rich or poor, a gentleman or a commoner, not excepting any estate or condition whatsoever.'

On hearing this his master replied:

'If only I had breath enough in my body to speak a few words to you at my ease, and if only this pain in my ribs would abate a little, so that I could make you understand, Panza, how wrong you are. Look here, you rogue: should the winds of fortune, hitherto so adverse, turn in our favour, driving the sails of our desire so that with a constant breeze behind us, and in perfect safety, we reach harbour on one of the islands I have promised you, what would become of you if, after conquering it, I made you its lord? Well, you would render things impossible for yourself, through not being a knight or even wanting to be one, or having the courage or the desire to avenge affronts and defend your dominions. For I would have you know that in freshly conquered provinces and kingdoms, the hearts of the natives are never so subdued or so well disposed towards their new master as to leave no fear that they might play some trick, to reverse the state of affairs once more and, as people say, try their luck again; and so the new master must have understanding to be able to govern, and courage to attack and defend in any crisis.'

'In this particular crisis we've just been in,' replied Sancho, 'I do wish I'd had that understanding and courage you're going on about, but I can swear, on my word as a poor man, that I'm in more of a state for plasters than for chit-chat. You try and see if you can get up, and we'll give Rocinante a hand, though he doesn't deserve it, because he was the main cause of all this battering. I never would have believed it of him, I always took him for a pure-minded character, and as peaceful as me. Still, as they say, you need time to get to know people, and there's nothing certain in this life. Who'd have said that after you'd cut that poor knight errant about like that, the follow-up was going to be this great storm of a thumping that's just rained down on our ribs?'

'Your ribs, Sancho,' replied Don Quixote, 'must at least be accustomed to such squalls; but it is clear that mine, nurtured as they were between cambric and holland-cloth, feel the pain of this misfortune more keenly. And if it were not that I imagine . . . – no, I do not imagine: I know for a certain fact – that all these discomforts are inseparable from the exercise of arms, I should be ready to die of sheer rage, here and now.'

To this his squire replied:

'Sir, seeing as how all these disasters are as you might say the harvest of chivalry, I'd be grateful if you'd tell me whether they happen very often, or just at certain set times, because to my mind after two harvests like this one we're going to be useless for the third, unless God in his infinite mercy helps us.'

'Let me tell you, friend Sancho,' replied Don Quixote, 'that the life of a knight errant is subject to a thousand dangers and misfortunes, and it is equally true that knights errant are potential emperors and kings, as is shown by the experience of many different knights, about whose histories I am fully informed. And I could tell you now, if the pain would allow me, about some who by the might of their arms alone have risen to the high estate I have just mentioned; and yet these selfsame knights, both before and afterwards, were engulfed in various calamities and misfortunes. The valiant Amadis of Gaul once found himself in the power of his mortal enemy the enchanter Arcalaus, who, it is attested, had him tied to a column in his courtyard and gave him more than two hundred lashes with the reins of his horse. And there is an anonymous author of no small credit who says that after the Knight of the Sun had been caught in a trap[1] by a door that opened under his feet in a certain castle, and found himself bound hand and foot in a deep pit underground, there he was given what is known as an enema, of snow-water and sand, which was nearly the end of him; and if he had not been succoured in that sore extremity by a sage who was a great friend of his, the poor knight would have fared very ill. So I can well have patience, being as I am in such good company; for they suffered greater affronts than those which we have undergone. And I would have you know, Sancho, that wounds received from weapons that happen accidentally to be in the assailants' hands are not dishonourable, and this is explicitly stated in the law of challenges: if a shoemaker hits a man with the last he is holding, that man cannot be said to have been birched, even if the last is made of this particular wood. I am only telling you this to prevent you from thinking that, just because we have taken a battering in this dispute, we have been dishonoured, for the arms borne by those men, with which they belaboured us, were only their walking-staffs, and none of them, so far as I can remember, was carrying a rapier, a sword or a dagger.'

'They didn't give me a chance to look into details like that,' replied Sancho. 'I'd hardly drawn my own trusty blade when they gave my shoulders such a thrashing with those pine trees of theirs that they knocked the sight out of my eyes and the strength out of my feet and left me where I'm lying now, and where wondering whether the beating was dishonourable or not doesn't bother me in the slightest – all that does bother me is the pain of those staff-blows, and they're going to be as deeply engraved in my memory as they are on my shoulders.'

'For all that, brother Panza,' replied Don Quixote, 'allow me to remind you that there is no memory that time does not efface, no pain that death does not destroy.'

'Well, what bigger disaster could there ever be,' retorted Panza, 'than the one that has to wait for time to efface it and for death to destroy it? If this mishap of ours was one of those that can be cured with a couple of plasters it wouldn't be so bad, but I'm beginning to think that all the bandages in a hospital aren't going to be enough to even begin to sort us two out.'

'Stop that talk, Sancho, and attempt to make the best of a bad business,' replied Don Quixote, 'because that is what I shall do; and now let us see how Rocinante is, because it seems to me that not the least part of this misfortune has fallen to the poor fellow's share.'

'There's nothing surprising about that,' retorted Sancho, 'seeing as how he's such a fine knight errant. But what does surprise me is that my donkey's still in the pink, while we're black and blue all over.'

'Fortune always leaves a door open in adversity, to provide a remedy,' said Don Quixote. 'I say this because that creature of yours can now replace Rocinante, and bear me to some castle where I can be cured of my wounds. Furthermore, I shall not count it dishonourable to ride on such a beast, for I remember reading that when good old Silenus, the tutor of the merry god of laughter, rode into the city of the hundred gates, he did so, much to his satisfaction, on a handsome ass.'[2]

'I expect it's true he rode on an ass, as you say,' replied Sancho, 'but there's a big difference between riding an ass and being slung across an ass's back like a sack of rubbish.'

To which Don Quixote replied:

'Wounds received in battle do not detract from honour, but bestow it; and so, friend Panza, stop answering me back and do as you are told, get up as best you can and put me on top of your donkey in the posture that most pleases you; and let us be gone from here before night falls and catches us in this wild place.'

'Well, well,' said Panza, 'I have heard you say that it's right and proper for knight errants to sleep on open plains and deserts for most of the year, and that they count themselves lucky to do it.'

'All that,' said Don Quixote, 'is when there is no alternative, or when they are in love; and this is so true that there have been knights who have remained on top of a crag, in sunlight and shadow and all the inclemencies of the heavens, for two whole years, unknown to their ladies. And one of these was Amadis, when he called himself Beltenebros and took up his quarters on the Peña Pobre, for eight years or eight months – I cannot quite remember which, but all that matters is that he was doing penance there for some vexation or other that the lady Oriana had caused him. But let us leave these matters, Sancho, and do make haste, before some misfortune like Rocinante's befalls the donkey.'

'Then there'd be the devil and all to do,' said Sancho.

And letting out thirty groans and sixty sighs and one hundred and twenty curses on the head of the person who'd brought him there, he hauled himself to his feet, but he was so exhausted that he stopped half way up, bent over in the form of a Turkish bow and incapable of straightening himself any further; yet despite all these troubles he harnessed his donkey, which had also taken advantage of the day's excess of liberty to go a little astray. Then he righted Rocinante, who, if he'd had a tongue to complain with, certainly wouldn't have been matched by Sancho or his master.

In short, Sancho settled Don Quixote on the ass, tied Rocinante behind and, letting the ass lead the way, set off towards where he thought the highway might be. And he hadn't gone a couple of miles when fortune, which was taking his affairs from good to even better, brought the road before him, and by the side of the road he saw an inn that, to his grief and Don Quixote's delight, was to be a castle. Sancho insisted that it was an inn, and his master insisted that it wasn't an inn but a castle; and their insisting went on for so long that they reached it before they'd finished, and Sancho walked in, without any further investigation, with his string of animals.

CHAPTER XVI

*About what happened to the ingenious hidalgo at the inn
that he took for a castle*

The innkeeper, seeing Don Quixote slumped across the ass, asked Sancho
what was wrong with him. Sancho replied that it wasn't anything much,
he'd just fallen off a rock and got a little bit spifflicated in the ribs. The
innkeeper had a wife who wasn't at all like most innkeepers' wives,
because she had a charitable nature and sympathized with others in their
calamities; and so she hurried to look after Don Quixote and made her
daughter, a very attractive girl, help her. Another girl was serving at the
inn: an Asturian lass[1] with broad jowls, a flat-backed head, a pug nose,
blind in one eye and not very sound in the other. It's true that the loveliness
of her body offset her other shortcomings: she didn't measure five feet
from her head to her toes, and her shoulders, with something of a hump
on them, made her look down at the ground more than she liked. This
comely wench assisted the innkeeper's daughter, and the two of them
prepared for Don Quixote a woeful bed in an attic that showed all the
signs of having served for many years in former times as a hayloft. A
muleteer was also staying at the inn, and his bed was a little beyond Don
Quixote's. Although it was made up of his mules' body pads and blankets,
it was far superior to Don Quixote's, which consisted of four bumpy
boards on top of two tortuous benches, a mattress so thin that it was more
like a bedspread, stuffed with what could be seen through rents in it to
be balls of wool but which felt so hard that they could have been taken
for pebbles, two sheets made of shield-leather and one blanket whose
every thread you could have counted without missing a single one.

On this wretched bed Don Quixote lay himself down, and then the
innkeeper's wife and daughter covered him in ointment from head to foot
while Maritornes, for this was the Asturian's name, held the lamp; and,
finding Don Quixote so badly bruised all over, the innkeeper's wife said
that it looked more like a beating than a fall.

'No, it wasn't a beating,' said Sancho, 'it's just that the rock had lots
of jags and sharp edges on it.'

And each of them had made its own bruise. And he added:

'I'd be grateful, lady, if you could see to it that there are a few bits of tow left over, because somebody else is going to need them – my back's a bit on the sore side, too.'

'So you fell off the rock as well, did you?' replied the innkeeper's wife.

'No,' said Sancho Panza, 'but from the shock of seeing my master fall my own body hurts so much it's just as if I'd been beaten black and blue all over.'

'That could well be so,' said the daughter. 'I've often dreamt about falling off a tower and never reaching the ground, and when I've woken up I've felt as weak and exhausted as if I really had fallen off it.'

'That's the funny thing about it, lady,' said Sancho Panza. 'I wasn't dreaming at all, I was wider awake than I am now, yet I'm almost as badly bruised as my master Don Quixote.'

'What did you say this gentleman's name was?' asked Maritornes the Asturian.

'Don Quixote de la Mancha,' replied Sancho Panza, 'and he's a knight adventurer, and he's one of the best and mightiest ones the world has seen for a long, long time.'

'What's a knight adventurer?' replied the wench.

'Are you so green you don't know that?' retorted Sancho Panza. 'Well, look here, my dear: a knight adventurer, to cut a long story short, is someone who's being beaten up one moment and being crowned emperor the next. Today he's the unhappiest creature in the world, and the poorest too, and tomorrow he'll have two or three kingdoms to hand over to his squire.'

'Well, you're the squire of this fine master,' said the innkeeper's wife, 'so how is it that, to judge from appearances, you aren't even a count?'

'It's early days yet,' replied Sancho, 'we've only been out looking for adventures for a month, and so far we haven't come across any worthy of the name. And sometimes you go looking for one thing and you find another. The fact is that if my master Don Quixote gets over his wounds or fall and it doesn't turn me into a cripple, I wouldn't swap my hopes for the best title in Spain.'

Don Quixote was listening to every word of this conversation and, sitting up in bed as best he could and taking the innkeeper's wife by the hand, he said:

'Believe me, beauteous lady, you may account yourself fortunate to lodge in this your castle such a person as I, whom I refrain from praising because, as is often said, self-praise is no recommendation; but my squire will inform you about me. All I do say is that I shall keep eternally engraved on my memory the service that you have rendered me, so as to remain grateful to you for so long as my life shall last; and if only it had pleased the high heavens that love had not so vanquished me and subjected me to its laws and to the eyes of that beauteous ingrate whose name I shall not speak aloud, the eyes of this fair maiden would have been the lords of my liberty.'

The innkeeper's wife and daughter and the worthy Maritornes were bemused by the knight errant's words, which they understood as well as if he'd spoken in Greek, although they did realize that he meant to compliment them and offer them his services; and since they weren't used to such language they stared at him in amazement, and thought that he wasn't at all like normal men; and then, thanking him for his offers in the most expressive innkeeperese, they left him, and Maritornes the Asturian went to see to Sancho, who was no less in need of help than his master.

The muleteer had agreed with her to have some fun and games together that night, and she'd promised him that as soon as the guests had settled down and her master and mistress were asleep she'd go to him and give him all the pleasure he could wish for. And it's said of this splendid wench that she never gave such a promise without keeping it, even if she gave it unwitnessed in the middle of a moor, because she prided herself on being a hidalga, and didn't consider it at all dishonourable to be serving at the inn, for she said that misfortune and unhappy events had reduced her to that situation.

Don Quixote's hard, narrow, wretched, perfidious bed was the first you reached as you entered that starlit barn, and next to it Sancho made his, which was just a rush mat and a blanket that looked more as if it were made of close-cropped hessian than of wool. After these two beds came the muleteer's, constructed, as described above, out of the body pads and all the trappings of the two best mules he possessed, although he owned twelve altogether, glossy, plump, superb creatures, because he was one of the rich muleteers of Arévalo,[2] according to the author of this history, who makes special mention of this man, because he knew him very well, some people even claiming that the two of them were related – quite apart from the fact that Cide Mahamate Benengeli was a careful and meticulous historian, something that's obvious enough, for he refused to pass in silence over the happenings related so far, even though they're so petty and trivial, which should serve as an example to those grave historians who recount events so very succinctly that we can hardly catch a taste of them and, out of carelessness, malice or ignorance, the most substantial part is left in their inkwells. All praise to the author of *Tablante de Ricamonte*, and to the author of that other book that narrates the deeds of Count Tomillas:[3] how minutely they do describe everything!

I was about to say that after the muleteer had visited his animals and given them their second feed, he stretched himself out on his body pads to wait for his dependable Maritornes. Sancho was poulticed and bedded down, and, although he was trying to sleep, the pains in his ribs wouldn't allow it; and Don Quixote's pains kept him staring into space like a hare. The whole inn was in silence, and there was no light except that of a lamp hanging in the porch.

This extraordinary stillness, and the thoughts, always occupying our knight's mind, of the events narrated at every turn in the books that had been his undoing, brought into his imagination one of the strangest whims that it's possible for anyone to imagine: he had arrived at a famous castle (as we know, all the inns at which he stayed were castles as far as he was concerned), the innkeeper's daughter was the daughter of the lord of the castle, and, overwhelmed by his charm, she had fallen in love with him and promised him to come that night, unknown to her parents, and lie with him for a good while; and, taking all these fancies that he'd constructed for the solid truth, he began to feel anxious and to ponder about the perilous predicament in which his virtue was about to find itself, and he resolved in his heart not to betray his lady Dulcinea del Toboso even if Queen Guinevere herself and her lady-in-waiting Quintañona appeared before him.

As he was mulling over such absurdities, the time arrived for the Asturian girl's visit and for trouble for Don Quixote: barefoot and in her shift, with her hair gathered in a fustian net, she tiptoed into the room where the three men were in their beds, in search of the muleteer. But hardly had she reached the door when Don Quixote heard her, sat up, in spite of all his poultices and the pains in his ribs, and stretched out his arms to receive his beauteous maiden. The Asturian girl, hunched up in silence, was creeping forward with her arms held out in front of her in search of her lover, when she bumped into Don Quixote's arms and he seized her by her wrist and pulled her towards him and made her sit on his bed, and she did not dare utter a word. He felt her shift and, although it was made of sackcloth, it was for him the sheerest sendal. On her wrists she was wearing glass beads, but for him they had the sheen of precious pearls of orient. Her hair was more like a horse's mane, but he saw it as strands of gleaming Arabian gold, the splendour of which made the very sun grow dim. And her mouth, which reeked of stale piccalilli, seemed to him to exhale the gentlest of aromas; and, all in all, he depicted her in his imagination with every attribute of that other princess he'd read about in his books who, overcome by love, came to see the sore wounded knight, arrayed in all the finery there described. And the poor hidalgo was so besotted that neither touch nor smell nor any of the good maiden's other attributes could make him notice his mistake, even though they'd have made anyone but a muleteer vomit; on the contrary, he thought that he was holding the very Goddess of Beauty in his arms. And as he clutched her he began to murmur in soft and loving tones:

'Would that I were in a condition, most beauteous and eminent lady, to be able to repay the singular favour that you have done me in allowing me the sight of your wonderful loveliness; but fortune, which never tires of persecuting the virtuous, has seen fit to lay me low in this bed, so weak and exhausted that, even if it were my desire to satisfy yours, such a thing would be impossible. Furthermore, to this impossibility is added another, which is the fidelity that I have promised to the peerless Dulcinea del Toboso, the sole mistress of my most secret thoughts; but if it were not for these obstacles, I should not be such a doltish knight as to let slip the happy opportunity that in your great goodness you have offered me.'

Maritornes was in a cold sweat of dismay at finding herself in Don Quixote's clutches, and, without understanding or even trying to understand the words he was directing at her, she struggled in silence to break loose. The good muleteer, who'd been kept awake by his wicked desires, had heard his woman as soon as she came in through the door, had been listening to Don Quixote's every word and, suspecting that the Asturian girl might have broken her promise to him in favour of another man, had crept up close to Don Quixote's bed and was waiting there to see where all that incomprehensible jabbering was going to lead. But when he saw the girl struggling to break free and Don Quixote doing what he could to cling on to her, he decided that he didn't like this little joke, raised one arm and delivered such a terrible punch to the amorous knight's lantern jaws that his mouth was bathed in blood; and, not content with this, he climbed up on top of his ribs and started to trot up and down from one end of them to the other.

The bed, being somewhat fragile and insecurely founded, couldn't bear the addition of the muleteer and came crashing to the floor and awoke the innkeeper, who immediately assumed that it must be some of Maritornes' goings-on, because he yelled out to her and there was no reply. So he got up and, lighting a lamp, went in the direction from which the racket was coming. The girl, realizing that her master was on his way and knowing what a fearsome fellow he was, took refuge, agitated and frightened, in the bed of the soundly sleeping Sancho Panza, and there she rolled herself up into a little ball. In came the innkeeper with the words:

'Where are you, you little tart? I know this is all your doing.'

Sancho awoke and, feeling that bundle almost on top of him and thinking he was in the middle of a nightmare, began to flail about with his fists and caught Maritornes with them several times; provoked by the pain, she threw modesty to the wind and gave him so many punches in return that he was soon wide awake, much against his will; and finding that some unknown enemy was treating him in this way, he struggled to his feet and grappled with Maritornes, and the two of them began the fiercest and funniest skirmish imaginable.

When, by the light of the innkeeper's lamp, the muleteer saw the plight that his lady was in, he left Don Quixote and went to give her the help she needed. The innkeeper went to her, too, but with a different intention – to punish the girl in the belief, no doubt, that she was the sole cause of all this harmony. And just as children chant that the cat chased the mouse, the mouse chased the rope, the rope chased the stick, so the muleteer thumped Sancho, Sancho thumped the girl, the girl thumped him, the innkeeper thumped her and they all thumped each other at such a rate that there wasn't a moment's rest for any of them; and the best part of it all was that the innkeeper's lamp went out and left them in the dark, and they all carried on thumping each other at random so mercilessly that wherever a fist fell something or other was broken.

As it happened, another guest at the inn that night was an officer of the Holy Brotherhood of Toledo who, also hearing the strange strains of the struggle, seized his staff of office and the tin box containing his warrants and burst into the dark room crying:

'Stay where you are in the name of the law! Stay where you are in the name of the Holy Brotherhood!'

And the first person he bumped into was the battered Don Quixote, who lay senseless on his back among the ruins of his bed; and the peace-officer felt for the knight's beard and grabbed it and kept shouting:

'Help an officer of the law!'

But realizing that the man he was holding didn't stir, he assumed that he was dead and that the others in the room were his murderers, and in a voice reinforced by this suspicion he yelled:

'Shut the inn door! Don't let anyone leave – a man's been killed!'

These shouts alarmed them all, and each abandoned his fight at whatever stage it had reached when he heard them. The innkeeper went back to his room, the muleteer to his body pads, the girl to her garret; only the hapless Don Quixote and Sancho couldn't budge from where they were. And now the peace-officer let go of Don Quixote's beard and went to look for a light to track down and arrest the delinquents; but he couldn't find one, because the innkeeper had taken the precaution of extinguishing the lamp in the porch when he went back to his room; and the peace-officer had to resort to the fireplace, where after much time and trouble he lit another lamp.

CHAPTER XVII

*In which a further account is given of the countless
hardships that the brave Don Quixote and his good squire
Sancho Panza underwent at the inn that, unfortunately for
him, he mistook for a castle*

By now Don Quixote had come to his senses and, in the same tone of
voice that he'd used the day before to call to his squire when lying in the
Vale of Staffs,[1] he called out to him with the words:

'Sancho, friend, do you sleep? Do you sleep, friend Sancho?'

'How am I supposed to sleep, damn it,' retorted Sancho boiling with
fury, 'when anyone would think all the devils in hell have been messing
with me?'

'You may well think that,' replied Don Quixote, 'because either I am
an ignoramus or this castle is enchanted. For I would have you know . . .;
but what I am about to tell you is something that you must swear to keep
secret until after my death.'

'I swear it,' answered Sancho.

'I am only saying this,' insisted Don Quixote, 'because I believe that it
is wrong to deprive anyone of her honour.'

'I'm telling you I do swear it,' Sancho repeated, 'and I will keep it a
secret until after you've died – and I hope to God I can spill the beans
tomorrow.'

'Do I harm you so much, Sancho,' replied Don Quixote, 'that you
would like so soon to see me dead?'

'It isn't that,' answered Sancho, 'it's just that I hate keeping anything
for very long – I wouldn't like it to go off.'

'Whatever the reason,' said Don Quixote, 'I trust your love and courtesy;
and I would have you know that I have this night experienced one of
the most curious adventures that I could ever celebrate; and, to be brief,
you must know that the daughter of the lord of this castle, who is the
most elegant and beauteous maiden to be found almost anywhere on
earth, came to me a short while ago. How can I paint for you the loveliness
of her person? How describe her fine intelligence? How delineate other

hidden charms that, to preserve the fidelity I owe to my lady Dulcinea del Toboso, I must leave untouched and in silence? I shall only tell you that – whether because the heavens were envious of the great boon that fortune had placed in my hands or (and this is more probable) because this castle is, as I have said, enchanted – just when I was engaged with her in the most tender and loving conversation, a hand attached to some arm of some enormous giant came down, without my seeing it or knowing whence it came, and delivered such a punch to my jaws that they are all bathed in blood; and then it so pummelled me all over that I am in an even worse state than yesterday, after the affair with those men from Yanguas who, because of Rocinante's excesses, inflicted on us the affront about which you know only too well. From this I conjecture that some enchanted Moor must be the guardian of the treasure of this maiden's beauteousness, and that it cannot ever be mine.'

'Nor mine neither,' said Sancho, 'because more than four hundred Moors have been giving me a going-over, and the hammering with the walking-staffs was chicken-feed beside it. But tell me, sir, how can you call it a curious and celebrated adventure, when we've ended up like this? You didn't do so badly, because you got your hands on that incomparable beauteousness you've just been on about, but what did I get out of it apart from the worst hiding I hope I'll ever be given in my life? Oh, what made my poor mother give birth to this miserable sinner? I'm not a knight adventurer and I'm never going to be a knight adventurer, yet I get more than my fair share of all the misadventures!'

'So you were beaten, too, were you?' replied Don Quixote.

'Isn't that what I've just been telling you, damn it?' said Sancho.

'Do not worry about that, my friend,' said Don Quixote. 'I shall now make the precious balsam that will heal us in the twinkling of an eye.'

The peace-officer had now managed to light the lamp, and he went to inspect what he thought was the corpse; and as soon as Sancho saw him walking into the room, in his shirt and nightcap, carrying the lamp and with an ugly look on his face, he asked his master:

'Sir, do you think this might be that enchanted Moor come to punish us again, with some extra punches he forgot to throw the first time?'

'It cannot be the Moor,' replied Don Quixote, 'because those who are enchanted do not allow anyone to see them.'

'Maybe they don't let anyone see them, but they let them feel them all right,' said Sancho. 'And if you don't believe me, just ask my ribs.'

'You could ask mine, too,' replied Don Quixote, 'but this is not sufficient evidence to make us believe that the man before us is indeed the enchanted Moor.'

The peace-officer approached and was amazed to find them coolly chatting to each other. It's true, though, that Don Quixote was still lying on his back, pummelled and plastered into immobility. The peace-officer went up to him and said:

'So how's it going then, you poor old fellow?'

'If I were you,' retorted Don Quixote, 'I should speak with greater courtesy. Is it the custom in this land to talk to knights errant in that way, you blockhead?'

The peace-officer couldn't tolerate being addressed so disrespectfully by such a sorry-looking wretch, and he raised his lamp, oil and all, and smashed it down on Don Quixote's head, leaving a good-sized dent there. The room returned to darkness, he hurried out and Sancho Panza said:

'I'm sure this is the enchanted Moor, sir, and he must be keeping the treasure for other people, and for us he just keeps his punches and his lamp-bastings.'

'You are right,' replied Don Quixote, 'and we must not heed these affairs involving enchantment, and it serves no purpose to grow angry about them: since they are invisible and chimerical, we shall not find anyone on whom to avenge ourselves, however hard we try. Get up, Sancho, if you can, and summon the governor of this castle, and have some oil, wine, salt and rosemary brought to me so that I can make the salutiferous balsam; I do believe I stand in much need of it now, because I am losing a great deal of blood from the wound that this ghost has inflicted on me.'

Sancho struggled to his feet with aching bones and groped his way in the dark towards the innkeeper's room; and bumping into the peace-officer, who was listening to find out how his enemy was faring, he said:

'Sir, whoever you are, please would you very kindly give us a little rosemary, oil, salt and wine that we need to heal one of the best knight errants in the world, who's lying in that bed over there sore wounded by the enchanted Moor that's staying at this inn.'

When the peace-officer heard this, he took Sancho for a madman; and, since day was beginning to dawn, he opened the inn door, called to the innkeeper and told him what this fellow had asked for. The innkeeper gave Sancho everything he wanted, and Sancho took it to Don Quixote, who was clutching his head in both hands complaining of the pain of the lamp-basting, which had done him no more harm than to raise two sizeable lumps; because what he thought was blood was only the sweat that had poured from him in the anguish of his latest storm.

So he took his ingredients and compounded them, mixing them well together and boiling them for a good while, until he thought they were done to a turn. Then he asked for a flask to put the mixture in, and, since there wasn't one of those in the house, he decided to pour it into an oil-bottle made of tin that the innkeeper gave him gratis. And then he said more than eighty Paternosters and as many more Ave Marias and Salve Reginas and Credos over the oil-bottle, and every word was accompanied by the sign of the cross, like a blessing. Sancho, the innkeeper and the peace-officer were present throughout, while the muleteer was calmly seeing to his animals' welfare.

Once Don Quixote had done all this, he was determined to test the virtues of that precious balsam, as he imagined it to be; and so he swallowed a couple of pints of what was left in the cooking-pot after filling the oil-bottle. Hardly had he done drinking than he began to vomit and didn't stop until there was nothing left in his stomach; and with all the retching and writhing he came out in a copious sweat, so he told them to wrap him up and leave him alone. They did so and he slept for more than three hours, at the end of which time he awoke feeling so soothed in his body and so much better from his beating that he considered himself cured. And he firmly believed he'd hit upon the recipe for the Balsam of Fierabras and that, provided with that remedy, he could now, without fear, undertake any fight, battle or devastation, however perilous they might be.

Sancho Panza, who also thought his master's recovery was a miracle, asked him for what was left in the pot, and there was plenty of it. Don Quixote granted the request and, taking up the pot in both hands, with great faith and even greater zeal, Sancho gulped down not much less than his master had swallowed. But the fact is that poor Sancho's stomach can't have been as delicate as Don Quixote's, and so, before he could vomit, he retched and gagged and sweated and swooned, and was fully convinced that his last hour had come; and in his anguish he cursed the balsam and the dog that had given it to him. Seeing him in this state, Don Quixote said:

'It is my belief, Sancho, that all your sufferings are caused by your not having been admitted to the order of chivalry, for it seems to me that this liquor does not benefit those who are not knights.'

'Well, I'll be damned, and all my kinsfolk too!' cried Sancho. 'If you knew that, why did you let me drink the stuff in the first place?'

But now the potion did its work and the poor squire began to gush at both ends at such a rate that neither the rush mat, on which he had lain down once more, nor the hessian blanket covering him could ever be used again. He was sweating and sweating, with such seizures and spasms that not only Sancho himself but all the others thought his end had come. This calamitous tempest lasted almost two hours, at the end of which he was left, not like his master, but so weak and exhausted that he couldn't stand.

But Don Quixote, who, as has been said, felt fit and well, decided to go out straight away in search of adventures, because he believed that every moment spent at the inn was time stolen from the world and from those in it who needed his favour and assistance, even more so with the sure confidence he felt in his balsam. And so, compelled by this desire, he himself saddled Rocinante and put the pack-saddle on the donkey, and helped his squire to dress and struggle on to the animal. Then he mounted and, riding over to a corner of the inn, seized a watchman's short pike leaning there, to use it as a lance.

All the people in the inn – there were more than twenty of them – were looking at him, among them the innkeeper's daughter; and he didn't take his eyes off her, every so often heaving a sigh that he seemed to wrest from the depths of his bowels, and that everyone thought was caused by the pains in his ribs. This, at least, was what was thought by those who'd seen him being anointed the night before. Once the two were mounted and stationed by the inn door, Don Quixote summoned the innkeeper and said in a calm, grave voice:

'Many and magnificent are the kindnesses, my lord governor, that I have received in this your castle, and I am under a great obligation to remember them with gratitude for the rest of my life. If I can repay you for them by taking revenge on your behalf on some insolent knave who has offered you some affront, I would have you know that my office is none other than to assist the helpless, avenge the offended and punish treachery. Search your memory, and if you find anything of this kind to entrust to me, you only have to mention it, for I promise you, by the order of chivalry that I have received, to bring you satisfaction and reparation to the utmost of your desire.'

The innkeeper replied in similarly tranquil tones:

'Sir knight, I don't need you to avenge any affronts for me, because I'm quite capable of taking whatever revenge seems fit when anyone insults me. All I need is for you to pay for your night's stay at my inn – your animals' straw and barley and your own suppers and beds.'

'What – is this an inn?' said Don Quixote.

'Yes, and a very respectable one,' replied the innkeeper.

'I have been in error all this time,' replied Don Quixote, 'for I truly believed it was a castle, and not a bad one at that; but since it turns out not to be a castle but an inn, the best procedure now will be for you to forgive me for not paying you, because I cannot contravene the order of knights errant, of whom I know for certain (never having read anything to the contrary) that they did not pay for their lodging or anything else at any inn where they stayed, because whatever hospitality they might receive is due to them as a right and a privilege, in recompense for the insufferable travails they undergo searching for adventures by night and by day, in winter and in summer, on foot and on horseback, thirsty and hungry, in the heat and in the cold, subject to all the inclemencies of the heavens and all the discomforts of the earth.'

'That hasn't got anything to do with me,' the innkeeper retorted. 'Just cough up what you owe, and don't come to me with tales about knights and errantry – all I'm interested in is being paid for my work.'

'You are a foolish, scurvy innkeeper,' replied Don Quixote.

And putting spurs to Rocinante and brandishing his pike, he rode out of the inn without anybody stopping him, and he continued for a good way without looking back to see if his squire was following.

Seeing Don Quixote leave without paying, the innkeeper hurried to extract the money from Sancho Panza, who said that since his master hadn't been willing to pay he wasn't going to either, because being as he was a knight errant's squire, the same rule applied to him as to his master about not paying in inns and hostelries. This enraged the innkeeper, who threatened that if he didn't hand over the money he'd make him pay in a manner he wouldn't relish. To which Sancho retorted that, by the law of chivalry his master had received, he wasn't going to pay a single farthing, even if it cost him his life, because the ancient and worthy custom of knight errants wasn't going to lapse through his fault, nor were the squires of the same yet to come into the world going to reproach him for the loss of such a just privilege.

As poor Sancho's bad luck would have it, among the people staying at the inn there were four cloth-teaselers from Segovia, three needle-makers from the Potro district of Cordova and two inhabitants of the Heria quarter in Seville,[2] cheerful, well-meaning, mischievous, playful fellows who, almost as if moved by a common impulse, sidled up to Sancho, pulled him from his ass, threw him into the blanket that one of them had run to fetch from the innkeeper's bed, looked upwards, saw that the ceiling was too low for what they had in mind, and decided to go out into the yard, whose limit was the sky. And there, with Sancho in the middle of the blanket, they began to toss him up and down and to amuse themselves at his expense, as people do with dogs at carnival time.

The wretched victim shouted so loud that his master heard him, and as he listened with rapt attention he thought some new adventure was looming, until he realized that the man who was shouting was his squire; so he turned about and rode back to the inn at a laborious gallop and, finding it shut, rode round it to see if he could find a way in, but before he reached the yard walls, which weren't very high, he saw the bad joke that was being played on his squire. He saw him rising and falling through the air so fast and so gracefully that, if his rage had allowed it, I do believe he would have burst out laughing. He tried to scramble from his horse on to the wall, but he was so weak and exhausted that he couldn't even get off the horse; and so, from where he was seated, he began to hurl such furious abuse at the men who were blanket-tossing Sancho that it's impossible to put it down in writing – but his cries didn't make them stop their laughter or their game, nor did flying Sancho stop his laments, sometimes mixed with menaces and sometimes with pleas, all of which served no purpose at all until the jokers stopped out of sheer fatigue.

They brought him his ass, sat him on it and threw his topcoat over his shoulders. And the tender-hearted Maritornes, seeing him so tired, thought it would be a good idea to come to his rescue with a jug of water, and she brought him one from the well, because the water was cooler there. Sancho took the jug and put it to his lips, but he stopped when he heard his master's cries:

'Sancho, dear Sancho, do not drink water! Do not drink it, dear Sancho, for it will kill you! Look, here I have the holy balsam,' – showing him the oil-bottle containing the potion – 'and with just two drops of it you will recover.'

At these words, Sancho rolled his eyeballs sideways in his master's direction and said, among other stronger words:

'Have you forgotten by any chance that I'm not a knight errant, or do you want me to spew up what guts I've got left inside me after last night? Keep your liquor, in the name of the devil, and leave me alone!'

Sancho's ending this speech and starting to drink was all one; but since at the first swallow he realized that it was water, he wouldn't drink any more, and asked Maritornes if he couldn't be brought some wine, which she was very happy to do, and paid for it herself; indeed it is said of her that, although she was of that old profession, there were some vestiges of a Christian about her.

As soon as Sancho had finished drinking he put heels to his ass, threw open the inn door and rode out, delighted at having had his way and not paid a farthing, even though it had been at the expense of his usual sureties, his ribs. It's true that the innkeeper kept Sancho's saddle-bags in lieu of what he was owed, but Sancho was so dazed that he didn't notice they were missing. Once the innkeeper had seen Sancho off, he went to lock and bar the door, but the tossers wouldn't allow it because even if Don Quixote had been one of the Knights of the Round Table these people wouldn't have cared a fig for him.

CHAPTER XVIII

*Which relates the conversation that Sancho Panza had
with his master Don Quixote, and other adventures
worth relating*

Sancho was so worn-out and droopy when he rode up to his master that
he couldn't even put heels to his ass. When Don Quixote saw him in this
state, he said:

'I am now altogether convinced, good Sancho, that the castle or inn is
enchanted, because what could those men who amused themselves with
you in such an atrocious way be but ghosts and creatures from the other
world? And I can confirm this by the fact that, when I was sitting beside
the yard wall beholding the acts of your sad tragedy, I could not climb
on to it, much less dismount from Rocinante, because they must have
enchanted me; for I swear, by my body and bones, that, had I been able
either to climb or to dismount, I should have exacted such revenge that
those arrant knaves would have remembered their prank for ever, even
though it might have meant contravening the laws of chivalry which, as
I have already told you several times, do not allow a knight to lay hands
on anyone who has not been knighted, except in defence of his own life
and person, in dire and urgent necessity.'

'I'd have had my revenge, too, if I could, regardless of the knighting,
but I couldn't, though to my mind them that were playing about with
me back there weren't the ghosts or enchanted men you say they were,
but men of flesh and blood like you and me – I heard them shouting to
each other while they were tossing me, and each of them had his own
name, one was called Pedro Martínez, and another Tenorio Hernández,
and I noticed the innkeeper was called cack-handed Juan Palomeque. So
you see, sir, not being able to get over the wall or even off your horse
was caused by something else, not enchantments. And what this makes
me think is that all these adventures we're looking for are going to end
up by getting us into so many misadventures that we aren't going to
know our left legs from our right. And what it would be best and most
sensible for us to do, in my humble opinion, is to go back to the village

now it's harvest-time and we ought to be looking to our own business, and stop gallivanting about from pillar to post and from the frying-pan into the fire, as they say.'

'How little you know, Sancho,' replied Don Quixote, 'about matters concerning chivalry! Come, say no more, and be patient, for the day will arrive when you will see with your own eyes how honourable it is to follow this profession. Or else just tell me this: what greater happiness can there be in the world, what pleasure can equal that of winning a battle and vanquishing an enemy? None whatsoever, none whatsoever.'

'That's as may be,' replied Sancho. 'I don't know, I'm sure. All I do know is that ever since we've been knight errants, or rather ever since you've been one, because I haven't got any reason to include myself in that honourable company, we haven't won a single battle, unless you count the one against the Basque, and you came out of that missing half an ear and half a helmet – and from then on it's been nothing but beatings and more beatings, punches and more punches, and I've got the advantage over you of one blanket-tossing, given by enchanted persons that I can't take my revenge on so as to find out how happy you feel when you beat an enemy, according to you.'

'That is what is worrying me and ought to be worrying you, too, Sancho,' replied Don Quixote, 'but from now on I shall endeavour to have at hand some sword made with such skill that whoever bears it cannot be subjected to any kind of enchantment; and it could even be that fortune brings my way the sword that belonged to Amadis, when he was known as "The Knight of the Burning Sword", which was one of the best that any knight ever possessed because, apart from having the power that I have just mentioned, it cut like a razor, and there was no armour, however strong and enchanted, that could withstand it.'

'Knowing my luck,' said Sancho, 'if that did happen and you did come across that sword, it'd only be of any use to knights, like that balsam, and the devil take the poor old squires.'

'Never fear, Sancho,' said Don Quixote. 'Heaven will deal better by you.'

As Don Quixote and his squire discussed these matters, Don Quixote saw that a huge, dense cloud of dust was approaching them along the road, and he turned to Sancho and said:

'This is the day, O Sancho, when will be seen the good that fortune has in store for me; this is the day, I say, when the might of my arm will be displayed as never before, and when I shall do deeds that will remain written in the book of fame for the ages to come. Do you see that cloud of dust rising up over there, Sancho? Well, it is being raised by a vast army from countless different nations, marching towards us.'

'In that case there must be two armies,' said Sancho, 'because opposite it, back there behind us, there's another dust cloud just like it.'

Don Quixote turned round and saw that Sancho was right; and then he was beside himself with joy, because he knew that these were two armies marching to clash in the middle of that broad plain. Every minute of every hour his imagination was filled with those battles, enchantments, adventures, extravagances, loves and challenges that books of chivalry recount, and everything he said, thought or did was channelled into such affairs. And the dust clouds were being raised by two great droves of sheep approaching from opposite directions along the same road, but the dust prevented the sheep from being seen until they came close. And Don Quixote was so insistent they were armies that Sancho believed him, and said:

'So what are we going to do now, sir?'

'What are we going to do?' said Don Quixote. 'Favour and assist the needy and helpless. And you should know, Sancho, that this army approaching from in front of us is led and directed by the great Emperor Alifanfarón, lord of the great island of Taprobana;[1] the other army coming up behind me belongs to his enemy, the King of the Garamantes,[2] known as Pentapolín of the Uprolled Sleeve, because he always goes into battle with his right arm bare.'

'But why do these two lords hate each other so much?' asked Sancho.

'They hate each other,' replied Don Quixote, 'because this Alifanfarón is a wild pagan, and he is in love with Pentapolín's daughter, who is a very beauteous and, moreover, charming lady, and a Christian, and her father will not give her in marriage to the pagan king unless this man first abjures the religion of his false prophet Muhammad and is converted to Christianity.'

'My eye!' said Sancho. 'Pentapolín's doing just the right thing, and I'm going to help him in every way I can.'

'Then you will be doing your duty, Sancho,' said Don Quixote, 'because to take part in battles of this kind it is not necessary to be knighted.'

'I'm very well aware of that,' replied Sancho, 'but where are we going to put this ass of mine so that we can be sure of finding it again once the fighting's over? Because I don't expect going into battle on something like this is what people usually do.'

'That is true,' said Don Quixote. 'What you can do with the ass is to leave it free to have its own adventures, whether it goes missing or not, because we shall possess so many horses when we emerge victorious that even Rocinante will be in danger of being replaced by another. But now pay attention to me and keep your eyes open, for I am going to inform you about the most important knights in these two armies. And so that you can see and observe them better, let us withdraw to that hill over there, from where both armies must be visible.'

This they did, and from the hill they would indeed have had a clear view of the two flocks that were armies for Don Quixote, if the clouds of dust they were raising hadn't interfered with the view. Yet seeing in his imagination what he didn't see and didn't exist, he began to proclaim:

'That knight you can see over there in yellow armour, with a crowned lion lying submissive at a damsel's feet on his shield, is the valiant Laurcalco, Lord of the Silver Bridge; the other one, with golden flowers on his armour, and on his shield three silver crowns on a blue field, is the much-feared Micocolembo, the Grand Duke of Quirocia; that other one on his right, with gigantic limbs, is the fearless Brandabarbarán de Boliche, Lord of the Three Arabias, wearing that serpent's skin for armour and, instead of a shield, bearing a door which is reputed to be one of the doors of the temple pulled down by Samson when in dying he avenged himself on his enemies. But look in the other direction and you will see at the front of the other army the ever victorious, never vanquished Timonel de Carcajona, the Prince of Nueva Vizcaya, with his armour quartered blue, green, white and yellow, and on his shield he has a golden cat on a tawny field with the word *Miau*, which is the beginning of his lady's name, for it is said that she is the peerless Miulina, the daughter of Duke Alfeñiquén of the Algarve; that other knight who burdens the back of that powerful steed, with armour as white as snow and white arms – that is to say a shield without any device on it – is a novice knight from France, called Pierres Papin, Lord of the Baronies of Utrique; that other one, striking his iron spurs into the flanks of that dazzling, fleet zebra, and with armour of blue vair, is the powerful Duke of Nerbia, Espartafilardo of the Wood, who bears on his shield the device of an asparagus plant, with a motto in Castilian that says: "Divine my fortune."'

And he went on naming imaginary knights from one army and the other and, swept along by the fancies of his unique madness, he improvised armour, colours, devices and mottoes for all of them; and without a pause he continued:

'This other army, facing us, is formed of people of many races: here are those who have drunk the sweet waters of famous Xanthus;³ mountaineers who tread the Massilian fields; those who sift fine gold dust in Arabia Felix; those who enjoy the famous, cool banks of clear Thermodon; those who bleed golden Pactolus along many different channels; and the Numidians, breakers of promises; the Persians, bowmen of great renown; the Parthians and the Medes, who fight as they flee; the Arabs, who move their dwellings; the Scythians, as cruel as they are pale; the Ethiopians, with pierced lips, and other infinite peoples, whose faces I see and recognize, even though I do not remember their names. In this other squadron come those who drink the crystalline waters of olive-bearing Betis; those who wash their faces in the liquor of the ever rich and golden Tagus; those who enjoy the beneficent waters of the divine Genil; those who tread the lush pastures of the Tartesian fields; those who take delight in the Elysian meadows of Jerez; men of La Mancha, rich and crowned with yellow ears of corn; men clad in iron, ancient relics of Gothic blood; those who bathe in the Pisuerga, renowned for the gentleness of its current; those who graze their flocks and herds on the broad meadows of winding Guadiana, famous for its secret course; those who shiver in the cold of the bosky Pyrenees and among the white snowflakes of the lofty Apennines: in short, all those whom Europe contains and encloses within its boundaries.'

Great God, how many provinces he mentioned, how many races he named, giving to each one of them, with wonderful readiness, its own attributes, steeped as he was in everything he'd read in his lying books! Sancho Panza was hanging on his every word, and didn't utter a single one himself, and every so often he'd turn his head to try to spot the knights and giants his master was naming; and since he couldn't see any of them, he said:

'Look sir, the devil can take any of those men or giants or knights you say there are hereabouts – at least I can't see them, perhaps it's all a magic spell, like those ghosts last night.'

'How can you say that?' retorted Don Quixote. 'Do you not hear the neighing of the horses, the sounding of the bugles, the beating of the drums?'

'All I can hear,' replied Sancho, 'is lots of sheep bleating.'

And he was right, because the two flocks were coming close.

'It is your fear, Sancho' said Don Quixote, 'that is preventing you from seeing or hearing properly; because one of the effects of fear is to muddle the senses and make things seem to be what they are not; and if you are so frightened, stand aside and leave me alone, for I am sufficient by myself to give the victory to whichever army I decide to support.'

As he said this he put spurs to Rocinante and, with his lance at the ready, he sped down the hill like a thunderbolt. Sancho shouted after him:

'Come back, come back, Don Quixote sir, I swear to God they're sheep you're charging! Come back! By the bones of my poor old father! What madness is this? Look, there aren't any giants or knights, or cats, or armour, or shields quartered or left in one piece, or blue vairs, or the devil. What are you doing? Lord have mercy on us sinners!'

But nothing would make Don Quixote turn back. Instead he galloped on, crying:

'Come, you knights, fighting beneath the banners of the valiant Emperor Pentapolín of the Uprolled Sleeve, follow me, and you shall see with what ease I give him his revenge over his enemy Alifanfarón of Taprobana!'

With this he rode into the army of sheep and began to spear them with as much fury and determination as if he really were attacking mortal enemies. The shepherds and farmers accompanying the flock were screaming at him to stop, but, seeing that this didn't have any effect, they drew their slings from their belts and started to salute him about the ears with stones the size of fists. Don Quixote didn't take any notice of the stones; instead he galloped this way and that, crying:

'Where are you, proud Alifanfarón? Come here: a lone knight am I, who wishes, in single combat, to try your strength and take your life, as punishment for the distress you have caused the valiant Pentapolín the Garamante.'

As he said this a large smooth pebble came and struck him in the side and buried two of his ribs in his body. This left him in such a state that he felt certain he was either dead or sore wounded and, remembering his remedy, he took out the oil-bottle, put it to his mouth and began to pour the liquor into his stomach; but before he could swallow what he considered to be a sufficient amount, another of those sugared almonds came and hit his hand and his bottle with such force that it smashed the bottle, taking out three or four teeth as well, and crushing two fingers.

Such was the first blow, and such was the second, that the poor knight couldn't stop himself from sliding off his horse. The shepherds came up to look at him, and thought they'd killed him, so they made haste to round up their flock, pick up the dead sheep, of which there were more than a few, and make themselves scarce, without looking any further into the matter.

All this time Sancho had been on the hill, watching his master's follies, tearing his beard and cursing the moment when fortune had brought them together. When he saw that Don Quixote was lying on the ground and that the shepherds had gone away, he ventured down the hill and approached him, and found him in a terrible state, although still conscious. And Sancho said:

'Didn't I tell you, Don Quixote sir, to turn back, because what you were attacking wasn't armies, it was flocks of sheep?'

'This just shows how my enemy, that scoundrel of an enchanter, can transform things and make them disappear. I would have you know, Sancho, that it is very easy for such people to make us look like whatever they want, and this villain who is persecuting me, envious of the glory he saw I was about to conquer in this battle, turned the armies of enemy forces into flocks of sheep. If you do not believe me, Sancho, I beg you to do something that will correct your mistake and make you see that I am telling you the truth: mount your ass and stalk them, and you will soon see how, once they have gone a little way, they turn back into what they were at first and, ceasing to be sheep, become real men again, just as I described them to you. But do not go yet, because I have need of your assistance: come here and see how many of my teeth are missing, for it seems to me that there is not one left in my mouth.'

Sancho came so close that his eyes were nearly inside his master's mouth; and by now the balsam had done its work in Don Quixote's stomach, and, just as Sancho was peering in, he discharged all its contents with the violence of a shotgun and they exploded in the face of the compassionate squire.

'Holy Mother of God!' cried Sancho. 'What's up now? The man's dying, he must be – he's spewing blood!'

But when he examined the evidence more closely he could tell from the colour, taste and smell that it wasn't blood but the balsam he'd seen him drinking from the oil-bottle, and this disgusting discovery so turned his stomach that he vomited his guts all over his master, and both of them were left in the same fine mess. Sancho staggered over to his ass to look in the saddle-bags for something with which to clean himself and see to his master's wounds, and when he couldn't find them he almost went insane. He cursed himself again, and decided in his heart to leave his master and go back home, even if that did mean forfeiting what he was owed for services rendered and his hopes of governing the promised island.

Don Quixote now struggled to his feet, with his left hand clapped to his mouth to stop his remaining teeth from falling out, took hold with the other hand of the reins of the faithful Rocinante, who was so loyal and good-natured that he hadn't budged from his master's side, and went over to his squire, who was leaning over his ass with his hand on his cheek, in the posture of a man overwhelmed by thought. And when Don Quixote saw all these signs of deep distress, he said:

'Allow me to remind you, Sancho, that no man is worth more than any other, unless he achieves more than the other. All these storms falling upon us are signs that the weather will soon clear and that things will go well for us; for neither good nor bad can last for ever, and from this we can deduce that since this bad spell has lasted for a long time, a good one cannot be far away. So you must not be distressed about the misfortunes that I undergo, for you have no part in them.'

'No part in them?' retorted Sancho. 'The bloke who got blanket-tossed yesterday – was he by any chance any other than my own father's son? And the saddle-bags I've lost today, with all my valuables in them – do they belong to any other than the same?'

'You have lost your saddle-bags, Sancho?' said Don Quixote.

'Yes I have,' replied Sancho.

'So we have nothing to eat today,' replied Don Quixote.

'We wouldn't have,' replied Sancho, 'if it wasn't for those herbs you say you know all about growing in the fields, the ones that unfortunate knight errants like you go and pick to make up for lack of food in fixes like this.'

'For all that,' replied Don Quixote, 'I would sooner have a two-pound loaf of white bread or indeed an eight-pound loaf of bran bread and a couple of dozen salted pilchards, than all the herbs described by Dioscorides, even in Dr Laguna's magnificent edition.[4] But anyway, climb on to your donkey, good Sancho, and follow me, because God, who is the provider of all things, will not fail us, especially since we are engaged in his service; because he does not fail the gnats in the air, or the worms in the earth, or the tadpoles in the water. And he is so merciful that he makes his sun rise on the evil and on the good, and sends his rain on the just and on the unjust.'[5]

'You'd have done better as a preacher,' said Sancho, 'than as a knight errant.'

'Knights errant have always known and still must know about everything, Sancho,' said Don Quixote, 'for there were knights errant in centuries past who would stop to preach a sermon or deliver a speech in the middle of a fair just as if they were graduates of the University of Paris; from which we can infer that the sword has never blunted the pen, nor the pen the sword.'

'All right, I'll take your word for it,' replied Sancho, 'and now let's get going and find somewhere to stay the night, and God grant it's a place where there aren't any blankets, or blanket-tossers, or ghosts, or enchanted Moors – because if there are any of those, I'll send this adventuring lark to the devil, lock, stock and barrel.'

'You must pray to God for that, my son,' said Don Quixote. 'And now guide us where you will, for on this occasion I wish to leave the choice of a lodging to you. But first lend me your hand and feel with your finger how many teeth are missing on this upper right side, because that is where I feel the pain.'

Sancho put his fingers in and, as he felt around, he asked:

'How many back teeth did you use to have on this side?'

'Four,' replied Don Quixote, 'apart from the wisdom tooth, all of them whole and sound.'

'Are you quite sure of what you're saying, sir?' said Sancho.

'Yes, four, if not five,' replied Don Quixote, 'because I have never had any teeth extracted, nor have any fallen out or been destroyed by decay or infection.'

'Well, down here below,' said Sancho, 'you've only got two and a half now, and up above not even half a tooth, it's as smooth as the palm of my hand.'

'Oh, unhappy me!' said Don Quixote as he heard the sad news his squire was giving him. 'I would rather have lost an arm, so long as it was not my sword arm. For I would have you know, Sancho, that a mouth without teeth is like a mill without a millstone, and that a tooth is much more worthy of esteem than a diamond. But those of us who profess the order of chivalry in all its severity are subject to this. Mount your donkey, my friend, and lead the way, and I shall follow at whatever pace you prefer.'

Sancho did so, heading towards where he thought they might find a place to stay without leaving the highway, which was uninterrupted in that part.

As they plodded along, because the pain in Don Quixote's jaws didn't give him any respite or any inclination to ride faster, Sancho tried to amuse him and cheer him up by chatting to him, and said, among other things, what is recorded in the next chapter.

CHAPTER XIX

About the intelligent conversation that Sancho had with his master, and their adventure with a corpse, together with other famous events

'What I think, sir, is that all these mishaps of the past few days must have been a punishment for the sin you've committed against the chivalry order, not keeping that vow you took ne'er at table to eat bread nor with the queen to lie, and all that other stuff that came afterwards and you swore to do until you'd taken that helmet off Malandrino, or whatever the Moor was called, I don't rightly remember his name.'

'You are quite right, Sancho,' said Don Quixote, 'but, to tell you the truth, it had altogether slipped my mind; and you can be equally certain that the business of the blanket which you underwent was your fault, for not calling my attention to it in time. But I shall make due amends, for in the order of chivalry there are ways and means of redressing all such lapses.'

'And what vows have I taken?' retorted Sancho.

'It does not matter that you have not taken any vows,' said Don Quixote. 'It is enough that I believe you could be under suspicion of being an accessory after the fact, and it will be as well to seek a remedy, just in case.'

'Well, if that's the way it is,' said Sancho, 'you'd better make sure you don't go and forget about that, too, as you did with the vow, because the ghosts might take it into their heads to have some more fun with me, and maybe with you as well, if they see how stubborn you are.'

As they talked away like this, night came on and caught them on the open road, without a sight of anywhere to stay, and what made it even worse was that they were dying of hunger, being without saddle-bags and therefore without a larder or provisions. And, to complete their misfortunes, they had an adventure that didn't need any contrivance to make it look like one. The night was dark but they rode on regardless, because Sancho thought that, being as they were on the king's highway, there must be an inn not more than half a dozen miles off.

As they plodded on through the blackness, the squire famished and his master with a healthy appetite, they saw coming towards them along the same road a myriad of lights that looked exactly like moving stars. Sancho was frozen with fear at the sight of them, and even Don Quixote had the wind up: the one tugged on his ass's halter, and the other pulled on his nag's reins, and there they both sat motionless, peering to make out what it could be, and they saw that the lights were coming closer and closer, and the closer they came the bigger they looked; and Sancho began to quiver like a rabbit, and the hair on Don Quixote's head stood on end. But plucking up a little courage he said:

'This, Sancho, must be the greatest and most perilous of adventures, in which it will be necessary for me to show all my valour and resolution.'

'Oh, dear, dear me!' cried Sancho. 'If this is another ghost adventure, as I'm beginning to think it is, where are the ribs that are going to be able to take it?'

'Ghosts though they may be,' said Don Quixote, 'I will not allow any of them to touch one thread of your clothes; for if they had their fun with you before, that was only because I could not climb over the yard wall; but now we are in open country, where I shall be able to wield my sword as I please.'

'And if they enchant you and put you out of action as they did the last time,' said Sancho, 'what'll it matter whether we're in open country or not?'

'All the same,' replied Don Quixote, 'I beg you, Sancho, to be of good courage, for the event will show you how courageous I am.'

'I will – if God helps me,' replied Sancho.

And standing a little to one side of the road, they peered again to try and make out what all those moving lights could be, and they soon saw a throng in white, a fearful vision that drained whatever courage remained in Sancho Panza, whose teeth began to chatter as if he had an attack of malaria; and they chattered even faster when he had a clearer view, because there were about twenty figures in white drapes, all mounted, with flaming torches in their hands, and behind them came a litter covered in mourning followed by another six mounted figures, in mourning too, right down to the heels of their mules – because it was clear, from their sober gait, that these were no horses. The men in white were murmuring in compassionate tones. This strange vision, at such an hour and in such a desolate place, was more than enough to strike fear into Sancho's heart, and even into his master's; and this could indeed have happened to Don Quixote, but not to Sancho, who didn't have any heart left for fear to be struck into. But what did happen to his master was the very opposite, because in his imagination he saw with total clarity that this was one of the adventures out of his books. He saw the litter as a bier on which must lie some sore wounded or dead knight, whose revenge was reserved for him alone, and without further thought he couched his pike, settled himself in his saddle, and with graceful and courageous bearing stationed

himself in the middle of the road where the men in white were going to
have to pass; and when they came up he said:

'Halt, you knights, or whatever you may be, and inform me who you
are, where you have come from, where you are going and what it is that
you are carrying on that bier; for it seems that either you have committed
some outrage or you have been the victims of one, and it is right and
meet that I should know this, either to punish you for the wrong you
have done or to avenge you for the wrong done you.'

'We're in a hurry,' replied one of the men in white, 'and the inn's a
long way off, and we haven't got time to stop for all that informing.'

And, putting spurs to his mule, he continued on his way. Don Quixote
was affronted by such a reply and, grasping the mule's bridle, he said:

'Halt, and mind your manners, and inform me of what I have asked. If
not, I challenge you all to mortal combat.'

The mule was a highly strung animal, and was so frightened at being
seized by the bridle that it reared up and fell back on its haunches and on
top of its rider. An attendant on foot, seeing the fall, started to shout insults
at Don Quixote, who, beside himself with fury, couched his pike again and
without more ado charged at one of the men in mourning and left him sore
wounded on the ground; and as he continued charging about among the
rest, it was wondrous to behold the agility with which he attacked them
and knocked them off their mules, and Rocinante's movements were so
swift and proud that it seemed as if he'd suddenly sprouted wings.

The men in white were timorous characters, and unarmed; and so they
were only too happy to flee from the skirmish and run away across the
plain with their torches blazing, looking for all the world like masked
figures at a midnight party rushing hither and thither. But the men in
mourning, swathed and tangled in their skirts and cassocks, couldn't run,
so Don Quixote gave them all a good beating with impunity and made
them quit the field much against their will, because they all thought he
wasn't a man but a devil from hell, come to steal away the dead body
they were carrying in the litter.

Sancho was watching it all, amazed at his master's courage, and saying
to himself:

'It's true, this master of mine is just as brave and strong as he says he
is.'

A torch was burning on the ground next to the man who'd fallen under his mule, and by its light Don Quixote could see him; and coming up to him he poked the tip of his pike at the man's face, ordering him to give himself up, or else he'd die. To which the fallen man replied:

'I've given up already – I can't move, one of my legs is broken. I beg you, if you're a Christian knight, not to kill me – you'd be committing a great sacrilege because I'm a master of arts and I've taken my first orders.'

'And what the devil brings you here,' said Don Quixote, 'if you are a man of the cloth?'

'What brings me here, sir?' replied the fallen man. 'My misfortune.'

'Another greater one awaits you,' said Don Quixote, 'if you do not give satisfactory answers to all the questions I asked you in the first place.'

'It'll be easy enough to satisfy you,' replied the master of arts. 'To start with, I ought to point out that although I said just now that I'm a master of arts, I'm really only a BA, and I'm called Alonso López; I'm a native of Alcobendas; I've come from the city of Baeza with eleven other priests, the ones that ran off with the torches; we're on our way to the city of Segovia with that litter containing the corpse of a gentleman who died in Baeza, where it's been deposited until now; and, as I said, we were taking his bones to be buried in his tomb in Segovia, his home town.'[1]

'And who killed him?' asked Don Quixote.

'God did, with a pestilential fever,' replied the bachelor of arts.

'That means,' said Don Quixote, 'that Our Lord has relieved me of the task I would have had of avenging his death, if anybody else had killed him; but seeing who it was that killed him, all one can do is shrug one's shoulders and be silent, for that is what I should do if he had killed me. And I would have you know, reverend sir, that I am a knight of La Mancha, Don Quixote by name, and my office and profession is to wander about the world righting wrongs and redressing grievances.'

'I'm not too clear about this righting of wrongs,' said the bachelor of arts, 'because I was all right, and you've done me the wrong of breaking my leg, which will never be right again in all the days of my life; and the grievance you've redressed in my case has been to leave me so grievously injured that I'll live in grief for ever; and it's been a terrible misadventure for me to come across you in search of your adventures.'

'Not all things,' said Don Quixote, 'follow the same plan. The trouble, my dear Alonso López BA, arose from your coming, as you did, by night, wearing those surplices, with your torches blazing, praying, and dressed in mourning, looking exactly like something evil from the other world; and so I could not fail to fulfil my obligation to attack you, and I should have attacked you even if I had known that you were the very devils from hell, which is what I took you for.'

'Since that's what my bad luck's arranged for me,' said the bachelor of arts, 'I entreat you, sir knight errant (whose errors I'm paying for), to help me out from under this mule, it's got my leg caught between the stirrup and the saddle.'

'But why didn't you say so in the first place?' Don Quixote exclaimed. 'How long were you intending to wait to inform me of your plight?'

He shouted for Sancho Panza, but Sancho Panza wasn't in any hurry to obey, because he was busy stripping the good gentlemen's supply-mule, loaded with food. Sancho turned his topcoat into a sack, crammed into it all the food he could, loaded his ass – and then he went to see why his master was shouting, and helped him to pull the bachelor of arts out from under his heavy mule, and sat him on top of it, and handed him his torch; and Don Quixote told him to follow his companions, whose forgiveness he begged for the grievance, which it had not been in his power to avoid. And Sancho said:

'If by any chance those gentlemen want to know the name of the valiant adventurer that did this to them, you can tell them he's the famous Don Quixote de la Mancha, also known as the Knight of the Sorry Face.'[2]

The bachelor of arts started riding away slowly, and Don Quixote asked Sancho why he'd called him the Knight of the Sorry Face, and at that moment in particular.

'All right, I'll tell you,' replied Sancho. 'I was just looking at you by the light of that poor bloke's torch and the truth is that at this moment you're the sorriest sight I've ever clapped eyes on. It must be because of being tired after your fight, or else losing all those teeth.'

'No, those are not the reasons,' replied Don Quixote. 'It is rather because the sage whose task it is to write the history of my exploits must have thought it right for me to take some appellation, as all previous knights have done: one was known as the Knight of the Burning Sword, another as the Knight of the Unicorn, another the Knight of the Damsels, yet another the Knight of the Phoenix, that one the Knight of the Griffin, that other one the Knight of Death;[3] and by these names and devices they were known all round the world. And so I believe that the sage I have mentioned must, a moment ago, have placed in your thoughts and on your tongue the appellation "The Knight of the Sorry Face", which is what I propose to call myself from now on; and to ensure that the title suits me all the better, I am resolved to have painted on my coat of arms, at the earliest opportunity, a very sorry face.'

'There's no need to go wasting time and money on a painting,' said Sancho. 'All you've got to do is lift your visor and let anyone looking at you see your face, and without any need of a picture or a shield they'll call you the Knight of the Sorry Face straight away. Believe you me, I'm telling the truth – I can promise you, sir (this is just my little joke, though) that what with being famished and not having any teeth your face is such a terrible sight that, as I just said, there's no need for any sorry painting.'

Don Quixote laughed at Sancho's little joke, but he still decided to call himself by that title as soon as he could have his round infantryman's shield painted as he'd said.

' – Oh, I almost forgot to tell you that you're excommunicated for laying violent hands on what is sacred, *iuxta illud: Si quis suadente diabolo,* etc.'[4]

'The Latin is beyond me,' Don Quixote replied, 'yet I know very well that it was not my hands but this pike that I laid on you; and furthermore I did not think I was attacking priests or anything to do with the Church, which I respect and adore as the good Catholic and faithful Christian that I am, but ghosts and phantoms from the other world. And even if I have done what you say, I can remember what happened to the Cid Ruy Díaz when he smashed the chair of that king's ambassador in front of His Holiness the Pope, who excommunicated him for what he had done; yet the good Cid's behaviour on that day had been that of a very honourable and valiant knight.'[5]

On hearing this the bachelor continued on his way, as described, without another word. Don Quixote would have liked to find out whether the corpse in the litter was a skeleton or not, but Sancho wouldn't allow it, saying:

'Sir, you've come out of this dangerous adventure more in one piece than out of any of the others I've seen, and, although you routed all those people, they could have spotted that it was just one person fighting them, which could make them feel ashamed, and they might pluck up courage and come back for us, and then we'd really have our work cut out. The donkey's well loaded, the mountains are near at hand, hunger's pressing and all we need to do is beat a dainty retreat and, as the saying goes, to the grave with the dead and the living to their bread.'

And pushing his ass along in front of him, he asked his master to follow; and Don Quixote, feeling that Sancho was right, obeyed him without a word. After walking a short distance between two hills they found themselves in a broad and secluded valley, where they stopped, and Sancho unloaded the donkey; and, stretched out on the green grass, they had breakfast, dinner, tea and supper all at once, accompanied by the best hunger-sauce, satisfying their stomachs from more than one lunch-box that the priests (such gentlemen seldom allow themselves to go short) had been carrying on their supply-mule. But another misfortune befell them, in Sancho's opinion the worst of all, and this was that they didn't have any wine to drink, or even any water to raise to their lips, and they were tormented by thirst. Seeing that the meadow where they were lying was thick with lush young grass, Sancho said what will be related in the next chapter.

CHAPTER XX

About the unprecedented and unique adventure undertaken
by the valiant Don Quixote de la Mancha, the one that with
the least danger was ever brought to a happy conclusion
by any famous knight in the world

'All this grass, sir, must be a sign that there's a spring or a stream near here watering it, so it'll be a good plan to carry on a little further, and we'll find somewhere we can quench this terrible thirst of ours – I'm sure thirst hurts even more than hunger does.'

Don Quixote thought this was good advice, and he took Rocinante by the reins, and Sancho loaded his ass with all the left-overs and took it by the halter, and they began to feel their way up the meadow, because the darkness of the night prevented them from seeing anything; but they hadn't gone a couple of hundred paces when a sound of thundering water reached their ears, as if it were crashing down from some great cliff. They were overjoyed at this but, when they stopped to work out where the sound was coming from, they suddenly heard another noise that diluted the pleasure of the water, especially for Sancho, with his timid, fearful nature. What they heard was a steady pounding and some sort of a clanking of iron and chains that, added to the water's furious roaring, would have struck fear into any other heart than that of Don Quixote.

In this dark night they'd wandered in among some tall trees whose leaves, blown by the breeze, rustled eerily; and the combination of the solitude, the surroundings, the darkness, the noise of the water and the rustling of the leaves filled them with fear and dread, all the more so when they found that the pounding didn't cease, the breeze didn't die down and the morning didn't come; and, on top of all this, they had no idea where they were. But Don Quixote, steeled by his intrepid heart, leapt upon Rocinante, grasped his little round shield, clasped his pike and said:

'Friend Sancho, I would have you know that I was born, by the will of heaven, in this iron age of ours, to revive in it the age of gold, or golden age, as it is often called. I am the man for whom dangers, great exploits, valiant deeds are reserved. I am, I repeat, the man who will revive the Knights of the Round Table, the Twelve Peers of France and the Nine Worthies, and who will consign to oblivion the Platirs, the Tablantes, the Olivantes and Tirantes, the Phoebuses and Belianises, together with the whole crowd of illustrious knights errant of olden times, by performing in this age in which I live such prodigies, such wonders, such feats of arms as to eclipse the most brilliant deeds that they ever accomplished. You are aware, faithful and trusty squire, of the darkness of this night, its unearthly silence, the confused and muffled hubbub of the trees, the fearsome roar of the water that we have come to seek and that seems to crash down from the heights of the Mountains of the Moon,[1] and the incessant pounding that assails and wounds our ears; all of which together, and indeed each by itself, would be enough to infuse fear and terror and dismay into the breast of Mars himself, let alone one unaccustomed to such occurrences and adventures. Now all of this that I depict for you is an incentive and a stimulant for my spirit, making this heart of mine burst in my breast with a desire to launch out on this adventure, however difficult it seems to be. So tighten Rocinante's girths a little, and God be with you, and await me here for just three days, after which, if I should not return, you may go back to our village, and from thence, as a favour and a service to me, you shall go to El Toboso, where you shall inform my incomparable lady Dulcinea that her hapless knight died attempting exploits which would make him worthy to call himself hers.'

When Sancho heard his master's words he began to weep tears of infinite tenderness and said:

'Sir, I don't know why you want to take on this fearful adventure – it's night now, nobody can see us here, we can easily ride the other way and avoid the danger, even if we have to go for three days without a drink, and since there's no one to see us, there's no one to think we're cowards, either. What's more, I've heard our village priest, who you know well, saying in a sermon that danger loved is death won,[2] so it isn't a good idea to go tempting God by taking on such a tremendous feat that you can only get out of alive by some miracle – you ought to be content with the ones that heaven worked on you when it stopped you from being tossed in a blanket, as I was, and when it brought you out safe, sound and victorious from among all those enemies that were riding with that corpse. And if all this doesn't move or soften that hard heart of yours, let's see if this does – just think that as soon as you've gone away I'll be ready to give up the ghost to whoever wants to take it, out of pure fear. I left my village and my children and my wife to come and serve you, in the belief that I'd be better for it rather than the opposite, but greed breaks the sack and it's broken all my hopes, because just when they were brightest and I thought I was going to get my hands on that damned island you've promised me so often, I find that instead you want to leave me in a place like this, far from all human company. In the name of the one true God, sir, let not this wrong be done unto me, and if you just can't hold yourself back from doing this daring deed, at least put it off till morning – according to the lore I learned as a shepherd, dawn can't be three hours away, because the Little Bear's mouth is on top of its head, and at midnight it's in line with its left arm.'

'But Sancho,' asked Don Quixote, 'how can you tell where that line goes, or where that mouth or small bear is, when the night is so dark that there is not a star to be seen in the sky?'

'That's true enough,' said Sancho, 'but fear has many eyes, and it can see things under the ground so it's got even more reason to see them up in the sky, but anyway you only need to use your head to realize that it isn't long till daybreak.'

'However long it is,' replied Don Quixote, 'it shall not be said of me, now or ever, that tears and pleas deflected me from acting as I should, in a true knightly fashion; so I beg you, Sancho, to hold your tongue; for God, who has placed in my heart the desire to undertake this unique and dreadful adventure, will be sure to watch over my well-being and console your grief. What you must do is to make Rocinante's girths as tight as may be, and wait here, for I shall soon return, alive or dead.'

Sancho realized that this was his master's final decision, and that tears, advice and pleas weren't having any effect, so he decided to make use of his cunning to force him to wait until daybreak, if he could: as he was tightening the horse's girths he took his ass's halter and, ever so carefully and quietly so as not to be noticed, he tied Rocinante's hind legs together, so that when Don Quixote tried to set off he couldn't, because the only way in which the horse could move was in fits and starts. When Sancho saw that his trick had worked, he said:

'There you are, sir – the heavens, moved by my tears and my prayers, have ordained that Rocinante can't move, and if you keep on spurring him again and again like that you'll only annoy fortune and, as they say, kick against the pricks.'

Don Quixote was close to despair, and the more he gave his horse the spur the less it budged; and, not suspecting the ligature, he resigned himself to calming down and waiting either for dawn to come or for Rocinante to move, ascribing the problem to everything except Sancho's cunning. And so he said:

'Since the fact is, Sancho, that Rocinante cannot move, I am content to wait until dawn smiles on us, even though I weep at her delay.'

'No, you mustn't weep,' replied Sancho. 'I'll keep you amused by telling you stories till daybreak, unless you'd rather get off your horse and lie down for a little nap on the green grass, as knight errants often do, so as to feel nice and fresh when day comes and it's time to go off on that enormous adventure that's in store for you.'

'What do you mean, get off my horse and lie down for a little nap?' said Don Quixote. 'Am I, perchance, one of those knights who repose in the midst of danger? You can sleep, for you were born to sleep – indeed you can do as you wish – but I shall behave as I consider befits my aspirations.'

'Don't be angry, sir,' replied Sancho, 'I didn't mean it like that.'

And coming up to him he held on to the front of his saddle with one hand and on to the back of it with the other, so that he was left embracing his master's left thigh, not daring to stir one inch from it, so scared was he of the pounding, which continued unabated. Don Quixote asked him to tell a story to while the time away, as he had promised, to which Sancho replied that he would, if his fear of what he was hearing let him.

'But in spite of that I will try my hardest to tell you a true story that, if I manage to tell it properly and don't get interrupted, is the best true story there ever was, and now you must pay attention because I'm about to begin. "Once upon a time and may good befall us all and evil come to him that evil seeks . . ." And you can see, sir, that in those ancient times they didn't start their stories any old way, but with a saying by Cato the Senseless of Rome,³ who says "And evil come to him that evil seeks", which just about fits the bill here, to persuade you to stay put and not wander off seeking evil, and let's go the other way instead, sir, because nobody's forcing us to carry on in this direction, with all these terrors putting the fear of God into us.'

'Continue with your story, Sancho,' said Don Quixote, 'and leave me to worry about the direction in which we are travelling.'

'I was saying, then,' continued Sancho, 'that in a village in Extremadura there once lived a goat-shepherd, in other words a man who looked after goats, and this shepherd or goat-shepherd my story's all about was called Lope Ruiz, and this Lope Ruiz was in love with a shepherdess called Torralba, and this shepherdess called Torralba was the daughter of a rich stock farmer, and this rich stock farmer . . .'

'If that is the way in which you tell your story, Sancho,' said Don Quixote, 'repeating everything you say, in two days' time you still will not have finished; either tell it straightforwardly, like a man of good sense, or do not tell it at all.'

'The way I'm telling it,' retorted Sancho, 'is the way tales are always told where I come from, and I don't know any other way to tell it, and it isn't fair to expect me to learn new habits.'

'Tell it however you like, then,' replied Don Quixote, 'and since fate decrees that I cannot avoid listening, you had better continue.'

'And so, my dear good sir,' continued Sancho, 'as I was saying, this herdsman was in love with Torralba the shepherdess, who was a plump lass, unruly and a bit mannish, because she had the beginnings of a moustache — I can almost see her even now.'

'So you knew her, did you?' said Don Quixote.

'I didn't know her as such,' replied Sancho, 'but the person who told me the story said it was so very true that when I told it to anyone else I could swear blind I'd seen it all for myself. So the days came and the days went and the devil, who doesn't sleep and meddles and muddles in everything, made the love that the herdsman felt for the shepherdess turn into deadly hatred, and the cause, so the gossips said, was a dose of jealousy-pangs she gave him, that went well beyond the pale; and the herdsman hated her so much from then on that, so as never to see her again, he decided to leave that land and go where he wouldn't ever clap eyes on her. As soon as Torralba saw that Lope scorned her, she fell in love with him, even though she'd never been at all fond of him before that.'

'That is the way with woman,' said Don Quixote: 'to disdain the man who loves her, and to love the man who disdains her. Continue, Sancho.'

'What happened,' said Sancho, 'was that the herdsman put his plan into action, and he drove his goats in front of him through the fields of Extremadura to cross over into the Kingdom of Portugal. The Torralba woman found out and went after him, and followed him at a distance on her bare feet, with her staff in her hand and her two satchels hanging from her neck and containing, so it's said, a piece of a mirror and a piece of a comb and some sort of jar of face lotion, but whatever it was she was carrying, and I'm not going to start trying to find that out now, all I will say is that it's said that the herdsman and his goats reached the River Guadiana, and it was swollen almost to overflowing, and there wasn't any ferry or any other boat to take him and his animals across, which put him in a tizzy because he could see that the Torralba woman was getting close and she was going to make a nuisance of herself with all her pleading and moaning, but he kept looking so hard that he saw a fisherman with a boat by his side, so small that there was only room in it for one person and one goat, and in spite of this he spoke to him and bargained with him and they agreed that the fisherman would ferry him and his three hundred goats across to the other bank. The fisherman climbed into his boat and took one goat across, and he came back and took another goat across, and he came back again and took another goat across. You've got to keep count of the goats that the fisherman takes across, because if you let just one of them slip from your memory the story will come to an end and I won't be able to tell you another word of it. To continue, then, I ought to say that the landing-stage on the other side was very muddy and slippery, and the fisherman was taking a long time going to and fro. All the same, he came for another goat, and another goat, and another goat . . .'

'Just assume that he has ferried them all across,' said Don Quixote. 'Don't keep coming and going like that – you won't get them to the other side in a year.'

'How many goats has he taken across so far?' asked Sancho.

'How the devil do you expect me to know that?' replied Don Quixote.

'That's just what I told you – to keep good count. Well, by God, the story's over, I'm not going on.'

'How can that be?' replied Don Quixote. 'Is it so essential to the story to know exactly how many goats have gone across that if we are so much as one out you cannot continue telling it?'

'No, sir, not at all,' replied Sancho. 'It's just that when I asked you to tell me how many goats had gone and you replied that you didn't know, at that very instant I clean forgot what I had left to say, and it was full of good things, I can tell you that much.'

'So your story is finished?' said Don Quixote.

'As sure as my mother is,' said Sancho.

'I can honestly say,' replied Don Quixote, 'that you have just told one of the most original tales, true or false, that anybody could ever have dreamed of, and that your way of telling it and concluding it is something never heard before nor to be heard again, although I did expect no less from your fine mind. But this does not surprise me, because that incessant pounding must have turned your brain.'

'That's as may be,' replied Sancho, 'all I know is, that's the end of my story – it finishes where you start to make mistakes in counting the goats.'

'It is welcome to finish wherever it wishes,' said Don Quixote. 'Now let us see if Rocinante can move.'

He set spurs to his horse again, and again the horse jumped and froze, for Sancho's knots were good knots.

It appears that at this moment, either because of the cold of the morning, which was fast approaching, or because Sancho had eaten something loosening for his supper, or because of natural processes (which seems most likely), he felt the urgent need to do the job of work that nobody could do for him; but so great was the fear which had entered his heart that he didn't dare to move as much as a hair's-breadth from his master's side. Yet not doing what he had to do wasn't a possibility, either; and so what he did, for the sake of peace and concord, was to draw his right hand away from the back of Don Quixote's saddle and use it with great stealth to loosen the running knot that was all that held his breeches up, at which they slid down and encircled his ankles like fetters. Then he lifted up his shirt as best he could, and thrust two ample buttocks into the night air. Once he'd done this, which he'd thought was all he needed to do to escape from his harrowing predicament, he found himself in another even worse plight: he thought that he wasn't going to be able to relieve himself in silence, and he began to grit his teeth and hunch his shoulders and hold his breath for as long as he could, but in spite of all these precautions he was unfortunate enough, in the end, to make a small noise, quite different from the noise causing him such great fear. Don Quixote heard it and said:

'What murmuring is that, Sancho?'

'I don't know, sir,' he replied. 'It must be some new business, because adventures and misadventures never come singly.'

He tried his luck again, and such was his success that, with no greater noise than the previous time, he relieved himself of the burden that had been weighing so heavily upon him. But since Don Quixote's sense of smell was as acute as his sense of hearing, and since Sancho was clinging so very close to him, it was inevitable that some of the fumes, rising almost in a straight line, would reach his nostrils, whereupon he went to their rescue by squeezing them between finger and thumb, and said in somewhat nasal tones:

'It seems to me, Sancho, that you are very frightened.'

'That I am,' replied Sancho, 'but what makes you notice it now more than at other times?'

'The fact that now, more than at other times, you smell, and not of ambergris,' replied Don Quixote.

'You could well be right,' said Sancho, 'but I'm not the one to blame – you are, for dragging me into such wild places at these unearthly hours.'

'Move three or maybe four places backwards, my friend,' said Don Quixote, without taking his hand from his nose, 'and from now on be more careful with your person and with what is due to mine; for it is my familiarity with you that has given rise to this contempt.'

'I bet you're thinking,' said Sancho, 'that I've done something with my person that I didn't ought to have done.'

'The more you stir it the worse it gets, friend Sancho,' replied Don Quixote.

In this and other similar conversations master and servant spent the night; but when Sancho saw that morning was fast approaching, he very quietly untied Rocinante and tied his breeches. Once Rocinante found himself free it seems that, although he wasn't a high-spirited animal, the after-effects of his confinement made him begin pawing, because prancing (begging his pardon) was beyond him. And when Don Quixote noticed that Rocinante could move again, he considered it to be a favourable sign indicating, he believed, that it was time for him to undertake that terrible adventure.

And now dawn broke at last, and objects began to be clearly visible, and Don Quixote saw that he was beneath some tall trees, chestnuts, which cast a deep, dark shade. He also noticed that the pounding didn't cease, but he couldn't see what was causing it; and so, without further delay, he let Rocinante feel the spur and, saying goodbye again to Sancho, told him to wait there for three days, at the most, just as he had told him before, and, if by the end of them he hadn't returned, to take it as certain that it had been God's will that he should end his life in that perilous adventure. He repeated his instructions about the message to be taken on his behalf to his lady Dulcinea, and told Sancho not to worry about the matter of the payment for his services, because he had made his will before leaving home and in it he had made full provision for wages covering the time served, *pro rata*; and he added that, if God brought him out of that peril safe and sound and ransomless, Sancho could count with total certainty on receiving the promised island.

Sancho wept again as he heard his good master's doleful words once more, and he resolved not to leave him until the absolute final end of that particular incident. From these tears of Sancho Panza's and from this honourable decision of his the author of this history concludes that he must have been of good family and, at the very least, of pure old Christian stock. And his master was moved by his feelings, but not so much as to make him waver in the slightest; on the contrary he hid his emotion as best he could and began to ride in the direction from which he thought the noise of the water and the pounding were coming. Sancho followed on foot, leading his donkey – his perpetual companion in prosperous and adverse fortune – by the halter, as he so often did; and after they'd advanced some way under those gloomy chestnut trees, they came to a little meadow at the foot of a high cliff from which a great waterfall came tumbling down. Beneath the cliff there were some roughly constructed buildings that looked more like ruins than anything else, and the two men realized that the ceaseless pounding din was coming from over there. Rocinante started at the racket of the water and the pounding, and Don Quixote soothed him and then inched his way towards the buildings, commending himself with all his heart to his lady and imploring her to favour him in this dreadful enterprise, and while he was about it he also commended himself to God and asked not to be forgotten by him. Sancho never strayed from his side, and he poked his neck out as far as he could and he peered as hard as he could between Rocinante's legs, to try to make out what it was that was filling him with such dread.

They must have advanced another hundred paces when, as they came round the side of a hillock, they saw, starkly exposed to their gaze, without any room for doubt, the cause of that hideous and, for them, horrendous din that had kept them so bewildered and scared throughout the night. And it was (please don't take this amiss, dear reader) six fulling-hammers making all the noise with their alternating blows.

When Don Quixote saw what it was he fell silent and stiffened from top to toe. Sancho looked up at Don Quixote and saw that his head was sunk on his breast in manifest mortification. Don Quixote looked down at Sancho and saw that his cheeks were puffed up and his mouth was filled with mirth, about to explode with it; and the knight's dejection was not so great that it could prevent him from laughing at the sight of Sancho, and when Sancho saw that his master had begun to laugh, he released his own captive so suddenly that he had to press his fists to his sides so as not to explode. Four times he calmed down, and four times he started laughing again, every bit as hard as the first time, and Don Quixote was becoming more and more enraged, particularly when he heard Sancho say by way of mockery:

'"I would have you know, friend Sancho, that I was born, by the will of heaven, in this iron age of ours, to revive in it the age of gold, or golden age. I am the man for whom dangers, great exploits, valiant deeds are reserved ..."'

And he went on to repeat most of what Don Quixote had said when they'd first heard the dreadful pounding. Seeing Sancho making fun of him, Don Quixote was so furious that he raised his pike and struck him two such blows that if they'd connected with his head instead of his shoulders there wouldn't have been any need to pay any wages, except to his heirs. Now that his jolly jest had turned into ugly earnest, and fearful that his master might give him some more of the same, Sancho grovelled:

'Calm down, do, sir, please – I swear to God I was only joking.'

'You may be joking, sir, but I am not,' retorted Don Quixote. 'Look here, my merry fellow: do you fancy that, if these were not fulling-hammers but some perilous new adventure, I should have failed to display the courage needed to undertake and conclude it? Am I, perchance, sir, obliged – being, as I am, a knight and a gentleman – to identify and distinguish between sounds, and tell whether they come from fulling-mills or not? And furthermore it could be the case, as indeed it is, that I have never seen such things in my life, just as you must have seen them often, being a miserable peasant, born and brought up among them. Or else, sir, you just turn these six hammers into six giants, and set them on me one by one or all together, and if I do not topple each and every one of them, then you can laugh at me as much as you please.'

'Enough said, sir,' said Sancho, 'I will admit I was a bit free with my giggles. But tell me, now we're at peace again, and may God get you out of all your adventures to come as safe and sound as out of this one – wasn't it a great joke, and won't it make a fine story, this enormous fear of ours? My fear I mean, because I'm aware you don't even know what fear is, sir, or what it feels like to be afraid.'

'I do not deny,' replied Don Quixote, 'that what has happened to us is worth laughing at; but it is not worth telling, because not all people are intelligent enough to see things in the right perspective.'

'At least you got your pike in the right perspective,' replied Sancho, 'aiming at my head and hitting my shoulders, thanks to God and the care I took to duck. But there we are, it all comes out in the wash, and I've often heard people say "you've got to be cruel to be kind", and what's more, when important gentlemen give their servants a good talking-to, they normally give them a pair of breeches afterwards, though I don't know what they give them after beatings, but maybe what knight errants give after beatings are islands, or kingdoms on dry land.'

'The dice could well fall in such a way,' said Don Quixote, 'that what you say comes true; and forgive me for what has just happened, because you are intelligent and so you understand that man's first impulses are beyond his control; and pay heed from now on to what I am about to say, so that you refrain from talking to me excessively: in all the books of chivalry I have read, an infinity of them, I have never come across any squire who talked to his master as much as you do to yours. And in truth I consider it a great fault in both you and me; in you, because you show me scant respect; in me, because I do not make you respect me more. Yes, indeed: Gandalin, Amadis of Gaul's squire, was the Count of the Firm Isle, yet we read that he always addressed his master cap in hand, with his head bowed and his body bent double, in the Turkish fashion. And what shall we say of Gasabal, Sir Galaor's squire, who was so quiet that to convey the excellence of his miraculous silence his name is only mentioned once in the whole of that great and true history? From all that I have said you should infer, Sancho, that a distance must be kept between master and man, between lord and lackey, between knight and squire. So from now on we must behave with more respect, and not indulge in our little jokes, for in whatever way I become annoyed with you, sir, take note that it is always the pitcher that is broken. The boons and favours that I have promised you will arrive in good time, and if they do not arrive you will not, at least, forfeit your wages, as I have already informed you.'

'All you say is very well said,' replied Sancho, 'but what I'd like to know, just in case the time of the favours never does come round and I have to fall back on wages, is how much knights' squires used to earn in those olden days, and whether they were hired by the month or on a daily basis like builders' labourers.'

'I do not believe,' replied Don Quixote, 'that such squires were ever paid wages: they depended upon favour. And if I have provided for you to be paid wages, in the sealed will I left in my house, that was only because of what might happen; for I do not yet know how chivalry will fare in these calamitous times of ours, and I should not want my soul to suffer in the other world for the sake of a mere trifle. For I would have you know, Sancho, that there is no profession in this world more hazardous than that of knight adventurer.'

'That's true enough,' said Sancho, 'because it only needed the sound of some hammers in a fulling-mill to strike fear and terror into the heart of a really brave errant adventurer like yourself. But you can take it from me that from this moment on I won't open my mouth to make fun of your doings, but only to honour you as my master and natural lord.'

'In that case,' replied Don Quixote, 'your days will be long on the face of the earth, because next to our parents, our masters should be respected as if they were our parents.'

CHAPTER XXI

Concerning the sublime adventure and rich prize of
Mambrino's helmet, and other things that happened to our
invincible knight

And now it began to drizzle, and Sancho wanted them to shelter in the fulling-mill. But the mockery that Don Quixote had just suffered had given him such a grudge against those hammers that he wouldn't go in there on any account, so they veered off to the right and came to a road like the one along which they'd been travelling on the previous day. A little later Don Quixote sighted a man riding towards them with something on his head that shone as if it were made of gold, and as soon as he saw this man he turned to Sancho and said:

'It appears to me, Sancho, that there is no proverb which is not true, because they are all maxims derived from experience itself, the mother of all knowledge: especially the one that says, "When one door closes, another opens." I say this because if last night fortune closed the door to the happiness for which we were searching when she deceived us with the fulling-mill, today she is throwing open another door to a better and surer adventure, and if I do not succeed in entering this door I alone shall bear the blame, and I shall not be able to ascribe it to a lack of information on the subject of fulling-mills, or to the darkness of the night. I say this because, if I am not mistaken, we are being approached by a man who bears on his head Mambrino's helmet, about which I swore that vow.'

'Just be careful what you're saying, and even more careful what you're doing,' said Sancho. 'All I hope is that it isn't some more fulling-hammers to finish off the job of pounding and beating us senseless.'

'The devil take you for your perversity!' replied Don Quixote. 'What has a helmet to do with fulling-hammers?'

'I haven't the faintest idea,' replied Sancho, 'but by my faith, if I was allowed to talk as much as I used to, maybe I'd say that which would make you see how wrong you are.'

'How can I be wrong, you doubting Thomas?' said Don Quixote. 'Tell me, do you not see that knight coming towards us, upon a dapple-grey steed, wearing a helmet of gold?'

'All I can make out,' replied Sancho, 'is a bloke on a donkey, brown like mine, with something shiny on his head.'

'Well, that is Mambrino's helmet,' said Don Quixote. 'Move aside and leave me alone with him: you will soon see how, without uttering a single word, so as to save time, I bring this adventure to a happy conclusion, and the helmet that I have so desired becomes mine.'

'I'll move aside all right,' replied Sancho. 'But I'll say it once again – pray God this is what you say it is, and not more fulling-mills.'

'I have already told you, sir, never even to think of mentioning fulling-mills again,' said Don Quixote, 'or I swear my most solemn oath that I shall mill your very soul out of your body.'

Sancho held his tongue, fearful that his master might fulfil the vow he'd sworn with such verve.

The explanation of the helmet, the steed and the knight that Don Quixote saw is as follows: in this area there were two villages, one of them so small that it had neither a chemist nor a barber, while the other, close to it, had both; so the barber of the larger village also looked after the smaller one, where there was a sick man who needed bleeding, and another who wanted a shave, and the barber was on his way there with his brass basin; and fate ordained that as he was riding along it started to rain and, to prevent his hat, which must have been a new one, from getting stained, he put his basin on his head; and since the basin was clean it shone from more than a mile away. He was riding a brown donkey, as Sancho said. And this was what made Don Quixote think he saw a dapple-grey steed, and a knight, and a helmet of gold, because he was so ready to accommodate everything he saw to his delirious chivalry and his errant thoughts. And when he saw this poor knight coming close, he set off without directing a single word at him, and charged at him at Rocinante's fastest pace, his pike couched low, with the intention of passing him through and through; and as he came close, without checking the fury of his charge, he cried:

'Either defend yourself, base caitiff, or hand me of your own free will what is so rightfully due to me!'

The barber, seeing such an apparition descending upon him when nothing had been further from his thoughts or his fears, could only dodge the pike by throwing himself from his donkey; and he'd hardly touched the ground when he sprang back up nimbler than a deer and sprinted away across the plain so fast that the wind itself couldn't have caught him. He left his basin on the ground, and Don Quixote was delighted and said that the pagan had been prudent indeed in behaving like the beaver, which, when cornered by huntsmen, bites off what, by natural instinct, it knows it is being hunted for.[1] He ordered Sancho to retrieve the helmet, and Sancho picked the basin up and said:

'By God this is a good basin – it's worth a piece of eight if it's worth a maravedí.'[2]

He gave it to his master, who put it on his head and then turned it round and round searching for the visor, and not finding one he said:

'The pagan for whose measurements this famous helmet was first forged must have had a very large head; and what is worst of all is that half of the helmet is missing.'

When Sancho heard the basin being called a helmet he couldn't restrain his laughter, but then he recalled his master's fury and checked himself in full flow.

'What are you laughing at, Sancho?' asked Don Quixote.

'What I'm laughing at,' Sancho replied, 'is the thought of the big head on that pagan who was the owner of this here helmet that looks for all the world exactly like a barber's basin.'

'Do you know what I think, Sancho? I think that this famous piece of this enchanted helmet must, by some strange accident, have fallen into the hands of a person who did not understand or appreciate its value, and, not knowing what he was doing, he must, on seeing that it is made of the purest gold, have melted down the other half to sell it, and with the remaining half made this, which seems, as you say, like a barber's basin. But let it be what it will; for me, who knows it well, its transformation is of no consequence; I shall have it corrected in the first village where there is a blacksmith, and in such a manner that it is not surpassed or even equalled by the helmet that the god of forges made for the god of battles,[3] and in the meantime I shall wear it as best I can, because something is better than nothing, particularly since it will certainly be adequate to protect me against stonings.'

'So long as they don't use slings, that is,' said Sancho, 'as they did in the battle between those two armies, when they gave you that blessing on your jaws and smashed the bottle of that very holy concoction that made me spew my guts up.'

'I am not excessively distressed at its loss,' said Don Quixote, 'for as you know, Sancho, I have the recipe in my memory.'

'I've got it in my memory, too,' replied Sancho, 'but let me be struck dead here and now if I ever make it or drink it again. What's more, I'm not intending to be in the way of needing it, because I'm going to use all my five senses to avoid being sorewounded, or sorewounding anyone else. As for being blanket-tossed again, I can't make any promises, because those kinds of mishap can't always be prevented, and if they do come your way there's nothing to be done but curl up, hold your breath, shut your eyes and let yourself go wherever fate and the blanket take you.'

'You are a bad Christian, Sancho,' this prompted Don Quixote to say, 'for once you take offence you never forget. Well, I would have you know that noble and generous breasts pay no heed to trivialities. What lame leg, what broken rib, what shattered skull have you been left with, to make that little jest so unforgettable? For when all is said and done it was only a jest, an amusement; if I did not regard it as such, I should have returned there and avenged you by wreaking more havoc than the Greeks did for the rape of Helen[4] – who, if she had lived in our times, or if my Dulcinea had lived in hers, could be certain that she would not enjoy such a reputation for beauty as she does.'

And here he heaved a sigh that echoed throughout the heavens. And Sancho said:

'It'd better pass as a jest, then, since it isn't going to be taken in earnest and avenged – but I'm the one who knows what those earnest jests were like, and I also know that they won't fade from my memory any more than the sting of them will go away from my ribs. But putting all that aside, please can you tell me what we're going to do with this here dapple-grey steed that looks just like a brown donkey, left all defenceless by that Martino fellow who you knocked over and who, to judge from the way he scarpered, isn't ever going to come back for it? And, my eye, the dapple's a fine animal all right!'

'I am not in the habit,' said Don Quixote, 'of despoiling those whom I vanquish, nor is it a custom of chivalry to take their horses and leave them on foot, unless the victor has lost his own horse in the fray, in which case it is legitimate to take the defeated knight's horse, as a prize won in lawful war. And so, Sancho, leave that horse, or donkey, or whatever you want to call it, for as soon as its master sees that we have gone he will return for it.'

'God knows I'd love to take it,' replied Sancho, 'or at least swap it for mine, because I don't think mine's such a good one. These laws of chivalry are really strict, if they won't even stretch to letting you swap one donkey for another – could you please tell me if I can at least swap the tackle?'

'I am not very clear about that,' replied Don Quixote, 'and as it is a doubtful case, I should say that until I am better informed you can swap it, if your need is very great.'

'It's so great,' said Sancho, 'that if I'd wanted the tackle to wear it myself I couldn't have needed it more.'

And, now that he'd been granted official permission, he performed his *mutatio capparum*[5] and refurbished his donkey, a very great change for the better. Then they breakfasted on the leftovers of the camp-provisions plundered from the priests' supply-mule, and they drank from the river that powered the fulling-mill, taking care not to look in that direction, so great was the loathing inspired by the fear it had struck into them. Once they'd dulled the pangs of hunger, and even the pangs of melancholy, they mounted and, not taking any particular direction, as is appropriate for knights errant, their progress was dictated by Rocinante's will, which carried along with it that of his master, and even that of the ass, which always followed wherever Rocinante led, in love and good fellowship. Despite all this, they found their way back to the main highway, which they followed at random and without any fixed plan. As they jogged along, Sancho said to his master:

'Sir, would you very kindly give me permission to say a few words to you? With that harsh order of silence you imposed on me, quite a number of things have rotted away inside my stomach, and there's one I've got on the tip of my tongue at this very moment and I wouldn't want it to go bad too.'

'Out with it, then,' said Don Quixote, 'and be brief, for long speeches are never enjoyable.'

'What I'm saying, sir,' Sancho replied, 'is that for some time now I've been thinking about how precious little there is to be got out of going around like this looking for these adventures of yours in these wastes and along these remote roads where, even if you triumph in the most dangerous ones, there isn't anybody to see them or know about them, and so they're going to be hushed up for ever, which goes against what you intend and the adventures deserve. And so I think it'd be preferable, saving your better judgement, for us to go off and serve some emperor or other bigwig who's fighting some war, and in his service you can show off your personal qualities, your great might and your even greater intelligence, because once the lord we go to serve sees all this he'll be bound to reward us, each getting what he deserves, and you won't be short of someone to write down all your exploits, to be remembered always. I can't say as much about mine, because they won't go beyond squirely limits, though I will say that if it's regular in chivalry to write about the deeds of squires, I'm not intending mine to be left out of the story.'

'There is something in what you say, Sancho,' replied Don Quixote, 'but before one reaches that stage one must wander about the world on probation as it were, in search of adventures, so that, by bringing some of them to a happy conclusion, one gains such fame and renown that when one does go to some great monarch's court one is known as a knight by one's deeds; and as soon as all the boys in the street see one riding through the city gates, they follow one and come swarming around one and shouting: "This is the Knight of the Sun" or of the Serpent or whatever device it is under which one has performed great exploits. "This," they will say, "is the man who in single combat defeated the enormous giant Brocabruno of the Mighty Strength, the man who freed the Great Mameluke of Persia from the long enchantment in which he had languished for almost nine hundred years." And so they will go on proclaiming one's deeds from mouth to mouth, and then, upon hearing the noise of the boys and the other people, the king of that kingdom will stand at the windows of his royal palace, and as soon as he sees the knight and recognizes him by his armour or by the device on his shield, he is bound to say: "Ho, there! Let all the knights at my court come hither to receive the flower of chivalry, who approaches yonder!" At this command they will all issue forth, and the king will advance halfway down the staircase, and will give him a warm embrace and the kiss of peace on his face, and then lead him by the hand to the queen's chamber, where the knight will discover the queen with the princess, her daughter, and it will be difficult to find a fairer or more perfect maiden anywhere on the face of the earth.

'What will happen next, without a pause, is that she will fix her eyes upon the knight and he will gaze into hers, and each will seem to the other more divine than human, and without understanding how it has happened they will find themselves caught and enmeshed in the tight-knit nets of love and with great anguish in their hearts, not knowing how they can contrive to speak and make their feelings and desires known to each other. From there he will most certainly be taken to some richly furnished chamber in the palace, where, once his armour is removed, a fine scarlet robe will be brought for him to wear; and if he looked well in his armour, he will look as well or even better in his jupon.[6]

'Once night has fallen, he will dine with the king, the queen and the princess, and he will not take his eyes off her, stealing glances at her when the others are not looking, and she will do likewise, taking the same precautions because, as I have said, she is a most intelligent maiden. The tables will be removed and a tiny, ugly dwarf will appear in the hall door with a beautiful lady following him between two giants and bringing a certain adventure-game contrived by a most experienced sage, and whoever succeeds in it will be held to be the best knight in the world. The king will then order that all the knights there present shall attempt it, and none of them will bring it to a happy conclusion save the guest, to the great enhancement of his reputation, and the princess will be overjoyed and well satisfied to have set her sights so very high. And the best part is that this king or prince or whatever is engaged in a desperate war with another monarch as powerful as he, and his guest the knight asks him, after he has been at his court for a few days, for permission to go off and serve him in this war. The king will grant it most willingly, and the knight will courteously kiss his hands for the favour conceded.

'And that night he will bid farewell to his lady the princess through the railings in a garden by the room in which she sleeps, where he has often spoken to her before thanks to the mediation of a lady-in-waiting, the princess's confidante. He will sigh, she will swoon, the lady-in-waiting will fetch some water and be sore distressed, because morning is approaching and she would not like them to be discovered, worried as she is about her mistress's honour. Finally the princess will come to herself and will extend her white hands through the railings, and the knight will kiss them a thousand times and bathe them in tears. The two will agree on how they are to convey their news, both good and bad, to each other, and the princess will beg him to make his absence as short as possible; he will promise to do so, with many vows; he will kiss her hands again, and take his leave in such grief that he will be close to death. From there he goes to his chamber, throws himself down on his bed, cannot sleep from the pain of the parting, rises very early, goes to say goodbye to the king, the queen and the princess; after he has taken his leave of the king and the queen they tell him that the princess is indisposed and cannot receive any visits; the knight believes that this is because of her sorrow at his departure, he is broken-hearted and almost betrays his deep distress. The lady-in-waiting is present, she takes note of everything and she goes to tell her mistress, who receives her with tears, and says that one of her greatest griefs is not knowing who the knight is, and whether he is of royal descent or not; the lady-in-waiting assures her that such courtesy, gentility and bravery can only be found in illustrious royal persons; the distressed damsel finds some consolation in this; she attempts to be of good cheer, so as not to give her parents any cause for suspicion, and after two days she reappears in public.

'The knight has taken his departure; he fights in the war, defeats the king's enemy, conquers many cities, triumphs in many battles, returns to court, meets his lady in the usual place, it is agreed that he will ask her father for her hand in marriage, in return for his services. The king refuses, because he does not know who the knight is; but in spite of that, whether they elope or however it happens, the princess does become his wife, and her father eventually considers it a most fortunate match, because it is discovered that the knight is the son of the valiant king of some kingdom unknown to me, not being, as far as I am aware, anywhere on the map. The father dies, the princess inherits, in brief the knight becomes king. And now comes the time for bestowing favours on his squire and all those who have helped him to rise to such high estate: he marries his squire to one of the princess's ladies-in-waiting, obviously the one who was the helpful confidante, the daughter of a very important duke.'

'That's what I want, and no messing about,' said Sancho. 'And that's what I'm counting on, because it's all going to turn out just as you said, now you're called the Knight of the Sorry Face.'

'Do not doubt it, Sancho,' replied Don Quixote, 'because in the way and by the steps I have related knights errant rise and always have risen to be kings and emperors. All that is needed now is to discover which Christian or pagan king is waging a war and has a beautiful daughter; but there will be time enough to think about that because, as I have told you, one must win fame elsewhere before appearing at court. There is something else lacking, too: supposing that a king with a war and a beautiful daughter is found, and that I have by then won incredible fame throughout the universe, I really do not know how it could be discovered that I am descended from kings, or am even an emperor's second cousin, because the king will not give me his daughter to be my wife without enquiring very carefully into all this, however meritorious my famous deeds may be, and I am afraid that through this shortcoming I might forfeit what my arm so richly deserves. It is true, of course, that I am a hidalgo of known family and a man of property, and that the law protects my good name with a fine of five hundred shillings; and it could happen that the sage who writes my history deals with my family background in such minute detail that he finds me to be a king's grandson five or six times removed. For I would have you know, Sancho, that there are two kinds of lineage in this world: those that sprang from princes and monarchs, and that time has gradually destroyed, and have ended in a point, like an upside-down pyramid; and others that began with low-born people, and have prospered little by little, until they have achieved the eminence of great lords. So the difference is that some were but no longer are, and others are who never were; and I might be one of the former, and it might be discovered that I had great and famous beginnings, which ought to be sufficient for the king my father-in-law-to-be; and, if not, the princess will be so enamoured of me that, in spite of her father – even if he has clear evidence that I am the son of some water-carrier – she will accept me as her lord and husband; and if this does not happen, it will be the moment to carry her off wherever I see fit, and either time or death will put an end to her parents' anger.'

'It will also be the moment,' said Sancho, 'for what some wicked people say, "Never ask as a favour for what you can get by force," although what's more to the point is "A clean pair of heels is better than a good man's pleas." I'm only saying this because if the king, your father-in-law, doesn't come round to letting you have my lady the princess, there's nothing for it but to cart her off and take her somewhere else, as you said. But the trouble is that until the war ends and you can enjoy your kingdom in peace and quiet, the poor old squire might well be starved of favours. That is unless the lady-in-confiding who's going to be the squire's wife goes away with the princess, and he shares his unhappy life with her until heaven decrees a change – because I suppose his master can give her to him as his lawful wedded wife if he wants.'

'Nobody can prevent it,' said Don Quixote.

'Well, in that case,' said Sancho, 'we'll just have to commend ourselves to God and let fortune take whatever course God wants it to.'

'May God provide,' said Don Quixote, 'as I wish and as you, Sancho, need; and he who thinks himself a wretch can stay a wretch.'

'I'll say amen to that,' said Sancho, 'because I'm of old Christian stock, and that's good enough for me to be a count.'

'It is more than enough,' said Don Quixote, 'and even if you were not, it would not signify; because as king I can make you a noble without your buying the title or serving me in any way. For once I make you count – there you are, a gentleman, say what they will; and, to be sure, they shall call you Lordship, whether they like it or not.'

'I bet I'd know how to live up to that handful all right!' said Sancho.

'I think you mean to say *handle*, not *handful*,' said his master.

'Whatever you like,' replied Sancho Panza. 'What I'm saying is that I'd be able to carry it off, because once, upon my soul, I was the beadle in a confraternity, and the beadle's uniform suited me so well that everyone said I had the presence to be the steward. So just imagine when I get the robes of a duke round my shoulders, or when I dress up in gold and pearls like all those foreign counts! I reckon people will come from hundreds of miles away to see me!'

'Yes, you will look well,' said Don Quixote, 'but you will have to shave frequently, because your beard is so thick, rough and unkempt that if you do not take a razor to it every second day at least, people will see in a trice what you are.'

'Why not just get a barber,' said Sancho, 'and keep him in the house on wages? And, if needs be, I'll even make him follow me around like a grandee's equerry.'

'And how do you know,' asked Don Quixote, 'that grandees are followed by their equerries?'

'I'll tell you how I know,' replied Sancho. 'A few years ago I was in the capital for a month, and there I saw a tiny little man that everyone said was a very big man because he was a grandee, going for a ride, and another man following him around on horseback wherever he went, as if he was his tail. I asked why this second man never caught up with the first one, but always rode behind him. They replied that he was his equerry, and that it was a habit of grandees to have these characters following them around. And that's how I know – I've known it so well ever since that I've never forgotten.'

'And I say that you are quite right,' said Don Quixote, 'and that you can take your barber with you in the same way; because customs did not arise all together, nor were they all invented at once, and you can be the first count to be followed by his barber; indeed, shaving a man's beard is an even more intimate duty than saddling his horse.'

'Let me see to the barber,' said Sancho, 'and you can see to becoming a king and making me a count.'

'So it shall be,' replied Don Quixote.

And raising his eyes, he saw what will be related in the next chapter.

CHAPTER XXII

About how Don Quixote freed many wretches who, much
against their will, were being taken where they would have
preferred not to go

Cide Hamete Benengeli, the Arab author from La Mancha, relates in this most grave, grandiloquent, meticulous, delightful and imaginative history that after the conversation between the famous Don Quixote de la Mancha and his squire Sancho Panza recorded at the end of the twenty-first chapter, Don Quixote raised his eyes and saw that some twelve men on foot, strung by the neck, like beads, on a great iron chain, and with shackles on their hands, were plodding towards them along the road. Two men on horseback and two others on foot were escorting them. The mounted men were carrying firelocks and the others swords and spears, and as soon as Sancho Panza saw them he said:

'Here comes a chain-gang of convicts, on their forced march to the King's galleys.'

'What do you mean, forced march?' demanded Don Quixote. 'Is it possible that the King uses force on anyone?'

'I don't mean that,' replied Sancho, 'just that they've been sentenced to serve the King in his galleys for their crimes, and they've got a long walk to get there.'

'In short,' replied Don Quixote, 'whatever the details may be, these people, wherever they are going, are being forced to march there, and are not doing it of their own free will.'

'That's right,' said Sancho.

'In that case,' said his master, 'this situation is calling out for the exercise of my profession: the redressing of outrages and the succour and relief of the wretched.'

'Look, sir,' said Sancho. 'Justice, and that means the King himself, isn't doing these people any outrages, only punishing them for their crimes.'

At this point the chain-gang came up, and Don Quixote, in courteous language, asked the guards to be so kind as to inform him of the reason or reasons why they were bearing those people off in that way. One of the guards on horseback replied that they were all convicts, detained at His Majesty's pleasure and on their way to the galleys, and that there was nothing else to be said and nothing else that he had any business to know.

'All the same,' said Don Quixote, 'I should like to hear from each one of them individually the cause of his misfortune.'

He added other such polite expressions to persuade them to tell him what he wanted to know that the other guard on horseback said:

'We do have here the documents and certificates with the sentences that each of these wretches has been given, but this is no time to stop to take them out and read them; so you'd better come and ask the men yourself, and they'll tell you if they want to – and they will want to, because these are fellows who really enjoy getting up to their evil tricks and bragging about them afterwards.'

With this permission, which Don Quixote would have taken for himself if it hadn't been given him, he approached the chain-gang and asked the first convict what sins had put him in that plight. The convict replied that he was there for being in love.

'For no more than that?' replied Don Quixote. 'If they send men to the galleys for being in love, I could have been rowing in them for a long time by now.'

'It isn't love of the sort you think,' said the convict. 'Mine was for a washing-basket that was chock-a-block with linen, and I loved it so much, and I hugged it so tight, that if the law hadn't taken it off me by force I still wouldn't have let go of it of my own free-will to this day. I was caught red-handed, there wasn't any need for torture, the trial's over and done with, they gave me a hundred of the best plus three in the tubs and that's that.'

'What are tubs?' asked Don Quixote.

'Tubs is galleys,' replied the convict.

He was a young man of maybe twenty-four, and he said he was a native of Piedrahita. Don Quixote put the same question to the second convict, who was so overcome by melancholy that he didn't offer a word in reply, but the first one answered for him and said:

'This one, sir, is here for being a canary-bird, that is to say for being a singer and musician.'

'What?' said Don Quixote. 'Do men go to the galleys for being singers and musicians, too?'

'Yes, sir,' replied the convict, 'because there's nothing worse than singing in your throes.'

'On the contrary,' said Don Quixote, 'I have often heard it said that one can sing away sorrows and cast away care.'

'Here it's the opposite,' said the convict. 'Sing just that once and you'll weep for the rest of your life.'

'I fail to understand,' said Don Quixote.

But one of the guards explained:

'Sir knight, among these ungodly people singing in your throes means confessing under torture. This sinner was tortured and he confessed to his crime – he's a prigger of prancers, in other words a horse-thief – and because he confessed he was sentenced to six years in the galleys and two hundred strokes of the lash, and these he's already been given; and he's always sad and lost in his thoughts, because the other criminals back there in prison and here in the chain-gang despise and mock and maltreat him and make his life impossible for confessing and not having the guts to keep saying no. They say, you see, that "nay" has no more letters in it than "aye", and that a delinquent's a lucky man if his life or death depends on his own tongue and not on witnesses or evidence, and it's my belief they aren't far wrong.'

'That is my understanding, too,' replied Don Quixote.

He moved on to the third convict and put the same question to him; the reply was ready and assured:

'I'm off to our old friends the tubs for five years, for the lack of ten ducats.'

'I will most gladly give you twenty,' said Don Quixote, 'to relieve you of such distress.'

'That looks to me,' replied the convict, 'like having money in the middle of the ocean when you're starving and there isn't anywhere to buy what you need. I'm saying this because if I'd had those twenty ducats you're offering me when I needed them, I'd have used them to grease the clerk's pen and liven up my lawyer's wits, and now I'd be in the middle of Zocodover Square in Toledo instead of in the middle of this road, like a greyhound on a leash. But God is good, and you've just got to be patient.'

Don Quixote went on to the fourth convict, a man with a venerable face and a white beard reaching below his chest who, when asked why he was there, began to weep and didn't reply; but the fifth convict acted as interpreter and said:

'This honourable man is going to the galleys for four years, having been paraded in state through the customary streets, all dressed up and on a fine horse.'

'That means, I think,' said Sancho, 'that he was exposed to public shame.'

'That's right,' said the convict, 'and the crime he was given this punishment for was stockbroking, or to be more exact bodybroking. What I mean to say is that this gentleman's here for being a pimp, and also for having a touch of the sorcerer about him.'

'If it were not for the touch of the sorcerer,' said Don Quixote, 'for being a pimp alone he does not deserve to go to row in the galleys, but rather to be the admiral in charge of them. Because the pimp's trade is no ordinary trade; it must be carried out by intelligent people and it is absolutely essential to any well-ordered society, and only the well-born should exercise it; and there should be an official inspector of pimps, as there is of other trades, and a maximum permitted number of them established and published, as is the case with stockbrokers, and this would be the way to forestall many evils that arise from the fact that this trade is in the hands of untrained and unqualified people such as little strumpets, page-boys and other scoundrels of no age or experience who, when at a critical moment some decisive action is called for, make a mess of the whole thing because they cannot tell their right hands from their left. I should like to go on to give the reasons why it would be advisable to make a careful selection of those who do such a necessary job in society, but this is not the place: one day I shall present my ideas to the proper authorities. All I shall say now is that the distress caused me by the sight of these white hairs and this venerable face in such a plight through his being a pimp is dissipated by the addition of his being a sorcerer. I know, of course, that there are no spells in the world that can control a person's will, as some simple people believe; for our free will is sovereign, and there is no herb or enchantment that can control it. What some silly little strumpets and deceitful rogues do is to make certain poisonous mixtures that they use to turn men mad, claiming that they have the power to make them fall in love, whereas it is, as I have just said, impossible to coerce the will.'

'Right you are,' said the old man, 'and honestly, sir, I wasn't guilty of being a sorcerer, though I couldn't deny the charge of being a pimp. But I never thought I was doing any harm, all I wanted was for everyone to be happy and live in peace and quiet, without any quarrels or sadness — but these good intentions weren't any use to prevent me from being sent where I don't expect to come back from, what with my advanced age and my bladder trouble, that doesn't give me a moment's peace.'

And here he started weeping again, and Sancho felt so sorry for him that he took a real from inside his shirt and handed it over. Don Quixote moved on to the next man and asked what was his crime, and he replied with no less brio than the last, indeed with rather more of it:

'I'm here because I fooled around too much with two girl-cousins of mine, and with two girl-cousins of somebody else's; and, in short, I fooled around so much with the lot of them that as a result the family tree's become so complicated that I don't know who the devil would be able to work it out. It was all proved against me, there weren't any strings for me to pull, I hadn't got any money, I was within an inch of having my neck stretched, I was sentenced to the galleys for six years and I accepted my fate: it's the punishment for my crime, I'm still young, long live life, while there's life there's hope. If, sir knight, you've got anything on you that you could spare for us poor wretches, God will repay you for it in heaven, and here on earth we'll take care to pray to God that your life and your health may be as long and as good as you obviously deserve.'

He was wearing a student's gown, and one of the guards said that he was a great talker and a first-rate latiner.

Behind all of these was a man of thirty, very good-looking except that he squinted a little. He was shackled in a different way from the others: he had a chain on his ankle so long that he'd wound it all round his body, and two neck-irons, one linking him to the other convicts and the other, one of the sort called a keep-friend or friend's foot, from which descended two bars to his waist, where his wrists were manacled to them with great padlocks, so that he could neither raise his hands to his mouth nor lower his head to his hands. Don Quixote asked why this man was wearing so many more fetters than the others. The guard replied that it was because he'd committed more crimes than all the others put together, and that he was so reckless and such a villain that, even though he was shackled up like that, they didn't feel at all safe with him, and feared he was going to escape.

'What crimes can he have committed, though,' asked Don Quixote, 'if he was not given a worse punishment than the galleys?'

'He's going for ten years,' replied the guard, 'which is civil death, more or less.[1] All you need to know is that this man is the famous Ginés de Pasamonte, also known as Ginesillo de Parapilla.'[2]

'Look you here, sergeant,' said the convict, 'just watch your step, and don't be in such a hurry to fix names and nicknames on to people. I'm called Ginés, not Ginesillo, and my family name is Pasamonte, not the Parapilla you said, and I'd advise you lot to stop poking your noses into other people's business.'

'Less impudence, you double-dyed villain,' replied the sergeant, 'unless you want me to shut your mouth for you.'

'It isn't hard to spot,' replied the convict, 'that at the moment I'm reduced to what God has seen fit to send me; but one day somebody's going to find out whether I'm called Ginesillo de Parapilla or not.'

'Isn't that what people call you, then, you liar?' said the guard.

'Yes, that's what they call me,' replied Ginés, 'but I'll stop them calling me that, or else I'll pull out every single hair from my I know what. If you've got something to give us, sir knight, let's have it, and then you can clear off, because you're beginning to get on my nerves with all your prying into other people's lives – and if you want to know about mine, let me tell you I'm Ginés de Pasamonte, and my life has been written by these very fingers here.'

'Now he's telling the truth,' said the sergeant. 'He's written his own life-history himself and a good one it is, too, and he pawned the book in prison for two hundred reals.'

'And I mean to redeem it,' said Ginés. 'And I would, even if I'd pawned it for two hundred ducats.'

'Is it as good as all that?' said Don Quixote.

'It's so good,' replied Ginés, 'that I wouldn't give a fig for *Lazarillo de Tormes*³ and all the others of that kind that have been or ever will be written. What I can tell you is that it deals with facts, and that they're such fine and funny facts no lies could ever match them.'

'And what is the title of your book?' asked Don Quixote.

'*The Life of Ginés de Pasamonte,*' replied the man of that name.

'And have you finished it?' asked Don Quixote.

'How can I have finished it,' he replied, 'if my life hasn't finished yet? What's written so far is from my birth to when I was sentenced to the galleys this last time.'

'Have you been to the galleys before, then?' asked Don Quixote.

'I have, serving God and the King for four years, so I know what biscuits taste like and I know what the lash tastes like,' replied Ginés. 'And I'm not too worried about going back, because it'll give me a chance to finish my book – there are lots of things left for me to say, and in Spanish galleys there's more than enough peace and quiet, not that I need much of that for what I've got left to write, because I know it all by heart.'

'You seem to be an able fellow,' said Don Quixote.

'And an unfortunate one, too,' replied Ginés, 'because misfortunes always pursue men of genius.'

'They pursue villains,' said the sergeant.

'I've already told you, sergeant,' replied Pasamonte, 'to watch your step – you weren't given that staff to ill-treat us poor wretches, but to guide and take us to where His Majesty commands. Otherwise – by the blood of . . . ! – all sorts of things might come out in the wash one day, like those stains that were made at the inn, for example. So everyone keep his mouth shut, and live a good life, and speak even better words, and let's get moving, because this little joke has been going on for far too long.'

The sergeant raised his staff to hit Pasamonte in reply to his threats, but Don Quixote thrust himself between them and begged the sergeant not to maltreat the fellow, for it was only to be expected that one whose hands were so tightly bound would loosen his tongue a little. And turning to the chain-gang he said:

'From everything that you have told me, dearly beloved brethren, I have gathered that, although it is for your crimes you have been sentenced, the punishments you are to suffer give you little pleasure, and that you are on your way to receive them with reluctance and against your will; and it could be that one man's lack of courage under torture, another's lack of money, another's lack of strings to pull and, to be brief, the judge's perverse decisions, were the causes of your downfall and of his failure to recognize the right that was on your side. All of which is now so powerfully present in my mind that it is persuading, telling and even obliging me to demonstrate on you the purpose for which heaven sent me into this world and made me profess in it the order of chivalry that I do profess, and the vow that I made to favour the needy and those oppressed by the powerful. But because I know that one essential part of prudence is never to do by force what can be achieved by consent, I hereby request these guards and this sergeant to be so kind as to release you and allow you to go in peace, for there will be no lack of other men to serve the King in happier circumstances, and it does seem excessively harsh to make slaves of those whom God and nature made free. What is more, guards,' added Don Quixote, 'these poor men have done nothing to you. Let each answer for his sins in the other world; there is a God in heaven who does not neglect to punish the wicked and reward the virtuous, and it is not right for honourable men to be the executioners of others, if they have no personal concern in the matter. I am making my request in this mild and measured manner so that, if you accede to it, I shall have reason for thanking you; but if you do not accede voluntarily, this lance and this sword and the might of my arm will force you to comply.'

'That's a good one that is!' said the sergeant. 'That's a fine joke he's come out with at long last! He wants us to hand the King's prisoners over to him, as if we had the authority to let them go or he had the authority to tell us to! You'd better clear off and make tracks, sir, and straighten that chamber-pot you've got on your head, and don't go around trying to put the cat among the pigeons.'

'You are the cat, and the rat, and the villain, too!' retorted Don Quixote. He matched his deeds to his words and his attack was such a sudden one that he tumbled the man to the ground with a pike-wound before he had a chance to defend himself; and it was fortunate for Don Quixote that this was the guard with the firelock. The other guards were amazed and disconcerted by this unexpected development, but they rallied, and those on horseback seized their swords, and those on foot their spears, and they all fell upon Don Quixote, who was calmly awaiting them; yet he'd have fared badly if the convicts, seeing their chance to be free, hadn't succeeded by breaking the chain on which they were threaded. The hurly-burly was such that the guards, trying both to control the convicts, who were unshackling themselves, and to attack Don Quixote, who was attacking them, chased around in circles and achieved nothing.

Sancho, for his part, helped with the freeing of Ginés de Pasamonte, who was the first to spring into action as he launched himself at the fallen sergeant, snatched up his sword and his firelock and, pointing this at one man and then at another, without firing it, made all the guards disappear as they fled both from the gun and from the stones being hurled at them by the escaped convicts.

This incident saddened Sancho, because he supposed that the fleeing men would go and inform the Holy Brotherhood, who would sound the alarm and come out in pursuit of the wrongdoers; and Sancho said so to his master, and begged him to agree to a quick getaway to hide in the forests in the nearby sierra.

'That is a good idea,' said Don Quixote, 'but there is something I must do first.'

And he called out to the convicts, who were creating a furore as they stripped the sergeant naked; they gathered around to see what he wanted, and he said:

'It is a mark of well-born people to be grateful for benefits received, and one of the sins most offensive to God is ingratitude. I am saying this because you have seen, gentlemen, manifest before your eyes, the benefit that you have received from me; in payment of which it is my wish and desire that you should set out without delay, bearing that chain that I have taken from your necks, for the city of El Toboso, and present yourselves before the lady Dulcinea del Toboso, and tell her that her knight, the Knight of the Sorry Face, presents his compliments, and relate to her, stage by stage, every detail of this famous adventure up to and including my restoration of the liberty that you so desired; and once you have done this you can go wherever you like, and may good fortune attend you.'

Ginés de Pasamonte replied on behalf of them all, and said:

'This that you order us to do, dear lord and liberator, is utterly and totally out of the question, because we can't travel together – we've got to split up and go alone, each along his own road, and try to find a way into the very bowels of the earth so as not to be caught by the Holy Brotherhood, who'll be coming out after us, for certain. What you can do and what it'd be right for you to do is to replace that toll or tax payable to the lady Dulcinea del Toboso by a certain number of Ave Marias and Credos, which we'll say for your kindness, and this is something that can be done by night and by day, running away and resting, in peace and in war; but to think that we're going back to the flesh-pots of Egypt,[4] in other words picking up our chain again and setting off for El Toboso, is like thinking it's night-time already when it isn't yet ten in the morning – it's like trying to get figs from thistles.'

'By my faith,' cried Don Quixote, by now in a fury, 'you little bastard, Don Ginesillo de Paropillo or whatever you're called – now you shall go there alone, with your tail between your legs and the whole chain on your back!'

Pasamonte wasn't a long-suffering sort, and from Don Quixote's absurd desire to set them free he'd realized that the man wasn't very sane, so when he found himself thus addressed, he tipped his companions the wink and they edged away and began to rain so many stones on Don Quixote that, however he ducked and dodged behind his little round shield, he couldn't fend them off; and poor Rocinante paid no more attention to the spurs than if he'd been made of bronze. Sancho sheltered behind his ass from the hailstorm falling on them both. Don Quixote couldn't prevent countless stones from hitting his body with enough force to knock him to the ground, and as soon as he did fall the student leapt on him, snatched the basin from his head and smashed it three or four times on his back and as many more times on the earth, pounding it almost to pieces. Then they stripped him of a surcoat he was wearing over his armour and would have stripped him of his stockings, too, if his leg armour hadn't made this impossible. They took Sancho's topcoat and left him in his shirtsleeves, and they shared the rest of the spoils of battle, and each went his own way, more concerned to escape from the dreaded Holy Brotherhood than to burden himself with the chain and go to present himself before the lady Dulcinea del Toboso.

The ass and Rocinante, Sancho and Don Quixote were left alone: the ass hanging its head, lost in its thoughts, flapping its ears every so often in the belief that the storm of stones wasn't yet over, because it was still raging inside its skull; Rocinante stretched out by his master's side, because he'd also been brought down by a stone; Sancho in his shirtsleeves and fearful of the Holy Brotherhood; and Don Quixote sulking at being left in such a sorry state by men for whom he had done so much.

CHAPTER XXIII

About what happened to the famous Don Quixote in the
Sierra Morena, one of the strangest adventures recounted
in this true history

Finding himself in this sorry state, Don Quixote said to his squire:

'I have always heard, Sancho, that to do good to low-born rabble is to cast water into the sea. Had I believed what you said, I should have avoided this vexation; but the damage is done now, so one must be patient and learn one's lesson for the future.'

'If you've learned your lesson for the future,' retorted Sancho, 'I'm a Turk. But since you're saying that if you'd believed me then you'd have avoided all this mayhem, just believe me now and you'll avoid worse –

because I'd like you to know that chivalry doings won't wash with the Holy Brotherhood, they don't care a fig for all the knight errants in the world, and let me tell you I can almost hear their arrows whistling towards me even now.'

'You are a coward by nature, Sancho,' said Don Quixote, 'yet to prevent you from claiming that I am obstinate and never do as you recommend, just this once I shall take your advice and keep my distance from the fury that so frightens you, but on one condition: never, in life or in death, will you tell anyone that I retreated from this peril out of fear, but rather acceded to your entreaties; and if you say anything else, you will be lying, and I give you the lie from now until then and from then until now, and I affirm that you lie and you will lie whenever you think or say it. And do not answer me back; for the mere thought that I am retreating from peril, especially this peril, which does appear to have some faint shadow of fear about it, is enough to make me take my stand here and await alone not only that Holy Brotherhood whose name you speak in such terror but the brothers of the twelve tribes of Israel, and the seven Maccabees, and Castor and Pollux,[1] and all the brothers and brotherhoods in the world.'

'Look here, sir,' replied Sancho, 'withdrawing isn't running away, and waiting isn't prudent when danger outweighs hope, and the wise man saves himself for tomorrow and doesn't risk everything on one day. And I'd just like to say that although I'm an uncouth peasant I do understand a bit about this business they call right conduct, so don't repent of having taken my advice, but climb on to Rocinante if you can, and if you can't I'll help you up, and follow me, because my old grey matter's telling me that at the moment one pair of heels is worth two pairs of hands.'

Don Quixote mounted without another word, and Sancho led the way on his ass into a nearby part of the Sierra Morena, his idea being to ride right across it as far as Viso or Almodóvar del Campo and hide out for a few days in that rough country, so as not to be found if the Holy Brotherhood did come after them. He was encouraged to do this by the discovery that the provisions on his ass had escaped untouched from the skirmish with the convicts, something that he considered miraculous, considering how they'd searched and pillaged.

As Don Quixote rode in among the mountains, his heart rejoiced because these seemed like ideal places for the adventures he was seeking. The marvellous events experienced by knights errant in similar lonely and rugged spots were returning to his memory. He rode along musing on all these matters, so absorbed and carried away by them that he didn't have a thought for anything else. And as soon as Sancho believed they were safe, his only concern was to satisfy his stomach with the remains of the clerical spoils, and along he rode behind his master, sitting side-saddle on his donkey, and out of the saddle-bag came the food and into his belly it all went; and so long as he had this to keep him busy, he wouldn't have given a brass farthing for another adventure.

But then he did raise his eyes, and saw that his master had stopped and was using the tip of his pike to try to prise up a bundle that was lying on the ground, so he hurried to help; and he reached him just as he was lifting on his pike-tip a saddle-pad with a travelling bag attached to it, half-rotten or rather entirely so and falling to pieces; but they were so heavy that Sancho had to dismount and take them from the pike, and his master told him to see what was in the travelling bag. Sancho hastened to do so and, although the bag was secured with a padlock and chain, it was so torn and decayed that he could see what was in it: four shirts of fine holland-cloth, other articles of linen, as exquisite as they were clean, and, wrapped in a handkerchief, a sizeable pile of gold escudos. When Sancho saw them he exclaimed:

'All heaven be blessed for sending us an adventure that pays!'

Some more rummaging yielded a richly bound notebook. Don Quixote asked for it, and told Sancho to take the money and keep it for himself. Sancho kissed his hands for the favour and removed all the linen to his provision bag. Don Quixote observed his actions and said:

'It seems to me, Sancho (and this is the only possible explanation), that some lost traveller must have wandered into this sierra, and been waylaid and killed by robbers, who brought his body here to this remote spot to bury it.'

'That can't be right,' replied Sancho, 'because if they were robbers they wouldn't have left all this money behind.'

'That is true,' said Don Quixote, 'so I cannot guess or imagine what has happened. But wait, let us see if there is anything written in this notebook that can help us to trace and discover what we want to know.'

He opened it, and the first thing he found written there, as if it were a draft, although very neatly set out, was a sonnet, which he read aloud for Sancho to hear, and found that it went like this:

> Love's blind – or, rather, ignorant, I'd say,
> Or cruelty must be his guiding passion;
> For it's unjust to make a lover pay
> With torture on the rack for indiscretion.
>   But if Love is a god, I must confess
> That he has boundless knowledge and, what's more,
> A god cannot be harsh and pitiless.
> Who, then, has sent this pain that I adore?
>   My Chlöe? No, that couldn't ever be:
> Such ills could never have a source so dear,
> Nor have the gods sent suffering to me:
> That I am soon to die is all that's clear.
>   For when the cause of the complaint's unsure,
> A miracle alone can bring a cure.

'We aren't going to discover anything from that rhyme,' said Sancho, 'unless that clue is something we can follow up.'

'To which clue do you refer?' said Don Quixote.

'I thought,' said Sancho, 'you mentioned something about his clue.'

'What I said was Chlöe,' replied Don Quixote, 'and this must be the name of the lady of whom the author of this sonnet is complaining; and to be sure he is a very fair poet, or I am no judge of that art.'

'So,' said Sancho, 'you know all about rhymes, too, do you?'

'More than you think,' replied Don Quixote, 'as you will see when you take a letter, written in verse from beginning to end, to my lady Dulcinea del Toboso. For I would have you know, Sancho, that all or nearly all the knights errant of past times were great troubadours and great musicians, because these two skills, or, to be more accurate, gifts, are essential to knights errant in love. It does have to be admitted, though, that the verses written by the knights of old are distinguished more by spiritedness than by elegance.'

'You go on and read some more,' said Sancho, 'I'm sure you'll find something to help us.'

Don Quixote turned the page and said:

'This is prose, and it looks like a letter.'

'A personal letter, sir?' asked Sancho.

'To judge from its opening it is a love-letter,' replied Don Quixote.

'Do read it out aloud, then,' said Sancho. 'I'm very fond of love stories.'

'Very well,' said Don Quixote.

And he read it out aloud, as Sancho had requested, and found that it went like this:

Your false promise and my true misfortune carry me to a place from whence you will sooner hear the news of my death than the sound of my complaints. You rejected me, ungrateful woman, for one more wealthy but not more worthy than I; yet if virtue were a valued treasure, I should not now be envying another's good fortune or lamenting my own misfortune. What your beauty raised up, your deeds have laid low: your beauty made me believe you were an angel, your deeds make me realize you are a woman. Peace be with you, who have sent war to me, and may heaven keep your husband's deceptions concealed for ever, so that you are not struck with remorse for what you have done, and I do not reap a revenge that I do not desire.

When Don Quixote had finished reading the letter, he said:

'All that one can discover from this and from the poem is that the man who wrote them is some slighted lover.'

And, thumbing through the book, he found other verses and letters, some of which he could read and others not, but they all contained complaints, laments, suspicions, longings and sorrows, favours and slights, some celebrated and others bemoaned.

While Don Quixote was going through the notebook, Sancho was going through the travelling bag, leaving not one corner of it or of the saddle-pad unsearched, unscrutinized or unexplored, not one seam unripped and not one tuft of wool unpicked, to make sure that he wasn't overlooking anything through haste or carelessness – such was the appetite that finding the escudos, of which there were more than a hundred, had stimulated. And although he didn't find anything else, he knew it had all been worthwhile – all the blanket-flying, the spewed-up balsam, the benedictions from the walking-staffs, the thumping from the muleteer, the disappearance of the saddle-bags, the theft of the topcoat, and all the hunger, thirst and exhaustion that he'd been through in his good master's service: all worthwhile because he'd been so well repaid by being allowed to keep that treasure trove.

The Knight of the Sorry Face was left with a great desire to know who was the owner of the travelling bag, and he conjectured from the sonnet and the letter, from the gold coins and the fine shirts, that they must belong to some lover of high rank, reduced to a desperate decision by his lady's disdain and ill treatment of him. But since there was nobody in that rugged and uninhabitable country to inform him, his only concern was to press on whichever way Rocinante wanted to go – in other words wherever Rocinante could manage to plod – always imagining that some wonderful adventure must be awaiting him among those briars and brambles.

As he rode along, then, with this idea in mind, he saw on a hill in front of him a man leaping with unusual agility from rock to rock and from bush to bush. He seemed to be half-naked, and he had a thick black beard, long hair tied in a pony tail, bare legs and feet; he wore short breeches that seemed to be of light brown velvet, but they were so torn that in many places his skin showed through. He was bareheaded. Although the man moved at such speed, the Knight of the Sorry Face took note of all these details, and he tried to follow him but without success because Rocinante's feebleness wouldn't allow him to gallop over such rough terrain, and furthermore he was a sedate and phlegmatic horse. It immediately occurred to Don Quixote that this man was the owner of the travelling bag and the saddle-pad, and he decided to go in search of him until he found him, even if this meant wandering through the sierra for a year; so he ordered Sancho to dismount from his ass and cut across one part of the hill, and he himself would go the other way, as by such measures they might find the man who had so swiftly disappeared from their sight.

'No, that'll be beyond me,' replied Sancho, 'because as soon as I leave your side the fear comes over me and attacks me with all kinds of alarms and visions. And what I'm telling you now can serve as a warning so that you never again expect me to budge so much as an inch from your side.'

'Very well,' said the Knight of the Sorry Face, 'and I am delighted that you are resolved to rely on my courage, which will not desert you, even if your very soul should do so. And now follow me slowly, or however you can, and keep your eyes peeled; we shall ride all round this hill and maybe come across that man we saw, who is beyond doubt none other than the owner of the objects we have just found.'

To which Sancho replied:

'It'd be much better not to look for him, because if we do find him and the money does turn out to be his, it's clear I'll have to give it back – so it'd be better not to go to all these uncalled-for lengths, and for me to keep the money in good faith until its real owner turns up in some other way, without so much poking around for him. And by then I might have spent it all, and the King would let me off.'

'You are deluding yourself there, Sancho,' replied Don Quixote, 'because now that we have formed a suspicion of who the owner might be – and he is virtually standing here in front of us – it is our duty to seek him out and return his money; and if we did not go in search of him, our strong suspicion that he is the owner would make us as guilty as if we were altogether certain that he is. So, Sancho my friend, you must not let searching for him grieve you, in view of how finding him would relieve me.'

So he put spurs to Rocinante, and Sancho followed him on his donkey, as usual, and after they'd ridden some of the way round the hill they found a dead mule lying in a stream, complete with saddle and bridle, half devoured by dogs and pecked by crows, which confirmed their suspicion that the man who'd run away from them was the owner of the mule and the saddle-pad. As they contemplated this sight they heard a whistling, like that of a herdsman rounding up his animals, and suddenly, to their left, a number of goats appeared and behind them on the top of the hill the goatherd, an old man. Don Quixote shouted to him and invited him to descend. He shouted back asking what had brought them to that place, seldom if ever visited by anything other than goats and wolves and other wild beasts that lived in those parts. Sancho replied that if he came down they'd explain everything. He did so and as he approached Don Quixote he said:

'I bet you're looking at that hired mule lying dead in that ravine. To be sure it's been there for a good six months now. Tell me, have you come across its owner?'

'We have not come across anyone,' replied Don Quixote, 'just a saddle-pad and a travelling bag that we found not far from here.'

'I found it too,' replied the goatherd, 'but I never picked it up or even went close to it, for fear that it might bring bad luck, and that I might have to return it as stolen property – the devil's a cunning one, and things are always showing up at a man's feet to make him trip and fall when he's least expecting it.'

'That's what I say, too,' replied Sancho. 'I found it as well, and I wouldn't have touched it with a bargepole, so I left it just where it was, and there it lies exactly as it did before – I don't want a dog with a bell round its neck.'

'Tell me, my good man,' said Don Quixote, 'do you know who is the owner of these articles?'

'All I can tell you,' said the goatherd, 'is that one day roughly six months ago, at a goat-fold about ten miles from here, a good-looking young man turned up riding the mule that's lying down there dead, with that same saddle-pad and travelling bag you say you found and didn't touch. He asked us which part of this sierra was the most rugged and remote, and we told him that this part was where we are now, and so it is, because if you went in another mile or two maybe you'd never find your way out again, and I'm astonished you've got this far, because there isn't any road or path to bring you here. Anyway, as soon as the young man heard our reply he turned his mule and went off in the direction we'd said, leaving us all admiring his good looks and amazed at his question and at the speed at which he'd ridden away towards the sierra, and we didn't see him again until a few days later he waylaid one of the goatherds and without a word came up to him and punched him and kicked him and then went over to our supply-donkey and took all the bread and cheese there was on it, and ran away at an incredible rate to hide in the sierra. When we found out about this, some of us goatherds went looking for him for almost two days in the remotest part of the sierra, and in the end we found him hiding in the hollow of a fine, stout cork-oak. He came out very quietly, with his clothes ripped and his face changed and sunburned so that we could hardly recognize him – except that his clothes, torn as they were, were the same ones we'd seen him wearing earlier and showed he was the man we were looking for.

'He greeted us courteously, and with a few well-chosen words he told us not to be surprised at seeing him going about like that, because he had to do so to fulfil a penance imposed on him for his many sins. We asked him to tell us who he was, but we couldn't get this out of him. We also asked him, when he needed food, to tell us where we could find him, because he couldn't survive without it and we'd be more than willing to take it to him, and, if he didn't like this idea either, at least to come and ask us for it rather than snatching it from us. He thanked us for our offer, apologized for his past attacks, and said that from then on he'd beg us for his food, without annoying anybody. As for his dwelling-place, he said he had none but whatever chance offered him when night fell, and he ended his words with such tender tears that those who'd been listening would have had to be of stone not to weep with him, considering how he'd looked before and how he looked now. As I said, he was a very handsome and well-graced young man, and in his courteous and thoughtful words he showed himself to be a real gentleman, so that, although all of us listening were simple country folk, even we could tell that he was a person of high rank.

'He was in full flow when he stopped and fell silent and stared down at the earth, and we all waited in a puzzled hush for a good while to find out how this trance was going to end, saddened to see him like that – because from the way he was opening his eyes wide, glaring and glaring at the ground without batting an eyelid, then suddenly shutting his eyes tight and clenching his lips and arching his eyebrows, it was easy to spot that he was in the grips of some fit of madness. And he soon showed that we were right, because he sprang in fury to his feet from where he'd slumped to the ground, and launched himself at the man nearest him with such wild determination that if we hadn't torn him away he'd have beaten and bitten him to death, and he was saying:

' "Ah, perfidious Fernando! Now, now you shall pay for the wrongs you've done me! These hands of mine will tear out your very heart, the den wherein all evil dwells, and the greatest of them trickery and deceit."

'And he added other words, all of them abuse of this man Fernando, calling him perfidious and a traitor. We managed to pull him off our companion and, without another word, he ran away and hid among the brambles and the thickets, and we couldn't follow him. We reckoned that the madness comes on him every so often, and that some man called Fernando must have done something terrible to him, something awful enough to have brought him to that state. It's all been confirmed since, on the many occasions he's come down from the hills, sometimes to ask the goatherds for food, at other times to take it from them by force, because when the fit of madness is upon him he won't let them give him food, even if they do so willingly, but punches them and takes it; when he's in his right mind he begs them for it in a courteous, restrained way, and gives profuse thanks and even sheds some tears. And to tell you the truth, sirs,' continued the goatherd, 'yesterday I decided with four young lads – two servants of mine and two friends – to go in search of him until we find him, and once we find him to take him, whether he wants to go or not, to the town of Almodóvar, twenty-five miles from here, and have him cured there, if there is a cure for his illness, or find out from him, when he's in his right mind, who he is, and whether he has relatives we should inform about his misfortune. This, sirs, is what I can tell you in reply to your question, and you can be sure that the owner of the things you found is the same person you saw running by so nimble and so naked' – because Don Quixote had told him how he'd seen the man leaping from crag to crag on the hill.

Don Quixote was amazed at what the goatherd had told him, and was even more anxious now to know who the unfortunate madman was, and decided to do what he'd been contemplating: search the whole sierra for him, leaving not a cave or a cranny unexplored until he'd found him. But fortune was kinder than he'd dared to hope, because at that very moment, in a gorge that opened on to the place where they were talking, the young man himself appeared, muttering words that were incomprehensible from close up, let alone from a distance. His clothes were as they've been described, except that when he came nearer Don Quixote noticed that a ragged suede jerkin he was wearing was perfumed with ambergris, further confirmation that a person wearing such clothes couldn't be of low rank.

The young man came up and greeted them in a hoarse, discordant voice, but with great courtesy. Don Quixote replied no less politely and, dismounting from Rocinante, walked with graceful elegance to embrace him, and held him for some moments in his arms, as if he knew him from distant times. The young man, whom, just as Don Quixote was the Knight of the Sorry Face, we can call the Ragged Knight of the Miserable Face, submitted to the embrace and then pushed Don Quixote a little away, gazing at him with his hands on the other man's shoulders as if trying to recognize him, perhaps no less astonished to see Don Quixote's face, figure and armour than Don Quixote had been to see him. In the end the first one to speak after this embrace was the Ragged Knight, and he said what will be recorded in the next chapter.

CHAPTER XXIV

In which the adventure in the Sierra Morena is continued

The history says that Don Quixote listened with rapt attention to the ill-dressed and ill-starred Knight of the Sierra, who continued:

'Most certainly, sir, whoever you are, for I do not know you, I thank you for your expressions of civility, and I wish I were in a position to serve you with more than my goodwill in return for that which you have shown me in the warm reception which you have extended to me; but my fortune does not allow me anything with which to respond to the kindnesses done me, other than the sincere desire to repay them.'

'Mine,' replied Don Quixote, 'is to serve you; so much so, that I had resolved not to leave this sierra until I had found you and discovered from you whether there was any remedy for the grief that, to judge from your extraordinary life here, afflicts you; and if it were necessary to go in search of such a remedy, to do so with the utmost possible diligence. And if your misfortune were of the sort that keeps the doors tight shut to all solace, it was my intention to join you, as best I could, in your tears and lamentations, for it is always a consolation in disaster to find someone who is sympathetic. And if my good intentions deserve to be acknowledged with any kind of courtesy, I beg you, sir, in the name of the abundance of that quality that I can see you possess, and I entreat you in the name of whomsoever in this life you love or have loved the best, to tell me who you are and what has brought you to live and die in this wilderness like a brute animal, because your dress and person show how alien to you is this present life of yours. And I swear,' added Don Quixote, 'by the order of chivalry that I, although unworthy and a sinner, have received, and by the profession of knight errant, that if you comply with this request, sir, I shall serve you with that earnestness to which I am obliged by being who I am, either by remedying your misfortune, if indeed it has a remedy, or by assisting you to bewail it, as I have promised.'

When the Knight of the Forest heard the Knight of the Sorry Face speak in this way, he only stared at him, and stared at him again, and stared at him once more from head to foot; and once he'd had a good stare, he said:

'If you people have anything to eat, let me have it, for God's sake, and once I've eaten I'll do everything you say, to express my gratitude for the kind intentions you've expressed.'

They immediately produced some food, Sancho from his saddle-bag and the goatherd from his pouch, and the Ragged Knight satisfied his hunger, eating what he was given like a man in a daze, so fast that there was no space between one mouthful and the next, because he didn't so much swallow them as shovel them down; and while he ate, neither he nor those watching him spoke a word. Once he'd finished, he signalled to them to follow him, which they did, and he took them to a green meadow behind a rock not far away. On reaching it he stretched himself out on the grass, and the others did the same, all without a word being spoken by anyone until the Ragged Knight, once he'd made himself comfortable, said:

'If you wish me, gentlemen, to tell you in a few words about the immensity of my misfortunes, you must promise that you won't interrupt the thread of my sad story with any question or any other intervention, because the instant you do so my narrative will end.'

These words brought into Don Quixote's memory the story that his squire had told him, when he'd failed to keep count of how many goats had crossed the river, and the story had been left unfinished. But to return to the Ragged Knight, he continued:

'I give you this warning because I'd like to pass quickly over the story of my misfortunes, since bringing them back to my memory only adds to them, and the fewer questions you ask the sooner I'll be finished; but I shan't leave anything important out, because I want to satisfy all your wishes.'

Don Quixote promised in the name of the whole company that he would not be interrupted, and with this assurance the Ragged Knight began:

'My name is Cardenio; I'm from one of the finest cities in Andalusia; my family's noble; my parents are wealthy; and my misfortune's so great that my parents must have wept and my family grieved over it, unable with all their wealth to remedy it, for the greatest of fortunes can do little to relieve the misfortunes sent by heaven. There lived on this earth a heaven in which love had placed all the glory that I could ever wish for: such is the beauty of Luscinda, a maiden as noble and wealthy as I, but luckier, and less constant than my honourable intentions deserved. This Luscinda I loved, worshipped and adored from my tenderest and earliest years, and she loved me too, with the simple affection and eagerness of youth. Our parents knew of our feelings, and they weren't opposed to them, because they could see that if they continued they could only lead to marriage, something almost required by the equality of our lineage and wealth. Our love increased as we grew up, and Luscinda's father thought himself obliged by good form to refuse me entry to his house, imitating the parents of that Thisbe so celebrated by poets.[1] This ban only added flame to flame and desire to desire because, although our tongues had been silenced, it was impossible to silence our pens, which tell the loved one more freely than do tongues about the hidden secrets of the soul; for the presence of the beloved often confuses and silences the most determined intention and the boldest tongue. Heavens, how many letters I wrote her! What delicate and modest replies I received! How many songs I composed, how many verses of love, in which my soul declared and revealed its feelings, depicted its burning desires, cherished its memories and relived its passion! Eventually, at my wit's end and with my soul consumed by desire to see her, I decided to put into effect once and for all what I thought was the most effective means to gain my longed-for and deserved prize, which was to ask her father for her as my lawful wife, and I did this; he replied that he was grateful to me for wanting to honour him and seeking to honour myself with his precious treasure, but that, since my own father was still alive, it was he who should by rights make the request, because Luscinda was not a woman to be taken or given in an underhand way without his full permission and approval.

'I thanked him for his kindness, thinking that he was right, and that if I told my father about my proposal he would agree to it; so I immediately went to inform him of my wish. When I walked into his room, I found him with a letter open in his hand, and before I could speak he gave it to me and said:

'"You will see from this letter, Cardenio, the favour that Duke Ricardo wishes to do you."

'This Duke Ricardo, as you must already know, gentlemen, is a grandee of Spain, whose estate lies in the best part of Andalusia. I took and read the letter, which was so insistent that I myself would have objected if my father had failed to do what it asked of him, which was to send me immediately to the Duke: he wanted me as a companion, not a servant, for his elder son, and he would undertake to situate me in accordance with the high opinion he had of me. I read the letter and was dumbfounded, even more so when I heard my father saying:

'"In two days' time you will depart, Cardenio, to do as the Duke wishes; and give thanks to God for opening a way for you to what I know you well deserve."

'To this he added some more pieces of fatherly advice.

'The moment of my departure approached, I spoke by night with Luscinda, I told her all that had happened and I told her father as well, and begged him to wait a few days and postpone settling her marriage until I found out what Ricardo wanted of me; he promised to do so, and she confirmed his promise with a thousand vows and a thousand swoons. So away I went to join Duke Ricardo. I was so well received and treated by him that envy immediately started to do its work and to possess his servants, for they thought that all the signs he gave of favouring me would be to their detriment. But the person who was most delighted at my arrival was the Duke's younger son, Fernando, a charming, attractive young man, of generous and amorous disposition, who soon wanted me to be such a close friend that everybody was gossiping about it; and although the elder son liked me and treated me well, he didn't go to Don Fernando's extremes of attention and affection.

'Now as there are no secrets between friends, and as the favour that Don Fernando showed me stopped being mere favour and turned into friendship, he told me all his thoughts, and in particular one relating to love that was worrying him somewhat. He loved a wealthy farmer's daughter, one of his father's tenants, and she was so beautiful, modest, intelligent and virtuous that nobody who knew her could decide which of these excellent qualities was most outstanding in her. And they raised Don Fernando's desires to such a pitch that he decided that to have his way with her and conquer her virginity he'd give her his word of marriage,[2] because to have tried any other approach would have been to attempt the impossible. Prompted by our friendship, I tried, with the best arguments I knew and the most eloquent examples I could find, to dissuade him and turn him aside from this course, but seeing that it was all in vain I decided to put the matter before Duke Ricardo, his father; Don Fernando, however, cunning and intelligent as he was, suspected and feared that I might do this, knowing that I was obliged, as a loyal servant, not to conceal something so prejudicial to the honour of my lord the Duke; and to mislead and deceive me he told me that he couldn't think of anything to take his mind off the beauty which had so captivated him other than going away for a few months, that he wanted to achieve this by staying with me at my father's house, and that the excuse the Duke would be given was that he was going to inspect and buy some excellent horses in my city, which breeds the best horses in the world.

'Moved by my own love, I should have welcomed his decision as soon as I heard it as one of the best imaginable, even if his motivation had been less laudable – because I could see what an excellent opportunity it gave me to see my dear Luscinda again. With this thought in mind I supported his ideas and encouraged his plan, advising him to carry it out as soon as possible, because absence was bound to have its effect, in spite of the strongest feelings. By the time he told me all this he had already, as later became apparent, enjoyed the girl's favours as her husband, and was looking for an opportunity to reveal all without having to pay the consequences, fearful as he was of what the Duke his father would do when he found out about his folly.

'It happened, then, that since love in young men is usually not love at all, but lust, which, since gratification is its sole aim, ceases to exist as soon as it is satisfied, and what had looked like love turns back because it cannot go any further than the limits fixed for it by nature, which does not establish any limits for true love ... what I'm trying to say is that as soon as Don Fernando had his way with the farmer's daughter his desires abated and his ardour cooled, and, if at first he'd pretended to want to leave so as to cure his desires, now he really did want to leave so as not to put them into effect. The Duke gave his permission and told me to go with him. We arrived in my city, my father accorded him the reception due to his rank, I went to see Luscinda, my passion was revived (although it had never been dead or even dormant) and I was unwise enough to tell Don Fernando of it, because I thought that the great friendship he professed for me forbad me to keep anything from him. I praised Luscinda's beauty, grace and intelligence, and my praise aroused in him a desire to contemplate a maiden adorned with such fine qualities. For my own misfortune I fulfilled his desire by letting him see her one night, by the light of a candle, at a window where we used to talk. He saw her in a chemise and forgot all the beauties he'd ever seen before. He was struck dumb, he lost his senses, he was spellbound and, in short, he fell as hopelessly in love as you'll see in the course of this tale of my misfortune. And the more to inflame his passion (which he hid from me and revealed to the heavens when he was alone) he happened one day to find a letter written by her, asking me to ask her father for her hand in marriage, which was so well expressed, so modest and so tender that he told me Luscinda brought together in herself the beauty and understanding that was shared among all the other women in the world.

'I do have to confess that, although I could see how justified Don Fernando's praises were, I disliked hearing them in his mouth, and I began to grow fearful and suspicious of him, because there was never a moment when he didn't want us to be talking about Luscinda, and he was always dragging her up as a subject for conversation; and this awoke a strange jealousy in me – not that I was worried that Luscinda's fidelity and virtue might crumble, yet her very assurances did make me fear for my future. Don Fernando always contrived to read the letters I sent Luscinda and also her replies, on the grounds that he derived great pleasure from the good sense we both showed. It happened, then, that Luscinda asked me for a book of chivalry to read, one that she was very fond of, *Amadis of Gaul* . . .'

No sooner had Don Quixote heard the words 'book of chivalry' than he said:

'If you had said at the beginning of your story that the lady Luscinda was fond of books of chivalry, no other praise would have been necessary to make me appreciate the sublimity of her understanding; for it would not have been as fine as you, sir, have said if she had lacked a taste for such palatable reading-matter: and so, as far as I am concerned, there is no need to employ any more words in describing her beauty, worth and understanding, for knowledge of her reading alone is enough to make me confirm her as the most beautiful and intelligent woman in the world. And I should have wished, sir, that you had sent to her with *Amadis of Gaul* the good *Sir Rugel of Greece*,[3] because I know that the lady Luscinda would have much enjoyed Daraida and Geraya, and the wise words of the shepherd Darinel, and his admirable bucolics, sung and performed by him with such grace, good sense and assurance. But a time may come when that omission can be remedied; and indeed the remedy will be delayed no longer than it takes you to be so kind as to come with me to my village, for there I shall be able to lend you a goodly number of books, my soul's dearest treasure and my life's delight; although it is my belief that I no longer possess any books at all, thanks to the wickedness of evil and envious enchanters. And you must forgive me for having broken our promise not to interrupt your discourse, but as soon as I hear anything about chivalry and knights errant it is as much in my power not to talk about them as it is in the power of sunbeams not to warm us or in the power of moonbeams not to moisten us.[4] So do forgive me, and please continue, for that is of most importance to us at present.'

While Don Quixote had been saying all this, Cardenio's head had slumped upon his breast, a sign that he was engrossed in thought. And although Don Quixote twice asked him to continue his history, he neither raised his head nor spoke a word in reply; but after some time he did look up and say:

'One thing I cannot get out of my head, and there is nobody in the world who can get it out of there, nor is there anyone who can make me believe otherwise, and anyone who does believe otherwise is a fool – that poxy scoundrel Master Elisabat was sleeping with Queen Madásima.'[5]

'No, never, by God!' replied Don Quixote in fury, with his usual oaths, 'and that is a most malicious or more precisely villainous thing to say! Queen Madásima was a most noble lady, and it is not to be believed that so great a monarch would take some quack as a lover; and whoever maintains otherwise lies like an arrant scoundrel. And I will force him to admit it, on foot or on horseback, armed or unarmed, by night or by day, or howsoever he pleases.'

Cardenio was peering at Don Quixote: a fit of madness had come over him and he was in no state to continue his history, nor would Don Quixote have heard it even if he had, so enraged was he by those allegations about Madásima. It was a strange business – Quixote stood up for her just as if she really were his own true lady, such was the state that his unholy books had put him into! I was about to say that since Cardenio had gone mad, and had heard himself called a liar and a villain and other such insults, he didn't appreciate the joke and picked up a stone that he found by his side, and struck Don Quixote such a blow on the chest that he tumbled over backwards. Sancho Panza, seeing his master sprawling on the ground, took his fist to the madman, and the Ragged Knight received him with a punch that left him spread-eagled at his feet, and then jumped on to him and trampled his ribs to his heart's content. The goatherd went to Sancho's defence and suffered the same fate. And once the madman had thrashed them all, he withdrew with elegant composure into his mountain thickets.

Sancho got up and, furious at his undeserved beating, went to avenge himself on the goatherd, claiming that he was the one to blame, for not warning them that the man went mad every so often – because if they'd known this, they'd have been on their guard and taken the necessary precautions. The goatherd replied that he had told them this, and if they hadn't been listening it wasn't his fault. Sancho made his reply to this, and the goatherd replied to Sancho, and all this replying ended up with them grabbing each other by the beard and exchanging such punches that if Don Quixote hadn't pacified them they'd have thumped each other to pieces. And as Sancho grappled with the goatherd he was saying:

'Please let me take him on, Sir Knight of the Sorry Face – he's just a peasant like me and he's never been knighted, so it's all right for me to get my own back in a good fisticuff fight, like a man of honour, for all the wrong he's done me.'

'That is true,' said Don Quixote, 'but I know that he is not to blame for what has happened.'

With this he pacified them, and then he again asked the goatherd if it would be possible to find Cardenio, because he was anxious to hear the end of the story. The goatherd repeated what he'd said at the beginning, which was that he didn't know exactly where Cardenio's lair was, but that if Don Quixote kept wandering about the area he was bound to come across him sooner or later, sane or mad.

CHAPTER XXV

Concerning the strange things that happened to the brave knight of La Mancha in the Sierra Morena, and his imitation of the penance of Beltenebros

Don Quixote took his leave of the goatherd and, remounting Rocinante, told Sancho to follow him, which Sancho did, with his donkey and with bad grace. They were slowly entering the craggiest part of the sierra, and Sancho was dying to talk to his master and longing for him to start the conversation, so as not to disobey orders. But unable to bear so much silence he broke out:

'Don Quixote sir, please give me your blessing and my discharge – I want to go back home to my wife and children, because with them at least I'll be able to chatter away to my heart's content, and expecting me to traipse along with you through all these God-forsaken places by day and by night without speaking to you when I feel like it is the same as burying me alive. If fate had let animals talk, as they did in the times of that Hyssop character, it wouldn't be so bad, because then I could chat as much as I wanted with my donkey, and grin and bear it like that, because it's a hard business, and more than a man's patience can take, to go about looking for adventures your whole life long and only find kicks and blanket-tossings, brickbats and punches, and then on top of it all you've got to keep your mouth tight shut without daring to say what's inside your heart, as if you were dumb.'

'I understand you, Sancho,' replied Don Quixote. 'You are dying for me to lift the ban that I have placed on your tongue. Well, you can consider it lifted, and you can speak as much as you like, on condition that the lifting only lasts for as long as does our wandering about this sierra.'

'Agreed,' said Sancho. 'I'll speak now, and God's decided what'll happen later, and so to start to make use of my safe conduct, what I say is why were you so concerned to stick up for that queen with bad asthma, or whatever you said? And what did it matter whether that abbot was her lover or not? If you'd let it pass, because you weren't being her judge or anything, to my mind that madman would have gone on telling his story, and we'd have been spared the stone, and the kicks, and more than half-a-dozen backhanders as well.'

'Upon my soul, Sancho,' replied Don Quixote, 'if you knew, as I know, what an honourable and noble lady Queen Madásima was, I am certain you would say that I showed great forbearance in not dashing to pieces the mouth that uttered such blasphemies. For it is a very great blasphemy indeed to say or even think that a queen could take a sawbones to her bed. The truth about the story is that the Master Elisabat whom the madman mentioned was a very prudent man and wise counsellor, and he was the Queen's tutor and physician; but to think that she was his mistress is an absurdity worthy of the severest punishment. And to realize that Cardenio did not know what he was saying you have only to observe that he had lost his reason by the time he made that claim.'

'That's just what I'm saying,' said Sancho, 'there wasn't any need to bother about the ravings of a madman, and if good fortune hadn't come to your aid, and had made the stone hit your head instead of your chest, a fine state we'd have been in now, for sticking up for her ladyship, God damn her. And I bet Cardenio would have got off scot-free for being mad!'

'Against sane men and madmen alike it is every knight errant's duty to defend the honour of all women, whoever they may be, and even more so if they are queens of such high degree and worth as was Queen Madásima, for whom I feel a particular affinity because of her excellent qualities: apart from being beauteous, she was also very prudent and long-suffering in her calamities, of which there were many; and the advice and the company of Master Elisabat were of great benefit and comfort to her, to help her to bear her trials with prudence and patience. And this was what induced the ignorant, malicious rabble to think and say she was his mistress. And they lie, I tell you, they lie two hundredfold, all those who say or think such a thing!'

'I'm not saying it or thinking it,' replied Sancho. 'That's up to them, and it's their own lookout. Whether they were lovers or not, they'll have answered to God for it by now. I've got other fish to fry, and I just don't want to know, I'm not fond of prying into other people's lives. Him that buys and denies, his own purse belies. What's more, naked was I born, and naked I remain, so neither lose nor gain. And if they were, so what? It's no skin off my nose. There are those that think they'll find bacon where there isn't so much as a hook to hang it from. Till you cage in the sky, the sparrows will fly. And if they gossiped about God, who won't they gossip about?'

'And God save us all!' said Don Quixote. 'What a string of absurdities you have come out with now, Sancho! What connection is there between what we are discussing and all those proverbs you have just threaded together? For goodness sake, Sancho, do keep quiet, and from now on concern yourself with putting spurs to your ass rather than with putting your nose into what is no business of yours. And understand, with all your five senses, that whatever I have done, am doing and shall do is totally reasonable and in conformity with the rules of chivalry, for I have a better knowledge of them than any knight who has ever professed them.'

'But, sir,' replied Sancho, 'is it a good rule of chivalry for us to be wandering about aimlessly, lost in these here mountains, looking for a madman who when we find him is as likely as not to take it into his head to finish off what he started? And I don't mean his story, but the smashing of your head and my ribs!'

'Be quiet, Sancho, I tell you,' said Don Quixote. 'And let me inform you that what brings me to these parts is not only my wish to find the madman, but also my desire to perform here a deed with which I shall gain perpetual renown all over the face of the earth, and it will be such as to set the seal on everything that can make a knight errant perfect and famous.'

'And is this deed a very risky one?' asked Sancho Panza.

'No,' replied the Knight of the Sorry Face, 'although the dice could roll in such a way that we score a double one rather than a double six. But it all depends upon your diligence.'

'My diligence?' said Sancho.

'Yes,' said Don Quixote, 'because if you return quickly from where I am going to send you, my grief will quickly end and my glory will as quickly start. And because it is not right to keep you any longer in suspense, waiting to see where my words are leading, I want you to know, Sancho, that the famous Amadis of Gaul was one of the most perfect knights errant there ever was. No, I was wrong to say "one of": he was the only one, the first, unique, the lord of all the knights in the world in his day. A fig's end for Don Belianis and for all those who say that he was in any way the equal of Amadis, because I swear they are mistaken. Let me add that when a painter wants to become famous for his art, he tries to copy originals by the finest artists he knows. And this same rule holds good for nearly all the trades and professions of importance that serve to adorn a society; and so what a man must do and what a man does if he wishes to achieve a reputation for prudence and long-suffering, is to imitate Ulysses, in whose person and labours Homer painted for us a living portrait of these two qualities, just as Virgil showed us in the person of Aeneas the courage of a dutiful son and the sagacity of a brave and able captain, not describing or revealing them as they were but as they should have been, to leave models of their virtues for future generations. In this same way Amadis was the pole star, the morning star, the sun of brave and enamoured knights, and we who serve under the banner of love and chivalry should all imitate him. If, then, this is so, as it is, I consider, friend Sancho, that the knight errant who best imitates Amadis will be the closest to attaining perfection in chivalry. And one of the ways in which this knight best demonstrated his prudence, resolve, courage, long-suffering, steadfastness and love was when he withdrew, disdained by the lady Oriana, to do penance on Peña Pobre, after changing his name to Beltenebros, a name most certainly significant and suited to the life that of his own free will he had chosen. And it is easier for me to imitate him like this than by cleaving giants asunder, beheading serpents, slaughtering monsters, crushing armies, routing fleets and breaking spells. Since this place is so suitable for such a purpose, there is no good reason to allow opportunity to slip by, now that she so conveniently offers me her forelock.'

'So what is it, then,' asked Sancho, 'that you're planning to do in this God-forsaken place?'

'Have I not already told you,' replied Don Quixote, 'that I intend to imitate Amadis, and to act the desperate, foolish, furious lover so as also to imitate the valiant Orlando, when he found signs by a spring that the fair Angelica had disgraced herself with Medoro,[1] and the grief turned him mad, and he uprooted trees, sullied the waters of the clear springs, slew shepherds, destroyed flocks, burned cottages, tore down houses, dragged away mares and performed a hundred other excesses, worthy to be recorded on the tablets of eternal fame? And although I do not intend to imitate Orlando, or Roland, or Rotolando (for he had all these three names) step by step in each and every one of the mad things he did, said and thought, I shall act out a résumé, as best I can, of those that seem most relevant. And it could even be that I might settle for imitating Amadis alone, because his madness did not involve doing any damage, but just weeping and being heartbroken, and he achieved as much fame as the best of them.'

'But to my mind,' said Sancho, 'the knights who did all that were pushed into it and had their reasons for their antics and their penances, but what reason have you got for going mad? What lady has scorned you, what signs have you found that the lady Dulcinea del Toboso has been up to tricks with some Moor, or some Christian for that matter?'

'That is the whole point,' replied Don Quixote, 'and therein lies the beauty of my enterprise. A knight errant going mad for a good reason – there is neither pleasure nor merit in that. The thing is to become insane without a cause and have my lady think: if I do all this when dry, what would I not do when wet? Besides, my long absence from my ever-beloved lady Dulcinea del Toboso provides me with abundant motivation, for, as you heard that shepherd fellow Ambrosio say, the absent lover feels and fears every ill. So, Sancho my friend, do not waste your time advising me not to perform such a rare, happy and unprecedented imitation. I am mad, and mad I shall remain until you return with the reply to a letter that I intend to send by you to my lady Dulcinea; and should that reply be such as is due to my fidelity, then my folly and my penance will be at an end; and should it be otherwise, I shall go truly mad, and feel nothing. So however she replies I shall be free of the conflict and travail in which you will leave me: either sane, and enjoying the bliss you bear, or mad, and oblivious to the misery you bring. But tell me, Sancho: have you been looking after Mambrino's helmet with due care? I saw you picking it up after that ungrateful fellow had tried to smash it to smithereens. But he could not do so, and that is an indication of the excellence of its temper.'

To which Sancho replied:

'In God's own name, Sir Knight of the Sorry Face, I just can't stand some of these things you come out with, making me think that everything you tell me about chivalries, and winning kingdoms and empires, and giving islands away and doing other favours and great deeds, as knight errants do, must all be empty lies, and a fraction or a friction or whatever it is you call it. Because anyone who hears you saying that a barber's basin is Mambrino's helmet, and sticking to your story for days on end – what's he going to think except that the man who says things like that must be queer in the head? Yes, I've got the basin in my saddle-bag, well dented, and the reason I've got it there is to take it home and mend it for trimming my beard, if God's good enough to let me see my wife and children again some day.'

'Look here, Sancho,' said Don Quixote, 'I swear to you by the same oath you have just sworn to me that you are the most dim-witted squire there ever was. Is it possible that in all the time you have been with me you have failed to realize that all things appertaining to us knights errant seem like chimeras, follies and nonsenses, because they have all been turned on their head? Not because that is their real state, but because we are always attended by a crew of enchanters who keep transforming everything and changing it into whatever they like, according to whether they have a mind to help us or destroy us; and so what looks to you like a barber's basin looks to me like Mambrino's helmet and will look like something else to another person. And the sage who is on my side showed rare foresight in making everyone take what is really and truly Mambrino's helmet for a barber's basin, because Mambrino's helmet is so highly esteemed that everyone would otherwise have pursued me to try to take it from me, but since they see that it is only a barber's basin they do not bother about it, as was clearly shown when that youth tried to shatter it and left it on the ground; to be sure, if he had recognized it he would never have left it behind. You can keep the helmet, my friend, because for the moment I have no need of it; on the contrary, I am going to remove all this armour, and be left as naked as the day I was born, if the urge takes me to imitate Orlando in my penance rather than Amadis.'

That evening they reached the very heart of the Sierra Morena, where Sancho thought they could spend the night, and even a few days more, at least as many as their rations lasted. And so they slept between two crags and among many cork-oaks. But destiny, which, in the opinion of those who lack the light of the true faith, guides, fashions and disposes everything as it wishes, decreed that Ginés de Pasamonte, the famous liar and thief who'd escaped from the chain thanks to Don Quixote's madness, impelled by fear of the Holy Brotherhood (of which he had good reason to be afraid), decided to hide in those mountains, and fortune and fear led him to the same spot where they'd led Don Quixote and Sancho Panza, early enough in the evening for him to recognize them and late enough for them to be settling down to sleep. And since the wicked are always ungrateful, and necessity makes men do what they ought not to do, and the needs of the moment take precedence over thoughts for the future, Ginés, who was neither grateful nor well-intentioned, decided to steal Sancho Panza's ass, not bothering with Rocinante, a creature that it would have been as impossible to pawn as to sell. Sancho Panza slept, Ginés stole his donkey and long before morning it was much too far away to be found. Dawn broke, bringing joy to the earth and grief to Sancho Panza when he missed his precious dun, and he began to make the most doleful lamentation in the world, awaking Don Quixote with his cries:

'O child of my bowels, born in my very house, my children's treasure, my wife's delight, the envy of my neighbours, the ease of my burdens and, lastly, the half of my maintenance, because the twenty-six maravedís a day that you earned did cover half my expenses!'

On seeing Sancho's tears and learning the cause, Don Quixote consoled him with the best words he could think of, begged him to be patient and promised to give him a warrant on presenting which Sancho would be given three donkeys of the five that Don Quixote had left at home. This comforted Sancho, who dried his tears, restrained his sobs and thanked Don Quixote for the favour.

As they discussed these matters they reached a high mountain that stood out among the many hills surrounding it, almost as if it had been hewn from the living rock. At its foot a gentle stream flowed, and all around this stream a meadow spread forth, so green and lush that it was a joy to behold. There were many woodland trees and some plants and flowers to add to the delights of the spot, which the Knight of the Sorry Face chose for his penance; and so, as soon as he saw it, he began to proclaim, as if he were mad:

'This is the place, O heavens, that I hereby choose and select to lament the misfortune into which you have plunged me. This is the place where the humours of my eyes will swell the waters of this stream, and where my profound and incessant sighs will never stop stirring the leaves of these woodland trees, in testimony and token of the grief that harasses my hapless heart. O you rustic deities, whosoever you may be, dwelling in this uninhabited place, give ear to the laments of this ill-starred lover, brought by a long absence and imagined jealousy to weep among these craggy wastes and to complain of the hard heart of that beauteous ingrate, the sum and perfection of all human loveliness! O you wood nymphs and dryads, who are wont to dwell in the depths of the forest: may the fickle and lascivious satyrs, by whom you are loved, although in vain, never perturb your sweet repose; and help me to lament my misfortune, or at least do not weary of hearing about it! O Dulcinea del Toboso, day of my night, glory of my grief, goal of my journeying, star of my fortune: may the heavens grant you prosperity in all that you ask of them; and consider the place and the state to which absence from you has brought me, and grant me the reward that my fidelity deserves! O lonely trees, who from this day will accompany my solitude, show in the gentle movement of your branches that my presence is not disagreeable to you! O you, my squire, pleasant companion in my most prosperous and my most adverse eventualities, impress on your memory what you will see me do here, so that you can relate and recite it to the sole cause of it all!'

And so saying he dismounted from Rocinante and stripped him of bridle and saddle; and slapping him on the haunches, he said:

'He who lacks liberty gives you yours, O steed as excellent for your exploits as you are unfortunate in your fate! Go hence where'er you please, for on your forehead it is written that neither Astolfo's hippogryph nor the renowned Frontino, who cost Bradamante so dear, was your equal in fleetness of foot.'[2]

When Sancho saw this he said:

'And hurray for whoever it is that's just saved us the trouble of taking the pack-saddle off my dun! To be sure it wouldn't have gone without its slaps on the back or its praises, either. But if it had been here I wouldn't have let anyone take its pack-saddle off, because there wouldn't have been any reason to – it wasn't a witness to a desperate lover's goings-on, because its master, in other words me when it so pleased the Lord, never was one of that sort. And to tell you the truth, Sir Knight of the Sorry Face, if my journey and your madness are going to be for real, it'll be better to saddle Rocinante again to make up for the lack of my dun, and save time in my travels – if I go on foot I just can't tell when I'll get there or when I'll get back, because the truth is I'm a very bad walker.'

'What I say, Sancho,' replied Don Quixote, 'is that you must do as you please, for your idea does not seem a bad one; and I also say that you shall depart three days from now, because I want you to spend this time witnessing what I do and say for her sake, so that you can tell her about it.'

'And what else have I got to see,' asked Sancho, 'apart from what I've seen already?'

'You are well informed about these matters, I must say!' Don Quixote retorted. 'Now I must tear my garments, scatter my armour and dash my head against these rocks, and perform other similar actions that will amaze you.'

'For God's sake,' said Sancho Panza, 'do be careful how you go around dashing your head, because you could pick on such a rock and hit it in such a place that you put paid to the whole penance business with the very first knock you gave it. And if you really think head-dashing's essential and this job can't be done without it, to my mind you ought to be content, since it's all make-believe, a fake and a sham, to dash your head against the water, or something soft like cotton, and leave the rest to me – I'll tell my lady you were knocking it against a jutting crag, harder than diamonds.'

'I am grateful to you for meaning well, friend Sancho,' replied Don Quixote, 'but I would have you know that I am doing all these things not in jest but very much in earnest; for to behave otherwise would be to contravene the commands of chivalry, which instruct one never to tell a lie, on pain of being punished as a recidivist; and to do one thing instead of another is the same as lying. So my blows on the head must be real, firm and effective, with no element of the sophistical or the fantastic about them. And you will have to leave me some lint to cure my wounds, for fate has left us without our balsam.'

'Losing the ass was worse,' replied Sancho, 'because the lint and all was lost with it. And I'd ask you very kindly not to bring that damned potion up again – just hearing it mentioned turns not only my stomach but my very soul inside-out. And I'd also ask you, as regards those three days you allocated for watching the crazy things you're going to do, to make believe they're over and done with, because I'll be happy to take them for granted as if seen and approved, and I'll tell my lady wonders. So you write your letter and then send me packing, because I'm longing to come back and get you out of this purgatory where I'm leaving you.'

'Purgatory you call it, Sancho?' said Don Quixote. 'You would do better to call it hell, or worse, if there is anything worse.'

'In hell,' replied Sancho, '*nulla est retentio*, so I've heard say.'[3]

'I do not understand what you mean by *retentio*,' said Don Quixote.

'*Retentio* means,' replied Sancho, 'that people in hell never get out, and can't get out. It'll be the reverse with you, though, so long as I get my heels working, if I'm wearing spurs to make Rocinante move, that is – and you just wait till I reach El Toboso, and come before my lady Dulcinea, and then I'll tell her such stories about the acts of madness and stupidity, which comes to the same thing, that you've done and are doing as will make her as sweet as a nut, even if she's as hard as a cork-oak when I start work on her. And I'll come back through the air like a sorcerer with her honeyed answer, and I'll rescue you from this purgatory that seems like hell but isn't, because there's a hope of getting out of it, which people in hell haven't got, as I've just said, and I don't suppose you'll want to disagree with that.'

'True,' said the Knight of the Sorry Face, 'but how are we going to manage to write that letter?'

'And that donkey-warrant,' added Sancho.

'It will all be included,' said Don Quixote, 'and, since we have no paper, it would be appropriate to write it, as the ancients did, on leaves from the trees, or on tablets of wax; yet it would be as difficult to find these now as paper itself. But I have just thought of a good place, indeed an excellent one, to write it: the notebook that used to belong to Cardenio, and you must take care to have it copied in a clear hand on to a sheet of paper in the first village with a schoolmaster, or else any sexton will copy it for you; but do not ask a clerk to copy it, because they use a corrupt and degenerate hand that Satan himself would not be able to read.'

'And what's to be done about your signature?' asked Sancho.

'The letters of Amadis are never signed,' replied Don Quixote.

'That's as may be,' replied Sancho, 'but the warrant must be signed, and if it's copied out they'll say the signature's a fake and I'll be left without my donkeys.'

'The warrant will be signed in the notebook, and when my niece sees it she will not raise any objections about complying with it. And as regards the love-letter, you will have it signed: "Yours until death, The Knight of the Sorry Face". It will matter little that it is signed in another hand, because as far as I remember Dulcinea cannot read or write, and she has never seen a letter written by me, because the love between us has always been platonic, never going beyond a modest glance. And even this has been so occasional that I can truly swear that, in the twelve years I have loved her more than the light of these eyes that the earth will one day devour, I have not seen her as many as four times; and it is possible that on those four occasions she has not even once noticed that I was looking at her, such is the reserve and seclusion in which her father Lorenzo Corchuelo and her mother Aldonza Nogales have brought her up.'

'Oho!' said Sancho. 'So Lorenzo Corchuelo's daughter is the lady Dulcinea del Toboso, also known as Aldonza Lorenzo, is she?'

'She is,' said Don Quixote, 'and she it is who deserves to be the mistress of the entire universe.'

'I know her well,' said Sancho, 'and let me tell you she pitches a bar as far as the strongest lad in all the village. Good God, she's a lusty lass all right, hale and hearty, strong as an ox, and any knight errant who has her as his lady now or in the future can count on her to pull him out of the mire! The little baggage, what muscles she's got on her, and what a voice! Let me tell you she climbed up one day to the top of the church belfry to call to some lads of hers who were in a fallow field of her father's, and even though they were a good couple of miles off they could hear her just as if they'd been standing at the foot of the tower. And the best thing about her is she isn't at all priggish, she's a real courtly lass, enjoys a joke with everyone and turns everything into a good laugh. And now I can say, Sir Knight of the Sorry Face, that not only is it very right and proper for you to get up to your mad tricks for her sake – you've got every reason to give way to despair and hang yourself, too, and nobody who knows about it will say you weren't justified, even if it does send you to the devil. And I wish I was on my way already, just to take a look at her, because I haven't seen her for days, and she must be changed by now, because women's faces get spoiled by always being out in the fields, in the sun and the wind. And I must be honest with you, Don Quixote sir – until now I've been completely mistaken, because I really and truly believed that the lady Dulcinea must be some princess you were in love with, or at least someone who deserved all those fine gifts you've sent her, that Basque and those convicts, and lots of others that there must have been, too, considering how many victories you must have won before I became your squire. But all things considered, what will the lady Aldonza Lorenzo I mean the lady Dulcinea del Toboso care whether the knights you defeat and send to her get down on their bended knees before her? Because when they turn up she might be combing flax or threshing wheat in the yard, and then they'd be all embarrassed and she'd burst out laughing and turn up her nose at the gift.'

'I have often told you before now, Sancho,' said Don Quixote, 'that you are a chatterbox and that, although you are a dim-witted fellow, you often try to be too clever by half; but, so that you can see how stupid you are and how intelligent I am, I want you to listen to a little story. There was once a widow who was beautiful, young, unattached, rich and, above all, carefree, and who fell in love with a certain lay brother, a well-fleshed, corpulent young man; his superior found out, and said to the good widow one day, by way of friarly reprehension:

'"I am surprised, madam, and not without good reason, that a woman of your quality, as beautiful and as wealthy as you are, should have fallen in love with such a low, vulgar and ignorant fellow, when in this house there are so many bachelors, masters and doctors of divinity among whom you could have chosen as among pears at a fruit-stall, saying: 'I'll have this one; no, not that.'"

'But she replied to him with wit and dash:

' "You are much mistaken, sir, and very old-fashioned in your ideas, if you think I have made a bad choice, however stupid he may seem to you; because for what I want of him he knows as much philosophy as Aristotle, and more."

'And so, Sancho, for what I want of Dulcinea del Toboso, she is as good as the most exalted princess in the world. Yes indeed, for not all poets who praise ladies under a name that they choose for them really have any such mistresses at all. Do you really believe that the Amaryllises, Phyllises, Sylvias, Dianas, Galateas, Alidas and others that fill books, ballads, barbers' shops and theatre stages were real ladies of flesh and blood, and the mistresses of those that praise and have praised them? No, of course not, the poets themselves invent most of them, to have something to write their poetry about, and to make people think that they are in love and that they have it in them to be lovers. And so it is enough for me to be convinced that the good Aldonza Lorenzo is beautiful and virtuous, and the question of lineage is not very important, because nobody is going to be enquiring into it to see whether she is entitled to robes of nobility, and for me she is the greatest princess in the world. For I would have you know, Sancho, if you do not know it already, that there are just two qualities that inspire love more than any others, and these are great beauty and good repute, and these two qualities are to be found in abundance in Dulcinea, because no woman can equal her in beauty, and few can approach her in good repute. And to put it in a nutshell, I imagine that everything I say is precisely as I say it is, and I depict her in my imagination as I wish her to be, both in beauty and in rank, and Helen cannot rival her, nor can Lucretia[4] or any other of the famous women of past ages, whether Greek, Barbarian or Roman, equal her. And people can say what they like, because if I am reproached by the ignorant for this, I shall not be punished by even the most severe judges.'

'And I say you're right as right can be,' replied Sancho, 'and I'm an ass – but I don't know why I'm talking about asses, because you don't mention ropes in the house of the man that hanged himself. Let's have the letter, though, and then I'll be off.'

Don Quixote took out the notebook and, drawing a little aside, he began with great deliberation to write the letter; and as he finished he called Sancho and said that he was going to read it aloud, so that Sancho could learn it by heart, in case he lost it on the way, because with his bad luck anything could happen. To which Sancho replied:

'You just write it down two or three times in the book and then let me have it, and I'll take good care of it – it's madness to think I'm going to learn it by heart, because my memory's so bad I often forget my own name. But read it to me all the same, I'll enjoy listening to it, because it must be a beauty.'

'Listen, then; it goes like this,' said Don Quixote.

Letter from Don Quixote to Dulcinea del Toboso

Sovereign and noble lady,

One sore-wounded by the dart of absence and lacerated to the very fabric of his heart, O sweetest Dulcinea del Toboso, wishes you the good health that he does not enjoy. If your beauteousness scorns me, if your worth does not favour me, if your disdain is my humiliation, I shall ill be able, albeit I am well furnished with longanimity, to suffer a grief that is not merely intense but protracted. My good squire Sancho will render you a full account, O lovely ingrate, O beloved enemy of mine, of the state to which I am reduced for your sake. If it be your wish to succour me, I am yours, and if not, do what you will, for by ending my life I shall satisfy your cruelty and my desire.

Yours until death,
THE KNIGHT OF THE SORRY FACE

'By my dear father's bones!' cried Sancho. 'That's the very finest thing I ever did hear! Damn it all, how well you say everything you want to say, and how well it all suits the signature "The Knight of the Sorry Face"! To be sure you're the very devil, there isn't anything you don't know!'

'Everything is needed,' replied Don Quixote, 'in the profession that I follow.'

'Come on, then,' said Sancho, 'turn over the page and write the warrant for the three donkeys, and sign it clear as clear, so they know your signature as soon as they see it.'

'Very well,' said Don Quixote.

And once he'd written it he read it out:

On receipt of this my first donkey-warrant, please order that three of the five that I left at home in your charge be given to my squire Sancho Panza. Which three donkeys I hereby order to be delivered to him and duly paid for, in return for the like number received from him here; and this bill, together with his receipt, will be sufficient for this transaction. Given in the heart of the Sierra Morena on the twenty-second of August of the current year.

'That's good,' said Sancho. 'Now sign it.'

'There is no need for me to sign it,' said Don Quixote. 'All I have to do is to append my flourish, which counts as a signature, and that is sufficient for three asses, and even for three hundred.'

'I'll believe you,' replied Sancho. 'Now let me go and saddle Rocinante, and you get ready to give me your blessing, because I'm leaving straight away, without waiting to see any of these antics you're going to get up to, though I'll tell her I saw you do so many of them that she'll be more than satisfied.'

'At least, Sancho, I want you, because it is essential – what I mean to say is that I want you to see me naked, performing a dozen or two dozen mad deeds, which will only take me half an hour, so that having seen them with your own eyes you can safely swear to any others that you may care to add; and I can assure you that you will not tell her of as many as I intend to perform.'

'For the love of God, sir, don't make me see you naked, I'll feel so sorry for you I shan't be able to help crying. And my head's in such a state after crying so much last night for my dun that I'm in no condition for any more tears, so if you want me to see some of your antics, do them with your clothes on – quick antics, just the most relevant ones. What's more, there isn't any need for all this as far as I'm concerned, and, as I said, it would mean I'd come back all the sooner with the news that you want and deserve to hear. If not, the lady Dulcinea had better look out, because if she doesn't reply as she ought to, I take my solemn oath that I'll kick and punch the right answer out of her guts. Because who can put up with a famous knight errant like you going mad, without any reason at all, for a . . . ? And the lady had better not make me say it, or else by God I'll upset the apple cart, and hang the consequences! And I can! She doesn't know what I'm like! If she did, she'd stand in fear of me, she would!'

'And so, Sancho,' said Don Quixote, 'it seems that you are no saner than I am.'

'No, I'm not as mad as you,' said Sancho, 'but I am angrier. Leaving all that aside, though, what are you going to eat while I'm away? Are you going to waylay goatherds and steal your food, like Cardenio?'

'You must not worry about that,' replied Don Quixote, 'for even if I had any food, all I should eat would be whatever herbs and other fruit of the land this meadow and these trees provide; for the beauty of my plan lies precisely in not eating and in other equivalent mortifications. And so goodbye.'

'But do you know what I'm scared of? Not finding the way back here where I'm leaving you, because it's so secluded.'

'You take good note of the landmarks, and I shall try not to move far off,' said Don Quixote, 'and I shall even take the precaution of climbing the highest of these crags here to see if I can spot you when you return. In addition, your surest way of not getting lost and missing me will be to cut some of this broom growing so abundantly hereabouts, and to drop a branch every so often until you reach the plain, and they will serve as guide-marks on your return, like the thread in Perseus's labyrinth.'[5]

'That's what I'll do,' replied Sancho Panza.

He cut some broom, asked his master for his blessing and, not without many tears on both sides, said goodbye. And climbing on to Rocinante, whom Don Quixote warmly entrusted to Sancho's safe-keeping, with the instruction to take as good care of him as of his own person, he headed off towards the plain, scattering broom-branches every so often, as his master had advised. And so he rode away, even though Don Quixote was still insisting that he should watch a couple of his wild deeds, at least. But Sancho hadn't gone a hundred steps when he turned and came back and said:

'I think you were right, sir, and to be able to swear with a clear conscience that I've seen you doing mad deeds, I'd better see one of them at least, although I must say I've seen a big enough one already – you staying here.'

'Did I not tell you so?' said Don Quixote. 'Just wait a minute, Sancho, I shall perform them in the saying of a creed.'

And pulling down his breeches as fast as ever he could, he stood there in his shirt and then did two leaps in the air followed by two somersaults, revealing things that made Sancho turn Rocinante so as not to have to see them again; and he felt fully satisfied that he could swear his master was mad. And we shall allow him to go his way until his return, which was speedy.

CHAPTER XXVI

In which a further account is given of the dainty deeds performed by the lover Don Quixote in the Sierra Morena

And turning back to what the Knight of the Sorry Face did once he was alone, the history says that when Don Quixote had finished his somersaults or handsprings naked from the waist down and clothed from the waist up, and had seen Sancho depart without caring to witness any more antics, he climbed to the top of a high crag, and again turned his thoughts to what had often occupied them without ever having led him to a decision: which would be better and more suitable, imitating Orlando and his outrageous madness, or Amadis and his melancholy madness? And he said to himself:

'If Orlando was such an excellent knight and as brave as everybody says he was, what is so surprising about that? After all, he was enchanted, and nobody could kill him except by stabbing a penny pin into his big toe, and he always wore shoes shod with seven iron soles.[1] Yet these tricks were of no avail against Bernardo del Carpio, who saw through them all and squeezed him to death at Roncesvalles. But leaving his courage aside, let us consider his going mad, which he most certainly did, because of the signs he found by the spring and the news given him by the shepherd that Angelica had enjoyed more than a couple of siestas with Medoro, a young Moor with curly hair, Agramante's page-boy. And if he believed that this was true and that his lady had played him false, it was a normal enough reaction to go crazy. Yet how can I imitate his mad deeds if I do not imitate their cause? I would venture to swear that my Dulcinea del Toboso has never seen a real Moor in real Moorish clothes in all her life, and that she is today as intact as the mother who bore her; and I should be doing her a manifest wrong if, imagining something different, I went mad after the fashion of Orlando Furioso. Furthermore, I can see that Amadis of Gaul, without going insane or performing any crazy deeds, achieved as much renown as a lover as the best of them; because, according to his history, all he did when scorned by his lady Oriana, who told him not to appear in her presence until she commanded it, was to withdraw to Peña Pobre with a hermit, and there he wept and commended himself to God to his heart's content until heaven came to his aid in the midst of his greatest tribulation. And if this is true, as indeed it is, why should I take the trouble to strip naked or torment these trees that have never done me any harm? Nor have I any need to sully the clear waters of these streams, which will provide for me when I am thirsty. Long live the memory of Amadis, and let him be imitated as well as is possible by Don Quixote de la Mancha, of whom it shall be said what was said of another: if he did not achieve great things, he died in the attempt. And if I am not rejected or scorned by Dulcinea del Toboso, it is enough, as I have said, to be separated from her. So now to work! Come to my memory, O exploits of Amadis, and show me how my imitation must commence! Yet I well know that what he most did was to pray and commend himself to God; but what can I use as a rosary, not having one on me?'

As he said this an idea came into his head for making one, and he tore a long strip from his shirt-tail hanging down behind him, and he tied eleven knots in it, one of them bigger than the others, and this he used as a rosary[2] all the time he was there, during which he said a million Ave Marias. And what was a great worry to him was not finding thereabouts any hermit who could confess and console him. So he amused himself by taking strolls around the meadow, and carving in the bark of the trees and tracing in the fine sand of the stream a great number of verses, all of them expressive of his sadness, and some of them in praise of Dulcinea. But the only complete and legible poem that was discovered after he had been found was this:

You trees, you herbs, you plants that show
Your splendour in this pleasant site
And tall and green and plenteous grow:
Although my ills give no delight,
Pray listen to my tale of woe.
  And let my grief disturb you not
Although you could not ever see a
Lover pay you on the dot
Or suffer like poor Don Quixote,
Who weeps here for his Dulcinea
   del Toboso.

Here, in this green and pleasant mead,
The truest lover ever known
Hides from his lady, in dire need:
He has been made to grieve and groan,
Not knowing whence his ills proceed.
  Love keeps him always on the trot,
A very wicked sort is he – ah!
Enough to fill the biggest pot
Are tears of doleful Don Quixote,
Who weeps here for his Dulcinea
   del Toboso.

He sought adventures as he pined
Among these crags and rocks and stones,
And cursed what made his maid unkind:
But this poor wretch, sad to his bones,
Could only misadventures find.
  Love laid his lash upon him hot:
No gentle thong – the very idea!
And when it touched his tender spot
Tears flowed from doleful Don Quixote,
Who weeps here for his Dulcinea
   del Toboso.

The addition of 'del Toboso' to the name of Dulcinea raised some giggles among those who found these verses, because they imagined that Don Quixote must have imagined that if, when he named Dulcinea, he didn't also say 'del Toboso', the stanza wouldn't be understood – and they were right, as he later confessed. He wrote many other lines of poetry but, as has been said, these three verses were all that was found complete and could be deciphered. In this, and in sighing, and in calling out to the fauns and sylvans of those woods, to the nymphs of the rivers, and to moist and mournful Echo,[3] to reply to him, comfort him and listen to him, he passed the time, and also in seeking herbs on which to live until Sancho's return; and had this taken three weeks instead of the three days it did take, the Knight of the Sorry Face would have been so ravaged that the very mother who'd borne him wouldn't have known him.

And it will be as well now to leave him wrapped in his sighs and his verses, so as to relate what happened to Sancho Panza on his mission. When he reached the highway he went in search of the road to El Toboso, and the next day he arrived at the inn where he'd suffered the mishap with the blanket; and no sooner had he glimpsed the place than he imagined himself flying through the air again, and he couldn't bring himself to go in, even though he'd come at an hour when he could and should have done so, for it was dinner-time and he was longing for something hot to eat, having had nothing but cold food for many days.

This craving forced him to approach the inn, still wondering whether to enter it or not. As he hovered there, two men came out and recognized him. And one of them said to the other:

'Look, reverend father, that man on the horse – isn't it Sancho Panza, the fellow our adventurer's housekeeper said had gone off with her master as his squire?'

'So it is,' said the priest, 'and that's our dear Don Quixote's horse.'

They recognized them immediately, being the priest and the barber of his own village, the two men who had carried out the interrogation and auto-da-fé of the books. Anxious for news of Don Quixote, they went up to him and the priest called him by his name:

'My dear friend Sancho Panza, where is your master?'

Sancho Panza recognized them at once, and decided to conceal the place and the circumstances in which he'd left his master; and so he replied that his master was busy in a certain place on a certain matter which was very important to him, and which he couldn't reveal, not for the very eyes in his head.

'No, no, Sancho Panza,' said the barber. 'If you don't tell us where he is we're going to imagine, as we already do, that you've murdered and robbed him, since you're riding his horse. You really must lead us to the nag's master, or it'll be the worse for you.'

'There isn't any need to come to me with your threats, I'm not one to go robbing or murdering people: let each man be killed by his own fate say I, or by the God that made him. My master's doing penance in the middle of these mountains, and loving every minute of it.'

And he reeled off an account of the state his master was in, the adventures he'd had and the letter to the lady Dulcinea del Toboso, Lorenzo Corchuelo's daughter, who he was up to his neck in love with.

They were both amazed at what Sancho Panza was telling them, because although they knew that Don Quixote was mad and they knew what sort of madness it was, whenever they heard about it again they were amazed again. They asked Sancho Panza to show them the letter he was taking to the lady Dulcinea del Toboso. He told them that it was written in a notebook, and that his master's orders were to have it copied on to a sheet of paper at the first village he came to; at which the priest asked to see it, saying that he would copy it out himself in a very good hand. Sancho Panza felt for the notebook inside his shirt, but he couldn't find it, and he wouldn't have found it if he'd kept searching for it to this day, because Don Quixote hadn't given him it, and he hadn't remembered to ask for it.

When Sancho realized that he couldn't find the notebook, a look of mortal horror crept over his face; and running his hands all over his body again, he confirmed that the notebook wasn't there, and then he clenched his hands and clutched at his beard and tore half of it out and gave himself half-a-dozen punches on the nose and the face, bathing them in blood. At this sight the priest and the barber asked him what had happened to make him treat himself so roughly.

'What do you think has happened?' said Sancho. 'Only that at one foul swoop and in a single instant I've been and gone and lost three donkeys as fine as three castles, that's all!'

'How can that be?' replied the barber.

'I've lost the notebook,' answered Sancho, 'with the letter for Dulcinea and a warrant signed by my master ordering his niece to give me three of the four or five donkeys he's got at home.'

And he went on to tell them about the theft of his dun. The priest comforted him, saying that as soon as he found Don Quixote he'd make him confirm the order and draw the warrant up again on a separate sheet of paper, as was the usual custom, because warrants written in notebooks were never accepted or honoured. This consoled Sancho, and he said that in that case he wasn't too concerned about the loss of Dulcinea's letter, because he had almost all of it in his memory, from where they could make a copy wherever and whenever they wanted.

'Let's hear it, Sancho,' said the barber, 'and then we'll make the copy.'

Sancho Panza dismounted to scratch his head and bring the letter back into his memory, balancing first on one foot and then on the other; sometimes he gazed at the ground, sometimes at the sky, and, after gnawing off half a finger-tip while those waiting to hear the letter stood there in suspense for an eternity, he said:

'By God, reverend father, the devil take all I can remember of the letter, though at the beginning it did say, "Noble and slobbered-on lady".'

'No, it won't have said slobbered-on lady,' said the barber, 'but sovereign lady, or maybe supreme lady.'

'That's it,' said Sancho. 'Then, if I remember rightly, it went on . . . , if I remember rightly, "One lastrated and well-finished with not sleeping and sore-wounded kisses your hands, beautiful and unknown ingrate", and then it said something about health and an illness he was sending her, and it went on and on and on like this, until it ended up, "Yours until death, The Knight of the Sorry Face".'

The two men were much amused by Sancho Panza's splendid memory and they praised it to the skies and asked him to recite the letter another couple of times so that they in their turn could commit it to memory and write it down in due course. Sancho went through it another three times, and on each occasion he came out with a further three thousand absurdities. He went on to relate his master's doings, but he didn't say a word about the blanket-tossing in that inn which he refused to enter. He also told them how, as soon as he brought his master good tidings from the lady

Dulcinea del Toboso, his master was going to set out to try to become an emperor or at least a monarch, and that was what they'd agreed between the two of them, and he could easily manage it, considering the worth of his person and the might of his arm — and as soon as this happened, his master was going to find a wife for him, because he'd be a widower by then, he couldn't fail to be, and his master would marry him to the empress's lady-in-waiting, the heiress to a big, rich estate on dry land — no islands or such-like for him, he didn't have any use for those any more.

Sancho said all this with such calm assurance, every so often wiping his nose with the back of his hand, and it was all so absurd, that both men were again struck with amazement as they considered how powerful Don Quixote's madness was, carrying this poor man's wits along with it. They decided not to give themselves the trouble of trying to persuade him of his error because, as they believed, it did no harm to his conscience and so it was better to leave him be; and anyway it would be jolly good fun to listen to all his nonsense. So they told Sancho to pray to God for his master's well-being because it was possible and indeed extremely likely that with the passing of time he might become an emperor, just as he had said, or at least an archbishop or some equivalent dignitary. To which Sancho replied:

'If fortune changed everything, sirs, and my master got the urge not to be an emperor but an archbishop, what I'd like to know next is what archbishop errants give their squires.'

'Usually,' replied the priest, 'they give them some benefice, with or without cure of souls, or they make them sextons, which yields a good fixed income, quite apart from the surplice fees, which are usually reckoned at as much again.'

'For that,' Sancho replied, 'the squire will have to be a single man, and know how to help at mass, at least, and in that case — unhappy me, married as I am and not knowing so much as the first letter of the ABC! What will become of me if my master takes it into his head to be an archbishop rather than an emperor, which is what's normal with knight errants?'

'Don't distress yourself, friend Sancho,' said the barber. 'The reverend father and I shall ask your master, and indeed advise him, and even put it to him as a case of conscience, to be an emperor and not an archbishop – this will be easier for him, because he is more brave than studious.'

'That's what I've always thought, too,' replied Sancho, 'though let me tell you he can turn his hand to anything. What I'm going to do for my part is to pray to our Lord to give him whatever job does him the most good and lets him do me the most favours.'

'You speak like a wise man,' said the priest, 'and you'll be acting like a good Christian. But what must be done now is to work out how to extricate your master from that pointless penance that you say he's doing; and so, to think how we're going to set about it, and to have our dinner, for it's high time we did that, we'd better go into this inn.'

Sancho said that they could go in and he'd wait outside, and later he'd tell them why it didn't suit him to enter, but please would they bring out something hot for him to eat and also some barley for Rocinante. They went in and left him, and a little later the barber brought him out some food. Then, when the pair put their heads together to work out the best way of achieving their aim, the priest thought of a plan that was ideally suited to Don Quixote's tastes and to the goal they had in mind. And he told the barber that his idea was that he himself would dress up as a maiden errant, and the barber would try his best to make himself look like a squire, and then they would go off like that to see Don Quixote, pretending that she was a damsel in need and distress come to beg a boon of him, which he, as a brave knight errant, could not refuse to grant. And the boon was to be that he should go with her whither she should carry him, to redress an injury done her by a wicked knight, entreating him likewise that he would not desire her to divest herself of her mask, nor enquire anything further concerning her, until he should have done her justice upon that wicked knight – and he could rely on Don Quixote doing every single thing he was asked, and in that way they'd get him out of there and take him back to the village, where they'd see if there was any remedy for his strange madness.

CHAPTER XXVII

*About how the priest and the barber achieved their aim,
and other matters worthy of being recounted in this
great history*

The priest's plan didn't seem a bad one to the barber – indeed he thought it so splendid that they put it into action without delay. They asked the innkeeper's wife for a frock and a head-dress, leaving as security a new cassock of the priest's. The barber made a long beard from a pale red ox tail in which the innkeeper used to stick his comb. His wife asked them what they wanted these things for. The priest gave her a brief account of Don Quixote's madness, and told her that the disguise was needed to get him out of his present quarters in the sierra. And then the innkeeper and his wife realized that this madman was their former guest, the man with the balsam, the master of the blanket-tossed squire, and they told the priest everything that had happened, including what Sancho had been so concerned to omit. So the innkeeper's wife dressed the priest and left him looking as pretty as a picture: she fitted him out with a woollen frock, covered with black bands of slashed velvet, as broad as your hand, and bodices of green velvet with white satin trimmings; and they must have been made – both the bodices and the frock – in the times of King Wamba.[1] The priest wouldn't let them touch his head, but instead donned his quilted cotton nightcap and bound his forehead with a black taffeta garter, and he used another garter as a travelling-mask to conceal his face and beard. He rammed his hat, which was so big it could have served as a parasol, on to his head, wrapped himself in his cape and mounted his mule side-saddle, and the barber climbed on to his own mule, with his beard down to his waist – a pale red beard, as described, made out of the tail of a sorrel ox. They said goodbye to everyone, including the good Maritornes, who promised to say a rosary, sinner though she was, so that God would give them success in the difficult Christian task they'd set themselves.

But the priest had hardly left the inn when a thought struck him: it was improper to have rigged himself out like that, indecent for a man of the cloth to dress in that way, even if so much did depend on it; and he said so to the barber and asked him to exchange clothes, because it was more appropriate for the latter to appear as the maiden in distress, and he himself would act the part of the squire, which was less of a profanation of his office – and if the barber wasn't agreeable to this, the priest was resolved to have nothing more to do with the affair, and to let the devil take Don Quixote.

And now Sancho appeared, and when he saw the two of them dressed like that his mirth was uncontrollable. The barber agreed to all the priest's demands, and they changed their plans and the priest instructed him on his demeanour, and on the words with which he was to try to persuade Don Quixote to come away with them and give up his occupation of the place he'd chosen for his vain penance. The barber replied that he didn't need any lessons to handle the affair to perfection. He didn't want to get dressed yet, not until they came close to where Don Quixote was, so he folded up his clothes and the priest put his beard away, and they rode on with their guide Sancho Panza, who told them all about what had happened with the madman they'd found in the sierra, keeping quiet, however, about the discovery of the travelling bag and what was in it: the servant might have been stupid, but he did have his fair share of greed.

The next day they reached the place where Sancho had strewn the branches to help him find his master again, and, once he recognized the spot, he told the other two that this was the way in, so they could get dressed if that was what was needed for the rescue. Because they had earlier told him that wearing those disguises was of vital importance for extricating his master from the bad life he'd chosen, so would he please be careful not to tell him who they were or even that he knew them; and if Don Quixote asked, which he would, whether Sancho had given Dulcinea the letter, he should say that he had but that, as she couldn't read, she'd replied verbally ordering Don Quixote, on pain of incurring her displeasure, to go and visit her forthwith, this being a matter of the utmost importance to her – and what with this and the things that they themselves intended to say to him they were sure he could be led back to a better life, and made to set out to become an emperor or a monarch, and there wasn't any need to worry about that plan to become an archbishop.

Sancho listened to all of this, and took it into his memory with meticulous care, and gave them hearty thanks for deciding to advise his master to be an emperor and not an archbishop, because to his mind, when it came to doing favours to their squires, emperor errants had more clout than archbishop errants. He added that it would be best if he went on ahead to look for his master and give him his lady's reply, because this alone would be enough to make him leave that place, without any need for them to go to so much trouble. They liked Sancho Panza's idea, and decided to wait until he returned with the news that he'd found his master.

Sancho rode off into the mountain ravines, leaving the other two men in another ravine through which flowed a gentle little stream in the cool, pleasant shade of the rocks and trees surrounding it. It was a hot August day, and August is hot indeed in those parts; it was three o'clock in the afternoon; and all this made the spot even more delightful, inviting them to await Sancho's return there, which they did.

As they rested in the shade, they heard a voice that, unaccompanied by any other instrument, was sweet and melodious; and they were astonished, this not seeming to be a place to come across someone singing so well – because although it's often said that shepherds with fine singing voices are to be found in the woods and fields, this is more an exaggeration of poets than a sober truth. And they were even more amazed when they realized that what they could hear being sung were verses not of rustic herdsmen but of intelligent courtiers. This was confirmed by the fact that the verses they heard were the following:

> What puts my patience to the test?
> Absence's jest.
> What aggravates my misery?
> Fierce jealousy.
> What turns my happiness to pain?
> Unkind disdain.
> If this is so, there is no cure
> For torments that I now endure,
> Since every hope of mine is slain
> By absence, jealousy, disdain.

And what repels my happiness?
Fortune's duress.
What is the cause of such dire throes?
Love's cruel blows.
And what confirms my misery?
Heaven's decree.
If this is so, the sole release
Is death, from such a strange disease,
Since all unite to harrow me:
Fortune, and love, and heaven's decree.

What can release me from my sadness?
No less than madness.
Where shall I find a speedy cure?
Cold death is sure.
What gains love's joys most readily?
Inconstancy.
If this is so, it makes no sense
From such attacks to seek defence,
Since there's no better remedy
Than madness, death, inconstancy.

The time of day, the weather, the solitude, and the voice and the skill
of the singer combined to astonish and delight the two listeners, who sat
still, hoping to hear some more; but as the silence dragged on they decided
to go in search of the man who sang so well. Just as they were about to
do so, the same voice held them back as it reached their ears, singing this
sonnet:

SONNET

O sacred Friendship, who in urgent flight,
And leaving here on earth your guileful ghost,
Exultant soared to that empyrean height
To dwell in glory with the heavenly host,
From there to show us, when you think it best,
Behind a veil that peace for which we long

– A veil that other times betrays a zest
For doing good, which then does vicious wrong:
　　　Come back from heaven, Friendship: don't agree
To the destruction of sincere intent
When Fraudulence parades your livery;
For if his base charade has your consent
Grim-visaged war will win the world again
And dark primeval anarchy will reign.

The singing ended in a deep sigh, and the two men waited attentively to see if it would be resumed; but when they heard that the music had dissolved into sobs and pitiful groans they agreed to go and discover who was this sad man with a voice as superb as his moans were sorrowful. They hadn't walked far when, as they came round a boulder, they saw a man who looked exactly like the one described by Sancho Panza when he told them about Cardenio's story; and when this man saw them he didn't seem frightened but stayed still with his head bowed over his breast like someone lost in his thoughts, not raising his eyes again to look at them after his first glance when they'd appeared so suddenly.

The priest, who was a man of ready speech and knew about Cardenio's misfortune because he'd recognized him from Sancho's description, went up to him and with brief but judicious words begged and advised him to abandon that wretched existence so as not to die in that place, which would be the greatest of all misfortunes. Cardenio was enjoying a spell of sanity, free of the fury that often drove him out of his mind, and he was surprised to see two men in clothes so very different from the ones worn by those who wandered about these lonely places, and even more surprised to hear his private life being discussed as if it were common knowledge – because this was the impression given by the priest's words. So Cardenio replied like this:

'I can clearly see, gentlemen, whoever you are, that heaven, which takes care to succour the virtuous and even the wicked as well, has sent to me, unworthy though I am, here into these remote places so far from all human society, people who, by placing a diversity of powerful arguments before me to show me how unreasonable it is to live as I do, seek to take me away from this existence to a better one; but since they

do not know, as I do, that if I escape from this affliction it will only be
to plunge into another still greater one, it may be that they take me for
a man of little sense or even what would be worse, one deprived of all
reason. And this would not be surprising, because I am aware that the
recollection of my misfortunes is so intense and has such power to destroy
me that, without my being able to do anything to prevent it, I sometimes
become as void of all sense and awareness as a stone; and I realize that
this is so when people tell me and show me proof of the things I do when
in the grips of those terrible fits, and all I can do then is express a futile
regret for what has happened and utter fruitless curses on my fate, and
offer as an excuse for my mad deeds an account of their cause to any who
will hear me; because once reasonable people know the cause they will
not wonder at the effects, and, if they cannot cure me, at least they will
not blame me, and their annoyance at my impudence will turn to pity for
my misfortunes. And if, gentlemen, you have come with the same intentions
as others, I beg you, before you proceed with your judicious persuasion,
to listen to the endless story of my misfortunes because, once you have
heard it, perhaps you will save yourselves the trouble of trying to console
me for an affliction that puts me beyond all consolation.'

The two men, who wanted nothing better than to hear the cause of
his grief from his own mouth, asked him to tell them about it and assured
him that in any attempts they might make to cure or comfort him they
wouldn't do anything against his will; and so this sad gentleman began
his piteous history, with almost the same words and events as when he'd
narrated it to Don Quixote and the goatherd a few days earlier, and, on
account of Master Elisabat and of Don Quixote's punctiliousness in
maintaining the decorum of chivalry, the story had been left unfinished,
as related in this history. But this time, fortunately, the fit of madness was
suspended and he was able to tell his story to its conclusion; and so, when
he reached the point at which Don Fernando found a letter among the
pages of *Amadis of Gaul*, Cardenio said that he could remember it well,
and that it went like this:

Luscinda to Cardenio

Each day I discover in you qualities that oblige and compel me to hold you in even higher esteem; and so, if you should wish to relieve me of this obligation without causing me to forfeit my honour, you can easily do so. I have a father who knows you and loves me, and who will not be going against my wishes when he accedes to those which you may justly have, if you esteem me, as you say and I believe.

'This letter encouraged me to ask for Luscinda's hand in marriage, as I've already told you, and it was also what established her in Don Fernando's opinion as one of the most sensible and intelligent women of the day; and it was this letter, too, that awoke in him the desire to destroy me, before my own desire could be fulfilled. I told Don Fernando of Luscinda's father's observation that it was my own father who should make the request, and that I didn't dare mention it to him, fearing that he'd refuse to do so, not because he wasn't well aware of Luscinda's rank, goodness, virtue and beauty, or of the fact that her qualities were sufficient to ennoble any family in Spain, but because I realized that he didn't want me to marry yet, not until it became clear what Duke Ricardo had in store for me. In short, I told him that I didn't dare tell my father about the matter, because of both this obstacle and many others that discouraged me, although I didn't know exactly what they were: all I did know was that it was looking as if what I so desired could never be achieved.

'To all this Don Fernando replied that he'd take it upon himself to speak to my father and persuade him to speak to Luscinda's father. Oh you ruthless Marius, you cruel Catiline, you wicked Sulla, you deceitful Ganelon, you treacherous Vellido, you vengeful Julián, you covetous Judas![2] Treacherous, cruel, vengeful, deceitful – what deeds of disloyalty had ever been committed by this poor man who so frankly revealed to you the joys and secrets of his heart? In what ways had I ever offended you? What words did I ever speak to you, what advice did I ever give you, but that which was designed to increase your honour and prosperity? Yet what am I complaining about, miserable wretch that I am? It's certain that when misfortune is brought by the movements of the stars, it comes crashing down from on high with such fury and violence that there's no power on earth that can stop it, no human contrivance that can hold it back. Who could have imagined that Don Fernando, an illustrious and intelligent gentleman, indebted to me for my services and powerful enough to secure for himself whatever his amorous inclinations desired, would sully his conscience, as they say, by stealing from me one ewe lamb, which was not even yet mine?[3] But let's leave these considerations aside, because they're vain and fruitless, and take up the broken thread of my tale of woe.

'I was going to say, then, that Don Fernando, finding my presence an obstacle to the execution of his false and evil plan, decided to make me go to his elder brother to ask for money to pay for six horses that, with the sole object of sending me away so that he could more readily carry out his perverse scheme, he bought on the same day that he offered to talk to my father. So I was to go for the money. Could I have foreseen this treachery? Could I even have imagined it? No, of course not: on the contrary, I most willingly offered to leave at once, delighted with the excellent bargain he'd made. That night I spoke with Luscinda and told her what I'd agreed with Don Fernando, and how she should firmly trust that our good and just desires would be fulfilled. Suspecting Don Fernando's treachery as little as I did, she told me to try to come back soon, because she believed that the accomplishment of our wishes would be delayed by no longer than our fathers' conversation. I don't know why, but when she finished saying this her eyes filled with tears and a knot seemed to form in her throat, stopping her from speaking any more of the very many words that she appeared to want to say to me.

'I was astonished at this strange faltering, because it had never happened before and, whenever good fortune and my diligence had allowed us to talk, we'd done so with great joy, without any tears, sighs, jealousy, suspicion or fear. I would dwell on my good fortune, because heaven had given her to me as my lady; I would extol her beauty, marvel at her merit and her understanding. She would return the compliments with interest, praising in me that which seemed to her, as a woman in love, worthy of praise. And we would tell each other a hundred thousand tales and pieces of gossip about our friends and neighbours, and the most I ever dared to do was to take, almost by force, one of her lovely white hands and press it to my lips as well as the close bars separating us would allow. But on the night before the sorrowful day of my departure she wept, sighed and moaned, and went away leaving me confused and fearful at having seen these sad new signs of deep grief in her; yet, so as not to dash my own hopes, I put it all down to the strength of her feelings for me and the pain that absence causes in those who are in love.

'So I left, dejected and sunk in thought, with my soul loaded down with suspicions and imaginings, yet not knowing what it was that I suspected and imagined: clear signs of the sad event and the misfortune reserved for me. I reached the town to which I'd been sent, I gave the letters to Don Fernando's brother, I was well received but my business was not well attended to, because he told me to wait, much to my displeasure, for a week, where the Duke could not find me, as his brother had written asking him to send money without his father's knowledge; and this was all part of the treacherous Don Fernando's plan, because this brother of his had the money and could have sent me back with it immediately. This was an order that I was very close to disobeying, because it seemed impossible to endure life for so long without Luscinda, particularly since I had left her in the state that I've described; but in spite of all that I obeyed as a dutiful servant, although I could see that it would be at the cost of my well-being.

'But four days after I'd arrived a man came for me with a letter, and by the address I could tell it was from Luscinda, because it was in her handwriting. I opened it in fear and trembling, for it had to be a serious matter to make her write when I was far away – she seldom wrote even when I was near. Before I read it I asked the man who had given it to him and how long it had taken him to come. He told me that he'd happened to be walking down a street in his city at midday when a very beautiful lady called out to him from a window, with her eyes full of tears, and blurted:

' "Brother, if you're a Christian, as you seem to be, I beg you for the love of God to make sure that this letter reaches without delay the place and the person to whom it's addressed – they're both well-known enough; and you'll be doing a great service to our Lord, and, so that you don't lack the means to do so, please accept the contents of this handkerchief."

' "And so saying she threw me a handkerchief out of the window, and tied into it were these hundred reals and this gold ring I have here, together with the letter I've just given you. And without waiting for a reply she moved back from the window, though not before watching me pick up the letter and the handkerchief and make signs that I would indeed do as she had asked. Because seeing that I was so well paid for whatever trouble it could give me to bring it, and seeing from the address that it was for you – I know about you, sir, very well – and compelled, too, by that beautiful lady's tears, I decided not to entrust it to anybody else but to bring it myself, and in the sixteen hours that have elapsed since I was given it I have made the journey here – some sixty miles, as you know."

'As the grateful special messenger was telling me all this, I was hanging on his every word and my legs were shaking so much that I could hardly stand. I opened the letter and read the following:

The promise that Don Fernando made you, to persuade your father to speak to mine, has been kept, but more for his gratification than for your benefit. You must know, sir, that he has asked for my hand in marriage, and my father, persuaded that Don Fernando will be a better match, has given his consent so eagerly that the wedding is to take place two days from now, in such secret that the only witnesses will be the heavens and some of the household. My present state is something that you can imagine for yourself; whether it is in your interest to come is something that you must decide for yourself; and whether I love you or not is something that the outcome of this affair will demonstrate to you. God grant that this may reach your hand before mine is joined with that of one who keeps his promises so badly.

'This, then, was what the letter said, and this is what made me set off straight away, without waiting any longer for a reply or for money; because I could clearly see that it had been the purchase not of horses but of his pleasure that had led Don Fernando to send me to his brother. My indignation and my fear of losing the treasure that I had won by so many years of service and desire lent me wings, and the next day I was back in my town at the hour when I could speak to Luscinda, almost as if I'd flown there. I rode in unobserved, I left my mule at the house of the fellow who'd brought me the letter, and it was my good fortune to find Luscinda at her window, behind the grating that was the witness to our love. Luscinda recognized me and I recognized her, but not as we should have recognized each other. Yet who in this world can claim to have penetrated and understood the confused mind and fickle nature of a woman? Nobody, nobody. I was about to say that as soon as Luscinda saw me she said:

'"Cardenio, I'm wearing my wedding dress: the treacherous Don Fernando and my covetous father are waiting in the hall with others who will be witnesses rather of my death than of my marriage. Don't be upset, my dear, but do make sure that you're present at this sacrifice: if my words can't prevent it, a dagger I have hidden on me can resist the strongest forces by putting an end to my life and a beginning to your understanding of my love for you."

'In my confusion I made a hurried reply, afraid that I might run out of time:

'"Let your actions, madam, make good your words; for if you carry a dagger to vouch for you, I carry a sword to defend you or kill myself, if fortune proves adverse to us."

'I don't believe she could have heard all I said, because urgent voices were calling out to her that the bridegroom was waiting. And the night of my sadness came, and the sun of my happiness set: there was no light left in my eyes, no sense left in my brain. I couldn't enter her house – I couldn't move; but then I reminded myself how important it was for me to be present because of what might happen, I nerved myself as best I could and went in; and since I knew all the ways in and out, and the house was in its secret upheaval, nobody noticed me; so I was able to slip unobserved into the recess formed by a window in the hall, covered by the borders of two tapestries, between which I could see, without being seen, everything that happened.

'Who could describe the fluttering of my heart as I stood there, the thoughts that came into my mind, the calculations that I made? There were so many of them, and they were of such a nature, that I can't describe them, nor would it be right to do so. Suffice it to say that the bridegroom walked into the hall wearing nothing finer than his everyday clothes. His best man was one of Luscinda's cousins, and the only other people in the hall were the servants.

'A little afterwards Luscinda came out of a side room accompanied by her mother and two maids, and she was as richly dressed and adorned as her rank and beauty deserved, the perfection of elegance and courtly poise. My amazement and trepidation didn't allow me to observe the details of her dress; I only noticed its colours, crimson and white, and the glinting of the jewels in her hair and on her clothes, all of it surpassed by the singular beauty of her lovely blond hair to such an extent that, in competition with the precious stones and the light of four torches that were burning in the hall, her light was the one that offered most brilliance to the eyes. O memory, the mortal foe of my repose! Why bring before me now the incomparable beauty of that adored enemy of mine? Won't it be better, cruel memory, to recall and picture to me what she did next so that, moved by such a manifest affront, I can at least, since vengeance is impossible, put an end to my life?

'Try not to be bored, gentlemen, by these digressions of mine: my tale of woe is not one of those that can or should be told in a few words, because each aspect of it seems to demand a full explanation.'

To this the priest replied that not only were they not bored listening to him but they were deriving great pleasure from all the details he was providing, because they shouldn't be passed over in silence and indeed merited as much attention as the main thread of his story.

'I was about to say, then,' Cardenio continued, 'that the people were standing there in the hall and the parish priest came in and took each by the hand to do what had to be done, and when he said, "Will you, Luscinda, take Don Fernando, here present, to be your lawful wedded husband, as our Holy Mother the Church commands?", I thrust my head and neck out between the two tapestries to listen, with straining ears and soul in turmoil, to Luscinda's reply, knowing that it would be either my death sentence or the confirmation of my life. Oh, why didn't I rush out, crying, "Luscinda, Luscinda! Think what you're doing, consider what you owe me, remember you're mine and can't be another's! Remember that your saying 'I will' and the end of my life will be one and the same thing. O treacherous Don Fernando, thief of my glory, death of my life! What do you want? What do you seek? Bear in mind that there is no Christian way in which you can satisfy your desires, because Luscinda is my wife and I am her husband."

'What madness! Now that I'm far removed from the danger, I'm saying that I should have done what I didn't do! Now that I've allowed my dear one to be stolen, I curse the thief, on whom I could have taken revenge if I'd had the courage to do so, as I have for complaining! In short, I behaved then like a fool and a coward; no wonder that I'm dying now ashamed, repentant and mad.

'The priest was waiting for Luscinda's reply, and she was taking a long time to give it, and just when I thought that she was going to draw her dagger and allow it to speak for her, or else loosen her tongue to undeceive them all and help my cause, I heard her whisper "I will", and Don Fernando said the same thing and gave her the ring, and they were joined in an indissoluble bond. The bridegroom went to embrace his bride, and she clutched her hand to her heart and fell fainting into her mother's arms. It only remains for me to say how I felt as I saw, in her consent, that my hopes were shattered, that all Luscinda's words and promises had been false, and that it would be impossible ever to recover the treasure that I had lost in an instant. I was left not knowing what to do, forsaken, as it seemed to me, by all heaven: the earth that supported me had become my enemy, air denied itself to me for my sighs, water for my tears, and only fire grew, so that all burned in fury and jealousy.

'Everyone was thrown into confusion by Luscinda's fainting fit, and, when her mother loosened her bodices, a folded piece of paper was discovered there, which Don Fernando snatched up and started to read by the light of one of the torches; and once he'd finished reading he sat on a chair and put his hand to his cheek like a man lost in his thoughts, not going to help with the attempts that were being made to bring his bride round from her swoon. With everyone in such a commotion I plucked up my courage and left, not caring whether I was seen or not, and determined that, if I was, I'd do such a desperate deed that they'd all learn from my punishment of the false Don Fernando or even of the fickle, swooning traitress how just was my indignation. But my fate, which must have reserved me for even worse evils (if there can be any worse), decreed that I should then have full use of an understanding that has since failed me; so I didn't take my revenge on my greatest enemies (which would have been easy, for all thought of me was far from their minds) but decided to give myself the punishment that they deserved, and perhaps an even more severe one than I'd have given them had I killed them, because with sudden death the suffering is soon over, whereas torture endlessly protracts the life that it's doing away with.

'So I left that house and returned to the one where I'd left the mule; I told the man to saddle it and, without stopping to take my leave of him, I mounted it and rode out of the city, not daring to look back, like another Lot;[4] and once I found myself alone in the countryside, with the darkness of the night hiding me and its silence inviting me to voice my complaints without fear of being overheard or recognized, I bellowed out curse after curse on Luscinda and Don Fernando, as if this were satisfaction for the wrong they'd done me. I called her cruel, ungrateful, false, thankless, but above all covetous, because my enemy's wealth had closed the eyes of her affection, taking it away from me and giving it to one with whom fortune had been more bountiful and generous; but even as I was most furiously cursing and abusing her I was also making excuses for her, saying that it wasn't surprising that a young girl, immured in her parents' house, accustomed to obeying them always, should have decided to fall in with their wishes, because they were giving her as a husband a gentleman who was so eminent, so rich and so noble that, if she'd refused him, it could have been thought either that she was out of her mind or that she had another lover, which would have been so prejudicial to her good name and honour.

'Then I'd change my tune and say that, even if she had declared that she and I were married, they'd have seen that her choice hadn't been such a bad one that they couldn't forgive her, because before Don Fernando put himself forward they themselves couldn't have wanted a better husband for their daughter, if they'd kept their expectations within reasonable limits; and that, rather than making that last fatal move, giving her hand to Don Fernando, she could easily have said that I'd already given her mine, because I'd have confirmed whatever story she'd made up for the occasion.

'So I concluded that a lack of true love and of good sense, and an excess of ambition and of thirst for grandeur, had made her forget the words with which she'd deceived, kept alive and sustained my firm hopes and honourable desires. Shouting and agonizing in this way I rode on through what was left of the night, and at daybreak I came to a pass leading into this sierra, through which I wandered aimlessly for another three days until I reached some meadows somewhere among these mountains and asked some herdsmen where the wildest parts lay. They sent me in this direction. I headed for this place at once, intending to end my life here, and as I reached it my mule dropped dead from exhaustion and starvation or, as I rather believe, to be rid of so useless a burden. So I was left on foot, at the mercy of nature, perishing with hunger, with nobody to help me and no thoughts of looking for help.

'I lay like that for some time, I don't know how long, and then I stood up, now not feeling at all hungry, and found some goatherds there who must have been the people who'd satisfied my needs, because they told me how they'd found me raving in such a way that it was clear I'd lost my reason; and since then I've realized that I'm not always in full possession of it, but so deranged at times that I perform a thousand mad actions, tearing my clothes, bellowing in these solitudes, cursing my fortune and vainly repeating my beloved enemy's name, with no other thought or plan than to end my life in screams; and then when I come back to my senses I feel so weak and exhausted that I can hardly move. My usual dwelling-place is the hollow of a cork-oak, large enough to shelter this miserable carcass of mine. The cowherds and goatherds who roam over these mountains, moved by charity, provide me with sustenance, placing food by the paths and rocks where they think I might pass and find it; and when I do, even at times when I've lost my reason, natural instinct makes me recognize the food and awakes in me the desire to go and fetch it and the will to take it up. When they come across me in my senses they tell me that at other times I waylay the herdsmen carrying food up from the village to the folds and take it from them by force, even though they're happy to give it to me.

'This is how I'm spending the last days of my wretched existence, until heaven is pleased to put an end either to it or to my memory, so that I do not remember Luscinda's beauty and treachery or the wrong done me by Don Fernando; for if heaven does this without ending my life, I'll turn my thoughts to a better course; if not, all that can be done is to beg heaven to have infinite mercy on my soul, because I don't feel in myself the strength or vigour to rescue my body from these desperate straits to which I've chosen to reduce it.

'This, gentlemen, is the dismal story of my misfortune: you tell me now whether it would have been possible to tell it with less emotion than I've shown – and don't trouble to advise or try to persuade me to do what your reason suggests as a remedy for me, because that would be as much use to me as the medicine prescribed by a famous doctor for the patient who refuses to take it. I don't want well-being without Luscinda and, since she has seen fit to belong to another, although she is or should be mine, let me give myself up to misfortune, although I could have been given up to happiness. She wished, with her fickleness, to make my ruin permanent; by seeking my own ruin I'll satisfy her wishes, and this can show posterity that I alone have lacked what other unfortunates possess in abundance; for to them the impossibility of being consoled is in itself a consolation, whereas it only brings me still greater misery, because I believe that my wretchedness will not be ended by my death.'

Here Cardenio ended his long discourse and his tale of love and sorrow; and as the priest was preparing to speak some words of comfort, he was checked by a voice that reached his ears, saying in plaintive tones what will be set down in the fourth part of this narration, because at this point the wise and circumspect historian Cide Hamete Benengeli put an end to the third.

Fourth Part of
the Ingenious Hidalgo
DON QUIXOTE
de la Mancha

CHAPTER XXVIII

*Concerning the unusual and agreeable adventure
undergone by the priest and the barber in the
Sierra Morena*

Most happy and fortunate were the times when that most daring knight
Don Quixote de la Mancha appeared on this earth, because it is thanks
to his honourable determination to revive and restore to the world the
lost and indeed almost defunct order of knight-errantry that we can now
enjoy, in this age of ours, so much in need of amusing entertainments,
not only the delights of his true history but also the stories and episodes
inserted into it, for in some ways they are no less agreeable or imaginative
or true than the history itself; which, resuming its thread (duly dressed,
spun and wound), relates that as the priest was preparing himself to
comfort Cardenio, he was checked by a voice that said in mournful tones:

'Oh God, is it possible that I've at last found a place that can serve as
a hidden tomb for the heavy burden of this body of mine, which I so
unwillingly bear? Yes, it is, if the solitude promised by these sierras doesn't
deceive me. Oh unhappy me, how much more agreeable company these
crags and thickets will be for my thoughts – since they'll give me the
opportunity to bewail my fate and tell heaven of my misery – than that
of any human being, because there isn't one on this earth from whom
one can expect advice in perplexity, comfort in lamentation or remedy in
distress!'

When the priest and those with him heard these words they realized that the voice wasn't far away and stood up to go and look for the speaker, and they hadn't gone twenty paces when they saw, sitting behind a rock at the foot of an ash tree, a lad in farmer's clothes whose face they couldn't see, because his head was bent over a stream that flowed there, in which he was bathing his feet; and they approached him so quietly that he didn't notice them, being so engrossed in bathing his feet, which looked like nothing so much as two pieces of white crystal lying among the other stones there. They were astonished at the whiteness and the beauty of those feet, which didn't look as if they were accustomed to treading the clods or trudging behind the plough and the oxen, as the lad's clothes indicated they were.

And so, seeing that they hadn't been noticed, the priest, who'd gone on ahead, motioned to the other two to crouch down and hide behind some rocks, which they did, watching every movement made by the lad, who was wearing a pale-brown rustic cape, tied tight round his waist with a strip of white towelling. He was also wearing pale-brown woollen breeches and gaiters, and a cap of the same colour. He'd hitched his gaiters halfway up his legs, which, of course, resembled the purest alabaster. He finished washing those beautiful feet and then dried them with a kerchief that he untied from under his cap; and as he did so he raised his face and the onlookers saw such peerless beauty that Cardenio whispered to the priest:

'Since this isn't Luscinda, it's no human creature but a divine one.'

The lad removed his cap and, as he shook his head from side to side, hair that the sun itself might have envied began to flow down and spread out. This made them realize that the person who'd seemed to be a farmer was a woman, and a well-favoured one at that, indeed the most beautiful woman that two of them had ever seen, and that Cardenio would have ever seen if he hadn't seen Luscinda, because he later affirmed that only Luscinda's beauty could match hers. Her long blond hair didn't just cover her shoulders but spread all around her, and so lush and abundant was it that only her feet could be seen. And now she combed it with her hands, and, if her feet in the water looked like pieces of crystal, her hands in her hair looked like pieces of firm snow. All this increased the astonishment of the three men and their desire to know who she was.

So they decided to show themselves and, as they stood up, the beautiful young woman raised her head and, parting her hair from her eyes with both hands, looked to see what was making the noise; as soon as she saw them she sprang to her feet, and without stopping to put on her shoes or tie up her hair, she snatched up a bundle lying beside her, which looked as if it contained clothes, and began to run away in confusion and alarm. But she hadn't taken half-a-dozen steps when her delicate feet, unable to bear the roughness of the stones, failed her and she fell to the ground. The three men stepped forward, and the priest was the first to address her:

'Stop, madam, whoever you are: those whom you see before you desire only to serve you. Please do not attempt to make so inopportune an escape, for neither will your feet withstand it nor will we allow it.'

In her bewilderment she made no reply. So they went up to her and the priest took her hand and continued:

'What your clothes deny, madam, is betrayed by your hair: a clear sign that it can have been no trivial reason that led you to disguise your beauty in such an unworthy habit and that brought you into such a lonely place, where it has been a stroke of good fortune to find you – if not to remedy your ills, at least to give advice, for no ill can be so oppressive or so extreme that, while life lasts, the sufferer refuses to listen to well-meant counsel. And so, my dear lady, or my dear sir, whichever you prefer to be, do dismiss the fears that seeing us has caused you, and tell us about your good or evil fortune; for in all of us together, or in each separately, you'll find sincere sympathizers.'

As the priest was speaking, the disguised girl seemed as if she had lost her senses, gazing at them all without moving her lips or saying a word, like the rustic villager who's suddenly shown strange objects that he's never seen before. But the priest said some more words to the same effect, and she breathed a deep sigh and broke her silence:

'Since the solitude of these sierras hasn't been sufficient to hide me, and the loosening of my dishevelled hair won't allow my tongue to lie, it would be futile to maintain a pretence that could only be accepted out of politeness. In view of this, gentlemen, I thank you for your offer, which has placed me under an obligation to comply with your request, even though I fear that the tale I shall tell of my misfortunes will cause you not only pity but grief, because you won't be able to find any cure to remedy them, or any consolation to alleviate them. But in spite of all this, and to dispel any doubts you might be entertaining about my honour now that you know I'm a woman and have seen me young, alone and in these clothes – circumstances that coming together or even taken separately would be enough to demolish any reputation – I feel bound to tell you what I'd rather keep secret if I could.'

The newly discovered beauty said all this with such a fluent tongue and in such a calm voice that they were as amazed at her intelligence as at her looks. And after further offers had been made, together with further requests to do as she'd promised, she made any more coaxing unnecessary by putting on her shoes with all due modesty, tying up her hair, sitting on a rock with the three men around her, trying to suppress the tears that welled into her eyes and in a clear, serene voice commencing her life history:

'There is in Andalusia a town from which a certain duke takes his title, and which makes him one of those known here in Spain as grandees. He has two sons: the elder is the heir to his estate and, so it seems, to his virtuous habits, and the younger is the heir to I don't know what, unless it's the treachery of Vellido and the deceit of Ganelon. My parents are tenants of this duke, of humble stock but so rich that if nature had been as generous with their pedigree as fortune has been with their wealth, they could have nothing more to desire and there would have been no risk of my finding myself in my present predicament; because it may be that my bad luck is born of theirs, in not having been born aristocratic. It's certainly true that they're not so low-born as to feel affronted by their rank, but neither are they so exalted as to rid my head of the thought that my disaster derives from their modest station. In short they're farmers, simple folk, of pure blood unmixed with that of any ill-sounding races and, as it's often put, dyed-in-the-wool old Christians – but so rich that thanks to their wealth and generosity they're beginning to be regarded as hidalgos and even as nobles. But their greatest wealth and nobility was, for them, having me as a daughter, and, both because they had no other heir and because they were loving parents, I was one of the most indulged of children. I was the mirror in which they contemplated themselves, the staff of their old age and the goal towards which they guided, under the direction of heaven, all their desires, which were so worthy that mine never diverged one iota from them. And I was the mistress not only of their affections but of all they owned. I was in charge of hiring and dismissing the servants, I controlled all the sowing and harvesting, and the olive-presses, the wine-presses, the size of the herds and flocks, even the quantity of beehives. In short, I managed everything that a very wealthy farmer like my father can and does possess, and I was both the stewardess and the mistress of it all, with so much diligence on my part and so much satisfaction on his that I couldn't begin to say how splendid everything was.

'The moments of each day that were left to me after I'd paid the shepherds, foremen and day labourers, I spent on occupations that are both proper and necessary for young ladies, such as those provided by the needle and the pincushion and often the distaff; and if I occasionally put these activities aside in search of some recreation, I would entertain myself by reading a book of devotion, or playing a harp, because experience showed me that music settles the distressed mind and eases the troubles that are born of the spirit. This, then, was the life I led in my parents' house, and I've described it in such detail not to boast or to demonstrate that I'm a wealthy woman, but so that you can see how little I deserved to fall from that happy state into my present misery.

'As I spent my life, then, with so much to keep me busy, and in a seclusion which could be compared to that of a nunnery, and unseen, or so I thought, by anyone except the servants, because when I went to mass it was so early in the morning, and I was so closely attended by my mother and other maidservants and so carefully veiled and withdrawn that my eyes hardly glimpsed anything other than the ground I trod . . . – but, despite all these precautions, loving eyes or, more accurately, idle eyes, which the eyes of the lynx cannot rival, did see me: the eyes of the importunate Don Fernando, for this is the name of the younger son of the duke of whom I spoke.'

The storyteller had no sooner named Don Fernando than the colour of Cardenio's face changed and he broke into a sweat, in such violent perturbation that when the priest and barber noticed it they feared he was about to have one of the fits of madness that they'd been told he suffered every so often. But Cardenio only sat there perspiring and gaping at the farmer's daughter and imagining who she was; and she, not noticing Cardenio's response, continued her story:

'And the moment those eyes of his caught sight of me (as he later said), he fell as deeply in love as his demonstrations of it were to indicate. But to shorten the true story of my woes, I'll pass in silence over the measures that Don Fernando took to declare his love to me. He bribed all the servants in my house, he gave presents and offered favours to my relations. Every day was a happy fiesta day in my street, and at night nobody slept, with all the serenades. The love-letters that came into my hands by unknown means were countless, full of words of passion and promises, and containing more offers and vows than signs of the alphabet. All of which not only failed to weaken my resistance, but steeled me, as if he were my mortal enemy and everything he did to win me over were done with the opposite intention; not that I disliked Don Fernando's gallantry, or thought him too importunate, because it gave me a very special thrill of happiness to be loved and esteemed by such an eminent gentleman, and I wasn't sorry to read his praises in his letters: however ugly a woman is, it seems she always likes to hear herself called beautiful.

'But my sense of virtue did object, and so did my parents, who kept giving me their advice – by now they knew all about Don Fernando's passion, because he didn't care if everybody knew about it. My parents would tell me that their honour and reputation depended upon my virtue and goodness alone, and that I must consider the difference in rank between Don Fernando and me, and that this would make me see that his intentions, even if he said otherwise, had more to do with his pleasure than with my welfare; and also that if I would erect some kind of obstacle to make him desist from his unjust pretensions, they would marry me without delay to any man I chose among the most eminent men in our town and those near by, because with their great wealth and my good name anything was possible. My parents' firm promises and the truths they were telling me strengthened my resolve, and I never replied to Don Fernando with a single word that could have given him the remotest hope of fulfilling his desire.

'All this reserve of mine, which I suppose he took for disdain, must have had the effect of arousing his lust to an even higher pitch – this is the name I must give to his passion, which, had it been what it should have been, you wouldn't be hearing about now, for there wouldn't have been any occasion to tell you of it. In the end Don Fernando found out that my parents were looking for a match for me, so as to make him lose his hopes of possessing me, or at least to provide me with more guards to watch over me; and this information, or suspicion, was the reason why he did what you will now hear. One night I was in my room accompanied only by a maid, with all the doors locked for fear that any carelessness might in some unimagined way endanger my virtue, and in the midst of all these defences and precautions, in the solitude of this silence and seclusion, I found him standing there before me, and the sight of him so shocked me that I lost my sight and my power of speech. So I couldn't shout out, and anyway I don't believe he'd have let me, because he hurried over to me, took me in his arms (as I've said, I was so shocked I had no strength left with which to defend myself) and began to say such things to me – I just don't know how it's possible for duplicity to possess such skill in constructing lies that they seem like evident truths. The traitor produced tears to support his words and sighs to vouch for his passion. I, poor thing, alone in my own house, unprepared for such a situation, began – I don't quite know how – to take all these falsehoods for truths, but his tears and sighs didn't move me to anything more than honest compassion. And so, once I'd recovered from the initial shock, I began to regain some of my lost vital spirits, and with more energy than I thought there was in me I said:

' "If, sir, as I am in your grip, I were in that of some fierce lion, and I could gain my freedom by doing or saying something to the prejudice of my chastity, it would be as possible for me to say it or to do it as it is for that which has been to cease to have been. For if you hold my body in your arms, I keep my soul secure in the purity of my intentions, which are very different from yours, as you will soon realize if you try to carry them into effect by force. I am your tenant but I am not your slave, and the nobility of your blood should not and does not give you the authority to despise and dishonour the humility of mine; and I hold myself, a lowly farmer's daughter, in quite as much esteem as you, a lord and gentleman, hold yourself. All your violence will have no effect on me, all your wealth will be powerless, all your words will not deceive me, all your sighs and tears will not move me. If the man my parents give me as a husband were to prevail upon me in this way, I should bow to his will, and my will would not exceed the bounds of his; so, if my honour were secured in this way, even if my pleasure were not, I should willingly surrender to you what you are striving so hard to attain. I have said all this because it is unthinkable that any man who is not legitimately married to me can gain anything from me."

' "If that's all you're concerned about, lovely Dorotea," (for this is the name of the hapless woman you see before you) the dutiless gentleman exclaimed, "look here, I'll give you my hand in marriage, and let the witnesses be heaven, from which nothing's hidden, and this image of our Lady you've got here." '

When Cardenio heard her say that her name was Dorotea, he showed fresh agitation as he found his original suspicions confirmed, but he didn't interrupt her story, being anxious to hear the ending, which he almost knew already.

'Dorotea is your name, madam? I have heard of another Dorotea who, perhaps, has suffered similar misfortunes. Please continue, and in due course I shall tell you of things that will amaze you as much as they will arouse your compassion.'

Dorotea considered Cardenio's words and his strange, ragged clothes, and asked him, if he had any information about her affairs, to tell her immediately, because if fortune had allowed her to retain one good quality it was her determination to face up to any disaster that could befall her, in the certain belief that none could make matters any worse than they already were.

'I would not omit to tell you, madam,' replied Cardenio, 'what I think, were I certain that it is the truth; but the opportunity to do so still remains, and you do not need to know quite yet.'

'Be that as it may,' replied Dorotea, 'what happens next in my story is that Don Fernando picked up a holy image that I had in my room and made it the witness of our wedding. With persuasive words and extraordinary vows he gave me his word of marriage even though, before he finished speaking, I told him to think what he was doing and consider how angry his father would be when he discovered that he was married to a peasant girl, one of his tenants; I told him not to be blinded by my beauty, such as it was, for it wasn't sufficient to provide an excuse for his blunder; I told him that if he wished to do me a kindness, because of his love for me, he should allow my life to run a course appropriate to my rank, because such uneven matches never retain for long the happiness of their first days.

'I put all these arguments to him, and many others that I don't remember, but they were powerless to make him change his mind: the man who never intends to pay isn't worried about any problems when he strikes his bargain. Then I reasoned to myself like this:

' "All right then, I shan't be the first girl to rise by means of marriage from humble to high estate, nor will Don Fernando be the first man to be led by beauty or, more likely, by blind desire, into taking a wife beneath his rank. Well, since I'm not going to be changing the world or creating some new custom, it'll be best to accept this honour that fortune's offering me, even if the love this man professes does last no longer than it takes him to have his way – for, after all, in God's eyes I'll be his wife. And if I scorn and reject him, I can see he's in such a state that he'll ignore his obligations and use violence, and I'll be dishonoured and left without the excuses that anyone who doesn't know how innocently I have come to this pass would otherwise have made for me. Because what arguments will be powerful enough to persuade my parents and others that this gentleman entered my room without my consent?"

'I turned all these diverse considerations over in my mind in an instant, but what most affected me and pushed me towards what was, although I didn't realize it, my ruin were Don Fernando's vows, the witnesses he invoked, the tears he shed and, in general, his gentlemanly behaviour, which, accompanied by so many signs of true love, would have conquered any heart as fancy-free and over-protected as mine. I called out to my maid, to have a witness on earth as well as the heavenly ones. Don Fernando repeated and confirmed his oaths yet again; he added a few more saints to his list of witnesses; he called down a thousand curses on himself if he failed to carry out his promises; he again moistened his eyes and deepened his sighs; he pressed me tighter in his arms, from which he'd never released me. And then my maid left, and I stopped being one, and he started being a deceiver and a traitor.

'The day after the night of my undoing didn't come as soon as I think Don Fernando wanted, because once lust has been satisfied the greatest pleasure is to escape from the scene of the fun. I say this because Don Fernando was in a great hurry to leave, and with the help of my maid –

she was the one who'd let him in – he was out in the street before daybreak. And when he said goodbye he also said (though with less ardour and vehemence than at the beginning) that I should feel certain of his faithfulness, and that his oaths were firm and true; and as further confirmation of his words he took a fine ring from his finger and put it on mine. So off he went, and I was left feeling I don't know whether sad or happy, but what I do know is that I was confused and pensive and almost beside myself at what had just happened; and I didn't have the heart, or it didn't occur to me, to scold my maid for her treachery in letting Don Fernando into my room, because I still couldn't decide whether what had just happened to me was good or bad. When he left I told him that he could come to me on other nights in the same way, until he wanted our marriage to be made public, for I was now his. But he only returned once more, on the following night, and I never set eyes on him for over a month, either in the street or at church – it was in vain that I searched and searched for him, even though I knew he was in town and went hunting (a sport he was very fond of) nearly every day.

'I well remember those were dismal days and wretched hours, and I also remember that I then began to doubt and even disbelieve Don Fernando's faithfulness, and I remember, too, that my maid did then hear the words of reproof for her effrontery that she hadn't heard before; and I remember that I had to control my tears and the looks on my face, so that my parents wouldn't ask me why I was unhappy and force me to invent a lie. But all this came to a sudden end as the moment arrived when the proprieties were cast aside and all thoughts of honour were abandoned, and when patience ran out and the secrets of my heart were revealed. And this happened because a few days later news spread through town that in a nearby city Don Fernando had married a young woman of great beauty and noble family, although not so very wealthy that her ›dowry could have led her to aspire to such a fine match. It was said that her name was Luscinda, and that all sorts of amazing things had happened at her wedding.'

When Cardenio heard Luscinda's name his only reaction was to hunch his shoulders, bite his lips, arch his eyebrows and, a few seconds later, let two springs of tears well from his eyes. But this didn't stop Dorotea from continuing her story and saying:

'When this sad news reached my ears, I could hardly say that it chilled my heart – on the contrary, my heart burned in such rage and fury that I was close to running out into the street to proclaim the evil treachery that had been done me. But the fury abated for the time being when I had the idea of doing what I did that very night: I dressed in these clothes, given me by a herdboy – as farmers call them – in my father's service, whom I told of my misfortune and asked to go with me to the city where I believed my enemy was to be found. Once he'd reproached me for my rashness and censured my decision and seen that I was resolute, he offered to go with me to the end of the world, as he put it. I immediately packed some of my clothes into a cotton pillow-case, together with jewels and money, to provide for any eventuality. And in the silence of that night, without saying anything to my treacherous maid, I left home, accompanied by my new servant and by many anxious thoughts, and I started out on foot for the city, lent wings by my need to be there, if not to prevent what I assumed was already done, then at least to make Don Fernando tell me how his conscience had allowed him to do it.

'In two and a half days I was there, and on the outskirts of the city I asked the way to Luscinda's parents' house, and the first man I asked replied with more details than I should have liked to hear. He told me where the house was and he told me everything that had happened at the wedding, an event of such notoriety in the city that groups of gossips had formed throughout it to discuss the details. He told me that on the night when Don Fernando married Luscinda, she fell into a deep faint after saying "I will", and, when her husband went to unbutton her bodices to give her air, he found a note written in her own hand, in which she declared that she couldn't be Don Fernando's wife, because she was already married to Cardenio, who the man told me was a noble gentleman of that city; and that if she'd agreed to be Don Fernando's wife, it was only so as not to disobey her parents. In short, he said that the note made it clear that she'd intended to kill herself once the ceremony was over, and set out her reasons for doing so, all of which is said to be confirmed by a dagger found in her clothing. When Don Fernando read the note he concluded that Luscinda had deceived and slighted and mocked him, and he fell upon her while she was still unconscious and tried to stab her with the dagger they'd found on her, and would have done so if her parents and the others hadn't stopped him. I was told more: Don Fernando left straight away, and Luscinda didn't recover from her faint until the following day, when she told her parents that she was truly married to that fellow Cardenio I mentioned before.

'I discovered still more: the said Cardenio, they claimed, had been present at the wedding, and once he'd seen Luscinda married, something he hadn't been expecting, he went from the city in despair, leaving her a letter in which he spoke of the wrong she'd done him and said he was going where no one could find him. Everybody in the city knew all about it, and everybody in the city was talking about it, and their tongues wagged even faster when it became known that Luscinda had gone missing from her parents' house and from the city, and wasn't anywhere to be found, and her parents were out of their minds with worry, and didn't know what they could do to trace her. This knowledge revived my hopes, and I thought it was better not to have found Don Fernando than to have found him properly married, because it meant that the door to reparation hadn't slammed on me; and it occurred to me that it might have been heaven that had put this impediment in the way of the second marriage, to make him remember his obligation to the first one and realize that he was a Christian and should have more regard for his soul than for mere human concerns. I turned all these ideas over in my imagination and tried to comfort myself by inventing feeble, distant hopes to sustain a life that I now abhor.

'So there I was in the city, not knowing what to do, because I couldn't find Don Fernando, when I heard a town-crier announcing a large reward for anyone who found me, stating my age and describing the clothes I was wearing. I heard someone saying it was rumoured I'd eloped with the lad who'd come with me, and this cut me to the quick, showing how low my credit had fallen – as if it weren't bad enough to have lost it by running away, everybody knew whom I'd run away with, someone so mean and unworthy of my affections. As soon as I heard the announcement I left the city with my servant, who was beginning to show signs of wavering in the loyalty he'd promised me; and that night, fearful of being discovered, we took refuge in the most densely wooded part of this sierra.

'But it's often said that misfortunes never come singly, and that the end of one is often the beginning of another still worse; and that's what happened to me, because once we were in these wilds my worthy servant, until then faithful and reliable, tried to take advantage of the opportunity that he thought these lonely places offered him, and, prompted more by his own wickedness than by my beauty, and bereft of all shame, fear of God and respect for me, he asked me for my love; and when he found that I responded to his insolence with just contempt, he abandoned the entreaties with which he'd thought he'd have his way, and turned to violence. But righteous heaven, which seldom if ever fails to watch over and favour good intentions, favoured mine, and with the little strength I have, and yet with little difficulty, I pushed him over a precipice, where I left him, whether dead or alive I don't know. And then, faster than could have been expected from my consternation and exhaustion, I made my way into these mountains, with no other thought or plan than to hide here from my father and from those whom he'd sent to look for me.

'I don't know how many months ago it was that I arrived here with this idea and came across a herdsman who took me as his servant to a village in the depths of the sierra, and I've been working for him as a herdboy all this time, always trying to stay out in the open so as to hide these locks of mine that have now so unexpectedly betrayed me. But all my cunning and all my precautions were futile, because my master found out that I'm not a man, and was seized with the same wicked desire as my servant; and since fortune doesn't always send the evil complete with its remedy, I couldn't find any precipice or ravine where I could put my master out of his misery, as I had my servant; and what seemed to be the lesser evil was to run away and hide once more in these wilds, rather than try my strength or my pretexts against him. So, as I said, I took to the forest again to look for a spot where I could, unhindered, implore heaven with sighs and tears to take pity on my plight, and grant me help and strength either to escape from it or to end my life in this wilderness, so that no memory remains of an unhappy creature who, through no fault of her own, must have provided grist for gossip in the place where she lives, and all around.'

CHAPTER XXIX

*Concerning the beautiful Dorotea's intelligence and other
delightful and entertaining matters*

'This, gentlemen, is the true history of my tragedy. Now you must judge
whether you mightn't have expected even more sighs than you have
listened to, even more words than you have heard, even more tears than
have fallen from my eyes; and, if you consider the nature of my misfortune,
you'll see that consolation is futile, because there is no possible remedy.
All I beg of you – and it's something that you can easily do, and should
do – is to tell me where I can spend my life without being tormented by
my dread of being found by those who are looking for me; because
although I know that my parents' deep love is an assurance of a kind
welcome from them, I'm filled with such shame just to think that I must
appear before them so different from how they had taken me to be, that
I prefer to banish myself for ever from their sight rather than look them
in the face in the knowledge that they see me deprived of the purity that
they must have expected me to defend.'

She fell silent, and her face was suffused with a colour that showed the
suffering and the shame in her soul. Those who had been listening to her
felt in their own souls as much pity as amazement at her misfortune, and,
although the priest was about to console and counsel her, Cardenio took
the initiative and said:

'And so you're the lovely Dorotea, the only daughter of wealthy
Clenardo?'

Dorotea was astonished to hear her father's name spoken by such a
low fellow – Cardenio's dress has already been described. So she said:

'And who might you be, my good man, to know my father's name? If
I remember rightly, I have not mentioned it once in the whole course of
my tale of woe.'

'I, madam,' replied Cardenio, 'am that unfortunate man to whom, as
you have told us, Luscinda said she was married. I am the unhappy
Cardenio, whom the villainy of the person who has reduced you to your
present state has left as you can see me, clothed in rags, half naked,

deprived of all human consolation and, what is worst of all, deprived of my reason, because I only enjoy its use when heaven sees fit to let me have it for a while. I, Dorotea, am the man who witnessed the wrong done me by Don Fernando, the man who stopped to hear Luscinda say "I will." I am the man who lacked the courage to wait to see how her fainting fit ended, or what were the consequences of the discovery of the note in her bodice, because my heart couldn't bear so much misfortune all at once; and so I abandoned patience and I abandoned her house, and I left a letter with someone with whom I'd often stayed, asking him to place it in Luscinda's hands, and I came away to these empty places, intending to end my life, which I hated from that moment as my mortal enemy. But fate wouldn't deprive me of it, and was content to deprive me of my senses, perhaps to save me for the good fortune of meeting you; because if everything that you have said is true, as I believe it is, it might even be that heaven has in store for us a happier ending to our misfortunes than we think. For given that Luscinda can't marry Don Fernando, because she's mine, and he can't marry her, because he's yours, as she has made perfectly clear, we can well hope that heaven will restore to us what is ours, because it's all still valid, it hasn't been alienated or damaged. And since we do have this consolation, not born of remote hopes, nor founded on wild imaginings, I entreat you, madam, to reconsider your original decision, as I shall mine, and prepare yourself to expect better fortune; for I swear by the faith of a gentleman and a Christian that I won't forsake you until I see you married to Don Fernando, and that, if I can't persuade him with arguments to acknowledge what he owes you, I will make use of the privilege to which every gentleman is entitled, and demand satisfaction for the wrong he has done you, setting aside the injuries he has done me, the avenging of which I leave to heaven so as to be able to attend to yours here on earth.'

Cardenio's words completed Dorotea's amazement and, not knowing how to thank him for such generous offers, she tried to seize his feet and kiss them, but he wouldn't allow it, and the priest replied on her behalf as well as his own and praised Cardenio's good thinking; and he particularly begged, advised and encouraged them to return with him to his village, where they would be able to stock up with all they needed, and where a method could be devised for finding Don Fernando, or restoring Dorotea to her parents, or doing whatever seemed best. Cardenio and Dorotea thanked him and accepted his kind offer. The barber, who had remained in silent bewilderment throughout, also spoke some fine words and offered with no less goodwill than the priest to serve them in whatever way he could. He went on to give them a brief account of what had brought him and his friend there, of Don Quixote's strange madness, and of how they were waiting for his squire, who'd gone in search of him. Cardenio recalled, as if from a dream, his fight with Don Quixote, and told the others about it, but he couldn't say what the cause of their disagreement had been.

And now they heard a shout and realized that it came from Sancho Panza, who, not finding them where he'd left them, was calling out to them. They went to meet him and in answer to their enquiries about Don Quixote he said he'd found him dressed only in his shirt, skinny, pale and half dead with hunger, and sighing for his lady Dulcinea; and that although he'd told him that she'd ordered him to leave that place and go back to El Toboso, where she was waiting for him, he'd replied that he was resolved not to appear before her beauteousness until such time as he should have performed such exploits as would render him worthy of her favour. And if all that palaver went on much longer, he was running the risk of never getting to be an emperor, as he damn well should, or even an archbishop, which was the least you could expect. So they had to put a scheme together to get him out of there.

The priest replied that Sancho mustn't worry – they would indeed get him out of there, whether he liked it or not. Then the priest told Cardenio and Dorotea about the plan for curing Don Quixote, or at least taking him back home. To which Dorotea replied that she could play the damsel in distress better than the barber, and, what was more, she had with her some clothes for making her performance totally convincing, and they could trust her to play the role precisely as was necessary for success in their plans, because she'd read lots of books of chivalry and knew exactly how damsels in distress turned their hands to begging favours of knights errant.

'Well, all we have to do now,' said the priest, 'is to put the plan into action without delay: fortune's clearly on my side, because a door has begun to open so unexpectedly to a solution to your problems, my friends, and the door that we needed has also been provided.'

Dorotea now took out of her pillow-case a frock of fine camlet and a bright green shawl, and out of a casket a necklace and other jewels, and in an instant she put them on and looked like a rich, fine lady. She said she'd brought all this and more from home, to provide for any eventuality, but hadn't needed to use it yet. They were all charmed by her grace, elegance and loveliness, and convinced that Don Fernando was a man of little judgement to reject such a beauty. But the person who was most amazed was Sancho Panza, because he thought, and he was right, that in all the days of his born life he'd never seen such a lovely creature; so he begged the priest to tell him who that very beauteous lady was, and what she was looking for in those God-forsaken parts.

'This beautiful lady, brother Sancho,' replied the priest, 'is no less a personage than the heiress in the direct male line of the great kingdom of Micomicón, and she's come in search of your master to beg a boon of him: that he would redress a wrong and grievance done unto her by an evil giant; and, attracted by the fame as an excellent knight that your master has conquered over the entire face of the earth, this princess has travelled here all the way from Guinea to find him.'

'That's good searching and good finding,' Sancho Panza interrupted, 'and even better if my master's lucky enough to redress that grievance and right that wrong by killing that bastard of a giant you just mentioned, and he will kill him if he catches up with him, so long as he isn't a ghost that is, because my master can't cope with ghosts. But there's just one thing I'd like to ask you to do, reverend sir, among others, so as to stop my master from getting the urge to become an archbishop, which is what I'm most frightened of – advise him to marry this here princess straight away, and then he won't be allowed to take archbishop's orders and then it'll be easy for him to get his empire and for me to get everything I want, because I've looked into it and I've worked out that it won't suit me for my master to be an archbishop, because I'm useless to the Church, being as I am married, and to go getting dispensations to let me have a living, with a wife and children and all, would be an endless job. So you see, sir, everything hangs on my master marrying that lady right away – nobody's told me what her name is yet, so I can't call her by it.'

'Her name,' replied the priest, 'is the Princess Micomicona, as indeed it would be, seeing that her kingdom is called Micomicón.'

'You're right there,' replied Sancho, 'because I've often known people to take their surnames from the towns where they were born, and call themselves Pedro de Alcalá, Juan de Úbeda, Diego de Valladolid and the like, and they must do the same in Guinea – queens taking their names from their kingdoms, I mean.'

'That must indeed be so,' said the priest, 'and as for your master's marrying, I shall do everything in my power to bring it about.'

This left Sancho as content as the priest was amazed at his simplicity and at the hold his master's nonsenses had taken of his imagination, because Sancho really did believe that Don Quixote was going to become an emperor.

By now Dorotea had mounted the priest's mule and the barber had stuck the ox-tail beard on to his face, and they told Sancho to lead them to Don Quixote, and warned him not to reveal that he knew the priest or the barber, because his master's becoming an emperor depended on his not recognizing them. But neither the priest nor Cardenio would go with them, because Cardenio didn't want Don Quixote to remember their fight, and the priest's presence wasn't needed yet. So they sent the others on ahead and followed slowly on foot. The priest didn't omit to tell Dorotea what she had to do, to which she replied that they needn't worry, everything would be done exactly right, just as the chivalry books described and demanded.

They'd have gone a couple of miles when they caught sight of Don Quixote amidst a maze of rocks, wearing his clothes now but not his armour; and as soon as Dorotea saw him and was informed by Sancho who he was, she whipped her palfrey onwards, followed by the bushy-bearded barber. When they reached Don Quixote, the squire sprang from his mule and ran to help Dorotea to dismount, and she did so most gracefully and fell on her knees before the knees of Don Quixote; and although he was striving to bring her to her feet she remained kneeling, and spake thus:

'I will not arise from this spot, O valorous and redoubtable knight, until your benevolence and courtesy vouchsafe me a boon that will redound to the honour and glory of your person and to the weal of the most disconsolate and aggrieved damsel that ever the sun beheld. And if it be that the strength of your formidable arm is correspondent to the voice of your immortal fame, you are obliged to favour this unhappy damsel who comes from far distant lands, attracted by the odour of your celebrated name, to seek from you a remedy for her woes.'

'I will not answer you one word, most beauteous lady,' answered Don Quixote, 'nor will I hear one circumstance more of your affairs, until you arise from the ground.'

'I will not arise, sir,' replied the damsel in distress, 'ere of your courtesy the boon I crave is first vouchsafed me.'

'I do indeed vouchsafe and grant it you,' replied Don Quixote, 'provided that it does not lead me to act to the detriment or disservice of my king, my country or her who holds the key of my heart and my liberty.'

'It is not to the detriment or disservice of any of those you've just mentioned, my good sir,' replied the doleful damsel.

And at this point Sancho Panza sidled up to his master and muttered in his ear:

'You can easily grant her this here boon she's craving, sir, it isn't anything special, only killing some enormous giant, and this here woman craving it is the high-up princess Micomicona, the queen of the great kingdom of Micomicón in Ethiopia.'

'Whosoever she may be,' replied Don Quixote, 'I will do my duty, as my conscience dictates, in conformity to what I have professed.'

And turning to the damsel, he said:

'Arise, arise, most beauteous lady, for I vouchsafe whatever boon you may wish to crave of me.'

'Well, what it is I'm craving,' said the damsel, 'is that your magnanimous person will come with me right now to where I'm going to take you, and will promise not to get involved in any other adventure or similar activity until you've taken vengeance for me on a traitor who, flouting all human and divine law, has usurped my kingdom.'

'I repeat that I do vouchsafe it,' replied Don Quixote, 'and so you can, my lady, from this day forward, dispel the melancholy that oppresses you, and allow your fainting hopes to gain fresh strength and vigour; for, with God's help and that of my arm, you shall soon see yourself restored to your kingdom and seated on the throne of your ancient and high estate, in spite and in defiance of all the wretches who would gainsay it. And let us set to work forthwith; for, as the saying goes, delays are dangerous.'

The damsel in distress strove and struggled to kiss his hands, but Don

Quixote, always a gallant and courteous knight, would by no means consent to this; on the contrary, he brought her to her feet and embraced her with great courtesy and gallantry, and he ordered Sancho to check Rocinante's girths and to arm him without a moment's delay. Sancho took the armour down from the tree on which it was hanging like some trophy, checked the nag's girths and in an instant slipped the armour on to his master, who said:

'Let us go from hence in God's name to succour this great lady.'

The barber was still on his knees, at great pains to smother his laughter and to stop his beard from falling off, which could have put paid to all their fine plans; and seeing that the boon had been granted and that Don Quixote was preparing so diligently to go and keep his word, he stood up and offered his free hand to his lady, and the two men helped her on to the mule. Then Don Quixote climbed on to Rocinante, and the barber settled himself on his mount, and Sancho was left on his feet, a predicament that renewed his grief for the loss of his dun; but he bore it all with good cheer because he considered that his master was at last well on the way to being an emperor, indeed right on the verge of it, because he was definitely going to marry that princess and become, at the very least, the King of Micomicón. He was only worried by the thought that this kingdom was in the land of negroes and that all the people he was going to be given as vassals would be black, but his imagination soon worked out a good solution, as he said to himself:

'Who cares if my vassals are negroes? All I'll have to do is ship them over here to Spain, sell them for hard cash, buy myself a title or some official position or other, and live at my ease for the rest of my days. Oh yes, I'm going to be caught napping, I am, and I won't have the wit or the savvy to see to things and sell thirty or ten thousand vassals in the twinkling of an eye, I won't! By God I'll shift them, as a job lot or however I can, and they can be as black as they like, I'll soon turn them into yellow gold and white silver! Come on, come on, I'm an innocent little thumb-sucker, I am!'

He was so engrossed in these thoughts, and so happy with them, that he forgot all about the distress of having to walk.

Cardenio and the priest were watching this scene from behind some bushes, wondering how they could contrive to join company with the others, but the priest was a great schemer and soon thought of a way: he took a pair of scissors out of their case and whipped Cardenio's beard off, and dressed him in a pale brown cape that the priest had been wearing, and also gave him his black cloak, which left the priest in his doublet and hose; and the transformation of Cardenio was such that he wouldn't have known himself if he'd looked in a mirror. Although the others had ridden on while Cardenio and the priest had been disguising themselves, it was easy for these two to reach the highway first, because the undergrowth and the uneven surface made the progress of riders slower than that of walkers. So they waited on the plain where it joins the sierra and, as soon as Don Quixote and his companions emerged, the priest stood gazing at him, indicating that he thought he knew him, and after a good long look he hurried over with open arms, crying:

'Well met, well met, O mirror of chivalry, my good neighbour Don Quixote de la Mancha, the very flower of politeness, the succour of the needy, the quintessence of knights errant!'

While he said this he was embracing the left knee of Don Quixote, who, astonished at what he was seeing and hearing the man say and do, peered down at him and eventually recognized him, and was full of wonder when he did so, and struggled to dismount; but the priest wouldn't let him, which led Don Quixote to say:

'Pray permit me to alight, sir, for it is not fit that I should be on horseback while so reverend a person as you is on foot.'

'I will by no means consent to that,' said the priest. 'You stay on your horse, for on your horse you carry out the greatest exploits and adventures that our age has ever beheld, and for me, although an unworthy priest, it will be enough to get up behind one of these gentlemen riding with you on their mules, if it isn't too much trouble for them. And it will even seem to me as if I'm prancing along on the steed Pegasus, or on the zebra or warhorse of the famous Moor Muzaraque, who lies to this day enchanted on the great hill of Zulema, not far from the splendid town of Compluto.'[1]

'That solution had not occurred to me, reverend sir,' replied Don Quixote, 'and I know that my lady the princess will, for my sake, be glad to order her squire to accommodate you on the saddle of his mule, and he shall ride behind you, so long as the mule can withstand it.'

'Yes, it can, I think,' replied the princess, 'and I know that I shan't need to order my dear squire to do this, because he's so courteous, not to say courtly, that he won't allow a man of the cloth to walk when he can ride.'

'Quite right,' replied the barber.

And alighting in an instant he offered his saddle to the priest, who accepted it without having to be asked a second time. But the problem was that as the barber was clambering up on to the crupper, the mule, a hired one, which is the same as saying a bad one, reared its hind quarters and sent its back legs flying in the air, and if it had sent them at Master Nicolás's chest or head he'd have sent Don Quixote and their trip to fetch him to the devil. Master Nicolás was so frightened that he tumbled to the ground, taking so little care of his beard that it fell off, and when he noticed his beardlessness all he could think of doing was to clutch both hands to his face and cry out that his teeth had been kicked in. When Don Quixote saw that hank of beard-hair, bloodlessly detached from its jaw and lying far from the fallen squire, he said:

'Good God, this is indeed a great miracle! The mule has plucked his beard clean from his face, just as if it had been shaved off!'

The priest, seeing that his plot was at risk of being discovered, snatched up the beard, hurried with it to where Master Nicolás lay still moaning, clasped the barber's head to his breast and stuck the beard back in place as he muttered some words that he described as a certain spell for beard-reattachment, as they would soon see; and having performed this operation he stepped aside, and the squire was as whole and as bearded as before, which astonished Don Quixote, who begged the priest to teach him the spell as soon as he had a moment to spare, for he reasoned that its power must extend beyond beard-reattachment since it was obvious that where a beard had been ripped off the flesh must be left torn and raw: so, since the spell had brought about a complete cure, it followed that it wasn't only good for beards.

'Quite right,' said the priest, and then promised to teach it to him at the earliest opportunity.

They all agreed that the priest would ride the mule to begin with and that the three of them would take turns on it until they reached the inn, which must be a half-a-dozen miles away. So with three of them mounted (Don Quixote, the princess and the priest) and three of them on foot

(Cardenio, the barber and Sancho Panza) Don Quixote said to the damsel:

'My lady: Your Highness must direct us whithersoever it most pleases you to go.'

Before she could reply, the priest said:

'Towards which kingdom does Your Excellency wish to direct us? Is it, perchance, the kingdom of Micomicón? I think it must be, or else I am a poor judge of kingdoms.'

She knew what she was doing and understood that it was up to her to agree, so she said:

'Yes, sir, my way lies towards that kingdom.'

'If that's the case,' said the priest, 'we shall pass through my home town, and from there you must head towards Cartagena, where you can embark, all being well; and if there's a favourable wind, a calm sea and no storms, in a little less than nine years you might be in sight of the great Urinals I mean Urals, which are slightly more than one hundred days' journey on this side of Your Highness's kingdom.'

'No, you are mistaken, my dear sir,' she said, 'because I left there not two years ago and I haven't really had any fine weather at all; but despite all that, I have succeeded in seeing what I so longed to see – Don Quixote de la Mancha, the news of whose deeds reached my ears as soon as I set foot in Spain and encouraged me to come in search of him to commend myself to his courtesy and commit my just cause to the might of his invincible arm.'

'That is quite enough: no more praise of me,' said Don Quixote, 'for I hate all flattery and, even if this is not flattery, such talk still offends my chaste ears. What I can say, my lady, is that whether I am mighty or not, such might as I do or do not possess shall be employed in your service even unto death; and now, leaving all that aside until later, I would beg you, reverend sir, to tell me what has brought you into these parts alone, without servants, and so lightly clad that you quite alarm me.'

'My reply will be brief,' the priest replied. 'You must know, sir, that I was on my way with Master Nicolás, our friend and barber, to Seville to collect some money sent me by a relative who settled in South America many years ago – no inconsiderable sum, in fact it was more than sixty thousand pesos in pure silver bars, worth double that amount once alloyed and coined; and yesterday, as we were riding through these parts, four highwaymen waylaid us and literally fleeced us; and so, finding himself without a beard, the barber thought it better to wear a false one, and they even left this young fellow here' (pointing to Cardenio) 'in the state in which you see him. And the best part of it is that everybody in these parts is saying that the men who attacked us were from a chain-gang that's said to have been released, almost on this very spot, by a man who's so brave that, in spite of the sergeant and the guards, he freed them all; and there can't be the slightest doubt that the fellow must be out of his mind, or perhaps he's another villain as bad as them, or someone without a soul or a conscience, letting the wolf loose among the sheep, the fox among the chickens, the fly among the honeycombs. He has defrauded justice and flown in the face of his king and natural lord, because he has flouted his king's just commands. He has, furthermore, robbed the galleys of their engines and disturbed the Holy Brotherhood, which had been reposing for many years. And he has done a deed that will lose him his soul and gain nothing for his body.'

Sancho had told the priest and the barber all about the adventure of the convicts, brought to such a glorious conclusion by his master, and this was why the priest had now laid it on so thick, to see what Don Quixote would do and say: his colour changed with every word, but he didn't dare admit that he had been those good people's liberator.

'These, then,' said the priest, 'were the men who robbed us. May God in his infinite mercy forgive whoever it was that prevented them from being taken to the punishment that they deserved.'

CHAPTER XXX

Concerning the amusing and ingenious plan to extricate our enamoured knight from the cruel penance that he had imposed upon himself

The priest had hardly finished speaking when Sancho said:

'Well by my faith, reverend sir, the one who did that there deed was my master, and not for any want of me warning him to be careful what he was getting up to, and telling him it was a sin to set them free, because they were all there for being terrible villains.'

'You blockhead!' exploded Don Quixote. 'It is not the responsibility of knights errant to discover whether the afflicted, the enchained and the oppressed whom they encounter on the road are reduced to these circumstances and suffer this distress for their vices, or for their virtues: the knight's sole responsibility is to succour them as people in need, having eyes only for their sufferings, not for their misdeeds. I came across a rosary of angry, wretched men, I did with them what my religion requires of me, and nothing else is any concern of mine; and to anyone who thinks ill of it – saving, reverend sir, your holy dignity and honourable person – I say that he is no judge of matters of chivalry, and that he is lying like a bastard and a son of a whore, and I swear by my gospel-oath that I will make him acknowledge this with my sword, at length and in extenso.'

As he said this he steadied himself in his stirrups and pulled his steel cap down tight, because the barber's basin, which in his reckoning was Mambrino's helmet, was hanging from the pommel of his saddle, awaiting repair after its maltreatment by the convicts. Dorotea was sharp-witted and full of fun, she knew all about Don Quixote's strange turns and that everyone was teasing him except Sancho Panza, and she didn't want to be left out, so seeing that he was in a temper she said:

'Sir knight, pray remember the boon that you have granted me and remember, too, that by its terms you cannot become involved in any other adventure, however urgent it may be; so calm your breast, for if the priest had known that it was your unconquered arm that freed the convicts, he would have put three stitches through his lips and would even have bitten his tongue three times rather than utter a single word that redounded to your disparagement.'

'I swear that's true,' said the priest, 'and I'd have pulled half my moustache off as well.'

'I will be silent, my lady,' said Don Quixote, 'and repress the just indignation that had risen in my breast, and I will ride with you in the utmost peace and quiet until I have accomplished the promised boon; but in return for my firm resolve I entreat you to tell me, if it is not too grievous for you, what is your woe and how many, who and of what sort are the people on whom I am, on your behalf, to take due, sufficient and complete revenge.'

'I'll be happy to do so,' replied Dorotea, 'so long as it doesn't bother you to hear about afflictions and misfortunes.'

'Not at all, my lady,' replied Don Quixote.

To which Dorotea answered:

'That being so, will you all give me your attention, please?'

She hadn't finished saying this when Cardenio and the barber hurried to her side, eager to hear how this quick-witted woman would go about making up her story, and so did Sancho, as fully taken in by her as his master. And once she'd made herself comfortable in her saddle and prepared herself by coughing and taking other preliminary precautions, she began to make merry:

'First of all, I'd like you to know, gentlemen, that my name is . . .'

And here she hesitated, because she'd forgotten the name with which the priest had christened her; but realizing what the trouble was he came to the rescue and said:

'It is no wonder, my lady, that Your Highness should be overcome by confusion and embarrassment as you relate your misfortunes, for their ravages often deprive victims of their memory to such an extent that they cannot even remember their own names, as has just happened to Your Majesty, who has forgotten that your name is Princess Micomicona, the legitimate heiress to the great kingdom of Micomicón; and with the help of this prompting Your Highness will now, no doubt, be able to recall to your buffeted memory everything you wish to tell us.'

'Right you are,' replied the damsel, 'and I don't think any more prompting's going to be needed for me to sail the flagship of my true history to a safe harbour. My father, the King, whose name was Tinacrio the Sage,[1] was very learned in what are named the magic arts, and he divined that my mother, whose name was Queen Jaramilla, was going to die before him, and that a little after that he too would depart this life and I'd be left an orphan. But he used to say that this didn't worry him as much as having discovered for a certain fact that an enormous giant, the lord of a big island almost bordering on our kingdom, whose name is Pandafilando of the Grim Visage, because it's a well-known fact that, although his eyes are perfectly normal, he always looks at you skew-whiff, as if he was cross-eyed, and he does this out of spite and to strike fear and terror into those he's looking at . . . I was saying that my father found out that as soon as this giant knew I was an orphan he was going to invade my kingdom at the head of a great army and take it from me, without leaving me so much as a tiny village to retire to, but that I could avoid all this ruin and disaster if I agreed to marry him; yet my father's understanding of the matter was that I would never agree to so ill-assorted a match, and in this he was quite right, because it has never even occurred to me to marry that giant, or any other, however vast and enormous he might be. My father also said that when, after his death, I saw that Pandafilando was beginning to invade my kingdom, I shouldn't stay to defend it, because that would be my ruin, but that I should let him have it without offering any resistance, if I wanted to avoid the death and total destruction of my good and loyal subjects, because I wasn't going to be able to defend myself against the giant's diabolical power. Instead I should set out immediately with a few followers for Spain, where I'd find the solution to my troubles as soon as I found a knight errant whose fame would have extended by this time over the whole kingdom and whose name would be, if I remember rightly, Don Biscuit, or Don Fixit, or Don Riskit.'

'Don Quixote he must have said, lady,' Sancho interrupted, 'also known as the Knight of the Sorry Face.'

'Right you are,' said Dorotea. 'And my father said something else, too: that this knight would be tall and thin-faced and that on the right side of his body under his left shoulder-blade, or thereabouts, he'd have a brown mole with long stiff hairs growing out of it.'

When Don Quixote heard this he said to his squire:

'Here, Sancho my son, help me to undress – I want to see if I am the knight that the wise king prophesied.'

'But why get undressed?' asked Dorotea.

'To see whether I bear the mole to which your father referred,' replied Don Quixote.

'There isn't any need for you to get undressed,' said Sancho, 'I know you've got a mole just like that halfway down your backbone, the sign of a strong man.'

'That's enough for me,' said Dorotea, 'there isn't any call to bother about such trifles among friends, and who cares whether it's on his shoulder or on his backbone – he's got a mole, and that's all that matters, wherever it is, because it's all the same flesh; and it's clear that my good father was right in everything he prophesied, and that I am right to put myself in the hands of Don Quixote, who is definitely the man my father said, because his face, at least, exactly matches what is trumpeted about this knight not only in Spain but throughout the length and breadth of La Mancha – no sooner had I landed at Osuna than I heard accounts of so many deeds of his that my heart told me straight away that this was the very man I was looking for.'

'But how could you have landed at Osuna, my lady?' asked Don Quixote. 'Osuna is not on the sea.'

Before Dorotea could reply, the priest stepped in:

'The Princess must mean that after she had landed at Malaga, the first place where she heard about you was Osuna.'

'Yes, that's what I meant,' said Dorotea.

'And that's more like it,' said the priest, 'and do continue, Your Majesty.'

'There's nothing more to say,' replied Dorotea, 'except that now I've had the great good fortune to find Don Quixote, I already look upon myself as queen and mistress of all my kingdom, for he, in his courtesy and magnificence, has granted me my boon and will go with me wherever I take him, and that will be to where he'll find himself face to face with Pandafilando of the Grim Visage, so that he can kill him and restore to me what has been so wrongfully usurped; and all this is going to work out to a T, because it's what my good father Tinacrio the Sage prophesied, and he also left it written in Chaldean or Greek letters that I can't read that if this knight in his prophecy, once he'd slit the giant's throat, wanted to marry me, I must immediately and without demur submit to be his lawful wife, and give him possession of my kingdom and my person.'

'What do you think now, friend Sancho?' Don Quixote exclaimed. 'Did you hear that? Did I not tell you so? You see, now we have our kingdom to reign over and our queen to marry!'

'I should damn well say so,' said Sancho, 'and the devil take the bugger that wouldn't marry her as soon as old Pandoflando's gullet's slit! And she's a bit of all right, she is, the Queen! I wouldn't complain if the fleas in my bed were like her!'

And as he said this he showed how delighted he was by leaping into the air a couple of times and slapping his shoe as he did so, and then he grasped the reins of Dorotea's mule to make it stop, threw himself to his knees before her and begged her to let him kiss her hands to show that he accepted her as his queen and mistress. How could the onlookers have failed to laugh as they witnessed the madness of the master and the simplicity of the servant? Dorotea held out her hands and promised to make him a great lord in her kingdom, as soon as heaven was so benevolent as to put her back in possession of it. Sancho expressed his thanks in words that sent them into fresh fits of laughter.

'This, gentlemen,' Dorotea continued, 'is my history. It only remains for me to tell you that of all the attendants I brought with me from my kingdom I have none left except this well-bearded squire, because the others drowned in a violent storm that overtook us within sight of harbour, and by some miracle he and I reached shore on a couple of planks; and indeed the whole of my life has been one great miracle or mystery, as you all must have noticed. And if I have been in any way immoderate, or have been less exact than I might, you must blame that on what the priest said at the beginning of my story: continual and extraordinary travails affect the memory of the person suffering them.'

'Mine will not be affected, O great and worthy lady,' said Don Quixote, 'by whatever travails I undergo in your service, however severe and unprecedented they may be; and so I again confirm the boon that I have vouchsafed you, and I promise to go with you to the end of the world until I confront your fierce enemy, whose haughty head, by the help of God and this arm, I shall cut off with the blade of this ... I cannot say good sword, thanks to Ginés de Pasamonte, who stole mine from me.'

He muttered these last few words to himself, and continued:

'And after I have cut it off and restored you to the peaceful possession of your realm, it shall be left to your own will to dispose of your person according to your pleasure; because so long as my memory is pervaded, my will enslaved, my understanding enthralled, by that ... I say no more ..., it is impossible for me even to contemplate marriage, even if it were to the Phoenix itself!'[2]

Sancho was so outraged by what Don Quixote had just said about not marrying that he cried out in fury:

'Damn and confound it all, Don Quixote sir, you can't be in your right mind! How can you have any doubts about marrying a high-up princess like this one? Do you think fortune's going to be offering you a stroke of luck like this round every corner you turn? Is my fine lady Dulcinea better-looking by any chance? No, of course she isn't, not by a long chalk, and I'd even go so far as to say that she can't hold a candle to this lady here. A fat chance I have of getting my earldom if you go reaching for the stars like that. Get married, get married as soon as you can, in the name of Satan, and grab that kingdom that's falling into your hands without you having to lift a finger, and once you're king make me a marquis or a governor – and then the whole show can go to the devil!'

Don Quixote couldn't bear to hear such blasphemies uttered against his lady Dulcinea and without one word of warning he raised his pike and dealt Sancho two blows that flattened him; and if Dorotea hadn't cried out to him to stop, he'd have ended his squire's life there and then.

'Do you imagine, you villainous wretch,' he said after a while, 'that you can always be cocking a snook at me, sir, and that we shall go on for ever like this with you misbehaving and me forgiving? Well, do not imagine it, you damned rogue; and indeed you are damned, for defaming the peerless Dulcinea. And do you not realize, you layabout, you miscreant, you brute, that if it were not for the might that she infuses into my arm I should not have the strength to kill a flea? Tell me, you viper-tongued scoffer, what do you think has conquered this kingdom and cut off this giant's head and made you into a marquis (I take all this for granted as if seen and approved, of course) but the might of Dulcinea, using my arm as the instrument for its exploits? In me she does battle and conquers, and in her I live and breathe and have my being.[3] O you villain, you bastard, what ingratitude you show: you find yourself raised up from the dust of the earth to be made a titled lord, and you repay such kindness by maligning your benefactress!'

Sancho's beating hadn't been severe enough to prevent him from hearing everything his master said, and he got up rather nimbly and positioned himself behind Dorotea's palfrey, from where he added:

'Just you tell me this, sir: if you've decided not to marry this great princess, it's clear the kingdom won't be yours, and if the kingdom isn't yours what favours can you do me? That's all I'm concerned about. Marry the queen, marry the queen, do, now that we've got her here heaven-sent out of the blue, and then afterwards you can go back to my lady Dulcinea – there must have been kings before now who've had a bit on the side. As for their beauty, I won't poke my nose into that, but to tell you the truth, if I've got to, they both seem all right to me, though I've never seen the lady Dulcinea.'

'How can you say that you have never seen her, you blasphemous traitor?' said Don Quixote. 'Have you not just brought me a message from her?'

'I mean I've never examined her so very closely,' said Sancho, 'as to see in detail how lovely she is, and size up her fair features one by one. But she looks all right to me, on the whole.'

'Now I can excuse you,' said Don Quixote, 'and you must forgive me for the annoyance I have caused you: man's first impulses are beyond his control.'

'I can see that all right,' replied Sancho, 'and as for me, my first impulse is always to talk, and I can't help saying, once over at least, whatever comes into my head.'

'All the same,' said Don Quixote, 'you had better be careful what you say, Sancho, because the pitcher goes so often to the well . . . I need say no more.'

'All right,' said Sancho, 'but God's up there in heaven, and he sees what we get up to, and he'll be the judge of who's worse – me for not being careful what I say, or you for not being careful what you do.'

'That's enough of that, now,' said Dorotea. 'Come on, Sancho, kiss your master's hand, and beg his forgiveness, and from now on do try to be more judicious with your praise and your condemnation; and don't speak ill of that lady Tobosa, of whom all I know is that I am her humble servant, and place your faith in God, who won't fail to provide you with an estate on which you can live like a prince.'

Sancho went up to his master with his head bowed and asked for his hand, which his master gave him with tranquil solemnity, and after Sancho had kissed it his master blessed him and said that he would like the two of them to move on a little ahead of the others, because he had some matters of great importance to ask about and discuss. Sancho did as he was told and the pair went on a short way in front, and Don Quixote said:

'I have not had an opportunity since your return to enquire about many interesting particulars concerning your mission and the reply that you brought back; and, now that fortune has granted us that opportunity, do not refuse to give me the happiness that your good news can bring me.'

'You go ahead and ask whatever you like,' replied Sancho, 'I found my way in and I'll find my way out. But please, sir, don't be so vindictive from now on.'

'Why do you say that, Sancho?' asked Don Quixote.

'I say that,' Sancho replied, 'because the beating you just gave me had more to do with the quarrel that the devil sparked off between us the other night than with what I said about my lady Dulcinea, who I love and revere like a relic although of course she's nothing of the sort, just because she's yours.'

'For goodness sake do not harp on that conversation, Sancho,' said Don Quixote. 'It is very upsetting for me. I have forgiven you for all that, but you know the saying: for a new sin a new penance.'

As they talked they saw a man riding a donkey towards them along the road, and when he came closer they thought he was a gipsy. Whenever Sancho Panza saw a donkey he riveted his eyes and soul on it; so as soon as he could take a good look at this man he realized that it was Ginés de Pasamonte; and putting two and two together he concluded that it was his own dun that Pasamonte was riding – and he was right. To avoid recognition and to sell the ass, the convict had dressed himself in gipsy clothes, because he could speak Romany, as he could speak many other languages, like a native. But Sancho did recognize him, as soon as he saw him, and he cried:

'Hey, Ginesillo, you thief! Leave my dearest alone, free my heart's content, unload the comfort of my life, leave my donkey be, leave my beauty alone! Clear off you bugger, go away you robber and give up what isn't yours!'

There wasn't any need for so many insults, because as soon as Ginés heard the first of them he jumped off the donkey and departed at a lively trot that might almost have been taken for a gallop, and in an instant he was far away.

Sancho went to his dun, and as he embraced it he said:

'And how have you been, my sweet, my darling dun, my boon companion?'

And he kissed it and caressed it as if it were a human being. The ass quietly accepted the kisses and the caresses without offering a word in reply. The others came and congratulated Sancho on finding his dun, in particular Don Quixote, who added that this wouldn't cause him to revoke his warrant for the three donkeys. Sancho thanked him for his generosity.

While the two of them were talking away like this, the priest told Dorotea that she'd put on an intelligent performance in the way she'd invented the story, kept it brief and made it follow the pattern of the books of chivalry. She said that she'd often whiled away the time reading such books, but didn't know where the different provinces and seaports were, and that was why she'd had to guess the bit about landing at Osuna.

'That's what I thought,' said the priest, 'and why I butted in to say what I did, and put things right. But isn't it extraordinary how this unfortunate hidalgo believes all these lies and fictions, just because they imitate the style and manner of the nonsense in his books?'

'Yes, it is strange,' said Cardenio, 'and the whole business is so weird and wonderful that I can't believe that if anyone wanted to invent such a story he'd be clever enough to do it.'

'And there's something else, too,' said the priest. 'If we leave aside the absurdities that the good hidalgo comes out with concerning his mania, in conversations on other subjects he talks with great good sense, and shows himself to have a clear and balanced judgement. So long as you don't get him going on his chivalry, nobody would say that he wasn't a man of excellent understanding.'

While they were engaged in this conversation, Don Quixote was continuing his with Sancho:

'Friend Panza, we must let bygones be bygones and forget about our quarrels, and now do tell me, leaving aside all anger and resentfulness: where, how and when did you find Dulcinea? What was she doing? What did you say to her? What did she reply? What look was on her face as she read my letter? Who copied it out for you? And tell me, too, everything else that you consider worth knowing, asking and answering; and you must not add anything or tell any lies to increase my pleasure, still less omit anything to detract from it.'

'To tell you the honest truth, sir,' replied Sancho, 'nobody copied the letter out, because I didn't have it on me.'

'Yes, it is just as you say,' replied Don Quixote, 'because two days after you had left I found the notebook in which I had written the letter, which caused me great sorrow because I did not know what you would do when you missed it; and I must say I thought you would return to me as soon as you did miss it.'

'And that's just what I would have done, too,' said Sancho, 'if I hadn't learned it by heart when you read it to me, so I repeated it to a sexton, who took it down from my memory so exactly that he said he'd never seen or read such a pretty letter in all the days of his born life, even though he'd read out lots and lots of letters of excommunication.'

'And do you still retain my letter in your memory, Sancho?' asked Don Quixote.

'No, sir,' replied Sancho, 'because once I'd said it to the sexton I could see it wasn't going to be of any more use, so I turned my mind to forgetting it. If there's anything I do remember it's that bit about your slobbered-on I mean sovereign lady and the ending, "Yours until death, The Knight of the Sorry Face". And in between I stuck more than three hundred darlings, dear hearts and lights of my eyes.'

CHAPTER XXXI

*About the delectable conversation between Don Quixote
and his squire Sancho Panza, and other events*

'All this does not displease me; do continue,' said Don Quixote. 'So you arrived; and what was that queen of beauty doing? No doubt you found her stringing pearls, or embroidering some emblem in gold thread for this her hapless knight.'

'All I found her doing,' said Sancho, 'was sieving a bushel or two of wheat in a yard.'

'Then you may well suppose,' said Don Quixote, 'that the grains of wheat became grains of pearl when touched by her hands. And did you look, my friend, to see whether it was white wheat or spring wheat?'

'Just buckwheat,' replied Sancho.

'Yet I can assure you,' said Don Quixote, 'that, sieved by her hands, it produced the finest white bread. But continue: when you gave her my letter, did she kiss it? Did she press it to her brow? Did she perform some similar ceremony worthy of such a letter, or what did she do?'

'When I went over to give it to her,' said Sancho, 'she was busy shaking a great sieveful of wheat, and she said: "Put the letter on top of that sack, love, I can't read it till I've done with this lot."'

'A wise lady!' said Don Quixote. 'That would have been so as to read it at her leisure, and savour it. Continue, Sancho: while she was about her task, what conversation passed between you? What did she ask you about me? And what did you reply to her? Come on, tell me everything, and do not omit the smallest detail.'

'She didn't ask any questions,' said Sancho, 'but I told her how as you were doing penance to serve her, naked from the waist up and stuck in these sierras like a savage, sleeping on the ground and ne'er at table eating bread or combing your beard, and crying, and cursing your fate.'

'You were wrong to say that I was cursing my fate,' said Don Quixote, 'because, on the contrary, I bless it and shall bless it all the days of my life, for having made me worthy to love so lofty a lady as Dulcinea del Toboso.'

'Yes,' replied Sancho, 'and she's so lofty I'll swear she's a good handsbreadth taller than me.'

'How do you know that, Sancho?' said Don Quixote. 'Did you measure yourself against her?'

'Yes,' said Sancho, 'and it happened like this – I went to help her load a sack of wheat on to a donkey, and we got so close to each other I could see she was more than a handsbreadth above me.'

'And truly,' exclaimed Don Quixote, 'the stature of her person is accompanied and graced by a thousand million spiritual gifts! But you will not deny me one thing, Sancho: when you approached her did you not notice a certain Sabaean[1] perfume, an aromatic fragrance, some undefinable sweetness that I cannot find words to express? I mean some sort of odour that might have made you think you were in a shop in which expensive gloves were being sold?'

'All I can say,' said Sancho, 'is that I noticed a mannish kind of smell, and it must have been that she was working so hard she'd got a bit runny like, a bit sweaty.'

'No, it would not have been that,' replied Don Quixote. 'Rather you must have had a cold in the head, or have been smelling yourself, for I well know the aroma of that rose among thorns, that lily of the field, that liquid ambergris.'

'You could be right,' said Sancho. 'I've often noticed that same smell I thought was coming out of her highness the lady Dulcinea coming out of me, but that's no wonder, one devil's much the same as another.'

'Well then,' continued Don Quixote, 'she has finished sifting her wheat and sending it off to the mill. What did she do when she read the letter?'

'She didn't read the letter at all,' said Sancho, 'because she said she couldn't read or write, and instead she tore it up into little bits and told me she didn't want anyone to read it to her and have her secrets known all over the village, and it was enough with what I'd mentioned about your love and the special penance you were doing for her sake. And she ended up by telling me to tell you that she sent her kind regards, and was keener to see you than to write to you and, having received yours of this inst., she begged and ordered you to leave these wastelands and stop playing the fool and set off straight away for El Toboso, if nothing else of greater importance happened, because she wanted to see you so much. She had a good laugh when I told her you were called the Knight of the Sorry Face. I asked her if that Basque had gone to see her, and she said he had, and he was a decent enough sort. I asked her about the convicts, too, but she said she hadn't seen any of those yet.'

'So far so good,' said Don Quixote. 'But now tell me this: what jewel did she give you when you bade her farewell, to reward you for the news you had borne her from me? For it is a common and ancient custom among knights and ladies errant to make to squires, dwarfs and damsels – the ladies to the former and the knights to the latter – a gift of some rich jewel, in gratitude for their errand.'

'I don't doubt it for a moment, and it seems like a good idea to me. But it must have been in times gone by when they did that, and all they give nowadays must be a hunk of bread and cheese, because that's what my lady Dulcinea gave me, over the yard wall, when I said goodbye to her. And what's more it was sheep's cheese.'

'She is a most generous lady,' said Don Quixote, 'and if she did not give you a jewel set in gold it must have been because she did not have one on her at the time. But better late than never: I shall see her about it, and all will be put right. Do you know what it is that astonishes me, Sancho? It is that you seem to have flown there and back, because it has taken you little more than three days to go to El Toboso and return here, and El Toboso is more than a hundred miles away. Which leads me to believe that the wise sorcerer who is in charge of my affairs and who is on my side – because there is one, there has to be one, on pain of my not being a good knight errant – this sorcerer, I say, must have helped you on your way without your realizing it; for there are sages of this sort who take a knight errant sleeping in his bed and, without the faintest idea how it has happened, he wakes up the following morning more than three thousand miles away from where he fell asleep. And if it were not for this, knights errant would not be able to assist each other when in danger, as they do, all the time. One might be fighting in the mountains of Armenia with some monster or fierce ogre, or with another knight, having the worst of the battle and about to be killed, and when one least expects it – hey presto, along on a cloud or a chariot of fire comes another knight, one's friend, who had been in England a moment earlier, to help one and save one from certain death, and by nightfall he is back at his inn, enjoying his supper; and the one place is usually eight or ten thousand miles away from the other. And all this is achieved by the cunning and the wisdom of these wise enchanters who look after these worthy knights. And so it is, friend Sancho, that I do not find it difficult to believe that in so short a time you have travelled to El Toboso and back again because, as I said, some friendly sage must have swept you through the air without your knowing it.'

'I expect you're right,' said Sancho, 'because, upon my soul, old Rocinante moved as if he was a gipsy's donkey with quicksilver poured into his ears!'

'Quicksilver, you say!' exclaimed Don Quixote. 'And a legion of devils besides, because they can move and make others move, without tiring, as fast as they like. But leaving all this aside, what do you think I should do now about this matter of my lady's command to go and see her? For although I appreciate that I am obliged to obey her, I also appreciate that I am prevented from doing so by the boon I have vouchsafed to the princess who is travelling with us; and the law of chivalry obliges me to put my promise before my pleasure. On the one side, I am pursued and hounded by my desire to see my lady; on the other, I hear the call of the faith I have pledged and of the glory I shall acquire in this undertaking. But what I intend to do is to hurry to wherever this giant is to be found, and when I arrive I shall cut off his head and restore the princess to the peaceful possession of her realm, and then I shall immediately return to behold the light that lightens my senses, and I shall present to her such excuses as will make her approve of my delay, for she will see that it all redounds to her greater glory and fame; because all the fame and glory I have achieved, do achieve and shall achieve by force of arms in this life springs from the succour that she affords me and from my being hers.'

'Oh dear me!' said Sancho. 'You really have gone off your head, haven't you just! Look here, sir – do you seriously intend to make this journey for nothing, and let a noble and money-spinning match like this one slip through your fingers? As a dowry you'll get a kingdom that I've heard, honestly, is more than seventy thousand miles round, and is full of everything needed to support human life, and is bigger than Portugal and Castile put together. Stop your nonsense, for God's sake, you ought to be ashamed of yourself – take my advice, if you'll kindly forgive me for speaking, and get married in the first village where there's a priest, or else make use of the one we've got with us, he'll do a very good job. I'm old enough by now, you know, to give advice, and this advice I'm giving you here is just what the doctor ordered, and a bird in the hand is worth two in the bush, because when the pig's offered you must poke open the hold.'

'Look here, Sancho,' replied Don Quixote, 'if you are advising me to marry so that once I have killed the giant and become king I shall be in a position to do you favours and give you what I have promised you, I would have you know that it will be easy for me to fulfil your desire without marrying; for before I go into battle I shall require as a further condition that once I am victorious, if I do not marry, I am to be presented with a part of the kingdom, so that I can give it to whomever I please; and, when I do receive it, to whom do you expect me to give it, if not to you?'

'Right you are,' replied Sancho, 'but just make sure you pick somewhere by the seaside so that if I don't like the way of life I can load up my black vassals and do with them what I said I would. And don't bother to visit my lady Dulcinea for the time being, go and kill the giant and get it over and done with – I've got a hunch, by God, that it'll bring us plenty of honour and profit.'

'And I say, Sancho,' said Don Quixote, 'that you are right, and that I shall accept your advice about going away with the princess before I visit Dulcinea. And let me warn you not to tell anyone, not even our companions here, about what we been discussing: since Dulcinea is so modest that she does not want her feelings known, it would not be right for me, or anyone else because of me, to reveal them.'

'Well, if that's the way it is,' said Sancho, 'why do you make all those defeated by your mighty arm go and present themselves before my lady Dulcinea, when that's like signing a statement to the effect that you love her and you're her sweetheart? And seeing as how you force them all to get down on their bended knees in her presence and say they've come on your behalf to swear obedience, how can you expect to hide what's going on between you?'

'Oh what a dunderhead, what a nincompoop you are!' said Don Quixote. 'Can you not see, Sancho, that all this redounds to her greater glory? For I would have you know that in this our way of chivalry it is a great honour for a lady to have many knights errant serving her without any other ambition than to serve her, merely because she is who she is, and without expecting any other reward for their manifold good services than the knowledge that she is content to accept them as her knights.'

'That's the kind of love,' said Sancho, 'that I've heard in sermons we're supposed to feel for our Lord – for his own sake, without being moved by hopes of glory or fears of punishment. Though I must say I'd prefer to love him and serve him for what he can do for me.'

'The devil take you, you peasant!' said Don Quixote. 'What good sense you sometimes speak! Anyone would think you'd been to university!'

'Well, I promise you I can't so much as read,' replied Sancho.

As they talked, Master Nicolás shouted out to them to wait a minute, because the company wanted to stop and have a drink at a nearby spring. Don Quixote stopped, and Sancho wasn't sorry about the interruption, being exhausted by all that lying and scared that his master might catch him in the net of his questions because, although he knew that Dulcinea was a peasant girl from El Toboso, he'd never seen her in his life.

By this time Cardenio had put on the clothes that Dorotea had been wearing when they found her, and although they weren't very good clothes they were a great improvement on those which they'd replaced. They all dismounted by the spring and, with the provisions that the priest had acquired at the inn, they did something, although not very much, about the ravenous hunger afflicting them all. As they sat there a lad happened to come along the road, and he stopped and stared at the people by the spring; and after a moment he charged at Don Quixote and hugged his legs and burst into tears and said:

'Oh, my lord! Don't you recognize me? Take a good look at me, I'm that lad Andrés you freed from the evergreen oak where I was tied.'

Don Quixote did recognize him, and taking him by the hand he turned to the others and said:

'So that you can see how important it is that there be knights errant in the world to redress the wrongs and outrages committed by the wicked and insolent men who live in it, I would have you know that some time ago I was riding through a wood when I heard cries and piteous shouts as of one afflicted and in distress; I hastened, as was my duty, to where I thought the sad sounds were coming from, and I found, tied to an evergreen oak, this lad you see before you, whose presence fills my soul with joy because he is a witness who will confirm everything that I say. He was tied to the evergreen oak, then, naked from the waist up, and a peasant, who I later learned was his master, was flaying him alive with the reins of his mare; and as soon as I saw this I enquired into the reason for this terrible flogging, and the brute replied that he was whipping the boy because he was his servant and a certain lack of care on his part had more to do with thieving than with simple-mindedness. Upon which the boy said:

'"Sir, the only reason he's flogging me is because I asked for my wages."

'His master replied with all kinds of bluster and excuses, to which I listened but which I did not accept. The end of the matter was that I made his master untie him and swear that he would take him away and pay him every single real he owed him, and with brass knobs on, too. Is this not all true, Andrés, my son? Did you not see how imperiously I issued my command, and how humbly he promised to carry out everything

I ordered and specified and required? Speak up; do not be embarrassed or hesitant; tell these people what happened, so that it can be seen and understood that the presence of knights errant on the road is as beneficial as I say it is.'

'Everything you've said is very true,' replied the lad, 'but it all ended up the opposite of what you think.'

'What do you mean, the opposite?' replied Don Quixote. 'Did the peasant not pay you, then?'

'Not only that,' replied the lad, 'but as soon as you were out of the wood and we were left on our own again he tied me back to the same oak tree and gave me a fresh flogging, and I was left skinned like another St Bartholomew. And each time he hit me he cracked a joke about how he was making a fool of you, and if I wasn't in such pain I'd have had a really good giggle at the things he said. To cut a long story short, he left me in such a state that I've been in hospital ever since, getting over the injuries he did me, that evil peasant. And you're to blame for it all, because if you'd gone on your way and hadn't come poking your nose into other people's business, my master would have been content to hit me a dozen or a couple of dozen times, and then he'd have untied me and paid me what he owed me. But since you threw all those pointless insults at him and called him all those names he got into a temper, and since he couldn't take it out on you he loosed his storm on me as soon as we were alone – and I don't think I'll be the same again as long as I live.'

'The trouble was,' said Don Quixote, 'that I departed, which I should not have done until he had paid you; for I should have known, from long experience, that no peasant keeps his word if he thinks that breaking it will profit him. But no doubt you remember, Andrés, that I swore that if he did not pay you I should go in search of him and that I should find him, even if he hid in the belly of the whale.'[2]

'That's true enough,' said Andrés, 'but it didn't do any good at all.'

'Now you will see whether it does any good or not,' said Don Quixote.

And as he said this he sprang to his feet and told Sancho to bridle Rocinante, who was grazing while they ate. Dorotea asked Don Quixote what he was planning to do. He replied that he was going in search of that peasant to punish him for his wicked behaviour, and to see that Andrés was paid to the last maravedí, in spite of all the peasants in the world. To which she replied that he must remember that, according to the vouchsafed boon, he couldn't be involved in any other enterprise until he'd completed hers, and as he knew this better than anybody he'd do well to calm down until he'd finished his business in her kingdom.

'That is true,' replied Don Quixote, 'and Andrés will have to be patient until I return, as you say, my lady; and I again swear to him and I promise him once more that I will not stop until I have seen him avenged and paid.'

'I don't believe all those oaths of yours,' said Andrés. 'At the moment I'd rather have what's needed to get me to Seville than all the vengeance in the world – so give me something to eat and something to take with me, if you've got anything, and God be with you and all knights errant. And I hope all their errantry does them every bit as much good as it's done me.'

Sancho took a hunk of bread and a lump of cheese from his supply and gave them to the lad with the words:

'Here you are, brother Andrés, each one of us has a share in your misfortune.'

'And what's your share, then?' asked Andrés.

'This share of bread and cheese I'm giving you,' replied Sancho. 'God in heaven knows whether I'm going to feel the want of it, because I'll have you know, my friend, that we knight errants' squires must face up to a lot of hunger and bad luck, as well as other things it's better not to talk about.'

Andrés grabbed his bread and cheese and, seeing that nobody was giving him anything else, bowed his head and, as they say, made himself scarce. It has to be added that as he left he addressed Don Quixote:

'Look here, mister knight errant, if you ever come across me again, even if you can see that I'm being torn to pieces, for God's sake don't come to my rescue – just leave me alone with my troubles, because they can't possibly be so great that your help won't make them much worse. And God's curses on you and on every single knight errant that ever was born.'

Don Quixote was rising to punish him, but he scampered away at such a pace that nobody tried to follow. Don Quixote was plunged into embarrassment by Andrés's tale, and the others had to stifle their laughter so as not to complete his discomfiture.

CHAPTER XXXII

*Concerning what happened to Don Quixote and his gang
at the inn*

The banquet was over, they saddled their mounts and nothing else worth
mentioning happened until on the following day they reached the inn that
was the dread and terror of Sancho Panza; and reluctant though he was to
go in, he couldn't avoid doing so. The innkeeper and his wife and daughter
and Maritornes saw Don Quixote and Sancho coming, and went out to
receive them with a great show of contentment, and Don Quixote accepted
their welcome with solemn gravity, and told them to prepare a better bed
than last time; to which the innkeeper's wife replied that if he paid for it
better than last time she'd give him one fit for a king. Don Quixote said he
would, so they made up a tolerable bed for him in the attic where he'd slept
before, and he retired immediately because he was both exhausted and upset.
No sooner had he locked the door than the innkeeper's wife descended on
the barber and, seizing him by the beard, exclaimed:

'By all that's holy, you aren't using my tail as a beard any more, you've
got to give it back to me, it's shameful how my husband's thingummy's
bandied about all over the place nowadays – I mean his comb that I used
to stick into my fine tail!'

The barber wouldn't part with it, however hard she tugged, until the
priest told him to let her have it back: the disguise wasn't necessary any
longer, he could show himself as he really was, and tell Don Quixote that
when the convicts had stripped him he had fled to the inn, and if Don
Quixote asked about the princess's squire he could be told that she'd sent
him on ahead to warn the people in her kingdom that she was on her
way there with the liberator of them all. So the barber willingly gave the
innkeeper's wife back her tail, and they also returned all the other
accessories she'd lent them for the freeing of Don Quixote. Everyone at
the inn was astonished by Dorotea's beauty and by the good looks of the
herdboy Cardenio. The priest ordered whatever food there was in the
house to be prepared, and the innkeeper, in hope of better payment, did
his very best to cook a passable meal; and all this time Don Quixote slept

on, and they thought it better not to awake him, because it would do him more good to sleep than to eat.

The conversation after the meal, with the innkeeper, his wife, his daughter, Maritornes and all the guests sitting round the table, was about Don Quixote's strange madness and how he had been found. The innkeeper's wife related the events involving the muleteer, and, after looking around to see if Sancho was present and not finding him there, she told them all about the blanket-tossing, which gave them no little merriment. And the priest's observation that the books of chivalry which Don Quixote had read had turned him mad prompted the innkeeper to say:

'I don't understand how that can be so, because to my mind there isn't a better read anywhere in the world – I've got two or three of them back there, with some other papers, and I can truly say they've given me new life, and plenty of other people besides. At harvest time, you see, lots of the reapers come in here on rest-days, and there are always some who can read, and one of them picks up one of these books, and more than thirty of us gather around him, and we enjoy listening so much that it takes all our worries away. Speaking for myself, at least, when I hear him describing all those furious and terrible blows that the knights deal one another I feel like doing the same thing myself, and I could go on listening day and night.'

'And so do I,' said the innkeeper's wife, 'because the only time I get any peace and quiet in this place is when you're sitting there listening – you're in such a stupor you forget all about yelling at me for a while.'

'You're right there,' said Maritornes, 'and I can tell you I love hearing about all those goings-on, they're wonderful, especially when it's about a lady lying under orange trees in her knight's arms, and this duenna standing guard over them, dying of envy and scared out of her wits. It's lovely, it really is.'

'And what about you, young lady, what do you think?' the priest asked the innkeeper's daughter.

'I don't know, sir, I'm sure,' she replied. 'I listen, too, and the honest truth is that even though I don't understand it, I do enjoy it. I don't enjoy those fights that my father likes, mind you, but the knights' laments when they're separated from their ladies – to tell you the truth they sometimes make me cry out of sheer pity for them.'

'So would you do something to put them out of their misery, young lady,' asked Dorotea, 'if it was you they were crying for?'

'I really don't know what I'd do,' the girl replied. 'All I do know is that some of those ladies are so cruel that their knights call them tigers and lions and thousands of other nasty names. Good Lord, I can't imagine how they can be so heartless, so remorseless, letting an honest man die or go mad rather than look at him! I can't see why they're so bashful – if it's for their virtue's sake, they can just get married, that's what the men are after.'

'Hush, my girl,' said the innkeeper's wife, 'you seem to be very well-informed about these matters – it isn't right for young women to know or say so much.'

'This gentleman here asked me the question,' her daughter replied, 'so I had to give him an answer.'

'And now,' said the priest, 'bring me those books, landlord, I want to see them.'

'Very well,' he replied.

He went into his room and came back carrying an old case, fastened with a chain, which he unlocked to reveal three large books and some manuscript papers written in an excellent hand. When the priest opened the first book he saw it was *Don Cirongilio of Thrace*, and the next was *Felixmarte of Hyrcania*, and finally the *History of the Great Captain Gonzalo Fernández de Córdoba, together with the Life of Diego García de Paredes*.[1] As the priest read the first two titles he turned to the barber and said:

'What we need here and now is my friend's housekeeper, and his niece.'

'No, we don't,' replied the barber, 'because I'm just as good as they are at carting books off to the yard – or to the fireplace, there's a good fire burning there.'

'Do you want to burn still more books?' said the innkeeper.

'Just these two,' said the priest. '*Don Cirongilio* and *Felixmarte*.'

'Are my books heretics, then, or phlegmatics,' said the innkeeper, 'to make you want to burn them?'

'You mean schismatics, my friend,' said the barber, 'not phlegmatics.'

'All right, then,' replied the innkeeper. 'But if you want to burn a book, burn this one about the Great Captain and that Diego García fellow. I'd sooner allow one of my children to be burned than either of the other two.'

'My dear friend,' said the priest: 'those two books are full of lies, absurdities and nonsense. But this other one about the Great Captain is a true history, because it narrates the deeds of Gonzalo Fernández de Córdoba, universally known for his many splendid exploits as the Great Captain, a famous and illustrious title, earned only by him; and Diego García de Paredes was an eminent gentleman from the city of Trujillo in Extremadura, a most courageous soldier and so strong that with one finger he could stop a millstone turning at top speed; and armed with a two-handed sword he stood at the approach to a bridge and prevented a vast army from crossing it. And he performed so many other feats of this kind that if, instead of recounting them himself with all the modesty of a gentleman who is his own chronicler, someone else had done so with dispassionate objectivity, his deeds would have relegated those of the likes of Hector, Achilles and Roland to oblivion.'

'Pooh, so that's all he did, is it?' said our innkeeper. 'Fancy getting all het up about somebody stopping a millstone! For God's sake, you ought to read about what Felixmarte of Hyrcania got up to – with just one back-stroke he cut five giants clean through the middle, as if they were those friar-dolls that children make out of bean-pods! And another time he charged at an enormous powerful army and defeated more than one million six hundred thousand soldiers all in armour from head to foot, and he routed the lot of them as if they were flocks of sheep. And what do you think about good old Don Cirongilio of Thrace, who was as brave and daring as you'll read he was in the book, where it says that once when he was sailing down a river a serpent of fire came out of the midst of the water and as soon as he saw it he flung himself on top of it and sat astride its scaly back and squeezed its throat so hard with both hands that the serpent realized it was being strangled and had no choice but to sink to the bottom of the river with the knight sitting on top of it because he wouldn't let go? And when they got to the bottom he found himself among such lovely palaces and gardens that they were wondrous to behold, and then the serpent turned into a an old old man who told him such things, you couldn't possibly imagine them. Come, say no more, sir – if all this was read out to you, you'd go mad with pleasure. A fig for the Great Captain and another for that Diego García character!'

When Dorotea heard this she whispered to Cardenio:

'Our host could almost play second lead to Don Quixote.'

'I agree,' replied Cardenio, 'because all the signs are he's convinced that everything in those books happened exactly as they say, and a churchful of discalced friars couldn't make him believe otherwise.'

'Look here, my friend,' the priest resumed, 'there never was any Felixmarte of Hyrcania or Don Cirongilio of Thrace or any of those other knights in those books of chivalry of yours, because it's all make-believe, fiction invented by idle minds for the purpose you've just mentioned, passing the time of day as your reapers do when they sit listening to it. I solemnly swear that such knights never existed and that such deeds or rather such nonsenses never took place.'

'You can go and throw that bone to another dog!' the innkeeper retorted. 'As if I didn't know how many beans make five, or where my own shoe pinches! Don't you come trying to feed me with pap – I wasn't born yesterday, by God! A fine thing it is for you to come telling me that everything in these good books is stuff and nonsense, when they were all published with their proper licences from the gentlemen on the Royal Council – as if those were the kind of people who'd allow a pack of lies to be printed, and all those battles and enchantments that fair turn you crazy!'

'I have already told you, my friend,' replied the priest, 'that this is only done to while away our idle moments; and just as in well-ordered societies such games as chess, tennis and billiards are permitted for the amusement of those who do not, should not and cannot work, so permission is also granted for the publication of such books, in the justified belief that there can't be anybody so ignorant as to read them as if they were true histories. And if it were timely to do so, and if those here present were to request it, I'd say a few words now about the qualities that books of chivalry need in order to be good books; and some people might find my words useful or even enjoyable. But I expect that a time will come when I can convey my ideas to a person in a position to do something about such matters; and meanwhile, landlord, you take me at my word, and here are your books – now you can find your own way among their lies and their truths, and much good may they do you, and God grant that you don't end up lame in the same leg that your guest Don Quixote halts on.'

'Don't you worry,' replied the innkeeper, 'I'm not so mad as to become a knight errant, and it's clear enough to me that things are different now from what they were then, when all those famous knights are supposed to have roamed about all over the world.'

Sancho appeared in the middle of this conversation and was plunged into thought and confusion when he heard that knight errants had fallen out of fashion and that books of chivalry were a pack of arrant lies; and he decided that he'd better wait and see how this latest trip of his master's turned out, and if it didn't turn out as well as expected, he'd leave him and go back home to his wife and his children and his everyday labours.

The innkeeper was taking his case away with the books in it when the priest said:

'Wait a minute, I want to have a look at those papers, they're written in such a fine hand . . .'

The innkeeper took them out and handed them over to the priest, who found eight folios and on the title-page the words, printed large: 'The Tale of Inappropriate Curiosity.' He read three or four lines to himself, and said:

'I must say this tale has rather a good title: I have a mind to read it through.'

To which the innkeeper replied:

'Well, you go ahead and do so, your reverence, because I can tell you some of our guests have read it and enjoyed it enormously, and begged me to let them take it away. But I wouldn't part with it, because I intend to return it to the man who left this case behind with these books and those papers – he might well come back for it some day and, although I know I'm going to miss the books, I'll hand them over to him all right. I might be an innkeeper, but I'm still a Christian.'

'That's very right and proper, my friend,' said the priest. 'If I like the tale, however, you must allow me to copy it out.'

'Most willingly,' replied the innkeeper.

While the two men had been talking, Cardenio had picked up the story and begun to peruse it, and, reaching the same conclusion as the priest, he asked him to read it aloud so that they could all hear.

'I'd be most happy to,' said the priest, 'except that our time would be better spent sleeping than reading.'

'It'll be wonderfully relaxing for me,' said Dorotea, 'to while away the time by listening to a story, because I haven't calmed down enough yet to be able to get to sleep.'

'Well, in that case,' said the priest, 'perhaps I will read it, if only out of curiosity. Who knows, maybe it'll prove curiously entertaining.'

Master Nicolás also urged him to do so, as did Sancho; the priest realized that he could give them all some pleasure, and receive some himself, and said:

'If that's so, pay attention all of you. The tale begins like this:'

CHAPTER XXXIII

Which tells the Tale of Inappropriate Curiosity

'In Florence, that rich and famous Italian city in the province of Tuscany, there once lived two wealthy and eminent gentlemen called Anselmo and Lotario, who were so close that all their acquaintances referred to them by way of antonomasia as "the two friends". They were bachelors, young men of the same age and the same habits, which is enough to explain the friendship that bound them together. It is true that Anselmo was somewhat more inclined towards amorous dallying than Lotario, whose favourite pastime was hunting; but when the occasion arose, Anselmo put his own interests aside and pursued those of Lotario, and Lotario did the same for Anselmo; and in this way their inclinations were so concordant that no clock could have been better regulated.

'Anselmo was madly in love with a beautiful young lady of high rank from the same city, the daughter of such excellent parents and so excellent, too, in her own right that he decided (after consulting Lotario, because he never did anything without Lotario's consent) to ask them for her hand in marriage, and this he did; the man entrusted with the mission was Lotario, who carried it out so much to his friend's satisfaction that he soon found himself in possession of the object of his desires, and Camila was so happy to have gained Anselmo as her husband that she never stopped thanking heaven and Lotario, whose mediation had brought her such joy.

'A wedding celebration is a time of happiness, so for the first few days Lotario continued to frequent his friend Anselmo's house, doing all he could to honour, regale and delight him; but once the celebrations were over and the congratulatory visits had abated, Lotario began to be careful to neglect to go to see Anselmo, because it seemed to him (as it would to any person of good sense) that a man shouldn't haunt his friends' houses once they're married as he used to do in their bachelor days; for although good, true friendship must be above all suspicion, the honour of a married man is so delicate that even a brother, it seems, let alone a friend, can damage it.

'Anselmo noticed the falling-off in Lotario's visits and made heated complaints about it, saying that if he'd known getting married was going to erect a barrier between them he would never have taken such a step; and that if their closeness as bachelors had earned them that fine reputation as "the two friends", Lotario mustn't allow a circumspection that was quite unnecessary and gratuitous to destroy such a famous and agreeable title; and that he therefore begged Lotario, if the use of such a word between them could be justified, to treat his house as his own again, and to come and go as before, with the assurance that his wife Camila had no pleasure or desire other than those that he wanted her to have; and that, knowing as she did how fond they were of each other, she couldn't understand why he had become so elusive.

'To all these and many other arguments that Anselmo used to persuade Lotario to visit him as often as he had before, Lotario replied with such prudence, good sense and sound judgement that Anselmo was convinced that his friend had the best of intentions, and they agreed that Lotario would go to dine with him just twice a week and on holy days; in spite of this, however, Lotario decided to do only what he considered was best for his friend's honour, which he held in higher esteem than his own. He would say, with good reason, that the man to whom heaven had granted a beautiful wife should be as careful over what friends of his he invited home as over supervising what friends of hers she talked to, because that which isn't arranged and indeed put into effect at market-places, churches, public festivities and devotions (which husbands can't always keep their wives away from), is arranged and put into effect in the houses of the wife's most trusted friends and relatives.

'Lotario would also say that every married man needs to have a friend to warn him about the shortcomings in his behaviour, because the great love a husband has for his wife can lead him not to want to annoy her and therefore not to tell her to do or refrain from doing certain things that can honour or shame him; and with the friend to warn him he can easily deal with this problem. But where can one find a friend as wise, loyal and true as Lotario had in mind? I certainly don't know, unless it was Lotario himself, who watched over his friend's honour with the greatest care and vigilance, and contrived to pare and whittle down the number of visiting-days agreed upon, to prevent the idle vulgar herd with their wandering, malicious eyes from gossiping about the visits of a well-born young gentleman with the qualities he believed he possessed to the house of a woman as beautiful as Camila; for although her worth and her virtue were enough to silence any wagging tongue, he still didn't want to put her good name or that of his friend at risk, and he found other occupations and activities, which he claimed were unavoidable, for most of the agreed visiting-days. And so it was that much of each day was spent in complaints on the one side and excuses on the other.

'Now it happened that once, when they were strolling in a meadow outside the city, Anselmo addressed the following words to Lotario:

' "No doubt you think, my good friend Lotario, that, given the favours which God has bestowed upon me in making me the son of such parents as mine and in heaping upon me what are known as the blessings of nature and the gifts of fortune, it is impossible for me to respond with a gratitude that equals the good I have received or exceeds that which he granted me in providing me with you as a friend and Camila as a wife, two treasures that I value, if not as much as I should, then as much as I can. Well, in spite of all these gifts, which are enough to fill most people with happiness, I'm the angriest and bitterest man in the world, because for I don't know how long now I've been assailed and tormented by a desire that's so peculiar and so unusual that I'm astonished at myself, and accuse and scold myself when alone, and try to stifle it and hide it from myself; but I've been as successful in repressing it as if my intention had been to tell the whole world about it. And since it must be revealed, I want this to happen in the total secrecy that I can expect from you, trusting that in this secrecy, and thanks to the care that you, as my true friend, will devote to relieving me, I shall soon be free of this anguish, and your concern will bring me as much joy as my madness has brought me misery."

'Anselmo's words bewildered Lotario, who couldn't imagine where such a long prelude or preamble was leading, and although he tried to imagine what desire this was that so disturbed his friend, he was always very wide of the mark; and to ease the agony of the suspense Lotario said it was offensive to their close friendship for Anselmo to search for roundabout ways to convey his most secret thoughts, because he well knew that he could count on his friend for either advice to dissipate them or help to put them into action.

'"You're right," replied Anselmo, "and with that assurance I can tell you, dear Lotario, that this desire that so disturbs me is the urge to find out whether my wife Camila is as virtuous and perfect as I think she is; and I can't convince myself of this truth except by putting her to the test in such a way as to reveal the purity of her virtue, as fire reveals the purity of gold. Because it's my belief, dear friend, that a woman is good only in proportion as she is or is not tempted, and that the only virtuous woman is the one who doesn't give in to promises, gifts, tears and all the advances of persistent suitors. For what thanks are due to a woman for being good," he went on, "if nobody is asking her to be bad? What merit is there in all her reserve and reticence, if she isn't given any opportunity to go astray, and if she knows that she has a husband who'll kill her if he catches her cutting loose even once? So I can't have the same regard for the woman who's virtuous out of fear or lack of opportunity as I'd have for the one who's tempted and pursued and emerges wearing the crown of victory. And for these reasons, and many others that I could give you to support and reinforce my ideas, I want my wife Camila to be put to this test, and to be proved and assayed in the flames of enticement and temptation by a man worthy to make her the object of his desires; and if she emerges from this battle with the palm of victory, as I believe she will, I shall account myself the luckiest of mortals. I shall be able to say that the cup of my desires is full; I shall say that the virtuous woman, of whom the wise man says 'Who can find her?'[1] has fallen to my lot. And if the outcome is the opposite of what I anticipate, the pleasure of seeing that I was right will enable me to bear without feeling it the pain that such a costly experiment could be expected to cause. And since no objections that you can raise to this desire of mine will prevent me from putting it into practice, I want you, my good friend Lotario, to make yourself ready to be the instrument that will carry into effect this plan on which I've set my heart; I shall provide you with the opportunities for doing so and ensure that you lack nothing that I consider necessary for seducing a virtuous, honourable, modest and high-principled woman. And what moves me, among other considerations, to entrust this arduous enterprise to you is the knowledge that if you do overcome Camila's resistance your triumph won't be carried to the ultimate extreme, but will simply consist, because of your respect for me, in establishing that you could have taken it that far; and in this way I shall only be wronged in the intention, and the offence will remain hidden in your virtuous silence, which I well know will be as eternal as the silence of death, in any affair of mine. So if you want me to enjoy a life worthy of the name, you must enter now into this battle of love, not in any half-hearted or dilatory way but with all the determination and diligence that my decision demands, and with the resolve of which I am assured by our friendship.'

'This was what Anselmo said, and Lotario listened so attentively that he didn't open his lips until his friend had finished, except to say the few words recorded earlier; and when Lotario saw that he had nothing more to say, he stood staring at him for a while, as if staring at something he'd never seen before, at something that amazed and terrified him, and then he spoke:

' "I can't persuade myself, my dear friend Anselmo, that what you've just said isn't a joke; and if I'd believed you were in earnest I shouldn't have allowed you to say as much as you did, and by refusing to listen I'd have cut short your lengthy harangue. I'm convinced that either you don't know me or I don't know you. And yet I do know that you're Anselmo, and you know that I'm Lotario; the trouble is that I don't think you're the Anselmo you used to be, and you must have thought that I'm not the Lotario I ought to be, because what you've just said doesn't come from my friend Anselmo, and what you've asked me to do can't be asked of the Lotario you know. Good friends should verify their friendship and help each other *usque ad aras*, as the poet put it;[2] which means that they mustn't use their friendship for purposes that are offensive to God. Now if this is what a pagan thought about friendship, how much more intensely must a Christian believe in the same principle, because he knows that the love of God mustn't be lost for the sake of any human love? And if a friend does go so far as to set aside his duty to heaven to attend to the duties of friendship, this mustn't be for petty, trivial matters, but for matters involving his friend's honour and his life. Now you tell me this, Anselmo: which of these two is in danger, to make me take the risk of trying to please you by doing this detestable thing you're asking of me? Neither of them, of course; on the contrary, what you're asking me, as far as I can see, is to do all I can to deprive you of your honour and your life, and to deprive myself of them at the same time. Because if I try to deprive you of your honour, it's clear that I shall also be depriving you of your life, since a man without honour is worse than a dead man; and if I'm the instrument, as you want me to be, of so much harm to you, am I not dishonoured too and, by the same logic, dead? No, no, listen to me, Anselmo, and have the patience not to reply until I've finished telling you how I feel about what this desire of yours is urging you to do, and there will be plenty of time afterwards for you to reply and for me to hear you out."

' "Very well," said Anselmo, "say what you like."

'And Lotario continued:

' "It seems to me, Anselmo, that your mind is in the same state as the minds of Moors, who can't be made to understand the error of their sect with references to Holy Scripture or with arguments involving intellectual speculation or based on articles of faith, but must rather be confronted with examples that are palpable, straightforward, easy to understand, demonstrable, indisputable – with mathematical proofs that can't be denied, such as 'If equal parts are taken from equal parts, the remainders are also equal'; and if they can't follow the verbal reasoning, as indeed is the case, they must be shown it all using one's fingers, and have it placed in front of their eyes, and even so nobody can persuade them of the truths of our holy religion. And I shall have to use the same approach and method with you, because this desire that has developed in you is so misguided and so far from any semblance of rationality that I believe I shall be wasting my time if I try to make you understand how silly you're being – for the moment I shall call it that; and I'm even inclined to abandon you to your folly, as a punishment for that evil desire of yours; but my friendship won't allow me to be so severe or leave you in such manifest danger of destroying yourself.

'"And to make it all clear to you, tell me, Anselmo, haven't you urged me to entice a woman who's modest, inveigle a woman who's virtuous, bribe a woman who's high-principled, court a woman who's prudent? Indeed you have. Now if you know that you have a wife who's modest, virtuous, high-principled and prudent, what more do you need to know? And if you believe she'll emerge victorious from all my attacks, as indeed she will, what finer names do you intend to call her afterwards than she already deserves, and in what way will she be a better woman than she already is? Either you don't believe her to be what you say she is, or you don't know what you're asking for. If you don't believe her to be what you say she is, why do you want to test her instead of dealing with her as you think best and as befits a wicked woman? But if she's as good as you say she is, it's inappropriate to go performing experiments on truth itself, because it can't have a greater value afterwards than it had in the first place. And so the conclusion we must reach is that to attempt things that are more likely to do us harm than good is an action of rash, unstable minds, even more so if we aren't forced into them and it's perfectly clear that it's madness to attempt them.

'"Difficult tasks are attempted for God's sake, or for the world's sake, or for both at the same time: those that are attempted for God's sake are the actions of saints, who try to live lives of angels in human bodies; those that are attempted for the world's sake are the actions of the men who pass across great expanses of water, through vast varieties of climates and among a bewildering diversity of peoples in order, as it is said, to make their fortunes; and the tasks that are attempted for the sake of both God and the world are the actions of brave soldiers, who no sooner see in the enemy's ramparts the small breach that a single cannon-ball can make than, casting all fear aside, without thinking, or paying any heed to the evident perils threatening them, carried forward on the wings of their desire to fight for their faith, their country and their king, they hurl themselves fearlessly into the midst of a thousand different deaths awaiting them. These are the tasks that men attempt, and it is honourable, glorious and beneficial to attempt them, even though they are full of difficulties and dangers; but the task that you say you want to carry out won't gain you the glory of God, or make you a fortune, or give you fame among men, because even if you do achieve what you seek you won't be any grander, richer or more honourable than you already are, and if you don't achieve what you seek you'll be left as wretched as it's possible for a man to be: it won't help to tell yourself that nobody knows about the calamity that has befallen you, because merely knowing about it yourself will be enough to torment and destroy you. As a confirmation of this truth let me quote a stanza from the end of the first part of the famous poet Luigi Tansillo's *Le lacrime di San Pietro*:[3]

> The grief is greater, greater is the shame
> In Peter once he sees the light of day
> And though he is alone he takes the blame
> And knows he's left the straight and narrow way:
> An upright, honest spirit feels the same
> Repentance, even if not seen to stray:
> The heart is filled with shame and misery
> When only heaven and earth are there to see.

' "So you won't avoid grief by keeping it secret; on the contrary, you won't stop weeping, if not tears of water from your eyes, then tears of blood from your heart, like that simple-minded doctor who, as the poet tells us, made the trial of the magic cup, which the prudent Reynald more wisely refrained from doing;[4] for although this is a poetic fiction it contains a hidden moral that should be observed and understood and imitated. All the more so since what I'm about to tell you will convince you once and for all that you're about to make a very great mistake.

' "Tell me this, Anselmo: if heaven or fortune had made you the lawful owner of a superb diamond, and every expert who examined it was convinced of its quality and value, and they all with one voice proclaimed that it attained the utmost perfection possible in such a stone, and you yourself were certain of this without a shadow of doubt – would it be reasonable to take it into your head to place that diamond between an anvil and a hammer and there, by the brute force of one blow after another, test it to see if it was as hard and excellent as everybody said? Wouldn't it be even less reasonable to put this desire into effect? For even if the stone could resist such an absurd test it wouldn't thereby gain in value or repute, and if it were destroyed, which is something that could well happen, all would be lost, wouldn't it? Yes, of course it would, and the diamond's owner would be left looking a fool in everybody's eyes. Now think of Camila, Anselmo my friend, as a superb diamond, in your opinion and in everybody else's, and think whether it's reasonable to expose her to the risk of destruction, because even if she does remain intact, she won't then be worth any more than she is now; and if she falters and can't withstand the trial, consider how you'd feel without her, and how justly you'd reproach yourself for having been the cause of her downfall and your own as well. Remember that there's no jewel in the world as valuable as a chaste and honourable woman, and that women's honour lies exclusively in their good reputations; and since your wife's reputation couldn't be better, as you know, why do you insist on calling this truth into question? Remember, too, my friend, that woman is an imperfect animal, and that obstacles shouldn't be placed before her to make her stumble and fall, but rather removed to free her way of pitfalls so that she can run on unhindered to achieve the perfection she needs, that of being virtuous.

' "Naturalists tell us that the ermine is a little animal with pure white fur, and that when huntsmen want to catch it they use the following stratagem: they trace its tracks and its haunts, and daub them over with mud, and then they frighten it into running in that direction, and as soon as the ermine reaches the mud it stops and allows itself to be caught rather than run over the mud and sully and lose its whiteness, which it treasures more than its liberty and its life. The pure, chaste woman is an ermine, and the virtue of chastity is whiter and purer than snow, and the man who wants her not to lose it, but on the contrary to keep and preserve it, shouldn't do as huntsmen do with ermine – he shouldn't place before her the mud of insistent suitors' gifts and offers, because it's possible or, more accurately, it's certain that she has insufficient natural strength and virtue to be able to overcome such obstacles unaided, and it's necessary to remove them for her, and place before her the purity of virtue and the beauty that good repute contains within itself.

' "A good woman is also like a mirror of clear, shining glass, but any breath that touches this mirror will cloud and dim it. She should be treated like a holy relic, adored but not touched. She should be guarded and prized like a beautiful garden full of roses and other flowers, whose owner doesn't allow anybody to walk in it or touch the blooms; it's enough for the visitors to enjoy their beauty and fragrance from afar, from behind its iron railings. And to summarize I'd like to recite some lines of poetry that I've just remembered and that I heard in a modern play, because they seem relevant to what we're discussing. A wise old man is advising another, a young woman's father, to keep her securely locked up at home, and among other reasons he adduces these:

> One never should experiment
> On Woman, who is made of glass,
> To see if she will break or not,
> For anything could come to pass.
> A breakage being probable,
> It's equally absurd and vain
> To put at such excessive risk
> What never can be joined again.
> To this belief let all assent,
> And reason strengthens what I say:
> Wherever there's a Danae
> A shower of gold will find its way.[5]

' "Everything I've said so far, Anselmo, relates to your part in all this, and now I ought to say something concerning my own interests in the matter; if I do so at some length you'll have to forgive me, because it's made necessary by the labyrinth into which you've strayed and from which you want me to extricate you. You consider me your friend, but you want to deprive me of my honour, something that flies in the face of all friendship; and not only that, but you want me to deprive you of your honour, too. That you want to deprive me of my honour is clear, because when Camila sees that I'm trying to seduce her, as you desire, it's obvious that she'll take me for a man without honour or scruple, because I shall be attempting and indeed doing something so contrary to the obligations of my breeding and your friendship. That you want me to deprive you of your honour is beyond doubt, because when Camila sees that I'm trying to seduce her she'll think that I've noticed some fickleness in her that encourages me to reveal my evil intentions to her, and in considering herself disgraced her dishonour will extend to you, as a part of her. And from this springs what so often happens: even though the adulterous woman's husband doesn't know that his wife isn't what she ought to be, hasn't given her any motives for being unfaithful, has never had it in his power to prevent his misfortune and hasn't contributed to it by any neglect or lack of precautions, he is nonetheless called by a vile and shameful name, and those who know about his wife's wickedness regard him with a certain contempt instead of compassion, even though they can see that it isn't his fault but his wayward companion's lust that has caused him such misfortune.

'"Now I'm going to tell you why a wicked woman's husband is justly dishonoured, even if he doesn't know that she's wicked, and isn't to blame, and hasn't contributed to her sin, and hasn't given her any motives for it. And don't grow tired of listening to me, because it's all for your own good.

'"When God created our first father in the earthly paradise, Holy Scripture says that he made Adam fall asleep and took one of the ribs from his left side, from which he created our mother Eve; and when Adam awoke and saw her he said, 'This is flesh of my flesh and bone of my bone.' And God said, 'For this cause a man shall leave his father and his mother, and they two shall be one flesh.'[6] And at that moment the divine sacrament of matrimony was instituted, with such bonds as only death can untie. And this miraculous sacrament has such power that it makes two different people into one flesh; and it does even more when two good people marry, because although they have separate souls they have only one will. It follows that, since the wife's flesh is the same as the husband's, anything that blemishes it, any defects it acquires, affects his flesh too, even if he hasn't, as I said, given her any cause to misbehave. For just as a pain in the foot or anywhere else is felt all over the body, because it's all the same flesh, and the head feels the pain in the ankle without having caused it, so the husband shares his wife's dishonour, because he and she are one and the same. And since all the honour and dishonour in the world springs from human flesh and blood, and this includes the disgrace of a bad wife, the husband is bound to share it and to be regarded as a man without honour even if he doesn't know about it.

' "So you can see, Anselmo, the danger in which you are placing yourself by seeking to disturb the tranquillity that your good wife enjoys; you can see how vain and inappropriate is the curiosity that leads you to want to stir up the passions that now lie quiet in her breast; you can see that you're giving yourself the chance of gaining very little, and that what you'll lose is so very much that I shan't attempt to assess it, for there are no words to express its value. But if everything I've said isn't enough to dissuade you from your wicked plan, you can go and look for another instrument to bring about your misfortune and disgrace, because I don't intend to do it, even if it means losing your friendship, the greatest loss I can imagine."

'The virtuous and wise Lotario stopped speaking, and Anselmo was left so confused and sunk in thought that for a while he couldn't reply; but finally he said:

' "I've been listening attentively, Lotario, as you've observed, to everything you've said, and in your arguments, examples and comparisons I've confirmed how much good sense you're blessed with, and what a true friend you are; and I do see and confess that if I don't agree with your opinions and I adhere to my own I'll be shunning good and pursuing evil. I acknowledge this, but you must consider that I'm suffering from the disease that sometimes affects women and makes them want to eat earth, plaster, coal and even worse things, disgusting to look at, let alone to eat; so some plan has to be devised to cure me, and this could easily be done by your beginning, in a half-hearted and make-believe way, to court Camila, who can't be so frail as to allow her virtue to collapse at the first encounter; and with this beginning I shall rest content, and you'll have done what's due to our friendship, by not only restoring me to good health but also persuading me not to strip myself of honour. And you have a duty to do this for one reason alone, which is that, since I'm resolved to carry out this test, you can't allow me to reveal my foolishness to anybody else, because that would be to place at risk the honour that you don't want me to lose; and if your honour isn't all it should be in Camila's opinion when she realizes that you're making advances to her, that's of little or no importance because very soon, once you encounter the firm resistance we expect, you'll be able to tell her the truth about our plan and your good name will be restored. And since you can give me so much happiness by risking so little, please don't fail me, however many objections you can see, because, as I've said, if you'll only make a beginning I shall regard the matter as concluded."

'Lotario realized that Anselmo had made up his mind, couldn't think of any other examples or arguments with which to dissuade him and saw that he was threatening to tell others about this evil desire of his, so he decided to keep him happy and prevent a greater ill by doing as he asked, with the intention of managing the affair so as to satisfy Anselmo without disturbing Camila's peace of mind; so he told him not to reveal his thoughts to anybody else, because he was going to take the matter in hand and make a beginning whenever Anselmo wished. Anselmo gave him a fond and tender embrace and thanked him for his offer, as if his friend had done him some great favour, and the two of them agreed that Lotario would set to work on the very next day. Anselmo would give him an opportunity to speak to Camila alone, and would provide him with money to offer her and jewels to give her. He advised him to serenade her and to write poetry praising her, and said that if Lotario didn't want to go to so much trouble he'd write it himself. Lotario agreed to everything, but not with the intention that Anselmo supposed. Having reached this understanding they returned to Anselmo's house, where they found Camila anxiously awaiting her husband, because he was later than usual that day.

'Lotario went home, leaving Anselmo as contented as he himself was troubled, wondering how he was going to manage to bring that inappropriate enquiry to a satisfactory conclusion. But that night he thought of a way to deceive Anselmo and not offend Camila, and on the following day he went for lunch with his friend and was made welcome by Camila, who always gave him a cordial reception, knowing how fond her husband was of him.

'They finished the meal, the table was cleared and Anselmo asked Lotario to stay with Camila while he went off on urgent business from which he said he'd return in an hour and a half. Camila begged him not to go, and Lotario offered to accompany him, but it was all to no avail; on the contrary, Anselmo insisted that Lotario must stay and wait for him, because they had to talk about a matter of the greatest importance. He also told Camila not to leave Lotario by himself while he was away. In short, he was so successful in feigning that heedless, needless need to absent himself that nobody would have realized that it was feigned. So Anselmo departed, and Camila and Lotario were left alone at table, because all the servants had gone away to their own meal. And Lotario found himself entering the lists, as his friend had planned, and facing an enemy who could have vanquished a whole squadron of knights in armour with her beauty alone. Lotario had good reason to fear her!

'But what he did was to lean his elbow on the arm of his chair and his cheek on his open hand, ask Camila to forgive his manners and say that he'd like to rest for a while, until Anselmo returned. Camila replied that he'd rest more comfortably on the cushions in the estrade than at the dining-table, and asked him to go in there to sleep. Lotario declined, and dozed where he sat until the return of his friend, who found Camila in her room and Lotario asleep and assumed that, since he'd been away so long, the two had had plenty of time to talk and even to nap; and he was longing for Lotario to wake up, so anxious was he to go out with him and ask what had happened.

'Everything fell out as he wished: Lotario woke up, they left the house together, Anselmo asked his questions and his friend replied that it hadn't seemed wise to be too blatant on the very first occasion, so he had only praised Camila's beauty and told her that nobody was talking in the whole city about anything other than her fine looks and her intelligence, because this had seemed an appropriate way to start gaining her confidence and making her ready to lend a willing ear the next time, using the trick that the devil uses when he wants to deceive those who are on their guard: he turns himself from an angel of darkness into an angel of light, presents a specious appearance of virtue, and finally reveals himself and achieves what he wants, so long as his deceit isn't discovered at the outset. Anselmo was well pleased, and said that he'd provide the same opportunity every day even if he didn't leave home, because he'd find things to do about the house in such a way that Camila wouldn't suspect their plot.

'Many days went by and Lotario didn't say a word to Camila, yet assured Anselmo that he'd talked to her and couldn't elicit the smallest hint of an agreement to do anything untoward, or make her give him the slightest shadow of hope – on the contrary, she'd threatened to tell her husband if he didn't give up his wicked designs.

'"Very well," said Anselmo. "So far Camila has resisted words, and now we must see how she resists deeds: tomorrow I shall give you two thousand gold escudos for you to offer or even give her, and another two thousand to buy jewels to tempt her, because women, particularly beautiful ones, are fond of dressing well and looking smart, however virtuous they are. And if she resists this temptation I shall rest satisfied and shan't trouble you any more."

'Lotario replied that now he'd started out on that business he'd see it through, even though he knew he was going to end up exhausted and defeated. On the next day he received the four thousand escudos, and with them four thousand headaches, because he couldn't think how he could lie his way out of this new predicament; but in the end he decided to tell Anselmo that Camila was as impervious to gifts and promises of gifts as she was to words, and that there wasn't any point in wearing himself out any more, because it was all a waste of time.

'But fortune, which had other plans, ordained that once Anselmo had left Lotario and Camila alone as usual, he should lock himself into a side room and watch and listen through the keyhole, and discover that in over half an hour Lotario didn't direct a single word at Camila, and wouldn't have done so if he'd sat there for a century; and Anselmo realized that everything his friend had told him about Camila's replies had been fiction and falsehoods. And to confirm his suspicion he walked out of the room, called Lotario to one side and asked him what news there was and what state Camila was in. Lotario replied that he wasn't going to address her on the subject ever again, because her answers were so brusque and surly that he wouldn't have the courage to say another word to her.

' "O Lotario, Lotario," cried Anselmo, "how badly you fulfil your duty and repay all the trust I've placed in you! I've been watching you through this keyhole and I've seen that you haven't said a word to Camila, from which I conclude that your very first words to her have yet to pass your lips; and if this is so, as I'm sure it is, why do you deceive me, why do you plot to deprive me of the means of carrying this desire of mine into effect?"

'Anselmo said no more, but he had said enough to cover Lotario with shame and confusion; and, as if he took being caught in this lie as a blemish on his honour, he swore that from that moment on he'd take the utmost care to do exactly as he was told and never lie again, as Anselmo would be able to corroborate if he spied on his every move, although he wouldn't need to put himself to any such trouble, because of the pains Lotario would take to raise himself above all suspicion. Anselmo believed Lotario and, to smooth his path and remove all risk of interruption, he decided to absent himself from home for a week by going to visit a friend who lived in a village not far from the city; and he persuaded this friend to summon him urgently, to provide Camila with an excuse for his departure.

'Unfortunate, ill-advised Anselmo! What are you doing? What are you plotting? What are you trying to bring about? Look here: you're doing yourself great harm, you're plotting your own dishonour and you're bringing about your own destruction. Your wife Camila is a good woman; you possess her in peace and security; nobody interrupts your contentment; her desires don't venture beyond the walls of her house; you're her heaven on earth, the goal of her desires, the fulfilment of her joys and the rule by which she measures her will, always adjusting it to your will and that of heaven. So if the mine of her honour, beauty, virtue and modesty yields up to you, without even needing to be worked, all the riches that it contains and that you can desire, why do you want to dig still deeper in search of yet more veins of new and unseen treasure, risking the collapse of the whole structure, which is supported only on the feeble props of her frail nature? Remember that the man who seeks the impossible may justly be denied the possible, or, as the poet expressed it better:

> I look to death in quest of life;
> I seek health in infirmity
> And freedom in captivity;
> I search for rest in bitter strife
> And faithfulness in treachery.
> But fortune always was unkind:
> I know that it has been designed
> By adverse fate and heaven's decree
> That, since I seek what cannot be,
> What can be I shall never find.[7]

'The next day Anselmo went off to the village, after telling Camila that Lotario would come to look after the house and dine with her while he was away, and that she should take care to treat Lotario as she would her own husband. Camila, being a sensible and honourable woman, was distressed by these orders, and asked him to bear in mind that it wasn't right for anybody to take his place at table while he was away, and that, if he was doing it because he was uncertain of her ability to manage the household affairs, he should give her this one chance to show him that she could cope with this and much greater problems. Anselmo replied that he'd made up his mind, and that she just had to bow her head and obey him. Camila said that she would do so, but much against her will.

'Anselmo left, and on the following day Lotario came to the house, where Camila gave him a warm but correct welcome. She avoided places where he might find her alone, seeking always to be attended by her servants, in particular a maidservant called Leonela of whom she was very fond, because the two of them had been brought up together in Camila's parents' house and, when she'd married Anselmo, Leonela had come with her. For the first three days Lotario didn't say a word to Camila, even though he had an opportunity to do so whenever the table was cleared and the servants went away for a hasty meal, as she had ordered. And Leonela had even received instructions to dine before Camila did, and then never to leave her side; but the maidservant's thoughts were intent on other matters concerning her own pleasures, and she needed time for her amusements, so she didn't always obey her mistress's orders, but left the two alone, as if that were what she'd been told to do. But Camila's modest manner, her gravity of expression and the composure of her person were enough to curb Lotario's tongue.

'Whatever good was done by Camila's virtues in silencing Lotario was outweighed, however, by the harm they did in other ways, because even if his tongue was stilled, his feelings were not, and he had the opportunity to gaze in awe at each one of Camila's perfections of goodness and beauty, which were enough to make a marble statue fall in love, let alone a human heart.

'Lotario would be looking at her when he should have been speaking to her, and he would be thinking how lovable she was, and this idea slowly began to make inroads on his consideration for Anselmo, and a thousand times he decided to leave the city and go where Anselmo would never see him again, nor he Camila; but he was held back by the delight he derived from looking at her. He struggled and struggled with himself to repress the pleasure that forced him to keep looking at Camila. When he was alone he condemned his folly; he called himself a false friend and even a bad Christian; he argued with himself and drew up comparisons between himself and Anselmo, and the conclusion was always that Anselmo's madness and rashness were worse than his own breach of trust, and that if what he was planning to do was as excusable before God as it was before men, he needn't fear any punishment for his sin.

'And so it was that Camila's beauty and goodness, together with the opportunity that her stupid husband had placed in his hands, overthrew all Lotario's loyalty; and, after three days during which he fought a continuous battle against his desires, he made his first pass at Camila without a thought for anything other than his pleasure, and in such a fluster and with such words of love that all she could do in her bewilderment was to come to her feet and walk to her room in silence. But this rebuttal, far from stifling Lotario's hopes, because love and hopes are always born together, only strengthened his feelings. Camila, for her part, had found in Lotario what she had never suspected was there, and she didn't know what to do. Considering it unsafe and improper to give him any more opportunities to talk to her, she decided to send a servant to Anselmo that very night with a letter in which she wrote:

CHAPTER XXXIV

In which the Tale of Inappropriate Curiosity is continued

Just as it is commonly said that an army is in a bad way without its general and a castle without its warden, so I say that a young married woman is very much worse off without her husband, unless the most pressing of reasons forces him to be absent. I am in such a bad way without you, and so unable to bear your absence, that if you do not come home soon I shall have to go and stay for a while at my parents' house, even though that would leave yours unguarded; because the guard whom you left me, if that is what he is meant to be, seems more concerned with his own pleasure than with your interest; and since you are an intelligent man I need say no more, nor would it be right for me to do so.

'When Anselmo received this letter he realized that Lotario had begun the campaign, and that Camila must have responded as he'd hoped she would; and, delighted with the news, he didn't write back but told the messenger to tell Camila on no account to leave the house, because he'd soon return. Camila was amazed at Anselmo's reply, which threw her into even greater confusion, because she didn't dare stay at home, still less go to her parents' house, since if she stayed her virtue was imperilled and if she left she would be disobeying her husband.

'She eventually decided to do what was the worst thing she could have done – to stay at home and not to avoid Lotario, so as not to give her servants food for gossip; and she was already regretting having written to her husband, worried that he might think Lotario had noticed some levity in her conduct that had encouraged him to abandon the respect he owed her. But she trusted her own virtue and put her faith in God and in her determination to resist all Lotario's advances in silence, without mentioning the matter again to her husband, so as not to create any trouble or conflict for him. And she was even searching for some way in which she could exonerate Lotario when Anselmo asked what had prompted her to write that letter.

'On the following day, armed with these resolutions, more honourable than wise or effective, she sat listening to Lotario, who was so insistent that her steadfastness began to weaken, and her modesty had to struggle to come to the rescue of her eyes and prevent them from betraying the loving compassion that Lotario's words and tears had awoken in her breast. Lotario observed all this, and it inflamed him even more. The moment arrived when he decided that he must intensify his siege of this fortress while the opportunity provided by Anselmo's absence lasted; so he attacked her pride by praising her beauty, because there's nothing that can demolish the fortified towers of a beautiful woman's vanity sooner than that vanity itself when deployed by flattery. And he mined away at the fort of Camila's integrity with such charges that even if she'd been made of bronze she'd have come toppling down. Lotario wept, he begged, he promised, he flattered, he insisted and he feigned with such feeling, with such shows of sincerity, that he overcame Camila's modesty and won the victory that he'd least expected and most desired.

'She surrendered; Camila surrendered; but what wonder, if Lotario's friendship didn't stand firm? A clear example showing that love can only be conquered by fleeing from it, and that nobody should engage with such a powerful enemy, because its human strength can only be defeated by divine might. Leonela alone knew about her mistress's frailty, because the two false friends and new lovers couldn't keep it from her. Lotario didn't see fit to tell Camila about Anselmo's scheme and reveal that he was the one who'd provided the opportunity for what had happened, wanting her not to disparage his love but to believe that his advances had been spontaneous, uncontrollable, unpremeditated.

'A few days later Anselmo returned to his house and didn't notice what was missing there: what he'd taken least care of, yet had most valued. He went at once to see Lotario, and found him at home; the two embraced each other, and one of them asked for the news that meant life or death for him.

'"The news I have for you, my dear friend Anselmo," said Lotario, "is that you have a wife worthy to be an example and a pattern for all good women. My words to her have gone with the wind; my promises have been disdained; my gifts have been rejected; she has mocked my crocodile tears. In short, just as Camila is the epitome of beauty, so she also is the treasure-house of chastity, propriety, and modesty and all the virtues that can make an honourable woman fortunate and praiseworthy. Here you are, my friend, take back your money: I haven't needed to touch it, because Camila's integrity doesn't yield to such wretched things as gifts and promises. Be satisfied with this, Anselmo, don't make any further trials, and, now that you've navigated unscathed the gulf of all the suspicions that can be and are entertained about women, don't venture again on to the deep sea of yet more problems, don't engage another pilot to test the soundness and strength of the ship that heaven has sent you for your passage across the ocean of this life, but rather consider yourself safe in harbour, and moor your ship to the anchors of proper respect, and stay there until you have to pay the debt that not even the noblest of mortals are exempt from paying."

'Anselmo was delighted with what Lotario had said, and he believed every word of it as if some oracle had been speaking. But this didn't prevent him from begging his friend not to abandon the campaign, even if only for the sake of curiosity and amusement, and using less urgent methods than hitherto; all Anselmo wanted Lotario to do now was to write some poetry praising Camila and calling her Chloris, because then he would tell her that their friend was in love with a lady to whom he'd given that name so that he could sing her praises with the propriety due to her good character. And if Lotario didn't want to take the trouble to write the verses, he would do so himself.

'"That won't be necessary," said Lotario, "because the muses aren't so hostile to me that they don't pay me occasional visits. Tell Camila about my love and her false name, just as you've suggested, and leave me to see to the verses, which will be the very best that I can manage, even if not as good as their subject deserves."

'This was what the inappropriately curious husband and his treacherous friend agreed; and when Anselmo returned home he asked Camila what she was astonished he hadn't asked already: to tell him what had prompted her to write that letter. Camila replied that Lotario had seemed to be rather freer with his looks than when Anselmo was present, but that she'd later realized she'd been mistaken: it must all have been in her imagination, because Lotario always avoided seeing her and being alone with her. Anselmo told her that she could indeed dismiss her suspicions, because he knew that Lotario was in love with one of the high-born young ladies of the city, whose praises he sang using the name Chloris; and that, even if he weren't in love with Chloris, Camila could have nothing to fear, given Lotario's uprightness and the close friendship that united the two men. If Camila hadn't been warned by Lotario that this love for Chloris was a pretence and that he'd told Anselmo all this so that he could while away the time writing in praise of Camila herself, she'd have fallen into the snare of despairing jealousy; but, being forewarned, she didn't so much as bat an eyelid.

'The next day, as the three sat round the table after dinner, Anselmo asked Lotario to recite some of those verses that he'd written about his beloved Chloris: since Camila didn't know her, he could safely say whatever he pleased.

'"Even if Camila did know her," replied Lotario, "I wouldn't keep anything back, because when a lover praises his lady for her beauty and reproaches her for her cruelty he can't do her good name any harm. But, be that as it may, I can tell you that yesterday I wrote a sonnet about my Chloris's ingratitude, and it goes like this:

SONNET

In the quiescence of the silent night,
As others dream in comforting repose,
To heaven and to Chloris I recite
The mean account of my abundant woes.
    And as Aurora rises and displays
On eastern balconies her rosy face
I sigh and stammer as I try to raise
My protest and submit my plaintive case.
    And then, as Phoebus, from his starry throne,
Casts down his rays upon the burning soil,
With aggravated grief I weep and moan.
And night's return renews my sorrow's toil.
But never, as I madly persevere,
Will heaven listen, or will Chloris hear."

'Camila liked the sonnet, but Anselmo liked it even more, and he praised it and declared that the woman who didn't respond to such evident truths was too cruel. To which Camila replied:

' "So everything that lover-poets say is true, is it?"

' "No, as poets they don't tell the truth," said Lotario, "but what they say as lovers is as understated as it is, indeed, truthful."

' "There's no doubt of that," replied Anselmo, to press Lotario's feelings on Camila, who was as unaware of Anselmo's stratagem as she was in love with Lotario.

'And so, since she took such delight in everything Lotario did, and even more because she knew that his verses and his desires were directed at her and that she was the real Chloris, she asked him to recite another sonnet or any other poem of his, if he could remember one.

' "Yes, I can," replied Lotario, "though I don't think it's as good or, rather, as tolerable as the first one. But you can judge for yourselves, because here it is:

SONNET

I know you're killing me! And I repeat,
Since, thankless beauty, you still doubt it's true,
You'll sooner see me dying at your feet
Than giving up my reverence for you.
      Then I'll be gone from human memory,
Bereft of glory, honour, life and grace,
And on my opened breast the gods shall see
The image of your captivating face.
      This is a relic that I shan't forsake
In that most desperate and dreadful strait
In which I'll be, for obstinacy's sake,
Made, by your rigour, still more obstinate.
Unhappy he who sails through storm-tossed night
And rock-strewn seas without a guiding light!"

'Anselmo praised this second sonnet as he had the first one; and so he went on adding link after link to the chain with which he was shackling himself and securing his own dishonour, because the more Lotario dishonoured him the more he told him that his honour was assured; and, in this way, every step Camila took down into the depths of disgrace was, as her husband saw it, a step that she climbed up towards the pinnacles of virtue and good repute.

'Once when Camila was alone with her maidservant, she said:

' "I feel ashamed, Leonela, when I consider how little I've valued myself, because I didn't even make Lotario spend any time to buy full possession of the favours I so quickly granted him. I fear he'll only remember how eagerly and easily I gave in to him, and not bear in mind the pressure he exerted to make himself irresistible."

' "You shouldn't worry about that, my lady," replied Leonela. "The value of a gift neither rises nor falls as a result of giving it quickly, so long as the gift is a good one and of value in itself. Indeed it's often said that she who gives quickly gives twice."

' "And it's also said," said Camila, "that what's cheaply bought is little valued."

'"But that doesn't apply to you," replied Leonela, "because love, I've heard, sometimes flies and sometimes walks, rushes along with one person and dawdles with another, cools some people down and heats some others up, wounds this one and slaughters that, ends the race of passion just about as soon as he's started it, lays siege to a fortress in the morning and overruns it in the evening, because there's no force that can resist him. And this being so, what is it that alarms you, what have you got to fear? Because this is what Lotario must have felt, too, once love had taken my master's absence as his instrument for overcoming both of you. And it was inevitable that, while Anselmo was away, what love had already made up his mind about was going to happen, without giving Anselmo time to return and curtail love's work, because love has no better minister to carry out his desires than opportunity: he makes use of opportunity in all his actions, particularly at the beginning. I know all this very well, more from experience than from hearsay, and one day I'll tell you all about it, ma'am, because I'm young, too, and made of flesh and blood.

'"What's more, my lady Camila, you didn't give in so soon that you couldn't first see Lotario's soul revealed in his eyes, in his sighs, in his words and his promises and his gifts – and you also saw there and in his virtues how worthy he was of your love. Now this being so, don't you go bothering your head with all those finicky and prudish scruples, just be assured that Lotario thinks as much of you as you do of him, and be thankful and happy that, given that you've fallen into the snare of love, your captor's a worthy and honourable man. He's sensible, solitary, solicitous and secretive, so he's got the four S's they say all good lovers must have – not only that, though, he's got a whole alphabet of qualities, and if you don't believe me you just listen and you'll soon hear how I reel it off! If I judge right he's appreciative, benevolent, chivalrous, dutiful, enamoured, firm, gallant, honourable, illustrious, judicious, kind, loyal, manly, noble, onest, princely, quantious, rich, the four S's of the saying, and then tacit, unattached, veracious, well-born, the X doesn't suit him because it's a rough old letter, the Y I've already done and as for the Z he's really zealous for your honour."

'Camila laughed at her maidservant's alphabet, and thought that she was more practised in matters of love than she'd admitted; and the girl confessed as much, revealing that she was seeing a well-born young man of that city, which worried Camila, who feared that this could put her own honour at risk. She insisted on being told whether the relationship had gone beyond words, and her maid replied without a blush that it had gone beyond words. It's clear that a lady's failings rob her maids of their shame, and when they see their mistress trip and fall they think nothing of stumbling – and letting her know all about it.

'All Camila could do was ask Leonela not to breathe a word about her mistress's affair to the man she said was her lover, and to manage her own affair in the utmost secrecy so that neither Anselmo nor Lotario found out about it. Leonela agreed, but the way in which she kept her promise confirmed Camila's fear that her servant was going to bring about the loss of her good name. Because once that brazen hussy Leonela became aware of the change in her mistress's behaviour, she had the effrontery to bring her own lover into the house, safe in the knowledge that even if her mistress saw him there she wouldn't dare expose him. The sins of any lady give rise to this evil, among many others: she becomes her own servants' slave, and has to cover up for their immorality and depravity, as did Camila, who realized dozens of times that Leonela was with her young man in a room in the house, yet not only didn't dare scold her but provided her with opportunities to let him in, and removed all obstacles from his path, to prevent her husband from seeing him. But she couldn't remove them successfully enough to prevent Lotario from seeing the young man as he left one day at dawn. At first, not recognizing him, Lotario thought he was a ghost, but when he saw him walk away muffling himself up with studied care, he abandoned that absurd notion for another which would have been the ruin of them all if Camila hadn't found a remedy. It didn't occur to Lotario that the man he'd seen leaving Anselmo's house at such an unseemly hour might have gone there for Leonela – Lotario didn't even remember that Leonela existed. All that came to his mind was that Camila had been an easy and rapid conquest for another man, just as she had been for him. These are the consequences of a sinning woman's behaviour. Her reputation is lost in the eyes of the man to whom she has surrendered after all his pleading and persuasion; and then he thinks that she will surrender to other men even more readily, and he is ready to believe every suspicion that finds its way into his mind. And at this point, it seems, all Lotario's good sense deserted him and all sound reasoning abandoned his head, because without pausing for a single judicious or even sane thought, blinded by the rage of jealousy gnawing at his entrails, and determined to avenge himself on Camila, who had done him no wrong, he ran to see Anselmo, who was still in his bed, and said:

' "I must inform you, Anselmo, that for many days now I have been battling with myself, struggling to avoid telling you something that it's neither possible nor right for me to conceal any longer. I must inform you that the fortress of Camila's virtue has surrendered, and that I can do with her as I please; and if I have been slow to reveal this truth to you, it's only because I wanted to see if it was merely some passing whim of hers, or if she was perhaps behaving as she was to test me and discover whether the advances I was making to her with your permission were seriously intended. I also believed that, if she was the woman she should be and we both thought she was, she would have told you about my approaches by now; but her delay forces me to recognize that she was telling the truth when she promised me that the next time you leave home she'll meet me in the garderobe where you keep your personal effects." (This was, indeed, their rendezvous.) "I don't want you to rush into taking your vengeance, because the sin is as yet committed only in thought, and, between now and the time of committing it in deed, Camila may change her mind and repent. And so, since you've always followed my advice at least in part, do take the advice I'm going to give you now so that you can, with a clear and cautious judgement unimpaired by error, decide on the best course of action to take. Pretend to go away for two or three days, as you sometimes do, and then conceal yourself in the garderobe — the tapestries and other hiding places there will make this easy; and then you'll see with your own eyes, and I shall see with mine, what is in Camila's mind, and if it's the wickedness that's to be feared rather than to be expected, you can inflict silent, prudent and judicious punishment for the wrong done you."

'Anselmo was left in stunned and bewildered amazement by Lotario's revelation, because it came when he was least expecting it: convinced as he was by now of Camila's triumph over Lotario's sham assaults on her virtue, he was beginning to enjoy the glory of victory. He remained silent for some moments, gazing at the floor without moving so much as an eyelash, until at length he said:

' "You have done everything, Lotario, that I expected of your friendship; I shall follow your advice; do as you please, but keep this secret as carefully as you can understand is necessary in this unexpected situation."

'Lotario promised to do so, but as soon as he left he realized how stupidly he'd acted, and repented of everything he'd said, because he could have taken revenge on Camila himself, and in a less cruel and dishonourable way. He cursed his lack of judgement, condemned his reckless action and racked his brains to find some way to undo what he'd done, or to save the situation. In the end he decided to make a clean breast of it all to Camila; there was no lack of opportunity for this, and he found her alone that same day; but when she saw that there was a chance to speak she was the one who did so:

' "I must tell you, my dear Lotario, that there's a grief so intense in my heart that it seems to be about to burst in my breast, and it will be a wonder if it doesn't; because Leonela's brazenness has reached such a pitch that every night she lets her lover into this house and he stays with her until morning, at great cost to my good name if anyone sees him leaving at such an unusual hour and reaches the obvious conclusion. And what most infuriates me is that I can't scold or punish her, because her knowledge of our affair stills my tongue and forces me to keep quiet about her affair, and I fear some harm will come of all this."

'At first Lotario thought this was a trick to persuade him that the man he'd seen leaving the house wasn't her lover; but her grief and her tears and her pleas for help made him see the truth, and this completed his confusion and remorse. Yet he replied to Camila that she shouldn't worry, because he would take measures to put an end to Leonela's insolence. He also told Camila what, in his jealous rage, he'd said to Anselmo, and how it had been agreed that Anselmo would hide in the garderobe and witness her infidelity for himself. Lotario begged her forgiveness for his folly and asked for her advice about how to put things right and extricate himself from the tortuous labyrinth into which his thoughtlessness had led him.

'Camila was appalled and infuriated by what Lotario had told her, and with many heated and well-chosen words she rebuked him and reviled his foul suspicions and his stupid action; but as women are naturally more quick-witted, for both good and evil, than men, though not when it comes to constructing coherent arguments, Camila hit there and then upon a way in which to solve such an apparently insoluble dilemma, and told Lotario to make Anselmo hide the next day where he'd said he would, and then she'd contrive to ensure that in future they'd be able to take their pleasure together without fear of interruption; and, without revealing any more of her plans, she instructed him, once Anselmo had hidden, to come as soon as Leonela called and to reply to everything she said exactly as he would reply if he didn't know that Anselmo was listening. Lotario pressed her to explain her scheme in full, so that he could make sure to do whatever he saw was necessary.

'"I'm telling you," said Camila, "that you have nothing to do except answer my questions," because she didn't want to forewarn him about her intentions, fearful that he might be unwilling to co-operate in the plan that seemed so excellent to her, and that he might develop other less effective plans of his own.

'Off went Lotario, and the next day Anselmo produced his excuse about going into the country to see his friend, made his departure, and returned to hide in the garderobe, which was easy for him to do because Camila and Leonela made it so. Anselmo lurked in his hiding-place with the trepidation of one waiting to see the bowels of his own honour torn to shreds, and on the brink of losing the supreme good that he'd once believed he possessed in his beloved Camila. Once Camila and Leonela were certain that Anselmo was installed, they walked into the garderobe, and no sooner had Camila set foot in it than she heaved the deepest of sighs and said:

'"Oh, my dear Leonela! Would it not be better, before I put into execution what I will not inform you of, so that you do not attempt to hinder me, if you took this dagger of Anselmo's, which I have just asked you to give me, and transfixed this infamous breast of mine with it? But no, no, do not do that; because it would not be right for me to receive the punishment for another's crime. First I must know what it was that Lotario's audacious and licentious eyes saw in me to make him dare to disclose his evil desire, both scorning his friend and dishonouring me. Go to that window, Leonela, and call him; he must be waiting out there, hoping to carry out his wicked design. But first mine, cruel yet honourable, will be put into effect."

'"Oh, my lady!" replied the wily and well-rehearsed Leonela. "What are you going to do with this dagger? Do you perhaps intend to take your own life, or to take Lotario's? Either of these actions will lead to the loss of your good name and reputation. It will be better to dissemble your wrong, and not give this wicked man the opportunity to enter this house and find us here alone. Remember, my lady, that we are weak women, and he is a man, and a determined one; and since he comes with that wicked intention, blinded by passion, perhaps before you can do whatever it is you have in mind he may do what would be worse for you than death itself. A plague upon my master Anselmo for giving this cutthroat such a free rein in his house! And when you have killed him, my lady, as I think you intend, what shall we do with him once he's dead?"

'"Do with him?" replied Camila. "Oh, we'll leave him for Anselmo to dispose of, because it's only right that he should enjoy the restful toil of burying his own infamy. Come now, call the man here, for every moment I delay my just revenge I seem to be failing in the loyalty I owe my husband." ·

'As Anselmo listened, his feelings changed with every word that Camila spoke. But when he heard that she was determined to kill Lotario, he made up his mind to come out and show himself, to avert such a disaster; he was held back, however, by his desire to see where all these brave words and virtuous sentiments would lead, and he decided to emerge later, in time to forestall any mischief.

'And now Camila was overcome by a violent fainting-fit and, as she threw herself on to a nearby bed, Leonela began to weep bitter tears and say:

'"Oh, woe is me that I should be so unhappy as to see dying here between my arms the flower of the world's chastity, the pick of pure women, the pattern of feminine virtue," and more to the same effect, and nobody could have heard her and not taken her for the most loyal and heart-broken maidservant in the world, and her mistress for another persecuted Penelope.[1]

'It wasn't very long before Camila came out of her fainting-fit, and as she did so she said:

'"Why do you not go, Leonela, to call the most faithful friend that the sun ever saw or the night ever hid? Come now, be quick, hurry, fly, lest the delay dampens the fire of my wrath, and the just revenge that I await is dissipated in threats and curses."

' "Yes, I am going to call him now, my lady," said Leonela, "but first you must give me that dagger, to prevent you from doing, while I am away, that which would leave all those who love you mourning for the rest of their lives."

' "Go, Leonela my friend, I assure you that I shall not do any such thing," replied Camila, "because even though it might be rash and stupid of me, in your eyes, to defend my honour, I am not going to be as rash and stupid as that Lucretia of whom it is said that she killed herself without having done anything blameworthy, and without first killing the man who caused her misfortune. I shall die if I have to, but I shall die revenged of him who made me come to this place to bewail his audacity, which sprang from no misconduct of mine."

'Leonela had to be coaxed again and again before she would go and call Lotario; but she went in the end, and while she was away Camila spoke, as if talking to herself:

' "God help me! Would it not have been better to send Lotario away, as I have on so many other occasions, than make him think, as must now be the case, that I am a loose and wicked woman, even if only until I correct him? Yes, it would, there is no doubt; but I should not achieve my revenge, and my husband's honour would not be upheld, if Lotario were allowed to stroll away unscathed from where his evil intentions have brought him. Let the traitor pay with his life for what his lust has led him to attempt. Let the whole world know (if it finds out) that Camila not only kept faith with her husband but avenged him on the man who presumed to offend him. Yet I do think, all the same, that it would be better to tell Anselmo about this; but then I tried to do so in that letter I sent him, and I suppose that the reason why he did nothing about the trouble to which it referred must have been because he is so good and trusting that he would not or could not believe that the breast of such a firm friend housed any feelings that went against his honour; and I myself did not believe it, either, for very many days, and would never have believed it if his insolence had not grown so great that his blatant gifts and splendid promises and never-ending tears made it plain. But why try to reason it all out now? Does a brave decision stand in need of arguments?

No, of course not. Begone, then, traitors! Draw nigh, revenge! Let the cheat enter, approach and die, come what may! I was pure when I came into the possession of the man that heaven gave me as my husband, and pure I shall be when I cease to be his; or, at worst, I shall be bathed in my own chaste blood and in the foul blood of the falsest friend the world has ever seen."

'As she talked she paced about the room brandishing the dagger, taking such enormous and irregular strides and making such gestures that she seemed to have lost her senses, and she looked more like some desperate villain than a gentle lady. Anselmo, hiding behind the tapestries, was watching it all in utter amazement, thinking that what he'd seen and heard was quite enough to refute even worse suspicions, and wishing that Lotario's part in the test could be avoided, because he feared a sudden disaster. He was about to emerge and embrace his wife and tell her the truth, yet he stayed where he was because he saw Leonela return leading Lotario by the hand; and when Camila saw him she drew a long line on the floor in front of her with the dagger, and said:

'"Lotario, listen to what I am going to say: if you should venture to cross this line or even approach it, as soon as I see what you are doing I shall plunge this dagger I hold deep into my breast. No, no, before you reply you must hear me out, and then you can say what you please. First of all, Lotario, I want you to tell me whether you know my husband Anselmo, and what you think of him; and then I want you to tell me whether you know me. Answer now, and do not be embarrassed or start weighing your words, because my questions are not difficult ones."

'Lotario wasn't so foolish that he hadn't realized, as soon as she'd told him to make Anselmo hide, what she was going to do; and he played along with such skill and good timing that the two of them could have persuaded anyone that their lie was more truthful than truth itself. He replied:

'"I did not suspect, lovely Camila, that you had summoned me to ask questions so far removed from the purpose that has brought me here. If you have done this to delay granting me the favour that you have promised me, you could have achieved that without making me come, because the nearer the prospect of possession the more eager we are to enjoy the desired good. But, so as not to be accused of refusing to answer your questions, let me say that I do know your husband Anselmo, and we have known each other since our tenderest years, and I will not say what you know only too well about our friendship, because I do not wish to bear witness to the offence that I am being forced to commit against it by love, a potent excuse for even greater sins. I do know you, too, and I hold you as dear as your husband does; or else I should not, for lesser charms than yours, be acting so contrary to my duty as a gentleman and to the holy laws of true friendship, which I have now violated and broken at the instigation of an enemy as dauntless as is love."

' "If you confess to that," replied Camila, "you mortal enemy of everything that truly deserves to be loved, how can you dare appear before the woman you know is the mirror into which gazes a man whom you should use as your mirror so that he could show you how little excuse you have for wronging him? But ah! unhappy me! now I realize what it was that led you to forget yourself: it must have been some indiscretion of mine – I will not call it immodesty, because it cannot have been deliberate, but rather one of those slips that we women are prone to make when we believe that we do not need to be on our guard. Or else just tell me this, O traitor! When did I ever respond to your appeals with any word or hint that could have awoken the slightest shadow of a hope of gratifying your infamous desires? When were your words of love not rejected and reproved with words of the harshest severity? When were your many promises ever believed, your even more abundant gifts ever accepted? And yet it is my belief that no man can persevere in his quest for love unless he is sustained by some glimmer of hope; so I shall blame myself for your insolence, because some thoughtlessness of mine must have kept your hopes alive, and I shall inflict on myself the punishment that you deserve. And so that you can see that if I am going to be so cruel to myself I cannot fail to treat you in the same way, I have brought you here to witness the sacrifice that I am going to offer to the offended honour of my most honourable husband, whom you have wronged to the utmost of your power, and whom I too have wronged by not taking sufficient care to avoid giving you the impression, if this is what I did, that I welcomed and applauded your wicked designs. I repeat that what most distresses me is my suspicion that it was some carelessness on my part that spawned such wild feelings in you, and this is what I most wish to

punish with my own hand, because if another executioner did so my guilt might become public; but I shall die killing, and take with me the one who will satisfy my desire for the vengeance that I long for – nay, now enjoy! – so that I can see, wherever it may be, the punishment that impartial, unbending justice metes out to the man who has reduced me to this desperate plight."

'As she spoke these words she sprang upon Lotario with unbelievable violence and agility, brandishing the dagger in such a show of determination to bury it in his chest that he himself almost wondered whether she was pretending or not, because he had to have recourse to all his strength and dexterity to prevent Camila from wounding him. She acted out her strange, unworthy deceit to such perfection that to make it even more realistic she decided to colour it with her own blood, and realizing, or pretending to realize, that she couldn't wound Lotario, she said:

' "Though fate denies me a full satisfaction of my just desires, at least it will not prevent me from satisfying them in part."

'And wresting the hand holding the dagger from Lotario's grasp she placed the point of the weapon where it could only make a shallow wound and slid it into her armpit, under her left shoulder, and then dropped to the floor as if she had fainted. Leonela and Lotario stood astonished at this development, still wondering whether what they were witnessing could be true, as Camila lay there on the floor, bathed in her own blood. Breathless with terror, Lotario ran to pull the dagger out, but when he saw how slight the wound was the fear that till then had possessed him was dispelled, and he was struck anew with amazement at the lovely Camila's cunning, prudence and quick wits; and, continuing to play his part, he began to make a long, sorrowful lament over her, as if she were dead, cursing not only himself but also the man who had put him in this position. And since he knew that his friend Anselmo was listening, his lamentations were such that anyone who heard him would have felt much sorrier for him than for Camila, even supposing her to be dead.

'Leonela took her up in her arms and laid her on the bed, entreating Lotario to go and bring someone who could look after her in secret. She also asked him for his advice about what they could tell Anselmo concerning her mistress's wound if he returned before it healed. Lotario replied that they could say whatever they liked, because he was in no state to give advice that would be of any use; he only told her to try to stop the bleeding, because he was going where nobody could find him. And with a show of enormous grief he left the house, and once he was alone where nobody could see him he crossed himself over and over again in wonder at Camila's ingenuity and Leonela's role-playing. He reflected on how convinced Anselmo must be that he had a second Portia for a wife,[2] and he couldn't wait to see his friend to rejoice together over the most perfectly dissembled lie and truth that could ever be imagined.

'So Leonela staunched the bleeding, which was no more copious than was necessary to lend credibility to the performance, washed the wound with a little wine and bound it up as best she could, uttering while she did so such words as, even if nothing had been said before, would have been enough to convince Anselmo that in Camila he possessed a pattern of chastity. Leonela's words were accompanied by others from Camila, as she called herself a spineless coward for having lacked courage when she most needed it, to take that life of hers that she held in such abhorrence. She asked for her maid's advice about whether she should tell her dear husband all about the incident, and her maid advised her not to, because that would compel him to avenge himself on Lotario, which he couldn't do without great risk, and it was the good wife's duty not to give her husband reasons to fight, but rather to keep him out of trouble as much as possible. Camila replied that this was sound advice and that she would follow it, but that at all events they were going to have to find some explanation for her wound, because Anselmo was bound to notice it; to which Leonela replied that she was incapable of telling a lie, even in jest.

'"And how capable do you think I am, my dear?" replied Camila. "I should not dare to invent or maintain a falsehood even if my life depended on it. So if we can think of no escape from this difficulty, it will be better to make a clean breast of it than have him catch us telling lies."

'"Do not worry, my lady," replied Leonela. "By tomorrow I shall have thought of something to tell him, and maybe, with the wound being where it is, it can be covered up so that he does not notice; and heaven will see fit, I am sure, to favour our just and honourable cause. Do calm down, my lady, and try to control your feelings, so that master does not realize that you are upset when he returns – and leave all the rest to me and to God, who always comes to the help of well-intentioned people."

'Anselmo had been watching and listening, with rapt attention, to the tragedy of the death of his honour, as it was performed by the players with such unusual and effective feeling that they seemed to have been transformed into the very characters they were acting. He was longing for night to come to give him the chance to slip away from home and go to see his good friend Lotario and rejoice with him over the precious pearl[3] that he'd discovered in the revelation of his wife's virtue. The two women took good care to give him an easy opportunity to escape, and he accepted it and slipped away, and went straight to look for Lotario; he found him, and words can't describe his embraces, his expressions of joy and his praise of Camila. Lotario listened to it all, unable to produce any expressions of joy at all, because he couldn't help thinking how deluded his friend was, and how inexcusable was his own treachery. And although Anselmo noticed that Lotario wasn't at all happy, he supposed that it was because Camila had been left bleeding on the floor and he had been the cause. And so, among other arguments, Anselmo told his friend not to worry about Camila – the wound was clearly not such a serious one, since the two women had agreed to keep it hidden, and this showed that there was nothing to fear, and they could rejoice and celebrate together; because thanks to Lotario's ingenious mediation Anselmo had been raised to the highest happiness that he'd ever dared to desire for himself, and the only pastime he wanted now was writing poems in praise of Camila to make her eternal in the memory of future generations. Lotario praised his friend's good intentions and said that he, for his part, would help to erect so glorious an edifice.

'This left Anselmo the most splendidly bamboozled man that the world had ever seen: he led home by the hand the man who had ruined his good name, believing that what he was taking there was the instrument of his glory. Camila greeted him with a grimace on her face and a smile in her heart. This deception lasted for some while until, a few months later, fortune turned her wheel, the artfully concealed intrigue was revealed and Anselmo's inappropriate curiosity cost him his life.'

CHAPTER XXXV

*Which brings the Tale of Inappropriate Curiosity
to an end*

Not much more of the tale remained to be read when Sancho Panza came running in a frenzy from the loft where Don Quixote had gone to bed, crying:

'Come on, come on, all of you, come and help my master, he's got himself into the roughest and toughest battle I've ever set eyes on. Great God, he's just taken his sword to that giant who's my lady Princess Micomicona's enemy, and he's topped him like a turnip!'

'What do you mean, my dear friend?' said the priest, putting aside what was left of the tale. 'Are you in your right mind, Sancho? How the devil can what you say be right, when the giant's a good seven thousand miles away?'

They heard a great uproar in the loft, and Don Quixote bellowing:

'Stay, robber, scoundrel, poltroon; I have you at last; and your scimitar shall not save you!'

It sounded as if he was slashing the walls. Sancho said:

'Don't just stand around listening, get in there and pull them apart, or give my master a helping hand, though that won't be needed any more, because the giant's dead by now, for certain, and answering to God for his evil past – I saw his blood flowing all over the floor, and his head cut off and lying on its side, and it's as big as an enormous wineskin.'

'I'll be hanged,' interjected the innkeeper, 'if Don Quixote or Don Devil hasn't been slashing at those skins of red wine I keep behind that bed, and the wine he's spilled must be what this character took for blood.'

And he burst into the loft, and the others followed him, and they found Don Quixote wearing the strangest outfit in the world. He was in his shirt, which wasn't long enough in front to cover his thighs, and was some six inches shorter behind; his legs were long and scrawny, hairy and none too clean; on his head he had a greasy red nightcap belonging to the innkeeper. Round his left arm he had wound the blanket from his bed, against which Sancho bore such a grudge, for reasons well known to himself; in his right hand he grasped his sword, with which he was letting fly in all directions as he shouted out as if he really were fighting with a giant. And the best part of it all is that his eyes were tight shut, because he was asleep and dreaming that he was battling against the giant: so intensely had he lived in his imagination the adventure in which he was going to be triumphant that he was dreaming he'd reached the kingdom of Micomicón and was at grips with the enemy. And he'd given the wineskins so many slashes, thinking he was slashing the giant, that the loft was flooded with wine. This sight so enraged the innkeeper that he flew at Don Quixote and began to rain so many punches on him that, if Cardenio and the priest hadn't dragged him away, he'd have put an end to the adventure of the giant there and then; yet the poor knight still didn't wake up, until the barber brought a large bucketful of cold water from the well and drenched him from head to toe, and then he did awaken, but not fully enough to be aware of his situation.

In view of Don Quixote's short and scanty apparel, Dorotea didn't care to go in to watch the battle between her protector and her adversary. Sancho was looking all over the floor for the giant's head and, not finding it, he said:

'Now I know that everything about this house is enchanted – last time, here, where I'm standing now, I got a good hiding and I never knew who gave it to me, and I never even saw anyone, and this time I can't find that head I saw cut off with my own two eyes, and the blood was gushing from the body like a fountain.'

'Blood and fountain my foot, you enemy of God and all his holy saints!' said the innkeeper. 'Can't you see, you idiot, that your blood and your fountain are none other than these wineskins here all full of holes and this red wine we're swimming in? And I'd like to see the soul of the man who spilled it all swimming too – swimming in hell!'

'I don't know anything about that,' replied Sancho, 'all I know is that I'm going to be so unlucky that just because I can't find this head my earldom's going to melt away like salt in water.'

And Sancho awake was worse than his master asleep, so besotted was he with his master's promises. The innkeeper was in despair at the squire's apathy and his master's handiwork, and swore it wasn't going to be like last time when they got away without paying – all the privileges of his chivalry weren't going to let him off coughing up for the two of them, right down to the cost of the patches for the perforated wineskins.

The priest was holding on to Don Quixote by his hands, and he, thinking that the adventure was over now and that he was standing before Princess Micomicona, fell to his knees in front of the priest, saying:

'O great and famous lady, Your Highness can from this day forward rest assured that this ill-born creature can do you no further harm, and from this day forward, too, I am released from the promise I made you, for, with the help of God on high and through the favour of her for whom I live and breathe, I have fulfilled it to perfection.'

'Didn't I tell you so?' said Sancho when he heard this. 'It's true, it's true, I wasn't drunk – my master's done for the giant good and proper! We're having a fiesta after all, my earldom's on its way!'

Who could have failed to laugh at the nonsense of these two, master and servant? And laugh they did, all except the innkeeper, who was cursing himself to the devil. But at length the barber, Cardenio and the priest managed to force Don Quixote down on to the bed, where, exhausted, he fell asleep. They left him there and went out into the porch to console Sancho Panza for not having found the giant's head, but it was a harder job to pacify the innkeeper, who was reduced to despair by his wineskins' sudden death. And his wife was screaming:

'In an evil hour that knight errant came into my house, and I wish I'd never set eyes on him, he's turned out so expensive. The last time he went off owing me for the night, supper, bed, straw and barley for him and his squire and a nag and a donkey, saying that he was a knight adventurer, and I hope God sends him plenty of misadventures, him and all the adventurers in the world, and he said that being one made him exempt from paying, because this was written up on all the knight-errantry price-lists. And then, thanks to him, this other character came and took my tail away, and he's given it back with more than half-a-real's damage, all the hair gone, and now it's no good for what my husband wants it for. And on top of all that, hacking my wineskins to pieces and spilling all my wine – I'd like to see all his blood spilled, I can tell you that much. Well, they aren't getting away with it – by the bones of my father and the eternal glory of my mother I swear they're going to pay me back, every single maravedí they owe me, or my name isn't what it is and I'm not my father's daughter!'

The innkeeper's wife went on railing away like this, with her good servant Maritornes seconding her. Her daughter kept quiet, and every so often she smiled. The priest calmed everyone down, promising to make good their losses as best he could – both the wineskins and the wine, and above all the tail, which they evidently held so dear. Dorotea consoled Sancho Panza by promising him that so long as it was confirmed that his master had indeed cut the giant's head off, and once her kingdom was restored to peace, she'd give him the very best earldom in her gift. Sancho took comfort from this, and he assured the princess that she could be dead certain he really had seen the giant's head and that if she wanted any more details he'd got a beard that went right down to his middle, and if the head didn't turn up it was because all the goings-on in that place were enchanted, as he'd found the other time he'd stayed there. Dorotea said she believed he was right, and he shouldn't worry, everything would go well and turn out to his heart's content.

Now that peace was restored, the priest thought it would be a good idea to finish reading the tale, because he could see that not much was left. Cardenio, Dorotea and all the others begged him to do so. He was eager to please everyone, and was enjoying the reading himself, so he continued:

'So Anselmo, convinced of Camila's virtue, led a happy and carefree life, and Camila took good care to glower at Lotario whenever she saw him, so that Anselmo should believe her feelings for him to be the opposite of what they were; and to provide even more confirmation Lotario begged leave not to return, because it was clear how upset Camila was by his visits; but the deluded Anselmo replied that by no manner of means should he absent himself. And so in a thousand different ways Anselmo was manufacturing his own dishonour in the belief that he was creating his own happiness.

'Meanwhile, Leonela's satisfaction at finding her love affair officially approved was such that she brushed all other considerations aside and pursued her pleasure with abandon, safe in the knowledge that her mistress was covering up for her and even advising her on how she could enjoy herself with little fear of detection. But finally, one night Anselmo heard footsteps in Leonela's room, and, when he tried to go in to see who it was, he found that the door was being held against him, which made him even more determined to open it; he forced it open and broke in to see a man jumping out of the window into the street, and, as he ran over to catch him or at least see who he was, Leonela prevented him from doing either by clinging on to him and crying:

' "Calm down, sir, don't get excited, don't follow him out of the window – it's my own affair, indeed he's my husband."

'Anselmo wouldn't believe her, and instead, in a blind rage, he drew his dagger and threatened her, saying that if she didn't tell him the truth he'd kill her. She was so terrified that she didn't know what she was saying when she said:

' "Don't kill me, sir, I'll tell you something more important than you can imagine."

' "I want to hear it now," said Anselmo. "If not, you're dead."

' "I can't, not now," said Leonela, "I'm too upset. Give me till tomorrow, and then I'll tell you something that'll amaze you. And believe me, the person who jumped out of the window is a local young man who's given me his hand in marriage."

'With this Anselmo regained his composure and agreed to the postponement, not suspecting that he was going to hear anything against Camila, about whose virtue he was so convinced; and so he left the room and locked Leonela into it, telling her that she wouldn't be allowed out until she said what she had to say.

'He went straight to Camila to inform her about what had happened and about the maid's promise of revelations of the utmost importance. There's no need to describe Camila's perturbation, for her fear was so great – believing, as she did and as she had every reason to, that Leonela was going to tell Anselmo all she knew about her mistress's infidelity – that she didn't have the courage to wait and see whether her suspicions were justified; and that very night, once she saw Anselmo was asleep, she collected together her finest jewels and some money and slipped unnoticed from the house and went to Lotario's and told him what had happened, imploring him to find a safe hiding-place for her or to run away with her to where Anselmo couldn't catch up with them. Camila's words plunged Lotario into such confusion that he couldn't reply, still less decide what to do. At length he resolved to remove Camila to a convent where one of his sisters was prioress. Camila agreed, and with all the urgency demanded by the circumstances Lotario took her to the convent and left her there, and departed from the city without telling anybody.

'At dawn the next day, Anselmo was so anxious to learn what Leonela had to tell him that he didn't notice that Camila was missing from his side when he got up and walked to the room into which he'd locked their servant. He opened the door and went in, but Leonela wasn't there; all he found were some sheets knotted together and hanging from the window, a sure sign of how she'd escaped. He went sadly back to tell Camila and was astonished not to find her in bed or anywhere in the house. He asked his servants where she was, but nobody could give him an answer.

'As he was searching for Camila he came across her jewel-boxes open and most of the jewels gone, and this made him realize the full extent of his misfortune and appreciate that Leonela wasn't the one to blame. He went off, still only half-dressed, lost in thought and stricken with grief, to tell his friend Lotario about the disaster. When he couldn't find him either, and Lotario's servants said he had departed that night and had taken all his money with him, Anselmo thought he'd go mad. And as the last straw, he returned home and found not one of his servants there, just an empty, deserted house.

'He didn't know what to think, say or do, and he was slowly losing his sanity. He found himself deprived at one blow of his wife, his friend and his servants, abandoned by the heavens above and, worst of all, dishonoured, because in Camila's disappearance he could see his own undoing.

'Eventually he decided to go to the village where his friend lived, and where he himself had stayed to make it possible to contrive this whole disaster. He shut up his house, mounted his horse and started out with a heavy heart; but he'd hardly gone halfway when, besieged by his own thoughts, he had to dismount and tie his horse by the reins to a tree, at the foot of which he dropped to the ground, breathing piteous sighs of sorrow; and there he lay until close to nightfall, when he saw a man coming on horseback from the city, and, after greeting him, he asked what was the news from Florence. The man from the city replied:

' "It's the strangest news that's been heard there for many a long day; because it's reported that Lotario, the great friend of rich Anselmo, who used to live in the San Giovanni area, ran away last night with Camila, Anselmo's wife, who's nowhere to be found. Camila's maidservant told the whole story, after being discovered last night by the Governor letting herself down by a sheet from a window in Anselmo's house. The fact is I don't know exactly what happened, all I do know is that the whole city is astonished, because this wasn't something to be expected from the close friendship between the two men, which is said to have been so remarkable that everyone called them 'the two friends'."

' "Is it known, by any chance," asked Anselmo, "which way Lotario and Camila went?"

' "Nobody knows that," said the man from Florence, "even though the Governor has ordered the most thorough searches to be made."

' "God be with you, sir," said Anselmo.

' "And with you," said the other, and rode away.

'This terrible news brought Anselmo to the verge of losing not only his reason but his life as well. He struggled to his feet and rode on to his friend's house; his friend didn't yet know about the disaster but, seeing Anselmo arrive looking pale, gaunt and haggard, he realized that something awful had happened. Anselmo asked to be put to bed and provided with writing materials. This was done, and he was left there by himself, for this was what he wanted, and he even asked for the door to be locked. Once he was alone all the details of the disaster crowded in on his brain and he knew he was dying, so he decided to leave an account of the reasons for his strange death; and he began to write but, before he could finish setting down all he wanted, he breathed his last and left his life in the hands of the grief that his inappropriate curiosity had brought upon him.

'When the master of the house saw that it was getting late and that Anselmo remained silent, he decided to go in to find out if he was any worse, and discovered him lying face down with half his body on the bed and half on the writing-tray, a paper with writing on it open in front of him and the pen still in his hand. He called out to his guest, then ran over and took his hand and, finding that there was no response and that he was cold, knew that he was dead. He was overcome by amazement and grief, and summoned his servants to come and see what a disaster had befallen Anselmo; and then he read the paper written, as he could see, in Anselmo's own hand:

A stupid and inappropriate desire has taken my life. If news of my death reaches Camila's ears, I want her to know that I forgive her, because she was under no obligation to work miracles, nor had I any need to expect her to; and since I manufactured my own dishonour, there is no cause to ...

'This was all Anselmo had written, showing that here his life had ended, before his letter could. On the following day Anselmo's friend sent news of his death to his relatives, who already knew of his misfortune, as well as to the convent where Camila was very close to accompanying her husband on that unavoidable journey, not because of the news of her husband's death but because of what she'd heard about her missing lover. It's said that although she was now a widow she would neither leave the convent nor take the veil until, not long afterwards, she received news that Lotario had died in a battle waged by Monsieur de Lautrec against the Great Captain Gonzalo Fernández de Córdoba in the kingdom of Naples,[1] where the tardily repentant friend had ended up; and then Camila did take the veil, and died shortly afterwards at the unforgiving hands of sadness and melancholy. These were the ends that the three of them came to, arising from such ridiculous beginnings.'

'This,' said the priest, 'seems like a pretty good tale to me, but I can't believe it's true; and if it's invented the author hasn't done his job in a very convincing way, because I can't believe there could ever be a husband so stupid as to want to carry out such a costly experiment. If it were presented as involving a lover and his mistress it might pass, but with a man and his wife it approaches the impossible. Yet the way in which it's told doesn't displease me at all.'

CHAPTER XXXVI

Concerning the fierce and prodigious battle that Don
Quixote fought against some skins of red wine, and other
things that happened to him at the inn

And now the innkeeper, standing by the door, said:

'Here's a fine troop of customers on their way – if they stop, we're going to have ourselves a party.'

'Who are they?' asked Cardenio.

'Four men,' replied the innkeeper, 'on horseback – short stirrups Arab-style, lances and leather shields, black travelling-masks – and with them a woman in white – high saddle complete with back and arms, face covered too – and two servants on foot.'

'Are they very near?' asked the priest.

'They're so very near,' replied the innkeeper, 'that here they are.'

When Dorotea heard this she veiled her face, and Cardenio disappeared into Don Quixote's room; and they hardly had time to do so before all the people described by the innkeeper came in. The four on horseback, who looked and behaved like men of breeding, dismounted and went to help the lady down from her high saddle; and one of them took her into his arms and sat her in a chair by the entrance to the room in which Cardenio had hidden. Neither she nor they had removed their travelling-masks or uttered a word; as the woman sank into the chair she only exhaled a deep sigh and let her arms drop to her side, like someone who was weak and ill. The foot-servants took the horses to the stable. The priest wanted to know what people these were who appeared in such garb and such silence, and he went to see the two servants and put his question to one of them, who replied:

'By God, sir, I can't tell you who they are, all I know is that they seem to be very high-up, specially that one who went over to take the lady in his arms, and I say this because all the others are full of respect for him and nothing ever gets done unless he says so.'

'And who is the lady?' asked the priest.

'I couldn't tell you that, either,' replied the servant, 'because I haven't set eyes on her face all the way here. I've heard her sigh all right, lots and lots of times, and groan away as if she was about to give up the ghost each time she groaned. And you mustn't wonder about us not knowing any more than this, because we haven't been with them for more than a couple of days – they came across us on the road and persuaded us to go with them to Andalusia and promised to pay us very good wages.'

'And have you heard any of their names?' asked the priest.

'No, never,' replied the servant, 'because they all ride along in such silence you wouldn't believe it, nothing to be heard except the poor lady sighing and sobbing, which makes us feel very sorry for her; and we're both convinced she's being forced to go wherever she's being taken, and as far as you can tell from her clothes she's a nun, or about to become a nun, which is more likely, and maybe it's because she isn't becoming a nun of her own free will that she's as sad as she seems to be.'

'That may well be the case,' the priest declared.

And he left them and went back to Dorotea who, moved by natural compassion when she heard the masked woman's sighs, drew near to her and said:

'What's wrong with you, my lady? If it's it something that another woman might be able to help you with, I'll do so with the best will in the world.'

But the grieving lady didn't answer, and although Dorotea repeated her offer with even greater insistence, she stayed silent; and then the masked man, the one whom the servant said the others obeyed, came over and said to Dorotea:

'Don't waste your time, madam, making this woman any offers, because it isn't her way to be thankful for what's done for her; and don't attempt to make her reply, unless you want to hear a falsehood.'

'I have never told lies,' the silent woman burst out. 'It's precisely because I'm so honest and incapable of lying that I'm so wretched now; and I call you as a witness to that, since it's my total truthfulness that forces you to lie and to cheat.'

Cardenio heard these words clearly, being so close to the speaker, because only the door of Don Quixote's room separated them, and he cried:

'Good God! What is this I hear? Whose voice is ringing in my ears?'

The lady looked round in alarm and, not seeing who could have shouted, stood up and went to enter the room; observing which the gentleman grasped her and prevented her from taking a step. In her agitation the taffeta travelling-mask slipped down, revealing a face of incomparable and miraculous beauty, although pale and terrified, as her eyes ranged all round the room so eagerly that she looked like a madwoman – behaviour that mystified Dorotea and the others, and filled them with pity. The gentleman was gripping the lady by the shoulders and was so concerned to hold on to her that he couldn't attend to his mask as it slipped down his face and eventually fell off; Dorotea, with her arms round the lady, looked up and saw that the man also holding her was her husband Don Fernando, and a sigh rose from the deepest depths of her being as she toppled over backwards – and if the barber hadn't been standing near by to catch her, Dorotea would have fallen to the floor.

The priest ran over to remove her veil and sprinkle water on her face, and as he did so Don Fernando recognized her and was thunderstruck, not that this made him release Luscinda, for she it was who was trying to struggle free from him, having in her turn recognized Cardenio from his cries, as he had her. And Cardenio had heard Dorotea's sigh as she'd fainted, and, in the belief that it was his Luscinda, he rushed in terror out of the loft, and what he first saw was Don Fernando with Luscinda in his arms. Don Fernando also recognized Cardenio, and the three of them, Luscinda, Cardenio and Dorotea, were struck dumb with amazement, hardly knowing what had happened to them. Speechless, they all gazed at each other: Dorotea gazed at Don Fernando, Don Fernando at Cardenio, Cardenio at Luscinda and Luscinda at Cardenio. The first to break the silence was Luscinda, who said to Don Fernando:

'Don Fernando: because of what you owe yourself as a gentleman, if no other duty sways you, you must allow me to go and cling to that wall on which I am the ivy, and lean on that support from which you have never been able to separate me with all your insistence, your threats, your promises and your gifts. See how heaven, working in ways strange and mysterious to us, has placed my true husband before me. And you know very well, from a thousand costly experiences, that only death would be strong enough to erase him from my memory. So let those lessons in disillusionment teach you, if you aren't capable of anything better, to turn love into rage, desire into murderous vindictiveness, and take my life, because if I yield it up in the presence of my dear husband I shall consider it well spent: maybe my death will convince him that I have remained faithful until the very last moments of my existence.'

In the meantime Dorotea had recovered consciousness and had been listening to everything Luscinda had said, from which she deduced who she was; and seeing that Don Fernando was still not releasing Luscinda or replying to her, Dorotea struggled to her feet and went to kneel before him and, as lovely, pitiful tears flowed from her eyes, she began:

'Unless, my lord, the rays of that sun that you are holding eclipsed in your arms have dazzled and blinded you, you will have perceived that the woman kneeling here at your feet is Dorotea, luckless and wretched for as long as you are pleased to have it so. Yes, I am that humble farmer's daughter whom you chose, out of your kindness or for your pleasure, to raise to the eminence of calling herself yours. I am the woman who, enclosed within the bounds of virtue, lived a contented life until she responded to the insistent calls of what seemed like true love, opened the doors of her chaste seclusion and handed you the keys of her freedom, a gift you thought very little of, as is made clear by my being reduced to the circumstances in which you find me, and by your being in the situation in which I find you. Yet in spite of all that I shouldn't wish you to imagine that I have come here driven by my dishonour: it is only the deep sorrow of being forgotten by you that has brought me. You wanted me to be yours and you were so successful that, even if you now want me to stop being yours, you can't stop being mine.

'Bear in mind, my lord, that my matchless love for you can be a compensation for the beauty and nobility of the woman for whom you want to desert me. You can't be lovely Luscinda's, because you're mine, and she can't be yours, because she's Cardenio's. And, if only you think about it, it will be easier for you to force yourself to love the woman who adores you than to persuade the woman who hates you to love you. You laid siege to my unsuspecting heart; you importuned my integrity; you were not unaware of my rank; you well know the circumstances in which I gave in to your desires: you can't claim that you were deceived into our bond. And if all this is so, as it is, and you are a Christian as you are a gentleman, why are you using all this evasion to delay making me as happy in the sequel as you did in the beginnings? And if you don't want me as what I am, your true and lawful wife, at least accept me as your slave, because so long as I'm in your power I shall consider myself a fortunate woman. Don't abandon me for the gossips to huddle together in their little groups and destroy my honour; don't give my parents such an unhappy old age, because it isn't what they deserve for the loyal services that, as good tenants, they've always rendered your parents.

'And if you believe that you'll destroy your blood if you mix it with mine, bear in mind that there are few, if any, noble families in the world who haven't travelled down this road, and that the women's blood is not what counts in illustrious pedigrees; what's more, true nobility consists in virtue, and if you forfeit that by denying me my just rights, I shall be left with better claims to nobility than you. And finally, sir, let me say that whether you like it or not I am married to you; your own words are witnesses, and they cannot and must not be false ones, if you pride yourself on possessing what you despise me for lacking; the signature you put on the document will be a witness, and so will heaven, because you called on heaven to be a witness to what you were promising me. And if all this doesn't move you, your own conscience won't fail to raise its silent voice in the midst of your joys, defending this truth that I've laid before you, and disturbing all your finest moments of pleasure.'

The afflicted Dorotea spoke these and other words with such feeling and accompanied by such tears that even the men with Don Fernando joined all the others in weeping with her. Don Fernando listened in silence until she stopped speaking and started sighing and sobbing so sorrowfully that only a heart of brass could have remained unmoved. Luscinda stood gazing down at her, no less afflicted by her grief than amazed by her beauty and good sense, and, although she wanted to hurry to her side with some words of comfort, Don Fernando was still holding her tight and preventing her from moving. He stood there staring at Dorotea in bewilderment and alarm, and after a while he opened his arms to release Luscinda and said:

'You've won, lovely Dorotea, you've won: nobody could have the heart to deny such an assemblage of truths.'

When Don Fernando released Luscinda she swooned and would have slumped to the floor, but Cardenio was close at hand, having placed himself behind Don Fernando so as not to be recognized, and he set fear aside and ventured all as he hurried to support Luscinda, and taking her into his arms he said:

'If merciful heaven is minded to grant you some repose at last, my steadfast, faithful and beautiful lady, I believe that nowhere can you rest more safely than in these arms that hold you now and held you once before, when fortune was pleased to let me call you mine.'

At these words Luscinda looked up at Cardenio, at first recognizing him by his voice and then confirming with her eyes that it was he; almost beside herself, and with no regard for the proprieties, she threw her arms around his neck and, pressing her face to his, said:

'You, my dearest, you are the true master of this your slave, however much adverse fate tries to prevent it, and however many threats are made against this life of mine, which depends on yours.'

This was a strange sight for Don Fernando and all the others, who stood in wonder at such an unusual occurrence. It seemed to Dorotea that Don Fernando had paled and was about to avenge himself on Cardenio, because she saw his hand moving towards his sword; and as soon as this idea struck her she clasped his legs and kissed them and held on to him, and as her tears flowed on down her cheeks she said:

'Don Fernando, my one and only refuge: what is it that you have in mind to do in this unexpected predicament? At your feet is your wife, and the woman you want to make your wife is in her husband's arms. Ask yourself whether it will be right or even possible to undo what heaven has done, or whether it will be better to raise up and make your equal the woman who, overcoming all obstacles and confirmed in her faithfulness and constancy, is gazing into your eyes and bathing in loving tears the face and breast of her lawful husband. For the good Lord's sake I beg you, for your own sake I implore you, not to allow this stark revelation of the truth to increase your wrath, but rather to quell it so that you can bring yourself in your tranquillity to allow these two lovers to enjoy peace together without any interference from you for as long as heaven sees fit to grant it to them; and in so doing you will be showing the generosity of your illustrious and noble breast, and all the world will be able to see that reason has more power over you than passion.'

As Dorotea was saying this, Cardenio continued to hold Luscinda in his arms, but he didn't take his eyes off Don Fernando, determined as he was that if he saw any hostile movement he'd defend himself and attack as best he could anyone who attacked him, even if it cost him his life. But now Don Fernando's friends, and the priest and the barber, who'd been present throughout, together with the good Sancho Panza, surrounded Don Fernando and entreated him to heed Dorotea's tears and, if what she'd said was true, as they believed it was, not to allow her legitimate hopes to be frustrated. He should reflect that it wasn't by chance, as it might appear, but by a special disposition of Providence, that they had all come together where nobody could have anticipated such a meeting. And the priest told him that only death could part Luscinda from Cardenio, and that even if they were separated by the blade of a sword, they'd count that a happy death; and that in these irremediable circumstances his wisest course would be to control and conquer himself and show a generous heart by allowing these two, of his own free will, to enjoy the happiness that heaven had now granted them; and he should also contemplate Dorotea's beauty, and he'd see that few if any women could equal let alone surpass it, and he should add to her beauty her humility and the great love she felt for him, and above all bear in mind that, if he prized himself on being a gentleman and a Christian, he had no alternative but to keep the promise that he'd made her; and that in this way he would be doing his duty to God and what was right in the eyes of all men of good sense, who well know that it's one of the prerogatives of beauty, even in a woman of low birth, so long as her beauty is united with virtue, to be capable of being raised to any height, without any disparagement to the man who thus raises it to equality with himself; and nobody can be blamed for responding to the powerful promptings of pleasure, so long as no sin is involved.

And to these words all those present added others, so many of them and so well chosen that Don Fernando's worthy heart – nourished, after all, with illustrious blood – relented and gave in to the truth, which he couldn't have denied even if he'd wanted to; and the sign he gave of having surrendered and accepted the excellent advice he'd been offered was to stoop down and embrace Dorotea, saying:

'Rise, my lady: it isn't right for the woman I hold in my heart to be kneeling at my feet, and if I've been slow to demonstrate that I believe this, perhaps it has been ordered by heaven, so that on seeing the constancy with which you love me I should be brought to hold you in the esteem you deserve. What I beg of you is that you don't reprimand me for my bad behaviour and my neglect, because the same force that impelled me to accept you as mine drove me to try to avoid being yours. And for proof that what I say is true, turn round and look into the eyes of Luscinda here, happy at long last, and in them you'll find an excuse for all my errors; and since she has found and achieved all that she desired, and I have found in you what I deserve, may she live secure and contented for many happy years with her Cardenio, and I shall pray heaven to allow me the same happiness with my Dorotea.'

And as he said this he embraced her again and pressed his face to hers with such warmth of feeling that he had to exercise great self-control to prevent his tears from giving final proof of his love and his repentance. But it wasn't so with Luscinda and Cardenio and indeed most of those present, because they began to shed so many tears, some for joy on their own account and some on the account of others, that anyone would have thought some awful disaster had befallen them all. Even Sancho Panza was weeping, although he was later to say that this was only because he could see that Dorotea wasn't Queen Micomicona, from whom he'd been expecting so many favours, as he'd thought she was. Their tears and their amazement took some time to dissipate, and then Cardenio and Luscinda went to kneel before Don Fernando and thank him for the favour he'd done them, in such courteous words that Don Fernando didn't know how to reply, so he brought them to their feet and embraced them with every mark of affection and courtesy.

He asked Dorotea how she'd come to that place, so far from her home. In a few, well-chosen words she told him what she'd earlier told Cardenio, and Don Fernando and his men so enjoyed what she said that they wished the tale had gone on longer, because she spoke so entertainingly about her misfortunes. And once she'd finished, Don Fernando described what had happened to him in the city after he'd found among Luscinda's bodices the paper declaring that she was Cardenio's wife and couldn't marry Don Fernando. He said that he'd meant to kill her and would have done so if her parents hadn't stopped him, and that he'd left the house in embarrassment and fury, determined to take his revenge at a more convenient moment; and the next day he'd learned that Luscinda had gone missing from her parents' house, and no one knew where she was, and finally, some months later, he'd been told she was in a convent, with the intention of staying there for the rest of her life if she couldn't share it with Cardenio; and he'd immediately picked those three men and ridden with them to the convent, but hadn't tried to speak to her because of his fear that if it was known he was there the guard would be redoubled; so one day he waited until the porter's lodge was left unmanned, and posted two of his men at the door as he went in with the other in search of Luscinda, whom they found in the cloister talking to a nun; and they seized her without giving her a chance to resist and took her to a place where they provided themselves with everything they needed for their journey. It had all been simple for them, because the convent was in the middle of fields, a long way from the city. On finding herself in his hands Luscinda had fainted, and even after recovering consciousness all she'd done was weep and sigh, without speaking a word; and so, accompanied by silence and tears, they'd arrived at the inn, which for Don Fernando was the same as arriving in heaven, where all the wretchedness of this earth comes to an end.

CHAPTER XXXVII

Which continues the history of the famous Princess
Micomicona, together with other amusing adventures

Sancho had been listening with a grieving heart as he saw all his hopes of an earldom going up in smoke, and the lovely Princess Micomicona turning into Dorotea before his very eyes, and the giant becoming Don Fernando, and his master still fast asleep and not in the slightest concerned about what was happening. Dorotea couldn't be certain that the happiness she'd attained wasn't all a dream. Cardenio was thinking the same thoughts, as was Luscinda. Don Fernando was thanking heaven for the benefit it had bestowed upon him in extricating him from that tortuous maze in which he'd been on the brink of forfeiting both his good name and the salvation of his soul; and everyone at the inn was rejoicing at this happy solution to such a convoluted and seemingly irremediable quandary.

The priest was speaking a few timely words, as the sensible man that he was, and congratulating them on the happiness they'd attained; but the most contented and delighted of them all was the innkeeper's wife, because of the promise made by Cardenio and the priest to pay all damages, plus all interest accruing, for losses sustained at the hands of Don Quixote. Only Sancho, as has been said, was heart-broken and grief-stricken, and so, with a woebegone look on his face, he went for his master, who had just woken up, and said:

'Yes, you can carry on sleeping, Sir Sorryface, as much as you like, and not bother your head about killing any giants or getting the princess's kingdom back for her – it's all over and done with.'

'I am certain you are right,' replied Don Quixote, 'because I have just been fighting against that giant in the most atrocious and dreadful battle that I ever expect to wage in all the days of my life, and with one backstroke, swish! – I sent his head flying to the ground, and so much blood came gushing out that it ran all over the earth like water from rivers.'

'Like red wine, you'd do better to say,' replied Sancho, 'and I want you to know, if you don't know it already, that the dead giant is a wineskin all full of holes, and the blood is twenty gallons of red wine he had in his belly, and the head you chopped off is the whore that brought me into this world, and the devil take the giant and all the rest of it!'

'What are you saying, you madman?' exclaimed Don Quixote. 'Can you be in your right mind?'

'Well, you get up,' said Sancho, 'and you'll see for yourself what a fine mess you've made and we've got to pay for, and you'll also see the queen changed into a private individual called Dorotea, and other doings that'll leave you dumb-struck, if you happen to understand what's going on.'

'That would not surprise me in the least,' replied Don Quixote, 'because, if you remember, that other time we were here I told you that everything that happens in this place is brought about by enchantment, and it would be no wonder if it were so now.'

'I'd believe every word you say,' replied Sancho, 'if my blanket-tossing had been like that, but it wasn't, it was the real thing all right, and I saw the very same innkeeper who's here today holding one corner of the blanket, and he was sending me up into the sky for all he was worth and enjoying himself too, laughing as hard as he was heaving. And when you start recognizing people it's my opinion, simpleton and sinner though I am, that it isn't an enchantment at all, but real bruises and real misery.'

'Well, well, God will provide a remedy,' said Don Quixote. 'Help me dress and I shall go out there, for I want to see these doings and transformations to which you refer.'

Sancho helped him dress and, while he was doing so, the priest told Don Fernando and the others about Don Quixote's escapades and the trick they'd used to extract him from Peña Pobre, where he'd imagined that his lady's disdain had taken him. The priest also recounted most of the adventures narrated by Sancho, which amazed and amused them no end, because they were of the same opinion as everybody else: this was quite the weirdest sort of madness that could attack a disordered brain. The priest added that, since Dorotea's happy resolution of her problems prevented them from going ahead with their scheme, they'd have to dream up another way to get him back to his village. Cardenio offered to continue what they'd started, with Luscinda taking over the part played by Dorotea.

'No,' said Don Fernando, 'you mustn't do that: I want Dorotea to carry on with her impersonation, and so long as the village where this worthy knight lives isn't too far away, I shall be delighted if there's something that can be done for him.'

'It's no more than two days' journey from here.'

'Well, even if it were further off, I'd be happy to go, for such a good cause.'

And now Don Quixote emerged, in full panoply, with Mambrino's helmet, battered as it was, on his head, his little round infantryman's shield on his arm, and leaning on his branch, or pike. Don Fernando and his party were astounded at the extraordinary figure he presented: his face, gaunt and pale and as long as a wet week, his ill-matching arms and armour, his sober demeanour. They waited in silence to see what he was going to say until, with great gravity and composure, and fixing his eyes on the beautiful Dorotea, he spoke:

'I am informed, lovely lady, by my squire here, that Your Highness has been annihilated and your being destroyed, because from the queen and great lady that you used to be you have been turned into a private individual. If this has been done by order of your father, the sorcerer king, because he feared that I should not give you the due and necessary assistance, I can only say that the man did not and does not know what he is talking about, and has little acquaintance with histories of chivalry; because if he had read and reread them as slowly and carefully as I have, he would have discovered on every page how other knights, of less renown than I, have brought more difficult enterprises to a successful conclusion; and killing some paltry giant, however proud he may be, poses few problems, for it was only a few hours ago that I tackled him, and ... yet I had better keep quiet, so as not to be accused of lying; but time, the revealer of all things, will tell, when we are least expecting it.'

'What you tackled was two wineskins not a giant,' put in the innkeeper.

Don Fernando told him to be quiet and on no account to interrupt Don Quixote's speech again, and he continued:

'I say, then, exalted and disinherited lady, that if it is for the reason I have mentioned that your father has performed this metamorphosis in your person, you must not believe what he says, for there is no peril on earth that my sword cannot brush aside, and with it, casting your enemy's head to the ground, I shall soon place the crown of your country upon yours.'

Don Quixote stopped speaking and waited for the princess to reply, and, in view of Don Fernando's determination to press on with the deceit until they took Don Quixote back home, she answered with waggish gravity:

'Whosoever told you, O worthy Knight of the Sorry Face, that I had been altered and transformed, did not tell you the truth, for I am the same woman that I was yesterday. It is the case, indeed, that some modification has been worked within me by certain strokes of good fortune which have brought the greatest happiness I could desire, but I have not stopped being who I was before, or continuing to hope, as always, that I can verily avail myself of the valour of your valorous and invenerable arm. And so, my dear sir, you must let the father who begot me have his honour back, and look upon him as a man of sagacity and foresight, because he used his great knowledge to find such a sure and straightforward way to remedy my misfortune – I do believe that if it were not for you, sir, I should never have attained the happiness I now enjoy, and when I say this I tell a truth to which most of those here present can stand as witnesses. All that remains is to set out tomorrow, because we would not be able to travel far in what is left of today, and as for the rest of what needs to be done to achieve the happy outcome I expect, I shall leave that to God and to the worth of your heroic breast.'

So spoke the quick-witted Dorotea, and when Don Quixote heard her words he turned in high fury to Sancho and said:

'Now let me tell you, Sancho you wretch, that you are the greatest little villain in the whole of Spain. Have you not just been claiming, you good-for-nothing rogue, that this princess had been turned into a private individual called Dorotea and that the head I believe I cut off a giant was the whore that brought you into this world, and other nonsenses that plunged me into the greatest bewilderment I have known in all the days of my life? By . . . ,' – and he raised his eyes to heaven and gritted his teeth – 'I have a good mind to work such havoc on you as will force some sense into the brainpans of all the lying squires of knights errant from now until the end of time!'

'Calm down, sir,' replied Sancho. 'I might have been mistaken about the alteration to my lady the Princess Micomicona, but as for the giant's head or rather the cutting-up of wineskins, and the blood that's really red wine, I'm not making any mistakes, as God's my witness, because the skins are there to be seen, all wounded at the head of your bed, and the red wine's turned the room into a lake, and if you don't believe me the proof of the pudding's in the eating – what I mean to say is you'll soon see, when our friend the innkeeper here charges you for all the damage. And as for the rest, about my lady the queen being just as she always has been, it warms the cockles of my heart, because I've got a stake in that, as much as any other father's son.'

'All I can say, Sancho,' said Don Quixote, 'is that you are a fool, and forgive me, and enough said.'

'Enough said, indeed,' said Don Fernando, 'and now let's drop the subject. And since my lady the princess says we should set off tomorrow, because it's too late today, so be it, and we can while away the night in pleasant conversation until dawn arrives, when we shall all accompany Don Quixote, for we want to witness the splendid and unheard-of deeds that he will perform in the course of this grand enterprise that he has undertaken.'

'I am the one who must serve and accompany all of you,' replied Don Quixote, 'and I am deeply grateful for the favour you are doing me and for the good opinion you have of me, which I shall attempt to justify, else it will cost me my life, and even more, if such a thing is possible.'

Many courteous words and offers of service were exchanged between Don Quixote and Don Fernando, but they were brought to an end by the sudden arrival of a traveller whose dress indicated that he was a Christian recently returned from the lands of the Moors, for he was wearing a blue woollen doublet with short tails, half sleeves and no collar; his cotton breeches were also blue, as was his cap; he had date-brown riding-boots and a scimitar was hanging from a broad strap that crossed his chest. Behind him, on a donkey, came a woman dressed in the Moorish style: a veil over her face, a brocade cap on her head and a cloak from her shoulders to her feet. The man had a fine, robust physique; he was a little over forty, swarthy, with a long moustache and a good beard; and his agreeable presence showed that if he hadn't been wearing the uniform of a slave of the Moors he'd have been considered a well-born person of high rank. As he walked in he asked for a private room, and when he was told that there weren't any available he seemed concerned, and went over to the woman who appeared from her dress to be Moorish, and lifted her down. Luscinda, Dorotea, the innkeeper's wife and daughter and Maritornes, attracted by the novelty of her clothes, the like of which they'd never seen before, surrounded her, and Dorotea, always charming, courteous and sensible, and seeing that both she and the man seemed troubled by the want of a room, said to her:

'Try not to be too worried, my lady, by the lack of comfort here, because that's what you must expect at any roadside inn; but, all the same, if you'd like to accept our company' – motioning towards Luscinda – 'you may find that you've met with worse welcomes in the course of your journey.'

The veiled woman didn't reply, but only rose from her seat and, with her hands crossed over her chest and her head bowed, leaned forward to indicate her gratitude. Her silence confirmed that she must be Moorish and couldn't speak Spanish. The former captive, who'd been busy with other matters, joined them, and, when he saw that they were all standing round his companion and that she wasn't replying to anything they said, he told them:

'Ladies, this young woman hardly understands our language and can only speak her own, and this is why she won't have answered and isn't answering your questions.'

'All we're asking her,' replied Luscinda, 'is whether she'd like to accept our company for the night and share our sleeping quarters with us, because we'll make her as comfortable as ever we can, with all the goodwill due to foreigners in need of help, particularly women.'

'On her behalf and my own,' replied the captive,' I kiss your hands in gratitude, madam, and highly prize, as I am bound to, the favour you have offered – in such circumstances, and coming from such people as you show yourselves to be, it must evidently be a very great one.'

'Tell me, sir,' said Dorotea, 'is this lady Christian or Moorish? Because her clothes and her silence are making us think that she's what we'd prefer her not to be.'

'Her clothes and her body are Moorish, but her soul is devoutly Christian, because she has the most fervent desire to become one.'

'So she hasn't been baptized?' asked Luscinda.

'There hasn't been an opportunity since she left Algiers, where she comes from,' replied the former captive, 'and she hasn't yet been in such danger of imminent death as to make it necessary for her to be baptized without first receiving instruction in all the ceremonies that our Mother the Holy Church requires; but, if it pleases God, she will soon be baptized with all the formalities due to someone of her rank, which is higher than her clothes and mine suggest.'

These words made all those who heard them eager to know who the Moorish woman and the former captive were, but nobody cared to ask them yet, this being more a time for helping them to rest than for asking them to recount their life histories. Dorotea took her by the hand and sat her by her side, and asked her to remove her veil. She looked towards the captive, as if to ask what they were saying and what she should do. He told her in Arabic that she was being asked to remove her veil, and that she should do so; she removed it, revealing a face so lovely that Dorotea thought her more beautiful than Luscinda, Luscinda thought her more beautiful than Dorotea and all the others thought that if any face could be compared to Dorotea's and Luscinda's it was the Moorish woman's, and there were even those who found hers somewhat superior. And since beauty enjoys the privilege and prerogative of reconciling hearts and attracting affections, they all surrendered forthwith to the desire to serve and cherish the beautiful Moor.

Don Fernando asked the former captive what her name was, and he replied that it was Lela Zoraida; but as soon as she heard his answer she realized what the question had been, and in a flurry of delightful distress she blurted:

'No, Zoraida no: María, María!'

These words and the warm feeling with which they were spoken drew tears from some of those listening, especially the women, by nature tender and compassionate. Luscinda gave her a loving embrace and said:

'Yes, yes, María, María.'

To which the Moor replied:

'Yes, yes, María: *Zoraida makanshe!* – meaning 'not Zoraida'.

Night was now falling, and by order of Don Fernando's men the innkeeper had taken the utmost pains to prepare the very finest meal of which he was capable. Suppertime arrived, and they all sat down at a long table like the ones servants eat at, because there wasn't a round or square one in the house. They sat Don Quixote at the head of it, in spite of his protestations, and he asked Princess Micomicona to sit beside him, since he was her protector. Next to her, Luscinda and Zoraida took their places, and opposite them Don Fernando and Cardenio, and then the former captive and the other gentlemen, and on the ladies' side the priest and the barber. And there they enjoyed their supper, and their pleasure was even greater when they saw Don Quixote stop eating, moved by an impulse similar to the one that had led him to discourse at such length after the supper with the goatherds, and begin to address them:

'In truth, ladies and gentlemen, if we reflect upon it, those who belong to the order of knight-errantry behold the most extraordinary and wondrous sights. Or else who in the whole wide world coming in now through the gates of this castle and seeing us sitting here would believe that we are who we are? Who could tell that this lady at my side is the great queen we all know her to be, or that I am that Knight of the Sorry Face who is so celebrated by the voice of fame? It is no longer possible to doubt that this profession of mine surpasses all those ever invented by mankind, and that it should be held in even higher esteem for being exposed to more dangers. Away with anyone who gives letters the preference over arms, for I say to him, whoever he may be, that he does not know what he is talking about. The argument that such people usually adduce and depend upon is that brain-work is superior to physical work, and that the exercise of arms involves the body alone, as if it were the business of market-porters, which needs nothing more than brute strength; or as if acts of fortitude requiring a keen intelligence were not involved in what we fighters call soldiership; or as if the warrior who is in charge of an army or the defence of a besieged city did not labour with his mind as much as with his body. Or else you tell me how mere bodily strength can enable one to assess the enemy's intentions, tactics and stratagems, size up the difficulties, and forestall the dangers – because all these are acts of the understanding, in which the body plays no part.

'Since it is the case, then, that arms need brains as much as letters do, let us go on to see which of the two brains, that of the scholar or that of the warrior, has more work to do. And this can be determined by the goal to which each is directed, because the intention that has the nobler goal in view must be more highly regarded. The goal of letters . . . and I do not now refer to sacred letters, whose goal is to conduct souls to heaven, for to an end as endless as this no other can be compared; I refer to human learning, the goal of which is to organize distributive justice and give to every man according to his deserts: to interpret and enforce the law. This is a goal that is certainly noble and generous and praiseworthy, but less so than the goal that arms have before them, which is peace, the greatest good to which men can aspire in this life. And so it was that the first good news the world and men received was proclaimed by the angels on that night which was our day, when they sang in the heavens "Glory to God in the highest, and on earth peace to men of good will;"[1] and the greeting that the greatest master on earth and in heaven taught his followers and disciples to give when they entered any house was "Peace be to this house;"[2] and on many other occasions he said to them "My peace I give unto you; my peace I leave with you; peace be unto you,"[3] like a precious jewel left us by him as a gift: a jewel without which there can be no well-being on earth or in heaven. This peace is the true goal of war; and war and arms are all one. Given, then, this truth, that the goal of war is peace, and that this is nobler than the goal of letters, let us now consider the bodily hardships of the man of letters and the man of arms, and see which are greater.'

Don Quixote was developing his arguments in such an orderly and lucid way that for the time being none of those listening to him could believe that he was a madman. On the contrary, since most of them were gentlemen and therefore much concerned with arms, they were delighted to sit there listening as he continued:

'I should say that the hardships of the student are these: above all poverty – not that they are all poor, but I am putting the strongest possible case for them; and having said that the student suffers poverty it seems to me that there is nothing more to add concerning his troubles, because he who is poor lacks everything that is good. He suffers this poverty in each of its facets: now hunger, now cold, now nakedness, now all of them together; but in spite of that, his hunger is never so great that he goes without eating, even if he does so a little later than other people, even if he eats leftovers from the tables of the rich, for it is the student's greatest suffering to beg his bread, as they themselves term it; and there is always somebody who will let them in to sit at the fireside or by the brazier, which, if it does not warm them, at least takes the edge off the cold, and they always sleep under a roof at night. I shall not descend to other details such as their lack of shirts or shortage of shoes, their thin and threadbare clothes, or how they gorge themselves with such gusto when good fortune sets a banquet before them.

'Along this road that I have described, rough and difficult, stumbling here and falling there, struggling to their feet and falling again, they gain the degree to which they aspire; and once they attain this, many are those we see who, having sailed over these shoals and between these Scyllas and Charybdises[4] as if borne on the wings of favourable fortune, govern and rule the world from an armchair, with their hunger turned into satiety, their pinching cold into cool comfort, their nakedness into finery and regalia, their nights shivering on rush mats into repose between holland-cloth and damask, the just reward for their virtue. But if their hardships are compared and contrasted with those of the militiaman or warrior, they fall very far short, as I shall now demonstrate.'

CHAPTER XXXVIII

Concerning Don Quixote's curious discourse about arms
and letters

Don Quixote continued:

'Since, in discussing the student, we began with his poverty and its different facets, let us now see if the soldier is any richer. And we shall observe that he is the very poorest of the poor, because he depends on his paltry pay, which he receives late or not at all, or on what he can loot at grave risk to his life and his conscience. And sometimes he is so short of clothes that a slashed jerkin has to serve him as both uniform and shirt, and in mid-winter he is often all too aware of the inclemency of heaven when he is out in the open field with nothing to warm him but his breath, which issues from an empty space and must therefore, I am sure, emerge cold, contrary to all the laws of nature. And now let us contemplate him waiting for night to arrive so that he can recover from all these discomforts in the bed that is ready for him and that will not be a painfully narrow one unless he has done something to deserve it: he will be able to measure out as much ground as he likes, and turn over and over to his heart's content, without a moment's worry about the sheets riding up.

'And then come the day and the time for his degree ceremony – a battle day, when he will have a doctor's cap placed on his head, made of lint to dress a bullet wound in the temple, unless he has received some other injury disabling a leg or an arm. And if this does not happen, if merciful heaven keeps him alive and whole, he might still be left as poor as ever, and it will need one engagement after another, one battle after another, and him triumphing in all of them, to make some improvement in his situation; but such miracles seldom occur.

'But tell me now, ladies and gentlemen, if you have ever considered it: how many men have been rewarded by war, compared with all those who have perished in it? You will have to reply that there is no comparison, and there is no counting those who have died, while those alive and rewarded can be reckoned in three figures. It is the very opposite with men of letters, because on their salaries, let alone the payments on the side, they can make ends meet well enough. So although the soldier's hardships are greater, his reward is much smaller. But to this it can be replied that it is easier to reward two thousand men of letters than thirty thousand soldiers, because the former are rewarded with jobs that have to be given to men of their profession, whereas the latter can only be rewarded from the property of the master they serve; and this fact only strengthens my case.

'But let us set all this aside, for it is a maze from which it is very difficult to find a way out, and return to the pre-eminence of arms over letters, a controversy that has yet to be decided, because the arguments on both sides are strong ones; and in addition to those I have mentioned, letters say that arms could not exist without them, because war too has its laws and is subject to them, and laws are the province of men of letters. To which arms reply that laws could not exist without them, because arms are responsible for defending nations, preserving kingdoms, guarding cities, keeping highways safe, clearing seas of pirates; and, in short, if it were not for arms, all states, kingdoms, monarchies, cities and journeys over land and sea would be subject to the cruelty and turmoil that war brings with it for as long as it lasts and is free to make use of its privileges and powers.

'And it is a proven truth that what costs most is and should be most valued. To become eminent in letters costs time, sleepless nights, hunger, nakedness, dizzy spells, indigestion and other related problems, some of which I have already mentioned. But to go through the various stages necessary to become a good soldier costs everything that it costs to be a student to such a greater degree that there is no comparison between the two, because at every step one is on the point of losing one's life. And what dread of poverty and want can afflict the student as much as the dread that the soldier feels when, on sentry duty on a ravelin of some besieged fortress, he realizes that the enemy is mining towards the place where he stands, and he cannot on any account abandon his post or flee from the danger that so imminently threatens him? All he can do is inform his captain of what is happening so that the situation may be remedied with a countermine, and stand his ground, wondering in fear when the moment will suddenly come for him to fly up to the clouds without wings and descend to the depths against his will. And if this seems but a trifling danger, let us consider whether it is equalled or surpassed when two galleys ram each other in the middle of the open sea, and once they are grappled together the soldier has no more room for his charge than the two-foot wide timber at the prow; and despite this, and seeing before him as many ministers of death threatening him as there are guns being aimed not a lance's length from him, and knowing that one slip of his feet will send him down to visit the depths of Neptune's dominions, he still, with an undaunted heart and sustained by the honour that inspires him, makes himself a target for all those harquebuses and tries to storm his way across such a narrow bridge into the enemy vessel. And what is even more astonishing is that as soon as one soldier falls, never to rise until doomsday, another takes his place; and, if this one also falls into the sea that awaits him like one more enemy, another and another replace him without a moment's pause between their deaths: the finest example of courage and daring to be found in all the extremities of war.

'A blessing on those happy ages that did not know the dreadful fury of these devilish instruments of artillery, whose inventor is, I feel sure, being rewarded in hell for his diabolical creation, by which he made it possible for an infamous and cowardly hand to take away the life of a brave knight as, in the heat of the courage and resolution that fires and animates the gallant breast, a stray bullet appears, nobody knows how or from where – fired perhaps by some fellow who took fright at the flash of the fiendish contraption, and fled – and in an instant puts an end to the life and loves one who deserved to live for many a long age. And when I think about this I am tempted to say that it grieves me to the depths of my soul that I ever took up this profession of knight-errantry in such a detestable age as this one in which we are living, because even though there is no danger that can strike fear into me I am concerned when I think that gunpowder and lead might deprive me of the opportunity to make myself famous all over the face of the earth by the might of my arm and the blade of my sword. But let heaven do what it pleases, for I shall be more highly esteemed, if I accomplish my aim, for having exposed myself to dangers greater than were ever faced by knights errant of centuries past.'

Don Quixote gave voice to this long digression while the others were eating their supper, yet he didn't remember to lift a single morsel to his mouth, even though Sancho Panza told him several times to eat up, there'd be plenty of time later to talk as much as he wanted. Those who'd been listening to him were again moved to pity on seeing that a man who seemed to have a good brain, and could argue clearly about everything he discussed, so totally lost his senses as soon as the talk turned to his detestable and damnable chivalry. The priest told him that he'd been quite right in everything he'd said in favour of arms and that, although he himself was a man of letters and a graduate, he shared his beliefs.

They finished their supper and the table was cleared, and, while the innkeeper's wife and daughter and Maritornes were tidying Don Quixote de la Mancha's attic, where it had been decided that only the women would sleep, Don Fernando begged the captive to tell them the story of his life, because it was bound to be unusual and entertaining, to judge from the first sample of it, his arrival there with Zoraida. To which the captive replied that he'd willingly do so, only he feared that they weren't going to like his tale as much as he'd wish; but, in spite of all that, so as not to appear disobliging, he would tell it. The priest and all the others expressed their thanks and added their entreaties. And, in the face of such unanimity, the captive said that they didn't need to beg what they could command.

'So listen carefully, and you'll hear a true story that could never, perhaps, be equalled by any of those fictional ones that people compose with such care and skill.'

This made them all settle down in total silence, and, once the captive saw that they were quiet and waiting to hear what he had to say, he began to speak in a calm and pleasant voice:

CHAPTER XXXIX

In which the captive tells the story of his life and adventures

'My family had its origins in one of the villages in the mountains of León, and was always more favoured with the blessings of nature than with the gifts of fortune, although in the general poverty of those parts my father had the reputation of being rich, and really would have been, if he'd been as good at looking after what he owned as he was at spending it. Being free with his money was a consequence of a youth as a soldier, because a soldier's life is a school in which the niggardly learn to be generous, and the generous to be prodigal; and if there are any miserly soldiers, they're like monsters that one seldom sees. My father exceeded the bounds of liberality and was close to being a spendthrift, which is of no benefit at all to a married man with children to inherit his name and his position. He had three grown-up sons. Since he realized that he couldn't cope with his character, as he put it, he decided to deprive himself of what was both the instrument and the cause of his prodigality, in other words to rid himself of his property, without which Alexander himself would have seemed tight-fisted. So one day, calling all three of us aside into a room, he spoke to us along the following lines:

'"My sons, to assure you that I love you dearly, no more needs to be known and said than that you are my sons; but for you to think that I don't love you at all, no more is needed than to observe that I'm not managing to cope with my character so as to keep your inheritance intact for you. Well, to make it clear that I do love you like a father, and that I don't want to destroy you like a stepfather, I intend to put into effect something that I've been thinking about for some time and have decided upon after careful consideration. You've all reached the age at which you should settle down in life, or, at any rate, choose a career that, with the passing of the years, will bring you honour and profit. And what I've decided to do is to divide all I own into four parts, and I shall give three of them to you, each receiving his due and no more, and I shall keep the fourth to live on for as long as heaven is pleased to spare me. But after you've taken possession of your shares, I should like each of you to take one of the paths I'm going to indicate. We have a proverb here in Spain, in my opinion a very true one, as they all are, being brief maxims arising from the wisdom of long experience; and this proverb says 'The church, the sea or the palace of the king', or, to spell it out more clearly, 'Whoever wants to prosper and be rich should either enter the church, or take up trading and go to sea, or serve a king in his palace', because, as they also say, 'Better the king's crumb than the lord's boon'. I say all this because what I want is for one of you to study to become a man of letters, another to go into commerce and the third to serve the king in his wars, since obtaining a position in his palace is difficult, and even though war doesn't bring much wealth, it does greatly increase one's worth and one's good name. In a week's time I shall give each of you his share in cash, not withholding a single maravedí, as you will see for yourselves. Now, tell me whether you are willing to follow the advice I'm offering you."

'He called on me, as the eldest, to reply first, and after I'd protested that he shouldn't part with his possessions but spend as much as he liked, because we were old enough to make our own fortunes, I concluded by saying that I'd do as he wished, and that my choice would be to follow the profession of arms, and serve God and my king in that way. My younger brother made a similar protest and chose to sail to America with merchandise that he'd buy with his share. The youngest, and, I think, the most sensible of us, said that he wanted to enter the Church, or go and complete his studies at Salamanca University. As soon as we'd reached this agreement and chosen our ways of life, my father embraced us; and he fulfilled his promise as quickly as he said he would, giving each of us his share, which was, as I remember, three thousand ducats, because an uncle of ours bought the entire estate and paid for it in cash, to keep it in the family, and on that same day all three of us said goodbye to our dear father; and thinking it inhuman to leave him in his old age with so little to live on, I made him take back two thousand of my three thousand ducats, because the rest was quite enough to provide me with all a soldier needs. My two brothers were moved by my example to give him a thousand ducats each. So my father was left with four thousand ducats in cash and three thousand more, which was, it seems, the value of the estate that fell to his share and that he didn't want to sell and had kept as land. In short, we said goodbye to him and to our uncle, with the tears of sorrow rolling down our cheeks, and they urged us to send them our news, whether good or bad, whenever we had a chance. We promised that we would, our father hugged and blessed us, and one son set out for Salamanca, another for Seville, and I left for Alicante, having heard that a Genoese ship was in that part loading wool for Genoa.

'It's twenty-two years now since I left my father's house, and in all this time, even though I've written letters, I haven't received any news about him or my brothers. And now I'll tell you briefly what has happened to me during these years. I embarked in Alicante, I had a good trip to Genoa, from there I went to Milan, where I equipped myself with arms and military clothing, and from there I decided to go to Piedmont to enlist; I was on my way to Alessandria when I heard that the great Duke of Alba was marching to Flanders.[1] I changed my plans, went to join him, served him in his campaigns, was present at the executions of Count Egmont and Count Hoorne,[2] rose to be an ensign under a famous captain from Guadalajara called Diego de Urbina,[3] and, a little after I reached Flanders, news arrived of the alliance that His Holiness Pope Pius V, of happy memory, had made with Venice and Spain against the common enemy, the Turk, whose fleet had just taken the famous island of Cyprus, which had been under the rule of Venice: a lamentable, disastrous loss.[4] It became known that His Serene Highness Don John of Austria, our good king Don Philip's half-brother, was to be the general in command of the allied armies. News spread of the massive preparations for war that were being made, and all this inflamed my desire to fight in the great battle that lay ahead; and even though I'd been given hints and almost firm promises that I was going to be promoted to captain at the earliest opportunity, I decided to drop everything and go back to Italy. And as my good fortune would have it, Don John of Austria had just reached Genoa on his way to Naples to join the Venetian fleet, which he later did at Messenia.[5] So, to be brief, I fought in that glorious battle,[6] having already been made a captain in the infantry, to which honourable rank I rose more by luck than through merit. And on that day, so happy for all Christendom, because it was when all the nations in the world learned how wrong they'd been to believe the Turks invincible at sea, on that day when

Ottoman pride was dashed to pieces, among all the happy men there – because the Christians who died were even happier than those who survived victorious – I alone was wretched: instead of the naval crown that I could have expected if these had been Roman times, I found myself on the night following that famous day with my feet fettered and my hands manacled.

'And it happened like this: after Alouk Ali, the King of Algiers, a bold and successful privateer, had rammed and overpowered the Maltese flagship and only three Knights of Malta were left alive on it, all badly wounded, Giovanni Andrea Doria's flagship, on which I was serving with my company, went to the rescue; and doing what was my duty at such a juncture I leapt aboard the enemy galley, which then sheered off from the galley ramming her, thus preventing my soldiers from following me and leaving me alone among my enemies – so many of them that I couldn't resist for long and was overpowered, covered in wounds. And as you'll have heard, gentlemen, Alouk Ali escaped with his entire squadron, so I ended up a captive in his power, the only sad man on a day when so many rejoiced, the only prisoner on a day when so many were set free, for on that day fifteen thousand Christians rowing in the Turkish fleet gained the liberty they'd been longing for. I was taken to Constantinople, where the Grand Turk Selim promoted my captor to admiral for having done his duty in the battle and having carried off, as proof of his bravery, the standard of the Knights of Malta.

'In the second year of my captivity, which was seventy-two, I was at Navarino,[7] rowing in the admiral's flagship with its three lanterns. I was a witness to the opportunity that was lost to catch the whole Turkish fleet in harbour – all the Turkish sailors and soldiers were convinced that they were going to be attacked there, and had their clothes and their passamackeys, or shoes, ready to flee over land without waiting for the assault, such was the terror that our fleet had inspired in them. But heaven decreed otherwise, not through any fault or negligence of our general but because of Christendom's sins and because it is God's will that there shall always be scourges to chastise us. And Alouk Ali took refuge on Modon, an island near Navarino, disembarked his troops, fortified the harbour entrance and waited there until Don John went away. In this campaign the galley called *The Prize*, whose captain was a son of the famous privateer Barbarossa, was captured by the flagship of Naples, called *The She-Wolf*, commanded by that thunderbolt of war, that father to his soldiers, that happy and never-defeated captain Don Álvaro de Bazán, the Marquis of Santa Cruz. And I don't want to pass over the events associated with the taking of *The Prize*. Barbarossa's son was so cruel and treated his captives so badly that as soon as the galley-men saw that *The She-Wolf* was closing in on them they all dropped their oars, pulled him down from the awning-bollard where he stood screaming at them to row faster and passed him along from bench to bench, from the stern to the prow, biting him all the way so viciously that he'd gone little further than the mast before his soul had gone down to hell, such was their hatred for him because of his ill-treatment.

'We returned to Constantinople, and the next year, seventy-three, news reached the city that Don John had taken Tunis and won the whole kingdom of Tunisia from the Turks,[8] and had handed it over to Muley Hamet, putting an end to the hopes that Muley Hamida, the cruellest and bravest Moor there's ever been, had cherished of regaining his throne. The Grand Turk felt this loss keenly and, with the sagacity characteristic of all his dynasty, he made peace with the Venetians, who wanted it much more than he did, and in the following year of seventy-four he attacked the Goletta and the fort that Don John had left half-built just outside Tunis.[9] In all these actions I was at the oar, without any hope of liberty; at least I didn't have any hopes of being ransomed, because I'd decided not to send news of my misfortune to my father.

'Both the Goletta and the fort eventually fell, in the face of seventy-five thousand regular Turkish soldiers and more than four hundred thousand Moors and Arabs from all Africa, and this vast army was supplied with all the munitions they could ever have needed, and with so many sappers that they could have buried the Goletta and the fort using their bare hands. The Goletta, until then believed impregnable, was the first to fall, through no fault of its garrison, which did everything that could and should have been done to defend it, but because it was easy, as the event proved, to throw earthworks up in that desert sand: in normal conditions water would be struck a spit deep, yet the Turks could dig down six feet without being hampered by it; and so, by piling up sandbags, they made the earthworks so high that they commanded the walls of the Goletta and the attackers could fire down at the defenders, which made it impossible for any of these to hold his ground or put up a defence.

'There was a widespread belief that our troops shouldn't have shut themselves up in the Goletta, but should rather have gone out to meet the enemy as it landed; those who say this are speaking from a safe distance and with little experience of such matters, because if there were hardly seven thousand soldiers in the Goletta and the fort, how could so few, no matter how valiant, have both taken the field and held the two fortresses against so many? And how is it possible not to lose a fortress that's never relieved, particularly when it's besieged by so many determined enemies in their own country? But many people thought, as I did, that it was a special favour granted by heaven to Spain to allow the destruction of that seedbed and cloak of iniquity, that glutton, that sponge, that canker consuming the endless money that was squandered there and that served no other purpose than to preserve the memory of its conquest by the most invincible Emperor Charles V of most happy memory, as if the support of all those stones were necessary to make his name eternal, as it is and always will be.

'The fort fell too, but the Turks had to take it inch by inch, because the soldiers defending it put up such a brave and fierce resistance that they killed more than twenty-five thousand of the enemy in twenty-two general assaults. Not one of the three hundred survivors was captured uninjured, clear and certain proof of their strength and resolution and of how well they'd defended themselves and maintained their positions. A small fort or tower in the middle of the lagoon, commanded by Don Juan Zanoguera, a gentleman from Valencia and a famous soldier, surrendered on the enemy's conditions. Don Pedro Puertocarrero, the commander of the Goletta, who'd done everything he could to defend it, was taken prisoner; he felt the loss so deeply that he perished of grief on the way to Constantinople. They also captured the commander of the fort, who was called Gabrio Cervellón, a gentleman from Milan, a great engineer and a brave soldier. Many people of note died in these two fortresses, among them Pagán Doria, a Knight of Malta and a generous man, as he showed in his liberality to his brother the famous Giovanni Andrea Doria; and what made his death all the more lamentable was that he perished at the hands of Arabs whom he had trusted when he saw the fort was lost, and who had offered to take him in Moorish clothes to Tabarca, an anchorage and station of Genoese coral-fishers; and these Arabs cut off his head and took it to the admiral of the Turkish fleet, who applied to them our Castilian proverb that says "Love the treason but hate the traitor", and so it is said that the admiral ordered the gift-bearers to be hanged for not having brought a live gift.

'Among the Christians captured in the fort was one called Don Pedro de Aguilar,[10] an ensign from somewhere in Andalusia, a soldier of distinction and a very clever man; he had a special gift for that business they call poetry. I mention him because he happened to be sent to my galley and my bench, and to be my own master's slave, and before we left the port this gentleman composed two sonnets in the style of epitaphs, one for the Goletta and the other for the fort. And I really must recite them, because I know them by heart and I think they won't displease you — you might even enjoy them.'

The moment the captive named Don Pedro de Aguilar, Don Fernando glanced at his companions, and all three of them smiled; and when he spoke of the sonnets, one of them said:

'Before you continue, please would you tell me what became of that Don Pedro de Aguilar you mentioned?'

'All I know,' replied the captive, 'is that after two years in Constantinople he disguised himself as an Albanian and escaped with a Greek spy, and I don't know whether he gained his freedom, but I think he did, because a year later I saw the Greek in Constantinople, though I couldn't ask him about the outcome of their journey.'

'No, Don Pedro wasn't recaptured,' the gentleman replied, 'because he's my brother, and he's alive and well in our village, wealthy and married with three children.'

'Thanks be to God for all the mercies he has shown him,' said the captive, 'because in my opinion there's no happiness on earth to compare with regaining one's liberty.'

'And what's more,' the gentleman went on, 'I know the sonnets my brother composed.'

'You recite them, then,' said the captive, 'you'll do it better than me.'

'Very well,' replied the gentleman. 'The one about the Goletta goes like this:'

CHAPTER XL

In which the captive's tale is continued

SONNET

'O happy souls, delivered and set free
By heroes in a sacrosanct campaign
From the dark prison of mortality
To soar aloft to heaven's supreme domain:
    Your breasts with noble zeal and fury glowed,
Your tireless sinews braved prodigious toil,
Your blood with that of Turks and Arabs flowed
To stain the sea and drench the dusty soil.
    Your earthly lives but not your courage failed
In bodies from which all the strength had flown,
Victorious though defeated and bewailed
On perishing between cold steel and stone;
Because for such a death before such foes
Its fame the world, its glory heaven bestows.'

'That's exactly the version I know,' said the captive.

'The one about the fort, if I remember rightly,' said the gentleman, 'goes like this:

SONNET

And from these ruins on the desert plain,
These scattered clods that heap this bloody site,
Three thousand soldiers' souls, alive though slain,
To happier regions winged their joyous flight,
    Yet not before they vainly had essayed
The vigour of their arms with dauntless zeal
Until, outnumbered and fatigued, they laid
Down their young lives to scimitars of steel.
    This is the place, and this the dismal ground,

That for men's hopes has offered but a tomb,
Through past and present centuries renowned
For evils spawned in its unloving womb.
From braver bodies never could there rise
Such saintly souls from earth to gain the skies.'

The company thought the sonnets weren't too bad, and the captive was cheered by the news of his companion. He continued his tale:

'Once the Goletta and the fort had fallen, the Turks set about demolishing the Goletta, because there was nothing left of the fort to knock down, and to save time and labour they mined it in three places; but they couldn't blow up what seemed to be the weakest part, the old walls, although all of what was left standing of the new fortifications built by Friar Puck[1] came down without any trouble whatsoever. To cut a long story short, the fleet returned to Constantinople triumphant and victorious, and a few months later my master Alouk Ali died – he was known as Alouk Ali Fartach, which in Turkish means "The Scabby Renegade", because he suffered from ringworm, and it's a custom among the Turks to name people after some defect or quality of theirs. And this is because there are only four families with their own surnames, all of them descended from the house of Ottoman, and everyone else, as I've just said, takes his name and surname from bodily defects or moral qualities. And this Scabby Renegade had rowed as a slave of the Grand Turk for fourteen years and, at the age of thirty-four, enraged at having his face slapped by a Turk while he was at the oar, had abandoned his faith so as to be able to avenge himself; and he was such an able man that, without resorting to the vile methods used by most of the Grand Turk's favourites to rise, he'd become the King of Algiers and then the Admiral of the Fleet, which is the third most important position in that empire. He was from Calabria, an upright man and very kind to his captives, and he amassed three thousand of them, who were divided after his death, as he'd ordered in his will, between his renegades and the Grand Turk, who counts as a son and heir of anyone who dies, and shares his wealth with the other sons; and I fell to the lot of a Venetian renegade who'd been captured by Alouk Ali when he was a deckhand and was so well-loved by him that he became one of his most pampered pages, and then turned into one of the cruellest renegades there ever was. He was called Hassan Aga, and he became very rich and rose to be King of Algiers; and I was quite happy to come with him from Constantinople because it brought me so close to Spain – not that I was going to write to anyone about my sad lot, but I did hope that fortune might be kinder to me in Algiers than in Constantinople, where I'd tried a thousand different ways of escaping, without ever having any luck; and it was my intention to seek in Algiers other means of achieving what I so desired, because the hope of gaining my freedom never forsook me, and whenever what I dreamt up and put into practice didn't have the intended result I would immediately, without despairing, seek out or invent some other grounds for hope, however feeble they might be, to sustain me.

'This was how I whiled the time away, shut up in a prison or rather a kind of compound called a *bagnio*, where they keep Christian captives belonging to the king and to private individuals, as well as those they call slaves of the Almazen, in other words those belonging to the town council and employed on public works and other similar jobs; and it's next to impossible for these captives to gain their freedom, because they're public property and have no single master, so there's nobody with whom they can agree their ransom, even if they can get the money. In these bagnios, as I said, private individuals often keep their captives, particularly those who are to be ransomed, because they can have them safely waiting there without working, until the money comes. The king's captives who are to be ransomed don't go out to work with the slave-gang, either, except when the money takes a long time to appear; in which case, to make them write asking for it with greater urgency, they are forced to work and go collecting firewood with all the others, and that's no laughing matter.

'I was classed as a ransomable captive: since it was known that I was a captain, even though I told them about my lack of means and my small chances of raising money, nothing could prevent them from placing me on the list of gentlemen-slaves to be ransomed. They put a chain on me, more as a mark of this than to secure me, and so I spent my time in that bagnio with many other gentlemen and important people chosen to be held for ransom. And although hunger and lack of clothes might have distressed us at times – in fact, nearly always – nothing afflicted us as much as hearing and seeing, all the time, my master's unimaginable cruelty to the Christians. Every day he hanged one, impaled another, cut the ears off a third, and all for such petty causes, or without any cause at all, that the Turks knew he did it for its own sake and because he was by nature a mass murderer. The only man who emerged unscathed from his hands was a Spanish soldier called something Saavedra,[2] who performed exploits that will stay in the memory of those people for many years, all for the sake of gaining his liberty, yet Hassan Aga never beat him or ordered him to be beaten, or even spoke a harsh word to him; and for the very least of his many doings we all feared that he was going to be impaled, and so did he, more than once, and if we weren't short of time I'd tell you of this soldier's exploits, and they would entertain and amaze you much more than my own story.

'I should mention that our prison yard was overlooked by the windows of a house belonging to a rich and eminent Moor – as is normal in Moorish houses, they were more like little holes than windows, and even so they were covered by dense and impenetrable grilles. And one day, when I was with three companions on a roof terrace in the prison, whiling away the time by seeing who could jump the furthest in our chains – we were alone because all the other Christians had gone out to work – I happened to look up and I saw a cane being poked out of one of those little latticed windows, and tied to the end of it there was a handkerchief, and the cane was being waved up and down as if to signal to us to go and take it. We considered the situation and one of the men with me went to stand under the cane to see if the person holding it dropped it, or what would be done with it; but when he went the cane was raised and waved from side to side like someone shaking their head. My companion rejoined us, and the cane was lowered again with the same movements as before. Another of my companions walked over to the cane, with the same result. Finally the third one went, and was similarly dismissed. Seeing all this, I wanted to try my luck as well, and as soon as I stationed myself under the cane it was dropped into the bagnio, at my feet. The handkerchief had been tied into a knot and I made haste to undo it, and inside I found ten zianyis, Moorish coins of gold alloy each worth ten of our reals. There's no need to tell you how happy I was with this windfall: my joy was matched only by my amazement as I wondered who could have sent that gift to us, or more precisely to me, because the fact that the cane had been dropped for me alone showed for whom the present was meant. I took the welcome cash, broke the cane into little pieces, returned to the roof terrace, looked up at the window and saw there a pure white hand being rapidly opened and closed. This gave us to understand or imagine that it must have been a woman living in that house who'd made us that gift, and to indicate our gratitude we made salaams in the Moorish way, lowering our heads and bowing with our arms held over our chests. A little after that a small cross made of cane appeared for an instant at the same window. This sign made us think that a Christian woman must be a captive in that house, and that it was she who had favoured us; but the whiteness of that hand and the bracelets it displayed soon dispelled this notion, though we did then imagine that she might be a Christian renegade, for these are often taken as wives by their masters, who even consider it a stroke of good fortune to be able to do so, because they hold Christian women in higher esteem than women of their own race.

'In all our speculations we were very far from the truth; and so from that day on we had no other pastime than to gaze up at that horizon or window at which the north star or cane had appeared, but for a good fortnight we didn't see it, or the hand, or any other sign. And although we did all we could during those days to find out who lived in that house and whether there was any renegade Christian woman in it, all we learned was that a rich and important Moor called Hajji Murad lived there, and that he'd been governor of Al-Batha,[3] a position of great importance. But when we were least expecting it to rain more zianyis, we saw the cane suddenly appear, and another handkerchief on it, tied into a bigger knot; and this happened at a time when the bagnio was, as before, empty except for us. We did as we had the first time, each of the three others going up before I did, but the cane was only surrendered to me, being dropped when I walked up. I undid the knot and found forty Spanish gold escudos and a piece of paper with Arabic writing on it, with a large cross drawn at the end of the text. I kissed the cross, I took the escudos, I went back to the roof terrace, we all performed our salaams, the hand appeared again, I signalled my intention to read the paper, the window was shut. We were all left bewildered and happy, and since none of us understood

Arabic, our desire to know what the paper said was very great, but our difficulty in finding someone to read it for us was even greater.

'In the end I made up my mind to confide in a renegade from Murcia who considered himself a close friend of mine and had given me certain pledges of his loyalty that forced him to keep any secret I entrusted to him. Some renegades who want to return to Christian lands take with them documents signed by important captives in which these captives certify as best they can that the renegade in question is an upright man who has always treated Christians well, and that it's his wish to escape at the very first opportunity to do so. Some of them procure these affidavits with honest intentions, and others to make opportunistic use of them in emergencies: if they happen to be shipwrecked or captured on their way to a raid into Christian territory, they produce their affidavits and say that these papers prove their real reason for coming was to stay behind in Christian lands, and that's why they're in the corsair with the Turks. In this way they're spared their captors' initial fury, and are readmitted to the Church, and nobody does them any harm; and as soon as they see their chance they go back to Barbary to be what they were before. There are others who procure these papers with good intentions and do stay in Christian lands. Well, one such renegade was this friend of mine, who had documents signed by all the captives in which we vouched for him in the highest terms, and if the Moors had found these papers they would have burned him alive. I discovered that he had an excellent knowledge of Arabic, written as well as spoken; before I took him fully into my confidence, however, I asked him to read me a paper that I'd found in a hole in my hut. He unfolded it, and spent some time examining and construing it, muttering to himself as he did so. I asked him if he understood it. He said that he did, perfectly, and that if I wanted an exact translation I should give him pen and ink to facilitate his task. This we did, and he worked his way through the paper, and once he'd finished he said:

' "What I've written here in Spanish, omitting not so much as a single letter, reproduces what is contained in this Moorish document, and please note that where it says *Lela Marien* it means 'Our Lady the Virgin Mary'."

'We read the paper, which went like this:

When I was a little girl, my father had a female slave who taught me Christian worship in my own language and told me many things about Lela Marien. The Christian slave died, and I know that it wasn't to the fire that she went but to Allah, because since then I have seen her twice, when she told me to go to the land of the Christians to see Lela Marien, who loved me very much. I don't know how I can go. Many Christians have I seen through this window, and none but you has seemed a gentleman. I'm very beautiful, and young, and I have much money to take with me. See if you can find a way for us to go, and there you'll be my husband if you want, and if you don't want I don't mind, because Lela Marien will give me a husband. I've written this myself; be careful whom you allow to read it: don't trust any Moor, because they're all treacherous. I'm very worried about this, and please don't tell anyone, because if my father finds out he'll throw me down a well and cover me over with stones. I shall fasten a thread on to my cane; you tie your answer to it; and if there isn't anybody to write Arabic for you, answer me in sign language, and Lela Marien will make me understand you. May she and Allah keep you, and this Cross that I kiss again and again, because it is what the slave told me to do.

'Consider, ladies and gentlemen, whether our wonder and delight at the contents of this letter were justified; and both were so evident that the renegade realized it hadn't been found by chance, but had been written to one of us; and so he asked us, if his suspicions were correct, to trust him and tell him the truth, because he would risk his life to give us our liberty. As he said this he drew a metal crucifix from inside his shirt, and with copious tears he swore by the God that the image represented, in whom he, though a wicked sinner, faithfully and devotedly believed, to be loyal to us and keep whatever secrets we entrusted to him, because he imagined and could almost guarantee that with the help of the woman who had written that letter both he and we would be freed, and he would achieve what he so desired: to be restored to the bosom of our Holy Mother Church, from which like a gangrenous limb he had been cut off because of his ignorance and sinfulness. The renegade said this with so many tears and such signs of repentance that we all agreed to reveal the truth to him; and we told him the whole story, not keeping anything back. We showed him the window at which the cane kept appearing, and he took note of the house and undertook to spare no effort to discover who lived there. We also agreed that we ought to reply to the Moorish woman's letter; and, since we had someone there who could do so, the renegade wrote down what I dictated to him, and I can give you the exact words, because not one of the material circumstances of that affair has faded from my memory, nor shall I forget them as long as I live. The reply to the Moorish woman went like this:

May the true Allah keep you, my lady, and also that blessed Marien who is the true Mother of God and has filled your heart with the desire to go to the lands of the Christians, because she loves you dearly. Pray to her to reveal how you can carry out what she has commanded, because she is so good that she will respond. For myself and all the other Christians here with me I can say that we will do everything we can for you, and die if necessary. Do not fail to write to me and tell me what you intend to do, because I will never fail to answer your letters: the great Allah has sent us a Christian captive who can speak and write your language well, as you can see from this letter. So you can, without fear, tell us anything you want. As for what you say about becoming my wife if you reach the lands of the Christians, I promise you as a good Christian that this shall be so; and remember that Christians keep their word better than Moors. May Allah and Marien, his mother, protect you, my lady.

'After this letter had been written and folded I waited two days for the bagnio to be left empty, as before, and then I went to the usual place on the roof terrace to see if the cane appeared, which it wasn't long in doing. As soon as I saw it, even though I couldn't see who was holding it, I held up my letter to indicate that the thread should be fastened to the cane; but it was already there, and I tied my letter to it, and a little after that our star showed again, with the white flag of peace – the knotted handkerchief. It was dropped into the bagnio, I picked it up, and inside I found more than fifty escudos in all kinds of gold and silver coinage, which multiplied our joy fifty times over and confirmed our hopes of gaining our freedom.

'That same night our renegade returned, and told us he'd discovered that the Moor we'd been told about, Hajji Murad, did indeed live there, that he was a man of unimaginable wealth, and had an only daughter, the heiress to all his estate, who was in the opinion of everyone in the city the most beautiful woman in all Barbary; that many of the viceroys who had served there had asked for her hand, but that she had never wanted to marry; and he'd also discovered that she'd once had a Christian slave, now dead. All of this agreed with the contents of the letter. We had a discussion with the renegade about how we could rescue the Moorish woman from her house and escape to Christian territory, and we finally agreed to wait for a second letter from Zoraida, because that was the name of the woman who now wants to be called María: we could well see that she and nobody else was the one who could find a solution to all our problems. After we'd decided on this, the renegade told us not to worry – he would set us free or die in the attempt.

'The bagnio was full for the next four days, and so there were no signs of the cane; then the bagnio emptied again and the handkerchief appeared, so very pregnant that it promised a most happy delivery. The cane and handkerchief bowed before me, and in it I found another piece of paper and one hundred escudos, all of gold. The renegade was there with us, and we returned to the seclusion of our hut and gave him the paper, which he translated as follows:

I don't know, sir, how to arrange for us to go to Spain, and Lela Marien hasn't told me, even though I've asked her; what can be done is for me to send you through this window many, many gold coins; then ransom yourself and your friends, and one of you go to Christian lands and buy a boat and come back for the others; and I shall be in my father's villa by the Bab Azzun gate, next to the seashore, where I must spend all the summer with my father and my servants. From there, at night, you'll be able to take me to the boat without fear of discovery; and don't forget that you are to be my husband, because otherwise I shall pray to Lela Marien to punish you. If there is no one you can trust to go for the boat, ransom yourself and go, because I know that you're more likely to come back than anybody else, since you're a gentleman and a Christian. Try to find out where the villa is, and when you walk about the roof terrace I shall know that the bagnio is empty and I shall give you lots of money. May Allah keep you, sir.

'This was what the second letter said, and on hearing it each of my companions offered to be the man ransomed, and promised to go to Spain and return exactly as agreed, and I made the same offer as well; but the renegade opposed all these suggestions, saying that he wouldn't allow anyone to go free until we all went together, because experience had taught him how remiss freed men were in keeping promises made in captivity – captives who were important men had often tried this remedy, ransoming someone who was to go to Valencia or Majorca with money to equip a boat and return for those who'd ransomed him, and not one of these had ever come back; because the new freedom and the fear of losing it erased from their memories all the obligations in the world. And as confirmation that what he said was true he briefly told us about what had happened not long before to some Christian gentlemen, the strangest affair that had ever occurred even there, where the most dreadful and amazing events are witnessed every day. His conclusion was that what could and should be done was for him to be given the money provided for the ransom, and he would buy a boat in Algiers itself, on the pretext that he was becoming a merchant and was going to trade in Tetuan and along the coast; and once he was the boat's owner it would be easy for him to find a way to get them all out of the bagnio and on to the boat. Even more so if the Moorish woman, as she had promised, provided enough money to ransom all of them, because once they were free it would be the simplest matter to embark, even at midday; but the biggest problem was that the Moors don't allow any renegade to buy or own a boat unless it's a large vessel for privateering, because they're afraid that he'd only want it to go back to Christian territory, particularly if he's Spanish; yet this renegade would overcome the difficulty by taking a Tagarene Moor as his trading partner, and with this blind he would become the boat's real owner, and the rest would be as good as done. And even though my companions and I had thought it preferable to send to Majorca for the boat, as the Moorish woman had suggested, we didn't dare contradict him for fear that if we didn't do as he said he might inform on us, and put our lives at risk, if he revealed our agreement with Zoraida, for whose life we would all have sacrificed our own; so we decided to place ourselves in God's hands and in those of the renegade, and we immediately replied to Zoraida saying that we'd do everything she suggested, because she'd advised us as well as if Lela Marien had told her what to say, and it was in her hands whether to delay the plan or put it into action straight away. I repeated my promise to marry her, and the next day, when the bagnio happened to be deserted, she used the cane and the handkerchief several times to send us two thousand escudos of gold, and a letter in which she said that on the following Juma, in other words Friday, she was going away to her father's villa, that before she went she would let us have some more money, and if it wasn't enough we should tell her so and she would give us as much as we needed, because her father was so wealthy that he wouldn't miss it, particularly since she held all the keys.

'We immediately gave the renegade five hundred escudos to buy the boat; I ransomed myself for eight hundred, handing the money over to a Valencian merchant who was in Algiers at the time and who ransomed me from the King by promising to pay the money on the arrival of the first ship from Valencia, because if he'd paid up straight away it would have made the King suspect that my ransom-money had been in Algiers for some time and that the merchant had kept quiet about it in order to speculate with it. And my master was so mistrustful that I didn't dare, on any account, have the money handed over immediately. On the day before the Friday when the lovely Zoraida was to go away to the villa she gave us another thousand escudos, told us of her departure and begged me, if I was ransomed, to locate the villa immediately and, come what might, to find an opportunity to go and see her there. I hurried to assure her that I would, and told her to take care to commend us to Lela Marien in all those prayers that the captive had taught her. Next, procedures were set in motion for the ransoming of my three companions, both to make it easier for us to leave the bagnio and in case seeing me ransomed and themselves not, although we had the money, made them alarmed and the devil put it into their heads to do something that could endanger Zoraida; for even though their breeding might have been a guarantee against this fear, I still didn't want to take any risks; so I had them ransomed by the same method that I'd used for ransoming myself, giving the merchant all the money so he could stand surety for them with certainty and confidence. But we never revealed our plan or our secrets to him, because that would have been too dangerous.

CHAPTER XLI

In which the captive gives us still more of his tale

'Within a fortnight our renegade had bought an excellent boat, with room for more than thirty people in it; and for the sake of greater credibility and security he decided to make a trip to a town called Cherchell, which is some sixty miles from Algiers going towards Oran, and does an extensive trade in dried figs. He made this journey two or three times with that Tagarene I mentioned. In Barbary they call the Moors of Aragon *Tagarenes*, and those of Granada *Mudéjares*, and in the kingdom of Fez they call the Mudéjares *Elches*, and these are the men most used by that king in his wars. Well, each time the renegade went by in his boat he cast anchor in a cove not a couple of bowshots from the villa where Zoraida was waiting, and there he would either, with great deliberation, set about performing his daily devotions with the young Moors who were rowing for him, or try out as if in jest what he was planning to do later in earnest, by going to Zoraida's villa and asking for fruit, and her father would give him some without knowing who he was; and although he would have liked to speak to Zoraida, as he later informed me, and tell her that he was the man who, on my orders, was going to take her away to the lands of the Christians, and that she could feel happy and safe with him, he was unable to do so, because a Moorish woman will never appear before a Moor or a Turk unless her husband or father tells her to. They don't mind Christian slaves keeping them company and talking to them, even more than might seem proper; and I must say I'd have been concerned if he had talked to her, because it could have raised all sorts of fears to find renegades discussing her affairs. But God had decided otherwise and didn't give the renegade any opportunities to put his good intentions into effect. Seeing that he could travel to and from Cherchell in complete safety and anchor whenever and wherever and however he pleased, and that his partner the Tagarene had no will of his own, and that I had by now been ransomed, and that it only remained to find some Christians to row the boat, he told me to consider which of these I wanted to take with me, apart from the ransomed ones, and to engage them for the following Friday, when he decided that we should set out. So I spoke to twelve Spaniards, all excellent oarsmen and free to leave the city whenever they pleased; and it was no small achievement to have found so many of them, because twenty vessels were out privateering and had taken all the rowers with them, and I wouldn't have found the men I did find if their master hadn't stayed behind that summer to finish a galliot in the shipyard. All I told them was that on the following Friday evening they should steal out of the city one by one, make their way towards Hajji Murad's villa, and wait for me there. I gave each man these instructions separately and told him that if he saw other Christians he shouldn't say anything other than that I'd instructed him to wait for me there.

'Once I'd seen to this, one more move remained to be made, the most important of them all: to let Zoraida know how matters stood so that she was forewarned and prepared and didn't become alarmed if we suddenly appeared before she imagined that the Christian boat could have had time to come. So I decided to visit the villa and see if I could speak to her, and a few days before our departure I went there pretending to be collecting wild salad leaves, and the first person I met was her father, who asked me in a language that's spoken between captives and Moors all over Barbary and even in Constantinople, and that's neither Arabic nor Castilian nor the tongue of any other country but a mixture of them all, and we all manage to understand each other using it – anyway, he asked me in this strange language what I was looking for on his property, and who was my master. I replied that I was one of Arnaute Mami's slaves[1] (I said this because I knew very well that these two men were close friends) and that I was looking for any leaves that would be suitable for a salad. Then he asked me whether I was up for ransom or not, and how much my master was asking for me. While we were busy with these questions and answers, the beautiful Zoraida, who'd been watching me for some time, wandered out of the house, and since, as I've said, Moorish women aren't particular about showing themselves to Christians and aren't at all coy with them, she didn't have any scruples about coming to where we stood; indeed, when her father saw her hesitant approach he called her over.

'I couldn't begin to describe Zoraida's beauty and grace or her rich and elegant attire when she came before me; all I will say is that there were more pearls hanging from her lovely neck, ears and tresses than hairs on her head. On her ankles, which, in the Moorish fashion, were bare, she was wearing two karkashes (that's what they call ankle-rings in Arabic) of the purest gold and set with so many diamonds that she later told me her father put their value at ten thousand doubloons, and her bracelets were worth the same amount. She was wearing all those superb pearls because for any Moorish woman they are the most splendid finery to be had, and this is the reason why there are more pearls and seed-pearls in Moorish hands than among all the other peoples in the world put together; and Zoraida's father had the reputation of possessing great numbers of the best pearls in Algiers, as well as two hundred thousand Spanish escudos. And all this was hers, then – and now all she has is me.

'You can imagine her beauty in prosperous times and when thus adorned from what remains of it now, after so much toil and trouble. Because we all know that some women's beauty has its days and its seasons, that circumstances can increase or diminish it and that it's natural for intense emotions to alter it for better or for worse, though they more often destroy it. As I was saying, then, at that moment she was so magnificently attired and so very beautiful that she seemed to me the loveliest woman that I'd ever seen, and when on top of this I considered how indebted I was to her, she seemed to me like a goddess from heaven who had come down to earth for my delight and deliverance. When she reached us her father told her in their language that I was a captive belonging to his friend Arnaute Mami and that I'd come to look for salad leaves. She took up the conversation and asked in that mixture of languages I've just described whether I was a gentleman and why I hadn't ransomed myself. I replied that I had, and that my master's esteem for me could be judged from the price I'd paid, one thousand five hundred sultanins. To which she replied:

'"To tell you the truth, if you belonged to my father I wouldn't let him part with you for twice as much, because you Christians never stop lying and pretending that you're poor, to cheat us Moors."

'"That might well be so, dear lady," I replied, "but the truth is that I dealt honestly with my master, as I deal and shall always deal with everybody."

'"And when are you leaving?" asked Zoraida.

' "Tomorrow, I believe," said I, "because there's a French ship here that sets sail tomorrow, and I intend to go in her."

' "Wouldn't it be better," replied Zoraida, "to wait for ships to come from Spain and go in one of those, rather than with the French, who are no good friends of you Spaniards?"

' "No," I replied, "although if the news I've heard that a Spanish vessel is on its way turns out to be true I'll wait for it – but it's more likely that I'll leave tomorrow, because my longing to be back in my own country with the people I love is so great that it won't allow me to wait long for another passage, however preferable it might be."

' "You must be a married man," said Zoraida, ' "and that's why you're so keen to go back, to be with your wife again."

' "No, I'm not married," I replied, "but I have given my word to marry as soon as I reach Spain."

' "And is the lady you've promised to marry very beautiful?" Zoraida asked.

' "She's so very beautiful," I replied, "that to convey how lovely she is I can only say that she looks just like you."

'At this her father burst out laughing and said:

' "By Allah, Christian, she must be beautiful indeed if she looks like my daughter, because my daughter is the most beautiful woman in this whole kingdom. If you do not believe me take a good look at her, and then you will see that I am telling the truth."

'Zoraida's father acted as interpreter for most of this conversation because, although she spoke in the hybrid language that, as I've said, is used there, she expressed herself more in gestures than in words, and he was more fluent in it. While we were engaged in this conversation, a Moor ran up and shouted that four Turks had climbed over the wall and were picking the fruit even though it wasn't yet ripe. This alarmed the old man, as it did Zoraida, because the fear that Moors feel for Turks is widespread and almost instinctive, and especially their fear for Turkish soldiers, who are so insolent and tyrannical to any Moors subjected to them that they treat them worse than slaves. So Zoraida's father said to her:

' "Return to the house, daughter, and lock yourself in, while I go and talk to these dogs; and you, Christian, can pick your salad and depart in peace, and may Allah bear you safely to your own country."

'I bowed, and he went to look for the Turks, leaving me alone with Zoraida, who made a show of doing as her father had ordered. But as soon as he'd disappeared among the trees in the garden, she turned to me with her eyes full of tears, and said:

'"*Ameshi*, Christian, *ameshi?*" – which means, "Are you going away, Christian, are you going away?"

'I replied:

'"Yes, dear lady, but most certainly not without you: expect me tomorrow, *Juma*, and don't be alarmed when you see us, because we're going to the lands of the Christians, I assure you."

'This I said in such a way that she understood everything I'd been telling her, and putting her arm over my shoulder she began to walk with faltering steps towards the villa; and as fortune would have it (with disastrous results, if heaven hadn't decreed otherwise), as we went along like this, her father, on his way back after sending the Turks away, saw how we were walking, and we saw that he'd seen us; but Zoraida, alert and quick-witted, didn't withdraw her arm but rather came closer to me, went limp at the knees and leaned her head on my chest to give a clear indication that she was fainting, while I, for my part, acted as if I were being forced to support her. Her father ran up to us and, seeing his daughter's distress, asked her what was wrong, but she didn't reply and he said:

'"The fright those dogs coming in here gave her must have made her faint."

'And taking her from me he held her to his breast, and she, sighing and with her eyes not yet dry from her tears, repeated:

'"*Ameshi*, Christian, *ameshi*!" – this time meaning, "Go away, Christian, go away!"

'To which her father replied:

'"There is no need for the Christian to go, daughter, he has not done you any harm, and the Turks have left. Do not be alarmed, there is nothing to be frightened of: as I said, the Turks went by the same way they came as soon as I told them to."

'"It was they who alarmed her, sir, as you thought," I said to her father. "But she's telling me to go away, and I don't want to upset her: peace be with you, and with your permission I shall come back here for salad leaves if I need them again, because my master says that there are none better to be found anywhere."

'"You can come whenever you like," replied Hajji Murad. "My daughter did not speak as she did because she dislikes you or any other Christian: she really meant to tell the Turks to go away, or maybe she thought it was time for you to go to look for your salad leaves."

'With this I said goodbye to them both, and she went off with her father looking as if her soul was being torn out of her; and under the pretence of searching for leaves I walked all round the grounds at my leisure. I studied the ways in and out, and the strengths and weaknesses of the house, and everything that could be exploited to expedite our plan. Then I went back and told the renegade and my companions what had happened, and looked forward with impatience to the time when I could enjoy untroubled the happiness that fortune was offering me in the lovely Zoraida.

'And in this way the time went by and the day that we had all been longing for arrived; and, since everyone put into practice with great precision the plans that we had so often and in such careful detail thrashed out, we achieved the success for which we had hoped; because the Friday after the day I spoke to the lovely Zoraida outside the villa, our renegade anchored his boat at nightfall almost directly opposite it. The Christians who were going to row the boat were ready and hiding in different places near by. They were awaiting me with anxious joy, eager to attack the boat they had before their eyes, because they didn't know the renegade's plan and thought they were going to have to fight for their freedom and kill the Moors who were on board. So as soon as my companions and I showed ourselves they all came out of their hiding-places and approached us. By this time the city gates had been shut, and there was nobody to be seen in that area of open country. Once we were all together, we wondered what it would be better to do first, go to fetch Zoraida or overpower the Moorish sailors who were the oarsmen in the boat. As we stood there hesitating, our renegade appeared and asked what we were waiting for – it was time to get moving and all his Moors were off guard, most of them asleep. We told him what we were undecided about, and he said that we should first take control of the boat, which could easily and safely be done, and then we could go for Zoraida. We all thought this was good advice and so, without further delay, he led us to the boat, climbed on board, drew his scimitar and shouted in Arabic:

' "None of you must move an inch unless you want to die."

'By this time most of the Christians were aboard. The Moors were a poor-spirited lot, and when they heard their captain speaking like that they were terror-stricken; not one of them reached for his weapon (hardly any of them had a weapon, anyway), and without making a sound they allowed their wrists to be bound by the Christians, who did so at speed as they threatened the Moors that if any one of them spoke so much as a single word they would all be put immediately to the sword.

'Once this had been achieved, half our number stayed to guard the Moors, and the rest of us, still led by the renegade, hastened to Hajji Murad's villa, and were lucky enough to find that when we went to force the gate in the wall it swung open as readily as if it hadn't been locked at all, and so we reached the house in tranquil silence and unnoticed by anyone. The lovely Zoraida was waiting for us at a window, and as soon as she heard people in the garden below she asked in a whisper if we were *Nizarani*, in other words if we were Christians. I replied that we were, and asked her to come down. She recognized me and didn't hesitate for an instant, but came down without a word and opened the door, revealing herself to all of us so beautiful and so wonderfully dressed that I couldn't begin to describe her. When I saw her I took her hand and kissed it, and the renegade did the same, and so did my two companions; and all the others, who didn't know what was happening, copied us, because they could see that we were thanking and acclaiming her as our liberator. The renegade asked her in Arabic if her father was in the house. She replied that he was, asleep.

' "We're going to have to wake him up," said the renegade, "and take him with us, and everything of value in this lovely villa."

' "No," she replied. "No one, no one is to touch my father, and there's nothing in this house except what I'm bringing with me, which is quite enough to make you all rich and happy. Just wait and see."

'And she went back into the villa saying she'd return in a moment and we must stay still and not make any noise. I asked the renegade what they'd been saying to each other, and he told me, and then I told him that nothing must be done unless Zoraida agreed to it; she was already approaching with a coffer full of so many gold coins that she could hardly carry it, but meanwhile her father had unfortunately awakened, heard the noise in the garden, hurried to his window and realized that all the men below were Christians; at which he began to bellow in Arabic:

' "Christians, Christians! Thieves, thieves!"

'These cries threw us all into the greatest confusion and trepidation. But the renegade, seeing the danger we were in and the importance of completing this operation undetected, rushed up to Hajji Murad's room followed by a few others – I didn't dare leave Zoraida, who'd fainted in my arms. To be brief, the men who'd entered the house did their job so well that in an instant they came down with Hajji Murad, bound and gagged, warning him that any further attempt to cry out would cost him his life. When his daughter saw him she covered her eyes to shut the sight out, and he was horror-struck, not knowing how willingly she had placed herself in our hands. But it was our feet that we needed to use, and we ran back to the boat, where those who'd remained on board were anxious for our return, fearing for our safety.

'We were all on the boat before two hours of the night had elapsed, and Zoraida's father's hands were untied and the gag was taken out of his mouth; but the renegade repeated the threat that he'd be killed if he uttered a single word. Seeing his daughter there he began to breathe piteous sighs, redoubled when he noticed that I was holding her tight and that she lay motionless in my arms, without making any attempts to resist or to protest or to struggle free; but he kept quiet, fearful that the renegade might put his many threats into effect. Finding herself on board, and the boat about to set off, and her father and the other Moors lying there with their ankles bound, Zoraida told the renegade to ask me to do her the favour of releasing them all, and her father with them, because she'd sooner throw herself overboard than have a father who'd loved her so dearly carried off as a captive in her presence and because of her. The renegade told me what she'd requested, and I replied that I gladly agreed. But he said that this would be unwise, because if we left them behind they'd immediately raise the alarm in the city and throughout the country, and then fast frigates would be sent out after us, leaving us nowhere to go on land or sea and making escape impossible; and he added that what we could do was to set them free on the first Christian territory we reached. We all agreed to this, and informed Zoraida of our decision and our reasons for not doing as she wished, and she was satisfied with the arrangement; and in a joyful silence and with a happy diligence each of our lusty rowers took his oar, and, commending ourselves to God with all our hearts, we began our journey to the Balearic Islands, the nearest Christian lands. But since a moderate northwester was blowing and the sea was choppy, it was impossible to keep a straight course for Majorca, and we had to coast in the direction of Oran, with heavy hearts because we feared we might be spotted from Cherchell, sixty miles from Algiers along that coast. We were also afraid that we might come across some galliot returning with merchandise from Tetuan, although each of us felt such confidence in himself and in the whole group that we were sure that if we did meet one of them, so long as it wasn't equipped for privateering, not only would we resist being taken but acquire a vessel in which to complete our journey in greater safety. As we pursued our course, Zoraida kept her head buried in my hands to avoid seeing her father, and I heard her calling on Lela Marien to help us.

'We would have gone a good thirty miles by the time dawn came, and we found ourselves about three musket-shots from land, which we could see was deserted, so nobody was going to detect us yet; but just to be on the safe side we rowed further out to sea, because it was now a little calmer, and after five or six miles the order was given to row by turns so that everyone could have a bite to eat, because the boat was well supplied with food; but the oarsmen said this was no time to be resting, and those who weren't rowing could feed them, because they certainly weren't going to abandon their oars. That's what we did, but then a strong crosswind began to blow, forcing us to hoist the sails, and stop rowing, and head for Oran, because it was impossible to steer any other course. This all happened very quickly, and once we were under sail we careered along at more than eight knots, fearing nothing except an encounter with some privateer. We fed the Moorish sailors, and the renegade offered them some comfort by telling them that they weren't being taken captive, and would be freed as soon as possible. Zoraida's father was given the same assurance, and he replied:

' "I could expect any other kindness from your liberality and courtesy, my Christian friends, but do not think me so stupid as to imagine that you are going to hand me my liberty: you did not take such risks to deprive me of it only to give it back so generously, knowing who I am and how much money you can make by selling it. And if you name your price, I will give you whatever you want for me and this unfortunate daughter of mine, or else for her alone, the greater and better part of my soul."

'As he said this he began to cry so bitterly that we all felt for him, and Zoraida couldn't help stealing a glance at him; and the sight of her father weeping so moved her that she rose from where she was sitting at my feet and went to hug him and, with their cheeks pressed together, they both wept with such loving tenderness that many of the rest of us shed tears with them. But when her father realized that she was wearing her finest clothes and so many jewels, he said in Arabic:

' "What does this mean, daughter? Yesterday evening, before this disaster overtook us, I saw you wearing your everyday indoor clothes; and now, even though you have not had time to change, and I have not brought you any good news to be celebrated by putting on finery and jewels, here you are sporting the very best clothes I was capable of giving you when fortune most favoured us. Let me hear your answer, because this astonishes and perturbs me even more than the predicament in which I find myself."

'The renegade told us what the Moor had said to his daughter, who offered not one word in reply. But when in a corner of the boat he saw her jewel-coffer, which he was certain she'd left in Algiers and hadn't taken to the villa, he was even more bewildered, and asked her how it had found its way into our hands, and what was in it. To which the renegade replied, before Zoraida could:

' "Don't weary yourself, sir, asking your daughter Zoraida so many questions, because by answering just one of them I can answer them all: let me tell you, then, that she's a Christian, and that she's the one who has broken our chains and freed us from captivity. She's here of her own free will, and she's as happy, I imagine, to find herself in this position as is anyone emerging from darkness to light, from death to life and from grief to glory."

' "Is what this man says true, daughter?" the Moor asked.

' "Yes, it is," replied Zoraida.

' "So you are a Christian," the old man said, "and you are responsible for putting your own father into his enemies' power?"

'To which Zoraida replied:

' "Yes, I am a Christian, but I am not responsible for putting you in this predicament, because it was never my intention to do you harm, only to do myself good."

' "And what is this good that you have done yourself, daughter?"

' "That," she replied, "is something you should ask Lela Marien, because she can tell you better than I could."

'As soon as the Moor heard this he hurled himself with extraordinary agility head first into the sea, where he would have drowned if his long, cumbersome robes hadn't kept him afloat. Zoraida cried out to us to rescue him and we all rushed to his aid and, seizing hold of his haik, hauled him out of the water half drowned and unconscious, and Zoraida was so distressed that she burst into a tender and sorrowful lament over him, as if he were dead. We turned him face downwards; he brought up a great quantity of water; he regained consciousness two hours later, during which time the wind changed and we had to go back inshore and then ply our oars to avoid running aground; but we were fortunate enough to come to a creek next to a small headland that the Moors call the Cape of *La Cava Rumia*, which means "the wicked Christian woman"; and there is a tradition among the Moors that *la Cava*, through whom Spain was lost,[2] is buried there, because in their language *cava* means "wicked woman" and *rumia* means "Christian"; and they look on it as a bad omen to be forced to anchor there – they'll never do so unless they have to, although for us it wasn't so much a wicked woman's haven as the safe anchorage of our salvation, so rough had the sea become. We posted sentries on shore, and the oars weren't relinquished for a moment as we ate what the renegade had provided, and prayed to God and our Lady with all our hearts to favour us and help us to bring to a happy conclusion what we'd so successfully started. At Zoraida's request we considered releasing her father and all the other Moors who were tied up in the boat, because her tender heart could no longer bear seeing him bound and her countrymen prisoners. We promised to do this when we set off again, since it wouldn't be dangerous to leave them in that uninhabited place. Our prayers weren't in vain: heaven heard them and turned the wind in our favour and calmed the sea, inviting us to resume our voyage in good heart. So we untied the Moors and put them ashore one by one, to their astonishment; but when we came to Zoraida's father, by now fully recovered, he said:

'"Why do you think, Christians, that this evil woman is so pleased to see me set free? Do you think that it is out of pity? No, not at all: it is only because my presence would be a hindrance as soon as she wants to gratify her wicked desires. And do not imagine that what has led her to change religions is any belief that yours is better than ours: it is only the knowledge that promiscuity is more freely practised in your country than in ours."

'And turning to Zoraida, while another Christian and I held his arms to prevent him from doing something desperate, he added:

'"Oh, you misguided girl, you infamous creature! Where do you think you are going, in your blindness and stupidity, and in the clutches of these dogs, our natural enemies? Accursed be the hour when I begot you, accursed be the delights and the luxuries among which I reared you!"

'I could see that he was intending to go on like this for some time, so I hustled him on to the beach and from there he continued screaming out his curses and his lamentations, calling on Muhammad to call on Allah to confound us and destroy us and exterminate us; and even when we had set sail and could no longer hear what he was saying, we could see what he was doing as he tore at his beard and hair and writhed on the sand. But at one point he shouted so loud that we could hear:

'"Come back, my darling daughter, come back to land, I forgive you for everything! Let those men have the money, for it is theirs now anyway, and come back to comfort your sorrowing father, who will die here on these empty sands if you forsake him!"

'Zoraida was listening, and grieving, and weeping, and all she could answer was:

'"May it please Allah, dear father, to have Lela Marien, who turned me into a Christian, comfort you in your grief. Allah knows that I couldn't have done otherwise, and that these Christians don't have to feel indebted to me for any particular goodwill towards them, because even if I hadn't wanted to come with them, but to stay at home, that would have been impossible, with my soul so eager to perform a deed that is as righteous in my opinion, beloved father, as it is wicked in yours."

'But when Zoraida said all this, her father couldn't hear her and we couldn't see him; and, as I comforted her, we all turned our attention to our voyage, now assisted by a favourable wind, so that we felt certain that by dawn the next day we'd be on the Spanish coast. But good seldom or never comes pure and simple, unaccompanied by some evil to throw it into disarray, and as our fortune would have it – or perhaps it was the curses that the Moor had hurled at his daughter, because any father's curses are to be feared – when we were well out at sea, and almost three hours of the night had elapsed, and we were racing along under full sail with our oars held at the ready because the favourable wind saved us the trouble of using them, we saw by the light of the clear moon a square-rigged vessel also in full sail, steering almost directly into the wind and across our bows, so close that we had to shorten sail to avoid a collision, while they clapped their helm a-starboard to give us room to pass. They'd gathered on the deck to ask us who we were, where we were going and where we'd come from, but since the questions were put in French, our renegade muttered:

' "Don't reply, any of you – these must be French privateers, and they plunder everything that comes their way."

'Thus warned, none of us said a word; but after we'd drifted a little further on and left their ship leeward of us, they suddenly fired two cannon, both of which must have been loaded with chainshot, because one cut our mast off and dumped it and the sail in the sea, and the other, seconds later, hit our boat amidships and staved her in without doing any further damage. We could see that we were sinking and we all began to shout for help, begging the men in the ship to take us on board because we were going under. They shortened sail and launched the skiff, in other words the ship's boat, and about a dozen well-armed Frenchmen climbed into it complete with their harquebuses and glowing fuses; they drew alongside and saw how few of us there were and how our boat was sinking, and they took us in, saying that all this had happened to us for not having had the courtesy to reply to them. When no one was looking, our renegade picked up Zoraida's jewel-coffer and dropped it into the sea.

'So we all joined the Frenchmen who, having extracted from us all the information they wanted, stripped us of everything we owned as if we were their mortal enemies, even taking Zoraida's ankle-rings. But I was less concerned about Zoraida's distress than about my fear that they might proceed from taking her exquisite and priceless jewels to depriving her of the most valuable jewel of them all, the one she prized above all the others. But those people's desires don't extend beyond money, and their lust for it is never satisfied, and it was then at such a pitch that they would even have stripped us of our captives' uniforms if they had been worth anything to them. There were those among them who thought that we should all be tied up in a sail and thrown overboard, because it was their intention to trade in Spanish ports pretending to be Bretons, and if they let us live and took us with them their theft would be discovered and they'd be punished. But the captain, the man who'd robbed my beloved Zoraida, said that he was happy with the prize he'd taken and didn't intend to call at any Spanish port, but slip through the Straits of Gibraltar by night, or in any way he could, and make for La Rochelle, from where they had set out. So they agreed to let us have the skiff and whatever else we needed for the short voyage that remained, as they did the following day, within sight of the Spanish coast; and as soon as we saw it we forgot all about our troubles and our hardships, as if they'd never happened – such is the joy of recovering lost liberty.

'It must have been about midday when they put us in the skiff with two barrels of water and some ship's biscuit; and the captain, moved by strange compassion, gave the lovely Zoraida forty gold escudos as she embarked, and stopped his men from taking these clothes she's wearing now. We climbed down into the skiff and thanked them for their kindness, showing that our gratitude outweighed our resentment; they sailed on towards the Straits; we rowed so hard, guided only by the shore before us, that by dusk we were near enough, we thought, to be able to land before the night was far advanced; but there was no moon, and the sky was dark, and we didn't know where we were, so it didn't seem safe to run the skiff ashore as many of us wanted, arguing that we should do so even though we might hit rocks and be far from any town, because in this way we should be relieved of the fear we naturally felt of the prowling vessels of the Tetuan corsairs, who leave Barbary at dusk, reach the Spanish coast at dawn, take some prize and go back home to bed; we resolved the difference of opinion by agreeing to approach the shore slowly and land wherever we could if the sea was calm enough to permit it. This we did, and it would have been a little before midnight when we arrived at the foot of a towering hill, which didn't fall quite so sheer into the sea but that it left us a little room to land in comfort. We ran the skiff on to the sand, climbed out, kissed the ground and with tears of infinite joy thanked the Lord God for his incomparable goodness. We took the provisions out of the skiff, hauled it up the beach and then climbed far up the hill; because even though we were where we were, we still couldn't calm the fears in our breasts, or persuade ourselves that it was Christian soil beneath us.

'Dawn came later, I think, than we'd have liked. We climbed to the top of the hill to see if we could make out any village or herdsmen's huts, but however hard we looked we couldn't spot any settlement, or human being, or road, or path. But we decided to press on inland, because we were bound before very long to come across somebody who could tell us where we were. What most pained me was seeing Zoraida trudging along over that rough ground, because although I took her on my back once or twice, my weariness was more wearisome to her than her rest was restful, and she wouldn't let me carry her any more, and on she walked, patient and looking happy, holding my hand. After nearly a mile the sound of a sheep-bell reached our ears, telling us that a flock wasn't far away, and as we all looked around for it we saw a shepherd-boy sitting at the foot of a cork-oak calmly whittling away at a stick. We called out to him and he looked up and jumped to his feet, and, as we later learned, the first people he saw were the renegade and Zoraida; and since they were in Moorish dress he thought that the whole of Barbary had come for him, and he sprinted into the wood with the loudest screams ever heard in this world:

'"Moors, the Moors have come! Moors, Moors! To arms, to arms!"

'Bewildered by these cries, none of us knew what to do; but realizing that the shepherd-boy's shouts would alarm the whole area and that the coastguards would soon come to see what was up, we agreed that the renegade should take off his Turkish robes and put on the captive's doublet that one of my companions handed him, even though that left him in his shirtsleeves; and, commending ourselves to God, we took the path we'd seen the shepherd-boy take, expecting the coastguards to appear at any moment. And our assumptions weren't mistaken, because before two hours had elapsed, when we'd emerged from the woodland on to an open plain, we saw about fifty coastguards galloping towards us; we stopped and waited for them, and, when they came up and, instead of the Moors they were looking for, only found a bunch of poor Christians, they were puzzled; and one of them asked us if we were by any chance the people who had caused a shepherd-boy to raise the alarm.

'"Yes," I said, and as I was starting to explain what had happened, and where we'd come from and who we were, one of the Christians with us recognized the horseman who'd asked the question and interrupted me:

'"Praise be to God, gentlemen, for bringing us to so fine a place. Because if I'm not mistaken this soil we're treading belongs to Vélez Málaga, and if my years of captivity haven't impaired my memory, you, sir, asking us these questions, are Pedro de Bustamante, my uncle."

'Hardly had the Christian captive finished speaking when the coastguard leapt from his horse and ran to embrace the young man, crying:

'"My dear, dear nephew, I can recognize you now: how I've wept for you, believing you dead, and my sister your mother too, and all your family – they're all still alive, and God has been pleased to spare them to give them the joy of seeing you again. We knew you were in Algiers, and judging from your clothes and those of your companions here, I can see you've had a miraculous deliverance."

'"Yes, we have," replied the young man, "and there'll be plenty of time to tell you all about it."

'As soon as the horsemen realized that we were Christian captives they dismounted and offered us their animals for the journey to the city of Vélez Málaga, about five miles away. We told them where we'd left the skiff, and some of them went to take it to the city; each of the others sat one of us behind him, and Zoraida rode behind our companion's uncle. The whole town came out to welcome us, because one of the coastguards had gone on ahead to spread the news of our arrival. They weren't surprised to see either Christian slaves who'd escaped or Moors who'd been captured, because everyone along that coast is used to seeing both, but what did astonish them was Zoraida's beauty, which at that time was in its full perfection, because the fatigue of the journey and the happiness of being at last on Christian soil without any fear of recapture had brought such a glow to her cheeks that, unless my love was deceiving me, I'd venture to say that there was no more beautiful creature in the whole world – not, at least, that I had ever seen.

'We went straight to church to thank God for the mercies we'd received, and as Zoraida walked in she said that there were faces there that looked like Lela Marien's faces. We told her that they were images, and the renegade explained as best he could what they signified, so that she could worship them as if each one really were the very same Lela Marien who'd spoken to her. Zoraida has a good mind and a clear and ready understanding, and immediately grasped what she was told about the images. From there we were taken to be lodged in various houses in the town, and our companion who lived there took the renegade, Zoraida and me to stay with his parents, who had their fair share of the good things of life, and they treated us with as much love as they did their own son.

'We stayed for six days in Vélez Málaga, at the end of which the renegade, having made his formal declaration of intentions to the authorities, went to the city of Granada to be restored to the sacred bosom of the Church through the good offices of the Holy Inquisition, all the other freed captives went their various ways and Zoraida and I were left alone, possessing only the escudos that the courteous Frenchman had given her. I used them to buy this donkey that she's riding, and with me acting so far as her father and her squire rather than as her husband, we're going to see if my own father is still alive and if either of my brothers has had better luck than I have – though since heaven has made me Zoraida's companion, I don't believe there's any other stroke of good fortune that I could ever prize more highly. She is enduring the discomforts of poverty with such patience, and is so determined to become a Christian, that I'm filled with amazement, and resolved to serve her all the days of my life, although the happiness of knowing that I am hers and she is mine is marred by not knowing whether I shall find any corner back home where we can find shelter, or whether time and death have made such changes in the fortunes and lives of my father and brothers that, if they are no longer in this world, there will hardly be anyone left who knows me.

'There's nothing more to tell you, gentlemen, and I'll leave it to your discernment to judge whether my story's an entertaining and curious one; all I can say is that I wish I could have been briefer, although my concern not to bore you has led me to omit several episodes.'

CHAPTER XLII

Concerning further events at the inn, and many other particulars worth knowing about

The captive stopped speaking, and Don Fernando said:

'Truly, captain, the way in which you have narrated these strange events has been every bit as extraordinary as the events themselves. The whole tale is curious, and surprising, and full of incidents that astonish the listener. And it has given us such pleasure that we'd be happy to hear it all over again, even if it took you until tomorrow morning to tell it.'

And then Cardenio and all the others offered to help the captain in every way they could, in such affectionate and sincere words that he was left in no doubt about their goodwill. In particular, Don Fernando said that if the captain would like to go with him he'd persuade his brother the Marquis to be godfather at Zoraida's baptism, and that for his own part he'd equip him to appear in his own town with all the dignity and decorum that was due to his person. The captain gave Don Fernando the most courteous thanks, but declined his generous offers.

The evening had moved on, and as night fell a coach drew up at the inn, accompanied by some men on horseback. They asked for a lodging, but the innkeeper's wife replied that there wasn't an inch of room left in the house.

'Well, even if that is true,' said one of the horsemen, who had entered the inn, 'some room will have to be found for His Honour the Judge.'

When she heard this title the innkeeper's wife became flustered and said:

'What I meant to say, sir, is that I haven't any beds; if His Honour has one with him, as I'm sure he must, he's more than welcome, and me and my husband will give up our own room for him.'

'That'll do,' said the squire.

By this time a man had alighted from the coach, and his clothes proclaimed the position he occupied: his long robe with loose slashed upper sleeves showed him to be a judge, as his servant had said. He led by the hand a girl who seemed about sixteen years old, dressed in travelling clothes, and so marvellously beautiful and graceful that everyone was dazzled by the sight of her and, if they hadn't seen Dorotea, Luscinda and Zoraida at the inn, they'd have believed it next to impossible to find another comparable beauty. Don Quixote was still sitting there when the judge and the girl walked in, and on seeing them he said:

'You can safely enter this castle, sir, and take your ease in it because, although it is cramped and uncomfortable, there is nowhere in the world so lacking in space and comfort that it does not make room for arms and letters, especially if arms and letters have beauteousness as their guide and leader, as letters, represented by you, sir, do in this beauteous maiden, before whom not only should castles open their doors and humble themselves, but rocks should split asunder, and mountains should gape and bow to welcome her in. Enter, sir, I say, into this paradise, because here you will find stars and suns for the heaven you bring with you: here you will find arms at their zenith and beauty in its prime.'

The judge was amazed at Don Quixote's speech, and looked him up and down, and was no less amazed at his appearance than at his words; and not finding any with which to reply, he was amazed yet again when he saw before him Luscinda, Dorotea and Zoraida, who, on hearing about the new guests and being given by the innkeeper's wife an account of the girl's beauty, had come to have a look at her and welcome her. Don Fernando, Cardenio and the priest greeted the judge with more normal and straightforward courtesies. So he entered the house in some bewilderment, both at what he saw and at what he heard, and the beauties at the inn welcomed the latest beauty to arrive. It was easy for the judge to tell that all the people at the inn were of high rank, but Don Quixote's figure, face and bearing bemused him; and after they'd all exchanged the usual courtesies, and questions had been asked and answered about the accommodation, what had previously been decided was decided again: all the ladies would sleep in the loft we know about, and the men would stay outside it on guard, as it were. And the judge was happy for his daughter to go with the other ladies, which she was very willing to do. And on a part of the innkeeper's narrow bed, and a half of the bed that the judge had brought with him, the ladies were more comfortable that night than they'd thought they'd be.

As soon as the captive saw the judge his heart throbbed with the suspicion that this was his brother, and he asked one of the servants who he was and where he was from. The servant replied that the judge was called Juan Pérez de Viedma, MA, and that he'd heard he was from a village in the mountains of León. This news, together with what the captive had seen, confirmed that the man who'd had just arrived was indeed his brother, the one who, following their father's advice, had studied to be a man of letters; overjoyed, he called Don Fernando, Cardenio and the priest aside, saying he was certain the judge was his brother. The servant had also said that his master was on his way to take up an important position in America, in the Supreme Court of Mexico; and that the girl was the judge's daughter, that her mother had died in giving birth to her and that the judge was a very wealthy man thanks to the fortune that his wife had settled on the child. The captive asked for their advice about how to reveal his identity, and how to find out first whether his brother, when he saw how poor he was, would feel affronted or welcome him back with open arms.

'Let me be allowed to discover that,' said the priest. 'But it's inconceivable, captain, that you won't be warmly welcomed, because the resolve and the wisdom that your brother reveals in his impressive presence don't make him seem at all like an arrogant man or one who disregards his obligations, or one who won't be able to relegate the vicissitudes of fortune to their proper place.'

'In spite of all that,' said the captain, 'I'd prefer not to make myself known to him all of a sudden, but in a roundabout way.'

'I've already told you,' replied the priest, 'that I'll manage it so that we're all happy with the outcome.'

By now supper was ready and they all sat down at the table except the captive and the ladies, who ate in their own room. Halfway through the meal the priest said:

'A companion of mine in Constantinople, where I was a captive for some years, had the same surname as you, Your Honour, and he was one of the best soldiers and captains in the whole of the Spanish infantry. But he was as unfortunate as he was resolute and valiant.'

'And what was the captain's name, my dear sir?' asked the judge.

'His name,' replied the priest, 'was Ruy Pérez de Viedma, and he was from a village in the mountains of León; and he told me a story about his father, his brothers and himself that, if he weren't such an honest man, I'd have taken for one of those tales that old wives tell each other round the fire in wintertime. He said that his father had divided all he had among his three sons and had given them better advice than Cato himself could have given. And let me tell you that the son who chose to become a soldier started out so well that in only a few years, thanks to his courage and determination, and without any patron other than his great virtue, he rose to be a captain in the infantry, and was on the very verge of being promoted to field officer. But fortune turned against him, because just when he might have expected to enjoy her favour she withdrew it from him, and he lost his liberty on that glorious day when so many others gained theirs, at the battle of Lepanto. I lost mine at the Goletta, and circumstances brought us together in Constantinople. From there he went to Algiers, where I know he had one of the strangest experiences that anyone could ever have had.'

The priest continued the tale, and provided the judge with a summary of his brother's adventures with Zoraida. The judge was all ears – never had he heard any case as attentively as he did this one. The priest stopped at the point where the French stripped the Christians in the skiff of all their possessions and left his companion and the beautiful Moorish woman in such dire poverty, and said that he didn't know what had happened to them after that – whether they'd made it to Spain or the French had taken them off to France. The captain was standing some distance away, listening to every word that the priest uttered and watching every movement made by his brother, who, seeing that the story had ended, sighed from the depths of his soul and said, as his eyes brimmed with tears:

'Oh, sir, if only you knew how very concerned I am about this news that you've brought me – I can't help showing it in these tears I'm shedding, in spite of all my cleverness and self-restraint! This brave captain about whom you've been talking is my elder brother, who, being stronger and more high-minded than my younger brother or I, chose the honourable and meritorious profession of arms, one of the three ways proposed to us by our father, as your companion told you in what you thought was an old wives' tale. I chose letters, and God and my own exertions have brought me to the position in which you find me. The younger of my brothers is in Peru and is such a wealthy man that with what he has sent back to my father and me he has more than repaid the money he was given, and provided plenty more for my father to indulge his natural generosity, and for me to pursue my studies in a more respectable and dignified way, and reach my present position. My father is still alive, but dying to receive news of his eldest son, and never ceasing to pray to God that death does not close his eyes until they have gazed upon those of that son. What does surprise me in a man of his good sense is that neither in his times of toil and trouble nor in his prosperity did he ever see fit to send his father any news; if we'd known what was happening, my brother wouldn't have had to wait for the miracle of the cane to obtain his ransom. But what I'm worried about now is whether those Frenchmen have released him, or killed him to cover up their robbery. And this means that I can't continue my journey joyfully, as I began it, but in deep grief. Oh, my beloved brother, how I wish I knew where you are now: I'd go and rescue you from all your troubles, whatever it cost me! Oh, how I wish I could take our dear old father the news that you're alive, even if in the deepest dungeons of Barbary – because his wealth and my brother's and mine would soon get you out of there! Oh, lovely and generous Zoraida, how I wish I could repay you for what you've done for my brother! How I wish I could be present at the rebirth of your soul, and at your wedding, both of which would give us all such great joy!'

The judge spoke these and many other similar words, so moved by the news about his brother that all who heard him joined him in manifestations of their tender concern for his sorrow. So the priest, seeing that he'd achieved what he and the captain wanted, decided not to keep these people in distress any longer, and he rose to his feet and walked into the ladies' room and returned holding Zoraida by the hand, followed by Luscinda, Dorotea and the judge's daughter. The captain was waiting to see what the priest was going to do next, and what he did was to go and take him by the hand, too, and walk with both of them to where the judge and the other men were sitting, and say:

'You can stop crying now, Your Honour, and enjoy the culmination of all your most cherished desires, because here before you stand your beloved brother and your dear sister-in-law. This man you see here is Captain Viedma, and this woman is the lovely Moor who did him such good. Those Frenchmen left them as poor as you see them so that you could show the generosity of your noble heart.'

The captain sprang forward to embrace his brother, who, however, kept him at arm's length with his hands on his shoulders to take a proper look at him; but once he'd recognized him he clutched him so tight and shed such tender tears of happiness that most of those present couldn't help weeping with him. The words the two brothers exchanged and the emotion they showed can, I think, hardly be imagined, let alone put down in writing. They exchanged brief accounts of their adventures; they demonstrated the finest brotherly feeling; the judge embraced Zoraida; he offered her all he possessed; he told his daughter to embrace her; and then the beautiful Christian and the lovely Moor caused everybody's tears to spring forth yet again. Don Quixote sat there watching, uttering not one word, pondering over such extraordinary events and putting them down to the chimeras of knight-errantry. It was agreed that the captain and Zoraida would go with the judge to Seville and tell their father about how he'd regained his freedom and been found, so that the old man could come as soon as possible to be present at the wedding and at Zoraida's baptism, since the judge had to press on with his trip, because he'd been given news that a fleet was leaving Seville in a month's time for Mexico and it would be most inconvenient to miss it.

So everyone was delighted with the happy ending to the captive's tale, and since by now almost two-thirds of the night had elapsed, they agreed to retire and rest for what was left of it. Don Quixote offered to mount guard over the castle to prevent attacks by giants and other villainous wretches, greedy for the precious treasure of beauty that it contained. Those who knew him thanked him for his kindness, and informed the judge about Don Quixote's whimsy, which he thought most amusing. Only Sancho Panza was unhappy, as he despaired of ever turning in, and only he made himself really snug afterwards, on his donkey's tackle – which was to cost him dear, as will be seen in due course. The ladies had retired to their room, the men settled down with as little discomfort as they could manage and Don Quixote marched out of the inn to his sentry duty, as he'd promised.

A little before dawn the ladies heard a voice which was so fine and tuneful that they all had to listen, particularly Dorotea, who was already awake and by whose side Doña Clara de Viedma, the judge's daughter, was fast asleep. None of them could imagine who it was singing so well, and unaccompanied. Sometimes the voice seemed to be coming from the courtyard, at other times from the stables; and as they lay there listening in bewilderment Cardenio came to their door and said:

'If any of you are awake, do listen and you'll hear a young footman singing. It's the most gorgeous sound: enchanting chanting, one might say.'

'We're already trying to listen, sir,' Dorotea replied.

So Cardenio crept away, and Dorotea, listening as hard as she could, heard that what was being sung was the following:

CHAPTER XLIII

Which relates the agreeable history of the footman,
together with other strange events at the inn

A mariner of love am I
Who, far from any strand,
Sails on, although without a hope
Of ever reaching land.

My eyes are on a distant star
That serves me as a guide,
More beautiful and bright than all
That Palinurus[1] spied.

I don't know where she's leading me,
And so, bemused, I steer,
My heart intent on watching her,
Careless and full of care.

> And her unkindly bashfulness
> And undue modesty
> Are clouds that hide her from my eyes,
> The girl I long to see.
> O Clara, clear and shining star,
> I fade beneath your light,
> And if you hide your beams from me
> I'll die in darkest night.

When the singer reached this point in his song, Dorotea thought it would be a pity if Clara missed hearing such a good voice, so she shook her awake and said:

'Forgive me for waking you up, my child, but I did it so that you can enjoy the finest voice perhaps you've ever heard.'

Clara was still half-asleep and couldn't at first make out what Dorotea was saying, so she asked her, and Dorotea repeated her words, and Clara began to listen. But hardly had she heard the next two lines of the song when she was seized with an strange trembling, as if she were having a violent attack of malaria, and clinging to Dorotea she said:

'Oh, my dear, dear lady, why did you wake me up? The greatest good that fortune could have done me was to have kept my eyes and ears shut, so as not to see or hear that unhappy singer.'

'What are you saying, my child? I'm told he's a mere footman, you know.'

'No, on the contrary, he's the lord of many manors,' replied Clara, 'and he's so securely in possession of the manor of my heart that so long as he doesn't give it up he'll never be ejected from it.'

Dorotea was amazed at the girl's passionate words, which seemed to indicate an intelligence far in excess of her years. She said:

'You talk in such a way, Doña Clara, that I cannot understand you: please explain yourself and tell me what you mean about your heart and manors and this singer whose song disturbs you so. But don't tell me anything yet, I'm not going to let worrying about your nervous turns deprive me of the pleasure of listening to him – he's starting up again, I think, with different words and a different melody.'

'Just as you wish,' replied Clara.

And to avoid hearing him she pressed both hands over her ears, which also surprised Dorotea, who listened avidly as the singer continued:

> O sweetest hope of mine,
> Breaking through all the barriers of despair
> To keep the firm straight line
> That you yourself imagine and prepare:
> Don't be dismayed to see
> That every step has death for company.
> No sluggard ever gained
> Triumphs or laurels to adorn his brow,
> And joy won't be attained
> By those who, faced by Fortune, tamely bow
> And yield their feeble arms
> To Indolence's comfortable charms.
> Love's glory's dear: that's fair
> And only as it should be, honest trade;
> For there's no gift as rare
> As one that has been properly assayed.
> What easy joy is prized?
> What's cheaply bought is soon to be despised.
> But Love will persevere
> And sometimes do what never can be done,
> And though I often fear
> I'm striving for the stars and for the sun,
> My hope is still to rise
> Impossibly from earth to gain the skies.

Here the song ended and Clara's sobs began afresh, all of which made Dorotea even more curious to know the cause of such sweet singing and such sad weeping. So she again asked the girl what she'd meant by what she'd said before. Clara, afraid that Luscinda might be listening, hugged Dorotea tight, brought her lips close to her new friend's ear so as to speak without fear of being overheard, and whispered:

'The singer, my lady, is the son of an Aragonese gentleman, the lord of two manors, who lives across the road from my father's house in the capital. And although my father covered the windows with oilcloths in the winter and lattices in the summer, I really don't know how it happened but this young man, who was a student, saw me, maybe in church or somewhere like that. And he fell in love with me, and told me so from the windows of his house with such signs and tears that I ended up believing him, and even loving him back, not knowing who I was in love with. Among the signs he made to me was one where he clasped his hands together to say that he wanted to marry me, and even though I'd have been very happy with that, I was motherless and alone and didn't know who to talk to about it, so I didn't make any response except, when both our fathers were out, to lift the oilcloth or the lattice a little and let him see me, which made him show such delight that it looked as if he was going mad.

'The time came for my father to leave, and the young man found out about it – not from me, though, because there wasn't any way I could tell him. I believe he fell ill with grief, so on the day we left home I couldn't see him to say goodbye, not even with my eyes. But two days after we'd set out, when we were going into an inn in a village a day's journey from here, I saw him standing by the door dressed as a footman, looking so much the part that if his features hadn't been engraved on my memory I could never have recognized him. But I did recognize him and I was astonished and delighted; and he stole glances at me when my father wasn't looking, and he always hides from him when we meet on the lanes and at the inns; and since I know who he is, and I believe it's for love of me that he's walking all this way and putting up with all this hardship, I'm heartbroken for him, and watch over every step he takes. I don't know what he's hoping to achieve, or how he could have run away from his father, who loves him deeply because he hasn't any other heir and because he deserves it, as you'll agree when you meet him. And I'll tell you something else: everything he sings comes out of his own head, because I've heard he's an excellent student and poet. And what's more, whenever I see him and whenever I hear him sing, I tremble all over and become so alarmed, because I'm frightened my father might recognize him and find out about our feelings for each other. I've never spoken to him, yet I love him so much that I'm not going to be able to live without him. And this is all I can tell you, my lady, about this singer whose voice you liked so much – and just by listening to it you can tell he's no mere footman, as you say, but a lord of manors and a lord of hearts, as I say.'

'Say no more, Doña Clara,' Dorotea broke in as she kissed her over and over again. 'Say no more, only wait for tomorrow to come, because it is my hope that with God's help I'll be able to set your affairs on course for the happy ending that such a virtuous beginning deserves.'

'But, madam,' said Doña Clara, 'how can it end, if his father's so high-up and so rich that he won't think me fit to be his son's servant-girl, let alone his wife? And getting married behind my father's back – I won't do that for anything in the world. All I want is for this lad to leave me alone and go back home – maybe with not seeing him and the great distance we're going to travel, this grief I'm feeling would ease off, though I must say this remedy I'm imagining isn't going to do me much good. I just don't know what the devil's happened or how this love I feel for him can have got into me – I'm still so young and he is, too, I do believe we're both the same age, and I'm not sixteen yet, because my father says I'll be sixteen come Michaelmas.'

Dorotea couldn't help laughing as she heard Clara's childish talk, and she said:

'Let's rest now, young lady, for what little is left of the night, and tomorrow will be another day, and things will improve – if I have anything to do with it.'

They settled down again, and there was silence throughout the inn. The only ones not asleep were the innkeeper's daughter and her servant Maritornes, who, knowing Don Quixote's weakness, and knowing that he was outside the inn mounting guard in armour and on horseback, decided to play a trick on him or, at any rate, to pass the time listening to his nonsense.

Now the fact is that there wasn't any outward-looking window in all the inn, except a large hole in a hay-loft for taking in the straw. The two demi-virgins posted themselves behind this hole and saw that Don Quixote was sitting on his horse, leaning on his pike and from time to time heaving such huge, mournful sighs that each one of them seemed as if it would tear his very soul out of his body. And they heard him saying in soft, delicate, loving tones:

'O my lady Dulcinea del Toboso, the perfection of all beauty, the acme and pinnacle of intelligence, the treasury of the finest wit, the depository of virtue and, in short, the exemplar of all that is beneficial, pure and delightful in this world! And what might you be doing now? Might you, perchance, be thinking of this your hapless knight, who to so many perils, only to serve you, voluntarily exposes himself? Bring me tidings of her, O three-faced luminary![2] Perhaps you are even now gazing down at her in envy as she strolls along a gallery beside her sumptuous chambers or, leaning over a balcony, considers how, without detriment to her chastity and nobility, she can calm the storm that this my aching heart endures for her own sake, and thinks what glory she can bestow on my sufferings, what rest on my cares, and, in short, what life on my death and what reward on my services. And you, O sun, hastening no doubt to harness your steeds and sally forth betimes to behold my lady: I entreat you, as soon as you behold her, to greet her on my behalf, but pray take care that when you do behold and greet her you do not kiss her on the face, for if you did so I should be more consumed by jealousy than you were when that wanton ingrate made you sweat on the plains of Thessaly or by the banks of Peneus – I cannot remember exactly where it was that you ran on that occasion, consumed by jealousy and love.'[3]

As Don Quixote reached this point in his pitiful monologue, the innkeeper's daughter began to psst him and to whisper:

'Hey, sir, do come over here, if you wouldn't mind.'

This summons made Don Quixote turn his head, and, by the light of the moon, shining at that moment at its brightest, he saw someone beckoning to him from the hole that he took for a window with the golden bars that any castle as splendid as this one must have on its windows; and then his wild imagination made him see that yet again, just like the last time, the beauteous maiden, the daughter of the lord of that castle, overwhelmed by her love, was making up to him; and so, not wanting to appear unmannerly or ungrateful, he turned Rocinante's head and rode up to the hole, and when he saw the two girls there he said:

'My heart goes out to you, beauteous lady, for having directed your amorous inclinations towards a quarter where it is not possible that they should find the response due to your great merit and grace; for which you should not blame this wretched knight errant, prevented by love from being able to yield his heart to any other than her whom, at the very moment when he first saw her, he made absolute mistress of his soul.

Forgive me, good lady, and retire to your room, and do not, by insisting on your requests, oblige me to appear still more ungrateful; and if the love that you feel for me can find in me anything, other than love itself, with which I can satisfy you, pray command it, for I swear by that absent sweet enemy of mine that I shall give it you forthwith, even were you to ask me for one of Medusa's[4] tresses, all of which were serpents, or indeed the very rays of the sun itself enclosed within a vial.'

'No, my mistress won't be needing any of all that, sir,' Maritornes interrupted.

'And what is it that your mistress does need, wise duenna?' Don Quixote replied.

'One of your lovely hands, that's all,' said Maritornes, 'so she can use it to relieve the immense desire that's brought her to this hole, putting her honour at such risk that if her father had heard her she'd have been lucky to get off minus an ear.'

'I should like to see him try!' replied Don Quixote. 'But he will take good care not to do any such thing, unless he wishes to meet the wretchedest end that any father in this world ever did meet, for laying hands on the tender extremities of his love-stricken daughter.'

Maritornes felt sure that Don Quixote was going to give her the hand that he'd been asked for, and, making up her mind what she must do, she climbed down from the hole and hurried to the stable, where she grabbed Sancho Panza's donkey's halter and then ran back to her hole, in time to find Don Quixote standing on Rocinante's saddle so as to reach the gold-barred window at which he believed the love-lorn maiden was pining; and as he gave her his hand he said:

'Take, dear lady, this hand, or rather this scourge of the malefactors of the world; take this hand, I say, which has never been touched by that of any woman, nay not even by her who has complete possession of my entire body. I do not present it for you to kiss, but rather for you to observe the structuring of its sinews, the conformation of its muscles, the size and prominence of its veins, from all of which you will be able to deduce the might of the arm to which such a hand belongs.'

'We'll soon see about that,' Maritornes muttered.

And she made a running knot in the halter, which she slipped round his wrist, and then she climbed down from the hole and tied the other end of the halter to the bolt on the hay-loft door. When Don Quixote felt the roughness of the rope on his wrist he said:

'You appear, madam, to be grating rather than greeting my hand; do not maltreat it so, for it is not to blame for the ill that my heart does you, nor is it right that such a small part of me should bear the whole brunt of your wrath. Pray consider that true love does not wreak such cruel revenge.'

But nobody was listening to Don Quixote any more, because as soon as Maritornes had tied him up she and the other girl had run away, bursting with laughter and leaving him so well-secured that it was impossible for him to release himself. So there he was, standing on Rocinante, with the full length of his arm thrust through the hole, tied by his wrist to the bolt on the hay-loft door and terrified by the thought that if Rocinante took just one step in any direction he'd be left hanging by his arm; so he didn't dare make the slightest movement, even though Rocinante was such a patient and sedate creature that he could well have been expected to stand there for a century without budging an inch.

So finding himself strung up in this way, without any sign of the ladies, Don Quixote assumed that it had all happened by magic, just like that other time when the enchanted Moor or muleteer had thrashed him in that same castle; and he cursed his own lack of sense and judgement in venturing into it again after having come off so badly the first time, because it's a precept among knights errant that if they are unsuccessful in an adventure this is a sign that it is not meant for them, but for others, and so they are not required to attempt it again. He did try a few tugs with his arm to see if he could free himself, but he was so well-lashed that all his attempts were in vain. It is true that his tugs were only tentative ones, so as to keep Rocinante from moving, and however much he longed to sit in his saddle he had to stay standing – unless he tore his hand off.

And then did he wish for Amadis's sword, against which no enchantment had any power; and then did he curse his ill fortune; dwell on how sorely his presence would be missed in the world for as long as he remained enchanted, as he had by now convinced himself he was; think again of his beloved Dulcinea del Toboso; call for his trusty squire Sancho Panza, who, buried in sleep and stretched out on his donkey's pack-saddle, hadn't a thought for anyone, not even the mother who'd borne him; call on the sages Lirgandeo[5] and Alquife to help him; invoke his good friend Urganda to rescue him: and eventually morning came and found him so desperate and bewildered that he was bellowing like a bull, because he didn't have any hope that day would relieve his plight, which he considered to be eternal, since he was enchanted. He was confirmed in this opinion by the fact that Rocinante never budged an inch, and he believed that he and his horse would remain in that position, without eating or drinking or sleeping, until the malign influence of the stars should have dissipated, or until another wiser enchanter should have disenchanted him.

But in this he was much mistaken, because just as day was dawning four well-dressed and well-equipped men on horseback arrived at the inn, their muskets resting on their saddle-bows. They banged on the inn door, which was still shut, whereupon Don Quixote shouted in imperious tones from where he remained on sentry duty:

'Knights, or squires, or whatever you are: you have no business to be knocking on the castle door, for it is evident that at such an hour those inside are either asleep or not in the habit of opening the fortifications until the sun's rays are extended over the surface of the earth. Draw back and wait outside until day comes, and then we shall see whether it is appropriate to open to you.'

'What bloody fortification or castle is this,' said one of them, 'to make us go through such ceremonies? If you're the innkeeper, just tell them to open up – we're on a long journey and only want to feed our horses and continue on our way, because we're in a hurry.'

'Do you really believe, sirs, that I look like an innkeeper?' retorted Don Quixote.

'I don't know what you look like,' replied the other, 'but I do know you're talking nonsense when you call this inn a castle.'

'A castle it is,' replied Don Quixote, 'and one of the finest in the province, too; and it houses one who has had a sceptre in her hand and a crown on her head.'

'It'd be better the other way round,' said the traveller. 'The sceptre in her head and the crown in her hand. But what's more likely is that there's some company of strolling players lodging in there, they often mess around with these crowns and sceptres you're on about – because in a place as small and dead as this I can't believe that anyone with a right to a real crown and sceptre can be lodging.'

'You know little of the world,' replied Don Quixote, 'because you are ignorant of events that are common in knight-errantry.'

The other travellers were growing tired of their companion's conversation with Don Quixote, and they renewed their banging on the door so furiously that the innkeeper awoke, as did everyone else, and got up to find out who it was. While this was going on, one of the travellers' horses happened to trot over to Rocinante to smell him as he stood there motionless, sorrowful and with drooping ears, supporting his lofty master; and since Rocinante was, after all, made of flesh and blood, even if he did seem to be carved out of a solid block of wood, he couldn't help weakening and repaying the compliment to the one who'd come to caress him; and he'd hardly moved an inch when both Don Quixote's feet slipped off the saddle, and he'd have tumbled to the ground if he hadn't been left hanging by his arm, which caused him such pain that he thought that either his hand was being severed or his arm was being torn off, because he was left dangling so close to the ground that he could just touch it with the tips of his toes, which made matters even worse because, feeling how near he was to being able to put his feet down, he stretched and struggled to do so, just like those who are tortured on the pulley and left with their toes similarly brushing the floor, and who increase their own agony in their determination to stretch, deluding themselves with the hope that by stretching just a little further they'll make it to the ground.

CHAPTER XLIV

In which a further account is given of the singular events at the inn

And Don Quixote made such a commotion that the innkeeper flung open the doors and rushed out in alarm to go and see who it was bawling away like that, and the men outside ran over to him as well. The din had also awoken Maritornes, who, guessing what had happened, hurried across to the hay-loft without anyone seeing her and untied the halter from which Don Quixote was dangling; and this sent him sprawling to the ground in front of the innkeeper and the travellers, who went up to him and asked what was the matter to make him shout so loud. He answered not one word, but removed the rope from his wrist, rose to his feet, mounted Rocinante, seized his shield, couched his pike, rode off to take up his position a good distance away and then cantered back with the words:

'If anyone claims that I was rightfully enchanted, I hereby – provided that my lady the Princess Micomicona gives me leave to do so – declare that he lies and is a traitor, and challenge him to single combat!'

The newcomers were astonished at these words, but the innkeeper dispelled their astonishment by telling them that this was Don Quixote, and they mustn't take any notice of him, because he was mad. They then asked the innkeeper whether a lad of about fifteen had by any chance turned up there dressed as a footman, and gave a description that fitted Doña Clara's admirer. The innkeeper replied that there were so many people at the inn that he hadn't noticed the one they were asking about. But one of the four had spotted the coach in which the judge had arrived, and said:

'Yes, he must be here, because this is the coach that he's said to be following. One of us will stay by the door and the others go in and look for him – it'll be better, though, if someone else rides round the outside of the inn to stop him from getting away over the yard wall.'

'That's what we'll do,' replied another.

Two of them went in, one stayed at the door and the other started off round the inn; as the innkeeper watched all this he couldn't imagine why these men were taking such measures, although he did realize that they must be looking for the lad they'd described. It was getting lighter by now and, both because of this and because of the row that Don Quixote had made, everyone was awake and getting up, the first among them Doña Clara and Dorotea, neither of whom had slept much that night, one from her excitement at knowing that her admirer was so close and the other from her eagerness to see what he looked like. Don Quixote, observing that none of these four travellers paid him the slightest attention or responded to his challenge, was seething with indignation and fury, and if he'd discovered in his chivalry statutes that a knight errant could legitimately undertake another venture after he'd given his word not to do so until he'd completed the one to which he was already pledged, he'd have charged the lot of them and forced an answer out of them. But since he considered that it wouldn't be right or proper to start out on a fresh enterprise until he'd restored Micomicona to her kingdom, he felt obliged to hold his tongue, stay where he was and wait to see the result of the travellers' search: one of them found the lad for whom he was looking, asleep beside a footman and little suspecting that anyone was searching for him, still less that they had found him. The traveller grasped the lad by the arm and said:

'I must say, Don Luis, the clothes that you are wearing are most suitable for your rank, and the bed in which I find you lying accords splendidly with the luxury amidst which your mother raised you!'

The lad wiped his sleepy eyes, stared up at the man holding him and soon realized that this was one of his father's servants; which gave him such a shock that he was speechless for a good while; and the servant continued:

'There's nothing for it, Don Luis, but for you to be patient and come back home, unless you want to send my master your father to his last home; because no other outcome is to be expected from the grief into which your absence has plunged him.'

'And how,' asked Don Luis, 'did my father find out that I was coming this way and that I was wearing these clothes?'

'From a student whom you told of your plans,' replied the servant. 'He was the one who gave you away, moved to pity by your father's laments when he found you'd gone. So he sent us four servants off to look for you, and here we all are at your service, happier than anyone could imagine at being able to return with such good news and restore you to his loving arms.'

'That'll be if I say so, or if heaven decrees,' retorted Don Luis.

'What can you say, and what can heaven decree, except that you're coming back with us? There's no other possible outcome.'

The footman lying beside Don Luis overheard this conversation and went away to find Don Fernando and Cardenio and the others, who were dressed by now, and to tell them what had happened, and how the man had called the lad *Don*, and all about the conversation they'd had, and how the man wanted to take him back to his father's house and the lad didn't want to go. And this, and what they knew about him, and the fine singing voice that God had given him, made them all long to find out exactly who he was, and even to help him if he was threatened with violence; so they walked over to where he was still talking and arguing with his servant. At that moment Dorotea was emerging from her room followed by Doña Clara in the utmost confusion, and Dorotea called Cardenio aside and summarized the history of Doña Clara and the singer, and then Cardenio told Dorotea about what had happened when the lad's father's servants had come for him, but didn't speak quietly enough to prevent Clara from overhearing, which made such an impact on her that she'd have slumped to the floor if Dorotea hadn't hurried to support her. Cardenio told Dorotea to take Clara back into their room and he'd try to sort everything out, and off the ladies went.

By now all the four men who'd come for Don Luis were inside the inn and had surrounded him to try to persuade him not to delay a moment longer but to return home to comfort his father. He replied that on no account could he do so until he'd settled a matter that involved his life, his honour and his soul. The servants insisted that they would not return without him – they were going to take him back whether he liked it or not.

'You'll do no such thing,' replied Don Luis, 'unless you carry me back dead – though whichever way you take me, I'll have lost my life.'

By now nearly everyone at the inn had come to listen to the argument, in particular Cardenio, Don Fernando, his companions, the judge, the priest, the barber and Don Quixote, who considered that there was no further need to mount guard over the castle. Cardenio, knowing the lad's history, asked the men who wanted to take him away why they were determined to do so against his will.

'To save his father's life,' said one of the four. 'This young gentleman going missing has put him in danger of losing it.'

At this Don Luis said:

'You haven't any business to be discussing my private affairs here. I'm free to do as I please, and I'll go back if I feel like it, and if I don't feel like it none of you is going to force me.'

'Reason will make you go back,' the man replied, 'and if that isn't enough for you, it's quite enough for us, and we'll do what we've come to do and what it's our duty to do.'

'Let's get to the root of all this,' put in the judge.

The man recognized him as a neighbour, and replied:

'Don't you know this young gentleman, Your Honour? He's your neighbour's son, and he's run away from home in clothes that are quite unworthy of his rank, as you can well see.'

The judge looked at the lad more closely, recognized him and embraced him, saying:

'What pranks are these, Don Luis, and what motive can have been powerful enough to make you come here like this, wearing clothes so unsuitable for someone in your position?'

Tears flooded into the lad's eyes and he couldn't reply. The judge told the four men to calm down, because a satisfactory solution would be found; and taking Don Luis by the hand he went to one side with him and asked what it was that had impelled him to come to the inn.

While he was putting this question and others, shouts came from the inn door, and the reason was that two guests who'd stayed there overnight, seeing everyone so busy finding out what the four men wanted, had tried to leave without paying their bill; but the innkeeper, more mindful of his own business than of other people's, grabbed them as they sidled out, and demanded his money, and reproached them for their wicked intentions with words that moved them to reply with their fists; and they started to give him such a thrashing that the poor man had to shout for help. His wife and daughter couldn't see anyone who wasn't too busy to help except Don Quixote, and the daughter said to him:

'Oh, sir knight, please use the mighty power God gave you, to help my poor father — two wicked men are beating the living daylights out of him.'

To which Don Quixote replied with leisurely composure:

'Beauteous maiden, I cannot at present grant your petition, because I am prevented from involving myself in another adventure until I have brought the one to which I have already pledged myself to a happy conclusion. But what I can do to serve you is what I shall now inform you of: you should run and tell your father to hold his own in this battle as best he can, and on no account to be vanquished, while I go to beg for Princess Micomicona's permission to succour him in his plight; and if she concedes it, you can rest assured that I shall rescue him.'

'God bless my sinning heart!' Maritornes broke in. 'By the time you get this permission of yours my master'll have gone to kingdom come!'

'Allow me, my lady, to obtain the permission to which I have referred,' replied Don Quixote, 'and, once I have done so, it will matter little that he has gone to kingdom come, for I will bring him back from there even if that whole kingdom opposes me; or, at the very least, I will wreak such vengeance upon those who will have sent him there that you will be more than moderately satisfied.'

And without another word he went to kneel before Dorotea and beg her in knightly and errantical terms that Her Highness would be pleased to concede him permission to aid and succour the lord of that castle, who was in a most grievous pass. The princess graciously granted it, and he took up his shield and drew his sword and marched to the inn door, where the two guests were still beleaguering the innkeeper; but when he arrived he stopped and stood there aghast, despite all the demands of Maritornes and the innkeeper's wife to know why he was holding back and wasn't running to help their master and husband.

'I am holding back,' said Don Quixote, 'because it is not licit for me to draw my sword against squirely characters; but summon my own squire Sancho, for this defence and revenge is a task for him to perform.'

As this discussion proceeded at the inn door, so did the punching and the pounding, much to the disadvantage of the innkeeper and the displeasure of Maritornes and the innkeeper's wife and daughter, who were in despair at Don Quixote's cowardice and the sufferings of their master, husband and father. But let's leave him there, because someone's bound to come to his rescue sooner or later – and if not, let him suffer in silence for biting off more than he can chew; and let's walk fifty paces into the inn to find out what Don Luis said in reply to the judge, whom we left standing aside with the boy and asking him why he'd come here on foot and in such disgraceful clothes. The lad, seizing the judge's hands, as if to indicate that his heart was oppressed by some great sorrow, and with the tears pouring from his eyes, replied:

'Oh, sir, all I can say is that from the very moment when heaven decreed and our being neighbours made it possible that I should set eyes on Doña

Clara, your daughter and my lady, I made her the mistress of my heart; and if you, my true lord and father, don't prevent it, we shall be married this very day. For her I left home, for her I put on these clothes, to follow her wherever she went, as the arrow seeks its target and the sailor the North Star. All she knows of my passion is what she might have deduced from sometimes seeing at a distance my eyes full of tears. You know, sir, of my parents' wealth and nobility, and you know that I am their only heir; if you believe that these are motives enough for you to venture to make me a perfectly happy man, accept me now as your son; and if my father has plans of his own for me and doesn't approve of this happiness I have found, time has more power to undo and change things than the human will.'

With this the young lover fell silent, and the judge was left bewildered, bemused and amazed, both at the intelligent way in which Don Luis had expressed his feelings and at finding himself with no idea how to react in such a sudden and unexpected situation; so he made no reply except to tell the lad to calm down and to procrastinate with his servants so that they didn't take him back that day, leaving time to consider what was best for all parties. Don Luis seized and kissed his hands and even bathed them in tears, which would have melted a heart of stone, let alone the heart of the judge, who was shrewd enough to have realized immediately how advantageous this marriage would be for his daughter; though, if possible, he wanted it to be done with the consent of Don Luis's father, who, he knew, was hoping to acquire a title for his son.

By now the two guests had made peace with the innkeeper because, thanks to Don Quixote's persuasion and fine words rather than any threats, they'd paid their bill in full, and Don Luis's servants were awaiting the outcome of the confabulation with the judge and the decision of their master, when the devil, who never sleeps, brought into the inn that barber from whom Don Quixote had taken Mambrino's helmet and Sancho Panza the ass's trappings that he'd exchanged for his own; and as the barber was taking his donkey to the stable he caught sight of Sancho Panza, who was mending something on the pack-saddle, and immediately recognized him, and made bold to charge at him, crying:

'Hey, you thief, I've got you now! You give me back my basin and my pack-saddle and all the rest of the tackle you stole off me!'

Sancho, finding himself so suddenly attacked and hearing such abuse being hurled at him, grabbed the pack-saddle with one hand and with the other delivered to the barber's mouth a punch that bathed his teeth in blood; but this didn't make the barber loosen the grip he'd taken on the pack-saddle – on the contrary he raised such an outcry that everyone flocked over to watch the new fight, as he yelled:

'Help, help, in the King's name, justice! First he steals my property and now he wants to kill me, the thief, the highwayman!'

'You liar!' Sancho rejoined. 'I'm no highwayman, my master Don Quixote won these spoils in a just war.'

Don Quixote had reached the scene by now, and was delighted to see how well his squire was defending himself and attacking the enemy; and from that moment on he deemed him a man of mettle, and he took the decision to knight him at the earliest opportunity, for he truly deserved to be received into the order of chivalry. The barber said many things in the course of the disagreement, among them:

'Look, all of you, this pack-saddle's as much mine as is the death I owe God, and I know it as well as if I'd given birth to it, and my ass over there in the stable will confirm my story, because if you don't believe me just try the pack-saddle on its back, and if it doesn't fit like a glove you can call me all the names you like. Not only that, the day it was stolen they also stole a brand-new brass basin, never used, worth a whole escudo.'

Don Quixote could contain himself no longer, and thrusting himself between the two to keep them apart, and depositing the pack-saddle on the floor in safe-keeping until the truth should be made manifest, he declared:

'Here you can perfectly clearly see for yourselves how mistaken this fellow is, calling a basin what was, is and shall be Mambrino's helmet, which I won from him in a just war and of which I thus became the true and lawful owner! With regard to the pack-saddle I shall not interfere: all I can say about that is that my squire Sancho requested my permission to remove the caparisons from this vanquished coward's horse and to adorn his own with them; I gave it, he took them, and if the caparisons have been converted into a pack-saddle I can only give the usual explanation, that these transformations do occur in the affairs of chivalry; for confirmation of which, Sancho my son, hurry and fetch the helmet that this fellow says is a basin.'

'By God, sir,' said Sancho, 'if we haven't got any better proof to support us than that, Malino's helmet is as much a barber's basin as this character's comparisons are a pack-saddle!'

'Go and do what I told you to do,' replied Don Quixote. 'Not everything in this castle can be governed by enchantment.'

Sancho went and fetched the basin, and as soon as Don Quixote saw it he took it into his hands and said:

'Consider, ladies and gentlemen, the sheer impudence of this squire in claiming that this is a basin and not the helmet I have specified; and I swear by the order of chivalry which I profess that this helmet is the same helmet I won from him, and I have not added or removed any part.'

'There isn't any doubt about that,' Sancho put in, 'because from the time my master won it up to now he's only fought one battle wearing it, when he freed those poor wretches in chains, and if it hadn't been for this here basinelmet he'd have had a bad time of it, because there was lots of stonethrowing on that occasion.'

CHAPTER XLV

In which the doubts about Mambrino's helmet, about the
pack-saddle and about other adventures are finally
resolved

'Now you all tell me,' said the barber, 'what you think about these fine gentlemen still insisting this isn't a basin but a helmet!'

'And I will make whoever says anything different,' said Don Quixote, 'admit, if he is a knight, that he is a liar, and if he is a squire, that he is a liar a thousand times over.'

Our own barber, having been present throughout these exchanges and being well acquainted with Don Quixote's disposition, decided to give his folly some encouragement and spin the joke out so that everyone could have a good laugh, and so he addressed the other barber:

'Mister barber or mister whoever you are: I'll have you know that I'm in the same line of business as you, and I've had my certificates these twenty years or more, and I know the tools of the trade, every one of them; on top of all that, as a young man I was a soldier, so I know what a helmet is, and I know what a morion is, and I know what a sallet is, and other matters concerning the militia, in other words the arms and armour used by soldiers; and what I'm saying, with all due respect of course and do correct me if I'm wrong, is that this object here before us in the hands of this good gentleman not only is not a barber's basin but is as far from being a barber's basin as black is from being white and as truth is from being falsehood; but I do also have to say that although it is a helmet it isn't a complete one.'

'No, of course not,' said Don Quixote, 'because half of it, the beaver, is missing.'

'That is indeed so,' said the priest, who'd realized what his friend the barber was up to. Cardenio and Don Fernando and his men backed him up, and, if the judge hadn't been so concerned with the Don Luis affair, he, too, would have done his bit to advance the joke; but the serious matters on his mind so preoccupied him that he was paying little or no attention to these pleasantries.

'Good God!' exploded the bantered barber. 'How can it be possible for all these respectable people to be saying that this here isn't a basin but a helmet? It's enough to confound an entire university, however brainy it might be! All right then: if this here basin's a helmet, then this here pack-saddle must be a horse's caparisons, just as the gentleman said.'

'To me it looks like a pack-saddle,' said Don Quixote, 'but then I have already stated that this is an affair in which I shall not interfere.'

'Whether it's a pack-saddle or a caparison,' said the priest, 'is something that only Don Quixote can decide, because in matters of chivalry all these gentlemen, and I too, bow to his superior knowledge.'

'By God, sirs,' said Don Quixote, 'so very many strange things have happened to me in this castle on the two occasions when I have lodged here that I dare not give a clear answer to any question about anything in it, because I imagine that everything that occurs here is carried out by enchantment. The first time I was much harassed by an enchanted Moor who lives here, and Sancho did not fare too well in an encounter with some of his henchmen, and last night I hung by this arm for nearly two hours, without the faintest idea how I came to suffer such a misfortune. So to start giving my opinion now about such a perplexing matter would be to commit the sin of making a rash judgement. As regards some people's opinion that this is a basin and not a helmet, I have already given my answer; but as for declaring whether this is a pack-saddle or a caparison, I dare not give a definitive decision: I can only leave it to your own good judgement. It is possible that, since you have not been knighted, as I have, the enchantments in this place do not affect you, and that your understanding is unclouded, and that you can form judgements about the affairs of this castle as they really and truly are, rather than as they appeared to me.'

'There's no doubt,' Don Fernando replied, 'that Don Quixote has just spoken most judiciously – it's up to us to reach a decision in this case; and, to ensure that our decision is a well-founded one, I shall now take a secret vote among these ladies and gentlemen, and give you all a full and clear account of the result.'

All this had those who knew about Don Quixote's foibles splitting their sides with laughter; but to those who didn't know about them it just seemed extremely silly – in particular to Don Luis's four servants and Don Luis himself, and to another three travellers who'd turned up at the inn and who looked like officers of the Holy Brotherhood, as indeed they were. But one man had been plunged into the deepest depths of despair, and that was the barber, whose basin, there before his very eyes, had turned into Mambrino's helmet, and whose pack-saddle, he was sure, was about to turn into the splendid caparisons of some handsome steed; but both those who were in the know and those who weren't chortled as they saw Don Fernando going from one person to the next, collecting votes and whispering into ears to obtain secret declarations as to whether the treasure that had been the cause of such strife was a pack-saddle or a caparison. And after taking the votes of those who knew Don Quixote, he declared:

'The fact is, my dear fellow, that I'm tired of sounding out so many opinions, because there isn't a single person I ask who doesn't say it's the height of absurdity to claim that this is a donkey's pack-saddle rather than a horse's caparison – and a thoroughbred's at that; so you'll just have to grin and bear it because, in spite of you and your ass, this is a caparison and not a pack-saddle, and you have pleaded and presented your case very poorly indeed.'

'May I never be presented in heaven,' cried the extra barber, 'if you aren't wrong, the whole lot of you, and as sure as I hope my soul will appear before God this looks to me like a pack-saddle and not a caparison, but then it's the lords that make the laws, and I'll say no more – and I'm not drunk, honestly I'm not, because I haven't had my breakfast yet and there's nothing inside me but my sins.'

This nonsense spoken by the barber caused no less mirth than the absurdities voiced by Don Quixote, who remarked:

'All that can be done now is for each to take what belongs to him, and may St Peter bless what God has given.'

One of Don Luis's four servants said:

'Unless this is some practical joke, I just can't fathom how men of good understanding, as these here present are or seem to be, can have the gall to keep saying that this isn't a basin and that that isn't a pack-saddle; but since this is exactly what they are saying, all I can suppose is that something mysterious is afoot when people insist on what's so contrary to what we can see with our own eyes to be the case; because I swear by . . .' – and the oath was a rich one – 'nobody in the whole wide world is going to tell me that this isn't a barber's basin and that that isn't an jackass's pack-saddle.'

'It could be a she-ass's,' said the priest.

'That doesn't matter,' said the servant. 'That isn't the point at issue – the point at issue is whether this is a pack-saddle or, as you all say, it isn't.'

When one of the newly arrived officers of the Holy Brotherhood, who had been listening to the argument, heard this, he cried in a blind fury:

'If that isn't a pack-saddle then my father isn't my father, and anyone who says anything different must be half-seas over.'

'You lie like a base villain,' Don Quixote replied.

And raising his pike, which was never out of his hands, he aimed such a blow at the officer's head that, if he hadn't ducked, it would have stretched him out at full length. The pike shattered on the ground and the other peace-officers, seeing their comrade assaulted, cried out demanding assistance for the Holy Brotherhood. The innkeeper, who was also a peace-officer, hurried to fetch his staff of office and his sword, and stationed himself by his comrades' side; Don Luis's servants surrounded the lad to prevent him from escaping in the confusion; the barber took advantage of the turmoil to grab his pack-saddle, and so did Sancho; Don Quixote drew his sword and attacked the officers; Don Luis was shouting at his servants to leave him be and go to help Don Quixote and also Cardenio and Don Fernando, both of whom had gone to Don Quixote's assistance; the priest was shouting, the innkeeper's wife was screaming, her daughter was moaning, Maritornes was weeping, Dorotea was bewildered, Luscinda was astonished and Doña Clara was fainting. The barber was pounding away at Sancho; Sancho was hammering away at the barber; Don Luis gave a servant who dared to seize one of his arms to prevent him from running away a punch that bathed his teeth in blood; the judge was defending the servant; Don Fernando had a peace-officer under his feet and was trampling away to his heart's content; the innkeeper cried out again demanding help for the officers of the Holy Brotherhood. So the inn was all tears, shouts, screams, confusion, fear, alarm, disasters, flashing knives, flying fists, flailing cudgels, pounding feet and flowing blood. And in the midst of this chaos, this labyrinth, this edifice of mischief, Don Quixote took it into his head that he was in the thick of the turmoil in King Agramante's camp,[1] and he cried in a voice that thundered throughout the inn:

'Stay still everyone; everyone sheathe his sword; everyone be calm; listen everyone, if you value your lives!'

At these stentorian commands everybody froze, and Don Quixote continued:

'Did I not tell you, sirs, that this castle is enchanted, and that some legion of devils must inhabit it? As proof of which I call on you to behold with your own eyes how the turmoil in King Agramante's camp has been transported into our midst. See how they are fighting there for the sword, here for the horse, there for the eagle, here for the helmet, and every one of us is fighting, and every one of us is at odds with his neighbour. Come then, Your Honour, and come, Your Reverence, and one of you can be King Agramante, and the other King Sobrino, and make peace among us because, by God Almighty, it is sheer villainy for such eminent personages as us to be killing each other for such petty causes.'

The men of the Holy Brotherhood, who didn't understand Don Quixote's diction and were having little success in their tussle with Don

Fernando, Cardenio and friends, weren't ready to be pacified; but the barber was, because both his beard and his pack-saddle had been destroyed in the struggle; Sancho obeyed his master's slightest word like a good servant; and Don Luis's four servants also stopped in their tracks, seeing that it wouldn't be a good idea not to. Only the innkeeper was insisting that this madman must be punished for his effrontery, throwing the whole house into an uproar every five minutes. So the din died down for the time being, the pack-saddle was left as a caparison until judgement day, and the basin remained as a helmet and the inn as a castle in Don Quixote's imagination.

With peace restored and everyone friends again thanks to the judge and the priest, Don Luis's servants insisted yet again that he must return home; and while he was busy with them the judge consulted Don Fernando, Cardenio and the priest about what he should do, and told them what Don Luis had told him. It was finally decided that Don Fernando would reveal his identity to the servants and tell them that he'd like Don Luis to go with him to Andalusia, where he'd receive from Don Fernando's brother the marquis the welcome to which his quality entitled him, because it had become clear that Don Luis was determined to allow himself to be torn limb from limb rather than return so soon to his father's arms. When the four servants were informed about Don Fernando's rank and Don Luis's resolution, they decided that three of them would go back and tell his father how matters stood, and that the fourth would stay to serve Don Luis and not leave his side until the others returned or his father's orders were known.

And so that edifice of dispute was pacified, by the authority of Agramante and the wisdom of King Sobrino; but the enemy of concord and adversary of peace, finding himself scorned and outwitted, and seeing how little it had benefited him to embroil them all in that labyrinth of confusion, decided to try his luck again by reviving old quarrels and disturbances.

What happened was that the peace-officers calmed down on overhearing the rank of the men who'd been fighting against them, and withdrew from the conflict realizing that whatever the result they were going to get the worst of it; but one of them, the one who'd been trampled and kicked by Don Fernando, recalled that among the warrants he had on him for the arrest of various criminals there was one for Don Quixote, whom the Holy Brotherhood had ordered to be detained for setting the convicts free, as Sancho had so rightly feared. With this in mind, the peace-officer decided to check whether the description of Don Quixote fitted the man before him, and he pulled a parchment folder out of his shirt and found the warrant he was looking for, and began to peruse it with the utmost deliberation, not being very good at reading, and looked up at Don Quixote at every word to compare his face with the description in the warrant, and found that this was most certainly his man. Once he'd reached this conclusion he put his folder away, took the warrant in his left hand, with his right hand seized Don Quixote so tight by the collar that he couldn't breathe, and cried:

'Help, help the Holy Brotherhood! And to see that I really mean it, just read this warrant, where it says that this highwayman must be arrested.'

The priest took the warrant and saw that the peace-officer was telling the truth and that the description did match Don Quixote, who, finding himself so roughly handled by that base caitiff, and at the highest pitch of fury, and with every bone in his body creaking, grabbed the officer by the throat with both hands and with all the strength he could muster; and if the officer's companions hadn't gone to his aid he'd have given up the ghost before Don Quixote had given up his prey. The innkeeper, obliged to assist a fellow officer, also ran to help him. The innkeeper's wife, seeing her husband involved in yet another fight, raised her voice again, and their daughter and Maritornes provided accompaniment as the three of them begged heaven and all those present for help. In view of what was going on, Sancho remarked:

'Good God, it's true what my master says about this castle being enchanted – you don't get a moment's peace and quiet in here!'

Don Fernando prised the peace-officer and Don Quixote apart and, much to the relief of both of them, unhooked their hands, one from a tabard collar and the other from a throat; but this didn't make the officers stop claiming their prisoner and demanding the assistance of the company, who were to tie him up and deliver him to their charge, as required in the service of the King and of the Holy Brotherhood, in whose name they repeated their demand for aid in detaining that thief and highway robber. But Don Quixote only laughed at these words, and declared with supreme composure:

'Look you here, you wretched and low-born rabble: is highway robbery your name for the liberation of those who are in chains, the release of prisoners, the succour of the unfortunate, the raising of the fallen, the relief of the needy? You infamous crew: your vile and paltry minds make you unworthy that heaven should reveal to you the worth that is in knight-errantry, or make you understand your sinfulness and ignorance in not revering the shadow, let alone the presence, of any knight errant! Look you here, you who are not officers of the law but officers of lawlessness, footpads licensed by the Holy Brotherhood: tell me, who was the ignoramus that signed a warrant of arrest against such a knight as I am? Who was it that did not know that knights errant are independent of all judicial authority, and that their law is their sword, their decrees are their prowess and their edicts are their will? Who was the numbskull, I repeat, who was unaware that there is no patent of nobility with as many privileges and prerogatives as the one that a knight errant acquires the very day he is dubbed and gives himself over to the rigorous exercise of chivalry? What knight errant ever paid tallage, excise, royal subsidies, septennial levies, tolls or ferry taxes? What tailor ever presented him with a bill for his labours? What lord of a castle ever made him pay for his sojourn? What king ever failed to sit him at his own table? What maiden ever failed to fall in love with him and give herself up to his will and pleasure? And, in short, what knight errant of the past, the present or the future would not have the spirit to deal four hundred cudgellings to any four hundred peace-officers confronting him?'

CHAPTER XLVI

About the notable adventure of the peace-officers, and the ferocity of our good knight Don Quixote

While Don Quixote was saying all this, the priest was explaining to the peace-officers that the knight was out of his senses, as they could see from his deeds and his words, and that it was futile to press the matter any further, since even if they did arrest him and take him away, he'd be released immediately as a madman; to which the one with the warrant retorted that it wasn't his job to judge whether Don Quixote was mad or not, but to carry out his superior's orders, and once he'd arrested him they could let him go three hundred times over for all he cared.

'All the same,' said the priest, 'I'm sure you'll let him off just this once – and anyway I don't think he'd allow anyone to arrest him, so far as I can tell.'

And the priest spoke so many fine words and Don Quixote performed so many mad deeds that the officers would have been even madder than he was if they hadn't acknowledged his weakness; and so they thought it best to calm down and even act as peacemakers between the barber and Sancho Panza, who were still wrangling away for all they were worth. As officers of justice, therefore, they mediated in the case and arbitrated to such effect that both parties were left if not completely content then at least reasonably satisfied, because pack-saddles were exchanged but not girths or headstalls. And as regards Mambrino's helmet, the priest, surreptitiously and behind Don Quixote's back, let the barber have eight reals for the basin, and the barber made out a receipt and a written promise not to claim that he'd been unfairly treated, now and for ever and ever, amen.

Now that these two disputes, the most serious ones, had been settled, it only remained for Don Luis's servants to agree that three of them would return home and the other one would accompany him to where Don Fernando wanted to take him; and since good luck and even better fortune had begun to smile on the lovers and the brave men at the inn and to smooth away obstacles for them, it decided to finish the job and produce a happy outcome for everyone, because the servants agreed to everything Don Luis wanted, which made Doña Clara so happy that nobody could see her face and not know of the joy in her soul. Although Zoraida didn't fully understand what was going on, she was vaguely sad or glad according to the looks she saw on people's faces, and in particular on the face of her Spanish man, on whom her eyes were fixed, and her heart and soul as well. The innkeeper, who hadn't failed to spot the priest making the barber his compensatory gift, demanded payment for Don Quixote's stay, together with the damage to his wineskins and the loss of his wine, swearing that neither Rocinante nor Sancho's donkey would leave the inn until he'd been paid to the last maravedí. The priest appeased the innkeeper and Don Fernando paid him, even though the judge had also hastened to offer the money; and they were all left in tranquillity and harmony, so that the inn no longer bore any resemblance to the turmoil in King Agramante's camp, as Don Quixote had claimed, but rather recalled the peace and calm of Octavian's time;[1] and it was the general opinion that they owed thanks for all this to the priest's goodwill and eloquence and to Don Fernando's incomparable generosity.

Now that Don Quixote was rid of all those disputes, both his squire's and his own, he thought it would be a good idea to continue the journey that he had begun, and conclude that great adventure for which he had been chosen and called; and so he advanced with firm and resolute tread to kneel before Dorotea, who wouldn't let him utter a word until he'd come to his feet; and, obeying her, he rose and said:

'It is a well-known proverb, beauteous lady, that diligence is the mother of good fortune, and in many grave matters experience has shown that the assiduity of the negotiator can bring a difficult dispute to a happy conclusion; but nowhere is this truth more evident than in war, in which speed and alacrity forestall the enemy's plans, and bring victory before he can defend himself. I say all this, eminent and lovely lady, because I believe that our stay in this castle is no longer beneficial, and indeed could cause us very great harm, as one day we might discover; for who knows whether your enemy the giant has, from diligent and hidden spies, discovered that I am on my way to destroy him and, in his own good time, is fortifying his position in some impregnable castle or fortress against which all my efforts and the might of my indefatigable arm would be of little avail? And so, my lady, let us forestall his plans, as I have suggested, by our diligence, and depart immediately in search of good fortune: Your Highness's finding it as you desire will take no longer than it takes me to confront your adversary.'

Don Quixote fell silent and waited in serene silence for the beauteous princess's reply: with a royal bearing, to match Don Quixote's style, she replied as follows:

'I am obliged to you, sir knight, for the desire that you express to succour me in my great necessity, like the true knight you are, whose care and concern it is to assist orphans and the distressed; and may heaven

427

grant that your desire and mine may be fulfilled, so that you may see that there are women on this earth who are capable of gratitude. And as regards my departure, let it be immediate, for I have no other will than yours: pray dispose of me according to your will and pleasure, for she who has once entrusted to you the defence of her person, and has placed in your hands the restoration of her domains, will not contradict whatever your wisdom may decree.'

'God's will be done,' said Don Quixote. 'And since a lady humbles herself thus before me, I will not let slip the opportunity of raising her up and placing her upon the throne that she inherited. Let us leave forthwith, for that expression about there being danger in delay is putting spurs to my desire to be on the road. And since heaven has never created nor has hell ever seen any danger that can strike fear into me, go, Sancho, and saddle Rocinante and make your donkey and the Queen's palfrey ready, let us take our leave of the lord of the castle and these other gentlemen, and be on our way.'

Sancho, who had been present all the time, shook his head and said:

'Oh, sir, there's more going on in the village than folks know about – with all due respect to your hard feelings, ma'am.'

'What can be going on in any village or in all the cities in the world that can be known about to my discredit, you peasant?'

'If you're going to get cross, now,' replied Sancho, 'I'll keep quiet about what it's my duty as a good squire to tell you, and what any good servant ought to tell his master.'

'You may say whatever you please,' replied Don Quixote, 'so long as it is not the intention of your words to strike fear into me; for if you are frightened, you are acting like the man you are, and if I am not frightened, I am acting like the man I am.'

'It isn't that, God bless my sinful heart!' replied Sancho. 'What it is, is that I know for a certain fact that this lady who's said to be the queen of the great kingdom of Micomicón is no more a queen than my mother was, because if she was what she says she is, she wouldn't go slobbering over a certain person whenever she gets a chance and thinks nobody's looking.'

Sancho's words brought Dorotea's face out in a blush, because it was true that her husband Don Fernando had occasionally, unseen by other eyes, taken with his lips a part of the prize gained by his love, and Sancho had spotted them and considered that this brazenness was more appropriate to a courtesan than to a queen of such a great kingdom; and Dorotea couldn't and wouldn't say a word in reply, but allowed Sancho to continue with his tirade:

'I'm only saying this, sir, because if after all that plodding on and on and on down highways and up byways, and putting up with bad nights and worse days, a certain person who spends his time having fun at the inn is going to come and gather the fruit of our toils, there isn't any reason for me to be in such a hurry to saddle Rocinante, put the pack-saddle on the donkey or get the palfrey ready – we'd better both sit on our backsides, and let the whores get on with their work, while we eat!'

God save us! How mighty was Don Quixote's anger when he heard his squire's disrespectful words! It was so great, I say, that his voice shook and his tongue faltered and fire darted from his eyes as he cried:

'Oh, you villainous peasant, lout, jackanapes, ignoramus, gibberer, foulmouth, malapert, backbiter, scandal-monger! How dare you speak such words in my presence and in that of these illustrious ladies, or allow such insolent indecencies into your disordered imagination? Begone from my presence, you monster of nature, depository of lies, storehouse of deceit, silo of knavery, inventor of evil, proclaimer of nonsense, enemy of the respect that is due to royal persons! Begone, get out of my sight, under pain of incurring my wrath!'

And as he said this he arched his eyebrows, blew out his cheeks, glared around in all directions and gave a great stamp on the ground with his right foot, all of which showed how mighty was the wrath in his bowels. In the face of these words and these furious gestures Sancho was so abashed and terror-stricken that he'd have been happy for the earth to open up at his feet and swallow him. And all he could think of doing was turning round and removing himself from his master's raging presence. But to temper his fury the quick-witted Dorotea, who by now knew Don Quixote's character so well, said:

'Be not wrathful, Sir Knight of the Sorry Face, at the absurdities uttered by your worthy squire; for perhaps he does not speak them without some cause, and a man with his good understanding and Christian conscience cannot be suspected of bearing false witness; so we must assume, indeed there can be no doubt about it, that since everything in this castle, as you yourself, sir, have said, proceeds by means of enchantment, it could be the case, I believe, that Sancho did see, by these diabolical means, what he says he saw, so much to the detriment of my virtue.'

'I swear by almighty God,' Don Quixote exclaimed, 'that Your Highness has hit the mark, and that some evil vision was placed before this sinner Sancho, which made him see what he could never possibly have seen by any means other than enchantment; for I know all about the goodness and innocence of this poor unfortunate, who is quite incapable of bearing false witness.'

'You're absolutely right there,' said Don Fernando, 'and so, Don Quixote, you must forgive him now and restore him to the bosom of your favour, *sicut erat in principio*,[2] before those visions turned his brain.'

Don Quixote replied that he did indeed forgive him, and the priest went to fetch Sancho, who returned in abject humility and, falling to his knees, asked his master for his hand; and his master acceded, allowed it to be kissed, blessed him and said:

'Now you must finally realize, Sancho my son, that what I have so often told you is true, and that everything that happens in this castle takes place by way of enchantment.'

'I believe you,' said Sancho, 'except for the blanket business – that definitely happened in the ordinary way.'

'You must not think that,' replied Don Quixote, 'for if it were the case, I should have avenged you then, and would even avenge you now; but neither then nor now has it been possible for me to do so, nor have I ever identified anybody on whom I could take vengeance for the injury done you.'

They asked what this blanket business had been all about, and the innkeeper gave them a meticulous account of Sancho's aerial acrobatics, which provided them with a hearty laugh and would have provided Sancho with as much embarrassment if his master hadn't assured him yet again that it had been a magic spell; though Sancho was never simple-minded enough to believe that it wasn't the absolute and verified truth, unadulterated by any trickery whatsoever, that he'd been blanket-tossed by men of flesh and blood and not by ghosts that he'd dreamed up and imagined, as his master believed and asserted.

That illustrious company had now been at the inn for two days, and, since they thought it was time they were leaving, they conceived a scheme that obviated the need for Dorotea and Don Fernando to go with Don Quixote to his village under the pretence of the restoration of Queen Micomicona, and made it possible for the priest and the barber to take him back, as they wanted, to try to cure his madness at home. And what they did was to agree with a man with an ox-cart who happened to come that way to carry Don Quixote off in the following manner: they constructed a cage with wooden bars, large enough to hold him comfortably, and then Don Fernando and his companions, Don Luis's servants, the peace-officers and the innkeeper, all taking their orders from the priest, masked their faces and disguised themselves, some in one way and some in another, to make Don Quixote think that they weren't the same people he'd seen at the inn. Then they all tiptoed in to where he lay recovering his strength after the recent skirmishes. They crept up to him, fast asleep and oblivious to what was going on, seized him and bound him hand and foot, so that when he awoke with a start he couldn't move or do anything other than gaze in bewilderment at all those deformed faces before him. And he believed what his tireless and delirious imagination was telling him, that all those figures were the ghosts of that enchanted castle and that he himself was obviously enchanted again, since he couldn't move or defend himself: exactly as the priest, the designer of the scheme, had thought would happen. Only Sancho, of all those present, was both in his right mind and in his right clothes, and, although he wasn't far from suffering from his master's disease, this didn't prevent him from recognizing the men through their disguises; but he didn't dare to part his lips until he saw what came of the attack and arrest of his master, and the victim didn't utter a word, either, as he, too, waited to see the upshot of this latest misfortune; and the upshot was that the masked figures brought in the cage and shut him up in it and nailed it down so firmly that it wasn't going to be broken open in a hurry. They hoisted it on to their shoulders, and as they marched out of the room a fearful voice was heard, or at least one as fearful as the barber – not the saddle-bag barber, the other one – could make it, and it was saying:

'O Knight of the Sorry Face! Be not abashed by the captivity to which you have been reduced, which is needful for the more speedy accomplishment of the adventure in which your valour has engaged you. And it will be accomplished when the livid lion of La Mancha shall lie with the white dove of El Toboso, once their lofty necks have been humbled by the gentle yoke of matrimony; from which unique coupling shall come into the light of the world brave cubs that will emulate the rampant claws of their valiant sire. And this will come to pass before the bright pursuer of the fugitive nymph shall have twice performed his round of visits to the luminous signs in his natural and rapid course.[3] And you, the most noble and obedient squire that ever had a sword in his belt, a beard on his face and a smell in his nose, be not dismayed or grieved to see the flower of knight-errantry thus borne away before your eyes; for ere long, if it so please the Fabricator of this world, you will find yourself so ennobled and exalted that you will not recognize yourself, and you will not be defrauded of the rewards promised you by your noble lord. And I assure you, on behalf of the sage Mentironiana,[4] that your wages will be paid, as you will duly see; so follow in the footsteps of the valiant and enchanted knight, for it is necessary that you travel together to the end of your journey. And because I am not permitted to say any more, God be with you. I am returning now to I know where.'

And as he reached the end of the prophecy he raised his voice and then lowered it again in such tender tones that even those who knew that it was all a joke were close to believing what they'd heard. The prophecy was a great comfort to Don Quixote, because he at once grasped its full meaning, and understood that it promised that he would be joined in holy and lawful matrimony with his beloved Dulcinea del Toboso, from whose fortunate womb would issue the cubs, in other words his sons, for the everlasting glory of La Mancha; and in this firm and steadfast belief he heaved a profound sigh and cried:

'O you, whoever you may be, who have prophesied such good for me! I beg that you will, on my behalf, ask the wise enchanter who is in charge of my affairs not to permit me to perish in this prison in which I am being borne away, until I have seen the fulfilment of the joyful and incomparable promises that have here been made me; for if this is granted, I shall consider the griefs of my captivity as glories, the chains that bind me as comforts, and these boards on which I am made to lie not as a hard battlefield but as a soft and happy nuptial couch. And as regards your consolation of my squire Sancho Panza, I trust that his goodness and integrity will not allow him to leave me, in prosperity or adversity. For if it so falls out that, because of his or my bad fortune, I cannot give him the island that I have promised him, or something equivalent, he will, at least, not lose his wages, since in my will I have declared what is to be given him, not I fear proportionate to his many good services, but rather to my own possibilities.'

Sancho Panza made him a bow expressive of deep respect and kissed both his hands, it being impossible to kiss only one of them, because they were tied together. The visions hoisted the cage back on to their shoulders, and then fixed it on top of the ox-cart.

CHAPTER XLVII

*About the strange way in which Don Quixote was
enchanted, and other famous events*

Finding himself caged on a cart, Don Quixote said:

'Many weighty histories of knights errant have I read, but never I have read, or seen, or heard of enchanted knights being carried off in this way or as slowly as these heavy, slothful beasts promise; for knights are always borne through the air, at extraordinary speed, wrapped in some dark, grey cloud, or on some chariot of fire, or on some hippogryph or similar beast; but for me to be carried off now on an ox-cart does, as God is good, throw me into the greatest confusion! Yet maybe the chivalry and the enchanting of these times of ours follow different paths from those of earlier days. And it could also be that, since I am a new knight in the world, and the first to resuscitate the forgotten exercise of knight-errantry, new forms of enchantment and other ways of carrying off the enchanted have been invented. What do you think, Sancho my son?'

'I don't know what I think,' replied Sancho, 'not being as well-read as you are in errantry writings – all the same I must say I haven't got much faith in these here visions.'

'Faith? Goodness gracious me!' replied Don Quixote. 'How could you have faith in them when they are all demons who have assumed fantastic bodies to come and do this to me and reduce me to this situation? And if you want to see that I am right, just touch them and feel them, and you will find that their bodies are only air, nothing but outward appearance.'

'I have touched them, sir, so help me God,' replied Sancho, 'and this devil that's fussing about here is as plump as a dumpling, and there's something else about him that's very different from what I've heard about demons – it's said they all stink of sulphur and other such muck, but this one reeks of ambergris from a couple of miles away.'

Sancho was referring to Don Fernando, who, being of such high rank, must have smelled of what Sancho said.

'You must not wonder at that, friend Sancho,' replied Don Quixote, 'because I can tell you, devils are crafty characters, and even if they carry smells with them, they themselves do not smell, because they are spirits, and if they do smell of anything it can never be pleasant, but foul and noxious. And the reason is that since they take hell with them wherever they go, and since they cannot receive any kind of relief from their torments, and since a good smell is pleasing and delightful, it is not possible for them to smell of anything wholesome. So if you think that demon to which you referred smells of ambergris, either you are deceiving yourself or he wants to deceive you and make you believe that he is not a demon.'

As master and servant conversed, Don Fernando and Cardenio, fearing that Sancho might tumble to their scheme, since he was on the very verge of doing so, decided to hasten their departure; and, calling the innkeeper aside, they told him to saddle Rocinante and put the pack-saddle on Sancho's donkey, which he hurried to do. In the meantime the priest had arranged for the peace-officers to accompany them back to the village for a daily payment. Cardenio hung the shield from one end of Rocinante's saddle-tree and the basin from the other, signalled to Sancho to mount his ass and take Rocinante's reins, and positioned two peace-officers with their muskets on either side of the cart. But before the cart moved off, the innkeeper's wife and daughter and Maritornes came out to say goodbye to Don Quixote, pretending to be shedding tears of grief at his misfortune, and Don Quixote addressed them:

'Weep not, good ladies; for all these calamities are the lot of those who profess what I profess, and if these disasters did not befall me I should not consider myself a famous knight errant: such things do not happen to knights of small repute, because nobody ever bothers about them. They happen to valiant knights, because their resolve and courage is envied by many men of high rank and by many other knights, who attempt by evil means to destroy these good men. But in spite of all that, virtue is so mighty that it will, unaided, and despite all the sorcery that the very first sorcerer, Zoroaster,[1] ever knew, emerge triumphant from every predicament, and give its light to the world as the sun gives its light to the sky. Forgive me, beauteous damsels, if, quite inadvertently, I have done you any mischief, for I have never harmed anyone wilfully or consciously; and pray to God that he deliver me from this captivity, to which some ill-intentioned enchanter has reduced me; for if I am one day freed, the favours you have done me at this castle will not escape my remembrance, that I may acknowledge, requite and repay them as they deserve.'

While the damsels of the castle were busy with Don Quixote, the priest and the barber said goodbye to Don Fernando and his companions, to the captain and his brother and to all the contented ladies, particularly Dorotea and Luscinda. They all embraced each other and agreed to keep in touch, and Don Fernando let the priest have his address so that he could write and tell him what happened to Don Quixote, as there would be no greater pleasure for him, he said, than to be informed about this; and Don Fernando in his turn would let the priest have any news that might interest him, about his wedding and Zoraida's baptism and the Don Luis affair and Luscinda's return home. The priest promised to do exactly as he was asked. They embraced again, and made each other some more promises. The innkeeper approached the priest and gave him a bundle of papers, saying that he'd found it in a pocket in the case where the 'Tale of Inappropriate Curiosity' had been discovered, and that since its owner hadn't come back the priest could have it, because not being able to read he didn't have any use for it himself. The priest thanked him, opened the bundle and saw written at the top of the first page: *The Tale of Rinconete and Cortadillo*;[2] from which he gathered that this was another work of fiction and that, since the 'Tale of Inappropriate Curiosity' had been a good one, perhaps this was too, because they might both be by the same author; so he put it in a safe place, intending to read it when he had an opportunity.

He mounted, and so did his friend the barber, both wearing their masks to prevent Don Quixote from recognizing them, and they started out behind the cart. And the procession set off as follows: first went the cart, led by its owner; on either side of it went the peace-officers, as we have said, with their muskets; then Sancho Panza on his ass, leading Rocinante by the reins. Bringing up the rear came the priest and the barber on their powerful mules, with their faces covered in the way described, and their bearing grave and sedate, since they couldn't ride any faster than the oxen would permit. Don Quixote was sitting in the cage with his hands tied and his legs stretched out in front of him, leaning against the bars, and his silence and his patience were such that he seemed more like a stone statue than a man of flesh and blood.

They rode on in this ponderous silence for half-a-dozen miles until they reached a valley that seemed to the carter like a good place to let his oxen rest and graze; but when he said so to the priest, the barber thought it would be better to ride on a little further, because he knew that behind a hill they could see not far away there was a valley with more and better grass than there was where they were thinking of stopping. The barber's advice was followed, and so they plodded on. As they did so, the priest looked back and saw approaching them some six or seven men, well dressed and equipped, who soon caught up with them because they weren't riding at the sedate and imperturbable pace of oxen but on canons' mules, and were anxious to reach the next inn, which could be seen only a couple of miles ahead, before the sun was intolerably hot. The speedy duly overtook the slow, and courteous greetings were exchanged; and one of the newcomers, who turned out to be a canon of Toledo and the man in charge of the group, on seeing the well-organized procession of cart, peace-officers, Sancho, Rocinante, priest and barber, and Don Quixote caged and imprisoned, couldn't resist asking why they were taking that man along in that way, although he'd already guessed from the peace-officers' insignia that he must be a wicked highwayman or some other delinquent for whose punishment the Holy Brotherhood was responsible. One of the officers, to whom the question had been put, replied:

'Sir, why this knight is being taken along in this way is something he'll have to tell you himself, because we haven't the faintest idea.'

Don Quixote overheard the conversation and said:

'Are you gentlemen by any chance versed and skilled in the matter of knight-errantry? If you are, I shall communicate my misfortunes to you, but if you are not, it would be pointless for me to bother to do so.'

By now the priest and the barber, seeing that the travellers were talking to Don Quixote de la Mancha, had ridden over to provide answers that wouldn't betray their scheme. The canon replied to Don Quixote:

'The fact of the matter, my dear friend, is that I know more about books of chivalry than about Villalpando's *Summaries*.³ So if that's the only problem, you can safely communicate whatever you like to me.'

'God's will be done,' replied Don Quixote. 'And in that case I should like you to know, sir knight, that I am travelling in this cage under a spell, because of the envy and deceit of evil enchanters, for virtue is more persecuted by the wicked than it is beloved by the righteous. I am a knight errant, not one of those whose names fame has never been concerned to perpetuate in her memory, but one who, in spite of envy itself, and of all the magicians Persia ever bred, all the Brahmans of India, and all the Gymnosophists of Ethiopia,⁴ shall write his name in the temple of immortality to serve for future ages as a pattern and example, by which knights errant will know the steps that they must follow if they wish to reach the peak and honourable summit of arms.'

'Don Quixote de la Mancha is speaking the truth,' the priest inserted here, 'for he is indeed travelling on this cart under a spell, not for his crimes and sins but because of the ill will of those who are annoyed by virtue and infuriated by valour. This, sir, is the Knight of the Sorry Face, of whom you may perhaps have heard, and whose valiant exploits and mighty deeds shall be engraved in durable bronze and eternal marble, however much envy may toil to obscure them and malice may labour to conceal them.'

When the canon heard both the prisoner and the free man speaking in this way, he was so amazed that he almost crossed himself, unable to imagine what had happened; and all those with him were similarly astonished. And Sancho Panza, who'd come over to listen to the conversation, said, just to add the finishing touch:

'Look here, sirs, I expect I'll make myself unpopular with what I'm going to say but the plain truth is my master Don Quixote's about as bewitched as my mother is: he's in his right mind and he eats and drinks and does his business just like anybody else, the same as yesterday before they put him in a cage. So how can anyone try and tell me he's enchanted? Because I've heard lots of people say that when you're enchanted you don't eat or sleep or talk, yet my master'll talk more than thirty lawyers if someone doesn't stop him.'

And turning to face the priest, he continued:

'Oh father, father! Did you think I don't recognize you, do you imagine I can't see where all these latest enchantments are leading? Well, let me tell you that I do recognize you, however much you cover up your face, and I can see through you, too, however much you try to cover up your tricks. But there we are, where envy rules virtue can't survive, and where meanness is king there isn't any room for generosity. Hell and damnation! If it wasn't for your reverence, my master would be married to Princess Micomicona by now and I'd be a count at least, because I couldn't expect anything less than that, what with my master of the Sorry Face being so kind and my services being so first-rate. But now I can see it's right what they say – the wheel of fortune goes round faster than a mill-wheel, and there you were up at the top yesterday and here you are down on the floor today. I'm sorry for the wife and for the children, because they could and should have expected to see their father walk in through the door as the governor of some island or the viceroy of some kingdom, and all they're going to see is a stable-boy. I've only said this, father, to urge your reverence to have second thoughts about this bad treatment of my master – and you'd better watch out in case God takes you to task in the next life for locking my master up like this, and makes you answer for all the rescues and other good deeds he's being prevented from carrying out all this time he's being held prisoner.'

'Strike a light!' the barber interrupted. 'Do you belong to your master's fraternity as well, Sancho? As God is good, I can see you're going to be keeping him company in his cage, and be as enchanted as he is, because of what you've caught of his character and his chivalry! An evil hour it was when you allowed yourself to be seduced by his promises, and an evil hour it was when the idea of that island you're so set on found its way into your brain-box.'

'I haven't been seduced by anyone,' retorted Sancho, 'and I'm not the sort of man to let himself be seduced, not even by the king himself, and I might be poor but I'm of old Christian stock, and I don't owe anybody anything, and if I'm set on islands others are set on worse, and deeds make the man, and being as I am a man I can get to be pope let alone governor of an island, and even more so with a master who's going to conquer so many of them that he'll run out of people to hand them out to. You be careful what you say, mister barber, there are other things in life than shaving beards, and each man's a little bit different from the next. I'm only saying this because we all know one another, and nobody's going to play against me with loaded dice. And as for this enchanting of my master, God knows the truth, and let's leave it at that, because the more you stir it the worse it gets.'

The barber didn't reply to Sancho, concerned as he was that any more absurdities might reveal what he and the priest were striving so hard to conceal; and this same fear had made the priest suggest to the canon that the two of them might ride a little ahead so that he could explain the mystery of the caged man and other matters that the canon would enjoy. The canon agreed and, after going on in front with his servants and with the priest, listened to everything the priest told him about Don Quixote's standing, life, madness and habits, as he provided a brief account of the beginnings and the cause of his folly, and of everything that had happened to him until they'd put him in the cage, and of their plan to take him back home to see if they could find some cure for his madness. The canon and his servants were again struck with amazement as they listened to the extraordinary history of Don Quixote, and when it was finished the canon said:

'The truth is, my dear sir, that I myself consider these so-called books of chivalry to be prejudicial to the public good. And although my idleness and poor taste have led me to start reading most of those that have been printed, I've never managed to reach the end of a single one, because it seems to me that they're all more or less the same as each other, without any important differences between them. In my opinion this kind of writing comes under the heading of Milesian tales,[5] which are absurd stories, concerned only to amuse and not to instruct, unlike apologues, which amuse and instruct at the same time. And even though the main aim of such books is to amuse, I don't know how they can succeed when they're full of so many monstrous absurdities, because the soul can only take delight in the beauty and harmony that it sees or contemplates in what the eyes or the imagination places before it, and nothing that contains ugliness or disorder can give us any pleasure. Because what beauty can there be, what proportion of the parts to the whole, or of the whole to the parts, in a book or story in which a sixteen-year-old lad slashes at a giant as tall as a tower and slices him in two as if he were made of marzipan, or in which a battle is described and after we've been told that there are a million warriors on the enemy's side we have to accept, like it or not, so long as the book's hero is opposing them, that this knight gains the victory by the valour of his mighty arm alone? And what can one say about the readiness with which a queen or empress-to-be falls into the arms of some unknown errant knight? What mind that isn't totally barbarous or uneducated can derive any pleasure from reading that an enormous tower full of knights sails on through the sea, like a ship with a favourable wind, and that tonight it's in Lombardy and tomorrow morning it's in Prester John's land in the Indies, or somewhere else never described by Ptolemy or seen by Marco Polo?[6]

'And if someone replies that the authors of such books write them as fictions and are therefore under no obligation to bother with subtleties or truths, I'd answer by saying that the more a lie looks like the truth the better a lie it is, and the more feasible it is the more it pleases us. Fictional stories should suit their readers' understanding and be written in such a way that, by making impossibilities seem easy and marvels seem straight-forward and by enthralling the mind, they amaze and astonish, gladden and entertain, so that wonder and pleasure go hand in hand; and none of this can be achieved by the writer who forsakes verisimilitude and imitation, because the perfection of all writing consists in these two qualities.

'I've never seen a book of chivalry that could be regarded as a whole body complete with all its members, and in which the middle corresponds with the beginning and the end with the beginning and the middle; on the contrary, their authors give them so many members that their intention seems more to produce a chimera or a monster than a well-proportioned figure. Apart from this, their style is harsh, their adventures are incredible, their loves are licentious, their civilities are uncouth, their battles are endless, their speeches are absurd, their journeys are preposterous, and, in short, there's no ingenious artifice about them, so they deserve to be thrown out of a Christian society as useless wastrels.'

The priest had been listening to the canon with rapt attention, and thought him a man of sound understanding who was making very good sense; so he told him that, being of the same opinion and sharing his dislike for books of chivalry, he had burned the whole of Don Quixote's large collection of them. And he described the scrutiny he'd made of them, and the ones he'd condemned to the flames and the ones he'd spared, at which the canon chortled heartily and then said that despite all his strictures on such books he did find one positive quality in them: they provided subject matter with which a good intelligence could express itself, because they made available a broad and spacious canvas on which the pen could wander unhindered, describing shipwrecks, storms, skirmishes and battles; portraying an exemplary captain with all the necessary characteristics – prudent in anticipating his enemies' tricks, an eloquent orator in persuading or dissuading his soldiers, mature in his decisions, quick to act, courageous both in awaiting an attack and in launching one; depicting now a lamentable and tragic event, now a happy and unexpected one, there a lovely lady, virtuous, intelligent and demure, here a Christian knight, brave and courteous, there a reckless braggart of a barbarian, here a worthy, polite and considerate prince; representing goodness and loyalty in vassals, grandness and generosity in lords. The author can show himself to be an astrologer, a skilled cosmographer, a musician, knowledgeable about affairs of state, and perhaps he will even have an opportunity to show himself to be a magician, if he so wishes. He can portray the wiles of a Ulysses, the piety of an Aeneas, the courage of an Achilles, the misfortunes of a Hector, the treachery of a Sinon, the friendship of a Euryalus, the generosity of an Alexander, the resolve of a Caesar, the clemency and honesty of a Trajan, the fidelity of a Zopyrus,[7] the wisdom of a Cato, and, in short, all the faculties that contribute to the perfection of an illustrious man, whether he unites them all in one hero or distributes them among several.

'And if all this is done in an agreeable style and with ingenious inventiveness, and comes as close as possible to the truth, it will most certainly weave a web of beautiful and varied threads which, once complete, will display such perfection and loveliness that it will attain the highest goal to which writing can aspire: giving instruction and pleasure together, as I have said. Because the openness of such books allows the author to display his talent for the epic, the lyric, the tragic and the comic, together with all the qualities of the sweet and pleasing arts of poetry and oratory; for epic can be written in prose as well as in verse.'

CHAPTER XLVIII

In which the canon continues on the subject of books of chivalry and on other matters worthy of his mind

'It's just as you say, sir,' said the priest, 'and this makes those who've written such books all the more blameworthy, disregarding all sound reasoning and all the rules of art, by which they could have been guided and helped to become famous for their prose, as the two princes of Greek and Latin poetry[1] are for their verse.'

'I myself,' replied the canon, 'have been tempted to write a book of chivalry, observing all those points I've just been making, and to tell the truth I've written more than a hundred pages of it. And to find out how accurate my own opinion of it was, I gave it to men who like reading such books and who are learned and intelligent, and also to others who are ignorant and only concerned with the pleasure they derive from reading nonsense, and I'm pleased to say that all of them have expressed their approval; in spite of that, however, I haven't written any more, both because it seems rather inappropriate to my profession and because I'm aware that there are more fools than wise men in the world and, although the praise of the wise few is more important than the mockery of the foolish many, I'm not willing to subject myself to the indiscriminate judgement of the fickle mob, the principal readers of such books. But what most made me put it aside and indeed put the idea of finishing it out of my head was an argument that I derived from those plays that are always being performed nowadays, and I said to myself:

' "If it's no secret that all or at least most of these fashionable plays, both the purely fictional ones and those based on historical fact, are so much stuff and nonsense, higgledy-piggledy hodgepodges, and yet the masses love them, and think they're splendid creations when they're the very opposite, and the authors who write them and the actors who perform them say that it can't be otherwise because that's how people want them and they wouldn't have them any other way, and that plays which are properly structured and plotted as art demands are only good for the half-a-dozen intelligent people who understand them, and all the rest are left in the dark about their subtleties, and that it's better to earn a living from the many than approval from the few – then all of that is exactly what would happen with my book, and after burning the midnight oil to make sure I observed all those rules I've been mentioning I'd end up like that proverbial tailor who sewed for nothing and provided the thread himself."

'And although on occasions I've tried to persuade the impresarios that they're wrong about all this, and that they'd attract larger audiences and gain more credit by putting on works of art rather than balderdash, they're so wedded to their own opinions that no amount of argument or evidence can make them change their minds. I recall that one day I said to one of these stubborn people:

' "You tell me this: don't you remember that a few years ago three tragedies written by a famous Spanish poet were performed in this country, and that they were so good they delighted, surprised and amazed all those who went to see them, both the simple-minded and the wise, both the riff-raff and the élite, and that those three plays alone made more money for the players than the best thirty that have been produced since?"

' "I'm sure you must be referring," said the impresario, "to *Isabella, Phyllis* and *Alexandra*."[2]

' "Yes, they're the ones I mean," I replied, "and you just tell me whether they observed the rules of art, and whether this prevented them from showing themselves to be the excellent works they are, or from pleasing everyone. So it isn't the masses who are to blame for demanding rubbish, but rather those who aren't capable of providing them with anything else. Yes, indeed: *Ingratitude Revenged* wasn't rubbish, nor was there any in *Numancia*, nor did anybody find any in *The Merchant Lover*, still less in

The Friendly Enemy[3] or a few others written by a handful of skilled poets who in this way added both to their own renown and to the profits of the players."

'I added some further considerations in my attempt to make him see how wrong he was, and I thought they left him somewhat bemused, though not convinced.'

'The subject you've broached, sir,' the priest interrupted, 'has awoken my old loathing for these fashionable plays, which is as great as my loathing for books of chivalry, because whereas drama should, as Cicero puts it,[4] be a mirror of human life, an exemplar of customs and an image of truth, these modern plays are just mirrors of absurdity, exemplars of folly and images of lewdness. Because what greater absurdity can there be in the theatre than having a baby in nappies appear in the first scene of the first act, who by the second scene has become a grown man with a beard? Or than presenting us with an old man who's courageous and a young one who's a coward, a lackey who's a great orator, a page who's a counsellor, a king who's a porter and a princess who's a cleaning-woman? And what can I say about their notion of how the actions they represent can or could be distributed into acts, except that I've seen a play in which the first act began in Europe, the second in Asia, the third ended up in Africa, and if there had been four acts the last would have finished in America, and so it would have been set in all four quarters of the globe? And if imitation is the principal feature expected of a play, how can anyone with the slightest intelligence be content with this other one I'm going to describe? The action is set in the times of King Pepin and Charlemagne, yet the protagonist is the Emperor Heraclius, who carries the Cross into Jerusalem and recovers the Holy Sepulchre, like Godfrey of Bouillon,[5] when in reality a whole age separated one event from the other; and although the play is based on fictitious actions, historical veracity is claimed for it, and bits and pieces of other histories involving different people and periods are mixed in, and without any attempt at verisimilitude, either, but with obvious mistakes that are quite inexcusable. And what's worst of all is that there are people ignorant enough to say that this is sheer perfection, and that to expect anything better is to ask for the moon and the stars.

'And what about plays on religious subjects? How many false miracles they invent, how many apocryphal and misunderstood events, with the miracles of one saint attributed to another! And even in the plays that aren't religious they make bold to insert miracles, without any respect or consideration – their only thought is that such and such a miracle or special effect, as they call them, would do very nicely there, to fill the ignorant rabble with amazement and persuade more of them to come and see the play; and all this works to the detriment of truth and to the prejudice of history, and even to the discredit of Spanish writers, because foreigners, who are most meticulous in obeying the rules of drama, consider us to be barbarous and ignorant when they see the absurdities and nonsenses in our plays.

'And it isn't a sufficient excuse to say that the main reason why well-ordered societies allow the public performance of plays is to entertain the community with some harmless recreation, and to keep at bay the bad temper that idleness sometimes produces, and that, since this end is achieved with any play, good or bad, there's no need to make laws or oblige those who write and perform plays to do so in the proper way because, as I said before, any old play will do the job. To this I'd reply that this end would be far, far better achieved with good plays than with bad ones, because the audience that has gone to see an ingenious and well-crafted play comes out at the end cheered by its jests, instructed by its truths, amazed at its action, wiser thanks to its speeches, warned by its roguery, shrewder for its examples, incensed against vice and enamoured of virtue; for a good play will provoke all these reactions in anyone who watches it, including the most slow-witted of yokels, and it's absolutely impossible for a play possessing these qualities not to cheer and entertain, satisfy and please far more than one that lacks them, as do nearly all of those performed nowadays.

'And the blame for this doesn't lie with their authors, because some of them know very well where they're going wrong and what they should be doing; but, since plays have been turned into goods for sale, playwrights say, and they speak the truth, that the players wouldn't buy them if they weren't of the kind I've described; so the writer tries to meet the demands of the impresario who's going to pay him for his work. The truth of what I'm saying can be seen in many, indeed countless plays written by a brilliant Spanish genius,[6] with such panache and wit, in such elegant verses, containing such excellent speeches and weighty maxims, and, in short, so rich in eloquence and loftiness of style, that he has filled the world with his fame; yet his urge to comply with the actors' taste has meant that not all his plays have reached the required pitch of perfection, although some certainly have. Others write their plays so thoughtlessly that the actors have to run away and hide after performances for fear of being punished, as they often have been, for scenes that insult kings or dishonour families.

'Now all these problems, and many others that I haven't mentioned, would be solved if there were some intelligent and sensible person in the capital to scrutinize all plays before they're performed, not only there but anywhere in Spain, and if no local authorities could permit the production of any play without his approval, seal and signature; and then the actors would make sure to send their plays off to the capital so as to be able to perform them safely, and the playwrights would devote much more care to their work because of their fear of this rigorous examination by someone who knew what he was doing; and in this way good plays would be written and their goals splendidly attained: not only the amusement of the people but also the good reputation of Spanish writers, the livelihood and security of the actors and the avoidance of the trouble of punishing them.

'And if another person, or even the same one, were given the job of scrutinizing any new books of chivalry that were written, some of these might well show the perfection that you've specified, enriching our language with the delightful, precious treasure of eloquence, eclipsing old books in the light of the new ones published for the innocent amusement not only of the idle but also of the busy, because the bow can't always be bent, nor can our frail human nature subsist without some honest recreation.'

As the canon and the priest reached this point in their conversation, the barber rode up to them and said to the priest:

'This is the place, sir, that I said would be a good one for us to rest while the sun is high and for the oxen to enjoy plenty of lush pasture.'

'I agree with you,' replied the priest.

He told the canon of their plans, and the canon decided to stay with them, attracted by the sight of a beautiful valley that opened up before them. So to enjoy the view and the priest's conversation, which he was growing to like, and to find out in more detail about Don Quixote's exploits, he told some of his servants to ride on to the inn, which wasn't far away, and to bring back all the food to be had there, so that everybody could eat, because he intended to take his rest where he was; to which one of his servants replied that their supply-mule, which must by then have reached the inn, had sufficient provisions, and all they'd need from the inn itself was barley.

'In that case,' said the canon, 'take all the animals on to the inn, and bring the supply-mule back here.'

While all this was happening Sancho saw his opportunity to speak to his master without those suspicious characters the priest and the barber breathing down his neck, for once, and he sidled up to his master's cage and muttered:

'Look, sir, I want to unburden my conscience and tell you what's what concerning this enchantment of yours – those two over there with their faces all covered up are the village priest and the barber, and I expect they've decided to carry you off like this because they're bursting with envy at you getting in ahead of them at doing famous deeds. Now if I'm right you aren't under a spell at all, but just a fool with the wool pulled over your eyes. And to prove it I'm going to ask you one question, and if you answer as I think you will, you'll rumble their trick for yourself and see you're more bamboozled than enchanted.'

'You ask whatever you wish, Sancho my son,' replied Don Quixote, 'and I shall do as you ask and give all the answers that you require. And as regards what you said about those two men riding hither and thither being the priest and the barber, our friends from the village, it may well be that they look like them; but you should not believe by any manner of means that they really are them. What you should believe and understand is that if they look like our friends, as you say they do, what must have happened is that those who have enchanted me have assumed their likenesses; because it is easy for enchanters to take on whatever appearance they please, and they must have taken on the appearance of our friends to make you think what you are thinking, and lead you into a maze of conjectures from which you would not be able to extricate yourself even if provided with the thread of Theseus. And they must also have done it

447

to befuddle my understanding so that I cannot fathom from where this harm has come; because if on the one hand you tell me that the village priest and barber are accompanying me and, on the other, I find myself in a cage and I know full well that no mere human powers, only supernatural ones, would be sufficient to put me here, what can you expect me to say or think except that the manner of my enchantment is more extraordinary than all those about which I have ever read in all the histories dealing with knights errant who have been enchanted? So you can rest assured and be certain that they are not who you say they are: if they are the priest and the barber, I am a Turk. And as regards your desire to ask me a question, ask away, Sancho, and I shall answer, even if your interrogation lasts from now until tomorrow.'

'God save us all and his Holy Mother too!' Sancho exclaimed. 'How can you be so thick-skulled and empty-headed that you can't see that what I'm saying is the plain truth, and that it's more through roguery than enchantment that you're in this mess and in this cage? But since that's the way it is I'm going to give you clear proof that you aren't enchanted. Just you tell me, then, as you'd have God save you from this pickle, and as you'd have my lady Dulcinea take you into her arms when you're least expecting it . . .'

'You needn't exorcize me,' said Don Quixote, 'just ask me your question. I have already said that I shall give you a complete and honest answer.'

'That's all I'm asking for,' replied Sancho, 'and what I want to know is for you to tell me, without adding anything or taking anything away, but giving me the whole truth, as can rightly be expected from all those who profess arms, as you profess them, with the title of knight errants . . .'

'I tell you I do not intend to lie,' replied Don Quixote. 'Do put your question to me; I really am beginning to grow tired of all these salvos, prayer-bells and preparatives, Sancho.'

'And I tell you I'm sure my master's a good and honest man, and so, being as it is very much to the point, what I'm asking, with all due respect, is whether maybe, in the time you've been shut up and, as you think, enchanted here in this cage, you've ever felt the need or urge to do number one or number two, as some people put it.'

'I do not understand what you mean by "doing numbers", Sancho; you must be more explicit if you wish me to give you a clear answer.'

'How can you not know about doing number one and number two? It's the very first thing you learn at school. Look, what I'm asking is if you've felt the urge to do what you've got to do.'

'Oh, now I understand you, Sancho! Yes, yes, often; indeed I am feeling it at this very moment. Do save me from my plight, for things in here are none too clean!'

CHAPTER XLIX

Which concerns the intelligent conversation that Sancho Panza had with his master Don Quixote

'Oho!' said Sancho. 'Now I've caught you! That's what I wanted to know, with all my heart and soul. Look here sir: can you deny that when someone's off colour people often say, "I don't know what's wrong with him, he won't eat or drink or sleep, or give a proper answer when you ask him a question, anyone would think he'd been bewitched"? You can see from this that people who don't eat or drink or sleep or answer the call of nature as I said before are enchanted, but not people who feel the urges you're feeling and who drink when they're given a drink, and eat when there's food's to be had, and reply to everything they're asked.'

'What you say is true, Sancho,' replied Don Quixote, 'but I have already told you that enchantment can take many different forms, and it could be that these have changed in the course of time, so that what happens nowadays is that the enchanted do all the things that I do, even though formerly they did not. So one cannot either argue against the customs of the times, or draw any conclusions from them. I know for certain that I am enchanted, and this is enough for the comfort of my conscience; because my remorse would be great indeed if I thought that I am not enchanted and that I am sitting here in this cage like an idler and a coward, depriving so many distressed and needy people of the succour I could be giving them, when they must at this very moment be in extreme need of my aid and protection.'

'All that's as may be,' said Sancho, 'but what I'm saying is that just to make doubly sure it'd be a good idea if you tried to get out of this prison, and what I'll do for my part is help you as much as I can, and even rescue you myself, and then you could try to get up on good old Rocinante — you'd think he's enchanted, too, he's so dejected and miserable. And once we'd done that we could try our luck at looking for more adventures, and if things didn't go well we'd be in plenty of time to come back to the cage, and I give you my word as a good and loyal squire that I'd lock myself up in it with you if you were so unlucky or I was so stupid that I couldn't do what I've said I'll do.'

'I am content to do as you say, brother Sancho,' replied Don Quixote, 'and, as soon as you spot an opportunity to contrive my release, I shall obey your every command; but you will see, Sancho, how mistaken you are in your assessment of my misfortune.'

The knight errant and his errant squire chatted away like this until they caught up with the priest, the canon and the barber, who'd dismounted and were waiting for them. The carter unyoked his oxen and set them free to wander in that green and pleasant place, whose coolness was an open invitation, not to enchanted people like Don Quixote, but to those as wide-awake and quick-witted as his squire, who asked the priest to let his master out of the cage for a while, because if he didn't it was going to end up less spick and span than was required for a respectable knight like his master. The priest understood his meaning, and said he'd most willingly do as asked if he weren't afraid that once Don Quixote found himself free he'd get up to his old tricks again and take himself off to where nobody could ever find him.

'I'll guarantee he won't run away,' replied Sancho.

'And so shall I,' said the canon, 'particularly if he gives me his word as a knight that he won't go anywhere unless we say so.'

'I do indeed give my word,' said Don Quixote, who'd been listening to the conversation, 'and in any case, a person who is enchanted, as I am, is not at liberty to dispose of his person as he wishes, because the man who enchanted him can prevent him from moving for three centuries on end, and if he flees he will bring him back in the twinkling of an eye.' And this being so they could well release him, since it would be to everyone's advantage, and if they didn't he could assure them that he wouldn't be able to help offending their noses, unless they kept their distance.

The canon took him by the hand, even though it was tied to the other one, and, after he'd given them his word of honour they uncaged him, and he was overcome by joy and delight to find himself out of the cage. And what he first did was to have a good stretch, and then he went over to Rocinante, gave him a couple of slaps on the haunches and said:

'I still trust in God and his Blessed Mother, O flower and mirror of steeds, that we two shall soon be as we would wish to be: you with your master on your back, and I mounted upon you, practising the profession for which God sent me into this world.'

And so saying, Don Quixote retired with Sancho to a far distant spot, from where he returned much eased and comforted, and with increased desires to put into execution whatever his squire should order him to do. The canon was gazing at Don Quixote and wondering at this strange, great madness of his, and at how he showed a fine understanding in all his remarks and replies, only taking leave of his senses, as has already been pointed out, when chivalry was the subject under discussion. And so, after everybody had sat down on the green grass to wait for the provisions, the canon, moved by pity, said to him:

'Can it really be possible, my dear hidalgo, that reading all those useless and pernicious books of chivalry has had such an effect on you as to make you mad enough to believe you're enchanted, and other such stuff and nonsense that's as far from being true as is falsehood itself? And how can any human understanding persuade itself that the world has ever contained such an infinity of different Amadises, and such a mob of so many famous knights, so many Emperors of Trebizond, all those Felixmartes of Hyrcania, all those palfreys, and maidens errant, and serpents, and monsters, and giants, and unique adventures, and enchantments of every kind, and battles, and terrible combats, and splendid costumes, and lovelorn princesses, and squires who become counts, and funny dwarfs, and love-letters, and amorous compliments, and valiant women and, in short, all those absurdities to be found in books of chivalry? Speaking for myself I can say that when I read them they give me some pleasure so long as I overlook the fact that they're all folly and falsehood; but as soon as I remember what they are, I dash the best of them against the wall, and I'd even hurl it into the fire if there were one handy, because they all deserve this punishment for being cheats and impostors and beyond the pale of common nature, for inventing new sects and a new way of life, and for inducing the ignorant rabble to accept as truths all the absurdities they contain. And such is their audacity that they even dare to unsettle the wits of intelligent and well-born hidalgos, as is clear from what they've done to you, because they've reduced you to such a state that it has proved necessary to shut you up in a cage and transport you on top of an ox-cart, as people wheel a lion or a tiger from one village to the next to exhibit it for money.

'Come now, Don Quixote, take pity on yourself, and restore yourself to the bosom of good sense, and make use of the generous amount of it that heaven has been kind enough to give you, by applying your splendid gifts of mind to different reading matter that will benefit your conscience and increase your honour! And if, following your natural inclinations, you still want to read books of adventure and chivalry, take the Scriptures and read the Book of Judges, and there you will find great truths and deeds as authentic as they are brave. Portugal had its Viriatus, Rome its Caesar, Carthage its Hannibal, Greece its Alexander, Castile its Count Fernán González, Valencia its Cid, Andalusia its Gonzalo Fernández, Extremadura its Diego García de Paredes, Jerez its Garci Pérez de Vargas, Toledo its Garcilaso and Seville its Don Manuel de León;[1] and reading about their meritorious deeds can entertain, teach, delight and amaze the finest minds. Now this would be reading matter worthy of your excellent understanding, my dear Don Quixote, and it will make you knowledgeable about history, enamoured of virtue, instructed in goodness, improved in your habits, brave but not rash; and all for God's greater glory, for your own benefit and for the renown of La Mancha, from where, I've been told, you hail.'

Don Quixote had been listening with profound attention to the canon's words, and when he realized that he'd finished, he sat staring at him for some time; and then he said:

'It seems to me, my dear hidalgo, that your speech was intended to give me to understand that there never have been any knights errant in the world, and that all books of chivalry are false, full of lies, harmful and of no use to society, and that I have done wrong in reading them, and worse in believing them, and worse still in imitating them and setting out to follow the rigorous profession of knight-errantry that they teach; and you deny that there ever were any Amadises, of Gaul or of Greece, in this world, or any of the other knights of whom the writings are full.'

'Yes, that is precisely what I meant,' said the canon.

To which Don Quixote replied:

'You went on to say that such books had done me great harm, inasmuch as they had made me take leave of my senses and had confined me to a cage, and that it would be better for me to mend my ways and change my reading, turning to other more truthful books that amuse and instruct more effectively.'

'Indeed I did,' said the canon.

'Well, for my part,' replied Don Quixote, 'I consider that it is you who are out of your senses and under some spell, for you have taken it upon yourself to utter such blasphemies against what has been so well received in the world and so widely accepted as the truth that anyone who denies it, as you do, deserves the same punishment that you say you inflict on books that annoy you when you read them. Because trying to persuade anyone that Amadis and all the other knights adventurers that pack the histories never existed is like trying to persuade him that the sun does not give out light, and that ice is not cold, and that the earth does not sustain us. For what mind can there be in the entire world capable of convincing another that there is no truth in the story about Princess Floripes and Guy of Burgundy, or about Fierabras at the Bridge of Mantible,[2] an event that took place in Charlemagne's time, and I swear is as true as that it is now daytime? And if that is a lie, it must also be a lie that there ever was a Hector, or an Achilles, or a Trojan War, or the Twelve Peers of France, or King Arthur of England, who still wanders about today transformed into a raven and is expected in his realms at any moment. And no doubt they will also attempt to persuade us that the history of Guerrino Il Meschino is false, and so is the quest for the Holy Grail, and that the loves of Sir Tristan and Queen Iseult and of Guenevere and Lancelot are apocryphal, even though there are people alive who almost remember seeing the duenna Quintañona, the best server of wine there ever was in the whole of Great Britain.[3] And the truth of this is shown by the fact that I remember my grandmother on my father's side saying, whenever she saw some aged duenna go by in her weeds: "That one over there, my boy, she could be old duenna Quintañona herself." From which I conclude that my grandmother must have known her, or at least have contrived to see some portrait of her. And who could deny that the history of Pierres and the fair Magalona is a true one, for to this very day one can see in the royal armoury the peg with which the brave Pierres guided the wooden horse as he rode through the air, and it is a little bigger than a cart-pole.[4] And next to the peg is Babieca's saddle, and Roland's horn is at Roncesvalles, the size of a large beam, from all of which we can deduce that the Twelve Peers did exist, that Pierres did exist, that the Cid and other such knights did exist

> And went, as people say,
> Adventuring their way.

'Or else let them try to tell me that it is not true that the brave Portuguese Juan de Merlo was a knight errant who went to Burgundy and did battle in the city of Arras with the famous lord of Charny called Monseigneur Pierres and later, in the city of Basle, with Monseigneur Henri de Remestan, emerging victorious and crowned with honour and glory from both exploits; and let them try to deny the adventures and challenges, also in Burgundy, of those courageous Spaniards Pedro Barba and Gutierre Quixada (from whose stock I am descended in the direct male line), who defeated Count St Pol's sons. They might as well also deny that Don Fernando de Guevara ever went to Germany in search of adventures, and fought against Messire George, a knight of the Duke of Austria's household. And let them claim that the jousts of Suero de Quiñones by the Honourable Pass never happened, and nor did the exploits of Monseigneur Louis de Falces against the Castilian knight Don Gonzalo de Guzmán, and many other deeds performed by Christian knights of these and foreign realms, all of which are so true and authentic that I repeat that anyone who denied them would be devoid of all reason and good sense.'[5]

The canon was amazed to hear the mixture that Don Quixote had concocted of real events and fictional ones, and to discover how well informed he was about everything connected with the exploits of his precious knight-errantry; and he replied:

'I can't deny, Don Quixote sir, that some of what you've said is true, particularly concerning Spanish knights errant; and I'll also concede that the Twelve Peers of France did exist, but I can't believe they did everything that Archbishop Turpin says they did, because the truth of the matter is that they were knights chosen by the kings of France, and were called peers because they were all equals in worth, rank and courage – or at least if they weren't they should have been – and it was like a religious order after the style of the present-day orders of Santiago and Calatrava, the members of which we presume are, or should be, worthy, courageous and high-born knights; and just as nowadays people refer to a knight of St John, or of Alcántara, in those times they used to talk about a knight of the Twelve Peers, because there were always twelve equals who'd been chosen for this military order. As regards the existence of the Cid, there can't be any doubt about that, or about Bernardo del Carpio, but there are very great doubts about whether they performed the exploits ascribed to them. And as for that other matter of Count Pierres' peg, which you say is next to Babieca's saddle in the royal armoury, I must confess my sin: I'm so ignorant, or so short-sighted, that although I've seen the saddle I've never spotted the peg, even though you say it's so big.'

'Yet it is most definitely there,' replied Don Quixote, 'and furthermore it is said to be kept in a calfskin cover to prevent it from becoming mouldy.'

'That's as may be,' replied the canon, 'but I'm as sure that I've never seen it as I am that I'm a priest. And even if I did concede that it is there, this wouldn't oblige me to believe the histories of so many Amadises or of that great mob of knights in the stories people tell; nor is it right for a man like you, honourable and talented and intelligent, to give any credit to the extravagant nonsense that's written in those ridiculous books of chivalry.'

CHAPTER L

*About the intelligent dispute between Don Quixote and
the canon, and other matters*

'Now that is a good one!' Don Quixote retorted. 'Books printed with
licences from kings and with the approval of those to whom they have
been submitted, read with universal delight and praised by great and small,
poor and rich, the educated and the ignorant, plebeians and gentlemen, in
short by all kinds of people of all ranks and circumstances – are they
likely to be lies, above all when they bear such an appearance of truth,
telling us about the father, mother, country, kindred, time, place and
deeds, detail by detail and day by day, performed by the knight or knights
in question? Hold your tongue, sir, and do not voice such blasphemies,
and believe me, I am advising you now to act as a man of good sense
should; only read them, and you will find out for yourself how much
pleasure they afford you. Or else tell me this: can there be any greater
delight than to see, as it were, here and now before us a vast lake of
bubbling pitch, and swimming about in it vast numbers of serpents, snakes
and lizards and many other kinds of fierce and fearsome animals, while
from the lake comes a plaintive voice:

'"You, O knight, whosoever you may be, beholding this dread lake:
if you wish to attain the good hidden beneath these black waters, you
must show the resolve of your dauntless breast and cast yourself into the
midst of its dark, burning liquid, else you will not be worthy to see the
mighty marvels contained in the seven castles of the seven fairies that lie
beneath its murky surface"?

'And what of our delight when the knight, almost before the fearful
voice has ceased, without giving his situation a second thought, without
stopping to consider the peril to which he is exposing himself, or even
shedding the burden of his heavy armour, commends himself to God and
to his lady and hurls himself into the boiling lake and, all of a sudden
when he least knows where he is bound, finds himself amidst flowery
meadows, far finer than the Elysian fields themselves? Here it seems to
him that the skies are clearer, and that the sun shines with a different

brightness; and here his gaze is regaled with a pleasant glade of such green and leafy trees that his eyes rejoice at the sight of them, and his ears are delighted by the sweet, artless song of the innumerable little brightly coloured birds that flit to and fro in the maze of branches. Here he espies a brook whose cool waters, like liquid crystal, lap over fine sand and white pebbles that resemble gold dust and perfect pearls; there he sees a cunningly wrought fountain of many-coloured jasper and smooth marble; in another place he finds another fountain adorned in the grotesque style, in which tiny clam shells and the curling yellow and white dwellings of sea-snails, placed in disordered order and mingling with pieces of glittering crystal and imitation emeralds, form so varied a composition that art, imitating nature, seems here to surpass it. And over there he suddenly beholds a mighty castle or splendid palace, with walls of solid gold, battlements of diamond and doors of jacinth; yet it is so admirably built that, although it is made of nothing less than diamonds, carbuncles, rubies, pearls, gold and emeralds, its workmanship is even more praise-worthy.

'And what more splendid sight, after seeing all this, than a bevy of damsels emerging from the castle gate, wearing such elegant and splendid apparel that if I started now to describe it as the histories do, I should never finish? And then she who appears to be the most important damsel takes the hand of the bold knight who cast himself into the boiling lake, and walks with him, without a word, into the sumptuous castle or palace, and has him strip as naked as the day he was born, and bathes him in warm waters, and then anoints his whole body with aromatic balsams and dresses him in a shirt of the finest sendal, perfumed and sweet-smelling, and another damsel comes and throws over his shoulders a cloak that is said to be worth at least as much as a city if not more! And is it not a marvellous sight when we are told that after all this he is taken to another hall where he finds tables laid with such orderly elegance that he is dazzled and amazed? And seeing him sprinkle his hands with the essence of ambergris and perfumed flowers? And then to see him seated on a chair of ivory? Seeing him being served by all the damsels in a wonderful silence? Being brought such a variety of foods, so exquisitely cooked, that the appetite is at a loss which to choose? Hearing the song that sounds as he eats, not knowing whence it comes or who is singing it?

And then when, once the meal is over and the tables have been cleared, as the knight lolls in his chair picking his teeth, as is the custom, through the door suddenly comes another damsel much more beautiful than any of the others, who sits by his side and begins to tell him what castle this is, and how she lives there under a spell, and other matters that amaze the knight and astonish the readers of his history?

'I shall not enlarge any further on this subject, because from what I have said it is clear that any passage from any history of a knight errant is bound to delight and amaze anyone who reads it. Only believe me and, as I said before, read these books, and you will soon see how they banish any melancholy you might be feeling, and improve your disposition, if it is a bad one. Speaking for myself, I can say that ever since I became a knight errant I have been courageous, polite, generous, well-bred, magnanimous, courteous, bold, gentle, patient and long-suffering in the face of toil, imprisonment and enchantment; and although so short a time ago I found myself locked into a cage like some madman, it is my intention, by the might of my arm, if heaven favours me and fortune does not oppose me, to become within a few days the king of some kingdom where I shall be able to demonstrate the gratitude and liberality contained in my breast. Because on my faith, sir, the poor man is prevented from showing the virtue of liberality towards anyone, even if he possesses it to a degree; and gratitude that is restricted to good intentions is as dead as faith without works. For this reason I do wish that fortune would soon offer me some opportunity to become an emperor, so that I can show my true nature by doing good to my friends, especially poor Sancho Panza here, my squire, who is the salt of the earth, and I should love to give him an earldom that I promised him a long time ago, except that I fear he will not have what it takes to govern his estate.'

Sancho overheard these last few words, and he said to his master:

'You set to work, Don Quixote sir, and get that earldom you've been promising me and I've been waiting for all this time, and what I can promise you is that I won't be found wanting in what it takes to govern it. And if I am found wanting, I've heard there are men that rent lords' estates from them, and give these lords money every year and govern the estates themselves, and the lord sits about with his feet up all day long having a good time on the rent he's paid and not worrying about anything at all – and that's what I'll do, and I won't bother to bargain, I'll just hand the whole lot over and enjoy my rent like a duke, and everyone else can go and get stuffed.'

'That, brother Sancho,' said the canon, 'might apply to enjoying the revenues, but the lord of the estate must concern himself with the administration of justice, and this is where his ability and good judgement come into play, and above all his honest determination to do what is right, because if this isn't present from the very beginning, things will go wrong in the middle and at the end; and that is why God favours the good intentions of the simpleton as much as he obstructs the evil intentions of the clever man.'

'I don't know about all that philosopherizing,' replied Sancho Panza, 'all I do know is that I wish I was as sure that I'm going to lay my hands on that earldom as I am that I've got what it takes to govern it – I have as much of a soul as the next man, and as much of a body as the best of them, and I'd be as good a king of my estate as anyone else, and that being so I'd be doing as I liked, and doing as I liked I'd be doing what I wanted to do, and doing what I wanted to do I'd be happy, and if you're happy you can't ask for more than that, and if I couldn't ask for more there's nothing more to say, and let's have my estate, and goodbye and I hope we'll be seeing each other soon, as one blind man said to the other.'

'That isn't bad philosopherizing, as you put it, Sancho; all the same, there's a great deal more that could be said on the subject of earldoms.'

To which Don Quixote replied:

'I am not so sure that there is any more to be said: I am simply guided by the example given me by the great Amadis of Gaul, who made his squire the Count of the Firm Isle; and so I can make Sancho Panza a count without any qualms of conscience, because he is one of the best squires that any knight errant ever had.'

The canon was astounded at the concerted nonsense spoken by Don Quixote, at his evocation of the adventure of the Knight of the Lake, at the effect on him of the premeditated lies in the books he'd read, and also at Sancho's simplicity and his longing to possess the earldom that his master had promised him.

The canon's servants were by now approaching with the supply-mule that they'd fetched from the inn; and turning a carpet they had with them and the green grass of the meadow into a table in the shade of some trees, they all sat and ate there so that the carter's oxen could continue to enjoy the advantages of the spot. As they were eating they suddenly heard a loud rustling and the clanking of a tin bell in a thicket of brambles near them, and at the same instant a handsome black, brown and white goat broke out of the thicket, followed by a goatherd who was calling to her in goatherds' language to stop or go back to the herd. The runaway, panic-stricken goat trotted over to the picnickers as if to implore their protection, and then halted. The goatherd followed her, seized her by the horns and addressed her as if she could understand his words:

'Oh Dapple, Dapple, you wild gadabout, how footloose you have become! What wolves are you running away from, my dear? Won't you tell me what's up, my beauty? But what can it be except that you're a female and can't settle down – and the devil take those ways of yours and the people you've copied them from! Come back, come back with me, my sweet, you'll be safer, even if you aren't as happy, in your fold or in the herd with your friends – and if you who are meant to be keeping order among them are so out of order yourself, what are they going to end up by doing?'

The goatherd's words delighted all those who heard them, especially the canon, who said:

'Do please calm down a little, my friend, and don't be in such a hurry to return the goat to her herd – since she's a female, as you put it, she's going to follow her natural instincts whatever you do to try to stop her. Have a bite to eat and a drop to drink, and that will make you simmer down, and in the meantime the goat can have a rest.'

And as he said this he speared a quarter of a cold rabbit on his knife and offered it to him. The goatherd took it and thanked him; he drank wine and calmed down, and said:

'I wouldn't like any of you to think me a simpleton because I spoke to this animal so seriously – the truth is that my words were a little strange. I may be a rustic, but not so much of one that I don't know the difference between talking to a human being and talking to a beast.'

'I don't doubt that,' said the priest, 'because I have found out for my-self that mountains breed scholars and herdsmen's huts house philos-ophers.'

'Or at least, sir,' replied the goatherd, 'they give shelter to men who've learned from bitter experience; and so that you can see for yourselves how true this is, even though I might seem to be forcing myself on you, I shall – so long as it isn't tiresome, gentlemen, and you're willing to lend me your ears for a while – tell you a true story that will confirm what this gentleman' – pointing to the priest – 'and I have just said.'

To this Don Quixote replied:

'Seeing that this seems to have some suspicion of a chivalry adventure about it, I for my part am most willing to listen to you, my friend, and so are all these gentlemen, for they are intelligent people and are keen to hear anything new and curious that amazes, delights and captivates the mind, as I am sure your story will. You may begin, my friend, for we shall all listen.'

'You can count me out,' said Sancho, 'I'm off to that stream over there with this pie I've got here, and I'm going to stuff myself enough to last me for three days, because I've heard my master Don Quixote say that a knight errant's squire must eat whenever he gets a chance to, until he can't eat any more, since what often happens is that they wander into such a thick forest that it takes them more than six days to find their way out, and if the squire wasn't full at the beginning, and his saddle-bags weren't full either, he might not get out at all, as often does happen, and be left there to turn into a mummy.'

'You are quite right, Sancho,' said Don Quixote. 'You go wherever you like, and eat as much as you can; I am fully satisfied already, and only need refection for my spirit, which I shall obtain by listening to this good fellow's story.'

'And that's what we'll all do,' said the canon.

And he asked the goatherd to do as he'd promised. He gave the goat, which he was still holding by the horns, a couple of slaps on the back with the words:

'You lie down here next to me, Dapple – there's plenty of time to go back to the herd.'

The goat seemed to understand him, because as her master sat down she quietly stretched herself out by his side, and looking up into his face she indicated that she was paying attention to what he was saying; and he began his story like this:

CHAPTER LI

Concerning what the goatherd told Don Quixote's kidnappers

'Ten miles from this valley there's a village which, though small, is one of the richest hereabouts, and in it there lived a farmer of great renown who, although honour always goes with money, was even more highly regarded for his goodness than for his wealth. But what made him happiest of all, he said, was having a daughter of such exquisite beauty, rare intelligence, elegance and virtue that anyone who knew her and beheld her was amazed to see the extraordinary qualities with which heaven and nature had endowed her. As a child she was pretty, and she continued to grow in beauty, so that by the age of sixteen she was lovely. The fame of her loveliness began to spread throughout the nearby villages – but why do I leave it at the nearby ones, when it spread to distant cities and even reached the halls of royal palaces and the ears of all kinds of people who came from every part to see her, as if she were some strange curiosity or miracle-working image?

'Her father stood guard over her virtue, and she stood guard over it herself, too, because there are no keys, locks or bolts that can protect a maiden better than her own modest reserve. The father's wealth and the daughter's beauty moved many men, both from the village and from elsewhere, to ask for her hand in marriage; but given the task of disposing of such a precious jewel, he was perplexed and couldn't decide which of the countless men who pestered him he should entrust her to. Among all those with this honourable intention I was one, and I was given great hopes of success by the knowledge that her father knew me to be of good family, from the same village, of pure Christian blood, in the prime of life, rich in worldly goods, and no less so in intelligence. Another man from the village, with the same qualities, also asked for her hand; and so her father couldn't make up his mind, because he felt that either of us would be a good match for her; and to resolve this difficulty he decided to refer the matter to Leandra herself (that's the name of the lady of fortune who has reduced me to wretchedness), because he realized that since there was nothing to choose between us it would be best to let his beloved daughter make up her own mind, an example that could well be followed by all parents in search of spouses for their children. I'm not saying that they should allow their children to choose among evil or base suitors, but that they should propose several good ones and give them a free choice among these. I don't know which was Leandra's choice; all I do know is that her father put us off with talk about how young she was and with generalities that neither put him under any obligation nor released us from ours. My rival is called Anselmo and I'm Eugenio, so now you know the names of the people involved in this tragedy, which hasn't ended yet, although it's plain enough that the ending is going to be calamitous.

'At about this time one Vicente de la Rosa, the son of a poor farmer from the village, returned from Italy and various other parts of the world where he'd been serving as a soldier. He'd gone off at the age of about twelve with a company that happened to come our way, and he returned twelve years after that, dressed as all soldiers like to dress, in a thousand different colours, covered in glass trinkets and little steel chains. One day he'd be wearing one piece of finery and the next another, all of them flimsy, artificial, tawdry, worthless. Village people, who are naturally malicious, and who with time on their hands turn into malice personified, took due note of this, started counting all his baubles and gewgaws, one by one, and found that he owned just three suits of clothes, of different colours, each with its garters and hose; but he rang the changes on his finery in such a way that if his clothes hadn't been counted anyone would have sworn that he'd displayed more than ten suits and more than twenty plumes. And don't imagine that what I'm telling you about his clothes is irrelevant or gratuitous, because they play an important part in this story.

'He used to sit on a stone bench under the great poplar tree in our village square, and we'd all sit around him with our mouths agape, hanging on the exploits he was telling us about. There wasn't a land in the world he hadn't been to, not a battle he hadn't fought in; he'd slaughtered more Moors than there are in Morocco and Tunis, had taken part in more single combats, according to him, than Gante y Luna,[1] Diego García y Paredes and thousands of others he named, and had been victorious in every one of them, without ever having been made to shed a single drop of blood. And then he'd show us scars that we couldn't see but that he said were from gunshot wounds received in various skirmishes and raids. And he had the unparalleled effrontery to address equals, and even those who knew what he was, as if they were inferiors, and declare that his arm was his father, that his deeds were his pedigree and that, being a soldier, he was second to nobody, not even the King himself. In addition to all this bravado, he had a smattering of music and could strum a guitar, and there were those who said that he could make it talk; and his talents didn't end here, because he could also write poems, and produced five-mile-long ballads about every single trifling incident in the life of the village.

'Now this soldier I've described, this Vicente de la Rosa, this hero, this man of fashion, this musician, this poet, was often seen and indeed gazed upon by Leandra from a window in her house that overlooked the square. She fell in love with his gaudy clothes; she was captivated by his ballads – he distributed twenty copies of every one; she heard all about the feats he claimed to have performed; and in the end – it must have been the devil's own work – she fell in love with the man himself, before he had the presumption to try his luck with her. And since in no affair of the heart do events proceed more smoothly than when the initiative comes from the woman, it was easy for Leandra and Vicente to reach an understanding, and before any of her suitors had the slightest inkling of her infatuation she had satisfied it by leaving the house of the father she loved so much (she has no mother) and running away with the soldier, who carried this venture to a more triumphant conclusion than any of the others to which he had laid claim.

'This event astonished the whole village and indeed all who heard about it; it left me dumbfounded, Anselmo thunderstruck, her father wretched, her relatives humiliated, the authorities alerted, the officers of the Holy Brotherhood astir: the roads were patrolled, the woods were searched, the whole countryside was scoured, and after three days they found the flighty Leandra in a mountain cave, wearing only a chemise, and all the money and the valuable jewels that she'd taken from the house had disappeared. They returned her to her forlorn father; they asked her what had brought about this disaster; she confessed without any coercion that Vicente de la Rosa had deceived her, promising to marry her and persuading her to run away from home: he was going to take her to the richest and most luxurious city in the whole world, Naples, and she'd been ill-advised and beguiled enough to believe him; after robbing her father she'd placed herself in the soldier's hands that same night when she'd gone missing; and then he'd taken her to a rocky mountain and shut her up in the cave where she'd been found. She also told them that the soldier had plundered her of everything she possessed except her honour, had left her in the cave and had gone away; and this detail was a cause of fresh amazement for everyone. It was hard to believe that the young man had been so restrained, yet she insisted on this earnestly enough to console her disconsolate father, who wasn't concerned about the riches that had been stolen, since his daughter had been allowed to keep that jewel which once lost can never be retrieved.

'The very same day that Leandra reappeared her father made her disappear again, taking her away to shut her up in a convent in a town not far from here, in the hope that time might efface a part of the bad reputation that she'd earned for herself. Leandra's tender years were some excuse for her lapse, at least in the eyes of those who had no personal interest in whether she was a good girl or not; yet those who knew just how clever and intelligent she was didn't put her sin down to ignorance but to her pertness and to the natural propensity of her sex for reckless impetuosity.

'Once Leandra had been locked away, Anselmo lost his sight – or at least was left with nothing to look at that could give him any joy; and I was plunged into darkness – for there was no light to guide me towards any pleasant goal. Leandra's absence increased our sorrow, wore away at our patience, made us curse the finery of the soldier and abominate the negligence of Leandra's father. In the end Anselmo and I agreed to leave the village and come to this valley, where he grazes a large flock of his sheep and I pasture a great herd of my goats, and we spend our time among these trees relieving our passions by together singing the praises or dispraises of the lovely Leandra and separately sighing and confiding our complaints to heaven. Many of Leandra's other suitors have copied us and have come to these rugged mountains with their animals, and there are so many of them that anyone would think the place has been converted into the pastoral Arcadia,[2] teeming with shepherds and goatherds and their folds, and there's no part of it where the name of the lovely Leandra can't be heard. This man fulminates against her and calls her flighty, fickle and wanton; that man condemns her forwardness and levity; a third absolves and pardons her, a fourth judges and condemns her; another praises her beauty, another rails at her wicked ways, and in short they all vilify her, and they all adore her, and the madness that affects them all is so great that there are those who bewail her disdain without ever having spoken to her, and others who complain of being afflicted by the raging disease of jealousy, when she can never have made anyone jealous because, as I said, her sin was discovered before anyone knew where her fancies lay. There's not a hollow in a rock, or the bank of a stream, or a shade under a tree that isn't taken up by some shepherd telling the air all about his misfortunes; wherever an echo can sound it repeats Leandra's name: "Leandra" the mountains ring out, "Leandra" murmur the streams, and Leandra has us all in suspense and under her spell, hoping against hope and fearing without knowing what it is that we fear.

'Among all these lunatics, the one who shows the least and at the same time the most sense is my rival Anselmo, who has so much to complain about yet only complains of her absence; and to the sound of his fiddle, which he plays admirably, he voices his laments in verses that display his great ability. I take an easier and, I think, the wisest course, which is to revile women's fickleness, their inconstancy, their double-dealing, their worthless promises, their broken faith and, in short, their lack of judgement in bestowing their affections. And this is the explanation, gentlemen, of the way in which I spoke to this goat earlier: since she's a female I don't have a very high opinion of her, even though she's the best goat in my herd.

'This is the story that I promised to tell you; and if I've been long-winded in the telling I shan't give you short shrift in hospitality – my fold isn't far away, and there I have fresh milk, delicious cheese and all kinds of ripe fruit no less pleasing to the eye than to the palate.'

CHAPTER LII

About Don Quixote's fight with the goatherd, and the
singular adventure of the penitents, which he brought to
a happy conclusion by the sweat of his brow

The goatherd's tale delighted all those who heard it, particularly the canon, who paid special attention to the way in which he told it, making him seem less like a rustic herdsman than a sharp-witted courtier; and so the canon declared that the priest had been quite right to say that mountains breed scholars. They all offered Eugenio their services, but the one who did so with the most expansive generosity was Don Quixote, who said:

'In truth, brother goatherd, if I were in a position to be able to embark on another adventure, I should without a moment's delay set about bringing yours to a happy conclusion; for I should rescue Leandra from the convent (where she is most certainly being held against her will) in spite of the abbess and of anybody else who attempted to prevent me, and I should place her in your hands so that you could deal with her exactly as you wished, always obeying, however, the laws of chivalry, which command that no mischief whatsoever be done to any damsel; yet I trust that by the grace of our Lord God the powers of an evil enchanter are not so great that they cannot be overridden by those of another better-disposed one, and I promise to give you all my assistance as soon as that should come about, as required by my profession, which is none other than to succour the needy and helpless.'

The goatherd looked at Don Quixote, and finding him such a sorry sight he asked the barber – who was sitting next to him – in some bewilderment:

'Who is this man, sir, that cuts such a figure and speaks in such a way?'

'Who should he be,' answered the barber, 'but the famous Don Quixote de la Mancha, the redresser of injuries, the righter of wrongs, the protector of damsels, the terror of giants and the victor in battles?'

'That sounds to me,' replied the goatherd, 'like what you read in books about knights errant, who used to do all those things you said this man does, but it's my opinion that either you're joking or some of the rooms in this character's upper storey are empty.'

'You are a villainous wretch,' Don Quixote burst out, 'and you are the one who is empty and a fool, and I am fuller than the whore of a bitch who bore you ever was.'

And with these words he snatched up a loaf and hurled it at the goatherd's face with such furious force that he flattened his nose; and the goatherd, who couldn't take a jest and found himself being assaulted in earnest, disregarded the carpet and the tablecloths and all the people who were eating, and leapt upon Don Quixote, seized him by the throat with both hands and wouldn't have hesitated to throttle him if Sancho Panza hadn't rushed over, grabbed the goatherd by the shoulders and flung him down on the table, breaking plates, smashing cups and overturning and scattering everything else. As soon as Don Quixote found himself free he jumped on top of the goatherd, who, bloody-faced and pounded by Sancho's feet, was crawling over the tablecloths in search of a knife with which to take some gory revenge, but the canon and the priest were making sure this couldn't happen; and then the barber intervened to enable the goatherd to climb on top of Don Quixote, at whom he flailed away until as much blood was pouring from the poor knight's face as from his own. The canon and the priest were laughing fit to burst, the peace-officers were jumping with joy, everyone was cheering the two men on as dogs are cheered on when they're fighting; only Sancho Panza was in despair, because he couldn't wriggle free of the grasp of one of the canon's servants who was preventing him from going to help his master.

In short, just when everyone was enjoying this festival of fun, except the two battered, scratching warriors, they heard a trumpet call, so mournful that it made them all turn towards where it seemed to be coming from; but the man who was most affected by the sound was Don Quixote who, although he was under the goatherd, much against his will and most severely mauled, said to him:

'Brother devil, for that is what you must be, since you have found the resolve and the strength to overpower me: I request that we agree on a truce for just one hour, because the sorrowful sound of that trumpet which we can hear appears to be summoning me to a new adventure.'

The goatherd, who by now was tired of thumping and being thumped, climbed off without more ado, and Don Quixote stood up and looked with the others in the direction of the sounds, and as he did so a horde of men dressed as penitents in white suddenly came into sight as they descended one of the sides of the valley. What had happened was that the clouds had withheld their moisture from the earth that year, and processions, public prayers and acts of penitence were being organized in all the villages in the area to entreat God to open the hands of his mercy and send down some rain; and to this end the people from a nearby village were coming in a procession to a holy chapel on one side of the valley. Don Quixote, seeing the processionists' strange dress, and not pausing to remember that he must have seen such penitents many times before, imagined that this was the subject for an adventure, and that it was his task alone, as a knight errant, to undertake it; and he was further confirmed in this belief when he saw a holy image swathed in mourning that they were carrying, and thought it was some eminent lady whom those arrant and insolent knaves were bearing off against her will; and no sooner had this idea found its way into his head than he charged over to where Rocinante was grazing, unhooked both the horse's bit and his own shield from the pommel, put the bit in its place in the twinkling of an eye, told Sancho to give him his sword, mounted Rocinante, took up his shield and cried to all present:

'And now, O doughty company, you shall perceive how important it is that knights who profess the order of knight-errantry should exist in the world; now, I say, you shall perceive, in the freeing of that good lady who is being carried away captive, whether or not knights errant are worthy of esteem.'

And as he said this he put thighs to Rocinante, because he wasn't wearing any spurs, and at a canter, because we don't read anywhere in this true history that Rocinante ever ventured on a full gallop, he advanced on the penitents, despite all the efforts of the priest and the canon and the barber to stop him; but it was impossible, and Sancho couldn't do anything to dissuade him, either, by yelling:

'What are you going to do now, Don Quixote sir? What demons have you got inside your breast egging you on against our holy Catholic faith? I'll be damned – look, look, that's a penitents' procession, and that lady they're carrying on the platform is the blessed image of the immaculate Virgin. Be careful, sir, what you're doing – this time I'm really sure it isn't what you think it is.'

But Sancho laboured in vain, because his master was so set on confronting the men in white and freeing the lady in black that he didn't hear a word; and even if he had heard one he wouldn't have turned back, not if it had been the King himself ordering him. So on he cantered towards the procession and then he halted Rocinante, who was by now ready to take a rest, and he cried in a hoarse and agitated voice:

'O you who hide your faces, perchance because you are evil: pay attention and listen to what I have to say to you.'

The first to stop were the men carrying the image, and one of the four priests chanting the litanies took one look at Don Quixote's strange figure, Rocinante's thinness and other ludicrous aspects of the knight's appearance, and replied with the words:

'If you want to say something to us, my good man, say it quickly, because our brethren here are tearing their flesh to shreds, and we cannot and must not stop to listen to anything unless it's brief enough to be said in a couple of words.'

'I shall say it all in one word,' replied Don Quixote, 'and it is this: you must at this very instant set free that beautiful lady, whose tears and sorrowful face are clear proof that you are bearing her off against her will and that you have done her some very great mischief; and I, who came into this world to redress such injuries, will not permit you to take one step forward unless you give her the liberty that she desires and deserves.'

These words made all those who heard them realize that Don Quixote must be some madman, and they burst into hearty laughter, which was like pouring gunpowder on to the fire of Don Quixote's wrath: without another word he drew his sword and charged at the platform. One of the men carrying it left his companions holding it up, came out to meet Don

Quixote brandishing the forked prop on which he helped to support it whenever they paused for a rest, used this prop to ward off a mighty sword-stroke that the knight aimed at him and that cut it in two and then, with the part left in his hand, delivered such a blow to the shoulder of his enemy's sword arm, which the shield couldn't protect against brute strength, that poor Don Quixote tumbled to the ground in dire straits. Sancho Panza, who came puffing after his master, saw him fall and cried out to his demolisher not to hit him again, he was only a poor enchanted knight who'd never done anyone any harm in all the days of his born life. But what stopped the peasant wasn't Sancho's shouts but seeing that Don Quixote wasn't stirring, not so much as a hand or a foot; and so, in the belief that he'd killed him, he hoisted his tunic up to his waist and ran away across the fields like a deer.

And now Don Quixote's companions arrived on the scene, as did the other processionists, who saw their opponents come running up with the peace-officers clutching their crossbows, feared the worst and swarmed around the holy image with their hoods raised from their faces, brandishing their scourges while the priests wielded their great processional candle-sticks, awaiting the assault in the determination to defend themselves and even attack their assailants if they could; but fortune treated them better than they'd thought it would, because all Sancho did was to throw himself upon his master's body and pour over him the most piteous and laughable lament ever heard, in the belief that he was dead. Our priest was recognized by one of the priests in the procession, and this calmed the fears that had developed in both squadrons. The first priest gave the second one a brief account of Don Quixote, and then he went with the throng of penitents to see whether the poor knight was dead, and they all heard Sancho Panza saying, with tears in his eyes:

'O flower of chivalry, whose well-spent life just one thump with a cudgel has done for! O pride of your family, honour and glory of all La Mancha and all the world – now that you've gone from it, it'll fill up with evil-doers who won't be frightened of being punished for their wicked ways! O you who were more open-handed than all the Alexanders, because for only eight months' service you said you'd give me the best island that ever had the sea all round it! O you who were humble to the haughty and haughty to the humble, tackler of dangers, taker of insults, in love without a cause, imitator of the good, scourge of the wicked, enemy of villains – in a word, knight errant, and that says it all!'

Sancho's cries and groans revived Don Quixote, and what he first said was:

'He who lives absent from you, sweetest Dulcinea, is subject to even greater calamities than this. Help me, dear Sancho, to climb on to the enchanted cart: I am no longer in any fit state to burden Rocinante's saddle, for this shoulder of mine has been smashed to smithereens.'

'I'll do that with a will, sir,' replied Sancho, 'and let's go back to our village with these gentlemen, who only want what's best for you, and there we'll work out a way to make another sally that'll bring us more profit and renown.'

'You are speaking sound sense,' replied Don Quixote, 'and it will be wise indeed to wait for the presently prevailing malign influence of the stars to dissipate.'

The canon and the priest and the barber told him that he would be quite right to do as he'd said; and so, having been most wonderfully entertained by Sancho Panza's absurdities, they put Don Quixote back on the cart. The religious procession formed up again, and went on its way. The goatherd said goodbye to everyone. The peace-officers refused to go any further, and the priest paid them what he owed them. The canon asked the priest to let him know what happened to Don Quixote, whether he recovered from his madness or continued in the same state, and then begged their leave to continue his journey.

And so the party split up and each followed his own road, leaving the priest and the barber, Don Quixote and Panza and the good Rocinante, as patient as his master in the face of everything he'd undergone. The carter yoked his oxen, put Don Quixote on top of a truss of hay, followed with his usual sedateness the route indicated by the priest; and six days later they reached their village, which they entered at noon, and as it happened to be a Sunday everybody was in the square, through the middle of which the cart trundled on its way. Everyone went over to see what was in the cart, and when they recognized their neighbour they were astonished, and a lad ran to tell the housekeeper and the niece that their master and uncle had come back, thin and pale, and lying on top of a pile of hay in an ox-cart. It was pitiful to hear the cries these two good ladies let loose, the slaps they gave themselves, the curses they again directed at those damned books of chivalry; all of which they renewed when they saw Don Quixote coming in through the door.

At the news of Don Quixote's arrival Sancho Panza's wife hurried to his house, because she had discovered that her husband had gone away with him as his squire, and when she saw Sancho the first thing she asked was whether the ass was well. Sancho replied that the ass was better than its master was.

'Thanks be to God for his great goodness to me,' she replied. 'And now tell me, husband, what have you got out of all this squiring of yours? How many fine skirts have you brought back for me? How many pairs of shoes for your children?'

'I haven't brought any of all that, wife,' said Sancho. 'But I've got other stuff that's much more special and important.'

'I'm very pleased to hear it, too,' his wife replied. 'Now show me this stuff that's so much more important and special, husband – I'd love to see it to cheer up this heart of mine that's been so sad and out of sorts all these ages that you've been away.'

'I'll let you see it when we get home,' said Panza, 'and meantime you can count yourself lucky, because if it's God's will for us to go off again in search of adventures you'll soon see me made an earl or the governor of an island, and not any old island either but the very best island there is.'

'May heaven grant it, husband, we need it badly enough. But tell me, what's all this about islands? I don't understand you.'

'Honey wasn't made for the mouths of asses,' Sancho retorted. 'You'll see in due course, wife, and you'll get a surprise, I can tell you, when you hear all your vassals calling you your ladyship.'

'What's this you're saying, Sancho, about ladyships, islands and vassals?' replied Juana Panza, for this was the name of Sancho's wife, not that they were blood relations but because it's the custom in La Mancha for women to take their husbands' surnames.

'Don't you be in such a hurry, Juana, to know about all these things; I'm telling you the truth, and that's enough for you, so shut up. All I will say, since I'm on the subject, is that there's nothing better in life than being an honest man who's the squire of a knight errant who goes in search of adventures. It is true that most of the adventures you find don't turn out as well as what you'd like them to, because out of a hundred you come across ninety-nine usually go skew-whiff. I know that from experience, because I've ended up blanket-tossed in some and beaten black and blue in others. But in spite of all that, it's great to be waiting to see what's going to happen next as you ride across mountains, explore forests, climb crags, visit castles and put up at inns as and when you like, and not the devil a farthing to pay.'

While Sancho Panza and his wife Juana Panza chatted away like this, Don Quixote's housekeeper and niece welcomed their master, undressed him and laid him on his ancient bed. He was peering at them through unfocused eyes, and couldn't fathom where on earth he was. The priest told the niece to make sure to pamper her uncle and have him watched so that he didn't escape again, and described what they'd had to do to bring him back home. And then the two women again raised the roof with their outcry; again they renewed their cursing of the books of chivalry; again they implored heaven to cast the authors of all those lies and absurdities into the depths of the bottomless pit. All this left them bewildered and fearful that as soon as their master and uncle felt a little better they'd lose him again; and that was indeed what happened.

But although the author of this history has searched with the most meticulous care for an account of the deeds performed by Don Quixote during his third sally, he hasn't been able to find any information about them, not at least in writings by reputable authors; tradition alone has preserved, in the memory of La Mancha, the belief that the third time Don Quixote left home he went to Saragossa, where he took part in some famous jousts and underwent experiences worthy of his courage and intelligence. But the author could not discover any information about how Don Quixote met his end, nor would he ever have even known about it if good fortune had not sent him an aged doctor who had in his possession a lead casket which, he said, had been found among the foundations of an old, ruined chapel that was being rebuilt. In this casket there were some parchments with texts written in Roman letters but in Castilian verse, describing many of his exploits and giving accounts of

Dulcinea del Toboso's beauty, Rocinante's looks, Sancho Panza's loyalty and Don Quixote's grave, in various epitaphs and eulogies about his life and works. And those that could be read and understood have been set down here by the trustworthy author of this original and matchless history, who only asks from his readers, in recompense for the immense trouble that he has taken to scrutinize and explore all the archives in La Mancha so as to be able to bring it to the light of day, that they give it the same credit that people of good sense give to books of chivalry, so highly prized by all; and this will make him feel well rewarded and satisfied, and encourage him to search out other histories, perhaps less authentic than this one but no less ingenious or entertaining.

The first words written on the parchment found in the lead casket were these:

THE ACADEMICIANS OF ARGAMASILLA, A VILLAGE IN LA MANCHA, DURING THE LIFE AND DEATH OF THE BRAVE DON QUIXOTE DE LA MANCHA[1]

HOC SCRIPSERUNT[2]

SAMBO, A MEMBER OF THE ACADEMY OF ARGAMASILLA, TO THE GRAVE OF DON QUIXOTE

Epitaph

This thunderpate who decked La Mancha's plain
With trophies more than Jason gave to Crete;[3]
This solid judgement of a weathervane
– And spindly, too, where potency was meet;
This arm so lengthened by its own vast might,
Extending to Gaeta from Cathay;[4]
This ugliest and wisest muse to write
A verse on sheet of bronze or slab of clay;

This man who left Amadis in his wake,
And thought but little of proud Galaor;
Who even made brave Belianis quake
And, faced by love and valour, stand in awe:
He who on Rocinante erring went
Lies here, beneath this cold stone monument.

FLUNKEY,
A MEMBER OF THE ACADEMY OF
ARGAMASILLA

IN LAUDEM DULCINEAE DEL TOBOSO

SONNET

She whom you gaze on here, this moon-faced dame,
Big-breasted and of energetic mien,
Was once Don Quixote de la Mancha's flame,
Fair Dulcinea, El Toboso's Queen.

For her alone he wandered far and wide
Across Sierra Morena (that Brown Hill),
To Montiel Plain, and grassy fields beside
Aranjuez, all on foot, and tired, and ill.

The fault was Rocinante's. O black doom
Of this Manchegan dame and errant knight
Unconquered, in his prime, her tender bloom!
For death destroyed her beauty at its height
And, though hard bronze records his every deed,
He never from love's wrath and wiles was freed.

FLIGHTY,
A WISE MEMBER OF THE ACADEMY OF
ARGAMASILLA, IN PRAISE OF ROCINANTE,
DON QUIXOTE DE LA MANCHA'S HORSE

SONNET

Upon his proud and diamond-studded throne,
Where mighty Mars once pressed his bloody heel,
The hero from La Mancha sits alone
And brandishes his flag with frenzied zeal.

He hangs up all his armour, hangs his swords
With which he used to ravage, hack and hew:
Unprecedented deeds! But Art accords
To champions that are new a style that's new.

And if Amadis is the pride of Gaul
And his brave sons have heightened Greece's fame,
Bellona now crowns Quixote in her hall
And, more than either, Mancha loves his name.
Forgotten, never: even Rocinante
Makes Brillador's and Bayard's verve⁵ seem scanty.

DECEIVER,
AN ARGAMASILLAN ACADEMICIAN,
TO SANCHO PANZA

SONNET

Here Sancho Panza lies, in body small,
In courage great – a miracle most rare;
The simplest and most guileless squire of all
That ever trod this earth, I vow and swear.

A count or earl he surely would have been,
Had not this wicked world conspired, alas,
To wound him with its insolence and mean
Contempt. It will not even spare an ass,

On which he rode (forgive this lowly word),
A meek, mild squire who plodded on behind
The mild steed Rocinante and his lord.
How vain are all the hopes of humankind!
How sweet our promises of comfort seem,
And yet they end in shadow, smoke and dream!

HOBGOBLIN,
A MEMBER OF THE ARGAMASILLA ACADEMY,
ON THE GRAVE OF DON QUIXOTE

Epitaph

Here lies a knight, a man of pluck,
Rich in thumpings, poor in luck,
Who, perched on Rocinante's back,
Rode up this path and down that track.
And Sancho Panza is the dolt
Who lies beside him in this vault:
The loyallest man in our empire
Who ever earned the name of squire.

DING-DONG,
A MEMBER OF THE ARGAMASILLA ACADEMY,
ON THE GRAVE OF DULCINEA DEL TOBOSO

Epitaph

Fair Dulcinea here is laid
And though she was a meaty maid
Death turned her into dust and clay
In his horrendous, dreadful way.
Of a true breed she surely came,
She was the great Don Quixote's flame,
She wore with style a lady's gown:
The glory of Toboso town.

These were the verses that were legible; since the others were worm-eaten, they were handed to an academician for him to decipher. It is reported that he has done so, after long vigils and much toil, and that he intends to publish them, as we await Don Quixote's third sally.

Forsi altro canterà con miglior plectio.[6]

FINIS

*Second Part of
the Ingenious Knight*
DON QUIXOTE
de la Mancha

PART II

PROLOGUE TO THE READER

Goodness me, how you must be longing to read this prologue, illustrious or perhaps plebeian reader, expecting to find retaliations, rebukes and railings against the author of the second *Don Quixote*, the one said to have been conceived in Tordesillas and born in Tarragona![1] But the fact is that I'm not going to give you that pleasure, because although insults awake anger in the humblest breasts, mine is going to be an exception to the rule. You'd like me to call him an ass, a numskull and an impudent monkey, but it has never occurred to me to do so: let his sin be his punishment, it's his own lookout – absolutely his own affair. What I couldn't help resenting is that he attacks me for being old and one-handed, as if it had been in my power to halt time and prevent it from ravaging me, or as if I had been maimed in some tavern brawl rather than at the greatest battle that past or present ages have ever seen or that future ages can ever hope to see.[2] If my wounds do not shine in the eyes of those who behold them, they are at least honoured in the estimation of those who know where they were received, because it is better for the soldier to die in battle than to be safe in flight; and I am so firmly of this opinion that, even if an impossibility were proposed and could be performed for me, I would choose to have fought in that prodigious confrontation rather than not suffer from these wounds and not have been there. The scars that the soldier displays on his face and his breast are stars that lead others to the heaven of honour and hopes of merited praise; and it should be noted that one does not write with one's grey hairs but with one's understanding, which often improves with the passing years.

I also resent the fact that he calls me envious, and then explains to me what envy is, as if I were some ignoramus; the truth is that of the two kinds of envy I only know the righteous, noble and well-meaning sort; and if this is so, as it is, I'm not going to start persecuting any priests, still less if they're familiars of the Holy Office as well;[3] and if when he said this he was thinking about the man I have in mind, he's completely mistaken, because I adore that man's creativity and I admire his works and his unceasing, virtuous virtuosity. Yet the truth is that I'm grateful to this gentleman for saying that my *Exemplary Tales*[4] are more satirical than exemplary, but that they're good; and they couldn't be good if they didn't contain a little of everything.

I expect you're telling me now that I'm showing great restraint and allowing myself to be held back by my modesty, in the knowledge that one shouldn't heap affliction on the afflicted, and that this gentleman's affliction must be great indeed, because he doesn't dare show himself in open country and in broad daylight, but covers up his name and lies about his birthplace as if he were guilty of high treason. If by any chance you meet him, tell him from me that I don't consider myself offended: I know very well what the devil's temptations are like, and that one of the greatest of them is to put it into a man's head that he can write and print a book that will earn him as much fame as money, and as much money as fame; and to confirm this I'd like you, in your own witty, amusing way, to tell him this story:

There was in Seville a madman who developed the funniest and most absurd obsession that ever affected any madman in the world. And it was this: he made a tube out of a cane sharpened at one end and, catching a dog in the street or wherever, he'd hold down one of its hind legs with his foot and use his hand to lift up the other, and fit the tube as best he could in the place where, by blowing, he made the dog as round as a ball; once he'd achieved this, he'd pat its belly a couple of times and let it go, saying to the onlookers, of whom there were always many:

'Do you think it's an easy task to inflate a dog?'

Do you think it's an easy task to write a book?

And if this story doesn't suit him, you must, dear reader, tell him this other one, which is also about a madman and a dog:

In Cordova there was another lunatic, who had the habit of carrying a piece of a marble slab, or a sizeable rock, on his head, and when he came across a dog off its guard he would stand by its side and discharge his burden on top of it. The dog, in a fury, would run barking and howling up three streets without stopping. It so happened that among the dogs on which he dropped his load there was one belonging to a cap-maker, much loved by its master. Down came the rock, catching it on the head, the battered dog screeched, its master saw the scene and was furious, he snatched up a measuring rod and beat the madman, leaving not one bone unbroken in his body; and with each stroke he said:

'You dog! You wretch! You'd hurt my whippet? Couldn't you see, you monster, that my dog's a whippet?'

And after repeating the word 'whippet' over and over again, he sent the madman on his way beaten to pulp. The madman had learned his lesson and hid himself, and didn't reappear for more than a month, after which time he returned with his old trick and a new load. He would approach a dog, examine it from head to tail and, not daring to drop his rock, say:

'This one's a whippet: stay clear!'

And indeed every dog he came across, even if it was a mastiff or a mongrel, he called a whippet; so he never dropped his rock again. Maybe it will be the same with this historian, who won't dare discharge the weight of his wit in the form of books that, if bad, are even harder than rocks.

You can also tell him that, as for his threat to deprive me of my earnings with his book, I don't care two hoots about it; and that, to borrow the words of that famous farce *La Perendenga*,[5] my reply is 'Long live my master the alderman, and the peace of Christ be with us all.' Long live the great Count of Lemos, whose well-known Christian virtue and generosity sustains me in the face of all the blows of my scant fortune, and long live the splendid charity of the Archbishop of Toledo, Don Bernardo de Sandoval y Rojas,[6] even if printing-presses cease to exist, and even if more books are published attacking me than there are letters in the ballads of Mingo Revulgo.[7] These two great men, unsolicited by any praise or flattery on my part, out of sheer kindness, have taken it upon themselves to protect and favour me, which makes me consider myself luckier and wealthier than if fortune had placed me on its highest pinnacle by more usual means. Honour is something that a poor man can have, but not a dissolute one; poverty can cast a cloud over nobility, but cannot hide it altogether; but if virtue gives out a glimmer of light, even if only through the chinks and straits of penury, it will be valued and therefore favoured by lofty and noble spirits.

And don't you say anything else to him, and I don't intend to say anything else to you, either, except to ask you to remember that this second part of *Don Quixote* that I'm offering you is cut by the same craftsman and from the same cloth as the first one, and that in it I give you Don Quixote prolonged and finally dead and buried, so that nobody can presume to produce any more evidence against him, because what has already been produced is quite enough, and it is also enough that an honourable man has provided information about these clever follies and doesn't want to go into them ever again: too much of something, even of a good thing, causes it to be valued less, and a scarcity, even of bad things, confers a certain value of its own. I almost forgot to tell you to look out for *Persiles*,[8] which I am now finishing, and for the second part of *Galatea*.

CHAPTER I

*About the discussion that the priest and the barber had
with Don Quixote concerning his illness*

Cide Hamete Benengeli recounts in the second part of this history, which
concerns Don Quixote's third sally, that the priest and the barber went
almost a month without seeing him, so as not to revive past events and
bring them back into his memory. But this didn't prevent them from
visiting his niece and his housekeeper, and telling them to make sure to
pamper him and give him nutritious food to strengthen his heart and his
brain, from where it was reasonable to assume that all his misfortunes
sprang. The women asserted that they were already doing so and would
continue to do so with all possible care and concern, because they could
see that their master was showing every sign of recovering his sanity; and
this news made the two men happy because it suggested that they had
been right to enchant him and bring him home on the ox-cart, as described
in the last chapter of the first part of this history, the excellence of which
is rivalled only by its authenticity. And so they decided to visit him and
put his recovery to the test, although they thought it almost impossible
that it could be real, and they agreed not to mention anything connected
with knight-errantry, to avoid the risk of tearing open stitches that were
closing so recent a wound.

So off they went to visit him, and they found him sitting up in bed
wearing a green flannel singlet and a knitted red Toledo cap, and he was
so withered and wizened that he could have been taken for a mummy.

He gave them a warm welcome, they inquired after his health and he provided a well reasoned and elegantly expressed account of his progress. And as the conversation developed they came to the subject that is sometimes called reason of state and methods of government, and they all corrected this abuse and condemned that one, and reformed one custom and forbad another, and each of the three men turned into a new legislator, a present-day Lycurgus or a modern Solon;[1] and they subjected society to such radical reforms that anyone would have thought they'd taken it to a forge and brought away a different one; and Don Quixote spoke with such good sense about every subject they discussed that his two examiners reached the firm conclusion that he was fully recovered and of sound mind. The niece and the housekeeper were present at the conversation, and they were tireless in thanking God for having restored their master to his senses; but the priest, changing his mind about not mentioning anything to do with chivalry, decided that the examination of Don Quixote's sanity should be a full and proper one, and, as the conversation proceeded, he inserted into it pieces of news that had arrived from Madrid, one of them being that it was considered certain that the Turk was on his way up with a mighty fleet, and nobody knew what his intentions were or where the storm was going to burst; and this fear had set the alarm bells ringing throughout Christendom, as happened almost every year, and His Majesty had fortified the coasts of Naples and Sicily and the island of Malta. To this Don Quixote replied:

'His Majesty has acted as a warrior of great prudence in fortifying his states in good time, so that the enemy does not catch him unawares, but if anybody listened to my advice I should suggest a precaution that as yet he must be far from considering.'

As soon as the priest heard this he said to himself:

'God help you, poor Don Quixote: it looks to me as if you're toppling from the peak of your madness into the abyss of your stupidity!'

And the barber, who'd had the same thought as the priest, asked Don Quixote what this precaution was that he believed should be adopted; perhaps it was suitable to be included on the long list of those inapposite pieces of advice so often sent to monarchs.

'My advice, mister shaver,' said Don Quixote, 'will not be inapposite, but the very opposite.'

'That isn't what I mean,' replied the barber, 'but rather that experience has shown nearly all the memoranda sent to His Majesty by armchair politicians to be impracticable, or nonsensical, or harmful to the King or the kingdom.'

'Well, my advice,' replied Don Quixote, 'is neither impracticable nor nonsensical, but the simplest, the most just and the most ingenious and expeditious advice that any such politician could ever conceive.'

'Yet you're taking a long time to tell us what it is, Don Quixote,' said the priest.

'I should not like,' said Don Quixote, 'to reveal it here and now, for it to reach the ministers' ears tomorrow morning and for someone else to receive the thanks and the reward for my labours.'

'As for me,' said the barber, 'I hereby give you my word before God that I shall not repeat whatever you say, to king or queen or rook, to bishop, knight or pawn, or any mortal man, which is an oath I learned from that ballad about the priest who in the first few lines warned the king about the thief who'd robbed him of his hundred doubloons and his mule that to wander far and wide did love.'

'I do not know about such stories,' said Don Quixote, 'but I do know that the oath is a valid one, because I know that the barber is an honest man.'

'And even if he wasn't,' said the priest, 'I'll be surety for him and guarantee that he'll keep as silent as a mute about the matter, under pain of paying the penalty as judged and sentenced.'

'And who will vouch for you, reverend sir?' asked Don Quixote.

'My profession,' the priest replied, 'which is to keep secrets.'

'For God's sake, then!' Don Quixote burst out. 'All His Majesty has to do is to order by public proclamation that all knights errant wandering in Spain must assemble in Madrid on a given day because, even if only half a dozen went, there could well be among them one who would destroy all the power of the Turk single-handed! Pay attention, now, so as to follow my argument. Is there, perchance, anything new in a knight errant destroying unaided an army of two hundred thousand men, as if they had but one throat between them or were made of barley sugar? Or else tell me this: how many histories are full of such marvels? The famous Don Belianis should be alive today – which would be unfortunate for me and maybe for others as well – or some of the innumerable descendants of Amadis of Gaul; for if any of these were indeed alive today and confronted the Turk, I swear I should not wish to be in the Turk's shoes. But God will care for his people, and will provide someone who, if not as ferocious as the knights errant of old, will not at least be inferior in spirit; and God understands my meaning, and I say no more than that.'

'Oh dear!' exclaimed the niece. 'I'll be blowed if my master doesn't want to be a knight errant again!'

To which Don Quixote replied:

'A knight errant I shall be until I die; and let the Turk be on his way up or down whenever he likes and with as much might as he can; for I repeat, God understands my meaning.'

The barber put in:

'Please may I have your permission, gentlemen, to tell you a little tale about something that happened in Seville, and that fits the bill so perfectly I've got the urge to tell it?'

Don Quixote gave him their permission, and the priest and the others gave him their attention, and he began like this:

'In the Seville madhouse there was a man whose relations had sent him there because he was out of his mind. He was a graduate in canon law from Osuna University;[2] but, in many people's opinion, even if he'd studied at Salamanca itself he'd still have been a madman. After a few years of confinement, this graduate persuaded himself that he'd recovered and was sane, and in this belief he wrote to the archbishop begging him in measured and well-chosen words to have him released from the wretched situation in which he was living, because God in his infinite mercy had restored his lost wits, although his relations were keeping him there so as to continue using the income from his property and, regardless of the truth, were determined that he'd stay mad until his dying day. The archbishop, impressed by so many well-reasoned, intelligent letters, told one of his chaplains to find out from the madhouse governor whether what the graduate claimed was true, to talk to the madman and, if he seemed to be sane, to have him released. The chaplain did as he was told and the governor informed him that the man was still mad: although he often spoke like a person with an excellent understanding, he always ended up by breaking out into absurdities that counterbalanced the sensible things he'd said at the beginning, in both quantity and quality, as anyone could find out for himself by talking to him. The chaplain decided to do this, he was put in with the madman and they spoke for upwards of an hour, during which time the madman didn't utter a single crazy or foolish word; on the contrary, everything he said was so rational that the chaplain was forced to conclude that the madman was sane. The madman said, among other things, that the governor remained hostile so as not to forfeit the presents that his relations provided for saying he was still mad, with lucid intervals; and that his greatest bane in his misfortunes was his wealth, because his enemies, to continue enjoying it, had recourse to criminal fraud and threw doubts upon the blessing that our Lord had bestowed upon him in turning him back from a beast into a man. In short, his words made the governor look suspicious, his relations covetous and heartless, and himself so full of good sense that the chaplain decided to take him away so that the archbishop could examine him and discover the truth for himself.

'The worthy chaplain, in all good faith, asked the governor to have the clothes in which the graduate had arrived returned to him; the governor again told the chaplain to watch his step, because the graduate was beyond a doubt still mad. None of the governor's warnings and advice not to take the graduate with him made any impression on the chaplain; the governor obeyed, seeing that the order came from the archbishop; the graduate was dressed in his own clothes, which were new and respectable ones. Finding himself dressed in his sanity and stripped of his lunacy, he asked the chaplain to be so charitable as to give him permission to go and say goodbye to his friends the madmen. The chaplain said that he would like to go with him and see the madmen in the house. So they all climbed the stairs with some other people who were present, and the graduate walked over to a cage containing a raging lunatic, although at that moment calm and collected, and said:

' "Is there anything I can do for you, my dear friend? I'm going home, because God has seen fit at last, in his infinite goodness and mercy, and without my having done anything to deserve it, to restore my sanity: I'm in my right mind again, because to all-powerful God nothing is impossible. You must put great hope and trust in him, because he has restored me to my former state and he'll restore you, too, if you have faith in him. I'll take good care to send you some fine food, and you be sure to eat it; because let me tell you, it's my opinion, having been through all this myself, that our madness comes from having our stomachs empty of food and our brains full of air. Take heart, take heart – letting your troubles get you down undermines your health and hastens your death."

'A madman in the cage opposite that of the raging lunatic overheard everything the graduate said; and, getting up from an old mat on which he was lying naked, he cried out asking who this fellow was that was going away in his right mind. The graduate replied:

'"It's me, my dear friend, who's going away – I don't have to stay here any longer, for which I give infinite thanks to heaven that has sent me this wonderful blessing."

'"You mind what you're saying, graduate, watch out for the devil and his tricks," the madman replied. "Control those itchy feet of yours and stay right here at home, and you'll save yourself the return journey."

'"I know I'm well," the graduate replied, "and I won't ever have to go on my rounds again."

'"You, well?" cried the madman. "We'll soon see about that. God go with you; but I swear by Jupiter, whose majesty I represent on earth, that just for this sin that Seville is committing today in releasing you from this house and considering you to be sane, I shall inflict a punishment on the city that will be remembered for ever and ever, amen. Don't you realize, you puny little wretch of a graduate, that I can do just that, because, as I have said, I am thundering Jupiter, and I hold in my hands the burning bolts with which I can and often do threaten and destroy the world? And yet I shall inflict only one punishment on this ignorant town: I shall not rain here or in this entire district for three whole years, counting from this day and this moment at which this threat is made. You free, you healthy, you sane – and me mad, me ill, me tied up? I'll hang myself sooner than start raining."

'The madman's bellowed words riveted everybody's attention; but our graduate, turning to the chaplain and gripping his hands, said:

'"Don't you worry, sir, and don't you take any notice of what this madman said, because if he's Jupiter and doesn't want to rain, I, Neptune, the father and the god of water, will rain as often as I like and as is required."

'To which the chaplain replied:

' "All the same, my lord Neptune, it will be not be a good idea to annoy my lord Jupiter: you stay here at home, and we'll come back for you another day at a more suitable moment, when we have more time."

'The governor and all the others laughed, which made the chaplain feel something of a fool; they stripped the graduate, he stayed at home and that's the end of the story.'

'And is that the tale, mister barber,' said Don Quixote, 'that fitted the bill so perfectly that you could not refrain from telling it? Oh mister shaver, mister shaver, how blind is the man who can see no further than the end of his nose! And is it possible that you do not know that comparisons made between one person's intelligence and that of another, or between their worth, or their beauty, or their pedigree, are always odious and unwelcome? I, mister barber, am not Neptune, the god of water, nor am I a madman trying to make people believe me sane; I am merely striving to make the world understand the delusion under which it labours in not renewing within itself those most happy days when the order of knight-errantry carried all before it. But these depraved times of ours do not deserve all those benefits enjoyed by the ages when knights errant accepted as their responsibility and took upon their shoulders the defence of kingdoms, the relief of damsels, the succour of orphans and wards, the chastisement of the arrogant and the rewarding of the humble. Most of the knights that one comes across nowadays rustle in damask and brocade and the other fine cloths they wear rather than rattling in chain mail; there is not one knight now who sleeps in the open fields, exposed to all the inclemency of the heavens, fully armed from head to foot; not one who, without removing his feet from the stirrups, leans on his lance and merely takes forty winks, as the saying goes, which is what knights errant used to do. There is not one knight now who rides out of this forest into yonder mountain-range, and from there to tread the barren, deserted shore of some sea that is usually rough and stormy, and, finding on the beach a little skiff without any oars, sail, mast or rigging, casts himself out with an intrepid heart on to the implacable billows of the deep, which now raise him up to the heavens and now plunge him down into the abyss; and braving the unyielding tempest, he finds himself, when he least expects it, ten thousand or more miles away from where he embarked, and after landing on a remote and unknown shore he has adventures that are worthy to be recorded not on parchment but on bronze. Nowadays, however, sloth triumphs over diligence, idleness over work, vice over virtue, arrogance over courage and the theory over the practice of arms, which only ever lived and shone in those golden ages and among knights errant. Or else you tell me who has there ever been more chaste and courageous than the famous Amadis of Gaul? Who more intelligent than Palmerin of England? Who more easygoing and manageable than Tirante the White? Who more gallant than Lisuarte of Greece?³ Who readier to hack and be hacked than Don Belianis? Who more intrepid than Perion of Gaul,⁴ who readier to face danger than Felixmarte of Hyrcania, who more sincere than Esplandian? Who bolder than Don Cirongilio of Thrace? Who fiercer than Rodamante? Who more prudent than King Sobrino? Who more daring than Reynald? Who more invincible than Roland? And who more debonair and well-bred than Ruggiero, from whom the present-day Dukes of Ferrara are descended, according to Turpin's *Cosmography*?⁵ All these knights, and many others I could mention, reverend sir, were knights errant, the light and the glory of chivalry. I only wish that these, or others like them, could be the ones referred to in my memorandum, for if they were, His Majesty would be well served and would save a vast expense, and the Turk would be left tearing his beard out; and so I am not willing to stay at home, even though the chaplain is not taking me away, and if Jupiter, as the barber said, does not rain, here am I who shall rain as often as I like. I am only saying this to let mister basinhead know that I understand what he is driving at.'

'Honestly, Don Quixote sir,' said the barber, 'I didn't mean it like that, and I said it with the best of intentions, so help me God – you mustn't get cross.'

'Whether I can get cross or not,' retorted Don Quixote, 'is something that I know best.'

At which the priest said:

'Although I've hardly spoken a word so far, I'd now like to unburden myself of a misgiving that has been gnawing away at my conscience as a result of what Don Quixote has been saying.'

'You are authorized, reverend sir,' replied Don Quixote, 'to do greater things than that, so you can well say what it is that is troubling you, because it is most disagreeable to have one's conscience being gnawed by misgivings.'

'Well, now that you've given your consent,' replied the priest, 'I can say that my misgiving is that I simply can't persuade myself, Don Quixote sir, that this crowd of knights errant you've been enumerating really and truly were people of flesh and blood who lived in this world: it seems to me, quite on the contrary, that it's all fiction, fables and lies – dreams recounted by men after they've woken up, or to be more accurate half woken up.'

'This is another error,' said Don Quixote, 'into which many people have fallen, refusing to believe that knights have ever existed; and I have often, on different occasions and with different people, attempted to expose this almost universal misconception to the light of truth; and although there have been times when I have not succeeded in my purpose, at other times I have done so, by supporting it upon the shoulders of truth: truth so palpable that I can almost say I have seen Amadis of Gaul with my own eyes – he was a tall man with a pale face, a splendid beard even if it was a black one, a look that hovered between gentleness and severity, and sparing of words, slow to lose his temper and quick to recover it; and just as I have described Amadis I believe I could describe every single knight errant in every single history in the world, because my realization that they were as their histories say they were, together with my knowledge of the deeds they did and the qualities they possessed, enables me to use logic to deduce their features, complexion and stature.'

'How tall, Don Quixote sir,' asked the barber, 'do you reckon the giant Morgante would have been?'

'With regard to giants,' replied Don Quixote, 'there are different opinions as to whether they ever existed or not; yet the Scriptures, which cannot be anything less than the absolute truth, show us that they did exist, by recounting the history of that immense Philistine, Goliath, who was seven and a half cubits tall,[6] a vast height. Besides, on the island of Sicily, shoulder-bones, arm-bones and leg-bones have been found, the size of which shows that they belonged to giants as tall as towers: geometry puts this truth beyond all doubt. Yet in spite of all this I cannot speak with certainty as to the size of Morgante, although I suspect that he cannot have been very tall; and I am inclined to this opinion by reading in the history where his exploits are described in detail that he often slept under a roof, and since he found houses in which there was room for him it is evident that he was not excessively large.'

'That's true enough,' said the priest.

He was relishing all Don Quixote's nonsense, so he asked him for his opinion about the faces of Reynald of Montalban and Sir Roland and the rest of the Twelve Peers of France, because they were all knights errant.

'As regards Reynald,' replied Don Quixote, 'I would venture to suggest that he was broad-faced, ruddy-complexioned, with darting and rather bulging eyes, excessively touchy and bad-tempered, friendly with thieves and ne'er-do-wells. As for Roland, or Rotolando, or Orlando, for he is given all these names in the histories, it is my considered opinion that he was of medium size, broad-shouldered, a little bandy-legged, dark face and red beard, hairy body, a menacing look in his eye, sparing of words, but very courteous and well-bred.'

'If Roland wasn't more of a gentleman than you say,' replied the priest, 'no wonder the fair Angelica scorned him and left him for the grace, dash and poise of the downy-cheeked little Moor to whom she surrendered her charms; and she was wise to love soft and gentle Medoro rather than rough old Roland.'

'That person Angelica, reverend sir,' replied Don Quixote, 'was a flighty, fickle and even somewhat wanton damsel, and she left the world as full of her indiscretions as of the fame of her beauty: she scorned a thousand lords, a thousand heroes and a thousand sages, and contented herself with a smooth-faced little page-boy, with no other wealth or renown than that which he gained for gratitude by his loyalty to his friend. The great singer of his beauty, the famous Ariosto, not caring or perhaps not daring to say what happened to this lady after her contemptible surrender, which would doubtless not make a very decorous story, left her with the lines:

> Another better bard may sing one day
> How she received the sceptre of Cathay.[7]

And it is evident that this was some sort of prophecy, because the poet is also called the *vates*, which means "fortune-teller". This truth is plain to see: since then a famous Andalusian poet has lamented and sung her tears, and another famous and unique Castilian poet has sung her beauty.'[8]

'Tell me, Don Quixote sir,' the barber broke in, 'hasn't any poet written a satire about that lady Angelica, among all those who've praised her?'

'I can well believe,' replied Don Quixote, 'that if Sacripante or Roland had been poets they would have given the damsel a good tongue-lashing; because it is only to be expected from poets who have been scorned and rejected by ladies who had pretended to be theirs – or whom the poets had pretended were theirs, after choosing them to be the mistresses of their thoughts – that they will take their revenge with satires and lampoons, a revenge, to be sure, unworthy of generous hearts; yet up to now I have not heard of any defamatory verse against the lady Angelica, who turned the world on its head.'

'What a miracle!' said the priest.

As he said this they heard the housekeeper and the niece, who had previously withdrawn from the conversation, shouting in the yard, and they went to see what the row was all about.

CHAPTER II

Concerning the extraordinary quarrel between Sancho Panza and Don Quixote's niece and housekeeper, and other amusing matters

The history relates that the shouts heard by Don Quixote, the priest and the barber came from the niece and the housekeeper, who were yelling at Sancho Panza as he tried to force his way in to see his master while they held the door against him:

'What does this vagrant want in this house? Go back to your own, chum – it's you, you alone that takes my master off and leads him astray and makes him wander to the back of beyond.'

To which Sancho replied:

'You devil of a housekeeper – I'm the one who's been taken off and led astray and made to wander to the back of beyond, not your master. He's the one who took me traipsing about all over the place, and you two women haven't got the faintest idea what's been happening – he tricked me away from home, by promising me an island that I'm still waiting for.'

'Let's hope you choke on your bloody islands, Sancho,' replied the niece. 'And what are islands, anyway? Something to eat, you great glutton, you greedyguts?'

'They aren't something to eat,' replied Sancho, 'but to govern better than any half-dozen high-court judges could ever govern any half-dozen cities.'

'That's as may be,' said the housekeeper, 'but you aren't coming in here, you sackful of mischief, you bundle of malice. Go and govern your own household and get some work done in your garden, and stop dreaming about islands or highlands or whatever it is you call them.'

The priest and the barber were enjoying this conversation, but Don Quixote, afraid that Sancho might unbutton his lips and blurt out a pack of malicious nonsenses and mention matters that were not at all to his credit, called out to him and told the two women to be quiet and let him in. Sancho entered the house, and the priest and the barber said goodbye to Don Quixote, despairing of his sanity because they could see how intent he was on his absurd ideas, how steeped he was in the idiotic errors of his errantry; and so the priest said to the barber:

'You'll see, my friend – when we're least expecting it our hidalgo's going to take wing again.'

'I don't doubt it for a minute,' replied the barber, 'but what astonishes me isn't so much the knight's madness as the squire's stupidity – he's got such faith in his island that however many times that bubble's pricked he won't put the idea out of his head.'

'God help them,' said the priest, 'and we must stay alert: we shall soon see where this great fabric of absurdities leaves this knight and this squire – anyone would think they'd been made in the same mould, and that the madness of the master wouldn't be worth a farthing without the foolishness of the man.'

'That's right,' said the barber, 'and I'd love to know what they're talking about at this very moment.'

'I can assure you,' replied the priest, 'that the niece or the housekeeper will tell us later, because they aren't the sort of women not to listen in.'

Meanwhile, Don Quixote shut himself up alone in his room with Sancho, and said:

'It grieves me deeply, Sancho, that you have said and still say that I turned your life upside-down, when you know full well that my own life has hardly been on a normal footing: together we left home, together we sallied forth, together we went on our pilgrimage; we shared the same fortune and the same fate, and, if you were blanket-tossed once, I was rib-basted a hundred times, and I have the advantage over you there.'

'Quite right too,' replied Sancho, 'because, from what you say, disasters are meant more for knight errants than for squires.'

'You are mistaken, Sancho,' said Don Quixote. 'According to the saying, *quando caput dolet*, etcetera.'[1]

'The only language I understand is my own one,' Sancho retorted.

'What I mean to say,' said Don Quixote, 'is that when one's head aches all one's limbs hurt, and I, being your lord and master, am your head, and you, being my servant, are a part of me, and for this reason any ill that affects me will hurt you, and vice versa.'

'That's just how it should be,' said Sancho, 'but when this limb here was being blanket-tossed, my head was sitting on the other side of the yard wall, watching me fly through the air and not feeling any pain at all – and if the limbs are supposed to suffer when the head's hurting, the head ought to suffer for them, too.'

'Are you now saying, Sancho,' replied Don Quixote, 'that I was not suffering for you when you were being tossed in the blanket? And if this is indeed what you are saying, please do not say it or even think it, for during those moments I was feeling more pain in my spirit than you were in your body. But let us leave this affair aside for the time being, because there will be opportunities to consider and resolve it later, and tell me, Sancho my friend, what are people saying about me out there in the village? What is my reputation amongst the common people, the hidalgos, the nobility? What are they saying about my valour, my exploits and my courtesy? What talk is there about the decision I have taken to revive and return to the world the forgotten order of chivalry? In short, Sancho, I want you to tell me everything that has reached your ears, without adding anything to the good news or substracting anything from the bad; for it is the duty of the loyal vassal to tell his master the truth, the whole truth and nothing but the truth, not allowing flattery to puff it up or misplaced respect to tone it down; and I would have you know, Sancho, that if the naked truth were to reach the ears of the top people, unclothed in flattery, we should see happier days, and other times would be considered iron ages, not ours, which I hold to be the gilded age of recent history. Let this warning assist you, Sancho, to convey to my ears, intelligently and faithfully, the truth, as you understand it, about what I have asked you.'

'I'll be happy enough to do that, sir,' replied Sancho, 'so long as you don't get cross about what I'm going to say, since you want it naked, or at least with no more clothes on than when I was told it.'

'I shall most certainly not be cross,' replied Don Quixote. 'You can speak freely, Sancho, without beating about the bush.'

'Well the first thing I'll say,' he said, 'is that the common people think you're a raging lunatic and I'm no better. The hidalgos are saying you're going beyond the proper limits for hidalgos, calling yourself "Don" and staking a claim to be a nobleman when all you own is a tiny vineyard, a couple of yokes of land and hardly a rag to your back. And the nobles are saying they'd rather you hidalgos didn't try to rival them, especially not the ones who are more like squires and who go over the cracks in their boots with soot and oil, and darn their black hose with green silk.'

'None of all that,' said Don Quixote, 'can possibly refer to me, because I am always well-dressed, never darned – worn, maybe, and that more from the chafing of armour than from the ravages of time.'

'And,' continued Sancho, 'as for your valour, courtesy, exploits and decision, opinions do differ – some say "Mad, but funny", others "Brave, but unlucky", still others "Polite, but a meddler", and on and on they go till not a bone is left unbroken in your body or in mine.'

'Look here, Sancho,' said Don Quixote, 'wherever virtue is found to a high degree it is persecuted. Few if any of the famous heroes of history have escaped the slander of malicious tongues. Julius Caesar, a most spirited, wise and courageous leader, was criticized for being over-ambitious and not as clean as he might have been, either in his dress or in his personal habits.[2] Alexander, whose exploits won him the name of "the Great", is said to have been something of a drunkard. Of Hercules, the hero of so many labours, it is rumoured that he was over-fond of his pleasures and creature comforts. Gossips say of Don Galaor, Amadis of Gaul's brother, that he was more lecherous than he had any need to be; and of his brother they say that he was a cry-baby. So you can see, Sancho, that among all these calumnies directed at heroes, those directed at me can well be tolerated, if they are no worse than those which you have mentioned.'

'And that's just the problem, by the bones of my father!' Sancho replied.

'Is your story still incomplete, then?' asked Don Quixote.

'I've still got the tail left to skin,' said Sancho. 'What I've said so far is chicken-feed, and if you want to know all the faults they're finding in you, I'll bring someone who'll give you the whole story here and now, not leaving out the tiniest scrap. Last night Bartolomé Carrasco's son came back home from Salamanca University, where he's passed his final exams, and when I went to welcome him he told me that your history's been put into a book called *The Ingenious Hidalgo Don Quixote de la Mancha*, and he says I'm named in it with my very own name of Sancho Panza, and the lady Dulcinea del Toboso too, and things are even mentioned when you and I were alone when we did them, which had me making the sign of the cross on myself as I wondered how that historian could have found out about them.'

'I can assure you, Sancho,' said Don Quixote, 'that the author of our history must be some wise enchanter, for to such people nothing of what they have a mind to write can remain hidden.'

'And what a very wise enchanter the author of our history must have been,' said Sancho, 'with a name, according to Sansón Carrasco, that young graduate I just mentioned, like Cide Hamete Brinjalcurry!'

'That is a Moorish name,' Don Quixote replied.

'I expect it is,' said Sancho, 'because I've often heard that the Moors are very fond of their brinjal curry.'

'I think, Sancho,' said Don Quixote, 'you must be mistaken about the surname of that fellow Cide, which in Arabic means "master".'

'I could be that,' Sancho replied, 'but if you want me to bring him here I'll go for him in a jiffy.'

'That will give me great pleasure, my friend,' said Don Quixote, 'for what you have just said has left me in some confusion, and I shall not be able to enjoy a single mouthful of food until I am fully informed about it.'

'I'll go for him then,' Sancho replied.

And he left his master and went to look for the young graduate, with whom he soon returned, and the three of them had a most amusing conversation.

CHAPTER III

About the ridiculous discussion between Don Quixote,
Sancho Panza and Sansón Carrasco, BA

Don Quixote remained deep in thought as he awaited the young graduate Carrasco, from whom he was expecting to hear news about himself published in a book, as Sancho had said; and he couldn't persuade himself that such a history existed – the blood of the enemies that he had killed was not yet dry on the blade of his sword, and people were already claiming that his noble deeds of chivalry had appeared in print! Despite this, though, it did occur to him that some sage, friendly or hostile, must have published his deeds by way of enchantment: if friendly, to exalt them and place them above the most renowned exploits ever performed by any knight errant; if hostile, to dismiss them and present them as being meaner than the wretchedest deeds that the basest squire had ever been described as doing, but then again (he said to himself), squires' exploits had never been recorded; and if it was true that this history did exist, the fact that it concerned a knight errant was a guarantee that it would be grandiloquent, lofty, illustrious, magnificent and true.

This thought offered him some consolation, but then he lost heart again when he remembered that the name Cide suggested that the author was a Moor, and not a word of truth was to be expected from any of those, since the whole lot of them are deceivers, liars and story-tellers. He was afraid that the author might have handled his love affair in an indelicate manner that would cause detraction and damage to the chastity of his lady Dulcinea del Toboso; he hoped that he had portrayed his faithfulness and the unswerving correctness of his behaviour towards her, snubbing queens, empresses and damsels of all ranks, and holding in leash the powerful urges of his natural passions; and in this state, engrossed in these and many other thoughts careering about his brain, he was found by Sancho and Carrasco, whom Don Quixote greeted with gracious courtesy.

Despite his name the new graduate wasn't a big man, although he was a great leg-puller; his complexion was dull but his wits were sharp; he'd have been about twenty-four, with a moon face, a snub nose and a large mouth, all signs that he had a waggish disposition and loved joking and jesting, as he showed when he saw Don Quixote by throwing himself on to his knees before him and saying:

'Pray give me your hands, Don Quixote de la Mancha; I swear by this habit of St Peter that I'm wearing, even though I've only taken minor orders, that you are one of the most famous knights errant that have ever existed or indeed ever will exist in the whole wide world. A blessing on Cide Hamete Benengeli for having written the history of your great deeds, and a double blessing on the diligent man who took care to have it translated from Arabic into our Castilian vernacular, for the amusement and entertainment of all.'

Don Quixote brought him to his feet and said:

'It is true, then, is it, that a history of me exists, and that it was a Moor and a sage who wrote it?'

'It's so true, sir,' said Sansón, 'that I'm to understand that more than twelve thousand copies of the history are in print at this moment; and if you don't believe me, just ask Portugal, Barcelona and Valencia, where they were printed; and there's a report that it's being printed now in Antwerp, and all the signs are that there's no language in the world into which it won't be translated.'

'One of the things,' Don Quixote put in, 'that must give the greatest happiness to a virtuous and eminent man is to find himself with a good name on everybody's lips, and in print, while he is still alive. I said "with a good name" because, if the opposite were the case, no death could equal it.'

'As far as good names and good reputations are concerned,' the young graduate said, 'you have gained the palm from all other knights errant, because the Moor in his language, and the Christian in his, took good care to depict most vividly for us your gallantry, your courage in confronting perils, your patience in adversity, your long-suffering in misfortune and when wounded, and your chastity and continence in that most platonic love-affair between you and my lady Doña Dulcinea del Toboso.'

'I've never heard anyone,' Sancho butted in, 'calling my lady Dulcinea Doña, but just the lady Dulcinea del Toboso — so the history's wrong about that, for starters.'

'That isn't an important objection,' Carrasco replied.

'Certainly not,' said Don Quixote, 'but tell me, sir, which of my deeds are most highly praised in the history?'

'About that,' the young graduate replied, 'opinions differ, as tastes do: some prefer the adventure of the windmills, which you thought were Briareuses and giants; others, the adventure of the fulling-mill; others, the description of the two armies that turned out to be two flocks of sheep; one man praises the adventure of the corpse being taken to Segovia to be buried; another says that the best one of them all is the freeing of the convicts; yet another that none of them equals the adventure of the two Benedictine giants and the fight with the brave Basque.'

'Could you please tell me, sir,' Sancho put in, 'whether they've included the adventure of the men from Yanguas, when good old Rocinante had the bright idea of reaching for the stars?'

'The sage didn't leave anything out,' replied Sansón. 'He includes and describes it all, even the capers cut by Sancho in the blanket.'

'I didn't cut any capers in the blanket,' Sancho retorted. 'I cut them in the air, and more of them than I'd have chosen to.'

'I suppose,' added Don Quixote, 'that every history that has ever been written has its ups and its downs, especially those that deal with chivalric exploits, for they cannot recount successful adventures alone.'

'For all that,' the young graduate replied, 'some of those who've read the history say that they'd have been happier if its authors had overlooked some of the countless beatings that Don Quixote received in various confrontations.'

'That's where the truth of the history comes in,' said Sancho.

'But they could, in all fairness, have kept quiet about them,' said Don Quixote, 'because there is no need to narrate actions that do not alter or undermine the truth of the history, if they are going to result in the discrediting of the hero. I am sure that Aeneas was not as pious as Virgil depicts him, nor was Ulysses as prudent as Homer says.'

'That's true,' Sansón replied, 'but it's one thing to write as a poet and quite another to write as a historian: the poet can narrate or sing events not as they were but as they should have been, and the historian must record them not as they should have been but as they were, without adding anything to the truth or taking anything away from it.'

'Well if this Moorish bloke's after telling the truth,' said Sancho, 'I bet the thumpings they handed out to me will be in there among the ones my master got, because they never took the measure of his shoulders without taking it of my whole body. But that's no surprise, because as my master says, all the limbs have got to share the headache.'

'You are a sly dog, Sancho,' replied Don Quixote. 'I must say your memory works well enough when you want it to.'

'Even if I did want to forget the thrashings I've been given,' said Sancho, 'the bruises wouldn't let me, still fresh here on my ribs.'

'Keep quiet, Sancho,' said Don Quixote, 'and stop interrupting our friend from the university, whom I entreat to continue telling me what is said about me in this history.'

'And about me, too,' said Sancho. 'They say I'm one of the main caricatures in it, too.'

'*Characters*, not *caricatures*, friend Sancho,' said Sansón.

'Oh no, not another blunders-expert!' said Sancho. 'If you two start up on that again, we'll all be here till the ends of our lives.'

'May God give me a bad life, Sancho,' replied the young graduate, 'if you aren't the second most important character in the history, and there are those who'd rather hear you talk than the finest of the others, even though there are also people who say you were too gullible in believing you could ever become governor of that island offered you by Don Quixote here.'

'All is not yet lost,' said Don Quixote, 'and as Sancho matures he will, with the experience that only the passing years can bring, become more suited and better qualified for the post of governor than he is at present.'

'For God's sake, sir,' said Sancho, 'the island I can't govern at my age I shan't be able to govern when I'm as old as Moses. The problem is that this island of yours is biding its time God only knows where, not that I haven't got the gumption to govern it.'

'Entrust the matter to God's good care, Sancho,' said Don Quixote, 'for everything will turn out well, better perhaps than you think: not a leaf stirs on a tree unless God wishes it to.'

'That's true enough,' said Sansón, 'and, if it is God's will, there shall be a thousand islands for Sancho to govern, let alone one.'

'I've seen governors about the place,' said Sancho, 'that to my mind can't hold a candle to me, yet, for all that, they get called my lord and they eat off plates of silver.'

'Those aren't governors of islands,' replied Sansón, 'but of other less demanding things; because those who govern islands must at the very least have some knowledge of syntax.'

'I could cope with the sin,' said Sancho, 'but I'll pass on the tax – it's something I haven't ever come to grips with. But to leave me being governor in God's hands, and may he send me where I can be of most service to him – what I say, Sansón Carrasco sir, is that I'm very very glad that the author of this here history has talked about me in such a way that what he says doesn't give offence, because I swear to you as a loyal squire that if he'd said anything that wasn't fit to be said about a pure-bred Christian, which is what I am, the deafest of the deaf would have heard what I'd have had to say to him.'

'That would have been a miracle,' Sansón replied.

'Miracle or no miracle,' said Sancho, 'everyone should watch out how he talks or writes about the next man and not just shove down the first thing that comes into his brain-box.'

'One of the faults that have been found in this history,' said the young graduate, 'is that the author included a tale called *Inappropriate Curiosity*; not that it's a bad one or badly told, but it's out of place and has nothing to do with the history of the great Don Quixote.'

'I bet,' replied Sancho, 'that the bastard's gone and made a right old hotchpotch.'

'I do now have to say,' said Don Quixote, 'that the author of my history is no sage but some ignorant prattler, who started writing it in a haphazard and unplanned way and let it turn out however it would, like Orbaneja, the famous artist of Úbeda, who, when asked what he was painting, replied: "Whatever emerges." On one occasion he was painting a cockerel so badly and so unlike a real cockerel that he had to write in capital letters by its side: "This is a cockerel." My history must be like that, needing a commentary to make it intelligible.'

'No, no,' replied Sansón, 'it's so very intelligible that it doesn't pose any difficulties at all: children leaf through it, adolescents read it, grown men understand it and old men praise it, and, in short, it's so well-thumbed and well-perused and well-known by all kinds of people that as soon as they see a skinny nag pass by they say: "Look, there goes Rocinante." And the people who have most taken to it are the page-boys. There's not a lord's antechamber without its *Quixote*: if one person puts it aside, another picks it up; some ask to be lent it, others run up and snatch it away. All in all, this history provides the most delightful and least harmful entertainment ever, because nowhere in it can one find the slightest suspicion of language that isn't wholesome or thoughts that aren't Catholic.'

'To write in any other way,' said Don Quixote, 'would be to write not truths but falsehoods, and historians who have recourse to falsehoods should be burnt, like counterfeiters; and I do not know what could have made the author turn to stories about other people when there was so much to write about me: I suppose he was relying on the saying, "It's all fish that comes to the net." Yet the truth of the matter is that just by recording my thoughts, my sighs, my tears, my worthy designs and my missions he could have written a volume bigger than all the works of El Tostado put together, or at any rate as big.[1] Be that as it may, my understanding of the matter, my dear sir, is that to write histories and other books one needs a fine mind and a mature understanding. To tell jokes and write wittily is the work of geniuses; the most intelligent character in a play is the fool, because the actor playing the part of a simpleton must not be one. History is, as it were, sacred, because it must be truthful, and where there is truth there is God, because he is truth; and yet, in spite of all this, there are those who toss off books as if they were pancakes.'

'There's no book so bad,' said the young graduate, 'that there isn't something good in it.'

'About that there is no doubt,' Don Quixote replied, 'but it often happens that men who have deservedly achieved and won fame by their writings lose it completely or find it diminished in part as soon as they publish them.'

'The reason for that,' said Sansón, 'is that printed works are read at leisure and their defects are easily spotted, and the more famous the author the more closely they're scrutinized. Men renowned for their genius – great poets, illustrious historians – are usually envied by those whose pleasure and pastime is to pass judgement on what others have written, without ever having published anything themselves.'

'That is not surprising,' said Don Quixote, 'because there are many theologians who cannot preach, yet are experts at identifying the faults and the excesses of those who can.'

'It is exactly as you say, Don Quixote,' said Carrasco, 'but I do wish that such critics were more forgiving and less censorious, and did not pay such attention to the spots on the brilliant sun of the work they grumble at; for if *aliquando bonus dormitat Homerus*,[2] they should also remember how very long Homer stayed awake to give us the light of his work with the least possible shadow; and it could even be that what they think are faults are in reality beauty spots, which often increase the loveliness of a face; so, you see, anyone publishing a book exposes himself to enormous risk, because it's absolutely impossible to write one in such a way that it satisfies and pleases all those who read it.'

'The book that has been written about me,' said Don Quixote, 'will not have pleased many people.'

'Quite the contrary: since *stultorum infinitus est numerus*,[3] innumerable are those who have relished this history. Some have found fault with the author's memory and accused him of deception because he forgets to tell us who was the thief that stole Sancho's dun – the incident isn't narrated and we just have to infer that somebody has stolen it, and a little later we find Sancho riding the very same donkey without having recovered it. They also say that the author forgot to state what Sancho did with the hundred escudos he found in the travelling bag in the Sierra Morena, which are never mentioned again; and there are many people who would like to know what happened to them, or what he spent them on, which is one of the essential points omitted from the book.'

Sancho replied:

'Right now, Señor Carrasco, I'm in no state to go into any accounts or explanations, because I've just gone all a-flutter in my tummy, and if I don't get a couple of swigs of the old stuff inside me to put it right I'll soon be nothing but skin and bone. I'll have to go home for it, and the wife's waiting for me – as soon as I've done eating I'll come back and answer all the questions you and anyone else want to put to me, both about the loss of the ass and about the spending of the hundred escudos.'

And without awaiting a reply or saying another word he went home. Don Quixote insisted that the graduate must share his humble board. The graduate accepted the invitation and stayed for the meal, a couple of squabs were added to the pot, the conversation at table was about deeds of chivalry, Carrasco played along with his host, the banquet came to an end, they had their afternoon nap, Sancho returned and the previous conversation was resumed.

CHAPTER IV

In which Sancho Panza provides the answers to the young graduate Sansón Carrasco's doubts and questions; together with other events worth knowing and telling

Sancho Panza returned to Don Quixote's house and to the previous conversation, and he said:

'To what Señor Sansón said about people wanting to know who stole my donkey, and how and when, it is my reply that on the very same night when we went to hide from the Holy Brotherhood in the Sierra Morena, after the adventure or misadventure of the convicts, and the other one of the dead body being taken to Segovia, me and my master rode into a clump of trees where my master leaned on his lance and I sat on my dun, both of us dead beat after the fights we'd had, and we dozed off just as if we were lying on half-a-dozen feather mattresses, and in particular I fell so very fast asleep that whoever it was managed to come and prop up the pack-saddle, with me sitting there and all, on top of four poles one in each corner, and get the dun out from underneath without me noticing a thing.'

'That is easy enough to do, and no new occurrence: it is what happened to Sacripante when he was at the siege of Albracca and that famous thief

Brunello removed his horse from between his legs using the same trick.'[1]

'Dawn broke,' Sancho resumed, 'and as soon as I gave myself a good shake the poles caved in and I came down with an almighty thump, and I looked around for my donkey and I couldn't find it, and the tears filled my eyes and I made such a lament that if the author of our history hasn't put it in he can take it from me he hasn't put anything worthwhile in. A few days later, I can't rightly remember how many, I was walking along with Princess Micomicona when I spotted my donkey, and on top of it wearing gipsy clothes was that character Ginés de Pasamonte, that crook, that great villain me and my master set free from the chain.'

'That isn't the mistake,' Sansón replied. 'The mistake is that before the ass has reappeared the author says Sancho's riding it!'

'I don't know what to say to that,' said Sancho, 'but maybe the historian got it wrong, or it might have been a slip of the printer's.'

'I'm sure you're right,' said Sansón, 'but what happened to the hundred escudos? Did they disappear into thin air?'

Sancho replied:

'I laid them out on the well-being of my person and of my wife and children, and those escudos are the only reason why my wife's putting up with me going off along all those highways and byways serving my master Don Quixote, because if after all that time I'd come back home penniless and donkeyless I'd have been in for it – and if there's anything else you want to know about me here I am, and I'll answer to the King himself in person, and there's no cause for anybody to be poking their noses into whether I brought money back with me or not and whether I spent it or not. Because if the thumpings I was given on my travels had to be paid for in hard cash, even if they were only priced at four maravedís apiece another hundred escudos wouldn't be enough to pay for the half of them, and people can put their hands on their hearts and say what they'd have done, and stop making out that what's white's black and what's black's white – each of us is how God made him and many are much worse.'

'I'll take care,' said Carrasco, 'to warn the author of the history that if he prints it again he mustn't forget what the worthy Sancho has just said – for this will carry it to even greater heights.'

'Are there any other features of this book that need correcting, my dear young graduate?' Don Quixote asked.

'Yes, there must be,' he replied, 'but none of them can be as important as those that I have mentioned.'

'And does the author,' Don Quixote asked, 'by any chance promise a second part?'

'Yes, he does,' Sansón replied, 'but he says he hasn't found it and doesn't know who's got it, so we can't tell whether it'll come out or not – and both because of this and because some people are saying, "Second parts are never any good," and others are saying, "What's already been written about Don Quixote is quite enough," there are doubts about the appearance of this second part; although other people who are jovial rather than saturnine say, "Let's have more quixotry – let Don Quixote charge and Sancho Panza talk, and that'll keep us happy, whatever he writes."'

'And what is the author's position?'

'He says,' Sansón replied, 'that as soon as he does find the history, for which he's searching with the utmost diligence, he's going to have it printed immediately, more for the profit he can make out of it than to win anybody's praise.'

At which Sancho remarked:

'So the author's hoping to make some money out of it, is he? That'd be a miracle, because it'll be hurry, hurry, hurry, like a tailor on the day before a fiesta, and rushed jobs are never as well done as they ought to be. That Moorish bloke, or whatever he is, had better take care to be on his mettle – me and my master are going to hand him such a supply of raw materials in the shape of adventures and all kinds of other doings that he'll be able to write not just one second part but a hundred of them. I suppose that character thinks we're resting on our laurels here – well, if he holds up our feet to be shod he'll soon see if there's anything wrong with our hooves. All I can say is that if my master took my advice we'd be out in the fields by now, redressing grievances and righting wrongs as all the best knight errants do.'

Sancho had hardly finished speaking when they heard Rocinante neighing, which Don Quixote took as a most happy omen, so he decided to make another sally in three or four days' time. He informed the young graduate of his decision, and asked his advice about where to start the campaign; and the reply was that they should travel to the kingdom of Aragon and the city of Saragossa, where solemn jousts were soon to be held to celebrate

St George's day² – and these would give Don Quixote the chance to outshine all the knights in Aragon, which would be the same as outshining all the knights in the world. Sansón commended Don Quixote's decision as a most honourable and courageous one, and warned him to be more cautious when he confronted dangers, because his life was not his own: it belonged to all those who needed his aid and protection in their misfortunes.

'That's where I've got a bone to pick, Señor Carrasco,' Sancho put in. 'Because my master attacks a hundred armed men like a greedy boy attacking half a dozen water melons. For God's sake, Señor Carrasco! There's a time to attack and a time to retreat, it can't always be "For St James, close, Spain!"³ What's more, I've heard it said, by my master himself if I remember rightly, that being brave is halfway between the extremes of being a coward and being foolhardy, and if that's right I don't want him to go running away when there isn't any reason to, or attacking when the odds are hopeless. But what I specially want to warn my master is that if he's going to take me with him, there's one proviso – he's going to do all his battling for himself and I'm not going to be forced to do anything more than look after his person and keep him clean and comfortable, and I'll mollycoddle him like nobody's business, but if he thinks I'm ever going to draw my sword, even against poxy peasants with their hatchets and their iron skullcaps, he's got another think coming. I'm not setting out to win myself a reputation as a hero, Señor Carrasco, but as the best and loyallest squire that ever served a knight errant, and if my master Don Quixote, out of gratitude for my many good services, decides to give me one of all those islands he says he's going to come across, I'll be duly grateful, and if he doesn't, I was born to suffer, and man mustn't make his fortunes depend on other men but on God, and what's more my bread will taste as good to me islandless as with an island, or better. And how am I to know that the devil hasn't been fixing up tripwires on those islands to make me stumble and fall and bash my teeth in? Sancho I was born and Sancho I shall die, but all the same if out of the kindness of its heart, without me having to put myself out or risk too much, heaven did let me have an island or something similar, I'm not such an idiot as to turn it down, because as they also say, "When you're offered a heifer make haste with the halter," and "When good fortune comes knocking at the door, hurry up and let her in."'

'Brother Sancho,' said Carrasco, 'you've spoken like a professor; but do put your trust in God and in Don Quixote, because he's going to give you a kingdom, not just an island.'

'Too much would be just as bad as too little,' Sancho replied, 'although I can tell you, Señor Carrasco, that if my master did give me a kingdom he wouldn't be pouring it down the drain – I've taken my own pulse and found myself in a good condition to rule kingdoms and govern islands, and so I've told my master more than once.'

'Be careful, Sancho,' said Sansón. 'Success can go to one's head, and it could happen that once you were governor you wouldn't want to know your own mother.'

'That,' said Sancho, 'might be true of people whose blood isn't as pure as it might be, but not of anyone with a good thick slab of the suet of an old Christian all round his soul, like me. A man of my calibre being ungrateful to anyone!'

'May God grant it,' said Don Quixote, 'and we shall see what happens when you take over the governorship: I do believe that it is very nearly in sight.'

Then he asked the young graduate, if he was a poet, to do him the favour of writing some verse about the way in which he intended to bid farewell to his lady Dulcinea del Toboso, and to take care to put at the beginning of each line one letter of her name, so that when the reader reached the end of the poem and put all the first letters together they would read: *Dulcinea del Toboso*. The young graduate replied that even though he wasn't one of the famous poets of Spain, of which there were said to be no more than three and a half, he wouldn't fail to write the poem, in spite of the fact that he could see one great difficulty in the task, because there were seventeen letters in the name, and if he made four stanzas of four lines each there'd be one letter left over, and if he used five-line or ten-line stanzas he'd be three letters short; but, in spite of all that, he'd squeeze the extra letter in as best he could, and make the name of Dulcinea del Toboso fit into four four-line stanzas.

'That is how it must be written, come what may,' said Don Quixote, 'for if the name is not there, clear for all to see, there is no woman on earth who will believe that the poem was composed for her.'

This was settled, and they agreed that they'd depart one week later.

Don Quixote instructed the young graduate to keep his intentions secret, particularly from the priest and Master Nicolás, and also from his niece and the housekeeper, so that they wouldn't prevent him from putting his honourable and courageous intentions into practice. Carrasco promised to do so. With this he took his leave, begging Don Quixote to send him all his news, both good and bad, whenever he had an opportunity; and so.they parted, and Sancho went away to make his preparations for their campaign.

CHAPTER V

About the intelligent and amusing conversation between
Sancho Panza and his wife Teresa Panza, together with
other events worthy of happy memory

As the translator of the history begins this fifth chapter, he says that he considers it to be apocryphal, because Sancho Panza speaks here in a way that is quite different from what could be expected from his dull wits, and makes incisive comments that seem beyond his capabilities; the translator adds, however, that, concerned as he is to do his job properly, he has decided not to leave it untranslated, and so he continues:

Sancho was in a jubilant mood when he reached home, so much so that his wife could tell at a glance how happy he was, and couldn't resist asking him:

'What's happened, Sancho my dear, to make you so cheerful?'

To which he replied:

'I can tell you this much, wife – if it so pleased God, I'd be well content not to feel as happy as I look.'

'I don't understand you, husband,' she replied, 'and I don't know what you mean when you say you'd be well content, if it so pleased God, not to feel happy – I mightn't be very clever but I don't know anyone who's happy at not being happy.'

'Look, Teresa,' Sancho replied. 'I'm happy because I've made up my mind to go back into service with my master Don Quixote, who's riding off in search of adventures for a third time, and I'm going with him again, because my needs force me to, together with the happy hope of finding another hundred escudos like the ones that have been spent, even though I'm sad at having to leave you and the children – but if it so pleased God to let me have enough to eat safe and sound here at home without dragging me along all those highways and byways, something he could do without much effort by just willing it to happen, it's clear that my happiness would be firmer and sounder, because this happiness I've got at the moment is mixed with sadness at leaving you. So I was right to say that I'd be well content, if it so pleased God, not to be happy.'

'Look, Sancho,' Teresa replied: 'ever since you've been a knight errant's limb you talk in such a roundabout way that nobody can understand you.'

'It's enough if God understands me, wife,' Sancho replied, 'because he's the understander of all things, and you just let it rest there, and take good note, woman, that you must cosset the dun these next three days, so it's ready to take up arms – give it double rations, and give the pack-saddle and the rest of the tackle a good overhaul, because we aren't going off to some wedding but to ride round the world and swap blows with giants, monsters and dragons, and hear hissings and roarings and bellowings and howlings, and all this would be chicken-feed if we didn't also have to deal with men from Yanguas and enchanted Moors.'

'I can well believe, husband,' replied Teresa, 'that squire errants don't get their bread for nothing, so I'll be praying to Our Lord to deliver you soon from all that hardship.'

'I can tell you this much, wife,' Sancho replied: 'if I wasn't expecting to be in control of an island before very long, I'd drop down dead on the spot.'

'No, don't do that, husband,' Teresa said, 'let the hen live on though she has got the pip, and you live on too, and the devil take all the controls in the world. You were out of control when you came out of your mother's belly, you've survived so far out of control, and when it's God's will you'll go to your grave, or rather you'll be carried to your grave, out of control. There are plenty of people who get by without control, and that doesn't stop them from living on and being counted as human beings like anyone else. Hunger's the best sauce there is, and since that's one thing the poor are never without, we always enjoy our food. But mind you, Sancho, if you do by any chance find yourself in control of an island, don't go and forget me and the children. Remember that Sanchico's fifteen now, and it'd be a good idea if he went to school, if his uncle the priest is going to make a churchman out of him. Remember too that your daughter Mari-Sancha won't exactly die of grief if we find a husband for her – she's showing signs of being as keen to get married as you are to be in control and, when all's said and done, better a poor husband than a rich lover.'

'Upon my word,' Sancho replied, 'if God does put me in control of something worthwhile, wife, I'll marry off Mari-Sancha so high-up that nobody will be able to get within sniffing distance of her without calling her your ladyship.'

'No, don't do that, Sancho,' Teresa replied. 'Marry her to someone who's her equal, that'd be wiser. If you take her out of her clogs and put her into fine ladies' shoes, and out of her skirt of grey-brown homespun and into a farthingale and bright silk petticoats, and turn her from "Marica" and plain "you" into "Doña" and "your ladyship", the poor girl won't know where she is, and she'll put her foot in it with every step she takes, and keep showing her true colours – which are humble grey and brown.'

'Enough of that, you silly woman,' said Sancho, 'all she needs is two or three years' practice, and then grand and grave manners will fit her like a glove – and if they don't, who cares? She'll be her ladyship, and nothing will alter that.'

'Stick to your own station, Sancho,' Teresa replied. 'Don't be looking to get above yourself, and remember the proverb that says: "Wipe the nose of the boy next door, and take him into your own house." A fine thing it would be to marry our María to a high and mighty earl or some other fine gentleman who when the fancy took him would drag her through the mud and call her peasant wench and clodhopper's and tow-spinner's brat! Over my dead body, husband! Do you think that's what I've raised my daughter for? You bring some money home, Sancho, and leave me to see to her marriage. There's Lope Tocho now, Juan Tocho's son, a strapping healthy lad, and one we know, and I'm sure he fancies the girl, and he's our equal and will make a good husband for her; and we'll always have her under our eye, and we'll all be as one, parents and children, grandchildren and sons-in-law, and peace and God's blessing will be with us – so don't you go marrying her at those courts and grand palaces of yours where nobody will understand her and she won't know what she's doing.'

'You look here, you dunce, you devil of a woman,' Sancho replied. 'Why on earth have you gone and taken it into your head, without rhyme or reason, to try and stop me from marrying my daughter to someone who'll give me grandchildren who'll be called your lordship? Look, Teresa, I've always heard my elders and betters say that if you don't make the most of good fortune when it comes your way you can't complain if it passes you by. So now that it's knocking at our door it won't do to shut it out – we'd better let ourselves be blown along by the fair wind.'

It was because of this way of expressing himself and because of what Sancho says a little later that the translator of this history declared that he considered this chapter to be apocryphal.

'Can't you see, you animal,' Sancho continued, 'that it'll be a good idea if I end up in control of something worthwhile that will pull us out of the mire? And then Mari-Sancha can marry whoever I say, and you'll soon see how they'll call you Doña Teresa Panza, and in church you'll sit yourself down on top of carpets and cushions and counterpanes, and snub your nose at all the hidalgos' wives in the village. But oh no, oh no, you want to stay as you've always been, never getting any bigger or smaller, like one of those figures on tapestries. And that's that – Sanchica's going to marry an earl, whatever you say.'

'Do you know what you're saying, husband?' replied Teresa. 'And I don't care what you say, I'm afraid this earldom of my daughter's is going to be her undoing. You go ahead and do what you like, make her a duchess or a princess if you please, but I can tell you it won't be with my goodwill or consent. I've always been in favour of equality, and I can't stand people getting above themselves for no good reason. Teresa I was christened, pure and simple, without any frills or flounces or titles stuck on the front, and Cascajo was my father's name, and just because I'm your wife I'm called Teresa Panza even though by rights I ought to be called Teresa Cascajo. But then it's the laws that make the lords, and I'm well content with my own name, without any doñas piled on top of it to make it too heavy for me to carry, and I don't want to give people seeing me dressed up as a countess or a governor's wife the excuse to say, as they very soon would: "Look what airs the slut's giving herself now! Only yesterday she was busy spinning her tow from morning to night and she had to pull her skirt over her head when she went to mass for want of a veil, and there she goes today in her farthingale and her brooches and her fine airs as if we didn't know who she is." If God keeps me in my seven senses or my five senses or however many of them I've got, I don't intend to expose myself to all that. You go off, my friend, to be a government or an island, and give yourself all the airs you like – but I swear by the eternal glory of my dear mother that me and my daughter aren't going to budge one inch from this village. A woman's place is in the home, and a modest maid's finest fiesta is a job well done. So off you go with your precious Don Quixote on your adventures, and leave the two of us here with our disasters – if we're good, God will provide a remedy. And I must say I don't know who gave that man the right to call himself Don – it's a title that neither his parents nor his grandparents ever had.'

'All I can say,' said Sancho, 'is that you must have some little devil in that body of yours. For God's sake, woman – stringing all that nonsense together, one piece of it after another, without any rhyme or reason! What can old Cascajo, brooches, proverbs and people giving themselves airs and graces have to do with what I'm talking about? Look you here, you dimwit, you ignoramus, and I've got every right to call you that, because you refuse to understand me and you're turning your back on good fortune – if I was telling my daughter to throw herself off some tower or take to the streets like Doña Urraca,[1] you'd be right not to go along with me, but when I'm saying that in a brace of shakes and in the twinkling of an eye I'll stick a doña and a ladyship on top of her and fetch her out of the stubble-fields and put her under an awning on a platform with more plush pillows on it than all the pilaus that all the Moors of Morocco ever had for dinner, why on earth won't you agree and fall in with my wishes?'

'You don't know why, husband?' Teresa replied. 'It's because of the proverb that says: "What covers you discovers you." People hardly even glance at a poor man, but they have a good look at anyone who's rich, and if he was once poor that sets off the gossiping and the nit-picking, and what's worst of all is that it goes on and on and on, because there are gossips everywhere in the streets like swarms of bees.'

'Look, Teresa,' Sancho replied, 'and listen to what I'm going to say to you – it's maybe something you haven't heard in all the days of your life, and I'm not just speaking for myself, because everything I'm going to say is taken from the holy father that came to the village to preach last Lent, and if I remember correctly he said that what we can see in front of us with our own two eyes comes into our mind, is present there and stays there much better and more clearly than what's in our past.'

These observations being made here by Sancho are the second reason why the translator says that he considers this chapter to be apocryphal, because they are beyond Sancho's capabilities. He continued:

'From which it follows that when we see someone who's smartly turned out and wearing fine clothes and with a train of servants, we seem to feel obliged to be respectful towards him, even though our memory may at that same moment recall to us some lowly condition in which we once saw him – a blot on his character that, whether it was a matter of money or of family, is a thing of the past and doesn't exist any more, because nothing exists except what we see in front of us. And if this person that fortune has pulled out of the snow of his pond (these were the selfsame words used by the holy father) to the height of prosperity is well-mannered, generous and polite to everyone, and doesn't go trying to vie with those who've been noble for ages, then you can be sure, Teresa, that nobody's going to remember what he used to be, but instead they'll stand in awe of what he is – all except envious people, and nobody's good fortune is safe from them.'

'I just don't understand you, husband,' Teresa replied. 'You do whatever you like, and stop making my head spin with all your highfalutin palaver. And if you're revolved to do as you say . . .'

'*Resolved* is the word, wife,' said Sancho, 'not *revolved*.'

'Don't you go picking quarrels with me, husband,' Teresa replied. 'I speak as God's pleased I should, and I don't believe in making things more complicated than they already are. And what I say is that if you're so set on being in control of an island, you should take your son Sancho with you, to start teaching him to be in control too, because it's a good idea for a son to learn and inherit his father's trade.'

'Just as soon as I'm put in control,' said Sancho, 'I'll send for him post-haste, and I'll send you money too, because I won't be short of that, since there's never any lack of people to lend it to controllers who are out of funds – and then you dress him to hide what he is and make him look like what he's going to be.'

'You just send me the money,' said Teresa, 'and I'll dress him up as pretty as a picture.'

'So we agree,' said Sancho, 'that our daughter's going to marry an earl.'

'The day I see her married to an earl,' Teresa replied, 'is the day I'll start digging her grave, but I'll say it yet again – you do as you please, because that's the burden we women were born with, obeying our husbands even if they are damn fools.'

And she began to cry as hard as if young Sancha were already dead and buried. Sancho comforted her by saying that even though he was going to marry the girl to an earl, he'd put it off as long as he could. This ended their conversation, and Sancho went to see Don Quixote and to make arrangements for their departure.

CHAPTER VI

About the conversation between Don Quixote and his niece and his housekeeper, one of the important chapters in this history

While Sancho Panza and his wife Teresa Cascajo were having this inappropriate conversation, Don Quixote's niece and housekeeper weren't sitting on their hands, either, because countless signs were leading them to the conclusion that their uncle and master was intending to slip away a third time and return to the exercise of what was in their opinion his errant chivalry, and they were trying in every way they could to deflect him from this absurd plan – but it was like preaching in the wilderness, or hammering away at cold iron. All the same, among many other points they put to him, the housekeeper said this:

'The honest truth is, sir, that if you don't get a grip on yourself and stay calmly here at home instead of gadding about up hill and down dale like a lost soul looking for what people say are called adventures but I call disasters, I'm going to take my complaints to God and the King and demand they do something about it.'

To which Don Quixote replied:

'My dear housekeeper, I do not know what God will reply to your complaints, nor can I tell what His Majesty's response will be: all I do know is that if I were the King I should refrain from replying to the countless irrelevant memoranda handed him every day; for one of the most tedious of the many, many chores of a monarch is having to listen to everybody and reply to everybody; so I should not like him to be bothered by my affairs.'

To which the housekeeper replied:

'Do tell us, sir: aren't there any knights at His Majesty's court?'

'Yes,' replied Don Quixote, 'very many of them, and so there should be, as embellishments of monarchs' magnificence and displays of royal majesty.'

'Well then,' she replied, 'couldn't you be one of those that take it easy serving their king and master at court?'

'Look here, my friend,' Don Quixote replied, 'not all knights can be courtiers, and not all courtiers can or should be knights errant: the world needs both kinds, and even if we are all knights there is a very great difference between one sort and the other; because courtiers, without leaving their chambers or the confines of the court, stroll all over the world just by perusing a map, which does not cost them a penny or cause them to suffer any heat or cold, or hunger or thirst; but we, the true knights errant, exposed to the sun, to the cold, to the air, to the inclemencies of the heavens, by night and by day, on foot and on horseback, measure the whole earth with our own paces; and we do not merely know our enemies from their portraits but in their own persons, and at every turn and on all occasions we attack them, without concerning ourselves over trifles like the laws of challenges: whether or not one lance or sword is longer than the other, whether the enemy has holy relics on him, or is practising some other form of covert trickery, whether or not the sun should be divided and carved up so that it shines into the eyes of neither, and other ceremonials of this sort that are involved in challenges between two individuals, which you do not know about and I do.

'And there is something else that you should know: the good knight errant – even when confronted by ten giants whose heads not only touch but pierce the clouds, and every one of them with two vast towers for legs, and arms like masts of mighty ships, and each eye like an enormous millstone burning brighter than a glass furnace – must not take fright on any account, but with gallant demeanour and an intrepid heart must charge and attack them and, if he can, defeat them and put them to flight in an instant, even if they wear as armour the shells of a certain sea-creature that are said to be harder than diamond, and even if in place of swords they bear keen knives of Damascus steel or clubs covered in spikes of the same metal, as I have seen on more than one occasion. I have said all this, my dear housekeeper, so that you can see what a difference there is between one sort of knight and the other; and it would be only right if there were no monarch who did not prize more highly this second kind, or to be more exact this first kind, of knight errant; for, as we read in their histories, there have been those who were the salvation not merely of one kingdom but of several.'

'Oh, sir!' the niece broke in. 'Look, everything you've said about knights errant is a fable and a fib, and if the histories written about them aren't burnt, each and every one of them deserves to be forced by the Inquisition to wear a scapular or some other sign showing it's a wicked corruptor of morals.'

'By the God who sustains me,' said Don Quixote, 'if you were not my niece, the daughter of my own sister, I should mete out to you such a punishment for the blasphemy you have just uttered that all the world would echo with it. How is it possible for a little missy who can hardly even manage a dozen bobbins when she is making lace to dare to traduce and find fault with the histories of knights errant? What would Sir Amadis say if he heard such a thing? Yet it is certain that he would forgive you, because he was the humblest and most courteous knight errant of his time and, furthermore, a great protector of damsels; but you could have been heard by someone who would not have let you off so lightly, because not all of them are courteous or considerate: there are some who are unmannerly ruffians. Not all those who are called knights are altogether knightly; for some are of gold, others are of alloy, and they all seem like knights, but not all of them can withstand the touchstone of truth. There are base fellows who are bursting to seem like knights, and there are grand knights who seem to be dying to be taken for base fellows; the former rise through ambition or virtue, the latter lower themselves through lack of spirit or through vice, and we must use our finest discernment to distinguish between these two sorts of knights, so similar in their titles and so different in their actions.'

'God bless me!' said the niece. 'You know so much, uncle, that if needs be you could climb up into any pulpit and preach away for all you were worth, yet you've got yourself into such a state of blind stupidity you believe that you're stout-hearted when the truth is you're old, that you're strong when you're ill, and that you right wrongs when you're bowed down by age – and, worst of all, that you're a knight when you aren't, because even if hidalgos can be knights it's certain that poor ones can't.'

'There is a great deal of truth in what you say, niece,' Don Quixote replied, 'and I could tell you things about noble families that would astonish you, but not wanting to mix the sacred with the profane I shall desist. Look, my dear friends: all the families in the world – please attend to what I am saying – can be reduced to four kinds, which are these: those that had humble beginnings, and extended and grew until they attained greatness; those that had splendid beginnings, and maintained this state and even now remain as they were at the outset; those that had splendid beginnings but tapered off, like a pyramid, after dwindling and decaying until they ended up in oblivion, like the tip of the pyramid, which compared with its base is nothing; and all the others, the vast majority, that had neither a good beginning nor an acceptable middle, and will have the same anonymous end, the lineage of common, plebeian people. Of the first kind, those who had humble beginnings and rose to the greatness that they preserve to this day, let the Ottoman house[1] serve as an example, for, springing from a humble, lowly herdsman, it has reached the heights where we contemplate it now. Of the second type, the family that had its origins in greatness and maintains it without adding to it, we can find examples in the many kings who have inherited their position and retain it without any expansion or contraction, being content to stay peacefully within the borders of their kingdoms. Of those who began in splendour and tapered away there are thousands of examples; because all the Pharaohs and Ptolemies of Egypt,[2] all the Caesars of Rome, together with the whole horde (if it is correct to give them this name) of countless Median, Assyrian, Persian, Greek and Barbarian princes, monarchs and lords, all these ancient dynasties and lineages have tapered away into nothingness and oblivion, both the families themselves and those who founded them, because it is impossible now to find any of their descendants, and even if we did find one it would be in some lowly and humble station. Of the plebeian stock all I can say is that it only serves to swell the ranks of the living, and its achievements deserve no more fame or praise than that.

'From all I have said I hope you will be able to gather, my dearly beloved dimwits, that there is a great confusion among lineages, and that the only families who show themselves to be great and illustrious are those that display these qualities in the virtue, wealth and generosity of their paterfamilias. I say virtue, wealth and generosity because the great man who is sin-ridden can only be a great sinner, and the wealthy man who is not generous will be nothing but a miserly beggar: the owner of wealth is not made happy by owning it but by spending it, and not by spending it capriciously, but by knowing how to spend it well. The poor gentleman has no means of showing that he is a gentleman other than by his virtue: being affable, well-bred, courteous and considerate and solicitous; not proud, not arrogant, not a gossip and, above all, charitable, because by cheerfully giving a pauper a couple of maravedís he will show himself to be as generous as the man who distributes alms to a fanfare of trumpets, and anybody who sees him adorned with these virtues of which I speak, even if he does not know him, cannot fail to consider that he is a man of good stock, and that it would be a miracle if he were not; and praise has always been virtue's reward, and the virtuous are bound to be praised.

'There are two roads, my daughters, to riches and honour: one is letters, the other is arms. I myself am more arms than letters, and, to judge from this inclination of mine, I must have been born under the influence of the planet Mars; so I am almost forced to follow that road, and by it I must travel in the face of all the opposition in the world, and you will be wearying yourselves in vain if you try to persuade me not to want for myself what heaven wants for me, what fortune ordains for me, what sound reason demands for me and, above all, what my own will desires for me; because knowing, as I do, the countless toils that are part and parcel of knight-errantry, I also know the innumerable benefits that it brings. And I know that the road of virtue is very narrow and the road of vice is broad and spacious.[3] And I know that they lead to very different ends and goals, because the broad and spacious road of vice leads to death, and the narrow and toilsome road of virtue leads to life, and not life that comes to a conclusion but life without end; and I know, too, as the great Castilian poet says, that

> This rough and rutted footpath is the way
> Up to the heights of immortality,
> Refused to all but those who do not stray.'[4]

'Oh dear, dear me!' cried the niece. 'My master's a poet, too! He knows everything, he can do anything he wants to, and I bet if he wanted to be a bricklayer he could build a house as easy as making a birdcage!'

'I can promise you, niece,' Don Quixote replied, 'that if thoughts of chivalry did not engage all my faculties, there would be nothing I would not make, no knick-knack I would not manufacture, in particular birdcages and toothpicks.'

Someone knocked on the door, and when they asked who it was the reply came from Sancho Panza; and the housekeeper ran away to hide, to avoid seeing him, so great was her hatred for the man. The niece opened the door, his master Don Quixote walked out to greet him with open arms and the two of them shut themselves up in his room, where they had another conversation, in no way inferior to the previous one.

CHAPTER VII

About Don Quixote's conversation with his squire,
and other famous events

The instant the housekeeper saw Sancho Panza shutting himself away with his master in his room she knew what they were up to, and supposed that the result of their discussion would be a decision to go off on a third sally; grief-stricken, she threw on her cloak and hurried away in search of the young graduate Sansón Carrasco, believing that being an eloquent man and her master's latest friend he'd be able to persuade him to desist from this act of folly. She found Carrasco strolling about his courtyard, and she threw herself at his feet, sweating with anguish. When he saw her in such sorrow and distress, he said:

'What's this, my dear housekeeper? What can have happened to make you look as if your very soul were being torn out of you?'

'Oh, Señor Carrasco sir, just that my master's breaking out, he's breaking out for certain!'

'And what is he breaking out through, madam?' Sansón enquired. 'Has a hole appeared in some part of his body?'

'What he's breaking out through,' she replied, 'is the gaping gate of his madness. What I mean to say, dear Señor Carrasco sir, is that he wants to go off again, for the third time, and wander around the world trying his fortune, as he puts it, though I can't understand how anyone can call it that. The first time, they brought him home draped over a donkey and beaten black and blue. The second time, he came back on an ox-cart, locked in a cage, thinking he was enchanted, and in such a state, poor fellow, that his own mother wouldn't have known him: thin, pale, his eyes sunk back into the depths of the attics of his brain, and it's cost me more than six hundred eggs to get him into some sort of shape again, as God knows and everyone else knows, too, as well as my hens, who'll confirm what I'm saying.'

'I can well believe it,' the young graduate replied, 'because they're such good hens, so plump and well-bred, that they'd die rather than fail to tell the truth. In short, my dear housekeeper, nothing worse has happened and there have been no greater disasters than the one it's feared Don Quixote has in mind?'

'That's right, sir,' she replied.

'Don't you worry, then,' the graduate replied, 'just hurry back home and make me something hot for my lunch, and on the way you can be saying St Apollonia's prayer if you know it; I'll soon join you, and then you'll witness miracles.'

'Oh dear me!' the housekeeper replied. 'You're telling me to say St Apollonia's prayer? That'd be fine if there was something wrong with my master's teeth, but his problem's in his brain-box.'

'I do know what I'm saying, my dear housekeeper; so off you go, and don't start arguing with me – you know I'm a BA from Salamanca, and you can't be much more of a BA than that,' Carrasco replied.

And with this the housekeeper left, and the young graduate went in search of the priest, to tell him what will be recorded in due course.

While Don Quixote and Sancho were shut up together, they engaged in the conversation that the history relates in truthful detail. Sancho said to his master:

'I've had a word with the wife, sir, and she's designed to letting me go wherever you want to take me.'

'*Resigned* is what you should say, Sancho,' said Don Quixote, 'not *designed.*'

'If I remember rightly,' Sancho replied, 'I've already asked you once or twice not to correct my words, if you understand what I mean by them – and if you don't understand, you can always say, "Sancho, you devil, I don't understand you," and if I still don't make my meaning clear you can correct me, because I'm so practible . . .'

'I don't understand you, Sancho,' Don Quixote interrupted. 'I don't know what *I'm so practible* means.'

'So practible,' Sancho replied, 'means that's just the way I am.'

'And now I understand you even less,' Don Quixote replied.

'If you don't understand me,' Sancho replied, 'I don't know what else to say – that's all I do know, so help me God.'

'Now I see your meaning!' Don Quixote replied. 'What you intend to say is that you're so tractable, pliant and docile that you will accept everything I say, and learn whatever I teach you.'

'I bet,' said Sancho, 'you knew exactly what I meant from the start, but you wanted to ruffle me so as to make me put my foot in it another few hundred times.'

'That may well be so,' Don Quixote replied. 'But tell me, what does Teresa say?'

'What Teresa says,' said Sancho, 'is I should watch my step with you, and let papers speak and beards stay still, and he who shuffles doesn't cut, and a bird in the hand is worth two in the bush. And what I say is that a woman's advice is seldom given and a man would be mad not to take it.'

'And that is what I say, too,' replied Don Quixote. 'Speak on, Sancho my friend; do continue, you are in sparkling form today.'

'The fact is,' said Sancho, 'that as you know better than I do we're all mortal beings, here today gone tomorrow, and the lamb goes to the spit as soon as the sheep, and nobody can count on living longer than God lets him, because death is deaf and when he comes knocking at the door of our life he's always in a hurry and nothing will stop him, no not pleas nor struggles nor sceptres nor mitres, as everyone knows only too well and as the priests up in their pulpits keep telling us.'

'That is all very true,' said Don Quixote, 'but I cannot fathom what you are driving at.'

'What I'm driving at,' said Sancho, 'is that I want you to settle some fixed wages that you'll pay me every month so long as I serve you, and I want you to pay these wages out of your regular income, because I don't want to depend on gifts and favours, they come too late, or get damaged on the way, or never arrive at all, and God help each of us to what is rightly his. In a nutshell, however much or however little I'm earning I want to know what it is, because it only takes one egg to get a hen to lay, and many a little makes a mickle, and something is always better than nothing. It's true that if you do give me that island you've promised me, which I don't believe or expect you ever will, I'm not so ungrateful or so worried about a farthing or two here or there that I'd oppose the income from the island being totted up and stopped from my wages, in due abortion.'

'Sometimes, friend Sancho,' Don Quixote replied, 'a *proportion* might be preferable to an *abortion*.'

'Yes, I know what you mean,' said Sancho. 'I bet I ought to have said proportion not abortion – but it doesn't matter you see, because you understood me.'

'And I understood you so well,' Don Quixote replied, 'that I penetrated into the innermost recesses of your thoughts, and I know what target you are firing at with the countless arrows of your proverbs. Look, Sancho, I should be most willing to establish a fixed wage for you if I had found in any of the histories of knights errant any example that could give me the slightest indication of what squires used to earn monthly or yearly; but I have read all or at least almost all their histories, and I do not recall ever reading that any knight errant did establish fixed wages for his squire. I only know that all squires were rewarded for their service with gifts, and that when they were least expecting it – if their masters had been blessed with good fortune – they found themselves rewarded with an island or something similar and, at the very least, were given a title and an estate of some sort. If with these expectations and perquisites you wish to return to my service, Sancho, you are most welcome to do so; but to imagine that I am going to unsettle and disrupt the ancient customs of knight-errantry is to imagine the unimaginable. And so, my dear Sancho, you go back home and inform Teresa of my intentions, and if she is happy for you to serve me for gifts, and you are happy to do so, *bene quidem,*[1] and, if not, we remain friends; for so long as the pigeon loft does not lack food, it will not lack pigeons. And remember, my son, that a good hope is better than a bad holding, and a good grievance is better than bad compensation. I am talking like this, Sancho, to show you that I, too, can rain proverbs. And finally I should like to say, and I shall say, that if you are unwilling to depend on my bounty and accept your share of my fortunes, then God go with you and make a saint of you; I shall not be short of squires who are more obedient, more solicitous, less clumsy and less talkative than you.'

When Sancho heard his master's firm decision his sky clouded over and the wings of his heart drooped down, because he'd believed that his master wouldn't depart without him for all the riches in the world; and as Sancho stood there, lost in the bewilderment of his thoughts, Sansón Carrasco came in with the housekeeper and the niece, who were anxious to hear how the young graduate was going to persuade their master not to go off again in search of adventures. The famous jester Sansón came up to Don Quixote and embraced him as he had the first time, and proclaimed:

'O flower of knight-errantry! O resplendent light of arms! O honour and mirror of the Spanish nation! May it please God Almighty, in all his infinite goodness and wisdom, that the person or persons who would impede or prevent your third sally may never extricate themselves from the muddled maze of their murky musings, and never accomplish their evil desires.'

And turning to the housekeeper, he added:

'You can stop saying the prayer of St Apollonia, madam: I know that it is the precise determination of the heavenly spheres that Don Quixote shall again put into execution his original and lofty designs; and it would be a heavy burden on my conscience if I did not urge and exhort this knight no longer to restrain and still the strength of his mighty arm and the valour of his brave heart, because his inactivity is depriving wrongs of their righting, orphans of their succour, maidens of their honour, widows of their consolation and wives of their solace, and other problems of this sort that affect, concern, depend and are incumbent upon the order of knight-errantry. Come, my dear Don Quixote sir, so fair and so brave: sooner rather than later you must set off again in all your greatness and splendour, and if anything is wanting for the execution of your resolve, here am I to provide it in my person and my estate; and if it were necessary for me to serve Your Excellency as your squire, I should count it the greatest of good fortune to do so!'

And here Don Quixote, turning to Sancho, put in:

'Did I not tell you, Sancho, that I should have squires to spare? Look who is offering himself for the position: no less than the extraordinary bachelor of arts Sansón Carrasco, the perpetual frolicker and entertainer of the quadrangles of the colleges of Salamanca, sound in body, agile of limb, quiet, long-suffering in heat and in cold, in hunger and in thirst – all the qualities needed to be a knight errant's squire. But heaven forbid that merely for my own pleasure I should demolish the column of letters and shatter the vase of science and fell the lofty palm of the fair and liberal arts. Let this new Samson[2] stay in his own country, and in honouring it honour the grey hairs of his aged parents, for I shall be content with any squire that comes to hand, given that Sancho does not deign to accompany me.'

'Yes I do deign,' Sancho replied, with tender tears welling up into his eyes. 'Nobody's going to say of me, dear master, that I bite the hand that feeds me – no, I don't come from an ungrateful breed, and the whole world knows, particularly in the village, what the Panzas I descend from have always been like – and what's more I've realized thanks to your many good deeds and even better words how keen you are to do me favours, and if I haggled just now about my wages it was only to please the wife, because once she puts her hand to getting you to do something, there isn't a mallet that tightens the hoops on a barrel as tight as she tightens the screws to make you do what she's set her mind on, but when all's said and done a man must be a man and a woman a woman, and since I'm a man wherever I am and I can't deny it, I'm going to be a man in my own house as well whoever objects, so all that's got to be done is for you to draw up your will complete with codicil so it can't be resinned, and let's get under way to stop Señor Carrasco's heart from breaking, saying as he does say that his conscience is telling him to tell you to go out into the world for a third time, and I'll renew my offer to serve you faithfully and loyally, as well as any squire ever served a knight errant in past or present times, or better.'

The young graduate was astonished to hear how Sancho Panza expressed himself, because even though he'd read the first volume of his master's history he'd never believed that Sancho was as funny as he's depicted there; but when he heard him talk about a will and codicil that couldn't be resinned instead of a will and codicil that couldn't be rescinded, he believed everything he'd read about him, and set him down as one of the greatest simpletons of modern times, and thought to himself that two such madmen as this master and servant could never have been seen before on the face of the earth. Finally Don Quixote and Sancho embraced and were friends again, and, with the approval and blessing of the great Carrasco, now their oracle, it was agreed that they would set out three days later, which gave them time to prepare what they needed for the journey and to look for a helmet with a visor, because Don Quixote declared that he was going to wear one of these, come what might. Sansón offered him one, because he knew that a friend of his who owned it wouldn't refuse to let him have it, even though it wasn't so much brilliant with the splendour of burnished steel as murky with the rust and mould festooning it.

Countless were the curses that the two women, niece and housekeeper, heaped on the young graduate: they tore their hair, clawed their faces and, in the style of those hired mourning-women who once used to accompany funerals, they lamented their master's departure as if it were his death. Sansón's reason – on the advice of the priest and the barber, with whom he'd discussed his plan – for encouraging Don Quixote to sally forth again is stated later in this history.

In short, in the course of those three days Don Quixote and Sancho equipped themselves with what they considered necessary, and, once Sancho had placated his wife and Don Quixote had assuaged his niece and his housekeeper, they started out at nightfall for El Toboso, unseen by anyone except the young graduate, who rode out with them for a mile or two; Don Quixote was mounted on his good Rocinante, Sancho on his usual dun with its saddle-bags well-stocked with comestibles and with the purseful of money that Don Quixote had given him to provide against any eventuality. Sansón embraced Don Quixote and begged to be sent news of his fortunes, both good and bad, to rejoice at the latter or grieve over the former, as the laws of friendship required. Don Quixote promised to do so, Sansón returned to the village and the other two rode on towards the great city of El Toboso.

CHAPTER VIII

Which relates what happened to Don Quixote when he was on his way to visit his lady Dulcinea del Toboso

'Blessed be almighty Allah!' says Hamete Benengeli at the beginning of this eighth chapter. 'Blessed be Allah!' he repeats three times, and he says that he's uttering these blessings because Don Quixote and Sancho are in the field again at last; and the readers of his delightful history can reckon that at this point the exploits and capers of Don Quixote and his squire begin: he asks them to forget all about the ingenious hidalgo's earlier knightly deeds and look out for those that are yet to come, starting here on the road to El Toboso just as the others started on the plain of Montiel, and he isn't asking much in comparison with what he's promising; and so he continues:

Don Quixote and Sancho were left alone, and no sooner had Sansón left them than Rocinante began to neigh and the dun to let loose sonorous sighs, something that both men, knight and squire, considered to be a good sign and a most happy omen; although, if the truth is to be told, the dun's sighing and braying exceeded the nag's neighing, from which

Sancho deduced that his own good fortune was going to surpass his master's, perhaps basing his opinion on some system of judicial astrology known to him, although the history doesn't say anything about this; he'd only been heard to comment that when he stumbled or fell he wished he'd never left home, because from stumbling or falling all he ever gained was a torn shoe or broken ribs – and in this, fool though he was, he wasn't far wrong. Don Quixote said:

'Sancho my friend, night is coming on faster and darker than suits our plans if we are to reach El Toboso by daybreak, and that is where I have resolved to go before embarking on any more adventures, to receive a blessing and gracious leave from the peerless Dulcinea, for with this her leave I intend to, and indeed consider it certain that I shall, bring any perilous adventure to a happy conclusion; because nothing in this life makes knights errant more courageous than being favoured by their ladies.'

'That's what I think, too,' replied Sancho, 'but you might find it hard to talk to her or see her, anywhere at least where she can give you her blessing, unless she lets you have it over the yard wall, where I saw her the first time, when I took her the letter about the antics and mad deeds I left you doing in the heart of the Sierra Morena.'

'Did you imagine that it was a yard wall, Sancho,' said Don Quixote, 'where or over which you saw her never sufficiently praised grace and beauty? No, it must have been balconies or galleries or porticos, or whatever it is that they are called, of splendid regal chambers.'

'It might have been any of all that,' Sancho replied, 'but to me it looked more like a yard wall, unless my memory's playing me up.'

'We shall go there, Sancho, nonetheless,' Don Quixote replied, 'for so long as I see her it is all the same to me whether I do so over a wall or through a window, or through the chink of a door or through the railings around a garden – for any ray that reaches my eyes from the sun of her beauty will enlighten my mind and strengthen my heart, so that I shall be unique and unequalled in intelligence and in courage.'

'Well, the honest truth is, sir,' Sancho replied, 'that when I saw that sun of the lady Dulcinea del Toboso it wasn't bright enough to give out any rays, and it must have been because she was sieving that wheat I mentioned, and all the dust she was raising floated up in front of her face and clouded it over.'

'So you still persist, Sancho,' Don Quixote said, 'in saying, thinking, believing and asserting that my lady Dulcinea was sieving wheat, even though this is a task and an activity far removed from everything that is done and indeed can be done by persons of quality, who are made and reserved for other activities and amusements that reveal their rank from a mile away! You seem to have forgotten, O Sancho, those verses by our Spanish poet in which he depicts the tasks performed in their crystal dwellings by those four nymphs whose heads emerged from their beloved River Tagus and who then sat in the verdant meadow to work those rich cloths that the imaginative poet describes, all woven and adorned with gold and silk and pearls![1] And my lady's labours when you saw her must have been of this sort, but the envy that some evil enchanter must feel for all my affairs transforms all things that can give me pleasure into shapes quite unlike their real ones; and so I fear that if perchance the author of the history of my exploits that is said to be in print is some hostile sage, he has no doubt altered everything, mingling a thousand lies with one truth, and straying from his subject to recount actions foreign to what is required by the narration of a true history. O envy, the root of countless evils, and the tapeworm of virtue! Every other vice, Sancho, offers some sort of pleasure, but envy brings only grief, hatred and rage.'

'That's just what I say, too,' Sancho replied, 'and it's my belief that in that reading-book or history about us that young Sansón Carrasco told us he'd seen, my honour must be dragged through the dirt and kicked from one end of town to the other, as they say. Well, I can swear as an honest man that I've never said a bad word about any enchanter, and I'm not rich enough for anybody to envy me – it's true I'm a bit of a sly old fox and I can be something of a villain at times, but it's all covered over by the broad cloak of my simple-mindedness, which is always natural, never affected. And even if my only good point was that I believe, as I do, firmly and faithfully in God and in everything the Holy Roman Catholic Church believes, and that I'm a mortal enemy, as I am, of all Jews, that should be enough to make the historians take pity on me and treat me well in their writings. But they can say what they like, because naked was I born and naked I remain so neither lose nor gain, though so long as I'm in books and being handed round the world from one person to another I don't care a fig about whatever they want to say about me.'

'That seems to me, Sancho,' said Don Quixote, 'rather like what happened to a famous poet of our time,[2] who wrote a malicious satire against all courtesans but did not include or name a certain lady about whom it could be doubted whether she was one of them or not; and seeing that she wasn't on the list she complained to the poet, asked what he thought was wrong with her to make him fail to include her with the others, and told him to extend his satire and put her into the extension – and if not, he'd better watch out for himself. The poet did what she had demanded, and threw mud at her to his heart's content, and she was well pleased to find herself famous for being infamous. Another relevant story is the one about the shepherd who set fire to the celebrated temple of Diana, one of the seven wonders of the world, and razed it to the ground, so that his name would live in future ages; and even though it was ordered that he should never be named and no mention should ever be made of him in speech or in writing, to prevent him from achieving his aim, it emerged that he was called Erostratus. Also relevant is the story about the great Emperor Charles V and a certain gentleman in Rome. The Emperor went to visit the Rotunda, which in antiquity was called the temple of all the gods and is now better dedicated, to all the saints, and is the best-preserved building of all those that were erected in pagan Rome, the one that most fully evinces the grandeur and magnificence of its founders. It takes the form of half an enormous orange, and it is brilliantly lit, even though the only light comes in through a window or rather a round lantern at the top, from which the Emperor surveyed the building by the side of a Roman gentleman who detailed all the subtlety and skill of that splendid construction and that memorable architecture; and when they had descended from the lantern, this gentleman said to the Emperor:

'"A thousand times, Most Sacred Majesty, I felt the urge to clasp you in my arms and hurl myself down with you from that lantern, to win eternal fame for myself."

'"I am grateful to you," the Emperor replied, "for not having put so wicked a thought into execution, and henceforth I shall avoid placing you in a position which is such a test for your loyalty: so I command you never to speak to me again, and never to be where I am."

'And with these words he made him a handsome present.

'What I am saying, Sancho, is that the desire for fame is a powerful motivator. What was it, do you think, that cast Horatius down from the bridge, wearing full armour, into the depths of the Tiber? What put Mucius's hand and arm to the fire? What impelled Curtius to hurl himself into the gulf of flames that opened up in the middle of Rome?[3] What, in the face of all the adverse omens, made Caesar cross the Rubicon?[4] And to turn to more recent examples, what scuttled the ships and left the brave Spaniards led by courteous Cortés stranded and isolated in the New World?[5] All these and many other great deeds were, are and shall be the work of fame, desired by mortals as the reward, the taste of immortality, that their exploits earn for them, even though we knights errant, Christian and Catholic, must be more concerned with the glory of the life to come, to be enjoyed throughout eternity in the ethereal and celestial regions, than with the vanity of the fame that can be achieved in this present transient life; for this fame, however long it lasts, will end when the world ends, at the time appointed. And so, O Sancho, our works must not stray beyond the limits imposed by the Christian religion that we profess. In slaying giants, we must slay pride; in our generosity and magnanimity, we must slay envy; in our tranquil demeanour and serene disposition, we must slay anger; in eating as little as we do and keeping vigil as much as we do, we must slay gluttony and somnolence; in our faithfulness to those whom we have made the mistresses of our thoughts, we must slay lewdness and lust; in wandering all over the world in search of opportunities to become famous knights as well as good Christians, we must slay sloth.[6] Here, Sancho, you have the means by which the high praise brought by fame can be achieved.'

'Everything you've said so far,' said Sancho, 'I've understood very well, but all the same I'd like you to dissolve one doubt that's just found its way into my head.'

'*Resolve* is what you mean to say, Sancho,' said Don Quixote. 'You are most welcome to ask, and I shall reply as best I can.'

'If you could please tell me, sir,' Sancho continued: 'all those Julys or Augusts, and all those deed-doing knights you said, all of them dead – where are they now?'

'The pagan ones,' Don Quixote replied, 'are obviously in hell, and the Christian ones, if they were good Christians, are either in purgatory or in heaven.'

'Very well,' said Sancho, 'but now you tell me this: those tombs where the bodies of all those bigwigs lie, have they got silver lamps in front of them, and are the walls of their chapels festooned with crutches, shrouds, wigs, and legs and eyes of wax? And if not, what are they festooned with?'

To which Don Quixote replied:

'The tombs of the pagan ones were for the most part sumptuous temples: Julius Caesar's ashes were placed on top of a vast stone obelisk now known in Rome as St Peter's Needle; the Emperor Hadrian had as his tomb a castle as large as a sizeable village that was named *Moles Hadriani* and is now the castle of St Angelo, in Rome; Queen Artemisia buried her husband Mausolus in a tomb that was considered to be one of the seven wonders of the world; but none of these tombs or any of the many others constructed for pagans were decorated with shrouds or other offerings or signs indicating that those buried in them were saints.'

'That's what I'm driving at,' Sancho replied. 'So now you tell me this: what's better, bringing a corpse back to life, or killing a giant?'

'The answer is as plain as day,' replied Don Quixote. 'It is better to bring the dead back to life.'

'And now I've got you,' said Sancho. 'From that it follows that the fame of the man who brings the dead back to life, gives sight to the blind, gets the lame walking and makes the sick healthy, and who has lamps burning in front of his tomb and his chapel full of devout folk on their knees adoring his relics, must be a better sort of fame, for this world and for the next, than all the fame of all the pagan emperors and knight errants there ever were and ever will be on the face of the earth.'

'I confess that there, again, you are right,' Don Quixote replied.

'Since the bodies and the relics of saints,' Sancho replied, 'have got this fame, this grace, this prerogative as it's called, and with the approval and permission of our Holy Mother Church they have lamps, candles, shrouds, crutches, paintings, wigs, eyes and legs that strengthen people's devotion and spread their own Christian fame, and kings carry the bodies of saints or their relics on their shoulders, kiss bits of their bones, bedeck their oratories and spruce up their favourite altars with them . . .'

'What do you want me to infer, Sancho, from all this you have just said?' said Don Quixote.

'What I'm trying to say,' said Sancho, 'is let's go in for being saints, and then we'll get the good reputation we're after much sooner – and remember, sir, only yesterday or the day before, it was such a short time ago you could put it like that, they canonized or else beatified two poor discalced friars, and already it's thought very lucky to touch and kiss the iron chains they girded and tormented their bodies with, and, as I just said, they're more venerated than Roland's sword in the armoury of our lord the King, God keep him. So you see sir, it's better to be a humble little friar of any order than a brave knight errant, and as far as God's concerned a couple of dozen strokes of the lash are worth more than a couple of thousand thrusts of the lance, whether given to giants, monsters or dragons.'

'That is all true,' Don Quixote replied, 'but we cannot all be friars, and many are the roads along which God leads his people to heaven; chivalry is a religion, and there are knights who are saints in glory.'

'Yes,' said Sancho, 'but I've heard there are more friars than knight errants in heaven.'

'That,' replied Don Quixote, 'is because the number of the religious is greater than the number of knights.'

'There are plenty of errants,' said Sancho.

'Yes,' replied Don Quixote, 'but few who deserve to be called knights.'

They spent that night and the following day in these and other similar conversations, and nothing worth mentioning happened to them, which caused Don Quixote no little distress. Finally, at nightfall, they espied the great city of El Toboso, a sight that made Don Quixote's spirits rise and Sancho's sink, because he didn't know which was Dulcinea's house, and had never seen her in his life, any more than his master had; so they were both anxious, one to see her and the other at not having seen her, and Sancho had not the faintest idea what he was going to do when his master sent him into El Toboso. In the end Don Quixote decided to enter the city by night, so they waited in an oak-wood close to El Toboso, and when the time came they rode into the city, where events befell them that were events indeed.

CHAPTER IX

In which is related what will be found in it

'Twas on the stroke of the midnight hour,[1]

or vaguely thereabouts, when Don Quixote and Sancho rode out of the wood and into El Toboso. The village lay in a tranquil silence, because all the inhabitants were sleeping like logs, as the saying goes. It was a moonlit night, even though Sancho would have preferred it to be a pitch-black one, so as to find in the darkness some excuse for his stupidity. Dogs barked and barked throughout the village, thundering in Don Quixote's ears and convulsing Sancho Panza's heart. Every so often a donkey would bray, pigs would grunt, cats would mew, and this multiplicity of noises was intensified by the silence of the night, all of which was taken by the enamoured hidalgo as a bad omen; yet in spite of that he said:

'Sancho my son: lead me to Dulcinea's palace; it is possible that we might find her awake.'

'What palace am I supposed to lead you to, for God's sake?' Sancho replied. 'Where I saw her highness was only a little tiny house.'

'That must have been,' replied Don Quixote, 'because she had retired to some secluded building in her castle grounds to relax alone with her maidservants, as is the custom of ladies of rank and princesses.'

'Look, sir,' said Sancho, 'if in spite of everything I say you will have it that my lady Dulcinea's house is a castle, is this a likely time, do you think, to find the door open? Will it be a good idea to go banging on the door to wake everybody up and make them let us in, raising a rumpus and setting tongues wagging? Have we come here by any chance to go off to the local brothel like regular customers who arrive and bang on the door and are allowed in however late it is?'

'Let us first and foremost find the castle,' Don Quixote replied, 'and then I shall tell you, Sancho, what it will be right for us to do. And look, Sancho, either my eyes are deceiving me or that great mass of shadow you can see over there must be Dulcinea's palace.'

'Well, you lead me there then,' Sancho retorted. 'Maybe you're right, but even if I see it with my own two eyes and touch it with my own two hands I'll believe it as much as I believe it's midday at this moment.'

Don Quixote led the way, and after they'd advanced a couple of hundred paces he reached the great mass of shadow and saw that it was a tall tower, and immediately realized that the building was no castle but the parish church. And he said:

'We have chanced upon the church, Sancho.'

'So I see,' Sancho replied. 'And God grant we don't chance upon our graves as well, because it isn't a good omen to be traipsing about churchyards at this time of night, and besides I've already told you, if I remember rightly, that this lady's house must be down some blind alley.'

'God damn you, you fool!' said Don Quixote. 'Wherever did you get the idea that royal castles and palaces are built down blind alleys?'

'Well, sir,' Sancho replied, 'every land has its own ways, and maybe here in El Toboso they're in the habit of sticking palaces and other big buildings down blind alleys, so I'd ask you to let me have a look down these streets or alleys here – who knows, I might find that bloody castle tucked away in some corner, and a plague on it for harassing us and making us traipse up and down like this.'

'Speak with respect, Sancho, when speaking of matters concerning my lady,' said Don Quixote, 'and do not spoil our party, or throw the helve after the hatchet.'

'Yes, I'll control myself,' Sancho replied, 'but how am I supposed to put up with you expecting me to recognize our mistress's house straight away and find it at midnight, when I've only seen it once and you yourself can't find it after the thousands of times you must have seen it?'

'You will drive me to despair, Sancho,' said Don Quixote. 'Look here, you heretic: have I not told you over and over again that in all the days of my life I have never seen the peerless Dulcinea, and have never crossed the threshold of her palace, and am enamoured only by hearsay of her fame as a beautiful and intelligent lady?'

'I heard you this time,' Sancho replied, 'and I'd just like to say that since you've never seen her, nor have I.'

'That cannot be,' replied Don Quixote. 'There is, at least, the time you said you saw her sieving wheat, when you brought back the reply to that letter you took to her from me.'

'Don't you take any notice of that, sir,' Sancho replied. 'I'd like you to know that seeing her and bringing back her answer was all done by hearsay, too – I've got as much idea of who the lady Dulcinea is as of how to punch the sky.'

'Sancho, Sancho,' Don Quixote replied, 'there is a time for joking and a time when joking is inappropriate and out of place. My saying that I have neither seen nor spoken to the lady of my life is no reason for you also to say that you have neither spoken to her nor seen her, when, as you know, the truth is the very opposite.'

As they chatted away like this they saw approaching them a man with two mules who, from the racket made by the plough as it dragged along over the ground, they assumed was a farm-hand who must have got up before dawn to go to his work in the fields, and they were right. The farm-hand was singing that doleful ballad that goes:

> An evil day it was, you French,
> The day of Roncesvalles.[2]

'I'll be damned, Sancho,' Don Quixote said as soon as he heard him, 'if any good fortune is coming our way tonight. Can't you hear what that peasant is singing?'

'Yes, I can hear him,' Sancho replied, 'but what's the Roncesvalles rout got to do with what we're up to? He might as well be singing the ballad of Calaínos[3] for all the difference it'd make to whether we manage to do what we want to do or not.'

The farm-hand came up to them, and Don Quixote said:

'God bless you and bring you good fortune, my friend. Can you tell me whether the palace of the peerless princess Dulcinea del Toboso is to be found hereabouts?'

'Look, sir,' the young man replied, 'I'm a stranger in these parts, and I've only been in the village a few days working in the fields for a rich farmer. But the village priest and sexton live in this house right here in front of us, and either of them will be able to inform you about that princess lady, because they've got the list of all the inhabitants of El Toboso, though it's my belief that there isn't any princess living anywhere here – lots of ladies there are, very fine ones too, and each one of them can be a princess in her own house.'

'Well, among them, my friend,' said Don Quixote, 'must be the lady about whom I am enquiring.'

'Could be,' the young man replied, 'and goodbye, dawn's on its way.'

And slapping his mules forward, he didn't wait for any further questions. Seeing that his master was perplexed and disgruntled, Sancho said:

'Sir, day's coming on apace and it won't be a good idea for us to be seen out here in the street when the sun rises, so it'll be better if we leave the city and you hide away in some nearby wood, and then I'll come back by day and search every single nook and cranny in this place for my lady's house or castle or palace, and I'd be very unlucky not to find it, and once I do find it, I'll talk to her and tell her where and in what a state you're waiting for her so as to arrange a meeting without harming her honour and good name.'

'You have spoken, Sancho,' said Don Quixote, 'a thousand wise maxims within the space of a few words; I welcome the advice that you have given me, and I accept it most willingly. Come, my son, let us look for somewhere for me to hide, and you shall return, as you have just said, to search for my lady and find her and talk to her, and from her good sense and courtesy I hope to receive miraculous, nay more than miraculous favours.'

Sancho was dying to get his master out of the village so that he couldn't discover the lie about Dulcinea's reply, taken back by him to the Sierra Morena; and so Sancho ensured that their departure was a hasty one, and two miles from the village they found a grove or wood, where Don Quixote hid while Sancho went back to the city to talk to Dulcinea, and during this mission he met with adventures that demand fresh attention and fresh credit.

CHAPTER X

Which describes Sancho's cunning enchantment of the lady
Dulcinea, and other events as ridiculous as they are true

As the author of this great history reaches the events that he narrates in
this chapter, he says that he'd have preferred to pass over them in silence,
fearing he wouldn't be believed, because here Don Quixote's mad deeds
approached the limits of the imaginable, and indeed went a couple of
bowshots beyond them. But in the end, and in spite of these fears and
misgivings, he described those deeds exactly as they happened, without
adding or subtracting one atom of truth or concerning himself with any
accusations that might be made that he was lying; and he was right to
do so, because the truth might be stretched thin but it never breaks, and
it always surfaces above lies, as oil floats on water.

And so, continuing his history, he says that as soon as Don Quixote
had hidden in the glade, wood or oak-grove close to El Toboso, he
ordered Sancho to return to the city and not to appear in his presence
again without having spoken on his behalf to his lady and besought her
to be so gracious as to grant her hapless knight an audience and deign
to bestow her blessing on him, so that he could hope for the greatest
success in all his undertakings and difficult enterprises, thanks to her.
Sancho agreed to do exactly as he was told, and to bring back as good
a reply as he had brought back the first time.

'On your way, then, my friend,' replied Don Quixote, 'and do not be
plunged into confusion when you find yourself in the presence of the
light of the sun of beauty that you are now going to seek. Happy are you
above all the squires in the world! Stay alert, and make sure that you do
not fail to observe the way in which she receives you: whether her colour
changes as you deliver my message; whether she seems disturbed or
disquieted on hearing my name; whether her cushion seems not to be
able to hold her, if perchance you find her seated upon the rich dais
proper to her dignity – and if she is standing, watch her to see whether
she shifts her weight from one foot to the other; whether she repeats her
answer maybe two or three times; whether she changes it from a kind

one to a harsh one, or from a cruel one to a loving one; whether she raises her hand to her hair to pat it into place, even though it is not untidy; and in short, my son, watch her every action, her every movement, because if you tell me about them I shall deduce how she feels in the most secret places of her heart about my love for her; for I would have you know, Sancho, if you do not know it already, that the external actions and movements made by lovers while the conversation concerns their love are messengers between them giving totally reliable accounts of what is happening in their souls. So off you go, my friend, and may better fortune than mine guide you and send you a happier outcome than that which I, here in this my bleak solitude, fear and expect.'

'Yes, I'm going, and I'll soon be back,' said Sancho. 'And do try and stop that poor little heart of yours from shrinking so, it must be about the size of a hazel nut by now, and remember what they say, a good heart conquers ill fortune, and where there isn't any bacon there aren't any hooks to hang it from and, as they also say, the hare leaps up where you least expect it to. I'm only mentioning all this because if we didn't find my lady's palace or castle last night, now it's daytime I do intend to find it, when I'm least expecting to, and once I've found it, you just leave her to me.'

'This I will say, Sancho,' said Don Quixote. 'I do hope that God gives me even better fortune in my aspirations than you have in choosing proverbs appropriate to our discussions.'

After this, Sancho turned away and gave his dun the stick, and Don Quixote was left sitting on his nag, resting in his stirrups and leaning on his lance, overwhelmed by sorrowful and confused musings, where we shall leave him and go off with Sancho Panza, who was no less pensive and bewildered than his master; so much so, that he was hardly out of the wood when, looking back and seeing that Don Quixote was no longer in sight, he climbed off his donkey, sat down at the foot of a tree, and began to talk to himself and to say:

'Pray be so good as to tell us, brother Sancho, where it is that you're going. To look for some donkey that you've lost? No, most certainly not. So what are you looking for? Oh, I'm just going to look for some princess, that's all, the sun of beauty and the whole of heaven in one person. And where do you expect to find all that, Sancho? Where? In the great city of El Toboso. Very well, and on whose behalf are you going to look for her? On behalf of the famous knight Don Quixote de la Mancha, who rights wrongs and gives food to the thirsty and drink to the hungry. That is all most commendable. And do you know where she lives, Sancho? My master says she must live in a royal palace or a splendid castle. And have you ever seen her by any chance? Neither me nor my master have ever clapped eyes on the woman. And do you think it would be right and proper for the men of El Toboso, if they found out that you're here intending to spirit away their princesses and raise a rumpus among their ladies, to come and give you such a going-over that they didn't leave a bone unbroken in your body? Yes, they'd be in the right, unless they bore in mind that I'm just an errand-boy, and

> You're but a messenger, my friend,
> You don't deserve the blame.[1]

No, you can't rely on that, Sancho, because the people of La Mancha are as hot-tempered as they're honourable, and they won't let anyone play around with them. God Almighty, if they suspect what you're up to, I can promise you a bad time of it! No, you can get lost, Old Nick, you're not catching me in a hurry! Oh yes, I'm going to go stirring up a hornet's nest for the sake of somebody else's pleasure, I am! What's more, looking for Dulcinea in El Toboso would be like looking for a student in Salamanca or a girl called María in Madrid. Yes, yes, it was the devil, the devil and nobody else that got me into this mess!'

The result of Sancho's soliloquy was that he talked to himself again, and said:

'On the other hand, there's a remedy for all things but death, under whose yoke we must all pass, like it or not, at the end of our lives. I've seen a thousand signs that this master of mine is a raving lunatic, and I'm not much better myself, because I'm even stupider than he is, following him and serving him as I do, if there's any truth in the proverb that says a man is known by the company he keeps, and that other one about birds of a feather flocking together. So him being as he is mad, and with a madness that usually makes him take one thing for another and think that white is black and black is white, as anyone could see when he said that those windmills were giants, and those friars' mules were dromedaries, and those flocks of sheep were enemy armies, and all sorts of other stuff like that, it won't be all that difficult to make him believe that some peasant girl, the very first one I come across, is lady Dulcinea – and if he doesn't believe it I'll swear she is, and if he swears she isn't I'll swear she is again, and if he insists I'll insist even more, and so I'll make sure I always have the last word, come what may. Maybe by insisting like this I'll make him stop sending me off on all these errands, seeing what a mess I make of them – or on the other hand maybe he'll think, as I expect he will, that one of those evil enchanters that he says hate him so much has changed her looks to spite him and do him harm.'

These thoughts calmed Sancho's breast, and he counted the business as good as settled; and he waited where he was until the afternoon, to leave enough time for Don Quixote to believe that he'd gone to El Toboso and come back; and events fell out so well for him that when he got up to climb on his dun he saw three peasant girls coming towards him from El Toboso on three jackasses, or she-asses, because the author isn't explicit on this point, though it's more likely that they were she-asses, this being what peasant girls usually ride on; but since it doesn't matter much one way or the other, there's no need to stop to elucidate the matter. So, to cut a long story short, as soon as Sancho saw the peasant girls he rode back to his master Don Quixote as fast as he could go, and found him sighing and breathing a thousand amorous laments. When Don Quixote saw Sancho he said:

'What news, Sancho my friend? Can I mark this day with a white stone or with a black stone?'[2]

'It'll be best,' Sancho replied, 'for you to mark it in bright red paint, like new professors' names on college walls, so that everyone who sees it sees it clearly.'

'That means,' said Don Quixote, 'that you bring good news.'

'Such good news,' Sancho replied, 'that all you've got to do to find the lady Dulcinea del Toboso is to clap spurs to Rocinante and ride out of the wood – she's on her way with two of her maids to see you.'

'Good God! What are you saying, friend Sancho?' said Don Quixote. 'You had better not be deceiving me, or attempting to beguile my real grief with false joy.'

'What would I gain from deceiving you?' Sancho replied, 'specially now I'm so close to showing you the truth of what I'm saying. Just get your spurs into action, sir, and come with me, and you'll see the princess, our mistress, on her way here, dressed and bedecked just like what she is. She and her maids are all one blaze of flaming gold, all spindlefuls of pearls, they're all diamonds, all rubies, all brocade more than ten levels deep, with their hair flowing over their shoulders like sunbeams playing with the wind, and what's more each of them's riding her piebald poultry, a sight for sore eyes.'

'I think you mean *palfrey*, Sancho.'

'There isn't that much of a difference,' Sancho replied, 'between poultry and palfrey, but whatever they're riding they're looking as spruce and ladylike as you could ever wish, specially my lady Princess Dulcinea – she fair takes your breath away, she does.'

'Let us go, Sancho my son,' Don Quixote said, 'and as a reward for this news, as splendid as it is unexpected, I hereby promise you the best spoils I win in the first adventure that I undertake, and if this does not satisfy you I promise you all the foals born this year to my three mares: as you know, they are awaiting the happy event on the village green.'

'I'll take the foals,' replied Sancho, 'because it isn't too clear that the spoils of the first adventure are going to be that brilliant.'

As he said this, they emerged from the wood and saw the three peasant girls not far away. Don Quixote surveyed the road to El Toboso, and since all he could see was these three peasants he became alarmed and asked Sancho if the ladies had been outside the city when he'd left them.

'What do you mean, outside the city?' Sancho replied. 'Do you keep your eyes in the back of your head or something, to stop you from seeing that they're these ladies here, shining like the very sun at noon?'

'All I can see, Sancho,' said Don Quixote, 'is three peasant girls on three donkeys.'

'God save my soul from damnation!' Sancho replied. 'Is it possible for three palfreys or whatever they're called, as white as the driven snow, to seem to you like donkeys? Good Lord, I'd pull out every single hair on my chin if that was true!'

'Well, I am telling you, friend Sancho,' said Don Quixote, 'that it is as true that they are asses, or maybe she-asses, as it is that I am Don Quixote and you are Sancho Panza; or at least this is how it seems to me.'

'Hush, sir,' said Sancho, 'you mustn't talk like that – open those eyes of yours and come and do homage to the lady of your life, now she's so close at hand.'

And as he said this he rode forward to greet the three peasant girls, and, dismounting from his dun, he seized one of their asses by the halter, fell to his knees and said:

'O queen and princess and duchess of beauty, may your highness and your mightiness be pleased to receive into your grace and goodwill this your hapless knight, standing over there like a marble statue, all flustered and flummoxed at finding himself in your magnificent presence. I am his squire Sancho Panza, and he is the harassed knight Don Quixote de la Mancha, also known as the Knight of the Sorry Face.'

Don Quixote had by now knelt at Sancho's side and was staring with clouded vision and bulging eyes at the woman whom Sancho called queen and lady; and since all he could see there was a peasant girl, and not a very pretty one at that, because she was moon-faced and flat-nosed, he was dumbstruck and didn't dare open his mouth. The peasant girls were equally astonished, at the sight of such an ill-assorted pair kneeling in front of one of them and impeding her progress. But she broke the silence and spoke with neither goodwill nor grace:

'Get out of the bloody way and let us through, we're in a hurry!'

To which Sancho replied:

'O princess and universal lady of El Toboso! How is it that your magnanimous heart is not melted by the sight of the column and foundation of knight-errantry kneeling here in your sublimated presence?'

When one of the other girls heard this, she said:

'Come to cast pearls before swine, have we? Look at these fine gents trying to make fun of us village girls, as if we didn't know how to take the piss as well! You two go on your way, and let us go on ours, if you want to stay in one piece.'

'Arise, Sancho,' Don Quixote put in. 'I can see that fortune, not content with my sufferings, has blocked all the roads along which some happiness might have come to this wretched soul contained within my flesh. And you, O perfection of all the excellence that the heart can desire, acme of human courtesy, the sole remedy of this afflicted heart that adores you: even though the malicious enchanter is hounding me, and has placed clouds and cataracts over my eyes, and for them alone and not for other eyes has altered and transformed your face of peerless beauty into that of some poor peasant wench, I beg you – so long as he has not also changed my face into that of some monster, to make me abominable in your sight – not to refuse to look on me with gentleness and love, seeing in my position of submission and prostration before your disguised beauty the self-humiliation of my soul's adoration.'

'Hark at old grandad!' the village girl replied. 'Don't I just love oily eyewash like that! Come on, shift over and let us through, thank you very much.'

Sancho shifted over and let her through, delighted to have extricated himself from that particular muddle. As soon as the peasant girl who'd played the part of Dulcinea found herself free she prodded her poultry with a nail on a stick that she was carrying and it broke into a canter across the field. And feeling the nail, which annoyed it more than usual, it started to prance and buck, and dumped Lady Dulcinea among the daisies; Don Quixote rushed to pick her up and Sancho hurried to put the pack-saddle, which had slipped round under the ass's belly, back into place. Once Sancho had done this, Don Quixote went to lift his enchanted lady in his arms and place her on the ass; but the lady saved him the trouble by jumping to her feet, taking a couple of strides backwards, bounding up to the ass, bringing both hands down on to its rump and vaulting, as swift as a falcon, on to the pack-saddle, where she sat astride as if she were a man; and then Sancho said:

'By holy St Roch, our lady and mistress is nimbler than a hobby-hawk, and she could teach the best rider from Cordova or Mexico how to jump on to a horse Arab-style! Over the crupper she went in one leap, and without any spurs she's making her palfrey gallop like a zebra. And her maids aren't being outdone, they're going like the wind, too.'

And Sancho was right, because once Dulcinea was mounted the other two girls spurred after her, not turning their heads back for more than a mile. Don Quixote pursued them with his gaze, and when they were out of sight he turned to Sancho and said:

'Sancho, what is your opinion about this grudge that the enchanters bear me? You can see how far their malice and hatred extend, for they have deprived me of the joy that I could have experienced on beholding my lady in her true being. I was indeed born to be a mirror of misfortune, the eternal target for the arrows of adversity. And you should also note, Sancho, that those traitors were not content just to transform my Dulcinea, but had to transform her into a figure as wretched and ugly as that peasant wench, and at the same time they took away from her what is so characteristic of fine ladies, the sweet smell that they derive from living among ambergris and flowers. Because I would have you know, Sancho, that when I went to replace Dulcinea on her palfrey (as you call it, although I thought it was a donkey), I was half suffocated by a blast of raw garlic that poisoned my very soul.'

'Oh you miserable wretches!' Sancho burst out. 'Oh you fateful and spiteful enchanters, I'd like to see you all hanging by your gills like pilchards on a string! Aren't you clever, aren't you powerful and aren't you bloody well active! You ought to have been happy, you villains, with turning those eyes of pearl of my lady's into oak-apples, and her tresses of purest gold into hairs from the tail of a sorrel ox, and, all in all, every one of her features from good to bad, without messing about with her smell, too – from her smell we'd at least have been able to work out what was hidden under that ugly outside although, to tell you the truth, I never did see her ugliness but only her beauty, which was boosted no end by a mole she had on the right side of her lip, a bit like a moustache, with seven or eight blond hairs like threads of gold growing out of it, more than a handsbreadth long.'

'According to the rules of correspondence between facial moles and bodily moles,' said Don Quixote, 'Dulcinea must have another mole on the thick of the thigh on the same side as the one on her face; but hairs of the length that you have indicated are very long indeed for moles.'

'Well, I can tell you,' Sancho replied, 'they were there all right, just as if she'd been born with them.'

'I believe you, my friend,' replied Don Quixote, 'because nature has given Dulcinea nothing that is not complete and perfect; and so, if she had a hundred moles like the one you have described, on her they would not be moles but moons – resplendent moons and shining stars. But tell me, Sancho, the object that seemed to me like a pack-saddle, which you straightened for her – was it an ordinary saddle or a lady's saddle with arms?'

'It was nothing less than a great tall Arab-style saddle,' Sancho replied, 'with a saddle-cloth so precious it's worth half a kingdom.'

'And to think that I could not see any of that, Sancho!' said Don Quixote. 'I say it again, and I shall say it a thousand times: I am the most unfortunate of men.'

The sly rogue Sancho had his work cut out to hide his laughter as he listened to the nonsense being blurted by his master, whom he had deceived with such finesse. In the end, after the two had talked for a good while longer, they remounted and followed the road that led towards Saragossa, where they planned to arrive in time for the solemn festivities held each year in that famous city. But before they arrived certain things happened to them, so many, so important and so strange, that they deserve to be written and read about, as will be seen in what follows.

CHAPTER XI

About the strange adventure undergone by the valiant
Don Quixote with the cart or wagon of the Parliament
of Death

Don Quixote was plunged into dejected thought as he went on his way, considering the bad joke that the enchanters had played on him by turning his lady Dulcinea into the vile shape of a peasant wench, and he couldn't imagine what might be done to turn her back into herself; and he was so carried away by these thoughts that, not knowing what he was doing, he dropped the reins, and Rocinante made the most of the liberty he was being given to stop at every step to munch the green grass that was plentiful in those fields. Sancho Panza roused Don Quixote from his reverie by saying:

'Look here sir, sorrows weren't made for animals but for men, yet if men let themselves be too affected by their sorrows they turn into animals – so you snap out of it and come to your senses, and pick up Rocinante's reins, and wake up and cheer up and show some of the dash and spirit that knight errants are supposed to show. What the devil's the meaning of this? Why be down in the dumps like this? You're a brave Spaniard you know, not some feeble Frenchman. Satan can take all the Dulcineas in the world – the well-being of just one knight errant is worth more than all the enchantments and transformations on the face of the earth.'

'Hold your tongue, Sancho,' replied Don Quixote, in not particularly languishing tones. 'Hold your tongue I say, and do not utter blasphemies against that enchanted lady; for I alone am to blame for her dire misfortune: her sad plight springs from the envy that the wicked bear me.'

'That's just what I'm saying,' Sancho replied. 'To see her now having seen her then, brings tears to the eyes of the hardest of men.'

'You may well say that,' replied Don Quixote, 'because you beheld her in the fullness of her beauty: the enchantment did not extend to clouding your vision or hiding her loveliness from you, for its powerful venom is directed only against me and my eyes. There is, however, one point that has occurred to me: the description you gave me of her beauty was inaccurate because, if I remember rightly, you said that her eyes were pearls; but the eyes that look like pearls are the eyes of a codfish, not the eyes of a lady, and it is my belief that Dulcinea's eyes must be green emeralds, almond eyes with rainbows for eyebrows; so you had better move those pearls from her eyes to her teeth, because it is clear that you have mistaken one thing for another, Sancho, and confused teeth with eyes.'

'That could well be,' Sancho replied, 'because her beauty stunned me as much as her ugliness flummoxed you. But we'd better leave it all in God's hands, because he's the great knower of everything that's going to happen in this vale of tears, in this wicked world of ours where there's hardly a thing that isn't besmirched by evil, deceit and villainy. There's just one thing I'm worried about, sir, more than about all the others, which is that I don't know what's going to happen when you defeat some giant or some other knight, and you order him to go and present himself before the beauteous lady Dulcinea – where's this poor giant or poor wretched defeated knight going to find her? I can see them now, wandering all over El Toboso like dummies, searching for my lady Dulcinea, and even if they bump into her in the middle of the street they won't know her any more than they'd know my father.'

'It is possible, Sancho,' Don Quixote replied, 'that the enchantment does not extend as far as removing recognition of Dulcinea from defeated and presented giants and knights; and so we shall experiment on one or two of the first of these whom I defeat and send to her, and then discover whether they find her or not, by ordering them to return and give me an account of what happens to them in this respect.'

'For myself, sir,' Sancho replied, 'I think that's a very good idea, a ruse that'll tell us all we want to know – and if it turns out that it's only you she's hidden from, it'll be more your loss than theirs, but then so long as the lady Dulcinea is happy and well, us two will sort ourselves out and enjoy ourselves as best we can, searching for our adventures and leaving time to do his work – he's the best doctor for this and other worse illnesses.'

Don Quixote was about to reply to Sancho Panza, but he was interrupted by a cart crossing the road in front of them, loaded with the most varied and extraordinary personages imaginable. Driving the mules and acting as carter was a hideous demon. The cart was open, without any sides or awning. The first figure that presented itself to Don Quixote's gaze was Death itself, but with a human face; next to it there was an angel with enormous many-coloured wings; to one side there was an emperor with a crown, seemingly of gold, on his head; at Death's feet was the god they call Cupid, without any bandage over his eyes but with his bow, quiver and arrows. There was also a knight in full armour, except that he wasn't wearing a helmet or even a morion, but instead a hat stuck with many-coloured feathers; and there were other personages with different clothes and faces. When all this suddenly appeared, Don Quixote was somewhat ruffled, and fear was struck into Sancho's heart; but Don Quixote was immediately cheered by the belief that here was some new and perilous adventure, and with this thought in mind, and his spirit ready to confront any danger, he planted himself in front of the cart and cried with menace in his voice:

'Carter, coachman or devil or whatever, tell me this very instant who you are, where you are going and who these people are whom you carry in this contraption of yours, which looks more like Charon's boat[1] than the sort of cart one usually encounters.'

To which the devil, stopping his cart, meekly replied:

'We, sir, are actors in Angulo el Malo's company; today being the last day of the Corpus Christi celebrations, we performed *The Parliament of Death*[2] this morning in a village behind that hill, and this afternoon we're going to perform it again in that other village you can see over there, and, since they're so close to each other and to save the trouble of undressing and dressing again, we're travelling in our costumes. That lad there is Death, that other one's an Angel; that woman, the manager's wife, is the Queen, that other man's a Soldier, that one's the Emperor and I'm the Devil, and I'm one of the play's protagonists, because in this company I play the main parts. If there's anything else you'd like to know about us, just ask, and I'll give you a detailed answer, because being as I am the Devil nothing's hidden from me.'

'On my faith as a knight errant,' Don Quixote replied, 'when I saw this cart I imagined that it heralded some great adventure, and now I do declare that appearances must be examined closely to discover the hidden truth. God be with you, good people, and go and celebrate your festivities, but first consider whether there is any way in which I can be of service to you; I shall do so with a joyful spirit and a happy heart, for as a boy I loved Thalia, and as a young man I could not tear my eyes away from Melpomene.'[3]

While they were talking, fate ordained that another member of the company should catch up with them dressed as a clown, with bells all over him, and a stick with three inflated cow-bladders tied to one end; and the clown, coming up to Don Quixote, began to brandish his stick and beat the ground with his bladders and leap into the air with a great jangling of his bells, and this horrendous sight so frightened Rocinante that Don Quixote was powerless to prevent him from taking the bit between his teeth and racing across the fields at a greater speed than would have been expected from his rickety skeleton. Seeing that his master was in imminent danger of being thrown, Sancho jumped off his dun and rushed to his aid; but by the time he arrived his master was already on the ground with Rocinante lying by his side, the two of them having fallen together – the usual conclusion to Rocinante's deeds of derring-do. But no sooner had Sancho leapt from his mount to help Don Quixote than the dancing devil with the bladders jumped on to it and began belabouring it with them, and the combination of fear and noise, more than the pain from the bladder-blows, made it race across the fields too, towards the village where the festivities were going to be held. Sancho gazed after his racing dun and then at his fallen master, and he didn't know which of the two necessities to attend to first. But he was a good squire and a good servant, and his love for his master prevailed over his affection for his donkey, even though every time he saw the bladders rise in the air and fall upon its haunches he felt the anguish and terrors of death, and he'd sooner have had those blows fall on his own open eyes than on one hair of his donkey's tail. Caught in this tribulation of perplexity he came up to where Don Quixote lay, more battered than he would have liked, and as he helped him back on to Rocinante he said:

'Sir – the devil's taken the dun.'

'What devil?' Don Quixote asked.

'The one with the bladders,' Sancho replied.

'Well, I shall recover it,' Don Quixote said, 'even if he locks himself up with it in the deepest and darkest dungeons of hell. Follow me, Sancho: the cart is slow, and with those mules I will make good the loss of the dun.'

'There isn't any need to go to those lengths, sir,' Sancho replied. 'Calm down – from what I can see, the devil's let the dun go now and it's coming back to its old quarters.'

And Sancho was right, because the devil and the dun had taken a tumble in imitation of Don Quixote and Rocinante, and the devil walked back to the village and the donkey returned to its master.

'All the same,' Don Quixote said, 'it will be as well to punish somebody on the cart for the devil's audacity, even maybe the emperor himself.'

'You put that idea right out of your head,' Sancho retorted, 'and take my advice, which is never to fight play-actors, they're a protected species. I've known of actors arrested for a couple of murders and let off without even paying costs. They're a cheerful crowd and they amuse people, you see, so everybody looks after them, everybody protects them and helps them and likes them, even more so if they belong to one of the official companies – from the way most of them dress and behave anyone would think they were all princes.'

'Despite all you say,' Don Quixote replied, 'that devil of an actor shall not walk away from here bragging, even if the whole human race protects him.'

And so saying he rode back towards the cart, which was by now close to the village. He was crying:

'Stop, wait, you merry and joyful mob: I intend to teach you how to treat donkeys and other such creatures that serve the squires of knights errant as mounts.'

Don Quixote shouted so loud that the people in the cart heard and understood him and, conjecturing his intentions from his words, out jumped Death followed by the Emperor, the Devil with the reins, and the Angel, with the Queen and Cupid not far behind, and they all armed themselves with stones and formed up in a line waiting to give Don Quixote a sharp-edged welcome. When Don Quixote saw this gallant squadron, arms raised in readiness to hurl the stones at him, he drew rein and paused to consider how to attack with least danger to his person. As he did so Sancho trotted up and, seeing him about to attack the well-organized squadron, said:

'It'd be really mad to try that. Just remember, sir, there's no protection in the world against the very nasty dose of gravel rash they can give you, except crawling in under a great big bell of solid bronze – and another thing you must bear in mind is that it's more foolhardy than brave for one man alone to attack an army that's got death on its side, as well as emperors fighting in person, and good and bad angels helping out, and if that thought doesn't make you hold back, maybe this will – you can be certain that even though there might be kings, princes and emperors among them, there isn't a single knight errant there.'

'Yes indeed, Sancho,' said Don Quixote, 'there you have hit upon the consideration that can and must sway me from the course of action which I had decided to take. I cannot and must not draw my sword, as I have so often informed you, against anyone who has not been knighted. This is your responsibility, Sancho, if you wish to take revenge for the affront suffered by your dun; and I shall remain here and assist you by cheering you on and offering you helpful advice.'

'There won't be any need, sir,' replied Sancho, 'to take revenge on anybody, because good Christians shouldn't go avenging themselves for affronts, and what's more I'll get my ass to leave its revenge to my discretion – and all I want is to live in peace and quiet for as long as heaven spares me.'

'Since that is your decision,' Don Quixote replied, 'good Sancho, wise Sancho, Christian Sancho, honest Sancho, let us leave these phantoms and return to our quest for better and worthier adventures, because by the look of it this country cannot fail to provide us with many most marvellous ones.'

He turned Rocinante, Sancho went to fetch his dun, Death and his flying squad returned to their cart and went on their way, and this was the happy ending to the dreadful adventure of the Cart of Death, thanks to the sound advice that Sancho Panza gave his master, who on the following day had another adventure, with an enamoured knight errant, which was no less amazing than this one.

CHAPTER XII

*About the valiant Don Quixote's strange adventure with
the brave Knight of the Spangles*

Don Quixote and his squire spent the night following the skirmish with death in a clump of tall, shady trees; but first, Sancho persuaded Don Quixote to eat some food from the supply on the dun's back, and during the supper Sancho said:

'Sir, how stupid it'd have been of me to choose as my reward the spoils from your first adventure instead of the foals from your three mares! Yes, yes, it's true what they say – a bird in the hand is worth two in the bush.'

'All the same,' replied Don Quixote, 'if you had allowed me to attack, Sancho, as I wished, you would have received as spoils at least the Empress's gold crown and Cupid's many-coloured wings, for I should have torn them off his back and placed them in your hands.'

'Sceptres and crowns of playhouse emperors,' Sancho retorted, 'are never made of pure gold, but of tin or tinsel.'

'You are right there,' Don Quixote replied, 'and indeed it would not be appropriate for stage finery to be precious and real: it must be counterfeit and illusory, like drama itself, with which I should like you, Sancho, to be on the best of terms, as you must also, in consequence, be with actors and dramatists, because they are all instruments with which great benefits are conferred on society, holding up to us at every step a mirror in which we can see the actions of human life most vividly portrayed; for there is no more realistic representation of what we are and what we are going to be than plays and players. Or else tell me this: have you never seen a play that includes kings, emperors and popes, gentlemen, ladies and other different characters? One actor plays the pimp, another plays the liar, this one the merchant, that one the soldier, another the fool who is wise, another the lover who is a fool; but once the play is over and they remove their costumes, all the players are equals.'

'Yes, I've seen a play like that,' Sancho replied.

'Well, the same happens,' said Don Quixote, 'in the play of this life, in which some act as emperors, others as popes and, in short, all the characters that there can be in a play; but when it is over, in other words when life ends, death strips them all of the costumes that had distinguished between them, and they are all equals in the grave.'

'That's a fine comparison,' said Sancho, 'only not so very original that I haven't heard it about a hundred times before, the same as that other one about the game of chess – so long as the game lasts, each piece has its own special job to do, but once the game is over they all get jumbled up together and put into a bag, which is the same as life ending in the grave.'

'With every day that passes by, dear Sancho,' said Don Quixote, 'you lose some foolishness and gain some sense.'

'Yes, some of your good sense is bound to stick on to me,' Sancho replied. 'Soil that left to itself would be poor and sterile gives good yields when you manure it and you till it. What I'm trying to say is that being with you is the manure that's been spread over the barren soil of my poor wits, and the tilling is all this time I've been with you, serving you, so I'm hoping to give wonderful yields that won't be unworthy to be piled up beside the paths of good breeding that you've trodden over this feeble understanding of mine.'

Don Quixote laughed at Sancho's affected talk, and thought that what he'd said about his own improvement was true, because he occasionally spoke in a way that amazed his master; even though usually when Sancho held forth in a scholarly and courtly manner his argument ended up by plummeting from the heights of his simplicity into the depths of his ignorance; but where he showed his elegance and his memory to the greatest advantage was in adducing proverbs, whether or not they had anything to do with the subject in hand, as will have been noticed in the course of this history.

They spent much of the night talking away like this, and then Sancho felt the urge to drop the sluice-gates of his eyes, as he said when he wanted to go to sleep, and undressing his dun he turned it loose to graze on the lush pasture. He didn't unsaddle Rocinante, because he'd received express orders from his master that when they were in the field and sleeping without any roof over their heads he must not do any such thing: it was an ancient usage established and observed by knights errant to remove the bridle and hang it from the pommel of the saddle, but remove the saddle itself? Never! And so Sancho obeyed, and gave Rocinante the same liberty that he'd given the dun, whose friendship with the nag was so very close that there is a traditional belief, handed down from father to son, that the author of this true history wrote chapters on this very subject but, to preserve the propriety and decorum due to such a heroic history, suppressed them, even though on occasions he forgets himself and says that as soon as the two animals were together they'd start scratching each other, and that when they were tired and had had their fill of this Rocinante would lean his neck over the dun's (it stuck out more than half-a-yard on the other side), and the two would stay in this position, staring at the ground, for three days, or at least for as long as they were allowed, or for as long as hunger didn't force them to go in search of food. I was about to say that it's said that the author had written that he'd compared their friendship to that of Nisus and Euryalus, and to that of Pylades and Orestes;[1] and if this is so it must have been evident, for universal admiration, how firm was the friendship between these two peaceful animals, to the shame of men, who are so bad at preserving friendship. This is why somebody once said:

> There's no love lost between dear friends:
> The game of canes becomes a mortal battle;

and then there's the other song:

> From friend to friend the bug is passed, etc.[2]

And nobody must think that the author was rather mistaken to compare the friendship of these animals to that of men, because men have received many lessons from animals and learned from them much that is important, for example: from storks, the enema; from dogs, emetics and gratitude; from cranes, watchfulness; from ants, providence; from elephants, chastity; and loyalty from the horse.[3]

Sancho finally fell asleep at the foot of a cork-oak, and Don Quixote dozed at the foot of a stout evergreen oak; but before very long he was awakened by a noise that he heard behind him, and he started up and looked and listened in the direction of the noise, and he saw that it came from two men on horseback, and that one of them, sliding down from his saddle, said to the other:

'Dismount, my friend, and unbridle the horses – it seems to me that this place provides all the grass that they can want, and all the silence and solitude that I can need for my thoughts of love.'

As he said this he stretched himself out on the ground to the creaking of the armour he was wearing, a clear sign to Don Quixote that this must be a knight errant; and tiptoeing over to the sleeping Sancho he seized him by the arm and, with some difficulty, brought him to his senses, and whispered:

'Brother Sancho, an adventure looms.'

'God make it a good one,' Sancho replied. 'And where might this precious adventure of yours be found, dear sir?'

'Where might it be found, Sancho?' Don Quixote replied. 'Just look over there, and you will see a knight errant lying on the ground, not, as far as I can tell, a particularly happy one, because I saw him throw himself from his horse and stretch himself out with all the appearance of despair, and as he dropped his armour creaked.'

'And how can you tell,' asked Sancho, 'that this here is an adventure?'

'I am not saying,' Don Quixote said, 'that this is a full adventure, but rather the beginnings of one, for that is how adventures start. But listen: it seems he is tuning a lute or a viol and, to judge from his way of spitting and clearing his throat, he must be making himself ready to sing.'

'You're right, he is,' Sancho replied, 'so he must be a knight in love.'

'There is no knight errant who is not in love,' said Don Quixote. 'Let us listen to him, because if he does sing we shall be able to judge the skein of his thoughts from the thread of his song; for the tongue speaks out of the fullness of the heart.'[4]

Sancho was about to reply to his master, but the voice of the Knight of the Forest, which was neither a very good voice nor a very bad one, prevented him, and the pair of them listened in amazement as they heard that what he sang was this sonnet:

> Tell me, my lady, which must be the way
> For me to live my life as you decree,
> And then my steadfast steps shall never stray
> From where your sovereign will dispatches me.
> If you want me to silence all my woe
> And die, your slightest word shall seal my fate;
> If you want me to find new ways to show
> My grief, Love shall himself the tale relate.
> Withstanding contradictions is my role,
> A man of softest clay and hardest stone;
> The laws of love administer my soul:
> Both soft and hard, my breast is all your own.
> You stamp or carve whatever you like there:
> There it will stay eternally, I swear.

With a sigh torn, as it seemed, from the very bottom of his heart, the Knight of the Forest ended his song, and after a pause he added in tones of the profoundest grief:

'O most beauteous ingrate on the face of the earth! How is it possible, most serene Casildea de Vandalia,[5] that you should allow this your hapless knight to waste away and perish in endless pilgrimages and in cruel and bitter labours? Is it not enough that I have had you acknowledged as the most beautiful woman in the world by all the knights of Navarre, of León, of Andalusia, of Castille, and finally by all the knights of La Mancha?'

'That is untrue,' Don Quixote whispered at this point, 'because I am of La Mancha and I have never acknowledged any such thing, nor could I or should I acknowledge anything so injurious to my lady's beauty; so you can see, Sancho, that this knight is delirious. But let us continue to listen: perhaps he will reveal some more of his thoughts.'

'He'll do that all right,' Sancho replied. 'It looks as if he's going to moan away for a month non-stop.'

But this didn't happen, because the Knight of the Forest had heard people talking and, cutting his lamentation short, he stood up and said in booming and courteous tones:

'Who goes there? Who is it? Are you perchance numbered among the happy, or among the afflicted?'[6]

'Among the afflicted,' Don Quixote replied.

'Then come unto me,' said the Knight of the Forest, 'and you will see that you are coming unto sadness and affliction itself.'

Given such an affectionate and courteous answer, Don Quixote came unto him, and even Sancho came unto him too. The lamenting knight seized Don Quixote by the arm, and said:

'Sit here, sir knight; for to know that you are a knight, and one of those who profess the order of knight-errantry, it is sufficient to have found you in this place, accompanied by solitude and by the damp night air, the natural bed and appropriate abode for a knight errant.'

To which Don Quixote replied:

'A knight I am, and of the order which you have mentioned; and although my soul is the seat of sorrow, misfortune and disaster, this has not banished from it the compassion which I feel for the misadventures of others. From what you stated a little earlier I gather that your misadventures are amorous ones: that is to say that they concern your love for the beautiful ingrate whom you named in your lament.'

By now they were sitting side by side on the hard ground, in peace and good fellowship, just as if when day broke they wouldn't be busy breaking each other's heads.

'Are you by any chance in love, sir?' the Knight of the Forest asked Don Quixote.

'I am, by an evil chance,' Don Quixote replied, 'although the sufferings that spring from well-placed affections should be considered as favours rather than as catastrophes.'

'You are right,' replied the Knight of the Forest, 'if disdain, which in excess can seem like revenge, did not muddle our thinking and our understanding.'

'I have never been disdained by my lady,' Don Quixote retorted.

'Certainly not,' said Sancho, standing near by, 'because my lady's as meek as a little lamb and softer than a pat of butter.'

'Is this fellow your squire?' asked the Knight of the Forest.

'He is,' answered Don Quixote.

'I have never,' replied the Knight of the Forest, 'seen a squire daring to speak while his master is speaking. This is true, at least, of my squire, who is old enough to be this man's father, and nobody will be able to prove that my squire has ever opened his mouth while I was speaking.'

'Well, just let me tell you this,' said Sancho, 'I've spoken before now and I can speak any time in front of any old . . . but I'd better leave it at that, because the more you stir it the worse it gets.'

The Squire of the Forest seized Sancho by the arm and said:

'Let's clear off, just the two of us, to somewhere we can have a nice squirely chat about whatever takes our fancy, and leave these masters of ours to their story-telling contests about the histories of their loves – depend upon it, day will dawn and they still won't have done.'

'I'll say yes to that,' said Sancho, 'and I'll tell you all about me, and you'll soon see whether or not I can hold my own with the most talkative squires there are.'

And off the two squires went, and they had a conversation as funny as their masters' was grave.

CHAPTER XIII

Which continues the adventure of the Knight of the Forest,
with the intelligent, novel and genial conversation that
took place between the two squires

Knights and squires had split up, the squires telling each other of their lives and the knights of their loves; but the history relates first the squires' conversation and then comes that of their masters, and so it says that after they'd moved a little way off, the Squire of the Forest said to Sancho:

'This is a wearisome life that we lead, sir, us squires of knight errants:

we really do eat our bread in the sweat of our faces, which is one of the curses that God laid on our first parents.'[1]

'You could also say,' Sancho added, 'that we eat it in the ice of our bodies, because who puts up with more heat and more cold than us poor squires of knight-errantry? It wouldn't be so bad if we got a bite to eat, because in all kinds of grief bread brings us relief, but there are times when we go for a day or for two days without ever breaking our fast with anything more than the wind that blows in our faces.'

'But you can stand all that,' said the Squire of the Forest, 'when you've got hopes of a prize, because if the knight errant you're serving isn't too unlucky, at least you'll be rewarded after a few adventures with a handsome governorship of some island, or a good-looking earldom.'

'As for me,' Sancho replied, 'I've told my master that I'll be happy with being the governor of an island, and he's so noble and generous that I don't know how many times he's promised me one.'

'As for me,' said the Squire of the Forest, 'I'll be well satisfied with a canonry for my services, and my master has already promised me one – and what a canonry it is, too!'

'Your master,' said Sancho, 'must be a churchly knight who can do favours of that sort to his deserving squires, but mine's just a lay one, though I do remember a time when certain clever but to my mind spiteful people were advising him to try and become an archbishop, even though he'd decided to be an emperor, and I was in fear and trembling that he might take it into his head to go into the Church, because I don't think I'm up to holding down a benefice – let me tell you, I might look like a man but I'd be an ass in the Church.'

'Well you're really making a mistake there,' said the Squire of the Forest, 'because not all island governorships are in good shape. Some of them are deformed, others are poor, others are depressed, and even the most straight-backed and best-disposed of them brings a heavy burden of worry and discomfort to the shoulders of the unfortunate man to whose lot it falls. It would be much better for those of us who are in this accursed service to go back home and amuse ourselves there with gentler activities, like for example hunting or fishing; for what squire is there in the world so poor that he hasn't got a hack, a couple of greyhounds and a fishing-rod to amuse himself with in the village?'

'I'm not short of any of that,' Sancho replied. 'It's true I haven't got a hack, but then I've got a donkey that's worth twice as much as my master's horse. God send me miserable fiestas, the very next ones there are, if I'd do a swap with him even if I got four bushels of barley thrown in on top. You must think I'm joking about what my dun's worth – that's my donkey's colour, dun. And greyhounds wouldn't be a problem, there's plenty of them in the village, and hunting's much more fun when it's at somebody else's expense.'

'To tell you the honest truth, squire,' the Squire of the Forest replied, 'I've made up my mind to turn my back on all these capers of these here knights, and to go back to my village, and to bring up my children – I've got three of them, like three pearls of orient.'

'I've got two,' said Sancho, 'fit to be presented to the Pope in person, specially a daughter I'm bringing up to be a countess, God willing, though her mother isn't.'

'And how old is this young lady who's being brought up to be a countess?' asked the Squire of the Forest.

'She's fifteen, give or take a couple of years,' Sancho replied, 'but she's as tall as a lance, and as fresh as an April morning, and as strong as a market porter.'

'With those assets,' replied the Squire of the Forest, 'she could be not just a countess but a very nymph of the greenwood. Oh the little whore, what muscles the little bastard must have on her!'

To which Sancho replied, somewhat peeved:

'She isn't a whore and nor is her mother and, God willing, neither of them ever will be while I'm still alive. And you'd better watch your language – considering you were brought up among knight errants, who are courtesy itself, I don't think those words of yours were in very good taste.'

'How little you know,' replied the Squire of the Forest, 'about the language of compliments, squire! Are you really not aware that when one of the horsemen in the bullring deals the bull a good lance-thrust, or when anyone else does something with great skill, people say: "He's a clever bastard, look how well the bugger did that!" and what might seem like insults are, in this setting, high praise? And you should disown, my dear sir, any sons and daughters who don't do deeds that earn praise like that for their parents.'

'Yes I do disown them,' Sancho replied, 'and at that rate you can pour the contents of a whole whore-house on top of me and my wife and children, because everything they do and say is second to none and well worthy of such praises, and to be able to see them again I pray God to deliver me from mortal sin, in other words from this dangerous job of squire that I've fallen into for the second time, tempted and tricked by a purse with a hundred ducats in it that I found one day in the heart of the Sierra Morena – and now the devil keeps dangling a bag full of doubloons in front of my eyes here and there and everywhere, and with every step I take I seem to be touching it and clutching it to my breast and taking it home and buying property to lease and rent out and living like a king, and when I'm thinking about this it's easy to put up with all my toils and sufferings with this fool of a master of mine who I well know is more of a madman than a knight.'

'That,' the Squire of the Forest replied, 'is why they say that greed breaks the sack; and, talking about madmen, there isn't a worse one in the whole world than my master, because he's one of those that make people say "It's other folks' burdens that break the ass's back": he's pretending to be mad for the sake of helping another knight who's lost his reason to regain it, and he's looking everywhere for what I'm not sure he's going to like the taste of once he finds it.'

'And is he in love by any chance?'

'Yes,' said the Squire of the Forest, 'he's in love with a certain Casildea de Vandalia, the chastest and most chased lady on the face of this earth; but at the moment it isn't the chastity that's on his mind, he's got other even worse nonsense rumbling away inside him, as we shall all see before very long.'

'There's no road so smooth,' Sancho replied, 'that there aren't a few potholes in it, and life is all toil and trouble and for me double, and madness keeps a greater retinue than good sense. But if it's true what they say, that it helps to share your problems, I'll find comfort in you, because you're serving a master who's just as stupid as mine.'

'Stupid, but valiant,' replied the Squire of the Forest, 'and even more villainous than either.'

'Mine isn't like that,' Sancho replied. 'I mean to say he isn't at all villainous, he's as innocent as the babe unborn, he couldn't hurt a fly, he only wants to do good to everyone, and there isn't an ounce of malice in him – a child could make him believe it's midnight at noon, and it's because he's so simple that I love him from the bottom of my heart, and can't bring myself to leave him, however many silly things he does.'

'That's all very well, brother,' said the Squire of the Forest, 'but if the blind lead the blind[2] they're both in danger of falling into the ditch. It'll be better for us to clear off at a good lively trot, and return to where we belong, because those that go in search of adventures don't always find them to their liking.'

Every so often Sancho spat out some sort of dry and sticky saliva, of which the charitable forestal squire took due note, and he said:

'It seems to me we've been talking so much that our tongues are sticking to the roofs of our mouths; but I've got something hanging from my saddle-bow that will be very good at unsticking them.'

He rose to his feet and returned a moment later with a great leather bottle full of wine and a pie half-a-yard square, which is no exaggeration because it had been made with a white rabbit so successfully fattened that as Sancho felt it he took it for not just a kid but a full-grown goat; and then Sancho said:

'This is the sort of food you always carry, sir?'

'So what did you take me for, then?' the other replied. 'Do you think I'm any old run-of-the-mill squire? No, I carry better provisions on the back of my horse than any general takes when he goes off on his campaigns.'

Sancho didn't need to be asked twice to tuck in, and down went mouthfuls of food the size of hobble-knots, in the dark of the night. And he said:

'Now you really are a faithful and loyal squire, always ready and willing, generous and bountiful, as this here banquet shows, because if it hasn't been brought to us by a magic spell it certainly looks as if it has. You aren't like me, a miserable wretch who hasn't got anything in his saddle-bags except a lump of cheese that's so hard you could split a giant's skull with it, with a few dozen carob beans for company, and about the same number of hazel nuts and walnuts, thanks to my master's slender means and the idea he's got and the rule he follows that knight errants mustn't eat anything apart from nuts and herbs.'

'On my faith, brother,' the Squire of the Forest replied, 'I haven't got a stomach for thistles or wild pears or roots. Let our masters bother their heads with their ideas and laws of chivalry, and eat whatever they like. I carry my own food boxes and this leather bottle hanging from my saddle-bow, just in case I have need of it; and I'm so devoted to it and I love it so dearly that I smother it with hugs and kisses all day long.'

And as he said this he handed it to Sancho, who put it to his mouth, tilted it, gazed at the stars for a quarter of an hour and, when he'd finished drinking, dropped his head on one side, heaved a deep sigh, and said:

'That little bastard's a drop of the real stuff all right!'

'Don't you see,' said the Squire of the Forest when he heard Sancho's *bastard*, 'how you praised the wine by calling it a bastard?'

'I will admit,' said Sancho, 'that I confess that I do recognize that it isn't dishonourable for somebody to be called a bastard, when it comes under the heading of meaning to praise him. But tell me, sir, by all that's dearest to your heart – this is Ciudad Real wine, isn't it?'

'What an expert!' replied the Squire of the Forest. 'That's exactly where it's from, and it's a good few years old, too.'

'You don't need to tell me that!' said Sancho. 'I suppose you weren't expecting someone like me not to be able to put my finger on it. What a fine thing it is, squire, to have a flair like mine for spotting wines, such a great and natural flair that you've only got to let me smell one and I can tell you the place, the pedigree, the taste and the vintage, and how it's going to mature, and all the other details appertaining! But that's no wonder, because two of my forebears on my father's side were the finest judges of wine that La Mancha has known for many a long year, and as a proof of that I'm going to tell you about what happened to them once. The two of them were given some wine from a barrel to taste, and asked for their opinion about its condition and quality – whether it was good wine or bad. One of them tasted it with the tip of his tongue, and all the other did was lift it to his nose. The first one said the wine tasted of iron, and the second one said it tasted more of Cordovan leather. The winemaker said that the barrel was clean, and that nothing had been added to the wine to make it taste of either iron or leather. But the two famous wine-judges stuck to their guns. Time passed, the wine was sold, and when they cleaned out the barrel they found a tiny little key on a thong of Cordovan leather. So now you can see whether someone who comes from that sort of stock has a right to give his opinion on a subject like this!'

'That's why I'm saying,' said the Squire of the Forest, 'that we should stop searching for adventures, and since we've got bread not go looking for biscuits, and return to our own cottages, and there God will find us when he wants to.'

'I'm going to serve my master until he reaches Saragossa, and then we'll have to see.'

And the two good squires talked so much and drank so much that sleep had to come and tie their tongues and abate their thirst, because to quench it would have been impossible; and so, both clutching the almost empty wine-bottle, with their food half-chewed in their mouths, they fell asleep, where we shall leave them for the time being, to recount the conversation between the Knight of the Forest and the Knight of the Sorry Face.

CHAPTER XIV

Which continues the adventure of the Knight of the Forest

Among many remarks exchanged between the two knights, the history says that the Knight of the Forest said to Don Quixote:

'In short, sir knight, I wish you to know that my destiny, or rather my free choice, led me to fall in love with the matchless Casildea de Vandalia. I call her matchless because she has no equal in bodily stature or in supremacy of rank and of beauty. This Casildea I'm telling you about repaid my honest affection and pure love by imposing on me, as Hercules' stepmother did on him, many different perilous labours,[1] promising me at the end of each of them that at the end of the next one I should attain the goal of my hopes; but the chain of my toils has grown link by link until there's no counting them, and I still don't know when I'll reach the last one, which will be the beginning of the fulfilment of my chaste desires. Once she ordered me to go and challenge that famous giantess in Seville called La Giralda, who's brave and strong and made of brass and, although she never moves from where she stands, is the most changeable and inconstant woman in the world. I came, I saw her and I conquered her,[2] and I made her remain settled and steadfast, because for over a week only the north wind blew. On another occasion Casildea sent me to go and lift those four ancient stones, the great Bulls of Guisando,[3] an exploit more suited to market porters than to knights errant. Once she told me to hurl myself into the Chasm of Cabra, a fearful and unprecedented peril, and take back to her a detailed account of what lies concealed in those dark depths.[4] I stayed the movement of La Giralda, I lifted the Bulls of Guisando, I threw myself into the Chasm and revealed what is hidden down there – and my hopes are as dead as ever, and her commands and her scorn are as alive as ever.

'To cut a long story short, her latest command is for me to travel throughout the provinces of Spain and to make all the knights errant roaming through them confess that she surpasses in beauty all women alive today and that I am the bravest and most happily enamoured knight in the world; and on this quest I have already travelled through most of the country, and I have defeated many knights who have dared to contradict me. But what makes me proudest of all is having defeated in single combat that famous knight Don Quixote de la Mancha and forced him to confess that my Casildea is more beautiful than his Dulcinea; and with this one victory I reckon that I've defeated all the knights in the world, because this Don Quixote I'm talking about has defeated them all and, since I've defeated him, his glory, fame and honour have devolved upon my person:

> The victor's good repute can only grow
> According to the glory of his foe.[5]

So the innumerable exploits of the said Don Quixote have been transferred to my account and have become mine.'

Don Quixote was astonished to hear what the Knight of the Forest was saying, and he was a thousand times on the point of saying that he was lying, and even now had that dreadful word on the very tip of his tongue; but he controlled himself as best he could, to make the man's own tongue convict him of falsehood, and so he calmly said:

'As regards your having defeated most of the knights errant in Spain and even in the world, sir knight, I have nothing to say; but as for having defeated Don Quixote de la Mancha, I do have my doubts. It could have been another man, who looked like him, even though there are few who do.'

'What are you saying?' replied the Knight of the Forest. 'I swear by the heavens above that I did fight Don Quixote and most certainly did defeat him; and he's a tall man with a wrinkled face, long skinny arms and legs, greying, an aquiline nose somewhat hooked, a big black droopy moustache. He campaigns under the name of the Knight of the Sorry Face, and his squire is a farmer called Sancho Panza; he burdens the back and rules the reins of a famous steed called Rocinante, and, finally, his lady-love is a certain Dulcinea del Toboso, formerly known as Aldonza Lorenzo, just as I call mine Casildea de Vandalia because her name is Casilda and she comes from Andalusia. If this description is not sufficient to confirm the truth of my words, here is my sword, which will make incredulity itself accept them.'

'Pray compose yourself, sir knight,' said Don Quixote, 'and listen to what I have to say. I would like you to know that this Don Quixote to whom you refer is the best friend I have in the world, so much so that I can affirm that I feel the same regard for him as for myself; and from the description that you have given me, so precise and exact, I am forced to believe that it is he whom you have defeated. But on the other hand I see with my own eyes and even feel with my own hands that it cannot have been him, unless what has happened is that, since he has many enemies who are enchanters (and in particular one who pursues him most of the time), one of these has taken on his appearance to allow himself to be defeated and rob the knight of the fame that his sublime deeds of chivalry have won for him all over the face of the earth. And as confirmation of this I would also have you know that those hostile enchanters, no more than two days ago, transformed the figure and person of the fair Dulcinea del Toboso into a coarse and vulgar peasant wench, and they must have transformed Don Quixote in a similar way; and if all of this is not sufficient to convince you of this truth that I am telling you, here before you stands Don Quixote himself, who will maintain it by force of arms on foot, on horseback, or however you prefer!'

And so saying he rose to his feet and gripped his sword, awaiting the reaction of the Knight of the Forest, who replied in a similarly calm voice:

'A good payer is a good pledger: he who could once defeat you when you were transformed, Don Quixote sir, can well hope to overcome you again in your true being. But since it is unseemly for knights to do their deeds in the dark like highwaymen and pimps, let us await day, so that the sun can witness our exploits. And it must be a condition of our battle that the vanquished shall be at the disposal of the victor, to deal with him as he pleases, so long as he commands him to do nothing unbefitting a knight.'

'I am more than happy with this condition and agreement,' replied Don Quixote.

And so saying they went to see their squires, and found them snoring in the positions in which sleep had pounced upon them. They woke them up and instructed them to make the horses ready, because at sunrise these two knights were to engage in bloody and unprecedented single combat; at which news Sancho was overcome by astonishment and fearful for his master's well-being, because of what he'd heard from the Squire of the Forest about his own master's deeds of bravery; but without uttering a word the two squires went for the animals. By now all three horses and the dun had had a good smell of each other and were standing together. On the way the Squire of the Forest said to Sancho:

'You must know, brother, that it's the custom of the fighting men of Andalusia, when they're seconds in some scrap, not to sit there twiddling their thumbs while the principals are swapping blows. I'm only saying this to give you due warning that while our masters are fighting we'll have to take up the cudgels as well, and smash each other to smithereens.'

'That custom, squire,' Sancho replied, 'might well hold good among those fighting men and riff-raff you're talking about, but you can forget it as far as knight errants' squires are concerned. At any rate I've never heard my master talking about any custom of that sort, and he's got all the rules and regulations of knight-errantry off by heart. But even if I do grant it's true that there's a clear rule that squires must fight while their masters are fighting, I'm not going to obey it, and instead I'll pay the fine dealt out to peaceable squires – it can't be more than a couple of pounds of wax, and I'm happy to pay that much, because I know it'll cost me less than the lint I'd need to bandage my head, all split in two down the middle as I'm sure it would be. And there's something else that stops me from fighting – I haven't got a sword, I've never put one on in my life.'

'I know a way round that,' said the Squire of the Forest. 'I've got two cotton bags here, both the same size – you take one, I'll take the other, and we'll have a bag-fight on equal terms.'

'That I can agree to,' Sancho replied, 'because a fight like that is more likely to dust down our jackets than break our bones.'

'No, it won't be quite like that,' the other replied, 'because into the bags, to stop the wind from catching them, we'll put half a dozen nice smooth pebbles, one lot weighing the same as the other, so we'll be able to wallop away without doing any harm.'

'By the body of my father!' Sancho replied. 'Look what sabre furs and what fluffy cotton balls he's going to put in the bags to save us from bashing our brain-boxes in and smashing all our bones to smithereens! Even if you filled them with silk cocoons I can tell you this much, squire – I'm not going to fight. Let our masters do the fighting and sort things out between themselves, and let us eat, drink and be merry, because Old Father Time will take good care to steal our lives away, without us looking for ways to encourage him to end them before their due time and season, when they'll drop from their own ripeness.'

'All the same,' the Squire of the Forest replied, 'we must fight, even if only for half an hour.'

'Certainly not,' Sancho replied. 'I'm not going to be so rude or ungrateful as to have even the tiniest quarrel with a man whose food and drink I've shared – and what's more I'm not feeling the slightest bit angry, and who the devil can bring himself to fight in cold blood, without any anger or provocation?'

'I know a way round that,' said the Squire of the Forest. 'Before we begin fighting I'll come smartly up to you and give you three or four wallops that'll lay you out flat at my feet, and they'll rouse your anger even if it's sleeping like a dormouse.'

'I've got another ruse,' Sancho replied, 'to counter that one with, and it's every bit as effective. I'll grab a cudgel, and before you can come and rouse my anger I'll send yours so soundly to sleep that it won't ever wake up again except in the other world, where I'm known as a man who doesn't let people monkey around with him. Let each mind his own business, and it'll be best to let anger sleep on, because nobody knows another man's heart, and there's many a one who's come out shearing and gone back shorn, and God blessed the peacemakers and cursed the peacebreakers, and if a cat that's chased and caught and caged turns into a raging lion, God only knows what I, a man, might turn into – and so I'm warning you now, squire, that you'll be the one to blame for any harm or damage arising from this here scrap of ours.'

'All right, then,' replied the Squire of the Forest. 'God will send us his light, and then we'll see.'

By now a thousand different kinds of little speckled birds were beginning to warble in the trees, and with their varied and happy songs they seemed to be hailing and welcoming cool Aurora, who was revealing the beauty of her face in the portals and balconies of the east, shaking from her tresses an infinite number of liquid pearls, and as the grasses of the field bathed in this gentle essence they in turn seemed to give forth a rain of tiny white pearl drops; the willows exuded delicious manna, the springs laughed, the streams murmured, the woods rejoiced and the meadows were enhanced by her coming. But as soon as the light of day allowed objects to be seen and distinguished, what first presented itself to Sancho Panza's gaze was the Squire of the Forest's nose, which was so large that almost all his body lay in its shadow. It is said to have been of vast size, hooked, and covered in warts, purple in colour like an aubergine, hanging down a couple of inches below his mouth; and its size, colour, warts and hook made the squire's face so ugly that when Sancho saw it his hands and feet began to tremble like a child with convulsions, and he resolved to take two hundred wallops before letting his anger be roused to make him fight that monster.

Don Quixote looked at his own adversary and found that his helmet was already in place with the visor down, so that he couldn't see his face, but he observed that he was a well-built man, not very tall. Over his armour he was wearing a surcoat or tabard of what seemed to be the finest cloth of gold, sprinkled with glittering spangles like little moons, which made him look extremely elegant and dashing; over his helmet fluttered many green, yellow and white plumes; and his lance, leaning up against a tree, was long and thick, and tipped with over a foot of steel.

Don Quixote looked at it all and took note of it all, and from what he could see he reached the conclusion that this knight must be a very powerful one; but this didn't make him frightened like Sancho Panza, and he addressed the Knight of the Spangles with gallant resolve:

'If, sir knight, your great desire for combat has not exhausted your courtesy, I beg you to be so kind as to raise your visor a little, so that I can see whether the nobility of your face matches that of your demeanour.'

'Whether you emerge victorious or defeated from this engagement, sir knight,' replied the Knight of the Spangles, 'you will then have more than enough time and opportunity to see me, and if I do not now satisfy your request it is because I regard it as a grievous affront to the fair Casildea de Vandalia to delay your confession of what you know that I demand, by even as long as it takes me to raise my visor.'

'Well, while we mount our horses,' said Don Quixote, 'you could at least tell me whether I am that same Don Quixote whom you claim to have defeated.'

'To that we make answer,'[6] said the Knight of the Spangles, 'that you and the knight whom I defeated look as alike as one egg and another; but since you say that he is pursued by enchanters, I cannot venture to affirm whether you are the aforesaid or not.'

'That is quite enough,' Don Quixote replied, 'to convince me that you were indeed deceived; to undeceive you totally, however, let our horses be brought, for in less time than it would take you to raise your visor, and with the help of God, my lady and my right arm, I shall see your face, and you will see that I am not the defeated Don Quixote you believe me to be.'

With this they broke off their conversation and mounted, and Don Quixote turned Rocinante to take as much ground as he needed to charge back at his adversary, and the Knight of the Spangles did likewise. But Don Quixote hadn't ridden twenty paces when he heard the Knight of the Spangles calling him, and, each returning halfway, the Knight of the Spangles said:

'Remember, sir knight, that the condition of our combat is, as I said earlier, that the vanquished shall be at the victor's disposal.'

'Yes, I know,' Don Quixote replied, 'so long as what the vanquished is commanded to do is not something that goes beyond the bounds of chivalry.'

'Just so,' the Knight of the Spangles replied.

At that moment Don Quixote caught sight of the squire's extraordinary nose, and he was no less amazed to see it than Sancho had been, so much so that he thought he must be some monster or some new species of man never seen on earth. When Sancho saw his master riding off to make his charge, he didn't like the idea of being left alone with the squire of the nose, fearing that just one flick of it delivered to his own nose would put an end to his fight and leave him stretched out on the ground from the force of the blow or of his fear; so he ran after his master, clutched one of Rocinante's stirrup-leathers, and, when he thought it was time for him to turn, he said:

'Please, master, before you turn round and charge could you kindly help me up into that cork-oak over there, so I can get a good view, a better one than from ground level, of this brave encounter you're going to have with this knight.'

'I do believe, Sancho,' said Don Quixote, 'that what you really want is to scramble up on to the terraces so as to be out of harm's way as you watch the bullfight.'

'To tell you the honest truth,' Sancho replied, 'I'm scared out of my wits by that squire's enormous nose, and I daren't stay with him all by myself.'

'It is indeed such,' said Don Quixote, 'that were I not who I am it would frighten me too; so come along and I shall help you up.'

While Don Quixote stopped to instal Sancho in the cork-oak, the Knight of the Spangles took as much ground as he thought necessary and, in the belief that Don Quixote had done the same, without awaiting any trumpet-blast or similar signal, he turned his horse (which was no swifter or better-looking than Rocinante) and at its top speed, which was a modest trot, he went to meet his enemy; but when he saw him busy with Sancho's ascent he drew rein in mid-course, for which his horse was deeply grateful, being incapable of budging another step. Don Quixote, who imagined that his enemy was flying full tilt at him, dug his spurs into Rocinante's lanky flanks to such effect that the history relates that this was the only time this horse was known to have advanced at something approaching a gallop, because on no other occasion could it manage more than a manifest trot; and with this unprecedented fury he bore down on the Knight of the Spangles, who was burying his spurs up to their buttons in his horse without being able to move it one inch from where its charge had come to a halt. It was in this pretty predicament that Don Quixote found his adversary, harassed by his horse and busy with his lance, which he hadn't lowered into its rest, either because he hadn't had time to, or because he didn't know how to. Don Quixote, who wasn't concerned about such problems, charged at the Knight of the Spangles, without the slightest danger to his own skin and with such force that he tossed him, much against his will, over his horse's crupper to fall so heavily that as he lay there stirring not a hand or a foot it looked as if he had given up the ghost.

As soon as Sancho saw him fall he shinned down from the cork-oak and ran to his master, who dismounted from Rocinante, strode over to the Knight of the Spangles, unlaced his helmet to see if he was dead and to give him air if he happened to be alive . . . and saw . . . Who could say what he saw, without awaking amazement, wonder and terror in those listening? He saw, the history says, the very face, the very visage, the very countenance, the very physiognomy, the very image, the very effigy of the young graduate Sansón Carrasco; and as soon as he did see him he cried:

'Come here, Sancho, and look at what you won't believe when you see it! Hurry, my son, to witness the powers of magic, the powers of wizards and enchanters!'

Sancho came, and when he saw the face of the young graduate Carrasco, he began to cross himself over and over and over again. All this while the fallen knight showed no signs of life, and Sancho said to Don Quixote:

'To my mind, sir, you ought to shove your sword right down the mouth of this character that looks like Sansón Carrasco, just in case — maybe you'll be killing one of your enemies the enchanters.'

'That is not bad advice,' said Don Quixote. 'The fewer the enemies the better.'

But as he drew his sword to put Sancho's advice into effect, the Knight of the Spangles' squire came running up, minus the nose that had made him so ugly, screaming:

'You look what you're doing, Don Quixote sir, that man at your feet is your friend Sansón Carrasco, and I'm his squire.'

When Sancho saw him shorn of his original ugliness, he said:

'Where's your nose?'

To which the other replied:

'Here in my pocket.'

And putting his hand into his right pocket he pulled out a lacquered papier mâché nose, as described above. Sancho stared and stared at him, and exclaimed in bewilderment:

'Holy St Mary in heaven preserve us! If it isn't Tomé Cecial, my neighbour and old mate!'

'Of course it's me!' said the unnosed squire. 'I'm Tomé Cecial, Sancho my old friend, and I'll soon tell you all about the ruses and tricks and ploys that brought me here, but meanwhile you beg your master not to touch or harm or wound or kill the Knight of the Spangles at his feet there – he really is the selfsame Sansón Carrasco from our village, the mindless madcap.'

At this point the Knight of the Spangles came to, and Don Quixote put the tip of his sword to his face and said:

'You are a dead man, sir knight, if you do not confess that the peerless Dulcinea del Toboso surpasses your Casildea de Vandalia in beauty; and in addition to this you must promise (if you survive this fight and this fall) to go to the city of El Toboso and present yourself before her presence on my behalf, so that she may do with you whatever she desires; and if she releases you, you must come back to search for me (the trail of my exploits will lead you to wherever I am), and inform me of what she has done with you; conditions which, as we agreed before our combat, do not go beyond the bounds of knight-errantry.'

'I confess,' said the fallen knight, 'that the dirty tattered shoe of the lady Dulcinea del Toboso is superior to all the hairs on Casildea's ill-combed but clean beard, and I promise to go into her presence and then return unto yours, and to give you a full and detailed account of everything you demand.'

'You must also both confess and believe,' Don Quixote added, 'that the knight you defeated was not and could not have been Don Quixote de la Mancha, but another who looked like him, just as I confess and believe that even though you look like the young graduate Sansón Carrasco you are not he, but another who looks like him and who has been put here in his shape and form by my enemies, to make me restrain and mitigate the surge of my wrath, and use moderation in the glory of my victory.'

'I confess, think and feel as you believe, think and feel,' replied the shattered knight. 'But do let me get up, please, if the tumble I took will let me – it's left me in a terrible state.'

He was helped to his feet by Don Quixote and by his squire Tomé Cecial, at whom Sancho couldn't stop staring as he asked him questions the replies to which gave manifest proof that he really was the Tomé Cecial that he said he was; but the effect on Sancho of his master's story about the enchanters changing the figure of the Knight of the Spangles into that of the young graduate Carrasco prevented him from believing what he could see with his own two eyes. In the end both master and servant were left with their delusions; and the Knight of the Spangles and his squire, wretched and disgruntled, limped away to look for some place where his ribs could be poulticed and strapped. Don Quixote and Sancho continued on the road to Saragossa, where the history leaves them, to provide information about the Knight of the Spangles and his protuberrant squire.

CHAPTER XV

*Which provides an account of the Knight of the Spangles
and his squire*

Don Quixote rode along, happy, proud and full of himself at having won his victory over such a brave adversary as was, in his opinion, the Knight of the Spangles, who had given his knightly word to inform his vanquisher whether his lady's enchantment continued: the vanquished man had to return, on pain of ceasing to be a knight, to give an account of what took place between him and her. But one thing thought Don Quixote, and another the Knight of the Spangles, because all he had on his mind at that moment was finding a place to be poulticed, as mentioned above.

The history states, then, that when the young graduate Sansón Carrasco advised Don Quixote to resume his interrupted chivalric exploits, he did this because he'd first sat in council with the priest and the barber to decide what steps could be taken to prevail on Don Quixote to stay quietly at home, undisturbed by this wretched quest for adventures; and the result of this confabulation was the unanimous acceptance of Carrasco's proposal that Don Quixote be allowed to sally forth, because it seemed impossible to stop him, and that Sansón waylay him disguised as a knight errant, and do battle with him, for there would be no lack of pretexts, and defeat him, which would be easy, and that the two should first solemnly agree that the vanquished would be at the mercy of the victor; and so, once Don Quixote had been defeated, the graduate knight would order him to return to his village and his home and not leave them for two years or until further notice; and it was obvious that Don Quixote, once defeated, would comply so as not to contravene the laws of chivalry, and it might be that during the period of his reclusion he'd forget about his vain nonsense, or an opportunity might arise to seek some suitable remedy for his madness. Carrasco accepted the mission, and Tomé Cecial, an old friend and neighbour of Sancho Panza's and a cheerful, hare-brained fellow, offered to be his squire. Sansón put on the armour described above, and Tomé Cecial donned his false nose over his real one to serve as a mask so that his old friend wouldn't recognize him when they met, and they rode off after Don Quixote, and were very nearly present at the adventure of the Cart of Death. And they eventually caught up with their quarry in the wood, where all the events that the discreet reader knows about happened; and if it hadn't been for the strange thinking of Don Quixote, who persuaded himself that the young graduate was not the young graduate, this gentleman would never have taken his master's degree, through not even finding nests where he'd gone looking for birds.

Tomé Cecial, seeing how far short the young graduate had fallen of his goal and what an unfortunate end his journey had come to, said:

'We've certainly got what we deserved, Señor Carrasco – it's easy enough to plan and set about a scheme, but it's usually much harder to pull it off. Don Quixote mad, us sane, away he goes hale and hearty and laughing, you're left black and blue and miserable. Just you tell me, then, who's madder – the man who's mad because he can't help it, or the man who chooses to be mad?'

To which Sansón replied:

'The difference between these two madmen is that the one who can't help it will be mad for ever, whereas the one who's mad by choice can stop whenever he likes.'

'That being so,' said Tomé Cecial, 'I was mad by choice when I decided to become your squire, and by choice I now intend to stop being mad and go home.'

'That's the best course for you,' Sansón replied, 'because if you think I'm going home until I've given Don Quixote a good hiding you've got another think coming; and what's going to make me search him out now isn't any desire for him to recover his senses but a desire for vengeance – this terrible pain in my ribs doesn't allow me to form any more charitable plans than that.'

And so they continued talking until they came to a village where they were lucky enough to find a bone-setter, who attended to the unfortunate Sansón. Tomé Cecial turned back and went away, and Sansón was left brooding on his revenge, and the history will return to him at the proper time, so as not to miss making merry now with Don Quixote.

CHAPTER XVI

About what happened to Don Quixote with an intelligent gentleman of La Mancha

Joyful, satisfied and proud, as related above, Don Quixote rode along, imagining from his recent victory that he was the bravest knight errant alive in the world; he counted every adventure that could ever come his way as already brought to a happy conclusion; he disdained all enchantments and enchanters; he didn't remember the innumerable beatings he'd received in the course of his chivalric exploits, or the stone that had knocked half his teeth out of his head, or the ingratitude of the convicts, or the insolence and the pounding staffs of the men from Yanguas. In short, he told himself, if only he could find some ways and means of disenchanting his lady Dulcinea, he wouldn't envy the greatest bliss ever enjoyed by the happiest knight errant of centuries past. He was lost in these musings when Sancho said:

'Isn't it odd, sir, that I can still see my old mate Tomé Cecial's extra-large, enormous nose?'

'And do you really believe, Sancho, that the Knight of the Spangles was the young graduate Carrasco, and that his squire was your good friend Tomé Cecial?'

'I don't know what to say to that,' Sancho replied. 'All I do know is that what he told me about my house, wife and children is something that only he could have told me, and that his face once his nose was off was Tomé Cecial's very own face, just as I've seen it time and time again in the village and over the garden wall, and that the tone of his voice was the same, too.'

'Let's have a little chat about that, Sancho,' Don Quixote replied. 'Look here: how is it to be conceived that young Sansón Carrasco should come as a knight errant, furnished with arms defensive and offensive, to fight me? Have I ever been his enemy? Have I ever given him cause to bear me a grudge? Am I his rival, or has he taken up the profession of arms, to make him envious of the fame that I have won with them?'

'But how can we explain, sir,' Sancho replied, 'the way that knight, whoever he is, looks just like young Carrasco, and his squire looks just like my old mate Tomé Cecial? And if it's all a spell, as you say, aren't there any other two men in the world they could have been made to look like?'

'It is all a ploy and a stratagem,' Don Quixote replied, 'of the malicious sorcerers persecuting me, who, predicting that I was going to emerge victorious from the combat, took the precaution of making the defeated knight display my friend the graduate's face, so that the affection which I feel for him should come between the blade of my sword and the rigour of my arm, and temper the just wrath in my heart, and the life be spared of the man who with tricks and ruses tried to deprive me of mine. As proof of this, Sancho, you know from your own experience, which will confirm for you what I am saying, how easy it is for enchanters to change one face into another, turning fair into foul and foul into fair, because not two days ago you saw the loveliness and grace of the peerless Dulcinea in all its fullness and natural conformation, and I saw it in the ugliness and wretchedness of an uncouth peasant girl, with cataracts in my eyes and with foul breath in her mouth; and so it would not be surprising if the perverse enchanter who had the audacity to carry out such a wicked transformation also transformed other men into Sansón Carrasco and your good friend, to snatch the glory of victory from my hands. But I am nevertheless comforted by the thought that, when all is said and done, I have vanquished my enemy, in whatever shape or form.'

'God knows the truth about everything,' Sancho replied.

And since Sancho knew that Dulcinea's transformation had been all his own work, he wasn't at all convinced by his master's imaginative theories; but he didn't reply, so as not to say something that might let the cat out of the bag.

They were discussing these matters when they were approached from behind by a man riding along the same road on a handsome dapple-grey mare; he was wearing a topcoat of fine green flannel slashed with tawny velvet, and a cap of the same material; his mare was in country trappings, with Arab-style short stirrups and high saddle, all of it also brown and green. A scimitar hung from the broad green-and-gold strap crossing the rider's chest, and his riding-boots matched his sword-strap; his spurs weren't gilded, but lacquered green, and they shone so brightly that, matching as they did the rest of his dress, they looked better than if they'd been coated in the purest gold. When the traveller reached them he gave courteous greetings and spurred his mule forward, but Don Quixote hailed him:

'If, fine sir, you are going our way and are not in too much of a hurry, I should consider it a great favour if you would ride with us.'

'To tell you the truth,' said the man on the mare, 'I would not have overtaken you as I did, had I not been afraid that your horse might become excited in the company of my mount.'

'Oh no, sir,' Sancho butted in, 'you can rein your mare in all right, because our horse is the most virtuous and well-behaved horse in the world. At times like this he's never done anything he shouldn't have done, and once when he was a naughty boy and did, me and my master paid for it seven times over. So as I said you can pull up if you want to – even if she was presented to him on a silver platter he wouldn't take her on.'

The traveller drew rein, amazed at Don Quixote's bearing and at his face, because he wasn't wearing his helmet, which Sancho was carrying as if it were a travelling bag, on the front pommel of his donkey's saddle-tree; and if the man in green gazed at Don Quixote, Don Quixote gazed even more at the man in green, thinking that he must be a fine upright citizen. He seemed to be about fifty, with not many hairs turned grey, the face of an eagle and a look that was half cheerful and half serious; altogether, his clothes and his demeanour made him seem like a man of admirable qualities.

What the man in green thought of Don Quixote de la Mancha was that he'd never seen anyone remotely like this in his life: he wondered at the length of the man's horse, at the lankness of his body, at the thinness and pallor of his face, at his arms and armour, at his deportment: such a sight hadn't been seen in those parts for many a long year. Don Quixote noticed the care with which the traveller was examining him, read in his look of surprise what it was that he wanted to know and, being so courteous and so concerned to please everyone, didn't wait to be asked any questions but anticipated them and said:

'The appearance that I present to you is so strange and out of the ordinary that it would not surprise me to learn that it has filled you with wonder; but your wonder will cease when I tell you, as I am indeed telling you now, that I am one of those knights

> Who go, as people say,
> Adventuring their way.

I left my village, I pledged my estate, I abandoned my domestic comforts and delivered myself into the arms of fortune, to be borne by her wherever she pleased to take me. I decided to revive the extinct order of knight-errantry, and for some time now, stumbling here, falling there, crashing headlong in one place, climbing back on to my feet in another, I have in large measure been fulfilling my desires, succouring widows, rescuing maidens, protecting wives, orphans and wards, the proper and natural occupation of knights errant; and thus, because of my many brave and Christian deeds, I have been deemed worthy to appear in print in most of the nations of the world. Thirty thousand copies of my history have been published, and there is every sign that there will be a thousand times as many more, if heaven does not intervene to prevent it. In short and to resume in a few words, or in just one word, I am Don Quixote de la Mancha, otherwise known as the Knight of the Sorry Face, and, even though a man's praises in his own mouth stink, I am sometimes obliged to utter them, when it happens that there is nobody else present who will do it for me; and thus, noble sir, neither this horse, nor this lance, nor this shield, nor this squire, nor any of my arms defensive or offensive, nor the pallor of my face, nor my extreme thinness should surprise you from henceforth, now that you know who I am and the profession I follow.'

Don Quixote fell silent, and the man in green took so long to reply that he seemed not to know what to say; but after a lengthy pause he did speak:

'You surmised correctly from my look of astonishment, sir knight, what I wanted to know, but you have not been so successful in dispelling the amazement that the sight of you has caused me; for even though, as you say, sir, knowing who you are should have achieved this end, that has not been the result: on the contrary, now that I know who you are I am even more amazed and astonished. Is it really possible that there still are knights errant in the world today, and that there are histories in print of authentic chivalric exploits? I cannot imagine that there is anyone on the face of this earth who protects widows, rescues maidens or honours married women or succours orphans; and I simply would not have believed it unless I had seen with my own two eyes a living example of it all in you. Heaven be praised, because the history that you say has been printed about your noble and true deeds of chivalry must have consigned to oblivion the countless histories of fictional knights errant that used to clutter the world, to the great detriment of sound customs and to the prejudice and discredit of good histories.'

'There is much to be said,' replied Don Quixote, 'as to whether the histories of knights errant are fictional or not.'

'But is there anyone,' the green man replied, 'who doubts that those histories are all lies?'

'I doubt it for one,' replied Don Quixote, 'but we had better let the matter rest there for, if we travel long enough together, I hope with God's help to make you understand that it has been wrong of you to drift with the current of those who are convinced that such histories are untrue.'

These last words made the traveller suspect that Don Quixote must be some sort of idiot, and he was waiting for further confirmation of the fact; but before the talk drifted on to other matters, Don Quixote asked him to state who he was, since he himself had provided an account of his own position in society and way of life. To which the man in the green topcoat replied:

'I, my dear Knight of the Sorry Face, am a hidalgo from a village where we shall take lunch today, God willing. I am more than moderately well-off, and my name is Don Diego de Miranda. I spend my time with my wife, my children and my friends; my pastimes are hunting and fishing, but I keep neither hawk nor hounds, just one or two tame decoy partridges and intrepid ferrets. I possess about six dozen books, some in Spanish and others in Latin, some historical and others devotional; books of chivalry have yet to cross the threshold of my house. I peruse my books of devotion less than the others, so long as these latter provide harmless entertainment, delighting the reader with their style and amazing him with their inventiveness – although there aren't many books like that in Spain. I occasionally eat in my friends' and neighbours' houses, and they very often eat in mine, where they find my table neat and clean, and not lacking in good things; I neither like to gossip, nor do I allow others to gossip in my presence; I make no scrutiny of others' lives, nor do I spy on their deeds; I hear mass every day; I distribute my wealth among the poor, without ever boasting about my good deeds, so as not to allow hypocrisy and vainglory into my heart, for they are enemies that steal into the wariest breast; I strive to make peace among those who have quarrelled; I am a devotee of Our Lady, and I trust forever in the infinite mercy of Our Lord God.'

Sancho had been hanging on every word of the hidalgo's account of his own life and works, and, since it seemed such a good and holy life that the man who led it must work miracles, he threw himself down from his dun, ran to grasp the hidalgo's right stirrup and with a devout heart and on the verge of tears kissed his feet over and over again. At which the hidalgo asked him:

'What are you doing, my man? What is the meaning of all these kisses?'

'Do let me kiss you,' Sancho replied, 'because to my mind you're the first saint riding Arab-style I've ever come across in all the days of my born life.'

'I am no saint,' the hidalgo replied, 'but a great sinner; you, my man, must indeed be righteous, to judge from your simple-mindedness.'

Sancho returned to his pack-saddle, having forced a laugh from the depths of his master's melancholy and aroused fresh amazement in Don Diego. Don Quixote asked him how many sons he had, and informed him that for the ancient philosophers, who lacked a true knowledge of God, among the sources of supreme happiness were the blessings of nature and the gifts of fortune, and having many friends and many good sons.

'I myself, Don Quixote,' the hidalgo replied, 'have one son, and if I did not have him I should perhaps consider myself happier than I am; not because he is wicked, but because he is less good than I could wish. He must be eighteen by now; he has been at Salamanca University for six years, learning Latin and Greek, and when I wanted him to move on to other disciplines I found him so obsessed with poetry (if poetry can be called a discipline) that I cannot make him take up law, which is what I wanted him to study, or the queen of them all, theology. I wanted him to be the pride and joy of the family, for we live in a world in which our kings give rich rewards to the virtuous scholar: because scholarship without virtue is like pearls in a dunghill. But he spends the whole day working out whether Homer did or did not express himself well in such and such a verse of the *Iliad*, whether Martial was being obscene or not in such and such an epigram and whether these lines of Virgil should be understood like this or like that. In short, he has time only for books by these poets and by Horace, Persius, Juvenal and Tibullus, because he hasn't much interest in modern vernacular writers; yet despite all his apparent dislike for poetry in Spanish, at the moment his mind's in a whirl because he's writing a verse gloss on a stanza he has been sent from Salamanca – I believe it's some sort of literary competition.'

To all of which Don Quixote replied:

'Sons, sir, are fragments of their parents' bowels, and so their parents must love them whether they are good or bad, just as we love the souls that give us life; it is the parents' task to direct their sons from their earliest days along the path of virtue, good breeding and correct Christian behaviour, so that when they grow up they can be the staffs of their parents' old age and their glory for the future; and as regards forcing them to study this or that discipline, I consider it to be a mistake, although there would be no harm in trying to persuade them to do so; and, if the student has no need to study for the sake of *pane lucrando*,[1] because he is lucky enough to have been provided by heaven with parents who give him an income, I should incline to the opinion that he be allowed to study the subject that he likes best – and even though the study of poetry is not so much useful as pleasurable, it is not one of those subjects that dishonour their practitioners.

'Poetry, my dear hidalgo, is, as it seems to me, like a young, tender, lovely maiden, whom other maidens, that is to say all the other branches of learning, have the task of enhancing, adorning and perfecting, and she must make use of them all, and all of them must derive their prestige from her; but this maiden is not to be pawed over, or paraded through the streets, or displayed in the corners of market-places or in palace antechambers.[2] She is made of an alchemy-gold of such excellence that anyone who knows how to treat her will turn her into pure gold of inestimable worth; he who has her in his charge must keep her under strict control, and not allow her to stray into lewd satires or baneful sonnets; on no account must she be sold, except in heroic poems, mournful tragedies and cheerful, well-contrived comedies; she must not be allowed into the company of rogues or the ignorant, vulgar crowd, incapable of recognizing or appreciating the treasures contained within her. And do not imagine, sir, that by "vulgar crowd" I mean only the humble lower orders: everyone who is ignorant, even if he is a lord and a pillar of the community, can and should be considered one of the vulgar crowd. And so the name of the man who manages and controls poetry in the way I have specified will be famous and esteemed in all the civilized nations of the world.

'As regards what you say, sir, about your son's low opinion of poetry written in Spanish, it is my belief that he is making something of a mistake, for the following reason: the great Homer did not write in Latin, because he was a Greek, and Virgil did not write in Greek, because he was a Roman. In short, all the ancient poets wrote in the languages that they were suckled on, and they did not go in search of foreign languages in which to express their noble concepts. This being so, it would be reasonable for this custom to be extended among all nations, and for the German poet not to be held in low esteem because he writes in his own language, nor the Castilian, nor even the Basque writing in his. But I imagine that your son, sir, does not dislike vernacular poetry as such but rather poets who only know their own vernacular, and have no access to other languages or branches of learning with which to adorn and stimulate and assist their natural inspiration; and even here he could be wrong. Because, as people rightly say, poets are born not made, in other words the natural poet emerges a poet from his mother's womb and, provided by heaven with this gift, and without any study of the art, he composes his works, thus showing the truth of the saying: *Est deus in nobis* . . .[3] But I also say that the natural poet who calls in art to his aid will be the better for it, and will have the advantage over the man who tries to be a poet by relying upon his knowledge of the art alone, and the reason is that art does not surpass nature but merely perfects it; so if nature and art, art and nature, are combined, the result will be a perfect poet.

'The conclusion to my discourse, my dear sir, must therefore be that you should allow your son to go where his star is calling him; for, being as good a student as I am sure he is, and having mounted the first rung of learning, the ancient languages, these will enable him to climb by himself to the peak of the humanities, which so suit a private gentleman, and adorn, honour and exalt him as mitres do bishops and robes do judges. You should reprimand your son if he writes satires that damage other people's honour – and you should punish him, and tear them up; but if he writes satires in the Horatian manner, disparaging vices in general, as Horace did with such elegance, you should praise him, because it is permissible for the poet to attack envy and speak ill in his verses of the envious, and the same applies to the other vices, so long as he does not name any individual; but there are poets who for the sake of making some malicious comment will put themselves at risk of being banished to the Isles of Pontus.[4] If the poet is pure in his habits, he will be pure in his verses as well; the pen is the tongue of the soul, and his writings will be as are the concepts engendered in his soul; and when kings and princes find the miraculous art of poetry in prudent, virtuous and serious men, they honour, esteem and enrich them, and even crown them with the leaves of the tree that is never struck by lightning,[5] as a sign that those who are honoured and whose temples are adorned with such crowns will never be attacked by anyone.'

The man in the green topcoat was astonished by Don Quixote's reasoning, so much so that the opinion he'd formed of him as some sort of idiot had been dissipating. But halfway through his discourse Sancho, not finding it much to his taste, had wandered away from the road to ask some shepherds who were milking their ewes to let him have a little milk and, as he did so, the hidalgo in green, by now fully convinced of Don Quixote's good sense and sound mind, was about to have his say, when Don Quixote looked up and saw a cart bedecked with royal banners proceeding towards them along the road; and in the belief that this must be some new adventure, he called to Sancho for his helmet. Sancho heard his cries, abandoned the shepherds, dug his spurs into his dun and hurried to his master, who now had a most dreadful and reckless adventure.

CHAPTER XVII

About events that revealed the very highest peak ever reached by Don Quixote's unprecedented courage, in the happily concluded adventure of the lions

The history says that when Don Quixote shouted to Sancho for his helmet, Sancho was buying some curds from the shepherds and, flustered by his master's urgency, he didn't know what to do with them or where to put them; and so, determined not to leave them behind, because he'd already paid for them, he decided to put them into the helmet and, once he'd taken this wise precaution, went to see what his master wanted. Don Quixote said:

'Give me that helmet, my friend; either I am a poor judge of adventures or what I can see over there is one that will require me to take up arms, and indeed is doing so at this very instant.'

The man in the green topcoat heard this and looked around in all directions, but all he could see was a cart coming towards them bearing two or three small flags, which gave him to understand that it must be carrying a load of the King's money, and this is what he said to Don Quixote; but Don Quixote wouldn't accept what he said, believing as always that everything that happened to him must be adventures and still more adventures, and so he replied to the hidalgo:

'He is wise who looks ahead, and nothing is lost by my looking ahead, because I know from experience that I have both visible and invisible enemies, and I do not know when, or where, or at what moment, or in what shape they will attack me.'

And turning to Sancho he again asked for his helmet; Sancho, with no time to remove the curds, had to hand it over as it was. Don Quixote took it and, not noticing what was inside, rammed it down on his head, which gave the curds a thorough pressing and sent the whey running down over his face and his beard, alarming him so much that he exclaimed:

'What can this be, Sancho? It is as if my brain-box were softening, or as if my brains themselves were melting, or as if I were perspiring from head to toe! And if I am perspiring, it is most certainly not from fear: I am quite sure now that the adventure about to befall me is a terrible one indeed. Give me something with which to wipe myself, if you have anything about you: all this perspiration in my eyes is blinding me.'

Sancho kept quiet and gave his master a cloth and God thanks that his master hadn't tumbled to what had happened. Don Quixote wiped his face and removed his helmet to see what it was that had given him a cold head, if not cold feet; and then he saw all that white pap in there, and then he lifted it to his nose, and as soon as he smelled it he said:

'By the life of my lady Dulcinea del Toboso, these are curds you've put in here, you treacherous, villainous, ill-mannered squire!'

To which Sancho replied with his imperturbable duplicity:

'If it's curds let's have them and I'll eat them. But better let the devil eat them, because it must have been him that put them in there. Would I have the cheek to besmirch your helmet? So we've found him out at last, the impudent so-and-so, have we? Good God, sir, from what I can see with his holy help, I must have my enchanters, too, pursuing me because I'm your creature and your limb, and they must have put that muck in there to make you lose your temper and beat me up, as you usually do. Well, this time they've missed their mark, that's for sure, because I put all my trust in my master's good sense, he knows full well that I haven't got any curds or milk or anything of the sort, and if I had I'd put them in my belly not your helmet.'

'What you say could be true,' said Don Quixote.

And the hidalgo in green was watching it all, and wondering at it all, particularly when, after Don Quixote had wiped his head, face, beard and helmet, he put the latter on again, steadied himself in his stirrups, checked his sword, seized his lance and declared:

'And now, come what may! Here I wait, ready to join battle with Satan himself in person.'

As he said this the cart with the flags rolled up, accompanied only by the carter, riding one of the mules, and by another man sitting on the front seat. Don Quixote planted himself before the cart and said:

'Where are you going, my good men? What cart is this, what are you carrying on it and what flags are these?'

To which the carter replied:

'The cart is mine; on it are two fierce lions in crates, which the general in Oran[1] is sending to court as a present for His Majesty; and the flags are the King's banners, showing that what we're carrying here belongs to him.'

'And are the lions large?' asked Don Quixote.

'They're so large,' said the man on the front of the cart, 'that none larger or even as large have ever been sent from Africa to Spain; and I'm their keeper, and I've brought other lions over in my time, but none like these. They're a male and a female; the male's in this first crate and the female's in the other one behind; and they're hungry, because they haven't eaten today, so you'd better move aside, we're in a hurry to get to some place where we can feed them.'

To which Don Quixote said with a smile:

'Lion-whelps now, is it? Is it now lion-whelps, and at this time of day? Well, by God, those fellows sending them here will soon see whether I'm the sort to be afraid of lions![2] Climb down, my good man and, since you're their keeper, open these crates and turn the animals out: here, in the middle of this field, I will show them what sort of a man Don Quixote de la Mancha is, in spite of all the enchanters who have sent them after me.'

'I see, I see!' the hidalgo in green said to himself. 'Now our worthy knight has shown what he's made of – the curds have indeed softened his brain-box and ripened his brains!'

Sancho came up to him and said:

'Oh sir, for God's sake do something to stop my master Don Quixote from fighting these here lions – if he does they'll tear us all to shreds.'

'Is your master so mad, then,' the hidalgo replied, 'as to make you fear and believe that he's going to fight such fierce beasts?'

'He isn't mad,' said Sancho, 'only reckless.'

'I'll soon put a stop to all that,' the hidalgo replied.

And going over to Don Quixote, who was telling the keeper to hurry up and open the crates, he said:

'Sir knight: knights errant should undertake adventures that offer some chance of success, and not those that are utterly hopeless; because courage that crosses the border into foolhardiness has more of insanity than fortitude about it. Furthermore, these lions have not come here to attack you, nothing could be further from their minds; they're a present for His Majesty, and it will not be a good idea to detain them or obstruct their journey.'

'Sir hidalgo,' Don Quixote retorted, 'pray go away and play with your tame decoy partridge and your intrepid ferret, and let others proceed with their own business. This is my business, and I know whether or not these lion fellows have come after me.'

And turning to the keeper he said:

'I swear by all that's holy, you villain, that if you do not open these crates this very instant I shall pin you to your cart with this lance!'

Seeing how determined this apparition in armour was, the carter said:

'Dear good sir, for pity's sake, please let me unyoke the mules and reach a safe place with them before the lions are unleashed, because if they kill them I'm ruined for life – all I own in the world is this cart and these mules.'

'O you of little faith!'[3] Don Quixote replied. 'Dismount and unyoke, and do whatever you like, and you will soon see that all your trouble was for nothing and that you could have spared yourself the effort.'

The carter jumped down and unyoked his mules at breakneck speed, and the keeper yelled:

'All of you here are witnesses of how I'm being forced against my will to open these crates and let these lions out, and of how I'm protesting to this gentleman that all the damage these animals do must be his sole responsibility, together with my wages and dues. You gentlemen take cover before I open the doors, I'm sure the lions won't harm me.'

The hidalgo in green again tried to persuade Don Quixote not to do anything so mad – it was tempting God to commit such folly. To which Don Quixote retorted that he knew what he was about. The hidalgo replied that he should consider carefully what he was proposing to do, because in his opinion it was a very great mistake.

'Listen, sir,' Don Quixote replied, 'if you do not wish to be present at what you think is going to be a tragedy, put spurs to your dapple-grey mare and take yourself off to safety.'

Sancho heard this, and with tears in his eyes he implored his master to desist from this venture, in comparison with which the windmills, the fearful fulling-hammers and, in short, all the exploits he'd undertaken in the whole course of his life had been so much chicken feed.

'Look, sir,' Sancho said, 'this isn't a magic spell or anything like that – I saw the claw of a real live lion poking out through a crack between the planks of the crate, and to judge from it I reckon the lion it belongs to must be mightier than a mountain.'

'Or at least your fear,' Don Quixote replied, 'must make it seem to you bigger than half the world. Go away, Sancho, and leave me alone; and if I should die here, you know our old agreement: you will visit Dulcinea, and I shall say no more.'

He added some more words which eliminated all hope that he might desist from his absurd project. The man in the green topcoat would have liked to force him to, but his weapons were no match for Don Quixote's, and he didn't think it sane to fight a madman, which is what he now took Don Quixote to be without a shadow of doubt. Don Quixote again told the keeper to hurry up, and repeated his threats, which made the hidalgo spur his mare, Sancho his dun, and the carter his mules, and they all hastened to put as much ground as possible between themselves and the cart before the lions were uncrated. Sancho was mourning his master's death, certain that this time it was bound to come in the claws of the lion, and cursing his fate and the unlucky hour when it had occurred to him to come back into service; but all his weeping and lamenting didn't prevent him from cudgelling his dun to distance it from the cart. When the keeper saw that the fleeing men were a good way off, he again urged and exhorted Don Quixote as he'd exhorted and urged him before, and Don Quixote replied that he wasn't deaf, that the keeper shouldn't bother with any more urgings or exhortations, they'd be quite fruitless, and that he should make haste. As the keeper opened the first crate Don Quixote was considering whether it would be better to fight on foot or on horseback, and he eventually decided to fight on foot, concerned that Rocinante would take fright when he saw the lions. So Don Quixote jumped down, hurled his lance away, took up his shield, drew his sword and advanced with a slow and steady step, with wonderful courage and with a valiant heart, to confront the cart, fervently commending himself to God and then to his lady Dulcinea.

It is noteworthy that when the author of this true history reaches this point he exclaims:

'O doughty and inexpressibly courageous Don Quixote de la Mancha, mirror for all brave men in the world, second Don Manuel de León, that honour and glory of Spanish knights![4] What words shall I find to relate this dreadful deed, what expressions are there to make it credible to future ages, what praises can there be that you do not deserve, even the greatest hyperboles ever uttered? On foot, alone, intrepid, magnanimous, bearing only a sword, and that not of the sharpest Toledo steel, and a shield which is not particularly bright or shining, you stand there awaiting the two fiercest lions ever bred in the jungles of Africa! Let your deeds themselves be your praise, O valorous man of La Mancha: I can only leave here a simple account of them, lacking words with which to extol them!'

Here the author's exclamation comes to an end, and he continues, picking up the thread of his history and saying that when the keeper saw that Don Quixote had taken up his position and that it was impossible to avoid releasing the lion, on pain of incurring the wrath of that bold and angry knight, he threw open the doors of the first crate, revealing a lion of extraordinary size and fearful and hideous aspect. What the lion first did was to turn round in its crate, in which it had been lying down, reach out a paw, and have a good stretch; then it opened its mouth and gave a long, long yawn, and unrolled a vast expanse of tongue to lick the dust out of its eyes and wash its face; after which it extended its head from the crate and looked all around with eyes like burning coals, the sight of which would have struck terror into temerity itself. And there stood Don Quixote alone, watching it, longing for it to spring down from the cart and close with him so that he could tear it to pieces. His unparalleled madness reached even this far. But the noble-hearted lion, more inclined to civility than to despotism, wouldn't take any notice of posturing or bravado; and, having looked this way and that, as described, it turned round, showed Don Quixote its backside and, with the utmost composure and deliberation, lay itself down again in its crate. This prompted Don Quixote to order the keeper to beat the animal and provoke it into coming out.

'No, that I won't do,' the keeper replied, 'because if I make it angry the first person it'll tear to pieces is me. You be content, sir knight, with what you've done; it's all anybody can ask for under the heading of bravery, and don't go tempting fortune a second time. The door of the crate is open, it's up to the lion to come out or not, but since it hasn't come out by now it won't come out all day. You've shown what a great-hearted man you are; no brave champion, as far as I can see, is obliged to do any more than challenge his enemy and await him in the field, and if his enemy doesn't present himself he's the one that's disgraced, and the one waiting for him wins the crown of victory.'

'You speak the truth,' Don Quixote replied. 'Close the door, my friend, and make me a sworn declaration, as best you can, of what you have seen me do here, namely: that you opened the lion's crate, I awaited it, it did not come out, I waited still, it still did not come out, and then it lay down again. I have done my duty, and the spell has been overcome, and may God protect right reason and truth and honest chivalry; and you shut the door as I said, while I signal to those people riding away, so that they can learn of this exploit from your own mouth.'

The keeper did as he was told, and Don Quixote fastened to the tip of his lance the cloth with which he'd wiped his face after the deluge of curds, and began to call out to the men who were still riding away and glancing back with every step, all in a troop and with the man in green bringing up the rear; but Sancho spotted the waving white cloth and said:

'I'll be blowed if my master hasn't beaten those wild beasts – he's calling out to us!'

They all stopped, and saw that it was indeed Don Quixote who was signalling; so, losing some of their fear, they edged back until his cries were clearly audible. Eventually they returned to the cart, and as they arrived Don Quixote said to the carter:

'You can yoke your mules again, brother, and go on your way. Give him two gold escudos, Sancho, for himself and the keeper, to make amends for the delay.'

'I'll be very happy to do that,' said Sancho, 'but what's happened to the lions? Are they dead or alive?'

And then the keeper gave his account, in great detail and with weighty pauses, of how the conflict had ended, extolling Don Quixote's courage to the utmost of his power and ability: the sight of him had so intimidated the lion that it hadn't dared to venture out of its crate, even though the door had been open for a good while; and since he'd told the knight that it would be tempting God to provoke the lion into coming out, which is what the knight had wanted him to do, the knight had, very much against his will, allowed the door to be shut.

'What do you say to that, Sancho?' said Don Quixote. 'Are there any enchantments that can contend with true valour? Those enchanters can take my happiness away from me if they like, but they can never deprive me of my resolve and courage.'

Sancho handed the escudos over, the carter yoked his mules, the lion-keeper kissed Don Quixote's hands for the favour received, and promised that when he reached the court he'd tell the King himself all about that brave deed.

'Should His Majesty by any chance enquire who performed it, you must tell him that it was the Knight of the Lions; for henceforth I wish the title I have hitherto borne, the Knight of the Sorry Face, to be transformed, transfigured and transmuted into this; and in so doing I am following the ancient usage of knights errant, who changed their names when they pleased, or when it suited their purpose.'

The cart continued on its way, and Don Quixote, Sancho and the man in the green topcoat continued on theirs.

All this time Don Diego de Miranda hadn't spoken a word, so concerned was he to observe what Don Quixote did and to listen to what he said, because he regarded him as a sane man with madness in him, and as a madman with sane tendencies. Don Diego didn't know about the first part of Don Quixote's history – if he had read it he would have known what sort of madness he suffered from, which would have prevented him from being amazed by his words and deeds; but not knowing about it, he sometimes thought him sane and sometimes mad, because what he said was coherent, elegant and well expressed, and what he did was absurd, foolhardy and stupid. And Don Diego said to himself:

'What greater madness could there be than putting a helmet full of curds on your head and thinking that enchanters are softening your brain-box? And what could be more foolhardy and absurd than trying to force lions to fight you?'

Don Quixote brought him out of his musings and his soliloquy by saying:

'Who can doubt, Don Diego de Miranda sir, that your opinion of me is that I am a man who is both foolish and mad? And it would be no wonder if you did, because it is the only conclusion to be drawn from my deeds. Well, in spite of all that, I should like you to observe that I am not as mad or as foolish as I must have seemed. It is a fine sight to see a gallant knight, in the presence of his king, in the middle of a great square, thrusting his lance with perfect aim at a brave bull. It is a fine sight to see a knight in shining armour entering the lists for merry jousts before the ladies, and it is a fine sight to see all those knights who in military exercises – or rather in exercises that seem military – entertain, cheer and, if it is legitimate to say so, honour monarchs' courts; but it is a far finer sight than all of these to see a knight errant who in deserts, in wildernesses, at crossroads, in woods and in forests goes in search of perilous adventures, bent on bringing them to a happy and successful conclusion, all to win glorious and lasting fame. It is, I repeat, a finer sight to see a knight errant succouring a widow in some lonely waste than a knight courtier dallying with a damsel in some great city. Every knight has his part to play: let the knight courtier serve the ladies, add lustre to his king's court with his retinue, maintain poor knights at his sumptuous table, organize jousts, celebrate tourneys and show himself to be important, generous, magnificent and, above all, a good Christian, and if he does all this he will be fulfilling his own particular obligations. But the knight errant must search out the remotest corners of the world, make his way into the most complex labyrinths, at every step attempt the impossible, withstand on desolate plains the burning rays of the midsummer sun and in the winter the harsh inclemency of winds and ice; he must not be alarmed by lions, or dismayed by monsters, or daunted by dragons, because seeking these, attacking those and defeating them all is his principal and proper occupation. Now since it fell to me to be one of the number of knights errant, I cannot fail to tackle anything that seems to me to come within the sphere of my duties, and attacking those lions a moment ago was therefore something that I had to do, even though I was well aware that it was foolhardy beyond measure, for I know what courage is, a virtue situated between two extremes, the vices of cowardice and foolhardiness; but it is less reprehensible for the man who is courageous to rise up as far as the extreme of foolhardiness than to sink down to the extreme of cowardice; for just as it is easier for the spendthrift than for the miser to be generous, so it is easier for the foolhardy man than for the coward to become a truly courageous man; and in this matter of undertaking adventures, Don Diego, believe you me, it is better to lose the game through scoring too many points than through scoring too few, because "such and such a knight is rash and foolhardy" sounds better in the hearer's ears than "such and such a knight is timid and cowardly".'

'All I can say, Don Quixote sir,' replied Don Diego, 'is that everything you have said and done has been weighed on the balance of right reason itself, and it's my belief that if the rules and regulations of knight-errantry were ever lost they could be recovered from your breast as from their own repository and archive. And now it's getting late, so let's make haste to reach my village and my house, where you'll be able to rest from your recent labours – if not labours of the body, then of the spirit, which often also make the body weary.'

'I consider your offer to be a great favour and kindness, Don Diego,' replied Don Quixote.

And, spurring forward at a better pace than before, by about two o'clock in the afternoon they reached the village and the house of Don Diego, whom Don Quixote called the Knight of the Green Topcoat.

CHAPTER XVIII

*About what happened to Don Quixote at the castle or
house of the Knight of the Green Topcoat, and other
unusual events*

Don Quixote found that Don Diego de Miranda's house was a spacious
one in village style, but with his arms, although carved in coarse stone,
over the street door, the wine cellar under the courtyard and the buttery
under the porch; all around there were enormous earthenware jars that,
having been made in El Toboso, revived Don Quixote's memories of his
enchanted and transformed Dulcinea, and, not thinking what he was
saying or what company he was in, he sighed and said:

'O lovely tokens, for my woe discovered,
So lovely and so happy, when God willed![1]

O jars of El Toboso, how you have brought back to my memory the
lovely token of my greatest bitterness!'

The student poet, Don Diego's son, who had come out with his mother
to greet their guest, heard these words, and both mother and son were
astonished at Don Quixote's strange appearance as he dismounted from
Rocinante and approached her with the utmost courtesy to beg to be
allowed to kiss her hands, while Don Diego said:

'Pray receive with your customary affability, my lady, Don Quixote de
la Mancha, standing here before you, a knight errant – the bravest and
the wisest one in all the world.'

The lady, whose name was Doña Cristina, greeted Don Quixote with
every sign of affection and courtesy, and Don Quixote offered her his
services in an abundance of polite and well-chosen words. Then he
exchanged almost the same civilities with the student, whom by his speech
Don Quixote judged to be sharp-witted and sensible.

At this point the author describes every detail of Don Diego's house –
all the contents of any rich gentleman farmer's dwelling; but the translator
of this history thought it better to pass in silence over these and other
similar minutiae, because they aren't relevant to the principal purpose of

the history, which derives its strength from its truthfulness rather than from dull digressions.

They ushered Don Quixote into a room where Sancho removed his armour and he was left in his baggy knee-breeches and his chamois-leather doublet, all filthy from the grime on his armour; his collar was a broad one that flopped down over his shoulders, like a student's, unstarched and lacking any lace trimmings; his leggings were date-brown and his shoes were waxed. He put on his trusty sword, hanging from a sealskin strap that crossed his chest diagonally from one shoulder,[2] because it's believed that he'd been suffering from kidney trouble for many years; he donned a short cloak of good light-brown flannel; but before he did any of these things he took five bucketfuls of water, or six, because there's some difference of opinion as regards the number of bucketfuls, and washed his hair and his face, and the water still went the colour of whey, thanks to Sancho's greed and his purchase of those foul curds that had turned his master so fair. Thus arrayed, and with graceful and gallant demeanour, Don Quixote strolled into another room, where the student was waiting to keep him amused while the tables were being laid: on the arrival of so noble a visitor Doña Cristina was determined to show that she possessed both the *savoir-faire* and the means to regale those who visited her house.

While Don Quixote had been removing his armour, Don Lorenzo, for this was the name of Don Diego's son, had taken the opportunity to comment to his father:

'Who on earth can this knight be, sir, that you've brought home with you? Mother and I are astonished at his name, his appearance and his claim to be a knight errant.'

'I really don't know what to say, my son,' Don Diego replied. 'All I do know is that I've seen him perform the actions of the greatest madman in the world, and heard him speak words of such good sense that they dissipate the effect of his deeds. But you talk to him, and test him to see how much he knows, and being a sensible lad you'll be able to form your own judgement about which of the two, good sense or stupidity, is uppermost – though, to tell you the truth, I do believe he's more mad than sane.'

And Don Lorenzo went off to amuse Don Quixote, as explained above, and in the course of their conversation Don Quixote said:

'Your father Don Diego de Miranda has informed me of your rare abilities and fine mind, and in particular he said that you are a great poet.'

'A poet I might well be,' Don Lorenzo replied, 'but a great one, never. It is true that I'm quite fond of poetry and of reading good poets, but that doesn't give me the right to be called great, as I apparently am by my father.'

'I find your humility not unattractive,' Don Quixote commented, 'because there is no poet who is not arrogant and does not consider himself the greatest poet in the world.'

'There's no rule without an exception,' Don Lorenzo replied, 'and there must be somewhere a poet who is great but doesn't think he is.'

'There are very few of them,' Don Quixote replied, 'but do tell me this: what are these verses that you have in hand and that your good father tells me are making you somewhat pensive and restless? For if they take the form of a verse gloss, I do have some slight understanding of that art, and I should be happy to hear them; and if they are intended for a literary competition, you should try to win the second prize; because the first prize is always given as a personal favour or in recognition of the poet's social status, the second prize is won on pure merit and the third prize is really the second prize – and the first prize, by this reckoning, is the third prize, just as happens with university degrees. But in spite of all that, the name "First" does cut a fine figure.'

'So far,' Don Lorenzo said to himself, 'I can't consider you a madman; let's move on.'

And he said:

'I have the impression that you're a university man: what subjects did you study?'

'I studied knight-errantry,' Don Quixote replied, 'which is as good a subject as poetry, and even perhaps a fraction better.'

'I don't know what subject that is,' Don Lorenzo said. 'Until now I'd never even heard of it.'

'It is a subject,' Don Quixote replied, 'that contains within itself all or most of the other subjects in the world, because the man who applies himself to it must be a jurist and know the laws of distributive and commutative justice, so as to give to each what belongs to him and is due to him; he must be a theologian, so as to explain the Christian faith that he professes, clearly and distinctly, whenever this is requested of him; he must be a physician, and especially a herbalist, so as to recognize in the midst of wastelands and wildernesses those herbs that have the power to cure wounds, because the knight errant cannot be forever stopping to look for someone to attend to them; he must be an astrologer, so as to tell by the stars how many hours of the night have passed, and what part of the world he is in; he must know mathematics, because he will be in constant need of them; and leaving aside the fact that he must be adorned with all the theological and cardinal virtues and descending to more trivial details, I can say that he must know how to swim as well as it is said that Pesce Cola could swim,[3] he must know how to shoe a horse and mend a saddle and a bridle; and, returning to higher matters, he must keep faith with God and his lady; he must be pure in his thoughts, chaste in his words, generous in his works, valiant in his deeds, long-suffering in his travails, compassionate towards the needy and, in short, a defender of the truth, even if it costs him his life to defend it. Of all these qualities, both great and small, a good knight errant is composed, so now you can see, Don Lorenzo, whether this is some sort of child's play that the knight who studies and practises it has to learn, or whether it can rub shoulders with the most highfalutin subjects taught in your colleges and your universities.'

'If all this is true,' Don Lorenzo replied, 'I do declare that this subject is superior to all the others.'

'What do you mean, if this is true?' retorted Don Quixote.

'What I mean to say,' said Don Lorenzo, 'is that I doubt whether there are now, or have ever been, knights errant adorned with so many virtues.'

'Many times have I said what I shall now say once again,' Don Quixote replied. 'Most people in this world are of the opinion that there never were any knights errant in it; and since it seems that if heaven does not miraculously reveal to them the truth that such knights did and do exist, any effort that one makes oneself will be in vain (as experience has often shown me), and I do not intend now to stop to disabuse you of the error that you share with so many others; what I shall do is to pray to heaven to do the disabusing and make you realize how beneficial and necessary knights errant were in past centuries, and how useful they would be in the present one, were they but in fashion; but people are so sinful that what triumphs now is sloth and easy living and gluttony and luxury.'

'Now he's flipped his lid, our guest,' Don Lorenzo said to himself. 'But he's a splendid madman all the same, and I'd be a feeble fool not to think so.'

Here they ended their conversation, because they were called to lunch. Don Diego asked his son what conclusions he'd reached about the state of their guest's mind. He replied:

'All the doctors and fine clerks in the world couldn't make a fair copy of that man by eliminating his blotches of insanity: he's mad in streaks, complete with lucid intervals.'

They went off to lunch, and the food was exactly as Don Diego had said, when they were travelling together, that the food he offered his guests always was: clean, plentiful and tasty; but what most pleased Don Quixote was the marvellous silence throughout the house, which made it seem like a Carthusian monastery.[4] Once the tables had been cleared, God thanked and hands washed, Don Quixote entreated Don Lorenzo to recite the verses that he'd written for the literary competition. To which Don Lorenzo replied that, so as not to seem like one of those poets who refuse to read their verses when asked, and when not asked vomit them out, 'I will recite my verse gloss for you, but I'm not expecting any prizes for it – I only wrote it to exercise my mind.'

'A friend of mine, and an intelligent one at that,' Don Quixote replied, 'was of the opinion that nobody should weary himself writing verse glosses, and the reason, he said, was that the gloss was bound to fall short of the text glossed, and that often, nearly always in fact, it was a long way from the purpose and intention of the original; and, furthermore, the rules governing verse glosses were too strict, not allowing questions, or *he said*, or *I shall say*, or using verbs as nouns, or changing the sense, together with all sorts of other restrictions that constrain the authors of glosses, as you must know only too well.'

'The truth is, Don Quixote sir,' said Don Lorenzo, 'that I'd love to catch you out in some really big blunder, but I can't, because you keep slipping through my fingers like an eel.'

'I fail to understand,' Don Quixote replied, 'what you mean, sir, when you refer to my slipping through your fingers.'

'I'll let you know in due course,' Don Lorenzo replied, 'and in the meantime you can pay attention to the lines glossed and the gloss itself, and they go like this:

> If only *was* were *is* for me,
> Without awaiting what *will be*,
> Or else if Time could speed its way
> With what must come to me one day . . . !

GLOSS

> Dame Fortune, once upon a day,
> Was generous to me, and kind;
> But what she gave she took away,
> For all things change: she changed her mind,
> And what she took she won't repay.
> O Fortune: for a century
> I've waited here on bended knee:
> Just make me lucky, I implore,
> I'd be a happy man once more
> *If only was were is for me.*

> No other prize I seek to gain,
> No triumph, glory or success;
> All that I want is to attain
> That precious, longed-for happiness
> That in my memory is pain.
> If you would make this gift to me,
> O Fortune, then I'd surely see
> The fury of my fire allayed,
> The more so if it's not delayed:
> *Without awaiting what will be.*

> It's hopeless, what I'm asking for:
> Time can't be put back to an hour
> At which it has been once before;
> That's something that no earthly power
> Has ever managed, to be sure.

Time runs along and flies away
And won't come back until doomsday,
And I well know it isn't right
To ask if Time could halt its flight
Or else if Time could speed its way.

I do not live: I agonize;
This life of hope, this life of dread
Is only death in thin disguise.
Perhaps, I think, by being dead,
I'd find relief: he rests who dies.
I tell myself that the best way
Would be to die, but then I say
I'm wrong: more thought makes it quite clear
That life fills me with holy fear
Of what must come to me one day.'

As Don Lorenzo finished reciting his gloss, Don Quixote came to his feet, grasped the young man's right hand, and said in a voice so loud that he seemed to be shouting:

'As God's in heaven above, my noble youth, you are the best poet in the world, and you deserve to be crowned with laurel, not by Cyprus or Gaeta, as the poet said and God forgive him for it,[5] but by the Academies of Athens, if they still existed, and by those that do exist today in Paris, Bologna and Salamanca! Heaven grant that the judges who will rob you of the first prize are transfixed by the arrows of Phoebus,[6] and that the muses never cross the thresholds of their homes. Now recite to me, sir, if you will, some pentameters, for I should like to feel the pulse of your admirable abilities in all their aspects.'

Isn't it rich that Don Lorenzo is said to have been delighted to be praised by Don Quixote, even though he thought he was a madman? O power of flattery, how far do you extend, and how wide are the frontiers of your pleasant realm! Don Lorenzo proved this truth by complying with Don Quixote's wish and request and reciting to him this sonnet about the fable or history of Pyramus and Thisbe:[7]

SONNET

The maid splits Pyramus's heart in two
And then she splits the intervening wall;
From Cyprus, Cupid hurries here to view
A breach that's as enormous as it's small.

Here silence speaks, for through this narrow rift
The boldest voice would never dare proceed;
But souls meet here, for Love enjoys the gift
Of making light of the most awesome deed.

The careless virgin patterns her own plight
As lust comes marching forth: her steps create
Her death as she pursues her own delight.
But both will be united in their fate:
One sword, one sepulchre, one memory
Kills, covers, gives its immortality.

'Heaven be praised,' said Don Quixote when he had heard Don Lorenzo's sonnet. 'Among the countless consumptive poets that there are in this world, I have at last come across a consummate one – for that is what you are, my dear sir: the skill with which this sonnet is composed demonstrates as much to me!'

For four days Don Quixote lived a life of luxury in Don Diego's house, and then he begged permission to leave, saying that he was grateful for all Don Diego's kindness and hospitality, but that since it did not become knights errant to give themselves over to leisure and luxury for too long, he wished to go and do his duty, looking for the adventures that, as he was informed, abounded in that land, where he hoped to employ his time until he went to the jousts at Saragossa, his ultimate goal. But first he intended to go down into the Cave of Montesinos, of which so many amazing stories were told in those parts, and he also had to investigate and discover the origins and true sources of the seven lakes commonly known as the Lakes of Ruidera.[8] Don Diego and his son praised Don Quixote's honourable decision, and told him to take from the house whatever he liked, because their only desire was to help him, as they were obliged to do by the worth of his person and the honourable profession that he followed.

At length the day of his departure arrived, as happy for Don Quixote as it was miserable and wretched for Sancho, who was much enjoying life amidst the plenty of Don Diego's house and didn't at all fancy the idea of going back to the hunger that was the norm in the woods and the wilds and to the austerity of his ill-stocked saddle-bags. But he filled them to bursting with what he considered most necessary, and when the two took their leave Don Quixote said to Don Lorenzo:

'I do not know whether I said this before, and if I did say it I shall say it again: if you wish to save labour and shorten the distance to be travelled to reach the inaccessible peak of the temple of fame, all you have to do is to leave the somewhat narrow path of poetry and strike out along the still narrower path of knight-errantry, which can make you an emperor in the twinkling of an eye.'

With these words Don Quixote settled the case against his madness, and doubly so with what he added:

'God knows I should like to take Don Lorenzo with me, to show him how to forgive the humble and subdue the proud and trample them underfoot, virtues inherent to the profession that I follow; but since his tender age makes this inadvisable, and his praiseworthy pursuits will not permit it, I shall limit myself to advising you that as a poet he might become famous if he allows himself to be guided more by the opinions of others than by his own, because there is no father or mother who thinks his own children are ugly, and with children of the mind the peril is even greater.'

Father and son again wondered at Don Quixote's interlarding of sense and nonsense, and at his mania for devoting himself heart and soul to the search for his adventures or misadventures, the aim and object of his every desire. The offers of service and the civilities were repeated and, with the gracious permission of the lady of the castle, Don Quixote and Sancho rode away on Rocinante and the dun.

CHAPTER XIX

*Which relates the adventure of the shepherd in love,
together with other truly amusing events*

Don Quixote hadn't ridden far from Don Diego's village when he came across two men who appeared to be priests or students and two farmers, all four of them on asses. One of the students was carrying what looked like some white cambric and two pairs of serge hose, wrapped in a piece of green buckram as if it were a travelling bag; the other only carried a new pair of fencing foils, with their buttons on. The farmers had other objects, which indicated that they were riding back to their village from some town where they'd bought them; and both the students and the farmers were struck with the same wonder that struck everyone on first seeing Don Quixote, and were dying to learn what man this was, so different from the normal sort. Don Quixote greeted them, and when he discovered which way they were going, the same as his own, he offered them his company, asked them to slow down, because their she-asses were moving faster than his horse, and obliged them with a brief account of who he was and what profession he followed – that of the knight errant, who roamed all over the world in search of adventures. He told them that his personal name was Don Quixote de la Mancha, and that he went under the title of the Knight of the Lions. For the farmers it was as if he'd addressed them in Greek or Double Dutch, but not for the students, who soon realized that Don Quixote was weak in the head; for all that, however, they regarded him with wonder and respect, and one of them said:

'If, sir knight, you aren't following any fixed route, as is the custom among those who go in search of adventures, do come with us: you will witness one of the finest and most sumptuous weddings that can ever have been celebrated in La Mancha or for many many miles around.'

Don Quixote asked whether this was some nobleman's wedding that he was extolling so.

'No,' the student replied, 'it's the wedding of a farmer and a farmer's daughter – he's the richest man in all these parts, and she's the most beautiful woman that any man has ever seen. It's going to be done with quite extraordinary and novel splendour, because it's to be held in a field near the bride's village – she's known simply as Quiteria the Fair, and her husband-to-be is Camacho the Rich, and she's eighteen and he's twenty-two, the two of them perfectly matched, although some busybodies who know everybody's pedigree by heart do say that lovely Quiteria's is better than Camacho's; but nobody worries about that sort of thing any more, because gold is a good solder for all sorts of cracks. And Camacho's a big spender, and he's taken it into his head to have the whole field roofed over with branches, so the sun's going to have its work cut out if it wants to get in and visit the green grass growing on the ground. Camacho has also arranged for there to be performances of both sword-dancing and bell-dancing, because there are men in his village who can brandish those and ring these like nobody's business; and as for the flamenco dancers, well, he's hired hordes of them; yet nothing of what I've mentioned and none of the many other things I haven't mentioned is going to do as much to make this wedding memorable as what I imagine the slighted Basilio's going to come and do. This Basilio is a shepherd who lives in the same village as Quiteria, indeed his house is right next door to her parents' house, which gave Cupid the chance to bring the forgotten love of Pyramus and Thisbe back into the world, because Basilio fell in love with Quiteria when he was still a boy of tender years, and she responded with a thousand innocent demonstrations of affection, so much so that people used to amuse themselves in the village by telling each other stories about the love affair of the two children, Basilio and Quiteria. As they grew up, Quiteria's father decided not to allow Basilio into his house any more and, to save being dogged by mistrust and suspicion, arranged for his daughter to be married to Camacho the Rich, because he didn't think it wise to marry her to Basilio, less well endowed by fortune with material wealth than by nature with personal qualities; because to leave envy aside and speak the honest truth, he's the nimblest lad we know, a great pitcher of the bar, a splendid wrestler and a superb pelota-player; he can run like a deer, jump further than a goat and knock the skittles down like magic; he sings like a lark, and when he plays the guitar you'd say he's making it talk, and, above all, he can fence with the best of them.'

'For that gift alone,' Don Quixote put in, 'this youth deserves to marry not only the fair Quiteria, but Queen Guinevere herself, if she were alive today, in spite of Lancelot and anybody else who tried to prevent it.'

'You go and tell that to the wife!' said Sancho Panza, who until then had been listening in silence. 'She thinks it's wrong for people to marry anyone except their equals, believing as she does in the proverb "Every Jack to his Jill". What I'd like to happen is for that bloke Basilio, who I'm beginning to take a liking to, to marry that lady Quiteria, and I just hope all those that stop people who love each other from marrying enjoy the life eternal and rest in peace – I don't think.'

'If everybody married the person they love,' said Don Quixote, 'parents would lose their power to marry their children when and to whom they should; and if it were left to daughters to choose their husbands as they pleased, one would pick her father's servant, and another a man she has seen walking down the street and who she thinks looks jaunty and dashing, even though he is in reality some wild swashbuckler; because love and fancy easily blind the eyes of the understanding, which are so necessary when making decisions about settling down in life, and with marriage there is such a danger of making mistakes, and great circumspection and the special help of heaven are needed to make the right choice. When a prudent man sets out on a long journey, he first looks for someone trustworthy and agreeable to keep him company. Well, should not someone setting out on the journey of life, with death as his destination, do the same, particularly since the person he chooses will keep him company in bed, at the table and everywhere else, as a wife does her husband? The companionship of one's wife is not some article of merchandise that can be returned or bartered or exchanged after it has been purchased; it is an inseparable appendage that lasts as long as life itself lasts. It is a noose that once placed round the neck becomes a Gordian knot,[1] never to be undone except by the scythe of death. There is much else that I could say on this subject, were I not constrained by my anxiety to know whether my friend the Master of Arts here has anything else to say about the history of Basilio.'

To which the student, whether a mere BA or a full MA as Don Quixote had called him, replied:

'All I've got left to say is that ever since the moment when Basilio found out that the fair Quiteria was marrying Camacho the Rich, nobody has seen him laugh or heard him speak sense, and he's always plunged in thought and dejected and talking to himself, clear and certain signs that he's gone mad; he hardly eats or sleeps, and all he does eat is fruit, and when he sleeps, if he sleeps at all, it's in the open, on the hard ground, like a brute beast; sometimes he gazes up at the sky, and at other times he stares down at the earth, so stupefied that he looks for all the world like a dummy wearing clothes blown to and fro by the wind. In short, he's showing every sign of a broken heart, and all of us who know him fear that tomorrow when the fair Quiteria says "I will" it'll be his death sentence.'

'God will find a remedy,' said Sancho, 'because he sends the ointment after the wound, and nobody knows what the future has in store for us – from now till tomorrow the hours are many, and in any one of them, or in just one moment, the house can come tumbling down, and I've seen it raining while the sun was shining, and a man can go to bed hale and hearty and wake up unable to stir. And you just tell me this – can anyone claim to have put a spoke in the wheel of fortune? No, of course not, and between a woman's yea and a woman's nay I wouldn't try to put the point of a pin, there wouldn't be room for it. You give me Quiteria head over heels in love with Basilio, and I'll give him a sackful of happiness, because love, so I've heard, looks through spectacles that make copper seem like gold, poverty like wealth, and water in the eyes like pearls.'

'And where is all that supposed to take us, Sancho, curse you?' said Don Quixote. 'Once you start stringing your proverbs and sayings together the only person who would wait to hear you out is Judas himself, may he take your soul. Tell me, you animal, what do you understand about spokes, or wheels, or anything else for that matter?'

'Oh, if nobody understands me,' Sancho retorted, 'it's no wonder if my words of wisdom are taken for nonsense. But it doesn't matter, I know what I mean, and I also know that there wasn't much that was stupid in what I just said – it's just that you're such a cricket, sir, of everything I say, as well as of everything I do.'

'*Critic* is what you should say,' said Don Quixote, 'not *cricket*, you corrupter of good language, God damn you.'

'You shouldn't turn on me like that,' Sancho replied, 'because you know I wasn't brought up in the capital or taught at Salamanca to be able to tell whether I change a few letters in my words here and there. Good God, man, you can't expect a country bumpkin from Sayago[2] to speak like a nob from Toledo, and there might even be people from Toledo who aren't that hot at talking posh.'

'That's very true,' said the student, 'because people brought up in the Tanneries or around Zocodover Square can't be expected to speak as well as people who spend most of their day strolling round the cathedral cloister – and they're all Toledans. Pure, correct, elegant and clear language is to be found among courtiers of good sense, even if they were born in a village like Majalahonda;[3] and I say "of good sense" because there are many courtiers of another kind, and good sense is the grammar of correct language, assisted by custom and usage. I, sirs, for my sins, studied canon law at Salamanca, and I take some pride in expressing myself in clear, plain and meaningful language.'

'If you didn't take more pride in how you wag those foils of yours than in how you wag your tongue,' said the other student, 'you'd have been top of the class list instead of bottom.'

'Look you here, Corchuelo, BA,' replied the MA, 'you're as wrong as it's possible to be if you believe that skill at fencing is a waste of time.'

'As far as I'm concerned it isn't a belief but an established truth,' Corchuelo retorted, 'and if you want me to prove it to you in practice, you have brought your foils, this is a convenient spot and I have a steady hand and a strong arm that, backed by my stout spirit, will make you confess that I am not mistaken. Get off your donkey, and try out all your precious measured steps and circles and angles and science, because I'm going to make you see stars at midday with my modern, uncouth swordsmanship, and I trust that with it, and with God's help, the man isn't yet born who can make me turn my back or whom I can't force to give ground.'

'As to whether you turn your back or not, that's no affair of mine,' the fencing master replied, 'although it might well be that your grave will open up for you at the very spot where you first place your foot – killed, I mean, by the science that you so despise.'

'We'll soon see about that,' Corchuelo replied.

And leaping from his donkey he snatched one of the foils that the MA was carrying.

'No, that is not the way!' Don Quixote exclaimed. 'I shall be the umpire of this contest and the judge of this long unsettled question.'

And dismounting from Rocinante and seizing his lance, he stationed himself in the middle of the road, as the MA, with fine elegance of bearing and measured step, advanced on Corchuelo, who came at him with his eyes darting fire, as the saying goes. The two farmers accompanying them remained on their she-asses, spectators of the mortal tragedy. Corchuelo's slashes, lunges, down-strokes, back-strokes and flicks were innumerable and came thicker than raw liver, more unremitting than hail. He would rush in like an angry lion, but would be met by a tickle on the teeth by the button on the end on the MA's foil that stopped him in the midst of his fury and made him kiss it as if it were some holy relic, although with less devotion than holy relics should be and usually are kissed. In the end, the MA gave every button on his cassock a twirl, cut his skirt to ribbons like the tentacles on an octopus, knocked his hat off twice and so exasperated him that in his vexation, anger and fury he took his foil by the hilt and flung it away with such force that one of the farmers who were present, who was also a notary, and who went to fetch it, later gave evidence that it had been thrown a good two miles, which only goes to show, with the utmost clarity, how brute strength is overcome by skill.

Corchuelo flopped down, exhausted, and Sancho walked over to him and said:

'By my faith, mister BA, if you take my advice you won't go challenging anyone to a fencing duel ever again, but to wrestling or pitching the bar, because you've got the youth and the strength for that – I've heard that these duellists as they call them can stick the tip of a foil through the eye of a needle.'

'I'm well pleased,' Corchuelo replied, 'to have tumbled to the truth, and to have learned from experience what I was very far from believing.'

And he got up and embraced the other student, and they were even better friends than before; and not wanting to wait for the notary who'd gone to fetch the foil, since they assumed it was going to take him some time to do so, they decided to continue on their way so as to reach Quiteria's village, where they all lived, in good time. On the way the MA told them all about the splendours of fencing, adducing so many conclusive arguments and geometric figures and mathematical proofs that they were all left well informed about the virtues of that science, and Corchuelo renounced his stubborn opposition.

Night was only just now falling, but as they approached the village it seemed as if a heaven full of countless shining stars were extended before them. They heard, too, the softly mingling tones of different instruments such as flutes, tabors, psalteries, shawms, tambourines and timbrels,[4] and as they drew near they saw that the branches in a great canopy that had been constructed beside the village were all full of little lanterns, undisturbed by the wind, which was blowing so softly that it didn't have the strength to stir the leaves in the trees. The musicians were the entertainers at the wedding, wandering in groups about that pleasant place, some dancing, others singing and others playing the different instruments already mentioned. And it really seemed as if joy and good cheer themselves were frolicking and leaping all over that meadow. Many other people were busy raising platforms so that on the following day they would be able to watch in comfort the plays and dances that were going to be performed in that place dedicated to the celebration of Camacho the Rich's wedding and Basilio's funeral.

Don Quixote refused to enter the village, even though both the farmer and the student begged him to; and he gave as his excuse, more than sufficient in his opinion, that it was the custom of knights errant to sleep in fields and forests rather than in towns, even if under gilded ceilings; and so he rode a little off the road, much against Sancho's will, because Sancho recalled the excellent lodging that he had enjoyed in Don Diego's castle or house.

CHAPTER XX

Which relates the wedding of Camacho the Rich and the incident of Basilio the Poor

Scarce had fair Aurora allowed shining Phoebus time to dry the liquid pearls on her locks of gold with the heat of his burning rays, when Don Quixote shook sloth from his limbs, rose to his feet and called to his squire Sancho, who was still snoring; seeing which, Don Quixote addressed him thus before awaking him:

'O happy you above all who dwell upon the face of the earth for, neither envying nor envied, you sleep with a tranquil spirit and without enchanters to pursue you or enchantments to alarm you! Sleep on, I say again, and so shall I say another hundred times, without any jealous thoughts of your lady to hold you in perpetual vigil, or any worries about how to pay your debts, or what to do so that you and your distraught little family can eat tomorrow, to keep you awake. Neither does ambition disturb you nor does the vain pomp of this world worry you, because the limits of your desires extend no further than the feeding of your donkey: looking after your person is a responsibility that you have placed upon my shoulders, a counterweight and burden that nature and usage have imposed on us masters. The servant sleeps and the master lies awake, worrying about how to maintain him, better him and favour him. The anguish of seeing the heavens turning to brass and refusing to succour the earth with their necessary moisture does not afflict the servant but only the master, who in times of barrenness and hunger must provide for one who ministered to him in times of fertility and abundance.'

Sancho didn't reply to all this, because he was fast asleep, and he wouldn't have awoken as soon as he did if Don Quixote hadn't revived him by prodding him with the butt of his lance. In the end he did wake up, stretching and yawning, and he said as he peered all around:

'From that canopy over there, if I'm not much mistaken, there's a beautiful smell coming that's got more to do with fried rashers than with galingale and thyme – by all that's holy, a wedding that starts with smells like this is bound to be a plentiful and lavish one!'

'Stop it, you glutton,' said Don Quixote. 'Come on, let us go and witness this wedding and discover what the rejected Basilio is going to do.'

'He can do whatever he likes,' Sancho replied. 'He shouldn't have been poor and then he could have married Quiteria. It's a fine thing, not a penny to his name and wanting to marry way up the ladder like that! By my faith, sir, to my mind a poor man ought to be happy with what he can get, and not go reaching for the moon and the stars. I'll bet my arm that Camacho could bury Basilio in reals, and if this is true, as I'm sure it is, Quiteria would be a right idiot to turn down the jewels and finery Camacho can give her and must already have given her, and go instead for Basilio's bar-pitching and fencing. You won't get so much as a half-pint of wine in a tavern for a good pitch of your bar or a neat thrust with your sword. Those are skills and gifts that aren't saleable, even if Count Dirlos[1] himself has them, but when gifts like that fall to someone with lots of money, oh my, don't they look fine then! On a good foundation you can build a good house, and the best foundation in the world is money.'

'For God's sake, Sancho,' Don Quixote expostulated, 'do stop this harangue of yours; it is my belief that if you were allowed to continue each time you start one, as you do every five minutes, you wouldn't have any time left to eat or sleep, because you'd spend all your time talking.'

'If you happened to have a good memory,' Sancho replied, 'you might have remembered the clauses we put in our agreement, before we left home this last time, and one of them was that you'd let me talk as much as I liked, so long as I didn't insult anyone or undermine your authority – and up till now it seems to me I haven't broken that clause.'

'I have no recollection, Sancho,' Don Quixote replied, 'of any such clause, and even if you are right I want you to keep quiet and come with me, because the instruments that we heard last night are beginning to enliven the valleys again, and no doubt the wedding will be celebrated in the cool of the morning rather than in the heat of the afternoon.'

Sancho did as he was told, and after he'd saddled Rocinante and put the pack-saddle on the dun the two men mounted and rode slowly into the canopied field. What first met Sancho's gaze was a whole ox spitted on a whole elm trunk, and where it was going to be roasted a fair-sized mountain of faggots were burning, and six cooking pots that stood around the fire hadn't been made in normal cooking-pot moulds, because they were six medium-sized vats, with room for a slaughterhouseful of meat in each of them; whole sheep disappeared in there without trace like so many pigeons; the skinned hares and plucked hens, strung up on the branches waiting to be buried in the cooking pots, were uncountable; the birds and other game of all kinds hanging from the trees for the breeze to keep them cool were infinite. Sancho counted more than sixty wineskins each holding a good fifty pints, and every one of them full, as became evident later, of fine, old wine; there were heaps of the whitest loaves, like the piles of grain by the side of a threshing floor; the cheeses, built up like interlocking bricks, formed a solid wall, and two cauldrons of olive oil, bigger than dyers' vats, were for frying doughnuts that were removed with two enormous paddles once they'd been cooked, and plunged into another cauldron full of warm honey. There were more than fifty cooks, of both sexes, all busy, spotless and jolly. Sewn into the ox's bulging belly were twelve juicy little sucking pigs to make it tasty and tender. The spices of many different kinds seemed not to have been bought by the pound but by the bushel, and they were all on show in a great chest. In short, the splendour of the wedding was a rustic splendour, but on a scale to feed an army.

Sancho Panza looked, gazed and fell in love. What first won his heart were the cooking pots, from which he would have been more than willing to take a decent-sized bowlful, then the wineskins took his fancy; and what finally captivated him was all that fruit of the frying pan, if such rotund cauldrons can be given such a humble name; and so, unable to bear it any longer and powerless to act otherwise, he sidled up to one of the busy cooks and in courteous and hungry words asked to be allowed to dunk a crust of bread in one of those pots. To which the cook replied:

'Today isn't a day when hunger holds sway, my friend – thanks to Camacho the Rich. You get down from your donkey and see if you can find yourself a ladle, and skim off a hen or two, and much good may they do you.'

'But I can't see any ladles,' said Sancho.

'Wait a minute,' said the cook. 'Goodness me, what a hopeless old fusspot you are!'

And so saying he grabbed a great stew-pan, plunged it deep into one of the vats, hauled it out with three hens and two geese inside and said:

'There you go, my friend, you can have these skimmings for your breakfast, to keep you going till lunchtime.'

'But I haven't got anything to put them in,' Sancho replied.

'Well you can just take the ladle and all,' said the cook, 'Camacho's riches and the good mood he's in will buy replacements for anything and everything.'

While Sancho was busy with the cook, Don Quixote was watching how on one side of the canopied field a dozen farmers in their best party clothes were riding in on twelve handsome mares decked out in splendid, showy rustic trappings with many little bells on their breast straps; and then they all raced, in an orderly troop, not just once but many times up and down the field, joyfully crying at the tops of their voices:

'Long live Camacho and Quiteria, he as rich as she is fair, and she the fairest maid in all the world!'

When Don Quixote heard this, he muttered:

'No doubt these people have not seen my Dulcinea del Toboso, because if they had seen her they would be more moderate in their praises of this Quiteria of theirs.'

A little after this, many different groups of dancers began to file into the canopied field from all sides, among them a group of sword-dancers – some two dozen handsome and spirited-looking lads, all dressed in fine-spun cotton of the purest white and wearing many-coloured silk headscarves; and one of the men on the mares asked the leader, a sprightly youth, if there had been any injuries yet.

'None so far, thank God – we're all still in one piece.'

And then he began to weave his intricate patterns with his companions, turning so often and so nimbly that although Don Quixote had seen many sword dances before he'd never seen one as fine as this. He also relished a dance performed by a group of lovely maidens, all in the prime of life, for none of them seemed younger than fourteen or as old as eighteen, all dressed in green Cuenca cloth,[2] with their hair partly plaited and partly loose, but all of it so golden that it could rival the sun itself, and on their heads they wore garlands of jasmine, roses, amaranth and honeysuckle. Their leaders were a venerable old man and an aged matron, much nimbler than their years suggested. The music was provided by a Zamora double pipe,[3] and the maidens, with modesty in their faces and in their eyes, and agility in their feet, showed themselves to be the best dancers in the world.

After this came another group dancing a set piece known as a spoken masque: there were eight nymphs, in two lines; the leader of one line was the god Cupid, and the leader of the other line was Wealth; the former was adorned with wings, a bow, a quiver and arrows; the latter wore many-coloured silk and gold. The nymphs following Love carried their names on their backs, written in large letters on white parchment. The first was called Poetry, the second Sound Sense, the third Good Family and the fourth Valour. The nymphs following Wealth were similarly identified: the first was labelled Liberality, the second Largesse, the third Treasure and the fourth Peaceful Possession. In front of all of them came a castle of wood, pulled by four wild men, all dressed in ivy and hemp dyed green, and looking so lifelike that they almost scared Sancho out of his wits. On the front of the float and on all four sides of the castle was written: The Castle of Virtuous Modesty. The music was played by four skilful performers on pipe and drum. Cupid began the dance, and after he'd completed two figures he stood there raising his eyes and bending his bow in the direction of a maiden who went to stand behind the castle battlements, and to whom he said:

> I am the mighty deity
> Who rules on land and in the air
> And in the broad and stormy sea;
> My power is awesome everywhere,
> For hell itself's subdued by me.
> Fear is a thing I never knew;
> All that I wish must needs come true
> Even if it's impossible:
> My motto is 'I can and will',
> I make and break, do and undo.

He finished his verse, shot an arrow over the castle, and went back to his place. Then Wealth stepped forward, and danced another two figures; the drums fell silent, and he said:

> I'm stronger still, Love must concede,
> Although what leads me on is Love;
> I'm born of quite the finest breed
> Sent down to earth from heaven above,
> Famous and powerful indeed.
> I'm Wealth, I triumph come what may;
> To use me well, few know the way,
> To do without me, fewer still;

And so, just as I am, I will
Be yours for ever and a day.

Wealth went back to his place, Poetry came forward and, after dancing his figures like the other two, he gazed up at the maiden in the castle and said:

> Now Poetry, tuneful and sweet,
> Sends you his soul, my lovely maid,
> In many a delicate conceit
> And in a thousand songs arrayed,
> All lofty, graceful and discreet.
> And if my persevering tune
> Does not annoy you, I shall soon
> Exalt your fortune to the skies,
> The envy of a million eyes,
> Above the circle of the moon.

Poetry stood aside, and from Wealth's file Liberality came forward, danced his figures, and said:

> What men call Liberality
> Consists in gifts without excess:
> No reckless prodigality
> And no weak-willed miserliness
> Or lack of cordiality.
> Now I'll be prodigal and free,
> An honoured vice, if vice it be,
> And fitting well the lover's part
> For he in giving shows his heart;
> So this will be my eulogy.

In this way each pair of characters from the two groups came out and then returned to their places after dancing their figures and saying their lines, some elegant and some ridiculous, but Don Quixote only committed to memory (he had an excellent one) the verses quoted; and then they all mingled in the dance, forming themselves into patterns and breaking up again with the most elegant grace and poise; and whenever Love passed in front of the castle he shot his arrows into the air, but Wealth smashed gilded piggy-banks against it. Finally, after they'd been dancing for some time, Wealth took out a great purse made from the skin of a striped cat, which seemed to be full of money, and hurled it at the castle causing the planks to come apart and fall down and leaving the maiden exposed and defenceless. Wealth approached her with his followers and, by putting a great chain of gold round her neck, they indicated that they were defeating her and taking her prisoner, but when Love and his retinue saw this they made to snatch her away, and all these movements were danced in a well-ordered manner to the beat of the side-drums. The wild men established peace among them again and rapidly reassembled the castle, the maiden shut herself inside it as at the outset, and with this the dance ended to the great satisfaction of all those who had watched it.

Don Quixote asked one of the nymphs who had composed and arranged the dance. She replied that it was a clergyman from the village, who had a real gift for making up shows like that.

'And I'll wager,' said Don Quixote, 'that this student or clergyman is on better terms with Camacho than with Basilio, and that he's fonder of satire than of vespers: he did a good job of introducing Basilio's abilities and Camacho's wealth into the dance!'

Sancho Panza, who was eavesdropping, said:

'My money's on the winner – I'm sticking by Camacho.'

'Well, well, Sancho,' said Don Quixote, 'it is easy to see that you are a peasant, and one of those who always shout "Long live the conqueror!" '

'I don't know what I'm one of,' Sancho retorted, 'but I do know that I'm never going to get such fine skimmings off Basilio's cooking pots as I did off Camacho's.'

And he showed his master the stew-pan full of geese and hens and, grabbing one of them, began to eat with a good grace and a better appetite as he said:

'Let all Basilio's talents try paying for this lot! You're worth as much as you've got, and you get as much as you're worth. There are just two families in the world, my old grandma used to say, the haves and the have-nots, and she always stuck by the haves, and nowadays, Don Quixote sir, you're more respected for having than for knowing – an ass laden with gold looks better than a horse carrying a pack-saddle. I've said it before and I'll say it again, I'm sticking by Camacho, because the rich skimmings off his pots are geese and hens and hares and rabbits, and what you skim off Basilio's pots, if it comes to hand, though it'd be better for your feet, is wish-wash.'

'Have you quite finished your harangue, Sancho?' Don Quixote enquired.

'I suppose I'd better have,' Sancho replied, 'I can see you aren't very pleased with it, but if all this here hadn't got in the way I'd have had enough to go on about for three days.'

'God grant, Sancho,' replied Don Quixote, 'that I may see you struck dumb before I die.'

'At the rate we're going,' Sancho retorted, 'I'll be chewing clay long before you're dead, and in that case it might well be that I'm struck so dumb that I won't speak another word till the end of the world, or till doomsday at least.'

'Even if that did happen, O Sancho,' Don Quixote replied, 'your silence in death will never be able to outstrip all the talking you have done, do and still have to do in life; and furthermore, it is in the order of nature that the day of my demise should come before yours; and so I never expect to see you struck dumb, not even when drinking or sleeping – which is what I find most admirable of all.'

'By my faith, sir,' Sancho replied, 'you can't rely on Old Madam Rattlebones you know, by which I mean death, she devours lambs as well as sheep, and I've heard our priest say that with equal foot she tramples on the tall towers of kings and the humble hovels of the poor. What that lady is is powerful, not finicky, and she isn't at all squeamish either, she'll eat anything and make do with anything and she fills her food-bags with all sorts of people, all ages, all ranks. She isn't a reaper who has a nap in the afternoon, she goes out reaping at all hours, she cuts down dry grass and green grass alike, and you'd say she doesn't chew but rather swallows whole whatever's put in front of her, because she's always as hungry as a wolf, and she's never full, and although she hasn't got a belly it's as if she's suffering from the dropsy, always thirsty to guzzle down the lives of all living beings, like someone drinking a pitcher of cold water.'

'That's quite enough, Sancho,' Don Quixote broke in. 'Stay just where you are, on firm ground, and don't go stumbling off into the mire, for truly what you have just said in your rustic language about death is no less than what an able preacher could have said. Let me tell you, Sancho: you have enough good sense and natural talent to take your pulpit in your hand and travel around the world preaching the most splendid sermons.'

'He preaches well that lives well,' Sancho replied, 'and that's all the theology I know.'

'And it's all you need to know,' said Don Quixote, 'but I simply cannot understand how it is that, the fear of the Lord being the beginning of wisdom,[4] you who are more afraid of a lizard than of him know so much.'

'You be the judge of your chivalries, sir,' Sancho replied, 'and don't go setting yourself up as the judge of other people's fear or courage, because I'm as good a fearer of the Lord as the next man. And now let me finish off these skimmings, because all the rest is idle talk that we'll have to account for in another life.'[5]

So saying he renewed his attack on his stew-pan, with such vigour that he made Don Quixote feel hungry, too; and he would have gone to Sancho's assistance if he hadn't been prevented by what must be recounted next.

CHAPTER XXI

Which continues Camacho's wedding, together with other agreeable events

While Don Quixote and Sancho were engaged in the conversation recorded in the previous chapter, they heard a great racket and hullabaloo, and it was made by the men on the mares as they galloped whooping to meet the bride and groom, who were on their way surrounded by hundreds of musicians and masques and accompanied by the priest, their relations and all the top people from the neighbouring villages, wearing their Sunday best. And when Sancho saw the bride he said:

'By my faith, she isn't dressed like a farmer's daughter at all, but like a fine palace lady! Good God, as far as I can see, the tin medallions you'd expect her to be wearing are fine coral necklaces, and the green Cuenca cloth is thirty-pile velvet! And it's all trimmed with little strips of white cotton, isn't it just, oh yes! Upon my soul it's satin! And look at her hands wearing their humble rings of jet, I don't think – I'll be blowed if they aren't rings of gold, and solid gold at that, set with pearls as white as curds, and each pearl must be worth a fortune. What hair the little bugger's got, and if it isn't a wig I've never seen longer or blonder hair in all my born days! Oh yes, I'm going to stand here finding fault with her looks and her grace, I am, and I'm not going to liken her to a palm tree swaying in the breeze and loaded with bunches of dates, because that's exactly what the jewels hanging from her hair and her neck do look like! I swear by my soul she's a fine figure of a girl, fit and ready to couch any man's lance.'

Don Quixote laughed at Sancho Panza's rustic praises. He himself thought he'd never seen a lovelier woman, apart from his lady Dulcinea del Toboso. Quiteria the Fair was looking rather pale – it must have been from the sleepless night that any bride spends preparing for her wedding. The couple was walking over to a platform that had been constructed on one side of the field and adorned with carpets and branches, where the ceremony was to take place and from where they would watch the dances and the masques. As they reached it, they heard shouts behind them:

'Wait a minute, you rash and thoughtless people!'

The cries made everyone look back, and they saw a man who seemed to be dressed in a loose black coat trimmed with pieces of red silk cut in the shape of flames. He was also wearing (as they soon noticed) a wreath of funereal cypress; he was carrying a long staff. As he came closer they all recognized the dashing Basilio, and they waited in bewilderment to see what would come of all his cries, fearing some evil consequence from his appearance at such a moment. He reached them at last, weary and breathless, stood in front of the bride and groom, rammed the steel spike on the end of his staff into the ground and, paling and with his eyes fixed on Quiteria, spoke these words in a hoarse and unsteady voice:

'You know very well, thankless Quiteria, that by the holy religion we profess you can't marry while I'm alive; neither are you unaware that while I've been waiting for time and my own efforts to increase my fortune

I haven't failed to observe the respect due to your honour; but you, turning your back on all you owe my pure love, want to make another man, whose riches bring him not only good fortune but supreme happiness, the master of what is mine. And now to complete his bliss – not that I think he deserves it, but because heaven will have it so – I, with my own hands, am going to destroy the hindrance or obstacle that could frustrate it, by removing myself from between you. Many years of happy life to Camacho the Rich and Quiteria the Ingrate, and death to Basilio the Poor, whose poverty has clipped the wings of his joy and laid him in his grave!'

And as he spoke he pulled at the stick that he'd thrust into the ground, and half of it remained there, revealing that it was a scabbard for the medium-length rapier hidden inside it; and he fixed what could be called the hilt in the earth and with speedy assurance and resolve threw himself on to it, and its bloody tip and half the steel blade emerged from his back, leaving the unhappy wretch stretched out on the ground, transfixed by his own weapon and bathed in his own blood. His friends, grief-stricken at this pitiful calamity, rushed to help him, and Don Quixote dismounted from Rocinante, went to his aid, took him into his arms and found that he had not yet expired. They were going to pull the rapier out, but the priest was of the opinion that they shouldn't do so until he'd made his confession, because his death would be the immediate consequence of removing the weapon. But Basilio began to show signs of life, and said in a faint and doleful voice:

'If you were willing, cruel Quiteria, to give me your hand as my bride in this last fateful moment, I could bring myself to believe that there might have been some excuse for my temerity, because it would have enabled me to attain the bliss of being yours.'

When the priest heard this he told Basilio to look to the well-being of his soul rather than to the pleasures of his body, and to implore God most earnestly to forgive him for his sins and for this deed of despair. To which Basilio replied that on no account would he make his confession unless Quiteria first gave him her hand in marriage, because the joy that this would bring him would stiffen his resolution and give him strength to make his confession. When Don Quixote heard the wounded man's request, he eloquently affirmed that what Basilio was asking was very just and reasonable, and practicable, too, and that Señor Camacho would be as honoured by receiving Señora Quiteria as brave Basilio's widow as if he received her from her father:

'It is merely a question of saying "I will", which can lead to nothing beyond itself, because the bridal bed of this wedding will be the grave.'

Camacho was listening to every word, and every word increased his bewilderment, unable as he was to decide what to say or do; but Basilio's friends were so insistent as they begged him to allow Quiteria to give Basilio her hand in marriage, so that he did not forfeit his soul by leaving this life in a state of despair, that they moved and even forced Camacho to say that if Quiteria wanted to marry Basilio he was happy for her to do so, as it was only putting off the fulfilment of his desires for an instant. Then they all turned to Quiteria and, some with entreaties, others with tears and others with weighty words, they implored her to give her hand to poor Basilio; but it seemed that she, harder than marble and more immovable than any statue, couldn't or wouldn't say one word in reply; and she would never have replied at all if the priest hadn't told her to hurry up and decide what she was going to do, because Basilio's weary spirit was hanging upon his lips, ready to take its leave, and there was no time to be wasted waiting for ditherers.

Then Quiteria the Fair, still silent, flustered and looking grief-stricken, went over to Basilio, who was by now showing the whites of his eyes, taking shallow, fast breaths, muttering the name of Quiteria and giving every indication that he was about to die like a heathen and not as a Christian. Quiteria came up to him and, kneeling by his side, asked him for his hand, using signs instead of words. Basilio turned down his eyeballs and, gazing at her, said:

'O Quiteria, relenting at a time when your pity is a knife that will deliver the coup de grâce to me, for I no longer have the strength to bear the glory that you bestow on me by choosing me to be yours, or to seek respite from this pain that is so rapidly covering my eyes with the fearful shadow of death: what I beg of you, O fatal star of my destiny, is that this request for my hand and desire to give me yours must be no mere matter of complaisance, or some new deceit, but that you declare that of your own free will you give it to me as your lawful husband, because it would be wrong for you to deceive me in a situation like this, or resort to falsehoods with one who has always been so sincere with you.'

As he spoke these words he kept fainting, and each time he did so the onlookers thought he was giving up the ghost. Quiteria, all modesty and bashfulness, took Basilio's right hand in hers and said:

'No force would be sufficient to bend my will; and so it is acting in total freedom that I give you my hand as your lawful wedded wife, and I accept your hand, so long as you, too, give it me of your own free will, and not impaired or deranged by the calamity that you have brought upon yourself by your wild ideas.'

'I give it you,' Basilio replied, 'being neither impaired nor deranged, but with the clear understanding that heaven was pleased to grant me; and so I hereby give myself to you to be your husband.'

'And I, to be your wife,' Quiteria replied, 'whether you live to a ripe old age or are carried from my arms to the grave.'

'Considering this young shaver's so badly wounded,' Sancho put in at this point, 'he's in a very chatty mood. You'd better get him to forget all his sweet-talk and see to his spirit – to my mind it's more in his tongue than on his lips.'

As Basilio and Quiteria held hands, the priest, tender and tearful, blessed them and prayed to God for the eternal repose of the soul of the bridegroom, who, as soon as he'd received the blessing, sprang to his feet and with extraordinary composure extracted the rapier that had been sheathed in his body. All the bystanders were astonished, and some of them, more simple-minded than inquisitive, began to cry:

'A miracle, a miracle!'

But Basilio replied:

'No miracle, no miracle: ingenuity, ingenuity!'

The priest, shaken and astonished, felt the wound with both hands, and found that the blade hadn't passed through Basilio's flesh and ribs but through a hollow iron tube that he'd fitted round them, full of blood that, as was later discovered, had been specially prepared so as not to congeal. In short, the priest and Camacho and most of the other onlookers considered that Basilio had made utter fools of them all. The bride didn't give any signs of annoyance at the ruse; on the contrary, when she heard someone saying that the marriage, being based on deceit, couldn't be considered valid, she reconfirmed it, from which they all deduced that the two of them had planned the trick together; and this made Camacho and his supporters feel so humiliated that they entrusted their vengeance to their own hands and, unsheathing their swords, fell upon Basilio, in whose defence as many more swords were immediately drawn. But Don Quixote, anticipating them, on horseback with his lance couched over his arm and his shield raised, made them all give way before him. Sancho, who never found any pleasure or comfort in such exploits, took refuge among the cooking pots from which he'd acquired his delectable skimmings, thinking of this place as sacred, and therefore one that would be respected. Don Quixote was shouting:

'Stop, sirs, stop: it is not right to take revenge for the wrongs done us by love; and remember that love and war are one and the same, and just as in war it is lawful and customary to use tricks and stratagems to defeat the enemy, so also in amorous conflict and rivalry it is considered permissible to resort to ruses and contrivances to attain the desired end, so long as they do not discredit or dishonour the loved one. Quiteria belongs to Basilio, and Basilio belongs to Quiteria, by heaven's just and beneficent disposition. Camacho is rich, and will be able to buy whatever he wants when, where and as he pleases. Basilio has nothing save this one little ewe lamb, and nobody, however powerful, must take her from him: what God has joined together let no man put asunder,[1] and anyone who tries to do so must first find his way past the tip of this lance.'

And here he brandished it with such vigour and agility that he struck fear into all those who didn't know him; and Quiteria's disdain made such a mark on Camacho's mind that it obliterated the lady herself from his memory in an instant; and so the persuasive words of the priest, a wise and well-meaning man, had their effect on him, and restored him and his followers to peace and tranquillity, as a sign of which they returned their swords to their proper places, considering Quiteria's fickleness more to blame than Basilio's ingenuity; and Camacho reasoned that if Quiteria had been in love with Basilio before their marriage she would have continued to love him afterwards, and that more thanks were due to heaven for having taken her from him than for having given her to him. Now that Camacho and his band had been consoled and pacified, all the men on Basilio's side calmed down as well, and Camacho the Rich, just to show that the trick hadn't affected him in the slightest and that he couldn't care less about it, decreed that the festivities should go ahead as if he really were going to be married; but Basilio and his wife and henchmen wouldn't stay, and off they went to Basilio's village, because the poor man who is virtuous and intelligent has people who will follow, honour and uphold him, just as the rich man has people to flatter and dance attendance on him. They took Don Quixote along with them, for they esteemed him as a man of mettle, a real man. Only Sancho's soul was plunged into gloom, through having to miss Camacho's splendid banquet and celebrations, which lasted into the night; and so, woe-begone and forlorn, he followed his master, who was riding with Basilio's party, and left the fleshpots of Egypt behind him, even though he was carrying them in his soul; and their skimmings in the stew-pan, by now almost consumed and spent, conjured up visions of the glory and the abundance of the good cheer that he was forsaking; and so, anguished and dejected, even though not hungry, he followed, without dismounting from his dun, in Rocinante's footsteps.

CHAPTER XXII

*Which relates the great adventure of the Cave
of Montesinos, in the heart of La Mancha, brought to
a happy conclusion by the valiant Don Quixote
de la Mancha*

Many and magnificent were the attentions lavished on Don Quixote by the bride and groom, indebted to him for the stand he'd taken in defence of their cause; and they rated him as highly in intelligence as in courage, and saw him as a Cid in arms and a Cicero in eloquence. The worthy Sancho enjoyed himself at their expense for three days, during which time it was discovered that Basilio's simulated suicide hadn't been a plot that he'd hatched with the connivance of the lovely Quiteria, but purely his own idea, from which he'd expected the result that they'd witnessed; although he did confess that he'd confided in some of his friends, so that when the time came they could give him their support, and his deception their backing.

'No, nothing that is directed at a virtuous end,' Don Quixote said, 'can or should be called deception.'

And for people in love to marry was the most excellent end of all, always bearing in mind that love's worst foe is hunger and incessant need, because love is pure joy, delight and happiness, even more so when the lover is in possession of the loved one, to all of which need and poverty are absolute and declared enemies; and he was saying all this to encourage Basilio to stop devoting his time to those special skills of his, which brought him much renown but did not make him any money, and to apply himself to earning a living by honest hard work, an option that is always available to diligent and prudent people.

'The honourable poor man with a beautiful wife (if it is possible for a poor man to be honourable) holds in trust something the loss of which brings about the loss and death of his honour itself. The woman who is beautiful and honourable and whose husband is poor deserves to be crowned with laurels and palms of victory and triumph. Beauty by itself attracts the desires of all those who see and recognize it, and it is a delectable lure upon which golden eagles and falcons will swoop; but if to beauty need and poverty are added, crows and kites and other such scavengers will attack it as well, and the woman who remains firm in the face of all these assaults fully deserves to be called a crown to her husband.[1]

'Look here, Basilio, my intelligent young friend,' Don Quixote continued, 'it was the opinion of a sage whose name eludes me[2] that in the whole world there was but one virtuous woman, and his advice was that every man should convince himself that this one virtuous woman in the world was his own wife, and in this way he would be happy. I am not married, and it has not yet occurred to me to marry; but despite this I should venture to give some advice to any man who asked me for it about how to choose a wife. In the first place I should advise him to be more concerned about her reputation than about her wealth, because a good woman does not gain a good reputation merely by being good, but by showing herself to be good; and public indiscretions do much more harm to a woman's honour than secret vices. If you bring a virtuous woman back to your house it will be easy for you to keep her as good as she is, or even improve her; but if you bring a wicked woman home, it will be hard work correcting her, because it is unlikely that she will be able to go from one extreme to the other. I do not say that it is impossible, but to me it seems difficult.'

Sancho had been listening, and he said to himself:

'Whenever I come out with things of pith and substance this master of mine says I could take my pulpit in my hands and travel around the world preaching the most splendid sermons, but what I'll say about him is that when he starts stringing his words of wisdom together and giving his advice, he couldn't only take up one pulpit in his hands but two on each finger and go round the market-places living on the fat of the land. The devil take you, mister knight errant, knowing as much as you do! The truth is I always thought he could only know about his chivalry doings, but there isn't a pie in the world he doesn't poke his finger into.'

As Sancho muttered this his master heard some of it, and asked:

'What are you muttering about, Sancho?'

'I'm not saying anything or muttering about anything at all,' Sancho replied. 'I was just thinking to myself that I wished I'd heard what you've just said before I got married, because if I had I might now be saying, "The lone ox licks himself at pleasure."'

'Is your Teresa as wicked as all that, Sancho?' Don Quixote asked.

'No, she isn't all that wicked,' Sancho replied, 'but she isn't all that good either – at any rate, she isn't as good as I'd like her to be.'

'It is wrong of you, Sancho,' said Don Quixote, 'to speak ill of your wife because, after all, she is your children's mother.'

'We're quits on that score,' was Sancho's reply. 'She has a good go at me, too, whenever she feels like it, specially when she's in a jealous mood – and then let Satan himself try to put up with her.'

To cut the story short, they stayed with the newly-weds for three days, and were treated and entertained like kings. Don Quixote asked the student swordsman to provide him with a guide to take him to the Cave of Montesinos, because he had a strong desire to enter it and see for himself whether there was any truth in the marvels that were related about it in those parts. The student said that a cousin of his, a famous scholar and very fond of reading books of chivalry, would be most willing to take him to the mouth of the cave, and to show him the Lakes of Ruidera, also famous throughout La Mancha, and even throughout Spain; and he added that his cousin would be entertaining company, because he was a young man who wrote books that were published and dedicated to very important people.

So the cousin came on a pregnant donkey with a colourful sackcloth cover over its pack-saddle. Sancho saddled Rocinante and put his pack-saddle on his dun, stocked his food-bags, which were accompanied on this occasion by those of the cousin, similarly well-packed, and, after commending themselves to God and saying goodbye to everyone, off they went in the direction of the famous Cave of Montesinos. Along the way Don Quixote asked the cousin about the nature and character of his pursuits, profession and studies. To which the cousin replied that his profession was humanism, and that his pursuits and studies consisted in writing books for publication, all of great social value, being both instructive and entertaining; one of them was entitled *The Book of Knightly Gala-Dress*, depicting seven hundred and three examples, all complete with their colours, mottoes and ciphers, from which courtier knights could choose whichever gala-dress they wanted at times of festivity and celebration, without any need to go begging them from anybody or to rack their brains, as people commonly say, wondering how to design them to suit their needs and intentions.

'Because I provide the man who is jealous, or scorned, or forgotten, or separated from his loved one with fiesta clothes to suit him right down to the ground. I've written another book which I'm going to call *Metamorfoseos, or the Spanish Ovid*, and its contents are most novel and unusual, because in it I imitate Ovid in a burlesque style and describe the Giralda in Seville and the Angel Weather-Vane on St Mary Magdalene Church in Salamanca, the Vecinguerra Sewer in Cordova, the Bulls of Guisando, the Sierra Morena, the Fountains of Leganitos and Lavapiés in Madrid, not forgetting the Fountain of the Louse, the Fountain of the Gilt Tap and the Fountain of the Prioress, complete with allegories, metaphors and similes to delight, amaze and instruct all at once. Another book of mine is called *Supplement to Polydore Virgil*,[3] dealing with the beginnings of things, packed with erudition and learning, because I investigate matters of substance that Polydore omitted, and I explain them with great elegance. Polydore Virgil forgot to tell us who was the first person in the world to catch a cold, and the first person to use ointment to treat the pox, and I give precise details about all this, and substantiate them with references to more than twenty-five authorities; so you can see how hard I've worked, and how useful the book will be to everyone.'

Sancho, who'd been hanging on the cousin's every word, said:

'Excuse me sir, and God send you the best of luck with the printers of your books – could you please tell me, and I'm sure you can, because you know everything, who was the first man to scratch his head? To my mind it must have been our father Adam.'

'Yes, it would indeed have been him,' the cousin replied, 'because there's no doubt that Adam had a head, with hair on it; and, this being so, and Adam being the first man in the world, he must have scratched it on some occasion.'

'That's what I think, too,' Sancho replied, 'but now tell me this: who was the first tumbler in the world?'

'The truth is, my man,' the cousin replied, 'that I can't exactly tell you that here and now, not having carried out any research on the matter. I shall do so when I return to where I keep my books, and give you the answer when we next meet, for I'm sure this won't be the last time we shall be together.'

'Oh look, sir,' said Sancho, 'you needn't bother to do that, because I've just tumbled to the answer to my own question. The first tumbler in the world was Lucifer, you see, when he was chucked or thrown out of heaven, and went tumbling down to the depths of hell.'

'You're quite right, my friend,' the cousin said.

And Don Quixote said:

'That question and answer are not your own, Sancho: you have heard them from someone else.'

'Not a bit of it, sir,' Sancho retorted, 'upon my soul, if I get going on questions and answers I shan't be done by tomorrow morning. Oh, no, to ask silly questions and give silly answers I don't need to go looking for anybody's help.'

'You have spoken a greater truth, Sancho, than you realize,' Don Quixote said, 'for there are some people who weary themselves discovering facts that, once discovered, are of no use whatsoever either to the understanding or to the memory.'

They spent the day in these and other agreeable conversations, and that night they stayed in a little village, where the cousin told Don Quixote that they were no more than half a dozen miles from the Cave of Montesinos, and that if he was planning to go into it he'd have to equip himself with rope so that he could be tied up and lowered into its depths. Don Quixote replied that even if he had to go down into the depths of hell, he was determined to reach the bottom of the cave; so they bought almost two hundred yards of rope, and the following day, at two o'clock in the afternoon, they reached the cave, the mouth of which yawns wide but is choked with buckthorn and wild fig trees, brambles and weeds, so thickly matted that they cover and block it. On coming within sight of it all three dismounted, and the cousin and Sancho tied the rope securely round Don Quixote, and as they were girding and swathing him, Sancho said:

'Now you watch what you're doing, sir, don't go burying yourself alive or sticking yourself in there like a bottle of wine put down a well to keep it cool. No, it isn't any business of yours to go exploring this hole – it must be worse than a dungeon.'

'Tie me up and hold your tongue,' Don Quixote replied, 'for this brave exploit, friend Sancho, is reserved for me alone.'[4]

And then the guide said:

'I entreat you, Don Quixote sir, to keep your eyes peeled and closely observe everything in there, because it might contain material that I could include in my *Transformations*.'

'The drum's in hands that know how to beat it,' Sancho Panza replied.

After this exchange and the completion of Don Quixote's trussing, which was done not over his armour but over his doublet, he said:

'It was careless of us not to acquire a small bell to tie to the rope next to me, for its sound would have indicated that I was still descending, and still alive; but since that is impossible now, I entrust myself to the guidance of the hand of God.'

And he sank to his knees and murmured a prayer, asking God to help him and give him success in that new and, as it seemed, perilous adventure; and then he said aloud:

'O mistress of all my actions and movements, illustrious and peerless Dulcinea del Toboso! If it is possible for the prayers and supplications of this your fortunate lover to reach your ears, I beg you in the name of your matchless beauty to listen to them; for their purpose is none other than to beg you not to deny me your favour and help, now that I stand so much in need of it. I am going to dive, plunge and sink into this abyss here before me, only so that the world will know that while you favour me there is no impossible feat that I will not attempt and complete.'

And as he said this he walked to the edge of the abyss and saw that he couldn't be let down or find any way in unless he pulled or hacked the vegetation away; and so he drew his sword and began to cut down the undergrowth covering the mouth of the cave, and the noise brought an infinity of enormous ravens and rooks flying out, so thick and so fast that they threw Don Quixote to the ground; and, if he had been as superstitious as he was a good Christian and Catholic, he would have taken it as a bad omen and refrained from immuring himself in such a place. But he eventually came to his feet and, seeing that no more crows were emerging, or birds of the night such as the bats that had flown out with the crows, the cousin and Sancho lowered him into the dreadful cave; and as he went in Sancho blessed him, made the sign of the Cross over him a thousand times, and said:

'God guide you, and Our Lady of the Rock of France too, as well as the Trinity of Gaeta,[5] you flower and cream and skimmings of knight errants! There you go, the finest bravo in the world, heart of steel, arms of bronze! I'll say it again – God guide you, and bring you back free, unharmed and without ransom to the light of this life that you're leaving to bury yourself in the darkness that you're seeking!'

And the cousin offered almost the same prayers and supplications.

As Don Quixote descended he kept shouting to them to let out rope and more rope, and they did so little by little, and when the shouts, coming out of the cave as if through a pipe, could no longer be heard, they had paid out the full two hundred yards, and thought that they had better pull Don Quixote up again, since there was no more rope to let down. But they waited for about half an hour, at the end of which they began to pull the rope in with great ease because there wasn't any weight on it, which made them suppose that Don Quixote had remained down below, and in this belief Sancho wept bitter tears and pulled the rope in at speed to learn the truth; but at a depth of what they calculated to be about a hundred and fifty yards they felt a weight, to their great joy. Eventually, at about twenty yards, they could clearly see Don Quixote, and Sancho called out to him:

'Welcome back, sir, we thought you were staying down there for keeps.'

But Don Quixote didn't utter one word in reply, and when they pulled him right out, they saw that his eyes were shut and that he seemed to be asleep. They laid him on the ground and untied him, yet he still didn't wake up. But then they rolled him back and forth and shook him to and fro so much that after a good while he did awake, and stretched himself as if emerging from deep and heavy sleep; and looking about him as if in alarm he said:

'God forgive you, friends, for taking me away from the most delicious and delightful life and sights that any man has ever lived or seen. Now indeed I have understood that all the pleasures of this life pass away like a shadow or a dream, wither like the flowers of the field. O hapless Montesinos! O sore wounded Durandarte! O unfortunate Belerma! O weeping Guadiana, and you, luckless daughters of Ruidera,[6] showing in your waters the tears shed by your lovely eyes!'

The cousin and Sancho listened to Don Quixote's words, uttered as if he were wrenching them in agony from his very bowels. They begged him to tell them what he meant, and to say what he'd seen in that hell.

'Hell you call it?' Don Quixote said. 'No, you must not call it that – it does not deserve such a name, as you will soon discover.'

He asked for something to eat, because he was very hungry. They spread the cousin's sackcloth on the green grass, ransacked the pantry in their saddle-bags, and the three of them sat there and had their lunch and supper all in one, in love and good fellowship. Once the sackcloth had been removed, Don Quixote de la Mancha said:

'Do not stir from where you are sitting, my sons, and pay attention to me.'

CHAPTER XXIII

About the amazing things that the magnificent
Don Quixote said he'd seen in the deep Cave of Montesinos,
the magnitude and impossibility of which cause this adventure
to be considered apocryphal

It would have been about four o'clock in the afternoon when the sun, veiled in clouds and giving out an attenuated light and rays of pleasant warmth, provided Don Quixote with the opportunity to relate to his illustrious listeners, free of heat and discomfort, what he'd seen in the Cave of Montesinos; and he began as follows:

'About twenty-five or thirty yards from the bottom of this dungeon, on the right-hand side, there is a concave space with room for a large cart and its mules. A dim light finds its way into it through some cracks or holes that extend right up to the distant surface of the earth. I spotted this concavity when I was feeling weary and frustrated from dangling at the end of the rope as I was let down into that region of darkness, not knowing where I was going; and so I decided to enter and rest a little. I shouted to you not to let out any more rope until I told you to, but you cannot have heard me. I gathered in the rope you were sending down, coiled it into a pile, and sat down on top of it, deep in thought as I wondered what I was going to do to reach the bottom without anybody to hold the rope; and as I sat there, pensive and confused, I was suddenly and without any intention on my part overcome by a deep sleep; and then, when I least expected it, with no idea how it had happened, I awoke and found myself in the middle of the most beautiful, pleasant, delightful meadow that nature could create or the liveliest human mind imagine. I opened my eyes wide, rubbed them and realized that I was not asleep, but wide awake; I nonetheless felt my head and my chest, to discover whether it was I myself sitting there, or some false, spurious apparition; but touch, feeling and the coherent reasoning in which I engaged all showed me that I was the same man then and there that I am now and here.

'What next came before my eyes was a sumptuous royal palace or castle, the walls of which seemed to be made of clearest crystal; two great doors opened wide and I saw that out of them came walking towards me a venerable old man wearing a cloak of purple flannel that trailed over the ground; draped over his shoulders and his chest he had a collegiate tippet of green satin; on his head he wore a round black Milan cap, and his grey beard reached below his waist; he was not bearing any arms, but he was carrying a rosary, with beads larger than the average walnut, and every tenth one about the size of the average ostrich egg; and his bearing, his gait, his gravity and his powerful presence, each separately and all of them in combination, astonished and bewildered me. He came up to me, and his first action was to give me a warm embrace, and then he said:

' "It has been a long time, valiant knight Don Quixote de la Mancha, that we who live enchanted in these lonely places have been awaiting your visit, so that you can inform the world about what is hidden and buried in the deep cave into which you have entered, known as the Cave of Montesinos: an exploit reserved only to be attempted by your invincible heart and admirable spirit. Come with me, illustrious sir, and I shall show you the marvels concealed in this transparent castle, of which I am the warden and perpetual head guard, for I am none other than Montesinos, from whom the cave takes its name."

'As soon as he told me that he was Montesinos I asked him whether there is any truth in what people in this world up here say: that he had taken a small dagger and cut his great friend Durandarte's heart out of his breast, and carried it to the lady Belerma, as Durandarte himself had ordered when he lay dying. Montesinos told me that everything they say is true, except as regards the dagger itself, because it had not been a dagger at all, not even a small one, but a keen poniard, sharper than an awl.'

'That there poniard,' Sancho butted in, 'must have been made by Ramón de Hoces, of Seville.'[1]

'I know nothing about that,' Don Quixote continued; 'but it cannot have been made by that particular poniard-manufacturer, because Ramón de Hoces was making them until very recently, and the Battle of Roncesvalles, where the calamity occurred, was fought many years ago; and anyway the enquiry is irrelevant, for it does not affect the truth or the development of the history.'

'Quite right,' said the cousin. 'Do continue, Don Quixote sir, I'm listening to your account with all the pleasure in the world.'

'With no less pleasure do I tell it,' Don Quixote replied. 'Well, the venerable Montesinos took me into the crystal palace, where in a room on the ground floor, wonderfully cool and made of alabaster, there was a marble tomb, constructed with consummate skill, upon which I saw that a knight was lying, not one of bronze, marble or jasper as there often are on other tombs, but of real flesh and real blood. His right hand, which seemed somewhat hairy and sinewy, a sign of great strength, was held over the region of his heart; and before I could ask Montesinos any questions, he saw me looking in amazement at the knight on the tomb, and said:

' "This is my friend Durandarte, the flower and mirror of the brave and enamoured knights of his time: he is kept here, enchanted, as I and many other men and women are also kept here, by Merlin, that French sorcerer[2] who is said to have been the devil's son; and it is my belief that he was not the devil's son but rather that he knew one trick more than the devil, as the saying goes. How and why he enchanted us, nobody can tell, but we shall find out in due course and indeed before very long, in my belief. What astonishes me is that I know, with as much certainty as I know that it is now daytime, that Durandarte breathed his last in my arms, and that after he died I cut out his heart with my own hands, and it must have weighed a good two pounds, because according to doctors a man with a large heart is endowed with more courage than a man with a small one: and if all this is so, and this knight really did die, how can he moan and sigh every so often, as if he were alive?"

'Once Montesinos had finished speaking, the wretched Durandarte cried out and said:

> "O my cousin Montesinos,
> Listen to my last request:
> When I'm lying dead before you
> And my soul's flown from my breast,
>   Take a poniard or a dagger,
> Cut my heart from out of me,
> Carry it to fair Belerma,
> To wherever she may be."[3]

'When the venerable Montesinos heard this he knelt before the afflicted knight and said with tears in his eyes:

' "But Sir Durandarte, my dear cousin, I did indeed carry out your request on the fateful day of our defeat; I did cut out your heart, as best I could, leaving not the tiniest scrap behind in your breast; I wiped it clean with a lace handkerchief; I left with it at top speed for France as soon as I had laid you in the bosom of the earth, weeping such abundant tears that there were enough of them to wash my hands clean of all the blood I had on them from rummaging around inside you; and what is more, my dear cousin, in the first village I came to after leaving Roncesvalles I sprinkled a little salt on your heart, to stop it from smelling, and bring it, if not fresh then at least pickled, into the presence of the lady Belerma, who, together with you, me, your squire Guadiana, the duenna Ruidera and her seven daughters and two nieces, and many others of your friends and acquaintances, has been kept here in enchantment by the sage Merlin for a very long time; and although more than five hundred years have now passed by, none of us has died: the only ones who are no longer with us are Ruidera and her daughters and nieces, because Merlin must have felt sorry for them when he saw them crying, and turned them into lakes which are now, in the world of the living and in the province of La Mancha, known as the Lakes of Ruidera; the seven daughters' lakes belong to the kings of Spain, and the two nieces' lakes to the knights of a most holy order known as the Order of St John.[4] Your squire Guadiana, also lamenting your misfortune, was changed into a river named after him which, when it reached the surface and saw the sun in another heaven, felt such deep sorrow at the thought of leaving you that it plunged back into the depths of the earth; but since it cannot avoid following its natural course, from time to time it emerges and shows itself where the sun and the people can see it. The lakes I have spoken of supply it with their water, and thanks to this and other help it enters Portugal swollen and pompous. But for all that, wherever it goes it reveals its sadness and melancholy, and it does not bother to breed delicate and highly prized fish in its waters, but only coarse and insipid ones, quite unlike those in the golden Tagus; and what I am telling you now, cousin, I have told you a thousand times, and since you do not reply I have to assume you do not believe me, or you cannot hear me, and only God knows how sad that makes me feel. And now I am going to give you some news that will maybe not ease your pain, but will at least not add to it in any way. I can reveal to you that here in your presence – and if you will just open your eyes you will be able to see him for yourself – stands the great knight about whom Merlin has made so many prophecies: I refer to Don Quixote de la Mancha, who has newly revived in the present age, and with great improvements over ages past, the forgotten order of knight-errantry, with the assistance of which it could happen that we might be disenchanted, because great exploits are reserved for great men."

'"And if not," replied the afflicted Durandarte, in a faint and feeble voice, "if not, cousin: shuffle the pack and deal again, you never know your luck."

'And turning on his side he sank back into silence, without uttering another word.

'And now there was a great weeping and wailing, with deep groans and anguished sobs; I turned my head and through the crystal walls I saw in another room a procession of two files of lovely damsels, all in mourning, wearing white turbans in the Turkish style. At the rear of the files came a lady, or at least that was what in her gravity she seemed to be, also wearing black, with white weeds so full and long that they brushed the floor. Her turban was twice as large as that of any of the damsels; her eyebrows met and she was somewhat pug-nosed; her mouth was big but her lips were bright red; her teeth, which she occasionally revealed, were far apart and ill-set, although they were as white as hulled almonds; in her hands she carried a piece of fine cambric and inside it, as far as I could make out, a heart that must have been mummified, to judge from its dry and shrivelled aspect. Montesinos told me that all the people in the procession were the servants of Durandarte and Belerma, enchanted together with their master and mistress, and that the lady at the end, carrying the heart wrapped in cambric, was the lady Belerma, who formed that procession four times a week with her damsels to sing, or rather wail, dirges over his cousin's body and afflicted heart; and that if she had seemed somewhat ugly, or not as beautiful as she was reputed to be, that was because of the terrible nights and even worse days she suffered in her enchantment, as I could observe in the great rings under her eyes and her sickly complexion.

' "And her pallor and the rings under her eyes are not caused by that problem women have every month, because it has been many months and even years since it last came knocking on her door, but by the pain which her heart feels for that other heart that she always clasps between her hands and that reminds her of the misfortune of her lover who died so young; for if this were not so, she could hardly be equalled in beauty, grace and spirit by the great Dulcinea del Toboso herself, so famous throughout this place and indeed throughout the world."

' "Hold on there!" I said. "Relate your history, Sir Montesinos, in the proper manner, for you are well aware that all comparisons are odious, and there is therefore no call to compare anyone with anyone else. The matchless Dulcinea del Toboso is who she is, and the lady Belerma is who she is, and who she has been, and let us leave it at that."

'To which he replied:

' "Don Quixote sir, do forgive me, for I confess that I was in the wrong, and I should not have said that the lady Dulcinea could hardly equal the lady Belerma, because realizing by some strange hunch that you are her knight ought to have been enough to make me hold my tongue rather than compare her to anything other than heaven itself."

'With this satisfaction that the great Montesinos gave me, my heart was put at ease after the shock I had received on hearing my lady compared to Belerma.'

'What amazes me,' said Sancho, 'is that you didn't jump the old fool and kick all his bones to pulp and yank out his beard till there wasn't a single hair left in his chin.'

'No, friend Sancho,' Don Quixote replied, 'it would not have been right for me to do that, because it is the duty of all of us to treat the elderly with respect, even those who are not knights, and particularly those who are knights and have been enchanted; and I know that we measured up well to each other in the many other questions and answers that were subsequently exchanged between us.'

The cousin commented:

'I can't understand, Don Quixote sir, how in such a short space of time as you were down there you could have seen so many things and had such a long conversation.'

'How long ago did I go down?' Don Quixote asked.

'A bit over an hour ago,' Sancho replied.

'That cannot be,' Don Quixote retorted, 'because while I was there night came and then it was morning, and again, three times altogether; so by my reckoning I have been three days in those remote parts hidden from our sight.'

'My master must be telling the truth,' said Sancho, 'because since everything that happens to him comes by way of enchantment, maybe what seems to us like an hour seems like three days and nights down there.'

'That must be the explanation,' Don Quixote replied.

'And have you had anything to eat all this time, sir?' asked the cousin.

'I have not had a single mouthful to break my fast,' Don Quixote replied, 'yet I have not felt hungry in the slightest.'

'And do the enchanted eat?' asked the cousin.

'No, they do not,' Don Quixote replied, 'nor do they have bowel movements, although it is believed that their nails, their hair and their beards do grow.'

'And do the enchanted sleep by any chance, sir?' Sancho asked.

'Certainly not,' Don Quixote replied. 'At least, during these three days that I was with them none of them had a moment's sleep, and nor did I.'

'There's a proverb that fits the bill here,' said Sancho. 'A man is known by the company he keeps – if you go hobnobbing with fasting and sleepless people under spells, no wonder you don't eat or sleep while you're with them. But you'll have to forgive me, sir, if I say the devil I mean God take me if I believe one word of all you've been saying.'

'What do you mean?' said the cousin. 'Are you suggesting that Don Quixote is lying? Even if he wanted to do that, he hasn't had time to make up such a vast quantity of falsehoods.'

'No, I don't think my master's lying,' Sancho replied.

'What do you think, then?' asked Don Quixote.

'What I think is this,' said Sancho. 'That character Merlin, or those enchanters who put a spell on that crowd you say you saw and talked to down there, stuffed your mind or your memory full of all that codswallop you've been telling us – and all the rest that's yet to come, as well.'

'Such a thing could happen, Sancho,' Don Quixote replied, 'but it has not happened in this case, because what I have recounted is what I saw with my own eyes and touched with my own hands. But I wonder what you are going to say when I tell you that, among countless other marvels that Montesinos showed me and about which I shall inform you at leisure and as appropriate in the course of our journey, because this is not the right time or place for some of them, he showed me three village girls leaping and frolicking in those delightful meadows like three goats, and as soon as I saw them I recognized one of them as the matchless Dulcinea del Toboso, and the other two as those same girls who were with her, to whom we spoke on the outskirts of El Toboso! I asked Montesinos whether he knew them; he replied that he did not, but that he supposed they must be some ladies of quality who had been enchanted, that they had appeared in those meadows a few days earlier, and that this should not surprise me because in those places there were many other ladies of past and present centuries, transformed by enchantment into all sorts of strange figures, among whom he had spotted Queen Guinevere and her duenna Quintañona, pouring out wine for Lancelot,

When from Brittany he came.'

When Sancho Panza heard his master say all this, he thought he'd go crazy or die laughing: since he knew the truth about Dulcinea's faked enchantment, he himself having been the enchanter and the concocter of evidence, he was now certain beyond any possible doubt that his master was as mad as a hatter, and so he said:

'It was an evil moment and a worse hour and a black day when you went down into the other world, dear master of mine, and an unlucky instant when you met mister Montesinos, who's done this to you. You were fine up here in your right mind, just as God gave it to you, speaking your words of wisdom and advice at every turn, not how you are now, coming out with the biggest pack of nonsense anyone could ever imagine.'

'Since I know you, Sancho,' said Don Quixote, 'I shall pay no attention to your words.'

'Nor will I to yours,' Sancho retorted, 'even if you do rough me up or kill me for what I said or for what I'm going to say if you don't change your tune. Tell me though, while we're still at peace, how did you recognize our mistress? And if you spoke to her, what did you say and what did she reply?'

'I recognized her,' Don Quixote replied, 'by the fact that she was wearing the same clothes as when you pointed her out to me. I did speak to her but she uttered not a word in reply; instead she turned her back on me and ran away so fast that a crossbow bolt could not have caught her. I wanted to follow her and I should have done so if Montesinos had not advised me not to bother, because it would have been in vain, and also because the time was approaching for me to leave the cave. He furthermore told me that, in due course, I should be informed of the means of disenchanting him, and Belerma, and Durandarte, and all the others down there; but of all the sad scenes I saw in that place, what made me feel sorriest was that when Montesinos was speaking these words to me, one of the hapless Dulcinea's companions sidled up without my seeing her come and, her eyes full of tears, murmured in a distraught voice:

' "My lady Dulcinea del Toboso kisses your hands and entreats you to do her the honour of informing her how you are; and, being in great need, she also entreats you from the bottom of her heart to be so kind as to lend her, on this new poplin petticoat, half a dozen reals, or as many as you have on you, and she gives you her word that she will return them without delay."

'This message was a source of great amazement to me, and turning to Montesinos I asked him:

' "Is it possible, Sir Montesinos, that enchanted persons of quality can be in need?"

'To which he replied:

' "Believe you me, Don Quixote de la Mancha, what people call need can be found everywhere, and it extends to all parts, and affects everybody, and does not even spare the enchanted; and since the lady Dulcinea del Toboso has sent to ask you for these six reals, and the pledge seems a good one, you have no option but to give them to her, for she must be in some desperate strait."

' "I cannot accept any pledge," I replied, "still less give her what she asks for, because I only have four reals on me."

'I gave them to her (they were the ones you let me have the other day, Sancho, as alms for any beggars we might come across at the roadside), and I said:

'"My dear friend: tell your mistress that it grieves me to my soul to hear of her troubles, and that I wish I were a Fugger to be in a position to remedy them;[5] and that I should like to inform her that I cannot and should not enjoy good health while deprived of her delightful presence and intelligent conversation, and that I entreat her from the bottom of my heart to be so kind as to allow this her captive servant and harassed knight to see and talk to her. You must also tell her that when she least expects it she will hear that I have sworn an oath, after the style of the one sworn by the Marquis of Mantua to avenge his nephew Baldwin when he found him dying on the mountain, which was ne'er at table to eat bread and certain inconsequential trifles that he appended, until he had avenged Baldwin; and I shall swear a similar oath never to rest, and to roam through the seven parts of the world more painstakingly than Prince Peter of Portugal ever roamed through them,[6] until I disenchant her."

'"All this, and more, you owe to my mistress," the damsel replied.

'And she took the four reals, and instead of curtseying she leapt five feet into the air.'

'God Almighty,' Sancho cried out. 'Can things like this really be going on in the world, and can enchanters and their spells have so much power as to change my master's good sense into raving lunacy? Oh sir, sir, for God's sake look out for yourself and for your good name, and don't set store by all this hocus-pocus that's been addling your wits!'

'You are only speaking in that way, Sancho, because you love me so well,' said Don Quixote, 'and, since you lack experience in the ways of the world, anything that is at all difficult to understand seems impossible to you; but the time will come, as I have told you, when I shall describe for you some more of what I saw down there, and it will make you believe what I have just been telling you, because there can be no disputing its veracity.'

CHAPTER XXIV

*Which relates a thousand trifles that are as inapposite
as they are necessary for a proper understanding of this
great history*

The translator from the original text of this great history written by its
first author Cide Hamete Benengeli says that when he came to the chapter
about the adventure of the Cave of Montesinos, he found inscribed in the
margin, in the hand of Hamete himself, the following words:

I cannot bring myself to believe that everything recorded in this chapter
happened to the brave Don Quixote exactly as described, and this is
because whereas all the previous adventures have been feasible and
credible, I cannot see my way to considering the adventure of this cave
to be a true one, for it goes so far beyond what is reasonable. Yet I can't
believe that Don Quixote was lying, because he was the most honest
hidalgo and the noblest knight of his time: he couldn't have told a lie to
save himself from being executed. Furthermore, I consider that he related
the incident complete with all the details recorded, and that he couldn't
have built such an enormous structure of absurdities in so short a time;
and if this adventure does seem apocryphal, that isn't my fault; so I merely
record it, without affirming either that it is false or that it is true. You,
wise reader, must make up your own mind, because I should not and
cannot do more than this; even though it is believed to be the case that
when he was dying he is said to have retracted it all and stated that he
had made it up because he thought it tallied well with the adventures
that he had read about in his histories.

And then he goes on to say:

The cousin was taken aback by both Sancho Panza's effrontery and
Don Quixote's forbearance, and assumed that his tolerance sprang from the
happiness he felt at having seen his lady Dulcinea del Toboso, even though
she was enchanted, because otherwise Sancho had spoken words that would
have justified a thorough good hiding; the cousin really believed that Sancho
had overstepped the mark with his master, to whom he said:

'I consider, Don Quixote de la Mancha sir, that my journey with you has been time well spent, because during it I have profited in four ways. First, I have made your acquaintance, which is a great happiness for me. Second, I have learned what is concealed in this Cave of Montesinos and all about the transformation of Guadiana and the Lakes of Ruidera, which will be useful for the *Spanish Ovid* that I am working on. Third, I now know how old playing cards are, or at least I know that they were in use by the time of the Emperor Charlemagne, as we can deduce from the words that you say Durandarte said when, after Montesinos had directed that long speech at him, he awoke and said, "Shuffle the pack and deal again, you never know your luck." He couldn't have learned that expression while he was enchanted, but earlier, in France and in the times of the Emperor Charlemagne. And this discovery is just exactly what I need for that other book I'm writing, the *Supplement to Polydore Virgil, on the Beginnings of Antiquities*; because I do believe that he didn't remember to include the beginnings of playing cards in his book, so I shall include the subject in mine, and it will be a matter of great importance, and even more so adducing an authority as weighty and reliable as Sir Durandarte. And fourth, I now know for certain about the source of the River Guadiana, hitherto a mystery to everybody.'

'You are right,' said Don Quixote, 'but I should like to know, always supposing that by God's favour you obtain permission to publish these books of yours (which I doubt), to whom you intend to dedicate them.'

'There are lords and grandees enough in Spain to whom they can be dedicated,' the cousin said.

'Not many,' Don Quixote replied, 'and not because they do not deserve it, but because they do not consent to it, so as not to feel that the author's labours and courtesy are obligations that have to be repaid. I know of one lord who can more than make up for all the rest,[1] to such an extent that if I ventured to give details I should perhaps arouse envy in many a noble breast; but let us leave this for another, more suitable occasion, and go and look for somewhere to stay tonight.'

'Not far from here,' said the cousin, 'there's a hermitage, and the hermit who lives there is said to have been a soldier, and he's considered to be a good Christian, and very intelligent and extremely charitable. By the side of the hermitage there's a little house that he's had built at his own expense, and although it's small there's room in it for guests.'

'Does this here hermit keep hens by any chance?' asked Sancho.

'Few hermits are without them,' Don Quixote replied, 'because the hermits one comes across nowadays are not like those in the deserts of Egypt who dressed in palm-fronds and lived on the roots of the earth. Let it not be supposed, however, that because I speak well of the hermits of old I would not speak well of modern ones; I merely say that the penance of today's hermits does not approach the strictness and austerity of the lives of their earlier counterparts, but that does not prevent them from being good men, all of them – at least I consider them to be good; and even when the waters do run muddy, the hypocrite who pretends to be virtuous does less harm than the flagrant sinner.'

As they talked they saw a man coming up behind them, walking fast and using his staff to beat a mule laden with lances and halberds. When he came alongside, he greeted them and went on ahead. Don Quixote said:

'Wait, my good man; you seem to be going faster than that mule would wish.'

'I can't stop, sir,' the man replied, 'because these arms you can see I have here are needed for tomorrow, and so I just can't stop, and goodbye. But if you want to know why I'm travelling with them, I'm planning to stay the night at the inn a little up the hill from the hermitage, so if you're going the same way that's where you'll find me, and I'll tell you all about some real marvels. And goodbye again.'

And he urged on his mule at such a pace that Don Quixote didn't have time to ask him what marvels these were that he intended to tell them all about; and being a somewhat inquisitive man, always anxious to discover new information, Don Quixote decided that they should press on and spend the night at the inn, without stopping at the hermitage as the cousin would have liked. Accordingly they all remounted and took the direct road for the inn, which they reached a little before nightfall. On the way the cousin asked Don Quixote if they could drop in at the hermitage for a little drink. As soon as Sancho heard this he pointed his dun in that direction, and Don Quixote and the cousin followed suit; but it seems that Sancho's ill-luck decreed that the hermit wasn't at home, or at least that was what an under-hermitess they found there told them. They asked her for some good wine; she replied that her master didn't keep any wine, but if they wanted some water, cheap, she'd let them have it, with pleasure.

'If it was water I wanted,' Sancho retorted, 'there are plenty of wells by the roadside. O Camacho's wedding and the plenty in Don Diego's house, how often I'm going to miss you!'

With this they left the hermitage and spurred on towards the inn, and after a little while they saw a young lad walking in front of them at no great speed, so they soon caught up with him. He was carrying his sword over his shoulder, and from it dangled a bundle or package containing, as it seemed, his clothes, which would have been his breeches, his cloak and a few shirts, because he was wearing a velvet jacket that shone like satin in places, and his shirt flapped loose beneath it; his stockings were of silk, and his shoes were square-toed, in the Madrid fashion; he'd have been eighteen or nineteen, with a cheerful face, and, it seemed, agile in his movements. He was singing seguidillas[2] to beguile the weariness of the way. When they drew alongside he'd just finished a verse that the cousin committed to memory, and it's said to have gone like this:

> It's only dire necessity
> That's taking me to war;
> And if I were a moneyed man
> I wouldn't go, for sure.

The first to address him was Don Quixote, who said:

'You're very scantily clad, my fine young sir. Where are you going, may we ask, if you are willing to tell us?'

To which the youth replied:

'Being scantily clad is because of heat and poverty, and where I'm going is to war.'

'What can poverty have to do with it?' Don Quixote asked. 'Heat, of course, is a good enough reason.'

'Look, sir,' the youth replied, 'here in this bundle I have some velvet breeches that go with this jacket; if I wear them on the road, I shan't be able to cut a dash in them when I get to a city, and I haven't got any money to buy another pair, so for this reason, and to keep cool, I'm travelling like this until I catch up with some companies of infantry that aren't forty miles from here, and then I'll join up, and there's bound to be some pack animal I can ride from there to where we'll embark,

Cartagena³ I've heard. I'd rather have the King as my lord and master, and serve him in the wars, than some penniless blighter in Madrid.'

'And have you got a commission lined up by any chance?' the cousin asked.

'If I'd served a grandee, or some other high-up person,' the youth replied, 'I certainly would have, because that's the advantage of serving good masters – you go from the servants' table to be an ensign or a captain, or you get a good parting gift; but I was unlucky enough to be always serving job-seekers and other outsiders, with such stingy allowances and wretched pay that half of it went on having a collar starched; and it'd be a miracle if any page of fortune like me was even moderately fortunate.'

'Come, come, tell me now, my friend,' said Don Quixote, 'is it really possible that in your years of service you never obtained a suit of livery?'

'I was given two,' the page replied, 'but just as you're stripped of your habit and your own clothes are returned if you leave a religious order before you profess, so my masters gave me my own clothes back once the business that had taken them to Madrid was finished and they went home, stripping me of the livery they'd only given me for show.'

'That's remarkable *spilorceria*,⁴ as the Italians put it,' said Don Quixote. 'But for all that you must consider yourself a happy man to have left Madrid with such excellent intentions, because there is nothing on earth more honourable and profitable than serving God, first, and then one's king and natural master, particularly in the profession of arms, in which one gains, if not more wealth then at least more honour than in letters, as I have so often said; for although letters have founded more great houses than have arms, those founded by arms have a certain indefinable superiority over those founded by letters, and a very definable splendour that sets them above all the rest. Remember what I am about to tell you, for it will be of great use and comfort in your trials and tribulations: do not allow your mind to dwell on the adversities that could come your way, because the worst of them is death, and if it is a good death then the best of them is death. That brave Roman emperor Julius Caesar was once asked which was the best death, and he replied that it was the sudden, unexpected, unanticipated one; and although he answered as a heathen, without any knowledge of the true God, he was right, because it is a death that spares our feelings; for even if you are killed in the very first engagement, by a cannon ball, or blown up by a mine, what does it matter? You die, and that is that; and, according to Terence, it is better for a soldier to die in battle than to survive unscathed in flight;[5] and the good soldier's reputation extends as far as does his obedience to his captain and all his superiors. And bear in mind, my son, that it is better for a soldier to smell of gunpowder than of civet, and that if old age catches up with you in this honourable profession, even if you are scarred and maimed and lame, it will at least not come upon you without honour, which poverty cannot lessen; and what is more, steps are now being taken to provide care and pensions for crippled old soldiers, because it is not right to deal with them like those people who grant their black slaves their freedom when they are old and no longer able to work, so that by throwing them out as free men they turn them into slaves to hunger, from which they can only ever hope to gain their freedom by dying. And for the moment I shall say no more, except to invite you to ride on the crupper of my horse as far as the inn, and there you shall dine with me, and in the morning you will continue on your way, and God speed you on it, as you well deserve.'

The page declined the invitation to the crupper but accepted the invitation to the supper, and it's said that this is when Sancho said to himself:

'God, what an incredible master I've got! Is it possible for a man who can say all those brilliant things he's just been saying to also say he's seen all that crazy nonsense he's been talking about the Cave of Montesinos? Well, well, we'll just have to wait and see.'

As he said this they reached the inn, at nightfall, and it didn't displease Sancho to see that his master considered it to be a real inn and not a castle, as he usually did. The instant they entered Don Quixote asked the innkeeper about the man with the lances and halberds, to which the reply was that he was in the stable attending to his mule. The cousin and Sancho did the same with their donkeys, and gave Rocinante the best manger and the best stall in the stable.

CHAPTER XXV

*Which begins the adventure of the bray, and the amusing
adventure of the puppeteer, together with the memorable
divinations of the fortune-telling ape*

Don Quixote was on pins and needles, as the saying goes, until he could
find out about the marvels promised by the arms transporter. He went to
look for him where the innkeeper had said, and found him, and begged
him to answer sooner rather than later the questions he had put to him
back there on the road. The man replied:

'The story of my marvels must be listened to at leisure, and certainly
not standing up: let me finish feeding my donkey, good sir, and then I'll
tell you things that will amaze you.'

'We must not let that detain us,' Don Quixote replied. 'Allow me to lend
a hand.'

And so he did, sifting the barley and cleaning out the manger, a gesture
of humility that obliged the man to tell him with a will what he wanted
to hear; and sitting down on a stone bench with Don Quixote beside
him, and with the cousin, the page, Sancho Panza and the innkeeper as
senate and audience, he began like this:

'I should tell you that in my village, some fifteen miles from this inn,
a jackass belonging to one of the councillors went missing, thanks to the
ingenuity and trickery of a servant girl of his, but that's another story –
and although the councillor looked far and wide for his jackass, he
couldn't find it anywhere. A fortnight must have passed, according to
what everyone says, since the jackass had disappeared, when another
councillor came up to his donkeyless colleague in the village square and
said:

'"I expect a reward for bringing you this news, neighbour – your
donkey's turned up."

'"I do indeed promise you a reward, and a good one, too, neighbour,"
the other councillor replied, "but first let's know where the donkey is."

'"I saw it in the wood this morning," the finder replied, "without its
pack-saddle or any gear at all, and so thin it made my heart bleed to see

it. I tried to drive it in front of me and bring it back to you, but it's already turned so fearful and wild that, when I went up to it, it fled into the thickest part of the wood. If you'd like us to go and fetch it, just let me take this she-ass of mine home, and I'll be back right away."

'"That would give me great pleasure," said the owner of the jackass, "and I shall try to repay you in the same coinage."

'All those who know the truth about this matter tell the story exactly as I am telling it now, and with all the same details. To be brief, the two councillors walked together to the wood, but when they reached the place where they expected to find the jackass it was nowhere to be seen, however hard they looked. Realizing, then, that their search was fruitless, the councillor who'd sighted the jackass said to the other one:

'"Look, neighbour: I've just thought of a plan for finding this animal, without fail, even if it has hidden itself away not just in the heart of this wood but in the very bowels of the earth: I do a superb bray, you see, and if you can bray a little, too, the donkey's as good as found."

'"Bray a little too you say, neighbour?" said the other councillor. "Good God man, I'm second to none, not even to donkeys themselves."

'"We'll soon see about that," replied the second councillor, "because my idea is for you to go round one side of the wood and me round the other, so that between the two of us we walk all the way round, and every so often you'll bray and I'll bray, and the jackass is bound to hear us and bray back, if it's still in the wood."

'To which the owner of the jackass replied:

'"All I can say, neighbour, is that the plan is perfect and worthy of your fine mind."

'They split up as agreed and, as it happened, both brayed at almost the same time, and each was taken in by the bray of the other, and off they went in search of each other in the belief that they'd found the jackass; and when they met, the donkeyless councillor said:

'"Can it be possible, neighbour, that it wasn't my jackass that brayed?"

'"It was none other than me," his friend replied.

'"I do declare," said the jackass owner, "that between you and a donkey, neighbour, there's no difference at all, as far as braying's concerned, because I've never in my life seen or heard anything more convincing."

'"No, neighbour," replied the planner, "you deserve all those praises and compliments much more than I do. By the God who made me, you could give a two brays start to the best and most expert brayer in the world: the sound you produce is properly high-pitched, and you sustain the phrase with the correct tempo and rhythm, and the cadenza is fast and beautifully ornamented, and, all in all, I admit defeat, salute you and hand you the palm for this extraordinary achievement."

'"All I can say," said the owner, "is that I shall have a higher opinion of myself from now on, and I'll reckon I know a thing or two, seeing that I have some talent; because even though I thought I could bray quite well, I never suspected I was as good as all that."

'"And all I can say," the other replied, "is that there are rare skills lost in this world, wasted on people who don't know how to make use of them."

'"Our skill," the owner said, "can only ever be of any use in cases like this one we're dealing with at the moment, and even so it's going to need God's helping hand for it to produce results."

'After this exchange they split up and started braying again, and they kept fooling each other and meeting in the wood, until they agreed that, by way of countersign to indicate that it was them braying and not the jackass, they'd each bray twice in quick succession. So they went all the way round the wood with redoubled brays but without the slightest reply from the lost jackass. And how could the poor, ill-fated animal reply, since they found it in the thickest part of the wood, half devoured by wolves? When he saw it, its owner said:

'"I did think it strange that it never replied, because if it wasn't dead it would have brayed back at us as soon as it heard us, or it wouldn't have been a donkey; but having heard you bray with such skill, neighbour, I consider myself well rewarded for my search, even though I did find my jackass dead."

'"No, no, pride of place belongs to you, neighbour," the other replied. "If the priest sings well, so too does the altar-boy."

'And back they walked, disconsolate and hoarse, to the village, where they told their friends, neighbours and acquaintances everything that had happened during the search for the jackass, each praising the other's braying skills; and the story spread among all the nearby villages. And the devil, who never sleeps, and loves sowing discord and spreading resentment, building squabbles in the wind and fabricating fights out of nothing, arranged for the people from other villages to bray as soon as they saw anyone from our village, taunting us with the braying of our councillors. And then all the young boys took it up, which was as if the mouths of all the devils in hell had taken it up, and the braying spread and spread from one village to the next, so that by now the people from the village of the bray are as well known and as set apart as blacks are from whites; and this dreadful mockery has gone so far that the mocked have often marched out in armed squadrons to do battle with the mockers, and nothing and nobody, not fear nor shame, can do anything about it. Tomorrow or the next day, I think, the men of my village, the village of the bray, are planning to take the field against another village a half a dozen miles away, one of our worst persecutors, and to make sure we're properly equipped I've bought the lances and halberds you saw. And these are the marvels I said I'd tell you, and if they don't seem like marvels to you, I don't know of any others.'

And so he finished his tale, and at that moment a man came in dressed in chamois leather – leggings, breeches, doublet – and roared:

'Have you got any room for the night, landlord? The fortune-telling ape and the puppet show about the freeing of Melisendra[1] are on their way here.'

'By Christ,' said the landlord, 'if it isn't Master Pedro! We've got a grand evening in store for us!'

I almost forgot to say that this Master Pedro had his left eye and almost half his left cheek covered with a patch of green taffeta, indicating that something was wrong with that part of his face; and the innkeeper continued:

'Welcome, Master Pedro sir. Where are the ape and the puppet show? I can't see them.'

'They aren't far away,' replied the man in chamois leather. 'I just came on ahead to see if there was any room at the inn.'

'I'd throw the Duke of Alba[2] himself out to make room for Master Pedro,' the innkeeper replied. 'Bring the ape and the puppet show right in, there are people here tonight who'll pay to see the show and the ape's skills.'

'That's all right by me,' said the man with the patch, 'and I'll cut my

657

prices, and be happy just to cover my expenses – so now I'll go back to fetch the cart with the ape and the show.'

And he turned and left the inn. Don Quixote asked who was this Master Pedro and what was this puppet show and ape he had with him. To which the innkeeper replied:

'He's a famous puppeteer who's been wandering around this Aragon end of La Mancha for some time now with a show about Melisendra being set free by the famous Don Gaiferos, one of the finest and best performed stories seen in these parts for many a long year. He's also got an ape with the most unusual skill ever seen among apes or conceived by men, because if it's asked a question it listens attentively and then jumps up on to its master's shoulder and whispers the answer into his ear, and then Master Pedro announces it; and it says much more about events in the past than about what lies in the future, and although it doesn't always get everything right, it's more often right than wrong, so we all think it's got the devil inside it. He charges two reals per question, if the ape replies, or rather if he replies on behalf of the ape after it's whispered into his ear; and people believe this Master Pedro has got very rich like this; and he's a gallant man and a boon companion, as they put it in Italy, and he lives it up like the best of them; he talks more than six men and drinks more than twelve, all paid for by his tongue and his ape and his puppet show.'

As the innkeeper said this, Master Pedro returned pushing a cart with the puppet show and the ape on it, large and tailless, with buttocks like old leather but a not unpleasant face; and when Don Quixote saw him he asked:

'Now you tell me this, my fine fortune-teller: *che pesce pigliamo*?[3] What will become of us? Here are my two reals.'

And he told Sancho to give them to Master Pedro, who replied on behalf of his ape:

'No sir, this animal doesn't answer or give any information about events in the future; he does know something about past events, and about present-day ones too.'

'By the dog of Egypt!' said Sancho. 'I wouldn't give half a brass farthing to be told what's happened to me in the past, because who can know that better than what I do already? And to give good money to be told what

I already know would be a very silly thing to do, but since he knows about the present as well here's my two reals and please can pretty mister monkey here tell me what my wife Teresa Panza's doing at the moment – what is she up to?'

Master Pedro refused to take the money, saying:

'I will not accept my fees in advance, before the services have been provided.'

And he tapped his left shoulder twice with his right hand and the ape jumped up on to it, brought its mouth close to its master's ear and rattled its teeth together at great speed; and after it had done this for about the length of a creed, it jumped down to the ground and Master Pedro ran to kneel before Don Quixote, hug his legs and say:

'These legs I embrace as if I were embracing the twin pillars of Hercules, O illustrious reviver of the forgotten order of knight-errantry! O never sufficiently praised Don Quixote de la Mancha, encourager of the faint-hearted, support of those about to fall, helping hand to the fallen, staff and comfort of all the unfortunate!'

Don Quixote was astonished, Sancho bewildered, the cousin amazed, the page astounded, the man of the bray nonplussed and, in short, all were dumbfounded by the puppeteer's words, and he continued:

'And you, O worthy Sancho Panza, the best squire in the world, serving the best knight in the world! Be of good cheer, for your worthy wife Teresa is well, and at the moment she is carding a pound of flax, and furthermore on her left side she has a jug with a broken rim holding a tidy drop of wine, to keep her spirits up as she works.'

'I can believe that all right,' Sancho replied, 'because she's a good old soul she is, and if she wasn't so jealous I wouldn't swop her for the giantess Andandona herself,[4] who my master says was a fine woman and a very worthy one too – and my Teresa's one of those who don't like to go without, even if their heirs do have to pay for it.'

'What I now say,' Don Quixote interrupted, 'is that he who reads and travels sees and learns. And I say this because who could have persuaded me that there are apes that practise divination, as I have seen here with my own two eyes? For I am indeed the very same Don Quixote de la Mancha that this worthy animal has named, even though it has been somewhat excessive in its praises; but whatever my qualities may be, I thank heaven for having given me a mild and compassionate nature, inclined always to do good to everyone, and never to do any harm.'

'If I had any money,' said the page, 'I'd ask mister monkey what's going to happen on this pilgrimage of mine.'

To which Master Pedro, who had risen from Don Quixote's feet, replied:

'I've already told you that this creature doesn't answer questions about the future, and if it did it wouldn't have mattered about the money, because to serve Don Quixote here present I'd forego all the money in the world. And now, because I'm in his debt, and to provide him with some pleasure, I'm going to set up my puppet show and entertain everyone at the inn without charging a penny.'

When the innkeeper heard this he was overjoyed and indicated where the puppet theatre could be set up, which was done in a trice. Don Quixote wasn't very happy with the ape's divination, because it didn't seem appropriate for an ape to divine either the future or the past; and so, while Master Pedro was fixing his theatre together, he took Sancho aside to a corner of the stable where, speaking so that nobody could overhear, he said:

'Look, Sancho, I have given careful consideration to this ape's strange skill, and I have reached the conclusion that this Pedro fellow, its master, must have made some pact with the foul fiend, explicit or implicit.'

'If he's made a pack and the foul fiend's pissed in it,' said Sancho, 'it must be filthy dirty – and what good are packs like that to Master Pedro?'

'No, Sancho, you don't understand: all I mean is that he must have come to some agreement with the devil, who provides the ape with this skill so that Master Pedro can make his living, and once he's rich he'll give his soul to the devil, which is what this universal enemy wants. And what makes me think this is the fact that the ape only answers questions about the past and the present, for this is as far as the devil's wisdom can extend, because he can only know about the future by guesswork, and even that not always, it being reserved to God alone to know the times and the seasons,[5] and for him there is no past or future, because all is present. And if this is so, as indeed it is, it's clear that this ape is speaking in the style of the devil; and I'm amazed that it hasn't been reported to the Holy Inquisition, and interrogated, and the whole truth extracted from it about who has given it this power of divination; because it's clear that this ape is no astrologer, and that neither it nor its master casts or would know how to cast these affairs they call horoscopes that are so popular in Spain nowadays, to such an extent that there isn't a housewife or a page-boy or a cobbler who doesn't claim to know how to cast a horoscope as if it were as simple as casting a stone, thus destroying the wonderful truths of that science with their lies and their ignorance. I know of a lady who asked one of these amateur astrologers whether a little lap-dog bitch of hers would become pregnant and have puppies, and how many and what colour they would be. The fellow cast the horoscope and replied that the bitch would indeed become pregnant and have three puppies, one green, another red and the third a mixture of the two, so long as the bitch was covered between eleven and twelve in the morning or at night, on a Monday or a Saturday; and the outcome was that two days later the bitch died of overeating and the amateur astrologer was left with the reputation in the village of an excellent horoscope-caster, as happens with nearly all of them.'

'All the same,' said Sancho, 'I'd like you to tell Master Pedro to ask his monkey if what happened to you in the Cave of Montesinos was true, because to my mind, with all due respect and begging your pardon, it was all tricks and lies, or at the very least a dream.'

'That is not impossible,' Don Quixote replied, 'but I shall do as you recommend, even though I have certain scruples about it.'

As he spoke Master Pedro came looking for him to say that the puppet show was ready, and please could he come to watch it, because it was well worthy of his attention. Don Quixote told him what was on his mind, and requested him to ask the ape straight away to tell him whether certain things that had happened in the Cave of Montesinos had been true or had been dreams, because he himself thought that some of both was involved. Upon which Master Pedro, without saying a word, brought the ape back and, standing in front of Don Quixote and Sancho, said:

'Look, master monkey, this gentleman wishes to know if certain things that happened to him in a cave known as the Cave of Montesinos were true or false.'

And after he'd made the usual sign the ape jumped on to his left shoulder and whispered, as it seemed, into his ear, upon which Master Pedro said:

'The ape says that part of what you saw or experienced in the said cave was false, and that part of it was credible, and that this, and nothing else, is all it knows concerning this question; and that if you want to know more, next Friday it'll reply to all the questions it's asked, because for the time being its powers are exhausted, and they won't return till Friday next, as it said.'

'I told you so,' said Sancho. 'Well, didn't I tell you I couldn't swallow the idea that everything you said, sir, about what went on in that cave was true, or even half of it?'

'The event itself will tell, Sancho,' Don Quixote replied, 'because time, the uncoverer of all secrets, leaves none that it does not bring out into the light of day, even if it is hidden in the bowels of the earth. And that's quite enough of this matter for now; so let us go and see Master Pedro's puppet show, for I imagine that it might offer a certain novelty.'

'What do you mean, a certain novelty?' Master Pedro replied. 'This puppet show of mine offers sixty thousand novelties – I'm telling you, Don Quixote sir, it's one of the sights most worth seeing in the whole wide world, but *operibus credite, et non verbis*,[6] so let's set to work, because it's getting late and we have a lot to do, and say, and show.'

Don Quixote and Sancho did as they were told, and walked over to where the puppet theatre had been erected and uncovered, glowing all over with wax tapers that made it a glittering, resplendent sight. Master Pedro disappeared inside it, because he was the one who worked the puppets, and in front of it stood a boy, Master Pedro's servant, to act as announcer and interpreter of the mysteries of the show: he held a pointer to indicate the puppets as they emerged. With everyone at the inn in front of the puppet theatre, some of them standing, and with Don Quixote, Sancho, the page and the cousin in the best seats, the announcer began to say what anyone who reads the next chapter or has it read to him will see or hear.

CHAPTER XXVI

Which continues the amusing adventure of the puppeteer,
together with other really very good things

The Tyrians and the Trojans all were silent,[1]
what I mean to say is that everyone in the audience was hanging, as it were, on the lips of the announcer of the marvels of the puppet show, when the sounds of war-drums and trumpets and artillery fire rang out from inside the theatre and suddenly died down again, and the boy proclaimed:

'This true history that is about to be performed before your very eyes has been taken word for word from the French chronicles and from the Spanish ballads that people sing, and boys too, in the street. It's about how Don Gaiferos freed his wife Melisendra, who was a prisoner of the Moors in Spain, in the city of Sansueña,[2] which is what Saragossa was called then; and here you can see Don Gaiferos playing backgammon, as that song goes:

> And Don Gaiferos, playing at the tables,
> Has not a thought for Melisendra now.

And that character coming into view over there with a crown on his head and a sceptre in his hands – he's the Emperor Charlemagne, Melisendra's foster father, who's angry at his son-in-law's laziness and negligence and is coming to scold him; and see with what warmth and feeling he does it, it looks as if he's going to bang him on the head half a dozen times with his sceptre, and some authorities reckon that's exactly what he did, good and hard; and after telling him all sorts of things about the danger his honour is in from not trying to free his wife, it's said that he said:

> I've said enough; see to it now.

You can also see how the Emperor turns away and leaves Don Gaiferos fuming, and now you see him in his rage hurling the backgammon board far from him and calling for his arms and armour, and he asks his cousin

Roland to lend him his sword Durandal, and Roland refuses, offering him instead his company in the difficult task ahead; but our angry hero will not accept this, and says he's quite capable of rescuing his wife alone, even if she's imprisoned deep in the centre of the earth; and then he goes away to don his armour and set off. Now look at that tower you can see over there, which we must imagine is one of the towers of Saragossa Castle, today called the Aljafería; and that lady in Moorish clothes on that balcony is the matchless Melisendra, who often used to come out on to it to gaze at the road to France, and to console herself in her imprisonment by daydreaming about Paris and her husband. And now watch out for a new incident that's about to happen, maybe never seen before. Can't you see that Moor sneaking up behind Melisendra with his forefinger over his lips? Well, now look how he gives her a kiss slap on the mouth, and how soon she spits and wipes her lips with the white sleeve of her blouse, and how she wails and tears her lovely hair in grief, as if her hair were to blame for that evil deed. And see that grave Moor on that balcony, King Marsilio of Sansueña: he spotted the Moor's insolent action and, even though the fellow was a relative and a great favourite of his, ordered him to be arrested and given two hundred lashes, after being paraded through the city along the customary streets,

> With squawkers before him
> And truncheons behind,[3]

and now you can see they're coming to carry out the sentence, and the crime's hardly even been committed yet, because the Moors don't go in for notification of the charge or detention on remand, as we do.'

'Come, boy,' exclaimed Don Quixote, 'proceed with your story in a straight line, and don't go wandering round bends or up side-roads; for to reach the truth about something like that, proof upon proof is needed.'

And Master Pedro said from inside the theatre:

'Look here, my lad, I don't want any flourishes, just do as the gentleman says, that'll be the wisest course – stick to plain chant without any counterpoint, and don't you go and spin the thread so fine you break it.'

'All right,' the lad replied, and he continued: 'this figure appearing here on horseback, muffled in a Gascon cape, is Don Gaiferos himself; and here his wife, avenged for the amorous Moor's effrontery, with a happier and calmer look on her face, has come out on to the tower balcony and is talking to her husband in the belief that he's some passer-by, and they had that conversation in that ballad that goes:

> Sir knight, if it's to France you go,
> Pray ask for Don Gaiferos.

But I shan't repeat the conversation now, because long-windedness breeds boredom; it's enough to see how Don Gaiferos reveals who he is, and from Melisendra's gestures of joy we're given to understand that she's recognized him, and even more so now that we see her letting herself down from the balcony to sit on the crupper of her good husband's horse. But oh how unlucky, look, the hem of her skirt's got caught on one of the balcony railings, and she's been left hanging in the air and can't reach the ground. But now you can see that merciful heaven sends aid at times of greatest need, because up comes Don Gaiferos and without worrying about tearing her fine skirt he seizes her and tugs her down whether she likes it or not, and with a leap he puts her on to the crupper of his horse, astride, just like a man, and tells her to hold on tight and put her arms over his shoulders and across his chest so as not to fall off, because madam Melisendra wasn't used to galloping around like that. Observe, too, how the neighing of the horse shows how happy it is with the burden of bravery and beauty it bears in the shape of its master and mistress. Observe how they turn and leave the city, and full of joy and happiness they take the road to Paris. Go in peace, O peerless pair of true lovers! May you arrive safely in your longed-for homeland, and may fortune raise no barrier to hinder your happy journey! May your friends and relations see you enjoying the remainder of your life in peace and tranquillity, and may your days be as many as Nestor's!'[4]

Here Master Pedro shouted out again:

'Keep it simple, boy, none of those flights of yours! Affectation's always bad!'

The announcer didn't reply, but continued:

'Idle eyes see everything, and there they were to see Melisendra getting down and then getting up, and off they went to tell King Marsilio, who ordered the alarm to be sounded, and look how fast – the whole city's shaking with the bells being rung from all the mosque towers!'

'No, no,' Don Quixote intervened. 'Those bells are a grave blunder by Master Pedro, because Moors do not use bells but kettle drums, and a kind of pipe rather like our shawm; and to have bells ringing in Sansueña is most definitely a gross absurdity.'

When Master Pedro heard this he stopped ringing his bells and said:

'Don't worry about trivialities, Don Quixote sir – you can't make anything without making mistakes. Aren't thousands of plays performed all the time full of thousands of blunders and absurdities, and despite that they have a good run and are greeted not only with applause but with admiration too? You carry on, my lad, and let them say what they like – so long as I fill my money bags it doesn't matter if I make more blunders than there are atoms in the sun.'

'That is true enough,' Don Quixote replied.

And the boy said:

'See all the resplendent cavalry riding out of the city in pursuit of the two Christian lovers; how many trumpets blaring, how many pipes rather like shawms playing, how many kettle drums and other sorts of drums beating. I'm afraid they're going to catch up with them and return with them tied to the tail of their own horse, which would be a horrendous sight.'

Seeing such hordes of Moors and hearing such a racket, Don Quixote thought it would be a good idea to help the fugitives, and he sprang to his feet and cried:

'Never while there is still breath in my body will I consent to such an insult being offered in my presence to such a famous knight and bold inamorato as Don Gaiferos. Desist, you low-born rabble; do not follow him, do not pursue him, or you shall do battle with me!'

And acting even as he spoke he drew his sword and with one leap positioned himself in front of the stage, and with speedy and unprecedented fury began to hack at the hordes of puppet Moors, knocking some over, beheading others, wrecking this one, destroying that; and one down-stroke among many others would have lopped Master Pedro's head off as easily as if it had been made of marzipan, if he hadn't ducked and crouched and made himself into a ball. Master Pedro was crying:

'Stop, stop, Don Quixote sir, look, these you're knocking down and smashing and killing aren't real Moors but papier mâché figures. I'll be damned, you're destroying everything I own in the world!'

But this didn't stop Don Quixote from raining down his cuts and thrusts and two-handers and fore-strokes and back-strokes. And in the time it takes to say a couple of creeds he left the whole show in a heap on the floor, with the puppets and the fittings cut into little pieces, King Marsilio critically injured, and the Emperor Charlemagne with his head and his crown split in two. The senate of spectators was in an uproar, the monkey escaped through the window on to the roof, the cousin was frightened, the page was panic-stricken and even Sancho Panza was petrified because, as he swore once the storm was over, he'd never seen his master in such a temper. Once the demolition of the puppet show was complete, Don Quixote grew somewhat calmer and said:

'I should like to have here before me all those who do not and will not believe how beneficial knights errant are to society: for look – if I had not been present, what would have become of the worthy Don Gaiferos and the lovely Melisendra? By now those dogs would most certainly have caught up with them and done them some mischief. Long live knight-errantry, then, above all else on earth!'

'Yes, long live knight-errantry,' Master Pedro commented, in feeble tones, 'and quick death to me, so wretched that I can well say with King Rodrigo:

> But yesterday the lord of Spain . . .
> Today not one embattlement
> That I can call my own![5]

Not half an hour ago, indeed not half a minute ago, I was the master of kings and emperors, and my stables, my coffers and my bags were full of countless horses and innumerable pieces of finery; and now I'm abject and desolate, poverty-stricken and a beggar and, what's worst of all, monkeyless, for I'll have to sweat blood to get that animal back, all because of the wrongheaded fury of this knight here, who's said to succour orphans, and right wrongs, and do other charitable works, yet only with me have his good intentions misfired – blessed and praised be heaven above in the highest of the high. I suppose it had to be the Knight of the Sorry Face who came to deface the faces of my puppets.'

Sancho was moved by Master Pedro's words, and said:

'Don't cry like that, Master Pedro, don't wail so, you're breaking my heart – and I can tell you my master Don Quixote's such a scrupulous and Catholic Christian that if he realizes he's done you any harm he'll say so and pay you double.'

'If Don Quixote paid me for just half the figures of mine he's disfigured I'd be happy enough, and that would clear his conscience – because there's no salvation for the man who's holding on to something against its owner's will and doesn't give it back to him.'

'That is true enough,' said Don Quixote, 'but I am not aware that I am retaining anything of yours, Master Pedro.'

'What do you mean?' replied Master Pedro. 'And all these relics scattered about this hard and sterile soil – what was it that smashed and scattered them if not the invincible power of that mighty arm of yours? And who did they belong to if not to me? And how did I support myself except with them?'

'Now I am utterly convinced,' Don Quixote inserted, 'of what I have many times thought might be true: the ploy of these enchanters who pursue me is to place before my eyes things as they are, and then change them into what they want them to be. I can assure you really and truly, all you who hear me, that I did believe that everything happening here happened exactly as it seemed to happen: that Melisendra was Melisendra, Don Gaiferos was Don Gaiferos, Marsilio was Marsilio and Charlemagne was Charlemagne. That is why I lost my temper and, to do what I had to do as a knight errant, I decided to aid and assist the people who were fleeing, and with that worthy aim in mind I did what you have seen me do; if it has all turned out the opposite of how I intended, that is not my fault, but the fault of the wicked ones who pursue me; and despite all this, although my mistake did not proceed from malice aforethought, I hereby award costs against myself: so Master Pedro must assess what he wants for his broken puppets, and I will pay for them in good current Castilian coin.'

Master Pedro bowed and said:

'I expected no less from the unprecedented Christian virtue of the brave Don Quixote de la Mancha, true help and support of all needy and distressed vagrants; and the good innkeeper and the worthy Sancho will be assessors and arbiters between you and me of what the broken puppets are worth, or rather were worth.'

The innkeeper and Sancho agreed to this, and Master Pedro picked up King Marsilio of Saragossa, minus his head, and said:

'You can see how impossible it is to restore this king to his original state; and so it seems to me, and subject to your better judgement, that for his sad demise and sorry end I should be given four and a half reals.'

'Continue!' said Don Quixote.

'And for this crack from top to bottom,' Master Pedro continued, picking up the broken Emperor Charlemagne, 'I wouldn't be asking very much if I asked for five and a quarter reals.'

'That's no small sum,' said Sancho.

'Not a large one either,' replied the innkeeper. 'Split the difference and give him five reals.'

'Give him the full five and a quarter,' said Don Quixote, 'because this notable misfortune is not to be measured in quarters of a real; and I wish Master Pedro would hurry up, it is time for supper and I am beginning to feel the pangs of hunger.'

'For this figure,' said Master Pedro, 'minus its nose and an eye, the figure of the lovely Melisendra, I want two reals and twelve maravedís, and that's only fair.'

'There will be the devil and all to do,' said Don Quixote, 'if Melisendra and her husband are not on the French border by now, at least, because I thought the horse they were riding was flying rather than galloping; so don't you come trying to sell me a pig in a poke, and presenting me with a noseless Melisendra when she must, if given half a chance, be frolicking in France with her husband to her heart's content. God help each of us to what is rightly his, Master Pedro, and let us all march on with a firm foot and honest intentions. Pray continue.'

Master Pedro could see that Don Quixote was beginning to rave again and to return to his earlier fixation, and didn't want to let him off the hook, and so he said:

'This one can't be Melisendra, then, but one of her maidservants, so if I'm given sixty maravedís for her I'll be happy enough.'

And in this way he put prices to many other wrecked puppets, which the arbitrators moderated to the satisfaction of the two parties, and it came to a total of forty and three-quarter reals; and on top of this sum, which Sancho paid out immediately, Master Pedro asked for two reals for the trouble of going for his ape.

'Give them to him, Sancho,' said Don Quixote, 'although what he'll go for with them has more to do with grapes than with apes; and I would give two hundred reals this very moment as a reward to anyone who could tell me for certain that Doña Melisendra and Don Gaiferos are in France among their own people.'

'Nobody will be able to tell us that better than my monkey,' said Master Pedro, 'but the devil himself wouldn't be able to catch him now; though I imagine that his affection for me, and his hunger, will force him to come back to look for me tonight – and God will send us his light, and then we'll see.'

So the storm over the puppet show died down and all had supper together in peace and good fellowship, at the expense of Don Quixote, who was an extremely generous man.

The man transporting the lances and halberds left before dawn, and once it was light the cousin and the page came to take their leave of Don Quixote, one to go back home and the other to continue on his way, as a help with which Don Quixote gave him a dozen reals. Master Pedro didn't want any more argy-bargy with Don Quixote, whom he knew all too well, and so he rose before the sun, took his monkey and the remains of his puppet theatre, and went off in search of his own adventures. The innkeeper, who didn't know Don Quixote, was as amazed at his capers as at his generosity. And Sancho paid him well, on his master's orders, and at a little before eight o'clock in the morning they left the inn and took to the road, where we shall leave them to go on their way, as we must in order to provide an opportunity to record other matters that are relevant to the narration of this famous history.

CHAPTER XXVII

*Which explains who Master Pedro and his ape were,
together with the unfortunate outcome of the adventure of
the bray, which Don Quixote did not conclude as he had
wished or intended*

Cide Hamete, the chronicler of this great history, begins this chapter with the words: 'I swear as a Christian and as a Catholic . . .'; to which the translator adds that when Cide Hamete swore as a Christian and a Catholic, being a Moor, as he most certainly was, he only meant to say that just as when the Christian and Catholic swears something he swears, or should swear, the truth, and he swears to tell the truth in everything he says, so Cide Hamete was also telling the truth, as if he were swearing as a Christian and a Catholic, in everything he wrote about Don Quixote, especially in his explanation of who was Master Pedro, and who was the fortune-telling ape that amazed all those villages with its divination. Cide Hamete says, then, that anybody who has read the first part of this history will remember that character Ginés de Pasamonte, whom Don Quixote freed together with other convicts in the Sierra Morena, a kindness for which he was given very poor thanks and even worse payment by that malicious and nefarious crew. This fellow Ginés de Pasamonte, whom Don Quixote called Ginesillo de Parapilla, was the man who stole Sancho's donkey, an incident which, because the explanation of how and when the theft took place was omitted from the first part through the printers' carelessness, has led many people to offer their opinions and blame the printing mistake on the author's poor memory. But, to be brief, Ginés stole it while Sancho Panza was sleeping on it, with the trick used by Brunello when, at the siege of Albracca, he took the horse from between Sacripante's legs; and later Sancho recovered it in the way described. This Ginés, then, was fearful that the authorities might catch up with him, because they were searching for him to punish him for his countless villainous crimes, which were so numerous and of such magnitude that he himself had written a great tome describing them; and so he decided to take refuge in the kingdom of Aragon, put a patch over his left eye and take up the trade of puppeteering, because at this and at sleight-of-hand he was an expert.

And then it was that he bought the ape from some Christians who'd been freed in Barbary and were returning home, and he trained it to respond to a certain signal by jumping on to his shoulder and whispering, or seeming to whisper, into his ear. Before going into a village with his puppet show and his ape, he'd find out in the previous village, or from the best source he came across, what notable events had happened there, and to whom, and he'd carefully memorize them; but the first thing he'd always do was to perform his puppet show, sometimes one story, sometimes another, but all of them jolly and cheerful and well-known. After this preliminary show he'd describe the ape's skills, telling the people that it could divine everything in the past and present, but that it couldn't manage the future. For each answer he charged two reals, and he sometimes lowered the price, depending on his assessment of the questioners' ability to pay; and whenever he walked by a house where there were people living about whom he'd received information, even if nobody asked any questions so as not to have to pay any money, he'd make the sign to the ape, and then say that it had told him this and that and the other, all of it tallying exactly with what really had happened. This would earn an incredible reputation for him, and from then on he'd be in great demand. At other times, being such a shrewd man, he'd reply by shaping his answers to the mould of the questions; and since nobody pressed him for an explanation of how his monkey could divine, he made monkeys of the lot of them, and filled his money bags.

As soon as he walked into the inn he recognized Don Quixote and Sancho, and this made it easy for him to amaze them both and everyone else as well; but it would have cost him dear if Don Quixote had aimed a little lower when he decapitated King Marsilio and destroyed his entire cavalry, as related in the previous chapter. And this is what needed to be said about Master Pedro and his ape.

And returning to Don Quixote de la Mancha, I should say that after leaving the inn he decided first to go to see the River Ebro and its environs before proceeding to Saragossa, because he had time enough and to spare before the jousts began. With this idea in mind he went on his way, and travelled for two days without anything happening worth recording; and on the third day, as he rode up a hill, he heard a great din of drums, bugles and muskets. At first he thought that some regiment of soldiers was marching past, and to see them he spurred Rocinante and rode to the top of the hill; and from there he saw, at its foot, what seemed like more than two hundred men carrying different sorts of weapons such as lances, crossbows, partisans, halberds and pikes, as well as a few muskets and many round shields. He rode down the hill and approached the squadron until he could pick out the flags, distinguish the colours and read the mottoes on them, especially one on a standard or pennant of white satin, with a very realistic depiction of a small donkey with its head up, its mouth open and its tongue out, in a braying position, and round it were written these two lines in large letters:

> Our mayors twain
> Brayed not in vain.

From this device Don Quixote deduced that these people were from the village of the bray, and he told Sancho so, and read out the words on the banner. He also observed that the man who'd told them about the affair had been wrong when he'd said that the two brayers were councillors since, according to the words on the banner, they were no less than mayors. To which Sancho Panza replied:

'There's no need to go bothering your head about that, sir, it could well be that the councillors who brayed became mayors in due course, so they can be called by both titles, and anyway it doesn't affect the truth of the history whether the brayers were mayors or councillors, so long as they really did bray, because a mayor's just as likely to bray as a councillor.'

To cut the story short, they discovered that the derided village was marching to do battle with another village that had mocked more than it should, and more than good neighbourliness requires. Don Quixote rode up to them, to Sancho's deep dismay, because Sancho had never been fond of taking part in campaigns of this sort. The men in the squadron received him into their midst in the belief that he was fighting on their side. Don Quixote raised his visor and approached the donkey flag with easy verve and graceful demeanour, and all the leaders of the army surrounded him to have a good look at him, struck with the amazement that overcame everybody when they saw him for the first time. When Don Quixote saw them gawping there without speaking or asking him any questions, he decided to make the most of their silence; so he broke his own silence by proclaiming:

'My dear good sirs, I beg you with all my heart not to interrupt a speech I wish to make to you, unless you find that it displeases or wearies you; and, if this happens, your slightest sign will make me seal my lips and gag my mouth.'

They all told him to say whatever he liked, because they'd be happy to listen. Granted this permission, Don Quixote continued:

'I, my dear sirs, am a knight errant, and my exercise is arms, and my profession is succouring the defenceless and relieving the needy. I discovered some days ago about this unfortunate affair that causes you to take up arms at every turn to avenge yourselves on your enemies. And having given the matter my attention not just once but many times, I find that, according to the laws of combat, you are mistaken to consider yourselves dishonoured, for no individual can dishonour a whole community, except when he challenges it as a collective traitor because he does not know who in particular committed the treasonable act in question. We find an example of this in Don Diego Ordóñez de Lara, who challenged the entire population of Zamora, because he did not know that Vellido Dolfos alone had committed the treachery of killing his king, and he therefore challenged them all,[1] and so the revenge and the response was something that concerned them all; although it does have to be admitted that Don Diego did rather overstep the mark, and indeed went far beyond the limits of a challenge, because there was no call to challenge the dead, the waters of the river, the loaves of bread, or the babes as yet unborn, or any of the other details that are listed there; but there we are – when anger overflows, the tongue wags unrestrained. Since it is the case, then, that no one person can dishonour a whole kingdom, province, city, town or village, it is clear that there is no requirement to take up the challenge for such an affront, because it is no affront at all; it would be a fine affair if the people of the town of the lady clock were fighting to the death at every turn with those who call them that, and the same goes for the stewpots, the eggplanters, the whale-calves, the soapies[2] and others with nicknames constantly in the mouths of young boys and sundry other riff-raff. A fine affair it would be, indeed, if all these illustrious towns became enraged and sought revenge, pulling their swords out like trombones at every disagreement, however petty! No, no, God forbid! There are four reasons for prudent men and well-ordered communities to take up arms, draw their swords and put their persons, their lives and their possessions at risk: first, to defend the Catholic faith; second, to defend their own lives, in accordance with divine and natural law; third, to defend their honour, their families and their possessions; fourth, in the service of their king in a just war; and if we wished to add a fifth reason, which would come second in the list, it would be to defend their country. To these five principal causes other just and reasonable ones can be added that oblige us to take up arms; but to take them up because of childish pranks and what was no affront but a joke, a piece of fun, hardly seems to be something for sane and rational beings to do, particularly since taking unjust revenge (and no revenge can be just) flies in the face of the holy religion that we all profess, which orders us to do good to our enemies and love those who hate us,[3] a commandment that, although it might seem somewhat difficult to keep, is only so for those who have less of God than of the world in them, and more of the flesh than of the spirit; because when Jesus Christ, true God and true man, who never lied, or could or can lie, gave us our laws he said that his yoke was easy and his burden light;[4] he was not, therefore, going to command us to do the impossible. So, my good sirs, you are obliged by both divine and human law to calm down.'

'The devil take me,' said Sancho to himself, 'if this master of mine isn't a theologian – or if he isn't he's as much like one as one egg's like the next!'

Don Quixote paused for breath and, observing that they were all still standing there in silence, he decided to continue with his speech, as he would have done if the nimble-witted Sancho hadn't intervened, seeing that his master had stopped and giving him a helping hand by saying:

'My master Don Quixote de la Mancha, who was once called the Knight of the Sorry Face and is now called the Knight of the Lions, is a very prudent hidalgo who knows Latin and Spanish like a BA, and he acts like a very good soldier in all his doings and advice, and he's got all the rules and regulations of what they call challenging off to a T, so there's nothing for it but to do as he says, and on my own head be it if this isn't good advice. And besides, you've already heard it's silly to get all het up just because of someone braying — I can well remember when I was a lad I used to bray myself whenever I felt like it, and nobody ever tried to stop me, and my brays were so artistic and lifelike that as soon as I did one all the donkeys in the village brayed back, and that didn't stop me from being the son of my parents, and very honourable folk they were too, and even though I was envied for my skill by more than a few stuck-up people in the village I never cared a hoot about that. And so that you can see I'm telling the truth, just you wait and listen to this, because this skill's the same as swimming, once you've learned it you never forget.'

And clapping his hand to his nose he began to bray with such power that all the nearby valleys resounded. But one of the men standing beside him, thinking that Sancho was making fun of them, raised the staff he was carrying and hit Sancho so hard that all he could do was slump to the ground. Don Quixote, seeing Sancho so ill-treated, made to attack his assailant with levelled lance, but so many men interposed themselves that revenge was impossible; and seeing that a storm of stones was raining down on him, and that he was threatened by a thousand crossbows pointing at him, and by no fewer muskets, Don Quixote turned Rocinante and, at the fastest canter he could manage, rode away from them, commending himself to God with all his heart, praying to be delivered from that peril and fearing with every step that a bullet would hit his back and emerge through his chest: every so often he held his breath to see if he was leaking. But the men in the squadron were content to see him taking to flight, and didn't shoot. As soon as Sancho came round, they slung him across his donkey and let him follow his master, not that he was conscious enough to guide it, but it followed in Rocinante's tracks because it couldn't bear to be parted from him for a moment. After Don Quixote had ridden a good distance he looked back and saw that Sancho was following him, and he waited, since nobody was following Sancho.

The men in the squadron stayed where they were until nightfall when, their enemies not having come to do battle, they returned to their village, full of joy and good cheer, and if they'd known about the custom of the ancient Greeks they'd have raised a trophy on the spot.

CHAPTER XXVIII

*Of certain matters that Benengeli says the reader will find
out about if he pays attention*

When the brave man flees, it's because he's spotted foul play; and the prudent man ensures that he lives to fight another day. These truths were verified in Don Quixote, who, giving way before the fury of the people and the evil intentions of that enraged squadron, took to Rocinante's heels and, without a thought for Sancho or the peril he was leaving him in, rode off as far as was necessary for him to feel safe. Sancho followed, draped across his donkey as described. He caught up with Don Quixote, having recovered the use of his senses, and as he arrived he slid off the donkey at Rocinante's feet, bruised and battered and in agonies of pain. Don Quixote dismounted to examine his squire's wounds but, finding him unmarked from head to foot, said in a fury of indignation:

'Whatever put it into your head to bray at that precise moment, Sancho? And where did you ever hear that it is a good idea to name a rope in the house of the man who hanged himself? What counterpoint do you expect to the music of the bray, except the descant of the stick? And you can thank God, Sancho, that you were given a benediction with a staff rather than a *per signum crucis*[1] with a cutlass.'

'I'm in no fit state to reply,' replied Sancho, 'because it feels as if the words are coming out through the holes in my back. Let's get mounted and clear off, and I'll put an end to my braying, but I'm not going to keep quiet about knight errants that run away and leave their worthy squires beaten to pulp or powder in their enemies' hands.'

'He who withdraws does not flee,' Don Quixote replied, 'because I would have you know, Sancho, that courage which is not based on prudence is called foolhardiness, and the achievements of the foolhardy man are more to be credited to good fortune than to his courage. And so I confess that I withdrew, but not that I fled, and in so doing I followed the lead of many brave men who have saved themselves for better times, and the histories are full of such cases, about which I shall not tell you now because it would be of no benefit to you and no pleasure to me.'

By now Sancho was back on his donkey, with the help of Don Quixote, who remounted Rocinante, and they plodded towards the shelter of a poplar grove that they could see a half a mile away. Every so often Sancho heaved profound sighs and uttered agonized groans, and when Don Quixote asked him why he was in such distress, he replied that the pain from the base of his spine all the way up to the nape of his neck was driving him crazy.

'The reason for that pain,' said Don Quixote, 'must obviously be that the staff with which you were struck was an extremely long one, and took in your entire back, with all those parts that are hurting you now; and if it had taken in more of you, more of you would hurt.'

'God Almighty!' said Sancho. 'That's a great mystery you've cleared up for me and explained so neatly! By my body and soul, was the cause of my pain so hard to find that I needed to be told that where the stick hit me it hurts? If it was my ankles hurting it might make some sense to be guessing why, but you don't need to be a great guesser to say that it hurts where I got thumped. By my faith, master, our neighbour's care is easy to bear, isn't it just? With every day that passes I find out more about how little I can expect to get out of sticking with you, because if you let them beat me up this time, the next time and the next few hundred times we'll be back to the old blanket-tossings and other such pranks, and if it's my back that's hurting now it's my eyes they'll have next. I'd do much better, except that I'm a dunderhead and I'll never put a foot right in all the days of my life, as I was saying I'd do much better to go back to my wife and children, and keep her and bring up them on whatever God was pleased to send me, and not come traipsing around after you along roads that aren't roads and paths that aren't paths for bad drink and worse food. And what about sleep, then! "Just you measure out six feet of earth for yourself, brother squire, and if you want any more you can take the same amount again, so do help yourself to as much as you require, and stretch yourself out to your heart's content" – I'd like to see the first man who started out on knight-errantry burned to ashes, or at least the first man who became the squire of the fools that the knight errants of days gone by must have been. I'm not talking about present-day knight errants, because you being one of them I respect them, and also because I know that you know one trick more than the devil himself, and that applies to everything you say and think.'

'I should be prepared to bet you a goodly sum, Sancho,' said Don Quixote, 'that now you are talking away without anyone to stop you, you do not feel a single pain anywhere in your body. Do talk on, my son, say everything that comes into your head and your mouth, because in exchange for your not being in pain I shall deem all the annoyance that your nonsense causes me to be a great pleasure. And if, sir, you are so keen to go back home to your wife and children, God forbid that I should stand in your way – you are carrying my money, so pray work out how long it is since we left the village on this our third sally, and how much you can and should earn per month, and be your own paymaster.'

'When I worked for Tomé Carrasco, Sansón Carrasco BA's father and a man you know well,' Sancho replied, 'I got two ducats a month, plus food. With you I don't know what I could earn, though I do know that a knight errant's squire has a worse time of it than a farmer's labourer, because when all's said and done those of us who work for farmers might be toiling away all day long but at the worst we do get a bowl of stew at night and sleep in a bed, which is something I haven't slept in all this time I've been serving you, except for those few days we spent in Don Diego de Miranda's house, and that fiesta I had with the skimmings off Camacho's pots, and the eating and the drinking and the sleeping I enjoyed in Basilio's house – but all the rest of the time I've slept on the hard earth, in the open air, subject to the inclemencies of heaven as they put it, existing on slices of cheese and crusts of bread, and drinking water from the streams and springs we come across in these God-forsaken places we go traipsing about in.'

'I confess,' said Don Quixote, 'that everything you say, Sancho, is true. How much more, pray, do you think I ought to give you than Tomé Carrasco did?'

'To my mind,' said Sancho, 'if you gave me an extra two reals a month that'd make me happy enough. Those are the wages for my labour, but in lieu of your promise to make me governor of an island, it'd only be right to add another six reals, making thirty in all.'

'That is most appropriate,' Don Quixote replied, 'and now to work out the wages you have adjudicated to yourself – we left the village twenty-five days ago, so you must calculate pro-rata what I owe you and, as I said, be your own paymaster.'

'By my body and soul!' said Sancho. 'You're way out there, because the compensation for the promise of the island has got to be counted from the very day you made the promise to this present moment.'

'And was it so very long ago, Sancho, that I made you the promise?' said Don Quixote.

'If my memory isn't playing me up,' Sancho replied, 'it must be more than twenty years, give or take a day or two.'

Don Quixote gave himself a sonorous slap on the forehead and roared with hearty laughter, and said:

'My stay in the Sierra Morena and the whole of our wanderings together have hardly occupied two months, and you're telling me, Sancho, that I promised you the island twenty years ago? I think you want to devote all that money of mine that you're holding to your own wages; and if this is so, if this is what you wish to do, I give it to you here and now, and much good may it do you, because to be rid of such an appalling squire I shall be delighted to be left utterly penniless. But tell me this, you violator of the regulations of knight-errantry regarding squires: where have you ever seen or read of any knight errant's squire confronting his master with "you must give me so much a month if you want me to serve you"? Launch out, launch out, you scoundrel, you wretch, you monster, for it seems that you're all of these – launch out, I say, on the great sea of their histories, and if you find that a single squire has ever said or thought what you have just said here, I want you to nail his words to my forehead and, in addition, to give me four fine fillips on the nose. Turn your dun's reins, or rather its halter, and go back home, for you are not taking one more step in my company. You bite the hand that feeds you! You are unworthy of the promises that I have made you! You have more of the beast than of the man about you! Now, now, just when I was about to raise you to a station in which, in spite of your wife, you would have been called Your Lordship, you abandon me? You leave me now, just when I had reached the firm and resolute decision to make you the lord of the best island in the world? Well, after all, as you have so often said yourself, honey was not made for the mouths of asses. An ass you are, an ass you will remain and an ass you will still be when you end your days on this earth, and it is my belief that when you come to breathe your last you still will not have grasped the fact that you are an animal.'

Sancho gaped at Don Quixote as he discharged all this abuse, and was overcome by such remorse that the tears welled into his eyes, and in doleful, feeble tones he said:

'Oh sir, I confess that all I need to be a complete ass is the tail, and if you want to hang one on me to my mind I've deserved it, and I'll serve you as a donkey for all the rest of my life. Forgive me, sir, and take pity on my ignorance, and remember that I don't know very much and if I do talk a lot that's more an illness than wickedness – and he who errs and mends, himself to God commends.'

'I should have been astonished, Sancho, if you hadn't worked some proverb or other into your discourse. Very well then, I do forgive you, so long as you mend your ways and do not show so much concern henceforth for your own profit, but try to take heart and be of good cheer in the expectation of the fulfilment of my promises, which has been delayed but is not impossible.'

Sancho replied that he would do so, even if it did mean having to draw strength from weakness.

With this they rode into the poplar grove and Don Quixote settled down at the foot of an elm, and Sancho at the foot of a beech, because these trees and others like them always have feet but never hands. Sancho had a painful night, because the damp air made his bruises ache all the more. Don Quixote spent the night with his ever-present memories; but for all that they both surrendered their eyes to sleep, and as the new day peeped out they continued on their way in quest of the banks of the famous River Ebro, where something happened that will be recounted in the next chapter.

CHAPTER XXIX

About the famous adventure of the enchanted boat

Two days after they left the poplar grove, proceeding with measured steps and a few unmeasured ones, Don Quixote and Sancho reached the River Ebro, and it gave Don Quixote great pleasure to see it as he surveyed its delightful banks, its clear waters, its tranquil flow and its abundant liquid crystal, the contemplation of which delights revived a thousand loving thoughts in his mind. More than anything else he dwelt on what he'd seen in the Cave of Montesinos, for although Master Pedro's monkey had told him that some of those things had been true and some false, he stood more by the true ones than the others, quite the opposite of Sancho, who was convinced that they were all part and parcel of the same great lie.

As Don Quixote rode along, his eyes alighted on a small boat, without any oars or other equipment, moored to the trunk of a tree that stood on the river bank. Don Quixote looked all around but he couldn't see anybody, and without further delay he dismounted from Rocinante and ordered Sancho to get off his dun and tie both animals securely to the trunk of a nearby poplar or willow. Sancho enquired into the reason for this hasty descent and ligation. Don Quixote replied:

'I would have you know, Sancho, that this boat moored here is calling and inviting me, with all urgency and without anything being able to prevent it, to go on board and sail in it to succour some knight or some other person of quality who needs my help and who must be in a serious plight, because this is the way of the histories of knight-errantry and of the enchanters who meddle and intervene in such affairs: when a knight is in difficulties and can only be saved by the hand of another knight, even if the latter is seven or ten or more thousand miles away, he is either snatched up into the clouds or provided with a boat to board, and is borne in the twinkling of an eye through the air or over the waves to where he is required and his help is needed. And so, O Sancho, this boat has been placed here for just such a purpose, as surely as it is now day; so before it stops being day tie the dun and Rocinante together to the tree, and may God's hand guide us, because a monastery-full of discalced friars will not prevent me from embarking.'

'If that's the way it is,' Sancho replied, 'and you will insist at every turn on making these what I shouldn't but will call gaffes, there's nothing for it but to bow my head and obey and think of the proverb, "Do as your master commands and sit down with him at table," but for all that, just to make my conscience easy, I'd like to point out that to my mind this boat here isn't one of the enchanted sort but one of the sort pertaining to fishermen, because here in this river they catch the finest shad in the world.'

Sancho was saying this as he tied the animals to the tree, leaving them to the protection of the enchanters, with much grief in his soul. Don Quixote told him not to worry about leaving the animals unattended, because he who was going to care for them on a voyage of such longinquity would see to their animals' sustenance.

'I don't know what you mean by longdrinkity,' said Sancho, 'and I've never heard such a word in all the days of my life.'

'Longinquity,' Don Quixote replied, 'refers to a very great distance, and it is no surprise that you do not understand it, because you are not obliged to know Latin, like some who pride themselves on knowing it and don't.'

'I've tied them up,' Sancho replied. 'What are we going to do next?'

'What are we going to do?' Don Quixote said. 'Cross ourselves and weigh anchor: in other words board the boat and cut the mooring rope.'

And he jumped on board, followed by Sancho, and he cut the rope, and the boat drifted slowly away from the bank, and when Sancho found himself a couple of yards off shore he started to tremble, fearing for his life; but nothing distressed him more than hearing the dun bray and seeing Rocinante struggle to free himself, and he said to his master:

'The dun's braying because it's so sad to be without us, and Rocinante's trying to get free to jump in after us. O my dearest friends, peace be with you, and let's hope the madness that's taking us from you sees the light and lets us come back to you again!'

And with this he began to cry so bitterly that Don Quixote barked at him in fury:

'What are you afraid of, you cowardly creature? What is it making you blubber, you butter-hearted baby? Who is pursuing you, who is hounding you, you mouse-spirited wretch, and what do you lack, claiming deprivation when you're living in the lap of luxury? Are you perchance tramping barefoot over the Riphean mountains[1], or are you sitting on a bench like an archduke, drifting along in the tranquil current of this pleasant river, from which before very long we shall emerge into the boundless ocean? But we must already have emerged, and travelled at least two or three thousand miles, and if I had here an astrolabe to take the altitude of the pole I should tell you the distance we have gone, although either I am a poor judge of such matters or we already have passed, or soon shall pass, the equinoctial line, which divides the opposing poles at an equal distance.'

'And when we get to that notch or line you said,' Sancho asked, 'how far will we have gone?'

'A very great distance,' Don Quixote replied, 'for of the three hundred and sixty degrees contained in the terraqueous globe, according to the estimates of Ptolemy, who was the greatest cosmographer known to man, we shall have covered one half when we reach the line that I mentioned.'

'Good God,' said Sancho, 'that's a fine character you've dredged up as a witness, with his sexy butts and his tomfoolery, and what's more a great pornographer, or whatever it was you said.'

Don Quixote laughed at Sancho's interpretation of the name and the estimates of the cosmographer Ptolemy, and said:

'You must know, Sancho, that for the Spaniards and others who embark in Cadiz to sail for the East Indies, one of the signs that they have crossed the equinoctial line I mentioned is that all the lice on every man aboard the ship die, and not a single one is left, and they wouldn't find a louse on the vessel even if they gave its weight in gold; and so you can pass your hand over your thigh, Sancho, and if you find any living creature there we shall have resolved our doubts, and if not we've crossed.'

'I don't believe a word of it,' Sancho replied, 'but I'll do as you say all the same, though I can't fathom why there's any need for these experiments, because I can see with my own two eyes that we aren't five yards from the bank, and we aren't two yards downstream from the animals, because there they are over there, Rocinante and the donkey, exactly where we left them – and taking my bearings as I'm doing now, I swear by all that's holy that we're moving slower than an ant.'

'Make the investigation that I specified, Sancho, and don't bother your head with any other, because you don't understand about colures, lines, parallels, zodiacs, ecliptics, poles, solstices, equinoxes, planets, signs, points and measurements of which the terrestrial and celestial globe is composed; for if you did understand all these matters, or some of them, you would realize how many parallels we've crossed, how many signs we've seen and how many constellations we've left behind and are leaving behind even now. So I repeat: feel yourself, go fishing for lice, because it's my firm belief that you're freer of them than a sheet of smooth white paper.'

Sancho slipped his hand gently in and slowly down towards the back of his left knee, and then he looked up at his master and said:

'Either the whole experiment's baloney or we haven't got to where you say, not by a long long way.'

'What?' asked Don Quixote. 'Have you found something?'

'Quite a few somethings,' Sancho replied.

And he shook his fingers and gave his hand a good wash in the river, along which the boat was gliding with the current, not propelled by any secret intelligence or hidden enchanter but by the flow of the water, as yet calm and smooth. And now they saw some large water-mills standing in the middle of the river, and Don Quixote cried to Sancho:

'Do you see? There, my friend, stands the city, castle or fortress that must hold some knight under duress or some distressed queen, infanta or princess, to succour whom I have been brought here.'

'What the devil do you mean, city, castle or fortress, sir?' said Sancho. 'Can't you see they're water-mills for grinding corn?'

'Hush, Sancho,' said Don Quixote. 'Although they look like water-mills, that is not what they are: I have already told you that enchantments transfigure all things and deprive them of their natural forms. I don't mean to say that they really convert them from one thing into another, but that it seems as if they do, as experience has shown in the transformation of Dulcinea, the only refuge of my hopes.'

As he said this, the boat, drifting into the middle of the stream, began to move less slowly than hitherto. The millers, seeing a boat approaching down the river and realizing that it was going to be sucked into the mill-race, came running out armed with long poles to stop it, and since their faces and their clothes were covered in flour they didn't make a pretty sight. They were shouting:

'You devils! Where do you think you're going? Do you want to get yourselves killed? What are you trying to do – drown and be hacked to pieces by these wheels?'

'Did I not tell you, Sancho,' Don Quixote commented, 'that we had come to where I shall show how far the valour of my arm extends? Look how many knaves and blackguards are sallying forth to do battle with me; look at all the monsters ranged against me; look at all the ugly faces grimacing at us – well now you shall see, you villains!'

And standing in the boat he began to hurl threats at the millers:

'You wretches, ill intentioned and worse advised – set free the person you are keeping prisoner in that fortress or jail of yours, whether of high or low estate, of whatever rank or degree; for I am Don Quixote de la Mancha, also known as the Knight of the Lions, for whom the happy conclusion of this adventure has been reserved by order of the highest heavens.'

And as he said this he drew his sword and began to brandish it in the direction of the millers, who heard but couldn't understand his nonsense, and held out their poles to stop the boat, by now entering the mill-race. Sancho fell to his knees, sending devout prayers up to heaven to deliver him from such a manifest peril – which it did, acting through the quick thinking of the millers, who thrust their poles up against the boat and stopped it but couldn't avoid overturning it and throwing Don Quixote and Sancho out into the water; it was as well for Don Quixote that he could swim like a goose, but even so the weight of his armour dragged him twice to the bottom; and if it hadn't been for the millers, who jumped into the water and hauled the two of them out, people might have been saying, 'Here once stood Troy.'[2] When they'd been dumped on dry land, soaked to the skin and not exactly dying of thirst, Sancho knelt and pressed his hands together and riveted his eyes on heaven and prayed God in a long and fervent petition to deliver him in future from his master's foolhardy plans and enterprises. Next the fishermen who owned the boat, which had been smashed to pieces by the mill-wheels, appeared on the scene, and when they saw the state it was in they started stripping Sancho and demanding payment for it from Don Quixote, who, with supreme calm, as if nothing had happened, told the millers and the fishermen that he would most gladly pay for the boat on condition that they handed over to him, free and without ransom, the person or persons imprisoned in that castle.

'What persons and what castle are you on about, you lunatic?' replied one of the millers. 'Or maybe it's the girls who bring their wheat here to be ground that you want us to let you have?'

'Enough!' said Don Quixote to himself. 'It would be preaching in the wilderness to try to persuade this rabble to perform any virtuous action. In this adventure two mighty enchanters must have clashed headlong, and one of them impedes whatever the other attempts: one provided me with the boat, the other knocked me out of it. May God send a remedy; for everything in this world is trickery, stage machinery, every part of it working against every other part. I have done all I can.'

And, raising his voice and gazing at the water-mills, he continued:

'My friends, whoever you are, still imprisoned in this jail, forgive me, because unfortunately for me as well as for you I cannot relieve your distress. This adventure must have been reserved and destined for another knight.'

Once he had said this he settled up with the fishermen, paying fifty reals for the boat, which Sancho handed over with bad grace, saying:

'One more boat ride like this one and our whole stock will sink to the bottom.'

The fishermen and the millers stared in amazement at these two figures whose ways seemed so unlike the ways of other men, and they couldn't make head or tail of what Don Quixote had said and asked; and dismissing the pair as madmen, they went away, the millers to their mills and the fishermen to their huts. As for Don Quixote and Sancho, they went back to their animals, and to being animals; and thus ended the adventure of the enchanted boat.

CHAPTER XXX

About what happened to Don Quixote with a
beautiful huntress

The knight and his squire were in a melancholy and peevish mood when they returned to their animals; particularly Sancho, for whom to break into their stock of money, as precious to him as his own two eyes, was to break his heart. In short, they remounted in silence and rode away from the famous river, Don Quixote deep in thoughts of his love, and

Sancho deep in thoughts of his promotion, which at that time seemed very far distant; because in spite of all his oafishness he was well aware that all or at least most of his master's deeds were absurdities, and he was looking for a chance to make tracks one day and go back home without bothering about accounts or farewells; but fortune ordained that events should fall out quite other than how he feared they would.

What happened was that on the following day, as the sun was setting and they were riding out of a forest, Don Quixote cast his eyes over a green meadow and at the far end of it he observed some people who, when he came closer, turned out to be falconers. He drew nearer still, and among them he saw a graceful lady on a pure white hack or palfrey with green trappings and a silver high saddle. She, too, was wearing green, and her attire was so splendid that she seemed like the very personification of finery. On her left hand she bore a goshawk, an indication to Don Quixote that she was some great lady and the leader of the party, as indeed she was, and so he said to Sancho:

'Hurry, Sancho my son, and tell that lady on the palfrey with a hawk on her hand that I, the Knight of the Lions, salute her wondrous beauteousness, and if Her Excellency grants me her leave I will go and kiss her hands and serve her in all that my strength permits and Her Highness commands. And mind, Sancho, how you speak, and take care not to slip any of those proverbs of yours into the message.'

'So we've found him out at last, the great slipper-in of proverbs into messages, have we?' Sancho retorted. 'Fancy saying a thing like that to me! This isn't the first time in my life I've taken messages to high and mighty ladies, you know!'

'Apart from the one you took to the lady Dulcinea,' Don Quixote replied, 'I am not aware that you have taken any, not at least while in my service.'

'That's true enough,' Sancho replied, 'but a good payer's a good pledger, and where there's plenty to put in the pot the dinner is soon enough got – what I mean to say is that there isn't any need for you to come to me with advice and warnings, I'm ready for anything and I know a bit about everything.'

'And I believe you, too, Sancho,' said Don Quixote, 'so off you go, and God guide your steps.'

Sancho went away at top speed, forcing the dun out of its usual pace, and rode up to the beautiful huntress; and he dismounted, knelt before her and said:

'Lovely lady: that knight over there called the Knight of the Lions is my master, and I'm a squire of his called Sancho Panza when I'm at home. This here Knight of the Lions, who not so long ago used to be called the Knight of the Sorry Face, has sent me to ask Your Excellency to be so kind as to grant him your leave so that, with your blessing, approval and consent, he can come and carry out his dearest wish, which is none other, as he says and I believe him, than to serve Your High-and-Mightiness and Beauteousness; and if Your Ladyship grants him it you will be doing something that will rebound to your advantage, and he will count it a most single favour and cause for joy.'

'I must say, my dear good squire,' the lady replied, 'you've delivered your message with all the ceremony that's appropriate on these occasions. Do rise from the ground, because it isn't right for the squire of such a great knight as the Knight of the Sorry Face, about whom we've already heard a great deal in these parts, to remain kneeling; rise, my friend, and tell your master that he's most welcome to come and be served by me and my husband the Duke in our nearby country house.'

Sancho rose, amazed as much by the fine lady's beauty as by her good breeding and courtesy, and even more by what she had said about having heard of his master the Knight of the Sorry Face – and if she hadn't called him the Knight of the Lions it must have been because he'd taken this name so recently. The Duchess, whose full title is not yet known, asked:

'Tell me, my dear squire: is this master of yours not a gentleman about whom a history has been printed, *The Ingenious Hidalgo Don Quixote de la Mancha*, and whose lady-love goes by the name of Dulcinea del Toboso?'

'The very same, my lady,' Sancho replied, 'and that squire of his who plays his part or ought to play his part in that there history and who's called Sancho Panza is me – unless they did a swop when I was in my cradle, by which I mean the printing press.'

'I'm so, so delighted by all I've heard,' said the Duchess. 'Go, my dear Panza, and tell your master that he must come to be made most welcome here on my estates, and that absolutely nothing else could give me greater pleasure.'

Overjoyed at this gracious answer, Sancho went back to his master and told him everything that the fine lady had said, and in his rustic language he praised her great beauteousness, charm and courtesy to the skies. Don Quixote sat himself up straight and stately in his saddle, made his feet firm in his stirrups, adjusted his visor, spurred Rocinante forward and rode with graceful demeanour to kiss the Duchess's hands; and meanwhile she had her husband the Duke called, and told him, while Don Quixote was riding up, all about his message; and since they'd both read the first part of this history and learned about Don Quixote's eccentric character, they waited with the utmost pleasure and eagerness to make his acquaintance, intending to play along with him, agree with everything he said and treat him as a knight errant for as long as he stayed with them, with all the ceremonies described in books of chivalry, which they'd read and were very fond of.

And now Don Quixote reached them with his visor raised and, as he made to dismount, Sancho went to hold his stirrup, but was unlucky enough to tangle his foot in one of the ropes on his pack-saddle as he hurried down from his dun, and he couldn't pull it free, but hung there with his mouth and his chest pressed to the ground. Don Quixote, who wasn't used to dismounting without somebody holding the stirrup, thought that Sancho must by now be there doing so, and swung himself off the saddle, which must have been insecurely girthed because he dragged it after him and both he and it ended up on the ground, to his shame and with many a muttered curse on the unfortunate Sancho, whose foot was still fettered. The Duke ordered his huntsmen to go to the rescue of the knight and his squire, and they picked Don Quixote up, much the worse for his fall, and he limped as best he could to kneel before the lord and lady; but the Duke would by no means allow this, and instead he dismounted, embraced Don Quixote and said:

'It's such a shame, Sir Knight of the Sorry Face, that the first time you've shown yours in my estates it should all have turned out so inauspiciously; but the negligence of squires often leads to even worse results.'

'The result for me of my meeting you, O valiant lord,' Don Quixote replied, 'could not possibly be a bad one, even if I had fallen into the depths of the bottomless pit, because the glory of having seen you would have raised me and brought me back even from there. My squire, God damn him, is better at loosening his tongue to babble mischief than at tightening a girth to secure a saddle; but in whatever state I find myself, fallen or risen, on foot or on horseback, I shall always be at your service and at that of my lady the Duchess, your worthy consort, and the worthy queen of beauty and paramount princess of courtesy.'

'Step carefully now, my dear Don Quixote de la Mancha!' said the Duke. 'Where there is a Dulcinea del Toboso to be reckoned with, it is not right that other beauties should be praised!'

Sancho had by now disentangled himself from his noose and was standing near by, and before his master could speak he said:

'There's no denying and anyone would have to say that my lady Dulcinea del Toboso is very beautiful, but the hare leaps up where you least expect it to, because I've heard that what they call nature is like a potter making vases out of clay, and anyone who can make one fine vase can make two or three or a hundred of them – I'm only saying all this because the fact is that my lady the Duchess is every bit as easy on the eye as my lady Dulcinea del Toboso.'

Don Quixote turned to the Duchess and said:

'I should like Your Highness to know that no knight errant in the world ever had a squire who was more talkative or more laughable than mine, and if Your Majesty is willing to make avail of my services for a few days he will prove the truth of what I say.'

To which the Duchess replied:

'I place the highest importance on the fact that the good Sancho is laughable, because this is a sure sign that he's bright; jokes and witticisms, my dear Don Quixote, as you well know, don't go with dull wits; so since the good Sancho is laughable and witty, I can be certain that he's terribly clever.'

'And talkative,' Don Quixote added.

'So much the better,' said the Duke, 'because a wealth of humour can't be expressed in a paucity of words. And we'd better not let words use up all our time – the great Knight of the Sorry Face must come . . .'

'Of the Lions Your Highness ought to say,' said Sancho, 'because there isn't any Sorry Face or sorry anything else any more.'

'Of the Lions be it, then,' the Duke continued. 'As I was saying, the Knight of the Lions must come to a castle of mine not far from here, where I shall give him the reception due to such an exalted personage – the reception that the Duchess and I give to all knights errant arriving there.'

By now Sancho had put Rocinante's saddle back on and had strapped it down tight; and Don Quixote remounted, and the Duke mounted a handsome steed, and off they rode on either side of the Duchess towards the castle. The Duchess ordered Sancho to ride with her, because she simply adored listening to his clever conversation. Sancho didn't have to be asked twice, and he wormed his way in among the three of them, turning the conversation into a foursome to the delight of the Duchess and the Duke, who held it a great stroke of fortune to be able to receive in their castle such a knight errant, and such an errant squire.

CHAPTER XXXI

Concerning many weighty matters

Sancho was overjoyed to find that he was, to his mind, one of the Duchess's own special favourites, because he thought that he was going to discover in her castle what he'd discovered in the houses of Don Diego and Basilio, fond as he was of good living and therefore quick to seize by the forelock every opportunity to indulge himself.

The history relates, then, that before they reached the country house or castle the Duke rode on ahead and gave all his servants instructions about how they were to treat Don Quixote; and when the knight arrived with the Duchess at the castle gates, two lackeys or grooms instantly appeared, wearing those ankle-length robes known as dressing-gowns, of finest crimson satin, and they swept Don Quixote up in their arms, saying:

'Your Highness must go and help my lady the Duchess to dismount.'

Don Quixote did so, and there was a great exchange of courtesies over the matter; but the Duchess's insistence triumphed, as she refused to descend from her palfrey in the arms of anyone other than the Duke, saying that she did not consider herself worthy to impose such a useless burden on such a great knight. At length the Duke came forward to help her off her horse, and as they walked into a great courtyard two beautiful maidens appeared and draped over Don Quixote's shoulders a large robe of the finest scarlet, and in an instant all the galleries around the courtyard were filled with menservants and maidservants crying:

'Welcome to the crème de la crème of knight-errantry!'

And then they produced flasks and sprinkled scented waters over Don Quixote and the Duke and Duchess, and Don Quixote was amazed by what was happening; and that was the first day when he was fully convinced that he was a real knight errant, not a fantasy one, seeing himself treated in the same way as he'd read that such knights used to be treated in centuries past.

Sancho abandoned his dun, glued himself to the Duchess and entered the castle; and then he felt pangs of conscience about leaving his donkey all by itself and went up to a venerable duenna who'd come out with others to greet the Duchess, and muttered to her:

'Señora González, or whatever it is you're called . . .'

'My name is Doña Rodríguez de Grijalba,' the duenna retorted. 'And what can I do for you, my good man?'

To which Sancho replied:

'I'd just like you to do me the favour of going out to the castle gate, where you'll find a dun donkey of mine – kindly have it taken or take it yourself to the stables, because it's rather a jittery animal the poor thing, and it won't be feeling at all happy on its own like that, not by any manner or means.'

'If the master's as clever as the servant,' the duenna replied, 'it's a fine pair we've got on our hands here! Off with you, my good man, and a plague on you and the person who brought you here, and you can look after your donkey yourself, because in this house we duennas are not accustomed to performing such chores.'

'Well the honest truth is,' Sancho replied, 'that I've heard my master, and he's a wizard at histories, telling that one about Lancelot,

> When from Brittany he came,
> Dames waited on that man of might,
> And duennas on his steed;[1]

and as for the fact that what I've got is a donkey, it's one that I wouldn't swop for Sir Lancelot's steed itself.'

'If you're some jester, my good man,' the duenna replied, 'you had better keep your jokes for those who'll be amused by them and pay you; from me you'll get nothing but a fig for them.'

'At least it'll be a good ripe fig,' Sancho retorted, 'because in the game of years you wouldn't lose by scoring too few points!'

'You bastard,' said the duenna, by now burning with fury. 'Whether I'm old or not is something I'll answer to God about, and not to you, you garlic-stuffed villain.'

And she said this so loud that the Duchess heard it, and, turning and seeing the duenna so agitated and with her eyes aflame, she asked whom she was having words with.

'I am having words,' the retainer replied, 'with this fellow here, who has urged me to go and take an ass of his from the castle gate to the stables, alleging as a precedent that this was done goodness knows where, and that dames waited on some character called Lancelot, and duennas on his steed – and on top of all that, just for good measure, he called me old!'

'I'd consider that insult,' the Duchess replied, 'to be quite the very worst one that could ever be hurled at me.'

And turning to Sancho she said:

'I'll have you know, friend Sancho, that Doña Rodríguez is a very young woman, and she's wearing those weeds more from custom and because of her authority than because of her years.'

'May all the years I've got left to live be bad ones,' replied Sancho, 'if I meant it that way – no, I only said it because I'm so very fond of my donkey that I thought there wasn't any kindlier person I could entrust it to than Doña Rodríguez.'

Don Quixote was listening to every word, and said:

'Is this an appropriate conversation, Sancho, for this place?'

'Look, sir,' replied Sancho, 'everyone's got to speak up about his needs wherever he is. It was here I remembered my dun, so it was here I spoke up about it, and if I'd remembered it in the stable then I'd have spoken up about it there.'

To which the Duke replied:

'Sancho's quite right, and he's in no way to blame; the dun's every need will be attended to, and Sancho has no cause to worry, because it will be treated every bit as well as its master.'

With these exchanges, enjoyed by all except Don Quixote, they reached the top of the stairs, and Don Quixote was taken into a hall decorated with rich cloth of gold and brocade; six maidens removed his armour and acted as pages, all of them trained and instructed by the Duke and Duchess as to what they had to do and how they should behave towards Don Quixote, to make him believe and see for himself that he was being treated as a knight errant. After Don Quixote's armour had been removed he was left in his narrow knee-breeches and his chamois-leather doublet; and as he stood there lean and long and lank, with his jaws meeting up and kissing inside his mouth, he cut a figure that, if the maidens hadn't striven so hard to suppress their giggles (which was one of the precise orders given them by their master and mistress), would have made them explode with laughter. They asked him to allow himself to be undressed so that a clean shirt could be put on him, but he would by no means consent to this, saying that modesty was as becoming in a knight errant as valour. However he told them to give the shirt to Sancho, and shutting himself with him in an inner room where a fine bed stood, he undressed and put the shirt on; and, now that he was alone with Sancho, he said:

'Tell me, yesterday's dunderhead and today's court jester: do you consider it correct to dishonour and insult a duenna who is as venerable and worthy of respect as that lady is? Was that the time to remember your dun, and are the Duke and Duchess the sort of people to allow animals to be neglected when they treat their owners so splendidly? For God's sake, Sancho, do control yourself, and don't give yourself away so that everybody realizes what coarse, peasant stuff you're made of. Look here, you sinner: the more honourable and well-born the servants, the higher the esteem in which their master is held, and one of the greatest advantages that great noblemen have over others is that they're waited on by servants as noble as themselves. Don't you realize, pitiful creature that you are and luckless wretch that I am, that if they see you're a base peasant, or a laughable half-wit, they'll think I'm some charlatan or humbug knight? No, no, Sancho my friend, steer clear of these pitfalls, steer clear of them; for he who stumbles as a talkative and funny fellow will soon catch his foot and fall headlong as an unfunny buffoon. Put a brake on your tongue, consider and chew over your words before they leave your mouth, and bear in mind that we have come to a place where, with the help of God and the might of my arm, we shall better our fame and wealth a very great deal indeed.'

Sancho promised with heartfelt sincerity to stitch up his mouth or bite off his tongue before he uttered a single inappropriate or ill-considered word, just as his master had ordered, and he shouldn't worry his head any more about it – nobody was going to find out from him what sort of people they really were.

Don Quixote dressed, put his sword-strap over his shoulder, draped the robe of scarlet around his body, donned a cap of green satin that the maidens had given him; and thus arrayed he strode out into the great hall, where he found the maidens standing in two equal lines, bearing the various implements necessary for the washing of hands, which was done with much bowing and curtseying and ceremony. Then twelve pages came with the butler to take him in to dinner, because his hosts were waiting for him. The pages surrounded him, and with great pomp and majesty they conducted him to another room, where a sumptuous table was laid with just four places. The Duke and Duchess came to the door to receive him, and with them came one of those grave churchmen who rule noblemen's houses: one of those who, not having been born noble themselves, never manage to teach those who are noble how to live up to their rank; one of those who want the greatness of the great to be measured by their own narrowness of mind; one of those who, in their attempts to teach the people they rule to avoid extravagance, turn them into misers; as I was saying, he must have been one of this sort, that grave churchman who came with the Duke and Duchess to receive Don Quixote. Many courtesies were exchanged, and then they took Don Quixote between them and went to sit at table.

The Duke invited Don Quixote to take the head of the table, and although he refused, the Duke was so very insistent that he was eventually obliged to accept it. The churchman sat opposite him, and the Duke and Duchess on either side. Sancho stood by, gaping in stupefied astonishment at all the honours being paid to his master by these aristocrats; and when he saw all the formalities and entreaties being exchanged between the

Duke and Don Quixote to persuade him to take the head of the table, Sancho said:

'If you'll give me your leave I'll tell you a story about something that happened in my village about this business of who sits where.'

As soon as Sancho said this Don Quixote began to tremble, certain that he was about to come out with some more of his nonsense. Sancho looked at him, read his thoughts and said:

'Don't you worry, sir, about me getting out of control, or saying anything but what's spot-on, because I haven't forgotten all that advice you gave me just now about speaking a lot or a little, and well or badly.'

'I have no recollection of any such thing, Sancho,' Don Quixote replied. 'Say whatever you like, but do say it quickly.'

'Well what I'm about to say,' said Sancho, 'is so true that my master Don Quixote here present will confirm I'm not lying.'

'As far as I'm concerned,' Don Quixote replied, 'you can lie, Sancho, as much as you like, and I shall do nothing to restrain you; but do think before you speak.'

'I've thought and thought so very much, that the man who rings the alarm has put himself furthest from harm, as you'll see once I get going.'

'It would be a good idea,' said Don Quixote, 'if Your Highnesses had this fool thrown out of here, because he is going to put his big foot in it again and again.'

'Upon my soul,' said the Duchess, 'Sancho shall not move one inch from my side: I love him dearly, because I know he's so terribly bright.'

'And may Your Holiness enjoy many bright days, too,' said Sancho, 'for having so much faith in me, even if I don't deserve it. And this is the story I'm going to tell you: a hidalgo in my village, a very rich and important man, because he was one of the Álamos of Medina del Campo, and he married Doña Mencía de Quiñones, who was the daughter of Don Alonso de Marañón, Knight of the Order of St James, who drowned in the Herradura disaster,[2] that there was that scrap about some years ago in the village, that I'm given to believe my master Don Quixote was mixed up in, and Tomàsillo the Mischief-Maker, the son of Balbastro the Blacksmith, got hurt . . . That's all true isn't it, sir? Say so, go on, do, so that these folk don't think I'm some lying chatterbox.'

'Hitherto,' said the churchman, 'I consider you more of a chatterer than a liar; but I do not know what I shall take you for henceforth.'

'You call on so many witnesses, Sancho, and provide such an abundance of detail, that I have no choice but to say that you must be telling the truth. But do press on with your story, and keep it brief, because at the rate you are going you will not have finished two days from now.'

'He most certainly shall not keep it brief,' said the Duchess, 'if he wants to please me; on the contrary, he must tell it in his own way, even if he does not finish it in six days, because if it did last that long they would be quite the best six days of my life.'

'What I was saying, then, ladies and gentlemen,' Sancho continued, 'was that this hidalgo, and I know him like the back of my hand, because it isn't a bowshot from my house to his, invited a poor but honourable farmer . . .'

'Do get a move on, my good man,' interrupted the churchman. 'If you continue like this there will be no end to your story until you are in the next world.'

'No, I'll finish before I'm halfway there, with God's help,' Sancho replied. 'So, as I was saying, when the farmer arrived at the house of that hidalgo I said who'd invited him, and may his soul rest in peace, because he's dead now, and what's more they say he died like an angel, because I wasn't there, I'd gone to Tembleque for the wheat harvest . . .'

'I beg you, my son, to return without delay from Tembleque and to finish your story without burying the hidalgo, unless you want to be the cause of further funerals.'

'The fact is, then,' Sancho replied, 'that when the two of them were about to sit down for the meal – I can see them now, plainer than ever . . .'

The Duke and Duchess were deriving huge pleasure from the displeasure with which the good churchman reacted to the leisurely pace of Sancho's story and all the pauses in it, while Don Quixote was consumed with fury and rage.

'As I was saying,' said Sancho, 'when the two of them were about to sit down for the meal, as I just said, the farmer insisted that the hidalgo had to take the head of the table, and the hidalgo insisted that the farmer had to take it, because in his house it was his orders that had to be obeyed; but the farmer, who prided himself on being polite and well-bred, wouldn't give in, until the hidalgo, pretty well fed up by now, put both his hands on his guest's shoulders and pushed him down into the seat, saying:

' "Sit down there, you nincompoop – wherever I sit will be the head of the table as far as you're concerned." '

'And that's the story, and to be honest with you I think it was pretty much to the point.'

Don Quixote turned a thousand different colours, which showed in the brown of his face like veins in marble, mingling with it; the Duke and Duchess smothered their laughter so as not to complete Don Quixote's embarrassment, because they'd followed the malicious drift of Sancho's story, and, to change the subject and prevent Sancho from coming out with any more of his nonsense, the Duchess asked Don Quixote what news he had of his lady Dulcinea, and whether he'd sent her any giants or scurvy knaves as presents recently, because he couldn't have failed to vanquish any number of them. To which Don Quixote replied:

'My dear lady: my misfortunes, although they had a beginning, will never come to an end. Giants I have vanquished, and caitiffs and scurvy knaves I have sent her, but where could they find her if she has been enchanted and turned into the ugliest peasant girl imaginable?'

'I don't know about that,' said Sancho Panza. 'To me she looks like the most beautiful woman in the world, or at least in niftiness and jumping I know there isn't a tumbler that could better her – by my faith, Duchess, she can leap from the ground on to the back of a donkey as if she was a cat!'

'Have you seen her when enchanted, Sancho?' asked the Duke.

'Haven't I just!' Sancho replied. 'Who the devil was it if not me that first hit on this enchantment lark? She's about as enchanted as my father is!'

When the churchman heard this talk of giants, caitiffs and enchantment, he realized that this man must be Don Quixote de la Mancha, whose history the Duke was always reading, for which the churchman had often remonstrated with him, saying that it was an absurdity to read such absurdities; and when the man of the cloth found his suspicions confirmed he turned to the Duke in fury and exclaimed:

'Sir: Your Grace will have to answer to our Lord for this fellow's doings. I imagine that this Don Quixote, or Don Idiot, or whatever his name is, is not as much of a fool as Your Grace would like to turn him into, by encouraging him to perform his preposterous and ludicrous antics.'

And turning to Don Quixote he said:

'And as for you, you simpleton: whoever has put it into your head that you are a knight errant and that you vanquish giants and capture scurvy knaves? Be off with you, for goodness sake, and take my advice: go back home, and see to the upbringing of your children if you have any, and look after your property, and stop wandering about the world frittering your time away and turning yourself into the laughing-stock of all who know you and all who do not know you. Wherever have you unearthed the notion that knights errant have ever existed or do exist? Wherever are there any giants in Spain, or scurvy knaves in La Mancha, or enchanted Dulcineas, or any of the rest of the nonsense written about you?'

Don Quixote listened attentively to the reverend gentleman's words; and when at last they ended, the knight, forgetting the respect due to the Duke and Duchess, his face convulsed with fury, rose to his feet and said . . .

But this reply deserves a chapter to itself.

CHAPTER XXXII

About the reply made by Don Quixote to his critic,
and other grave and funny incidents

Don Quixote stood there, quivering from head to foot, and he spluttered:

'The place where I am, the company in which I find myself, and the respect I feel and have always felt for your calling, all hold and bind the hands of my just fury; and both because of this and because I know that everyone knows that men of letters attack with the same weapons as women, their tongues, I shall employ my own tongue and engage in equal combat a man from whom one might have expected good advice rather than infamous insults. Pious and well-intentioned reproof requires other circumstances, other settings: at any rate, reproving me so harshly in public goes far beyond the limits of benevolent reproof, because this is better founded on gentleness than on harshness, and it is not right, without any knowledge of the sin, to call the sinner a fool and an idiot. Or else tell me this: for which of the idiocies that you have observed in me do you condemn me and insult me and tell me to go back home to take charge of my household and my wife and children, without knowing whether I have either? Is it appropriate to go bursting into other men's houses to rule their lives, or for certain people, brought up in the narrow confines of some hall of residence, and having seen no more of the world than that part of it lying within fifty or a hundred miles around, to take it upon themselves to lay down the laws of chivalry and pass judgement on knights errant? Is it perchance an empty nonsense or a waste of time to wander about the world in search not of pleasure but of the rough and rutted footpath up which the virtuous climb to the heights of immortality?[1] If I were considered a fool by knights, by grandees, by noblemen, by the high-born, I should hold it to be an irreparable affront; but to be thought stupid by scholars who have never ventured along the paths of chivalry does not concern me one iota: a knight I am and a knight I shall die, if it pleases the Lord above. Some take the broad road of proud ambition; others that of servile, lowly flattery; others that of deceitful hypocrisy; a very few that of true religion; but I, guided by my star, follow the narrow path of knight-errantry, in which exercise I scorn wealth but not honour. I have redressed outrages, righted wrongs, punished insolence, vanquished giants and felled monsters; I am a lover, merely because it is obligatory for knights errant to be lovers, yet I am not one of those debauched lovers but one of the platonic and continent sort. My intentions are always directed towards worthy ends, that is to say to do good to all and harm nobody; and whether the man who believes this, puts it into practice and devotes his life to it deserves to be called a fool is something for Your Graces, most excellent Duke and Duchess, to determine.'

'God, that was well said!' said Sancho. 'But you don't need to put in any more good words for yourself, sir, because there's nothing at all left to say, or think, or go on and on about. And what's more if this here gentleman denies as he does deny that knight errants exist or have ever existed, it isn't surprising that he doesn't know what he's talking about, is it now?'

'Are you by any chance, my good man,' said the churchman, 'that

Sancho Panza I have heard mentioned, whose master has promised him an island?'

'That's me,' Sancho replied, 'and I deserve it every bit as much as the next man. Keep good men company and you'll be one of the number – that's me. Not who you were bred with but who you are fed with – that's me. Well protected shall he be who finds himself a leafy tree – that's me. I've found myself a good master, sir, and I've been going around with him for months and months now, and I'm going to be just like him, God willing, and long life to him and to me as well – he's not going to have any shortage of empires to rule, and nor am I of islands to govern.'

'No, of course not, friend Sancho,' the Duke put in. 'Because in the name of Don Quixote I hereby promise you the governorship of an island that I have to spare, and not at all a bad one either.'

'Go down on your knees, Sancho,' said Don Quixote, 'and kiss His Grace's feet for the favour that he has just bestowed upon you.'

Sancho did as he was told, and when the churchman saw all this he jumped up from the table, beside himself with rage, exclaiming:

'By this habit that I wear, I am on the very verge of declaring that Your Grace is as much of a fool as this pair of sinners. How can they fail to be mad when sane men sanction their madness? Your Grace can keep them for yourself; so long as they are in this house I shall stay in mine, and spare myself the trouble of reproving what I cannot remedy.'

And without uttering another word or eating another mouthful he stormed out, and the pleas of the Duke and Duchess were powerless to stop him, not that the Duke said very much, hindered as he was by the laughter that the priest's untimely anger had stirred in him. Once he'd done laughing, he said to Don Quixote:

'You have answered so absolutely splendidly for yourself, Sir Knight of the Lions, that there is no need for you to seek further satisfaction for what might seem to be an offence but is in reality no such thing, because just as women cannot give offence, nor can churchmen, as I am sure you know better than I do.'

'That is indeed so,' Don Quixote replied, 'and the reason for this is that the person who cannot be offended cannot give offence. Women, children and churchmen cannot defend themselves if they are attacked, and so they cannot be affronted. Because between an offence and an affront there is this difference, as I am sure Your Grace knows better than I do: the affront comes from someone who can commit it, who does commit it and who maintains it; but the offence can come from any quarter, without constituting an affront. To take an example: a man is standing in the street, off his guard; ten armed men appear and give him a cudgelling, and he draws his sword and does what he is bound to do; but he is overwhelmed by sheer numbers and prevented from attaining his goal, which is to avenge himself; this man is offended but not affronted.

'Another example will confirm my point: a man stands with his back turned; another man comes up behind him and gives him a cudgelling and runs away; the other man runs after him but cannot catch up with him; the cudgelled man has been offended but not affronted, because an affront must be maintained. The man who dealt the blows did so in an underhand way, but if he had then drawn his sword, stood his ground and faced up to his enemy, the cudgelled man would have been both offended and affronted: offended, because he received a treacherous cudgelling; affronted, because the man who cudgelled him maintained what he had done, stood his ground and did not take to flight. And so, according to the laws of that accursed business called the duel, I might have been offended a moment ago, but not affronted, because children are not affected by matters of honour and nor are women, nor can they flee, nor have they any need to stand their ground, and the same applies to men who are consecrated to the service of religion, because these three categories of people lack arms offensive and defensive; and so, although nature compels them to defend themselves, it gives them no urge to attack. And although I have just said that I might have been offended, I now say that this is not so, not at all, because he who cannot be affronted cannot affront anybody else; for which reasons I should not be, and indeed am not, affected by what that person said to me; I only wish he had stayed a little longer so that I could have made him understand how wrong he is to think and to say that knights errant have never existed; for if Amadis or any of his infinite progeny had heard him say such a thing, I am sure he would have had a hard time of it.'

'I bet he would,' said Sancho. 'They'd have taken their swords to him and split him open from top to toe like a pomegranate or a nice ripe melon. Oh yes, they were just the sort to put up with being mucked about with like that, they were! By all that's holy, if Reynald of Montalban had heard what that little runt just said he'd have given him one on the chops that would have kept him quiet for the next three years. Oh yes, he should have taken them on all right, and then he'd have seen how lightly he got off!'

The Duchess was ready to die with laughter as she listened to Sancho, whom she considered to be even funnier and madder than his master, and there were many people at that time who shared her opinion. In the end Don Quixote calmed down, the meal was finished and, once the tablecloths had been removed, four maidens appeared, one with a silver bowl, another with a jug also of silver, another with two luxurious, pure white towels over her shoulder and a fourth with her arms bare to the elbow, and in her white hands (yes, quite definitely white hands) a ball of Naples soap. The maiden with the bowl came forward, and with jaunty gracefulness she slipped it under Don Quixote's chin; not speaking a word, astonished at this ceremony, assuming that in these parts it must be the custom to wash beards after a meal instead of hands, he thrust out his chin as far as it would go, and at that same moment the jug began to rain forth its contents, and the maiden with the soap rubbed it on to his beard as fast as her hands would go, building up piles of snowflakes – for the lather was no less white than this – not only on the beard but all over the obedient knight's face and eyes as well, so that he was forced to shut them. The Duke and Duchess, who hadn't been warned about any of all this, were waiting to see how these extraordinary ablutions were going to end. Once the barber had raised a good few inches of lather, she pretended that she had run out of water and told the maiden with the jug to go for more – Don Quixote wouldn't mind waiting. She went, and Don Quixote was left sitting there, the strangest and most ridiculous figure imaginable. All those present, and there were many of them, were gazing at him; and seeing him with his half a yard of neck, considerably browner than average, his eyes tight shut and his beard smothered in soapsuds, it was a miracle and a supreme act of discretion that they were able to suppress their laughter; the maidens who were responsible for the joke kept their eyes lowered, not daring to look at their master and mistress, who, with both anger and laughter playing inside them, couldn't decide what to do: whether to punish the girls for their audacity or to reward them for the pleasure provided by seeing Don Quixote in that plight.

The maiden with the jug returned at last, and they finished washing Don Quixote, and then the maiden with the towels wiped him dry with great deliberation, and the four of them together made a deep curtsey but, just as they were about to leave, the Duke, to prevent Don Quixote from realizing that it had all been a joke, called to the maiden with the bowl:

'You must all come over here and wash me, and be careful not to run out of water.'

She was a quick-witted and diligent lass, and she hurried over and clapped the bowl to the Duke's chin, just as she'd done to Don Quixote, and they hastily gave him a good wash and lathering and, after leaving him clean and dry, curtseyed and left. It was later known that the Duke had sworn that if they didn't wash him as they had Don Quixote he would punish them for their audacity, a fate they'd cleverly avoided by lathering him.

Sancho had been peering at the ceremony of the ablutions, and he said to himself:

'Great God! What if it's the custom in these parts to wash squires' beards as well as knights'? Upon my soul, God knows mine could do with a wash, and it'd be even better if they shaved it off for me.'

'What's that you're muttering to yourself, Sancho?' the Duchess enquired.

'I was just saying, lady,' he replied, 'that I've always heard that at other noblemen's courts once the tablecloths are taken away they bring water to wash your fingers, but not lye to scour your beard, but then they who live longest see most, though it's also said that long life brings long misery – yet having a good wash like that must be more of a pleasure than a hassle.'

'Don't you worry, dear Sancho,' said the Duchess, 'I'll get my girls to wash you, and even to boil you in bleach, too, if necessary.'

'The beard'll be enough,' said Sancho, 'for the time being at least. As for the future, God's already made up his mind about that.'

'Butler,' said the Duchess, 'see what the good Sancho desires, and carry out his wishes in every particular.'

The butler replied that Señor Sancho would want for nothing, and then went away to eat, taking Sancho with him and leaving Don Quixote at table with the Duke and the Duchess, discussing many different matters, all connected with the exercise of arms and of knight-errantry. The Duchess begged Don Quixote, since he seemed to have such a splendid memory, to delineate and depict the beauty and the features of his lady Dulcinea del Toboso, because, to judge from what fame proclaimed about her loveliness, she must be quite the loveliest creature in all the world, and even in all La Mancha. Don Quixote sighed when he heard the Duchess's request, and said:

'If I could pluck out my heart and lay it before Your Grace's eyes, here, upon this table on a plate, I should relieve my tongue of the toils of describing what can hardly be conceived, because Your Grace would see her perfectly portrayed in it; but to what purpose should I set out to delineate and depict, detail by detail and feature by feature, the beauty of the peerless Dulcinea, when this is a burden worthy of better shoulders than mine, an undertaking to be entrusted to the brushes of Parrhasius, Timanthus and Apelles and to the chisels of Lysippus,[2] to paint her on wood and sculpt her in marble and bronze, and to Ciceronian and Demosthenic rhetoric to praise her?'

'What does Demosthenic mean, Don Quixote sir?' the Duchess asked. 'It's a word I've never heard in all the days of my life.'

'Demosthenic rhetoric,' Don Quixote replied, 'means the rhetoric of Demosthenes, just as Ciceronian rhetoric is the rhetoric of Cicero, and they were the two greatest rhetoricians in the world.'

'Quite so,' said the Duke, 'and it wasn't very bright of you to ask such a question. But in spite of what Don Quixote has just said, he'd give us great pleasure if he did portray her for us; I'm sure that even if he only does a rough sketch, it will be such as to excite envy in the most beautiful of women.'

'I would do so, of course,' Don Quixote replied, 'had her image not been erased from my mind by the misfortune that fell upon her not long ago, so terrible that I am more disposed to mourn for her than to describe her; because I should have Your Graces know that when I went some days ago to kiss her hands and receive her blessing, approval and consent for this third sally, I found a woman quite different from the one I was seeking: I found her enchanted and turned from a princess into a peasant, from a beauty into a scarecrow, from an angel into a devil, from a fragrance into a stench, from a model of eloquence into a rustic, from a sedate young lady into a jack-in-the-box, from light into darkness and, in short, from Dulcinea del Toboso into some bumpkin from Sayago.'

'God save us!' the Duke interrupted with a shout. 'Who is it that has done the world such evil? Who has deprived it of the beauty that cheered it, the wit that amused it, the virtue that honoured it?'

'Who do you think?' replied Don Quixote. 'Who could it be except one of the many malicious, envious enchanters that persecute me? An accursed breed, born into the world to obscure and obliterate the exploits of the good, and to light up and exalt the doings of the wicked! I have been persecuted by enchanters, I am persecuted by enchanters and I shall be persecuted by enchanters until they have hurled me and my noble deeds of chivalry into the deep abyss of oblivion; and they wound me where they know it hurts me most, because to deprive a knight errant of his lady is to deprive him of the eyes with which he sees, the sun by which he is lighted and the food by which he is sustained. I have said it many times before, and now I shall say it yet again: the knight errant without a lady is like a tree without leaves, a building without foundations and a shadow without the body that throws it.'

'Well, that's that, then,' said the Duchess. 'But still, if we're to believe the history of Don Quixote that came out not long ago to the general approbation of the public, we understand from it, if my memory serves me correctly, that you've never seen the lady Dulcinea, and that no such person exists, but that she's a creature of fantasy whom you conceived and to whom you gave birth in your mind, and provided with all the charms and perfections that you chose.'

'There is a great deal to be said on that count,' Don Quixote replied. 'God knows well enough whether Dulcinea exists or not, and whether she is a creature of fantasy or not; and these are not the kinds of matters into which a complete investigation can or should be carried out. I neither conceived nor gave birth to my lady, although I do see her as being exactly as a lady ought to be if she is to possess all the qualities needed to make her famous throughout the world, that is to say: beautiful without blemish, dignified without pride, amorous yet modest, gracious from courtesy, courteous from good breeding and, in short, noble because of her pedigree, since loveliness shines and displays itself with a higher degree of perfection when set off by good blood than in beauties of humble birth.'

'Quite so,' said the Duke, 'but you're going to have to allow me, Don Quixote sir, to say what the history of your exploits that I've read forces me to say, because from it we can infer – even if it is conceded that Dulcinea does exist, in El Toboso or out of it, and even if she is as amazingly beautiful as you say – that as regards blueness of blood she isn't the equal of the Orianas, or the Alastrajareas,³ or the Madásimas, or others of this ilk, of whom those histories that you know so well are full.'

'To that I can reply,' replied Don Quixote, 'that Dulcinea is the daughter of her works, and that virtues ennoble the blood, and that a virtuous person of humble extraction is worthier of regard and esteem than a depraved aristocrat. And what is more, Dulcinea has qualities that can raise her to be a queen, complete with her crown and her sceptre; for the merits of a beautiful and virtuous woman extend as far as working even greater miracles than that, and virtually, even if not formally, she has still greater good fortune stored up within her.'

'All I can say, Don Quixote sir,' said the Duchess, 'is that in everything you say you do pick your steps, and keep, as the saying goes, your weather eye open, and that from now on I shall believe and make everyone in my household, even including the Duke my husband if necessary, believe that Dulcinea del Toboso does exist, and that she is alive today, and is beautiful, and high-born, and worthy to have a knight like Don Quixote to serve her, which is the highest praise that I can possibly offer her. But I can't help worrying a little on one count, and bearing a certain grudge against Sancho Panza: and my worry is this, that the aforesaid history declares that when the said Sancho Panza took the said lady Dulcinea a missive on your behalf he found her sieving a sack of wheat, and what's more it says that it was buckwheat, something that forces me to have my doubts about the nobility of her pedigree.'

To which Don Quixote replied:

'My dear lady: Your Grace must know that everything or nearly everything that befalls me goes beyond the ordinary bounds of what happens to other knights errant, whether because it is directed by the inscrutable will of the fates or because it is ordered by the malice of some envious enchanter. And since it is an established fact that all, or most, famous knights errant have some special gift — one that of being immune from enchantment, another that of being made of such impenetrable flesh that he cannot be wounded, like the famous Roland, one of the Twelve Peers of France, of whom it is said that he could only be sore wounded in the sole of his left foot, and that this had to be done with the point of a thick pin, and not with any other weapon; and so, when Bernardo del Carpio slew him at Roncesvalles, seeing that he could not wound him with steel, he lifted him up from the ground between his arms and squeezed him to death, remembering how Hercules had killed Antaeus, that fierce giant who was said to be a son of the Earth . . . I infer from what I have just said that perhaps I might have some gift of this sort, not that of being invulnerable, because experience has often shown me that I am made of soft and not at all impenetrable flesh, nor that of being immune from enchantment, because I have found myself shut up in a cage, where the whole world would not have had the power to put me, except by force of enchantment; but, since I freed myself from that spell, it is my belief that there is no other that can harm me; and so, now that these enchanters have realized that they cannot practise their wicked arts on my person, they take their revenge on what I most love, and they try to take away my life by spoiling that of Dulcinea, for whom I live; and so I believe that when my squire took her my message, they turned her into a peasant girl engaged in such a lowly chore as sieving wheat; yet I have already said that the wheat was not buckwheat or indeed any other kind of wheat, but grains of pearl of orient; and as proof of this fact, let me tell Your Graces how, as I was passing through El Toboso not long ago, I simply could not find Dulcinea's palace, and on the following day, although my squire Sancho saw her in her true form, which is the most beautiful form that there is in the world, she seemed to me like an uncouth, ugly village yokel, and not at all well-spoken, whereas Dulcinea is urbanity itself. And since I am not enchanted, and all sound reasoning proves that I cannot be enchanted, she it is who has been enchanted, smitten and altered, changed and transformed, and it is in her person that my enemies have avenged themselves on me, and for her I shall live in perpetual tears until I see her restored to her pristine state.

'I have said all this to prevent anyone from heeding what Sancho said about Dulcinea's sifting or sieving; because since they altered her for me, it is no wonder if they transformed her for him. Dulcinea is noble and well-born; of the aristocratic families in El Toboso, which are many, ancient and of the highest quality,[4] I am certain that no small part has entered into the peerless Dulcinea's pedigree, and, thanks to her, that town will be famous and renowned in the centuries to come, as Troy was because of Helen, and Spain because of La Cava, although on better grounds and with a more estimable fame.

'I should also like you to know that Sancho Panza is one of the most amusing squires that ever served knight errant; on occasions he speaks such shrewd nonsense that it is enjoyable to wonder whether he is nonsensical or shrewd; he has wicked ways that condemn him as a villain, and he makes blunders that confirm he is a fool; he doubts everything and he believes everything; just when I think that his stupidity is about to bring him crashing to the ground, he comes out with sound good sense that raises him to the skies. In short, I would not exchange him for any other squire, not even with a whole city into the bargain; and so I have my doubts whether it will be a good idea to send him to that governorship with which Your Grace has favoured him, although I do see in him a certain aptitude for governing, because with some slight adjustments to his thinking he could manage to govern anything at all, by sheer dogged perseverance. Furthermore, we know from repeated experience that neither great ability nor great learning is needed to be a governor, because there are dozens of them who can hardly read, yet they govern like angels; the main point is that they should mean well and desire always to do what is right, for they will never lack people to help them and guide them as to what they should do, like those governors who are knights and not men of letters and who reach their decisions with the help of advisors. As for my own advice, it would be this: all bribes to refuse, but insist on your dues, and sundry other particulars that are buried deep inside me at the moment but will emerge in due course, for the benefit of Sancho and to the advantage of the island that he is to govern.'

The Duke, the Duchess and Don Quixote had reached this point in their conversation when they heard a great shouting and hullabaloo, and

Sancho burst into the room, scared out of his wits and with an ashes-cloth for a bib, and behind him came a throng of under-chefs or, to be more exact, scullions and others of the lowest of the low, and one of them was carrying a trough of what from its colour and filthiness was evidently dishwater; he was chasing after Sancho, and doing his best to thrust the trough under his beard, which another scullion was trying to wash.

'What is the meaning of this, you people?' the Duchess demanded. 'What's the meaning of this? What are you trying to do to this good man? Are you forgetting that he is a governor elect?'

To which the scullion-barber replied:

'This gent won't let himself be washed, as is the custom, and as his master and my lord the Duke have been.'

'Yes, I will,' Sancho retorted in a fury, 'but I'd like cleaner towels, clearer lye and less filthy hands, because there isn't so much difference between me and my master for him to be washed in angel-water and me in devils' piss. The customs of different lands and princes' palaces are all very well so long as they don't give umbrage, but the washing-custom they have here is worse than lashing yourself as a penitent. My beard's clean, and I don't need any cooling-down of that sort, and if anyone comes near me to wash me or touch a single hair of my head, of my beard I mean, with all due respect I'll give him a wallop that'll leave my fist stuck fast in his brain-box – these sermonies and soapings are more like bad jokes than ways of welcoming guests.'

The Duchess was ready to die of laughter as she contemplated Sancho's wrath and listened to his speech; but Don Quixote didn't derive much pleasure from seeing him so foully festooned in his streaky towel, and surrounded by so much kitchen riff-raff; and, with a deep bow to the Duke and Duchess, as if to request their permission to speak, he addressed the rabble in a composed voice:

'Hey there, my fine gentlemen! Be so kind as to leave my servant alone, and go back the way you came, or another way if you prefer; my squire is as clean as the next man, and those troughs are for him of no more use than fiddly little wine flasks. Take my advice and leave him be, because neither he nor I have a very good sense of humour.'

Sancho took over where his master had left off, and added:

'Oh yes, why don't you just try coming to have a bit of fun with this here country bumpkin, and I'll stand where I am and put up with it all, I will, as sure as it's now night! You go and fetch a comb or whatever you like and run it through this beard of mine, and if you find anything in it that gives offence you can give me a convict's crop.'

The Duchess, still laughing, interrupted:

'Everything Sancho Panza has just said is absolutely spot on, as will be everything he ever does say: he is clean, and, as he points out, he doesn't stand in any need of a wash, and, if our customs don't agree with him, on his own head be it; what's more, you ministers of cleanliness have been most remiss and negligent – I might even say presumptuous – in bringing to such a personage, and to such a beard, your wooden troughs and your dishcloths instead of bowls and jugs of pure gold and towels of the finest foreign make. But, after all, you are evil and ill-born, and, being the scurvy knaves you are, you can't help showing the grudge you bear against the squires of knights errant.'

The ministering scullions, and even the butler, who'd come with them, thought the Duchess was being serious, and so they slipped the ashes-cloth from Sancho's neck and slunk away in some confusion and even shame; and, when Sancho found himself liberated from what seemed to him a fearful peril, he ran and fell on his knees before the Duchess, and said:

'From great ladies we can hope for great favours, and I can only repay this favour that you have bestowed upon me by my wish to be made a knight errant so that I can devote all the days of my life to serving such a fine lady. A farmer I am, Sancho Panza by name, married with children and serving as squire – and if with any of all this I can be of service to Your Grace, it'll take you longer to command than me to obey.'

'It's easy to see, Sancho,' the Duchess replied, 'that you've learned to be courteous in the school of courtesy itself; what I mean to say is that it's obvious you've sucked at the breasts of Don Quixote, who must be the cream of courtesy and the flower of ceremony, or sermony as you put it. The best of luck to such a master and to such a servant, for the one is the lodestar of knight-errantry, and the other is the luminary of squirely fidelity. Arise, friend Sancho: I shall repay your courtesy by prevailing upon my lord the Duke to fulfil his promise of a governorship at the earliest opportunity.'

With this the conversation came to an end, Don Quixote retired to take his siesta, and the Duchess begged Sancho, if he wasn't feeling too excessively sleepy, to come and spend the afternoon with her and her maidens in a lovely cool room. Sancho replied that although he did usually sleep four or five hours on a summer afternoon he would, for her goodness's sake, try with all his might not to sleep for a single hour that particular afternoon, and would obey her command; and then he disappeared. The Duke gave fresh orders about how Don Quixote was to be treated as a knight errant without the slightest deviation from the way in which the knights of old are said to have been treated.

CHAPTER XXXIII

*About the delectable conversation that the Duchess
and her maids had with Sancho Panza, worthy to be
read and heeded*

The history records, then, that Sancho didn't sleep that afternoon but, to keep his promise, went to see the Duchess as soon as he'd done eating; and she, who adored listening to him, made him sit down on a stool beside her, although Sancho was so well-bred that he was reluctant to do so; but the Duchess told him to sit as a governor and speak as a squire, although under both headings he deserved to occupy the famous bench of the Cid Ruy Díaz, the Campeador.[1] Sancho shrugged and obeyed and sat down, and all the Duchess's duennas and maids gathered round him in profound silence, waiting to hear what he would say; but the Duchess was the first to speak:

'Now that we're alone, and no one can overhear us, I should like the Governor to settle certain doubts I have arising from the history of the great Don Quixote that has recently been published, one of the said doubts being that since the worthy Sancho never saw Dulcinea, by which I mean the lady Dulcinea del Toboso, and never took Don Quixote's letter to her, because it was left behind in the notebook in the Sierra Morena, how did he dare invent her answer, and all those details about finding her sieving wheat, the whole story being a hoax and a falsehood, so damaging to the peerless Dulcinea's good name, and quite at odds with the character and loyalty of a faithful squire?'

At these words, and without offering one in reply, Sancho got up from his chair and prowled round the room, his body bent and one finger over his lips, lifting up the hangings; and then he returned to his stool and said:

'Now I've seen that nobody's listening on the sly apart from present company, lady, I'll reply without fear or trembling to what I've been asked and whatever anyone else wants to ask me – and what I'll say first is that I reckon my master Don Quixote is stark raving mad, though sometimes he does say things that to my mind and everyone else's listening to him are so clever and to the point that the devil himself couldn't have said them better, but in spite of all that I'm sure he's an idiot, really I am. And because I've got this idea in my head I've also got the nerve to make him believe all sorts of stuff without any rhyme or reason to it, like all that about the reply to his letter, and what happened a week or so ago and isn't in the history yet, in other words the enchanting of my lady Dulcinea – I made him think she's enchanted, though that's a right old cock-and-bull story, that is.'

The Duchess implored him to tell her about that enchantment or hoax, and Sancho narrated it just as it had happened, which was great fun for all the listeners; and then the Duchess continued:

'Concerning all these things that the worthy Sancho has been telling me there's a certain misgiving tossing and turning in my soul, and a whisper reaching my ears and saying:

'"Since Don Quixote de la Mancha is a poor wretch, a fool, and a madman, and his squire Sancho knows it and still serves and follows him and has faith in his vain promises, it's abundantly clear that the squire must be even more of a fool and a madman than the master; and if this is so, as it is, it only spells trouble for you, my dear Duchess, to give this fellow Sancho Panza an island to govern, because how can somebody who can't govern himself govern others?"'

'By God, lady,' said Sancho, 'that there Miss Giving's dead right, and you'd better tell her to speak up as clearly as she likes because I can see she's telling the truth, and if I had any sense I'd have left my master long ago. But then that's just my rotten luck for you, I can't help it, I must follow him – we're from the same village, I've eaten his bread, I'm very fond of him, he's grateful to me, he gave me his donkeys and above all I'm a faithful fellow, so nothing's ever going to part us except the pick and the shovel. And if Your High and Mightiness doesn't want me to be given the island I've been promised, God made me without it, and perhaps not getting it would be for the good of my conscience – I might be a fool, but I do understand the proverb that says "The ant had wings to her hurt", and it might even be that squire Sancho will get to heaven sooner than governor Sancho would. There's as good bread baked here as in France, and in the dark all cats are grey, and unhappy is he who hasn't breakfasted by three, and no man's maw is a span bigger than any other man's, and you can always fill it, as they say, with hay and with straw, and the fowls of the air have their heavenly Father to feed them,[2] and four yards of Cuenca shoddy will keep you warmer than four of Segovia worsted, and when we quit this world and start swallowing clay the prince has got as narrow a path to tread as the labourer, and the Pope's body doesn't take up any more room in the churchyard than the sexton's, even if one is taller than the other, because when we go to our graves we all have to shrink and fit, or else we're made to shrink and fit whether we like it or not – and then goodnight to you all! And I'll say it again – if Your Grace doesn't give me the island because I'm stupid, I'll be wise enough not to let that bother me, because I've heard that the devil lurks behind the Cross, and all that glitters isn't gold, and from among oxen, ploughs and yoke-gear they took the farmer Wamba to be King of Spain, and from among brocades, entertainments and riches they took King Rodrigo to be eaten by snakes, if the words of the old ballads don't lie.'

'Of course they don't lie!' exclaimed the duenna Doña Rodríguez, who was among the audience. 'There's that ballad that says they stuck King Rodrigo, alive and kicking, into a tomb full of toads, and snakes, and lizards, and two days later the King inside the tomb said in a faint, anguished voice:

> They're gnawing me, they're gnawing me,
> In the parts that sinned the most.

And so this gentleman is quite right to say that he'd rather be a farmer than a king, if he's going to be devoured by vermin.'

The Duchess couldn't contain her laughter as she listened to the nonsense spoken by her duenna, or her astonishment as she listened to Sancho's arguments and proverbs, and she said to him:

'My dear Sancho knows very well that once a knight has made a promise he strives to keep it, even if it costs him his life. Now my lord and husband the Duke mightn't be all that errant but that doesn't stop him from being a knight, so he'll keep his word about that island he's promised you, in the face of all the envy and malice in the world. Let Sancho be of good cheer – when he's least expecting it he's going to find himself sitting on the throne of state of his island, and he'll take charge of his government, and may he soon move on to even greater things. What I'd urge on him is that he must be careful how he governs his vassals, bearing in mind that they're all loyal and well-born people.'

'All that about being a good governor,' Sancho replied, 'is something I don't need any urging about, because I'm kind by nature and feel sorry for the poor, and from him who kneads and bakes don't try to steal the cakes, and by all that's holy nobody's going to play against me with loaded dice, I'm an old dog and I'm not easily caught, and I can stir myself when I need to, and nobody's going to pull the wool over my eyes, because I know well enough where the shoe pinches – and I'm only saying all this because I'll be hand in glove with all the good folks, corroborating like, but the baddies won't even get a foot in the door. And to my mind in this governing game it's just a question of getting going, and it could well be that after a fortnight at the job I'll give my right arm to carry on, and know more about it than about farming, that I was brought up on.'

'You're quite right, Sancho,' said the Duchess, 'because no man is born learned, and bishops are made out of men, not out of stones. But to return to the discussion we were having earlier about the enchantment of the lady Dulcinea, I'm absolutely convinced that this notion of Sancho's that he hoaxed his master, and made him believe that a peasant girl was Dulcinea and that if he didn't recognize her it was because she was enchanted, was itself the work of one of those enchanters who persecute Don Quixote; because I know for certain, from a totally reliable source, that the wench who leapt on to the donkey was and is Dulcinea del Toboso, and that the worthy Sancho, who thinks he's the deceiver, is the deceived; there's no more reason to doubt the truth of this than of anything else that we've never seen; because I would have Señor Sancho Panza know that we, too, have our enchanters here, who look kindly upon us, and tell us what's happening in the world, purely and simply, without any deceit or trickery; and Sancho can believe me when I tell him that the leaping peasant girl was and is Dulcinea del Toboso, who's every bit as enchanted as the mother who bore her; and just when we're least expecting it we're going to see her in her own true form, and then Sancho will be disabused of the illusion under which he presently labours.'

'You could be right,' said Sancho Panza, 'and now I can believe my master's story about what he saw in the Cave of Montesinos, where he says he saw the lady Dulcinea del Toboso in the selfsame clothes I said I saw her in when I enchanted her just for the fun of it – and it all must be the opposite of what I thought it was, just as you say, lady, because nobody has any business to imagine that my poor wits could have dreamed up such a clever trick in the twinkling of an eye, and what's more I don't believe my master's mad enough to be led by my feeble arguings to believe something as far beyond the pale as that. But it wouldn't be right, lady, for Your Goodness to think that I'm a bad man – a dunderhead like me can't be expected to see into the wicked thoughts of those terrible enchanters, and I only made it all up to avoid being hauled over the coals by my master Don Quixote, and not with any idea of offending him – and if it's turned out topsy-turvy there's a God in heaven who judges our hearts.'

'Quite right, too,' said the Duchess, 'but now do tell me, Sancho, what's all this about the Cave of Montesinos – I'd simply love to know.'

And Sancho Panza gave her a painstaking account of that adventure, as already related. Having heard it, the Duchess said:

'From this episode we can infer that since the great Don Quixote says he saw down there the very same peasant girl that Sancho saw on the outskirts of El Toboso, she most certainly is Dulcinea, and that the enchanters are being very clever indeed, and all too officious.'

'That's just what I say, too,' said Sancho Panza, 'and if my lady Dulcinea del Toboso's enchanted, that's her bad luck, and it isn't up to me to take on my master's enemies, plentiful and spiteful as they seem to be. The plain truth is that the girl I saw was a peasant, I thought she was a peasant and I set her down as a peasant, and if she was Dulcinea that's nothing to do with me and it isn't my fault, and people had better heed what I'm saying or else. Oh yes, I'll let them all go on at my expense every five minutes I will, with their backbiting and their tittle-tattle, "Sancho said this, Sancho did that, Sancho went back and Sancho returned," as if Sancho was some nobody, and not the same Sancho Panza that's going all over the world in books, so Sansón Carrasco told me, and he's been bachelored at Salamanca he has, and people like that can't lie except when they feel like it or it's very much in their interest. So there's no need for anyone to come picking quarrels with me, and since I've got a good name and according to what I've heard my master say a good name is better than great riches,[3] they can just shove me on to that island and they'll see wonders, because he who has been a good squire will be a good governor.'

'All the worthy Sancho's observations,' said the Duchess, 'are Catonian maxims, or at any rate drawn from the very bowels of Michael Verino, *florentibus occidit annis.*[4] When all's said and done, and to speak as Sancho speaks – under a foul cloak there's often a fine drinker.'

'To tell you the honest truth, lady,' Sancho replied, 'I've never drunk just for the sake of drinking. Out of thirst, maybe – I'm no hypocrite, I do drink when I feel like it, and when I don't feel like it as well, and when I'm offered a drink too, so as not to seem choosy or rude, because if a friend drinks your health who could be so stony-hearted as not to drink his back? But even though I wear trousers I don't mess in them, and what's more knight errants' squires drink water most of the time, because they're always traipsing around woods, forests and meadows, mountains and crags, and they can't find a pittance of wine, not even if they give their eyes for it.'

'That I can well believe,' the Duchess replied. 'And now Sancho had better go and have a rest, and we'll speak at greater length by and by, and make arrangements for him soon to be shoved, as he puts it, on to his island.'

Sancho kissed the Duchess's hands again, and begged her to be so kind as to make sure that his dun was well looked after, being as it was the light of his life.

'What dun is this?' asked the Duchess.

'My ass,' Sancho replied, 'and so as not to call it by a nasty name like that I call it my dun, and when I came into the castle I asked this duenna here to look after it, and she got as het up as if I'd said she was ugly or old, when it ought to be more right and proper for duennas to feed asses than stand around decorating castle halls. God Almighty, how a certain hidalgo in my village hated females like that!'

'No, he must have been some peasant,' said the duenna Doña Rodríguez, 'because if he had been a well-born hidalgo he would have praised them to the skies.'

'Come now,' said the Duchess, 'no more of this: I want Doña Rodríguez to keep quiet, and Señor Panza to calm down, and the dun's comfort can be entrusted to me – since it's so terribly precious to Sancho I'll place it in my esteem above the very apple of my eye.'

'Just place it in the stable, that'll do,' Sancho replied, 'neither me nor my dun are fit to be above the apple of Your Grace's eye for a single moment, and I'd as soon give myself a good knifing as stand for that, because although my master says that in the game of courtesy it's better to bust than fall short, when being courteous to asses and donkeys you've got to tread very warily indeed.'

'Let Sancho take his dun with him to his government,' said the Duchess, 'and there he'll be able to make it just as comfortable as he pleases, and even pension it off.'

'Don't you imagine, Duchess, that you've said anything special there,' said Sancho. 'I've seen a few asses go into government before now, so if I took mine with me that wouldn't be anything new.'

Sancho's words plunged the Duchess into further giggles of delight, and then she sent him away to sleep and went to tell the Duke all about their conversation; and these two plotted a hoax to play on Don Quixote, so contrived as to achieve renown and perfectly match the chivalresque style; and in this same style they played many other hoaxes on him, so appropriate and clever that they're the very best adventures in this great history.

CHAPTER XXXIV

Which tells of the information that was received
about how the peerless Dulcinea del Toboso was to be
disenchanted, one of the most famous adventures
in this book

The Duke and Duchess were highly amused by their conversations with Don Quixote and Sancho Panza, which confirmed their intention to play hoaxes that would seem just like adventures; and Don Quixote's description of his adventure in the Cave of Montesinos gave them an idea for one that was bound to become famous. Yet what most astonished the Duchess was that Sancho was so very simple-minded as to have been made to believe as absolute truth that Dulcinea del Toboso had been enchanted, when he himself was the enchanter and the hoaxer. And so, six days later, after giving their servants instructions about what they were to do, the Duke and Duchess took Don Quixote hunting, with an array of beaters and hunters of which any crowned monarch would have been proud. They gave Don Quixote a hunting outfit and Sancho another, of the finest green worsted; but Don Quixote refused his, saying that he soon had to return to the harsh exercise of arms, and that he could not encumber himself with either wardrobes or stores. Sancho took what he was given, intending to sell it at the earliest opportunity.

So the appointed day came, Don Quixote donned his armour and Sancho put on his hunting outfit and, riding his dun, which he refused to leave behind despite being offered a horse, he joined the gang of beaters. The Duchess emerged, sumptuously dressed, and Don Quixote, courteous and gallant as always, took the reins of her palfrey, although the Duke did not want him to; and they eventually reached a wood between two great hills where, once all the hides and ambushes beside the tracks had been occupied and the hunters had been sent to their stations, the hunt began amidst such a racket and so much shouting and hallooing that people couldn't hear each other talk, what with the barking of the dogs and the blaring of the horns. The Duchess dismounted and, carrying her sharp spear, stationed herself where she knew wild boar often passed. The Duke and Don Quixote also dismounted, and stood on either side of her; Sancho placed himself behind all the others, without getting off his dun, which he didn't dare to leave for fear that it might come to some harm.

And scarcely had they taken their stand in a line with several of their servants when they saw a vast boar rushing towards them, hard pressed by the hounds and chased by the huntsmen, gnashing its teeth and its tusks and spraying foam from its mouth; and as soon as Don Quixote saw it he took up his shield, drew his sword and stepped forward to meet it. The Duke did likewise, clutching his spear; but the Duchess would have beaten them all to it if the Duke hadn't stopped her. Sancho alone, on seeing the great beast, abandoned his mount and ran away as fast as his legs would carry him, and tried to climb a tall evergreen oak – without success, because when he was halfway up it, clinging on to a branch and struggling to reach the top, he had the great misfortune to break the branch and, as he came crashing down, to be hooked on a snag in the tree and left dangling there, unable to reach the ground. And finding himself in this plight, with his green coat being ripped open, and imagining that if the fierce beast came that way it would reach him, he started to scream so loud and to shout for help so insistently that all those who heard him but couldn't see him thought that he was in the jaws of some wild creature. The long-tusked boar was run through by the many spears levelled at it, and Don Quixote looked in the direction of the screams, which he'd recognized as Sancho's, and saw him hanging head down from the evergreen oak, with his dun beside him, because it wouldn't abandon him in his plight; and Cide Hamete Benengeli says that he seldom saw Sancho without seeing his dun, and seldom saw the dun without seeing Sancho, such was the friendship and loyalty that bound the two together. Don Quixote went over and unhooked Sancho, who, once free and standing on the ground, examined the rents in his hunting coat, and they grieved him to the depths of his soul, because he'd believed the coat was worth a fortune.

Meanwhile they slung the great boar across a mule, covered it with rosemary plants and myrtle branches and bore it off, the spoils of victory, to some great marquees that had been erected in the middle of the wood, where they found the tables laid and the meal ready, an enormous and sumptuous spread that was a clear reflection of the importance and magnificence of the man providing it. Sancho, showing the Duchess the wounds in his torn outfit, said:

'If it'd been hares or sparrows we'd been hunting, my coat would have been safe from getting into this mess. I just can't see what can be the fun in lying in wait for an animal that can do for you if it catches you with its tusk, and I remember hearing someone singing an old ballad that says:

> May you be eaten by the bears,
> Like far-famed Fávila.'[1]

'That was a Gothic king,' said Don Quixote, 'who went hunting and was eaten by a bear.'

'That's just what I'm saying,' Sancho replied. 'I'd prefer it if lords and kings didn't put themselves at risk like that just for the sake of some fun that to my mind shouldn't be fun at all, because all you do is kill an animal that hasn't committed any crimes.'

'No, you're mistaken there, Sancho,' the Duke replied, 'because the sport of hunting bears and boars is more suitable and indeed necessary for kings and lords than any other. Hunting is an image of war: it involves stratagems, ruses and traps to defeat the enemy in safety; while practising it, one suffers extreme cold and intolerable heat, one scorns idleness and sleep, one strengthens one's body and increases the agility of one's limbs, and, in short, it's a sport that can be practised without harming anybody while giving pleasure to many; and what's best of all about it is that it isn't a sport for every Tom, Dick and Harry, as many other kinds of hunting are, except hawking, which is also reserved for kings and great lords. So, my dear Sancho, you'd better change your mind and, when you're a governor, practise hunting and you'll soon see how you reap the benefit.'

'Not likely,' Sancho replied. 'A governor's place is in the home. A fine thing it'd be if people came to see him on business, tired out from their journey, and he was out in the countryside having himself a good time! A pretty pickle the government would be in if he went and did that! On my faith, sir, hunting and such pastimes are more for loafers than for governors. How I'm going to amuse myself is playing brag at Easter and Christmas, and skittles on Sundays and fiesta-days – that hunting lark doesn't suit my nature or sit easy on my conscience.'

'May it please God, Sancho, that you do as you say, though there's many a slip twixt the cup and the lip.'

'There can be as many slips as you like,' Sancho replied, 'but a good payer's a good pledger, and God's help is better than early rising, and the guts support the feet and not the feet the guts – what I mean to say is that if God gives me a hand, and I do what I ought to do and my intentions are good, I'm bound to govern like an angel. Oh yes, they can come and stick their fingers in my mouth they can, and they'll soon see whether I bite or not!'

'God and all his holy saints damn you, Sancho you wretch!' said Don Quixote. 'When will the day come, as I have asked many times before, when I can hear you develop a straightforward, coherent argument without proverbs? Your Graces had better leave this idiot to his own devices, or he will grind your very souls between not just two but two thousand proverbs, and God grant him – and me too, if I tolerate any more of them – as long a life as his proverbs are appropriate and timely.'

'Sancho Panza's proverbs,' said the Duchess, 'may be more numerous than those collected by the Greek commander,[2] but they are no less worthy of esteem for that, because of their pithiness. Speaking for myself, I can say that they give me greater pleasure than others that are more timely and appropriate.'

With this and other amusing talk they left the marquee and went back into the wood, and in the inspection of hides the rest of the day soon passed and night fell, not as clear or calm a night as the season, midsummer, would have led one to expect, because a certain chiaroscuro about it was of great assistance to the schemes of the Duke and Duchess; and so, as night descended, a little after dusk, it suddenly seemed as if the entire wood were on fire, and then countless bugles and other military instruments were heard sounding out, here, there and everywhere, as if several troops of cavalry were riding through the wood. The blaze of the fires and the sound of the martial instruments almost blinded the eyes and deafened the ears of the bystanders and indeed of everybody in the wood. Next, innumerable cries of *la Ilaha ill'Allah*[3] rang out, as of Moors going into battle; trumpets and clarions blared, drums boomed, fifes shrilled, all at the same time, and so fast and continuously that only a person with no sense at all could have failed to lose it in the pandemonium created by all those instruments. The Duke was amazed, the Duchess was astonished, Don Quixote was dumbfounded, Sancho Panza was trembling and, in short, even those who knew the secret were alarmed. Fear imposed its silence, and then a post-boy in devil's garb rode before them, playing not a bugle but a vast hollow horn that emitted a fearful, raucous noise.

'Hullo there, my fine messenger!' said the Duke. 'Who are you, whither are you bound and what soldiers are these riding through this wood?'

To which the messenger replied in bold and blood-curdling tones:

'I am the devil; I am looking for Don Quixote de la Mancha; the people who are riding through the wood are six troops of enchanters, bearing the peerless Dulcinea del Toboso upon a triumphal chariot. She is enchanted and she has come with the gallant Frenchman Montesinos to give instructions to Don Quixote about how the said lady is to be disenchanted.'

'If you were the devil, as you say and your appearance indicates, you would have recognized the knight Don Quixote de la Mancha by now, because he stands here before you.'

'I swear to God, and upon my conscience be it,' the devil replied, 'that I just wasn't paying attention – I've got so much on my mind I was forgetting all about the main matter in hand.'

'This here devil,' said Sancho, 'must be an honest citizen and a good Christian, because if he wasn't he wouldn't have said "I swear to God, and upon my conscience be it." Now I can believe that even in hell there must be some good folks.'

Then the devil, without dismounting, directed his gaze at Don Quixote and said:

'To you, O Knight of the Lions (and clutched between their claws may I see you), the hapless but valiant knight Montesinos has sent me, and has instructed me to tell you on his behalf that you are to await him where I found you, because with him he brings the lady called Dulcinea del Toboso, to instruct you on what must be done to disenchant her. And since that's all I've come about I shan't stay any longer; may devils like me watch over you, and good angels over these other people.'

And so saying he blew a blast on his enormous horn, turned away and rode off without awaiting a reply.

All this produced further amazement in everyone, particularly Sancho and Don Quixote: in Sancho, because he could see that, in defiance of the truth, they were still insisting that Dulcinea was enchanted; in Don Quixote, because it was now even more difficult to decide whether what had happened in the Cave of Montesinos was real or not. And while he was absorbed in these thoughts the Duke said:

'Do you intend to wait, Don Quixote sir?'

'Do you expect me not to?' Don Quixote replied. 'Here I shall indeed wait, strong and intrepid, even if all hell comes charging at me.'

'Well if I see another devil and hear another horn like that one, I'll no more wait here than I would in Flanders,'[4] said Sancho.

With this, the night darkened and lights and more lights began to flit about the wood, much as the gaseous exhalations of the earth flit about the sky and look to us like shooting stars. At the same time a dreadful din was heard, like that made by the solid wheels of ox-carts, from which relentless creaking and groaning it's said that wolves and bears flee, if there are any in the vicinity. To this great tempest of sound was added another that was greater still, because it truly seemed that in the four corners of the wood four separate battles were being fought at the same time: on one side the harsh racket of fearsome artillery rang out, on another countless muskets were being fired, not far away the shouts of the combatants could be heard and in the distance the Moorish war-cries were being repeated. In short, the bugles, the horns, the clarions, the trumpets, the drums, the artillery, the muskets and, above all, the fearsome creaking of the ox-carts made together such a chaotic and horrendous clangour that Don Quixote had to summon up all his courage to endure it; but Sancho's failed him, and left him fainting on the Duchess's lap, where she let him lie and hurriedly ordered cold water to be splashed on his face. This was done, and Sancho came to, just as one of the carts with the creaking wheels was approaching the hide in which they sat. It was pulled by four ponderous oxen, all swathed in black hangings; to each of their horns was tied a flaming wax torch, and on the cart was a high chair and on this a venerable old man was seated, with a beard that was whiter than snow, and so long that it reached below his waist; he was dressed in a long robe of black buckram – since the cart was festooned with lights, it was easy to see exactly what was on it. It was driven by two ugly demons also clad in buckram, with such hideous faces that

Sancho, having seen them once, shut his eyes so as not to see them again. The cart rolled up to the hide, and the venerable old man rose to his feet and cried:

'I am the sage Lirgandeo.'

And the cart rolled on, without another word. After it another similar cart appeared, with another enthroned old man who, ordering his cart to be halted, said in a voice no less solemn:

'I am the sage Alquife, the great friend of Urganda the Unknowable.'

And the cart rolled on. Then another cart approached in the same manner; yet the person sitting on the throne wasn't old like the other two, but was a large, powerful man, a nasty-looking type; and as he arrived he stood up as the others had and said in an even hoarser and more devilish voice than theirs:

'I am the enchanter Arcalaus, the mortal enemy of Amadis of Gaul and all his tribe.'

And he moved on. These three wagons halted a short distance away, and the grating noise of their wheels ceased, and then what was heard was no noise at all, but the sounds of gentle, harmonious music, which cheered Sancho, who took it as a good sign; and he said to the Duchess, from whose side he hadn't stirred an inch:

'Lady, where there's music there can't be mischief.'

'Nor where there are lights and it is bright,' the Duchess replied.

To which Sancho answered:

'Flames give out light, and it's bright where there are bonfires, as we can see from all these around us, and they could well burn us – but music is always a sign of happiness and fiestas.'

'That remains to be seen,' said Don Quixote, who had been listening.

And he was right, too, as the next chapter shows.

CHAPTER XXXV

In which the information given to Don Quixote about Dulcinea's disenchantment is continued, with other amazing events

They could see that to the accompaniment of this agreeable music one of those vehicles called triumphal chariots was on its way towards them, drawn by six brown mules covered, however, with white drill; and on each mule a penitent was seated, also dressed in white, with a flaming wax torch in his hand. This chariot was twice or even three times as big as the carts, and upon its sides were another twelve penitents all as white as snow and all bearing lighted torches, a sight both amazing and terrifying; and on a high throne a nymph was seated, wearing a thousand pieces of silver cloth, with countless spangles glittering all over them, which made her if not magnificently then at least showily dressed. Her head was covered with a diaphanous veil, but the threads in its warp couldn't prevent a lovely maiden's face from being glimpsed between them, and the many lights made it possible to perceive not only her beauty but her age as well, for she seemed no older than twenty nor younger than seventeen. Next to her was a figure wearing one of those long garments called a dressing-gown, with his head covered by a black veil; but at the moment when the chariot came before the Duke, the Duchess and Don Quixote, the music of the shawms ceased, and soon the harps and lutes being played in the chariot fell silent as well; and the figure in the robe came to his feet, threw open his robe, removed his veil and stood revealed as Death itself, fleshless and hideous: which disquieted Don Quixote, scared Sancho and elicited signs of fear from the Duke and Duchess. This living death stood there and, in a sleepy voice and with a tongue only half awake, began to speak:

> Merlin am I, of whom the histories
> State that I had the devil for my sire
> (A lie that passing years have authorized):
> The prince of magic and the treasure-house

And monarch of the Zoroastic science,
The enemy of ages and of times
That seek to cover up the splendid deeds
Of dauntless errant knights, for all of whom
I've always had a soft spot in my heart.
And though the nature of us sorcerers
And wizards and enchanters normally
Is rigorous, relentless and severe,
Yet mine is tender, kind and affable
And fond of doing good to one and all.

  In gloomy Hades' darkest caves, my soul,
To try to while away those endless hours,
Was drawing rhombuses and characters,
When came the mournful voice of that fair maid
The peerless Dulcinea del Toboso.
I learnt of her enchantment and her woes,
And how, from high-born lady, she was turned
Into a village wench. I felt so sad
I clothed my spirit in the hollow shell
Of these dry bones, so fearful and so dire,
And rummaged in a hundred thousand books
Of this, my diabolical, foul science;
And now I come to bring the remedy
For such a grief, for such catastrophe.

  O you, the glory of all those who wear
Tunics of steel and coats of diamond,
O light and lantern, path, lodestar and guide
Of those who cast away ignoble sleep
And, leaping from the lazy down, embrace
That which is more than flesh and blood can bear,
The exercise of heavy, bloody arms:
To you I say, O hero never praised
Enough, to you, Don Quixote sir, O man
Of courage and of wisdom intertwined,
You splendour of La Mancha, star of Spain:
In order to recover and restore

Your peerless mistress to her pristine state,
Your squire, your Sancho, has to lash himself
Three thousand times and then three hundred more
On both his buttocks, big and bold and bare
Unto the air exposed, in such a way
That they will smart and sting and vex him sore.
For this has been decided by all those
Who worked the spells that cost the maid so dear;
And this, my noble lords, is why I'm here.

'By all that's holy!' blurted Sancho. 'I'm not talking about three thousand strokes of the lash, I won't give myself so much as three of them – I'd as soon stab myself three times as that! The devil can take that way of disenchanting a person! I don't see what my bum has got to do with magic spells! By God, if Señor Merlin hasn't found a better way than that to disenchant the lady Dulcinea del Toboso, she'll have to go enchanted to her grave!'

'I am going to take you,' said Don Quixote, 'you garlic-stuffed peasant, and tie you to a tree, naked as the day you were born, and give you not just three thousand three hundred but six thousand six hundred lashes, and I'll lay them on so thick that you won't be able to get rid of them, not if you rub your backside three thousand three hundred times. And don't you answer me back, or I'll tear your very soul out of your body.'

When Merlin heard this he said:

'No, that will not do, because the worthy Sancho must take his lashing of his own free will, not by force, and at a time of his own choosing, for no deadline has been established; but he is allowed, if he wishes to abate his atonement by one half of the thrashing, to have it administered by another hand, although it must be a somewhat heavy one.'

'No hand's going to touch me,' Sancho retorted, 'not someone else's nor my own, not heavy nor light. Was it me that gave birth to the lady Dulcinea del Toboso by any chance, for my bum to have to pay for her sins? My master's the one who's accountable, every five minutes he's calling her his life and his soul and his support and his stay, so he can and should do everything that's needed to disenchant her – but as for me taking the lashes, I announce them and all their works.'[1]

Sancho had hardly finished speaking when the spangled nymph by Merlin's side rose to her feet, lifted her diaphanous veil from her face, revealing it to be an exceedingly beautiful one in everybody's opinion, and addressed Sancho Panza with virile assurance and in not very feminine tones:

'O wretched squire, soul of lead, heart of cork, bowels of flint and granite! If you were being commanded, you thieving cutthroat, to hurl yourself to the ground from some high tower; if you were being asked, you enemy of human kind, to eat a dozen toads, two dozen lizards and three dozen snakes; if you were being urged to kill your wife and children with some fearsome, keen-edged scimitar: it would not be remarkable if you were reluctant and squeamish. But to be concerned about three thousand three hundred lashes, something that no boy in any orphanage, however wretched he may be, fails to receive every month, astounds, amazes and astonishes all the tender-hearted people listening to you, as well as all those who will come to learn of it in the course of time. Rest, O miserable, callous animal, rest, I say, those eyes of a frightened little mule upon the pupils of my eyes that emulate the glittering stars, and you will see them weeping thread after thread and skein after skein, wearing furrows, tracks and pathways through the beautiful meadows of my cheeks. Relent, you sly and spiteful monster: my blooming youth (I am still in my teens, I am nineteen, not quite twenty) is being consumed and withered away beneath the coarse exterior of a rustic peasant girl – and if I don't look like one right now, this is a special favour conceded by Señor Merlin, here present, so that my loveliness can move you, for the tears of a grieving beauty turn crags into cotton, tigers into lambs. Come on, lash that fat carcass of yours, you untamed beast, and arouse that slothful spirit that only moves you to eat and eat again, and set free my smooth flesh, my gentle character and my lovely face; and if you will not relent or come to any reasonable terms for my sake, do it for that poor knight by your side: do it for your master, I say, whose very soul I can see stuck in his throat, not ten inches from his lips, for it is awaiting your answer, cruel or kind, either to depart through his mouth or to go back down inside him.'

When Don Quixote heard this he felt his throat and said, turning to the Duke:

'By God sir, Dulcinea has spoken the truth: my soul is indeed stuck in my throat, just here, like the nut on a crossbow.'

'And what do you say to all this, Sancho?' the Duchess asked.

'What I say, lady,' Sancho replied, 'is what I said before – as for the lashes, I announce them and all their works.'

'*Renounce* is what you should say, Sancho, and not what you said,' said the Duke.

'You let me be, Your Grace,' Sancho replied. 'I'm in no state at the moment to worry my head about little details or a few letters here or there, because I'm so bothered about these lashes I'm going to be given or I'm going to give myself that I don't know what I'm saying or doing. But what I should like the lady Dulcinea del Toboso to tell me is where she learned how to get people to do her favours – here she comes asking me to tear my flesh open with a lash, and then she calls me soul of lead and untamed beast and a whole string of bad names, and the devil can put up with that. Is my flesh made of bronze by any chance, or have I got anything to lose or gain from her being disenchanted or not? What basketful of linen, shirts, headgear and socks, though I never wear any of those, has she brought to win me over? No, it's just one insult after another, knowing as she must do those proverbs about an ass laden with gold soon climbing to the top of the mountain, and about gifts breaking rocks, and about God being a good worker but he loves to be helped, and about how he gives twice who gives quickly. And then this master of mine, who ought to be patting my back and coaxing me to make me soft as wool and carded cotton, says that if he catches me he's going to tie me naked to a tree and double my dose of stripes, and these softhearted folk ought to bear in mind that they're not just asking for a squire to be lashed but a governor – gilding the lily as you might say. Well, they can all bloody well go away and learn how to ask for a favour – and learn some manners too, because times change and a man isn't always going to be in a good mood. Here I am ready to burst with grief because my green coat's all torn, and they come asking me to lash myself of my own free will, when I'd as soon do that as turn into an Indian chief!'

'Well, the plain truth is, friend Sancho,' the Duke said, 'that if you don't turn softer than a ripe fig, you won't get your hands on that governorship. A fine thing it would be for me to send my islanders a cruel governor with bowels of flint, who refuses to relent in the face of the tears of damsels in distress or the pleas of wise, ancient, imperious enchanters and sages! In short, Sancho: either you lash yourself or are lashed, or you shan't be governor.'

'Please, sir,' said Sancho, 'couldn't I have a couple of days' grace to think about what would be best for me?'

'No, of course not,' said Merlin. 'Here, at this instant and on this spot, the outcome of this affair must be settled: either Dulcinea will return to the Cave of Montesinos and to her pristine state as a peasant girl, or she will be borne in her present state to the Elysian Fields,[2] where she will wait until the correct number of lashes has been administered.'

'Come on, Sancho,' the Duchess said, 'be of good spirit, and show your gratitude for the bread given you by Don Quixote, whom we should all serve and humour, because of his splendid character and his noble deeds of chivalry. Give your consent, my son, to this flogging, and let the devil go to the devil, and leave fear to the faint-hearted – a good heart conquers ill fortune, as you well know.'

Sancho's reply to these words was the following nonsense, addressed to Merlin:

'Please would you explain this to me, Merlin sir – when that messenger devil came, he gave my master a message from Sir Montesinos, telling him to wait here because he was on his way to say how the lady Dulcinea del Toboso could be disenchanted, yet so far we haven't caught a glimpse of Montesinos or anyone like him.'

To which Merlin replied:

'The devil, friend Sancho, is an ignorant fool and a thorough scoundrel: I sent him in search of your master with a message not from Montesinos but from me, for Montesinos is sitting in his cave planning or, more precisely, hoping for his disenchantment, because he still has the tail to skin. If there's anything he owes you, or you have any business to do with him, I shall bring him here and put him wherever you choose. But for the time being just consent to this penance because, believe you me, it will be of the greatest benefit to you, both body and soul: good for your soul because of the charity with which you will perform it, and good for your body because I know that you are of a sanguine temperament, so it will do you no harm to lose a little blood.'

'What a lot of doctors there are in the world – even enchanters are doctors now,' Sancho replied. 'But since everyone's saying the same thing, even though I still can't see it for myself – all right, I'll agree to give myself the three thousand three hundred lashes, providing I can do it whenever I feel like it, without any time limits, and I'll do my best to pay off the debt as soon as I can, so everyone can enjoy the lady Dulcinea's beauty, because it's beginning to look as if she really is beautiful, in spite of what I thought. And there's another condition, too – I'm not to have to make myself bleed, and if some of the lashes turn out to be more like swatting flies they're still valid. One more thing – if I lose count, Merlin here, who knows everything, must do the counting and tell me how many too few or too many I've done.'

'There won't be any need to tell you about too many,' Merlin replied, 'because at the precise moment when you reach the correct number Dulcinea will be disenchanted and will come in gratitude to look for the worthy Sancho, to give him her thanks and even perhaps a reward for his good deed. So you don't need to worry about too many or too few, and heaven forbid I should cheat anyone of even a hair of his head.'

'All right then, God's will be done!' said Sancho. 'I agree to my bad luck – I mean to say I accept my penance, on the conditions that I said.'

Hardly had Sancho finished speaking when the music of the shawms sounded out again, and countless muskets were fired once more, and Don Quixote draped himself around Sancho's neck, smothering him in kisses on the forehead and the cheeks. The Duchess and the Duke and all the others showed signs of the greatest satisfaction, and the chariot began to move; and as the lovely Dulcinea went by she bowed her head to the Duke and Duchess and made a low curtsey to Sancho.

And now the happy, smiling dawn came on apace; the flowers in the fields all raised their heads and stood erect, and the liquid crystal of the streams, murmuring among pebbles brown and white, flowed along to pay its tribute to the expectant rivers. The happy earth, the bright sky, the clean air, the serene light – each and all gave the most manifest signs that the day that came treading on the skirts of the dawn was going to be calm and clear. And the Duke and the Duchess, happy with their hunt and with having achieved their aims so cleverly and successfully, returned to their castle, determined to play some more jests – because nothing done in earnest could provide them with more amusement.

CHAPTER XXXVI

Which relates the strange and indeed inconceivable
adventure of the Dolorous Duenna, alias the Countess
Trifaldi, and a letter that Sancho Panza wrote to his
wife Teresa Panza

The Duke had a butler, a wag with a ready wit, who'd played the part of Merlin, made all the arrangements for the recent adventure, written the poem and persuaded a page to play Dulcinea. And with the help of his master and mistress the butler prepared another adventure, the strangest and funniest and most ingenious adventure imaginable.

On the following day the Duchess asked Sancho whether he'd begun his task, the penance he had to carry out to disenchant Dulcinea. He replied that he had – during the night he'd given himself five lashes. The Duchess asked him what he'd hit himself with. He replied that he'd hit himself with his hand.

'That,' the Duchess replied, 'is more like slapping yourself on the back than lashing yourself. It's my belief that the sage Merlin won't be content with such softness; the good Sancho is going to have to make himself a spiked scourge or a cat-o'-nine-tails, because if you spare the rod you spoil the child, and the freedom of so great a lady as Dulcinea isn't to be won on the cheap like that; and Sancho must bear in mind that works of charity performed in a lukewarm and half-hearted way have no merit or value whatsoever.'[1]

To which Sancho replied:

'You let me have some whip or halter that'll do the job, Your Grace, and I'll hit myself with it providing it doesn't hurt too much, because let me tell you, I might be a peasant but what my flesh is made of is more like cotton than esparto grass, and it won't be a good idea for me to go doing myself a mischief for somebody else's benefit.'

'I welcome the suggestion,' the Duchess replied, 'and tomorrow I'll give you a whip that will suit you to a T, and that will go as well with your tender flesh as one twin goes with another.'

To which Sancho replied:

'I'd like Your Highness to know, my dear lady, that I've written a letter to my wife Teresa Panza, telling her all about what's been happening to me since I left home, and here it is inside my shirt, because it only needs the address being written on it – I'd like Your Wise Excellency to read it, because to my mind it's in tune with the governing, what I mean to say is it's written as governors ought to write.'

'And who dictated it?' the Duchess asked.

'Who do you think was going to dictate it if not this here sinner?' Sancho retorted.

'And did you write it down, too?' the Duchess said.

'Of course I didn't,' Sancho replied, 'I can't read or write, though I can sign my name.'

'Let's see it, then,' said the Duchess, 'because I'm sure it displays the quality and clarity of your mind.'

Sancho pulled an unsealed letter out of his shirt, and when the Duchess took it she saw that this was what it said:

Letter from Sancho Panza to his wife Teresa Panza

If I've had a good hiding, I've had some good riding upon a fine horse, as the thief said to the executioner;² what I'm saying is that if I've been given some good governing, it's costing me a good lashing. You won't understand this, Teresa my dear, for the time being, but you will later on. I'll have you know, Teresa, that I've decided you'll go about in a coach, because that's the proper way – any other way of going about is like going on all fours. The wife of a governor is what you are, so just think what the backbiting's going to be like! I'm sending you a green hunting outfit that my lady the Duchess gave me – make it up into a skirt and some bodices for our daughter. My master Don Quixote, according to what I've heard in these parts, is a sane madman and a funny fool, and I'm just as bad. We've been in the Cave of Montesinos, and the sage Merlin has got me to lend a hand with disenchanting Dulcinea del Toboso, known as Aldonza Lorenzo where she comes from – with the three thousand three hundred lashes, minus five, that I've got to give myself she'll be left as disenchanted as the mother that bore her. You mustn't tell anybody about this, because if you give gossip an hour's start you'll never overtake it. In a few days' time I'm going off to my governing, where I'm really looking forward to making some money, because I've been told that all new governors go with the same idea — I'll sniff about a bit and then I'll tell you whether to come or not. The dun is well, and sends its fondest regards, and I'm not going to leave it, not even if they take me away to be the Great Turk. My lady the Duchess kisses your hands a thousand times — make sure you return the favour by kissing hers two thousand times, because my master says there's nothing that costs less or comes cheaper than good manners. God hasn't seen fit to let me have another travelling bag with a hundred escudos inside it, like the previous one, but don't you worry about that, Teresa my dear, because the man who rings the alarm has put himself furthest from harm, and it'll all come out in the wash when I'm governor, but it's just that I'm very worried because I've been told that once I have a go at governing I'll give my right arm to carry on, and if that's so it isn't such a good bargain after all, though it is true that invalids and one-armed people do have a cushy little number as beggars — so one way or another you're going to have riches and good fortune. May God grant you it, as he can, and keep me to serve you. From this castle, 20th July 1614.[3]

Your husband the Governor,
SANCHO PANZA

When the Duchess had finished reading the letter, she said to Sancho: 'The worthy Governor has gone a little astray in two respects: firstly, in saying or hinting that the governorship has been given him in return for the flogging he is to give himself, when he knows full well and cannot deny that when my lord the Duke made his promise nobody had even dreamed of any such flogging; secondly, he reveals himself to be very covetous, and I'd rather he wasn't that sort of a person, because greed breaks the sack, and the covetous governor does poor justice.'

'I didn't mean it like that, lady,' Sancho replied, 'and if you think my letter isn't all it ought to be we'll just have to tear it up and write another one, and it could well be that if it's left to my own efforts it'll turn out even worse.'

'No, no,' the Duchess replied, 'the letter's fine, and I want the Duke to see it.'

With this they walked out into a garden where they were going to have lunch that day. The Duchess showed Sancho's letter to the Duke, who thought it frightfully amusing. They ate, and once the tables had been cleared and everyone had been entertained for a good while by

Sancho's delightful conversation, they suddenly heard the mournful tones of a fife and a raucous, tuneless drum. They all showed signs of being thrown into confusion by this sad, chaotic martial music, particularly Don Quixote, who was so alarmed that his chair couldn't contain him; as for Sancho, all that needs to be said is that his fear carried him to his usual refuge by the Duchess's side or in her lap, because the sound they heard was really and truly dismal and doleful.

As they all sat there in amazement, they saw two men come into the garden dressed in clothes of mourning so full and so long that they brushed the ground; these two men were beating large drums, also draped in black. By their side came the fife-player, all in black like the other two. These three were followed by a gigantic personage, blanketed rather than dressed in a pitch-black cassock, the skirts of which were similarly vast. Over his cassock his body was crossed diagonally by a broad sword-strap, also black, from which hung an enormous scimitar with a black cross-guard, in a black scabbard. His face was covered by a transparent black veil, through which it was possible to glimpse a long, long beard, as white as snow. He paced along to the sound of the drums with ponderous solemnity. In short, his size, his gait, his blackness and his escort could have astonished and indeed did astonish all those who saw him and didn't know him. He came, slow and stately, to kneel before the Duke, who rose to his feet with all the others to greet him. But the Duke would by no means allow him to speak until he had also risen. The prodigious apparition did so, and once he was on his feet he lifted the veil from his face and revealed the most horrendous, longest, whitest and thickest beard that human eyes had ever gazed upon, and then he wrenched and wrested from his broad and swelling breast a solemn, sonorous voice as he fixed his eyes upon the Duke, and said:

'Exalted and mighty sir, my name is Trifaldín,[4] he of the White Beard; I am the squire of the Countess Trifaldi, otherwise known as the Dolorous Duenna, from whom I bring for Your Grace a message, which is to beg Your Grace to see fit to grant permission for her to come to tell you of her plight, which is one of the most unusual and amazing plights that the most plight-ridden thought on the face of the earth can ever have thought of. But first she desires to know whether the brave and never vanquished knight Don Quixote de la Mancha is in this your castle, for she has come in search of him on foot and without breaking her fast from the kingdom of Kandy[5] to this your realm, something that can and should be set down to a miracle or enchantment. She stands at the gate of this fortress or country house, and is only awaiting your permission to enter. I have spoken.'

And then he coughed, and ran both hands over his beard from top to bottom, and with great composure awaited the Duke's reply, which was:

'For many days now, worthy squire Trifaldín of the White Beard, we have known of the misfortune of my lady the Countess Trifaldi, whom enchanters have caused to be called the Dolorous Duenna; yes, squire extraordinaire, do bid her enter, and tell her that here awaits the valiant knight Don Quixote de la Mancha, from whose generous disposition every aid and assistance is to be expected – and you can also tell her on my behalf that if she needs my succour she shall not find it wanting, for merely being a knight obliges me to extend it to her, it being a knight's concern and duty to succour women of all kinds, particularly widowed duennas, wronged and dolorous, as her ladyship must be.'

When Trifaldín heard this he bent his knee to the ground, made a sign to the players of fife and drum to start up, and departed from the garden to the same sounds and at the same pace as when he'd entered it, leaving everyone amazed at his presence and composure. And the Duke turned to Don Quixote and said:

'So there we are, famous knight: the darkness of malice and ignorance can't hide or obscure the light of courage and virtue. I say this because Your Excellency has only been in this castle for six days, and the sad and the afflicted are already coming in search of you from remote and far distant lands, and not in carriages or on dromedaries but on foot and fasting, confident of finding in that mighty arm of yours the remedy for their trouble and distress, thanks to your magnificent exploits, news of which has spread far and wide all over the face of the earth.'

'I do wish, my lord Duke,' Don Quixote replied, 'that the blessed man of the Church who at table the other day showed so much ill will and such a grudge against knights errant, were here to see with his own eyes whether or not such knights are needed in this world; at the very least he would have found out for himself that people in extremes of distress and despair, in uncommon adversity and enormous misfortune, do not go for help to the houses of scholars, or of village sextons, or of the gentleman who has never ventured beyond the boundaries of the parish in which he lives, or of the indolent courtier who is more concerned to find news to repeat and chatter about than to perform deeds for others to talk and write about: remedy for distress, relief in necessity, succour for maidens, consolation for widows, are never so readily to be found as in knights errant, and for being one I give infinite thanks to heaven, and I consider any mishap or hardship that may befall me in this honourable profession to be well worth undergoing. So let this duenna come forward, and ask what she will, for I shall confide her relief to the might of my arm and the dauntless resolve of my doughty spirit.'

CHAPTER XXXVII

Which continues the famous adventure of the Dolorous Duenna

The Duke and Duchess were delighted to find Don Quixote responding so well to their tricks, and then Sancho broke in:

'I wouldn't like this duenna woman to come and get in the way of the governing I've been promised, because I once heard a chemist from Toledo who could talk like a goldfinch say that nothing good could ever come of any business that duennas had a hand in. Great God, how he hated them, that chemist! What this makes me think is that since all duennas, of every kind and description, are pests and nuisances, what are they going to be like if they're dolorous too, as the man said this Countess Three-Skirts or Three-Tails is? Because where I come from skirts and tails, tails and skirts, is all one and the same thing.'

'Hush, friend Sancho,' said Don Quixote. 'Since this duenna has come from such distant lands in search of me, she cannot be one of those that the chemist had in mind; what is more she is a countess, and when countesses are in service as duennas it must be queens and empresses that they are serving, because in their own houses they themselves are exalted ladies served by other duennas.'

Doña Rodríguez was also present, and she retorted:

'My lady the Duchess has certain duennas in her service who could have been countesses if fortune had so willed it; but it's the lords that make the laws, and let nobody say so much as a single word against duennas, particularly those who are elderly spinsters, because although I myself am not one of these I can well appreciate the advantage that an unmarried duenna has over a widowed one; and whoever did the shearing still has the shears in his hand.'

'All the same,' Sancho replied, 'there's so much shearing to be done on duennas, according to what my barber says, that it'll be better not to stir the rice, even if it does stick.'

'Squires have always been our enemies,' Doña Rodríguez retorted. 'They haunt antechambers and are always watching us, so they spend all the time they don't spend saying their prayers – and that is a very great deal of time indeed – gossiping about us, digging the skeletons out of our cupboards and burying our good names. Well, they can all go to the galleys as far as I'm concerned, because whether they like it or not we duennas are going to live on in the world and in the houses of the top people, even if we are dying of hunger and covering our more or less delicate bodies with black habits like those of nuns, as a dung-heap is covered with a carpet on procession-days. By my faith – if I were allowed to, and if the time were right, I'd show not only all those present but everyone in the world that there's no virtue not to be found in a duenna.'

'I'm sure my good Doña Rodríguez is right, absolutely right,' said the Duchess, 'but it will be better if she waits for a more appropriate occasion on which to defend herself and duennas in general, and to refute the wicked ideas of that evil chemist, and to root out the enmity in the breast of the great Sancho Panza.'

To which Sancho answered:

'Now I can give myself the airs of a governor I've forgotten about the headaches of a squire, and I don't care a fig's end for all the duennas in the world.'

They'd have continued this donnish conversation of theirs if they hadn't heard the fife and drums striking up again and telling them that the Dolorous Duenna was making her entrance. The Duchess asked the Duke whether they hadn't better go out to receive her, since she was a countess, an eminent personage.

'Being as she is a countess,' Sancho replied before the Duke could, 'I'd agree to Your Graces going to meet her, but being as she is a duenna I think you shouldn't budge an inch.'

'Who told you to butt in like that, Sancho?' said Don Quixote.

'Who told me, sir?' Sancho replied. 'I butted in all by myself, as well I can, being a squire who's learned courtesy in your school, the school of the most courteous and well-bred knight in all courteousness – and in these matters, as I've often heard you say, as much is lost by a point too many as by a point too few. And a word to the wise is enough.'

'It is just as Sancho says,' said the Duke. 'We shall first see what this countess looks like, and thus judge the degree of courtesy appropriate to her.'

At this moment the players of fife and drum made their entrance as before. And here the author ended this short chapter and began another, continuing the same adventure, which is one of the most notable adventures in this history.

CHAPTER XXXVIII

Which relates the account given by the Dolorous Duenna of her misfortune

Behind these melancholy musicians about a dozen duennas filed into the garden in two lines, all dressed in ample nuns' habits made, it seemed, of milled serge, with white widows' weeds of fine muslin, so long that only the hems of their habits showed beneath them. Behind these duennas came the Countess Trifaldi, led by the hand by her squire Trifaldín of the White Beard, and she was dressed in the finest unnapped black flannel that, if it had been napped, would have shown knots as big as the best Martos[1] chick-peas. Her skirt or tail, or whatever it's called, had three pointed trains, borne by three pages, also in mourning, forming an impressive geometrical figure with the three acute angles made by the points, so that all who saw the spiky dress realized that this must be the reason why the woman was called the Countess Trifaldi, which is the same as saying the Countess of the Three Skirts; and Benengeli says that this is true, and that her proper title was the Countess Lupine, because of the many wolves bred in her earldom, and if instead of wolves they had been goats or other horned beasts she'd have called the Countess Horny, because it's the custom in those parts for the lords to be named after whatever is most abundant on their estates; nonetheless this countess, to highlight the novelty of her skirt, left off Lupine and took on Trifaldi.

The twelve duennas and their mistress entered at a processional pace, and their faces were covered with black veils that weren't transparent like Trifaldín's, but so closely woven that nothing could be seen through them. As soon as this squadron of duennas appeared, the Duke, the Duchess and Don Quixote stood up, as did all the others watching the slow procession. The twelve duennas stopped and formed a corridor along which the Dolorous Duenna advanced, still holding Trifaldín's hand; and at this the Duke, the Duchess and Don Quixote stepped forward some twelve paces to receive her. Sinking to her knees, she said in a voice that was not at all soft and delicate – coarse and rough, more like:

'May it please Your Graces to use less courtesy with this your manservant I mean handmaid, because I'm so dolorous that I'm not going to be able to give you the right answers, due to the fact that my strange and unheard-of misfortune has driven my wits clean out of my head and I don't know where they've gone, but it must be somewhere a long way off because the more I look for them the less I find them.'

'The person would have to be witless indeed, my lady Countess,' the Duke replied, 'who could not instantly see your quality in your person – worthy, without any need for further enquiry, of the very cream of courtesy, the very flower of polite ceremony.'

And he took her hand, brought her to her feet and escorted her to a chair next to the Duchess, who also received her with the utmost courtesy. Don Quixote was silent, and Sancho was dying to see Trifaldi's face and those of some of her many duennas; but this would be impossible until they themselves chose to lift their veils. All were waiting in a tranquil silence to see who would break it, and it was the Dolorous Duenna, with the following words:

'I am confident, most powerful lord, exceptionally lovely lady and eminently wise company, that my extremely wretched affliction will find in your exceedingly brave breasts a reception that will be no less placid than generous and dolorous; for my woe is so great that it is enough to soften the marble, mollify the diamonds and melt the steel of the hardest hearts in the world; but before it is brought into the domain of – I won't say your ears but your hearing faculties, I should like you to apprise me of whether, in this fraternity, circle or company, I can find the immeasurably undefiled Don Quixote de la Manchissima, and his singularly squirely squire Panza.'

'Panza's over here,' said Sancho before anybody else could reply, 'and Don Quixotissimo, too, and so, Dolorousissima Duennissima, you can say what positively ever you decidedly like, because here we all are, incredibly ready and unbelievably prepared to be your amazingly humble servants.'

At this, Don Quixote rose to his feet and addressed the Dolorous Duenna:

'If your afflictions, distressed lady, can hope to find any relief in any valour or strength possessed by any knight errant, here is mine which, although feeble and inadequate, will be entirely devoted to your service. I am Don Quixote de la Mancha, whose profession it is to assist the needy of every kind, and this being so, you do not need to win over my benevolence or have recourse to preambles, but can simply and without circumlocutions tell me of your griefs; because he who listens will, if he cannot cure them, at least share them with you.'

When the Dolorous Duenna heard this she manifested an urge to throw herself down at Don Quixote's feet, and indeed that is exactly what she did, and striving to embrace them she said:

'Before these feet and legs I cast myself, O never vanquished knight, because they are the plinths and pillars of knight-errantry; these feet I must kiss, because on the steps they take hangs and depends the entire remedy of my misfortune, O brave errant whose veritable deeds outstrip and obscure the fabulous exploits of all Amadises, Esplandians and Belianises!'

And turning away from Don Quixote and towards Sancho Panza, she seized him by the hands and said:

'O you, the loyallest squire that ever served a knight errant in present or past centuries, longer in goodness than the beard of my attendant Trifaldín here present! Well may you pride yourself on serving, in the great Don Quixote, the whole troop of knights that have ever handled arms in this world, all rolled into one. I conjure you, by all you owe to that most loyal goodness of yours, to be an effective intercessor for me with your master, so that he soon succours this surpassingly humble and superlatively unhappy countess.'

To which Sancho replied:

'As for my goodness being as big and long as your squire's beard, lady, that's something that doesn't mean much to me – I just hope there's beard and moustache enough on my soul when I quit this life, as the smooth-jowled man said when they laughed at him, because that's what matters, and the beards of this world don't worry me in the slightest. I don't need any wheedling or prayers to get me to ask my master, who I know is very fond of me and even more so now he needs my help in a certain piece of business, to favour and help you as much as he can. So you just unload your problem, and tell us all about it, and leave the rest to us – we'll know what to do all right.'

The Duke and Duchess were bursting with laughter as they listened to these exchanges, and so was everyone else who knew what was going on in this latest adventure, and they passed admiring comments on the sharp wits and the clever dissimulation of Trifaldi, who sat herself down again and said:

'The famous kingdom of Kandy, which lies between great Taprobana and the South Sea, two leagues beyond Cape Comorin,[2] was ruled by Queen Maguncia, the widow of King Archipiela, her lord and husband, and the issue of their marriage was Princess Antonomasia, the heiress to that kingdom; the said Princess Antonomasia was brought up under my tutelage, since I was her mother's longest-serving and most eminent duenna. The days came and the days went, and little Antonomasia reached the age of fourteen, such a perfect beauty that there was no detail in which nature could have made the slightest improvement. And her wits weren't exactly those of a new-born babe, either! She was as clever as she was lovely, and she was the loveliest girl in the world, and she still is if the envious and hard-hearted fates haven't cut the thread of her life. But this cannot have happened, because heaven will not permit anyone to do such evil to earth as to cut from the loveliest vine growing in the ground its bunch of grapes before it has ripened.

'Countless noblemen, both native and foreign, fell in love with this beauty, so inadequately extolled by my fumbling tongue, and among them one private knight who was at court dared to raise his aspirations to the heavens of such loveliness, trusting in his youth and his dash, his many skills and charms, his sharp and ready wit; because let me tell Your Graces, so long as I'm not boring you, he could play a guitar so well he made it talk, and what's more he was a poet, and a wonderful dancer, and so expert at constructing bird-cages that he could have made a living at it if he'd been reduced to utter poverty – and all these charms and accomplishments are enough to move a mountain, let alone a tender young maiden. But all his dash and wit and all his charm and skills would have done little or nothing to conquer the fortress of my girl's virtue, if that thieving cutthroat hadn't had recourse to the trick of winning me over first. Yes, first that scoundrel, that heartless vagabond, set about procuring my goodwill and securing my affections to make me, bad custodian that I was, hand over the keys of the fortress I was guarding. So he praised my mind, and he conquered my will with all sorts of trinkets and knick-knacks that he gave me, but what chiefly brought me down and led to my fall was a song I heard him singing one night while I was sitting in a window overlooking an alley where he lived, and if my memory serves me right it went like this:

> My soul is wounded by the pain
> Sent by my darling enemy:
> For greater grief, it's her decree
> I suffer and do not complain.[3]

'His words seemed to me prettier than pearls, and his voice sweeter than syrup, and from that there moment till this, I mean ever since then, considering the mischief that has come my way through this and other similar poems, I've always believed that poets ought to be banished from all well-ordered societies, as Plato recommended[4] – or at least the lustful poets should, because they write such verses, not like the ones about the Marquis of Mantua, which delight women and children and make them cry, but witty ones that slide right into your soul like soft thorns, and wound you there like thunderbolts, without leaving any mark on your clothes.

'And another night he sang:

> Come, death, and come with gentle tread;
> Don't let me be aware of you
> In case I'm made to live anew
> By the delight of being dead.[5]

And other verses and ditties of this kind, enchanting to listen to and amazing to read. And what can I say about when they condescended to write a kind of song in fashion at that time in Kandy that they called seguidillas? They made your very soul leap and dance, the laughter frolic about inside you, your whole body go a-tingle – in short, quicksilver in all your senses. And that's why I'm saying, ladies and gentlemen, that it would be right to banish all such troubadors to the Islands of Lizards.[6] Though they themselves aren't to blame, but the simpletons who praise them and the foolish women who believe them. If I had been the good duenna I should have been, those stale conceits wouldn't have moved me, and I shouldn't have believed all that stuff about "Dying I live, in ice I burn, in fire I shiver, in despair I hope, I leave and I stay", and other impossibilities of the same strain, which their writings are full of. And what can I say about when they promise you the Phoenix of Arabia, the crown of Ariadne, the coursers of the Sun, the pearls of the South Sea, the gold of Tibar and the balsam of Panchaia?[7] This is where the ink flows most freely, since it isn't much of a hardship for them to promise what they never intend to carry out, and indeed never could carry out. But how I'm digressing! Woe is me, luckless wretch that I am! What madness or what folly leads me to insist on the faults of others, when there is so much to be said about my own? Woe is me, I repeat, hapless creature that I am! What conquered me wasn't the poetry but my own simple-mindedness; what softened me wasn't the music but my own levity; it was my ignorance and my negligence that opened the way and smoothed the passage for Don Clavijo,[8] because that's the name of the knight to whom I'm referring; and using me as go-between he visited Antonomasia's bedroom not just once but many times, and it wasn't he but I that tricked her; but first he did give his solemn word to be her true husband, because although I'm a sinner I wouldn't have allowed him to touch so much as the sole of her slipper without that. No, no, most certainly not: marriage must always be the outcome of any affair of this kind that I take in hand!

There was only one problem in this business, the disparity of rank, because Don Clavijo was just a private knight and Princess Antonomasia was, as I said, the heiress to the kingdom.

'For some time my cautious management of the affair kept it hidden and secret, until it seemed to me that it was speedily being revealed by a certain swelling in Antonomasia's stomach, and the fear this caused made us put our three heads together, and we agreed that before the mischief came to light Don Clavijo would ask for Antonomasia's hand in the presence of the Vicar-General, on the strength of a written promise to be his wife that the Princess had made him, drawn up by me so ingeniously and in such cast-iron terms that all the power of Samson couldn't have made a dent in it. Our plan was put into effect, the Vicar-General looked at the document, he heard the lady's confession, she made a full one, he ordered her to be detained in the house of a very honourable policeman . . .'

Sancho interrupted:

'So there are policemen, poets and seguidillas in Kandy, too – I swear it makes me think the world's the same all over. But do hurry up, Señora Trifaldi, it's late and I'm dying to hear the end of this long history.'

'Indeed I will,' the Countess replied.

CHAPTER XXXIX

In which Trifaldi continues her stupendous and
memorable history

Every word uttered by Sancho delighted the Duchess as much as it drove Don Quixote to despair, and once he'd told him to keep quiet the Dolorous Duenna continued:

'In short, after much questioning and answering, and seeing that the Princess always stood her ground, without varying or departing from her original declaration, the Vicar-General pronounced in favour of Don Clavijo, and handed her over to him as his lawful wife, which so enraged Queen Maguncia, Princess Antonomasia's mother, that within three days we buried her.'

'I suppose she must have died, then,' said Sancho.

'Of course she died!' Trifaldín replied. 'In Kandy we don't bury the living you know, only the dead.'

'It wouldn't be the first time, squire,' Sancho retorted, 'that a person in a faint has been buried because they thought he was dead, and it struck me that Queen Maguncia ought to have fainted rather than dying, because while there's life there's hope, and the Princess's blunder wasn't so enormous she needed to take it like that. If the lady had married one of her page-boys or some other servant, as lots of others have, so I'm led to believe, the harm would have been past repair – but getting married to a knight who's as much of a gentleman and as skilful as we've just been told he is? To tell you the honest truth even if it was a silly thing to have been and gone and done, it wasn't as awful as people think, because according to my master's rules, and he's with us now and will confirm the truth of what I'm saying, just as scholars can become bishops, knights, specially if they're errant ones, can become kings and emperors.'

'That is quite correct, Sancho,' said Don Quixote, 'for a knight errant, given a modicum of luck, is on the very threshold of being the greatest lord in the world. But let the Dolorous Lady continue her narration, because I have a suspicion that she has yet to recount the bitter part of this hitherto sweet history.'

'You can say that again!' the Countess replied. 'It's so bitter that bitter-apples are sweet and oleander is good to eat in comparison. So the Queen was dead, then – not in a faint – and we buried her, and no sooner had we covered her with earth and made our last farewells when, *quis talia fando temperet a lacrimis?*,[1] sitting on top of a wooden horse on the Queen's grave we saw the giant Malambruno, Maguncia's cousin, who besides being a cruel man was an enchanter, and to avenge his cousin's death and punish Don Clavijo for his audacity, and indignant at Antonomasia's brazenness, he used his magic arts to put them both under a spell there on top of the grave itself – she was turned into a brass monkey, and he into a fearsome crocodile of some unknown metal, while between the two of them stands a column, also of metal, with an inscription in Syriac which, translated into Kandian and now into Spanish, states:

These two foolhardy lovers will not regain their original form until the brave man of La Mancha engages with me in single combat; for his mighty courage alone the Fates reserve this unparalleled adventure.

'Next Malambruno drew a vast, broad scimitar from its sheath, grabbed me by the hair and made as if to slit my gullet and slice off my head. I was distraught, my voice stuck in my throat, I was frightened to death; and yet I summoned up all my strength and in faltering and piteous tones spoke such words to him, and so many of them, that he suspended the execution of such a cruel punishment. Finally he had all the duennas in the palace brought before him, all these here present, and after dwelling on the enormity of our offence and denouncing duennas' characters, their evil ways and worse intrigues, and laying on all of us the blame that was mine alone, he said he was not going to inflict capital punishment on us, but another sort, long-drawn-out, that would mean unending civil death for us; and at the very moment he stopped speaking we all felt the pores on our faces opening up, and it was as if needles were pricking us all over them. We put our hands up to our faces, and found ourselves as you will see us now.'

Here the Dolorous Duenna and the other duennas raised their veils and revealed their faces, all bristling with beards – some blond, others black, others white, others streaked – at which spectacle the Duke and Duchess showed their surprise, Don Quixote and Sancho their amazement and all the others their astonishment. And Trifaldi continued:

'This is how that malevolent knave Malambruno punished us, by covering the silky smoothness of our visages with these coarse bristles; would to heaven that he had struck off our heads with his enormous sword instead of darkening the light of our faces with this stubble all over them, because if we give the matter due consideration, ladies and gentlemen (and what I'm about to say now is something that I'd like to say with my eyes flowing like fountains, but what with brooding over our misfortune and the oceans they've wept already, they're as dry as straw by now, so I'll say it tearlessly): where, I ask you, can a duenna with a beard go? What father or mother will take pity on her? Who will help her? If even when her skin is smooth and her face has been tortured with a thousand different concoctions and cosmetics she can hardly find a soul who likes her, what can she do when she displays a face that has been turned into a forest? O duennas, my friends, in an evil moment were we born, in an unlucky hour did our parents beget us!'

And as she said this she seemed to be fainting away.

CHAPTER XL

About matters relevant to this adventure and to this memorable history

All those who enjoy histories like this one should really and truly be grateful to its first author, Cide Hamete, for his meticulousness in telling us about all its most minute particulars, never neglecting to bring every little detail, however trivial, clearly to light. He depicts characters' thoughts, reveals their fancies, answers unspoken questions, clears up doubts, brings arguments to their proper conclusion: in short he reveals every last atom of information that the most curious reader could ever want to know. O celebrated author! O happy Don Quixote! O famous Dulcinea! O funny Sancho Panza! May all of you together and each of you in your own right live on for ever, for the pleasure and entertainment of everyone in the world!

The history says, then, that when Sancho saw the Dolorous Duenna fainting, he said:

'I swear on my faith as an honest man and on the eternal life of my forebears the Panzas that I've never heard or seen an adventure like this one, nor has my master ever told me about one like it, nor could he ever have imagined one like it. Not wanting to curse you, being as you are an enchanter and a giant, a thousand devils help you, Malambruno, and couldn't you have found any punishment for these sinners apart from bearding them? Wouldn't it have been better, and more what they deserve, to cut off the bottom half of their noses, even if it did make them speak funny, than to stick beards on them? I bet they haven't got the money to pay for all the shaving.'

'That's quite right, sir,' replied one of the twelve. 'Indeed we don't have the money to be shaved, so some of us have adopted an economical remedy, using patches or sticking-plasters that we put on our faces and when we rip them off we're left as smooth as the bottom of a stone mortar; because although there are women in Kandy that go from house to house removing hair, plucking eyebrows and doing other such hocus-pocus associated with women, we duennas of my lady's household have never been willing to let them in, because most of them have a distinct whiff of those who have ceased being principals in their particular game and have turned to being third parties; so if we're not relieved by Don Quixote, we'll be carried to our graves in our beards.'

'I shall go to the lands of the Moors and pluck mine out there,'[1] said Don Quixote, 'if I do not rid you of yours.'

Trifaldi suddenly recovered from her fainting fit and said:

'The distant echo of your promise, valiant knight, reached my ears in the midst of my swoon, and was enough to bring me out of it and restore all my senses; and so I again beseech you, illustrious errant, indomitable sir, to put your gracious promise into effect.'

'For my part I will do whatever is needed,' Don Quixote replied. 'Please tell me, my lady, what that is, for my spirit is most willing to serve you.'

'The fact is,' said the Dolorous Duenna, 'that from here to the kingdom of Kandy, by land, it's five thousand leagues, give or take a couple; but by air, in a straight line, it's three thousand two hundred and twenty-seven. What you should also know is that Malambruno mentioned that whenever fortune sent me our knight and liberator, he himself would send a mount that would be much better and have fewer faults than the ones you hire, because it would be that very same wooden horse on which the brave Pierres carried off the fair Magalona, a horse controlled by a peg in its forehead that acts as a bridle, and it flies through the air so fast that you'd say it was being borne along by all the devils in hell. This horse, according to ancient tradition, was constructed by that sage Merlin; he lent it to Pierres, who was his friend and who made long journeys on it, and upon it bore away the fair Magalona, as I said, carrying her through the air on its crupper, and leaving all those watching them from earth dumbfounded; and Merlin only lent it to people he was very fond of or who paid him well, and from when the great Pierres rode it to this moment in time nobody else is known to have mounted it. But now Malambruno, with his magic arts, has spirited it away, and he's in charge of it, and uses it on his trips, because he's always travelling through different parts of the world, and now he's here, and tomorrow he's in France, and the next day he's in Peru; and the best thing of all is that the horse doesn't eat or sleep or use horseshoes, and as it ambles through the air, without any wings, it gives such a smooth and easy ride that whoever's on it can carry a cupful of water in his hand without spilling a single drop; and for this reason the fair Magalona loved riding it.'

At this Sancho said:

'For a smooth and easy ride there's nothing like my dun, even though it doesn't go through the air – but on land I'll back it against any other ambler in the world.'

They all laughed, and the Dolorous Duenna continued:

'And if Malambruno does want to put an end to our misfortune, this horse will be here within half an hour of nightfall; because he explained that the sign with which he'd let me know that I'd found the knight I was looking for would be to send me the horse, wherever I was, with all speed and dispatch.'

'And how many people is there room for on this here horse?' Sancho asked.

The Dolorous Duenna replied:

'Two: one on the saddle and the other on the crupper, and usually these two are the knight and his squire, so long as the knight hasn't got any borne-away maidens with him.'

'What I'd next like to know, Dolorous Lady,' said Sancho, 'is what's this horse's name?'

'Its name,' the Dolorous Duenna replied, 'is not that of Bellerophon's horse, called Pegasus, or that of Alexander the Great's horse, Bucephalus, or Orlando Furioso's Brigliadoro, or Bayard, the name of Reynald of Montalban's horse, or Frontino, like Ruggiero's, or Boötes or Pirithoa, said to be the names of the horses of the Sun,[2] nor is it called Orelia, like the horse on which the unfortunate Rodrigo, the last Gothic king of Spain, rode into the battle in which he lost his kingdom and his life.'

'I bet,' said Sancho, 'that since it wasn't given any of those famous names of well-known horses, it wasn't named after my master's horse

Rocinante either, even though that name's more fitting than any of the others you've said so far.'

'That is true,' the bearded countess replied, 'but its name still suits it quite well, because it's called Clavileño[3] the Swift, which reflects the fact that it's made of wood and has a peg in its forehead and goes fast; and so, as regards its name, it can well compete with the famous Rocinante.'

'The name isn't bad,' Sancho replied, 'but what bridle or halter do you control it with?'

'I have already said,' Trifaldi replied, 'that it is controlled with the peg – by turning it one way or the other the knight riding it makes it go wherever he likes, either high in the sky, or skimming and almost brushing the ground, or following the middle course that is sought and should be taken in all well-ordered actions.'

'I can't wait to see it,' Sancho replied, 'but you might as well go looking for figs on thistles as think I'm going to get on to it, on either the saddle or the crupper. That's a fine thing I must say – I can hardly manage to stay on my dun, on a pack-saddle that's softer than silk, and now they're expecting me to sit on a crupper of wood, without so much as a pad or a cushion! Good God, I'm not intending to give myself a pounding like that to rid anyone of her beard – let each of them get her own shave as best she can, because I'm not going with my master on a long journey like that. What's more, I can't be needed for the shaving of these here beards, as I am for the disenchanting of my lady Dulcinea.'

'Oh yes you are, my friend,' Trifaldi replied, 'and you're needed so much that without you, I believe, we'll achieve nothing.'

'Oh, no – help, help!' cried Sancho, 'What have squires got to do with their masters' adventures? Is it right for them to get all the fame for the successful ones, and us all the hard work? By my body and soul! It wouldn't be so bad if the historians wrote, "Such and such a knight brought such and such an adventure to a happy ending, but only with the help of his squire named so and so, and without him he couldn't have done it." But no, all they do is write, "Sir Paralipomenon of the Three Stars triumphed in the adventure of the six monsters," without so much as a mention for his squire, who'd been there all the time – just as if he didn't exist! So, ladies and gentlemen, I'll say it again – my master can go by himself, and much good may it do him, because I'm staying right here with my lady the Duchess, and it could well be that when he comes back he finds the lady Dulcinea's cause bettered no end, because in my spare time I'm planning to give myself such a good hiding that not a single hair will ever sprout on my body again.'

'In spite of all that, you shall go with him if necessary, worthy Sancho, because there are good people who will beg you to; and these ladies' faces can't be left so bushy just because of your idle fears: that would certainly be most unfortunate.'

'Help, help, help!' was Sancho's reply. 'If this act of charity was to be done for orphaned maidens or charity-girls, a man could take on any task, but to go through it all just to rid duennas of their beards – not bloody likely! I'd sooner see the whole lot of them bearded, from the biggest to the littlest, from the fussiest to the finickiest.'

'You are indeed on bad terms with duennas, friend Sancho,' said the Duchess, 'and you're excessively influenced by the opinion of that chemist from Toledo. Well, you really are wrong, you know – there are duennas in my household who are the very models of duennas, and my Doña Rodríguez here won't let me say otherwise.'

'You go ahead and do so all the same, Your Excellency,' said Rodríguez, 'because God knows the truth about everything; and whether we duennas are good or bad, bearded or smooth, we are our mothers' daughters like other women, and since God brought us into the world he knows why he did it, and I put my trust in his mercy and not in anybody's beard.'

'Nevertheless, Señora Rodríguez, Señora Trifaldi and company,' said Don Quixote, 'I trust in heaven that it will look with kindly eyes on your distress; for Sancho will do my bidding if Clavileño appears here and I fight Malambruno. I know that there can be no razor that will shave you ladies with greater ease than my sword will shave Malambruno's head from his shoulders: God suffers the wicked, but not for ever.'

'Oh, oh!' the Dolorous Duenna broke in. 'May all the stars in the celestial regions look down upon you, valiant knight, with kindly eyes, and infuse into your spirit all courage and strength to make you the shield and protector of the abused and downtrodden order of duennas, loathed by chemists, gossiped about by squires and wheedled by page-boys: woe betide the trollop who in the prime of her life doesn't become a nun rather than a duenna! What unhappy women we duennas are; for even if we are descended in a direct male line from Hector of Troy[4] himself our mistresses still can't desist from addressing us like the scum of the earth if this makes them feel like queens! O giant Malambruno, you may be an enchanter but you do keep your promises: send us without delay the peerless Clavileño so that our misfortune can be brought to an end, because if the hot weather sets in and these beards of ours are still on our faces, what a pickle we'll be in then!'

Trifaldi spoke with such feeling that she drew tears from the eyes of all present, and even filled Sancho's eyes to the brim; and he resolved in his heart to go with his master to the uttermost ends of the earth if that was what had to be done to shear the wool from those venerable faces.

CHAPTER XLI

About the coming of Clavileño, and the end of this protracted adventure

As they spoke night came, and with it the moment for the arrival of the famous horse Clavileño, the delay in which was already troubling Don Quixote, because he supposed that since Malambruno was taking so long to send it, this must mean either that he was not the knight for whom this adventure was reserved, or that Malambruno did not dare to meet him in single combat. But, lo and behold, four wild men burst into the garden, all clad in green ivy, bearing on their shoulders a great wooden horse. They lowered it to the ground and one of them said:

'Let he who has the courage to do so climb up on to this contraption.'

'Not me,' said Sancho, 'I haven't got any courage and I'm not a knight.'

And the wild man continued:

'And let his squire, if he has one, take the crupper, and let him place his trust in the valiant Malambruno, for by no sword save Malambruno's, nor by any other threat, shall he be assailed. And all he has to do is to turn this peg in the horse's neck, and it will carry them through the air to where Malambruno awaits them; but to prevent the high altitude from making them dizzy, they must remain blindfolded until the horse neighs, which will be the sign that their journey has reached its end.'

With these words the wild men left Clavileño and went back, with graceful demeanour, the way they had come. As soon as the Dolorous Duenna saw the horse she exclaimed, almost in tears:

'O valiant knight: Malambruno has kept his promise, the horse is here, our beards are growing and each one of us with every single hair in them begs you to shear and shave us, because all you have to do is climb on to it with your squire and make a happy start on your novel journey.'

'I will do so, my lady Countess Trifaldi, with the greatest of pleasure and the best of goodwill, without even stopping to find a saddle-pad or put on my spurs, so as not to delay matters: such is my desire, dear lady, to see you and all these good duennas smooth and shorn.'

'But I won't do so,' said Sancho, 'not with goodwill nor with badwill nor with any other kind of will, and if this here shaving can't be done without me getting up on to that there crupper, my master can go and look for another squire to ride with him, and these ladies can look for another way of smoothing their faces – I'm not some witch to enjoy flying through the air. And what are my islanders going to say when they hear their governor's riding about in the sky? And another thing – it's three thousand odd leagues from here to Kandy, so if the horse gets tired or the giant gets angry we'll take a good half dozen years to come back and then there won't be any islanders or any highlanders left to come back to, and since it's often said that the danger's in the delay, and when you're offered a heifer make haste with the halter, these ladies and their beards are going to have to forgive me because St Peter's all right in Rome, what I mean to say is that I'm all right in this house where I'm treated so well and whose master I expect to do me such a good turn as to make me a governor.'

To all of which the Duke replied:

'Friend Sancho: the island I have promised you is neither moveable nor fugitive; it has such deep roots, struck down into the deepest profundities of the earth, that it isn't going to be very easily torn up or budged from where it is; and since you well know that there isn't any position like this, of the first importance, that isn't obtained with a bribe of one kind or another, the bribe I require for this island is for you to go with your master Don Quixote to bring this memorable adventure to a successful conclusion; for whether you return on Clavileño with the promptitude promised by its fleetness, or adverse fortune brings you back on your own two feet like a pilgrim from hostel to hostel and from inn to inn, whenever you return you shall find your island where you left it, and you shall find your islanders with the same desire to welcome you as their governor that they have always had, and my goodwill shall also be what it's always been – and don't you entertain the slightest doubt about this truth, Señor Sancho, for that would be a great insult to my desire to serve you.'

'Say no more, sir,' said Sancho. 'I'm just a poor squire and I can't take all that courtesy – my master can get on the horse, you can blindfold me and commit me to God's care, and I'd just like to know if once we're riding along up there in the sky it will still be all right for me to commend myself to Our Lord and call on the angels to help me.'

To which Trifaldi replied:

'Yes, Sancho, you can most certainly commend yourself to God or to whomever you fancy, because although Malambruno's an enchanter he's a Christian too, and he casts his spells with the greatest of care and consideration so as not to cause annoyance.'

'All right then,' said Sancho. 'God help me, and the Holy Trinity of Gaeta too!'

'Never since the memorable adventure of the fulling-mill,' said Don Quixote, 'have I seen Sancho as frightened as he is now, and, if I were as superstitious as some people are, his faint-heartedness would give rise to a certain wavering in my own courage. Come here, though, Sancho: with these good people's permission, I would like to have a word or two with you in private.'

And taking him aside, among some trees in the garden, and grasping both his hands, he said:

'You can see, brother Sancho, what a long journey lies ahead of us, and you must realize that God alone knows when we shall come back or how much leisure or time off this business is going to allow us; so I would like you now to retire to your room, as if you were going to look for something that you need for the journey, and in the twinkling of an eye, in part payment of the three thousand three hundred lashes to which you're committed, give yourself five hundred of them at least, and that will be five hundred less to suffer later on; because well begun is half done.'

'For God's sake!' said Sancho. 'You must be out of your mind! It's like that saying, "You can see that I'm pregnant and you expect me to be a virgin!" Now that I've got to ride along sitting on a bare board you expect me to do an injury to my bum? It just isn't right, and that is the honest truth. Let's go off to unbeard the duennas, and when we get back I promise you, on my word of honour, I'll be in such a hurry to do my duty that you'll be well pleased – and that's all there is to say.'

And Don Quixote replied:

'That promise is a great comfort to me, good Sancho, and I do believe you will keep it, for the fact is that although you're a fool you're a true-blue sort of fellow.'

'No, I'm not blue, I'm brown,' said Sancho, 'but even if I was a mixture of the two I'd still keep my word.'

And with this they walked back to mount Clavileño, and when Don Quixote was about to do so, he said:

'Have yourself blindfolded, Sancho, and up you go, Sancho; because one who sends for us from such remote lands cannot be doing so to deceive us for the sake of the paltry glory to be gained from tricking those who trust him; and even if everything did turn out the opposite of how I believe it will, no amount of malice will be able to obscure the glory of having undertaken this exploit.'

'Yes, let's go, sir,' said Sancho, 'because I've really taken those ladies' beards and tears to heart, and I shan't enjoy another mouthful of food till I see them made nice and smooth again. But you get on and put your blindfold on first – if I've got to ride on the crupper it's clear that the one in the saddle must mount before me.'

'Quite so,' Don Quixote replied. And taking a handkerchief from his waist-pouch, he asked the Dolorous Duenna to blindfold him with the utmost care; and once she had done so he pulled the blindfold off and said:

'If my memory is not playing tricks on me, I have read in Virgil about the Palladium of Troy, a wooden horse that the Greeks presented to the goddess Pallas, and it was pregnant with armed knights who then brought about the downfall of that city. So it will be a good idea to see what Clavileño has inside its stomach before we set off.'

'There's no need for that,' said the Dolorous Duenna. 'I'll answer for the horse and I know there's nothing tricky or treacherous about

Malambruno; you climb on, Don Quixote sir, without fear, and on my head be it if you come to any harm.'

It seemed to Don Quixote that anything he could reply concerning his safety would cast doubts upon his courage, and so, without any further argument, he mounted Clavileño and tried its peg and found it easy to turn; and since there were no stirrups and his legs dangled loose he looked like nothing so much as a figure on a Flemish tapestry depicting some Roman triumph. Sancho came up to climb on, in slow motion and with bad grace, and, settling himself as best he could on the crupper, he found it much less soft than he would have liked, so he asked the Duke if he could be provided with a saddle-pad or a cushion, even if it had to be taken from his lady the Duchess's drawing-room or from some page-boy's bed, because that horse's crupper seemed more like marble than wood. To this Trifaldi replied that Clavileño couldn't endure any trappings or any other kind of accoutrement, but what Sancho could do was to sit side-saddle, and then it wouldn't feel so hard. Sancho did this, and said goodbye and allowed himself to be blindfolded and, once this had been done, he pulled the blindfold off and, gazing down on everyone in the garden with tender, brimming eyes, begged them to help him in his plight by each saying some Paternosters and Ave Marias, so that God would provide somebody to say some for them whenever they were in a similar pickle. To which Don Quixote said:

'You scoundrel – are you standing on the scaffold by any chance, or breathing your last, to resort to pleas like that? You wicked, cowardly creature – are you not in the very same place occupied by the fair Magalona, from which she did not descend into her grave but rose to be Queen of France, if the histories are to be believed? And I, who ride with you – can I not compare myself with the brave Pierres, who sat where I sit now? Cover your eyes, you spiritless animal, and do not allow the fear that fills your body past your lips, not in my presence at least.'

'They'd better blindfold me, then,' Sancho replied, 'and if you won't let me commend myself to God or even get someone else to do the commending, is it any wonder if I'm frightened that there might be some legion of devils wandering about the place waiting to dump us right in front of the execution squad at Peralvillo?'[1]

The pair were blindfolded again, and once Don Quixote was satisfied that all was in order he felt for the peg, and as soon as he touched it the duennas and everyone else cried:

'God guide you, valiant knight!'

'God be with you, intrepid squire!'

'There you go through the air, cleaving it swifter than any arrow!'

'There you go, amazing and astonishing all who are watching you from earth!'

'Hold on tight, brave Sancho, you're wobbling! Be careful not to fall – if you do, it'll be worse than when that rash youth tried to drive the chariot of his father the Sun!'[2]

When Sancho heard the cries he snuggled up close to his master and wrapped his arms around him, saying:

'Sir – how is it they're saying we're so high up when we can hear their voices and it sounds just as if they're right here by our side?'

'Pay no attention to that, Sancho: since these affairs and these flights are so out of the ordinary course of events, you'll be able to see and hear whatever you please, even from a thousand leagues away. But don't hug me so tightly, you're pulling me off; I really don't know why you're so worried and so frightened, because I'd venture to affirm that never in all the days of my life have I mounted a horse that gave a smoother ride. Anyone would think that we were sitting in the same place all the time! Banish your fears, my friend; everything is going just as it should, and we have the wind astern.'

'You're right there,' Sancho replied, 'because there's such a strong wind back here where I am that it's just as if they were blowing a thousand bellows at me.'

Which was true, because people were indeed pumping air at him from several great bellows: the adventure had been so well planned by the Duke and the Duchess and their butler that no detail was lacking to make it perfect. When Don Quixote felt the blast he said:

'There can be no doubt, Sancho, that we must be reaching the second region of the air, where hail and snow are born; thunder, lightning and thunderbolts are born in the third region, and if we continue to climb like this we shall soon come to the region of fire – and I just don't know how to work this peg so that we don't fly up to where we'll both be roasted alive.'[3]

As he said this their faces were being warmed from a good distance with tow, easy to light and extinguish, hanging from a cane. When Sancho felt the heat he said:

'I'll be blowed if we aren't in that place of fire already, or really close to it, because a great chunk of my beard has just been singed, and I have a good mind to take off my blindfold, sir, and see where we are.'

'Do no such thing,' Don Quixote replied. 'Remember that true story about Dr Torralba, who with the help of devils flew through the air on a cane with his eyes shut, and reached Rome in twelve hours, and alighted at the Torre di Nona, a street in that city, and witnessed the assault, and the sack, and the death of Bourbon, and the next morning was back in Madrid, where he described everything he'd seen; well, he also said that as he was flying through the air the devil ordered him to open his eyes, and he did open them, and he found that he seemed to be so close to the horn of the moon that he could have held it in his hand, and he didn't dare look down at the earth for fear of fainting.[4] And so, Sancho, it would serve no good purpose to remove our blindfolds, for he whose charge we're in will care for us, and it may well be that we're circling and climbing so that we can swoop down on the kingdom of Kandy like a falcon hunting a heron, ensuring that it can catch its prey however much it tries to gain height; and even though it doesn't seem half an hour since we left the garden, we must have come a long long way, believe you me.'

'I don't know I'm sure,' Sancho Panza replied, 'all I can say is that if that lady Magellan[5] or Magalona was happy with this crupper, her flesh can't have been all that delicate.'

As the Duke and the Duchess and all the others in the garden listened to this conversation between the two heroes, they were delighted with it; but they decided to bring the extraordinary and well contrived adventure to an end, and they set fire to Clavileño's tail with some tow and, since the horse was packed with firecrackers, it flew into the air with an enormous racket, hurling Don Quixote and Sancho Panza to the ground, scorched and singed.

By this time the entire bearded squadron of duennas had disappeared from the garden, as had Trifaldi herself, and the other people stretched themselves out on the grass, as if they had fainted. Don Quixote and Sancho staggered to their feet, and when they looked around they were astonished to find themselves in the very same garden from which they'd flown, and to see so many people lying on the ground. And their astonishment grew even greater when on one side of the garden they saw a great lance thrust into the earth, and hanging from it by two green silk cords a smooth white parchment on which was written in large golden letters the following:

The illustrious knight Don Quixote de la Mancha has successfully completed the adventure of the Countess Trifaldi, otherwise known as the Dolorous Duenna, and company, by merely attempting it.

Malambruno regards himself as utterly and completely satisfied, and the duennas' chins are now shorn and smooth; and King Clavijo and Queen Antonomasia have been returned to their pristine state. And once the squirely thrashing has been completed, the white dove shall be delivered from the pestiferous gerfalcons pursuing her, and nestle in the arms of her own true love; for this has been ordained by the sage Merlin, the protoenchanter of all enchanters.

When Don Quixote read the parchment, it was clear to him that it referred to the disenchantment of Dulcinea, and thanking heaven for enabling him to carry out so mighty a deed in such safety and restore the original complexions to the faces of those venerable duennas, who were no longer to be seen, he went over to where the Duke and Duchess lay, still unconscious, and, seizing the Duke's hand, he said:

'Come now, good sir, take heart, take heart, there's nothing to worry about! The adventure's over without anyone being hurt, as is clearly shown by the document on that pillar over there.'

The Duke slowly came back to life, like someone awaking from a deep sleep, as did the Duchess and all the others lying in the garden, with such displays of terror and bewilderment that they almost persuaded themselves that what they were so good at acting in mere jest had happened in real earnest. The Duke read the notice with his eyes half closed, and then, with his arms wide open, he went to embrace Don Quixote and tell him that he was quite the finest knight ever seen in any age.

Sancho was looking everywhere for the Dolorous Duenna to find out what her face was like without a beard, and whether she was as beautiful when beardless as her charming disposition had promised; but he was told that as soon as Clavileño had come down in flames from the sky and crashed to the ground, Trifaldi and her whole squadron of duennas had disappeared, and were now clean-shaven and bristleless. The Duchess asked Sancho how he had fared on his long journey. To which Sancho replied:

'I felt us going up, lady, just as my master told me, flying through the region of fire, and I wanted to peep out from under my blindfold, though when I asked my master for his permission he wouldn't let me – but I'm a bit on the curious side, keen to know what I'm not supposed to know, so on the sly and so no one would see me I pulled the blindfold aside next to my nose and looked down towards the earth, and it didn't seem any bigger than a mustard seed, and the men walking around on it were hardly any bigger than hazelnuts – so you can see how high up we must have been by then.'

To this the Duchess replied:

'Mind what you're saying, Sancho my friend: it seems that you didn't see the earth at all, but only the men walking on it; for clearly, if the earth looked like a mustard seed, and each man looked like a hazelnut, one man alone would have covered the entire earth.'

'That's true enough,' Sancho replied, 'but I got a side view, and saw all of it like that.'

'Look here, Sancho,' said the Duchess, 'a side view doesn't show everything of what one is looking at.'

'I don't know about all this looking,' Sancho replied, 'all I do know is that it'd be a good idea if your ladyship realized that since we were flying by magic, by magic I could see all the earth and all the men, whichever way I looked. And if you don't believe that, you won't believe this either – when I pulled the blindfold aside next to my eyebrows, I saw I was so close to the sky there weren't a couple of handsbreadths separating us, so I can swear, lady, it's really really big. And, as it so happened, we were going along by the side of the Seven Sisters, that we also call the Seven Little Goats in my part of the world, and I swear to God and my immortal soul that having been as I was a goatherd as a little lad, as soon as I saw them I felt the urge to go and play with them a bit. And if I hadn't satisfied that urge I reckon I'd have burst. So what am I going to do about it then? Without a word to a soul, or to my master either, I slipped as quiet as quiet from off Clavileño and I went to play with the goats, and they're as pretty as petunias or as flowers, for nearly three-quarters of an hour, and Clavileño didn't budge an inch from where it was standing.'

'And while the worthy Sancho was amusing himself with the goats,' the Duke asked, 'how was Don Quixote amusing himself?'

To which Don Quixote replied:

'Since all these affairs and all these events are so out of the ordinary course of nature, it is not surprising that Sancho speaks as he does. For my part I can say that I did not peep out from behind my blindfold, either upwards or downwards, and that I did not see the sky, the earth, the sea or the shore. It is true, however, that I felt I was passing through the region of the air, and was indeed coming very close to the region of fire, but I cannot believe that we went any further than that, because the region of fire lies between the sphere of the moon and the upper region of the air, so we could not have reached the sphere where the Seven Little Goats, as Sancho calls them, are located, without being burned to cinders; and since we did not go up in flames, either Sancho is lying or Sancho is dreaming.'

'I'm not lying and I'm not dreaming either,' Sancho retorted. 'If you people don't believe me, just ask me what those goats look like, and you'll see from my answer whether I'm telling the truth or not.'

'Go ahead, then, Sancho,' said the Duchess.

'Two of them,' Sancho replied, 'are green, two are red, two are blue and one's a mixture.'

'That's a new kind of goat,' said the Duke, 'and in this region of the earth such colours don't exist – by which I mean to say that goats of such colours don't exist.'

'That's obvious enough,' said Sancho. 'You'd expect there to be a difference between the goats of the sky and the goats of the earth.'

'Tell me, Sancho,' the Duke asked, 'were any of those goats wearing nice long horns?'

'No, sir,' Sancho replied, 'but then I've heard it said that none of that sort ever get beyond the horns of the moon.'

They didn't care to ask him anything else about his journey, because he seemed to be in the mood to roam throughout the heavens and give an account of everything that happened in them, without ever having stirred from the garden.

This was the end of the adventure of the Dolorous Duenna, which gave the Duke and Duchess so much to laugh about, not just at the time but throughout their lives, and gave Sancho enough to have talked about for centuries, if only he had lived that long; and Don Quixote went up to him and whispered into his ear:

'Sancho, since you want people to believe what you saw in the sky, I want you to believe what I saw in the Cave of Montesinos. I say no more.'

CHAPTER XLII

About the advice that Don Quixote gave Sancho Panza
before he went to govern his island, together with other
carefully considered matters

The Duke and Duchess were so delighted with the successful and amusing outcome of the adventure of the Dolorous Duenna that they decided to continue with their jest, seeing that they had such a suitable subject, which ensured that it would be taken in earnest; and so, having told their servants and tenants how to behave to Sancho during his governorship of the promised island, on the day following Clavileño's flight the Duke told Sancho to dress and make himself ready to go and be a governor, because his islanders were yearning for him as for rain during a drought. Sancho bowed and said:

'Ever since I came down from the heavens and ever since I looked down from the top of them at the earth and saw it was so small, that great urge I had to be a governor has been cooling off a bit – what's so marvellous about ruling over a mustard seed, and what's so lordly or important about governing half a dozen men the size of hazelnuts? Because it seemed to me there weren't any more than that on the whole earth. If Your Lordship could see your way to giving me a little bit of heaven, even if only a couple of miles or so of it, I'd be happier with that than with the biggest island in the world.'

'Look here, friend Sancho,' the Duke replied, 'I can't give anyone a bit of heaven, not even an inch of it – for God alone such graces and favours are reserved. I'm giving you what I can give you, a real live island, round and well-proportioned, most extraordinarily fertile, where if you play your cards right you can win both the riches of the earth and the riches of heaven.'

'All right then,' Sancho replied, 'let's have that there island, and I'll do my best to be such a governor that I get to heaven in spite of all the rogues standing in my way. Not because of any craving to leave my proper station and get above myself, mind, but just because of this urge I've got to find out what it feels like to be a governor.'

'Once you try it, Sancho,' said the Duke, 'you'll give your right arm to continue, because it's a splendid thing to issue orders and to be obeyed. And depend upon it, when your master becomes an emperor, about which there's not the slightest doubt whatsoever, to judge from the way in which his affairs are developing, it won't be easy to oust him from the position, and he'll be grieved to the depths of his soul that so many years elapsed before he became one.'

'To my mind, sir,' replied Sancho, 'it must always be good to be in charge, even if only of a herd of goats.'

'You're a man after my own heart, Sancho, you have such a fine understanding,' the Duke replied, 'and I'm sure you'll be as good a governor as your sound sense promises, so let's leave it at that; and remember that tomorrow, without fail, you're to go to govern your island, and this afternoon you'll be fitted out with the proper uniform that you're to wear, and with everything else necessary for your departure.'

'They can dress me up as they please,' said Sancho. 'Whatever clothes they put me in I'll still be Sancho Panza.'

'Quite so,' said the Duke, 'but one's clothes must suit the position that one occupies, because it wouldn't be right for a lawyer to go around dressed as a soldier, or a soldier as a priest. You, Sancho, will go dressed half as a scholar and half as a captain, because on the island I'm giving you, arms are needed as much as letters, and letters as much as arms.'

'Letters,' replied Sancho, 'aren't exactly my strong point, seeing as how I still don't even know my ABC – though I do remember that big cross on the first page of the primer, and that's enough to be a good governor. As for arms, I'll fight with the ones I'm given till I fall, and then God's will be done.'

'With such a good memory,' said the Duke, 'Sancho can't possibly go wrong.'

And now they were joined by Don Quixote, and when he learned what was happening and how soon Sancho was going away to be governor, with the Duke's permission he took his squire by the hand and went with him to his room, to advise him about how to behave in office. Once they were in the room Don Quixote shut the door behind him and almost pushed Sancho down into a chair by his side; and in a tranquil voice he said:

'I give infinite thanks to heaven, Sancho my friend, that before I myself have met with any prosperity, good luck has come to find and favour you. I, who was confiding the payment of your services to my own future good fortune, am still at the beginning of my advancement, and you, long before your time and contrary to all reasonable expectation, are rewarded with your heart's desire. Others bribe, importune, solicit, rise early, entreat, persist, and still do not achieve their aim; and then along comes some other fellow and, without the faintest idea about how it has happened, he finds himself occupying the position that so many had been seeking. And here that proverb is to the point: Fortune to one is mother, to another is stepmother. As far as I am concerned, you are, without the slightest shadow of doubt, a dunderhead, yet without rising early or staying up late, or taking any trouble whatsoever, thanks only to some of the spirit of knight-errantry that has rubbed off on to you, you find yourself the governor of an island no less, just like that. I say all this, Sancho, so that you do not attribute the favour you have received to your own merits, but rather give thanks to God, who disposes matters with such benevolence, and next you must give thanks to the greatness inherent in the profession of knight-errantry. So with your heart ready to believe what I have told you, pay attention, my son, to this your Cato, whose desire it is to advise you and be the guide to lead you to a safe harbour from this stormy ocean into which you are about to venture; for these positions of great responsibility are nothing but a deep gulf of confusion.

'First, my son, you must fear God, for in the fear of God lies all wisdom, and if you are wise you cannot ever err.

'Secondly, you must always remember who you are, and try to know yourself, which is the most difficult knowledge of all to acquire. Knowing yourself will stop you from puffing yourself up as did the frog that wanted to be the equal of the ox; because if you do this the fact that you were once a swineherd will remind you of your folly, just as the peacock's foul feet make it ashamed of its pride in its fair feathers.'[1]

'True enough,' Sancho replied, 'but that was when I was a lad. Later, once I'd grown up a bit, it was geese I kept not pigs. But to my mind all this hasn't got anything to do with it, because not all governors are descended from kings.'

'True,' Don Quixote replied, 'and for this reason those governors who are not of noble extraction should temper the solemnity appropriate to their position with a gentle mildness, exercised with prudence, to deliver them from slanderous gossip, from which no station in life is exempt. Glory in your humble stock, Sancho, and do not be ashamed to say that you are descended from peasants; because when people see that this does not embarrass you, nobody will try to make you embarrassed about it; and take pride in being a humble and virtuous man rather than a lofty and sinful one. There are innumerable men who, born of low stock, have risen to the highest positions, both pontifical and imperial, and of this I could provide you with enough examples to weary you. For look here, Sancho, if you make virtue your method, and you take pride in doing virtuous deeds, you will not have to envy those descended from lords and noblemen; because blood is inherited, and virtue is acquired, and virtue has in itself a value that blood lacks. This being so, as it clearly is, if any of your relations go to visit you while you are on your island, do not turn them away or humiliate them; on the contrary, you must make them welcome, lavish attentions on them and give them royal treatment; for in this way you will please God, who wants nobody to disdain what he has created, and you will be doing what the harmony of nature requires of you.

'If you take your wife with you (because it is not a good idea for those who govern for long periods to be without their wives), teach her, instruct her, polish all that natural coarseness off her, because everything that is gained by an intelligent governor is often lost and wasted by a foolish, boorish wife. If by any chance you are widowed (something that could well happen), and thanks to your high office you acquire a better wife, do not take one to act as your fishing rod and hook, the friar's cowl left conveniently open on his shoulder; for verily I say unto you, everything the judge's wife receives has to be included by her husband in his final account of his doings, and then he will pay fourfold in death for all sums not accounted for in life.[2]

'Never make your whim the measure of the law, a step popular among ignorant people who think that they are clever.

'Let the poor man's tears move you to greater compassion, but not to greater justice, than the rich man's allegations. Try to discover the truth as much among the rich man's gifts and promises as among the poor man's sobs and entreaties.

'Whenever leniency can and should play its part, do not apply the full rigour of the law to the delinquent, for the cruel judge does not enjoy a better renown than the compassionate one. If you do bend the rod of justice, let it not be with the weight of a gift but with the weight of mercy.

'When you have to judge a case involving one of your enemies, forget all about your grievances and concentrate on the facts of the matter. Do not let your own feelings blind you to others' claims; for most of the mistakes that you make will not be reversible, and if they are it will be at the cost of your reputation or even of your pocket.

'If a beautiful woman comes to seek justice, turn your eyes away from her tears and your ears from her lamentations, and ponder over the merits of her plea, unless you want your reason to be drowned in her tears and your integrity in her lamentations.

'If you are going to have a man punished with deeds, do not batter him with words, because the suffering that the wretch is to undergo is enough, without the addition of any vilification.

'Think of the culprit whose case comes before you as one worthy of pity, subject to all the propensities of our depraved nature, and, as far as you can, without prejudice to the contrary party, be compassionate and lenient; for although all God's attributes are equally excellent, mercy shines out and catches the eye more than justice.

'If you follow these rules and precepts, Sancho, your life will be long, your fame eternal, your rewards abundant, your happiness indescribable; you will marry your children to whomsoever you please, they and your grandchildren will have titles, you will live in peace and enjoy everyone's approbation; and as you come to the end of your days death will overtake you in your tranquil, ripe old age, and your great-great-grandchildren will close your eyes with their tender, delicate little hands.

'The instructions I have given you so far are for the embellishment of your soul; listen now to instructions for the embellishment of your body.'

CHAPTER XLIII

About the second set of instructions that Don Quixote gave Sancho Panza

Who could have heard this discourse of Don Quixote's and not considered him to be a man of sound mind and excellent disposition? But, as has so often been pointed out in the course of this great history, he only talked nonsense when people led him on to the subject of chivalry, and when discussing all other matters he showed a clear and confident understanding, so that his actions were always discrediting his ideas, and his ideas his actions; but in these second instructions that he gave Sancho he showed a ready wit and raised both his good sense and his madness to a high level. Sancho listened with rapt attention, trying to store his master's advice in his memory, because he was determined to follow it and with its help bring the pregnancy of his government to a successful delivery. And Don Quixote went on to say:

'As regards your government of yourself and your household, Sancho, my first piece of advice is to be clean, and to cut your fingernails, and not to let them grow long, as some people do, moved by their ignorance to believe that long nails make their hands look beautiful, as if those appendages, those excrescences that they leave uncut had any right to be called fingernails at all, because they are more like the talons of a kestrel: a monstrous and filthy abuse.

'Do not go around, Sancho, with your clothes loose and flapping about you; for untidy dress is a sign of a lackadaisical spirit, unless this slovenliness and lassitude is a form of cunning, as it was thought to be in the case of Julius Caesar.

'Put out discreet feelers to discover what your new position might be worth; and if it will allow you to give your servants liveries, let them be modest and practical ones, not spectacular and showy, and divide them between your servants and the poor: what I mean to say is that if you have a mind to give clothes to six pages, give them to three pages and three poor men, and in this way you will have pages on earth and pages in heaven. This new system of giving livery is one to which the vainglorious cannot aspire.

'Do not eat garlic or onions, so that people do not notice from your smell that you are a peasant.

'Walk sedately, speak with deliberation, but not so that you seem to be listening to yourself; for affectation is always bad.

'Eat little for lunch and even less for dinner, because the health of the entire body is forged in the smithy of the stomach. Be temperate in your drinking, and bear in mind that wine keeps neither secrets nor promises. Be careful, Sancho, not to chew on both sides of your mouth at the same time, and do not eructate when in company.'

'I don't know what eructate means,' said Sancho.

And Don Quixote said:

' "To eructate", Sancho, means "to belch", and this is one of the most vulgar words in our language, even though it is very expressive; so well-spoken people have had recourse to Latin, and they now call belching eructating, and belches eructations; and if certain others do not understand these terms it does not matter much, because usage will make them more and more familiar, so that they will be readily understood, and this enriches the language, which is in the control of the people and of usage.'

'Honestly, sir,' said Sancho, 'one of the warnings and pieces of advice that I'm planning to keep in my memory is that one about not belching, because it's something I often do.'

'Eructating, Sancho, not belching,' said Don Quixote.

'Eructating's what I'll say from now on,' Sancho replied, 'and I promise I won't forget.'

'Also, Sancho, you must not mix that multitude of proverbs into everything you say; for although proverbs are brief maxims, you often drag them in so inappropriately that they seem more like nonsenses.'

'Only God can do anything about that,' Sancho replied, 'because I know more proverbs than will fill a book, and so many of them come crowding into my mouth when I'm talking that they're all fighting against each other in there to get out, but my tongue just pushes out the first ones it comes across, even if they aren't all that apt. But I'll be careful from now on to say the ones that go well with the gravity of my job, because where there's plenty to put in the pot the dinner is soon enough got, and he who shuffles doesn't cut, and the man who rings the alarm has put himself furthest from harm, and it's a clever one who can have his cake and eat it.'

'That's right, Sancho!' said Don Quixote. 'Cram your proverbs in, thread them together, string them out; nobody's going to stop you! Mother whips me, and I whip my top! I'm telling you to avoid proverbs, and in one instant you've delivered a whole litany of them with as much to do with what we're talking about as walking down a blind alley at midnight. Look here, Sancho, I'm not saying that a proverb's a bad thing when it's relevant; but loading everything that one says with them, stringing them together without rhyme or reason, makes one's discourse flimsy and vulgar.

'When you ride on a horse, do not lean back in the saddle, or stiffen and stretch your legs so that they stick out from the horse's flanks, but do not relax so much, either, that you look as though you were riding your dun; for going on horseback turns some men into knights and others into stable-boys.

'Moderate your sleep; for he who does not rise with the sun does not enjoy the day; and remember, Sancho, that diligence is the mother of good fortune, and that its opposite, sloth, never attained any worthwhile goal.

'And although this last piece of advice that I am going to give you does not contribute to the embellishment of your body, I want you to bear it constantly in mind, for I believe that it will be of no less use to you than those I have given you so far: and it is that you must never become involved in arguments about pedigrees, not at least when they are being compared with each other, because in such comparisons one family is bound to emerge as superior, and you will be hated by the family that you disparage, and you will not be rewarded in any way by the family that you exalt.

'As for clothes, you should wear full breeches, a long coat, a somewhat longer cloak; knee-breeches most certainly not, because these are suitable neither for knights nor for governors.

'And this, Sancho, is all the advice that occurs to me for the moment; time will move on, and my future instructions will be designed to suit the event, so long as you take care to keep me informed about your circumstances.'

'Sir,' said Sancho, 'I can well see that everything you've said is good and holy and helpful, but what use is it going to be if I can't remember any of it? It's true that the bits about not letting my nails grow long and about marrying again if I get the chance won't slip my mind, but as for all the rest of that great mish-mash and hotch-potch you came out with, I can't and shan't remember any more about it than about last year's clouds, so it'll have to be given me in writing, because although I can't read or write I'll hand it over to my confessor so he can hammer it into my head when needed.'

'Ah, sinner that I am!' replied Don Quixote. 'How ill it becomes a governor not to be able to read or write! For I would have you know, Sancho, that if a man cannot read, or is left-handed, this argues one of two things: either he was the son of the very lowest and wretchedest of parents, or he was so wicked and badly behaved that neither good habits nor a good education could find their way into him. This defect of yours is a very grave one, and so I should like you to learn to sign your name at least.'

'I can sign my name all right,' Sancho replied, 'because when I was steward of the confraternity back in the village I learned to draw some letters like the ones men mark their bundles with, and people said they spelt my name – and anyway I'll pretend I've hurt my right hand and I'll make someone else sign for me, because there's a remedy for all things but death, and I'll have the power and I'll have the cudgel so I'll do whatever I like, and besides, the judge's son goes safe to his trial. And when I'm governor, which is higher up than judge – roll up, roll up, and take a look at her! Oh yes, they can just try pooh-poohing me and calling me names, they can, because if they think they're coming out to shear me they'll find themselves going back shorn, and well thrives he whom God loves, and rich men's nonsense passes for wisdom in this world, and if

I'm rich, a governor and generous with it, as I plan to be, nobody will find anything wrong with me. Oh yes, I'm going to make myself all honey, aren't I, so the flies can eat me up, and you're worth what you've got, as my old grandma used to say, and a rich man can do no wrong.'

'God damn you, Sancho!' Don Quixote broke in. 'Sixty thousand devils take you and your proverbs! You've spent the last hour stringing them together, and torturing me with every single one. You mark my words, these proverbs of yours will take you to the gallows one day; your subjects will remove you from power because of them, or rise up in rebellion. Tell me, where do you find them all, you ignoramus, and how do you bring them to bear on what you're saying, you blockhead? If I want to use one in an appropriate way I have to work and sweat as if I were digging a ditch.'

'For God's sake, master,' Sancho replied, 'what silly little things you do moan about. Why the devil get all worked up about me using my own property? Because I haven't got any more property or riches than proverbs and more proverbs. And I've just thought of a few more of them that would have fitted in here like pears in a basket, but I'd better not come out with them, because silence is golden.'

'No wonder you're poor, then, Sancho,' said Don Quixote, 'because you don't know what silence is, you're all gossip, gossip and more gossip; but in spite of all that I should like to know what are these proverbs that come to your mind as being relevant here, because I'm ransacking my memory, which is a good one, and I can't find any.'

'What could be better,' said Sancho, 'than "Never stick your thumb between two wisdom teeth", and "To 'Get out of my house' and 'What do you want with my wife?' there's no reply", and "Whether the pitcher strikes the stone or the stone the pitcher, it's bad for the pitcher", all of which really fit the bill? Nobody had better pick a quarrel with his governor or anyone else above him, because he'll get hurt, like anybody who puts his finger between two wisdom teeth, and even if they aren't wisdom teeth so long as they're teeth it comes to the same thing. And to what your governor says there's no answer, any more than to "Get out of my house" and "What do you want with my wife?" And as for the pitcher and the stone, a blind man can see that. So anyone who can see a mote in another's eye had better see the beam in his own,[1] otherwise people will start talking about the dead woman who was frightened of a corpse, and, as you well know, a fool knows more in his own house than a wise man in another's.'

'No, that at least is not true, Sancho,' Don Quixote replied, 'a fool knows nothing, either in his own house or in another's, for on a foundation of folly no edifice of good sense can ever be constructed. Let us leave it at that, Sancho: if you govern badly, the blame will be yours and the shame will be mine; but I comfort myself with the knowledge that I have done my duty in advising you as sincerely and as sensibly as I can; and so I have discharged my obligation and kept my promise. May God guide you, Sancho, and govern you while you govern, and rid me of this fear I still have that you're going to turn the whole island on its head, something I could avoid by telling the Duke all about you: by informing him that that fat little body of yours is nothing but a sackful of proverbs and mischief.'

'Sir,' Sancho replied, 'if you don't think I'm up to this governing, I'll give it up here and now, because I'm more concerned about the smallest snippet of my soul than the whole length of my body, and I can stay alive as plain Sancho on bread and onions just as well as I can as governor on partridges and capons, and what's more when we're asleep we're all the same, great and small, rich and poor. And if you think about it you'll realize that you were the one who put me up to this here governing lark in the first place, because I don't know any more about governing islands than a vulture does, and if you think I'm going to sell my soul to the devil for the sake of being a governor let me tell you I'm more interested in going as Sancho to heaven than as a governor to hell.'

'By God, Sancho,' said Don Quixote, 'I think you're worthy to be governor of a thousand islands just for those last few words you've spoken: you're a good-natured fellow, and, without that, no amount of knowledge is of any use; commend yourself to God, and try not to err in your main resolve; what I mean is that you must always set out with the clear objective of doing right in every matter with which you deal, for heaven always favours good intentions. And now let's go to eat, because I believe these good people are waiting for us.'

CHAPTER XLIV

*How Sancho Panza was taken to his governorship,
and the strange adventure that happened to Don Quixote
in the castle*

It is said that in the original manuscript of this history one reads that when Cide Hamete came to write this chapter his translator did not render it as the Moor had written it, with some sort of complaint against himself for having undertaken such a dry and limited history as this one about Don Quixote, always feeling himself restricted to talking about him and Sancho, never daring to venture out into any digressions or more serious and entertaining episodes; and Cide Hamete added that to have his mind, his hand and his pen always constrained to writing about one subject and speaking through the mouths of so few characters was intolerable drudgery, which yielded nothing to the author's advantage, and that to avoid this problem he had in the first part had recourse to certain tales, like those of *Inappropriate Curiosity* and the *Captive Captain*, which stand, as it were, apart from the main story – although the other tales narrated there are events in which Don Quixote himself was involved and which could not be omitted. Cide Hamete also thought, he says, that many people, with all their attention engrossed by the deeds of Don Quixote, might not have any attention left for the tales, and might leaf through them in haste or exasperation, without noticing their elegance and artistry, which would have been plain to see had they been published by themselves and not as mere adjuncts to Don Quixote's mad antics and Sancho's tomfoolery. And so in this second part he decided not to include any disconnected or even tagged-on tales, but rather some similar-looking episodes developing, however, out of the events of the true history itself, and even these would be limited in number and told in no more words than were strictly necessary; and since he restricts himself to the narrow confines of the narrative, even though he has the ability, capacity and intelligence to deal with the entire universe, he begs not to be rewarded with scorn for his labours, and to be praised not for what he writes but for what he has refrained from writing.

And then the history continues, saying that once Don Quixote had finished eating on the day he gave Sancho his advice, he handed him that very afternoon a written version so that he could get someone to read it to him; but no sooner had Sancho received the papers than he dropped them and they found their way into the hands of the Duke, who showed them to the Duchess, and the two of them were struck by new astonishment at Don Quixote's madness and ingenuity; and so, to continue with their hoaxes, that afternoon they sent Sancho off with a great retinue to the town that for him was to be an island. And it so happened that the man in charge of this operation was a butler of the Duke's, very intelligent and very humorous (for there can be no humour without intelligence), who had played the part of the Countess Trifaldi with such panache; and thanks to these qualities, and to being coached by his master and mistress in handling Sancho, he had been so wonderfully successful. And as soon as Sancho saw this butler he thought he was looking at the face of Trifaldi herself, and turning to his master he said:

'Sir, the devil can whisk me off in two shakes of a lamb's tail from where I'm standing now if you don't admit that this butler of the Duke's here present has got exactly the same face as the Dolorous Duenna.'

Don Quixote took a close look at the butler, and then replied to Sancho:

'There will be no need for the devil to whisk you off, Sancho, with or without the shakes of a lamb's tail (a reference that I fail to understand); for the Dolorous Duenna's face is indeed the butler's, but this does not mean to say that the butler is the Dolorous Duenna; for if he were, this would imply a major contradiction, and now is not the time to make such enquiries, which would take us into inextricable labyrinths. Believe me, my friend, we must pray most earnestly to Our Lord to deliver us from wicked sorcerers and evil enchanters.'

'This isn't some joke I'm playing on you, sir,' Sancho replied, 'I heard him speak a little while back and it sounded exactly as if it was Trifaldi's voice I had in my ears. All right, I'll shut up about it, but I'll be keeping my eyes peeled from now on to see if he gives any other signs that back up or do away with this suspicion of mine.'

'Yes, that is what you must do, Sancho,' said Don Quixote, 'and you must keep me informed about everything you discover concerning this matter, and indeed about everything else that happens to you in your government.'

So off Sancho went at last, accompanied by a great retinue. He was dressed in scholar's clothes, and over them he wore an ample topcoat of tawny watered camlet with a cap of the same material, and he was riding with Arab-style short stirrups on a mule; and behind him, by order of the Duke, came his dun in asinine accoutrements of flaming silk. Sancho would turn his head every so often to gaze at his ass, in whose company he felt so happy that he wouldn't have changed places with the Emperor of Germany. On saying goodbye to the Duke and Duchess he had kissed their hands, and had accepted his master's blessing, given with tears and received with a whimper.

Now let the good Sancho go in peace and prosperity, kind reader, and be prepared for two bushels of laughter, which is what you can expect when you learn how he behaved in office, and meanwhile pay attention to what happened to his master that night; for if it doesn't make you laugh, at least you will spread your lips in a simian grin, because Don Quixote's doings have to be received with either astonishment or laughter.

It is recorded, then, that no sooner had Sancho left than Don Quixote began to miss him, and if he'd been able to revoke Sancho's commission and deprive him of his governorship he would have done so. The Duchess noticed how melancholy he was and asked him why he was sad: if it was because of Sancho's absence, there were squires, duennas and maids in her house to wait upon him and satisfy his every desire.

'The truth is, my lady,' Don Quixote replied, 'that I do miss Sancho, but this is not the principal motive for my appearing to be sad; and of all the offers that Your Excellency is making me I only accept that of the goodwill with which they are made and, for the rest, I beg Your Excellency to allow me to wait upon myself in my own room.'

'Truly, Don Quixote sir,' said the Duchess, 'this cannot be – you'll be waited on by four of my maids, as beautiful as flowers.'

'As far as I am concerned,' replied Don Quixote, 'they will not be flowers, but thorns stabbing my soul. They shall as soon enter or even approach my room as fly. If Your Grace insists on doing me unmerited favours, pray permit me to be alone, and to wait upon myself inside my own room, and to build a wall there between my desires and my virtue; I am unwilling to relinquish this habit for all the generosity that Your Grace wishes to extend to me. In short, I shall sleep in my clothes rather than allow anyone to undress me.'

'Say no more, Don Quixote sir, say no more,' the Duchess replied. 'For my part I assure you that I'll give orders that not one fly must enter your room, let alone a maid; I'm not the sort to bring about the impairment of Don Quixote's respectability, because from what I've been able to observe the most resplendent of his many virtues is his chastity. You undress and dress yourself alone and in your own way, however and whenever you like: there will be nothing to stop you, because in your room you will find all the chamber-pots needed by the person who sleeps behind locked doors, so that no call of nature will oblige you to open them. May the great Dulcinea del Toboso live for a thousand centuries, and may her name be spread over the entire surface of the globe, for meriting the love of such a brave and chaste knight; and may the benevolent heavens infuse into the heart of Sancho Panza, our governor, a desire to complete his self-punishment without delay, so that the world can again enjoy the beauty of such a splendid lady.'

To which Don Quixote said:

'Your Highness has spoken like the person you are; for no lady who is not excellent has any place in an excellent lady's mouth, and Dulcinea will be more fortunate and more famous throughout the globe because Your Grace has praised her than for all the praises that the most eloquent orators in the world could bestow upon her.'

'Well now, Don Quixote sir,' replied the Duchess, 'it's nearly time for dinner, and the Duke must be waiting; come with me and let's eat, and then you'll go early to bed; because your journey from Kandy yesterday wasn't such a short one that it didn't leave you feeling slightly shattered.'

'I do not feel at all shattered, my lady,' Don Quixote replied, 'because I would venture to swear to Your Grace that never in my life have I mounted a more sedate or easy-paced horse than Clavileño, and I really do not know what can have moved Malambruno to discard such a swift and graceful steed, and burn it like that, for no reason at all.'

'One can well imagine,' the Duchess replied, 'that he repented of the wrong he'd done to Trifaldi and company, and to other people as well, and of the evil deeds he must have committed as a sorcerer and enchanter, and therefore decided to do away with the tools of his trade; and that he burned Clavileño because it was the principal one of these, which made him most restless in his wanderings from land to land; and its burnt ashes and the trophy with the placard ensure that the great Don Quixote de la Mancha's valour lives eternally.'

Don Quixote thanked the Duchess again, and once he'd finished his dinner he retired alone to his room, not allowing anyone in to wait upon him: so fearful was he of finding opportunities that could induce or oblige him to abandon the chastity that he preserved for his lady Dulcinea's sake, with his thoughts always fixed on the virtue of Amadis, the flower and mirror of knights errant. He locked the door behind him and he undressed by the light of two wax candles, and, as he was taking off his stockings – such a disaster happened, so unworthy of such a personage! He burst out, not in sighs or anything else that could have thrown doubts upon the perfection of his manners, but rather in one of his stockings, where a couple of dozen stitches came undone, turning it into something resembling a window-lattice. The worthy gentleman was distraught, and he would have given an ounce of silver for a length of green silk: I say green because that was the colour of his stockings.

Here Benengeli exclaims:

'O poverty, poverty. I do not know what could have moved the great poet of Cordova to call you

Most holy, unappreciated gift![1]

Although I am a Moor, I well know, from conversations I have had with Christians, that holiness is made up of charity, humility, faith, obedience and poverty; but even allowing for all that, I do declare that anybody who can manage to be happy, being poor, must have much of God in him, unless it is that kind of poverty about which one of their greatest saints says: "Possess all things as if you did not possess them";[2] and this they call poverty of spirit; but you, that other poverty about which I am speaking – why do you choose to batter hidalgos and well-born people more than others? Why do you reduce them to smearing lampblack on their shoes, and to wearing coat-buttons some of which are of silk, others of twisted horsehair and others of glass? Why must their collars always be narrow, floppy and irregularly ruffled, rather than broad, starched and properly supported on a frame?'

In this detail it will be observed that the use of broad collars and starch is an ancient one. And he continues:

'What a wretch is the well-born man who feeds his honour by dining badly alone, making a hypocrite of the toothpick armed with which he goes out into the street after not having eaten anything that makes him need to use one! What a wretch, I repeat, is he whose honour is so easily alarmed that he thinks the patch on his shoe, the perspiration marks on his hat, the coarse threads in his cloak and the hunger in his stomach can be seen from a mile away!'

Such thoughts were revived in Don Quixote when the stitches came undone, but he was comforted when he saw that Sancho had left him some riding boots, which he decided to wear the next day. Finally he lay himself down, deep in thought and sorrowful, both because he was missing Sancho so much and because of the irreparable disaster to his stocking, which he wished he could have darned, even with silk of a different colour – one of the clearest signs of wretchedness that a hidalgo can give in the midst of his grinding penury. He blew out the candles, it was hot and he couldn't sleep, he got up and eased open the window, with a grille on it, looking out on to a beautiful garden, and as he opened it he heard people moving about and talking below him. He listened. The people started speaking louder, so that he could hear these words:

'Don't insist, O Emerencia, on my singing, because you know that ever since the moment this stranger entered the castle and my eyes alighted on him, I haven't been able to sing, but only weep; and, what's more, my mistress is such a light sleeper, and I shouldn't want her to find us here for all the treasure in the world. And even if she stays asleep and doesn't wake up, my song would be wasted if this new Aeneas, who has come to my land to make a mockery of me,³ also stays asleep and doesn't wake up to hear it.'

'Don't keep saying that, dear Altisidora,' was the reply, 'I'm sure the Duchess is indeed asleep, and everyone else in the house too, except the lord of your heart and rouser of your soul: just now I heard him opening the window with the grille in his room, so he must be awake. Sing, my darling sufferer, softly and quietly to the sound of your harp, and if the Duchess hears us we'll blame the heat.'

'That isn't the point, O Emerencia!' Altisidora replied, 'but rather that I shouldn't want my song to reveal the secrets of my heart so that I'm thought a fickle and flighty maid by those who don't know about the mighty force of love. But come what will: better a blush on your face than a blot in your heart.'

And as she said this Don Quixote heard the gentle tones of a harp. He marvelled, because in that instant his memory was crowded with the infinite number of similar adventures involving windows, grilles and gardens, serenades, sweet nothings and fainting fits that he'd read about in his vain books of chivalry. He immediately assumed that one of the Duchess's maidservants was in love with him, and that her modesty forced her to keep her passion secret; he was afraid of being conquered by her, but he made a firm resolution not to yield and, commending himself with all his soul and all his might to his lady Dulcinea del Toboso, he decided to listen to the music; and so, to let them know that he was there, he pretended to sneeze, which gave the maids great pleasure because they wanted nothing better than for Don Quixote to be listening. Now that she'd run her fingers over her harp's strings and tuned them, Altisidora began singing this ballad:

> O you, stretched out upon your bed
> In sheets of holland, yawning
> And sleeping soundly as a log
> All night long till morning,
>   The bravest and the best of knights
> That Mancha ever bore,
> More pure and simple, finer far
> Than all Arabia's ore:
>   Now listen to a mournful maid,
> Full grown and partly whole:
> The light of your two blazing suns
> Has fired her very soul.
>   You roam in search of derring-do
> But find another's plight;
> You deal out wounds and then refuse
> To cure and put them right.
>   So now you tell me, valiant youth
> – And may your pangs be sped –
> Were you conceived on Libyan sands?

On Jaca's[4] mountains bred?
    And was it snakes that suckled you?
And was your babyhood
Tended upon horrendous heights?
In the wildness of the wood?

    Your Dulcinea may well take pride,
So stout and strong and smart,
On conquering a fearsome beast,
Taming a tiger's heart.

    For this she will be far renowned
From Jarama to Henares,
Pisuerga to Arlanza, and
Tagus to Manzanares.[5]

    If only I could take her place
I'd gladly have her dressed
In a gown of mine, all trimmed with gold,
One of my very best.

    I'd love to be held in your arms
Or, sitting by your bed,
Caress your locks, and scratch away
The dandruff from your head.

    I ask too much, and don't deserve
So notable a grace;
To be allowed to scrub your feet
Is a humble woman's place.

    How many nightcaps I'd give you!
How many silver shoes!
How many damask breeches, and
Fine capes of many hues!

    How many pearls, and each so big
It's more a gall than a gem!
You'd call these pearls unique, except
There's such a lot of them.

    Don't gaze from your Tarpeian Rock
On this fire that's burning me,
O Mancha's Nero of the world,

Or fan it with cruelty.[6]
> I am a maid, a tender lass,
Not yet fifteen years old,
Just fourteen and three months I am,
I swear it on my soul.

> My legs are straight, I am not lame;
My arms are very sound;
My lily-white tresses are so long
They trail upon the ground;

> My nose is rather flat, it's true;
My mouth is aquiline;
My teeth, though, are of best topaz
And make my looks divine;

> My voice, you'll note, if listening,
Can well compete with any;
My character, I do declare,
Is quite as good as many:

> Such graces are your quiver's spoils;
Take them, or you'll be poorer;
A maiden in this house am I;
My name's Altisidora.

Here ended the song of the sore-wounded Altisidora, and here began the alarm of the tenderly wooed Don Quixote who, heaving a deep sigh, said to himself:

'To think that I'm such an unhappy knight errant that not a maid who sets eyes upon me fails to fall in love with me! To think that the peerless Dulcinea del Toboso is so hapless that she isn't allowed to enjoy alone this incomparable constancy of mine! What do you want of her, you queens? Why do you persecute her, you empresses? Why do you hound her, you fourteen- and fifteen-year-old maids? Allow the poor wretch to rejoice, glory and triumph in the lot that love has bestowed on her with the conquest of my heart and the surrender of my soul! Look here, you enamoured crew: for Dulcinea alone I am puff pastry and almond paste, and for all other women I am flint; for her I am honey, and for you aloes; for me Dulcinea alone is beautiful, intelligent, virtuous, graceful and well-born, and all other women are ugly, stupid, immoral and low-born; to be hers, and no other's, nature brought me into this world. As for Altisidora, let her weep or let her sing; as for that little madam whose fault it was that I was thrashed in the castle of the enchanted Moor, let her despair: Dulcinea's must I be, harassed, embarrassed, pure, well-born and chaste, in spite of all the powers of sorcery in the world.'

And with this he slammed the window shut and, indignant and sorrowful, as if some disaster had overtaken him, he lay down on his bed, where we shall leave him for the time being, because the great Sancho Panza is summoning us, anxious to make a start on his famous governing.

CHAPTER XLV

About how the great Sancho Panza took possession of his island, and began to govern it

O perpetual discoverer of the Antipodes, torch of the world, eye of heaven, sweet swayer of wine-coolers, Thymbrius[1] here, Phoebus there, now archer, now physician, father of poetry, inventor of music; O you who always rise and never set, despite all appearances! On you I call, O Sun, with whose help man begets man; on you I call to help me and lighten the darkness of my wits so that I can proceed step by step through the narration of the great Sancho Panza's governorship; for without you I feel tepid, feeble and uncertain.

Let me say, then, that Sancho arrived together with his retinue at a town of about five thousand inhabitants, one of the best towns that the Duke owned. He was told that it was called the Island of Barataria, which is to say Hankypanky Island – this was perhaps because of the way in which he'd acceded to power, though it's also true that the name of the town was Baratario. The town was a walled one, and when Sancho reached the gates the entire council came out to receive him; the bells were rung and all the inhabitants showed every sign of joy, and he was taken amidst great pomp to the parish church to give thanks to God, and then in a comical ceremony he was given the keys of the town and made

Perpetual Governor of the Island of Barataria. The new governor's clothes, beard, corpulence and shortness amazed all those who weren't in the secret, and even all those who were – and of these there were many. Next they took him out of the church and into the courtroom, where they sat him on the judge's bench, and the Duke's butler said:

'It is an ancient custom on this island, my lord Governor, that the man who comes to take possession of this famous island must answer a question that is put to him and that has to be a somewhat complicated and difficult one; and from the reply the islanders can gauge their new governor's wits and, as a consequence, either rejoice in his arrival or bewail it.'

While the butler was speaking, Sancho was peering at the many large letters written on the wall in front of him, and not being able to read he asked what all those paintings on that there wall were. The reply was:

'Sir, it is an inscription recording the day on which Your Lordship took possession of this island, and it says "On this day, the —th day of the month of — in the year —, Don Sancho Panza took possession of this island, and long may he enjoy it."'

'And who's this man they call Don Sancho Panza?' Sancho asked.

'Why, it's Your Lordship!' the butler replied. 'The only Panza who has ever set foot on this island is the one sitting on that bench.'

'Look you here then, my man,' said Sancho. 'I'm not a don, and there's never been one of them in my family – plain Sancho Panza is what I'm called and Sancho was what my father was called and Sancho was what my grandfather was called before him, and they were all Panzas without any dons tagged on in front or behind, and I'm thinking there must be more dons on this island than pebbles – but enough said, God in heaven knows what I mean, and it could even be that if I last five minutes in this job I'll give all these dons a good thinning-out, because there must be such a swarm of them as to be as much of a nuisance as mosquitoes. Now the butler can go ahead with his question, and I'll answer the best I can, and the islanders can bewail or not just as they please.'

At this point two men walked into the courtroom, one of them in farmer's clothes and the other in those of a tailor, with his scissors in his hand, and the tailor said:

'My lord Governor, me and this farmer here come before you because yesterday he went to my shop (I'm a qualified tailor, begging your pardon and God be blessed), and he put a piece of cloth into my hands and asked:

' "Is there enough cloth here, sir, to make a hood?"

'I sized up the cloth and told him that there was. I was thinking that he was thinking, and I was right, that I was planning to filch some of the cloth, on the grounds of his suspicious nature and us tailors' bad reputation, and his reply was to ask me to see if there was enough cloth for two hoods. I guessed what he was up to and I told him that there was, and he went on riding the hobby-horse of his first nasty suspicion and kept adding hoods to which I kept adding yeses till we reached five, and a few moments ago he came for them. I have them ready for him, but he won't pay me for my work – quite the opposite, he wants me to pay him, or give him back his cloth.'

'Is this all true, my man?' asked Sancho.

'Yes, sir,' the farmer replied, 'but now make him show you the hoods he made for me.'

'With pleasure,' said the tailor. And pulling his hand out from under his cape he displayed five hoods, one on each finger, and said:

'Here are the five hoods that this character requires, and I swear to God that there wasn't any cloth left over, and I'm happy for my work to be examined by the official inspectors of the trade.'

Everyone laughed at the profusion of hoods and the novelty of the case. Sancho pondered for a while, and said:

'I don't think there's any need for long delays in this case – what's needed is an on-the-spot commonsense verdict, so my decision is that the tailor will forfeit his pay and the farmer his cloth, and the hoods will be given to the prisoners in jail, and there's an end to it.'

If the decision about the herdsman's purse was to fill the spectators with amazement, this one excited their laughter; but the governor's orders were obeyed. Two old men now appeared before him; one of them was carrying a cane that he used as a walking stick, and the one without a cane said:

'Sir, a good while ago I lent this fellow ten gold escudos, as a special favour, on condition that he repaid them when I asked for them. For a long time I didn't ask for them, so as not to put him in even greater difficulties than he was in when I lent him them; but it seemed to me that he wasn't as eager as he might be to pay me back, so I've asked him for my money again and again, and not only does he not repay me – he denies the debt and says I never lent him the ten escudos in the first place, and that if I did lend him them he's returned them. There aren't any witnesses to the loan or the repayment – because he hasn't repaid me. I'd like you to take his oath, and if he swears he has repaid me I'll let him off the debt before the world and before God.'

'And you, old man with the stick, what do you say to all this?' said Sancho.

To which the old man replied:

'Sir, I admit that he did lend them to me, so if you'll lower your staff of office – since he makes it all depend on my oath – I'll swear I've really and truly repaid him.'

The governor lowered his staff, and as he did so the old man with the stick handed it to the other old man to hold while he was swearing his oath, as if it were a great encumbrance, and then he placed his hand on the cross on the top of the staff and said it was true he'd been lent the ten escudos he was being asked for; but he'd returned them into the hands of the other man, who didn't realize this and kept asking for them back. This prompted the great governor to ask the creditor what he had to say to that; and what he said was that his debtor must of course be telling the truth, because he considered him to be an upright citizen and a good Christian, and he himself must have forgotten all about how and when the money had been returned, and he would never ask for it again. The debtor took his stick back, bowed and left the courtroom. When Sancho saw him hurrying away like that, and when he considered the patience of the plaintiff, he bent his head over his chest, placed the index finger of his right hand along the side of his nose and up to his eyebrows, and sat there in this pondering position for a while, after which he looked up and ordered the old man with the stick to be brought back. This was done, and Sancho said:

'Give me your stick, my good man – I need it.'

'With pleasure,' the old man replied, 'here you are, sir.'

And he handed it over. Sancho took it, gave it to the other old man, and said:

'Now you can go, and God be with you – you've been repaid now.'

'What, sir?' the old man replied. 'Is this cane worth ten gold escudos, then?'

'Yes, it is,' said the governor, 'or I'm the greatest blockhead in the world. Now they'll see whether I've got what it takes to govern a kingdom.'

And he ordered the cane to be split open, there in front of them all. This was done, and inside it they found ten gold escudos. Everyone was amazed, and regarded their governor as a second Solomon. He was asked how he'd deduced that the ten escudos were in the cane, and he replied that when he saw the old man give his stick to his adversary to hold while he swore that he really and truly had returned them and, once he'd finished, ask for it back again, it occurred to him that the requested payment must be in there. From which you could deduce that even though governors might be fools, sometimes God guides them when they're reaching their decisions, and what's more he'd heard the village priest talking about a case just like it, and he himself had such a fine memory that if it wasn't for the fact that he forgot everything he wanted to remember, there wouldn't be another memory like it on the whole island. Finally the two old men left, one abashed and the other satisfied, all those present were lost in astonishment, and the man who was recording Sancho's words, deeds and movements couldn't make up his mind whether to regard and describe him as a simpleton or as a sage.

Once this case was concluded a woman burst in, dragging with her a man wearing the clothes of a wealthy herdsman, and she was screaming:

'Justice, my lord Governor, justice, and if I don't find it on earth I'll go up to heaven to look for it there! O my dear lord Governor, this wicked man caught me out in the fields, and he used my body as if it was a dirty rag, and, woe is me, he took away from me what I'd kept intact these twenty-three years and more, defending it against all and sundry; and there I was, always as unyielding as an oak tree, keeping myself as whole as a salamander in the flames, or as a tuft of wool on a bramble, just for this fellow here to come and make a clean sweep of my most precious asset.'

'That's yet to be found out — whether this fine fellow's sweep was a clean one or not,' said Sancho.

And turning to him he asked him what he had to say for himself in response to the woman's complaint. In a flutter of confusion the man replied:

'Gentlemen, I'm a poor herdsman dealing in pigs, begging your pardon, and this morning I was leaving this town after selling four of them, and in taxes and backhanders I had to cough up not much less than what they were worth. I was going back to my village, I came across this woman along the way and the devil, who's always messing and meddling, made us lie together. I paid her the usual amount but she wasn't satisfied with that, and she grabbed hold of me and wouldn't let go till she'd landed up with me here. She says I raped her, but she's lying, and I'll swear to that on oath – and that's the whole truth and I haven't kept the smallest scrap of it back.'

Then the governor asked him if he had any silver on him. He replied that he had about twenty ducats inside his shirt, in a leather purse. Sancho ordered him to produce his purse and give it, just as it was, to the plaintiff; he did so, trembling; the woman took it, made a thousand profound curtseys to everyone and besought God to watch over the life and health of the lord Governor, who took such good care of needy, orphaned maidens; and with this she hurried out of the courtroom clutching the purse in both hands, but not without first checking that the coins in it really were silver ones. As soon as she had left, Sancho said to the herdsman, whose eyes and heart had followed his purse out of the room and who was now giving way to tears:

'Now my good man, you follow that woman and take your purse off her, however much she resists, and bring her back here.'

The man didn't need to be told twice, and shot off like a thunderbolt to do as he'd been told. All the people were waiting in bewilderment to see what the outcome of the case would be, and a little later the man and the woman returned, even more tightly locked together than the first time, she clutching the hem of her skirt to her body with the purse in the fold, he struggling to pull it away from her; but this was impossible, so tenacious was the woman's defence, and she was screaming:

'Justice, in God's name! Justice, everybody! Look, look, my lord Governor, how shameless, how brazen this evil man is – in the middle of town, in the middle of the street, he tried to take back the purse you ordered him to give me.'

'And did he succeed?' the governor asked.

'What?' the woman retorted. 'I'd sooner let them take my life than let them take this purse. Me, stand for that sort of thing? They'd better find some fiercer dog to set on me than this revolting little wimp! Hammers and pincers and mallets and chisels couldn't tear this purse from my clutches, no and not lions' claws either – they'll get the soul out from the middle of my body first!'

'Yes, she's right,' said the man, 'and I admit she's got me beat, and I confess I haven't the strength to take my purse off her, so I give up.'

Then the governor said to the woman:

'And now, honourable and brave lady, let's see that purse again.'

She handed it over, and the governor returned it to the man, and said to the forceful and unforced maiden:

'If, my good woman, you'd shown the same grit and spirit in defending your body as you have in defending that purse, or even half of it, all the strength of Hercules couldn't have raped you. Off you go, confound you, and don't you stay anywhere on this island or within twenty miles of it, under pain of two hundred lashes. Get out, now, I say, you fraud, you swindler, you brazen little hussy!'

The woman took fright and slunk away disgruntled and hanging her head, and the governor said to the man:

'And now, my man, off you go to your village with your money – and from now on, if you don't want to lose it, try not to get the urge to lie with anybody.'

The man thanked him as worst he could, and went away, and everyone was again struck with amazement at their new governor's verdicts and decisions. All of this was recorded by the chronicler and sent to the Duke, who was eagerly awaiting it. And the good Sancho will also have to wait now, because his master is urging us to hurry back to him, thrown into turmoil by Altisidora's music.

CHAPTER XLVI

About the dreadful goat-bell scare and cat-fright
suffered by Don Quixote in the course of the enamoured
Altisidora's wooing

We left the great Don Quixote engrossed in the thoughts that had been aroused by the enamoured maiden Altisidora's music. They accompanied him to his bed where, as if they were fleas, they didn't allow him a moment's sleep or rest, especially when backed up by memories of the ladder in his stocking; but since time is a fast mover, and there isn't a ravine that can check its course, he rode along on the back of the hours, and morning soon came. And then Don Quixote abandoned the soft feathers of his bed and, not wasting a moment, donned his chamois-leather doublet and hose, and his riding boots, to hide the disaster to his stockings; he threw on his cloak of scarlet and clapped on his head a cap of green velvet, adorned with silver braid; he hung from his shoulder his sword-strap, with its fine, keen sword; he picked up a large rosary that he always carried with him; and he swaggered with great pomp and ceremony into the antechamber, where he came across the Duke and Duchess, already dressed and apparently waiting for him. And as they walked along a gallery he found Altisidora and her friend stationed there, and the instant Altisidora saw Don Quixote she pretended to faint, while her friend took her into her lap and hastened to unlace her bodices. Don Quixote saw all this, came up to them and said:

'I know what causes these attacks.'

'Well, I don't,' the friend replied, 'because Altisidora is the healthiest maid in this house, and I've never heard as much as a single sigh from her all the time I've known her; and the devil take all the knights errant in the world if they're equally unappreciative. Be off with you, Don Quixote sir, because this poor girl won't come to her senses with you around.'

To which Don Quixote replied:

'Please have a lute placed in my room tonight, and I shall console this afflicted maid as best I can; for when love is dawning, to be soon undeceived is the best cure.'

And he walked on, so as not to be criticized by anyone watching. As soon as his back was turned, Altisidora recovered from her faint and said to her friend:

'We'd better let him have his lute – it looks as if Don Quixote wants to give us some music, and coming from him it can't be bad!'

So they went straight off to tell the Duchess what had happened and how Don Quixote had asked for a lute, and she, absolutely delighted, plotted with the Duke and her maids to play a joke that would provide them with heaps of harmless fun, and they looked forward eagerly to the night, which came as quickly as the day had come, thanks to delightful conversations with Don Quixote. And that day the Duchess really did dispatch a page of hers (the one who'd played the part of the enchanted Dulcinea in the forest) to Teresa Panza with her husband Sancho Panza's letter and the bundle of clothes he'd left to be sent to her, instructing the page to bring back a full account of their conversation.

Once this had been done, it was soon eleven o'clock at night, and Don Quixote found a guitar in his room; he ran his fingers over the strings, opened the window and heard people moving about in the garden and, after adjusting the frets and tuning the instrument as best he could, he cleared his tubes, spat, and, in a voice that was somewhat hoarse but well-pitched, he sang the following ballad, which he'd composed himself that day:

> The soul, by Love's most mighty power,
> Can often be upset
> If Love can count on careless sloth
> To aid and to abet.
> Much sewing and embroidery
> And ceaseless occupation
> Are antidotes to the virulence
> Of amorous inclination.
> For if a modest maid aspires
> To be a wedded wife,
> Her dowry and her highest praise
> Will be her blameless life.
> Those errant knights who roam the world

And those who err at court
Will dally with the flighty ones
But marry the chaste sort.
    There's love between two inn-guests
That arose when the sun rose;
The time soon comes for it to set;
They go, and so love goes.
    For love that comes today and that
Tomorrow will depart
Will never leave its images
Engraved upon the heart.
    When paint is painted over paint,
It leaves no mark or trace,
And where one beauty reigns supreme,
Another has no place.
    Toboso's Dulcinea
Is indelibly portrayed
Upon the canvas of my heart
And never will she fade.
    True constancy in lovers
Is what all lovers prize:
It makes Love work his miracles
And raise them to the skies.

Don Quixote had reached this point in his song, to which the Duke, the Duchess, Altisidora and almost all the other people in the castle were listening, when suddenly, from a balcony immediately above his window, a rope with more than a hundred goat-bells tied to it was let down; and then a great sackful of cats, with smaller bells tied to their tails, was emptied after it. The clanking of the goat-bells and the screeching of the cats made such a din that although the Duke and Duchess had concocted the joke it scared even them; and Don Quixote was flabbergasted with fear. And as luck would have it, two or three of the cats scrambled in through the grille, and as they raced around the room it seemed as if a whole legion of devils was in there. They extinguished all the candles that were burning in the room as they charged about searching for a way out. The bell rope was being shaken up and down all the while; most of the people in the castle, who didn't know what was happening, were bemused and astonished.

Don Quixote sprang to his feet, drew his sword and began to make thrusts with it through the grille and to cry:

'Away with you, you evil enchanters! Away with you, you rabble of sorcerers; for I am Don Quixote de la Mancha, against whom all your wicked aspirations are powerless, impotent!'

And turning to face the cats that were rushing to and fro in his room, he slashed at them again and again; they raced over to the grille and clambered out, but one of them, hard pressed by Don Quixote's sword, hurled itself at his face and clung on to his nose with its claws and its teeth, the pain of which made him cry out as loud as he could. When the Duke and the Duchess heard him they guessed what was happening and rushed to his room, and when they unlocked the door with their master key, they found the poor knight struggling with all his strength to tear the cat off his face. They ran in with their candles aloft and saw the prodigious battle; the Duke moved in to break it up, but Don Quixote yelled:

'No, nobody must pull him off! Let me fight hand-to-hand with this devil, this sorcerer, this enchanter, and I will show him what Don Quixote de la Mancha is made of!'

But the cat disregarded these threats, and clung on, snarling. The Duke finally pulled it off and threw it out of the window. Don Quixote was left with a face riddled with holes and a less than perfect nose, but furious at not having been allowed to finish the battle in which he'd been locked with that knave of an enchanter. They sent for oil of hypericum, and Altisidora herself bandaged all his wounds with her own fair hands, and whispered to him as she did so:

'You only get into all this trouble, you hard-hearted knight, because of your sinful callousness and obstinacy; and I hope to God that your squire Sancho forgets all about lashing himself, so that your precious Dulcinea is never released from her enchantment and you never enjoy her or take her to the marriage bed, not at least while I'm alive – because I adore you.'

To all of this Don Quixote gave no answer except a deep sigh, and then as he stretched out on his bed he thanked the Duke and Duchess for their kindness, not because he had been afraid of that feline bell-clanking rabble of enchanters, but because he recognized that his hosts had come to help him with the best of intentions. The Duke and the Duchess went away to let him rest, regretting the unfortunate outcome of their hoax, because they hadn't imagined that this adventure was going to prove so tiresome and costly to Don Quixote, who was confined for five days to his room and his bed, where he had another adventure, more agreeable than this one, which his chronicler will not recount now, so that we can return to Sancho Panza and his droll and diligent governing.

CHAPTER XLVII

*Which continues the account of how Sancho Panza
conducted himself in government*

The history says that Sancho Panza was taken from the courtroom to a splendid palace, where in a great hall a sumptuous and spotless table was spread; and, as soon as he entered the hall, shawms started playing, and four pages advanced with water for his hands, which he received with profound solemnity. The music stopped, and Sancho sat at the head of the table because that was the only chair there was and the only place that was laid. A personage who later turned out to be a doctor came and stood at his side with a whalebone pointer in his hand. Then a fine white linen cloth was removed, revealing fruit and a multiplicity of different dishes; someone who looked like a student said grace, and a page tied a frilly bib round Sancho's neck; another man, playing the part of steward, placed a plate of fruit in front of him, yet hardly had Sancho taken one bite when the man with the pointer tapped the plate and it was whisked away; but the steward brought him another plate with some different food. Sancho was about to try it but before he could taste or even touch it, it had been tapped by the pointer and a page had removed it as quickly as the other had taken the fruit. Sancho was bewildered by all this, and he looked round at everyone in the hall and asked if this was a meal that had to be eaten like a conjuring trick. To which the man with the pointer replied:

'It merely has to be eaten, my lord Governor, according to the manner and custom of other islands where there are governors. I, sir, am a doctor, and I am employed on this island to look after its governors, and I take much more care of their health than of my own, studying by night and by day, and gauging each governor's constitution so as to be able to cure him when he falls ill; and my main task is to be present at all his lunches and dinners, and to allow him to eat that which appears to me to be suitable, and to take away from him that which I believe will do him harm and be injurious to his stomach; so I ordered the plate of fruit to be removed, because fruit is too moist, and I ordered the other dish to be taken away because it was too hot, containing as it did a profusion of spices, which increase thirst; for he who drinks copiously consumes and destroys the radical humour,[1] wherein life consists.'

'So that dish of roast partridges over there that don't look at all over-spiced won't do me any harm, will it?'

To which the doctor replied:

'My lord Governor shall not eat that, as long as there is still breath in my body.'

'Why not?' said Sancho.

And the doctor replied:

'Because our master Hippocrates, the light and guide of medicine, says in one of his aphorisms: *Omnis saturatio mala, perdicis autem pessima.*[2] Which means "All excess is bad, and that of partridges is the worst."'

'If that's the way it is,' said Sancho, 'perhaps the doctor would be kind enough to take a look at all these dishes on this here table and see which of them will do me most good and which will do me least harm, and let me eat them without any of his tapping, because I swear by the soul of a governor, and God let me live to enjoy being one, that I'm starving to death here, and not letting me eat, whatever the doctor says and with all due respect, won't make me live longer – it'll kill me off.'

'You are right, my lord Governor,' the doctor replied, 'and so it is my opinion that you must not eat those stewed rabbits over there, because that is a food from a furry animal. If that veal had not been roasted and served in that succulent sauce, you might have tried some of it; but as it has, it is out of the question.'

And Sancho said:

'That great big steaming dish in front of it looks like olla podrida to me, and since that sort of hotch-potch stew has got so many different foodstuffs in it, I can't fail to come across one that I'll like and will do me good.'

'*Absit!*' said the doctor. 'Far from us be any such base thought! There is no more unhealthy food in the world than olla podrida. Let your canons and your heads of colleges and your peasants at their weddings keep their olla podrida, and leave governors' tables, where all must be elegance and delicacy, undefiled by such stuff. And the reason for this is that simple medicines are more highly regarded than compounds, at all times, in all places, by all people, because with simple medicines one cannot go wrong, whereas with compounds one can, by erring in the quantities of the ingredients; but what I know the governor must eat now to conserve and fortify his health is a hundred wafer-tubes and a few very thin slices of quince jelly, to settle his stomach and aid his digestion.'

When Sancho heard this he leaned back in his chair and glared at the doctor, and asked him in sombre tones what his name was and where he had studied. To which he replied:

'I, my lord Governor, am Dr Pedro Recio de Agüero, from a village called Vamos,³ which lies between Caracuel and Almodóvar del Campo on the right-hand side, and I have the degree of doctor from the University of Osuna.'

'Well, now, this here Doctor Pedro Recio de Bloody Agüero, from Vamos, a village on the right-hand side as we go from Caracuel to Almodóvar del Campo, and a graduate of Osuna, had better get out of my sight at once, and if he doesn't I swear by all that's holy that I'll grab a cudgel and thump every single doctor off this island, starting with him – all those I consider ignorant that is, because wise, prudent and sensible doctors I'll honour and revere like divines. And I'll say it just once more – this Pedro Recio had better get out of here, because if he doesn't I'll grab this chair where I'm sitting and I'll smash it over his head, and they can ask me about it when I hand in my final report if they like, because I'll clear myself by saying I did God good service by killing a bad doctor, a scourge of society. And now let's have something to eat, otherwise you can stuff this governing lark, because a job that doesn't even keep you in food isn't worth having.'

Seeing the governor so enraged threw the doctor into a panic, and he started vamoosing out of the hall, but at that very moment a post-horn sounded in the street and the steward looked out of the window and turned back with the words:

'It's a messenger from my master the Duke, and the message he's bringing must be an important one.'

The messenger ran in, sweating and flurried, and taking a letter from inside his shirt he placed it in the governor's hands, and Sancho placed it in the butler's hands, and told him to read the address, which said: 'To Don Sancho Panza, Governor of the Island of Barataria, to be delivered to him personally or to his secretary.' Hearing which Sancho said:

'Which of you's my secretary?'

And one of them replied:

'I am, sir, because I can read and write – and I'm a Basque.'[4]

'With that tagged on,' said Sancho, 'you could be secretary to the Emperor himself. Open the letter and see what it says.'

The newborn secretary did so, and when he'd read the letter he said that it was a matter to be discussed in private. Sancho ordered the hall to be cleared and nobody to remain except the butler and the steward; and everyone else left, including the doctor, and the secretary read the letter, which said:

It has come to my knowledge, Señor Don Sancho Panza, that some enemies of mine and of your island are going to launch a furious assault on it one night; you must stay awake and alert, so as not to be taken unawares. I have also learned, from trustworthy spies, that four persons have entered the town in disguise to take your life, because they are afraid of your intelligence; keep your eyes open, be careful about who comes to speak to you, and do not eat any food that is given you as a present. I shall take care to assist you if you are in difficulties, and you must always act as one would expect a man of your calibre to act. From this town, on the sixteenth of August at four o'clock in the morning,

Your friend,
THE DUKE

Sancho was astonished, and the other three men seemed to be astonished as well, and turning to the butler Sancho said:

'What has to be done now, without delay, is to stick Dr Recio in a dungeon, because if anyone's going to kill me it's him, with the most horrible and adminicular death of all – starvation!'

'I also think,' said the steward, 'that you shouldn't eat any of the food on this table, because it was a gift from some nuns and, as people say, the devil lurks behind the Cross.'

'I don't deny that,' Sancho replied, 'and for the time being you can let me have a hunk of bread and about four pound of grapes, because there can't be any poison in them – the fact is I can't go without food, and if we're to be prepared for these battles threatening us we've got to be well nourished, because the guts support the heart and not the heart the guts. And you, secretary, can reply to my lord the Duke and tell him that his orders will be obeyed exactly as issued, and kiss my lady the Duchess's hands for me and tell her not to forget to send a messenger with my letter and my bundle to my wife Teresa Panza, I'll consider that a great favour and I'll take good care to serve her with everything in my power, and while you're about it you can stick in a hand-kissing for my master Don Quixote de la Mancha so that he can see I'm a grateful servant – and since you're such a good secretary and such a good Basque you can add whatever else you like that fits the bill. And now clear those tables and give me some food, and then I'll see off all the spies and killers and enchanters that come pitching into me and my island.'

At this point a page came in and said:

'There's a farmer here, come on business, and he wants to talk to you about a matter that he says is of supreme importance.'

'They're very strange,' said Sancho, 'these people who come on business. Can they really be so thick they don't realize this isn't the right time to come? Aren't we governors, we judges, men of flesh and blood who've got to be allowed to rest for as long as we need to – or do they think we're made of marble? I swear to God that if this governing of mine lasts, which it won't as far as I can see, I'll put the screws on more than one of these people coming here on business. Now go and tell that fellow to come in, but have him checked first to make sure he isn't one of those spies, or my killer.'

'No, he isn't that, sir,' the page replied, 'because he looks like a simple soul, and unless I'm very much mistaken he's as good as gold.'

'Have no fear,' said the butler, 'we're all here with you.'

'Might there be a chance, steward,' said Sancho, 'that now that Dr Pedro Recio isn't here I could eat something solid and substantial, even if it's only a hunk of bread and an onion?'

'Tonight, at dinner, the lack of a lunch will be made up for, and Your Lordship will be fully satisfied,' the steward said.

'God grant it,' said Sancho.

And the farmer came in, a man of good presence, and anyone could tell from miles away that he was a decent, honest soul. The first thing he said was:

'Which of you is the lord Governor?'

'Which do you think?' the secretary replied. 'The one sitting in the chair, of course.'

'I shall humble myself in his presence, then,' the farmer said.

And sinking to his knees, he begged Sancho for his hand so that he could kiss it. Sancho refused, and told him to get up and say what he wanted. The farmer obeyed, and said:

'Sir, I'm a farmer, from Miguel Turra, a village seven miles from Ciudad Real.'

'We've got another Vamos here!' said Sancho. 'Get on with it, my man – what I can say for my part is that I know Miguel Turra very well, because it isn't far from my own village.'

'It's like this, then, sir,' the farmer continued. 'By God's mercy I was married by the prescribed rites and rituals of the Holy Roman Catholic Church; I have two sons, both students, the younger studying for his BA and the elder for his MA; I am a widower, because my wife has died, or to be more accurate an incompetent doctor killed her by purging her when she was pregnant, and, if it had pleased God that the child had been born and it had been a boy, I should have had him study for his doctorate so that he didn't feel envious of his brothers the BA and the MA.'

'It seems, then,' said Sancho, 'that if your wife hadn't gone and died, or been killed, you wouldn't be a widower.'

'No, sir, certainly not,' the farmer replied.

'So that's cleared that up, then!' Sancho replied. 'Get a move on, my man, this is a time for sleep not business.'

'What I was saying,' said the farmer, 'is that this son of mine who's going to be a BA fell in love with a girl in the same village called Clara Perlerina, the daughter of Andrés Perlerino, a farmer of great wealth; and this surname Perlerino isn't inherited from their ancestors, but comes from the fact that everyone in the family's paralytic, and people call them the Perlerinos to make it sound better, although if truth is to be told that girl is just like a pearl of orient, and looked at from the right-hand side she's like a flower of the field – not so much from the left, because the eye's missing on that side, it popped out when she had the smallpox; and although she's got these big pock-marks all over her face, her admirers say they aren't pock-marks at all but graves where her lovers' souls are buried. She's such a clean girl that to avoid dirtying her face her nostrils are as you might say rolled up, and look just as if they were running away from her mouth, and yet she's a real good-looker, because she's got a big mouth and if it wasn't for the missing ten or a dozen teeth it could stand out among the very best mouths there are. I won't say anything about her lips, because they're so slender and delicate that if you could wind lips like yarn you could make a whole skein out of them; but since their colour is different from what's usual in lips, they're like miraculous lips, because they're streaked blue and green and purple; and my lord Governor must forgive me for painting in such detail the qualities of the young woman who will one day be my daughter, because I love her dearly and she doesn't seem at all bad-looking to me.'

'You can paint whatever you like,' said Sancho, 'because I'm really enjoying the picture – if I'd had any lunch, there wouldn't be any better pudding for me than what you're painting.'

'I haven't served you the pudding yet,' the farmer replied, 'but if it isn't being served now, it soon will be. As I was saying, sir, if I could paint her stature and her gracefulness it would amaze you; but this isn't possible, because she's bent double with her knees rammed up against her mouth, yet in spite of that it's easy to see that if she could stand up she'd hit her head on the ceiling; and she'd have given my BA son her hand in marriage by now, only she can't open it up, because it's withered; but in spite of that anyone can see what a fine and well-formed hand it is from her long, furrowed nails.'

'Very well,' said Sancho, 'and now just make believe, my man, that you've painted her all the way from head to foot. What is it you want? Come to the point without beating about the bush or sidestepping, without cutting anything out or adding anything on.'

'What I would like, sir,' the farmer replied, 'is for you to do me the favour of writing a letter of recommendation to her father, asking him to allow this marriage to go ahead, for we aren't unequal in either the gifts of fortune or the blessings of nature – because to tell the truth, my lord Governor, my son is possessed of the devil, and there isn't a day when he isn't tormented three or four times by the evil spirits; and as a result of falling into the fire his face is all crinkled like parchment, and his eyes are a bit weepy and bleary; but he's as good-natured as an angel, and he'd be a real saint if he didn't cudgel and punch himself so much.'

'Is there anything else you want, my good man?' Sancho replied.

'Yes, there is something else I'd like,' the farmer replied, 'only I daren't say what it is – but no, I will come out with it, whether it goes down well or not, because I don't want it rotting away inside of me. It's just this, sir – I'd like you to give me three or six hundred ducats towards my BA's dowry, what I mean to say is towards setting up his house, because after all they'll live on their own, so as not to have to put up with their in-laws meddling.'

'Are you quite sure there isn't anything else you'd like?' said Sancho. 'Don't you go and hold it back through being bashful or shy.'

'No, that's all,' the farmer replied.

As he said this, the governor rose to his feet, grasped the chair in which he'd been sitting and said:

'I swear by all that's holy, you boorish, inconsiderate bumpkin, that if you don't take yourself out of my sight I'll break your head open with this chair! You villain, you bastard, you painter of the devil himself – you come asking me for six hundred ducats at this time of day? And where have I got six hundred ducats, you evil-smelling wretch? And why should I give them to you, even if I did have them, you wheedler, you blockhead? And what do I care about Miguel Turra, or the whole tribe of Perlerinos? Get out I say, and if you don't I swear by the soul of my master the Duke that I'll do as I said! I don't think you're from Miguel Turra at all, you're some wheedler sent here from hell to tempt me. You scoundrel, I haven't been governor for a day and a half and you expect me to have six hundred ducats?'

The steward signalled to the farmer to leave the hall, which he did with his head bowed and looking frightened that the governor might turn his fury into action, because the rogue had played his part with great conviction. But let's leave Sancho with his fury, and may peace reign again among them all; and let's return to Don Quixote, whom we left with his face bandaged and treated for his feline wounds, from which he still hadn't recovered eight days later, and on one of those days he had an experience that Cide Hamete promises to relate with all the precision and truthfulness with which he relates everything, however trivial, in this history.

CHAPTER XLVIII

About what happened to Don Quixote with Doña
Rodríguez, the Duchess's duenna, and other events worthy
to be recorded and remembered eternally

The sore wounded Don Quixote was exceeding fretful and melancholy, with his face bandaged and marked not by the hand of God[1] but by the claws of a cat – such are the mishaps incidental to knight-errantry. He didn't appear in public for six days, and on one of the nights, when he couldn't sleep as he brooded on his misfortunes and on Altisidora's persecution of him, he heard someone unlocking the door of his room and imagined that the enamoured maid was coming to assail his chastity and expose him to the temptation of failing in the fidelity that he owed to his lady Dulcinea del Toboso.

'No,' he said, persuaded that everything he'd just imagined was true, and speaking in a voice loud enough to be heard. 'The greatest beauty in the world shall not be able to make me renounce my adoration of her whose image is printed and engraved in the centre of my heart and in the depths of my bowels – whether, my lady, you have been transformed into an uncouth peasant wench, or into a nymph of golden Tagus weaving cloth of gold and silk, or whether Merlin or Montesinos hold you wherever they will; because you are mine everywhere, and everywhere I have been and shall be yours.'

As he ended this speech the door opened. He rose to his feet on his bed, wrapped from head to foot in a yellow satin bedspread, with a nightcap complete with earflaps on his head, and bandages on his face and moustache – on his face because of the scratches, and on his moustache to stop it from drooping – and in this costume he looked like the weirdest ghost imaginable. He riveted his eyes on the door and, expecting to see the infatuated, lovelorn Altisidora walk in, what he did see was a venerable duenna wearing white widow's weeds with braided hems, so long that they swathed her from head to toe. In the fingers of her left hand she was holding half a lighted candle, and with her right hand she was shading her face to keep the glare out of her eyes, which were covered by an enormous pair of spectacles. Her tread was light and her feet moved softly.

Don Quixote peered down at her from his watch-tower, and when he saw her clothes and took note of the silence of her movements he thought that some witch or sorceress had come in that garb to do some evil deed, and he began to cross himself at speed. The vision came closer, and when she was in the middle of the room she raised her eyes and saw Don Quixote crossing himself as fast as he could; and if he was frightened when he saw her she was petrified when she saw him, so tall and so pale, in his bedspread and his disfiguring bandages, and she screamed:

'My God! What is this I see?'

And the shock made her drop her candle, and finding herself in the dark she turned to run away, but in her alarm she tripped over her skirts and crashed to the floor. The terrified Don Quixote blurted:

'I conjure you, you ghost or whatever, to tell me who you are and what it is you want from me. If you are a lost soul, tell me so; I shall do everything within my power to help you, for I am a Christian and a Catholic and only want to do good to everybody; and to this end I have received this order of knight-errantry that I profess, the exercise of which extends even as far as doing good to souls in purgatory.'

The duenna, bewildered to hear herself being conjured, guessed from her own fear how frightened Don Quixote must be feeling, and she replied in a low and doleful voice:

'Señor Don Quixote (if indeed you are Don Quixote): I am not a ghost, or a vision, or a soul in purgatory, as you appear to think, but Doña Rodríguez, my lady the Duchess's duenna of honour, and I have come to you with one of those urgent needs that you frequently remedy.'

'Tell me, Señora Doña Rodríguez,' said Don Quixote, 'have you by any chance come on go-between's business? Because I would have you know that I am of no use whatsoever to any woman, thanks to the peerless beauty of my lady Dulcinea del Toboso. In short, Doña Rodríguez, what I am saying is that, so long as you put aside any message of love, you can go and light your candle, and return here, and we shall discuss whatever you say, whatever you like – with the exception, as I said, of any arousing blandishments.'

'Me, with other people's messages, sir?' the duenna replied. 'How little you know me: I am not, indeed, so very ancient as to need to resort to such capers because, thank God, there is still plenty of spirit in my body, and all my teeth are in my mouth, only excepting a few that have been usurped by catarrhal coughing, so common in this land of Aragon. But you wait for me here a little; I shall go away and light my candle, and return in an instant to tell the tale of my woes to the healer of all the woes in the world.'

And without stopping for a reply she groped her way out of the room, where Don Quixote was left, calm again, and thoughtful, as he awaited her; but then a thousand thoughts came crowding into his brain concerning this new adventure, and he considered that he had judged and acted most unwisely in putting himself at risk of breaking the faith that he had pledged to his lady, and he said to himself:

'Who can tell whether the devil, who's so subtle and crafty, is trying to trick me with a duenna, having failed with empresses, queens, duchesses, marquesses or countesses! For I've often heard it said, by intelligent people, that if he can get away with it he will always give you foul instead of fair. And who can tell whether this solitude, this opportunity, this silence, will awake my dormant desires, and as I approach the end of my days make me fall where I have never even stumbled before? And in such a quandary it's better to flee than to await the battle. But I can't be in my right mind, thinking and saying all these absurdities, because it's impossible for a beanpole of a bespectacled duenna in white weeds to give rise to any lustful feelings in the most depraved breast in the world. Can there be a single duenna on the face of this earth with any flesh on her? Can there be a single duenna in this world who isn't insolent, cantankerous and priggish? Away with you, then, you rabble of duennas, useless for all human pleasure! Oh, what a good idea that lady had when, so they say, she ordered two dummy duennas with their spectacles and their pin-cushions to be stationed in one corner of her drawing-room, as if they were sewing, and they did as much to lend an air of propriety to the place as any real duennas!'

As he said this he jumped out of bed with the intention of locking the door to stop Señora Rodríguez from entering; but by the time he reached it she was already on her way in, holding a lighted candle of white wax, and when she saw Don Quixote from closer up, wrapped in the bedspread, with his bandages and his nightcap complete with earflaps, she felt frightened again, and starting a couple of paces back she said:

'Is one safe here, sir knight? Your having risen from your bed does not argue the purest of intentions.'

'I could well put the same question to you, madam,' Don Quixote replied, 'and so I do put it to you – am I quite safe from attack and ravishment?'

'From whom, and about whom, do you request that assurance?' the duenna retorted.

'I request it from you and about you,' said Don Quixote, 'because I am not made of marble and you are not made of bronze, and it is not now ten o'clock in the morning but midnight or even a little later, I suspect, and we are in a room that is more secluded and secret than the cave where the treacherous, audacious Aeneas lay with the beautiful, tender-hearted Dido. But give me your hand, my lady, for I need no greater assurance than my own continence and modesty, and that which is offered by those venerable weeds of yours.'

And so saying he kissed his own right hand and took hers, which she offered him after performing the same ceremony.

Here Cide Hamete inserts a parenthesis, swearing by Muhammad that he would have given the better of the two haiks he possessed to see the pair of them walking hand in hand from the door to the bed.

Finally Don Quixote climbed into his bed and Doña Rodríguez sat on a chair some way from it, without removing her spectacles or putting down her candle. Don Quixote snuggled down until only his face could be seen, and as soon as they had both regained their composure the first to break the silence was Don Quixote, who said:

'Now, my lady Doña Rodríguez, you may unbosom yourself and ventilate everything in your hapless heart and your bleeding bowels, for you will be heard by me with chaste ears, and succoured with compassionate deeds.'

'That is indeed what I believe,' the duenna replied, 'for from your gallant and agreeable presence such a Christian answer was only to be expected. The fact is, Señor Don Quixote, that although you see me sitting in this chair here in the middle of the kingdom of Aragon, and in the habit of a duenna, harassed and crushed, I am from Asturias, and from a family that is allied with many of the best families in that province. But my bad luck and the negligence of my parents, who were reduced to poverty long before they should have been, without anyone knowing how it had happened, took me to the capital, to Madrid, where, for the sake of peace and to avoid greater disasters, my parents put me into service as a seamstress in the household of a great lady – and I should like you to be aware that never in my whole life have I come across anyone who could beat me at hemstitch or linen-work. My parents left me in service and went back home, and a few years later they died and must have gone to heaven, because they were exceedingly good Christians and Catholics. I was left an orphan, depending on the wretched wages and miserable favours given to maidservants in palaces, and, just at that time, without any encouragement whatsoever on my part, a squire in that household fell in love with me, a man advanced in years, full-bearded and of good presence and, above all, as much of an aristocrat as the King himself, because he hailed from the ancient hills of León.[2] We weren't so very secretive about our love that our lady didn't find out about it, and to prevent tittle-tattle she had us married according to all the rules and rituals of our Holy Mother the Roman Catholic Church, and from this marriage a daughter was born to put an end to all my good fortune, if I'd ever had any – not that I died in childbirth, because it was a straightforward one, and came at the right time, but because a little later my husband died from a certain shock that he received, and if there were time to tell you about it I know you would be amazed.'

And here she began to weep tender tears, and then she said:

'Do forgive me, Don Quixote sir, I can't help it, because whenever I remember my prematurely deceased husband my eyes brim with tears. God Almighty! The magnificence of the man as he rode along with my lady behind him on that powerful mule, as black as jet itself! Because in those days people didn't ride about in carriages or litters, as they say is the fashion now; and ladies rode on their squires' cruppers. And there's just one thing that I cannot refrain from telling you, so that you may appreciate what a well-bred and punctilious man my husband was. As they were riding into the Calle de Santiago, in Madrid, a rather narrow street, one of the city councillors happened to come riding out of it with two alguacils in front of him, and as soon as my beloved squire saw him he turned the mule's reins, indicating that he was going back to accompany the councillor home. My lady, on his crupper, whispered:

'"What are you doing, you wretch? Don't you realize I'm riding here behind you?"

'The councillor, out of politeness, drew rein and said:

'"Pray continue on your way, sir: it is I who should accompany my lady Doña Casilda," for this was my mistress's name.

'My husband still insisted, hat in hand, on accompanying the councillor to his house; and this prompted my lady, beside herself with rage, to take a large pin or maybe it was a bodkin from her needle-case and plunge it into my husband's loins, and he screamed and writhed, which sent my lady tumbling to the ground. Two of her lackeys came to pick her up, as did the councillor and his alguacils; Guadalajara Gate was in uproar, by which I mean to say that the idlers hanging about it were. My mistress walked home, and my husband staggered into a barber's shop saying that his bowels had been pierced through and through. News of my husband's act of courtesy spread throughout the town, so much so that boys would chase after him in the street, and because of this and because he was a little short-sighted my lady the Duchess dismissed him, and the grief of this I'm certain was the death of him.

'I was left a poor forsaken widow, and with a daughter on my hands growing in beauty like the foam on the waves of the sea. In the end, since I had a good reputation as a seamstress, my lady the Duchess, then recently married to my lord the Duke, brought me with her here to the kingdom of Aragon, and she brought my daughter, too; the days came and the days went, and my daughter grew up, with all the graces in the world: she sings like a lark, she dances in the ballroom like the wind, she capers in the country-dance like a wild thing, she reads and writes like a schoolmaster, she counts like a miser. Her cleanliness is beyond words, for running water isn't purer, and she must now be, if I remember rightly, sixteen years, five months and three days old, give or take one or two.

'To cut the story short, the son of a wealthy farmer who lives in one of my lord the Duke's villages not far from here fell in love with this girl of mine. And in due course they came together, I don't know how it happened, and by promising to marry her he seduced her, and now he refuses to keep his promise, and even though my lord the Duke knows all about it, because I've complained to him not just once but often and asked him to order this farmer's son to marry my daughter, he always turns a deaf ear and hardly even listens to me; and the reason is that the seducer's father is a wealthy man and keeps lending the Duke money and standing surety for his other debts, so the Duke doesn't want to annoy or upset him in any way. And what I would like you to do, my dear sir, is to undertake to redress this wrong, either by pleas or by arms, because according to what everybody says you were born into this world to right wrongs and rectify abuses and succour the unfortunate. Consider my fatherless daughter and her charms and her youth and all the other fine qualities about which I have told you, because I solemnly swear before God that of all my lady's maids there isn't one who can hold a candle to her; and that girl they call Altisidora and look upon as the most charming and elegant of the lot, compared with my daughter, doesn't come within half-a-dozen miles of her. And I'd like you to know, my dear sir, that all that glitters is not gold, because this girl Altisidora has more vanity than good looks, and more brazenness than modesty, besides not being very healthy: there's an objectionable quality about her breath that makes it unbearable to stay close to her for a single moment. And even my lady the Duchess ... but I'd better keep quiet about that, because they say that walls have ears.'

'Upon my soul, Doña Rodríguez – what is wrong with my lady the Duchess?' demanded Don Quixote.

'When one has been besought in such a way,' the duenna replied, 'one cannot fail to respond with the whole truth to what one has been asked. Can you envisage, Don Quixote sir, my lady the Duchess's beauty, that complexion, comparable to the face of a bright, burnished sword, those cheeks of milk and carmine, with the sun in the one and the moon in the other, and that elegance of hers as she treads the ground as if she scorned it, so that she seems to be scattering good health wherever she goes? Well, just let me tell you she can thank God for all that in the first place, and in the second place she can thank those two flowing fountains in her legs, those issues that drain out of her all the noxious fluids the doctors say she's full of.'

'Holy St Mary!' said Don Quixote. 'Can it be possible that my lady the Duchess has such drain-holes in her? I should not have believed it if all the discalced friars in the world had told me so; but if Doña Rodríguez says that she has, it must be true. Yet such fountains, in such places, must give forth not noxious fluids but liquid amber. Truly, you have just convinced me that the opening of issues must be vital for good health.'

Hardly had Don Quixote finished speaking when the doors of the room burst open and the shock made Doña Rodríguez drop her candle, and the room was left as dark as the mouth of a wolf, as the saying goes. Then the poor duenna felt two hands seizing her by the throat with such force that she could hardly breathe, while someone else, without saying a word, hoisted her skirts and with what seemed to be a slipper gave her so many slaps that anyone would have felt sorry for her; but although Don Quixote did feel sorry, he didn't stir from his bed, and he couldn't imagine what was happening, and he stayed there still and silent, even fearing that the thumping and the clumping might come his way next. And his fears were not idle ones, because once the silent executioners had finished with the duenna, who didn't dare to cry out, they turned to Don Quixote, and, unwrapping him from the sheet and the bedspread, they pinched him so hard and so often that he had no choice but to defend himself with his fists, all in the most amazing silence. The battle lasted for almost half an hour; and then the ghosts departed and Doña Rodríguez gathered up her skirts and walked out bemoaning her disaster without a word to Don Quixote who, pinched and aching, bewildered and plunged in thought, was left by himself, where we too shall leave him longing to discover who was the perverse enchanter that had reduced him to such a state. But this will have to wait until later, because Sancho Panza is calling out to us, and for the sake of the proper organization of this history we must answer his call.

CHAPTER XLIX

About what happened to Sancho Panza when he made his rounds of the island

We left the great governor fuming with rage at that wheedling, portrait-painting farmer who, coached by the butler, who in his turn had been coached by the Duke, had made fun of him; but Sancho held his own against them all, foolish, uncouth and fat though he was, and he said to everyone present, including Dr Pedro Recio, who, now that the secret reading of the Duke's letter was over, had come back into the hall:

'Now I really do see that judges and governors ought to be and need to be made of bronze, so as not to be worn out by all the pestering from these folks who come on business and expect you to be listening to them and dealing with them at all hours of the day and night, and attending only to their affairs, come what may. And if the poor old judge doesn't listen to them and deal with them, either because he can't or because that isn't the time fixed for audiences, they soon start cursing him and gossiping about him and backbiting him, and even going into all sorts of details about his family. So, all you fools and idiots coming on business: don't be in such a hurry, wait until the proper time, don't come when it's time for me to be eating or sleeping, because judges are made of flesh and blood, and must give to nature what nature naturally needs – all except me that is, because I can't give my nature any food, thanks to Dr Pedro Recio Vamos here present, who wants me to die of hunger and then claims that this death is life, and God send the same fate to him and all his breed, by which I mean all bad doctors, because the good ones deserve palms and laurels.'

All those who knew Sancho Panza were amazed to hear him speaking with such elegance, and they didn't know how to account for it, unless it could be put down to the fact that posts of responsibility and importance quicken some wits and deaden others. In the end Dr Pedro Recio Agüero from Vamos promised to allow him to eat some dinner that evening, even if it did mean transgressing all the aphorisms of Hippocrates. This cheered the governor up, and he looked forward to the dinner hour with an intense desire; and although it seemed to him that time was standing still, the longed-for moment did eventually arrive and he was given cold beef and onions drenched in oil, and boiled calves-feet, the calves being somewhat advanced in years. Sancho tucked in with more gusto than if he'd been given francolins from Milan, pheasants from Rome, veal from Sorrento, partridges from Morón or geese from Lavajos, and as he ate he turned to the doctor and said:

'Look here, doctor, from now on don't bother to give me choice food or dainty dishes, because that'd only unhinge my stomach – it's used to goat-meat, cow-meat, fat bacon, salt beef, turnips and onions, and if it's ever given palace food it's a bit squeamish about that, and sometimes even goes all queasy. What the steward can do is bring me these great messes of pottage they call ollas podridas, and the messier they are the better they look, and he can shove into them whatever he likes as long as it's edible, and I'll thank him for that and pay him back for it one day, and don't anyone try to pull the wool over my eyes, so let's get on with it – long live us, and let's eat together in peace and good fellowship, because when God sends the dawn he sends it for everyone. As I govern this island, all bribes I'll refuse but insist on my dues, and everyone had better watch out and mind their own business, because I'll have them know the devil's among the tailors and if I'm given cause people are going to see marvels. Oh, yes, I'm going to make myself all honey, aren't I, so the flies can eat me up!'

'Truly, my lord Governor,' said the steward, 'what you say is quite correct, and I hereby offer in the name of all the islanders on this island to serve you with all diligence, love and goodwill, because the mild style of government that you have adopted from the outset leaves them no room for doing or thinking anything that could redound to your disservice.'

'Right you are then,' Sancho replied, 'and they'd be fools if they did or thought anything different. And I'll say it again – you take very good care over what I'm given to eat, and what my dun is too, because that's the most important part of this whole business, and when the time comes let's make our rounds: I'm planning to rid this island of all sorts of rubbish and tramps and idlers and layabouts, because I'll have you know, my friends, that useless, lazy people in a society are like drones in a beehive, eating up the honey that the worker bees produce. I'm planning to help farmers, keep hidalgos' privileges, reward the virtuous and above all respect religion and the honour of the clergy. What do you think about that, my friends? Is there anything in what I say, or am I beating my brains out for nothing?'

'There is so much in what you say, my lord Governor,' said the butler, 'that I am astounded to see that a man as untaught as you are, being, I believe, totally illiterate, can make so many observations full of wise maxims and good counsel, so different from what those who sent us here and we who have come here had been given to expect from your mind. In this world every day brings a new surprise; jests turn into earnest, and jesters find the tables turned upon them.'

So night had come, and the governor had eaten his dinner, by Dr Pedro Recio's leave. They made ready to go on their rounds, and Sancho left with the butler, the secretary, the steward, the chronicler whose task it was to record his deeds, and alguacils and clerks: there were so many people that they could have formed a decent-sized battle-squadron. Sancho strutted along bearing his staff of office in the middle of the group, a sight for sore eyes, and after they'd walked down a few streets they heard the sounds of a knife fight; they ran to see what was up, and found that it was only two men fighting, who stopped when they saw the authorities on their way; and one of them cried:

'Help, help, in the name of God and the King! Is it something they let people do here, holding others up in the middle of the town, robbing them in the street?'

'Calm down, my good man,' said Sancho, 'and tell me what's caused this scrap, because I'm the Governor.'

The man's adversary said:

'My lord Governor, I shall explain briefly. The fact is that this fine fellow here has just won more than a thousand reals in that gaming house over there, and God in heaven knows how he did it, and I was watching the game and decided more than one dispute in his favour, against all the dictates of my conscience; he got up with his winnings, and just when I was expecting him to give me an escudo or two at the very least, as a tip – because it's the normal custom to give one to leading citizens like myself who are there to earn a precarious living, and to support injustice and avoid disputes – he pocketed his money and walked out. This infuriated me and I followed him, and in polite and civil language I asked him to give me eight reals at least, because he knows I'm an honest man and I haven't any job or income, because my parents never taught me the one or left me the other; and the cunning blighter, who's not much worse a thief than Cacus or much more of a card-sharper than Andradilla,[1] was only prepared to give me four reals – so you can see, my lord Governor, what a shameless and remorseless character he is! But I swear that if you hadn't come I'd have made him cough up his winnings, and then he'd have found out how many beans make five.'

'What do you have to say to all this?' Sancho asked.

And the other man replied that everything his adversary had said was true, and he hadn't been willing to give him more than four reals because he was always giving him something, and anyone waiting for a tip should be courteous and happy to accept whatever he's given, without haggling with successful gamblers unless he knows for certain that they're cheats and their gains are ill-gotten; and there was no better proof that he was an honest man and not the thief he'd been made out to be than the fact that he hadn't been prepared to give him anything, because swindlers always pay their dues to the onlookers who know them.

'That's true enough,' said the butler. 'Now you must decide, my lord Governor, what is to be done with these men.'

'What's to be done is this,' Sancho replied. 'You, the successful gambler, whether a good man or a bad one or an indifferent one, will give your knifer here a hundred reals, and then you'll unload thirty more for penniless prisoners. And you, without a job or an income, scrounging your way through life on this island, will take these hundred reals, and tomorrow without fail you will leave this island, under sentence of banishment for ten years, on pain of completing it in the next life if you violate it, because I'll hang you from the pillory or at least order the executioner to. And don't either of you answer me back or he'll feel the weight of my hand.'

The one disbursed, the other pocketed; he left the island and the first man left for home, and the governor went on to say:

'Either I'm not much good as a governor or I'll shut these gaming houses down, because to my mind they do a lot of harm.'

'This one, at least,' said a clerk, 'you won't be able to close, because it's run by a very important person and, furthermore, what he loses each year on the cards is far in excess of what he wins. But you'll be able to flex your muscles on other, lesser gambling dens, they're the ones that do the most damage and cover up the most iniquities: in the houses of high-ranking gentlemen and nobles, famous card-sharpers don't dare to get up to their tricks, and since the vice of gambling has become such common practice it's better for it to happen in top people's houses than at some tradesman's place where they'll trap a poor wretch in the small hours and flay him alive.'

'Now, thanks to the clerk,' said Sancho, 'I can see that there are lots of ins and outs to this question.'

And now a constable came up clutching a young man, and he said:

'My lord Governor, this youth was proceeding in our direction, and as soon as he saw that it was the authorities he turned around and ran away for all he was worth, a sign that he must have been up to no good. I pursued him, and if he had not tripped and fallen I should never have apprehended him.'

'So why were you running away, my lad?' asked Sancho.

To which the youth replied:

'To avoid having to answer all the questions that the authorities always ask you, sir.'

'What is your trade?'

'Weaver.'

'And what do you weave?'

'Iron lance-heads, by your leave, sir.'

'So we've got a witty one here, have we? You think you're quite a joker, don't you? All right, then – where were you going just now?'

'To take the air, sir.'

'And where do you people take the air on this island?'

'Wherever it's blowing.'

'Very well – you give good straight answers, don't you? You're a clever young lad, but now you can just reckon that I'm the air and I'm blowing up your poop and puffing you off to jail. Hey, grab hold of him and take him to prison – that's where he's going to sleep tonight, without any air at all.'

'I swear by God,' said the lad, 'that you'll as much make me sleep in prison as make me king!'

'And what's going to stop me from making you sleep in prison?' Sancho retorted. 'Haven't I got the power to arrest you and release you whenever I feel like it?'

'However much power you've got,' the lad said, 'it won't be enough to make me sleep in prison.'

'Won't it, now?' Sancho replied. 'Take him to where he'll see with his own two eyes how wrong he is, and all the jailer's self-seeking generosity won't do him any good – because I'll give him a fine of two thousand ducats if he lets you take so much as one step out of prison.'

'This is too ridiculous for words,' the lad replied. 'The plain fact is that all the people in the world couldn't make me sleep in prison tonight.'

'Tell me, you devil,' said Sancho, 'have you got some guardian angel who's going to come and take off the fetters I'm planning to have you clapped into?'

'Ah now, my lord Governor,' the youngster replied with the best of humour, 'let's be reasonable and come to the point. Suppose you have me taken to prison, and there they clap me in fetters and chains, and stick me in a dungeon, and threaten the jailer with an enormous fine if he lets me out, and then let's suppose he obeys all his orders – regardless of all that, if I don't want to sleep, and I decide to stay awake all night long without closing an eye, will you be capable, with all your power, of making me sleep if I don't want to?'

'No, of course not,' said the secretary, 'and the young man has proved his point.'

'So,' said Sancho, 'if you stay awake it'll only be because that's what you want to do, not because you're determined to disobey me?'

'No, sir,' said the lad, 'of course not.'

'Well, then, off with you,' said Sancho. 'You can go and sleep in your own house, and God send you sound sleep, because I don't want to rob you of it, but my advice is that from now on you don't make fun of the authorities – you'll come across those as will make you pay for your japes with a cracked skull.'

The lad disappeared, and the governor continued on his rounds, and a little later two constables came up holding a man, and said:

'My lord Governor, this person who looks like a man isn't one, but a woman, and not a bad-looking woman either, wearing man's clothes.'

They raised a couple of lanterns to her face, and by their light they saw the features of a woman who seemed to be sixteen or so, with her hair gathered into a net of gold thread and green silk, and she was as lovely as a thousand pearls. They looked down at the rest of her, and saw that she was wearing red silk stockings with white taffeta garters fringed with gold and seed-pearls; her breeches were of green cloth of gold, and she had a loose open cape of the same material, under which she wore a doublet of the finest white cloth of gold, and her shoes, man's shoes, were also white. She wasn't carrying a sword, but only a splendid dagger, and there were many fine rings on her fingers. In short, they all thought the girl looked lovely, and none of them recognized her, and the townspeople said they couldn't think who she might be, and those who knew about the hoaxes being played on Sancho were the most amazed of all, because this event, this meeting, hadn't been planned, and so they were perplexed as they awaited the outcome. Sancho was struck by the girl's beauty, and he asked her who she was, where she was going and what it was that had made her dress up like that. With her eyes fixed on the ground in maidenly bashfulness she replied:

'I can't reveal in public, sir, something I was so concerned to keep secret; but one thing I do want to make clear to everyone: I'm not a thief or any other kind of criminal, but an unfortunate young girl driven by jealousy to disregard the decorum required of a respectable woman.'

When the butler heard this he said to Sancho:

'Tell the people to go away, my lord Governor, so that this lady can say whatever she likes without feeling embarrassed.'

The governor did so; they all went away, except the butler, the steward and the secretary. And then the girl continued:

'Gentlemen, I am the daughter of Pedro Pérez Mazorca, who administers the wool-tax in this town, and often comes to my father's house.'

'No, that will never do, my lady,' said the butler, 'because I know Pedro Pérez very well, and I know he hasn't got any children, male or female; and what's more you say he's your father and then you add that he often comes to your father's house.'

'I'd spotted that as well,' said Sancho.

'I'm so flustered, gentlemen, that I don't know what I'm saying,' said the girl. 'The truth is that I'm the daughter of Diego de la Llana, whom you all must know.'

'Now, that's more like it,' the butler replied, 'because I know Diego de la Llana, and I know that he's an important and wealthy hidalgo, and that he has a son and a daughter, and ever since he's been a widower nobody in this town can claim to have ever set eyes on the daughter, because he keeps her so shut away that he doesn't even give the sun a chance to glimpse her, and in spite of all that she has the reputation of being extremely beautiful.'

'That's all true,' the girl replied, 'and I am that daughter you speak of; and now you've found out for yourselves whether my reputation for beauty is justified or not, because you've all seen me.'

And she began to weep softly. The secretary whispered into the steward's ear:

'Something serious must have happened to this poor girl to make her walk the streets in those clothes and at this time of night, and she's from such a good family, too.'

'There can't be any doubt about that,' the steward replied, 'and what's more her tears confirm your suspicion.'

Sancho comforted her with the best words he could find, and asked her not to be afraid to tell them what had happened, because they were all going to try their very hardest to help her in every possible way.

'The fact is, gentlemen,' she replied, 'that my father has kept me shut away these past ten years, ever since my mother was laid in her grave. Mass is said at home in a beautiful oratory, so in all this time I've only ever seen the sun in the sky by day and the moon and the stars by night, and I don't know anything about streets or squares or churches or even men, except my father and my brother and Pedro Pérez the wool-tax man, who visits the house so often that I had that bright idea just now of saying he was my father so as not to say who my real one was. Being locked up like this and never allowed to leave home, not even to go to church, has been making me feel depressed for a long, long time; I wanted to see the world, or at least the town I was born in, and I didn't believe this wish infringed the decorum that young ladies of rank are supposed to observe. Whenever I heard talk about bullfights and mock battles and plays, I asked my brother, who's a year younger than me, to tell me about these things, and about others that I've never seen; he explained it all as best he could, but this only made me long even more desperately to see it for myself. In the end, to cut short the story of my undoing, I have to tell you that I begged and entreated my brother, and I wish I'd never begged or entreated him to do any such thing . . .'

And she burst into tears again. The butler said:

'Do continue, my lady, and finish telling us what has happened, because your words and your tears are keeping us all in suspense.'

'I have few more words to say,' the girl replied, 'though many a tear to shed, because that's the only return to be had from badly invested desires.'

The girl's beauty had made a deep impression on the steward's heart, and he held his lantern up again to take another look at her, and he thought it wasn't tears she was shedding but seed-pearls or meadow-dew, and then he promoted them and called them pearls of orient, and he was hoping against hope that her misfortune wasn't as very great as her tears and her sobs suggested. The governor was in despair at the way the girl was spinning out her story, and he told her to relieve them all of their suspense, because it was late and there was still a lot more of the town to patrol. And between gasping sobs and broken sighs she said:

'This is my misfortune, this is my calamity: I asked my brother to dress me as a man in one of his suits, and take me out to see the town, while our father was asleep. I pestered my brother so much that he agreed to what I wanted, dressed in these clothes and himself put on an outfit of mine that suits him down to the ground, because he hasn't a single hair on his face and looks just like a lovely young woman; and tonight, it must have been about an hour ago, we left home, and borne along by our youthful and misguided ideas we've walked all round the town, and just when we were about to go home we saw a great crowd of people on their way towards us, and my brother said:

' "This must be the authorities on their rounds, my girl – put wings on your feet and run after me, so that they don't recognize us, or we'll be in for it."

'And as he said this he turned and started running – no, he started flying, but I hadn't gone half a dozen paces before the fright of it all made me fall over, and then the officer of the law came up and brought me before you, to be shamed before all these people as a flighty, wicked young thing.'

'So, my young lady,' said Sancho, 'there haven't been any other disasters, and it wasn't jealousy that made you leave home at all, as you said it was at the start of your story?'

'No, nothing else has happened, and it wasn't jealousy that made me leave home but the urge to see the world, which didn't go any further than seeing the streets of this town.'

And the truth of what the girl had said was confirmed when the constables appeared with her brother as their prisoner, caught by one of them after he'd abandoned his sister in his flight. He was wearing nothing less than a splendid skirt, over his shoulders a blue damask mantilla with fine gold trimmings, his head unadorned by any veil or anything else apart from his own tresses, as fair and curly as rings of gold. The governor, the butler and the steward took him aside so that his sister couldn't hear, and asked him why he was wearing such clothes; and he, no less embarrassed and ashamed, told them the same story, which filled the enamoured steward with joy. But the governor said:

'To be sure, my young friends, this has been a very childish prank, and to explain this silly escapade of yours there wasn't any need for all that stalling and sighing and sobbing, because if you'd just said, "We're so-and-so and so-and-so, and we left our parents' house to have a bit of fun, in these disguises, just out of curiosity, without any other thought in mind," that would have been that, without any whining or blubbering or going on and on and on.'

'You're quite right,' the girl replied, 'but you must remember that I was in such a state I simply couldn't stay as composed as I should.'

'No harm done,' Sancho replied. 'Come on then, we'll take you home, maybe your father hasn't missed you. And in future don't behave like little children, and don't be so anxious to see the world – a lass's place is in the home, and women and hens are lost by gadding, and the woman who wants to see wants to be seen. That's all I've got to say.'

The youth thanked the governor for his kind offer to take them home, and they set off to walk the short distance to it. When they arrived the brother threw a pebble up at a grille over a window, and a maidservant who'd been waiting for them came straight down and opened the door, and in they went, leaving everyone amazed both at their charm and beauty and at their desire to see the world, by night and without leaving town; but they put it all down to their youth.

The steward was left with his heart transfixed, and he resolved to ask her father for her hand in marriage the very next day, certain that this wouldn't be denied to one of the Duke's own servants; and Sancho even felt the inclination to marry his daughter Sanchica to the lad, and decided to raise the matter for discussion when the time was right, in the belief that no prospective husband could be refused to a governor's daughter.

And this ended the night's rounds, and two days later the governorship itself ended, which upset and destroyed all Sancho's plans, as will be seen later.

CHAPTER L

Which reveals the identities of the enchanters and
executioners who beat the duenna and pinched and scratched
Don Quixote, and also what happened to the page who
took the letter to Sancho Panza's wife, Teresa Sancha

Cide Hamete, that painstaking investigator of the most minute details of this true history, says that when Doña Rodríguez left her room to go to see Don Quixote, her room-mate heard her and, since all duennas are fond of knowing about everything, finding out about everything and sniffing into everything, followed her, keeping so very quiet that the good Rodríguez didn't notice; and as soon as the duenna saw where she'd gone she scuttled off to let her lady the Duchess know that Doña Rodríguez was in Don Quixote's room, just to keep alive the universal custom of tale-bearing that characterizes all duennas. The Duchess told the Duke and asked his permission for her and Altisidora to go to see what that duenna Rodríguez wanted with Don Quixote. The Duke gave it, and the two women inched their way along on tiptoe until they were outside Don Quixote's door, so close to it that they could hear everything being said inside the room; and when the Duchess heard Rodríguez opening to the public the secret garden of flowing fountains in her legs she couldn't restrain herself, and nor could Altisidora; and so, burning with rage and thirsting for revenge, they burst into the room and riddled Don Quixote and thrashed the duenna in the way described; because insults directed against women's beauty and their pride in it arouse all fury within them and inflame the desire for revenge.

The Duchess told the Duke what had happened, which he found frightfully amusing; and, pressing on with her plans to play hoaxes on Don Quixote and be entertained by him, she sent the page who'd played Dulcinea when the disenchanting arrangements were made (long since driven out of Sancho Panza's head by the cares of government) to Teresa Panza with her husband's letter, another from the Duchess herself and a long string of fine corals as a present. The history states that this page was intelligent and sharp-witted, and that, anxious as he was to serve his master and mistress, he was happy to travel to Sancho's village; and just before reaching it he saw a group of women doing their washing in a stream and asked them if they could tell him whether one Teresa Panza lived there, the wife of a certain Sancho Panza, the squire of a knight called Don Quixote de la Mancha; and on hearing the question a young lass who was washing jumped up and said:

'That Teresa Panza you said is my mother, and that Sancho's my father, and that knight's our master.'

'Well, come with me, young lady,' said the page, 'and take me to your mother; because I bring her a letter and a present from that father of yours.'

'I'll be very happy to, sir,' replied the lass, who seemed to be about fourteen. And leaving the clothes she was washing with one of her companions, and without putting anything on her head or her feet – she was barefoot and dishevelled – she jumped out in front of the page's horse and said:

'You come with me – our house is at the beginning of the village, and my mother's at home, and she's very sad because she hasn't had word from my father for ever so long.'

'Well, I bring such very good news for her,' said the page, 'that she'll have to give God hearty thanks for it.'

And leaping, running and skipping along, the girl eventually reached the village, but rather than going into her house she shouted from the door:

'Come here, mother, Teresa, come here, come here, there's a gentleman here with letters and other things from Daddy.'

These shouts brought her mother Teresa Panza to the door, spinning a distaff of tow, and wearing a brown skirt, which was so skimpy that it looked as if she'd been punished by having it shortened at the placket.[1] She wore a bodice, also brown, and an open-necked blouse. She wasn't very old although she seemed to be past forty, but she was strong, erect, wiry and weatherbeaten; and when she saw her daughter, and the page on his horse, she said:

'What's this, girl? What gentleman is this?'

'A servant of my lady Doña Teresa Panza,' the page replied. And as he spoke he leapt down from his horse and went humbly to kneel before Señora Teresa, saying:

'Give me your hands, Señora Doña Teresa, as the lawful wedded wife of Señor Don Sancho Panza, rightful Governor of the Island of Barataria.'

'Oh, sir, get away with you, don't do that!' Teresa replied. 'I'm not a palace sort at all, just a poor farming woman, a clodhopper's daughter and a squire errant's wife, not the wife of any governor!'

'Madam,' the page replied, 'you are the most worthy wife of a most eminently worthy governor, and as proof of this fact be so good as to accept this letter and this present.'

And he took from his pocket a string of corals with a gold bead every couple of inches, put it round her neck and said:

'This letter is from my lord the Governor, and another letter I bring and this string of corals are from my lady the Duchess, who has sent me to you.'

Teresa was dumbfounded, and so was her daughter, who said:

'I'll be blowed if our master Don Quixote isn't mixed up in all this – he must have given Daddy that government or earldom he'd promised him so often.'

'You're quite right,' the page replied. 'It's thanks to Don Quixote that Señor Sancho is now the governor of the Island of Barataria, as you will be able to confirm in this letter.'

'Do read it out to me, good sir,' said Teresa, 'because although I can spin I can't read a thing.'

'Me neither,' added Sanchica, 'but you two wait here and I'll go and fetch somebody to read it, the priest maybe, or that student Sansón Carrasco, and they'll be only too happy to come, to hear news of my father.'

'There's no need to fetch anyone: I can't spin, but I can read, and so I'll read it out.'

And he did read it out, but since it has already been given it isn't repeated here; and then he fished out another letter, from the Duchess, and it said:

My dear Teresa,

Your husband's most excellent qualities of goodness and cleverness have moved and indeed obliged me to ask my husband the Duke to give him the governorship of one of the many islands that he possesses. I'm told he's governing like a perfect angel, which makes me so very happy, and as a consequence my lord the Duke is happy as well, and so I give the most fulsome thanks to heaven that I wasn't mistaken when I chose him for the governorship; because I want Señora Teresa to know that it's no easy matter to find an able governor nowadays, and may God treat me as well as Sancho governs.

With this I'm sending you, my dear, a string of corals with gold paternosters; I do wish they could have been pearls of orient, but then it's the thought that counts, isn't it? The time will come when we'll get to know each other personally and converse together, but only God knows the future. Give my kindest regards to your daughter Sanchica, and tell her from me to hold herself in readiness, because I intend to marry her to a man of high rank when she least expects it.

I'm told that there are fine fat acorns to be had in your village; do send me a couple of dozen of them, as it's a gift that I shall prize most highly, coming from you; and write me a long letter telling me how you are and how everything is with

you; and if there's anything you need you only have to say so, and your every word
will be my command, and God keep you. From this town,

Your ever loving friend,

THE DUCHESS

'Oh!' said Teresa. 'What a good, straightforward, down-to-earth lady. Give me ladies like that any time, not the hidalgos' wives you get in this village, thinking that just because they are hidalgos' wives the very wind hasn't got any right to blow on them, and they put on such airs and graces when they go to church that anyone would take them for queens, and they seem to think it's beneath them to even look at a working woman. And now this good lady, a duchess and all, calls me her friend and treats me as an equal – equal to the highest bell-tower in all La Mancha, that's where I'd put her. As for the acorns, sir, I'll send Her Ladyship a whole gallon of them, and they're so fine and fat they're a sight for sore eyes. And the first thing to do now, Sanchica, is to make sure that this gentleman's properly looked after – see to his horse, get some eggs from the stable, cut off a good big hunk of nice fat bacon, and let's get him a meal fit for a king, he deserves it for all the good news he's brought us and for that lovely face of his, and in the meantime I'll go and give the neighbours the happy news, and the priest and Master Nicolás the barber too, they're so good to your father and always have been.'

'Yes, mother,' Sanchica replied, 'but you're going to have to give me half that string of corals, mind, because I don't take my lady the Duchess for such a fool as to send it all to you.'

'It's all yours, my dear,' Teresa replied, 'but let me wear it for a few days, it truly seems to gladden my heart.'

'You'll also be glad,' said the page, 'when you see the bundle in this bag: an outfit of the finest worsted that the governor only wore for one day's hunting, all for Señora Sanchica.'

'May he live a thousand years!' replied Sanchica. 'And the same goes for the man that brought it, or even two thousand, if need be.'

Teresa hurried out of the house carrying the letters and with the string of corals round her neck, and she was drumming her fingers on the letters as if they were a tambourine; and coming across the priest and Sansón Carrasco she started dancing and yelling:

'We aren't the poor relations any more, oh no! We've got a government, we have! Oh yes, the finest of your fine hidalgos' wives can come looking for trouble, she can, and I'll leave her looking just like new, I will!'

'What's the meaning of this, Teresa Panza? What madness is this, and what papers are these?'

'The madness is only that these here are letters from duchesses and governors, and what I've got round my neck is fine coral, the avemaries that is, and the paternosters are made of beaten gold, and I'm a governess!'

'God alone can understand you, Teresa – we certainly don't know what you mean.'

'You can read all about it here,' Teresa replied.

And she gave them the letters. The priest read them aloud for Sansón Carrasco to hear, and Sansón and the priest glanced at each other with looks of amazement at what the letters said, and the young graduate asked who had brought them. Teresa replied that if they came home with her they'd see the messenger for themselves – he was a young lad as pretty as a picture, and he'd brought another present worth even more. The priest took the string of corals from her neck, looked at them and then looked at them again; satisfying himself that they were good ones, he was again struck with amazement, and said:

'I swear by this habit I'm wearing that I just don't know what to say or think about these letters and these presents; on the one hand I can see and feel the excellence of this coral, and on the other hand I read that a duchess writes to ask for a couple of dozen of acorns.'

'Stuff and nonsense!' Carrasco interrupted. 'But let's go to see the bearer of this letter – he'll solve the problem for us.'

This is what they did, and Teresa went with them. They found the page sieving some barley for his horse and Sanchica slicing off a chunk of fat bacon to mix with scrambled eggs for the page's dinner. His looks and his fine clothes pleased both men; and, after the exchange of courteous greetings, Sansón asked for news of Don Quixote and Sancho Panza, because although they'd read the letters written by Sancho and her ladyship the Duchess, they were still confused and couldn't fathom this business of Sancho's governorship, of an island what was more, when all or nearly all the islands in the Mediterranean Sea belonged to His Majesty. To which the page replied:

'As regards Señor Sancho's being a governor, there can't be any doubt about that; as regards whether or not it's an island he's governing, that's no concern of mine, but it's quite enough for it to be a town of more than five thousand inhabitants; and as regards the acorns, I can tell you my lady the Duchess is so straightforward and down-to-earth,' he continued, 'that she doesn't just write to a farmer's wife to ask for acorns, she's even been known to ask a neighbour to lend her a comb. Because I'd have you know that even though the ladies of Aragon are just as high-ranking as Castilian ladies, they aren't as punctilious or haughty; they're more informal in their dealings with other people.'

In the middle of this conversation Sanchica burst in with an apronful of eggs and asked the page:

'Tell me, sir, does my father wear long breeches now he's a governor?'

'I haven't looked to see,' the page replied, 'but I expect he does.'

'God!' replied Sancha. 'And what a sight it must be to see my father in those! Isn't it funny, ever since I was born I've wanted to see my father in long breeches!'

'You'll see him wearing all those sorts of clothes, if you live long enough,' the page replied. 'God Almighty, he's well set to ride around in a travelling mask like all the top people if he stays in office for another couple of months!'

The priest and the young graduate could easily see that the page was pulling her leg; but the excellence of the corals and the hunting outfit that Sancho had sent and that Teresa had shown them threw them into confusion. They didn't refrain from laughing at Sanchica's wish, and even more when Teresa said:

'Reverend sir, please could you look around to see whether there's anyone from these parts about to go to Madrid or Toledo so they can buy me a nice round farthingale, one in fashion, best quality, because I've got to do my husband's government as much credit as ever I can, and even if it does irk me I must go to the capital and get myself a carriage like all the other women – a lady with a governor for a husband has every right to keep a carriage.'

'Hasn't she just, mummy!' said Sanchica. 'And God grant it comes sooner rather than later, even if the people who see me sitting next to my fine mother in our carriage do say, "Just look at the little pipsqueak, the daughter of that garlic-stuffed peasant, lolling about in that carriage as if she was the Pope himself!" But then they'll be tramping through their mud and I'll be riding in my carriage with my feet well clear of the ground. A thousand plagues on all the gossips in the world – and if I'm nice and warm in my smock who cares if they all laugh and mock! Isn't that right, mummy?'

'Of course you're right, my dear!' Teresa replied. 'And my good Sancho did tell me that all this good fortune, and even better, was on its way, and you'll soon see, my girl – he won't let up till he's made me a countess, it's all a question of starting to get the luck coming your way, and as I've often heard your dear father say, who's just as much the father of proverbs as he's the father of my children, when you're offered a heifer make haste with the halter – so when you're offered a government grab it, when you're offered a countship collar it and when they say "Come here boy" with something worth eating, go and get your teeth round it. Oh yes, I'm going to be caught napping, I am, and I won't answer the door when all this good fortune comes knocking, oh no!'

'And what do I care,' Sanchica added, 'if people who see me all stuck-up and snooty do say, "Dress a dog in fancy linen," and so on, if that's what they feel like saying?'

When the priest heard this, he said:

'I can only believe that every member of this breed of Panzas was born complete with a sackful of proverbs inside him; I haven't met a single one who doesn't reel them off at all hours of the day and in all his conversations.'

'That is true,' said the page, 'because my lord Governor Sancho comes out with them all the time, and although lots are off the point they're still good to listen to, and my lady the Duchess and the Duke are delighted with them.'

'And do you still assert, my dear sir,' said the graduate, 'that this story about Sancho being governor is true, and that there actually is a duchess who sends his wife presents and writes to her? Because even though we have handled the presents and read the letters, we still can't believe it, and we think this must be another of those escapades of our neighbour Don Quixote, who fancies that everything is done by enchantment; and so I'm on the verge of saying that I'd like to touch and feel you too, to see whether you're a fantasy messenger or a man of flesh and blood.'

'All I know, gentlemen,' the page replied, 'is that I am a real messenger, and that Señor Sancho is a genuine governor, and that my master and mistress the Duke and Duchess can give and have given him the governorship, and that I have heard that the said Sancho Panza is performing his duties most admirably. Whether or not there's any enchanting mixed up in all this is something that you'll have to argue out among yourselves; because that's all I know, and I swear it on the lives of my parents, who are still alive and whom I love dearly.'

'That could all well be true,' the graduate replied, 'but *dubitat Augustinus*.'[2]

'I don't care who doubts it,' said the page, 'because what I've just said is the honest truth, which will always prevail over any lie, as oil floats on water; and if you don't believe me, *operibus credite, et non verbis:* one of you come back with me and your eyes will see what your ears don't believe.'

'Bags I go,' said Sanchica. 'Do take me with you, sir, on the crupper of your horse, I'd love to go and see my dear father.'

'Governors' daughters must not travel alone along the highways, but attended by coaches and litters and great retinues of servants.'

'For God's sake,' Sancha replied, 'I can go on a donkey as well as in any carriage. So we've found her at last, the finicky little prude, have we?'

'Keep quiet, girl,' said Teresa, 'you don't know what you're saying, and this gentleman's quite right, because circumstances alter cases – when it was Sancho it was Sancha and now it's governor it's my lady. I don't know if what I'm saying makes any sense.'

'Señora Teresa is making more sense than she realizes,' said the page, 'and now I'd like something to eat – and see to it quickly, because I intend to return this afternoon.'

To which the priest replied:

'You must come to share my humble board; Señora Teresa is more amply provided with goodwill than with a dinner service to do justice to such a fine guest.'

The page refused the priest's offer; but he had to relent, because it was the better one, and the priest was happy to take him home, because this provided the opportunity to ask at leisure about Don Quixote and his doings. The graduate offered to write Teresa's answers to her letters; but she didn't want the graduate poking his nose into her affairs, because she thought he was rather too fond of pulling people's legs, so she gave one bread roll and two eggs to an altar boy who knew how to write, and he penned two letters for her, one to her husband and the other to the Duchess, all her own work, and they aren't the worst letters in this great history, as will be seen in due course.

CHAPTER LI

About the progress of Sancho's government, and other most excellent events

Day dawned after the night of the governor's rounds, a sleepless night for the steward, with his thoughts engrossed by the face, the dash and the beauty of the girl in disguise; and the butler spent what was left of it writing to his master and mistress about what Sancho Panza said and did, as amazed at his sayings as at his doings, because of the mixture of intelligence and stupidity in his words and deeds. The governor eventually arose from his bed and on the orders of Dr Pedro Recio was given for his breakfast a little candied fruit and half a dozen sips of iced water, something that Sancho would have been pleased to exchange for a hunk of bread and a bunch of grapes. But seeing that it was a question of compulsion rather than choice he submitted to it, with desolation in his soul and tribulation in his stomach, because Pedro Recio had persuaded him that a tiny amount of delicate food sharpened the mind, this being what was needed by people appointed to govern and to fill positions of responsibility in which it is not so much their physical as their mental powers that they have to employ. All this sophistry kept Sancho hungry, so much so that he secretly cursed the governorship and even the person who had presented him with it; but he went to work on his candied fruit and his hunger, and he began his judging, and what he first had to consider was a problem posed by a stranger in the presence of the butler and his henchmen, and it was this:

'Sir, a great river divided a lord's estate into two parts – do pay attention, please, it's an important case and rather a difficult one. I was about to say, then, that there was a bridge across this river and at one end of it a gallows and some sort of a court-house, in which sat four judges to administer a law imposed by the owner of the river, the bridge and the estate, and the law went like this:

If anybody wishes to cross this bridge, he must first state under oath where he is going and for what purpose; and if he tells the truth he is to be allowed to cross it, and if he tells a lie he is to be hanged on the gallows that stand there, without any possible reprieve.

'Despite knowing about this law and its rigorous enforcement, many people used the bridge, and it immediately became clear that their state-ments were true, and the judges allowed them across. But it so happened that one man took his solemn oath and then stated that his purpose was none other than to die on those gallows standing there. The judges considered his statement and said:

' "If we allow this man to go free and cross the bridge, then his statement was a false one and according to the law he must die; but if we hang him, he stated that he was going to die on those gallows, and according to the same law he should go free."

'You are asked, my lord Governor, what the judges should do with this man; because to this day they remain perplexed and undecided. And having heard about your fine, incisive mind, they've sent me to beg you for your opinion about such a complex and puzzling case.'

To which Sancho replied:

'I must say these judges who've sent you to me could have spared themselves the trouble, because I'm not one of your incisive sorts at all – thick, more like. Still, you tell me the story again in words I can understand – who knows, I might hit upon an answer.'

The problem-poser repeated again and again what he'd said the first time, and finally Sancho said:

'I reckon I can sum up this whole rigmarole in a brace of shakes like this: this bloke says under oath he's going to die on the gallows, and if he does die, he's told the truth, and according to the law he deserves to go free and cross the bridge; and if they don't hang him, he's told a lie, and according to the same law he deserves to be hanged.'

'It is precisely as my lord Governor says,' said the messenger, 'and as far as a full understanding of the case goes, his account leaves nothing to be desired or open to doubt.'

'What I say, then,' Sancho replied, 'is that they ought to let the part of the man that told the truth go across the bridge, and hang the part of the man that told the lie – and in this way they'll fulfil the conditions to the letter.'

'But, my lord Governor,' the problem-poser replied, 'that will make it necessary to divide the man into two parts, the deceitful part and the truthful part, and if this is done he's bound to die, and so none of what the law demands will be achieved, and it's of vital necessity to comply with it.'

'Look here, my man,' Sancho replied, 'either I'm a blockhead or it'd be as reasonable to kill that traveller of yours as to let him live and cross the bridge, because if the truth he told saves him, his lie condemns him just as much – and if this is so, which it is, I reckon you should tell those gentlemen who sent you here that since the reasons for condemning him and for acquitting him balance each other out, he should be let free to cross the bridge, because doing good is always more highly praised than doing harm, and I'd give you this decision under my hand and seal if I knew how to sign my name. And in this case I haven't been speaking out of my own head, because what came into my mind was one of the rules that along with lots and lots of others my master Don Quixote laid down for me on the night before I came to be governor of this island, and it was that when there were any doubts about justice I should go for leniency and mercy, and it pleased God to let me remember it now, because it fits this case like a glove.'

'Quite so,' the butler replied, 'and it's my belief that Lycurgus himself, who gave the Lacedaemonians[1] their laws, couldn't have given a better decision than the one that the great Panza has just given. And with this let this morning's audience be closed, and I shall arrange for my lord Governor to eat a lunch that he will greatly enjoy.'

'Yes, that's what I want, and no messing about,' said Sancho, 'let me have some food, and then cases and problems can rain down on me for all they're worth, and I'll sort them out in mid-air.'

The butler was as good as his word, because he thought it would be a burden on his conscience to starve such a wise governor; and what's more he was planning to be rid of him that same night, by playing the last hoax with which he'd been charged. And after the governor had lunched that day against all Dr Vamos's rules and aphorisms, as the tables were being cleared, a messenger came with a letter from Don Quixote for the governor. Sancho ordered the secretary to look through it and, if it contained nothing secret, to read it out aloud. Once the secretary had examined it he said:

'It can most certainly be read aloud, because what Don Quixote writes here deserves to be printed in letters of gold, and this is what it says:

Letter from Don Quixote de la Mancha to Sancho Panza, Governor of the island of Barataria

Whereas I was expecting to receive news of your negligence and your blunders, friend Sancho, I have had reports of your intelligent behaviour, for which I have given particular thanks to heaven, which can lift the needy out of the dunghill and turn fools into men of good sense. I am told that you govern as if you were a man, and that you are a man as if you were an animal, because your behaviour is so humble; and I want you to bear in mind, Sancho, that it is often advisable and necessary to oppose the humility of one's heart for the sake of the dignity of one's position; because the fine apparel worn by the person in a post of great responsibility must accord with the requirements of this post and not with the preferences of his own humble disposition. Wear good clothes: dress up a stick and it does not look like a stick. I am not saying that you should wear trinkets or regalia, because you are a judge, not a soldier; but that you should wear the clothes that your office requires, ensuring that they are clean and tidy.

To gain the goodwill of the people you govern there are two things that you must do, among others: in the first place, be polite to everybody, although I have already told you about that, and secondly try to ensure a plentiful supply of food, because nothing wearies the hearts of the poor as much as hunger and deprivation.

Do not publish too many edicts, and ensure that those you do publish are good ones and above all that they are observed and obeyed, for edicts that are not obeyed might as well not exist; they serve only to indicate that the ruler who has the intelligence and authority to publish them lacks the courage to enforce them, and laws containing threats that are not carried out are like the log that was the king of the frogs, and that frightened them at first; but in time they came to scorn it and climb on top of it.[3]

Be a father to virtue and a stepfather to vice. Do not always be severe, or always mild, but choose the middle way between these two extremes; herein lies the essence of wisdom.

Visit the prisons, the butchers' shops and the markets, for the governor's presence in such places is of the greatest importance: he is a comfort for the prisoners, who are led to expect an early release; he is a bogeyman for the butchers, who have to use accurate weights for a while; and he is a bugbear for the market-women, for the same reason.

Do not show yourself to be covetous, a womanizer or a glutton, even if you are (which I do not believe to be the case); because as soon as the people and those who have dealings with you discover your weakness, they will concentrate their attacks on that point, until they topple you down into the depths of perdition.

Consider and reconsider, think and think again about the advice and instructions I wrote out for you before you left for your governorship, and you will see that you can find there, if you heed them, a contribution towards suffering the trials and tribulations that beset governors at every turn.

Write to your patrons to show how grateful you are; for ingratitude is the daughter of pride and one of the greatest sins there are, and the person who is grateful to those who have done him favours indicates thereby that he will also be grateful to God, who has done him and continues to do him so very many favours.

My lady the Duchess has sent a messenger with your outfit and another present to your wife Teresa Panza; we are expecting a reply at any moment.

I have been a little indisposed from a certain cat-clawing that I underwent at some slight expense to my nose, but it was nothing, for if there are enchanters to ill-treat me there are others to defend me.

Let me know whether that butler who is with you had anything to do with the Trifaldi affair, as you suspected; and keep me informed about everything that happens to you, because the distance separating us is so small; what is more, I intend soon to abandon this idle life that I am living, because I was not born for it.

A certain matter has arisen that will, I believe, cause me to fall out of favour with my lord and lady. But although this is of great concern to me, it is of no *concern to me at all, because when all is said and done I must comply with my profession rather than with their pleasure, in accordance with what is often said: amicus Plato, sed magis amica veritas.*[4] *I include this Latin maxim because I suppose that now you are a governor you will have learned that language. And God be with you and keep you from being pitied by anyone.*

Your friend,
DON QUIXOTE DE LA MANCHA

Sancho listened attentively to the letter, which was praised for its sound sense by all who had heard it, and then he rose from the table, called to the secretary and shut himself up with him in his room, and without delay he set about answering his master Don Quixote. He told the secretary to write down what he dictated, without adding or taking away a word; the secretary did so, and Sancho's reply went like this:

Letter from Sancho Panza to Don Quixote de la Mancha

I'm so busy with all the things I must deal with that I haven't even got the time to scratch my head or cut my nails and so they've got very long, heaven help me. I'm only saying this, my dear master, to stop you from being worried because until now I haven't written to tell you about how well or badly things are going for me in my governing, where I'm hungrier than when us two used to wander through the forests and the wilds.

My lord the Duke wrote to me the other day, warning me that some spies had come on to the island to kill me, and so far the only one I've discovered is a certain doctor who's employed in this town to kill all the governors that come here, he's called Dr Pedro Recio and he's from Vamos, and who wouldn't fear death at his hands, coming from a village with a name like that. This doctor says he doesn't cure illnesses when people are ill, but stops them from getting ill in the first place, and the medicines he gives you are diets and more diets, until he reduces you to skin and bone, as if being thin wasn't even worse than being overheated. In short, he's starving me to death, and anyway I'm dying of dejection, because I thought I was coming to this government to eat hot food and drink cool wine and relax between sheets of holland on feather beds, but the truth is I've come to do penance as if I was some hermit, and since I'm not doing it of my own free will I think I'm going to end up going straight to the devil.

So far all bribes I've refused and I haven't caught sight of any dues, and I can't think what's the point of this, because I've been told that all the other governors that come to this island take lots of money from the islanders in gifts or loans even before they arrive, and that this is the normal practice with anyone who's made a governor, not just here.

Last night when I was on my rounds I came across a beautiful young girl in man's clothes and a brother of hers in woman's clothes. My steward fell in love with the girl and chose her in his mind to be his wife, so he's told me, and I chose the lad to be my son-in-law, so today both of us are going to put our plans into effect with their father, a man called Diego de la Llana, a hidalgo and as much of an old Christian as anyone could want.

I visit the markets as you said, and yesterday I came across a stallholder selling fresh hazelnuts, and I found she'd mixed a bushel of new nuts with a bushel of old ones, empty and rotten — I confiscated them for the children in the orphanage, who won't have any trouble sorting them out, and I sentenced her to not setting foot in the market for a fortnight. I've been told it was a brave decision, and I can tell you everyone here says there are no people more wicked than these market-women, because they're a shameless, heartless, brazen lot, and I can believe it too, to judge from the ones I've seen in other towns.

What you say about my lady the Duchess writing to my wife Teresa Panza and sending her the present you mention makes me really pleased, and I'll try to show how grateful I am when the time comes, and please kiss her hands for me and tell her from me that her kindness isn't going to slip my mind, and I'll give her proof of that. I wouldn't want you to have any nasty rows with my lord and lady, because if you cross swords with them it's clear that I'll suffer for it, and it wouldn't be right for you to be advising me to be grateful and then not be grateful yourself to people who have done you all those kindnesses and treated you so royally in their castle.

The bit about the catting I don't understand, but I suppose it must have been one of those nasty tricks that wicked enchanters keep playing on you, and I'll find out when we meet.

I'd like to send you something, only I don't know what, except for some enema tubes for using with bladders, they make very neat ones on this island, though if I last at this job I'll find something to send, by hook or by crook.

If my wife Teresa Panza writes to me, you pay to have the letter brought here, because I'm longing to know how things are with my house, my wife and my *children. And so may God deliver you from evil-minded enchanters and bring me safe and sound out of this governing – though I doubt it, because I'll be lucky to get out of here alive, the way I'm being treated by Dr Pedro Recio.*

Your servant,

THE GOVERNOR SANCHO PANZA

The secretary sealed the letter and sent the messenger packing, and Sancho's hoaxers put their heads together and made their arrangements for sending Sancho packing from his governorship; and Sancho spent that afternoon making some by-laws concerning the smooth running of what he believed to be an island, and he ordered that no food be sold by anyone other than its producer, and that wine be permitted to be brought from all parts provided that the place of origin was declared so that a price could be fixed according to its popularity, quality and reputation, and anyone who watered it down or sold one wine for another would pay for his crime with his life. He lowered the price of all footwear, in particular shoes, because he considered it exorbitant. He established limits for servants' wages, which were galloping headlong down the road of self-interest. He imposed severe penalties on anyone singing lewd and disorderly songs, by night or by day. He ordered that no blind man sing his couplets about miracles unless he had solid evidence authenticating them, because he considered that most of the miracles that blind men sing about are fictitious, and bring discredit on the true ones. He created the post of overseer of beggars, not for this official to persecute them but rather to examine them to ensure that they really were unable to work, because feigned mutilations and false sores are covers for thieving arms and sound-bodied drunkenness. In short, Sancho made such excellent by-laws that they have remained in force in the town to this day, and they are called *The Ordinances of the Great Governor Sancho Panza.*

CHAPTER LII

Which relates the adventure of the second Dolorous or Anguished Duenna, otherwise known as Doña Rodríguez

Cide Hamete relates that once Don Quixote had recovered from his scratches the life he was leading in that castle seemed to him to be quite contrary to the order of chivalry that he professed, so he decided to request the permission of the Duke and Duchess to leave for Saragossa, as the fiestas there were drawing near and he intended to win the jousting prize, a complete suit of armour. But one day when he was at table with the Duke and Duchess, and beginning to put his intention into effect and ask for their permission, lo and behold, the door of the great hall was flung open and two women (as it later transpired) walked in, draped in mourning from head to foot, and one of them came up to Don Quixote, threw herself flat on the floor at his feet with her lips pressed to them and poured out such sorrowful, profound and painful sighs that all who could see and hear her were thrown into consternation; and although the Duke and Duchess thought this was some hoax that their servants were playing on Don Quixote, the anguished insistence with which the woman sighed and groaned and sobbed made them feel uncertain, until the compassionate Don Quixote raised her from the floor and begged her to remove the veil from her tearful face. She did so, and revealed what never could have been suspected – because what came into view was the face of the duenna Doña Rodríguez, and the other woman in mourning was her daughter, deceived by the rich farmer's son. All those who knew her were astonished, and the Duke and Duchess more than anyone else; because although they considered her a simple soul, they hadn't thought her quite so stupid as to perform such antics. Finally Doña Rodríguez turned to her master and mistress and said:

'Please will Your Excellencies be so kind as to give me permission to converse briefly with this knight, because this is what I have to do in order to extricate myself from the dilemma created for me by the presumption of an evil-minded peasant.'

The Duke said she had his permission and could converse with Don

Quixote as much as she liked. She turned to face Don Quixote and addressed him:

'Some days ago, most valiant knight, I gave you an account of the treacherous wrong that a wicked farmer perpetrated on my deeply beloved daughter, this unfortunate creature standing here before you, and you promised to support her cause and redress the wrong that she has suffered; but now it has come to my attention that you intend to depart from this castle in quest of whatever good fortune God may send your way; and so, before you slip off along those highways, I should like you to challenge this untamed rustic and compel him to marry my daughter in accordance with the promise he made her, before he lay with her, to be her husband; because to expect my lord the Duke to do us any justice is to go looking for figs on thistles, for the reason of which I have already informed you in private. And may our Lord grant you good health and not deprive us of his protection.'

To these words Don Quixote replied with great gravity and ceremony:

'Good duenna, temper your tears, or, rather, wipe them away, and spare your sighs, for I hereby make myself responsible for succouring your daughter, who would have done better not to be so ready to believe lovers' promises, which are for the most part quick in the making and slow in the keeping; and so by my lord the Duke's leave I will depart immediately in search of that heartless youth, and I will find him, and I will challenge him, and I will kill him should he refuse to fulfil his promise; for the principal occupation of my profession is to forgive the humble and punish the arrogant; that is to say, to succour the wretched and destroy the cruel.'

'There isn't any need,' the Duke replied, 'for you to go to the trouble of looking for the rustic that this good duenna's complaining about, nor is there any need for you to ask for my permission to challenge him: I consider him challenged already, and I will make it my personal responsibility to ensure that he's aware of this challenge and accepts it, and comes to answer for himself to this my castle, where I shall provide the two of you with a fair field, observing all the conditions that are and must be observed on such occasions, and ensure that equal justice is done to each party, as is required of all those noblemen who make lists available to those who engage in combat within the bounds of their territories.'

'Given that assurance, then, and by Your Grace's kind leave,' Don Quixote replied, 'I can declare that for just this one occasion I set aside my rank as hidalgo and lower myself to the level of the offender, and make myself his equal, thus enabling him to fight me; and so, although he is absent, I hereby challenge him, on the grounds that it was wicked of him to deceive this poor young woman who was once a maiden and now, because of him, is not, and that he must either keep the promise he gave her to be his lawful wife or die in single combat.'

And pulling off a glove he hurled it into the middle of the hall, and the Duke went and picked it up saying that, as he'd already said, he accepted this challenge on his vassal's behalf; and he fixed the date for the encounter as six days later, and the place as the castle courtyard, and the arms as those customary among knights: lance and shield and plate armour and the normal accessories, without any fraud, trickery or use of lucky charms, all this to be checked and inspected by the judges of the combat.

'But above all it's necessary for this good duenna and this naughty damsel to agree to place their cause in Don Quixote's hands; because otherwise nothing can be achieved, nor can the challenge be carried into due effect.'

'I agree,' the duenna replied.

'So do I,' her daughter added, all tearful, bashful and fretful.

Now that this formality had been settled and the Duke had worked out how he was going to handle the affair, the women in mourning withdrew, and the Duchess ordered that from then on they were not to be treated as her servants but as ladies in distress who had come to her house to beg for justice; and so they were given their own room and waited on like strangers, to the astonishment of the other maidservants, who couldn't think where the folly and impudence of Doña Rodríguez and her unfortunate daughter were going to lead.

As all this was going on, and just to add the finishing touch to the party and bring the meal to a fine conclusion – lo and behold, the page who'd taken the letters and presents to Teresa Panza, the wife of the governor Sancho Panza, walked into the hall, which delighted the Duke and Duchess, who were longing for news of his journey; and when they asked him about it he replied that he couldn't answer in public or in a few words, but requested their excellencies to be so kind as to wait until the three of them could be alone together, and in the meantime they could derive some entertainment from the letters. And he produced two letters and placed them in the Duchess's hands. The address on one of them said *Letter to my lady the Duchess Whatshername of I Don't Know Where*, and the other said *To my husband Sancho Panza, the Governor of the Island of Barataria, and God prosper him longer than me*. The Duchess was on tenterhooks, as they say, waiting to read her letter, and after opening it and glancing through it and seeing that she could read it aloud for the Duke and everyone else to hear, she did so:

Letter from Teresa Panza to the Duchess

It made me really really happy, my lady, to get the letter Your Grace wrote me, I'd been looking forward to it ever so much. The string of corals is a very fine one, and my husband's hunting outfit's every bit as good. Your Ladyship making my husband Sancho governor has cheered everyone in the village up no end, even though nobody believes it, in particular the priest and Master Nicolás the barber and Sansón Carrasco the graduate – but I don't care about that, because so long as it's true, which it is, they can all say what they like, though to tell you the honest truth if it wasn't for the corals and the outfit I wouldn't have believed it myself, because in this village everyone thinks my husband's a blockhead, and they can't imagine what he could be any good at governing apart from a herd of goats. God grant it, and point him in the direction that'll be best for his children.

I've decided, my dear lady, by your leave, not to sit here waiting for opportunity to knock twice, and to go up to the capital to loll about in a carriage and put the thousands of people who already envy me's noses out of joint. So I'm asking Your Excellency to tell my husband to send me a bit of money, a good fair bit, everything's dear in the capital – a loaf costs a real, and meat thirty maravedís a pound, it's unbelievable. And if he doesn't want me to go please tell him to say so in good time, my feet are itching to get on the road, because my friends and neighbours all tell me that if me and my daughter go about all proud and pompous in the capital my husband will get to be more well-known through me than me through him, because lots of people are bound to ask, 'Who are those ladies in that coach?' and then one of my servants will reply, 'The wife and daughter of Sancho Panza, the Governor of the Island of Barataria,' and in this way Sancho will get to be well-known, and I'll be thought highly of, so let's press on regardless.

There haven't been any acorns in the village this year and I'm as sorry as sorry can be about that, but all the same I'm sending Your Grace about half a gallon of acorns that I went into the woods to look for, and I couldn't find any bigger – I'd have liked them to be as big as ostrich eggs.

Don't forget to write, Your High and Mightiness, and I'll make sure to reply and tell you how I'm keeping and give you all the news from the village, where I'm praying to our Lord to look after Your Grace and not to forget about me. My daughter Sancha and my son both kiss your hands.

Your servant, who's even keener to see Your Ladyship than to write to you,

TERESA PANZA

Everyone was tremendously delighted to listen to Teresa Panza's letter, in particular the Duke and Duchess, and the Duchess asked for Don Quixote's opinion about whether it would be right to open the letter addressed to the governor, because she imagined it must be absolutely topping. Don Quixote said that he would indeed open it, just to please them, and he did so and saw that this was what it said:

Letter from Teresa Panza to her husband Sancho Panza

I got your letter, dearest Sancho, and I can promise you and I can swear to you as a Catholic and as a Christian that I was within an inch of going mad I was so happy. Look here, my dear – when I heard you're a governor I thought I'd drop dead there and then from the sheer bliss of it, because as you well know they say sudden joy can kill you just as much as awful pain can. Your daughter Sancha was so happy she wetted herself without noticing what she'd done. Here I was, with the outfit you sent in front of me, the corals my lady the Duchess sent round my neck, the letters in my hands, the lad that brought it all standing there, and yet I really did think that everything I was seeing and touching was a dream – who'd have thought a goatherd could get to be a governor of islands? You know what my mother used to say, my dear, the longer we live the more we learn – and I'm only coming out with this because I'm hoping to learn a bit more if I live a few more years, and I'm not intending to stop until you're an exciseman or a tax-collector, because although they're jobs that send you straight to the devil if you take unfair advantage, the fact is you do get your hands on some real money. My lady the Duchess will tell you how very much I want to go to the capital

843

— you ponder it over and let me know what you think, and I'll try to do you credit by going around in a carriage.

The priest, the barber, the graduate, even the sexton can't bring themselves to believe you're a governor, and they say it's all a trick or something done with magic spells like everything connected with your master Don Quixote, and Sansón says he's going to go looking for you to get this idea of being governor out of your head, and get the madness out of Don Quixote's brain-box too — but I just laugh, and I look at my string of coral beads, and I work out how I'm going to make an outfit for our daughter out of that suit of yours.

I sent some acorns for my lady the Duchess, I only wish they'd been made of gold. You send me a few strings of pearls, if people wear pearls on your island.

The news from the village is that the Berrueca woman has married her daughter to a bungling painter who came here to paint whatever came his way. The council told him to paint His Majesty's arms over the town hall door, he asked for two ducats, which they let him have in advance, he worked away for a week at the end of which he still hadn't painted a thing, and then he said he couldn't manage all those baubles and frippery — he gave the money back but in the meantime he'd got himself married in the character of a good tradesman, though it's true he's put his paintbrush aside for a spade, now, and goes out into the fields looking like a right gentleman. Pedro de Lobo's son has taken minor orders in the hope of becoming a priest, and when Mingo Silvato's granddaughter Minguilla found out she sued him for breach of promise — the gossips say he's put her in the family way, but he denies it flat.

There aren't any olives this year, and there isn't a drop of vinegar to be had in the whole village. A company of soldiers came through, they took three of the village girls off with them, I'm not going to tell you which ones, they might come back and there won't be any lack of men to take them as wives, with all their blemishes, however virtuous or otherwise.

Sanchica's making lace, she's earning eight clear maravedís a day that she puts in a piggy bank towards her trousseau, but now she's a governor's daughter you'll give her her dowry and she won't have to work for it. The fountain in the square's dried up and the pillory's been struck by lightning, and I couldn't care less.

Awaiting your reply and decision about me going to the capital, and God keep you for longer than me, or as long, because I wouldn't want to leave you in this world without me,

Your wife,
TERESA PANZA

The two letters provoked applause, laughter, praise and amazement, and as a finishing touch the messenger arrived with the letter sent by Sancho to Don Quixote, which was also given a public reading, and cast doubts upon the governor's stupidity. The Duchess went off with the page to discover what had happened to him in Sancho's village, and he provided her with a full account without omitting a single detail; he gave her the acorns and a cheese that Teresa had given him because it was a very fine one, even better than Tronchón cheeses. The Duchess was delighted to receive it, and we'll leave her in this state so that we can describe the end of the governorship of the great Sancho Panza, that flower and mirror of all island governors.

CHAPTER LIII

About the troubled conclusion to Sancho Panza's
governorship

To think that anything in this life will remain for ever in the same state is an idle fancy; on the contrary, it seems that life goes round and round like a wheel: spring chases summer, summer chases harvest, harvest chases autumn, autumn chases winter and winter chases spring, and time turns and turns again in this continuous circle; only human life rushes on to its end faster than time itself, without any hope of renewal except in the other life, which has no bounds to limit it. Thus speaks Cide Hamete, the Muslim philosopher; because many people, without the illumination of faith, guided by their own natural lights, have understood the brevity and transience of our present life and the permanence of the eternal life to come; but here our author is speaking in this way because of the speed with which Sancho's government was undone, ended and destroyed, and vanished into shadow and smoke.

He was lying in bed on the seventh night of his governorship, sated not with bread or with wine but with sitting in judgement and giving opinions and making decrees and by-laws, and, in spite of his hunger, sleep was beginning to close his eyelids, when he heard such a hullabaloo of bells and shouts that anyone would have thought the whole island was sinking into the sea. He sat up in bed and listened hard, to try to make out the cause of this uproar; not only did he not succeed, but his bewilderment and his terror were increased when to the shouts and the bells was added the din of countless bugles and drums; and he clambered out of bed, put on a pair of slippers because of the dampness of the floor, and not even pausing to grab a dressing gown or anything similar he rushed out of the door of his room in time to see more than twenty people approaching along the gallery carrying swords and flaming torches and crying:

'To arms, to arms, lord Governor, to arms! Hordes of enemies have invaded the island, and we're lost if your skill and courage don't come to our rescue.'

Amidst all this noise, this frenzy, this pandemonium, they charged up to where Sancho stood stupefied and fascinated by what he was seeing and hearing, and one of them said:

'Arm yourself at once, Your Lordship, unless you want to be destroyed and the whole island with you!'

'What do you mean arm myself?' said Sancho. 'What do I know about arms or rescues? It'll be better to leave all this to my master Don Quixote, he'll see to it good and proper in a brace of shakes, because I swear as I'm a sinner I haven't got the foggiest about what to do in tight corners like this.'

'Oh, my lord Governor!' said another. 'This is no joking matter! Arm yourself, we've brought arms offensive and defensive, and come out into the main square and be our guide and our captain, because that's your place by right, as our Governor.'

'You'd better get my armour on, then,' Sancho replied.

And they brought out two full-length wooden shields with which they'd come provided, and clapped them on him over his shirt without letting him put any other clothes on, one shield in front and the other behind, with his arms sticking out through holes that they had made, and they bound him tight with rope so that he was boarded up and walled in, as stiff as a distaff, unable to bend his knees or stir a single step. They put a lance in his hand, and he leaned on it to prevent himself from falling over. Once they'd made him ready they told him to march onward, and lead them, and inspire them all, because if he was their guide, their lantern and their lodestar all would be well.

'And how do you expect me to march, poor wretch that I am?' Sancho replied. 'I can't get my knee-joints working, with these here boards clamped on to my body like this. What you'll have to do is carry me out and put me at one of the posterns, propped upright or wedged across it, and I'll guard it with this lance or with my body.'

'Come now, lord Governor,' said another, 'it's more your fear than the boards that keeps you from walking. Get a move on, for goodness sake – it's late, and the shouts are getting louder, and danger's pressing.'

This urging and these insults stung the poor governor into trying to move, and the result was that he fell to the floor with such a crash that he thought he'd been broken into little pieces. There he lay like a turtle in its shell, or like a side of bacon being salted between two kneading-trays, or like a boat stranded on the sand; but seeing him down there didn't make his hoaxers feel at all sorry for him – on the contrary, they extinguished their torches, redoubled their cries and repeated 'To arms!', trampling back and forth over poor Sancho and hacking away with their swords at his shields; and if he hadn't shrunk himself up small and pulled his head in between those boards, things would have gone very badly for the unfortunate governor who, squashed into that narrow space, was sweating rivers and begging God with all his heart to deliver him from that peril. Some stumbled over him and others fell, and there was even one who stood on top of him for a good while and from there, as from a watch-tower, issued orders to the troops, crying:

'Here, boys, here, this is where the enemy's pressing hardest! Guard that gate, shut that other one, prise those ladders off the walls! Bring fire-pots, pitch and resin in cauldrons of burning oil! Barricade the streets with mattresses!'

And he reeled off the names of every single piece of rubbish and every instrument and implement of war used to repel an attack on a city, and the battered Sancho, listening to it all and enduring it all, was saying to himself:

'Oh, if only the Lord would let the island be lost once and for all, and I was dead or out of this agony!'

Heaven heard his plea and, when he was least expecting it, he heard people shouting:

'Victory, victory! The enemy's attacks are abating! Here, lord Governor, get up and come and enjoy the triumph and share out the booty that has been captured from the enemy by the might of that invincible arm of yours!'

'Just pick me up,' the aching Sancho groaned.

They helped him to his feet, and then he said:

'You lot can take any enemy I've beaten and nail him to my forehead, as far as I'm concerned. I'm not going to share out any booty, but just beg some kind friend, if I've got any of those, to let me have a mouthful of wine, because I'm drying up, and to wipe away all this sweat, because I'm turning into water.'

He was mopped down, given some wine, released from the shields, and then he sat down on his bed and fainted from fear, shock and fatigue. By now the hoaxers felt sorry that they'd taken things so far, but Sancho's return to consciousness mitigated the sorrow that his faint had caused them. He asked what time it was, and the answer was that day was dawning. He didn't reply, and uttering not another word he began to dress, buried in his silence, and everyone gazed at him wondering why he was in such a hurry to put his clothes on. Once this was achieved he hobbled little by little, because his battering prevented him from hobbling much by much, to the stable, followed by all the others, and he went up to his dun, hugged it, gave it a kiss of peace on the forehead and, not without shedding some tears, said:

'Come here, my companion and my friend, and my fellow-sufferer in my toils and my woes: when I was content with your company and hadn't got anything to think about except remembering to mend your tackle and feed your body, my hours, my days and my years were happy ones, but ever since I left you and I climbed the towers of ambition and pride, my soul has been invaded by a thousand miseries, a thousand woes and four thousand vexations.'

As he said this he was putting the pack-saddle on to the donkey, and nobody spoke a word to him. Once the pack-saddle was in place he struggled up on to his dun and, addressing the butler, the secretary, the steward, Dr Pedro Recio and all the many others present, he said:

'Now make way, gents, and let me go back to my old freedom. Let me go and look for my past life, so that it can deliver me from this present death. I wasn't born to be a governor or defend islands or cities from the enemies that choose to attack them. I know more about ploughing and digging, about pruning and layering vines, than about making laws or defending provinces or kingdoms. St Peter's all right in Rome – in other words each man's all right doing the job he was born for. It suits me better to have a reaper's sickle than a governor's sceptre in my hand, I'd rather guzzle my bread-and-meat soup than be in the clutches of a mean and meddling medical man who starves me to death, and I'd sooner lie in the shadow of an evergreen oak in the summer and snuggle up inside a nice thick sheepskin coat in the winter, and be free, than be tied down by being governor and lie between sheets of holland and dress up in savoury fur. Goodbye to you all, then, and tell my master the Duke that naked I was born and naked I remain, so neither lose nor gain – in other words I hadn't got a penny when I was made governor and I haven't got a penny now I'm stopping being one, very different from governors of other islands. And now make way for me, let me clear off, I'm going to get some plasters on – to my mind every single one of my ribs is bruised, thanks to all those enemies who've been going for walks on top of me.'

'There will be no need for that, my lord Governor,' said Dr Recio, 'for I shall give you a potion for falls and batterings that will immediately restore you to your pristine health and vigour; and, as regards food, I promise to mend my ways and allow you to eat in abundance whatever you want.'

'*Tarde piaches*,' Sancho replied, 'you're a bit late in cheeping, as the Galician soldier said to the chicken that hatched from the egg he'd just swallowed. I'd as soon turn Turk as stay here. This isn't the sort of jape you put up with twice. By God, I'd as soon stay in this government or take on another one, even if I was given it on a plate, as fly to heaven without wings. I'm a Panza I am, we're all stubborn and once we say no, no it is, come what may, in the face of the whole world. The ant's wings can stay here in the stable – they were what lifted me up into the air to be eaten by swifts and other such birds, so let's start walking the earth again with firm feet, and if they aren't adorned with fancy Cordovan leather shoes they won't go short of rough old rope-soled sandals. Every ram with its ewe, and don't stretch your legs out any further than your sheet will reach, and let me out, it's getting late.'

To which the butler said:

'But my lord Governor, we should most willingly allow you to depart, even though we shall be very sorry to lose you, because your fine mind and your Christian behaviour force us to want you to stay. Yet it is common knowledge that every governor, before he leaves the place he has been governing, must give an account of his administration; you must do so for your ten days in power, and then you can go, and God's peace go with you.'

'Nobody can demand that from me,' Sancho replied, 'except someone ordered to by my lord the Duke. I'm going to be seeing him, and I'll give him a full account, and what's more since I'm leaving empty-handed, as I am, no further proof's needed to show that I've governed like an angel.'

'By God, the great Sancho's right!' said Dr Recio. 'And it's my opinion that we should let him go, because the Duke is going to be delighted to see him.'

They all agreed to this and allowed him to leave, first offering him their company and anything else he needed for the well-being of his person and the comfort of his journey. Sancho said that he only wanted a bit of barley for his dun and half a cheese and half a loaf for himself, because the journey was a short one and he didn't have any call for more or better provisions. They all embraced him and, weeping, he embraced them all, and he left them lost in amazement, at both his words and his firm and wise decision.

CHAPTER LIV

Concerning matters relevant to this history, and not to any other

The Duke and Duchess decided that the challenge issued by Don Quixote to their vassal for the reason given should go ahead; and since the young man was in Flanders, where he'd fled to avoid having Doña Rodríguez as a mother-in-law, they made arrangements for a Gascon lackey called Tosilos to take his place, and first gave him a thorough course of training in everything he had to do. Two days later the Duke told Don Quixote that four days after that his opponent would arrive and present himself at the lists, armed as a knight, and would maintain that the girl was lying in her throat, and even in her beard, if she said that he'd promised to marry her. Don Quixote was overjoyed at the news, and promised himself to work miracles in this affair, and counted himself fortunate indeed to be offered an opportunity to show the Duke and Duchess what the might of his valorous arm was capable of achieving. And so he waited in raptures of joy for the four days to pass, and, measured by his impatience, they seemed to him like four hundred centuries. We shall let them pass by, just as we let many other things pass by, and go off to ride with Sancho, who felt half happy and half sad as he came on his dun in search of his master, whose company he enjoyed more than being governor of all the islands in the world.

It happened, then, that he hadn't travelled far from the island that he'd governed (though he'd never bothered to find out whether what he was governing was an island, a city, a town or a village) when he saw coming along the road towards him six pilgrims with staffs, the foreign sort who sing songs for alms, and when they reached him they arranged themselves in a line and, raising their voices all together, started singing in their own language something that Sancho couldn't understand, except one word that clearly meant 'alms', from which he concluded that it was alms they were asking for in their song; and since, according to Cide Hamete, he was a most charitable man, he took out of his saddle-bags the half cheese and half loaf that were his provisions and handed them over, signalling that he didn't have anything else to give them. They were happy to accept the food, and said:

'*Geld! Geld!*'

'I don't understand what you're asking me for, my good people,' Sancho replied.

Then one of them took a purse out from inside his shirt and showed it to Sancho, from which he understood that they were asking for money, and then he put his thumb on his throat and extended his hand upwards to indicate that he didn't have a farthing on him, and spurring his dun he broke through their line; but, as he did so, one of them, who'd been peering intently at him, rushed up and threw his arms round his waist and said in a very loud and a very Spanish voice:

'Lord Almighty! What's this I see? Is it possible that I'm holding my dear friend and good neighbour Sancho Panza in my arms? Yes, it is, there can't be any doubt about it, because I'm not asleep and as yet I'm not drunk!'

Sancho was astonished to hear himself addressed by his name and to see himself hugged by this foreign pilgrim, and after staring at the man without uttering a word he still couldn't recognize him; but when the pilgrim saw how bewildered Sancho was, he said:

'You don't mean to tell me, brother Sancho Panza, that you can't recognize your neighbour Ricote the Morisco, the village shopkeeper?'

Then Sancho Panza scrutinized him more closely and began to see the similarity, and in the end he realized who he was and, without dismounting from the donkey, he threw his arms round his neck and said:

'How the devil could I recognize you, Ricote, in those clown's clothes you're wearing? But tell me now – who's turned you into a bloody foreigner, and what made you do such a silly thing as come back to Spain? If they catch you and identify you, you'll be in for it.'

'So long as you don't give me away, Sancho,' the pilgrim replied, 'I'm sure nobody's going to spot me in these clothes. And now let's get off the road and go over to those poplars where my companions want to eat and rest, and you can eat with them, and you'll see they're a harmless enough lot. And that'll give me a chance to tell you what's happened to me since I left the village, obeying that edict of His Majesty's with all those terrible threats against the unfortunate people of my race.'[1]

Sancho did as he was asked, and after Ricote had spoken to the other pilgrims they all walked over to the poplar grove, a good distance from the highway. They threw their staffs to the ground, some took off their capes and others their long cloaks, and they stood there in doublet and hose; and all of them were handsome young men except Ricote, who was well on in years. Each had his two satchels hanging from his neck, and every one of the satchels seemed to be well-stocked, if only with those pungent foods that summon thirst from half-a-dozen miles away. They stretched themselves out on the ground and they used the grass as a tablecloth as they spread out on it bread, salt, knives, walnuts, wedges of cheese and ham-bones that didn't allow of any chewing but couldn't prevent themselves from being sucked. They also produced a black food that's said to be called caviare, made of fishes' roes, a great summoner of the leather bottle. There was no lack of olives, though they were dry and without any dressing, yet tasty and beguiling. But the stoutest campaigners on that field of banquet were six leather wine-bottles, one emerging from each of the pilgrim's satchels; even the worthy Ricote, who'd turned himself from a Morisco into a German, produced his, which could compete in size with the other five. They began to eat with the most intense pleasure, very slowly, savouring every morsel, which they took with the tips of their knives, very little of each; and then, all together at the same moment, they lifted their arms and their bottles into the air, and with their mouths pressed up against the mouths of their bottles and their eyes riveted on the sky it looked as if they were aiming at it; and they remained for some time in this position, moving their heads from side to side as a sign of the pleasure they felt as they emptied the entrails of those vessels into their own stomachs.

Sancho was watching, 'and he felt no grief or pain'² – on the contrary, just to obey the proverb, which he knew very well, 'When in Rome do as the Romans do,' he asked Ricote for the use of his bottle and took aim with the others, and with no less pleasure. The bottles withstood four hoistings but the fifth was impossible because by now they were as dry as esparto grass, which suppressed the good cheer that had prevailed until then. Every so often one of the pilgrims would grasp Sancho's right hand and say:

'*Espagnol et tudeski, tuto uno, bon compagno.*'

And Sancho would reply:

'*Bon compagno, jura Di!*'³ and he'd explode in a burst of laughter that lasted an hour, without a thought for what had happened during his governorship: because cares and worries don't wield much power while we're eating and drinking. The end of the wine was the beginning of a drowsiness that seized them all, and they fell asleep on their tables and their table cloths. Only Ricote and Sancho stayed awake, because they'd eaten more and drunk less; and Ricote took Sancho aside and sat down with him at the foot of a beech tree, and, leaving the other pilgrims buried in their sweet slumbers, Ricote spoke as follows in pure Castilian, without once lapsing into his Morisco language:

'You well know, Sancho Panza, my dear friend and neighbour, how the proclamation that His Majesty commanded to be published against those of my race filled us all with terror and dismay; or at least it terrified me so much that I do believe my children and I were feeling the rigours of the prescribed punishment before the time allowed for us to leave Spain had elapsed. So I made arrangements, prudently I believe (like the man who knows that on a certain date he's going to be thrown out of his house and who finds another one to move to) – as I was saying, I made arrangements to leave the village by myself, without my family, and to go to look for somewhere I could take them in comfort and without the haste of other Moriscos. Because I could clearly see, and all our elders could see, that these proclamations weren't just idle threats, as some people said, but real laws that were going to be enforced at the appointed time. And I was obliged to believe that this was true by my knowledge of my people's absurd and base intentions, so absurd that I do believe it was divine inspiration that moved His Majesty to put such an excellent decision into effect – not that we were all guilty, because some Moriscos were firm, true Christians; but there were so few of them that they couldn't stand up to the others, and it's unwise to nourish a viper in your bosom and keep enemies in your house. So in the end we were justly punished with exile, a mild enough penalty in some people's opinion, but for us the most terrible punishment that could have been inflicted upon us. Wherever we are we weep for Spain – after all we were born here, it's our native country. Nowhere have we found the welcome we long for in our misfortune, and it's in Barbary and everywhere else in Africa, where we'd thought we'd be accepted, welcomed and feasted, that we're most insulted and ill-treated. We didn't know our good luck until we'd lost it, and now the longing that nearly all of us have to return here is so great that most of those many Moriscos who can speak the language, as I can, do come back here, and abandon their wives and children, such is their love for Spain; and now I know and feel in my bones the truth of the saying that the love of one's country is sweet.

'As I was saying, then, I left the village and went to France, and although we were well received there I wanted to see the world. I moved on to Italy and then Germany, and it seemed to me that we could live in greater freedom there. Those people don't bother much about niceties: everyone lives as he pleases, because in most of the country there's freedom of conscience. I rented a house in a village near Augsburg; then I joined this group of pilgrims – lots of Germans come to Spain each year to visit shrines here, because for them they are what the Americas are for us, rich pickings and certain profits. They wander over almost the whole country, and there isn't a village they leave without having been wined and dined, as the expression is, and without a real at least in small change; and at the end of their travels they leave with more than a hundred escudos that they've saved, and that, converted into gold, they smuggle out of this country and into their own, hidden in hollows in their staffs or sewn into the patches on their cloaks or in whatever way they can devise, despite all the precautions that are taken in the custom-houses where money has to be declared.

'And now it's my intention, Sancho, to dig up the treasure I left buried, and since it's outside the village I'll be able to do so safely, and then write or go myself from Valencia to Algiers, where I know my wife and daughter are, and find a way to bring them to some French port, and from there to Germany, where we shall wait and see what God decides to do with us; because I know, Sancho, that my daughter Ricota and my wife Francisca Ricota are Christians and Catholics, and although I'm not much of one myself I'm still more of a Christian than a Moor, and I'm always praying God to open the eyes of my understanding and show me how I can serve him. But I can't for the life of me fathom why my wife and daughter went to Barbary instead of France, where they could have lived as Christians.'

To which Sancho replied:

'Look, Ricote, that can't have been their own decision, because they left the village with Juan Tiopieyo, your wife's brother, and him being one of your wily Moors I suppose he went where it suited him best to be, and there's something else I should tell you – I think your trip to look for what you buried is going to be in vain, we had news that lots of pearls and gold coins had been confiscated from your brother-in-law and your wife because they hadn't declared them.'

'That might well be true,' Ricote replied, 'but I know, Sancho, that they didn't touch my hoard, because being afraid of skulduggery I never told them where it was; and so, Sancho, if you'd like to come and help me dig it up and hide it on me, I'll give you two hundred escudos, which will solve a lot of your money problems, and you know I know you've got a lot of those.'

'And I'd do it, too,' said Sancho, 'only I'm not the grasping sort, because if I was I wouldn't have walked out of a job this morning where I could have built the walls of my house in solid gold, and where before six months were out I could have been eating off silver platters – and because of this and because to my mind I'd be betraying my king by helping his enemies, I wouldn't go with you even if instead of promising me two hundred escudos you'd given me four hundred of them here and now in ready cash.'

'And what's this job you've just walked out of, Sancho?' Ricote asked.

'I've just walked out of being the governor of an island,' Sancho replied, 'and such an island it was that I'd swear nobody will find another like it in a hurry.'

'And where is this island?' Ricote asked.

'Where is it?' Sancho replied. 'It's six miles from here, and it's called the Island of Barataria.'

'Come off it, Sancho,' said Ricote, 'islands are in the middle of the sea, there aren't any of them on dry land.'

'What are you talking about?' Sancho replied. 'I'm telling you, Ricote my friend, that I left it this morning, and only yesterday I was governing it as I pleased like a Sagittarian, but in spite of that I gave it up, because to my mind it's a risky job being a governor.'

'And what did you get out of governing?' Ricote asked.

'What I got out of governing,' Sancho replied, 'was finding out that I'm no good at governing anything except a herd of goats, and that any profit you get out of this governing business comes at the price of your rest and your sleep and even your food, because it looks as if governors of islands can't eat much, specially if they've got doctors to look after their health.'

'I don't understand what you're on about, Sancho,' said Ricote, 'but it's my belief that it's all balderdash, because who on earth would give you an island to govern? Was there any shortage of men more skilled than you at being governors? Shut up, Sancho, and come to your senses, and consider again whether you'd like to go with me, as I said, to help dig up my buried treasure – there really is so much of it that it's well worthy to be called a treasure, and as I said I'll give you quite enough to live on.'

'I've already told you, Ricote,' said Sancho, 'that I'm not going to do any such thing. I shan't turn you in, and you'd better be satisfied with that, so you just go on your way, for God's sake, and leave me to go on mine – I'm well aware that our honest gains we'll lose, and our dishonest ones will lose us into the bargain.'

'I shan't insist, Sancho,' Ricote replied. 'But tell me, were you in the village when my wife, my daughter and my brother-in-law went away?'

'Yes, I was,' Sancho replied, 'and I can tell you your daughter was looking so beautiful that everyone in the village came out to see her, and they all said she was the loveliest creature in the world. She was crying and she was hugging all her friends and acquaintances and everyone who'd come to see her, and she asked them all to commend her to God and our Lady his Mother, and with such feeling that it made me cry too, and I'm not normally a cry-baby. And the honest truth is that many a one felt the urge to hide her away, and ride after them and carry her off, but they were all afraid to flout the King's orders, and this held them back. The one who looked most smitten was Don Pedro Gregorio, that rich young heir you know only too well, and they say he was head over heels in love with her, and once she'd left he was never seen in the village again, and we all thought he'd gone after her to steal her away, but nothing more has been heard about it.'

'I always felt in my bones,' said Ricote, 'that that young gentleman was in love with my daughter; but trusting as I did in my Ricota's strength of character I'd never worried about it; because you'll have heard, Sancho, that Morisco girls have seldom if ever become involved in love affairs with men from old Christian families, and I'm sure that my daughter, who, I believe, was more interested in being a Christian than in being in love, wouldn't have paid any attention to that rich young heir's advances.'

'God grant you're right,' Sancho replied, 'because it would have been a bad business for both of them. And now let me be off, Ricote my friend – I want to be back with my master Don Quixote tonight.'

'God go with you, dear Sancho – these friends of mine are beginning to stir, and it's time for us to be on our way, too.'

And they hugged each other, and Sancho climbed on to his dun, and Ricote clutched on to his staff, and they parted.

CHAPTER LV

*About things that happened to Sancho on the road,
and others, excellent beyond compare*

Dallying with Ricote prevented Sancho from reaching the Duke's castle that day, but he came within a couple of miles of it by the time night fell – a rather dark and cloudy night. But as it was summer this didn't worry him very much, so he moved a little off the road with the intention of waiting until morning; but as his wretched luck would have it, he was looking for somewhere to make himself comfortable when he and his dun tumbled into a deep, pitch-black hole between two old buildings, and as he fell he commended himself to God with all his heart, imagining that he wasn't going to stop until he'd reached the bottom of the pit of hell. But this didn't happen, because after about five yards the dun hit the ground, and Sancho was still on top of it, unscathed. He ran his hands all over his body, and he held his breath to see if he was still in one piece or had a hole in him somewhere, and, finding himself sound in wind and limb he thanked the Lord God over and over again for his mercy, because he'd felt certain he must be broken into a thousand pieces. He also ran his hands over the sides of the hole, to find out if it would be possible to climb out of it unaided; but they were all smooth and lacking any handholds, which grieved him to his heart, particularly when he heard his dun moaning in pained and piteous tones; and this wasn't surprising, nor was it complaining without good reason, because the fact is that it was in a bad way.

'Oh, dear!' said Sancho. 'What unexpected things keep happening to people who live in this wretched world! Who'd have said that the man who yesterday was sitting on a throne as the governor of an island bossing his servants and his vassals around would today be buried in a hole in the ground without anyone to rescue him or any servant or vassal to come to his aid? Me and my donkey are going to starve to death down here if the donkey doesn't die first from its bruising and battering and me from my sorrow and grief. At any rate I'm not going to be as lucky as my master Don Quixote de la Mancha was when he went down into the cave of that there enchanted Montesinos, and found people to look after him better than in his own home – anyone would think he'd gone as a paying guest. And he saw fair and pleasant visions there, he did, and what I'm going to see here, as far as I can tell, is toads and snakes. What a poor unlucky devil I am, and look what all my follies and my fancies have come to! When it pleases heaven for somebody to find me they'll take away my bones, all fleshless and white and smooth, and the bones of my good dun with them, and that will tell them who we are – anyone, at least, who knows that Sancho Panza never parted from his ass, nor his ass from Sancho Panza. I'll say it again – what poor wretches we are, our bad luck hasn't let us die in our own village and among our own people, where, even if there wasn't any remedying our disaster, at least there'd have been someone to lament it and to close our eyes when we breathe our dying breath! O my friend and companion, how badly I've paid you for your good services! Forgive me and beg fortune, as well as you can, to get us out of this miserable plight we're in, and I promise to put a crown of laurel on your head so that you look like any poet laureate – and I'll put you on double rations, too.'

Thus did Sancho Panza lament, and his donkey listened without offering one word in reply, such was the distress and anguish that the poor creature was in. After a night spent in piteous moanings and lamentations, day finally came, and by its resplendent light Sancho saw that it was out of the question to climb unaided out of that pit, and he began to groan and shout, in case there was anyone to hear him; but he was crying in the wilderness, because there was nobody in the whole area, and then he did give himself up for dead. The dun was lying on its back, and Sancho Panza managed to get it to its feet although it could hardly stand; and taking a hunk of bread out of the saddle-bags, which had suffered the same fate and fallen with them, he gave it to the donkey, to whom it was not unwelcome, and Sancho said, as if it could understand him:

'In all kinds of grief bread brings us relief.'

As he said this he spotted a gap on one side of the hole, sizeable enough to take one person if he stooped and made himself small. Sancho Panza did so and found it broad and spacious inside – he could see it because through what could be called its ceiling a sun-ray shone in and lit it up. He could also see that it opened out into another extensive cavity, so he went back to where he'd left the donkey and used a stone to knock away the earth round the edges of the gap, and before long he'd made it big enough for the donkey to go through, which it did; and leading it by the halter he started walking through the cavern to see if he could find a way out. Sometimes he was in half-gloom, sometimes without any light at all; but never without fear.

'God Almighty help me!' he was saying to himself. 'This that's a disaster for me would have been better as an adventure for my master Don Quixote. He'd have taken these pits and dungeons for floral gardens and palaces of Galiana,[1] he would, and he'd be expecting to come out from this dark narrow hole into some meadow full of flowers. But poor old me, without any luck, without anyone to tell me what to do, without any courage – every step I take makes me imagine that another even bigger hole's going to open at my feet and swallow me up good and proper. We can bear without a groan any ill that comes alone.'

Thinking all these thoughts, he imagined that he must have walked about a couple of miles when he made out a dim light that looked like the light of day finding its way in somehow, and indicating that this road into the other world, as he had conceived it, led to some opening into this one.

At this point Cide Hamete Benengeli leaves Sancho and returns to Don Quixote, who in raptures of joy was awaiting the day of the battle that he was to wage against the man who had deprived Doña Rodríguez's daughter of her honour, so as to right the dastardly wrong he'd done her. And it so happened that Don Quixote rode out one morning to train and practise for the combat in which he was to be engaged on the following day, and when he urged Rocinante into a charge or gallop the horse stepped so close to a pothole that if Don Quixote hadn't tugged on the reins it would have been impossible to avoid falling in. But he did manage to halt his horse and he didn't fall into the hole, and edging a little closer, without dismounting, he peered into those depths, and as he peered he heard shouts inside, and by straining his ears to the utmost he could make out the words:

'Hey you up there! Is there anyone listening, any charitable knight to feel sorry for a sinner that's been buried alive, an unhappy unruly ruler?'

Don Quixote thought it was Sancho's voice he was hearing, which filled him with confusion and bewilderment, and raising his own voice as much as he could he called out:

'Who is it down there? Who is it lamenting so?'

'Who do you think it is down here lamenting so,' came the reply, 'if not poor harassed Sancho Panza – the governor, for his sins and his misfortune, of the Island of Barataria, and once upon a time the squire of the famous knight Don Quixote de la Mancha?'

When Don Quixote heard this, his amazement was redoubled and his astonishment was triplicated as it occurred to him that Sancho must be dead and that his soul was in torment down there; and borne on the wings of this notion he said:

'I conjure you by everything by which I can conjure you as a Catholic and a Christian to tell me who you are; and if you are a soul in torment, pray tell me what you want me to do for you; for just as it is my profession to aid and assist the needy in this world, so I shall also obey its precepts by assisting and aiding the needy in the other world, who cannot help themselves.'

'In that case,' came the reply, 'you up there speaking to me must be my master Don Quixote de la Mancha – by the sound of your voice you can't be anyone else, that's for certain.'

'Don Quixote I am indeed,' replied Don Quixote, 'he whose profession it is to aid and succour both the living and the dead in their hour of need. So do please tell me who you are, because you have plunged me into bewilderment. For if you are my squire Sancho Panza, and you are dead, and the devils have not carried you off, and by God's mercy you are in purgatory, then our Holy Mother the Roman Catholic Church can perform ceremonies sufficient to remove you from where you now languish, and I shall entreat the Church to do so, employing every penny at my disposal; so you must now bring yourself to tell me who you are.'

'I swear by all that's holy,' came the reply, 'and by the birth of anyone you like, Don Quixote de la Mancha sir, that I am your squire Sancho Panza and I've never died in all the days of my born life – but after I left my governing, for reasons I'd need more time to explain, last night I fell into this hole where I'm lying now, and the dun fell in with me, and it'll back me up in what I'm saying because here it is by my side.'

And what's more it appears that the donkey did understand what

Sancho had said, because it began to bray with such power that the whole cave reverberated.

'What a splendid witness!' said Don Quixote. 'I know that bray as well as if I myself had given birth to it, and it is indeed your voice that I can hear, dear Sancho. Wait where you are; I shall go to the Duke's castle, not far from here, and I shall bring someone to pull you out of this hole into which your sins must have cast you.'

'Yes, off you go, sir,' said Sancho, 'and do come back soon, for God's sake – I can't stand being buried alive down here, I'm dying of fright.'

Don Quixote hastened to the castle to tell the Duke and Duchess what had happened to Sancho Panza, which surprised them both no end, although they realized that he must have fallen into the far entrance of that cave that had been there since time immemorial; but what they couldn't understand was how he'd left his governorship without their being informed that he was on his way back. People eventually went for him with ropes and aye with cables, as the ballad puts it, and, with much labouring of many arms, Sancho and his dun were brought up from those murky depths into the light of day. Seeing which a student said:

'Yes, that's the way for all bad governors to leave office, the way it seems this sinner's coming out of the depths of his pit – starving, pale and penniless.'

Sancho heard him and said:

'It was eight or ten days ago, my loose-tongued young friend, that I went to govern the island I was given, and in all that time my belly has never once been full of bread, I've been persecuted by doctors, my bones have been pounded by enemies and I haven't had a single chance to bribes refuse or insist on my dues – and this being so, as it is, I don't believe that I did deserve to leave office like this. But man proposes and God disposes, and he knows what's best for everybody, and times change and us with them, and you never know what the future has in store, because where you think there's bacon there aren't even any hooks to hang it from, and God understands what I mean and that's enough for me, and I shan't say any more even though I could.'

'Don't you be worried or annoyed, Sancho, about any comments you hear, or there will never be an end to them. Keep a safe conscience and let people say what they like: trying to still gossips' tongues is like putting up doors in open fields. If the governor leaves office rich they say he's a thief, and if he leaves it poor they say he's a milksop and a fool.'

'This time,' Sancho replied, 'they're going to say I'm a fool not a thief, that's for sure.'

As they talked away like this they reached the castle, and boys and many other people flocked around them, and the Duke and Duchess were waiting in a gallery for Don Quixote and Sancho, who wouldn't go up to see the Duke until he'd made his dun comfortable in the stable, because he said that it had had a bad time of it in the place where they'd lodged the night before; and then he went up to see his master and mistress and said, on his knees before them:

'My Lord and Lady, because Your Graces insisted on it and not because of any merits of my own, I went to govern your island of Barataria, and naked I went and naked I remain, so neither lose nor gain. As to whether I've governed well or not, there are plenty of witnesses who'll say whatever they think fit. I've settled doubts and decided lawsuits, starving all the time, because that was what was ordered by Dr Pedro Recio, from Vamos, the island-governor doctor. We were attacked by enemies by night, and after they'd got us into a really tight corner the islanders said that we had come off victorious and free thanks to the might of my arm, and God grant them as much prosperity as there is truth in that particular tale.

'To cut a long story short, all this while I've been trying out the burdens and obligations that governing involves, and I've found out for myself that my shoulders can't take them, that they aren't a load for my back or arrows for my quiver – so before being governor could finish me off I thought I'd finish off being governor, and yesterday morning I left the island just as I'd found it, with all the same streets, houses and roofs as when I went there. I haven't borrowed any money off anyone and I haven't been involved in any business deals, and although I planned to make some useful by-laws I didn't make any at all in the end, because I was frightened they wouldn't be obeyed, and then they might just as well never have been made in the first place. I left the island, as I've said, with nothing but my donkey, I fell down a hole, I walked through it till this morning by the light of the sun I saw the way out, but it wasn't easy to reach and if heaven hadn't sent my master Don Quixote in my direction I'd have been left there till the end of the world. So there you are, Duke and Duchess, here's your governor Sancho Panza, and what he's got out of governing for ten days is knowing that he doesn't care a hoot about being governor, not just of an island but of all the world. And now I've made my mind up about that, I'll just kiss your feet and copy children playing who shout, "Jump and let me have it," and I'll jump out of my government and go back to serve my master Don Quixote because, when all's said and done, so long as I'm with him even though I do eat my bread in a state of alarm at least I get to fill my belly, and as far as I'm concerned so long as I'm full I don't care whether it's carrots or partridges.'

And here Sancho ended his long speech, throughout which Don Quixote had been dreading that he'd blurt a thousand absurdities; and when he concluded after coming out with so few of them his master gave silent thanks to heaven, and the Duke embraced Sancho and told him he was so frightfully sorry he'd relinquished being governor so soon, but he'd make arrangements for some less onerous and more profitable position in his territories to be given him. The Duchess also embraced him and ordered that he should want for nothing, because he gave every sign of being badly bruised and battered.

CHAPTER LVI

About the prodigious and unparalleled battle fought between Don Quixote de la Mancha and the lackey Tosilos, in defence of the duenna Doña Rodríguez's daughter

The Duke and Duchess didn't repent of the hoax they'd played on Sancho Panza by giving him the governorship, particularly since their butler returned that same day and gave them a precise account of virtually every word and deed that Sancho had uttered and performed during that time, concluding with a panegyrical narration of the attack on the island, Sancho's abject fear and his departure, all of which they relished.

Next, the history relates that the day appointed for the battle came, and that the Duke, having given his lackey Tosilos repeated instructions about how to deal with Don Quixote so as to defeat him without killing or wounding him, ordered the iron tips to be removed from the lances, telling Don Quixote that his Christian principles, on which he prided himself, didn't permit the battle to be fought with so much risk and danger to life, and that he must be content to be given a field of battle in the Duke's territories even though this contravened the decree of the Council of Trent forbidding all such challenges; so he mustn't seek to take this cruel combat to the utmost extremity. Don Quixote said that His Excellency must arrange the affair as seemed best to him, and he would obey his every command.

And so the dreadful day arrived, and the Duke had ordered a spacious platform to be erected on one side of the castle square for the judges of the lists and the plaintiff duennas, mother and daughter; and countless people had arrived from all the nearby towns and villages to watch this novel battle, for nothing like it had ever been seen or even heard of in that land, by the living or the dead. The first to enter the lists was the master of the ceremonies, who rode up and down the field surveying it to ensure that nobody was attempting any sharp practice and that there were no hidden obstacles to cause a trip and a fall. Then the duennas came and sat on their chairs, up to their eyes and even down to their chests in veils, showing every sign of great grief. A little after Don Quixote had presented himself, the large lackey Tosilos made his appearance on one side of the square to a fanfare of trumpets, riding a powerful horse with thundering hoofs; his visor was down and he was stiffly encased in strong and gleaming armour. The horse was a Friesland, broad and dapple grey; from each fetlock hung half a hundredweight of wool. This brave combatant had been carefully coached by his master the Duke to deal with the valiant Don Quixote de la Mancha, and warned on no account to kill him, but to find a way to elude the first clash, which must cause the man's death if they met at full tilt. He rode round the square and when he came to where the ladies were seated he stared for some time at the one who wanted him for her husband. The master of the field summoned Don Quixote, already in the square, and with Tosilos by his side he asked the duennas whether they consented to Don Quixote de la Mancha defending their cause. They confirmed that they did, and that they would accept whatever action he took on their behalf as correct, valid and binding. By this time the Duke and Duchess had taken their places on a balcony overlooking the lists, which were surrounded by countless people waiting to watch this unprecedented, cruel battle. The conditions of the combat were that if Don Quixote was victorious his opponent would marry Doña Rodríguez's daughter, and if he was defeated his opponent was quit of any such pledge, and need give no further satisfaction. The master of the ceremonies allocated to each man his position, ensuring that neither had the sun of the other. Drums rolled, trumpet blasts filled the air, the ground quaked under foot; the hearts of the gazing multitude were in suspense, some fearing and some hoping for a happy or a sad ending. And Don Quixote, commending himself with all his heart to our Lord God and his lady Dulcinea del Toboso, was waiting for the signal to charge. But our lackey had other thoughts – he was only thinking what I shall now reveal:

It seems that while he was staring at his fair enemy he was thinking that she was the most beautiful woman he'd ever seen in all his life; and that little blind boy, commonly known by the name of Love, didn't like to waste this opportunity of triumphing over a lackey's soul and placing it on his list of trophies; so creeping up on him unseen he plunged an arrow six feet long into the poor lackey's left side and pierced his heart through and through, which he was able to do at his ease because Love is invisible and comes and goes wherever he likes without anyone asking him what he's up to. So, as I was about to say, when the signal was given to charge, our lackey was in ecstasies as he thought about the beauty of the woman whom he'd made the mistress of his heart, and he didn't pay any attention to the trumpet-blast, unlike Don Quixote, who charged towards his enemy the instant he heard it, at the fastest speed that Rocinante could manage; and when his good squire Sancho saw him go, he bellowed:

'God guide you, cream of knight errants! God give you victory, because right is on your side!'

And although Tosilos could see Don Quixote coming at him, he didn't move one step from his post; instead, he shouted for the master of the field, and, when this gentleman came to see what he wanted, he said:

'Sir, isn't this battle being fought about whether I do or do not marry that lady?'

'That is so,' came the answer.

'Well,' the lackey said, 'I'm concerned about my conscience, and I'd be laying a heavy burden on it if I went ahead with this battle, so I declare myself defeated and I want to marry the lady at once.'

The master of the field was amazed at Tosilos's words, and since he was one of those who were in the secret he didn't know how to reply. Don Quixote stopped in mid-career when he saw that his enemy wasn't charging at him. The Duke didn't know what had prevented the battle from going ahead, and the master of the field went to explain what Tosilos had said, which both bewildered and infuriated the Duke. While all this was going on, Tosilos rode over to Doña Rodríguez and cried:

'My lady, I want to marry your daughter, and I don't want to accomplish through strife and struggle what I can achieve in peace and without risk to life.'

The valiant Don Quixote heard him and said:

'This being so, I am released and absolved of my promise; let them marry and good luck to them, and St Peter bless what the Lord has given.'

The Duke had come down into the castle square, and he went up to Tosilos and said:

'Is it true, sir, that you are surrendering, and that, driven by your uneasy conscience, you intend to marry this young lady?'

'Yes, sir,' Tosilos replied.

'Quite right, too,' Sancho Panza interrupted. 'Give to the cat what you were going to give to the mouse, and save yourself some trouble.'

Tosilos was unlacing his helmet as he walked away, and he begged for somebody to come quickly to help, because there was hardly any air left for him to breathe and he couldn't bear being shut up for so long in those cramped quarters. The helmet was soon off his head, and the face of a lackey was revealed for all to see. At this sight Doña Rodríguez and her daughter cried:

'This is a fraud, this is a fraud! Tosilos, my master the Duke's lackey, has been put in the place of my real husband! Justice, in the name of God and the King, against such mischief, not to say villainy!'

'Do not be distressed, ladies,' said Don Quixote, 'for this is neither mischief nor villainy; or if it is, it has not been the Duke's work, but rather that of the wicked enchanters who pursue me and who, envious of the glory I was going to gain in this victory, have converted your future husband's face into that of this man who you say is the Duke's lackey. Take my advice, and marry him despite all my enemies' mischief: there cannot be any doubt that he is the man whom you desire to obtain as a husband.'

When the Duke heard this, his fury almost dissipated in laughter, and he said:

'The things that happen to Don Quixote are so extraordinary that I myself am on the verge of believing that this lackey of mine isn't my lackey at all – but let's try this ruse: let's put the wedding off for, say, a fortnight, and we'll keep this dubious character locked up, and in this period he might possibly return to his pristine form, because the hatred those enchanters feel for Don Quixote surely won't last that long, particularly when they realize that it's of so little avail to practise these tricks and transformations.'

'Oh, sir!' said Sancho. 'It's something these scoundrels do all the time, changing all the things to do with my master from one into another. A knight he beat some time ago, called the Knight of the Spangles, they changed him into the shape of the young graduate Sansón Carrasco, from our village and a great friend of ours, and my lady Dulcinea del Toboso, well, they turned her into a rough peasant girl – so to my mind this here lackey's going to die a lackey and live a lackey all the days of his born life.'

To which Rodríguez's daughter said:

'This man who wants me for his wife can be whoever he likes – I'm grateful to him all the same, because I'd rather be the lawful wife of a lackey than the cast-off mistress of a gentleman, though the man who cast me off isn't one of those.'

To be brief, the upshot of all these doings and sayings was that Tosilos was to be locked up to await the outcome of his transformation; everybody acclaimed Don Quixote's victory, although most people were dejected and depressed because the participants in the long-awaited combat hadn't hacked each other to pieces, just as boys are disappointed when the condemned man they've been awaiting doesn't come out to be hanged, because he's been pardoned either by the aggrieved party or by the judge. The crowds went away, the Duke and Don Quixote returned to the castle,

Tosilos was locked up, Doña Rodrìguez and her daughter were overjoyed that in one way or another the affair was going to end in marriage, and Tosilos was hoping for no less.

CHAPTER LVII

Concerning how Don Quixote took his leave of the Duke, and an incident involving the Duchess's maid, the sharp-witted, brazen Altisidora

Don Quixote thought it was high time to put an end to his lazy life in the castle, because he imagined that his person was being sorely missed as a result of allowing himself to remain shut up and idle amid the countless luxuries and delights that the Duke and Duchess lavished upon him as a knight errant, and he felt that he was going to have to render a detailed account to heaven of such indolence and seclusion; so one day he requested the permission of the Duke and Duchess to leave. They granted it, displaying deep distress at his departure. The Duchess gave Sancho Panza his wife's letters, and he wept over them and said:

'Who'd have thought that all these great hopes raised in my wife Teresa Panza's breast by the news of me being governor were going to end up with me going back to those plaguey adventures with my master Don Quixote de la Mancha? All the same though, I'm glad to see my Teresa behaved herself and sent those acorns to the Duchess, because if she hadn't I'd have been put out and she'd have shown herself to be ungrateful. And it's a comfort to know that her gift can't be called a bribe, because I was already a governor by the time she sent it, and it's only right and proper for those who've been done a kindness to show that they're grateful, even if only with trifles. The truth is I was naked when I became a governor and naked when I stopped being one, so I can say with a clear conscience, which is something not to be sniffed at, "Naked was I born and naked I remain, so neither lose nor gain."'

All this is what Sancho said to himself on the day of their departure; and that morning, having taken his leave of the Duke and Duchess the night before, Don Quixote rode out in his armour into the castle square. All the people in the castle were gazing down at him from the balconies, and the Duke and Duchess also came out to look at him. Sancho was sitting on his dun, complete with saddle-bags, travelling bag and provisions, beside himself with glee because the butler who'd played Trifaldi had given him a purse containing two hundred gold escudos to cover their expenses, and Don Quixote didn't know about it yet. As all the people gazed down, a voice suddenly sounded out among the Duchess's duennas and maids, and it was the sharp-witted, brazen Altisidora, declaring in doleful tones:

> Draw rein awhile, you evil knight,
> Attend to what I plead;
> Stop wearying those tortured flanks
> Of your unruly steed.
>
> Look, traitor: you're not fleeing now
> From snakes that poison you,
> But from a gentle little lamb,
> Long years from being a ewe.
>
> You have deceived, you hideous fiend,
> The loveliest of maids
> That Venus gazed at in her woods,
> Diana in her glades.
> *Vireno,*[1] *Aeneas: all heartless you flee;*
> *Barabbas go with you for fine company!*
>
> All wickedly you're stealing
> In your talons and your nails
> The bowels of a lass in love,
> A humble maid's entrails.
>
> Three lovely nightcaps have you nicked,
> Two garters, black and white,
> From legs so smooth they can compare
> With marble shining bright.
>
> You're bearing off two thousand sighs
> And they could well destroy
> In greedy flames two thousand Troys,

If there was that much Troy.[2]
Vireno, Aeneas: all heartless you flee;
Barabbas go with you for fine company!

May your squire Sancho's heart and bowels
Become so hard and cold
That Dulcinea ne'er regains
Those forms she had of old.

May the consequences of your crime
Be reaped by that sad maid;
Because for sinners, in this land,
The just have often paid.

May terrible catastrophes
Dog all your finest schemes,
Your faith become forgetfulness,
Your pleasures, wistful dreams.
Vireno, Aeneas: all heartless you flee;
Barabbas go with you for fine company!

May you, from Seville to Marchena,
For bad faith gain renown,
From Loja to Granada,[3] from
England to London Town.

And if you play at whist or bridge,
Canasta or picquet,
May not one ace or king or queen
Ever come your way.

And when you have your corns cut off
May there be blood galore,
And when you have your teeth pulled out
May the stumps rot in your jaw.
Vireno, Aeneas: all heartless you flee;
Barabbas go with you for fine company!

While the grieving Altisidora had been voicing her lament in this way, Don Quixote had been staring up at her, and then, without answering a word, he glared at Sancho and said:

'I conjure you, Sancho, by the eternal salvation of your forebears, to answer one question truthfully. Tell me, are you by any chance in possession of the three nightcaps and the two garters to which this lovelorn maiden refers?'

To which Sancho replied:

'I've got the three nightcaps, but as for the two garters, I don't know what you're talking about.'

The Duchess was amazed at Altisidora's impudence, because although she knew that the girl was forward, witty and brazen, she hadn't thought she'd dare go as far as all that; and since the Duchess hadn't been warned about this hoax, her amazement was all the greater. The Duke felt like carrying the joke still further, and he said:

'I cannot, sir knight, but deplore the fact that, after receiving in this my castle the warm welcome that has been extended to you here, you have had the audacity to carry off at the very least three nightcaps belonging to my maid, and at the very worst a pair of her garters as well; these are signs of a false heart, behaviour that ill becomes your good name. Return her garters forthwith; if you do not, I hereby challenge you to mortal combat, without any fear that scoundrelly enchanters will transform my face, as they did that of my lackey Tosilos, who entered the lists with you.'

'God forbid,' Don Quixote replied, 'that I should unsheathe my sword against your illustrious person, from whom I have received such favours. I shall return the nightcaps, because Sancho says he has them; the garters, impossible, because they have never been in my possession or in his, and if this maiden of yours would like to rummage among her drawers I am sure she will find them. I, my lord Duke, have never been a thief, and I never intend to become one, so long as God does not forsake me. The maiden speaks (as she herself says) as one in love, something for which I am not to blame; so I have done nothing for which I must beg to be forgiven by her or by Your Excellency, whom I beg to think more highly of me, and again to give me leave to continue on my way.'

'And may God smooth it for you, Don Quixote sir,' said the Duchess, 'so that we always hear splendid news of all your exploits. And now goodbye, for the longer you tarry the fiercer the fire you kindle in the breasts of the maids who contemplate you. And my own maid I shall punish so severely that she will never again make free with either her eyes or her words.'

'Hear just one word of mine, O valorous Don Quixote!' Altisidora blurted. 'I beg your pardon about the theft of the garters, because by God and my immortal soul I'm wearing them, and I made the mistake of the man who was looking everywhere for the donkey he was riding.'

'I told you so,' said Sancho. 'I'm a fine one to go covering up for crime, I am. If I'd wanted to go thieving I had all the chances I wanted when I was governor.'

Don Quixote lowered his head and then bowed to the Duke and Duchess and everyone else, and turning Rocinante, with Sancho following on his dun, he rode out of the castle on his way to Saragossa.

CHAPTER LVIII

*Showing how adventures came crowding in on
Don Quixote without so much as a breathing-space
between them*

When Don Quixote found himself in open country, free at last from Altisidora's amorous advances, he felt that he was in his own element again, and that his spirits were reviving for the fresh pursuit of his chivalresque goals; and turning to Sancho he said:

'Freedom, Sancho, is one of the most precious gifts bestowed by heaven on man; no treasures that the earth contains and the sea conceals can compare with it; for freedom, as for honour, men can and should risk their lives and, in contrast, captivity is the worst evil that can befall them. I am saying all this, Sancho, because you are well aware of the luxury and abundance that we have been enjoying in the castle which we have just left; well, in the midst of all those delectable banquets, those snow-chilled drinks, I felt just as if I were undergoing all the tribulations of hunger, because I could not enjoy such luxuries with the same freedom as if they had been my own: the obligation to repay benefits and favours received is a bond that prevents the spirit from campaigning freely. Happy is he to whom heaven has given a crust of bread and who is under no obligation to thank anyone for it except heaven itself!'

'All that's as may be,' said Sancho, 'but it wouldn't be right for us not to be thankful for the two hundred gold escudos that the Duke's butler has just given me in a purse for emergencies and that I've got down in here over my heart like a mustard-plaster or a poultice – we aren't always going to be finding castles where they treat us, and we might even come across inns where they beat us.'

The two errants, knight and squire, were chatting away like this when, after they'd ridden for some three or four miles, they saw about a dozen men in farmers' clothes sitting on their cloaks on the grass of a green meadow, eating. Near them there were what looked like white sheets draped over various large objects scattered all over the ground, some upright and some horizontal. Don Quixote rode up to the men, delivered a courteous greeting and enquired what was under the sheets. One of the men replied:

'Under these sheets, sir, are some images carved in good hard wood for the altarpiece we're making in our village; we've covered them up to stop them from losing their sheen, and we're carrying them on our shoulders to stop them from getting broken.'

'If you would be so kind,' Don Quixote replied, 'I should like to see them, because images that are being transported with such care must be good ones.'

'Yes, they're good ones all right!' said another man. 'Their price is proof of that – truly there isn't one of them that didn't cost more than fifty ducats, and if you want to find out how right I am, just wait a jiff and you'll see with your own two eyes.'

And coming to his feet he left his food and went to take the cover off the first image, which turned out to be St George on horseback, with his lance thrust into the mouth of a coiled serpent at the horse's feet, all depicted with the usual ferocity. The whole piece looked like one great blaze of gold, as the saying goes. When Don Quixote saw it he said:

'This knight was one of the finest errants in the heavenly army; his name was St George and what is more he was a defender of maidens. Now let's see this other one.'

The man uncovered it, and it emerged as St Martin on horseback, dividing his cloak with the beggar. And as soon as Don Quixote saw it he said:

'This knight was another of the Christian adventurers, and in my opinion he was more generous than courageous, as you can observe, Sancho, in the fact that he is dividing his cloak and giving the beggar half of it; and it must have been winter at the time because he was so charitable that otherwise he would have given the beggar all of it.'

'No, it wouldn't have been that,' said Sancho, 'but rather he must have been minding that proverb – "It takes a wise man to have his cake and eat it." '

Don Quixote laughed and asked for another sheet to be removed, and under this one appeared a statue of the patron saint of Spain, on horseback, wielding a bloody sword, trampling Moors to the ground, stamping on their heads; and when Don Quixote saw it he said:

'Now this one really is a knight, belonging to Christ's own squadrons; he's called St James the Moor-killer, one of the bravest saints and knights who once lived in this world and now live in heaven.'

Then another sheet was taken off and from under it emerged St Paul falling from his horse, with all the details normally found in depictions of his conversion. When Don Quixote saw it, so lifelike that anyone would have said that Christ was speaking and Paul was replying, he said:

'This man was the greatest enemy that the Church of our Lord God had in his time – and also the greatest defender that it will ever have, a knight errant in life and a steadfast saint in death, a tireless worker in the vineyard of the Lord, the teacher of the Gentiles,[1] with heaven as his school and Jesus Christ himself as his Master.'[2]

There were no more images, so Don Quixote told the man to cover them up again, and said to those who were carrying them:

'I consider it a good omen, my friends, to have seen what I have just seen, because these saintly knights professed, as I myself profess, the exercise of arms; but the difference between them and me is that they were saints, and fought in the manner of angels, and I am a sinner, and fight in the manner of men. They conquered heaven by force of arms, for heaven suffers violence,[3] and so far I do not know what I conquer by force of toils; but if my Dulcinea del Toboso were to be delivered from her own toils, it could well be that my luck would change and my understanding would improve, and I should direct my steps along a better road than I am following at present.'

'God hear what you said and the devil be deaf,' Sancho interposed.

The men were astounded by both Don Quixote's appearance and his words, half of which they didn't understand. They finished their meal, heaved their images on to their shoulders, said goodbye to Don Quixote and went on their way. For Sancho it had been like meeting his master for the first time, and he was lost in admiration for his erudition, and thought that there couldn't be a single history or incident in the whole wide world that he hadn't got at his fingertips and stamped on his memory; and then he said:

'Truth to tell, master, if this that's just happened to us can be called an adventure, it's been one of the gentlest and mildest ones we've ever had in the whole course of our wanderings – we got out of it without a thumping or even any scares, we haven't laid hands on our swords or battered the earth with our carcasses or even been left hungry. God be blessed for letting me see such a marvel with my own two eyes.'

'You're quite right, Sancho,' said Don Quixote, 'but you should bear in mind that times are not all one nor do they run the same course, and what the common herd often calls omens, which are not based on any natural process of causation, should be regarded by intelligent people as mere happy coincidences. One of these superstitious fellows gets up in the morning, leaves home, comes across a friar of the order of the blessed St Francis – and then turns round and hurries back home as if he'd met a griffin. Another of them spills the salt on the table, and gloom spills throughout his heart, as if nature were obliged to give warnings of coming disasters with such trivial events. The wise Christian shouldn't pry into what heaven intends to do. Scipio lands in Africa, stumbles as he leaps ashore, and his soldiers consider it a bad omen; but he embraces the ground and says, "You won't be able to run away from me, Africa, because I'm holding you tight between my arms."[4] So as you can see, Sancho, coming across those images was for me just a most happy coincidence.'

'That's what I think, too,' Sancho replied, 'and now I'd just like you to tell me why it is that when Spaniards are about to go into battle they call on that St James the Moor-killer and yell, "St James, and close Spain!" Is Spain open, then, and needing to be shut – otherwise why all the fuss and bother?'

'You're a very simple fellow, Sancho,' Don Quixote replied. 'Look here,

God has given Spain this great knight with his red cross to be her patron saint and protector, particularly in the cruel wars that Spaniards have waged against Moors; so Spaniards call upon him as their defender in all the battles that they fight, and he has often been clearly seen in them, overthrowing, trampling, destroying and massacring the Muslim hordes; and I could adduce many examples of this fact that are related in the true histories of Spain.'

Sancho changed the subject and said:

'I'm flabbergasted, sir, at how brazen the Duchess's maid Altisidora was – she must have been really badly wounded by that character love, who's said to be a blind boy that, even though he's bleary-eyed or rather can't see at all, only has to take someone's heart as his target, however small it is, to pierce it through and through with his arrows. I've also heard that love's arrows are dulled and blunted on young girls' reserve and modesty, but on this Altisidora girl they seem to have been sharpened more than blunted.'

'Do bear in mind, Sancho,' said Don Quixote, 'that love knows no respect and does not proceed according to sound reason, and its behaviour is like that of death: it attacks both the lofty palaces of kings and the humble huts of shepherds, and once it has taken possession of a soul the first thing it does is to strip it of all fear and shame; and so Altisidora, having lost her shame, declared her feelings, which gave rise in my breast more to confusion than to pity.'

'How very very cruel of you!' said Sancho. 'How most terribly ungrateful! I can say for myself that the slightest word of love from her would have turned me into her humble slave. Bugger me, what a heart of marble, what bowels of bronze, what a soul of cement! But I can't think what this girl saw in you to bowl her over like that, what elegance or what dash or what wit or what looks – which of these or all of them combined made her fall in love? Because to tell you the honest truth I often stop and look at you from the tips of your toes to the topmost hair on your head and I see more to put the wind up a young girl than to put love into her heart, and since I've also heard say that beauty's the main feature that inspires love, I just don't know what it is that the poor girl fell in love with, because you aren't at all beautiful.'

'You should remember, Sancho,' said Don Quixote, 'that there are two kinds of beauty: beauty of the soul and beauty of the body; the beauty of the soul shines out in one's intelligence, one's virtue, one's right behaviour, one's generosity and one's good breeding, and all these qualities can well be found in an ugly man; and when it is this beauty of the soul and not the beauty of the body that is the object of admiration, love arises impetuously and with a special intensity. I know very well, Sancho, that I am not beautiful, but I am also aware that I am not deformed, and it is sufficient for a good-natured man not to be a monster to be well-loved, so long as he possesses the qualities of the soul that I have just mentioned.'

As they talked and talked they were riding into a wood by the side of the road, and suddenly, without realizing what had happened, Don Quixote found himself entangled in nets of green thread hanging between the trees; and unable to imagine what this could be, he said to Sancho:

'It is my belief, Sancho, that these nets must be the beginning of one of the strangest adventures imaginable. I'll wager my life that those enchanters who pursue me are now trying to ensnare me and halt my progress, in revenge for my severity with Altisidora. Well, I can assure them that even if these nets weren't made of green thread but of the hardest diamonds, or were stronger than the net in which the jealous god of blacksmiths[5] enmeshed Venus and Mars, I should break through them as if they were made of sea-rushes or cotton-shreds.'

But as he went to press forward and break the nets, two beautiful shepherdesses emerged from behind some trees in front of him; or rather two young women dressed as shepherdesses, except that their jackets and frocks were of fine brocade – or, to be more precise, their frocks were splendid gowns of gold tabby. Their hair flowed loose over their shoulders, and it was so golden that it could compete with the rays of the sun; it was crowned with garlands woven from green laurel and red amaranth. The girls seemed no younger than fifteen and no older than eighteen. This was a sight that amazed Sancho and astonished Don Quixote, made the sun stop in its course to gaze down at them and kept all four people in an extraordinary silence. Eventually the first to speak was one of the shepherdesses, who said to Don Quixote:

'Please stay still, sir knight, and don't break the nets – they're hanging there for our amusement, not to harm you; and since I know you're going to ask why they've been put there and who we are, I'll tell you in a few words. In a village half a dozen miles from here, where many people of rank and hidalgos and rich people live, a group of friends and relations agreed that we should come with their sons, wives and daughters, neighbours, friends and relatives, to enjoy ourselves in this place, one of the pleasantest spots in the whole area, creating a new pastoral Arcadia, with all us youngsters dressing up as shepherds and shepherdesses. We've learned two eclogues, one by the famous poet Garcilaso and the other by the superb Camões[6] in the original Portuguese, but we haven't performed them yet. We first came here yesterday; we've pitched some tents that they say are called marquees, among the trees on the bank of a flowing stream that waters all these meadows; last night we hung these nets from the trees to catch any innocent little birds that we can scare into flying in this direction. If, sir, you'd like to be our guest, you'll be entertained with courteous generosity, because for the present no sadness or grief is going to find its way into this place.'

She stopped, and remained silent. Don Quixote replied:

'To be sure, most lovely lady, Actaeon's wonder and amazement when he chanced to spy Diana bathing in the waters[7] can have been no greater than my astonishment on seeing your beauty. I commend your choice of entertainment and I thank you for your invitation, and, if I can serve you, you can command me in the certainty of being obeyed; for my profession is none other than to be grateful and to do good to people of all kinds, and particularly to those of high rank, as you clearly are; and if these nets, which cannot extend very far, stretched all the way round the world, I should search for new worlds so as to pass by without breaking them; and, so that you can give some credence to this slight exaggeration of mine, I would have you know that he who gives you this assurance is none other than Don Quixote de la Mancha, if this name has reached your ears.'

'Oh my dearest darling,' the other shepherdess broke in, 'what an enormous stroke of luck we've had! You see this gentleman standing here before us? Well, let me tell you he's quite the most valiant, the most passionate and the most courteous man in the whole world, unless a history of his exploits that's been printed and I've read is all lies and deceit. And I bet that this fine fellow with him is a certain Sancho Panza, his squire, who says such funny things – they're quite matchless.'

'You're right enough there,' said Sancho. 'I'm that funny squire you said, and this gent's my master, the very same Don Quixote de la Mancha in that there history book.'

'Oh!' said the other girl. 'Do let's entreat him to stay, darling, our parents and brothers and sisters will be so delighted, because I've also heard about his being valiant and funny, as you said, and what everyone declares is that he's quite the most steadfast and faithful lover known to mankind, and his lady's a certain Dulcinea del Toboso, who carries away the palm of beauty throughout the length and breadth of Spain.'

'And so she should,' said Don Quixote, 'unless your own unequalled beauty puts the matter in some doubt. But do not attempt to detain me, ladies, because the requirements of my profession will not allow me to rest in any place.'

At this moment the brother of one of the two shepherdesses came up, dressed in shepherd's clothes that were every bit as splendid and showy as those of the girls. They told him that the man with them was the valiant Don Quixote de la Mancha and that the other one was his squire Sancho, about both of whom he already knew, because he'd read their history. The gallant shepherd offered his services and asked Don Quixote to accompany him to the marquees, Don Quixote had no choice but to agree, and off they went. Now it was time to catch the birds, and the nets were filled with different varieties that, deceived by the colour of the thread, fell into the danger from which they were fleeing. More than thirty people assembled there, all gorgeously attired as shepherds and shepherdesses, and in a moment they were informed about who Don Quixote and his squire were, which delighted them all, because they, too, already knew about him from his history. They all walked to the marquees, they found the tables laid – sumptuous, plentiful and spotlessly clean; they honoured Don Quixote by giving him pride of place; everyone was staring at him, amazed to be seeing him.

At the end of the meal, once the tables had been cleared, Don Quixote cleared his throat and spoke up:

'Although some people say that the worst sin men commit is pride, I say that it is ingratitude, bearing in mind what is often said: hell is full of ingrates. This sin is one that I have tried to avoid as far as I have been able, ever since I have been capable of rational thought; and if I cannot repay good deeds done me with other good deeds, I put in their place my desire to do them; and if this is insufficient I make them publicly known, because anyone who makes the good deeds done him generally known shows that he would repay them with others if he could; for those who receive are usually inferior to those who give, and this is why God is above everyone, because he gives to everyone, and man's gifts cannot equal God's gifts – there is an infinite distance between them; but this inadequacy, this deficiency is, to some extent, compensated for by gratitude. I, then, grateful for the favour done me here, and unable to respond in like measure, restricted by the narrow limits of my powers, offer what I can, the special contribution that I am able to make: and so I declare that I shall maintain, for two whole days, in the middle of the highway leading to Saragossa, that these two damsels disguised as shepherdesses are the most beautiful and courteous maidens in the world, only excepting the peerless Dulcinea del Toboso, the sole mistress of my thoughts, and by this I mean no offence to any of the ladies and gentlemen listening to me.'

Sancho had been listening, with rapt attention, and when he heard all this he gave a great shout and said:

'Can there really be people in this world who dare to say and to swear that this master of mine's a madman? Just tell me this, you shepherds – is there a village priest, however clever and studious, who could say what my master's just said, and is there any knight errant, however famous for being brave, who could make the offer my master's just made?'

Don Quixote, his face flushed with fury, turned to Sancho and said:

'Can there really, Sancho, be anyone on the whole globe who does not say that you are made of solid folly, double-lined with the same material and trimmed with your own special variety of knavery and villainy? Who has told you to go meddling in my affairs and deciding whether I am clever or stupid? Keep your mouth shut and don't answer back, and go and saddle Rocinante if he has been unsaddled; we are off to fulfil my promise, and since right is so clearly on my side you can reckon all those who contradict me as already defeated.'

And seething with rage he rose from his chair, leaving all the people amazed and wondering whether to consider him mad or sane. In the end, after they had tried to persuade him not to go ahead with his plan, because they felt fully assured of his desire to express his gratitude and no new demonstrations of his doughty spirit were necessary since those related in the history of his exploits were quite sufficient, Don Quixote nevertheless insisted on putting his intentions into effect; and mounted on Rocinante, having taken up his shield and his lance, he stationed himself in the middle of a highway not far from the green meadow. Sancho followed on his dun, together with all the people in the pastoral flock, longing to see where this arrogant and unprecedented gesture was going to lead. Planted, then, in the middle of the road (as I've already said), Don Quixote rent the air with words to this effect:

'O you, travellers and wayfarers, knights, squires, people on foot and on horseback, who pass along this road or shall pass along it during the next two days! Know that Don Quixote de la Mancha, a knight errant, is here to maintain that all beauty and courtesy in the world is exceeded by that which is contained within the nymphs who inhabit these woods and meadows, only excepting the mistress of my soul Dulcinea del Toboso. So let anyone of the contrary opinion present himself at this place, where I await him!'

Twice he repeated these words, and twice there was no adventurer available to hear them. But fortune, which was making his affairs progress from good to even better, so ordered events that a little later they saw approaching along the road a crowd of men on horseback, many of them with lances in their hands, riding fast in a tight bunch. As soon as the people accompanying Don Quixote saw these men they turned and took themselves a good distance away, because they knew that if they stayed there they might be exposed to danger. Only Don Quixote, with an intrepid heart, remained where he was; and Sancho Panza cowered behind Rocinante's rump. The throng of lancers approached, and one of them, riding on ahead of the others, screamed at Don Quixote:

'Get off the road, you stupid devil, these bulls are going to trample you to pieces!'

'Pooh!' Don Quixote replied. 'I care nothing for bulls, you wretches, even if they are the fiercest bulls ever bred on the banks of the Jarama. Confess, you knaves, without a second thought, that what I have just declared is true; or else you shall do battle with me.'

The herdsman didn't have a chance to reply, nor did Don Quixote have a chance to get off the road, even if he had wanted to; and so the whole herd of fierce bulls led by tame oxen, together with the crowd of herdsmen and others who were taking them to be penned in a town where there was to be a bullfight on the following day, charged over Don Quixote and over Sancho and over Rocinante and over the dun, sending them all sprawling to the earth. There lay Sancho mauled, Don Quixote horrified, the dun thrashed and Rocinante much the worse for wear; but they eventually hauled themselves to their feet and Don Quixote started running after the herd of bulls, stumbling here and falling there, and crying:

'Stop, stay, you scurvy knaves: it is but one solitary knight awaiting you, a knight who shares neither the character nor the opinion of those who say that one should build a bridge of silver for a fleeing enemy!'

But this didn't make the hasty travellers stop, and they paid no more attention to his threats than to last year's clouds. Exhaustion brought Don Quixote to a standstill; and more enraged than avenged he sat in the road to wait for Sancho, Rocinante and the dun. They came; master and servant remounted; and without turning back to say goodbye to the make-believe Arcadia, and feeling more shame than satisfaction, they continued on their way.

CHAPTER LIX

Relating the extraordinary event, which can count as an
adventure, that happened to Don Quixote

For the dust and the weariness that were the consequences of the bulls' inconsiderate behaviour they found a remedy in a clear, clean spring that they discovered in a cool copse, and the harassed master and servant sat down on its bank, having left Rocinante and the dun to roam free, without bridle or halter. Sancho examined the larder in his saddle-bags, and took out from them what he called his grub; he rinsed his mouth, Don Quixote washed his face and with this refreshment their flagging spirits revived.

But Don Quixote wasn't eating a single mouthful, out of sheer exasperation, and Sancho wasn't daring to touch the food, out of sheer good manners, as he waited for his master to take the first bite; but seeing that he was so carried away by his musings that he hadn't a thought for putting food in his mouth, Sancho didn't open his own mouth to speak but, breaking every rule of good breeding, to cram bread and cheese into his stomach.

'Yes, you eat up, friend Sancho,' said Don Quixote, 'sustain life, which is of more interest to you than to me, and let me die at the hands of my thoughts and in the grasp of my misfortunes. I was born, Sancho, to live dying, and you were born to die eating, and so that you can see that I am telling you the truth just consider my case: in print in histories, renowned for my skill in arms, courteous in my actions, respected by nobility, wooed by maidens – and after all that, just when I was expecting palms, triumphs and crowns, well-earned and deserved by my valiant deeds, I have this morning found myself trampled and kicked and battered by the hoofs of unclean, vile animals. This reflection blunts my teeth, clamps my jaws and numbs my hands, and takes away my appetite, so I intend to allow myself to die of hunger, quite the cruellest of all deaths.'

'So,' said Sancho, without any interruption to his munching, 'you can't think much of that proverb that goes, "Let them kill young Kelly, but first let him fill his belly." I'm not planning to kill myself, not me. Instead I'm going to do what the shoemaker does, stretching out the leather with his teeth till he makes it reach where he wants it to, and I'll stretch out my life by eating until it reaches the end that heaven has fixed for it – and you mark my words, sir, there isn't any greater madness than the one that leads people to want to take their own lives, as you do, and you'd better believe me, and after you've had a bite to eat lay yourself down on the green mattress of this grass and have a little nap, and you'll soon see how you feel a bit better when you wake up.'

Don Quixote lay down, because he thought Sancho spoke more like a philosopher than a fool, and he said:

'If, Sancho, you would like to do for me what I am about to explain, my improvement would be more assured and my dejection less oppressive, and it is this: while, obeying your advice, I sleep, I should like you to go some way from here and, exposing your flesh to the air, give yourself with Rocinante's reins three or four hundred lashes in part payment of the three thousand odd that you must give yourself to disenchant Dulcinea; because it is a great shame that the poor lady is still enchanted just because of your gross negligence.'

'There's quite a lot I could say on that subject,' said Sancho. 'But let's both sleep now, and God's already decided what'll happen after that. I'll tell you this much, though – this lashing yourself in cold blood is a tough assignment, even tougher if the lashes fall on a body that's underfed and badly nourished, so my lady Dulcinea's going to have to be patient, and when she's least expecting it she'll find me riddled like a sieve with lashings, and we're all alive until we die, what I mean to say is I'm still alive and I still intend to do what I promised to do.'

Don Quixote thanked him and ate a little food, and Sancho ate a lot of food, and they both lay down to sleep, leaving those two inseparable friends and companions Rocinante and the dun to graze in utter freedom and as they pleased on the lush grass that filled the meadow. It was quite late by the time they awoke, and they remounted and continued on their way, hurrying to reach an inn that they could see about three miles distant. I say it was an inn because that's what Don Quixote called it, contrary to his habit of calling all inns castles.

So they reached it and asked the landlord if there was any room. The answer came that there was indeed, and with all the comforts and luxuries that they could ever find in Saragossa itself. They dismounted and Sancho took his larder away to their quarters, to which the landlord handed him the key; then he took the animals to the stable, gave them their fodder and went back to see what Don Quixote, who was sitting on a stone bench by the door, wanted him to do, offering up special thanks to heaven that his master hadn't taken this inn for a castle. Suppertime came round; they retired to their room; Sancho asked the landlord what he had on offer. To which the landlord replied that Sancho's every word was his command, so he should go ahead and ask for whatever he fancied: the inn was stocked with the birds of the air, the fowls of the ground and the fish of the sea.

'We won't be needing all that,' Sancho replied, 'and if you'll just roast a couple of chickens for us that'll be enough, because my master's a delicate man and doesn't eat a lot, and I'm not that much of a greedy-guts.'

The landlord replied that chickens were off, the kites had done for them.

'Well, then, landlord,' said Sancho, 'have a nice tender pullet roasted for us.'

'A pullet? Upon my soul!' the landlord replied. 'I have to be honest – only yesterday I sent more than fifty of them off to town to be sold, but apart from pullets, you go ahead and ask for whatever you like.'

'That can't be a reason,' Sancho said, 'for not having any veal or kid.'

'At the present moment in time,' the landlord replied, 'we haven't, we've run out, but there'll be plenty next week.'

'That's a fat lot of good to me!' Sancho retorted. 'But I bet all those items you haven't got are made up for by the lashings of eggs and bacon you have got.'

'For God's sake!' the landlord replied. 'This guest here's got a good sense of humour! I tell him I haven't any pullets or hens, and he expects me to have eggs? Dream up still further delicacies if you like, but do stop asking me for hens.'

'Bloody hell!' said Sancho. 'Let's sort this out. Just tell me once and for all what you have got – and you can leave the dreaming out of it, landlord!'

The innkeeper said:

'What I really and truly have got is a pair of cow-heels just like calves' feet, or a pair of calves' feet just like cow-heels; they've been stewed with plenty of chick-peas, onions and salt pork, and at this very moment they're saying, "Come and eat me, come and eat me!"'

'Bags I have them,' said Sancho, 'and don't let anyone touch them – I'll give you more than anyone else for them, because I can't think of anything I'll enjoy more, and I don't give two hoots whether they're feet or heels.'

'Nobody's going to touch them,' said the innkeeper, 'because the other guests staying here are so high-up that they've brought their own cooks, stewards and provisions with them.'

'If it's being high-up we're talking about,' said Sancho, 'there's nobody higher-up than my master, but the job he's doing doesn't let you have pantries or larders, so we just lie down in the middle of a field and stuff acorns and medlars.'

This was all the conversation that Sancho had with the innkeeper, because he was unwilling to answer the next question: what on earth was this job of his master's?

So suppertime came round, Don Quixote retired to his room and the landlord brought the stew, just as it was, and Don Quixote sat down to eat it with a will. It seems that in a room next to Don Quixote's, divided from it only by a flimsy partition, he heard someone saying:

'I beg you, Don Jerónimo – while dinner's being fetched do let's read another chapter of the second part of *Don Quixote de la Mancha*.'[1]

The instant Don Quixote heard his name he started to his feet and pricked up his ears to listen to what these people were saying, and he heard Don Jerónimo's reply:

'Why do you want to us read all that nonsense, Don Juan? Nobody who has read the first part of the history of Don Quixote de la Mancha can possibly derive any pleasure from reading this second part.'

'All the same,' said Don Juan, 'it'll be as well to read it, because there's no book so bad that there isn't something good in it. What I most dislike about this one is that it describes Don Quixote as no longer in love with Dulcinea del Toboso.'

When Don Quixote heard this he flared up and cried:

'If anyone claims that Don Quixote de la Mancha has forgotten or can forget Dulcinea del Toboso, I shall, with equal arms, force him to acknowledge that he is very far from the truth, because neither can the peerless Dulcinea del Toboso be forgotten, nor is Don Quixote capable of forgetting. His motto is constancy, and his profession is to observe this principle with ease and without constraint.'

'Who is that answering us?' came the reply from the other room.

'Who do you think it is,' Sancho replied, 'if not the very same Don Quixote de la Mancha? And he'll make good everything he's just said and everything he hasn't said yet, too, because a good payer's a good pledger.'

Hardly had Sancho finished speaking when two gentlemen, as they gave every sign of being, walked in through the door, and one of them put his arms round Don Quixote's neck and said:

'Neither can your presence belie your name, nor can your name fail to accredit your presence: there can be no doubt that you, sir, are the real Don Quixote de la Mancha, guide and lodestar of knight-errantry, in spite and in defiance of the one who has attempted to usurp your name and obliterate your deeds, as has the author of this book I have here.'

And taking a book from his companion he handed it to Don Quixote, who began to thumb through it in silence, and after a short while he returned it with the words:

'In the little I have seen I have found three aspects of this author's work that are worthy of rebuke. First, certain statements in the prologue;[2] secondly, the fact that the language is Aragonese, because he often omits the article; and thirdly, and this is what most confirms his ignorance, he blunders and strays from the truth in the most central feature of the whole history, because he says here that my squire Sancho Panza's wife is called Mari Gutiérrez, when she is called nothing of the sort, but Teresa Panza; and if someone can make a mistake about such an important matter we can well fear that he is mistaken in everything else that he says in his history.'

To which Sancho added:

'That's a fine thing in a historian! He must be really clued up on our doings if he calls my wife Teresa Panza Mari Gutiérrez! Take another look at the book, sir, and see if I'm in it, and if he's changed my name too.'

'From what I have heard, my friend,' said Don Jerónimo, 'you must be Sancho Panza, Don Quixote's squire.'

'That's me,' Sancho replied, 'and proud of it.'

'Well the fact is,' the gentleman said, 'that this novice author doesn't treat you with the scrupulosity that you display in your person: he represents you as a glutton, and simple-minded, and not at all funny, very different from the Sancho described in the first part of the history of your master.'

'God forgive him,' said Sancho. 'He should have left me in my corner and forgotten all about me, because you've got to know your strings before you pluck them, and St Peter's all right in Rome.'

The two gentlemen asked Don Quixote into their room to share their dinner, as they were well aware that there was no food to be had at that inn fit for him to consume. Don Quixote, courteous as always, acceded to their request and dined with them; Sancho was left with the stew, absolute lord and master of it all, and sat himself at the head of the table, and by his side sat the innkeeper, no less fond than Sancho of his heels and of his feet.

During dinner Don Juan asked Don Quixote what news he had of his lady Dulcinea del Toboso: whether she had married, whether she had given birth or was pregnant, or whether on the contrary she was still intact and still remembered (always preserving her decorum and propriety) Don Quixote's amorous intentions. To which he replied:

'Dulcinea is indeed intact, and my intentions are firmer than ever; our communications are as unsatisfactory as they ever were; her beauty has been transformed into that of a coarse peasant girl.'

And he went on to give a detailed account of Dulcinea's enchantment, and what had happened in the Cave of Montesinos, together with the arrangements made by the sage Merlin for her to be disenchanted, in other words Sancho's self-flagellation. It gave the two gentlemen great pleasure to hear Don Quixote narrating the strange events of his own history, and they were as astonished by his mad antics as by the elegant manner in which he described them. One minute they thought him an intelligent man, the next minute he skidded off into absurdity, and they couldn't decide where to place him between sound sense and madness.

Sancho finished his supper and, leaving the innkeeper pie-eyed and tangle-footed, he went through to the room where his master was, and as he walked in he said:

'I'll be blowed, gents, if the author of that book you've got there doesn't want to get on bad terms with me – and if he calls me a greedy-guts, as you say he does, I only hope he doesn't call me a boozer into the bargain.'

'Oh yes he does,' said Don Jerónimo, 'but I don't remember his exact words, although I do know that they're offensive ones and, what's more, quite untrue, as I can plainly see from the physiognomy of the worthy Sancho who stands before me.'

'You mark my words,' said Sancho, 'the Sancho and the Don Quixote in that there history can't be the same as the ones in the history by Cide Hamete Benengeli, which is us – my master, brave and wise and in love, and me, a down-to-earth funny man, and not a greedy-guts or a boozer either.'

'That's what I think, too,' said Don Juan, 'and if it were possible a law ought to be passed that nobody should presume to write about the doings of the great Don Quixote, except the first author Cide Hamete, just as Alexander ordered that nobody should presume to represent him on canvas except Apelles.'

'Anyone who so wishes can represent me,' said Don Quixote, 'but not misrepresent me; for patience often fails when it is overloaded with insults.'

'No insult can be offered to Don Quixote,' said Don Juan, 'that he cannot avenge, unless he wards it off with the shield of his patience, which, in my belief, is large and strong.'

They spent a great part of that night in conversation of this sort, and, although Don Juan would have liked Don Quixote to read some more of the book, to see what other comments he made, they couldn't persuade him to, and he said that he took it as read and assumed that it was absurd through and through; for if by any chance the author discovered that he had held it in his hands, he was unwilling to give that man the pleasure of knowing that he had read it; because our thoughts, and still more our eyes, must be kept aloof from everything lewd and obscene.

They asked Don Quixote where he was intending to go next. He replied that he was on his way to Saragossa, to take part in the jousts for the suit of armour that are held in that city each year. Don Juan told him that the new history related how Don Quixote, or whoever it was, had participated there in the riding at the ring,[3] an episode depicted without imagination, with poor mottoes, even poorer costumes, and rich only in absurdities.

'Well, for that very reason,' Don Quixote replied, 'I shall not set foot in Saragossa, and thus I shall announce that novice historian's lie to the whole world, and people will be made aware that I am not the Don Quixote about whom he writes.'

'That will be an excellent move,' said Don Jerónimo, 'and they hold other jousts in Barcelona, where Don Quixote will be able to display his prowess.'

'And that is what I intend to do,' said Don Quixote, 'and now, with your permission, it is time for me to retire to bed, and please count me in the number of your firmest friends and most devoted servants.'

'Me too,' said Sancho, 'who knows, I might come in handy sometime.'

And so they said goodnight, and Don Quixote and Sancho returned to their room, leaving Don Juan and Don Jerónimo lost in amazement at the mixture that the knight had contrived of sound sense and sheer madness; and they felt quite certain that these, and not the pair described by the Aragonese author, were the real Don Quixote and Sancho.

Don Quixote rose early next morning and, knocking on the partition, said goodbye to the men in the other room. Sancho showered wealth upon the innkeeper and advised him that in future he should either be less boastful about the provision at his inn, or keep it better provided.

CHAPTER LX

*About what happened to Don Quixote on his way
to Barcelona*

It was a cool morning, and it looked as if it was going to be a cool day, too, when Don Quixote left the inn after asking which was the most direct route to Barcelona without going through Saragossa – so great was his determination to prove that the novice historian who was said to have denigrated him was a liar. What happened next was that for more than six days nothing happened, nothing at least worth writing about; and at the end of that time, while he was riding off the road, night overtook him in a dense copse of evergreen oaks or cork-oaks – on this point Cide Hamete isn't as meticulous as usual. The master and his servant dismounted and each settled down against a tree-trunk, and Sancho, who that day had enjoyed an afternoon meal, slipped without knocking through the doors of sleep; but Don Quixote, kept awake by his imagination much more than by his hunger, couldn't manage to drop off, and he wandered in his thoughts through thousands of different places. Now he was in the Cave of Montesinos; now he was watching Dulcinea, transformed into a peasant girl, vaulting on to her donkey; now he could hear the sage Merlin's words ringing in his ears, telling him of the conditions to be met and the actions to be taken to disenchant Dulcinea. It made him despair to consider Sancho's lassitude and lack of charitable feeling, because it was his belief that his squire had only given himself five lashes so far, a ridiculously small number in comparison with all those that still remained, and this made him so furious that he reasoned to himself as follows:

'If Alexander the Great cut the Gordian knot saying, "To cut is as good as to untie," and if that didn't prevent him from becoming the lord and master of all Asia, the same could apply to the disenchantment of Dulcinea if I lash Sancho whether he likes it or not; because if the condition is that he must receive three thousand odd lashes, what do I care whether he applies them himself or someone else does so for him, since what matters is that he must receive them, wherever they come from?'

With these thoughts in mind he went over to Sancho, having first taken Rocinante's reins and fashioned them into a whip, and began to loosen the laces that held Sancho's breeches up, although it is believed that there was only the one lace, the front one; but hardly had he begun when Sancho was wide awake and crying:

'What's this? Who's touching me, who's unlacing me?'

'It is I,' Don Quixote replied, 'come to make up for your deficiencies and to remedy my woes: I have come to lash you, Sancho, and to discharge in part the debt into which you have entered. Dulcinea is languishing, you are living on regardless, I am dying of desire – so now undo your breeches yourself, because what I am going to do now that we are alone is to give you two thousand lashes at least.'

'Oh no you're not,' said Sancho, 'you just stay where you are, because if you don't I swear to the one true God that even the deaf are going to hear us. The lashes I said I'd give myself have got to be voluntary ones, not forced on me, and right now I don't feel like lashing myself. It's enough if I promise to give myself a good hiding or at least a good swatting just as soon as I get the urge.'

'No, it can't be left to your goodwill, Sancho,' said Don Quixote, 'because your heart is hard and, although you're a peasant, your flesh is soft.'

And as he spoke he was struggling to untie him, to which Sancho responded by jumping to his feet, hurling himself at his master, grappling with him and then sticking a leg in, to leave him lying face upwards on the ground; and then Sancho clamped his right knee to his master's chest and held his wrists to the ground so that he couldn't move and could hardly even breathe. Don Quixote was gasping:

'What, you traitor? You defy your own natural lord? You raise your hand against the man who feeds you?'

'I don't make the king or break the king,' Sancho replied, 'I only help my master[1] – in other words me. You promise to leave me alone, and not try to lash me yet, and I'll let you go, but if not,

> You'll die here and now, you traitor,
> Doña Sancha's enemy.'[2]

Don Quixote made his promise, and swore by his life not to lay a finger on him, and to leave it to him to choose with absolute freedom when to lash himself. Sancho stood up and took himself a good way off, and as he went to lean against another tree he felt something touching his head; he raised his hands and they came into contact with two feet in their shoes and stockings. He shuddered with fear and went to another tree, and the same thing happened there. He screamed to Don Quixote for help. Don Quixote came and when he asked Sancho what had happened and what he was frightened of, Sancho replied that all those trees were full of human feet and legs. Don Quixote felt them, and immediately realized what the cause might be, and said:

'There's no need to be afraid, these legs and feet that you can feel and cannot see must belong to outlaws and bandits who have been hanged from these trees; in these parts the authorities hang them twenty or thirty at a time when they catch them, from which I deduce that we must be near Barcelona.'

And he was quite right, too. As they were leaving, they raised their eyes and saw the fruit that was hanging from those trees: bandits' corpses. Day was breaking, and if the dead bandits had frightened them, they were no less distressed when more than forty live bandits suddenly surrounded them, telling them in Catalan to stay where they were and not to move an inch until their captain arrived. Don Quixote was standing, his horse unbridled, his lance leaning against a tree, and, in short, was utterly defenceless, so he thought it best to fold his arms and bow his head, saving himself for a better opportunity.

The bandits hurried to ransack the dun and empty the saddle-bags and the travelling bag, and it was fortunate for Sancho that the Duke's escudos and the money they'd brought with them from the village were safe in a waist-pouch he was wearing; but for all that, these fine fellows would have skinned him to see if there was anything hidden between his hide and his flesh, if their captain hadn't arrived at that very moment; he was a man of maybe thirty-four, and was robust, of larger than average build, with a stern look in his eye, and dark in complexion. He was riding a powerful horse, wearing a steel coat of mail and had four little carbines (known in those parts as *pedreñales*) at his sides. He saw that his squires, as those of that profession are called, were about to take all Sancho Panza's possessions; he ordered them to stop, and was instantly obeyed; so the waist-pouch escaped. The captain was astonished to see a lance leaning against the tree, a shield lying on the ground and Don Quixote standing there dressed in armour and sunk in thought, with the most forlorn and dejected face that sadness itself could ever have worn. He rode over to the knight and said:

'Don't be so sad, my dear good fellow – you haven't fallen into the hands of some cruel Osiris, but into those of Roque Guinart,[3] and about them there's more of kindness than cruelty.'

'My sadness,' Don Quixote replied, 'is not caused by having fallen into your power, O valiant Roque, whose fame knows no bounds on this earth, but by having been so negligent that your soldiers caught me horseless, whereas I am obliged by the order of knight-errantry that I profess to be always on the alert, at every moment of the day my own sentry; for I would have you know, great Roque, that had they found me on my horse, bearing my lance and my shield, it would not have been easy for them to overcome me, because I am Don Quixote de la Mancha, he whose exploits resound throughout the world.'

Roque Guinart could tell at once that Don Quixote's weakness was more a question of insanity than of courage, and although he'd heard him mentioned on a few occasions, he'd never thought that his exploits were real, nor had he been able to persuade himself that such a humour could prevail in any man's heart; and so he was overjoyed to have come across the knight, because he could now probe from close up what he'd heard from afar, and he said:

'Valiant knight, do not take umbrage or consider the present setback as some piece of ill luck, because it could well happen that this stumble straightens the crooked path of your fortune; for heaven, in strange, mysterious, roundabout ways, inconceivable to man, raises the fallen and makes the poor wealthy.'

Don Quixote was about to thank him when they heard behind them a noise like a troop of horse, although it was only one animal, ridden at a furious gallop by a youth who seemed to be about twenty, wearing green damask with trimmings of gold, knee-breeches and loose open cape, his hat worn aslant and feathered in the Walloon style, tight-fitting waxed boots, spurs, dagger and sword, all gilt, a small musket in his hands and two pistols at his sides. Roque turned his head at the noise and saw this handsome figure, who said as he drew close:

'I've come in search of you, O brave Roque, hoping to find in you if not a remedy then at least some comfort in my misfortune; and not wanting to keep you in suspense, because I can see you haven't recognized me, let me tell you who I am: I'm Claudia Jerónima, the daughter of Simón Forte, your special friend and the deadly enemy of Clauquel Torrellas, who's your enemy too, because he belongs to the opposite faction; and, as you know, this Torrellas has a son called Don Vicente Torrellas, or at least he had a son of that name not two hours ago. This man has caused me great misfortune, and to cut short my tale of woe I'll tell it in few words. He saw me, he wooed me, I heeded him, I fell in love with him, all behind my father's back, because there's no woman, however secluded the life she lives, however demure she is, who hasn't more than sufficient time to put her unbridled desires into effect. In a word, he promised to marry me, and I made him the same promise – but we didn't go any further than that. Yesterday I discovered that, forgetful of his pledge to me, he was about to marry another woman, and that this morning he was going off for the ceremony, news that overwhelmed and infuriated me; and since my father wasn't at home I had the opportunity to put on the clothes you see me wearing, and by riding hard on this horse I caught up with Don Vicente about three miles from here, and, without waiting to make any accusations or listen to any excuses, I fired this musket at him and these two pistols as well, and I think I must have put more than two bullets into his body, opening in it doors through which my honour, dripping with his blood, could gain its freedom. There I left him surrounded by his servants, who didn't dare do anything to defend him – nor did I give them the chance. I've come to look for you so that you can take me to France, where I have relations I can live with, and also to ask you to protect my father and stop Don Vicente's many relatives from taking cruel revenge on him.'

Amazed at the lovely Claudia's forthrightness and courage, her striking presence and the events she'd related, Roque said:

'Come with me, madam, and let's go and find out whether your enemy is dead – and then we'll see what's best for you.'

Don Quixote, who had been listening carefully to what Claudia said and Roque Guinart replied, spoke up:

'Nobody need take the trouble to defend this lady; I undertake to do so; give me my horse and my arms, and wait for me here, because I will go in search of that knight and force him, dead or alive, to keep the promise that he made to this beautiful woman.'

'And nobody should doubt that, either,' said Sancho, 'because my master's a dab hand at matchmaking – not many days ago he forced this other bloke to marry this maiden after he too had refused to keep his promise, and if it wasn't for the fact that the enchanters that pursue him turned the bloke's face into a lackey's face, by now the maiden wouldn't be a maiden any more.'

Roque's mind was focused on the lovely Claudia's predicament rather than on what the master and his servant were saying, and he didn't hear them; he ordered his squires to return to Sancho everything that they'd taken off his dun, and to go back to where they'd spent the night, and then he left with Claudia at top speed to look for the wounded or dead man, Don Vicente. They reached the place where she'd caught up with him, and all they found was recently spilt blood; but looking around in all directions they made out some people on a hillside and rightly assumed that it must be Don Vicente being carried away dead or alive to be buried or treated; they hastened to catch up with them and, as the group was moving slowly, it was easy for them to do so. They found Don Vicente in his servants' arms, begging them in a weak and weary voice to allow him to die where they were, because the pain of his wounds made it impossible for him to go any further. Claudia and Roque jumped from their horses and ran up to him, the servants cringed in Roque's presence, Claudia flustered in Don Vicente's presence, and, caught between pity and severity, she went up to him and, taking his hands in hers, she said:

'If you'd given me these hands as we'd agreed, you would not be in this plight.'

The wounded gentleman's eyes were half-closed; he opened them and, recognizing Claudia, said:

'I can now see well enough, lovely and deluded lady, that you're the one who has killed me, a punishment I never deserved, because neither in my intentions nor in my actions have I ever offended you.'

'Isn't it true, then,' said Claudia, 'that you were on your way this morning to marry Leonora, rich Balvastro's daughter?'

'No, it isn't true,' Don Vicente replied. 'It must have been my evil fortune that brought you that rumour so that in your jealousy you would take my life; but dying as I am in your arms I count myself lucky. And to show you that I'm telling the truth, I want you to press my hand and accept me as your husband, if you will, because I haven't any better satisfaction to offer for the wrong you imagine that I've done you.'

Claudia wrung his hand, which so wrung her own heart that she fainted on Don Vicente's bloody breast, and then he was seized by the spasm of death. The bewildered Roque didn't know what to do. The servants went for water to splash on to the lovers' faces. This brought Claudia round, but not Don Vicente: he was dead. When Claudia realized that her darling husband was no longer alive, she rent the air with her sighs, wounded the heavens with her lamentations, tore her hair and let it blow loose in the wind and mauled her face, together with all the other demonstrations of grief and suffering that could ever be expected from an afflicted breast.

'O cruel and thoughtless woman!' she cried. 'How ready you were to put your evil intentions into practice! O raging force of jealousy, to what a desperate end you lead those who take you into their bosoms! O my husband, whose wretched fortune, making you my own darling, has taken you from the bridal bed to the grave!'

Such were Claudia's doleful lamentations, and they drew tears from Roque's eyes, even though he was a man who never wept. The servants were crying, Claudia fainted again and again, and the whole area seemed like a field of sorrow and a place of misfortune. Eventually Roque Guinart ordered Don Vicente's servants to take his body to his father's village, which was close by, to be buried. Claudia told Roque that she wanted to go to a convent where an aunt of hers was abbess, to live out the rest of her days there, in the company of another better and more eternal husband. Roque commended her pious intent and offered to accompany her wherever she pleased, and to defend her father against the dead man's relatives and against the whole world, if it tried to attack him. But Claudia would not on any account allow him to accompany her and, thanking him for his offer in the best words she could muster, she took her leave in tears. Don Vicente's servants carried his body away, Roque went back to his men and that was the end of the love of Claudia Jerónima. No wonder, since the web of her lamentable story was woven by the cruel and indomitable hands of jealousy.

Roque Guinart found his squires where he'd ordered them to stay, and Don Quixote in their midst, mounted on Rocinante and making a speech in which he was trying to persuade them to give up that way of life, so dangerous both for the body and for the soul; but since most of them were Gascons, unruly peasants, Don Quixote's speech made little impression on them. When Roque arrived he asked Sancho Panza if his men had returned all the prized possessions that they had taken from the dun. Sancho replied that they had, except three nightcaps that were worth three cities.

'What are you saying, man?' said one squire. 'I've got them here, and they aren't worth three reals.'

'True enough,' said Don Quixote, 'but my squire values them as he does because of the person who gave them to me.'

Roque Guinart commanded them to be returned forthwith, and then he told his men to form up in a line, and ordered all the clothes, jewels, money and everything else that they'd stolen since the last distribution to be brought forth; and making rapid calculations and putting cash in the place of whatever couldn't be divided, he shared it out it among his company so wisely and fairly that nobody was given one farthing more or less than what distributive justice requires. Once this had been done, leaving everyone perfectly happy and satisfied, Roque said to Don Quixote:

'If one weren't so meticulous in one's dealings with these people, it would be impossible to live with them.'

To which Sancho said:

'From what I've seen here, justice is such a fine thing that it's needed even among thieves.'

One of the squires heard him and raised his musket by its barrel, and would have smashed Sancho's head open if Roque Guinart hadn't shouted at him to stop. The flabbergasted Sancho promised himself never to unbutton his lips again while he was among these people. At that moment various other squires appeared, men posted as sentries along the roads to observe the people passing by and keep their leader informed of the situation, and they said:

'Sir, not far from here, on the road to Barcelona, a great crowd of people is on its way.'

To which Roque replied:

'Did you notice whether they're the sort that come looking for us, or the sort that we go looking for?'

'The sort we go looking for, definitely,' the squire said.

'Off you go, then, all of you,' Roque replied, 'and bring them to me here immediately, and don't let a single one of them escape.'

They obeyed him, and Don Quixote, Sancho and Roque were left alone, waiting to see what the squires brought back; and during this interval Roque said to Don Quixote:

'This life of ours must seem strange to you, Don Quixote – strange adventures, strange incidents, and all of them dangerous; and I'm not surprised if it does, because I do have to confess that there's no way of life more uneasy or troubled than ours. I was driven to it by some sort of desire for revenge, a feeling that's powerful enough to convulse the most placid heart. I am by nature a compassionate and well-intentioned sort of fellow; but, as I said, the desire to avenge myself for an affront that I suffered so overturns all my better impulses that I still persist in this way of life, even though I know I shouldn't. And since deep calls unto deep,[4] and one sin calls forth another sin, one revenge has linked up with another in such a chain that I don't only attend to my own revenges but to those of other people as well. But although I'm buried in the labyrinth of my own confusion, God has allowed me not to lose all hope of emerging safely from it one day.'

Don Quixote was amazed to hear Roque speaking such good, sound sense, because it had been his belief that among those involved in the business of robbery and murder there couldn't be anyone capable of clear thinking, and he said:

'Señor Roque, the beginning of good health lies in knowing the disease and in the patient's willingness to take the medicine prescribed by the doctor. You are ill, you know what your disease is and heaven or, more accurately, God, who is our Doctor, will give you medicines to cure you – medicines that cure gradually, not all of a sudden by some miracle; what is more, intelligent sinners are closer to being cured than foolish ones, and since you have shown your good sense in the words that you have just spoken, you only have to be of good spirit and hope for an improvement in the disease of your conscience. And if you want to take an easy short cut to the road of your salvation, come with me and I shall teach you how to become a knight errant, and you will suffer so many trials and tribulations that if they are regarded as penances they will put you in heaven in a brace of shakes.'

Roque laughed at Don Quixote's advice and, changing the subject, told him about the tragic episode of Claudia Jerónima, which brought grief to Sancho's heart, because he thought that the beautiful, forthright, spirited girl was a bit of all right.

And now the squires arrived with their prize: two gentlemen on horseback, two pilgrims on foot and a coachful of women with half-a-dozen servants accompanying them on foot and on horseback, and a pair of footmen travelling with the gentlemen. The squires surrounded them all, and both victors and vanquished kept a profound silence, waiting for the great Roque Guinart to speak. He asked the two gentlemen who they were and how much money they had on them. One of them replied:

'We're captains in the Spanish infantry, sir; our companies are in Naples and we're on our way to embark on one of four galleys that are said to be in Barcelona with orders to sail for Sicily. We have about two or three hundred escudos and they make us feel rich and happy, because the poverty that we soldiers are used to doesn't allow us any greater treasures than this.'

Roque put the same question to the pilgrims, and the answer was that they were on their way to embark for Rome, and that between them they might have about sixty reals. Roque went on to ask who was travelling in the coach, and where they were going, and how much money they had, and one of the servants on horseback said:

'My mistress, Doña Guiomar de Quiñones – the wife of the President of the Naples Tribunal – and her young daughter, and a maid and a duenna are the occupants of this coach; there are six of us servants with them, and the money amounts to six hundred escudos.'

'And so,' said Roque Guinart, 'we have here nine hundred escudos and sixty reals; my soldiers must number about sixty; someone work out how much each of them gets, because I'm no good at figures.'

When the highwaymen heard this they raised their voices and cried:

'Long live Roque Guinart, in spite of all those thieving murderers who want to do for him!'

Faced by the confiscation of their property, the captains showed their distress, the judge's wife was plunged into sorrow and the pilgrims weren't at all pleased. Roque kept them in suspense for a short while; but not wanting to prolong their suffering, evident from a mile away, he said, turning to the captains:

'Please be so kind, captains, as to lend me sixty escudos, and perhaps the judge's wife will lend me eighty, to keep these men happy, because the priest dines on his singing; and you can continue on your way free and unmolested, with a safe conduct that I shall give you so that if you come across any others of my squadrons scattered about these parts they won't do you any harm; it isn't my intention to offend soldiers or women, particularly those of high rank.'

With countless well-turned phrases the captains thanked Roque for being so courteous and so generous, as they saw it, as to let them keep some of their own money. Doña Guiomar de Quiñones tried to throw herself from the coach to kiss the great Roque's hands and feet, but he wouldn't allow her to do any such thing; on the contrary, he begged her forgiveness for the wrong that he was doing her, forced as he was to comply with the obligations of his wicked calling. The judge's wife ordered one of her servants to hand over the eighty escudos assessed as her contribution, and the captains had already paid out their sixty. The pilgrims were about to surrender their miserable pittance, but Roque told them to stop and, turning to his men, he said:

'It works out at two escudos each, with twenty left over; give ten to these pilgrims, and the other ten to this worthy squire, so that he can speak well of this adventure.'

Writing materials, with which he always kept himself provided, were brought, and he handed out safe conducts to be presented to the leaders of his squadrons; and then he said goodbye and let them all go free, amazed at his nobility, his gallant disposition and his unusual behaviour, and regarding him as more of an Alexander the Great than a notorious robber. One of the squires muttered in his mixture of Gascon and Catalan:

'This here captain is fitter to be a friar than a bandit – if he wants to be so generous again, he'd better do it with his own money, not ours.'

The wretch hadn't spoken softly enough to prevent Roque from hearing, and he raised his sword and almost split the squire's head in two, saying:

'That's how I punish insolence and effrontery.'

All his men were dumbfounded, and none of them dared utter a word, such was their obedience.

Roque drew aside and wrote a letter to a friend of his in Barcelona, saying that he had with him the famous Don Quixote de la Mancha, the knight errant about whom people were talking so much, and that he was the funniest and most intelligent man in the world; and in four days' time, on St John the Baptist's day, he would be left in the middle of the city beach, in full armour, on his horse Rocinante, with his squire Sancho on an ass, and please would he tell Roque's friends the Niarros about this, so that they too could have some fun with him; he'd have liked his enemies the Cadells to be deprived of this pleasure, but that was going to be impossible, because Don Quixote's mixture of madness and sound sense, and his squire Sancho Panza's drollery, couldn't fail to delight everybody. Roque sent this letter off with one of his squires, who changed from his bandit's clothes into those of a farmer, went to Barcelona, and delivered it.

CHAPTER LXI

*About what happened to Don Quixote as he rode into
Barcelona, together with other events with more truth than
good sense about them*

Don Quixote stayed with Roque for three days and three nights, and if
he'd stayed with him for three hundred years he wouldn't have run out
of things to see and marvel at in his way of life: they'd be in one place
at dawn, eat lunch somewhere else, sometimes they'd be running away
from an unknown pursuer, at other times they'd be lying in wait for an
unknown prey. They slept on their feet, breaking their sleep to move on
from one spot to another. They were forever sending out spies, listening
to sentries, blowing on the fuses of their muskets, although there weren't
many of these, because they all had their carbines. Roque spent the nights
away from his men in places that they couldn't find out about, because
all the edicts published by the Viceroy of Catalonia putting a price on
his head kept him nervous and apprehensive, and he didn't dare trust
anybody, in the fear that his own men might either kill him or hand him
over to the authorities: a truly wearisome, wretched life.

Finally, using unfrequented roads, short cuts and secret paths, Roque,
Don Quixote and Sancho, with another six squires, made their way to
Barcelona. They reached the beach on the night before St John the
Baptist's day, and Roque embraced Don Quixote and Sancho, to whom
he gave the ten escudos he'd promised but not yet delivered, and left
them, after exchanges of a thousand offers of future service. Roque went
away; Don Quixote was left to wait for the day, just as he was, on
horseback, and it wasn't long before the white face of the dawn began
to peep from the balconies of the East, gladdening the plants and the
flowers rather than the ear, although to gladden that too there came the
sound of shawms and drums, and of horse-bells, the 'Mind your backs,
mind your backs, make way, make way!' of outriders who seemed to be
emerging from the city. The dawn yielded to the sun, which, with a face
broader than a buckler, was easing itself above the horizon.

Don Quixote and Sancho gazed all around them; they gazed at the sea, which they'd never seen before, and it seemed vast, endless, much bigger than those Lakes of Ruidera that they'd seen in La Mancha; they saw galleys moored off the beach, which lowered their awnings and displayed themselves decked with pennants and streamers that fluttered in the wind and kissed and caressed the water. Bugles, trumpets and shawms rang out inside them, and filled the air near and far with melodious warlike notes. The galleys began to move and to make as if to launch an attack as they glided over the still waters, and the appearance of a great number of gentlemen who rode out of the city on handsome horses, wearing magnificent gala-dress, was the response on land. The soldiers on the galleys were firing countless cannon, and those on the city walls and in the forts were replying with heavy artillery fire that rent the air with its dreadful roar, to be answered in turn by the cannon on the decks of the galleys. The happy sea, the joyful earth, the clear air, just occasionally smudged with artillery smoke, seemed to be inspiring a sudden gaiety in all the people.

Sancho couldn't imagine how those huge hulks moving about on top of the sea could have so many feet.

And now the gentlemen in gala-dress galloped cheering and yelling and whooping to where Don Quixote sat on his horse in confusion and bewilderment, and one of them, the one to whom Roque had written, cried to Don Quixote:

'Welcome to our city, O mirror, beacon and lodestar of all knight-errantry – and it's gospel every word! Welcome I say, O valiant Don Quixote de la Mancha – not the fraudulent, fictitious, apocryphal one recently displayed to our gaze in false histories, but the true, genuine and legitimate knight described for us by Cide Hamete Benengeli, the flower of historians.'

Don Quixote made no answer, and the gentlemen didn't wait for him to do so, but, wheeling and whirling about with all their followers, they careered around him in a labyrinthine spiral, and he turned to Sancho and said:

'They recognized us immediately: I'll wager they've read our history, and even the other one recently published by that Aragonese fellow.'

The gentleman who had spoken to Don Quixote came back and said:

'Be so kind, Don Quixote sir, as to accompany us; we're all your servants, and great friends of Roque Guinart.'

To which Don Quixote replied:

'If courtesy breeds courtesy, yours, sir knight, is the child or at least the close relative of that of the great Roque. Take me where you please, for I shall have no other will than yours, even more so if you wish to employ it in your service.'

The gentleman replied in no less courteous terms, and they all clustered around Don Quixote and, to the sounds of the shawms and drums, rode with him to the city; and, as they entered it, the evil one, the source of all the evil in this world, and the boys, who are more evil than the evil one – or, to be more exact, two of them, particularly bold and mischievous – wormed their way through the crowd and one lifted up the dun's tail and the other Rocinante's, and they rammed under each a handful of gorse. When the poor creatures felt the pricking of this original variety of spur they pressed their tails down, which increased their torment so much that they bucked and bucked until they threw their riders to the ground. Don Quixote, shamed and humiliated, went to remove this plumage from his poor old nag, and Sancho did the same for his dun. Those who were riding with Don Quixote would have liked to punish the boys for their insolence, but this was impossible because they disappeared among the hundreds of others who were following.

Don Quixote and Sancho remounted and, with the same pomp and music, they reached their guide's house, a large and stately one, as befitted a wealthy gentleman; and we shall leave him in it for a moment, because that is what Cide Hamete wants us to do.

CHAPTER LXII

Concerning the adventure of the enchanted bust, together with other trivialities that cannot be left untold

Don Quixote's host was called Don Antonio Moreno, and he was a wealthy, intelligent gentleman, fond of good, wholesome entertainment; and now that he had Don Quixote in his house he started looking for ways in which, without doing him any harm, he could reveal his capers to the public, because a jest that hurts is no jest, and no sport is any sport at all if it damages others. So what Don Antonio first did was to have the armour taken off Don Quixote and to display him, wearing the tight chamois-leather doublet and hose in which we've described him on other occasions, on a balcony overhanging one of the main streets in the city, in full view of the people and the boys, who stared up at him as if he were a monkey. The men in the magnificent gala-dress galloped past again as if they had donned it for him alone rather than to celebrate that festive day, and Sancho was overjoyed because he believed that he'd stumbled in some mysterious way upon another wedding like Camacho's, another house like Don Diego de Miranda's, another castle like the Duke's.

Some of Don Antonio's friends lunched with him that day, and they all honoured Don Quixote and treated him as a knight errant, and he was puffed up with pride and bursting with delight. Sancho came out with so many funny comments that all the servants in the house and indeed all the people listening to him were hanging on his every word. As Sancho waited at table, Don Antonio said:

'We've heard here, good Sancho, that you're so fond of chicken blancmange[1] and meatballs that if there's any left over you save it for the following day inside your shirt.'

'No, sir, that isn't true,' Sancho replied, 'because I'm cleaner than I'm greedy, and my master Don Quixote here present knows that us two often get by for a week on a handful of acorns or walnuts. It is true that if they happen to give me a heifer I do make haste with the halter – what I mean to say is that I eat what I'm given and I take things as they come, but if anyone's been saying I'm some champion eater and not at all clean with it, let me tell him he's wrong, and I'd have used a different word to say so if it wasn't for my respect for present company.'

'To be sure,' said Don Quixote, 'the frugality and the cleanliness of Sancho's eating habits are worthy to be engraved on sheets of bronze to remain in the eternal memory of the centuries to come. It is true that when he is hungry he might seem to be something of a glutton, because he eats at speed and chews on both sides of his mouth at the same time; but in cleanliness he leaves nothing to be desired, and during the time when he was governor he learned such fastidious table-manners that he ate grapes and even pomegranates with a fork.'

'What?' exclaimed Don Antonio. 'Sancho has been a governor?'

'Yes,' Sancho replied, 'of an island called Barataria. For ten days I was a top-notch governor, but I lost my peace of mind and learned to scorn all the governing in the world, so I ran away and fell into a cave where I gave myself up for dead, and it was a miracle I got out alive.'

Don Quixote then gave them a detailed account of all the incidents in Sancho's governorship, to the delight of his listeners. Once the tables had been cleared, Don Antonio took Don Quixote by the hand and walked with him to a distant room, where there was no furniture other than a slab, apparently of jasper, on a pedestal of the same material, and on the slab there was a bust, after the style of those of Roman emperors, which seemed to be of bronze. Don Antonio walked with Don Quixote all round the room, and several times round the pedestal, after which he said:

'Now that I am sure, Don Quixote sir, that nobody is listening to us, and that the door is locked, I am going to tell you about one of the strangest adventures, or, more accurately, novelties, that it is possible to imagine, on condition that you consign what I am about to tell you to the innermost recesses of secrecy.'

'I swear that I will do so,' Don Quixote replied, 'and even seal it in with a flagstone to make it all the more secure, because I would have you know, Don Antonio sir,' (he had discovered his host's name by now) 'that you are speaking to a man who has ears to hear but not a tongue to speak; so you can safely transfer what lies in your breast into mine, in the knowledge that you are casting it into the very abysses of silence.'

'Reassured by that promise,' Don Antonio replied, 'I shall fill you with amazement at what you are about to see and hear, and also give myself some relief from the sorrow that I suffer through not having anyone with whom to share my secrets, because they are not to be entrusted to just anybody.'

Don Quixote was on pins and needles as he awaited the outcome of all these precautions. Next Don Antonio took his hand again and passed it all over the bronze bust, the jasper slab and the jasper pedestal on which it stood, and then he said:

'This bust, Don Quixote sir, was made by one of the greatest enchanters and sorcerers the world has ever known, a man who was, I believe, a

Pole, and a disciple of the famous Escotillo,[2] about whom so many marvels are told; he stayed here in my house, and for a thousand escudos he made this bust, which has the property and the virtue of replying to all questions spoken into its ear. He looked to his rhombuses, drew his characters, observed his stars, studied his cardinal points, and eventually brought it to the pitch of perfection that we shall behold tomorrow; because on Fridays it is silent, and since today is a Friday it will make us wait until tomorrow. In the meantime you can be thinking about what questions to ask it; I know from experience that it always tells the truth.'

Don Quixote was astonished at the bust's virtue and property, and was on the verge of disbelieving Don Antonio. But seeing how little time he had to wait before putting it to the test, he only replied that he was grateful to have been allowed to share such a great secret. They walked out of the room, Don Antonio locked the door and they returned to the hall, where the other gentlemen were waiting. In the meanwhile Sancho had been telling them all about the adventures and incidents in which his master had been involved.

That afternoon they took Don Quixote out for a ride, not in his armour but in civilian clothes, wearing a long robe of tawny worsted that would have made ice sweat at that time of year. They made arrangements for their servants to keep Sancho amused and not to allow him to leave the house. Don Quixote wasn't riding Rocinante but a great, easy-paced mule with fine trappings. They robed him and, taking care that he didn't notice, stitched a parchment on his back, on which they had written in large letters: 'This is Don Quixote de la Mancha.' As they began their ride the placard caught the eyes of all who came to look at him, and when they read out aloud, 'This is Don Quixote de la Mancha,' he was astonished to find that everyone who saw him knew him and kept repeating his name; and turning to Don Antonio, riding by his side, he observed:

'Great is the prerogative that is inherent to knight-errantry, because it makes the man who professes it well known and indeed famous throughout the world. If you doubt what I say just look, Don Antonio sir: even the boys of this city know me without ever having seen me before.'

'Yes, you are right, Don Quixote sir,' Don Antonio replied. 'Just as fire cannot be hidden or shut away, virtue cannot fail to be recognized; and the virtue achieved in the profession of arms outshines and outclasses all others.'

But what happened next was that as Don Quixote rode along in state, as described, a man from Castile who read the placard on his back cried out:

'The devil take you, Don Quixote de la Mancha! How on earth have you managed to survive as long as this, and not died from all those beatings you've been given? You're a madman, and if you'd been mad by yourself and behind the closed doors of your own insanity it wouldn't have been so bad; but you have the ability to turn everyone who has anything to do with you mad and stupid just like you, and if you don't believe me you can confirm it in these people riding with you. Go back home, you fool, and look after your property and your wife and children, and drop all this nonsense that's eating your brain away and skimming all your wits off your mind.'

'Look here, my good man,' said Don Antonio, 'you go on your way and stop giving advice to those who haven't asked you for it. Don Quixote de la Mancha is extremely sane, and we who are accompanying him are no fools; virtue must be honoured wherever it is found, so get along with you and a plague on you, and stop poking your nose into other people's business.'

'You're right, by God,' the Castilian replied. 'Giving advice to this man is like kicking against the pricks, but even so it makes me sorry to think that the good sense the fool is said to display in all other matters is draining away down the ditch of his knight-errantry; and may that plague you wished on me infect me and all my descendants if I ever again give anyone any advice, even if I live longer than Methuselah,[3] and even if I'm asked for it.'

The adviser went away; the group moved on; but there was such a scrimmage of boys and people to read the placard that Don Antonio had to remove it, pretending to be removing something else.

Night fell and they went back home; a ball was held there, because Don Antonio's wife, a fun-loving, beautiful and intelligent lady of high rank, had invited other ladies, friends of hers, to come and honour her guest with their company and to enjoy his extraordinary antics. Some ladies came, there was a sumptuous dinner and the ball began at nearly ten o'clock. Among the ladies there were two who were full of mischief and fond of pulling people's legs, and although they were very virtuous, they were also a little over-familiar in their search for harmless amusement. These two kept Don Quixote dancing so continuously that they wearied not only his body but his very soul as well. It was a sight to see the figure cut by Don Quixote, lank, stiff, thin, pale, in clothes too small for him and, worst of all, by no means nimble. The two young ladies flirted with him on the sly, and he repulsed them in a similarly surreptitious way; but finding that there was no respite from all this flirtation he raised his voice and exclaimed:

'*Fugite, partes adversae!*[4] Leave me in peace, unwelcome thoughts; manage your desires as best you can, ladies; for she who is queen of mine, the peerless Dulcinea del Toboso, suffers none but hers to vanquish and enslave me.'

And so saying he sat down on the floor in the middle of the hall, exhausted from so much dancing. Don Antonio ordered him to be carried to his bed, and the first man to take hold of him was Sancho, who said:

'What on earth put it into your head, master, to go dancing? Do you fancy all brave men can dance and all knight errants are good at hoofing it? I can tell you this much – if you do, you're wrong. There's many a man would rather kill a giant than cut a caper. If it was clog-dancing I could have helped you out, because I can bang away at that like an angel, but as for ballroom dancing I can't do it to save my life.'

With these and other words Sancho gave everyone at the party a good laugh, and then he deposited his master in bed, covering him up to make him sweat out the chill he'd caught dancing.

On the following day Don Antonio thought it would be a good idea to give the enchanted bust its trial, and he locked himself into the room where it was kept, with Don Quixote, Sancho, another two friends and the two young ladies who had made Don Quixote drop with exhaustion at the dance, and who had stayed the night with Don Antonio's wife. He told them all about the strange property it possessed, bound them to secrecy and informed them that this was the first time that its powers were to be put to the test. Only Don Antonio's two friends knew the secrets of the enchanted bust, and if he hadn't told them how it worked they would have been struck with the same amazement as the rest of them, no other reaction being possible: such was the immense skill with which it had been constructed.

The first to approach the bust was Don Antonio himself, who spoke into its ear in a low voice, but not so low as not to be audible to all:

'Tell me, bust, by the virtue inherent in you: what am I thinking at this moment?'

And the bust replied, without moving its lips, in a clear and precise voice that all could hear:

'I do not divine thoughts.'

Everyone was dumbstruck at this, all the more so because there was nobody in the room or anywhere near the pedestal who could have replied.

'How many of us are there here?' Don Antonio asked.

And the answer came in the same quiet tone:

'You and your wife, with two friends of yours and two of hers, and a famous knight called Don Quixote de la Mancha, and a squire of his whose name is Sancho Panza.'

And now there was fresh amazement; now their hair stood on end with pure terror. Don Antonio stepped aside and said:

'This is enough to convince me that I was not deceived by the man who sold you to me, O wise bust, talking bust, answering bust, admirable bust! Now someone else come up and ask whatever they like.'

And since women are generally impatient and inquisitive, the first person to come forward was one of his wife's two friends, and her question was:

'Tell me, bust: what must I do to become very beautiful?'

And the reply was:

'Be very virtuous.'

'I'm not asking you anything else,' said the questioner.

Next her friend came up and said:

'I'd like to know, bust, whether my husband loves me or not.'

And the bust replied:

'Consider how he behaves to you, and you will find out for yourself.'

The married lady went away saying:

'There was no need of a question to get that answer, because it's obvious that a person's behaviour reveals his feelings.'

Next one of Don Antonio's friends stepped forward and asked:

'Who am I?'

And the reply was:

'You know that.'

'That isn't what I'm asking you,' the gentleman replied. 'I want you to tell me whether you know me.'

'Yes, I do,' came the reply, 'you are Don Pedro Noriz.'

'That's all I need to know, because it's enough to convince me, O bust, that you know everything.'

And he stood aside and Don Antonio's other friend went up and asked:

'Tell me, bust: what does my elder son want?'

'I have already said,' came the reply, 'that I do not divine thoughts; but all the same I can tell you that what your son most wants is to bury you.'

'That's right,' said the gentleman. 'It stands out a mile, doesn't it? And that's all I'm asking.'

Don Antonio's wife came up and said:

'I really don't know what to ask you, O bust – I'd just like you to tell me whether I'm going to enjoy my good husband's company for many years to come.'

And the reply was:

'Yes, you will, because his health and his temperance promise many years of life, which many men cut short by their intemperance.'

And then Don Quixote stepped forward and asked:

'Tell me, O you that answer so well, was what I describe as having happened in the Cave of Montesinos the truth or a dream? Will my squire Sancho's lashing ever come to be? Will Dulcinea ever be disenchanted?'

'About that cave,' came the reply, 'there is much to be said: there is a little of both in it; Sancho's lashing will take some time; Dulcinea's disenchantment will be accomplished in due course.'

'That is all I want to know,' said Don Quixote, 'because if I see Dulcinea disenchanted I shall reckon that all the good fortune I can desire has alighted upon me.'

The last questioner was Sancho, and what he asked was:

'Am I going to be given another government by any chance, O bust? Am I ever going to escape from this miserable life of a squire? Am I going to see my wife and children again?'

To which the reply was:

'You will govern in your own house, and if you go back there you will see your wife and children, and once you stop serving you will cease to be a squire.'

'That's good, by God!' said Sancho Panza. 'I could have told myself all that. The great prophet Stan Streason couldn't have done any better!'

'You animal!' said Don Quixote. 'What do you expect it to say? Isn't it enough that the replies this bust has given correspond to the questions put to it?'

'Yes, it is,' Sancho replied, 'but I'd just like it to be a bit more forthcoming and tell me some more.'

And this ended the questions-and-answers session. Yet it didn't put an end to the astonishment that possessed them all, except Don Antonio's two friends who were in on the secret. But Cide Hamete Benengeli explains it at once, so as not to hold the world in the amazed belief that there was some extraordinary magical mystery enclosed within the bust; and so he says that Don Antonio Moreno had made it at home to amuse himself and amaze the ignorant, in imitation of one he'd seen in Madrid, the work of an engraver; and it was constructed like this: the slab was made of wood, painted and varnished to look like jasper, and the pedestal on which it rested was of the same material, as were four eagles' feet projecting from it to support the weight more securely. The bust, resembling the effigy of a Roman emperor, the colour of bronze, was hollow, and it fitted into a hole in the slab so perfectly that the join was invisible. There was also a hollow in the pedestal, exactly under the hollow in the bust, and all this opened into the room underneath. Through this system of holes in the bust, slab and pedestal, a tin tube was neatly fitted so that nobody could see it. In the room below, the man who was to reply was stationed, with his mouth to the tin tube, and the voice downstairs went up it, and the voice upstairs came down it, as clearly articulated as through an ear trumpet, and so it was impossible to discover the trick. The answerer was a nephew of Don Antonio's, a sharp-witted, intelligent student, and since his uncle had told him who would be going into the room with him that day, it was easy for him to give a quick and precise answer to the first question; and he improvised answers to the others and, being intelligent, did so intelligently. And Cide Hamete adds that this marvellous invention lasted for about ten or twelve days; but then, as news spread through the city that Don Antonio had in his house an enchanted bust that replied to anyone who asked it a question, he was afraid that it might reach the ears of the watchful sentinels of our faith, so he told the inquisitors about it himself and they ordered him to dismantle it and never to use it again, to prevent the ignorant rabble from being scandalized; but in the opinion of Don Quixote and Sancho, the bust remained an enchanted and responsive one, more to Don Quixote's satisfaction than to Sancho's.

To please Don Antonio and honour Don Quixote and to give him another opportunity to perform his antics, the gentlemen of the city organized a riding at the ring to take place six days later, but it never happened, because of an event that will shortly be described.

Don Quixote had an urge to wander through the city without ceremony and on foot, fearing that if he went on horseback the boys would chase after him; so he and Sancho went out for a walk with two servants that Don Antonio provided for him. As they strolled down a street, Don Quixote happened to look up and he saw written in large letters over a door the words 'Books Printed Here', which pleased him no end, because he'd never seen a printing-house and was keen to know what they were like. In he went with all his retinue, and he saw men printing in one place, correcting in another, setting up the type over there, revising over here, and, in short, all the different activities of a large printing-house. Don Quixote would approach one compartment and ask what was being done there; the workmen told him, he expressed his amazement, and moved on. In another area he went up to a man and asked him what he was doing. The workman replied:

'This gentleman here, sir,' and he indicated a man of good appearance and presence, and a certain solemnity, 'has translated an Italian book into our Castilian tongue, and I'm setting it up to be printed.'

'What is the book's title?' Don Quixote asked.

To which the author replied:

'In Italian, sir, the book is called *Le Bagatelle*.'[5]

'And what does *Le Bagatelle* mean in our language?' Don Quixote asked.

'*Le Bagatelle*,' said the author, 'means something like *Trifles*; and although the book has a humble title, it contains excellent material of real substance.'

'I have a smattering of Italian,' said Don Quixote, 'and I pride myself on being able to sing a few verses by Ariosto. But please tell me, sir, and I am not asking this out of any desire to test your knowledge, but merely out of curiosity: have you found the word *pignatta* in your text?'

'Yes, often,' the author replied.

'And how do you translate it?' Don Quixote asked.

'"Cooking pot",' the author replied, 'how else?'

'God's body!' said Don Quixote. 'You are advanced in Italian! I should be prepared to bet a tidy sum that where it says in Italian *piace* you say "pleases", and where it says *più* you say "more", and that you translate *su* by "above", and *giù* by "beneath".'

'Yes, I do,' said the author, 'because these are their proper equivalents.'

'I would venture to swear,' said Don Quixote, 'that you are not a well-known man, for the world is always loath to reward fine minds and praiseworthy labours. Such skills going to waste! Such talents neglected! Such virtues scorned! And yet it seems to me that translating from one language into another, except from those queens of languages, Greek and Latin, is like viewing Flemish tapestries from the wrong side, when, although one can make out the figures, they are covered by threads that obscure them, and one cannot appreciate the smooth finish of the right side; and translating from easy languages is no indication of talent or literary ability, any more than transcribing or copying a document on to another piece of paper is. By this I do not mean to say that the exercise of translation is not to be given any credit, because there are worse and less profitable things that a man can do. From all this I exclude two famous translators: one is Dr Cristóbal de Figueroa, for his *Pastor Fido*, and the other is Don Juan de Jáuregui, for his *Aminta*,[6] translations which are so felicitous that they leave one wondering which is the translation and which is the original. But please tell me this: are you having this book printed on your own account, or have you sold the rights to a bookseller?'

'I'm printing it on my own account,' the author replied, 'and I'm hoping to make a thousand ducats, at least, from this first printing, of two thousand copies, because they'll sell like hot cakes at six reals each.'

'Your accounts are in a fine way, I must say!' Don Quixote replied. 'You do not seem to know anything about printers' credits and debits, or the agreements that they make with each other. I can promise you that when you find yourself loaded down with two thousand copies of your book you'll soon be so exhausted that it will frighten you, particularly if the book is at all abstruse and lacking in raciness.'

'What do you mean?' said the author. 'Do you want me to let a bookseller have it, and give me three maravedís for the copyright, and think he's doing me a great favour? I don't print my books to achieve fame, because my deeds have already made me well-known; profit is what I want, because without it fame isn't worth a farthing.'

'God send you good luck,' Don Quixote replied.

And he moved on to another compartment, where he saw that they were correcting a sheet of a book entitled *Light of the Soul*,[7] and when he saw it he said:

'Although there are already many books of this sort, they are the ones that ought to be printed, because there are many sinners in this world, and countless lights are needed for so many who are in the dark.'

He walked on and saw people correcting another book, and, when he asked what its title was, they replied that it was called *The Second Part of the Ingenious Hidalgo Don Quixote de la Mancha*,[8] written by somebody from Tordesillas.

'Yes, I have heard about that book,' said Don Quixote, 'and I really and truly did believe that it had been burned to ashes for its insolence; but it will have its Martinmas, like all hogs;[9] because fictional histories are good and entertaining in so far as they approach the truth or what looks like it, and true histories are the better the truer they are.'

With these words he stalked out of the printing-house, looking cross. And on that same day Don Antonio made arrangements for him to see the galleys that were moored off the beach, which delighted Sancho, because he'd never been on board a galley. Don Antonio informed the commodore that he was going to take a guest of his to see them that afternoon – the famous Don Quixote de la Mancha, about whom the commodore and all the inhabitants of the city had heard; and what happened on board will be related in the next chapter.

CHAPTER LXIII

*About the disaster that happened to Sancho Panza on
his visit to the galleys, and the strange adventure of the
beautiful Morisco girl*

The answer that the enchanted bust had given Don Quixote led him to
many different speculations, not one of them, however, hitting on the
secret of the trick, and all of them ending up with the promise, for him
a true one, of Dulcinea's disenchantment. To this thought he returned
again and again, and he rejoiced in the belief that he would soon see its
fulfilment; and as for Sancho, although he'd hated being governor, he
still longed to command and be obeyed again, a misfortune inseparable
from the exercise of power, even mock power.

To cut the story short, that afternoon their host Don Antonio Moreno
went with his two friends and Don Quixote and Sancho to inspect the
galleys. The commodore had been notified of their visit, which he
welcomed because of the chance it gave him to see two such famous men
as Don Quixote and Sancho, and as soon as they set foot on the beach
all the galleys lowered their awnings and sounded their shawms; then the
pinnace was launched, swathed in rich carpets and cushions of crimson
velvet, and as Don Quixote boarded it the flagship fired the cannon on
her deck, and the other galleys did likewise, and as Don Quixote climbed
the starboard ladder all the galley-slaves greeted him as they always greet
any very important personage who comes on board, crying 'Hoo, hoo,
hoo!' three times. The admiral (for that is what we had better call him),
a high-ranking gentleman from Valencia, shook hands with Don Quixote
and then embraced him, saying:

'I shall mark this day with a white stone, because it is one of the
happiest that I ever expect to enjoy, this day when I behold Don Quixote
de la Mancha: an occasion and a sign showing that in him is contained
and epitomized all the worth of knight-errantry.'

Don Quixote, overjoyed to find himself treated in such a lordly manner,
replied in no less courteous terms. They all went to the poop, which was
finely adorned, they sat on the benches there and the boatswain walked

on to the midship gangway and piped the order to strip, which was done in an instant. Sancho was astonished to see so many half-naked men, and was even more astonished when he saw the awning being raised at such a speed that it seemed to him that all the devils in hell were at work there; but this was small beer compared with what I shall narrate next.

Sancho was sitting on the awning-bollard by the starboard stroke who, following instructions previously given, seized him and raised him aloft, upon which all the galley-slaves, standing ready, rolled him along on upstretched arms from bench to bench along the starboard side, so fast that the poor man couldn't see what was happening and felt certain that all those devils from hell were flying away with him; and they didn't stop until they'd passed him back along the port side and deposited him on the poop. Poor Sancho was left panting, sweating and exhausted, unable to imagine what had happened to him.

Having witnessed Sancho's wingless flight, Don Quixote asked the admiral whether this was a ceremony undergone by all those who came aboard a galley for the first time; because if by any chance it was, he, who had no intention of taking up that particular career, was unwilling to perform such exercises, and he swore to God that if anyone approached him to seize him and roll him along he would kick his soul out of his body; and as he said this he came to his feet and grasped his sword. At that moment they lowered the awning and brought the lateen-yard down from the top of the mast to the bottom, with a deafening racket. Sancho thought that heaven was coming off its hinges and was about to fall on his head; and, petrified, he doubled up and tucked it between his knees. Don Quixote wasn't his usual self, either, and he shuddered and hunched his shoulders as the colour drained out of his face. And now the galley-slaves hoisted the lateen-yard again, making as much of a racket as when they'd lowered it, but always without uttering a single word, as if they didn't have any voices or any breath in their throats. The boatswain gave the signal to weigh anchor and, leaping into the middle of the gangway with his lash, he began to tickle the galley-slaves' ribs, and the vessel slowly put out to sea. When Sancho saw all those red feet, as he took the oars to be, moving all together, he said to himself:

'Now these really are magic spells, and not the ones my master goes on about. Whatever can these poor wretches have done to be whipped like that, and how can this one man, walking around the place whistling, dare to whip so many men? Now I know that this is hell, or purgatory at least.'

Don Quixote saw how closely Sancho was observing what was happening, and he said:

'Ah, friend Sancho, how quickly and at what little cost to yourself you could, if you so wished, strip to the waist and join these gentlemen, and complete the disenchantment of Dulcinea! For immersed in the pain and the grief of so many, you'd hardly be aware of your own; and, what's more, it might well be that the sage Merlin would consider each of these lashes, since they're delivered with a hard and heavy hand, to be worth ten of the ones you'll have to give yourself in the end.'

The admiral was about to ask what were these lashes and this disenchantment of Dulcinea, when the pilot called:

'Montjuich[1] is signalling that there's a vessel with oars on the coast, to the west.'

On hearing this the admiral jumped into the gangway and cried:

'Come on, my lads, don't let her get away! It must be some pirate brigantine from Algiers that they're warning us about from the watchtower.'

The other three galleys came alongside the flagship to receive their orders. The admiral told two of them to put out to sea, and he and the other galley would hug the coast, so that the vessel wouldn't be able to escape. The slaves plied their oars, driving the galleys forward at such speed that they seemed to be flying. When the two that had put out to sea were about two miles offshore they sighted a vessel that they judged to be of fourteen or fifteen oars, as indeed she was; and when she saw the galleys she took to flight in the hope that her speed might save her; but it wasn't to be, because the flagship was one of the fastest vessels on the sea, and gained on her so rapidly that the men on the brigantine realized that escape was impossible, and her captain told his men to drop their oars and surrender, so as not to annoy the man in charge of our galleys. But fortune had other ideas, and ordered that just as the flagship was close enough for the men on the brigantine to hear the shouted orders to surrender, two *torakis*, that is to say two drunken Turks, who were in the brigantine with a dozen others, fired their muskets and killed two soldiers on our forecastle. Seeing this, the admiral swore not to leave a single man on the brigantine alive, but as he went in at top speed to ram her she slipped away under the oars. The galley careered on past the other vessel, whose crew could see that there was no hope for them, but they made sail while the galley was turning and they took to flight again, propelled now by their canvas as well as by their oars; but their rashness did them more harm than their diligence did them good, because the flagship overhauled them within half a mile, clapped her oars on top of them and took them all alive. The other two galleys now sailed up, and all four of them returned with their prize to the beach, where a vast crowd was waiting to see what they would bring back. The admiral anchored close in, and saw that the Viceroy of Catalonia was waiting on the beach. He ordered the pinnace to be sent to fetch him, and the lateen-yard to be lowered so as to hang from it, without the slightest delay, the captain and the other Turks captured on the brigantine, some thirty-six in all, fine-looking men, most of them musketeers. The admiral asked who was the captain of the brigantine, and the answer came in the Castilian language from one of the galley-slaves, who later turned out to be a Spanish renegade:

'This lad you can see here, sir, he's our captain.'

And he pointed to one of the most handsome and elegant young men imaginable. He seemed to be under twenty. The admiral asked him:

'Tell me, you ill-advised dog, what led you to kill my soldiers, when you could see that escape was impossible? Is that the sort of respect to be shown to flagships? Don't you know the difference between temerity and courage? Faint hopes should make men brave, but not foolhardy.'

The captain was about to reply; but the admiral could not then listen to his answer, because he had to go and welcome the Viceroy, who was climbing aboard with some of his servants and with worthies from the city.

'That was good hunting, admiral,' said the Viceroy.

'Yes,' replied the admiral, 'and Your Excellency is soon going to see just how good, in the shape of the game hanging from this yard-arm.'

'What do you mean?' the Viceroy asked.

'They have killed,' the admiral replied, 'two of the best soldiers in these galleys, flouting the law, all good sense and the accepted practice of war, and I've sworn to hang everyone I capture, in particular this young man, the captain of the brigantine.'

And he pointed to the lad, with his hands already bound and the rope round his neck, awaiting death. The Viceroy looked at him and, on seeing him so handsome there, and so elegant, and so submissive, such beauty was like a letter of recommendation and he felt the desire to save the lad, and he asked:

'Tell me, captain, are you a Turk, or a Moor, or a renegade?'

To which the lad replied, also in Spanish:

'I am neither a Turk, nor a Moor, nor a renegade.'

'What are you, then?' the Viceroy asked.

'I am a Christian woman,' said the lad.

'A woman, and a Christian, in those clothes and in such a predicament? That's something sooner to be wondered at than believed.'

'Please suspend my execution, gentlemen,' said the lad. 'You haven't much to lose by postponing your revenge for as long as it takes me to tell the story of my life.'

What heart could be so hard as to fail to be softened by such words, for long enough at least to hear what the unhappy youth had to say? The admiral told him to say whatever he liked, but not to expect to be pardoned for his flagrant crime. With this permission the youth began to speak:

'I was born of that race, unhappy and unwise, upon which a sea of misfortune has recently poured down – yes, I was born of Morisco parents. Caught up in the torrent of their misfortune I was taken by an uncle and an aunt of mine to Barbary, and it was in vain that I told them I'm a Christian as, indeed, I am, and not one of those false, specious Christians either, but a true Catholic. It didn't serve any purpose to tell the truth to those in charge of our unhappy banishment, and my uncle and aunt also refused to believe me; on the contrary, they thought it was a lie that I'd made up so as to stay in the land of my birth, and they forced me to go with them. I had a Christian mother and a father who was a man of sound sense and a Christian too; I sucked the Catholic faith with my mother's milk, I was brought up to be well-behaved, and neither in my speech nor in my manners have I ever given any signs of being a Morisco, so far as I am aware. As these virtues (for that is what I believe them to be) grew in me, so did my beauty, if indeed I am beautiful; and although the reserve and seclusion of my life was great, it wasn't great enough to prevent a young gentleman called Don Gaspar Gregorio, the eldest son of the lord of a nearby village, from finding opportunities to see me. How he saw me, how we spoke, how he fell madly in love with me – and I wasn't much saner in my feelings for him – would make too long a story, particularly at a time when I'm fearing that this cruel rope threatening me is about to jam itself between my tongue and my throat; so I'll only say that Don Gregorio decided to go with us into exile. He mingled with the Moriscos leaving other villages, because he speaks the language very well, and during the journey he became friends with my uncle and aunt. For as soon as my father, a prudent and far-sighted man, had heard the first edict ordering us into exile, he'd left the village to look for somewhere abroad where we could all live; and he left many pearls and gems of great value, as well as money in the form of gold cruzados and doubloons, buried in a hiding-place known only to me. He told me not to touch this treasure on any account if we were exiled before he returned. I obeyed him and, with my uncle and aunt, as I've said, and with other relations, we went to Barbary and settled in Algiers, which was the same as settling in hell.

'The King heard of my beauty, and rumour told him of my wealth – which proved in some ways to be fortunate for me. He summoned me, asked me what part of Spain I came from, and what money and jewels I'd brought with me. I gave him the name of our village and said that the jewels and the money were buried there, but that they could easily be retrieved if I went back for them. I told him all this in the hope that he might be blinded more by his covetousness than by my beauty. While we were talking someone came to tell him that one of the most handsome and graceful young men imaginable had come to Algiers with me. I immediately realized that he was referring to Don Gaspar Gregorio, whose good looks exceed those of the most praised Adonises in the world. This threw me into confusion as I considered the danger that Don Gregorio was facing, because among those barbaric Turks a handsome boy or youth is much more highly prized than any woman, however beautiful she may be. The King ordered the young man to be brought so that he could take a look at him, and asked me whether what had been said about him was true. As if inspired by heaven, I said that it was, but that I also had to tell him that this wasn't a young man at all but another woman; and I begged him to allow me to go and dress her in her proper clothes so that she could display her full beauty and be less embarrassed to appear in his presence. He told me that I was welcome to do so and that on the following day we would talk about how I was to return to Spain to recover the hidden treasure.

'I talked to Don Gaspar, I told him how dangerous it would be to reveal that he was a man, I dressed him as a Moorish woman, and that same afternoon I took him into the presence of the King, who was thunderstruck when he saw her, and decided to keep her as a present for the Great Turk; and to avoid the danger that she must face in his own harem, because he didn't trust himself, he had her lodged in the house of some Moorish ladies of high rank, where she could be guarded and waited upon, and she was taken there straight away. What our feelings were (I can't deny I love him) is something that can be left to the imagination of all separated lovers.

'The King then arranged for me to return to Spain in this brigantine and to be accompanied by two native Turks, the ones who killed your soldiers. This Spanish renegade' (pointing to the man who'd spoken first) 'also came with me, and I know that he's a secret Christian and that his plan is to stay in Spain, not to return to Barbary; the rest of the crew are Moors and Turks who are only here to row. The two Turks, greedy and insolent, disregarded the orders that we'd been given for me and this renegade to be landed, wearing the Christian clothes with which we'd been provided, as soon as we reached Spain, and chose instead to make raids along the coast and take some prize if they could, fearing that if they put us ashore something might occur that would make us reveal that the brigantine was still at sea, and then if there happened to be any galleys along this coast it would be captured. Last night we sighted this shore and, not knowing about these four galleys, we were discovered; the rest you know.

'To sum up: Don Gregorio is still dressed as a woman and living among women, in the most extreme danger, and here am I, with my hands tied, awaiting or to be more precise fearing the loss of my life, of which I'm weary by now. This, gentlemen, is the end of my sad story, as true as it is wretched; all I ask is that you allow me to die as a Christian because, as I've said, I haven't played any part in the crimes that the people of my race have committed.'

And she fell silent, her eyes swollen with tender tears, and many of those present wept with her. The Viceroy, moved by tender compassion, went up to her without a word and with his own hands removed the rope that bound her beautiful hands together. While this Christian Morisco had been telling her extraordinary story, an old pilgrim who had boarded the boat with the Viceroy had been gazing at her, and the instant she stopped speaking he threw himself at her feet and, hugging them, cried in words broken by a thousand sobs and sighs:

'O Ana Félix, my poor unhappy daughter! I'm your father Ricote, come back to look for you because I couldn't live without you, my darling.'

At these words Sancho opened his eyes and raised his head, which had been bowed as he brooded over his dreadful trip round the galley; and when he looked at the pilgrim he recognized the very same Ricote that he'd met on the day when he'd stopped being governor, and he was certain the young woman was his friend's daughter; and she, now unbound, hugged her father and mingled her tears with his, while Ricote said to the admiral and the Viceroy:

'This, gentlemen, is my daughter, less happy in her adventures than in her name. Her name is Ana Félix, and her surname is Ricote, and she is as famous for her own beauty as for my wealth. I left my native land to search abroad for some place that would accept and shelter us, and having found it in Germany I came back in these pilgrim's clothes with some Germans to look for my daughter and dig up the treasure that I'd buried. I didn't find my daughter but I did find the treasure, which I have with me; and now, in this strange roundabout way you have seen, I've found the treasure that's the most precious of them all, my beloved daughter. If our lack of blame, and her tears and my tears, can, without contravening your system of justice, open doors to mercy, do be merciful to us, because we have never had any intention of doing you harm, and have never connived with our people, who have quite justly been thrown into exile.'

And then Sancho said:

'I know Ricote well, and I know that what he's saying about Ana Félix being his daughter is true – though as for all that other stuff about coming and going and having good or bad intentions, I won't go poking my nose into that.'

All were amazed at this extraordinary series of events, and the admiral said:

'Your tears do indeed prevent me from fulfilling my vow: go free, lovely Ana Félix, and live all the years that heaven has allotted you; but the insolent and foolhardy wretches who committed the crime must pay the penalty.'

And he ordered the two Turks who had killed his soldiers to be hanged at once from the yard-arm; but the Viceroy entreated him not to do so, because theirs had been more an act of madness than of valour. The admiral did as the Viceroy had asked, because it is not easy to take revenge in cold blood. Next they tried to work out how to rescue Don Gaspar Gregorio from the danger in which he'd been left; and Ricote offered more than two thousand ducats in pearls and other jewels. Many schemes were suggested, but none as likely to succeed as the one proposed by the Spanish renegade, who offered to go back to Algiers in a small boat of perhaps six oars, manned by Christians, because he knew when, how and where he could and should land, nor was he ignorant of the house where Don Gaspar was being held. The admiral and the Viceroy doubted whether they could rely on the renegade or trust him with a crew of Christians, but Ana Félix made herself answerable for him, and her father Ricote undertook to pay the Christians' ransom if they were captured. Once they'd agreed on these plans the Viceroy went ashore, and Don Antonio Moreno took the Morisco woman and her father home with him, after the Viceroy had asked him to treat them with the utmost kindness and consideration; as for himself, he offered for their pleasure everything his house contained. So great was the benevolence and sympathy that Ana Félix's beauty had inspired in his breast.

CHAPTER LXIV

Concerning the adventure that caused Don Quixote more grief than any of the previous ones

Don Antonio Moreno's wife, the history says, was overjoyed to have Ana Félix in her house. Won over by her beauty and her intelligence, because the Morisco girl was remarkable for both, she gave her a warm welcome, and everyone in the city came to see her as if summoned by church bells.

Don Quixote told Don Antonio that the decision they'd reached about freeing Don Gaspar hadn't been a wise one, because the plan was too dangerous to be practicable; and it would be better to land him in Barbary with his arms, his armour and his horse, and then he'd rescue the young man in the teeth of all the Moorish hordes, just as Don Gaiferos had rescued his wife Melisendra.

'Don't you forget,' said Sancho when he heard this, 'that Don Gaiferos rescued his wife on dry land and took her back to France over dry land too[1] – but if we do by any chance rescue Don Gregorio, we won't have any way to bring him back to Spain, because the sea's in between.'

'There is a remedy for all things but death,' Don Quixote replied. 'Once the boat comes up to the beach we shall be able to climb aboard even if the whole world tries to stop us.'

'You make it all sound as easy as pie,' said Sancho, 'but there's many a slip twixt the cup and the lip, and I'm all for the renegade – he seems a good sort to me, kindhearted.'

Don Antonio said that if the renegade was unsuccessful they would adopt the expedient of sending the great Don Quixote to Barbary.

Two days later the renegade left in a fast boat with six pairs of oars and an excellent crew, and two days after that the galleys sailed for the East, once the admiral had asked the Viceroy to keep him informed about the freeing of Don Gregorio and about the Ana Félix affair. The Viceroy undertook to do so.

And one morning, as Don Quixote went out to ride along the beach in full armour because, as he so often said, arms were his bed-hangings and his rest the bloody fray, and he never felt comfortable without them, he saw a knight approaching him, also in full armour, with a shining moon painted on his shield; and once this knight was close enough to be heard he shouted to Don Quixote:

'Illustrious knight and never sufficiently praised Don Quixote de la Mancha! I'm the Knight of the White Moon I am, and my unprecedented exploits have perhaps brought me to your attention: I've come to fight you and to test the strength of your arm, so as to make you recognize and confess that my lady, whoever she happens to be, is far more beautiful than your precious Dulcinea del Toboso; and if you confess this truth good and proper you'll save your life, and save me the trouble of taking it, too; and if you fight and I defeat you, the only satisfaction I demand is for you to put aside your arms, stop looking for your adventures, go back to your village for a year and stay there without ever touching your sword, in peace and quiet and beneficial tranquillity, because this is what's needed for the increase of your wealth and the salvation of your soul; and if you defeat me, my life will be at your mercy, and my armour, arms and horse will be your spoils, and the fame of my exploits will pass from my name to yours. Think about what's best for you, and let's have a speedy reply, because I've only got a day to do this bit of business.'

Don Quixote was plunged into bewilderment both by the arrogance of the Knight of the White Moon and by his reason for challenging him, and he replied with severe serenity:

'Knight of the White Moon, whose exploits had not until this moment come to my attention: I would dare to swear that you have never seen the illustrious Dulcinea, because if you had seen her, I know that you would have taken good care not to venture upon this issue, since the sight would have undeceived you of the notion that there ever has existed or can exist any beauty comparable with hers. And so, without saying that you lie, but merely that what you claim is incorrect, I accept your challenge on the conditions that you have stipulated, and I do so with instant effect, so as not to exceed the one day to which you are restricted; and I only exclude from the conditions the transfer of the fame of your exploits to me, because I do not know exactly what these exploits are; I am quite content with my own exploits, exactly as they are. So choose your ground; I shall do the same; and may St Peter bless what God bestows.'

The Knight of the White Moon had been noticed by people in the city, and the Viceroy had been informed that he was talking to Don Quixote de la Mancha. The Viceroy, thinking this must be some new adventure fabricated by Don Antonio Moreno or another gentleman in the city, rode out at once to the beach accompanied by Don Antonio and many others, just as Don Quixote was wheeling Rocinante round to go and take up his position. When the Viceroy saw both men about to turn and charge, he planted himself between them and asked what was the cause of such a sudden combat. The Knight of the White Moon replied that it was a question of pre-eminence in beauty, and he summarized what he had said to Don Quixote, together with the acceptance by both parties of the conditions of the combat. The Viceroy rode over to Don Antonio and asked him in a whisper whether he knew who the Knight of the White Moon was, and whether this was some hoax being played on Don Quixote. Don Antonio replied that he didn't know who the man was, or whether the challenge was in jest or in earnest. This reply left the Viceroy undecided about whether to allow them to go ahead or not; but he couldn't imagine that it was anything other than a hoax, and so he drew aside, saying:

'If there's nothing for it, gallant knights, but to confess or die, and if Don Quixote sticks to his guns and the Knight of the White Moon adheres to his cannon, so be it, and off you go.'

The Knight of the White Moon thanked the Viceroy in polite and well-chosen words for his kind permission, and so did Don Quixote; who, commending himself to heaven with all his heart, and to his Dulcinea (as was his custom before all battles), wheeled about to take up a little more ground, seeing that this was what his adversary was doing; then, without a blast from a trumpet or any other martial instrument to give them the signal for the charge, they both at the same instant turned their horses; and since the Knight of the White Moon's horse was faster, he hurtled into Don Quixote two-thirds of the way along the course with such power that, even though he didn't touch him with his lance (he raised it, it seems, on purpose), he sent Rocinante and Don Quixote toppling over in an alarming fall. He was upon him in a trice, and putting his lance to his opponent's visor he said:

'You are vanquished, sir knight, and you are a dead man unless you confess what we agreed in our challenge.'

Don Quixote, battered and stunned, did not raise his visor but spoke as from inside a grave, in a feeble, faltering voice:

'Dulcinea del Toboso is the most beautiful woman in the world, and I am the most unfortunate knight in it, and it would not be right for my weakness to obscure that truth. Drive your lance home, sir knight, and take away my life, since you have taken away my honour.'

'I shall do no such thing,' said the Knight of the White Moon. 'Long live, unobscured, the fame of the lady Dulcinea del Toboso's beauty; I shall be content if the great Don Quixote retires to his village for a year, or until further notice, as we agreed before engaging in this battle.'

The Viceroy and Don Antonio and many other people heard all this, and they also heard Don Quixote reply that so long as he was not asked to do anything to the prejudice of Dulcinea, he would comply as a true and dutiful knight. Now that Don Quixote had made his confession, the Knight of the White Moon turned his steed and, bowing his head to the Viceroy, rode at a canter into the city. The Viceroy told Don Antonio to follow him and be sure to find out who he was. Don Quixote was hauled to his feet and his face was uncovered, colourless and sweating. Rocinante was in such a sorry state that he couldn't move. Sancho, in the depths of despondency, had no idea what to say or do: he fancied it was all a dream or something worked by magic. Here was his master, defeated and forbidden to take up arms for a whole year; and he saw the light of the glory of his master's exploits dimmed, all the hopes of his latest promises wafted away like smoke before the wind. Sancho feared that Rocinante might be left crippled, or his master with a broken skull – though if this made it a bit less thick it would be no bad thing. Eventually Don Quixote was carried to the city in a sedan chair that the Viceroy sent for, and the Viceroy himself rode back there, longing to discover the identity of the Knight of the White Moon, who had buried Don Quixote in the slough of despond.

CHAPTER LXV

Which gives information about the identity of the Knight of the White Moon, and the rescue of Don Gregorio, and other events

Don Antonio Moreno followed the Knight of the White Moon, who was also pursued and even persecuted by a crowd of boys, until they cornered him at an inn, inside the city. Don Antonio entered to find out who this knight was. A squire appeared, to receive the knight and remove his armour; the two men walked into a private room on the ground floor, followed by Don Antonio, raring to discover the knight's identity. Seeing, then, that this gentleman wasn't going to leave him alone, the Knight of the White Moon said:

'I know well enough, sir, why you have come – to discover who I am; and since there isn't any reason not to inform you, I shall do so, without straying one iota from the truth, while my servant is removing my armour. I would have you know, then, that my name is Sansón Carrasco, BA; I'm from the same village as Don Quixote de la Mancha, whose madness and folly make all of us who know him feel sorry for him, and I'm one of those who've felt sorriest of all; and in the belief that his well-being depends upon his resting, and staying in his own village and his own home, I worked out a scheme to achieve this, and so it must have been about three months ago that I took to the road as a knight errant, calling myself the Knight of the Spangles, and intending to fight him and beat him, without hurting him, after establishing as a condition for our combat that the defeated knight would be at the disposal of the victor; and what I was intending to require of him (because I regarded him as defeated already) was that he must go back to his village and not leave it for a year, during which time he might be cured. But fortune managed things differently, because he knocked me off my horse and defeated me, so my plan failed. He went on his way and I went home, defeated, humiliated and battered by my fall, which was a particularly dangerous one; but that didn't make me any less determined to come back in search of him and defeat him, as you've seen today. And since he's so meticulous about observing all the ordinances of knight-errantry, there's no doubt at all that he'll keep his word and do what I've told him to do. This, sir, is how the matter stands, and I have nothing more to tell you: I entreat you not to reveal my identity or tell Don Quixote who I am, so that my good intentions can take effect and a man who has an excellent mind, if only all this chivalry nonsense is cleared out of it, can have it restored to him.'

'Oh, my dear sir!' said Don Antonio. 'God forgive you for the offence that you've committed against the whole world in attempting to restore the funniest madman in it to his senses! Don't you see, sir, that the benefits of Don Quixote's recovery can't be compared with the pleasure that his antics provide? But I suspect that all your ingenuity, my dear young graduate, won't be sufficient to make such a raving lunatic sane again, and if it weren't uncharitable to do so I'd say that I hope Don Quixote never recovers, because if he does we won't only lose his antics but those of his squire Sancho Panza as well, any one of which is enough to make melancholy itself merry. I'll keep quiet, all the same, and I shan't say a word to him, just to see whether I'm right in my suspicion that all Señor Carrasco's efforts will be fruitless.'

Sansón replied that at all events the matter was now well in hand, and he anticipated a happy outcome. After Don Antonio had placed himself at his disposal, the graduate said goodbye, and with his arms and armour tied in a bundle on a mule he left the city immediately, on the horse that he'd ridden into battle, and he went back home, without anything else happening to him that needs to be recorded in this true history.

Don Antonio reported to the Viceroy what Carrasco had told him, and the Viceroy was not very pleased to hear it, because Don Quixote's retirement meant the end of the entertainment enjoyed by all those who knew about his mad doings.

Don Quixote stayed in bed for six days, dejected, depressed, broody and in the worst of spirits, turning the disastrous events of his defeat over and over in his mind. Sancho tried to console him, and among other things he said:

'Do hold up that head of yours, sir, and cheer up, too, if you can, and give thanks to heaven that even if you were tumbled to the ground you didn't break any ribs, because as you know we can all expect to be given a dose of our own medicine every so often, and there isn't always bacon where there's hooks to hang it from, so a fig's end for the doctor, you don't need him to cure you of this illness of yours, and let's go back home and stop looking for adventures in lands and towns we don't know — after all, if you think about it, I'm the one with the most to lose, even though you're the one who's worst off at the moment. When I stopped governing I also stopped wanting to be a governor ever again, but I didn't stop wanting to be a count, and that'll never happen if you stop being a knight errant and don't become a king — and then all my hopes go up in smoke.'

'Enough of that, Sancho: as you know, my retirement and reclusion will only last for one year, and then I shall return to my honourable profession, and I shan't be short of a kingdom to conquer and an earldom to give you.'

'God hear what you said and the devil be deaf,' said Sancho. 'I've always heard that good hope is better than bad holding.'

As they were talking, Don Antonio walked in, showing all the signs of great joy and saying:

'Splendid news, Don Quixote sir: Don Gregorio is on the beach with the renegade who went for him! What am I saying, on the beach? He's in the Viceroy's house, and he'll be right here in a moment.'

Don Quixote showed some of the signs of a little joy, and said:

'I have to admit that I am on the very verge of saying that I should have been happy had things turned out otherwise, so that I was obliged to sail for Barbary, where by the might of my arm I should have released not only Don Gregorio but all the Christian captives being held there. But what am I saying, poor wretch that I am? Am I not the one who has been defeated? Am I not the one who has been overthrown? Am I not the one who cannot take up arms for a year? So what can I promise? What am I bragging about, when it is fitter for me to handle a distaff than a sword?'

'No more of that, sir,' said Sancho. 'Let the hen live on though she has got the pip, it's your turn today and it's my turn tomorrow, and you mustn't let yourself be affected by these combats and these thumpings, because he who's down one day can be up the next, unless he really wants to stay in bed that is – I mean just let his spirits drain away and never pluck up fresh courage for fresh fights. And now you get yourself up and welcome Don Gregorio, it sounds as if everyone's excited, so he must be in the house.'

And Sancho was right, because once Don Gregorio and the renegade had reported back to the Viceroy about the expedition, the former, anxious to see Ana Félix, had come with the renegade to Don Antonio's house; and although when he was rescued from Algiers he was wearing woman's clothes, he'd exchanged them on the boat for those of a captive who'd been released with him; but regardless of what clothes he happened to be wearing, he would have shown himself to be a person worthy to be sought out, served and respected, because he was exceedingly handsome, and he seemed to be about seventeen or eighteen years old. Ricote and his daughter went to welcome him, the father with tears and the daughter with due demureness. There were no embraces, because where there is great love there is often little display of it. The beauty of Ana Félix and Don Gregorio, standing there side by side, amazed all those who saw it.

Silence was the lovers' spokesman, and their eyes were the tongues that proclaimed their pure and joyful feelings. The renegade described the ways and means that he'd employed to rescue Don Gregorio; Don Gregorio told them about the difficulties and dangers he'd faced among the women with whom he'd been left, not in a long speech but in a few words, which indicated good sense in excess of his years. Finally, Ricote made handsome payment both to the renegade and to the oarsmen. The renegade was restored to the bosom of the Church, and from being a rotten limb was made whole and clean by penance and repentance.

Two days later the Viceroy discussed with Don Antonio how it might be arranged for Ana Félix and her father to stay in Spain, because they thought there couldn't be any harm in allowing such a Christian daughter and such an apparently well-meaning father to remain there. Don Antonio offered to try to negotiate a solution in Madrid, because he had to go there on other business, and he indicated that many difficulties could be overcome there by means of favours and gifts.

'No,' said Ricote, present at this conversation, 'we can't place our hopes in favours or in gifts, because the great Don Bernardino de Velasco, the Count of Salazar,[1] to whom His Majesty has entrusted our expulsion, won't heed any appeals, or promises, or gifts, or lamentations: although it is true that he tempers justice with mercy, he can see that the whole body of our race is tainted and rotten, and so he applies to it the cautery that burns rather than the ointment that soothes; and thus, with wisdom, sagacity, diligence and the fear that he inspires, he has borne upon his broad shoulders the weight of this great project and duly put it into effect; and all our tricks, stratagems, pleadings and deceptions haven't been able to blind his Argus eyes,[2] always on the alert so that not one of our people remains hidden from him like a root buried in the ground that later sprouts and bears poisonous fruit in a Spain now cleansed and free from the fears in which our rabble kept it. What an heroic decision by the great Philip III, and what unprecedented prudence to have entrusted it to the said Bernardino de Velasco!'

'At all events, once I'm there I'll do all I can – and then let heaven do what it will,' said Don Antonio. 'Don Gregorio will come with me to relieve the anxiety that his parents must be feeling at his absence; Ana Félix will stay with my wife in my house, or else in a convent, and I'm sure that the Viceroy will be happy for the worthy Ricote to stay with him until we see the result of my negotiations.'

The Viceroy agreed to everything that Don Antonio had proposed; when Don Gregorio was informed of the plan, however, he said that on no account could he or would he leave Doña Ana Félix; but then, with the idea of going to see his parents, and subsequently devising some way of returning for her, he agreed to the proposal. Ana Félix stayed with Don Antonio's wife, and Ricote stayed in the Viceroy's house.

The day came for Don Antonio's departure, and two days after that Don Quixote left with Sancho, because his fall hadn't allowed him to leave any sooner. There were tears, sighs, fainting fits and sobs when Don Gregorio said goodbye to Ana Félix. Ricote offered Don Gregorio a thousand escudos, if he needed them; but he didn't accept them, and only borrowed five from Don Antonio, promising to repay them in Madrid. And with this the two men departed, and Don Quixote and Sancho left later, as stated: Don Quixote out of his armour, in travelling clothes, and Sancho off his dun, because it was carrying the armour.

CHAPTER LXVI

Concerning what he who reads it will see, and what he who has it read to him will hear

As they left Barcelona, Don Quixote turned back to gaze at the place where he had fallen, and said:

'Here once stood Troy! Here my bad luck, and not my cowardice, deprived me of the glory I had won; here did I feel the fickleness of fortune; here the lustre of my exploits was obscured; here, in short, my joy came crashing to the ground, never again to rise!'

When Sancho heard this, he said:

'It's up to brave hearts, sir, to be patient when things are going badly, as well as being happy when they're going well – and that I know from my own experience, because when I was a governor I was happy and now that I'm a squire on foot I'm not sad. For I've heard say that what

934

they call fortune is a flighty woman who drinks too much, and, what's more, she's blind, so she can't see what she's doing, and she doesn't know who she's knocking over or who she's raising up.'

'You're in a very philosophical mood, Sancho,' Don Quixote replied, 'and you're speaking like a man of sense; I really don't know who can have taught you all this. What I can tell you is that there's no such thing as fortune, and whatever happens in this world, good and bad, does not occur by chance, but by special providence of heaven; and for this reason it is often said that every man is the architect of his own fortune. And I have been the architect of mine, but not with the necessary prudence, and so my presumption has led to disaster; because I should have realized that my feeble Rocinante couldn't stand up to the mighty bulk of the horse of the Knight of the White Moon. But I took him on, I did what I could, I was overthrown and although I lost my honour I did not lose, nor can I lose, the virtue of having kept my word. When I was a knight errant, brave and bold, I used to verify my own deeds with my arm and my actions, and now that I am a common squire I shall verify my own words by keeping the promise that I made. Forward then, Sancho my friend, and we shall spend our year of mortification in our own land, and in our seclusion we shall gain new strength to return to the profession of arms, which I shall never forget.'

'Sir,' Sancho replied, 'walking isn't such a very great pleasure for me that it makes me feel at all inclined to go on long marches. Let's leave all this armour hanging up on some tree instead of a bandit, and then with me on my dun's back and my feet off the ground we can travel as far each day as ever you please; because if you think I'm going to walk on and on and on you've got another think coming.'

'Well said, Sancho,' Don Quixote replied. 'Let my armour be hung up as a trophy, and at its feet, or all around it, we shall carve in the tree-trunks what was written under the trophy of Orlando's arms and armour:

> Let no one move this armour or this sword
> Who will not prove his prowess with their lord.'

'That sounds like a really good idea,' replied Sancho, 'and if it wasn't for the fact that we wouldn't do very well without him on the journey home, we could hang Rocinante up too.'

'I will not have either Rocinante or the armour hanged,' said Don Quixote, 'for people to say, "What a bad reward for good service!"'

'Right you are,' Sancho replied, 'because, as sensible people say, the pack-saddle shouldn't take the blame for what the donkey did – so since you're the one to blame for all this you'd better punish yourself and not vent your anger on your armour, because it's broken and bloody enough already, or on poor meek and mild Rocinante, or on my tender feet, making them walk more than what's right or proper.'

They spent the whole of that day in similar conversations, and then another four days, without anything happening to impede their progress; but as they entered a village on the fifth day they found a crowd of people at an inn door enjoying themselves, because it was a fiesta day. As Don Quixote rode up, a farmer shouted:

'One of these two gents here can tell us what's to be done about this wager of ours, because they don't know the parties.'

'I shall most certainly do so,' said Don Quixote, 'with the utmost rectitude, so long as I can manage to understand it.'

'Well, it's just this, good sir,' said the farmer. 'One of the villagers, who's so fat he weighs twenty stone, has challenged another man, a neighbour of his, who only weighs nine stone, to a race. The agreement is that it's to be a hundred yards' race, each of them carrying equal weight; and when the challenger was asked how the weights were going to be evened up he said that the man he'd challenged, weighing nine stone, should carry eleven stone of iron, and in this way the twenty stone of the thin man would equal the twenty stone of the fat man.'

'No, that isn't right,' Sancho butted in before Don Quixote could answer. 'And it's up to me to settle these doubts and give my opinion when there's a disagreement, because it was only a few days ago that I gave up being a governor and a judge, as everybody knows.'

'You go ahead and reply, Sancho my friend,' said Don Quixote. 'I'm not fit to feed a cat, my brain's so confused and out of order.'

Given this permission, Sancho addressed the farmers, who clustered around him with mouths agape as they awaited his verdict:

'What the fat man wants, my friends, simply won't do, and there isn't any justice about it at all, because if what I've heard said is true and it's up to whoever is challenged to choose the weapons, it isn't right for the other bloke to make a choice that means his opponent can't win. So to my mind the fat challenger should prune, trim, lop, polish and smooth eleven stone of his flesh away, from this part of his body and from that, just as he pleases, and then he'll be left weighing nine stone, the same as his opponent, and they'll be able to race on equal terms.'

'By all that's holy,' said a farmer who heard Sancho's verdict, 'this gentleman has spoken like a saint and given judgement like a canon! But it's certain that the fat man won't part with an ounce of his flesh, let alone eleven stone of it.'

'It'll be best for them not to race at all,' commented another, 'and then the thin man won't be ground into the dust by the iron nor will the fat man lose any flesh – so let's spend half the wager on drink and take these gents to the tavern with the best wine, and on my own head be . . . my hat when it rains.'

'Gentlemen,' said Don Quixote, 'I am grateful to you; but I cannot stop for an instant, because certain sad thoughts and events oblige me to appear discourteous and to depart without delay.'

And spurring Rocinante he rode on, leaving the farmers amazed at having seen such a strange figure and sampled the shrewdness of his servant, for that was what they judged Sancho to be. And another of the farmers said:

'If the servant's that clever, what must the master be like! I bet if they go and study in Salamanca they'll be high-court judges in a brace of shakes, because you're wasting your time unless you study and study and you can pull strings and you also have a bit of luck, and then when you're least expecting it you find a mace in your hand or a mitre on your head.'

Master and servant spent that night out in the fields, under the stars, and as they continued their journey on the following day they saw a man walking towards them, with two satchels hanging from his neck and a javelin or pike in his hand, all of which made him look like a foot-messenger; when he came close to Don Quixote he quickened his pace, trotted up to him, and, embracing his right thigh because he couldn't reach any higher, he said, with every sign of great joy:

'Oh, Don Quixote de la Mancha sir, what happiness it will bring to the heart of my master the Duke when he knows that you're returning to his castle – because he's still there with my mistress the Duchess!'

'I do not recognize you, my friend,' Don Quixote replied, 'and I cannot tell who you are unless you inform me.'

'I'm Tosilos, Don Quixote sir,' the messenger replied, 'my master the Duke's lackey, the one who refused to fight you about the marriage of Doña Rodríguez's daughter.'

'Good God!' said Don Quixote. 'Can you really be the man whom my enemies the enchanters turned into that lackey you have just mentioned, to rob me of the honour of victory in that combat?'

'No, no, good sir,' replied the messenger, 'there wasn't any enchantment or face-changing – I was as much the lackey Tosilos when I entered the lists as I was when I left them. I wanted to marry without a fight, because I liked the look of the lass, but it all went wrong – as soon as you left our castle my master the Duke ordered me to be given a hundred strokes of the birch for disobeying the orders he issued to me before the battle, and the upshot of it all is that the girl's a nun now, and Doña Rodríguez has gone back to Castile, and I'm on my way to Barcelona to take a bundle of letters from my master to the Viceroy. If you'd like a swig of wine, the real stuff though a bit warm, I've got a gourdful of the best here, and some slices of Tronchón cheese that'll be a good waker-up of your thirst if it happens to be asleep.'

'Yes, I'll see your cards,' said Sancho, 'and let's forget about the courtesy stakes – so start pouring, good old Tosilos, and a fig to all the enchanters in the Indies.'

'In a word, Sancho,' said Don Quixote, 'you are both the greatest glutton and the greatest ignoramus on this earth, because you refuse to be persuaded that this messenger is enchanted, that this Tosilos is a sham. You stay with him and fill your belly; I shall go on slowly ahead, and wait for you.'

The lackey laughed, unsheathed his gourd, unpacked his cheese-slices and took out a small loaf, and he and Sancho sat down on the lush grass; and in peace and good fellowship they gobbled up the contents of the satchels, with such an appetite that they even licked the bundle of letters, because it smelled of cheese. Tosilos said to Sancho:

'I reckon that master of yours, Sancho my friend, is short of a few marbles.'

'What do you mean?' Sancho retorted. 'He isn't short of anything –

he always pays on the dot, specially if the coinage is madness. I can see it clearly enough and I tell him so clearly enough, but what's the use? And he's even worse now, because he's been defeated by the Knight of the White Moon.'

Tosilos begged Sancho to tell him what had happened; but Sancho replied that it was bad manners to keep his master waiting, and there'd be time enough to tell him some other day, if ever they met again. And after shaking the crumbs off his smock and out of his beard, he pushed his dun on ahead of him, said goodbye, left Tosilos and caught up with his master, who was waiting for him in the shade of a tree.

CHAPTER LXVII

About the decision that Don Quixote took to become a shepherd and lead a rustic life until the year of his promise elapsed, together with other truly excellent and entertaining events

If there were many thoughts troubling Don Quixote's mind before he was vanquished, there were many more of them afterwards. He was waiting in the shade of the tree, as stated, and there, like flies to honey, thoughts came crowding in upon him and stinging him: some of them concerned Dulcinea's disenchantment, others the life that he was about to lead during his enforced retirement. Sancho appeared and praised the generosity of the lackey Tosilos.

'Can it be possible, Sancho,' said Don Quixote, 'that you still believe that man to be a real lackey? It appears you've forgotten all about seeing Dulcinea transformed into a peasant girl, and the Knight of the Spangles changed into the young graduate Carrasco, both of which were the work of the enchanters who pursue me. But now tell me: did you ask that fellow Tosilos, as you call him, how God has dealt with Altisidora — has she wept over my absence, or has she abandoned in the hands of oblivion those thoughts of love that tormented her in my presence?'

'The thoughts in my mind,' Sancho replied, 'weren't such as to give me any time to go asking silly questions. Bloody hell, sir! Is prying into other people's thoughts, particularly their thoughts of love, what you're up to now?'

'Look here, Sancho,' said Don Quixote, 'there's a great difference between deeds done out of love and deeds done out of gratitude. It's perfectly possible for a knight not to be in love, but it's quite impossible, strictly speaking, for him to lack gratitude. Altisidora loved me, as it seems; she gave me the three nightcaps about which you know, she wept when I left and, casting shame to the winds, she publicly reproached me, insulted me, cursed me: all signs that she adored me, because lovers' anger is often expressed as curses. I had no hopes to give her or treasures to offer her, because my hopes I have entrusted to Dulcinea, and the treasures of knights errant are like fairy gold, false and illusory; and all I can give her are these mementoes of hers that I keep, without prejudice, however, to my memories of Dulcinea, whom you are wronging by your remissness in lashing yourself and chastising that flesh of yours, which I would like to see eaten by wolves, and which you would rather save for the worms than use to succour that poor lady.'

'Look, sir,' Sancho replied, 'to tell you the truth I just can't swallow the idea that thrashing my bum has got anything to do with breaking magic spells — it's the same as saying, "If you've got a headache, rub some ointment on your knees." At least I'd be ready to swear that in all those books you've read about knight errants you haven't come across anyone who's been disenchanted by lashing but, just in case, I will lash myself — when I feel like it and when I've got enough time.'

'May God grant it,' Don Quixote replied, 'and may heaven give you the grace to realize that you are under an obligation to aid my lady, who is your lady too, since you belong to me.'

They were plodding along, chatting away like this, when they came to the place where they'd been trampled by the bulls. Don Quixote recognized it, and said:

'This is the meadow where we came across those charming shepherd-esses and gallant shepherds who were reviving and imitating the pastoral Arcadia, an original and intelligent idea that I should like us to imitate in our turn, Sancho, if you are agreeable, and turn ourselves into shepherds, at least for the time during which I am obliged to withdraw from the world. I shall buy some sheep, and all the other requisites for pastoral practice, I shall call myself "the shepherd Quixotiz" and you will be "the shepherd Panzino", and we'll wander around the hills, the woods and the meadows, singing here, lamenting there, drinking the liquid crystals of the springs or of the pure streams or of the mighty rivers. The evergreen oaks will give us their sweet fruit with generous hands; the trunks of the hard cork-oaks will offer us seats, the willows will provide shade; the roses, scent; the broad meadows, carpets of a thousand matching colours; the clean pure air, breath; the moon and the stars, light, despite all the darkness of the night; song will afford us pleasure, weeping will yield joy, Apollo will inspire verses and love will elicit conceits with which we shall be able to make ourselves famous and indeed eternal, not just in present times but for centuries to come.'

'Great God!' said Sancho. 'That kind of life suits me all the way down to the ground, and what's more as soon as the graduate Carrasco and Master Nicolás the barber see what it's like they're going to want to take it up and turn into shepherds too – and we'd better pray to God that the priest doesn't get it into his head to climb into the fold with us, being as jovial and fond of a giggle as he is.'

'You have spoken very well,' said Don Quixote, 'and if the graduate Sansón Carrasco joins the pastoral fraternity, as he most certainly will, he can call himself "the shepherd Sansonino" or alternatively "the shepherd Carrascón"; Nicolás the barber can call himself "Miculoso", just as that Boscán of old was called "Nemoroso";[1] I don't know what name we can give to the priest, except some derivative like "the shepherd Curiambro". As for the shepherdesses whose lovers we are going to be, we shall be able to pick and choose their names just as we please; and since my lady's name is as suitable for a shepherdess as for a princess, I needn't bother to look for another better one; and you, Sancho, can give your lady whatever name you like.'

'I don't intend,' said Sancho, 'to give her any other name than "Teresona", which will go well with her fatness and her real name, Teresa, and what's more when I praise her in my rhymes it'll be a sign of my chaste desires, because I'm not going round other men's houses in search of better bread than what is made from wheat. The priest had better not fix himself up with a shepherdess, though, because he's supposed to give a good example, and if the graduate wants one, on his own head be it.'

'My God!' said Don Quixote. 'What a life we're going to lead, Sancho my friend! All those shawms regaling our ears, all those Zamora pipes, all those tabors, all those tambourines, all those rebecs! And maybe amidst all these different sounds the albogues will ring out! Then we shall have nearly all the pastoral instruments.'

'What are albogues?' Sancho asked. 'I've never heard of them or seen one in all the days of my life.'

'Albogues,' Don Quixote replied, 'are thin plates rather like brass candle-holders, and when you strike them against one another on the concave side they make a sound which, if not very agreeable or harmonious, is not altogether unpleasant, and blends well with the rustic tones of the pipe and tabor; and this word *albogues* is of Morisco origin, as are all the words in our language that begin with *al*, such as: *almohaza, almorzar, alfombra, alguacil, alhucema, almacén, alcancía* and others like them, of which there can't be many more; and there are just three words in our language that are Morisco ones and end in *í*, and they are *borceguí, zaquizamí* and *maravedí. Alhelí* and *alfaquí*[2] are recognizable as Arabic words both by their initial *al* and by their final *í*. I have told you this in passing because mentioning albogues brought it to mind; and the facts that, as you know, I am something of a poet, and that the graduate Sansón Carrasco is an excellent one, will be of great assistance to appear to perfection in this profession. I say nothing of the priest, but I will wager that he's a dab hand at poetry; and I don't doubt that Master Nicolás is, too, because all barbers or at least nearly all of them play the guitar and compose songs. I shall complain of absence; you will sing your own praises as a constant lover; the shepherd Carrascón, as a scorned one; the priest Curiambro, as whatever suits him best; and we shall all have the most wonderful time.'

To which Sancho replied:

'I'm such an unlucky man, sir, that I'm afraid the day will never come when I can do all those things you said. Oh, what smooth, smooth spoons I'm going to make for myself when I'm a shepherd! All that custard, all that cream, all those garlands, all those other pastoral knick-knacks that mightn't make my name as a wise man but will get me known as a nifty one! My daughter Sanchica will bring our food to us to the fold. But watch out, though! She's a good-looker she is, and there are shepherds out there who aren't so much simple souls as out-and-out scoundrels, and I wouldn't want her to come out shearing and go home shorn, because there's as much of this lovey-dovey stuff and wicked urges out in the fields as inside the cities, in shepherds' huts as in royal palaces, and if you take away the opportunity you take away the sin, and out of sight out of mind, and a clean pair of heels is better than good men's pleas.'

'No more proverbs, Sancho!' said Don Quixote. 'Any one of those that you've quoted is sufficient to make your meaning clear; and I've often advised you not to be so prodigal with your proverbs, and to exercise some restraint with them; but I seem to be preaching in the wilderness, and mother whips me, and I whip my top.'

'To my mind,' said Sancho, 'you're like the one about the kettle calling the pot burnt-arse. You're telling me not to come out with any more proverbs, and then you go stringing them together two by two.'

'But look here, Sancho,' Don Quixote replied, 'the proverbs that I use are relevant ones, and fit the matter in hand like a ring on a finger; but you drag and force yours into your discourse rather than fitting them there; and if I remember correctly I've told you on other occasions that proverbs are brief maxims, derived from the experience and speculation of the wise men of former times, but the proverb that isn't relevant isn't a maxim but an absurdity. Let's drop the subject now, though, and since night is approaching let's move a little way off the road, and God has already decided what will happen tomorrow.'

They left the highway and had a late and inadequate supper, much against Sancho's will, and he was reminded of all the hardship of knight-errantry in the woods and the hills, even though on occasions there was abundance in castles and houses, such as Don Diego de Miranda's and Don Antonio Moreno's and the wedding of Camacho the Rich; but he remembered that neither day nor night could last for ever, and so he spent that night fast asleep, and his master spent it wide awake.

CHAPTER LXVIII

About Don Quixote's hairy adventure

The night was rather dark, because even though the moon was up it was nowhere to be seen: for sometimes the lady Diana goes for a stroll to the Antipodes, and leaves the hills dark and the valleys gloomy.[1] Don Quixote yielded to the demands of nature and had a brief first nap, without going back to sleep again after it, quite unlike Sancho, who never had to go back to sleep again, because his first nap always lasted from night until morning, a reflection of his healthy constitution and lack of worries. Don Quixote's cares kept him so wide awake that he woke Sancho up and said:

'I am astonished, Sancho, at your independence of spirit. I imagine you must be made of marble, or of hard bronze, and incapable of passion or feeling. I watch while you sleep; I weep while you sing; I faint from fasting while you are sluggish and torpid out of pure satiety. It is up to good servants to share their masters' griefs and feel their sorrows, even if only for the sake of appearances. Take note of the serenity of this night, the solitude that surrounds us, inviting us to intersperse our sleep with some vigil. Do please get up, move some distance away and with a willing spirit and courageous gratitude give yourself three or four hundred lashes in part payment of those that you must receive to disenchant Dulcinea, and this is something that I am begging of you; because I don't want to fight you like the last time, for I know that you have a heavy hand. Once you've lashed yourself, we'll spend what's left of the night singing, I of my separation and you of your constancy, thus making a start on the pastoral life that we shall lead in the village.'

'Sir,' replied Sancho, 'I'm not some monk to get up in the middle of my sleep and start scourging myself, and to my mind you can't go from the one extreme of the pain of a lashing to the other of music-making, just like that. You let me sleep, and stop harassing me about that lashing, or you'll make me swear on oath never again to lay hands on a single hair of my smock, let alone the hairs on my body!'

'Oh, you stony-souled creature! Oh, you pitiless squire! Oh, what a waste of the food and the favours I have lavished on you, and still intend to lavish on you! Thanks to me you have been a governor, and thanks to me you cherish hopes of being a count in the near future, or of acceding to some similar title, and the fulfilment of this will not be delayed by any longer than the end of this year; because *post tenebras spero lucem.*'[2]

'I don't know what that means,' Sancho replied, 'all I do know is that so long as I'm asleep I'm rid of all fears and hopes and toils and glory, and long live the man who invented sleep, the cloak that covers all human thoughts, the food that takes away hunger, the water that chases away thirst, the fire that warms the cold, the cold that cools the heat and, in short, the universal coinage that can buy anything, the scales and weights that make the shepherd the equal of the king and the fool the equal of the wise man. There's only one drawback about sleep, so I've heard – it's like death, because there's very little difference between a man who's asleep and one who's dead.'

'I've never heard you speak, Sancho,' said Don Quixote, 'with such elegance; and now I can appreciate the truth of that proverb that you sometimes quote, "Not who you were bred with, but who you are fed with."'

'Damn it all, master!' Sancho retorted. 'I'm not the one stringing proverbs together now, they're pouring out of your mouth two by two faster than out of mine, but there must be one difference between mine and yours – yours come at the right time and mine at the wrong time, but then they're all proverbs.'

As they talked they heard a dull rumble and then a strident cacophony spreading throughout the surrounding valleys. Don Quixote stood up and grasped his sword, and Sancho huddled under his dun, with the bundle of armour on one side of him and the pack-saddle on the other, as full of fear and trembling as Don Quixote was of excitement. The noise was growing and growing and coming closer and closer to the two frightened men, or rather to the one frightened man, because we know all about the courage of the other.

What was happening was that some men were taking more than six hundred pigs to sell them at a fair, and, as they drove them along, the din of the trampling and the grunting and the snorting was so great that it deafened Don Quixote and Sancho, who couldn't make out what it was. The far-spread grunting herd stampeded up, and, showing no respect for Don Quixote's authority, or for Sancho's, they trampled over the two of them, destroying Sancho's bulwarks and toppling not only Don Quixote but Rocinante as well. This grunting, stampeding herd of unclean animals appearing from nowhere threw the pack-saddle, the armour, the dun, Rocinante, Sancho and Don Quixote into confusion and on to the ground. Sancho picked himself up as best he could and asked his master for his sword, saying that he wanted to kill half a dozen of those great unmannerly swine, because by now he'd realized what they were. Don Quixote said:

'Let them be, my friend: this affront is a chastisement for my sin, and it is heaven's just punishment of a vanquished knight errant for jackals to eat him, wasps to sting him and pigs to trample him.'

'It must also be heaven's punishment of vanquished knight errants' squires,' Sancho replied, 'for flies to bite them, lice to eat them and hunger to wage war on them. If we squires were the sons of the knights we serve, or some sort of close relations, it'd be fair enough if we got lumbered with the punishment for their sins down to the fourth generation, but what have the Panzas got to do with the Quixotes? Never mind though, let's settle down again and sleep for what little's left of the night, and God will send his light and then we'll see.'

'You sleep, Sancho,' Don Quixote replied, 'you were born to sleep; and I, who was born to keep vigil, will, in the time between now and daybreak, give free rein to my thoughts, and vent them in a little madrigal that, unbeknown to you, I composed in my head last night.'

'To my mind,' said Sancho, 'there can't be all that many thoughts that you can use for making up rhymes. You rhyme away as much as you like, though, and I'll sleep away as much as I can.'

And then he chose his ground and huddled up and slept like a log, undisturbed by debts or bonds or aches or pains. Don Quixote, leaning against the trunk of a beech or a cork-oak (Cide Hamete Benengeli doesn't specify which it was), sang as follows, to the accompaniment of his own sighs:

> When, Love, I pause to heed
> The anguish that you deal me with your blows,
> In search of death I speed,

And hope to find an end there to my woes;
. But as I reach my goal,
My haven in this stormy sea of pain,
Such joy pervades my soul
I turn away, for I feel strong again.
So living ends my life
And dying gives me back my vital breath:
A paradox of strife
That keeps me dead in life, alive in death![3]

He accompanied each line with a spate of sighs and a torrent of tears, as one whose heart had been pierced by the grief of his defeat and his separation from Dulcinea. And now the day came, and the sun sent its rays down on to Sancho's eyes, and Sancho awoke and roused himself, shaking and stretching his sluggish limbs; he examined the ravages wrought to his pantry by the pigs, and cursed the whole herd of them, and more besides. Before long the pair resumed their journey, and towards dusk they saw some ten men on horseback and four or five on foot approaching them. Don Quixote's heart flinched and Sancho's quailed, because the men coming closer and closer were carrying lances and shields, and looked ready for war. Don Quixote turned to Sancho and said:

'If, Sancho, I could make use of my weapons, and my promise had not tied my hands, I should consider this array descending upon us as very small beer indeed; but it could be something quite different from what we fear.'

The men on horseback rode up and, brandishing their lances, they surrounded Don Quixote without uttering a word, and thrust them at his back and his chest, threatening him with death. One of the men on foot, with a finger over his lips to warn the knight to keep quiet, took Rocinante by the bridle and led him off the road, and the others, driving Sancho and his dun in front of them, all in an extraordinary silence, followed the man with Don Quixote, who tried two or three times to ask where he was being taken and what they wanted of him; but no sooner had he opened his lips than his captors closed them again with the tips of their lances; and the same thing kept happening to Sancho, because whenever he showed signs of talking one of the men on foot prodded him with a goad, and then did the same to the dun, as if the animal were trying to speak as well. Night fell, they quickened their pace, the two captives' fear increased, all the more so when every so often they heard:

'Get a move on, you troglodytes!'

'Keep quiet, you barbarians!'

'We'll make you pay, you cannibals!'

'Don't complain, you Goths, and don't open your eyes, you murderous Polyphemuses,[4] you bloodthirsty lions!'

And other similar names, with which they tormented the ears of the wretched master and servant. Sancho was thinking to himself:

'Us, chomping lice? Us, baboons and animals? Us, goats and hippopota-muses? I don't like these names at all. It's an ill wind that's going to winnow this pile of grain – all our troubles are coming together, like a thumping to a dog, and let's hope this terrible adventure ends in nothing worse than a thumping!'

Don Quixote was in a daze, and however hard he thought about it he couldn't fathom what might be the meaning of all those insults being directed at them – all he could conclude was that no good was to be hoped from them, and plenty of evil was to be feared. And now, about an hour into the night, they reached a castle, which Don Quixote realized was the Duke's, where he'd stayed a little earlier.

'Goodness me!' he said to himself when he recognized the building. 'What's happening now? In this house, indeed, all is courtesy and kindness; but for the vanquished good turns to bad, and bad to worse.'

They entered the main courtyard of the castle and saw it decked out in a way that increased their amazement and redoubled their fear, as will be seen in the next chapter.

CHAPTER LXIX

About the strangest and most singular experience
undergone by Don Quixote in the whole course of this
great history

The horsemen dismounted and they and the men on foot swept Don Quixote and Sancho up in their arms and carried them into the courtyard, around which about a hundred torches were blazing, fixed in their holders, and on the gallery around the yard there were more than five hundred lanterns, so that although the night was a dark one, nobody missed the light of day. In the middle of the courtyard there was a catafalque, raised about two yards above the ground, and over it there was a great canopy of black velvet under which, on the steps, white wax candles were burning in more than a hundred silver candlesticks; and on the catafalque itself lay the corpse of such a lovely young woman that she made death itself seem beautiful. Her head, crowned with a garland of sweet-smelling flowers of different sorts, rested on a brocade pillow, and her hands were crossed over her breast with a frond of the yellow palm of victory between them.

On one side of the courtyard a platform had been erected, with two seats on which sat two personages who, with crowns on their heads and sceptres in their hands, looked as if they were kings, real or fictitious. By the side of this platform, which had steps leading up to it, there were another two chairs, upon which the men who had captured Don Quixote and Sancho made them sit down, without speaking a word and with signs that they too must stay silent. But they didn't need any signs to make them do so, because their amazement at what they were beholding kept them tongue-tied. And now two persons of distinction, at once recognized by Don Quixote as his hosts the Duke and Duchess, walked up on to the platform, attended by a great retinue, and seated themselves on two magnificent chairs by the side of the two men who seemed to be kings. Who wouldn't have been amazed at all this? What was more, Don Quixote had realized that the corpse on the catafalque was that of the lovely Altisidora. As the Duke and Duchess mounted the platform, Don Quixote and Sancho rose and made them a deep bow, and they responded with a little nod. Then a servant appeared from one side of the courtyard, and coming up to Sancho, he swathed him in a robe of black buckram with flames painted all over it, and removing his peasant's hood put in its place a cardboard cone like those worn by people condemned by the Holy Inquisition, and whispered in his ear that if he unbuttoned his lips they'd either ram a gag into his mouth or kill him. Sancho looked himself up and down and saw that he was on fire, but since the flames weren't burning him he didn't care a hoot about them. He took off his cardboard cone, saw that it had devils painted on it and put it back on, saying to himself:

'Just as well the flames aren't hurting me and the devils aren't carting me off.'

Don Quixote was also looking at him and, although befuddled with fear, he couldn't help laughing at the figure Sancho cut. And now, apparently from beneath the catafalque, came a gentle, pleasant music of flutes which, uninterrupted by any human voice, because in that place even silence kept silence for itself, sounded soft and peaceful. Then, by the pillow of what seemed to be the dead body, a handsome youth suddenly appeared, dressed as a Roman, and to the accompaniment of a harp that he played himself he sang these two stanzas in a sweet, clear voice:

> And now, while fair Altisidora, slain
> By cruel Quixote, tries to reawake;
> And while, in this enchanted court, a train
> Of ladies in their sackcloth weep and ache;
> And while Her Grace's doleful duennas deign
> To dress in serge and baize for her own sake:
> I'll sing the praises of this hapless maid
> In sweeter sounds than Orpheus ever played.
>
> I can't believe this sacred duty will
> Be mine only in life; for, when my tongue
> Within my mouth is dead and cold and still,
> I shall repay my debt to you in song.
> And once my soul is freed from its mean cell

And, celebrating you, it sails along
The Stygian lake, its plaintive tones will slow
And halt Oblivion's unrelenting flow.[1]

'Enough!' exclaimed one of the two men who looked like kings. 'Enough, divine singer; for it would be an endless task to depict for us the death and the charms of the peerless Altisidora – not dead, as the ignorant world believes, but alive in the tongues of fame, and in the punishment that Sancho Panza, here present, must undergo to recall her to the light that she has lost. And so, O Rhadamanthus, you who sit in judgement with me in gloomy Hades' darkest caves, you who know everything determined by the inscrutable fates concerning this maiden's return to life: speak up and reveal it now, so that the good that we expect from her restoration is not delayed.'

No sooner had Minos,[2] Rhadamanthus's fellow-judge, spoken these words than the latter rose to his feet and exclaimed:

'Come now, all you servants in this house, high and low, great and small: come one by one to give Sancho twenty-four fine fillips on his nose, twelve pinches on his arms and six pinpricks in his loins, for this is the ceremony required to achieve Altisidora's well-being.'

When Sancho Panza heard this he broke his silence and cried:

'I swear by all that's holy that I'll as soon turn into a Moor as let them give me fillips on my nose and paw all over my face! Bloody hell! What's pawing my face got to do with bringing this girl back to life? Give a clown your finger and he'll grab your hand. Dulcinea gets enchanted, and I get thrashed so that she can be disenchanted. Altisidora dies from some illness that God saw fit to send her, and for her to be brought back to life I've got to be given twenty-four fillips on the nose and have my body riddled with pinpricks and my arms pinched till they're black and blue! Well you can go and try those tricks on your brother-in-law, because I'm an old fox and I'm not so easily snared.'

'You shall die!' Rhadamanthus shouted. 'Relent, you tiger; humble yourself, proud Nimrod,[3] and suffer in silence, for you are not being asked to do the impossible. And do not enquire into the difficulties of this task: filliped you shall be, pricked you shall wince, pinched you shall groan. Come now, you servants, obey my command; or else, on my word as an honest man, I will make you regret that you were ever born!'

At this, some half-a-dozen duennas appeared in the courtyard in a procession, in single file, four of them wearing spectacles, and all of them with their right hands raised high and four inches of wrist revealed to make their hands look longer, as is the current fashion. As soon as Sancho saw them he bellowed like a bull:

'All right, I'll let everyone paw me over – but have duennas touch me? Never! You can give my face a good cat-scratching as they did my master's in this very same castle, and you can stick sharp daggers through my body, and you can tear the flesh off my arms with red-hot pincers, I'll put up with it all, or I'll do whatever else these gentlemen like, just to oblige them – but I won't have duennas touching me, not if the devil himself carries me away.'

Don Quixote also broke his silence and said to Sancho:

'Be patient my son, and oblige these gentlemen, and thank heaven for having given your person such powers that by martyring it you can disenchant the enchanted and resurrect the dead.'

The duennas had by now drawn close to Sancho, and he, more tractable and resigned, settled himself in his chair and offered his face and his beard to the first of them, who delivered a splendid fillip to his nose, and then a deep curtsey to his person.

'Let's have less courtesy and less face-lotion, duenna,' said Sancho, 'your hands stink of vinegar-wash, by God.'

To be brief, all the duennas filliped him, and other members of the household pinched him; but what he couldn't bear was the pricking of the pins; and so he started from his chair in a rage and, grabbing a blazing torch from beside him, he charged at the duennas and all his other tormentors, crying:

'Away with you, servants of hell – I'm not made of bronze, so as not to feel this terrible martyrdom!'

At this point Altisidora, who must have been feeling tired from lying flat on her back for so long, rolled over on to her side; seeing which the onlookers cried almost with one voice:

'Altisidora is alive! Altisidora lives!'

Rhadamanthus told Sancho to calm down, because the desired end had been attained. As soon as Don Quixote saw Altisidora stirring, he went to kneel before Sancho with the words:

'Now is the time, my dearly beloved son – not merely my squire – to give yourself some of the lashes that you must undergo to disenchant Dulcinea. Now, I say – when your virtue has been matured and made ready to work the good that is expected of you.'

To which Sancho replied:

'That wouldn't be so much gilding the lily as piling codswallop on top of stuff and nonsense. A fine thing it'd be if after a pinching, a filliping and a pinpricking I got a lashing as well. All you lot need to do is get a nice big stone, tie it to my neck and chuck me down a well, which wouldn't bother me much if to sort out other people's problems I've got to be the general scapegoat. You just leave me alone, or else I'll upset the apple cart, by God, and hang the consequences!'

By now Altisidora had sat up on the catafalque, and as she did so the shawms sounded out, accompanied by the flutes and the voices of all, crying:

'Long live Altisidora! Long life to Altisidora!'

The Duke and Duchess and the Kings Minos and Rhadamanthus came to their feet and all of them together with Don Quixote and Sancho went to receive Altisidora and help her down from the catafalque; and, pretending to have no strength in her body, she curtseyed to the Duke and Duchess and the Kings and, directing a sidelong glance at Don Quixote, said to him:

'God forgive you, loveless knight, because through your cruelty I have been in the other world for what seems like more than a thousand years; yet to you, the most compassionate squire in all the world, I give thanks for the life I again possess. From henceforth, friend Sancho, six of my shifts are yours – I promise you them so that you can have six shirts made, and if they are not all undamaged at least they are all clean.'

Sancho kissed her hands in gratitude, with his cardboard cone in his hand and his knees on the ground. The Duke ordered the cone to be taken from him and his hood to be returned and his smock to be put back on and the fiery robe taken off. Sancho begged the Duke to be allowed to keep his robe and his mitre, because he wanted to take them back home with him as keepsakes to remind him of that incredible adventure. The Duchess replied that he could indeed keep them, for he well knew what a very great friend of his she was. The Duke ordered the courtyard to be cleared, and everybody to retire to their rooms, and Don Quixote and Sancho to be taken to where they'd slept before.

CHAPTER LXX

Which follows sixty-nine and deals with matters that are indispensable for the comprehension of this history

Sancho slept that night on a truckle-bed in the same room as Don Quixote, something he'd have avoided if he could, because he knew only too well that his master wasn't going to let him sleep with all his questions and answers, and he himself didn't feel much like talking, because the pains of his recent martyrdom were still with him and didn't let his tongue flow freely; and it would have suited him better to sleep alone in a hovel rather than with someone else in that splendid room. His fears were so well founded and his suspicions so accurate that no sooner had his master climbed into bed than he said:

'And what is your opinion, Sancho, about tonight's events? Great indeed is the power of indifference and disdain, as you have seen with your own eyes in Altisidora, slain by no other arrows or sword or other instrument of war or deadly poison than the thought of the severity and scorn with which I have always treated her.'

'She was welcome to die when and how she liked, and to leave me be,' Sancho replied. 'I never made her fall in love or scorned her in all my born days. I just don't know and can't fathom how the welfare of that Altisidora girl, with more flightiness than good sense about her, can have anything to do with the martyrdom of Sancho Panza, as I've pointed out before. Now I really can see that there are such things as enchanters and magic spells, and may God deliver me from them, because I don't know how to deliver myself. All the same, I'd ask you very kindly to let me sleep and not fire any more questions at me, unless you want me to throw myself out of the window.'

'Sleep away, friend Sancho,' Don Quixote replied, 'if the pinpricks and the pinches and the fillips you've been given will let you.'

'None of all that pain,' said Sancho, 'was as bad as the insult of being filliped – because it was duennas that did it, confound the lot of them. And I'll again ask you very kindly to let me sleep, because sleep gives relief from the woes that we have when awake.'

'So be it,' said Don Quixote,' 'and may God watch over you.'

And the pair did fall asleep, and during this interval Cide Hamete, the author of this great history, decided to explain what it was that had moved the Duke and Duchess to rig up all the paraphernalia just described. And he says that the graduate Sansón Carrasco hadn't forgotten about how the Knight of the Spangles had been toppled and defeated by Don Quixote, which spoiled all his plans, and he decided to try again, hoping for a happier outcome. And so, having discovered Don Quixote's whereabouts from the page who'd taken the letter and the present to Sancho's wife Teresa Panza, he looked out some more armour and another horse, and painted the white moon on the shield, and then took it all off on a mule led by a farmer – not his former squire Tomé Cecial, to avoid recognition by Sancho or Don Quixote.

So Sansón reached the Duke's castle, and the Duke informed him of the route that Don Quixote had taken, intending to participate in the jousting at Saragossa. The Duke also told him about the hoaxes that had been played on Don Quixote, and about the arrangements for Dulcinea's disenchantment, at the expense of Sancho's backside. And finally the Duke gave an account of the hoax played by Sancho on his master, making him believe that Dulcinea had been enchanted and turned into a peasant girl, and of how his wife the Duchess had made Sancho believe that he was the one who had been deceived, because Dulcinea really had been enchanted; all of which provoked deep amazement and hearty laughter in the young graduate as he pondered on Sancho's combination of sharp wits and simplemindedness, and on Don Quixote's extremes of madness. The Duke asked him, if he found the knight, and whether he defeated him or not, to return to the castle to tell him what had happened. The graduate did so: he went off in search of Don Quixote, he didn't find him in Saragossa, he continued his quest, and the remainder has already been narrated.

He returned to the Duke's castle and told him the whole story, complete with the conditions of the combat, and he added that Don Quixote was on his way back to keep his promise, as a good knight errant, to retire to his village for a year, during which time it was hoped that he might recover from his madness; for this was the intention that had moved the young graduate to assume his disguises, as it was a great pity that such an intelligent hidalgo as Don Quixote should be a madman. With this he took his leave of the Duke and returned to his village, to wait there for Don Quixote, who was following on behind.

This was what had given the Duke the chance to play his latest hoax, because he so enjoyed everything about Sancho and Don Quixote; and he had all the roads, near and far, along which he imagined Don Quixote might return, patrolled by his many servants, on foot and on horseback, so that they could bring him to the castle, whether he wanted to come or not, if they found him. They did find him and they sent news to the Duke, who, having already decided everything that was to be done, ordered the torches and the lanterns to be lit in the courtyard and Altisidora to be placed on the catafalque, with the accessories that have been described, all so lifelike and so well contrived that the scene was little different from reality.

And Cide Hamete says even more: he considers that the perpetrators of the hoax were as mad as the victims, and that the Duke and Duchess, going to such lengths to make fun of two fools, were within a hairsbreadth of looking like fools themselves.

Of the former pair one was fast asleep, buried in his dreams, and the other was wide awake, immersed in his thoughts, when day and the desire to be out of bed caught up with him; for Don Quixote, whether vanquished or victorious, never took any pleasure in the slothful feathers. Altisidora, brought back to life, in Don Quixote's opinion, and continuing her master and mistress's joke, walked into Don Quixote's room crowned with the same garland that she'd worn on the catafalque, dressed in a dalmatic of white taffeta decorated with flowers of gold, her hair flowing loose over her shoulders, and leaning on a black staff of finest ebony; thrown into the utmost confusion by her presence, he huddled himself up in his bed and hid under the sheets and counterpanes, his tongue paralysed, incapable of offering one word of greeting. Altisidora sat on a chair by the head of his bed and, after heaving the deepest of sighs, she said in a faltering, tender voice:

'When women of high rank and demure maidens disregard honour and allow their tongues to break through all barriers, making public the secrets hidden in their hearts, they are indeed in desperate straits. I, O Don Quixote de la Mancha, am one such, beset, vanquished and overcome by love, but long-suffering and chaste for all that; so much so that my silence made my very soul burst and I lost my life. For two whole days, tormented by the thought of the severity with which you,

Harder than hardest marble to my moans,[1]

O callous knight, have treated me, I lay dead or at least considered dead by those who saw me. And if love hadn't taken pity on me and made my recovery hinge on the martyrdom of this good squire, I'd have remained for ever in the other world.'

'Love could just as well have made it hinge,' said Sancho, 'on the martyrdom of my donkey, and I'd have been very grateful for that. But tell me one thing, lady, so heaven send you a more tender-hearted lover than my master – what was it you saw in the other world? What is there in hell? Because it's down there that anyone who dies in despair is bound to end up.'

'To tell you the honest truth,' Altisidora replied, 'I can't have died completely, because I didn't go right into hell: if I had, I couldn't ever have got out again, however much I wanted to. The fact is that I reached the gate, where about a dozen devils were playing pelota, all stripped down to doublet and hose, with broad, floppy collars trimmed in Flanders lace, and ruffles of the same material serving as cuffs, and displaying four inches of arm to add length to their hands, in which they were holding rackets of fire; and what most amazed me was that instead of balls they were serving books, full of wind and stuffing, an extraordinary, unheard-of thing. But this didn't astonish me as much as seeing that, although it's natural for the winners at games to be happy and the losers to be glum, in that game they were all grumbling, quarrelling and cursing each other.'

'That's no wonder,' Sancho retorted, 'because devils, whether they're playing games or not, can never be happy, win or lose.'

'Yes, that must be it,' Altisidora replied, 'but there's something else that amazes me, or rather that amazed me when I was there, which is that there wasn't one ball that could withstand the first volley or was in any condition to be served again, and so books old and new came in quick succession, an extraordinary sight. One of them, brand-new and well bound, was given such a thump that its guts poured out and its leaves flew all over the place. One devil said to another:

'"Go and see what book that is."

'And the other devil replied:

'"It's the second part of the history of Don Quixote de la Mancha, not written by Cide Hamete, its first author, but by some Aragonese person who says he comes from Tordesillas."

'"Remove it," replied the other devil, "and consign it to the depths of hell; I never want to see it again."

'"Is it as bad as all that?" the other one asked.

'"It's so bad," replied the first devil, "that if I'd tried my very hardest to write a worse one the task would have been beyond me."

'They continued their game, serving and returning other books, and once I'd heard the name of Don Quixote, whom I love so dearly, I did my best to retain this vision in my memory.'

'Yes, a vision, that is what it must have been,' said Don Quixote, 'for there is no other I in the world; and that other history is passed on from hand to hand to the next but never stays long in any of them, because everyone gives it a taste of his feet. It has not disturbed me to learn that I wander in a fantastic shape through the shades of hell or the clear light of earth, because I am not the person described in that history. If any history is good, faithful and true, it will enjoy centuries of life, but if it is bad the road from its birth to its burial will not be a long one.'

Altisidora was about to resume her complaints about Don Quixote when he addressed her:

'I have often told you, my lady, that I am sorry you have directed your affections towards me, because you can expect no response but gratitude from mine; I was born to belong to Dulcinea del Toboso, and the fates (if they exist) have dedicated me to her; and to think that any other beauty can occupy the place that she has in my soul is to think the impossible. This is sufficient disabuse to make you retire within the bounds of your chastity, because nobody can be forced to do what is impossible.'

When Altisidora heard this she bridled up and exclaimed:

'Good God! You cold codfish, with a soul like a granite mortar and a heart like a date-stone, more stubborn and unyielding than any peasant once he's made up his mind – just let me get at you and I'll tear your eyes out of your head! You aren't by any chance imagining, are you, you defeated and cudgelled wretch, that I died because of you? Everything you saw last night was a sham – I'm not a woman to let so much as my little finger ache for an old camel like you, let alone die for one.'

'I can believe that all right,' said Sancho. 'All this stuff about people dying of love is a joke. They might well say it, but as for doing it – they'd better try pulling the other one.'

As they talked, the musician, singer and poet who'd sung the two stanzas quoted earlier walked in, and making a deep bow to Don Quixote he said:

'Please count and include me, sir knight, among the number of your most faithful servants, because for some time now I have been a great admirer of yours, on account of both your fame and your deeds.'

Don Quixote replied:

'Please tell me who you are, so that my courtesy can correspond to your merits.'

The lad replied that he was the musician and panegyrist of the previous night.

'To be sure,' Don Quixote replied, 'you have a fine voice; but what you sang does not seem to me to have been altogether appropriate: what have Garcilaso's stanzas to do with this lady's death?'

'You mustn't be surprised at that,' the musician replied, 'because it's normal nowadays for novice poets to write however they please and steal from whomever they like, whether it's to the point or not, and there isn't an absurdity they sing or write that isn't put down to poetic licence.'

Don Quixote would have replied, but the Duke and Duchess prevented this by coming in to see him, and they all had a long and agreeable conversation during which Sancho displayed such wit and such shrewdness that the two were again left amazed at his combination of acuteness and simplicity. Don Quixote begged their leave to depart that same day, because it was fitter for vanquished knights like him to live in pigsties than in royal palaces. They were happy to grant his request, and the

Duchess asked him whether Altisidora was now in his good books. He replied:

'Madam, I would have Your Ladyship know that all this maiden's problems are born of idleness, the remedy for which is honest and constant occupation. She has just informed me that lace is worn in hell, and since she must know how to make it, let her apply herself to this activity; because so long as she is busy with her bobbins, the image or images of her desires will not be busy in her mind, and this is the truth, this is my opinion and this is my advice.'

'Mine too,' Sancho added, 'because I've never in all my life seen a lacemaker that died of love – busy girls think more about finishing the job in hand than about their boyfriends. I'm speaking from experience, too, because while I'm digging I haven't got a thought for my better half, by which I mean my Teresa Panza, and I love her more than these lashes over my eyes.'

'You're absolutely right, Sancho,' said the Duchess, 'and from now on I'll see to it that my Altisidora's kept busy with some needlework – she's incredibly good at it.'

'There's no need, my lady,' Altisidora replied, 'to have recourse to that remedy, because the thought of this gormless oaf's cruelty to me will be quite enough to blot him out from my memory. And by Your Grace's leave I'd like to get out of here so as not to have to put up with the sight not just of his sorry face but of his whole hideous, abominable appearance.'

'That reminds me,' said the Duke, 'of what they often say:

> A lover who's railing
> Is close to forgiving.'[2]

Altisidora made a show of wiping away her tears with a handkerchief, curtseyed to her master and mistress, and left the room.

'What I can promise you, you poor girl,' said Sancho, 'is bad luck, because you're tangling with a man whose soul is made of esparto grass and whose heart is made of oak. By God, if it was me you were tangling with it'd be a different story!'

The conversation ended, Don Quixote dressed, dined with the Duke and Duchess, and left that same evening.

CHAPTER LXXI

*About what happened between Don Quixote and his
squire Sancho Panza on their way back to their village*

The vanquished and harassed Don Quixote rode along sunk in gloomy
thought in one respect, and overjoyed in another. His sadness was caused
by his defeat, his happiness by thinking about Sancho's magical powers
as displayed in the resurrection of Altisidora, although it was only with
some reservations that he persuaded himself that the enamoured maiden
had really been dead. Sancho was not in the slightest overjoyed, only
dejected at Altisidora's failure to keep her word and give him those shifts;
and, after turning this grudge over and over in his mind, he said to his
master:

'The truth is, sir, that I must be the unluckiest doctor in this world,
where there are other doctors who after killing their patients expect to
be paid for their work, and all they do is sign a little form for a few
medicines, and it isn't even them that make them up, but the chemist –
and there you are, the swindle's complete. Yet I give other people their
health back, and it costs me blood-lettings, fillips, pinches, pinpricks and
lashes – and nobody gives me a brass farthing. Well, I swear by all that's
holy that if some other patient's put into my hands he'll have to grease
my palms before I treat him, because the priest dines on his singing, and
I can't believe that heaven's given me this power of mine just for me to
let others have its benefits free, gratis and for nothing.'

'You're quite right, Sancho my friend,' Don Quixote replied, 'and it
was most remiss of Altisidora not to give you the shifts that she had
promised you; and even though your power is *gratis data*, because you
didn't have to study to acquire it, being martyred is even worse than
studying. What I can say for myself is that if you had wanted payment
for the lashes required for the disenchantment of Dulcinea, I should have
been happy to pay you handsomely; and yet I'm not sure that the payment
is compatible with the cure, and I wouldn't like the reward to prevent
the medicine from working. Despite all that, I don't think we can lose
anything by trying: so you decide, Sancho, how much money you want,

and then lash yourself, and pay yourself in ready cash, since you are carrying my money.'

At these offers Sancho's eyes and ears gaped open, and he inwardly agreed to lash himself with a will, and he said:

'Very well, sir, I'm agreeable to going along with what you want, if there's something in it for me – because my love for my dear wife and children forces me to seem grasping. So tell me this – how much will you give me for each lash I give myself?'

'If I were to pay you, Sancho,' Don Quixote replied, 'in proportion to the magnitude and quality of this cure, all the treasure in Venice and all the silver-mines of Potosí[1] would be too small a recompense; but look and see how much of my money is left, and then put a price on each lash.'

'The lashes,' Sancho replied, 'number three thousand three hundred odd, and I've given myself about five of them so far, so all the rest are still to come. The five can count as the odd ones, so we're left with three thousand three hundred, which at a quarter of a real each, and I won't take any less even if the whole world tells me to, makes three thousand three hundred quarter-reals, and the three thousand makes one thousand five hundred half-reals, which makes seven hundred and fifty reals, and the three hundred makes one hundred and fifty half-reals, which makes seventy-five reals, and adding them on to the seven hundred and fifty makes eight hundred and twenty-five reals in all. These I'll pocket from this money of yours I've got here, and I'll walk into my house a rich and happy man, though a well-lashed one too, because you can't catch trout and keep your breeches dry, and that's all I need say.'

'O blessed Sancho! O kindly Sancho!' Don Quixote replied. 'Dulcinea and I shall be under an obligation to serve you for as long as heaven spares us! If she recovers her lost self (and no other outcome is possible), her misfortune will have been good fortune, and my defeat a most happy victory. And now consider, Sancho, when you want to start the scourging – to encourage you to make short work of it I'll add a hundred reals to the figure.'

'When do I want to start?' Sancho replied. 'This very night, without fail. You make sure we spend it out in the fields under the stars, and I'll cut my flesh to ribbons.'

Night came, longed for by Don Quixote with all the impatience in the world, as he imagined that the wheels on Apollo's chariot must have broken and that the day was longer than usual, just as happens to lovers, who can never balance the accounts of their desires. At length they took shelter among some welcoming trees a little way off the road where, vacating Rocinante's saddle and the dun's pack-saddle, they stretched themselves out on the green grass and supped from Sancho's stores; and then, after turning the dun's halter and headstall into a powerful and flexible whip, Sancho walked about twenty paces away from his master and ended up among some beech trees. Don Quixote, seeing him march off with determination and spirit, called out:

'Be careful, my friend, not to cut yourself to pieces; give yourself a rest between one series of strokes and another; don't be in such a hurry that you breathe your last before you are half done; what I am trying to say is that you mustn't hit yourself so hard that you kill yourself before you reach the number stipulated. And to ensure that you don't lose the game through scoring too few or too many points, I shall stay here where I am, counting the lashes on this rosary of mine. May heaven help you, as your noble intentions deserve.'

'A good payer's a good pledger,' Sancho replied. 'I'm planning to hit myself so that it hurts but doesn't kill me – that must be the secret of this miracle.'

And he stripped to the waist, seized the rope and began to flail himself, while Don Quixote began to count the strokes. By the time he'd given himself six or eight he decided that this joke was in bad taste and its price too low, and he paused and called out to his master that he'd decided it wasn't a fair bargain – each of those lashes was worth half a real, not a quarter.

'You continue, Sancho my friend, and do not flinch,' said Don Quixote. 'I'll double the stakes.'

'In that case,' said Sancho, 'God's will be done, and let it rain lashes.'

But the sly rogue stopped hitting his back and instead hit the trees, heaving such sighs from time to time that it seemed as if every stroke was tearing his very soul out of his body. The tender-hearted knight, fearful that Sancho might drop down dead and he through Sancho's recklessness not achieve his goal, called out:

'Upon my soul, friend, do let the matter rest now; this medicine seems a very drastic one, and it will be better if you take your time: Rome wasn't built in a day. You've given yourself more than a thousand lashes, if I've been counting correctly; that's enough for the time being: an ass, if I may use a vulgar expression, endures its burden, but not more than its burden.'

'No, no, sir,' Sancho replied, 'nobody's going to say about me, "The money paid, the work delayed." Move a bit further away and let me give myself another thousand lashes at least – in a couple of bouts like this we'll have finished this little consignment, and there'll still be some merchandise left over.'

'Since you are in such a compliant mood,' said Don Quixote, 'may heaven help you, and you carry on flailing yourself; I'm going away.'

Sancho resumed his task with so much fervour that he soon stripped many trees of their bark, such was the severity with which he lashed himself. At one point he dealt a beech tree a ferocious slash and screamed:

'Here Samson and the Philistines shall die!'

When Don Quixote heard the piteous cry and the crack of the implacable lash, he rushed over and grasped the doubled-over halter that Sancho was using as a whip, with the words:

'Let's not run the risk, Sancho my friend, of your losing your life for the sake of my pleasure, because your life must be used to support your wife and children: Dulcinea can wait for a more suitable occasion, and I shall contain myself within the bounds of hope soon to be fulfilled, and wait for you to recover your strength so that this affair can be concluded to everybody's satisfaction.'

'If that's the way you want it, sir,' Sancho replied, 'all well and good, and just put your cape round these shoulders of mine – I'm sweating and I wouldn't like to catch cold, a danger that novice penitents are exposed to.'

Don Quixote did so and was left in his shirtsleeves, and he wrapped Sancho up, and Sancho slept until the sun awoke him, and then they resumed their journey, which they finished for the day in a village ten miles further on. They dismounted at an inn, which Don Quixote recognized as such and not as a castle with its deep moat, towers, portcullises and drawbridge; because now that he'd been defeated his judgement on all subjects was sounder, as will soon be shown. He was lodged in a ground-floor room where in place of leather hangings there were old painted cloths of the sort common in villages. On one of them some clumsy hand had painted the rape of Helen, at the moment when the audacious guest carried her off from Menelaus, and on another was the story of Dido and Aeneas, she on a high tower, apparently signalling with half a sheet to the fugitive guest[2] who was escaping across the sea in a frigate or a brigantine. Don Quixote noted that Helen wasn't too sorry to be stolen away, because she was laughing to herself on the sly, but the lovely Dido was shedding tears the size of walnuts. As he looked at the paintings he said:

'These two ladies were most unfortunate not to have been born in the present age, and I am even more unfortunate not to have been born in theirs: had I confronted these gentlemen, neither would Troy have been burned nor Carthage destroyed, because by my simply killing Paris all those calamities would have been avoided.'

'I bet,' said Sancho, 'that before long there won't be a single eating-house or roadside inn or hostelry or barber's shop where there isn't a painting of the story of our deeds. But I'd like it to be done by a better artist than the one who painted these.'

'You're right, Sancho,' said Don Quixote, 'because this artist is like Orbaneja, a painter who lived in Úbeda and who when asked what he was painting would reply, "Whatever emerges"; and if he happened to be painting a cockerel he'd write underneath it, "This is a cockerel," to stop people from thinking it was a vixen. It seems to me, Sancho, that the painter or writer – it comes to the same thing – who published the history of this new Don Quixote that has just appeared must be just such a person, painting or writing whatever emerged; or maybe he was like a certain poet called Mauleón who was to be found hanging about the capital in recent years, and who used to improvise an answer to any question that was put to him; and when someone asked him what *Deum de Deo*[3] meant, he replied: "They'll underpay you." But leaving all that aside, tell me, Sancho, whether you're intending to have another session tonight, and whether you want to have it indoors or out in the open.'

'By God, sir,' Sancho replied, 'for the flogging I'm planning to give myself it doesn't matter whether I'm inside or out – but on second thoughts, I would like to be among some trees, they seem to keep me company and are such a wonderful help to me in my plight.'

'No, Sancho my friend, that isn't the way,' Don Quixote replied. 'To give you a chance to recover your strength we shall wait until we are back in the village, where we shall arrive, at the latest, the day after tomorrow.'

Sancho replied that Don Quixote could do whatever he liked, but he himself would like to finish that job off while his blood was up and the millstones were grinding well, because the danger lies in the delay, and God helps them that help themselves, and he gives twice who gives quickly, and a bird in the hand is worth two in the bush.

'No more proverbs, Sancho, for God's sake,' said Don Quixote. 'You seem to be going back to *sicut erat in principio*; use plain, straightforward language without complications, as I've so often told you, and you'll soon see how you reap the benefit.'

'I don't know why I have to be so unlucky,' said Sancho, 'that I can't make a point without quoting a proverb, or quote a proverb that to my mind doesn't make a point, but I'll mend my ways, if I can.'

And with this he stopped talking, for the time being.

CHAPTER LXXII

Concerning the arrival of Don Quixote and Sancho at their village

Don Quixote and Sancho spent all that day at the village inn, waiting for nightfall: one of them to bring his exercise in flagellation to a conclusion in the open air, and the other to witness its completion and with it the accomplishment of his desires. Meanwhile a traveller arrived on horseback with three or four servants, one of whom said to the man who seemed to be their master:

'You can rest here, Don Álvaro Tarfe sir, while the sun is high – the inn seems clean and cool.'

When Don Quixote heard this he said to Sancho:

'Look, Sancho, when I thumbed through that book containing the second part of my history, I think I came across the name Don Álvaro Tarfe.'

'You could be right,' Sancho replied. 'Let's wait for him to dismount and then we'll ask him.'

The gentleman dismounted, and the innkeeper's wife gave him a ground-floor room opposite Don Quixote's, decorated with painted cloths of the same sort. The recent arrival went to change into more comfortable clothes and, strolling out into the cool, spacious porch, where Don Quixote was pacing up and down, he asked:

'And where might you be bound for, my dear sir?'

And Don Quixote replied:

'To a village near here, where I live. And where are you going?'

'I am on my way to Granada, sir,' the gentleman replied, 'my home town.'

'And a very fine town it is, too!' Don Quixote replied. 'But please be so kind as to tell me your name; because I think it is going to be of more interest to me to know it than I can well explain.'

'My name is Don Álvaro Tarfe,' the guest said.

To which Don Quixote replied:

'I do believe you must be the very same Don Álvaro Tarfe who appears in the second part of the *History of Don Quixote de la Mancha*, recently printed and published by a novice author.'

'Indeed I am,' the gentleman replied, 'and that man Don Quixote, the protagonist of the history, was a very close friend of mine, and I was the one who took him away from home, or at least I persuaded him to travel to Saragossa to take part in jousts held there, where I was going; and the truth of the matter is that I did him many favours and prevented the executioner from tickling his ribs for his recklessness.'

'And please tell me, Señor Don Álvaro, am I at all like that Don Quixote to whom you refer?'

'No, certainly not,' the guest replied, 'not in the slightest.'

'And did that Don Quixote,' said our one, 'have with him a squire called Sancho Panza?'

'Yes, he did,' Don Álvaro replied, 'and although he had the reputation of being a comical fellow, not one of his attempts to be funny that I heard ever succeeded.'

'I can believe that all right,' Sancho butted in, 'because not everybody's good at being funny, and that Sancho you're talking about, my good sir, must be some great scoundrel, as much a crook as he's unfunny; I'm the real Sancho Panza, and I'm so funny it's as if fun had rained down on me from heaven, and if you don't believe me just give me a try, and follow me around for a year or so, and you'll see how the fun gushes out of me at every turn, so much of it and such high quality that even though most of the time I don't know what I'm saying I make everyone listening to me laugh. And the real Don Quixote de la Mancha, the famous one, the brave and wise one, the lover, the righter of wrongs, the guardian of minors and orphans, the protector of widows and the slaughterer of maidens, the one whose only lady is the peerless Dulcinea del Toboso, is this gentleman here present, who's my master. All other Don Quixotes and all other Sancho Panzas besides us two are so much jiggery-pokery, figures from dreamland.'

'And I believe you too, by God!' Don Álvaro Tarfe replied. 'Because you've said more funny things, my friend, in the half-a-dozen words you've just spoken than the other Sancho Panza managed in all the words I heard from him. He was better at gorging himself than at talking, and was more foolish than funny, and I consider it a certain fact that the enchanters who pursue Don Quixote the Good have been chasing after me with Don Quixote the Bad. But I don't know what to say – I'd go as far as to swear that I left him in the Toledo madhouse awaiting treatment, and now another Don Quixote pops up here, quite different from mine.'

'I do not know,' said Don Quixote, 'whether I am good, but I do know that I am not the bad Quixote, as proof of which I should like you to know, Don Álvaro Tarfe sir, that I have never in my life set foot in Saragossa; on the contrary, having been told that the fantasy Don Quixote had taken part in the jousts in that city, I refused to go there, to prove to all the world that he is a fraud; and so I went straight on to Barcelona, the storehouse of courtesy, the refuge of strangers, the hospital of the poor, the homeland of the brave, the avenger of the affronted and the appreciative returner of firm friendship, unique in its setting and its beauty. And although what happened to me there was not very pleasant, indeed was most disagreeable, I can bear it all without heaviness of heart, just for the sake of having seen Barcelona. In short, Don Álvaro Tarfe sir, I am the Don Quixote de la Mancha of whom fame speaks – not that wretch who sought to usurp my name and exalt himself with my thoughts. I entreat you, sir, as you are a gentleman, to be so kind as to make a formal declaration before the mayor of this village to the effect that you have never in all the days of your life seen me until now, and that I am not the Don Quixote who appears in the second part, nor is this squire of mine Sancho Panza the man whom you knew.'

'I shall be delighted to do so,' Don Álvaro replied, 'even though it amazes me to see two Don Quixotes and two Sancho Panzas at the same time, as identical in name as they are antithetical in action; and I repeat and confirm that I have not seen what I have seen and that what has happened to me has not happened.'

'I'm sure,' said Sancho, 'that you must be under a spell too, like my lady Dulcinea, and would to God I could get rid of it for you by giving myself another three thousand odd lashes like the ones I'm giving myself for her – and I'd do it without expecting anything for it, either.'

'I don't understand this talk of lashes,' said Don Álvaro.

And Sancho replied that it was a long story, but he'd tell it if they happened to be going the same way. By now it was time for lunch; Don Quixote and Don Álvaro ate together. The village mayor happened to walk into the inn with a notary, and to the said mayor Don Quixote presented a petition to the effect that it was his wish and right that Don Álvaro Tarfe, the gentleman who was there present, should depose before His Worship that the said deponent did not know Don Quixote de la Mancha, who was also there present, and that the said Don Quixote was not the man who appeared in print in a history entitled *The Second Part of Don Quixote de la Mancha* written by one Avellaneda, from Tordesillas. And the mayor took all the appropriate steps: the deposition was drawn up with all the legal requisites, as is proper in such cases, which delighted Don Quixote and Sancho, as if such a deposition were vital to their welfare, and as if their deeds and their words didn't clearly show the difference between the two Don Quixotes and between the two Sanchos. Many courtesies and offers were exchanged between Don Álvaro and Don Quixote, in the course of which the great man of La Mancha displayed such good sense that he disabused Don Álvaro of his error; and Don Álvaro reached the conclusion that he must indeed have been enchanted, since he'd seen with his own eyes two such contrasting Don Quixotes.

Evening came, they left the village and after a couple of miles the road forked, one way leading to Don Quixote's village and the other to where

Don Álvaro was going. In this short interval Don Quixote told him about his calamitous defeat, and about Dulcinea's enchantment and disenchantment, all of which filled Don Álvaro with fresh amazement; and then he embraced Don Quixote and Sancho and went on his way, as did Don Quixote, who spent that night among some more trees, to give Sancho the opportunity to complete his penance, which he did as he had on the previous night, at the expense of the bark of the beeches rather than the skin of his back, of which he took such good care that the lashes wouldn't have brushed a fly off it if there had been one there. The deluded Don Quixote didn't fail to count a single stroke, and found that together with the previous night's score the total was three thousand and twenty-nine. It seems that the sun rose early to witness the sacrifice, and by its light the pair continued on their way, discussing Don Álvaro's delusion and what a good idea it had been to have him make his deposition before the proper authorities in such a correct and formal manner. That day and that night they pressed on, and nothing worth mentioning happened to them, except that during the night Sancho completed his task, to Don Quixote's unutterable joy, and he waited eagerly for daylight, to see if he could find his lady Dulcinea along the way, disenchanted; and as he rode there was not a woman whom he did not approach to examine her and discover whether she was Dulcinea del Toboso, because he was absolutely certain that Merlin's promises could not be false. Full of these thoughts and expectations they climbed a hill, from the top of which they could see their village, and Sancho fell to his knees, exclaiming:

'Open your eyes, my longed-for village, and see your son Sancho Panza returning, not very rich but very well lashed. Open your arms, too, to welcome your son Don Quixote, who has been conquered by another's arm but comes here as the conqueror of himself; and that, he's told me, is the best conquering you can wish for. I've got some money with me, because if I've been given a good lashing I've had a ride on a good horse, as the thief said to the executioner.'

'Stop all that nonsense,' said Don Quixote, 'and let's put our best feet forward as we make our entry into the village, where we'll give free play to our imaginations and settle our plans for the pastoral life that we're going to lead.'

And with this they went down the hill towards their village.

CHAPTER LXXIII

*About the omens that Don Quixote encountered as he
entered his village, together with other events that adorn
and authenticate this great history·*

As they approached it, according to Cide Hamete Benengeli, Don Quixote
saw two boys squabbling on the threshing floor, and one said to the
other:

'Don't keep on, Periquillo – that's something that's never ever going
to happen.'

Don Quixote overheard him, and said to Sancho:

'Didn't you hear, friend Sancho, what that boy said – "that's something
that's never ever going to happen"?'

'And who cares,' said Sancho, 'what the boy said?'

'Who cares?' replied Don Quixote. 'Can't you see that if you apply
these words to my hopes, they mean that I'll never see Dulcinea
again?'

Sancho was about to reply when he was stopped by the sight of a hare
dashing across the fields, chased by many greyhounds and huntsmen, and
in its terror it sought shelter and squatted between the dun's feet. Sancho
picked it up and presented it to Don Quixote, who was saying:

'*Malum signum! Malum signum!*[1] Hare flees, greyhounds chase: Dulcinea
appears not!'

'You're a strange one,' said Sancho. 'Let's suppose that this here hare
is Dulcinea del Toboso and those there greyhounds chasing it are the
knavish enchanters that turned her into a peasant girl – she runs away, I
grab her and put her into your charge, and now she's in your arms and
you're caring for her, so how can that be a bad sign, and what bad omen
can you see in that?'

The two squabbling boys came to look at the hare, and Sancho asked
one of them why they'd been quarrelling. The answer came from the one
who'd said 'that's something that's never ever going to happen' – he had
taken a cricket cage from the other boy and was never ever going to give
it back to him. Sancho took four quarter-reals out of his waist-pouch and

gave them to the boy for the cage, which he placed in Don Quixote's hands, saying:

'Here you are, sir – your omens foiled and come to nought, and I might be a fool but to my mind they haven't got any more to do with our affairs than last year's clouds. And if I'm not much mistaken, I've heard the village priest saying that sensible Christian persons shouldn't pay any attention to such nonsense, and you yourself told me the same thing a few days back, and showed me that all Christians who heeded omens were idiots. But there's no need for me to keep on about it – let's go into the village.'

The huntsmen came up and asked for their hare, and Don Quixote gave it back to them; the pair continued, and in a meadow on the outskirts of the village they found the priest and the graduate Carrasco at their devotions. It should be mentioned that Sancho Panza had draped over his dun and the bundle of armour, as a kind of sumpter-cloth, the buckram robe with flames painted all over it that he'd been made to wear in the Duke's castle on the night Altisidora came back to life. And he'd also put the inquisitional cardboard cone on the donkey's head, the most original transformation and adornment ever effected on any ass in the world. The pair were immediately recognized by the priest and the graduate, who ran over to them with open arms. Don Quixote dismounted and embraced them warmly, while the village boys – boys' lynx eyes see everything – spotted the donkey's head-gear and came to stare at it, calling to each other:

'Come over here, lads, if you want to see an ass looking as spruce as a sparrow and an old hack as skinny as a skeleton – and then you can have a good giggle at the dun and Rocinante, too.'

Finally, surrounded by boys and accompanied by the priest and the graduate, they entered the village and went to Don Quixote's house, and at the door they found the housekeeper and the niece, who'd already been told of his arrival. So too had Teresa Panza, Sancho's wife, who, dishevelled and half naked, clutching her daughter Sanchica by the hand, hurried out to meet her husband; and when she saw that he wasn't as smart as she thought a governor ought to be, she said:

'Why are you looking like that, husband? I'd say you've come here on foot and it hasn't done your feet much good either – you look more unruly, than a ruler.'

'Shut up, Teresa,' Sancho replied. 'Often where there are hooks there isn't any bacon to hang on them, so let's go home, and then you'll hear marvels. I've brought some money back with me, and that's what counts, and I've earned it with my own wiles, without doing any harm to anybody.'

'So long as you've brought some money back, good husband,' Teresa said, 'you can have earned it this way or that for all I care – however you've earned it you won't have started up any new customs in the world.'

Sanchica hugged her father and asked him if he'd brought anything for her, she'd been longing to see him like rain in a drought; and with her hanging on to one side of his belt and pulling his dun along behind her, and his wife holding his hand, they made for their house, leaving Don Quixote in his, in the care of his niece and his housekeeper, and in the company of the priest and the graduate.

Without a moment's delay, Don Quixote took the graduate and the priest aside and gave them a brief account of his defeat and of the promise that he'd made not to leave the village for a year, which he intended to keep to the letter, without breaking it in the slightest detail, as became a true knight errant, bound by all the discipline and order of knight-errantry – and he added that his intention was to become a shepherd for the year, and amuse himself in the solitude of the fields, where he could give free rein to his thoughts of love as he practised that virtuous pastoral way of life, and that he entreated them, if they didn't have too much to do and weren't prevented by more important matters, to consent to be his companions; he'd buy sheep enough to qualify them as shepherds, and he could tell them that the most essential part of the business was already settled, because he'd provided them with names that would fit like gloves. The priest told him to say what they were. Don Quixote replied that he himself was going to be called the shepherd Quixotiz, the graduate the shepherd Carrascón, the priest the shepherd Curambro and Sancho Panza the shepherd Panzino.

They were both astonished at Don Quixote's latest delusion; but to prevent him from wandering away from the village again on his chivalric exploits, and in the hope that during the year he might be cured, they consented to his new project, acclaimed his folly as sound sense and agreed to join him in his new way of life.

'And what's more,' said Sansón Carrasco, 'as everybody knows, I'm a

973

famous poet and at every turn I'll write pastoral verse or courtly verse or whatever verse best suits my purpose, to keep us amused in the God-forsaken places where we're going a-wandering; and what's most essential, gentlemen, is for each of us to choose the name of the shepherdess he's going to honour in his verses, and for us not to leave a single tree, however hard the wood, where her name isn't carved, as is the habit and custom among shepherds in love.'

'That is most fitting,' Don Quixote replied, 'even though I have no need to search for the name of a fictitious shepherdess, because I already have the peerless Dulcinea del Toboso, the glory of these riverbanks, the ornament of these meadows, the mainstay of beauty, the cream of all the graces, and, in short, one worthy to receive all praise, however hyperbolical it might appear to be.'

'Quite right too,' said the priest, 'but the rest of us will look for nice obliging shepherdesses who'll be just what the doctor ordered.'

To which Sansón Carrasco added:

'And if they haven't got appropriate names, we'll give them the names of the shepherdesses that come printed in all those books – the world's full of them: Phyllises, Amaryllises, Dianas, Fléridas, Galateas, Belisardas; and since they're sold in the market squares, we've got every right to buy them and keep them for ourselves. If my lady or, more accurately, my shepherdess happens to be called Ana, I'll sing her praises under the name of Anárda; if she's Francisca, I'll call her Francenia; if she's Lucía, Lucinda; and so on and so forth. And if Sancho Panza is going to join the club, he can sing his wife's praises with the name Teresaina.'

Don Quixote laughed at the invention of the name, and the priest lauded his virtuous and honourable decision, and again offered to accompany them for as long as he could spare from his unavoidable duties. With this they took their leave and advised and begged him to take care of his health, and to indulge in everything that was good for him. As fate would have it, his niece and housekeeper overheard the conversation between the three men, and as soon as Don Quixote was alone they walked in, and the niece said:

'What's all this, uncle? Just when we were thinking you'd come back home to stay, and to live a quiet and honourable life here, you want to go off into yet more labyrinths, turning yourself into a

Little Shepherd, coming, coming,
Little Shepherd, going, going?[2]

Well, the plain fact is the straw's a bit old for making whistles.'

To which the housekeeper added:

'And are you going to be able to put up with the heat of the summer afternoons, the damp of the winter nights, the howling of the wolves, out there in the country? Of course not – that's a job for strong men, brought up and hardened to it pretty well since they were babes in arms. And of the two evils it's better to be a knight errant than a shepherd. Look, sir, take my advice, which I'm not giving you on a belly full of bread and wine but on an empty stomach and fifty years of experience – stay at home, look after your property, go often to confession, give alms to the poor, and on my conscience be it if I'm wrong.'

'Hush, my daughters,' Don Quixote replied, 'I know what's good for me. Take me to my bed now, because I don't feel very well, and rest assured that, whether an actual knight errant or a would-be shepherd, I shall never fail to provide for your needs, as you will see for yourselves.'

And his good daughters (as the housekeeper and the niece surely were) took him to his bed, where they gave him some food and lavished all possible attentions on him.

CHAPTER LXXIV

*Concerning how Don Quixote fell ill, the will that he
made, and his death*

Since what is human is not eternal, but is in continuous decline from its beginnings to its conclusion, this being particularly true of men's lives, and since Don Quixote's life had not been granted any special privilege by heaven to halt the course of its decline, it reached its end when he was least expecting it to; because, either out of the depression brought on by his defeat or by divine ordination, he was seized by a fever that kept him in bed for six days, during which time he was often visited by his friends the priest, the graduate and the barber, while his good squire Sancho Panza never left his bedside. In the belief that dejection at his defeat and the disappointment of his hopes for Dulcinea's deliverance and disenchantment had brought him to this state, they tried in every way they knew to raise his spirits; and the graduate told him to cheer up and get out of bed to make a start on the pastoral life, for which he'd already written an eclogue that would be bad news for all the eclogues Sannazaro had ever produced – and with his own money he'd bought two splendid dogs to keep watch over the flock, one of them called Barcino and the other Butrón, which a herdsman from Quintanar had sold him. But none of this roused Don Quixote from his melancholy.

His friends called in the doctor, who felt his pulse and wasn't happy with what he found, and said that to be on the safe side he should look to the well-being of his soul, because the well-being of his body was in some danger. Don Quixote listened with great composure, but not so his housekeeper, his niece and his squire, who started to weep tender tears as if he were already lying dead before them. The doctor's opinion was that depression and despondency were killing him. Don Quixote asked to be left alone, because he needed a little sleep. They did as he asked, and he slept for more than six hours at a stretch, as the saying goes: indeed he slept for so long that the housekeeper and the niece thought that he was going to die in his sleep. But he did eventually awake, and he bellowed:

'Blessed be Almighty God, who has done me such good! Indeed his mercy knows no bounds, and the sins of men do not lessen or obstruct it.'

The niece paid careful attention to her uncle's words, and they seemed more rational than usual, during his recent illness at least, and she asked him:

'What are you saying, sir? Has something happened? What's this mercy you're on about, and these sins of men?'

'The mercy, niece,' Don Quixote replied, 'is that which God has this instant shown me, unobstructed, as I said, by my sins. My mind has been restored to me, and it is now clear and free, without those gloomy shadows of ignorance cast over me by my wretched, obsessive reading of those detestable books of chivalry. Now I can recognize their absurdity and their deceitfulness, and my only regret is that this discovery has come so late that it leaves me no time to make amends by reading other books that might be a light for my soul. It is my belief, niece, that I am at death's door; I should like to make myself ready to die in such a way as to indicate that my life has not been so very wicked as to leave me with a reputation as a madman; for even though this is exactly what I have been, I'd rather not confirm this truth in the way in which I die. Call my good friends, my dear: the priest, the graduate Sansón Carrasco, and Master Nicolás the barber, because I want to confess my sins and make my will.'

But she was saved her trouble by the entrance of all three. As soon as Don Quixote saw them he said:

'You must congratulate me, my good sirs, because I am no longer Don Quixote de la Mancha but Alonso Quixano, for whom my way of life earned me the nickname of "the Good". I am now the enemy of Amadis of Gaul and the whole infinite horde of his descendants; now all those profane histories of knight-errantry are odious to me; now I acknowledge my folly and the peril in which I was placed by reading them; now, by God's mercy, having at long last learned my lesson, I abominate them all.'

When the three heard all this they were certain that he was in the grips of some new madness. And Sansón said:

'Now that we've had news, Don Quixote sir, that the lady Dulcinea has been disenchanted, you come out with all that? Now that we're on the point of becoming shepherds, to spend all our time singing and living like lords, you want to turn yourself into a hermit? Stop it for goodness sake, and come to your senses, and forget all that idle nonsense.'

'The nonsense in which I have been involved so far,' Don Quixote replied, 'has been real enough as regards the harm it has done me, but my death will, with heaven's help, turn it to my benefit. Gentlemen: I can feel that I am dying, and dying quickly; please leave jests aside and bring me a confessor to confess me and a notary to write down my will, because at times like this a man must not trifle with his soul. And so I implore you to send someone for the notary while the priest confesses me.'

They looked at each other, amazed at Don Quixote's words, and although they didn't know what to think they ended up by believing him; and one of the signs that led them to conclude that he really was dying was the ease with which he had turned from a madman into a sane man; for to what he had already said he added some more that was so well expressed, so Christian and so coherent that it removed all doubt from their minds and convinced them that he was indeed sane.

The priest ordered everybody out of the room and was left alone with him, and confessed him.

The graduate went to fetch the notary and returned a little later with him and with Sancho Panza, who had been told by the graduate about the state his master was in and who, finding the housekeeper and the niece in tears, began to pucker his lips and shed some of his own. The confession ended and the priest emerged, saying:

'Alonso Quixano the Good really is dying, and he really is sane; we'd better go back in so that he can make his will.'

This news was a terrible stimulus for the housekeeper's, the niece's and the good squire Sancho Panza's swollen eyes, so much so that it made the tears burst from them, and a thousand deep sighs burst from their breasts; because the truth is, as has been said before, that while Don Quixote was plain Alonso Quixano the Good – and while he was Don Quixote, too – he was always of gentle disposition and affable behaviour, and well loved not only by his own household but by everybody who knew him. The notary went in with the others, and once he had drawn up the heading and Don Quixote had disposed of his soul with all the necessary Christian formalities, they reached the part concerning the disposal of property, and he said:

'Likewise it is my will that with respect to certain monies in the possession of Sancho Panza, whom in my madness I made my squire, inasmuch as between the two of us there has been a certain amount of haggling, of give and take, he should not be held accountable for them, nor should any claim be made against him, but that, if anything remains after he has paid himself what I owe him, it should all be his, although there will be little enough of it, and much good may it do him; and if, just as when I was mad I helped to procure for him the governorship of an island, I could now that I am sane make him the ruler of a kingdom, I would do it, because the straightforwardness of his character and the fidelity of his conduct deserve it.'

And turning his face towards Sancho, he said:

'Forgive me, my friend, for making you seem mad, like me, and for making you fall into my own error of believing that knights errant ever have existed or do exist.'

'Oh no, don't die, master!' Sancho replied, crying. 'Take my advice and live for a long long time, because the maddest thing a man can do in this life is to let himself die, just like that, without anybody killing him or any other hands except the hands of depression doing away with him. Come on, don't be lazy, get out of that bed of yours, and let's go off into the countryside dressed up as shepherds as we said we would – and perhaps behind some bush or other we'll find the lady Dulcinea, disenchanted and looking as pretty as a picture. If you're dying from sadness because you were defeated, you just blame me and say you were knocked down because I didn't girth Rocinante properly – and what's more you must have read in your books of chivalry that it's an everyday event for knights to knock each other down, and for the one who's defeated today to be the victor tomorrow.'

'Very true,' said Sansón, 'and the worthy Sancho Panza has hit the nail right on the head.'

'Not so fast, gentlemen,' said Don Quixote: 'you won't find this year's birds in last year's nests. I was mad, and now I am sane: I was Don Quixote de la Mancha and now, as I said, I am Alonso Quixano the Good. May my repentance and my sincerity restore me in your eyes to the esteem in which I used to be held, and let the notary continue taking down my will:

'Likewise I bequeath all my estate in its entirety to my niece Antonia Quixana, here present, once what is needed for my other bequests has been deducted from the most readily disposable part of it; and it is my will that the first of these shall be the payment of the wages that I owe my housekeeper for all the time that she has been serving me, and in addition twenty ducats for a dress. I appoint the priest and the graduate Sansón Carrasco, here present, to be my executors.

'Likewise it is my will that if my niece Antonia Quixana should wish to marry, it must be to a man about whom it has first been formally established that he does not so much as know what books of chivalry are; and if it is discovered that he does, and, despite that, my niece still insists on marrying him, and she does so, she is to forfeit everything that I have left her, and my executors can distribute it in pious works as they see fit.

'Likewise I request the aforementioned gentlemen, my executors, if they are fortunate enough to meet the author who is said to have written a history that is circulating under the title of *The Second Part of the Exploits of Don Quixote de la Mancha*, to beg him on my behalf, as earnestly as they can, to forgive me for unintentionally having provided him with the opportunity to write all the gross absurdities contained in that book; because I am leaving this life with scruples of conscience for having given him an excuse for writing them.'

Here he ended his testament, and was overcome by a fainting fit that prostrated him on his bed. The company was thrown into alarm and hurried to help him, and during the three days that he lived after making his will he fainted frequently. The whole house was in turmoil; but still the niece ate, the housekeeper toasted and Sancho Panza enjoyed himself; because inheriting always does something to dispel or temper in the heir the thoughts of the grief that the dead man will, of course, leave behind him.

Eventually Don Quixote's last day on earth arrived, after he had received all the sacraments and had expressed, in many powerful words, his loathing of books of chivalry. The notary was present, and he said that he'd never read in any book of chivalry of any knight errant dying in his bed in such a calm and Christian manner as Don Quixote, who, amidst the tears and lamentations of everybody present, gave up the ghost; by which I mean to say he died.

At which the priest asked the notary to write out a certificate to the effect that Alonso Quixano the Good, commonly known as Don Quixote de la Mancha, had passed on from this life, and died from natural causes. And he said that he was requesting this certificate to deprive any author other than Cide Hamete Benengeli of the opportunity to bring him falsely back to life and write endless histories of his exploits.

This was the end of the Ingenious Hidalgo of La Mancha, the name of whose village Cide Hamete couldn't quite recall, so that all the towns and villages of La Mancha could fight among themselves for the right to adopt him and make him their own son, just as the seven cities of Greece contended for Homer. The lamentations of Sancho, the niece and the housekeeper are omitted from this account, as are the fresh epitaphs that were placed upon his tomb, although Sansón Carrasco did have this one put there:

> This is a doughty knight's repose;
> So high his matchless courage rose
> That, as it's plain enough to see,
> He granted death no victory,
> Not even when in death's last throes.
> This world he didn't ever prize:
> He was a scarecrow in its eyes,
> And yet he was its bugbear, too.
> He had the luck, with much ado,
> To live a madman, yet die wise.

And the sage Cide Hamete said to his pen:

'Here you shall rest, hanging from this rack on this length of brass wire, O quill of mine – whether well trimmed or not I do not know – and here you shall live on for many centuries, unless presumptuous and knavish historians take you down to profane you. But before they touch you, you can warn them and tell them as best you can:

> "Hands off, hands off, you paltry knaves;
> My noble king, let none
> Attempt this enterprise: you know
> It's kept for me alone."[1]

For me alone was Don Quixote born, and I for him; it was for him to act, for me to write; we two are as one, in spite of that false writer from Tordesillas who has had and may even again have the effrontery to write with a coarse and clumsy ostrich quill about my valiant knight's deeds, because this is not a burden for his shoulders or a subject for his torpid wit. And you can warn him, if you do happen to meet him, to leave Don Quixote's weary mouldering bones at rest in his tomb, and not to try to take him, in the face of all the prerogatives of death, to Old Castile, making him rise from the grave where he really and truly does lie stretched out at full length, quite incapable of any third sally or fresh campaign;

because to make fun of all those campaigns waged by so very many knights errant his two are quite sufficient, such has been the approval and delight of all those who have known of them, both in Spain and in foreign realms. And so you will have carried out your Christian mission, giving good advice to one who wishes you ill, and I shall feel proud and satisfied to have been the first author to enjoy the full fruit of his writings, as I desired, because my only desire has been to make men hate those false, absurd histories in books of chivalry, which thanks to the exploits of my real Don Quixote are even now tottering, and without any doubt will soon tumble to the ground. Farewell.'

NOTES

PART I

PROLOGUE

1. *St Thomases*: St Thomas Aquinas (1225–74), the great Italian philosopher and theologian.

2. *Xenophon and Zoilus or Zeuxis*: The Greek historian, writer and military leader (*c.* 435–*c.* 354 BC); the Greek grammarian (*c.* 400–*c.* 320 BC) chiefly known for the acerbity of his attacks on Homer; and the Greek painter who flourished in the late fifth century BC.

3. *Prester John ... Trebizond*: Legendary medieval Christian king of Asia, and one of the four parts into which the Byzantine Empire was divided in the early thirteenth century, often mentioned in books of chivalry; it fell to the Turks in 1461.

4. *Non ... venditur auro*: 'Freedom should not be sold for all the gold in the world', from the version by Walter Anglicus (twelfth century) of Aesop's fable of the dog and the wolf.

5. *Pallida ... Regumque turres*: 'Pale Death with impartial foot knocks at the doors of poor men's hovels and of kings' palaces' (Horace, *Odes*, I, 4b).

6. *Ego ... diligite inimicos vestros*: 'But I say unto you, Love your enemies' (Matthew 5. 44). (Here and below the Authorized Version is quoted.)

7. *De ... cogitationes malae*: 'Out of the heart proceed evil thoughts' (Matthew 15. 19).

8. *Donec ... solus eris*: 'When you are happy you have many friends, but if the weather becomes cloudy you are alone' (Ovid, *Tristia*, I, 9). Cervantes replaces Ovid's (not Cato's) *sospes* with its synonym *felix*, possibly a sly allusion to the dramatist Lope Félix de Vega Carpio, known as Lope de Vega (1562–1635), whom he attacks in this prologue and elsewhere (see note 21 below).

9. *where you'll find it written*: 1 Samuel 17. The passage is in the Book of Kings in the Vulgate, the Latin Bible of the Roman Catholic Church.

10. *Cacus*: Legendary son of Vulcan, who stole oxen from Hercules and was killed by him.

11. *Bishop . . . and Flora*: In one of his *Epístolas familiares*, Antonio de Guevara, the Bishop of Mondoñedo (1480–1545), tells the story of these three ladies.

12. *Medea . . . Circe*: Medea, the legendary enchantress who helped Jason to escape with the Golden Fleece by killing the boy Apsyrtus and cutting his body into pieces, and later caused various other gory deaths (Ovid, *Metamorphoses*, VII). Calypso, the legendary daughter of Atlas who lived on the island of Ogygia and became Odysseus' mistress after he was wrecked there (Homer, *Odyssey*, X). Circe, the sorceress who lived on the island of Aeaea and became Odysseus' mistress, and turned his men into pigs, after he was cast ashore there (Virgil, *Aeneid*, VII).

13. *a thousand Alexanders*: In Plutarch's *Parallel Lives*. Alexander the Great (356–323 BC), the Macedonian warrior and empire-builder.

14. *Leone Ebreo . . . full measure*: Real name is Judah Abarbanel (*c.* 1460–*c.* 1521); his seminal *Dialoghi d'Amore* (1535) expounds the neoplatonic theory of love.

15. *On the Love of God*: Cristóbal de Fonseca, *Tratado del amor de Dios* (1592).

16. *St Basil . . . Cicero*: An early Doctor of the Church (*c.* 330–79), and the famous Roman statesman, orator and writer (106–43 BC).

17. *the Plain of Montiel*: The plain, in the present-day provinces of Ciudad Real and Albacete, on which Don Quixote's village stands.

18. *Urganda the Unknowable*: Benevolent enchantress, the friend of the famous knight Amadis of Gaul, who was the hero of the most famous and influential Spanish romance of chivalry, immensely popular throughout Europe in the sixteenth century. The earliest known edition of *Amadís de Gaula*, a version by Garci Rodríguez de Montalvo, dates from 1508. Urganda is unknowable because of her frequent self-transformations.

These verses are in a form that enjoyed some transitory popularity in Spain at the time of writing, with the last unstressed syllable of each line omitted, for the reader to fill it in (*versos de cabo roto*). Only the final stressed vowels rhyme, in the pattern abbaaccddc (the *décima*).

19. *In Béjar*: Cervantes dedicated Part I of *Don Quixote* to the Duke of Béjar.

20. *Ladies and arms, loves and knights e—*: The opening line of *Orlando Furioso* (1532), a reworking of the Charlemagne legends, by Ludovico Ariosto (1474–1533).

21. *on your fine scu—*: Lope de Vega, with whom Cervantes was not on good terms, was fond of including elaborate shields of arms in the frontispieces of his books, as well as prefacing them with arrays of complimentary sonnets and including many shows of erudition. See also n. 8 above.

22. *Álvaro de Lu— . . . Dame Fortune's stu—*: Don Álvaro de Luna (1390–1453), the favourite of Juan II, held absolute power at court for thirty years until he was disgraced and beheaded. After Hannibal saw his immense power collapse he killed himself in 183 BC. Francis I of France was captured by the Spaniards at the battle of Pavia (1525), and held captive in Spain.

23. *Juan Lati*—: Juan Latino (d. *c.* 1573), humanist and son of an African slave.

24. *Peña Pobre's rugged face*: A desolate island to which Amadis retreated after a tiff with his lady Oriana.

25. *so long . . . in the fourth sphere*: In terms of Greek mythology, so long as the sun comes out each day. The universe was believed to consist of a number of concentric spheres.

26. *Sir Belianis of Greece*: Irascible protagonist of the romance of chivalry *Don Belianís de Grecia* (1547 and 1579), by Jerónimo Fernández.

27. *The Lady Oriana*: Mistress and later secret wife of Amadis of Gaul, who lived in Miraflores Palace, two leagues from London, where she became pregnant and shunned all company.

28. *Villadiego . . . is divi*—: In Act XII of Fernando de Rojas's *Tragicomedia de Calisto y Melibea* (1502), popularly known as *La Celestina*, the cowardly servant Sempronio tells his colleague Pármeno to 'put on Villadiego's breeches', in other words to flee, a proverbial expression referring to some now lost comic tale about a man who fled in such a hurry that he did not stop to put his breeches on.

29. *the great Babie*—: Babieca was the horse of the legendary eleventh-century Castilian hero Rodrigo Díaz de Vivar, El Cid, immortalized in the epic *Poema de mio Cid* (1207?).

30. *Lazari*— . . . *to his blind ma*—: The first picaresque novel, *La vida de Lazarillo de Tormes* (1554), by an unknown author; in the first chapter Lazarillo's wary blind master clutches the jar of wine, but the boy uses a straw to drink some.

31. *harried By sweet Angelica*: In Ariosto's *Orlando Furioso*, Angelica, the Princess of Cathay, sends the hero mad, by her preference for the young Moor Medoro.

32. *Moor and . . . Scythian foe*: Moors and Scythians were legendary for their fierceness in battle.

33. *The Knight of Phoebus*: One of the protagonists of the chivalry romance *Espejo de príncipes y caballeros* (1555), by Diego Ortúñez de Calahorra. In it, Claridiana is the daughter of the Emperor of Trebizond.

34. *Solisdán*: Not found in any of the chivalry books, and presumably Cervantes's invention.

CHAPTER I

1. *as many of them as he could find*: The popularity of romances of chivalry and other prose fiction was considered a very grave social and moral problem. A petition to Charles I and V at the Valladolid parliament of 1555 complains about

the damage done to 'men, youths and girls and other kinds of people' by 'books of lies and nonsense like Amadis and all its imitations', because youngsters of both sexes become so absorbed in these fictional accounts of deeds of arms and love that 'when something similar presents itself to them in real life they give themselves over to it in a more unbridled way than if they had not read about it'. The petitioner requested that such books be burned, so that young people would be 'left with no alternative but to read religious books to edify their souls and reform their bodies'. (*Cortes de los antiguos reinos de León y de Castilla* (Madrid: Real Academia de la Historia, 1903), V, pp. 687–8.) The king took the petition seriously, replying that a decree had been drawn up to remedy the problem and would soon be published. What is curious is that Cervantes was behind the times (or maybe this is part of the joke): by the early seventeenth century the romances of chivalry were no longer fashionable or therefore seen as a threat. And it was young women, not old men like Don Quixote, who had been regarded as being most at risk from their influence.

2. *Feliciano de Silva*: Notorious hack (1492?–1558?), who wrote various romances of chivalry. See note 4.

3. *Sigüenza . . . Palmerin of England*: A very small minor university 120 km north-east of Madrid, and Palmerin of England is the protagonist of the *Libro del muy esforzado caballero Palmerín de Inglaterra* (1547), the Spanish translation of a Portuguese chivalry romance by Francisco de Moraes Cabral.

4. *Knight of the Burning Sword*: Amadis of Greece, the protagonist of one of de Silva's efforts, *The Ninth Book of Amadis of Gaul* (1530).

5. *Bernardo del Carpio . . . with a bear-hug*: Bernardo del Carpio was a legendary Castilian hero, who, in a Spanish continuation (1555) of Ariosto's *Orlando Furioso* by Nicolás Espinosa, defeats Roland at Roncesvalles. Antaeus, in Greek legend, was a Libyan giant, the son of Poseidon, invincible at wrestling until overcome by Hercules.

6. *giant Morgante . . . well-mannered*: The protagonist of the poem *Morgante maggiore* by Luigi Pulci (1432–84), in which he is converted to Christianity by Roland.

7. *Reynald of Montalban*: Hero of French epic and Spanish ballads. Spanish legend has him participate in the events at Roncesvalles.

8. *the traitor Ganelon in the dust*: According to Carolingian legend, he caused the disaster at Roncesvalles.

9. *Gonella's . . . ossa fuit*: Pietro Gonella was the Marquis of Ferrara's court jester in the fifteenth century, often appearing in sixteenth-century joke-books. The Latin means 'was all skin and bone' (Plautus, *Aulularia*, III, 6, 28).

10. *Caraculiambro*: Strong overtones of 'Arse-face'.

CHAPTER II

1. *My arms . . . the bloody fray*: Opening lines of a popular Spanish ballad of the time. The innkeeper completes the stanza.
2. *the Playa district of Sanlúcar*: A notorious centre of Spanish picaresque life.
3. *And never . . . whose name*: Opening lines of a popular Spanish ballad about Lancelot, with appropriate alterations.

CHAPTER III

1. *Percheles . . . and Ventillas in Toledo*: List of disreputable districts in various Spanish towns and cities.
2. *Doña Tolosa*: Only members of the aristocracy were entitled to affix the titles 'Don' and 'Doña' to their names. Quixote himself, as a mere hidalgo, has no business to do so, and drops the title as soon as he regains his sanity. In Part II, chapter XVI, Diego de Miranda is another pompous hidalgo who calls himself 'Don'.

CHAPTER IV

1. *You dare to use that word in my presence*: The mention of the verb 'to lie' was considered an insult not just to the one accused but to any high-ranking person who was present, particularly if he had taken the side of the accused.
2. *St Bartholomew*: Apostle said to have been flayed alive in Armenia.
3. *Guadarrama spindle*: The Sierra de Guadarrama is a mountain range to the north of Madrid. Nobody has been able to explain why Don Quixote claims that spindles made there are particularly straight.

CHAPTER V

1. *the story of Baldwin . . . forest*: Don Quixote again remembers a popular Spanish ballad rather than a chivalry book. It relates the killing by Carloto, Charlemagne's son, of the Marquis de Mantua's nephew Baldwin.
2. *Diana*: The first pastoral romance, written in Spanish by its Portuguese author, and published in 1558 or 1559.
3. *the Twelve Peers . . . the Nine Worthies as well*: The Twelve Peers of France were

a body of the most famous knights at the court of Charlemagne. The Nine
Worthies were three Christians (King Arthur, Charlemagne and Godfrey of
Bouillon), three Jews (Joshua, David and Judas Maccabeus) and three Gentiles
(Alexander, Hector and Julius Caesar).

4. *Barabbas*: The robber whom Pilate released from prison to the Jews instead of
Christ (John 18. 40), traditionally regarded as hardly less evil than the devil
himself. See also Part II, chapter LVII.

5. *the famous sage Squiffy*: The enchanter Alquife is the husband of Urganda the
Unknowable in *Amadis of Gaul*.

CHAPTER VI

1. *hyssop*: A small bushy aromatic herb used for sprinkling holy water.

2. *the very first chivalry romance . . . Spain*: Although it was the most influential one,
Amadis (see Part I, Prologue, note 18) was not the first, which was *Tirant lo Blanc*
(see note 14).

3. *The Exploits of Esplandian*: *Las sergas de Esplandián*, also by Garci Rodríguez de
Montalvo, and published in 1510.

4. *of that same family*: The success of *Amadis of Gaul* provoked many continuations
by other hands.

5. *Don Olivante de Laura*: (1564) by Antonio de Torquemada. His *Jardín de flores
curiosas* was published in 1570.

6. *Florismarte of Hyrcania*: *Primera parte de la grande historia del muy animoso y esforzado
príncipe Felixmarte de Yrcania y de su estraño nascimiento* (1556) by Melchior de Ortega.
The protagonist, called both Florismarte and Felixmarte, is born on a mountain.

7. *The Knight Platir*: *Crónica del muy valiente y esforzado caballero Platir, hijo del
Emperador Primaleón* (1533), its author unidentified.

8. *The Knight of the Cross*: Probably *La Crónica de Lepolemo, llamado el Caballero de la Cruz,
compuesta en arábigo por Xartón y trasladada en castellano por Alonso de Salazar* (1521). The
claim that his book had been 'composed in Arabic . . . and translated into Castilian'
could have given Cervantes the idea for the developments in chapter IX.

9. *The Mirror of Chivalry . . . true historian Turpin*: *Primera, segunda y tercera parte de
Orlando Enamorado*. *Espejo de Caballerías* (1586), a prose adaptation of *Orlando
Innamorato*, by Matteo Boiardo (1441–94), which inspired Ariosto to write *Orlando
Furioso*. Turpin was Archbishop of Rheims in the eighth century, and a prominent
figure in the French epics about Charlemagne. He was claimed to be the author
of the twelfth-century Latin chronicle about the exploits of Charlemagne and
Roland that came to be known as the pseudo Turpin.

10. *turning it into Castilian*: The first of the sixteenth-century Spanish translations

of *Orlando Furioso* was by Captain Jerónimo de Urrea, published in 1549.

11. *Bernardo del Carpio*: *Historia de las hazañas y hechos del invencible caballero Bernardo del Carpio* (1585), by Agustín Alonso: see also Part I, chapter I, note 5.

12. *Roncesvalles*: *El verdadero suceso de la famosa batalla de Roncesvalles* (1555), by Francisco Garrido Villena.

13. *Palmerin of Oliva*: *Libro del famoso y muy esforzado caballero Palmerín de Oliva*, the first in this popular series, was published in 1511, and widely believed to have been written by King John II or III of Portugal.

14. *Tirante the White*: *Tirant lo Blanc* (1490), the Catalan romance of chivalry by Johanot Martorell and Johan de Galba, first published in Spanish translation in 1511.

15. *enchanted water*: Lovers with problems went to the enchantress Felicia, who gave them a potion the consumption of which led to new pairings.

16. *the second part . . . Gil Polo*: Continuations of *Diana*: *Segunda parte de la Diana de Jorge de Montemayor* (1564), by Alonso Pérez, and *Diana enamorada* (1564), by Gaspar Gil Polo, of considerable literary quality.

17. *Lofraso, a Sardinian poet*: Another pastoral romance, *Los diez libros de Fortuna de Amor* (1573).

18. *The Shepherd of Iberia . . . The Undeceptions of Jealousy*: Three more pastoral romances: *El pastor de Iberia* (1591), by Bernardo de la Vega; *Primera parte de las ninfas y pastores de Henares* (1587), by Bernardo González de Bobadilla; and *Desengaño de celos* (1586) by Bartolomé López de Enciso. The first is the most recently published book mentioned in this chapter.

19. *The Shepherd of Filida*: *El pastor de Fílida* (1582), by Luis Gálvez de Montalvo.

20. *The Treasury of Divers Poems*: *Tesoro de varias poesías* (1580), by Pedro de Padilla.

21. *López Maldonado's Book of Songs*: *Cancionero* (1586), including two poems by Cervantes. López Maldonado, Padilla and Gálvez de Montalvo were friends of Cervantes.

22. *Galatea . . . Cervantes*: The *Primera parte de la Galatea* (1585), his own pastoral romance; he kept promising a second part, but never produced it.

23. *Araucana . . . Monserrate*: Three works of heroic poetry: *La Araucana* (three parts, 1569–89), *La Austríada* (1584) and *El Monserrate* (1587).

24. *The Tears of Angelica*: *Primera parte de la Angélica* (1586), by Luis Barahona de Soto; it continues the story of Angelica and Medoro from *Orlando Furioso*. The same author's *Acteón* paraphrases Ovid's *Metamorphoses*.

CHAPTER VII

1. *Carolea . . . Luis de Ávila*: The two parts of *La Carolea* (1560), a heroic poem by Jerónimo Sempere about the exploits of Charles I and V; *La Primera y Segunda Parte de El León de España* (1586), a similar poem by Pedro de la Vecilla. Luis de Ávila wrote a factual prose chronicle about Charles's deeds (1584), *Comentarios . . . de la guerra de Alemaña, hecha de Carlos V*, published in Venice in 1548, but no poem; Luis Zapata did, however, write one, *Carlo famoso* (1566).

2. *Frestón*: The enchanter in *Don Belianís de Grecia* is Fristón.

CHAPTER VIII

1. *the giant Briareus*: A Titan in Greek and Roman mythology, Briareus had fifty heads and a hundred arms.

2. *Diego Pérez de Vargas . . . many Moors*: At the battle of Jerez, 1233.

3. *Agrages*: Character in *Amadis of Gaul*, fond of menacing people with these words.

CHAPTER IX

1. *Who go . . . their way*: Probably from some old ballad, now lost. Quoted again in Part I, chapter XLIX and Part II, chapter XVI.

2. *Platir*: The exploits of the hero of *The Knight Platir* are presented as having been recorded by the sage Galtenor.

3. *better and older language*: Hebrew.

4. *Cide Hamete Benengeli*: Cide is a title, meaning 'My Lord'; Hamete is the Spanish version of the Arabic personal name Hamed, meaning 'he who praises'; and Benengeli is a comic invention suggesting the idea of 'aubergine-eater', via the Spanish *berenjena*, 'aubergine', popularly considered at the time to be the favourite food of the people of Toledo.

5. *Azpetia*: Present-day Azcoitia, in the province of Guipúzcoa.

CHAPTER X

1. *the Holy Brotherhood*: La Santa Hermandad, the rural police, who were invested with the power to judge and punish those they arrested. They had a reputation for cruelty, corruption and cowardice.

2. *the Chaldeans*: In the Old Testament, feared enemies of the Israelites (Jeremiah 32. 28–9, 43. 3).

3. *the Balsam of Fierabras*: In Carolingian legend, a balsam, in which Christ had been embalmed, with miraculous healing properties when drunk. It was stolen in two barrels by the Saracen giant Fierabras when he conquered Rome (in another version, Jerusalem) and later returned to Rome by Charlemagne.

4. *Mambrino's helmet, which cost Sacripante so dear*: In Boiardo's *Orlando Innamorato* (see Part I, chapter VI, note 9), Mambrino is a Moorish king whose enchanted helmet Reynald of Montalban wins in battle. In Ariosto's continuation *Orlando Furioso* it is Dardinel, not Sacripante (Angelica's lover), who is defeated and killed by Reynald, thanks to the helmet.

5. *fell upon Albracca to carry off the fair Angelica*: In *Orlando Innamorato*. Agricane besieges the castle of Albracca, where Angelica is being held by her father, with an army of twenty-two hundred thousand knights.

6. *the kingdom of Soliadisa*: There is a Princess Soliadisa in *Clamades y Carmonda* (1562), and a kingdom of Sobradisa in *Amadis of Gaul*.

CHAPTER XI

1. *he that humbleth himself shall be exalted*: Luke 18. 14.

2. *another Cretan labyrinth*: Don Quixote refers to the labyrinth constructed, according to legend, at Knossos in Crete to house the Minotaur.

CHAPTER XII

1. *the mystery plays for Corpus Christi*: *Autos sacramentales*, plays on religious themes, were traditionally performed as part of the celebrations that took place during the week following Corpus Christi (the commemoration of the Eucharist on the Thursday after Easter Sunday).

CHAPTER XIII

1. *Quintañona*: Spanish addition to Arthurian myth.

2. *Let no man . . . their lord*: Ariosto, *Orlando Furioso*, canto 24.

3. *Augustus Caesar . . . Mantuan poet ordered in his will*: Virgil is said to have ordered his *Aeneid* to be burned, because he had not been able to perfect it. Augustus Caesar refused to heed Virgil's will, and ordered the poem to be published.

CHAPTER XIV

1. *the much-envied owl*: In popular belief, birds of prey attacked owls' eyes out of envy for their size and beauty.

2. *Father Tagus' banks . . . Betis'*: The Tagus, rising in the mountains of eastern Spain and reaching the Atlantic near Lisbon, is the longest river in the Iberian peninsula; Betis is the Roman name for the Guadalquivir, the great Andalusian river that flows by Cordoba and Seville, through the Tartesian plains, to reach the Atlantic near Cadiz.

3. *Tantalus . . . you sisters toiling night and day*: The Danaids, like Tantalus, Sisyphus, Tityus and Ixion, were figures from classical mythology, each with his or her own special torment in Hades. The Danaids had to fill a leaky jar with water.

4. *three-faced guardian of the dreadful gate*: Cerberus, the monstrous watchdog with three heads, who stood guard over the gate to hell.

5. *ride roughshod . . . her father Tarquin*: Tullia's father, over whom she drove her chariot, was Servius Tullius, not Tarquin, who was her husband.

CHAPTER XV

1. *after the Knight of the Sun had been caught in a trap*: This curious incident is Don Quixote's creation. It is not narrated in any of the romances of chivalry about the Knight of the Sun.

2. *Silenus, the tutor . . . on a handsome ass*: Bacchus' tutor rode into the Thebes in Boeotia, not the Thebes in Egypt (the city of the hundred gates).

CHAPTER XVI

1. *an Asturian lass*: Asturias is a region in north-west Spain, whose inhabitants had in earlier times a reputation for being wild and uncouth.

2. *muleteers of Arévalo*: Most muleteers were Moriscos. It is not known why a special mention is made here of Arévalo, a town near Ávila, in central Spain.

3. *Tablante de Ricamonte . . . deeds of Count Tomillas*: *La corónica de los nobles caballeros Tablante de Ricamonte y de Jofre hijo del conde Donason* (1513), a translation of a French chivalry romance; and *Historia de Enrique Fi de Oliva* (1498), a version of a French epic poem, in which Count Tomillas is a secondary character.

NOTES

CHAPTER XVII

1. *in the Vale of Staffs*: The narrator refers to the beating by the men from Yanguas by quoting from an old ballad about the Cid.
2. *the Heria quarter in Seville*: Places of ill repute.

CHAPTER XVIII

1. *the great island of Taprobana*: Sri Lanka. Alifanfarón and most of the other warriors are Don Quixote's inventions, as well as some of the places that they come from.
2. *King of the Garamantes*: In ancient times the Garamantes were a barbarous and ferocious African people.
3. *Xanthus*: Don Quixote moves from his fantasy chivalresque heroes to real peoples, first of Asia and Africa and then of Spain, mostly identified by the rivers flowing through their territories, as in Homer and Virgil and some romances of chivalry. The Xanthus was a river in Troy; the Massilian fields were in Africa; Arabia Felix was one of the three Arabias (Happy, Desert and Stony) mentioned above; the Thermodon was a river in Cappadocia (Turkey); the Pactolus was a river in Lydia, in Asia Minor, said to be rich in gold because Midas had bathed in it. The Genil runs by Granada; the Elysian Fields were thought by some ancient writers to be near Jerez de la Frontera; the Pisuerga, the old boundary between León and Castile, has its source in Palencia and flows into the Duero near Valladolid; the Guadiana flows through La Mancha, some of the way underground, and figures in the episode of the Cave of Montesinos (Part II, chapter XXIII).
4. *Dr Laguna's magnificent edition*: Andrés Laguna (1499?–1560) was a famous doctor, whose heavily annotated translation of the Greek physician's treatise on the medicinal properties of over six hundred plants was published in 1555.
5. *sends his rain on the just and on the unjust*: Cf. Matthew 5. 45.

CHAPTER XIX

1. *I've come from . . . his home town*: They are on a long and difficult journey: Baeza is 290 kilometres to the south of Madrid, Segovia is 70 kilometres to the north of it. Alcobendas is a town near Madrid.
2. *the Knight of the Sorry Face*: A knight in the chivalry romance *Don Clarian de*

Landanis (1524) is called 'El Caballero de la Triste Figura', because the face of a beautiful weeping damsel appears on his shield.

3. *Knight of the Burning Sword . . . Knight of Death*: The titles assumed by Amadis of Greece, Belianis of Greece, Florandino of Macedonia, Florarlan of Thrace, the Count of Arenberg (who lived during the reign of Philip II) and, again, Amadis of Greece.

4. *Si quis suadente diabolo, etc.*: The bachelor of arts quotes a canon approved at the Council of Trent, excommunicating 'according to where it says anyone who, persuaded by the devil', attacks a priest or a monk.

5. *Cid Ruy Díaz . . . honourable and valiant knight*: Incident narrated in one of the ballads of the Cid cycle.

CHAPTER XX

1. *the Mountains of the Moon*: It was believed in ancient times that the source of the Nile was in the Mountains of the Moon, in Ethiopia.

2. *danger loved is death won*: Ecclesiasticus 3. 27.

3. *Cato the Senseless of Rome*: Cato the Censor, since medieval times considered an authoritative source of maxims and proverbs.

CHAPTER XXI

1. *the beaver . . . being hunted for*: Allusion to an old myth about the beaver, hunted for the medicinal qualities of the castor in its genital organs.

2. *piece of eight . . . maravedí*: The maravedí was the smallest coin in common use; 68 maravedís were worth 1 silver real, 1 piece of eight was 8 silver reals and 5 silver reals were worth 1 escudo. A ducat was a gold coin, worth approximately the same as an escudo. Sancho says, in Part I, chapter XXV, that his daily maintenance costs him 52 maravedís, and, in Part II, chapter XXVIII, that he earned two ducats a month plus food when he worked as a farm labourer.

3. *the god of forges . . . the god of battles*: Vulcan and Mars.

4. *Greeks . . . the rape of Helen*: In Greek mythology, the abduction of Helen, the wife of Menelaus and the most beautiful woman in the world, by the Trojan prince Paris led to the ten-year siege of Troy and its sacking by the Greeks.

5. *mutatio capparum*: The Easter ceremony at which the cardinals exchanged their winter capes of fur for summer ones of silk.

6. *jupon*: Tight-fitting tunic worn under body armour.

CHAPTER XXII

1. *civil death, more or less*: The removal of all rights.
2. *Ginesillo de Parapilla*: The diminutive endings add a derogatory shade of meaning.
3. *Lazarillo de Tormes*: The picaresque novel, see Part I, Prologue, note 30.
4. *the flesh-pots of Egypt*: A life of abundance: see Exodus 16. 3.

CHAPTER XXIII

1. *twelve tribes of Israel . . . Castor and Pollux*: The brothers of the twelve tribes of Israel were Jacob's sons (Genesis 49); the killing of the seven Maccabees is narrated in 2 Maccabees; in classical mythology, Castor and Pollux were the twin sons of Leda.

CHAPTER XXIV

1. *that Thisbe so celebrated by poets*: In Roman mythology a Babylonian girl, the lover of Pyramus. The sonnet in Part II, chapter XVIII tells their story.
2. *give her his word of marriage*: Secret marriages by oral or written pact had been forbidden by the Council of Trent, yet the practice still continued, and there are several examples of it in *Don Quixote*.
3. *Sir Rugel of Greece*: *Crónica del muy excelente príncipe don Florisel de Niquea, en la cual trata de las grandes hazañas de los excelentísimos príncipes don Rogel de Grecia y el segundo Agesilao* (1535), by Feliciano de Silva, the eleventh of the Amadis romances.
4. *to moisten us*: The moon was believed to be a humid planet.
5. *Queen Madásima*: There are three Madásimas in *Amadis of Gaul*, none a queen and none involved with Elisabat.

CHAPTER XXV

1. *Medoro*: *Orlando Furioso*, cantos 19 and 23.
2. *Astolfo's hippogryph . . . in fleetness of foot*: Astolfo's winged horse is in *Orlando Furioso*, canto 4, and Frontino, which belonged to the female warrior Bradamante, is in canto 23.
3. *nulla est retentio, so I've heard say*: Sancho garbles a line from the burial service, *Quia in inferno nulla est redemptio* (He who is in hell cannot be redeemed).

4. *Lucretia*: In Roman legend, the wife of Lucius Tarquinius Collatinus. Her rape by Sextus Tarquinius led to her suicide and the founding of the Roman republic.

5. *Perseus's labyrinth*: It should be Theseus's labyrinth, where he killed the Minotaur, finding his way out with the aid of the thread. Later editions make the correction. For Perseus, see Part I, chapter XXXIII, note 5.

CHAPTER XXVI

1. *seven iron soles*: Don Quixote confuses Orlando with his enemy the giant Ferragut, who wore seven iron plates over the only place where he could be wounded, his navel. He goes on to say that Medoro was Agramante's page, but he was Dardinel's.

2. *from his shirt-tail . . . a rosary*: From the second edition onwards, this passage is amended so that Don Quixote makes his rosary out of oak galls. Nobody knows who decided that Cervantes's disrespect for Roman Catholic ritual had gone too far this time.

3. *moist and mournful Echo*: Because of the tears she sheds when rejected by Narcissus.

CHAPTER XXVII

1. *King Wamba*: Proverbial king of the Goths in Spain.

2. *Marius . . . Judas*: Gaius Marius was a Roman general and statesman, ever thirsty for power; Lucius Sergius Catilina led a life of conspiracy and intrigue; Lucius Cornelius Sulla, as absolute master of Rome and Italy, imposed a reign of terror; Vellido Dolfos treacherously killed King Sancho II of Castile at the siege of Zamora; Count Don Julián was blamed in legend for the loss of Spain to the Moors (see Part I, chapter XLI, note 2); Judas Iscariot was the apostle who betrayed Christ to the Jewish authorities in return for thirty pieces of silver.

3. *Stealing from me . . . was not even yet mine*: Reference to the parable in 2 Samuel 12, with which the prophet Nathan upbraids David for taking Uriah's wife.

4. *not daring to look back, like another Lot*: Genesis 19. When Lot and his family were allowed to escape from the destroyed city of Sodom, his wife disobeyed orders and looked back. She was turned into a pillar of salt.

NOTES

CHAPTER XXIX

1. *Pegasus . . . town of Compluto*: Pegasus is the famous winged horse of Greek mythology. Muzaraque seems to be Cervantes's own invention, although Zulema Hill exists, near Alcalá. Compluto is the Latin name for Alcalá de Henares, near Madrid, where Cervantes was born.

CHAPTER XXX

1. *Tinacrio the Sage*: Enchanter who appears in various romances of chivalry. All the other names in the story are invented ones.
2. *the Phoenix itself*: Mythical bird, the only one of its kind, which burns itself on a funeral pyre and rises from the ashes to live again.
3. *and in her . . . have my being*: Very reminiscent of Paul's words, referring to God, in Acts 17. 28.

CHAPTER XXXI

1. *Sabaean*: From Saba or Sheba, in Arabia.
2. *in the belly of the whale*: Reference to the prophet Jonah, who tried to disobey God's command to preach in Nineveh by escaping in a boat, was thrown overboard and swallowed by a great fish.

CHAPTER XXXII

1. *Don Cirongilio . . . Diego García de Paredes*: *Los cuatro libros del valeroso caballero don Cirongilio de Tracia* (1545), by Bernardo de Vargas. The third book is not a chivalry romance but an account of the exploits of the Great Captain, a famous Spanish general of the early sixteenth century. It was published in 1559, but the first edition to include the life of the valiant soldier García de Paredes came out in 1580.

CHAPTER XXXIII

1. *the wise man . . . her*: See Proverbs 31. 10.

2. *usque . . . as the poet put it*: Plutarch ascribes the phrase ('as far as the altar') not to a poet but to the orator Pericles.

3. *Le lacrime di San Pietro*: Religious poem, first published in 1585, and in Spanish translation in 1587.

4. *simple-minded doctor . . . refrained from doing*: Lotario fuses two incidents in Ariosto's *Orlando Furioso* (cantos 42 and 43) involving a magic cup that spills its contents if the drinker's wife has been unfaithful to him.

5. *a modern play . . . find its way*: The play has not been identified. In Greek mythology, Danae was the daughter of Acrisius, king of Argos, imprisoned by him in a tower in an attempt to evade a prediction that she would bear a son who would kill him. But Zeus visited her in the form of a shower of gold and she conceived Perseus, who was to kill Acrisius by accident.

6. *For this . . . one flesh*: Cf. Genesis 2. 23.

7. *I look . . . shall never find*: The poem and poet have not been identified.

CHAPTER XXXIV

1. *Penelope*: In Greek mythology, Odysseus' wife, beset by unsuccessful suitors when her husband did not return after the fall of Troy. A symbol of wifely fidelity.

2. *Portia for a wife*: Wife of Marcus Brutus, who killed herself by swallowing red-hot coals when her husband died.

3. *the precious pearl*: See Matthew 13. 45–6.

CHAPTER XXXV

1. *battle waged . . . in the kingdom of Naples*: Probably the battle of Cerignola, 1503.

CHAPTER XXXVII

1. *Glory to God . . . good will*: Cf. Luke 2. 14.

2. *Peace to be this house*: Luke 10. 5; see also Matthew 10. 12.

3. *My peace . . . peace be unto you*: Cf. John 14. 27, and see also John 20. 19.

4. *Scyllas and Charybdises*: In Greek mythology, Scylla was a sea monster who devoured sailors when they tried to navigate the narrow channel between her cave and the whirlpool Charybdis. In later legend they were identified with two dangerous rocks on either side of the Strait of Messina.

CHAPTER XXXIX

1. *Duke of Alba was marching to Flanders*: The Duke of Alba, Fernando Álvarez de Toledo, arrived in Brussels with ten thousand men on 22 August 1567, having marched from Alessandria, a city some 80 kilometres south-west of Milan.

2. *the executions of Count Egmont and Count Hoorne*: In Brussels, 5 June 1568.

3. *Diego de Urbina*: Under whom Cervantes fought at Lepanto. The captive's tale is based on Cervantes's own experiences as a soldier and slave – but when he returned to Spain he was not accompanied by a Moorish woman.

4. *the alliance . . . a lamentable, disastrous loss*: In 1570–71. The alliance was the Holy League, formed 25 May.

5. *Don John of Austria . . . later did at Messenia*: He reached Genoa, from Barcelona, on 26 July 1571, and Messenia, in the south of the Peloponnese, on 23 August.

6. *that glorious battle*: The naval battle of Lepanto, 7 October 1571, in which an alliance of Mediterranean Christian states defeated a large Turkish fleet, and Cervantes lost the use of his left hand.

7. *Navarino*: Port in the Gulf of Messenia.

8. *taken Tunis . . . from the Turks*: 11 October 1573.

9. *the Goletta . . . just outside Tunis*: The Goletta, the fort at the mouth of the bay of Tunis, was taken by the Turks on 23 August 1574. It had been occupied by a Spanish garrison since Charles V and I had captured it in 1535.

10. *Don Pedro de Aguilar*: A fictional creation, unlike the other people mentioned in the captive's tale.

CHAPTER XL

1. *Friar Puck*: 'El fratín', the nickname given to the Italian engineer Giacome Paleazzo.

2. *something Saavedra*: I.e. Miguel de Cervantes Saavedra.

3. *Hajji Murad . . . Al-Batha*: An important Moor of this name (a renegade, in fact) who was living in Algiers at this time, and a fortress near Oran, on the Mediterranean coast of Algeria.

CHAPTER XLI

1. *Arnaute Mami's slaves*: Arnaute Mami was the Albanian renegade who captured Cervantes in September 1575.
2. *La Cava Rumia . . . Spain was lost*: According to medieval legend, Count Julián, the governor of Ceuta (see Part I, chapter XXVII, note 2), allowed the Moors to conquer Spain to avenge himself on King Rodrigo, who had seduced Count Julian's daughter Florinda, 'la Cava'.

CHAPTER XLIII

1. *Palinurus*: Pilot of Aeneas's fleet.
2. *three-faced luminary*: The moon, in classical tradition. The faces are waxing, full and waning.
3. *wanton ingrate . . . consumed by jealousy and love*: In Greek mythology, the nymph Daphne fled from Apollo (the sun) over the plains of Thessaly, and the river Peneus, her father, turned her into a laurel bush to save her from him.
4. *Medusa*: In Greek mythology, one of the Gorgons, three sisters with snakes for hair, who had the power to turn anyone who looked at them to stone.
5. *Lirgandeo*: Enchanter, the mentor of the Knight of Phoebus (see Part I, Prologue, note 33).

CHAPTER XLV

1. *the turmoil in King Agramante's camp*: In *Orlando Furioso*, canto 27, Agramante is the chief of the Moors who besiege Charlemagne in Paris. The Archangel Michael sends discord into the Moorish camp, but Agramante and Sobrino restore order.

CHAPTER XLVI

1. *the peace and calm of Octavian's time*: The proverbial peace enjoyed by Rome under its first emperor (63 BC–AD 14).
2. *sicut erat in principio*: 'As it was in the beginning', from the *Gloria Patri*.
3. *the bright pursuer . . . in his natural and rapid course*: Before Apollo or the Sun, the pursuer of Daphne (see Part I, chapter XLIII, note 3) has twice visited all the signs of the zodiac; in other words within two years.

4. *the sage Mentironiana*: Not taken from any chivalry book or classical myth. The name has implications of 'liar'.

CHAPTER XLVII

1. *Zoroaster*: Or Zarathushtra, the Persian king who reformed his country's religion in about 800 BC, but who came to be popularly regarded as the inventor of magic.
2. *Tale of Rinconete and Cortadillo*: Story by Cervantes in the picaresque tradition, published as one of his *Novelas ejemplares* in 1613. They are a collection of twelve short tales loosely modelled on the Italian *novelle* of the fifteenth and sixteenth centuries, and their subject matter ranges from adventure and intrigue to realistic studies of contemporary low life.
3. *Villalpando's Summaries*: Gaspar Cardillo de Villalpando, *Summa summularum* (1557), a university textbook.
4. *the Gymnosophists of Ethiopia*: The Greeks' and Romans' name for the Brahmans of India.
5. *Milesian tales*: A classification developed in antiquity; such tales were associated with the city of Miletus, in Asia Minor.
6. *Ptolemy . . . Marco Polo*: The famous Greek astronomer and geographer of the second century, and the Italian explorer of the East (*c.* 1254–*c.* 1324).
7. *Sinon . . . Zopyrus*: Sinon persuaded the Trojans to take the wooden horse into their city; Euryalus was a Greek warrior famous for his friendship with Nisus (Virgil, *Aeneid*, V, 286–361); Zopyrus was a Persian nobleman who mutilated himself as a trick to enable his king Darius to capture a besieged city.

CHAPTER XLVIII

1. *the two princes of Greek and Latin poetry*: Homer and Virgil.
2. *Isabella, Phyllis and Alexandra*: *La Isabela*, *La Filis* and *La Alejandra*, by Lupercio Leonardo de Argensola, thought to have been written between 1581 and 1584.
3. *Ingratitude Revenged . . . The Friendly Enemy*: *La ingratitud vengada*, by Lope de Vega; *La Numancia*, by Cervantes; *El mercader amante*, by Gaspar de Aguilar; *La enemiga favorable*, by Francisco Agustín Tárrega, all plays written in the late sixteenth or early seventeenth centuries.
4. *as Cicero puts it*: According to Donatus in his commentaries on Terence, V, 1.
5. *King Pepin . . . Godfrey of Bouillon*: Pepin was Charlemagne's father, and reigned until 768; Charlemagne reigned until 814. Heraclius, the Byzantine Emperor,

reigned from 610 to 641. Godfrey of Bouillon was the leader of the first crusade, and won Jerusalem in 1099.

6. *a brilliant Spanish genius*: Lope de Vega.

CHAPTER XLIX

1. *Viriatus . . . Don Manuel de León*: Viriatus was a Portuguese hero in the resistance against the Romans; Count Fernán González fought in the tenth century for the independence of Castile; for Gonzalo Fernández (or Hernández), the Great Captain, see Part I, chapter XXXII, note 1; Diego García de Paredes fought under the Great Captain and was a hero in the Naples campaign against the French (see the same note); Diego García Pérez de Vargas fought heroically under Fernando III at the siege of Seville (1248); Garcilaso de la Vega is not the soldier-poet of the early sixteenth century but one of his fifteenth-century ancestors, a knight who fought in the taking of Granada from the Moors; Manuel Ponce de León was another hero in the war of Granada, a legendary figure in the ballads.

2. *Princess Floripes . . . Bridge of Mantible*: An episode from Carolingian legend: Floripes was the sister of the good giant Fierabras (see Part I, chapter X, note 3) and the wife of Guy of Burgundy, a nephew of Charlemagne and one of the Twelve Peers; the Bridge of Mantible was defended by the ferocious giant Galafre but carried by Charlemagne with the help of Fierabras.

3. *Guerrino il Meschino . . . of Great Britain*: Guerrino il Meschino is the hero of the Carolingian romance by Andrea de Barberino (*c.* 1370–*c.* 1431), which was published in Spanish translation in 1527; the Grail, Tristan and Iseult, Guenevere and Lancelot all belong to Arthurian myth, with the Spanish addition of Quintañona.

4. *Pierres . . . a cart-pole*: The wooden horse does not appear in the story of these lovers, the *Historia de la linda Magalona, hija del Rey de Nápoles, y de Pierres, hijo del Conde de Provenza* (1519, translated from the French), but in another popular love story, *La historia del muy valiente y esforzado caballero Clamades, hijo del rey de Castilla, y de la linda Clarmonda, hija del rey de Tuscana* (1521, also from a French original).

5. *of all reason and good sense*: In this paragraph Don Quixote has moved on to list some real Spanish knights of the early fifteenth century, whose exploits are recorded in the *Crónica del Rey Juan II*. The jousts of the Honourable Pass (1434) were among the most famous chivalric exploits of the Middle Ages. Suero de Quiñones, a Leonese knight, had sworn to wear an iron ring round his neck every Thursday in honour of his lady. To free himself of this promise he undertook to hold the bridge of Órbigo, between León and Astorga, with nine followers, for

thirty days. Sixty-eight knights presented themselves and three hundred lances were broken.

CHAPTER LI

1. *Gante y Luna*: Not traced.

2. *the pastoral Arcadia*: The mountainous region of the Peloponnese, the pastoral paradise for classical and Renaissance writers, most notably Jacopo Sannazzaro (1458–1530), whose prose romance *Arcadia* was first published in 1504, and in Spanish translation in 1547.

CHAPTER LII

1. *ARGAMASILLA ... DE LA MANCHA*: There are two villages in La Mancha with this name, Argamasilla de Alba and Argamasilla de Calatrava. It has traditionally been assumed that one of these, or the two fictionally fused, is the village that the narrator claims not to remember in the famous first sentence of the novel: amateur poets are fond of writing poems in praise of the local celebrity; furthermore, *argamasa* means 'mortar, plaster' and *masilla* means 'putty' (just as *mancha* means 'stain'), so it would not be surprising if the narrator conveniently forgot that his hero came from a place with such humble connotations.

2. *HOC SCRIPSERUNT*: Latin: 'wrote this'.

3. *than Jason gave to Crete*: In Greek mythology, Jason was a hero from Thessaly, not Crete, who led the Argonauts in their quest for the Golden Fleece.

4. *Gaeta ... Cathay*: Port near Naples, and the name by which China was commonly known in the Middle Ages.

5. *Bellona ... Brillador's and Bayard's verve*: Bellona was the Roman goddess of war; Brigliadoro was Orlando's horse; Bayard was Reynald's horse.

6. *Forsi ... miglior plectio*: *Orlando Furioso*, canto 30, l. 16: 'perhaps another will sing with a better plectrum'.

NOTES

PART II

PROLOGUE TO THE READER

1. *born in Tarragona*: The spurious second part, *Segundo tomo del ingenioso hidalgo don Quixote de la Mancha . . . compuesto por el licenciado Alonso Fernández de Avellaneda, natural de la villa de Tordesillas*, published in Tarragona in 1614. 'Avellaneda' is a pseudonym, and the author has not been identified.

2. *greatest battle . . . hope to see*: The battle of Lepanto: see Part I, chapter XXXIX, note 6.

3. *familiars of the Holy Office as well*: Reference to the prolific playwright Lope de Vega (see Part I, Prologue, note 21), who became a priest in 1614 and was notorious for his many love affairs.

4. *Exemplary Tales*: Cervantes's *Novelas ejemplares*: see Part I, chapter XLVII, note 2.

5. *La Perendenga*: This play has not been traced.

6. *the great Count of Lemos . . . Don Bernardo de Sandoval y Rojas*: Respectively, the dedicatee for Part II of *Don Quixote* and Cervantes's protector.

7. *the ballads of Mingo Revulgo*: Anonymous fifteenth-century satirical verse attacking Henry IV of Castile.

8. *Persiles*: Cervantes did not complete *Los trabajos de Persiles y Sigismunda* (published posthumously, in 1617).

CHAPTER I

1. *a present-day Lycurgus or a modern Solon*: Legendary legislator of Sparta (ninth century BC), and Athenian legislator (*c.* 630–*c.* 560 BC).

2. *Osuna University*: A minor university in the province of Seville, founded in 1549, and a frequent object of satire. Salamanca, on the other hand, was Spain's oldest and most famous university, founded over three hundred years earlier.

3. *Lisuarte of Greece*: The son of Esplandian and grandson of Amadis.

4. *Perion of Gaul*: Amadis's father.

5. *Ruggiero . . . Turpin's Cosmography*: Ruggiero is a character in *Orlando Furioso*. Don Quixote is alone in attributing a *Cosmography* to Turpin (see Part I, chapter VI, note 9).

6. *Goliath . . . seven and a half cubits tall*: Don Quixote exaggerates, because 1 Samuel 17. 4 tells us that the Philistine giant killed by David was six cubits and a half tall. A cubit was an ancient measurement of length, approximately the length of a forearm.

7. *Another, better . . . of Cathay*: *Orlando Furioso*, canto 13, quoted at the end of Part I.

8. *famous Andalusian . . . has sung her beauty*: *Primera parte de la Angélica* by Barahona de Soto (see Part I, chapter VI, note 24), and *La hermosura de Angélica* (1602) by Lope de Vega.

CHAPTER II

1. *etcetera*: The Latin aphorism, *Quando caput dolet, caetera membra dolent*.

2. *Julius Caesar . . . his personal habits*: Suetonius reports that, when young, Julius Caesar affected untidy dress, to win the favour of the plebs. See also Part II, chapter XLIII.

CHAPTER III

1. *El Tostado . . . at any rate as big*: Alfonso de Madrigal, the Bishop of Ávila (d. 1450), was proverbial for his productive pen.

2. *aliquando bonus dormitat Homerus*: Version of the statement by Horace in his *Ars Poetica*, l. 359: 'from time to time good Homer slumbers.'

3. *stultorum infinitus est numerus*: Ecclesiasticus I. 15: 'of fools the number is infinite'.

CHAPTER IV

1. *Sacripante . . . using the same trick*: For the siege of Albracca, see Part I, chapter X, note 5. The Brunello episode is narrated in *Orlando Furioso*, canto 27, verse 84.

2. *St George's day*: 23 April.

3. *For St James, close, Spain*: The traditional Spanish battle-cry. 'Close' means 'close with the enemy'.

CHAPTER V

1. *Doña Urraca*: The daughter of Ferdinand I, who threatens in a ballad to disgrace him, on finding herself omitted from his will, by taking to a disreputable life.

CHAPTER VI

1. *the Ottoman house*: The famous dynasty that ruled the Turkish empire.
2. *the Pharaohs and Ptolemies of Eygpt*: The Ptolemies were the descendants of Ptolemy I (360–283 BC), the general of Alexander the Great who took charge of Egypt after the latter's death, and declared himself king in 304 BC, replacing the previous rulers, the Pharaohs.
3. *the road of virtue . . . broad and spacious*: Paraphrase of Matthew 7. 13–14.
4. *This rough . . . do not stray*: Garcilaso de la Vega (c. 1503–36), *Elegía I*, 202–4.

CHAPTER VII

1. *bene quidem*: In Latin, 'very well'.
2. *Samson*: The Israelite leader, famous for his strength (Judges 13–16); in Spanish, *Sansón*.

CHAPTER VIII

1. *those verses . . . silk and pearls*: Garcilaso de la Vega, *Égloga III*, 53ff.
2. *poet of our time*: Possibly Vicente Espinel, *Sátira contra las damas de Sevilla* (1578).
3. *cast Horatius . . . in the middle of Rome*: Incidents narrated by Livy: Horatius Cocles held the bridge over the Tiber against Porsena, King of Clusium, in 507 BC to prevent him from entering Rome, and then escaped by swimming the river; Gaius Mucius Scaevola burned off his own right hand after the failure of his attempted assassination of King Porsena, during the latter's subsequent siege of the city; in 362 BC Manlius Curtius rode his horse into an abyss that had opened up in the Forum and that, according to the soothsayers, could only be filled by throwing into it Rome's greatest treasure (the flames are Don Quixote's contribution).
4. *Caesar cross the Rubicon*: When Julius Caesar crossed this stream in 49 BC, thus precipitating civil war, the omens, according to Suetonius, were favourable.
5. *scuttled the ships . . . in the New World*: Cortés ordered his boats to be burned in 1519 during the discovery and conquest of Mexico, to make retreat impossible.
6. *slay pride . . . sloth*: Don Quixote refers to the seven deadly sins, suppressing avarice (a sin that could never even tempt a knight errant), and adding somnolence.

CHAPTER IX

1. *'Twas on the stroke of the midnight hour*: The first line of an old ballad about the Count Claros de Montalbán, which had become a proverbial expression.
2. *An evil-day . . . Roncesvalles*: The first lines of the ballad of Count Guarinos, very popular in the sixteenth century. It concerns events following the defeat (by Moors in poetry, by Basques in reality) of the French in a mountain pass in the Pyrenees (778).
3. *Calaínos*: Ballad about a Moor who defeated Baldwin and was killed by Roland; it had become a proverbial expression to denote irrelevant talk.

CHAPTER X

1. *You're but . . . the blame*: Much-quoted lines from a popular ballad about the legendary hero Bernardo del Carpio.
2. *white stone . . . black stone*: The Roman practice, to indicate lucky and unlucky days.

CHAPTER XI

1. *Charon's boat*: Charon, the mythical son of Erebus and Nyx, ferried the souls of the dead across the river Styx.
2. *The Parliament of Death*: Possibly *Auto sacramental de las Cortes de la Muerte*, by Lope de Vega. Angulo was a well-known theatrical manager of the late sixteenth century.
3. *Thalia . . . Melpomene*: Greek muses of comedy and tragedy.

CHAPTER XII

1. *Pylades and Orestes*: In Greek mythology, Pylades helped Orestes avenge his father Agamemnon's murder, and married his own sister, Electra.
2. *the bug is passed, etc.*: From an unidentified song. The lines quoted earlier are from an old ballad.
3. *lessons from animals . . . from the horse*: Ideas deriving from Pliny the Elder's *Historia naturalis*, and repeated in several sixteenth-century Spanish books.
4. *the tongue . . . the fullness of the heart*: Matthew 12. 34 and Luke 6. 45.

5. *Vandalia*: Andalusia was overrun by the Vandals in the fifth century, and was for a while known as Vandalitia.

6. *among the happy . . . the afflicted*: He is quoting from Garcilaso de la Vega's *Égloga II*, 95–7.

CHAPTER XIII

1. *eat our bread . . . our first parents*: See Genesis 3. 19.

2. *if the blind lead the blind*: Cf. Matthew 15. 14.

CHAPTER XIV

1. *Hercules' stepmother . . . perilous labours*: In Roman mythology, Juno, the wife of Jupiter, hated her stepson Hercules and imposed on him the twelve tasks or labours.

2. *famous giantess . . . I came, I saw her and I conquered her*: La Giralda is the enormous brass weathervane, depicting faith, on Seville cathedral. The famous 'Veni, vidi, vici' is attributed to Julius Caesar on the conclusion of his Pontic campaign.

3. *Bulls of Guisando*: Four ancient misshapen granite figures about four feet high and six feet long, not far from Ávila.

4. *Chasm of Cabra . . . those dark depths*: Chasm in the Sierra de Cabra, province of Cordova.

5. *The victor's . . . his foe*: Misquoted from Alonso de Ercilla, *La Araucana* (see Part I, chapter VI, note 23).

6. *To that we make answer*: 'A eso vos respondemos' was the formula at the beginning of the King's answers to petitions at the Castilian parliament.

CHAPTER XVI

1. *pane lucrando*: Latin for 'earning his bread'.

2. *in palace antechambers*: Don Quixote is referring to pasquinades: lampoons or satires displayed in public places such as these.

3. *Est deus in nobis*: 'God is in us' (Ovid, *Fasti*, VI, 5, and *Ars amandi*, III, 549).

4. *the Isles of Pontus*: In the Black Sea, where Ovid was exiled and died.

5. *the leaves . . . never struck by lightning*: The laurel, which the ancients believed to have this virtue.

CHAPTER XVII

1. *Oran*: Port on the Mediterranean coast of Algeria, then a Spanish garrison.

2. *the sort to be afraid of lions*: Many heroes of chivalric romances confront fierce lions, as does the Cid in his poem.

3. *O you of little faith*: The words addressed by Jesus to Peter as he walked on the sea in the storm (Matthew 14. 31).

4. *glory of Spanish knights*: One of Don Manuel de León's legendary feats was to recover a lady's glove from a lions' den.

CHAPTER XVIII

1. *O lovely . . . when God willed*: The first lines of Garcilaso de la Vega's much-quoted Sonnet X.

2. *a sealskin strap . . . diagonally from one shoulder*: To avoid the pressure of an ordinary belt, and because sealskin was believed to be good for kidney trouble.

3. *Pesce Cola could swim*: Legendary amphibious creature of medieval folklore.

4. *Carthusian monastery*: The Carthusians were a contemplative Christian order (founded by St Bruno in 1084), who led a hermitic way of life of great austerity.

5. *not by Cyprus . . . forgive him for it*: Allusion to a sonnet by Pedro Liñán de Riaza (d. 1607) attacking a contemporary minor poet for making these extravagant claims about himself, and for being ignorant enough to mistake the Italian port Gaeta for Creta (Crete).

6. *the judges . . . the arrows of Phoebus*: In other words that they be executed for their crimes by Apollo, the father of the muses and the protector of the arts, just as the Holy Brotherhood executed criminals by shooting them with arrows.

7. *Pyramus and Thisbe*: The myth related by Ovid in his *Metamorphoses* (IV, 55–465). Forbidden to meet by their parents, they speak through a crack in the wall dividing their houses. They arrange to meet at the tomb of Ninus to elope, but Thisbe, who arrives first, runs away from a lioness, dropping her veil, which the lioness tears to pieces with its bloody jaws. Pyramus finds the veil, thinks that Thisbe is dead and kills himself with his own sword. When she returns and finds his body, she takes the sword and kills herself.

8. *Cave of Montesinos . . . Lakes of Ruidera*: The Cave of Montesinos, which takes its name from Spanish balladry, and the Lakes of Ruidera are in the province of Ciudad Real.

CHAPTER XIX

1. *Gordian knot*: Intricate knot tied by King Gordius of Phrygia. Whoever untied it would, it was prophesied, become the ruler of Asia. Alexander the Great cut through it with his sword.
2. *Sayago*: Region in north-west Castile, made proverbial by sixteenth-century Spanish theatre for its rustic buffoons.
3. *Majalahonda*: Now Majadahonda, a village near Madrid.
4. *flutes ... timbrels*: Rustic musical instruments. Tabors are small drums; psalteries are string instruments similar to dulcimers; shawms are double-reed wind instruments; and timbrels are instruments similar to tambourines, but with no parchment stretched over the hoop.

CHAPTER XX

1. *Count Dirlos*: Figure in Spanish ballads of the Carolingian cycle.
2. *green Cuenca cloth*: Cloth that was commonly used by peasants for their party clothes. Cuenca is a city and province in central Spain.
3. *Zamora double pipe*: Similar to an oboe, but with two tubes. Zamora is a city and province in the extreme north-west of Castile.
4. *fear of the Lord ... wisdom*: Cf. Psalms 111. 10 and Proverbs 1. 7.
5. *account for in another life*: See Matthew 12. 36.

CHAPTER XXI

1. *what God ... put asunder*: Matthew 19. 6, as quoted in the marriage service.

CHAPTER XXII

1.; *a crown to her husband*: See Proverbs 12. 4.
2. *a sage*: His name has also eluded all of Cervantes's commentators.
3. *Polydore Virgil*: Author of *De inventoribus rerum* (1499; Spanish translation 1550), a popular work containing much futile erudition.
4. *is reserved for me alone*: Notion common in the romances of chivalry.
5. *Our Lady of the Rock of France ... Trinity of Gaeta*: Place of pilgrimage between

Salamanca and Ciudad Real; and monastery overlooking the Gulf of Naples, and venerated by sailors.

6. *Montesinos ... daughters of Ruidera*: Montesinos, Durandarte and Belerma are characters from Spanish ballads of the Carolingian cycle. Squire Guadiana, the duenna Ruidera and her daughters and nieces do not appear in the traditional ballads. See also Part II, chapter XVIII, note 8 and chapter XXIII, note 4.

CHAPTER XXIII

1. *Ramón de Hoces, of Seville*: Not identified. Maybe one of Sancho's little jokes: *hoces* means 'scythes'.
2. *Merlin, that French sorcerer*: The Arthurian enchanter is described as French because the Arthurian legends came to Spain through France.
3. *O my ... she may be*: From a ballad now lost, or perhaps written by Cervantes.
4. *the order of St John*: The King of Spain did indeed own the Lakes of Ruidera, except for two which were the property of the Knights of the Order of the Hospital of St John of Jerusalem, (founded during the first crusade, 1096–9), who owned property in Spain and other European countries as a consequence of donations and privileges.
5. *a Fugger ... to remedy them*: The Fuggers, Augsburg traders and bankers, were proverbial for their wealth.
6. *ever roamed through them*: Allusion to the *Libro del infante don Pedro de Portugal, que anduvo las cuatro partidas del mundo* (1547).

CHAPTER XXIV

1. *one lord who can more than make up for all the rest*: Don Quixote is probably referring to the Conde de Lemos. See Part II, Prologue, note 6.
2. *seguidillas*: The stanza form characteristic of the folk music of the south of Spain, of four (or sometimes seven) lines of five, six or seven syllables.
3. *Cartagena*: Major Mediterranean seaport in the south of Spain.
4. *spilorceria*: Meanness.
5. *according to Terence ... unscathed in flight*: This maxim is not to be found in Terence.

CHAPTER XXV

1. *the freeing of Melisendra*: The story of the rescue by Don Gaiferos of his wife Melisendra, held captive by the Moors, was told in a popular ballad that had been incorporated from a Germanic source into the cycle of medieval Spanish ballads concerned with the exploits of Charlemagne and his followers.

2. *Duke of Alba*: Fernando Álvarez de Toledo, Duke of Alba (1508–83), was a famous soldier and a member of one of Spain's noblest families. He fought with distinction in Germany and Italy and in 1567 was appointed Governor of the Netherlands.

3. *che pesce pigliamo*: What fish shall we catch?

4. *the giantess Andandona herself*: An ogress in *Amadis of Gaul*.

5. *the times and the seasons*: Cf. Acts 1. 7.

6. *operibus credite, et non verbis*: 'Believe the works, and not the words', an allusion to John 10. 38.

CHAPTER XXVI

1. *The Tyrians . . . were silent*: The first line of Book II of Virgil's *Aeneid*, which appeared in Spanish translation in 1555.

2. *Sansueña*: From the French 'Sansoigne', Saxony, but popularly identified in Cervantes's time with Saragossa.

3. *With squawkers . . . truncheons behind*: From one of the low-life ballads by Francisco de Quevedo (1580–1645), referring to the parading of a convicted criminal to his public punishment, preceded by town criers proclaiming the crime and followed by policemen.

4. *days be as many as Nestor's*: Nestor, from Homer's *Iliad*, was proverbial for longevity.

5. *But yesterday . . . my own*: Much-quoted lines from a popular ballad about King Rodrigo and the loss of Spain (see Part I, chapter XLI, note 2).

CHAPTER XXVII

1. *Don Diego Ordóñez de Lara . . . challenged them all*: Don Quixote refers to a famous event in Spanish history, much celebrated in medieval epic and balladry, when King Sancho II of Castile, besieging his sister Doña Urraca in the northwestern city of Zamora, was treacherously killed in 1072.

2. *the town of the lady clock . . . the soapies*: The town of the lady clock (el pueblo de la Reloja) was Espartinas, in Andalusia, whose inhabitants were claimed to have asked for the town clock to be a female one so that she could give birth to other clocks; the stewpots (los cazoleros) were the inhabitants of Valladolid, because of their fondness for this dish; the eggplanters (los berenjeneros) were those of Toledo for a similar reason; the whale-calves (los ballenatos) were those of Madrid, who went out with arms one day to slay a whale in the tiny River Manzanares that flows through their town – the whale turning out to be an ass's pack-saddle; the soapies (los jaboneros) were those of Seville, where much soap was made and used.

3. *do good . . . hate us*: See Matthew 5. 44 and Luke 6. 35.

4. *yoke was easy and his burden light*: Cf. Matthew 11. 30.

CHAPTER XXVIII

1. *per signum crucis*: 'by the sign of the Cross'.

CHAPTER XXIX

1. *Riphean mountains*: Snow-covered mountains located by the ancient geographers in the northernmost part of Scythia, an empire extending from southern Russia to the borders of Persia.

2. *Here once stood Troy*: Proverbial saying deriving from Virgil's *Aeneid*, II, 11.

CHAPTER XXXI

1. *When from . . . his steed*: Sancho makes a convenient alteration to the text of the old ballad. See Part I, chapter II, note 3.

2. *the Herradura disaster*: In October 1562, a squadron of Spanish galleys was wrecked in a storm in this port near Malaga, and more than four thousand people were drowned.

CHAPTER XXXII

1. *rough and rutted . . . the heights of immortality*: Don Quixote is remembering the lines of Garcilaso de la Vega that he quoted earlier: see Part II, chapter VI.
2. *Parrhasius . . . Lysippus*: Famous artists of ancient Greece.
3. *Alastrajareas*: Alastrajarea appears in *Don Florisel de Niquea*, one of the Amadis series.
4. *the aristocratic families . . . the highest quality*: In reality El Toboso was a village of Moriscos; according to the notions of pedigree to which Don Quixote adheres, the families could not by definition possess any of the characteristics that he ascribes to them.

CHAPTER XXXIII

1. *the Campeador*: Ivory bench that the Cid won from the Moors at Valencia (*Poema de mio Cid*, 3114ff.), proverbial as a seat of honour.
2. *the fowls of the air . . . to feed them*: See Matthew 6. 26.
3. *a good name . . . great riches*: Cf. Proverbs 22. 1.
4. *Michael Verino, florentibus occidit annis*: 'Died in the flower of his years', from an epitaph composed by Angelo Poliziano on Verino (1469–87), who wrote a book of moral maxims for the instruction of children, after the manner of Dionysius Cato's *Disticha de Moribus ad Filium*. Both were used as school textbooks. Verino's book was first published in Spain in 1489, and frequently reprinted.

CHAPTER XXXIV

1. *May you be eaten . . . like far-famed Fávila*: A proverbial curse. Fávila was the son and successor of Pelayo, the hero of the Spanish resistance to the Moorish invasion. He was killed by a bear in the mountains of León in 739.
2. *collected by the Greek commander*: *Refranes o proverbios en romance* (1555), a collection of over six thousand proverbs by Hernán Núñez de Toledo y Guzmán, a professor of Greek and Knight Commander of the Order of St James.
3. *la Ilaha ill'Allah*: 'There is no God but Allah', the Moorish war-cry.
4. *Flanders*: The Spanish army was heavily engaged in Flanders at the time when Cervantes wrote his novel.

CHAPTER XXXV

1. *I announce them and all their works*: Sancho misremembers and misapplies the words in the baptism service with which the child's godfather renounces the devil.
2. *Elysian Fields*: According to Greek mythology, the fields at the end of the earth to which heroes, exempted from death, were conveyed by the gods.

CHAPTER XXXVI

1. *works of charity . . . no merit or value whatsoever*: This comment does not appear in any Spanish edition between 1616 and 1863, and was censored in the *Index* of 1632, presumably being regarded as an unacceptably frivolous application of a Christian precept.
2. *If I've had a good hiding . . . the executioner*: Convicted criminals were paraded through the streets on donkeys.
3. *20th July 1614*: This is believed to be the date when Cervantes wrote this part of the novel.
4. *Trifaldín*: Truffaldin, from *truffare*, 'to deceive', is a character in *Orlando Innamorato* and *Orlando Furioso*.
5. *the kingdom of Kandy*: Present-day Sri Lanka.

CHAPTER XXXVIII

1. *Martos*: Andalusian town, near Jaén.
2. *Taprobana . . . two leagues beyond Cape Comorin*: Parody of the absurd exotic geography that was characteristic of the romances of chivalry. Taprobana, like Kandy, is the modern Sri Lanka; Cape Comorin is the southern tip of India, to the west of Sri Lanka.
3. *My soul . . . do not complain*: Song lyric originally composed in Italian by Serafino dell'Aquila (1466–1500).
4. *as Plato recommended*: In his *Republic*, III, 398.
5. *Come, death . . . being dead*: Adapted from a well-known poem by the fifteenth-century Valencian poet Escrivá.
6. *the Islands of Lizards*: Mythical desert islands.
7. *crown of Ariadne . . . balsam of Panchaia*: Ariadne, the daughter of King Minos, gave Theseus the thread that enabled him to enter the labyrinth and kill the Minotaur, and Vulcan made her a crown of gold and Indian gems, which was

exalted into a constellation; in Greek mythology, the sun was Apollo's chariot, whose horses pulled it round the earth once every day; Tibar was the ancient name for a river in Arabia, famous for its fine gold dust; Panchaia was a region of Arabia Felix, celebrated for its frankincense.

8. *Clavijo*: *Clavija* means 'peg', 'plug'.

CHAPTER XXXIX

1. *quis talia fando temperet a lacrimis*: 'Who, hearing this, will be able to contain his tears?' (Virgil, *Aeneid*, II, 6–8).

CHAPTER XL

1. *the lands of the Moors and pluck mine out there*: Among the Moors, being beardless was a mark of infamy. In Spain, plucking a man's beard was a traditional form of humiliation.

2. *said to be the names of the horses of the Sun*: But not their names – Boötes is the name of a constellation, and Pirithous was the friend of Theseus.

3. *Clavileño*: *Clavo* means 'nail', *leño* means 'wood'.

4. *Hector of Troy*: Legendary warrior, son of Priam and Hecuba and husband of Andromache.

CHAPTER XLI

1. *execution squad at Peralvillo*: Village near Ciudad Real, the centre of the Holy Brotherhood's jurisdiction, where they killed malefactors with arrows.

2. *rash youth . . . his father the Sun*: Phaëthon asked his father the Sun to let him drive his chariot across the heavens for one day. The youth was too weak to control the horses, which came so close to the earth that it was almost set on fire, and Zeus killed him with a thunderbolt.

3. *the second region . . . be burned alive*: In Ptolemeic cosmography, each of the four elements, earth, water, fire and air, prevailed in its own region. Don Quixote is referring to a version of it according to which the region of the air was divided into three subregions.

4. *Dr Torralba . . . for fear of fainting*: During his trial (1528–31) by the Cuenca Inquisition, Dr Eugenio Torralba claimed to have witnessed the sack of Rome (1527) in this way.

5. *Magellan*: Famous Portuguese navigator (1480–1521).

CHAPTER XLII

1. *frog . . . its fair feathers*: Don Quixote uses as examples first one of Aesop's fables and then a popular belief of the time.
2. *pay fourfold . . . in life*: Paraphrase of 2 Samuel 12. 5–6.

CHAPTER XLIII

1. *see a mote . . . the beam in his own*: See Matthew 7. 3.

CHAPTER XLIV

1. *Most holy, unappreciated gift*: Juan de Mena, *Las trescientas* (1444), verse 227.
2. *as if you did not possess them*: Paraphrase of 1 Corinthians 7. 3.
3. *this new Aeneas . . . a mockery of me*: Virgil in the *Aeneid* (IV, 590) has Dido, who founded Carthage, complain in these terms and then stab herself after her desertion by Aeneas.
4. *Jaca's*: Town in the Spanish Pyrenees.
5. *From Jarama . . . to Manzanares*: Spanish rivers: the Henares flows into the Jarama, the Arlanza into the Pisuerga and the Manzanares into the Tagus.
6. *Don't gaze . . . with cruelty*: According to an old Spanish ballad, Nero, infamous for his cruelty, stood on the Tarpeian Rock to contemplate burning Rome.

CHAPTER XLV

1. *Thymbrius*: Epithet for Apollo.

CHAPTER XLVII

1. *the radical humour*. In medieval philosophy, the humour or moisture naturally inherent in all animals, its presence being a necessary condition of their vitality. It was often identified with semen.

2. *perdicis autem pessima*: The usual form was '*panis autem pessimá* – 'that of bread is the worst'.

3. *Vamos*: In the original the doctor is from a village called Tirteafuera ('clear off'), which does exist where specified.

4. *I'm a Basque*: The Basques enjoyed a reputation for faithfulness and for being of pure Christian stock, and many became secretaries to kings and nobles. See also Part II, chapter XLVIII, note 2.

CHAPTER XLVIII

1. *marked not by the hand of God*: It was said of people born with physical defects that they had been marked by the hand of God.

2. *the ancient hills of León*: People from this remote northern region, like the Basques, prided themselves on their pure Christian stock, untainted by Moorish blood.

CHAPTER XLIX

1. *Andradilla*: Not identified.

CHAPTER L

1. *shortened at the placket*: Cut short in front, a traditional punishment to shame dissolute women.

2. *dubitat Agustinus*: 'St Augustine doubts it', an expression used by students to express doubt about an idea expressed by an opponent in a dispute.

CHAPTER LI

1. *Lacedaemonians*: Spartans.

2. *lift the needy out of the dunghill*: Cf. Psalm 113. 7.

3. *the log . . . climb on top of it*: Aesop's fable about the frogs who asked to be given a king.

4. *amicus Plato, sed magis amica veritas*: Classical adage, 'Plato is my friend, but truth is a greater friend.'

CHAPTER LIV

1. *the unfortunate people of my race*: The Moriscos, Moors who remained in Spain after 1492 – in theory converted to Christianity – were expelled in proclamations issued between 1609 and 1613.

2. *he felt no grief or pain*: From the old ballad about Nero watching Rome burn: see Part II, chapter XLIV, note 6.

3. *Espagnol et tudeski . . . jura Di*: 'The Spaniard and the Germans, all one, good company . . . Good company, I swear to God!' (in the pidgin spoken by the pilgrims).

CHAPTER LV

1. *Galiana*: Moorish princess of medieval legend and balladry, who lived in a sumptuous palace on the banks of the Tagus near Toledo.

CHAPTER LVII

1. *Vireno*: In *Orlando Furioso*, cantos 9 and 10, Vireno, the Duke of Zelandia, abandons his mistress Olympia on a desert island.

2. *Troy*: See Part I, chapter XXI, note 4.

3. *Seville to Marchena . . . Loja to Granada*: Marchena is about fifty kilometres from Seville, and Loja is the same distance from Granada.

CHAPTER LVIII

1. *the teacher of the Gentiles*: 1 Timothy 2. 7.

2. *his Master*: Galatians 1. 11–12.

3. *heaven suffers violence*: Cf. Matthew 11. 12.

4. *Scipio . . . stumbles . . . my arms*: An action more often attributed to Julius Caesar. Frontinus alone makes Scipio Africanus the protagonist of the anecdote.

5. *the jealous god of blacksmiths*: Vulcan, who caught the adulterers Venus and Mars in a net to expose them to the mockery of the gods (*Odyssey*, VIII, 266–366).

6. *Camões*: Luis de Camões (*c.* 1524–80), the great Portuguese poet famous above all for *The Lusiads* (1572).

7. *Actaeon's wonder . . . bathing in the waters*: In Greek mythology, Actaeon was a

hunter who accidentally saw Diana bathing and was punished by being transformed into a stag and killed by his own hounds.

CHAPTER LIX

1. *the second part of Don Quixote de la Mancha*: Avellaneda's spurious one – see Part II, Prologue, note 1.

2. *certain statements in the prologue*: Presumably the personal attacks on Cervantes mentioned in the prologue to this second part.

3. *the riding at the ring*: Competition in which each knight rides at a metal ring suspended on a ribbon and attempts to carry it off on the tip of his lance.

CHAPTER LX

1. *I don't make the king . . . help my master*: Proverbial expression, said to have arisen from words used by the French captain Bertrand du Guesclin when he intervened to help Henry of Trastamara in a fight with his half-brother King Peter the Cruel, in 1369.

2. *You'll die . . . Doña Sancha's enemy*: The last lines of a popular old ballad.

3. *Osiris . . . Roque Guinart*: Osiris is a blunder by the bandit chief for the mythical Egyptian king Busiris, proverbial for his cruelty, who sacrificed foreigners to the gods. It is an understandable mistake, because Busiris was also the Greek name of the shrine of the Egyptian god Osiris. Roque Guinart is a portrait drawn from life: Perot Roca Guinarda was born in 1582, and became a legend in his own time; he lived as a bandit between 1602 and 1611, when he was pardoned and went to live in Italy.

4. *deep calls unto deep*: Cf. Psalms 42. 7.

CHAPTER LXII

1. *chicken blancmange*: One of the most esteemed medieval dishes, prepared from hens' breasts shredded and boiled into a pulp with rose water, goats' milk, rice powder and sugar.

2. *the famous Escotillo*: Probably Scoto or Scotillo of Parma, the sixteenth-century necromancer. But Michael Scot, the thirteenth-century philosopher, was represented by Dante as a magician (*Inferno*, XX, 115).

3. *Methuselah*: Patriarch, the grandfather of Noah, said to have lived for 969 years (Genesis 5. 27).

4. *Fugite, partes adversae*: 'Flee, enemies!', a formula of exorcism.

5. *Le Bagatelle*: No such book has been traced.

6. *Dr Cristóbal de Figueroa . . . Aminta*: Giovanni Battista Guarini's *Il Pastor Fido* (1590) was translated into Spanish by Cristóbal Suárez de Figueroa (1602). The translation by Juan de Jáuregui of Torquato Tasso's *Aminta* (1580) was published in 1607.

7. *Light of the Soul: Luz del alma cristiana*, by the Dominican friar Felipe de Meneses, first published in 1554, eleventh and last edition, 1594.

8. *correcting another book . . . de la Mancha*: This second edition of Avellaneda's *Quixote* is fictitious. The book was not published again until 1732.

9. *like all hogs*: Pigs are traditionally killed at Martinmas (11 November).

CHAPTER LXIII

1. *Montjuich*: Castle to the south of Barcelona, where there was a post of observation.

CHAPTER LXIV

1. *Don Gaiferos . . . over dry land too*: See Master Pedro's puppet show, Part II, chapter XXVI.

CHAPTER LXV

1. *Don Benardino de Velasco, the Count of Salazar*: He was indeed put in charge of the expulsion of the Moriscos from Castile, La Mancha, Extremadura and Murcia, between 1609 and 1614.

2. *his Argus eyes*: The mythical monster Argus had a hundred eyes, of which only two slept at a time.

CHAPTER LXVII

1. *Miculoso . . . Nemoroso*: It was believed that the shepherd Nemoroso in Garcilaso de la Vega's 'First Eclogue' was to be identified with Garcilaso's friend the poet Juan Boscán, since both Latin *nemus* and Spanish *bosque* mean 'wood'. Miculás was a rustic variant of Nicolás.

2. *almohaza . . . alfaquí*: almohaza, 'curry-comb'; almorzar, 'to lunch'; alfombra, 'carpet'; alguacil, 'policeman'; alhucema, 'lavender'; almacén, 'storehouse'; alcancía, 'money-box'; borceguí, 'buskin'; zaquizamí, 'garret'; alhelí, 'wallflower'; alfaquí, 'a priest of Islam'.

CHAPTER LXVIII

1. *Diana . . . and the valleys gloomy*. In Roman mythology the goddess associated with hunting and virginity, and identified with the moon.

2. *post tenebras spero lucem*: 'After darkness I expect the light' (cf. Job 17. 12). These words appear as a motto on the emblem of the publisher Juan de la Cuesta, which is printed on the frontispiece to the early editions of the *Quixote*.

3. *When, Love . . . alive in death*: Don Quixote has not written this madrigal, as he claims, but has translated one by Pietro Bembo (1470–1547).

4. *you murderous Polyphemuses*: In Greek mythology, Polyphēmus was the Cyclops who loved the sea-nymph Galatea, and in jealousy killed his rival Acis.

CHAPTER LXIX

1. *I can't believe . . . unrelenting flow*: The second stanza is from Garcilaso de la Vega's Third Eclogue. The Styx was the lake or river across which Charon ferried the souls of the dead; the Lethe was another river of the underworld, whose waters when drunk made the dead forget their life on earth.

2. *Rhadamanthus . . . Minos*: In Greek legend, the brothers Rhadamanthus and Minos, together with their half-brother Aeacus, were appointed judges of the underworld.

3. *Nimrod*: The mighty hunter before the Lord (Genesis 10. 8–9).

CHAPTER LXX

1. *Harder . . . to my moans*: Garcilaso de la Vega's *Égloga I*, l. 57.
2. *A lover . . . to forgiving*: From an old ballad.

CHAPTER LXXI

1. *Potosí*: City in southern Bolivia, standing at the foot of Cerro Rico, a hill from which the Spaniards extracted vast amounts of silver.
2. *the audacious guest . . . the fugitive guest*: Paris carried off Helen (see Part I, chapter XXI, note 4); and Aeneas, whose abandonment of Dido, Queen of Carthage, caused her to kill herself, according to Virgil's account in the *Aeneid*.
3. *Deum de Deo*: Words from the Nicene Creed, 'God of God'.

CHAPTER LXXIII

1. *Malum signum*: It was said to be the practice of doctors to declare the discovery of a 'bad symptom' in Latin, so that the patient would not understand.
2. *Little Shepherd . . . going, going*: From a popular Christmas carol.

CHAPTER LXXIV

1. *Hands off . . . for me alone*: From a ballad about the siege of Granada.

A CHOICE OF CLASSICS

Leon B. Alberti	On Painting
Ludovico Ariosto	Orlando Furioso (in two volumes)
Giovanni Boccaccio	The Decameron
Baldassar Castiglione	The Book of the Courtier
Benvenuto Cellini	Autobiography
Miguel de Cervantes	Don Quixote
	Exemplary Stories
Dante	The Divine Comedy
	La Vita Nuova
Machado de Assis	Dom Casmurro
Bernal Díaz	The Conquest of New Spain
Niccolò Machiavelli	The Betrothed
Eça de Quierós	The Maias
Sor Juana Inés de la Cruz	Poems, Protest and a Dream
Giorgio Vasari	Lives of the Artists (in two volumes)

and

The Poem of the Cid
Two Spanish Picaresque Novels
  (Anon / **Lazarillo de Tormes**; de Quevedo / **The Swindler**)